THE DEVIL DANCERS

By

T. Thurai

DISCLAIMER
Primary characters in this book are entirely fictional and any similarity between any of them and real individuals is entirely coincidental and unintentional. While I have tried to make the historical background as authentic as possible, this book is a historical novel, not a textbook. I have therefore allowed myself a degree of fictional latitude, putting my own interpretation on events. I have, nevertheless, tried to remain as true to historical facts as possible and to treat the historical characters fairly and impartially. In the case of Vimala Wijewardene, I have not, as some writers have done, described her as Buddharakkita's mistress. While some material exists from which such a relationship might be inferred, I do not believe that this provides conclusive proof of an affair and that their association could just as easily be explained by a mutual passion for politics.

DEDICATION
For my husband and my mother without whose inspiration, encouragement, technical skill and unfailing support this book would never have been written.

THE DEVIL DANCERS' WEBSITE:
Additional historical, cultural and biographical information relating to the book can be found at: **www.thedevildancers.com** and **www.facebook.com/The.Devil.Dancers**

FOR READERS' INFORMATION:
A Glossary of Terms and Bibliography appear at the end of this book.
Cover illustration and design © Hot Monkey Publishing 2011

ACKNOWLEDGEMENTS
Grateful thanks for their help, advice, proof-reading, constructive comments, marketing expertise and general support: my family; my mother-in-law and my husband's family; Barbara; Leland; Winnie; Helen; Agnes; Michael; Megan; Aruni; Madeleine; Tim; Wendy; Tom; Declan, Georgia; Jonny; Angelo; Dinesh; Sarah; Tracey; Angela; Bridget; Sidia; Ricci and family; Maria, Franco and family.

Published by:  **HOT MONKEY PUBLISHING**

e-mail: dd-contact@hotmonkeypublishing.com

Part 1: 1968
The patient

9 a.m. The sun is already at its height, the air humid and thick. In the street below, morning has erupted, an explosion of noise, colour and heat.

Watched by a crowd of eager customers, a man on the pavement is cooking hoppers on a charcoal stove. The aroma of food wafts under the noses of passers-by, a humble reminder of life's pleasures. A pedlar lurches past, strings of clashing saucepans strapped to his back like fish scales. Shoppers haggle shrilly with traders; neighbours shout greetings from doorways; bicycle bells trill urgently as riders dodge pedestrians and animals. Like dragonflies, women in jewel-coloured saris dart through the crowd, hovering around market stalls before disappearing in a flash of blue or green.

Ripples of sound drift in through the window, but all other intrusions from outside are blocked by heavy blinds. Inside the lightless room everything is still, even the small figure on the bed is motionless, one wasted hand stretched across its breast.

Outside, time runs like sand but, in here, it lingers. Seconds coalesce, gathering into minutes that fall, heavy and reluctant, like drops of water from a twig. The final hours of a life are being measured out, one by one, each longer than the last and, as that life draws to a close, it pulls others towards it: like planets around an imploding star.

Footsteps approach from the hallway. They stop. There is a murmur of voices and then the door swings inwards, pushed open by a heavily pregnant girl, her eyes ringed with black shadow and her face pale from lack of sleep. A man enters carrying a doctor's bag which he places on a table by the bed.

"How are you today?"

The question is a formality. The doctor is not inquiring after his patient's health, but the degree to which she is still alive. At this stage, the only prognosis is her proximity to death.

The figure on the bed stirs, raising the tips of its fingers in greeting. The face is expressionless, a mask robbed of identity. The doctor has seen it many times. Death transforms the dying, rendering them unrecognisable.

"Give me your hand."

Gently, he performs the ritual: taking her pulse, listening to the weak fluttering of her heart.

The woman closes her eyes, appearing to sleep. His ministrations finished, the doctor snaps his bag shut and pads softly to the door where the girl is waiting. As he leaves, she pulls the door to behind him, leaving it slightly ajar.

"It won't be long now," he says in a low voice. "I'll come again tonight and if she is in pain, I'll give her another shot of morphine. Just give her a drink if she wants it. There's nothing more you can do."

The girl motions with her head to show that she has understood. Quietly, they pass along the passage to the front door. The doctor passes out of the gloomy hallway onto the sunlit porch where he expels the sick-room air from his lungs, glad to be back among the living.

***

Alone in her room, the patient slips in and out of consciousness, until she can no longer distinguish between sleeping and waking, dream and thought. Sometimes, she hears voices and is unsure whether they come from the street or within her head. A great silver plane glides across the room, the sunlight glinting on its wings. It circles overhead several times then melts through the wall.

Bang. The front door slams. More feet approach. Another visitor. She hasn't the energy. Closing her eyes, she feigns sleep. Then, a voice. One that she recognises. She opens her eyes and he is standing there, at the end of the bed. A little older, a little fatter but still recognisable as the man she loves. For a second, she feels a surge of longing, a desire for life, then it ebbs away like every other impulse in her failing body.

He walks around the bed, takes her hand and gently presses it. She tries to smile but is beaten by fatigue.

"Just try to rest."

Exhausted, she closes her eyes. He thinks she wants to sleep and, replacing her hand on her breast, he turns and walks towards the door. She wants to call after him but lacks the energy. She watches him, retreating from the room, kissing the pregnant girl who has come to greet him, his arm around her thickened waist.

The patient groans.

The girl looks sadly at her mother. "She's in pain. I'll call the doctor."

The woman falls silent again, pretending to sleep.

"No. I think she was dreaming. Let her rest."

The man guides the girl from the room. The patient breathes her gratitude. She wants a clear head to think. Something has been trying to breach her consciousness for days, but every time it breaks the surface they give her morphine and she forgets. This time she will remember.

And then it comes to her. The secret that she has carried for ten years. What must she do? Tell or keep silent? There is not much time and she must make a decision.

Sleep is coming but she does not welcome it. It has lost the power to heal. She winces. Pain is scattered through her, embedded in her flesh like shrapnel. Her body is at war with itself.

"*... Only you ...*"

The faint strain of the record-player reaches her from the front room. It is him. He often does this when he visits, playing songs that he knows she will recognise, whose significance will be understood only by her. It is their song. A secret code. She struggles to keep awake, to think, but sleep rolls in like a mist and, with it, come memories.

***

"*... Only you...*"

Dimpled heat of summer. Carefree crooning from the record-player. In the still, dark warmth of the backroom, cries of passion stifled by the heavy furnishings. A room, rarely visited, where the woman meets her lover.

After passion, he sleeps deeply. She is watchful, head tilted on her arm, fingers absently twisting the sheet while she broods on a remote angle of the window. From a dark recess, a spider inches towards its prey. Frantic at first, the small moth struggles, then tires, succumbing to its attacker's venomous embrace. The spider inspects its victim, trussed in silk, then retreats to a corner. The woman averts her eyes.

Her lover stirs, murmuring in his sleep. From his mouth come wisps of dream talk. He raises his arm, covers his face, sighs. Then, he is quiet again, breathing deeply. His hand slips back onto the pillow. She leans over him, staring at the sleeping face. This is a time for quiet exploration.

Stretching out her hand, she tries to brush a damp curl from his forehead. The curl slips onto her finger, encircling it, like a ring. She lets it stay there while she maps his body with her eyes: a faint scar on the upper lip, a mole on the forearm, small round nipples the colour of pomegranates. A fierce glow surrounds her heart as she admires him. He is fair-skinned with a curved nose, fine brows and a bow-shaped mouth. The history of the island is reflected in his face.

Ceylon. A teardrop in the vast Indian ocean. For centuries, it has been both lure and landfall. Invaders, traders, buccaneers, missionaries, colonists, all laid claim to it and were then subsumed: just as the jungle swamps villages and swallows graves. Largely forgotten, these adventurers left little of note, except their names; Pereira, Fernandez, De Silva, and their religion; Buddhists, Hindus, Catholics, Moslems.

The island is a rich stew of blood and dogma. Occasionally, relics of a forgotten ancestry will appear in a face: an olive skin, an Arab nose, blue eyes. Like driftwood from a sunken ship, strange features rise to break the surface in a distant generation. Her lover has such a face. He is beautiful, beyond compare.

The woman examines herself, critically: looks down at her overripe breasts, runs fingers across her belly, soft after the birth of two children and catches sight of herself in the mirror, hair tumbled over her face. She can still pass as a young woman. In a certain light.

The web shivers. The spider creeps back to claim its prey. The woman shudders. Is she the same? No, she tells herself. She is not. She has taken advantage of no-one. But she knows that others would blame her for what she has done. She looks inside herself, scrutinises her thoughts, searches for signs of remorse or shame. But she can find none. Only a primitive joy. Closing her eyes, she bathes in contentment. A shaft of sunlight pierces the window, catching the lovers in its beam, like creatures trapped in amber.

**

" *Only you ...*"

Another memory. One that washes her further into the past, like a wave rolling a pebble. Helplessly, she drifts with the tide.

Part 2: 1955
The meeting

At last he has arrived. She has been waiting for hours, concealed behind her window. Now she watches as he struggles from the bus at the end of the street. The vehicle, squat and vividly painted, shudders from the motion of its engine as it waits for the man to alight.

He pays the driver, takes his leave of the other passengers and extricates his cases from the pile of hoes, sacks, spades and caged chickens piled inside the door. It is market day and the peasants are returning home with their spoils.

Amid squawks from protesting hens, he pulls his luggage free, spilling some loose change that ricochets into the road. With his view obscured by two large, cardboard suitcases, he emerges from the bus, feeling carefully for the steps with the toe of his shoe. Having descended, he drops the baggage at his feet and stands a while with his head down, as if trying to catch his breath.

With a potent blast of fumes, the bus crawls off like a giant insect, heading into the mountains with its cargo of farm implements, peasants and livestock. The man watches the bus disappear, gazing into the distance until the horizon is blank and there is nothing more to see.

Watching from her window, the woman wonders what he is thinking. She cannot see his face, eclipsed by the wide brim of his Panama hat. He is young; she has already guessed that from his letter. Although not tall, his slenderness lends him height. He wears a tropical white suit and shoes that were shiny when he left the city. He is an exotic sight in this remote place where men wear the traditional sarong, pleated at the waist and nothing on their feet. Even children, in their prim white uniforms, walk barefoot to school.

With fingertips resting on the glass, she leans forward to get a better look, sees other women, at the store across the street, looking sideways at the stranger, their eyes darting away when he glances in their direction.

Drawing a slip of paper from his pocket, he reads it slowly then, with the note clamped between two fingers, he heaves up his cases and steps over the coins that lie glittering in the dust. She cannot say why, but the carelessness of that gesture impresses the woman watching from the window.

The women at the hardware store follow him with their eyes. He passes them, unaware of their curiosity, his jacket slung over one shoulder, the turn-ups of his trousers flapping as he walks, his arms taut under the weight of the cases. Drawing near to the house, he sets down the cases and looks up. Too late. She has forgotten to withdraw. Is caught staring at him. For long seconds they eye each other, wary as cats. Then he smiles. A quick, lightening smile. A boy's face. Hopeful. Wanting to be liked. She smiles back. Feels a pang of sympathy, a desire to protect and comfort. He looks like a lost child.

She steps back into the shadows. In the kitchen, her mother Sunny is preparing the evening meal. Two curries: one meat, one vegetable; boiled rice, lentils and a pile of small, triangular poppadums. The rich smell of gravy and spices wafts through the house accompanied by a chorus of clattering pans. But what does he eat? She hasn't thought to ask.

And now she is afraid. She thinks of the spare room that she has prepared for him: a room built through her husband's folly and never used; a room that must pay for itself if they are to repay their debt to the builder. Harsh words have been exchanged and the dispute is still simmering. Can that room, with its quarrelsome history and second-hand furniture, be a fitting home for anyone? And this stranger is not just anyone. He is Mr Arjun Kumaran, special assistant to the Government Agent; an exalted position in this little town.

"What have I done?" she murmurs, suddenly terrified of the young man in European clothes.

Rat-tat. There is a sharp knock at the door. It is too late to change her mind. He is here and she must let him in. Diving into the silty gloom of the hallway, she stops to check her appearance. The convex mirror distorts her reflection, spitefully twisting her face out of shape. The nose appears large, the chin, too small. A stranger's face floats into view. With parted lips, it gapes at her from the airless glass.

"I look like a goldfish," she thinks, smoothing her hair.

She takes a deep breath, a few steps to the door, and her hand is on the latch. As she opens the door, light rushes in like a wave, pours over her, splashes onto the floor, laps at the walls.

He stands on the step, still wearing his hat.

"Mrs Neleni Chelvam? I am Arjun Kumaran. You are expecting me, I believe."

He holds out his hand. She takes it, reluctantly. Women do not usually shake hands with men, but perhaps this is a sign of a more cosmopolitan upbringing and she does not wish to appear ignorant.

"Come in. Was your journey long?

"About five hours."

He does not elaborate, omits to tell her about the drunk on the bus who lurched up and down, threatening the air with his fists. Finally, the man passed out, flopping face down in the aisle where he lay contented, soaked in his own piss. The other passengers, mostly country people and labourers, smiled benignly, exposing teeth stained red with betel.

He steps into the hallway and hands her his hat. She takes it and notices a small hole in the crown. Despite its superior weave, the Panama is second-hand. As she reaches up to hang it on the hat-stand, she catches a breath of scent. Not the cloying odour of hair oil, the sort that her husband uses, but something sharper, more subtle. It reminds her of something pleasant. No. Someone. She inhales, tries to recall who it was and becomes lost in a wilderness of memory.

"Mrs Chelvam?"

She has lingered too long.

"I'm sorry. Please follow me."

She stoops to pick up one of his cases but he is too quick for her. It is unthinkable for a woman to carry his baggage. It is not the mark of a gentleman. He clamps his hand around the worn handle of the suitcase. She notices that he wears no rings, in fact, no jewellery at all, except for a wrist watch with a steel strap. A good choice. Leather rots quickly in this humid country.

She walks slowly ahead, leading him across the hall. As they approach the kitchen, warmth and a tantalizing smell of food bloom from the open door. There is a sudden crash of pans. Sunny is signalling her disapproval. A traditional woman, she considers it unseemly for her daughter to converse with a man who is not her husband. Particularly if she is unaccompanied. That is how trouble starts.

"Neleni!" The old lady summons her daughter in a shrill voice.

"Yes," Neleni is unwilling to be drawn into the kitchen.

"I can't find the garlic."

"It's where it always is."

"I can't find it. How can I cook with no garlic?"

"I'll be there in a minute, Amma. Why don't you come and meet our guest?"

A wrinkled face with thick pebble glasses appears at the kitchen door.

"This is Mr Kumaran. Our new lodger. Mr. Kumaran, this is my mother."

"Hello, Aunty."

Using the familiar title for older female relatives, the young man steps forward to greet her, his hand held out.

"Hmmph!"

Snorting with disgust, the old lady disappears. Further complaints and turbulent rattling of saucepans soon follow. Flushed with rage, Neleni murmurs an apology.

"I'm sorry. She's old. She'll get used to you."

"Don't worry. My grandmother is just the same."

He grins. He is amused. Now she thinks of it, so is she. Laughing at her mother's eccentricities is a daring and original strategy, not one she has tried before, and it works. Both laugh, Neleni stifling her giggles behind her hands like a naughty child.

"I'd better show you to your room," she says, once they have recovered their breath.

She leads him into a long, narrow passage, illuminated only by the dim light that overflows from adjoining rooms. On the walls, photographs are packed so tightly that sepia figures seem to emerge from the plaster. All fix the newcomer with the same sombre stare. Arjun shudders at the silent sentinels who keep watch over the corridor. Yet his landlady regards them tenderly.

"This is my father aged twenty-two. He was the eldest of three brothers."

She speaks in the past tense. An indication that her father is deceased. Gently she wipes dust from the picture frame with the tip of her finger. Arjun squints in the gloom. The man in the photograph is like her, but his skin is even paler. Arjun guesses that her father was a burgher, of mixed European and Ceylonese descent.

"I bring them all my news," she says, now inspecting a photograph of schoolgirls encircled by nuns. She sighs but the significance is lost on him.

She is standing beside him, speaking softly. She has changed from the woman who met him at the door. Then, she was distant, aloof, her face immobile and mask-like, as impenetrable as one of her photographs. But now all that she thinks can be read there. He guesses, rightly, that she is sensitive and that her feelings run deep. Swift-moving, momentary expressions flit across her face; mood clouds; windswept notions, memories, ideas; subtle nuances of shade and colour, like light shining through a prism; merging, refracting, constantly changing. When she smiles, she is beautiful.

A sudden commotion scatters their thoughts. A cat in search of scraps has infiltrated the kitchen and is being sternly repulsed by Sunny.

"Ai, Ai. Filthy thief. Get out of my house or I will hammer you with this pan."

The cacophony reaches a crescendo as Sunny, shrieking and hissing, crashes two saucepan lids together.

"I'm afraid that happens at least once a day. After a while, you won't notice it."

"Is it your cat?"

"No. A stray. She threatens to kill it one minute, then feeds it the next. She thinks I don't know. Come."

She beckons him to follow her, leading him to a sharp turning at the end of the landing. Three steps up and another, shorter passage, narrow and gloomy, with one room at the end. The gable cuts across steeply, forcing them to walk slantwise to avoid the sloping ceiling. The air is thick and stagnant.

At the end of the passage, is a small, dark door. Neleni grasps the handle pulling it towards her as she jiggles the key in the lock. Daytime heat and cool night air have warped every door in this house and it requires the artfulness of a burglar to prise them open.

The key scrapes and squeaks, grinding against the unresponsive metal until, finally, it slips into place and, without further complaint, trips the lock. Neleni pushes the door, easing it open.

Against the outer wall is a metal-sprung bed covered with a green quilt. Next to it is a school desk, its ancient lid gouged by compass points and bruised with ink. The sloping, lean-to roof makes it necessary to lower one's head when approaching either.

Daylight squeezes through a porthole-shaped window, a contribution from Neleni's husband, Raj, who found it on a scrap heap. It funnels a meagre stream of daylight into the room and cannot be opened because Neleni has accidentally sealed the hinges with paint. In the corner is a wash-stand with a china basin, a clean towel and a cube of soap. Above that, a small mirror, the shape and size of a roti, has been fixed to the wall. It is so small that when Arjun shaves, he will have to work a square inch at a time.

The room is as cramped as the grave and almost as dark. Arjun is reminded of Poe's story, The Pit and the Pendulum. He will have to sleep with the door open.

"I hope it's all right," Neleni enquires, anxiously.

It was her idea to convert the abandoned room into a lodging. Surprisingly, Raj told her that, if she did the work, this could be her enterprise, he would not interfere. Neleni was surprised at his decision. Raj is a traditional man and does not like his wife to have any interests outside the home, or even within it, but the need to pay the builder has swayed him. Nevertheless, Neleni is grateful. For years, she has longed for an opportunity to prove herself, to be something more than a housekeeper.

Clearing the room has taken days of single-handed effort: sorting the contents of boxes, removing rubbish, dusting, cleaning, polishing and painting. Her back still aches and there are cuts on her hands. At first, she was proud of the result, but now she is ashamed. Cramped and tawdry, this room is inappropriate for a man of Arjun's status: a special assistant to the Government Agent. She has misled him and made herself look foolish. She stings with shame.

Seeing her distress, Arjun is reminded of his mother. He remembers the thousand humiliations she suffered just to keep the family afloat while his father squandered their money on horses. He recognizes the expression on Neleni's face; hope competing with despair. He cannot disappoint her.

"It's a lovely room. I shall be very happy here."

"Thank you."

She clasps her hands, slightly bowing her head. He is touched by her gratitude, and a little embarrassed. He has done nothing to deserve it. But to Neleni, his chivalry is a revelation. Her husband, simple, good-natured but uneducated, is insensitive to her feelings. He would have made fun of her mistake, made her look a fool, and she would have hated him. She knows because it has happened many times.

"Dinner will be ready in a couple of hours. I will send someone to fetch you. You can meet everyone then."

It is an awkward closure to their conversation, but she does not know what else to say. Pulling the door shut behind her, she walks slowly along the passage, smiling at the photographs as she passes.

1955: Arjun's room

Arjun tests the bed with his hand. It is a rickety contraption and the footboard leans inwards at a perilous angle. Propping himself against it, he pushes the bed hard against the wall in an attempt to stabilize the iron frame. A small puff of dust rises from the mattress; it has a musty smell and he wonders how many births, deaths, dramas and dreams it has witnessed.

He explores the room, acquainting himself with unfamiliar objects. The lodging, which initially disappointed him, begins to take on a more pleasing aspect. It is larger than he thought, the impression of smallness being due to the lack of air. He grapples with the window, trying to wrench the handle open, but it will not budge. Sweating with the effort, he resumes his inspection of the room.

Facing the bed is a wardrobe, old but capacious, the handles of its doors secured with a loop of string to prevent them from opening unbidden. Inside, metal hangers are strung from a piece of dowelling which looks new: its bleached colour does not match the dark, varnished interior of the wardrobe which smells strongly of camphor.

Having closed the wardrobe doors, Arjun completes his tour, returning to the desk in the corner. Its lid is scored with scratches and words have been tattooed into the soft wood with ink. A slot, drilled into the top of the desk, still bears the original inkwell; a pot made of thick, white porcelain. Arjun examines the contents with his finger. Small scales of dried ink adhere to his skin but, apart from a powdery residue, the ink-pot is empty.

Lifting the lid of the desk, he inhales the odour of old books, crayons and wood. It is the smell of school. With a pang, he remembers morning lessons when the lazy buzz of flies almost lulled him to sleep, followed by long afternoons, playing cricket. He resolves to re-fill the ink-pot and work at this desk.

He is about to close the lid, when he notices an old exercise book, wedged at the back of the desk. Easing it out of its hiding place, he flicks through its pages. They are filled with poems in childish writing, copied for homework or, possibly, for private pleasure. The corner of one well-thumbed page has been turned down to mark what was obviously a favourite: 'The Lady of Shalott'. Small drawings have been inked in the margin: a princess, her mirror, the knight, his horse, all executed with a firm and skilful hand. The artist had considerable talent. Arjun lays the book on his bedside table, intending to read it when he takes a rest. But, first, he must wash.

It is so hot in here. If only he could open that window. He splashes his face with tepid water from the basin, scooping it up with his hands and dousing his head and neck. He has spent five hours on the bus, cooped up between the window and a snoring, malodorous peasant. He can still smell the man's sweat on his own clothes.

Stripping to the skin, Arjun washes himself with the small cube of soap. It smells of carbolic, a good clean smell which also reminds him of school. Refreshed, he wraps himself in a sarong, not bothering to dry himself too thoroughly, hoping that the dampness of his skin will cool him.

Wearily, he lowers himself onto the edge of the bed where he sits for a while, elbows resting on his knees, contemplating the floor, then slowly lifting his legs, he swings them round until he is lying flat. The bed sways dangerously. Cautiously, he aligns his limbs, allowing the soft mattress to fold around him like water.

As he contemplates the ceiling, a series of vivid scenes swirl round his head like jewels in a kaleidoscope: kissing his mother goodbye; the rickshaw ride through swarming streets; a temple roof lit by the morning sun; pilgrims bearing lotus flowers; a professional beggar, contorting his arm behind his back; a cow ambling across a street, trailing its tether; the drunk on the bus; spilt coins glittering in the road; his landlady.

Then, darker things creep in. Doubt enters. It has tormented him for days, stealing in on his thoughts, like a thief through a window. What is he doing here, far from his family and those who love him? Is this the first step in a promising career? Or has he been the victim of an elaborate ruse?

Questions multiply, outnumbering answers. He shifts restlessly from side to side and the bed creaks in response, its springs resonating like metal cicadas. Then, with half-closed eyes, he revisits the events that have led him to a place as foreign as the moon.

1955: Arjun's story

For generations, Arjun's family had traded in rice and coir and his father and uncles had inherited a small, but profitable, business. The uncles made the deals, negotiating the best prices from suppliers and re-selling at a comfortable profit, while Arjun's father ran the office and dealt with the finances.

Everything seemed to be going well until, one day, Arjun's father was out of the office and one of the uncles opened the post. To his horror, he discovered a letter from the bank manager, threatening to foreclose, demanding to know why the business had not kept up with its repayments on a substantial loan. The uncle laughed, incredulous. What loan?

Things moved quickly after that. There were arguments and recriminations and Arjun's father was forced to admit that, not only had he entered the loan agreement without the knowledge of his brothers but that he had also been borrowing money from the business. His frequent absences from the office were due to his passion for horse-racing: the loan, to his love of gambling.

But discovery came too late. The business failed and the brothers, furious at the loss of their livelihood, had severed all ties with Arjun's father. Yet, a few years later, one uncle had had second thoughts and, prompted by compassion for the family of his errant brother, had done what he could to help them.

Arjun was just out of school: a bright young man with aspirations to enter the law. However, being the eldest son, he was expected to provide for his family which included six brothers and sisters, all of whom required money for education or dowries. After many discussions with his uncle, he was finally persuaded to give up his idea of becoming a lawyer and to enter the civil service.

"It is perfect for you. You are well-educated, you speak English and you are Tamil. The civil service is full of Tamils. It is run by them. You will have no trouble."

The uncle argued his case forcefully.

"I know a man. A katcheri worker. I will speak to him, if you like."

Reluctantly, Arjun agreed.

***

Arjun's uncle and the katcheri worker, Pius, had been schoolmates, attending the same Catholic college to which Arjun had later won a scholarship and, although their paths had diverged after school, they had stayed in touch.

Through family connections, Pius had attained a position of considerable influence: the head of a katcheri, or government department. Although unglamorous, it was a lucrative sinecure, entailing the gift of many valuable contracts. But Pius's favour came at a price.

When Arjun's uncle first suggested to Pius that he should employ his nephew, Pius had protested vigorously. What of his reputation? He had many enemies who would seize on the slightest opportunity to disgrace him. And he had prospects. Promotion to a position of even greater influence had been mentioned. No, no, he had too much to lose. It was too risky.

Bowing his head, the uncle had looked at his shoes and apologized profusely. He had not meant to impose on their friendship, but the boy was intelligent, a hard worker. Pius would not be disappointed. But his protestations had been met with stony silence. Something more was required.

"I will show you my gratitude," said the uncle, staring deep into Pius's eyes.

One never said exactly what one meant in these situations. It was implied. The uncle was answered by a twitch of the mouth, a tiny spark of interest in the other man's eye. To Pius, gratitude was a commodity which could be bought or sold. Finally, a price was agreed and Pius's reservations were overcome. Arjun was offered the position of junior clerk.

Indebted to his uncle and eager to prove himself, Arjun performed his duties with painstaking thoroughness, filling in forms, copying reports, filing papers, often working late into the night while Pius, with exquisite punctuality, finished work every day at precisely 4 p.m.

The boy's diligence provided the perfect foil for his master's intrigues. While Arjun ran the office, Pius devoted himself to more pressing matters. Holding court at his desk, he interviewed a steady stream of contractors, dispensing or withholding favours with feudal grandeur.

Leaning back in his chair, his fat hands folded over his paunch, Pius would roll a cheroot from one corner of his mouth to the other, exhaling slow streams of smoke as he weighed up each petitioner's request. Sometimes his eyelids would droop and flicker, an indication that greater generosity was required to keep him awake. Ingratitude was guaranteed to send him to sleep. If an offer proved too paltry, he would lapse into unconsciousness and, head thrown back, snore loudly until his guest took the hint. Thus, with minimum effort, he extracted maximum returns from suppliers although little benefit found its way into the public purse.

When not entertaining clients, Pius would devote himself to what he termed OB – Other Business – giving strict instructions that he was not to be disturbed. Once the door of his office was closed, he would settle down to work. With his feet on the table and, a cheroot clamped between his lips, he would close his eyes in order to give departmental affairs his undivided attention. Such was his dedication to duty that he rarely stirred from his chair, even taking meals at his desk. Tiffin boxes got the same treatment as official papers: once opened, their contents were consumed and they were then piled in the box marked 'Out'.

No-one in the katcheri dared to question their superior's conduct. He was an important man. With connections. Like a number of high-ranking civil servants, Pius owed his position more to family influence than innate ability. One of his uncles was a Government minister and, while he held office, Pius was invulnerable. But, one day, the unthinkable happened. The uncle had a seizure and died. Within hours of the corpse being laid in its coffin, the hunt was up for Pius and his valuable sinecure.

It was at this point, that a chance remark altered the course of Arjun's career. A senior official, Mr Rathnapathy, had requested some information from Pius's department. As usual, Arjun had replied on behalf of his superior, impressing the elder civil servant with the speed and accuracy of his work. Meeting Pius by chance a few days later, Mr Rathnapathy praised the outstanding ability of his clerk.

"A fine young fellow. You'd better watch out. He'll soon be running the katcheri."

Intended as a joke, the remark stung Pius's heightened sensibilities. Until his uncle's death, he had treated his staff with affable disinterest. However, fear now made him snappish and vindictive. He found fault where there was none, reversing his orders as soon as they were given, or worse, once they had been executed. In short, Pius's paranoia soon had the katcheri by its heels and none suffered more than Arjun.

Suspicious of his clerk's intentions, Pius began to watch Arjun out of the corner of his eye, convinced that the clever young upstart was plotting against him. It became his custom to berate Arjun on a daily basis, before withdrawing to his office to contemplate his options, aided by a bottle of whisky. One day, the door of the inner sanctum flew open. Irascible and red-eyed, Pius bore down on his clerk like an avenging demon.

"Is this what I asked you to do? Who told you to go to that file? You are spying on me. Spying!"

His voice rose to a hysterical crescendo as he snatched a file from Arjun's hands and lobbed it across the room. As it hit the ground, the file sprang open, spewing its contents over the floor. The other clerks scattered, seeking sanctuary behind desks and filing cabinets, abandoning Arjun to his fate.

"You should not have done that," Arjun retorted, his patience finally exhausted.

"What! What! Is my clerk now telling me how to run my department? Perhaps you would like my office, too. Is that it? Do you want my job?"

There followed an ugly scene in which Pius accused his junior of treachery and which left Arjun pale and shaking with rage. Unable to tolerate the stunned silence and averted eyes of his colleagues, Arjun strode angrily into the corridor where he collided with Mr Rathnapathy who happened, coincidentally, to be standing on the other side of the door.

"Goodness," said Mr Rathnapathy, dabbing at the corner of his mouth with a handkerchief. "What a commotion. Are you all right, my boy?"

Arjun opened his mouth, then shut it again, unable to speak.

"Ah," exclaimed Mr Rathnapathy, wisely, nodding his head. "Come with me."

He led the young man to his office where he plied him with tea and liberal doses of sympathy. Had Arjun not been so naïve or so distracted by the injustice of his treatment, he might have noticed a reptilian gleam in his mentor's eye. Others, with more experience, might have been less forthcoming. However, Arjun's innocence was his undoing. Brimming with anger, he told Mr Rathnapathy everything.

Mr Rathnapathy listened, patiently, betraying no emotion, although his heart exulted. He, too, had a nephew in need of preferment and Pius's post was just what was needed. While outwardly professing concern for Arjun's plight, Mr Rathnapathy was secretly plotting to usurp his master. But how? The question had tormented him for weeks. Suddenly, the answer presented itself. The key to the puzzle was sitting in front of him, pouring out his heart. An innocent vessel. A poisoned chalice. Eager to be alone, Mr Rathnapathy dismissed Arjun with a few words of comfort, then settled back in his chair, softly drumming his fingers on the table as he worked out the details of his plan.

***

A few days later, Mr Rathnapathy drew Pius aside to inform him of a post that had just become vacant, one that would be ideal for his clerk, a young man overdue for promotion. The post of special assistant to the Government Agent at Polonnaruwa had two advantages: it was ideally suited to Arjun's talents and it was a long way away. As expected, Pius took the bait. Mr Rathnapathy congratulated himself. Pius's paranoia would rob him of his only protection. Without Arjun, the katcheri would lapse into chaos and, without the protection of his uncle, Pius could be extracted like a rotten tooth.

Within the hour, Arjun was summoned to Pius's office and the good news broken to him.

"Well, what do you think?" snapped Pius, testily.

The head of the katcheri was sitting behind his desk his feet, for once, firmly planted on the ground. He attempted to lean forward but, restrained by his great girth, managed only to crane his neck, an attitude that lent him the aspect of an inquisitive turkey.

Despite the obvious advantages of the proposal, its timing unsettled Arjun. Coming so soon after his disagreement with Pius, promotion seemed more like a punishment than a reward.

"Come on, come on, what do you say? Someone does you a favour and you can't even open your mouth!" Pius was losing patience; the wattles below his cheeks were quivering.

Hoping to avoid further discord, Arjun accepted without enthusiasm, a fact that either escaped Pius or did not concern him.

"Good. That's settled. Here's the paperwork. Fill it out yourself. I'll sign it when you've finished."

And with that, Arjun was effectively dismissed from Pius's service.

***

Lying on the bed in Neleni's spare room, Arjun considers the tortuous fate that led to his promotion. Despite the envy of colleagues, his elevation has the taint of disgrace. It feels not like success, but failure. Moreover, his feeling of dejection is compounded by guilt. Before leaving the city, he learned of Pius's final humiliation: the nepotism that raised him, having been used to humiliate him. He has been replaced by Mr Rathnapathy's nephew.

"Poor Pius," murmurs Arjun. "It was all my fault."

And, indirectly, it was.

1955: Sunny's kitchen

In the kitchen, Sunny is stirring a large pot of mutton curry.

"I don't like him."

"Amma, keep your voice down."

Neleni quickly shuts the door to prevent her mother's shrill remarks from reaching the ears of her lodger.

"What do you mean, you don't like him? You've hardly met him. And you weren't so polite yourself."

"Who does he think he is, trying to shake my hand? I never shake hands with men."

"Amma, he comes from the city. Things are different there. Times are changing."

"Oh. Is that your excuse for spending so long alone with him?"

"We were only talking. He's just arrived in a strange place and he's miles from home. It's a long way from Kandy. And anyway, he's our lodger. He's going to be living under the same roof, eating the same meals with us. I can't just ignore him."

"I don't like him." The old lady sticks out her lower lip in protest.

"At the moment, Amma, it doesn't much matter whether you like him or not. We need the money. If the men in our lives hadn't been so ..."

She stops to search for a word:

"... so careless, then we wouldn't be in this position. But there it is. They have been and we are."

"Your father wasn't careless."

Neleni is briskly scraping potatoes at the kitchen sink. She keeps her head down, intent on her task. This argument has been rehearsed many times. She knows she is being unjust. No-one can help dying, even if it was the silliest accident. In order to photograph a dove on its nest, her father had climbed a temple tree. Everyone knows that the branches of the frangipani tree are treacherous, but he climbed it just the same. The branch snapped beneath his weight, and he fell, breaking his neck; and Neleni's fate was sealed, all because of a photograph. If that wasn't careless, what was?

"Your father was a good man," Sunny persists.

"I know, but if he hadn't died, I wouldn't be here, arguing with you about a stranger. Things would have been different."

The last comment is cryptic, but Sunny knows what it means. In fact, the two women understand each other so well that they often speak in telegraphic sentences whose meaning is clear only to them. At no time is this more apparent than when they are arguing.

"Raj is a good man, too," Sunny retorts defiantly. She knows that Neleni has been referring to her marriage, one that was arranged by her mother. Secretly, Sunny admits that it was a mistake, but what choice did she have? Beggars cannot be choosers and the death of Neleni's father left them practically destitute.

Neleni does not reply. Her scraping of the potatoes has now become so frantic that pieces of peel and juice are being sprayed far beyond the kitchen sink. Both women continue their tasks in silence; both angry, more at the blow which fate has dealt them, than with each other. They frequently vent their frustration in this way because no-one else understands.

16

After a few minutes, their angry silence is broken by a faint mewing from outside. Without a word, Sunny reaches into a dish beside the stove, extracting a handful of fat and gristle, off-cuts from the mutton that she has prepared for dinner. Assuming that no-one can see her, she shuffles towards the door where the stray cat is waiting to be fed. It is a daily ritual in which Sunny observes a truce with her detested enemy. Neleni, as usual, pretends not to notice.

Arjun awakes to a soft, shuffling sound. With a quickening heart, he parts his eyelids a fraction, spying through the narrow ellipse without appearing to be awake. At the end of the bed are two small girls, engaged in silent combat. The taller one, about ten years old, holds her sister in a vice-like grip: one hand clamped tightly around the little girl's wrist, the other clutching a hank of her hair. Squirming, the captive struggles to get free, picking determinedly at the fingers which hold her.

Arjun stirs and, rubbing his eyes, makes a pretence of waking up. He yawns, stretching his arms above his head then, swinging himself around, rises to his feet. Startled, the smaller girl peers at him uncertainly, then begins to whimper. The older one stares, unflinching as an owl, lips pressed tightly together. "Shut up" she orders her sister, still with her eyes on the stranger. Petrified, the younger child freezes, tears suspended from her eyelids in two pendulous pools.

"What is your name?" Arjun asks the elder child.

Self-possessed, eyes still fixed on him, she gives it some thought.

"Rani. She's Saro".

Another silence. Then, suddenly, questions topple from her mouth like dominos.

"What's your name? What are doing here? Have you come to live with us? Can I call you uncle? Do you want to see my dolls? Will you play with me?"

Exploiting this distraction, Saro wriggles free of her sister's hands. Scrambling onto the bed, she struggles to her feet then starts to bounce up and down, using her small arms like paddles. Suddenly, with a great leap, she hurls herself into space. For a second, she floats in mid-air then, legs and arms flailing, plummets to the ground like a shot bird. Temporarily winded, she gazes up at Arjun, waiting for sympathy. But he will not give it, withholding the signal to cry. He knows this game, has younger brothers and sisters of his own.

"Get up," he says matter-of-factly. Obediently, she hops to her feet then dashes past him to reclaim her position on the bed. Too late. Rani has taken possession and, in turn, is leaping into the air, flapping her arms to gain height.

Undeterred, Saro scrambles aloft and starts to run around the bed, closer and closer to Rani, in the hope of dislodging her. Serenely ignoring her sister, Rani continues to jump, forcing herself higher and higher until her head brushes the ceiling. The bed creaks and groans menacingly. Arjun is about to intervene, but is saved the trouble. The girls collide, falling in a heap, a tangled mass of limbs like two puppets whose strings have been cut.

Extricating her legs, Rani brushes down her skirt, then gives Saro a sharp slap on the head. Before hand has met scalp, Saro screams. With regal composure, Rani climbs off the bed and leaves the room. Saro continues to scream, shrill and unrelenting, hardly pausing for breath, her nose and eyes running in a display of unquenchable grief.

Arjun tries to calm her, but she will not be consoled. She kicks her little feet and clenches her fists. *Temper*, he thinks. When his brothers behaved like this, he smacked them. But they were boys and this is a girl, and a stranger's child. What is he to do? Picking up the exercise book from the bedside table, he sits down and pretends to read, but Saro keeps up the momentum. Arjun is becoming desperate when Neleni appears in the doorway, trailed by Rani.

"What is happening? What have you been up to?"

Arjun blushes. For a moment, he thinks she is speaking to him. Her mother's intervention prompts another squall of tears from Saro, who raises an arm and points accusingly at Rani.

"Bad girls. I told you not to come in here. Come with me where I can see you."

Neleni holds out a commanding hand to Saro who continues her mewling protest.

"What is that you are reading?"

Momentarily distracted, Neleni steps into the room. Arjun feels like a thief, caught in the act.

"I found it in the desk. I hope you don't mind."

"Oh no."

Her face is as inexpressive as a mask, just as it was when she welcomed him into the house. He does not know whether she is flattered, insulted, or simply disinterested.

Herding the girls towards the door, Neleni speaks over her shoulder: "Dinner is in half an hour."

They leave the room and Arjun can hear Neleni chastising the girls in the corridor, her voice growing fainter as she leads them to the kitchen. Disquieted, he hopes that she does not hold him responsible for their behaviour. She spoke sharply, a trace of annoyance in her face. Is she angry with him?

Realizing that he is still holding the exercise book, he returns to the desk and, lifting the lid, again savours the smells that transport him back to his schooldays. He replaces the book with a sense of guilty pleasure. Trespassing on his landlady's past has been as exciting as stealing mangoes from a neighbour's garden. He has acquired something to which he has no right. He had forgotten how satisfying that could be.

Wandering over to the window, he peers through the glass. The view of the street beyond is partially obscured by a temple tree, heavy with lemon-coloured flowers whose overlapping petals ensure a graceful, spiralling descent when they fall from the branch. A few blooms can scent a whole room, overpowering the smell of mildew, a common feature of the Island's humid climate. A whiff of dampness clings to the room which was closed for days before Arjun's arrival.

Returning to the bed, Arjun sits down, but cannot sleep. His mind is too restless; his thoughts, like cats and dogs, chasing each other, round and round. He must do something. He gets up, searches for a clean shirt, then realises that he has not yet opened his case. Pressing the metal studs that release the two latches, he lifts the lid, feels carefully inside and, without disturbing the contents, teases a fresh shirt from the top layer of clothes. The cuffs are slightly frayed.

"Not a good start," he thinks, disappointed. He had wanted to create more of an impression. Still, it cannot be helped. There has been no time to unpack properly and, if he does not take care, he will crease the clothes which his mother has spent two days washing and ironing. That would be sacrilege.

As he leans over the case, he smells the comforting odour of home and his heart aches with loneliness.

1955: The evening meal

At dinner, there is an unseasonal air of festivity as all the family, except Sunny, compete for the attention of the new guest. As Arjun enters the room, the girls cease playing and fix him with huge, expectant eyes; Neleni, fresh jasmine pinned into her hair, appears from the kitchen, although the meal is not yet ready, and a man, with a grin like a crescent moon, rises from his seat at the table.

"Raj," says the man, patting his chest, as if explanation were necessary. The geometry of his face is remarkable for its lack of planes and sharp angles. Every feature – eyes, cheeks, nose, lips, chin – is round, comprised of arcs or circles, lending him an aspect of perpetual jollity.

Raj blunders around the table, knocking into chairs; a moth attracted to a flame. After wiping his hand on his shirt, he offers it to Arjun. The palm is damp with sweat, the fingers plump and fleshy, like sausages. Putting his arm around Arjun's shoulders, Raj propels him to a seat, next to his own, squeezed between the table and the wall.

"Welcome, Machan. Sit here. Now we can talk."

Raj has beaten off the competition and won the guest's attention. His rivals drift back to their previous activities. Neleni disappears into the kitchen where Sunny is chattering shrilly to herself and the girls resume their game, although their noisy disputes are accompanied by frequent glances in Arjun's direction.

The dining room is a small, airless annex to the kitchen, with no windows and little ventilation. Lit by two kerosene lamps, and heated by the cooking next door, it is the hottest room in the house, guaranteed to gently stew anyone who overdresses. In a long-sleeved shirt, Arjun begins to baste in his own sweat.

"Drink, Machan?"

It is less a question than a command. Raj produces a bottle from under the table and fills a glass which he plants on the table with a purposeful thud. Still wrapped in the brown paper bag in which it was purchased, the bottle cannot be identified by its label, but Arjun guesses that it is arrack, a powerful spirit distilled from the fermented sap of palm flowers. He is not used to alcohol and wonders how to dispose of the liberal quantity which Raj has poured for him.

"Down the hatch, old boy."

Raj does a passable imitation of a British accent, the sort that characterises army officers and planters. It is an old joke but it amuses the children who have forgotten all pretence of a game and are watching the adults in anticipation of some new entertainment. Raj refills his own glass, sloshing some of the liquor on the tablecloth.

"Ooohh, Amma will kill me!"

Raj rolls his eyes in mock terror.

"We won't tell her, will we? It's our secret."

Saro nods urgently. Rani smirks. Raj leans closer to his guest. When he speaks, his breath, rank with raw liquor, blows hot in Arjun's face.

"So. Where are you from, Machan? What brings you here?"

A captive to his landlord's tipsy camaraderie, Arjun launches into a detailed account of his debacle with Pius. Nervousness loosens his tongue and he tells Raj more than he should. Later, he will regret it. But, it is difficult not to respond to Raj's wide-eyed attentiveness. He pounces on every detail with sympathetic exclamations: "No! The scoundrel! Outrageous! Tell me again!"

Like a lonely pye-dog, drawn to the warmth of a fire, Arjun laps up these crumbs of kindness.

"Oh. He was a bad man. A very bad man. That's not to say that anyone in his position would not be tempted …"

Raj pauses momentarily, contemplating what he would have done in Pius's position. Or Arjun's, for that matter. But his imagination does not stretch that far. He shrugs.

"Anyway, you're best off here. With friends. We'll take care of you, won't we Neleni?"

His wife, who is helping her mother in the kitchen, does not reply. She often ignores Raj's questions although she has the irritating habit of replying to comments not intended for her. To test whether she is really listening, Raj retaliates by making provocative statements. It is like dropping a depth charge. One must wait several seconds for a response. Raj raises his voice, aiming his comment at the kitchen door.

"Neleni is a wonderful woman but Oh! What a temper!"

"What is that? What is he saying about me?"

Neleni's voice rises from the kitchen.

"I was just telling our guest how wonderful you are, darling."

Nudging Arjun, Raj giggles under his breath: a naughty schoolboy, challenging teacher. Wedged into his seat, Arjun wishes he could escape. He does not wish to take sides in any dispute. The heat and the liquor, of which he has taken a few sips, add to his discomfort.

Her brow slightly furrowed, Neleni enters the room carrying a large bowl of rice which she places in the middle of the table. As she reaches past him, Raj grabs his wife, squeezing her around the waist.

"Stop it!"

Neleni darts away, making the children her excuse. A squabble over a doll has escalated into a flurry of pinches and slaps. Saro begins to whimper.

"Time to eat. Sit up."

Saro is lifted into a chair and pushed fast against the table, without room for manoeuvre or escape. Rani is left to fend for herself. Pulling one of the heavy chairs out from under the table, she climbs up, balances on her knees, then slides into a sitting position. However, with feet dangling a few inches above the floor, she is unable to push herself back to the table and so, remains at an awkward angle. No-one notices.

Neleni hurries back into the kitchen, putting a hand up to the back of her head. Arjun notices that her hair has been disarranged by Raj's playful embrace and that several strands of jasmine have been shaken loose. Unaccountably, those stray flowers annoy him, making him angry with Raj.

Sunny emerges from the kitchen. Perching on a chair, she inspects the lodger from the depths of her thick glasses, her eyes expanding or shrinking with every bird-like turn of her head. Arjun smiles at her cautiously. Sunny mutters something inaudible.

Neleni re-appears with the remaining dishes and, having removed the lids, spoons the food onto the plates: plain rice; mutton curry; buttered dhal; kankun fried with coconut; poppadums. Arjun is served first, then Raj, next the girls, then Sunny and, last of all, herself. It is an established sequence, followed at every meal except that, today, the place of honour has been accorded to Arjun, a fact that does not escape the attention of Sunny.

There is no western-style cutlery except for the serving spoons. Everyone eats in the traditional manner, mixing rice and curry into a ball with the fingers of the right hand and deftly scooping it into the mouth. The children are fed by the women: Saro by Neleni, Rani by Sunny. Like two fledglings, they wait for food to be dropped into their mouths by hands crowned with many clinking, gold bangles. It is an image of childhood, shared by every Islander, regardless of creed or social status.

"Come on, drink up."

Raj points to Arjun's glass.

Unable to avoid it, Arjun takes another sip of the arrack. It is a cheap, local variety, as unforgiving as a plateful of hot chillies. The raw liquor bites into his throat. He coughs and flushes, his eyes watering.

"Ah, you city-dwellers. Can't take your drink," jeers Raj.

"Always watering everything down with ice cubes and soda. You must learn to drink like us."

"Not everyone drinks as you do," remarks Neleni, quietly. She pours boiled water from a glass pitcher and passes the glass to Arjun who is struggling to catch his breath.

"Come, come, old fellow."

Raj thumps Arjun on the back with such force that he is winded.

"Stop! You're making it worse."

Neleni speaks sharply, as if to a naughty child. There is silence. Raj looks angry and sheepish. He has been shamed in front of his guest.

With a supreme effort, Arjun recovers himself, not wanting to be the cause of discord between his landlady and her husband

"I'm fine," he croaks. "Really. It just went down the wrong way. I'm so sorry."

His apology brings them to their senses.

"No, no. Don't worry."

Raj pats Arjun on the shoulder, gingerly, as if he might shatter under the impact. For a few seconds, no-one speaks. Then, with a stroke of inspiration, Raj asks:

"What do you think of Colin Cowdrey's batting?"

It is a question guaranteed to evoke a positive response, for every Islander is a passionate supporter of the game. Soon, the two men are immersed in a discussion of various cricketers' merits. Finally, Arjun enthrals Raj with an admission that he captained his school cricket team.

"Neleni, did you hear that? We have a cricketer in the family!"

Raj beams at his wife. All animosity is forgotten. Neleni smiles, distracted by thoughts of her father who was an avid follower of the game. Sometimes, he took her to matches. She liked that; enjoyed having him to herself, because he spoiled her. She misses him. Still cries, sometimes, when she is alone. Even though, in death, he betrayed her.

Quietly observing Neleni from the other side of the table, Arjun wonders what has made her so wistful. Lost in another world, she has ceased to listen to her husband. Raj prattles on, unaware of Neleni's mood, scuttling crab-wise from one topic to another, oblivious to the changing currents around him.

Firmly wedged into the narrow space between table and wall, Arjun is unable to move. He finds Raj's conversation increasingly difficult to follow and is starting to develop cramp in one leg. He wants to stretch but is unable to leave the table for fear of appearing rude. He is distracted by a slight pressure on his arm. Rani has slipped from her chair and quietly made her way over to where he is sitting. She is leaning against him, although she does not look at him.

Earlier that day the girls were marched from his room, all the way to the kitchen, before receiving a slap for disturbing the new guest. Usually, punishment is meted out on the spot. With childish cunning, Rani has concluded that there is something about this man's presence that prevents her mother from behaving normally. She does not want to offend him. Rani wonders how far her mother will go to keep the peace. She decides to test her.

"Rani, come here."

Neleni speaks gently, but there is a note of anxiety in her voice. Rani stares back at her sullenly then, in an audacious move, she wriggles sideways so that she is half-leaning, half-sitting on Arjun's knee. He is looking at her mother. Feeling aggrieved, Rani wriggles up onto his lap. He looks down at her, laughing, a little surprised. It is worth it, just to see the look on her mother's face.

Rani is not a beautiful child. Even at this age, she has a flamingo-like gawkiness with legs so thin they look like pieces of string with knots for the knees. Unlike her sister, whose pretty coyness is always rewarded, Rani knows that, in her case, flirtatiousness will not win favours from adults. However, on this occasion, prompted by the impish whisperings that frequently lead her into trouble, she decides to make up to the stranger just to see what will happen, her principal aim being to annoy her mother who punished her so severely this afternoon.

For a few seconds, she sits quite still, making sure of her position. Then, gazing into Arjun's eyes, with a look and manner borrowed from her sister, she lisps:

"Are you a prince?"

The effect on her mother is just what she planned. Neleni is staring anxiously at her eldest daughter, wondering what she will say next. Arjun smiles, a little puzzled.

"No," he says, simply.

Intoxicated by his attention, Rani pursues her line of enquiry.

"Do you live in a castle?"

"Tchaa," snorts Raj. "That child reads too much. Poor little Rani-poo thinks she is going to marry a prince. Ha, ha, ha! The closest she'll get to a prince is me!"

Slapping his knees, he laughs until his eyes fill with tears. The spell is broken. Playfully, he pinches his daughter's cheek. Another assault on her dignity. Determined not to cry, Rani bites her lip. Her most trusted friend has exposed her to ridicule. The cruelty of adults is difficult to fathom.

"Bed-time!" Neleni sweeps gracefully around the table.

"Off with her head," thinks Rani, wishing that she was a real queen. "And as for you ..."

She is trying to think of a suitable punishment for her father, when she is prised from Arjun's knee and dragged off by the arm. Arjun tries not to laugh at the cross little cat-face glancing back at him. If Rani had claws, they would be kneading her mother's flesh.

Once Neleni has disappeared with the girls, Raj tries to lure Arjun into a discussion of his favourite topic: politics. Leaning forward on his elbows and staring intently at his guest, Raj poses the question that currently causes him most agitation.

"What do you think of Bandaranaike? Will he get in do you think?"

"I don't know. I hadn't really thought about it."

It is an awkward moment. Arjun feels as if, somehow, he has let the side down. Like Raj and his family, he too, is a Tamil. Ceylon gained Independence from the British less than ten years ago. The constitution of the new state is a cause of anxiety for everyone, especially the powerful minority of Tamils; but Arjun has been too occupied with office politics to give much thought to who will win the forthcoming elections.

"Well, my boy," says Raj, portentously, "trouble is coming. I guarantee it. Especially if that bastard Bandaranaike gets in."

And with this gloomy prediction, Raj launches into a diatribe against politicians, some by name, some by party, all as a breed. Then, having exhausted this subject, and the last of the arrack, he begins to reminisce: old friends, family connections, memories that are meaningless to a stranger. Arjun becomes sleepy, his attention wanders; then, Sunny does something remarkable.

Getting up from her seat, the old lady shuffles to a dresser in the corner of the room. Standing on tiptoe, she reaches for a pottery jar, pulls it off the shelf and extracts a small clay pipe, a paper bag and a box of matches. Returning to the table, she perches on a chair, then rummages in the bag, mashing its contents with her fingers. Finally, she produces a large pinch of brown shreds and stuffs it in the pipe, tamping it down with her thumb. It is obviously some sort of tobacco but Arjun does not recognise it. He is intrigued.

"What are you putting in the pipe, Aunty?"

"Broken cigars. They last longer."

A reply, so matter-of-fact, that he feels ignorant for asking.

A match flares and Sunny draws on her pipe. Veiled in smoke, her shrunken face radiates contentment. Like most women of her generation, she never enters the conversation if men are present. It is easy to overlook her. She is a relic of the past, haunting the house like a family ghost.

But, although her presence is often ignored, Sunny sees everything, misses nothing. Neleni took special care with her appearance tonight. Her hair was pinned up, smooth and elaborate. She wore one of her better saris, pleated and tucked in such a way that it flattered her figure, and there was a trace of rouge on her cheeks.

Sunny also noticed Neleni's intolerance of her husband's tipsy ramblings which, if they do not exactly amuse her, have at least been treated in the past with detached leniency. Tonight, she became flustered and angry, embarrassed by him. Yet, she fussed excessively over Arjun; paying him small attentions, flushing when he looked at her. No lodger warrants this fuss.

Who is he, anyway? A boy from the city who wears European clothes and works in an office. How easily her daughter's head is turned. Still, Sunny consoles herself, he is no threat. He will not last long here. The ambling pace of this hill town will be too slow for him, its people too simple and unrefined.

Despite his efforts to look interested, Arjun was quickly bored by Raj's conversation this evening. And that is all he will get, night after night: Raj's political monologues and interminable reminiscences of times past or imagined. Sometimes, the same story will be repeated twice in one night, particularly when Raj has broached a second bottle of arrack. Just as he has done now.

No, this boy will not last. Soon, he will be on his way, back to the teeming ant-heap of the city. She gives him six months at most. Then everything will return to normal. He will pass out of memory, like a breeze over water, leaving nothing by which to remember him.

1955: Hooniyam's shrine

It is the hour before work and business is brisk at the shrine. Having left their shoes outside, office workers, stall-keepers, cooks and tradesmen press through the doors, eager to pay their respects to the god, Hooniyam. A constellation of oil lamps are placed before his image, prayers are offered, promises made, all in the hope of winning Hooniyam's favour.

After performing their devotions, the pilgrims depart as swiftly as they arrived, swarming down the steps and into the street, leaping onto buses, rickshaws or bicycles, or simply running, helter-skelter, through the choking traffic fumes. In the rush, some forget their shoes, leaving them behind in the courtyard.

The unclaimed shoes cause endless speculation; a conundrum that exercises the imagination of the shrine's priests. What happens to the owners of those sandals, ten or twenty of which are abandoned every week? And what of the owners who relinquish their slippers, not in pairs, but singly? No-one can recall a throng of one-legged pilgrims, yet the evidence suggests that they visit the shrine in scores.

Is it possible that one can leave for work suitably shod yet return home barefoot or, perhaps, wearing only one slipper? Or have the owners of unclaimed footwear been overtaken by catastrophe? Life can end abruptly in this country and Hooniyam is not always mindful of his flock. Quite the reverse. He still exhibits the capricious temper of a demon, for, until recently, that is exactly what he was.

***

The tide of visitors has subsided. The shrine is quiet, deserted except for a monk who is sweeping the courtyard. Swish! Swish! The twig broom whisks dust from crevices between the flagstones, collecting it into a neat pile. The monk sweeps the dust into a metal pan, then flings it back into the street.

He notices something tucked behind the gatepost. With a deft flick of the broom he propels the object out of its hiding place then bends over to pick it up. A single shoe. He inspects the dark corner carefully. Yes. There is the other. Rubber sandals, worn down at the heel, but they belong to someone. He places them carefully on the top step, so that they may be seen from the street. If they are not claimed within two days, it is the shrine's policy to distribute such shoes to the poor: if, that is, the poor have not already helped themselves.

Having cleaned the yard, the monk props his broom against the wall and washes his hands at a standpipe. The water clatters through a heavy metal drain as the monk performs his ablutions, washing his face and head, arms, hands and feet. He must be clean before entering the shrine. Hooniyam demands respect and, once his duties are finished, the monk has a special favour to ask.

Inside, the shrine is as dark as a cave. Most of the devotional lamps have gone out and those that are left throw a feeble, flickering light over the god's image. One could almost imagine him to be real. It is not a sight to comfort the faint-hearted for, despite his promotion to divine status, Hooniyam has retained his demonic features: the matted hair; the boar's tusks; the carmine lips suggestive of fresh blood and the seething belt of snakes, wound about his body.

After removing the guttered lamps, the monk lights others and re-arranges those that are still burning, filling any unsightly gaps. Offerings of faded flowers are thrown onto the rubbish heap behind the shrine, then the monk brushes the floor, paying particular attention to the area around Hooniyam's image. As he sweeps around the base of the statue, the monk can feel the god's eyes upon him, following every movement.

A shadow passes out of the door. The last worshipper leaves. The monk is alone. He must be quick. Laying down his broom, he reaches inside his robe and withdraws a small pouch, tied with string. Inside is a concoction of his own making, following principles learned from his father; an Ayurvedic doctor and a man versed in plant lore. The son has learned from the father, although the monk has put his knowledge to a different use.

But Hooniyam will understand. Because, before he became a deity, Hooniyam was king of sorcerers. The god has an intimate knowledge of the substances that cause suffering, as well as those that heal. Reaching behind the statue, the monk places the pouch in a space under the god's foot, where it will not be seen.

"Hooniyam, lord. I make you an offering. Invest these herbs with your power. Grant me success."

The monk needs no sign from the god to know that his wish has been granted. His faith is profound, complete, and unshakeable.

The shrine begins to fill again; pilgrims, drifting in at random, like dead leaves collecting in a courtyard. The monk resumes his sweeping although, every so often, he pauses and looks towards the road, as if he is expecting someone. A car pulls up. An official-looking limousine with a driver. It is not what the monk was expecting but he stops sweeping, waiting to see who will get out. He has a strange feeling of anticipation, as if he is bound, in some way, to the occupant of the car.

The driver walks round to the passenger side and opens the door. A man gets out. He is in his forties, well-groomed with neat, wire-rimmed glasses. He looks like a lawyer although, instead of a business suit, he wears a traditional white sarong, albeit one of superior fabric.

The man hesitates before entering the shrine. He is composing himself, trying to empty his mind of images that jostle for attention: faces, voices, endless meetings. A few months ago, victory was only an aspiration, incalculable and remote; now, it is close, but not yet within his grasp. He knows this feeling, has learned not to trust it. Success has eluded him before. He used to hold a position of prominence in the Government believing, for years, that he was in line for the premiership, only to learn that the Prime Minister, D.S. Senanayake, was grooming a relation, Sir John Kotelawela, to be his successor. No bond in this country is stronger than that of family.

He thinks bitterly of the argument with the Prime Minister's protégé that prompted his own resignation: polite words replete with venom, each man watching the other carefully as he spoke, like two snakes poised to strike. Somehow, a fragment of their conversation was leaked to the press, but it was reported as a piece of pantomime, conveying none of the original vitriol.

The politician had approached his rival, Sir John Kotelawala, hoping to persuade him to stand aside.

"Before he dies, my elderly father wants me to become Prime Minister."

But Sir John had family considerations of his own.

"Before departing this life, my aged mother wishes to see *me* as Prime Minister."

In the event, both were disappointed. The Prime Minister was succeeded by his own son. That was five years ago. Since then, Sir John has supplanted his cousin as Prime Minister and his exasperated opponent has formed his own political party. It has been a time of great uncertainty but, now, a new opportunity has arisen.

Conscious of his own party's waning popularity, Sir John has been panicked into calling a general election next year. It could be a fatal mistake. For that same year will mark the 2,500th anniversary of Buddha's death, the parinibbana. The country's Buddhist majority holds the view that nothing, not even elections, should interfere with the celebration of this important event. Sir John's decision has caused grave offence. There is a powerful groundswell of resentment which, if harnessed, will carry its rider to power. But how?

The politician has asked his advisers to devise a strategy; some have suggested an alliance with one party, some with another, but no plan has emerged. Sensing opportunity slipping away and tiring of the divisions among his supporters, the politician now seeks divine aid. A last resort, perhaps, but not an unusual one in this country of many faiths.

So, the politician, Mr Solomon West Ridgeway Dias Bandaranaike – more commonly known as S.W.R.D. Bandaranaike – has decided to petition Hooniyam for help.

***

As Mr Bandaranaike climbs the steps to the shrine, his sarong chafes his legs. It is the national costume of his country, particularly of the lower-class Sinhalese who he is hoping to woo, but he is unused to it and it makes him feel uncomfortable. Like many of his peers, Mr Bandaranaike has studied abroad, gaining a degree at Oxford University before qualifying as a barrister.

If he is honest, he feels more at home in the stiff, starched collars of western dress, the trousers and jackets. Deprived of his suit, he feels exposed with just a length of cloth to cover his bare legs. It is a primitive dress, despised by most of his western-educated contemporaries but, to prove that he is a man of the people he must wear it. The cloth shifts at his waist. He hopes that he has tied it properly and that it will not come undone. To be subjected to such humiliation would be worse than death for a man in his position.

He approaches a man selling votive lamps. Searching for coins, Mr Bandaranaike reaches for his pocket, only it is not there. How do these people carry their money? He is seething with frustration. He has come all this way to worship at the shrine and has no money to pay for an offering. There is no time to return to the house, he has an important meeting in just over an hour. He will have to ask his driver to lend it to him.

He is about to turn and walk out of the shrine when the lamp-seller smiles, displaying a row of red, betel-stained teeth. He holds out a lamp.

"There is no need for money, Mahayathaya."

"Thank you, brother."

Mr Bandaranaike takes the lamp. It is heart-warming to be recognised by the lamp-seller. The man must have seen one of his posters. Perhaps his campaign is working after all. But he pulls himself up short. He must not get complacent. This is just one man. Mr Bandaranaike needs the votes of thousands, no, scores of thousands, if he is to win.

He lights the lamp and places it at Hooniyam's feet, bowing humbly before the garish image. Mr Bandaranaike is a devout Buddhist but there is no restriction on praying to other gods. And many important people attend this shrine: Cabinet ministers, governors of banks, even Mr Bandaranaike's wife, Sirimavo, who will one day become Prime Minister herself. But that is in the future and, just now, Mr Bandaranaike has his own election to worry about.

He takes a deep breath, presses his hands together and whispers a prayer to Hooniyam.

1955: Hooniyam speaks

Ceylon is governed by belief. There are many faiths and even more gods; over thirty million in the case of Hindus. Every deity has a stake in the destiny of this nation. The gods are like family. They sit at your table, they eat your food, they direct your life. A god's disapproval is fatal, it will destroy you. But his favour will make you invincible. In this country, there is no room for scepticism – even amongst those who are educated. As everyone knows, including politicians, it is perilous to ignore the gods.

***

Mr Bandaranaike is still praying. Every so often, he peers up at the statue of the god that, distorted by the flickering heat of the candles, seems to dance on its pedestal. He closes his eyes and prays even harder. *Help me, Lord. Help me, Lord.* The same words, repeated over and over, until they roar in his ear.

"Out with it then. What do you want?"

Startled, Mr Bandaranaike looks around to see who has spoken. The closest person to him is a monk who is quietly sweeping the floor. But it could not have been him. He is too far away.

"For a politician, you don't pray with much conviction!"

There it is again. Right in his ear. But he can see no-one. Mr Bandaranaike's stomach quivers unpleasantly. Perhaps he has eaten something that disagreed with him, something that is causing him to hallucinate, hear voices. Perhaps he is going mad. The last weeks have been an unbearable strain.

"Well, come on. You asked me to listen, so here I am. Listening."

"Lord Hooniyam?"

"Who else?"

Mr Bandaranaike cannot believe his ears, or his luck. He has prayed many times in the past but never received a direct response. In fact, his faith has been waning recently. But today, he is conversing with a divinity. It is a miracle, an omen.

"Lord, teach me how to win the hearts of men."

"What makes you think I can teach you that?"

"Because, because ..."

Mr Bandaranaike falters. It is difficult to be both diplomatic and truthful.

"Because you think that, if a hairy demon, like me, can become a god, then there must be hope for a man, like you, to win an election?"

"Er, well, I wouldn't have put it quite like that."

"Of course not, you're a politician. You wrap up the truth, which is often uglier than I am, in candy-coated words. Much easier for the electorate to swallow!"

There is a deep subterranean gurgling. The god is laughing. His chuckling arouses the snakes, coiled about his waist, causing them to hiss softly. One, a great python, eyes Mr Bandaranaike hungrily.

"Very well. I'll tell you something that may help. My life story. Listen carefully. You might learn something."

The god shuffles about on his pedestal until he is comfortable. He relishes a new audience just as he used to relish human flesh. Of course, these days he is vegetarian. Well, almost. It is obligatory for gods. And, even he has to admit, that it is good sense. It would be bad manners, not to say bad business, to devour one's worshippers.

Hooniyam runs his tongue around his mouth, moistening his scarlet lips, then licking his tusks. They are as sharp as ever, honed to a fine point; but, nowadays, deprived of human bones, he has to use a file. It is a small vanity and a jealously-guarded secret. Only his friends, the snakes, know but, if they become a little loose-tongued from time to time, no harm is done. No-one with any sense waits around to listen to a snake.

Hooniyam casts an appraising eye over Mr Bandaranaike, assessing this new supplicant much as he used to weigh up human prey. Prime of life, good brain, reasonably fit, plenty of energy. It would take considerable effort to wear this one down. Involuntarily, Mr Bandaranaike's hand slips to where his pocket-watch would have been if he had been wearing a suit. As his fingers make contact with the soft folds of material, he frowns. No pocket. Hooniyam sees it all. Crowing inwardly, he pounces on this sign of weakness. The man is uncomfortable in these clothes and he is impatient, eager to be gone. Hooniyam decides to relate the full, unabridged version of his life story.

Hooniyam narrows his eyes. It is a warning. One does not anger the gods. Mr Bandaranaike composes his face, but finds it difficult to attain the right blend of enthusiasm and patience. Hooniyam is not fooled. After a leisurely inspection of his nails, he laces his fingers together and cracks his knuckles then, taking a deep breath, he proclaims:

"In the beginning ..."

His face contorted with adoration, Mr Bandaranaike sighs inwardly. But, this time, the god ignores the thoughts of his disciple. He is looking elsewhere, gazing into the past, reliving ancient slights, examining old wounds. It is a common pastime; one rapidly gaining popularity with Islanders.

"Like you, I was an aristocrat. Born to royal parents, I had a promising future, until someone started a vicious rumour. You know how news travels in this country? Rumour. A hint here, a whisper there. It was as true then as it is now. Gossip infects every conversation and is swallowed along with the truth. But everyone believes it because they heard it from a friend, or a relative. No-one ever checks the facts.

"Anyway, the story began to spread that my mother had consorted with a snake and that I was the result of their union. Of course, there was nothing in it. It was just a story, cooked up by my father's enemies. But it began to circulate and, soon, everyone had heard it, and many believed it. Even my father got to hear of it. It was never the same between my parents after that and my father never treated me with the same affection as he had before.

"Then came the final blow. An interfering old Brahmin told my father that when I grew up, I would murder my family. No-one would be spared. Already convinced that I was a freak and now, thoroughly terrified, my father banished me from the court.

"It was terrible. Imagine. A young child, abandoned by his family, driven out into the wilderness and left to die."

The god's voice quavers and he brushes away a tear with the back of his hand. Mr Bandaranaike shifts uncomfortably from foot to foot. He has left his watch at home in his jacket, but he knows that time is passing swiftly and he has an important meeting to attend. He wonders how long it will take Hooniyam to get to the point.

Without appearing to notice his guest's impatience, the god continues.

"I wandered without direction, begging food where I could until, finally, I found myself on the edge of a great forest. I was tired and hungry and the darkness offered me shelter and a respite from prying eyes and pointing fingers. So, I took refuge under the trees, living off snakes and wrapping them around my body to cover my nakedness. Serpents became my food, my friends and my counsellors."

Hooniyam's great python blinks sleepily and, tightening its grip around the god's waist, gives its master an affectionate squeeze that momentarily deprives him of speech. Hooniyam slaps the creature's head, forcing it to relax its grasp. The python hisses and lunges angrily at Mr Bandaranaike, forcing him to step back.

"Manners," says the god, mildly, tapping the python's flat skull. The snake recoils, still eyeing the politician malevolently.

"Don't worry. He won't harm you. Come closer so you can hear."

Gingerly, Mr Bandaranaike steps forward. The snake is only inches from his face, but now its head is in the crook of Hooniyam's arm and the god is stroking it affectionately. Although, the serpent looks as if it is sleeping, a sliver of yellow eye is still visible under its lowered lid. Mr Bandaranaike begins to sweat. He has always hated snakes.

"Now where was I? Oh, yes."

Hooniyam clears his throat and resumes his narrative.

"For many years, I roamed the forest, weeping and talking to myself, shouting curses that were swallowed by the hot, still air, until, one day, I arrived at a village. A stream ran beside it and I could hear the women singing as they washed their clothes. Their voices were like music. Hungry and desperate for the company of my own kind, I tried to approach them but, when they saw me, they screamed and ran away.

"I ran after them, trampling over the clothes that they had dropped in their haste. I followed them into the village and there, in front of me, seated on a bench and blind with age, was the old Brahmin whose lies had turned me into an outcast.

"Rage boiled inside me until I thought I would burst. I hated all humans, especially him. They had cheated me of my birthright and I wanted revenge. So I killed everyone in that village, tearing them apart with my bare hands and bathing in their blood.

"But I spared the Brahmin. I made sure he heard the screams of his children and grandchildren as they died. Then I left him, sitting on his bench, surrounded by carnage and broken bones and the terrible silence that follows death."

Mr Bandaranaike shivers. Hooniyam glows with pleasure. His disciple is suitably impressed.

"As I left that village, I laughed. I no longer needed love or acceptance. I had discovered something stronger. Power. After that, I revelled in my freedom, murdering and torturing as the mood took me.

"I hid in hollow trees beside deserted roads, waiting for lone travellers. As they passed, I'd leap out, shaking my shaggy mane and shrieking until the forest resounded with the noise of my unearthly howls. It was hilarious. The silly creatures were completely mesmerised. If they had run, they might have escaped, but they lost their legs to fear. They just stood there, gawping, too frightened to move, their eyes bolting from their heads like rabbits. I sucked the marrow from their bones and scattered the remains across the road for their friends to find. I killed without mercy or remorse, and everyone feared me. And then I met the boy with the twisted leg."

Hooniyam pauses and sighs, wistfully. Mr Bandaranaike, who has begun to wonder where all this is leading, is getting restless. He shuffles his feet and coughs, hoping that the god will soon get to the point. But Hooniyam will not be hurried.

"Yes, that boy was quite a character. He used to follow his friends to school. He could never keep up, always lagged behind. He seemed like easy prey, so I decided to have fun with him. I leapt out, did my dance, howled like a banshee, you know, all the scary stuff. But he just stood there, looking at me, slightly disdainful.

""What do you want?" he said. He might not have been able to run but he had a quick tongue and plenty of courage.

"For once, I was lost for words. Not that I talked to anyone any longer. I didn't know what to do. So, for want of a better plan, I scooped him up and took him back to my lair. As soon as we arrived, I could see he was unimpressed. I think it was the remains of my victims he objected to. You see, I used to arrange their bones in tasteful displays around my home. But the boy didn't appreciate my artistry. He told me to clean the place up and stop living like a pig. So I did. I threw out all my trophies just to please him. I'd never have done that for anyone else."

***

The god's voice trails off into a whisper. Mr Bandaranaike begins to nod. The gentle hum of other worshippers' prayers and the warmth from the many oil lamps has a soporific effect. Mr. Bandaranaike's eyelids are irresistibly heavy. He has had many late nights recently and often he is so busy that he simply forgets to eat. He thinks how nice it would be to take a nap. Mr Bandaranaike stifles a yawn, which does not go unnoticed by the god. Hooniyam commits that yawn to memory. It will not go unpunished. But for now, it will go unheeded. Pretending not to notice, Hooniyam rambles on.

"Following his abduction, the child and I talked a lot; nice, civilised conversation. He made me laugh and he reminded me what it was to be human. Ultimately, it weakened me. I began to fantasise about returning to society, living again with people.

"I roamed around the countryside for miles, daydreaming. When I saw people, I hid, but no longer with the intention of ambushing them, but of listening to their voices which were sweeter to me than birdsong. Then, one day, I discovered a lake, one of the irrigation tanks created by the old kings, the sort of thing my father would have built. I walked along the shore for miles. It was a beautiful day, not a ripple on the water and I was filled with new hope, having convinced myself that it was possible to become human again. Then, wandering down to the water's edge, I caught sight of my reflection.

"I hadn't seen myself for years and what I saw shocked me. My wild hair could be cut and combed, and I could send the snakes packing, but I could do nothing about my demon's tusks. I flew into a rage, uprooting trees and flinging them into the lake, and I cursed the child for awakening such pain in me.

"I can't remember what happened next, but a few days later I woke up in my cave with the boy's half-eaten body lying across my knees. That night, the forest echoed with demonic howls, but this time I was not play-acting. I wept until I could weep no more, then, to distance myself from what I could never have, I killed every human in sight. Soon, there was not a living person within fifty miles. At first, I enjoyed the peace, but then I got bored and a bit hungry so I began to travel, expanding the scope of my depredations.

"That's what got me into trouble. The gods had never been too bothered as long as I kept well out of their way. But I strayed into their territory. I used to hang around temples, picking off lone pilgrims. That really annoyed them. Then, one day, I saw Buddha preaching to his disciples. His voice resonated within me until I felt as if my head would explode. I could not stand it, so I charged into the crowd, intending to kill him. But his followers caught me and tied me to a pillar. I wriggled and squirmed, trying to get free, but the knots were too tight. My captors started to beat me, but Buddha stopped them.

"He asked me what I wanted. I raged and gnashed my teeth: "Blood sacrifices," I yelled.

"I expected him to be disgusted, in fact, I wanted him to be, but instead, there was pity in his eyes. He tried to reason with me but I was too steeped in my demonic ways to be talked round. I stubbornly resisted all persuasion so, reluctantly, Buddha banished me to Ceylon where I took up residence in a rock which still bears the stain of my victims' blood.

"For a long time, I lived as a demon until, eventually, human flesh began to lose its savour and I grew tired of the silly screams of village maidens. It didn't matter if I killed one or twenty; I got no pleasure from it. I was tired of cheap thrills. I began to think of the crippled boy and our conversations. I craved company, but no-one speaks to you if they think you're going to bite their head off!

"Tired of my life, I withdrew to the forest where the god Vishnu found me and made me protector of villages. Ha, Ha! What an irony. Poacher turned gamekeeper, that's what I was. Of course, Vishnu forbad me to take any more sacrifices but he made up for it by appointing me commander of all demons and protector of the Island's temples. And that was the beginning of my transformation. I reported regularly to the gods on the doings of men. It was important work. Only I could do it."

The god pauses and puffs out his chest. It is the cue for praise.

Hooniyam taps his foot, impatient for a response. But Mr Bandaranaike's attention has wandered. Distracted by the admiring whispers of two elderly ladies, he has turned to acknowledge them with his best patrician smile.

"Am I boring you?" Hooniyam snaps.

"No, Lord, of course not."

Mr Bandaranaike senses danger. He must not offend Hooniyam, or there will be no answer to his question, no divine intervention, and a whole morning will have been wasted. Bowing low, he presses his hands together in prayer.

"Please continue, Lord. Your story is most instructive."

Hooniyam leans forward and whispers confidentially.

"Although I am a god, I have retained some of my yakkha's powers. As a demon, I specialised in stomach ailments. I can play some wonderful pranks. At weddings and feasts, I creep up behind important people and, just by clicking my fingers, I can make them shit in front of their guests. You should see their faces when they feel the sudden movement of their bowels!"

"Very amusing, Lord."

Mr Bandaranaike forces a thin, unconvincing smile. Hooniyam might have royal blood in his veins, but he has spent too much time in the company of peasants.

"I don't suppose there's someone you would like me to humiliate? Some opposition politician, perhaps."

Hooniyam peers hopefully at Mr Bandaranaike.

"Er, well, tempting as that is, Lord, I actually came to ask a different favour?"

"Oh, and what might that be?" Hooniyam replies, tetchily.

It is rare for him to offer his help, and even rarer for it to be rejected. Like all those with demon blood, he has a remarkably thin skin where his own feelings are concerned.

"I, er, wondered if you would help me in the coming election?"

"Oh, yes. That. I'd forgotten. Well, you won't win by wearing those ridiculous clothes!"

Mr Bandaranaike winces. The god can be spiteful when he chooses.

"I quite agree, Lord. It requires divine wisdom to win the hearts of men. I thought, perhaps …"

"… you thought I would do your work for you. Well, I won't."

Crossing his arms, the god turns his head away. He has resumed the frozen posture of a statue. Panic-stricken, Mr Bandaranaike drops to his knees.

"No, no, Lord. Please don't go. Not yet. I desperately need your help."

"Got him," thinks Hooniyam, smiling slyly, his face rippling in the heat cast up from the oil lamps at his feet. "He's mine."

And just to make the politician squirm, Hooniyam holds his statue-pose for a few seconds more. He would increase the suspense if he could but wisps of jasmine-scented smoke float upwards and tickle his nostrils. He feels a sneeze coming on. Hooniyam sniffs, waves his hand in front of his nose and makes a face.

"Ugh. Whoever brought that stuff? Disgusting!"

He looks down at Mr Bandaranaike, who is still on his knees, staring up at the god hopefully. Hooniyam casually inspects his nails.

"Of course, what you need is someone like Visuddhananda."

"Who?"

"Visuddhananda. Extraordinary to think how one Buddhist monk single-handedly transformed a rustic demon, like me, into a god. He certainly turned this place around. Rebuilt the shrine, dedicated it to me, and knocked those silly old priests right off their perch. This shrine was going nowhere with them in control. You need someone to do the same for you."

"Could Visuddhananda help me?"

"Good heavens, no. He's too busy looking after me. Anyway, it'll take more than one man to dislodge this Government. You need someone with influence, who can lend you his own army of supporters."

"Oh dear. I can't think of anyone." Mr Bandaranaike is crestfallen, his disappointment so intense that it is visible to Hooniyam as a purple aura.

Hooniyam shrugs, as if to say "Too bad". It is fun, playing this powerful man like a fish on a line. But Hooniyam already has someone in mind. A Buddhist monk, a man both powerful and proud who, for now, supports the politician. Hooniyam begins to formulate an amusing plan, full of twists and turns, tricks and deceit; a plan that will further his own ambitions as well as paying back humanity for the suffering it has caused him; a plan that the other gods must not discover.

"Now I think about it," says Hooniyam, teasingly, "there is one who might help you. I believe Buddharakkita Thera is quite interested in politics."

Buddharakkita Thera, the abbot of Kelaniya monastery. Why has Mr Bandaranaike not thought of this before? Buddharakkita wields enormous influence. He is Secretary of the Buddhist monks' party and has supported several of Mr Bandaranaike's colleagues in previous elections.

"Do you really think he would help me?"

"You'd better ask him, hadn't you?"

"I will. Thank you, Lord. An excellent idea. I will do as you suggest."

Mr Bandaranaike makes his obeisance to Hooniyam, this time with a proper show of respect but, in his excitement, he lets his thoughts run unguarded, allowing the god to read his mind. Hooniyam uncovers desires that the politician hardly dares to admit to himself.

"Well, well," muses the god, "You're more ambitious than I thought. Your desire for power is almost as limitless as my own. It doesn't stop at winning the election, does it?"

He watches Mr Bandaranaike walk slowly from the shrine: the politician's posture, the carriage of his head, every movement is studiedly modest but nothing can conceal his love of adulation from the god's all-seeing eye. Awed by the presence of this illustrious man, other worshippers halt their devotions to watch him pass. Some even pursue Mr Bandaranaike down the steps to press him for help, treating him with the reverence normally reserved for a god, their hands pressed together in prayer. By common instinct, they scent success and are drawn, ineluctably, towards it.

Consumed with jealousy, Hooniyam forgets how he, too, once stole the worshippers of other gods. With narrowed eyes, he watches the politician as, surrounded by an adoring crowd, he holds court at the gates of the shrine.

"Infernal cheek!" growls the god. "I see that nothing short of divinity will satisfy you. Well, in that case, I shall help you achieve your goal."

And, chuckling maliciously, Hooniyam places Mr Bandaranaike at the centre of his plan, weaving his schemes around the politician as a spider spins silk around a fly.

Despite the politician's presumptuous behaviour, Hooniyam experiences a perverse depression after Mr Bandaranaike's departure. Truth to tell, without politics, duplicity, and surreptitious plans for insurrection, life has few worthwhile distractions, even for a deity.

Witness Hooniyam's daily case-load: seven demands for curses (minor ailments, nothing fancy); five requests for hexes to be lifted (all but one imaginary); twelve tales of marital infidelity (a higher number than usual, probably due to the combined effects of cheap arrack and a recent festival); two sagas of crop failure (thankfully less of these since Hooniyam has taken up residence in town), and one plea from a weeping child to find his pet squirrel (surreptitiously swallowed by Hooniyam's python).

At present, the god is occupied with a woman whose husband has deserted her; a story that is repeated at least six times a day with little variation regarding either the sex, age or general unattractiveness of its narrator. Weeping and beating her scrawny breast, the woman exhorts the god to curse her errant spouse. However, she is not so far gone in grief as to have overlooked all eventualities. In case the god proves deaf to her entreaties, she has brought along an ancient priest to intercede on her behalf.

"As if I could ignore her," groans Hooniyam, screwing a finger into his ear to muffle the woman's shrieking. But, no sooner has he stopped up one ear, than the other is assaulted by a loud droning from the priest. Stone deaf, the old man compensates for his lack of hearing with heightened volume, shouting imprecations which drown the restrained murmurings of other worshippers.

"Oh Lord Hooniyam, show us your mercy. Grant this woman's prayer. Use your sword of justice to punish her husband's wickedness."

There follows a lengthy incantation of the woman's woes which ends with a request for her husband to be visited with leprosy.

"Leprosy!" snorts Hooniyam. "That's not my speciality. You should have done your research before you came. What an insult! I'm not surprised your husband left you, you ugly old witch. And look at the priest you've brought with you. A charlatan if ever I saw one. He pretends to speak to me but he's not even looking in the right direction. Totally blind in one eye. And he certainly can't hear me. Deaf old fool, your breath stinks of garlic. May you step on a scorpion!"

The serpents around Hooniyam's waist writhe and flames leap from his mouth as he roars in the old man's ear. The priest continues to shout his prayers, his one good eye fixed on the wall above Hooniyam's head. Defeated, the god sighs.

"Oh, all right. I give up. I'll curse your unfortunate husband, but it'll be dysentery, not leprosy. Next time go to Kali."

By chance, the old priest chooses to end his prayers at this point; which is lucky, because if he had continued, Hooniyam would have treated both supplicants to a nasty dose of enteritis.

Exhausted, the god leans back on his pedestal and turns his eyes to heaven. He longs for a real challenge, some excitement. A god's life is comfortable, but dull. As one's status increases, so the real extent of one's power diminishes, and it is the exercise of power that Hooniyam misses. The only enjoyment he derives from performing miracles is a mild tingling of the scalp, not the all-consuming thrill he enjoyed as a yakkha wreaking devastation, answerable to no-one.

It is as if his blood supply is slowly being cut off. What he now wields is not the untrammelled power of a demon, real, raw, red-blooded potency, but a finite power, subject to conditions, hedged about by regulations and, worst of all, subject to the consensus of a million other deities. In Hooniyam's view, power-sharing is not power at all.

Of course, he can still cast spells, but if someone asks him nicely to lift his curses then, as a god, he is bound to obey. What sort of power is that? What Hooniyam craves is unfettered, elemental power, the kind that should be wielded by a king of the yakkhas. *King, rajah* ... the word sounds sweet in any language – even Tamil.

Hooniyam savours it for a second, letting it roll sweetly over his tongue like honey from a wild bees' nest. For too long the demons have been held in thrall to the gods, but if his plans come to fruition ... Hooniyam is distracted by a snuffling sound at the base of the altar. Looking down, he sees the former governor of a national bank running around on all fours.

"Oh god, he's pretending to be a pig again! No wonder he got the sack. He seems to think these farmyard antics amuse me. Moron! Come back when you've got something intelligent to say."

Wiggling his ample posterior in the air, the man begins to root through offerings of flowers with his nose.

"Oh really, this is too much!"

Hooniyam raises his hand and begins to murmur a spell. He is about to subject the man to an excruciating bout of the squits when something in the crowd catches his eye.

"Hello. What's this?"

Huddled in a quiet corner of the shrine are three men, their heads together, whispering intently.

"A conspiracy unless I am much mistaken," murmurs the god.

1955: The conspiracy

Hooniyam leans forward to get a better look. The group comprises a monk, a policeman, and a third man wearing the sarong and dirty vest of a labourer.

"Wait a minute, that one looks familiar. Of course, it's the monk from the shrine. The one that left me a present this morning. Haven't had time to open it yet. I've always had a soft spot for him. He's a true believer. He can't see me yet, but he hears me. Shows promise. I could work with him."

As if sensing the god's attention, the monk looks up, staring directly at Hooniyam. At that moment, the slumbering python awakes. Stretching its head in the monk's direction, it tastes the air with its forked tongue then, turning back, nudges Hooniyam's arm excitedly.

"Yes, yes. I know. His eyes. Pale like yours. He's a descendant of the Naga people, the serpent tribe, or I'm much mistaken. Not that he'd ever admit it, even if he knew. They originated in India, and he thinks of himself as pure Sinhalese. But he will suit my purpose very well. Now, let's have a look at the other two."

Hooniyam scrutinises the policeman.

"Hmm. Quite high-ranking. An Assistant Superintendent of Police, no less."

The god prides himself on his knowledge of the modern world.

"I like the look of him. Reminds me of myself when I was a yakkha. I'll bet he's merciless with prisoners. No scruples whatever. Not averse to torture although he probably calls it interrogation. Excellent. Now, what about this one?"

At the very moment that Hooniyam turns his attention to the third man, the fellow wanders over to one of the god's lesser images and inspects the carving with evident distaste.

"Ugh, a non-believer. What's he doing here?"

Hooniyam recoils as if stung.

"This is worse than that pig-worshipper. At least he pays his respects. Unbelievers have such bad manners. Never even acknowledge you. Look how the fellow stares about him like some sort of tourist. Disgraceful."

Hooniyam snarls, baring his monstrous fangs but the man in the sarong can neither see nor hear him. Even Hooniyam's curses are powerless against an unbeliever. In the good old days, as a yakkha, Hooniyam could have torn him limb from limb, but now he is impotent. The god has no option but to curb his temper and amuse himself by eavesdropping on the conversation now taking place between the policeman and the monk.

"If you're going to do it, it will have to be soon," says the policeman in a low voice.

"I've got a contact in the Government Agent's office. He says there is going to be an investigation. Once that starts we'll have lost our opportunity."

"And you still think this man is the right target?"

"Yes. His workers haven't been paid for months. They won't lift a finger to help him. And the location is sufficiently remote for you to work unhindered. It's an ideal opportunity for us. He's a Tamil. One who is known to have abused his position. No-one really cares about him, not even his own people. This is exactly what we need to rally support in the countryside."

The monk makes no reply. He is thinking. The policeman draws a handkerchief from his pocket and wipes the corners of his mouth. He is sweating and there are dark stains around the armpits of his khaki shirt.

Hooniyam nods his head in approval. "Here's a man whose promotion has already outstripped his moral capabilities. And he still wants more. I can smell his greed from here, oozing from every pore. No wonder he sweats so much."

The policeman mops his face. He is becoming impatient.

"And what about your friend over there? What does he say?"

With a slight motion of the head, he indicates the man in the sarong.

"He's not sure."

"Not sure? That's typical. These student-types are full of big ideas, but when it comes to doing anything, they always sit on the fence."

"That's not true. You don't know what you're talking about. He's one of our best men. Never thinks of himself. Totally dedicated to the cause. He'll do the job. Whatever it is."

A pale flame flickers in the monk's eyes, rendering them luminous in the gloom, his thin face becomes taut and a nerve twitches at the corner of his mouth. He is like a creature readying itself to strike. The policeman is either ignorant of his danger, or does not care.

"As I said, student-type. Can't trust any of them. How's he know so much anyway?"

"He got himself a job, shadowing our target. For the past month, he's been working as site foreman. He knows everything that goes on there. Not bad for a student-type."

This sarcasm is lost on the policeman. He makes a face, a shrug of the eyebrows, a spasm of the lips, to show that he is unimpressed.

"So what's he found out?"

"We won't have any trouble from the workmen, but our target has got some influential connections."

"Ha!" the policeman exclaims in a loud voice. Startled, several worshippers turn their heads, but when they see the source of the disturbance, they quickly look away.

"Not so loud," hisses the monk, but his warning does little to stem the policeman's mirth. The man's thick lips spread in a slow, lascivious smile, one of the few to lighten that pock-marked face and he chortles. It is a deep, hollow sound, devoid of humour.

"So, your target has influential connections, has he?"

The policeman lays particular emphasis on the word "target", emphasising his disdain for the theatricality with which civilians approach secret work.

"Yes."

The monk seems disinclined to elaborate, so the policeman helps him.

"If, by 'connections', you mean a certain politician with interests in a number of rubber and coconut plantations, then you need not worry. I spoke to him last week and he made it clear to me that he no longer has any interest in protecting your target. With the elections coming up, he can't afford to be associated with someone of such questionable morality."

Hooniyam, who has been listening avidly to their conversation, roars with laughter. Politicians, they are all the same! Morality only features on their agenda as a variable affecting success.

"What's happening?"

The man in the sarong has rejoined the monk and the policeman. At first sight, he is unremarkable: a tall, rangy fellow in his late twenties with short, stubbly hair that looks as if he has been recently shorn. It is his eyes that mark him out from the ordinary, shining from the depths of their dark sockets with a wilful intelligence that signifies either genius, or madness.

"I was discussing our plans with the Superintendent here."

The monk's tone loses some of its former asperity as he addresses the newcomer. He treats the man in the sarong with a deference bordering on awe, a fact not lost on either Hooniyam or the policeman.

"Is that wise?"

The man in the sarong speaks disdainfully.

"I would have thought that more secrecy would have been advisable. I don't know why you called a meeting here. It's hardly private. We need some out-of-the-way, godforsaken spot. Besides this place gives me the creeps. It positively reeks of desperation."

"How can you say that? Mr Bandaranaike was here just before you arrived," the monk parries, defensively.

"That just proves my point. He's clutching at straws because, at the moment, he hasn't got a hope of winning. I'm sick of hearing that saying: ' *the Buddha for refuge, the gods for help*'. Every useless politician repeats it like a mantra to cover his own inadequacies. What we need is action, not some forlorn hope of divine intervention."

"What! I've never heard such blasphemy."

Scandalised, Hooniyam throws up his hands in horror while the snakes at his waist spit their disgust. Even the monk, who seems to be in awe of the other man, murmurs his disapproval.

"Oh well, have it your own way. I'm going now. You know where to find me."

With a cursory nod to the policeman, the man in the sarong turns and strides out of the shrine. Pale with indignation, the policeman turns to his companion.

"So that's the kind of company you keep. I hope you know what you're doing. He seems highly unreliable to me."

"He's not," says the monk passionately, then, lowering his voice he repeats: "He's not. He's the best."

"Hm. Wish I could agree. Tell me what you decide to do. I'll be ready."

With that, the policeman departs while the monk lingers at the shrine. Approaching Hooniyam's image, he looks over his shoulder to see if he is being observed, then, reaching forward, removes the pouch he placed under Hooniyam's foot earlier that morning. Closing his hands in prayer around the bag, the monk bows to Hooniyam's image.

"Hey, that's mine," the god protests. "You're not supposed to take it back."

"Oh Lord, grant me your favour. Bless this offering and invest it with your divine potency."

Hooniyam is intrigued.

"That's the second time you've asked for my blessing. It must be important. Well, come on then. Let's see what's inside the bag!"

Opening his hands, the monk holds the bag up before him as he bows his head in prayer. Unable to contain his curiosity, Hooniyam dips a finger inside, then licks it.

"Ooh hoo, oh, uh!"

Hooniyam coughs until he nearly chokes and his eyes water.

41

"Good heavens. That's a strong one. Where did you learn to make that? Of, course. Your father was an Ayurvedic doctor, wasn't he? But that stuff's hardly going to cure anyone. Quite the opposite. What do you want it for, I wonder?"

For a second, Hooniyam is able to penetrate the monk's thoughts but, just as suddenly, they are concealed within a whirling magenta cloud. The monk has begun to chant his prayers.

"Damn! Just when it was getting interesting. Well, my son, I won't be put off so easily. If you want my help, I must know what you're up to. And, if you won't tell me, I must find out for myself."

Having finished his devotions, the monk turns to leave. But Hooniyam is determined to follow. Slipping quietly from his pedestal, he leaves his statue in charge of the remaining worshippers and creeps stealthily after the monk.

1955: Sunny's dilemma

Sunny holds a match to the kerosene lamp and watches as the flame glows, dully at first, then brighter, its light creeping across the kitchen, illuminating pans and glass jars ranged along the shelves. She fills the kettle at the stone sink then, bending under its weight, she hobbles to the stove where she heaves the cumbersome vessel onto the hob and lights the gas.

Having completed these tasks, she leans against the table for a few seconds, catching her breath, noting how, every day, she needs more time to recover from these simple chores. But she does not resent them. These are the rituals that give substance to her life and which she performs every morning, rising before dawn to enjoy a brief dominion over the silent house before the others are awake.

The battered old kettle emits a puff of steam from its spout then, as the water boils, it begins to rock on the hob, its lid jiggling and rattling while small bubbles foam around the rim. The water is not for her. It is for Raj who is usually the next to get up. He likes hot water for shaving.

If either of them wants tea, Sunny will make it in a saucepan, boiling water, tea, spices and milk together to make a strong, aromatic brew. However, Sunny's husband Edward used to make tea the English way, using this very kettle. Boiling the water every morning reminds her of him.

Having recovered her breath, Sunny makes her way to the dresser where she retrieves her smoking paraphernalia from the pottery jar. Clutching the pipe, matches and tobacco bag to her chest, she slowly skirts around the kitchen, guiding herself around the table and chairs with her free hand, occasionally stopping if her breath comes too slowly or her heart beats too fast.

Her joints are still rigid from the inactivity of sleep, a stiffness that eases a little as the day wears on but which rarely leaves her entirely. It is as if her body is preparing itself for the final rigor of death: without her consent, it follows a secret protocol, conniving at its own destruction. In some respects, it is a comfort. Sunny is required to do nothing but wait.

The kettle sputters angrily.

"Ahh!" Sunny waves her hand dismissively. She hasn't the energy to walk all the way back to the stove to turn it off. Anyway, Raj will be up soon.

As she slowly covers the short distance to the back door, Sunny reflects that, in old age, movement no longer consists of the effortless direction of one's limbs but a time-consuming process of pushing, pulling and coaxing them into submission. The body that was once her vehicle is now her burden and, increasingly, she longs to be free of it.

Having dragged herself to the door, Sunny rattles the big iron key in its lock, clutching it with her frail, bird-like fingers, willing it to turn, concentrating all her effort into a single action that others find easy but which has become so difficult for her.

Finally, the lock yields. Feebly pushing the door away from her, Sunny manoeuvres herself onto the step outside where she stands, leaning against the lintel for support, as she expertly fills her pipe with one hand.

The morning air is refreshing and she can smell the scent of the large temple tree at the front of the house although she cannot see it. She breathes in slowly, her eyes shut, savouring the smell. She wore those flowers on the day that she met her husband.

"Good morning, Edward," she whispers, listening for his answer on the quiet morning air.

As she draws on her pipe, she smiles. She greets her husband every morning, although she cannot see him and he has been dead for many years. Still, it cannot hurt, just to mention his name; here, where it is quiet and no-one else is listening. If Edward can hear her, he will know that she has not forgotten, that she still loves him.

But will Edward still love her? Would he even recognize the wizened bag of bones that was once his wife, the withered old woman, so different from the beautiful girl that he fell in love with? Could he see beyond his wife's failing flesh to what lies inside; a tenderness as fresh and sweet as the day they were married? It is a question with which she has become increasingly preoccupied.

"When I die, will you be there to meet me, Edward?"

She always believed that he would but, recently, her faith has been shaken by unforeseen events.

***

For years after Edward's death, Sunny contrived to re-create his presence. She made a small shrine in her bedroom consisting of his photograph, two candles, one on either side of the picture frame, and a small vase of fresh flowers. After saying her prayers, night and morning, she would meditate on Edward's face, summoning him to her until she was able to conjure his image at will and carry it with her wherever she went.

Thus, Edward became her constant companion. The perfect gentleman, he always appeared as he had on their wedding day; dressed in his best suit, a flower in his buttonhole, young, smiling and happy, without the trace of sadness that haunted him in later years. She would talk to him in the kitchen as she leant over the stove or picture him, sitting next to her at meal-times. Sometimes, his presence seemed so real that she would even set an extra place at table – a fact dismissed by her family as the effect of age and forgetfulness.

In this way, Sunny derived much comfort from her deceased husband, particularly when her influence in the family began to wane. Removed from domestic politics, he was always there by her side, silent, gracious and smiling. Together, they would sit, observing, listening, forgotten, a pair of ghosts whose opinion was never sought and whose advice, if it had been given, would have been ignored.

"You see," she would murmur to him. "We are alike. Invisible. No-one sees us."

With Edward for company, Sunny was happy, convinced that she was more spirit than flesh, inhabiting a realm divorced from the passions and petty cares of life. But, in recent months, something has happened to rob her of his presence.

Although removed to the fringes of family life, Sunny is keenly aware of its changing dynamics. She still has eyes in her head and she misses nothing. Since Arjun's arrival six months ago, her daughter has undergone a subtle change, the kind of thing that only a mother notices.

Neleni now pays attention to her appearance. Her hair is no longer wispy and unkempt; she wears one of her better saris, even for housework, and her cheeks are artfully dusted with rouge, relieving them of their normal pallor and lending her complexion a peach-like hue. It cannot be denied. She is radiant. But she is also acutely sensitive to Arjun's presence. Recognising his footfall before others can even hear it, she straightens her sari, looks at herself in the mirror, smoothes her hair.

Sunny wonders if her son-in-law has noticed. Probably not. But Sunny has noticed and what she has seen has caused her profound disquiet. Her first reaction was to summon Edward, ask him what he thought. He would know what to do, but the image that she invoked only smiled at her; a sweet, kindly, vacuous smile devoid of intelligence or understanding. The face of her husband had no more substance than that of his photograph. Her inability to make Edward speak forced Sunny to admit that the image with which she had comforted herself all these years did not have an independent existence, but was simply a fabrication of her own making.

And so began a period of profound anxiety in which she was tormented by questions; questions of the utmost importance because they concerned her journey to the next life. Sudden doubt gave rise to a recurrent dream in which she saw the dead as a mass of faceless souls, countless anonymous entities milling around like sago in a tub. How would Edward ever find her, or she him?

She was so disturbed by that dream that she sought the advice of the local priest, and instantly regretted it. Still fresh from his studies, the young man had a disturbing tendency to resort to the letter of scriptural text. Having misunderstood Sunny's fears, he told her that there was no male or female in heaven. In other words, the search for Edward was futile. Intended as comfort, the priest's words filled Sunny with despair.

With her belief in Edward's presence in this life shattered, Sunny lost any hope of being reunited with him in the next. The thread which she had relied on to guide her through death had been cut and she was adrift. Fearful and angry, she blamed both Neleni and Arjun for her anguish.

Ironically, it was Raj who comforted her. Normally dismissed by everyone, including his wife, as insensitive and unfeeling, Raj was the only one to notice Sunny's listlessness and to guess at its cause.

"Come on, Aunty," he had said one day, after finding her sitting forlornly in the kitchen. "Come outside with me and have a smoke."

He had guided her out onto the step and waited while she lit her pipe then, quite unexpectedly, he had said:

"My mother used to have a saying: 'There are more things in heaven and earth'. I think she was right. We can't expect to know everything."

Then, without another word, he had kissed her gently on the forehead and left for work. Sunny had continued to smoke as she watched the sun and, inexplicably, she had felt closer to Edward in those quiet moments than she ever had with his image before her.

Since that day, she has followed the same routine every morning, squatting on the step with her pipe, whispering her greetings to the sky. It is like putting a message in a bottle and casting it out to sea. It is enough to send the letter. She needs no reply. She has learned that faith cannot be confirmed by knowledge or the senses: it depends, not on certainty, but the courage to step alone into the dark. Today, as she exhales, releasing a slow stream of smoke from her lips, she wonders if this is how the soul will leave her body. It is a pleasant thought.

A crescent of light shimmers on the horizon. The sun is rising. In a few minutes, the night-time darkness will be utterly consumed then Sunny will hold her face up to the sky and let the warm rays caress her skin. The house will gradually come to life, its inhabitants waking to throw themselves into preparations for a ridiculous picnic; one planned by Arjun and Neleni. Sunny wonders if Raj will accompany them. She wants to warn him, but she knows that he will not listen to her. He will never hear anything against Neleni, even from her mother.

"Are you all right there, Aunty?"

Raj pokes his head out of the door. His hair is rumpled and his eyes puffy from sleep.

"Of course. Why shouldn't I be?"

Sunny's prickly tone is guaranteed to prevent further enquiry.

"No reason."

As if dodging an invisible bullet, Raj quickly pulls his head back through the door.

"Poor man," thinks Sunny.

1955: Preparing a picnic

It is a holiday and Neleni is scurrying about the kitchen, packing food for the picnic. But, already, she is panicking. She does not know if there will be enough curry to go around and the rice is taking longer than usual to cook. It is hot and she is becoming flustered.

They are going on a trip to Sigiriya, a historic site with many artistic treasures. It was Arjun's idea. Somehow, he persuaded his boss to lend him a car and a driver for the day so that they could all travel in comfort. Neleni was enraptured when he first told her of his plan. For weeks she has been able to think of nothing else, but today she feels disappointed and ashamed.

Her enthusiasm is not shared by the others. Saro has thrown a tantrum and is being comforted by her grandmother; Sunny has flatly refused to accompany them and Raj is still undecided. Only Rani shares her mother's excitement. Embarrassed by her family's lukewarm response, Neleni is determined to make the day a success.

***

Mangoes, watermelon – she knows they are here somewhere. But where? She bought them in the market only yesterday. Sunny must have put them away, or hidden them. Nothing that Sunny does these days surprises Neleni. Her mother's behaviour is becoming increasingly eccentric and, most difficult of all, she has developed an irrational hatred of Arjun which she makes no attempt to hide.

Neleni discovers the fruit, wrapped in newspaper, and stowed in a dark corner under the sink. On her hands and knees, she grapples with the makeshift parcel, which falls apart as she lifts it, spilling ripe mangoes onto the floor and bruising their soft flesh.

"Why did she do that?" thinks Neleni, angrily.

"She knows I never keep fruit here. And wrapped in paper! I might not have found them until they were rotten. Silly, silly old woman!"

For once, she has no guilt about the animosity which she sometimes feels towards her mother.

***

Having packed the fruit into a basket, Neleni begins to fill tiffin boxes and containers with cooked food. Yesterday, she prepared a batter from rice and split peas, leaving it to ferment overnight and, this morning, having spooned it into small moulds, she has cooked it in a steamer to make idlis; small white cakes, spongy in texture, which fit perfectly into the palm of one's hand.

She has also made sambar, a hot spicy sauce like thin soup, which can be poured over the idlis, and a vegetable curry made from okra. It is unusual for her family to eat purely vegetarian food but they will be joined at Sigiriya by Raj's cousin. The cousin's family are strict Hindus who eat no meat. The cousin's wife has offered to bring her own food but Neleni will not hear of it. One does not invite others to a picnic and expect them to feed themselves. However, secretly, she is beginning to regret her generosity.

47

Having fastened the metal clips around the lid of the last container, Neleni stretches, straightening her back and rubbing her neck. She is already tired and the day has hardly started. Now she must wash and dress the children, feed them, and get herself ready. Sunny would normally help with such chores but this morning she has made herself scarce.

"Just when I need her," thinks Neleni, bitterly. Picking up a clean tea-towel, she buries her face in it, rubbing her palms over her eyes which are stinging with perspiration.

"A waste of time!"

Neleni drops the towel from her eyes and sees her mother, a small crooked shadow outlined in the doorway.

"What do you mean?"

"You are wearing yourself out with all this work. And for what?"

"So that we can have a day out. And enjoy ourselves."

"Hah!"

"It was very kind of Arjun to have asked us. The girls will love it."

"Saro won't. She says she doesn't want to go."

"She will enjoy it when she gets there."

"She won't. She is still crying."

Pursing her lips, Neleni busies herself with the various baskets containing food, trying to divert the conversation from its present, dangerous course. But Sunny will not be distracted.

"It's not fair."

"What isn't?"

"You are forcing her to go just to please yourself."

"What?"

"You're the only one who wants to go. Saro doesn't want to go, I don't want to go, Raj doesn't want to go."

"Oh!"

Neleni throws down the tea-towel and turns her back on her mother, gripping the sides of the sink as she tries to rein in her anger. Then, having taken a deep breath, she speaks as slowly and calmly as possible.

"Amma, you are not going anyway, Saro is just being a chump and Raj can never make up his mind about anything until the last minute. This is the way it always is. So tell me why I am being unfair."

"Because that man is not your husband."

Speechless, Neleni turns to face her mother.

"Would you have been so quick to accept if Raj had suggested this picnic?"

"Amma, you say some wicked things."

"Well, would you?"

"I don't know because Raj has never suggested it. He never does anything, he never decides on anything and, if he does, it's a disaster. I have to think for both of us, constantly. You don't know how tired that makes me."

"He's still your husband," persists the old lady.

Taking off her apron, Neleni lays it wearily over the back of a chair, then says quietly:

"Don't worry, Amma. That is something I can never forget."

1955: Rani's disgrace

The picnic party winds its way along the dusty track: the adults, laden with provisions, stopping frequently to chat or admire the view, while the children run ahead, the little ones trying to keep up with those who have longer legs, sometimes stumbling and crying, at other times halting suddenly, their attention caught by treasures lying in the road that no-one else seems to appreciate; a shiny bottle-top, a pebble, a piece of coloured thread.

The two eldest children, a girl and a boy race towards the bridge where, half-way across, they hang over the rail, staring into the glass-green depths of the moat.

"There are skeletons in there," whispers the boy.

"I can't see any," says the girl. "Where are they?"

"At the bottom, stupid! At night, they rise from the water and creep through the gardens. You can't see them, because they are wrapped in green mist but, if you listen carefully, you can hear the sound of their bones. Click, click, click."

"No," the girl is thrilled. "How do you know?"

"Father told me. He says, if they find anyone living, they drag them down to the bottom of the moat to join the other skeletons."

Peering into the water, all the girl can see is her own reflection, squinting back at her. Releasing her foothold and stretching her legs out behind her, she pulls herself forward on the railing so that she is balancing on her pelvis, the top half of her body suspended above the water. Wrapt in fantasy, she does not hear her father creeping up behind. With a sudden movement, he grabs her around the waist, lifts her up and swings her legs over the railing.

"Ha. I'm going to throw you to the crocodiles."

Shrieking, the girl kicks wildly. "No, Appa, no."

Failing to appreciate the fun, the girl's small sister, starts to bawl, pointing with one chubby hand at her sister as she runs back to her mother for help.

"Raj, stop it! You're upsetting her."

Neleni scowls at Raj as she tries to comfort Saro who uses the opportunity to scramble into her mother's arms. Sheepishly, Raj sets Rani down on the bridge.

"Here. Carry this."

Without meeting Raj's eye, Neleni thrusts the picnic basket into his arms. Already tired after the morning's exertion, she is suddenly, unspeakably angry. It is a feeling that took root earlier this morning, as a result of the conversation with her mother, but which has been exacerbated by Raj's last-minute decision to attend the picnic.

Inclining her face towards Saro so that she does not have to look at her husband, Neleni hurries past Raj and Rani. She snapped at Raj, intending to hurt him, her actions prompted, not by anxiety at Saro's distress, but by resentment: she does not want him here at all.

Sometimes, she detests Raj for his stupidity but, today, she hates him for his unquestioning love. Such devotion is like a noose around her neck, as soon as she tries to move in any direction it tightens until it threatens to choke her. As a girl, she was told that love was a gift, but she knows from experience that it is a burden.

Raj's love is like a canker in her soul, a debt that can never be repaid. It makes her feel sick, diminished. But even greater than her hatred for Raj, is her own self-loathing. Shamed by her ingratitude and acts of cruelty, Neleni hates herself. Tired, exhausted and drained, she wishes, just now, that she was dead.

"Here, let me carry her."

Saro is lifted gently from Neleni's arms. Effortlessly, Arjun swings the whimpering child onto his shoulders, jogging her up and down until she shrieks with laughter. Round and round they spin, Saro clutching on tightly at first then, as her confidence grows, stretching out her arms to catch at the leaves that flutter overhead. Neleni laughs, too, her dark thoughts dispelled by their antics.

Watching them from the bridge, Rani slips her hand into her father's.

"I'm glad you came, Appa."

"So am I," he says. "See how your mother is enjoying herself. I haven't seen her laugh so much for a long time. It does me good to see her like this."

Squeezing his hand, Rani bites her lip, tears rising to her eyes. How can he be so generous when her mother has already spoilt his fun? She wants to hug her father, wishing that she was big enough to protect him, instead of the other way around. No-one ever seems to appreciate what a good man he is. She would not have forgiven Neleni so easily.

"I hate her," she says, stamping her foot so hard that the bridge rattles.

Aghast, Raj stares at her as if he has never seen her before, as if he has suddenly discovered that his daughter is a changeling child; then, bending over, he wags a finger in her face, so close that it nearly brushes her nose.

"Wicked, wicked," is all he can say, then, straightening up, he turns and walks away, leaving Rani alone on the bridge.

Determined not to beg his forgiveness, at least not yet, Rani climbs onto the bottom rung of the wooden railing and leans over, letting her tears fall unchecked in the water, fascinated by the tiny dimples they make in its surface. Then, as grief abates, she begins to plot her revenge. Staring balefully into the moat, Rani tries to pierce its murky depths, willing the skeletons to rise and punish her mother.

1955: Sigiriya

They have come to Sigiriya, fortress of King Kasyapa who, in the 5th century, snatched the throne from his father after burying the old man alive in his own tomb. Fearing retribution from his brother, the rightful heir to the throne, Kasyapa abandoned the ancient capital of Anuradhapura, building himself a new stronghold in the jungle. Sigiriya is a marvel of nature, a vast pillar of granite, towering above the forest: but it is also a tribute to human ingenuity.

The rocky walls are adorned with delicate paintings and poetry, while at the summit are the remains of a citadel. Cisterns, bathing pools, throne rooms, workshops and streets can still be seen. All formed part of Kasyapa's royal residence where ambassadors, courtiers, soldiers, blacksmiths, scribes and courtesans were received, after ascending to the giddy heights of the palace by a system of ladders, ropes and stairs.

At ground level, there are elegant gardens with sweeping lawns, shady trees, fountains and stone watercourses: at the summit, Kasyapa's fortress commands panoramic views of the countryside. In its day, his palace was unassailable: the final ascent to the royal eyrie controlled by a single, stone staircase.

However, it was the arch at the entrance to those steps, carved in the likeness of a gigantic lion's mouth, that gave Sigiriya its name. The symbol of kings, the lion still has significance for the Sinhalese people, for it is from a legendary lion that they claim their descent.

Following independence from the British, the Sinhalese lion has been revived and now struts proudly across the country's newly-devised flag. But it only represents the majority: the Sinhalese. The fate of minorities in this new utopia is less certain. As Kasyapa knew well, there is only room for one king in the political jungle.

But while past rivalries threaten to haunt the future, thoughts of violence and turmoil are not uppermost in the visitors' minds; particularly not that of Neleni. For while Sigiriya's sheer walls were intended as a defence against enemies, they also served a more peaceful purpose.

Here, artists found a natural canvas and poets, an indelible sheet for the inscription of their verse. While their authors have long since disappeared, both paintings and poems remain, as fresh as the day they were created. Timeless memorials to an ancient culture, their tale is one of love, not war. In this place, passion speaks and history comes to life. The granite walls of Sigiriya resonate with whispers from the past.

1955: The picnic

Surrounded by children, who dart back and forth like mayflies, the adults stroll through Sigiriya's ancient gardens; the men discussing cricket, politics and old acquaintances; the women, chattering, sharing news of betrothals and illnesses, comparing recipes, politely congratulating each other on their children's achievements and, more energetically, commiserating over their failures.

Neleni's party has been joined by Raj's cousin, Prashanthan, the proprietor of a rackety private bus who has taken a day off work, using his own vehicle to transport his family: his wife, Ana, a plump, comfortable woman; their five children; Ana's sister, her husband and their two children; an elderly aunt who lives with the family; a couple of young male cousins who talked incessantly of girls, and an elderly man, thought to be a relative (although no-one is quite sure) who is regularly included in family outings.

"You came by car?" the cousin's wife, Ana, inquires of Neleni. "That big, shiny one that we saw in the car park?"

"Yes. Mr Kumaran, our lodger, works for the Government Agent. The GA thinks very highly of him. He loaned him a car for the picnic. And a driver."

"A driver, too? Oh, that is very smart. I would love to be driven in a car like that. You are very lucky."

Although taking no credit for this borrowed affluence, Neleni blushes happily. Life has changed since Arjun joined their household. Here they are, being chauffeur-driven to a picnic: something that would have been unimaginable six months ago. More importantly, the increase in family income will allow Neleni to employ a maid. Arjun, himself, suggested it.

At last, after years of struggling, Neleni has finally acquired a degree of comfort, a little self-respect. Although not a snob, she basks in Ana's gentle envy. It is pleasant to feel like a woman of means, however modest, or temporary. Just for today, she can enjoy a subtle elevation in status; one that Raj could never achieve.

***

With Neleni trailing behind, the group weaves towards a shady place under the trees where the picnic will be spread out on the grass. Their earlier differences resolved, Raj and his daughter walk hand in hand; Rani chattering, her father pretending to listen. The other children run past them, shrieking as they chase each other up and down the long, rectangular stretch of greensward, splashing through the stone-flagged water-courses.

Deserted by Saro, Arjun finds himself alone with the other men. Occasionally, he tries to enter their conversation but, for the most part, he is silent, unable to speak a language of mutual acquaintance and shared experience. Although they are all Tamils, he has an overwhelming sense of his own foreignness in this tight little group.

He steals a glance at Neleni. She returns his attention with a ready smile, as if she has been waiting for him to look at her. Struck by her beauty, he wonders how she came to marry a man like Raj: a good sort, undoubtedly; good-humoured, when he has not drunk too much; kindly; loyal to family and friends, but without either the education or intelligence to match his wife.

As yet, Arjun has learned little of Neleni's past. She rarely mentions it and, when she does, she speaks of her younger self as one might speak of someone who has died. Her voice conveys a sense of loss; regret for something that cannot be recovered. Hope, perhaps. Or, ambition. He cannot tell.

However, he knows that she has had a good education, taught in a western-style Catholic school, as he was. She still retains a vestige of that learning, occasionally expressing an interest in art and literature, sometimes quoting Keats or Shelley.

But how can she possibly discuss such things with Raj, whose conversation, at best, consists of lambasting politicians or dissecting the latest cricket score? She is like a mermaid caught in a fisherman's net; an exotic creature struggling for breath in an alien environment; an enigma. Increasingly, Arjun's thoughts stray back to her.

He, too, is mirrored in Neleni's thoughts. Like a pulse of cool air, Arjun has revived her, awakening her from a malaise that started with the death of her father and deepened on her marriage to Raj. For years, her senses have been so dulled as to exclude all feeling and she has often imagined herself to be sleep-walking through the real world. Now, quite suddenly, she has entered a heightened state of awareness in which even small things, such as a flower drifting from a temple tree, can transport her to the verge of ecstasy. But such joy has its price.

As she awakens to life's opportunities, Neleni is increasingly aware of the extent of her mismatch to Raj. It is like surveying a once-fertile plain and seeing nothing for miles but desert. Unrelieved barrenness stretches before her, touching the horizon in every direction. She has been given a life sentence without hope of reprieve.

These days her desperation frequently resolves itself into rage, especially towards the man who has become her jailer. In the past, she trained herself to appreciate Raj's good points, even imagining a mild fondness for him, which she presumed to be love. But now all she feels is resentment. Her intolerance of him has increased to such a degree that she has to stop herself from screaming when he touches her.

She nurtures the hope that, one day, he might simply disappear; a separation effected without pain or trauma, without guilt on either side. However, when she is provoked, this hope escalates into a passionate desire for Raj's removal: instantly; by death, if necessary.

Neleni had such thoughts today. Back there, on the bridge, she used her tongue to strike at her husband's heart. Her words hit home. She saw the pain on his face and felt a momentary gratification. How could she have hurt him like that?

The only person to relieve her suffering was Arjun. He had made her laugh and Raj, seeing her smile, had laughed, too. It was a kind of absolution: a relief from pain that neither could give to the other. She steals another glance at Arjun and her heart quickens.

It is not right. Stricken with guilt, Neleni is filled with self-loathing. She is wicked, ugly, evil. Perhaps, after all, she deserves her fate. It is her punishment. She wishes that she were more like her mother. Then, she could be cleansed through confession. But such relief is only available to true believers, and she is not one.

***

Neleni approaches the group of adults and children, now seated under the trees. They are listening to Raj's cousin, reciting the tale of King Kasyapa, the visionary, whose brilliance was tarnished by an unforgiveable crime. Sitting on the grass, Neleni leans against a tree and closes her eyes, allowing the story to wind its way through her thoughts like a dark thread of smoke.

Disappointment is a slow poison that can eat a man alive. Neleni has felt its destructive force. She understands its corrosive power, how it wears one away from the inside. Yet the sufferer must keep it secret, concealed under a cloak of normality. For few sympathise with this disease. Neleni knows. For years, she has smothered her own feelings, holding them in check with such rigid control that she feels more akin to the dead than the living.

She empathises with Kasyapa: a man of passion and energy, passed over in favour of a mediocre brother because that was what convention dictated; his frustration resolving itself into anger, then hatred, finding a target in the man who probably loved him the most: his father. Neleni recognises that anger in herself. In suppressing her own desires, she has tasted the hunger that leads to desperation and, ultimately, madness. Without the restraint of reason, one can easily justify acts condemned by others.

Kasyapa was a victim who suffered defeat long before his death on the battlefield. Sigiriya was not a testament to a victorious ruler, but the refuge of a man consumed by fear and self-doubt. By immersing himself in the pleasures of this world, Kasyapa tried to postpone his terror of the next. Sigiriya was not the stronghold of a successful king, but a refuge hidden from view, where those enjoying the exquisite gardens were concealed by jungle and bathers in the palace pools had only clouds for company.

In the shadow of the Rock with its crevices, caverns and secret places, its history and symbolism, time knits together, bridging the centuries. Neleni holds her breath. He is here. Kasyapa has emerged from the past and is seeking her. So strong is her impression of his presence, that she opens her eyes and looks around, expecting to catch sight of him, wandering alone in the garden. Then, shutting her eyes again, she reaches out her hand, imagining that he is beside her.

She can almost feel him, laying his head in her lap, confessing to his pain and regret because she, alone, can understand him. He is reckless, handsome and youthful, a man with the heart of a poet, haunted by evil deeds. Knowing that he is doomed, he seeks solace with her. Entranced by this vision, Neleni turns her face towards the Rock. It draws her towards it, promising further discoveries, weaving its romance around her.

The other women are laying out the picnic, but she must go. Now. Kasyapa is waiting. He is close. She can feel his presence.

"Raj. Will you climb the Rock with me?"

Her husband, reclining on his elbow, is watching hungrily as the food is spread out before him. Despite what he said earlier to Rani in defence of her mother, Raj is secretly annoyed that his wife scolded him in front of the others.

"What now?" he says, pettishly. "We're about to eat."

The children are circling the food like a gang of hungry pye-dogs. Occasionally, one tries to steal a morsel from one of the tiffin boxes, receiving a sharp slap on the hand in reward.

"When?"

"When what?"

"When will you climb the Rock with me? This afternoon?"

Raj flaps his hand, dismissively.

"We'll see, we'll see. Maybe after I've had a sleep."

But Neleni knows that, once Raj has eaten, there will be no moving him. Deflated, she hangs her head, pretending to examine the hem of her sari, hoping that the others will not see how her eyes have filled with tears. How stupid, to be so upset over such a little thing, but then, it matters such a lot to her.

"I'll go with you."

Arjun has appeared at her side.

"Do you mind?"

He turns to Raj, seeking his approval.

"No, no. You go ahead."

Raj settles himself back on the grass, his hands behind his head. His broad smile indicates his approval of the arrangement. At heart, he is indolent and happy to let others perform tasks that he regards as onerous. It is an arrangement that suits everyone. He can see nothing wrong in it.

"Shall we go now … or later?"

Neleni has already sprung to her feet, but then realising that they have not yet eaten, thinks that she should offer Arjun the choice.

"No, I'm not hungry. Let's go now."

"Enjoy yourself, my boy. Make sure you see the Maidens! All naked. Very naughty!"

Raj rolls his eyes lasciviously, making a gesture with his hands to suggest the curves of a woman's body. He speaks loudly, attracting the attention of the others. The two young cousins nudge each other and giggle.

Neleni's cheeks flame with embarrassment. Raj is such an idiot! In private, she can ignore his tasteless remarks but today, with Arjun present, she is mortified.

Fortunately, Arjun has already started to walk away from the group. She hopes that he did not hear Raj's quip but, when she catches up with him, she realises that he did. His cheeks, like hers, are flushed.

"I'm so sorry. Raj says such silly things. He doesn't mean to offend. It's just that …"

She pauses, not knowing what else to say.

"Don't worry. It doesn't matter."

He stops and turns to look at her.

"I am only embarrassed if you are."

"Really!"

She lowers her head, not knowing what to say, both flattered by the attention and alarmed by the feelings it arouses in her. She struggles to focus on Kasyapa. After all, it is him that she has come to find.

Sensing her discomfort, Arjun tactfully changes the subject.

"I've always wanted to see this place. It's even more beautiful than I imagined."

Neleni laughs.

"This is nothing. Wait until you get to the Mirror Wall. There are poems, cut into its surface. They are over a thousand years old and most were written in praise of the Maidens."

"The Maidens?"

Arjun looks a little blank. Neleni has been talking with such enthusiasm that, for one moment, he thought that she was talking about living people.

"Yes. The Maidens of Sigiriya. The women painted in the frescoes!"

She looks up at him eagerly, her face dazzling with enthusiasm: the eyes liquid and warm, the pale skin flushing with colour. It is like watching someone who has been frozen in ice, coming back to life.

Tee, hee, hee! Behind them, the two young cousins continue to giggle, whispering into their hands as they watch Neleni and Arjun. One pulls the other towards him and murmurs something in his ear. It is not the mischief of children, but the lascivious talk of young men whose imagination, far outstripping their experience, exceeds all possibility.

Neleni cannot hear what they are saying, but there is no need. Their nudgings and gurglings are enough. Neleni's heart begins to pound.

Carried away by her enthusiasm, she had forgotten a crucial fact. The women in the frescoes are naked to the waist, their femininity erotically exaggerated. What will Arjun think of them? What will he think of her? Although there is no great difference in their ages, he is still a boy, innocent, untouched by the world.

Other doubts swarm in. Should she accompany Arjun alone? She knows what her mother would say. But, then, Raj has given them his blessing. Surely, that is enough. But a voice in her head says it is not.

She considers making an excuse. She could pretend to have a headache, return to the group. But that would be unfair. She has agreed to this trip and, without her, Arjun will have no-one to guide him around the site. He will see none of Sigiriya's treasures and the excursion will have been a waste of time. She must go.

Up there, someone, or something, awaits her; a truth that only she can discover. Kasyapa. She catches her breath as she looks up at the Rock, towering above her. Up there, she will be free, away from prying eyes and people telling her what to do. For once, she will be her own mistress, ordering her thoughts, controlling her actions, answerable to no-one.

A dove coos seductively from a branch overhead. It is a sign. She knows it. He is summoning her.

Together, Arjun and Neleni enter a narrow defile cut through the base of the rock. On either side, the walls are pitted with holes, large enough to hold a human foot. When she was a child, someone told Neleni that these hollows used to form a rough stairway, but they are too randomly placed for even the most agile climber. Perhaps they were never intended for human feet at all. No-one has yet provided a convincing explanation. But it is better that way. Some mysteries should never be solved.

A little further on, a set of wide granite steps leads to an iron staircase; a modern addition that, in places, consists of little more than narrow iron rungs driven into the rock-face. With a speed and agility that defies commonsense, visitors squeeze past each other on vertiginous angles where the steps are only a few inches wide and a fall to the ground would be fatal. As they pass each other, they smile politely and stop to chat, admiring the view while those behind wait patiently for them to move along.

Many wear only the flimsiest footwear: flip-flops or dainty sandals, while others prefer to go barefoot. In fact, no concessions are made in the matter of dress, particularly by the women, whose flowing saris lap around their ankles and whose scarves billow out behind them, fluttering like pennants in the breeze.

At one of the narrowest points, where tiny steps have been nailed into an outcrop of rock, Neleni and Arjun flatten themselves against the crag to let an old lady pass. With the folds of her sari clutched in one hand, and a large black brolly to shade her from the sun in the other, the little, white-haired woman steps nimbly past them. She is at least seventy years old.

As Neleni shrinks into the rock-face, her arm presses against Arjun. There is no help for it. There is nowhere else to stand. As she waits for the woman to pass, Neleni closes her eyes. A breath of air plays over her face and she can feel the taut flesh of Arjun's arm beneath his shirt. High above them, an eagle cries, remote and lonely, like a lost soul.

Neleni imagines herself standing next to Kasyapa, alone together, staring at the horizon where the green ocean of forest meets the sky. Kasyapa, the wind in his face, his hair streaming behind him, enjoying a moment of freedom before the end; his life, short and tragic, but full of passionate intensity. Neleni tries to picture his face. But all she can see is the face of the man beside her, standing so close that she can feel the quiet motion of his breathing.

High on the rock-face, the walls of an ancient, hand-hewn gallery resonate with excited chatter.

"The old devil, he's at it again!"

The woman giggles, clapping her hands in delight.

"What is it, Yaani? What are you talking about?"

Her friend leans closer, the jewels in her earrings glittering almost as spitefully as her narrow, cats' eyes.

"I saw him. This morning. Sneaking down into the garden to spy on the visitors. He thinks no-one can see him. But I can. The fool!"

The woman laughs again; a harsh, dry laugh, like the cracking of glass.

"Stop it, you two. You're always making fun of him. It's not fair."

A young girl, carrying a tray of flowers, rebukes the women.

"Oh, listen to her, bleating on. Always defending him."

The woman called Yaani rolls her eyes.

"Anyone would think she was in love."

"Well, isn't she? Just a little."

Head to one side, the cat-eyed woman pinches her thumb and forefinger together to show what 'a little' means.

The girl is undeterred.

"If it wasn't for him, you wouldn't be here."

"Hah! Precisely. I've got better things to do with my life than entertain his guests!"

Yaani tosses her head disdainfully, causing the pendants in her headdress to click together.

"She's right. You should show more respect."

A woman with a frangipani flower, delicately poised between her fingers, joins the conversation. Several years older than the others, she is still beautiful, although her jaw has lost the firmness of youth.

"Oh, I don't believe this. Why are you defending him, Shalini? After the way he treated you!"

Yaani throws up her hands in despair.

"Because," says the older woman, "it is my duty. I don't deny that it hurt me greatly when he ran after other women, especially you, Yaani; but I taught myself to forgive and I am happier for it."

"Tosh!" retorts Yaani.

"Tosh!" echoes another girl with slow, dreamy eyes. "That word went out with the British. Surely, no-one says tosh these days."

Yaani's eyes glint maliciously and she is just about to deliver a stinging insult when a young woman with golden skin and the body of a dancer steps into the group.

"Sisters, stop quarrelling! We have little enough time to ourselves. Don't spoil it by arguing."

"She's right," echo the others.

Outnumbered, Yaani sulks. There is a bad-tempered silence.

"Anyway," says her friend, gallantly trying to revive the conversation, "you still haven't told us what our silver-tongued deceiver was up to."

A murmur, resembling a giggle, passes around the group.

"He's got a new paramour."

Yaani almost spits the words at Shalini, watching for her reaction.

"What! Surely not! Not after all this time!" Shalini's lip trembles.

"Why not?" Yaani gloats. "He can no longer enjoy a woman but he can still get one into trouble. And I tell you, he's got a new victim."

"You've seen her?"

"Yes. I told you. I followed him."

"Where?"

"Down in the garden. Under the old neem tree where he used to sit with us. You remember it?"

The others nod sadly.

"What was she like?" asks the girl with the flower basket.

"A commoner, like you."

The flower girl looks as if she might cry. Shalini puts her arm around her. Old rivalries are beginning to surface.

Yaani continues.

"Actually, she was just his type. She wouldn't look out of place with us. She came here with her husband. A low-born oaf. But there was another man …. One who would have been worthy of any of us."

She wiggles her hips provocatively but her tale is cut short by the sound of footsteps approaching from the stairwell.

"Shhh! Back to your places. I'll tell you later."

In a tumultuous scramble, the women re-arrange their jewellery, flatten their hair and assume their positions in readiness for the next visitors.

1955: The gallery

The sound of footsteps gets louder until two people, a man and a woman, emerge at the top of the stairs. They pause while the woman recovers her breath, the young man waiting patiently at her side, although the swift movement of his eyes betrays his eagerness to explore.

Neleni and Arjun have climbed to the gallery that houses the Sigiriya Maidens; twenty-three mysterious women whose portraits, protected by the overhanging rock, remain as fresh as the day they were painted some 1,500 years ago. Crowned with tall, filigree headdresses, the Maidens are decked out with elaborate jewellery: gold armbands, bracelets, ropes and collars, medallions set with rubies and emeralds, and hooped earrings of such size that they reach nearly to the shoulder.

Two, in particular, catch Arjun's eye. They seem to be engaged in animated conversation: one, a voluptuous creature with amber-coloured skin, is making elegant gestures with her arms; the other, her head inclined to one side, appears to be listening politely, although her smile, intended to be gracious, hints at a smirk.

"She's spiteful, that one," says Arjun, pointing to the second figure. Neleni, who has lingered behind, draws level and looks to where he is pointing.

"Oh, I don't know."

Neleni's experiences with her own daughters have taught her that the one who looks innocent is usually the troublemaker. Overt expressions of naughtiness usually belong to the accomplice.

"But that one," says Arjun, catching his breath as he points to the woman with graceful arms. "Now she's beautiful."

"Troublemaker!" thinks Neleni.

The Maiden's face is perfectly-proportioned: straight, chiselled nose; gracefully-arched eyebrows, a strong but sensuous mouth, neither too large, nor too small; but it is a man's idea of perfection. No doubt the artist was in love with his subject, a woman far beyond the scope of his ambition.

He had probably only seen her from a distance, perhaps at a sitting, or in passing, but his passion prompted him to record her for posterity. Hanging precariously from bamboo scaffolding, hundreds of feet above ground, he had lovingly applied her image to the rock face with his paints, reckless of the danger, absorbed in his task.

Did he ever see her again? Or was he left only with the memory of a woman so remote that she appeared to him from the clouds, as this one did; a celestial beauty with voluptuous breasts, the lower half of her body obscured by vapour; a divine creature who, having aroused desire, denied its consummation.

Neleni views the painting critically. At first glance, the Maiden appears inscrutable; but a closer inspection reveals clues to her personality. The delicate, curved eyebrows are raised a fraction too high and the eyes, under their lowered lids, appear to be laughing. If one looks long enough, the face, at first glance serene and expressionless, becomes haughty and disdainful.

"Isn't she beautiful?" murmurs Arjun.

"No," retorts Neleni. "She's cruel. I don't like her at all. I prefer this one over here."

And she points at the figure holding a frangipani flower between her fingers. Although this Maiden's contours are not as firm as those of her youthful companion, she is gentle, thoughtful and wise. *True beauty withstands the test of time*, thinks Neleni, who sometimes grieves over the subtle changes that age has brought to her own face.

"Goodness. That one looks like the Queen Mother," says Arjun, looking over her shoulder. "She's old. She's not really your favourite, surely?"

"Yes. She is," replies Neleni, vigorously. There is a sharpness in her voice and Arjun blushes, thinking that he has offended her.

"I'm sorry," says Neleni, regretting her outspokenness. "I love painting. Art. But it's a long time since I discussed it with anyone. It's difficult to be detached."

He laughs, a little awkwardly.

"Shall we go?"

His suggestion seems slightly abrupt. But, perhaps, it is for the best.

"Good idea. There's still a lot to see."

Arjun stands aside politely, letting Neleni go first. As she passes the painting of the young Maiden, a breeze tugs spitefully at Neleni's hair, dislodging a strand that drifts wilfully across her eyes; then, as she is about to leave the gallery, she hears a faint, mocking laugh and the words "Queen Mother!"

Yaani is still laughing.

"Queen Mother!"

Shalini is hurt by that remark. She tries to hide it, but Yaani sees her flinch at Arjun's thoughtless words.

"Serve her right," thinks Yaani. "Thinks she's the queen bee. But not any longer. Not here among us, and not in his affections. I'm head courtesan now, and she'll have to admit it, sooner or later".

She relaxes her pose, wiggling her hips flirtatiously, although there is no-one to see her. The others are talking amongst themselves. The little flower girl is murmuring words of comfort to Shalini, who discreetly wipes away a tear as she pretends to examine her frangipani flower.

And then another thought occurs to Yaani. One that angers her. Kasyapa has found a new favourite. The woman who, only a few moments ago, stood right here and openly declared her dislike for Yaani.

"If she had lived in my time, I would have dealt with her," thinks Yaani savagely.

In her day, it was not unusual for Kasyapa's lovers to disappear overnight. Yaani always told him that girls from the lower classes could not be relied on. Sooner or later, they would always run off. And he was content to believe her.

Of course, he was always heartbroken when one of them disappeared, but Yaani was always there to comfort him. As he lay in her arms, she would smile to herself in the dark, knowing that her rival's body lay safely disposed of, under the roots of a tree, or at the bottom of a tank. But now, Kasyapa has a new favourite. Neleni. Yaani knew it as soon as she saw her. Although much younger, she has the soft beauty of Shalini, Yaani's only serious rival; the one she could never touch.

While Kasyapa might have had his suspicions about the disappearance of minor courtesans, Yaani always chose her victims with care. None of them ever mattered enough to warrant any serious investigation. But Shalini was different. Kasyapa loved her in a way that he never loved Yaani. And, all these centuries later, it still galls her.

Yaani hates Shalini for her goodness, because it is the one thing to which she cannot aspire. Shalini whose devotion led her to commit suicide on her lord's death while Yaani ran away to live the life of a common prostitute, plying her trade in a distant town in the hope that no-one would recognise her. Even that common little painter, the one who daubed her image on the rock-face, would have been preferable to some of the men who laid hands on her after Kasyapa's defeat. She shudders. The memories are bitter.

She seeks revenge for past humiliation in the present but, like her lord Kasyapa, she is a living memory, a form without substance who must live out her dreams and desires through others. Neleni and Arjun offer interesting possibilities.

Humming to herself, Yaani practises the moves to a dance, one that she performed often for Kasyapa. It never failed to please him. Through that dance, and what followed, she became the richest and most powerful courtesan in the king's harem. For a while. These are the memories that she prefers to dwell on. Not the penniless indignity of her later years.

"That young man…," she sways seductively as she thinks of Arjun, weaving her hands gracefully through the air.

"Kasyapa sees a reflection of himself in that boy. Actually, there is a similarity."

Yaani pauses. A thought has suddenly occurred to her.

"… and that woman, the one who was here just now, the one who looks like Shalini when she was younger. Oh, now I know his plan. Kasyapa is plotting a new conquest. Only he can't do it for himself. He must use someone else. Yes, that's it. That woman is Kasyapa's new favourite. Well, we'll see about that. It may not turn out quite as he expects."

Yaani is invigorated by the prospect of fresh intrigue. Her life with Kasyapa has become a game of chess, played with human pawns and this will be the most exacting contest of all. Reliving their passion through others, Kasyapa and Yaani will both strive for dominion. And Kasyapa, as usual, will underestimate the cunning of his chief courtesan. For Yaani still has the power to dispense with her rivals.

As Arjun climbs the winding staircase, he neither sees the mountains, hazy with heat, nor the breath-taking expanses of sky and forest, but the alluring faces of the Maidens. In his mind, they have come to life. He imagines their voices, musical and sweet, and he longs to hear them for himself, tarry a little so that he can listen to them speaking of poetry and love, especially the beautiful girl that Neleni so disliked.

He smiles. On the subject of that Maiden, Neleni expressed herself with unusual forcefulness and what sounded like jealousy. He cannot understand it. Why should she feel so threatened by what is, after all, only an image from the past? Neleni is beautiful in her own right and would compare favourably with any of the Maidens. He wonders if he should tell her so. She seems so lacking in self-esteem. But what would she think of him, if he did?

She is in front of him now, bending slightly forward, her sari hitched up in front to prevent her from tripping. The taut cloth clings to her hips and, as she climbs, the swaying of her body reminds Arjun of the Maidens, their glowing skin and voluptuous breasts.

Despite their elaborate headdresses, jewellery, gold and gems, all of the Maidens are naked to the waist. No man could resist their erotic beauty. Their radiant faces, luminous skin and sensuous curves have worked an ancient spell on Arjun, awakening desire, making him restless for pleasure. He has never experienced feminine sensuality and is ill-prepared for the challenge. As he follows the gentle swaying of Neleni's hips, a transformation takes place.

He has never been so aware of a woman's body, or of his own. It is as if he perceives her, not with his eyes, but with every fibre of his being. The rustle of her sari becomes the music of stringed instruments; the tap of her foot, the delicate beat of drums. He hears laughter and someone whispering in his ear: a man's voice, urging him to take her because here, high above the common platform of the world, he is untouchable. Dizzy with desire, he has a sudden urge to push her against the rock wall … and then? He does not know.

He can no longer deny his attraction to Neleni, a feeling which has slowly been taking shape in his mind but which, until now, has not communicated itself to his body. He struggles to make sense of how this subtle change has been effected. Perhaps, it is simply the fact that he finds himself alone with her, out of earshot and out of sight of their companions, removed from all normal constraint. Or, perhaps it has something to do with the Maidens. He realises that, unconsciously, he has been comparing them to Neleni: her eyes have the same dreamy quality; her lips have their enigmatic smile; while her skin is suffused with a similar velvety glow.

He is rocked on a warm tide as sibilant voices murmur in his ear. He can kiss Neleni if he wants. There is no harm. No-one will see. Just a kiss. And then, he hears a man's voice, harsher, more commanding, ordering him to do what he would normally find unthinkable. And yet, he wants to obey. He wants to touch her, pull her towards him, commit acts he has never dreamt of before.

He grasps the railing, trying to catch his breath, but all he can see is the swaying of her hips and all he can hear is the quiet tapping of her feet. She is within inches of his grasp and there is no-one to see them. He must have her or go mad. The man's voice is insistent, taunting, wheedling, urging him on.

And then another voice speaks, sweet and reasonable, a woman's voice. "Wait. Wait and see. There will be others. Do not do something you will regret."

"It is my conscience speaking," thinks Arjun, with relief.

Relaxing his grip on the railing, he fills his lungs with air and, as the madness passes, he thanks God and all the saints for saving him from sin.

If Arjun had the sight of an immortal, he would see two figures looking down on him from a rocky incline: one, a man, clothed in silver-scaled armour that glints in the sunlight; the other, a woman, the Maiden who, a few minutes ago, won Arjun's admiration.

The man's black hair flows about his shoulders while, from one ear, hangs a huge emerald, the size of a pigeon's egg. A bloody sword hangs from his side and on his head is a crown, tall, like the Maiden's headdresses, and encrusted with gems. His arms are crossed and he scowls.

"Yaani. I should punish you for that!"

"How can you? I am like you, a thought, a thing of air, a memory. I cannot be touched. No, Kasyapa. You can no longer frighten me with threats of violence. I am my own woman now."

"No!" Kasyapa shouts. "You are my woman."

"I ceased to belong to you when you committed suicide."

"It was a matter of honour."

"And what about my honour? Did you think of that?"

"Hmph!" Kasyapa turns away.

"And what do you think it does for my dignity, or my reputation with the others, when you run after mortal women?"

"It's none of your business what I do."

"Mmm," Yaani examines her nails. "That's what I said when you found me in the arms of that painter. Remember?"

Kasyapa growls: "Common little upstart. I had him thrown off the top of the Rock."

"You certainly made it your business to interfere in my affairs," says Yaani, archly.

"I'm the king. It's my right."

"You *were* the king," she reminds him, sweetly.

"I don't care what you say, Yaani. You won't interfere in this. I forbid it."

And, snapping his fingers at her, Kasyapa disappears. Yaani remains, arms crossed, watching Arjun and Neleni, the fingers of one, elegant hand, beating on her arm.

"We'll see," she murmurs. "We'll see who's the cleverest. And, perhaps, this time, I will have my revenge."

1955: Arjun and Neleni

He is not looking at her. They have been sitting together for several minutes, and he has not spoken. After leaving the Maidens, they climbed in silence to the place where they are now sitting, a stretch of level ground, the size of a cricket pitch, worn down by many feet. Perhaps, in the past there were lawns here, too, but now there is just a layer of hard earth where grass should be.

It is a convenient resting place before the last leg of the journey and some visitors, who are better prepared, have stopped to take refreshment, unpacking small packs of rotis and flasks of tea. Neleni has found a place to sit on one of the stone slabs that forms the footing of an ancient wall. Arjun sits nearby, at a respectful distance. But he has not spoken since they arrived.

Assuming his silence is due to embarrassment, Neleni berates herself. Like her, Arjun has had a strict Catholic upbringing. Although a grown man, he is still innocent. By indulging her passion for art and history, she has embarrassed him. What must he think of her?

Her confidence wanes. She should not have brought him here. What possessed her? And why did Raj let her come, unaccompanied? *So typical of him*, she thinks angrily. He only responds to his immediate desires; food, drink, sleep … She shudders, trying not to think of the other things that require her participation, carnal acts so perfunctory that they resemble the mating of animals. There is no tenderness, no pleasure – at least not for her.

In fact, her experience of physical love is so devoid of passion, so functional and so starved of beauty, that she is convinced that the eroticism personified by the Maidens can only be a figment of the artist's imagination. She regards the paintings as impotent relics, like the photographs on her wall at home.

Having convinced herself that the Maidens are unconnected to human passion, Neleni has fallen into a trap. An object may be neutral; but the viewer, conditioned by upbringing and beliefs, lends it meaning. Centuries ago, the naked beauty of the Maidens inspired awe. However, time and the influence of Christian missionaries have diminished their power. No longer understood, they have become the subject of seedy jokes and salacious comments.

Successive waves of invaders have cut the Islanders adrift, alienating them from the past. Many have lost their cultural compass. Perhaps Arjun is one of them. And there is something else.

Neleni underestimated the Maidens' ability to excite emotion in herself. Her reaction was unexpected, violent and shocking. When Arjun expressed admiration for the Maiden with the flawless face, Neleni snapped at him. And it was not just that she disagreed with him. She was jealous, angry at his admiration for a painted face. One that was not her own.

Cold-hearted whore! She is not sure whether the words are her own, or someone else's. She certainly hears them as clearly as if they had been whispered in her ear. Distracted, her thoughts take a different turn. Poor Kasyapa! Fancy having to cope with all those women, vying for his attention.

One of her uncles had a saying: 'Spoons in a drawer will rattle together' which he used to quote when her aunts squabbled in the kitchen. No doubt, it was the same at Kasyapa's court. Poor man! Had anyone truly loved him and, if they had, did he know? Neleni considers how terrible it would be to die without truly experiencing love. She is overcome by sadness.

67

"Are you all right?"

Arjun is leaning towards her, frowning, not with anger, but anxiety. He is still her friend. She is so grateful that, in her relief, she could kiss him. She wants to. Instead, she looks down at her lap, where her fingers have been picking anxiously at a loose thread in her sari.

"I'm fine, thank you. Just a little out of breath, or rather, I was when we arrived."

"You're sure?"

He reaches out his hand as if to touch her arm, but then, thinks better of it. Neleni is warmed by his concern. Raj would not notice if she dropped dead in front of him. Just as long as his food was on the table.

"I'm sure."

They sit back in mutual silence, enjoying the coolness of the air.

"Look. An eagle."

Neleni points, directing Arjun's gaze.

With wings outstretched, the bird cruises the air, rising and falling as it rides the thermals around the rock. Then, it draws near, so close that they can distinguish the ruff of feathers around its neck and the curve of its beak. They hold their breath, waiting to see what will happen next. Turning its head, the bird takes a long look at them then, tilting its wings, glides away, borne up by a column of air.

"How wonderful," says Arjun. "I've never seen anything like that before. I've never been anywhere like this. It's just ... wonderful."

Lost for words, he repeats himself. Neleni laughs.

"You haven't seen it all yet. Come with me. I'll show you how Sigiriya got its name."

She leads him across the baked, red earth to a set of stairs, flanked by two enormous lion's paws. The claws alone are the height of an average man. Passing between the mighty stone paws, the stairs narrow and disappear into darkness.

"There used to be an archway here. A lion's mouth. Sigiriya means 'Lion Mountain'."

Arjun is awestruck. With pleasure, Neleni watches him as he tilts his head back to get a better look, his eyes travelling slowly past the great carved feet, seeking the summit of the Rock which is obscured from below by the overhanging cliff.

"The royal lion was the symbol of Kasyapa's power. By passing through the lion's mouth, visitors were forced to acknowledge his sovereignty."

How typical of Kasyapa to make such a grand statement when his hold on the throne was so tenuous. Once again, Neleni is aware of his presence. He is so close, it feels as if he is standing next to her.

"You bring it to life," says Arjun. "I can see it, just the way it used to be."

Neleni is not used to being listened to. But, in Arjun, she has found an attentive pupil. He shows an interest to which she is unaccustomed and his appreciation begins to revive something that she has long forgotten; enthusiasm, a part of her that was quietly packed away on marriage.

It is like trying on favourite clothes, worn in youth, and finding that they still fit. Although, over the years, she has lost touch with the part of herself which she liked the most, it is still there and, underneath, she is still the same person that she used to be: a confident, happy girl who lived for art and who had the power to involve others in her interest. She realises that it is not her old self that is unfamiliar, but the new one.

***

They mount the granite stairs, climbing slowly until they emerge at the summit. *Like two souls arriving in heaven*, thinks Neleni. The seamless blue sky is within inches of their fingertips and the eagle that they observed from the lower platform, has shrunk to a tiny black dot. Far below, the jungle flows out from the base of the Rock, covering the land for miles in a dense green carpet, a vast emerald expanse broken only by the paler, jade rectangle of Kasyapa's water gardens.

They make a leisurely tour of the citadel and Neleni, for Arjun's amusement, gives full rein to her imagination, describing workshops, throne-rooms, porticos, arches and stairways, raising the palace from its ruined foundations. With words alone, she crowds the empty streets with merchants and artisans, soldiers and nobles, giving a vivid account of life in Kasyapa's fortress. And, all the while, Arjun listens, enraptured.

"You bring this place to life. You paint in words."

"I used to paint with colour."

"Were you good?"

"Yes."

"Don't you paint any more?"

"No."

"Why not?"

She shrugs, unwilling to admit to her wasted life or the bitterness that has poisoned her happiness. Some things cannot be spoken. Once out, the truth would destroy her.

"Look, those are the steps to one of the sentry posts."

Running towards the edge of the Rock, she points to a set of narrow footholds, carved into the vertical face of the rock that leads to a hollow no wider than a coffin. It is a distraction from Arjun's questions. Neleni describes how any sentry who fell asleep on duty paid a terrible penalty, plunging hundreds of feet to his death.

Then, she shows him the tanks and reservoirs which provided the court with water for bathing, cooking and washing. The reflections in the pools of still water are so clear that it looks as if bright patches of sky have been embedded in the dark rock. They remind Neleni of a story that her mother used to tell.

"Amma said that the king's harem bathed here; but that the king was so jealous of his women that he would only allow them to bathe at night. Only the stars were allowed to see them naked."

"The Maidens?"

"Perhaps. No-one really knows who they were. But I'm sure they were Kasyapa's women."

As she speaks, Arjun hears a faint echo: the whispering of female voices. He breathes deeply. The air up here is sweeter and fresher than any he has ever known. A soft breeze teases the curls on Neleni's neck. She is so close. He wants to touch her, feel her skin.

"I wish life could always be like this," he murmurs.

She smiles, then looks away, afraid of what she might see. There is a wistful note in his voice, a hint of longing. Is there some hidden meaning in his words? Has she caught a look in his eye, something that should not be there, but which she would not be displeased to see? She tells herself she is imagining things. This place exerts a powerful magic and she is falling under its spell. Soon, it might suggest possibilities that she is not in a position to contemplate.

"We'd better be going," she says. "It's getting late. The others will be wondering where we are."

But still, she lingers.

At the bottom of the Rock, they drift slowly through the water gardens. Reluctant to rejoin their party, they take a detour, passing through a copse of trees whose lower branches are inhabited by rhesus monkeys. Some are dozing, long tails trailing from the branches like vines, while others graze on the trees, tearing off handfuls of berries which they stuff into their mouths and chew energetically, much like old men chewing betel.

The more energetic members of the troupe are playing on the ground and several scuttle forward, rising up on their hind quarters to stare at the visitors. They are used to begging for food and have no fear of humans whom they have learned to terrorise.

Neleni is approached by an older monkey, a bad-tempered, drunken-looking creature with a red face and yellow teeth. She opens her hands to show that she is not concealing any food. In a fit of pique, the monkey takes a swipe at her skirt, grabbing the fine mesh of the sari between his fingers.

"Naughty monkey, let go!"

She deals him a slap across the nose that sends him scampering back to the trees. Arjun laughs, impressed by her courage. A bite from a monkey is not only painful but it can be dangerous, leading to blood poisoning or infection. From the safety of the branches, the vanquished monkey hurls abuse at the intruders, baring his teeth in a display of aggression.

"Oh, shoo! Silly creature."

Neleni waves her hand airily, as if the monkey is of no more consequence than a fly although, inside, she is quaking. She has never done anything so daring, or foolhardy, before. If she had been with Raj, she would probably have shrieked and clung to his arm but, in Arjun's company, she takes control, feeling somehow responsible for him. She catches the look of admiration in his eye and the blood races wildly to her head. She feels confident. It is a new sensation, as if she had stepped into a new body.

By now, they are at a safe distance from the troupe of monkeys and Arjun turns to take another look at them. Light shines through the low-growing branches of the trees, illuminating the broad green leaves and covering the ground with pools of liquid gold. The monkeys eat, sleep, fight and play, much as they have done for centuries. It is a timeless scene, untouched by man.

"The kingdom of the monkeys," muses Arjun. "It's like a scene from Rudyard Kipling."

"I read "Jungle Book" to the children. It used to be my favourite as a child."

"Mine too. But what do you like to read now?"

He turns to look at her. She lowers her gaze, not so much through modesty, but embarrassment at her long period of inertia.

"Oh, I don't read much any more."

"Why not?"

"No time," she replies evasively, walking half a step ahead of him.

The truth is that she has lost the desire to read, because reading encourages her to think and thinking will disclose the extent of her own unhappiness. Thinking is a dangerous pursuit and best avoided. These days, Neleni limits her reading to a pile of old magazines stored under the bed. Pictures of happy women in pretty dresses are no challenge. In fact, they put her in the right mind for sleep; the only state of consciousness in which she finds peace.

"How about poetry?" Arjun persists.

"No, not that either."

"But at one time. You must have had a favourite."

"Oh, I can't remember."

"All right," he says triumphantly. "I'll tell you what it was: "The Lady of Shalott".

Neleni pauses, trying to remember lines from the poem that she used to know by heart.

"Yes. Now you mention it. That was my favourite. I learned it, the whole thing, and I recited it at a concert. I was twelve, maybe thirteen."

"I knew it."

"But how?"

"The exercise book in the old school desk. You know, the one in my room. Someone had copied out the poem. And there were some beautiful drawings. Did you do those?"

She seems to be struggling with her memory, delving into the past and, when she speaks, her voice is soft, distant.

"Yes. I'd forgotten. But they were just sketches. Nothing special."

"I think you have talent."

"Had," she corrects him. "I told you. I don't paint any more. And I don't read. There's no time."

She quickens her pace, increasing the distance between them so that he cannot see her face.

As they approach the picnic group, they hear the children squealing as they chase each other through the trees: then Raj's voice, rising above the rest, loudly debating politics with his cousin.

"There's too much bloody history in this country. Look at this place. Supposed to be one of the wonders of the world. But who built it? A bloody murderer."

The two men have not moved from their position under the trees, where they have been sharing a bottle of arrack. The cousin, whose role is always to play devil's advocate, starts to protest, but Raj interrupts.

"No, Machan. I'm telling you. All this historical stuff, all these paintings and legends and temples, it's dangerous."

"Why?"

"Because it's ammunition for the Sinhalese."

In his excitement, Raj has begun to shout, attracting the attention of other picnickers. The cousin winces, motioning with his hand for Raj to lower his voice.

"You see. That's what I mean. We're already scared of the buggers."

"Explain what you meant about history," says the cousin, trying to deflect Raj from an even more explosive subject.

"The nationalists always rake up history in support of their cause. You only have to look at that new flag. What is it? The Sinhalese lion and a lousy stripe for each of the minorities. That's what the Tamils are now. A stripe on someone else's flag. Don't you see? They're telling us that we don't belong here."

"Well, now you put it like that ..."

There is no scope for argument. The cousin has to agree. The debate begins to flounder. Raj takes a noisy swig of arrack and refills his glass.

"If you ask me," he continues," they should burn all the books, blow up the temples and pull places like this down. We need to look forward, towards the future, not back over our shoulders."

Neleni opens her mouth to protest. Raj rolls over onto his side with his back to her. Her views are not welcome. However, his statement has had the desired effect. The cousin is suitably incensed and enters the argument with new vigour.

"You're joking, Machan. Can you imagine what trouble that would cause? Just think what would happen if someone bulldozed the Temple of the Tooth? It would cause a riot, if not a war!"

The cousin adopts a look of outrage.

"Trouble is coming anyway," mumbles Raj, a spot of saliva clinging to his lip. "That bloody Bandaranaike. I don't trust him."

"He comes from a good family. He's clever, a lawyer."

The cousin speaks dismissively, trying to wind up the debate. After his fifth glass of arrack, he is beginning to feel sleepy. He no longer has the energy for their mock argument and, anyway, the discussion is getting serious, straying into areas that he would rather not think about. But Raj is looking at him with a petulant expression that says he will sulk if he doesn't get his own way. Drink can turn him nasty, so the cousin is forced to continue. He aims for a neutral remark, something that cannot be contested.

"Bandaranaike is an educated man. He studied at Oxford."

"So why does he dress like a peasant?"

"To get more votes, I suppose."

"Exactly."

"But, isn't that what Gandhi did?"

"No. Gandhi wanted to represent all Indians. But Bandaranaike's only interested in the Sinhalese. And Gandhi didn't turn his back on his religion. Bandaranaike was brought up as a Christian, now he claims to be a Buddhist. He pretends to be all things to all men, but in the end, he'll do whatever the nationalists want so he can win the election. As long as they are happy, the rest of us can go to hell."

A fly lands on Raj's nose, momentarily distracting him. He sweeps it away clumsily with the back of his hand then, to Neleni's relief, wipes the saliva from his lip. The mood of playful sparring has disappeared. The group has fallen silent. The cousin, now serious, speaks quietly.

"You think he'll get in, then?"

"I'm sure of it."

Raj and his cousin lapse into gloomy silence. A cloud hangs over them although, overhead, the sky is a peerless blue. Neleni, having lost interest in their conversation, has wandered over to where the cousin's wife Ana is sitting with Saro, asleep in her lap. Fresh from the excitement of Sigiriya, Neleni would have mounted a passionate defence in favour of art. How could Raj suggest destroying it? But she was not given the chance to speak. She never is.

Standing some feet away from the men, Arjun has observed a startling transformation. The clever woman, whose company he found so beguiling, has turned into a passive mute. The new Neleni does not look at him, or smile. The other woman has been quietly buried.

The women have packed up the remains of the picnic and, strung out like a skein of geese, the visitors are making their way back along the cinder track to the road. Somewhat the worse for drink, Raj shambles forward in an oblique line; a kind of staggering Morse code with uneven bursts of activity punctuated by pauses. For a few seconds, he breaks into a fast shuffle, only to halt abruptly and stare at his feet, as if to check that they are still attached to his legs. Ignoring Neleni's protests, he has insisted on carrying Saro who, despite her father's jolting progress, lies asleep in his arms with her cheek pressed against his shoulder.

Neleni follows closely behind, tracking Raj's uncertain footsteps, reaching out when he stumbles, ready to catch her daughter if he falls. The walk back to the car seems interminable and the afternoon sun shines hot on Neleni's cheek. With every step, old cares close in, piling up around her like grains of sand. Her former self, momentarily rediscovered, lies abandoned in Kasyapa's fortress, cast off like an empty skin.

Her thoughts speed ahead to the dull reality that awaits her. Thoughts of her mother fill her with apprehension. Will Sunny have forgotten their argument or will she continue to sulk? She does not have the gift of sarcasm, but something much worse: the propensity to speak truth in anger. Her remarks about Arjun caused much pain. Neleni sighs. Thoughts of home close around her heart like a cage.

The bridge over the moat rattles under the weight of many feet. Neleni is halfway across, when something catches her eye. A flash of colour. She leans over the railing to get a better look.

A huge dragonfly has emerged from the rushes, sparks of sunlight issuing from its brilliant carapace. In a glimmer of jade and turquoise, it skims the moat, then alights on a reed. The broad, green blade dips slightly, bending under the weight of the insect. Restlessly, the dragonfly moves from side to side, trying to get its balance.

A sudden breeze. The reed shudders. The creature straightens its wings, as if to take off then, quite suddenly, it is still. Beneath it, the moat glows with a dull sheen, silver on lead, its surface inscrutable, like liquid mercury. With monstrous eyes, the dragonfly scans its surroundings then bows to the water, admiring its reflection.

As still as stone, Neleni is praying: "Come closer, come to me."

The dragonfly sways upon the reed. Suddenly, its wings melt in a frenzy of motion and it is borne aloft. It approaches, wheels around and passes within an inch of Neleni's face. A breath of air fans her cheek and she hears the mechanical whirring of wings. Undecided, the creature hovers then, abruptly, drops to the rail and settles, an inch away from her hand. She watches it, unblinking, until her eyes smart, marvelling at the iridescent body and the transparent wings with their delicate tracery of veins. Colour so intense that it passes right through her: a dart of ecstasy, piercing her soul. She has been touched by divinity.

Her lips move without sound. *Thank you.*

"Neleni. Over here!"

Ana is waving to her, calling shrilly. Distracted, Neleni makes a slight movement, startling the dragonfly. It whisks away, sinking down over the water, then disappearing into the reeds.

"Neleni!"

Ana walks on, still calling, her voice now faint and distant, like that of a passenger on a departing ship.

Reluctantly, Neleni turns to join the others. She does not notice Arjun, who having made the excuse to take a last look at Sigiriya, has been watching her from his position on the bank.

1955: Restless

Sweating, Arjun awakes. He has heard a man and a woman arguing. Not Neleni and Raj, but people in his dreams, people from the past. He thought he knew them, although he has forgotten their names. And they were arguing over him. He remembers a dream in which a woman's limbs slithered around him, snake-like and sinuous, gripping him as tight as a climbing fig, until he felt that he would suffocate.

"Love me, love me," she whispered; then laughed, her voice as musical as tinkling bells. Beset by desire, he restlessly sought satisfaction, but was denied. The object of his passion resembled the Maiden Yaani but, with the intuition of a dreamer, he knows that her image is a metaphor for someone else. It is Neleni that he desires.

Lying in darkness on the creaking bed, Arjun flings back the sheet. Now fully awake, sleep eludes him. The air in the small room is stifling despite the fact that he has left the door open. The room lacks the row of vents usually featured above the doors and windows of a tropical house. Why? Because this room was originally intended for storage. At least, that's what Raj told him, although Arjun suspects that his disagreement with the builder was more to blame. Whoever built this room intended the occupant to suffer.

Restless and hot, Arjun turns on the light and struggles to his feet. He unknots then reties his sarong, hitching up the material and tucking the hem into the waistband so that his legs are exposed below the knee. Then, walking over to the wash-stand, he splashes his face with tepid water. It makes no difference. If anything, he feels hotter than before. He must get the window open. But hasty painting has sealed the frame and brute force alone will not open it. He has tried on several occasions.

Then, he remembers his pen-knife, a treasure from childhood, little used, but which accompanies him everywhere. It lies in the school-desk, next to Neleni's old exercise book. Arjun retrieves it and, on a whim, takes out the schoolbook as well, placing it on the floor near the window.

Opening the pen knife, he applies its sharp point to the sealed joints around the window. After several minutes of scraping and gouging, he eventually manages to prise the frame apart. The window creaks open, showering the floor with particles of rust from its hinges. Cool air rushes in bringing with it the scent of the temple tree.

Gratefully, Arjun lets the draft play over his skin. In the street outside, figures flicker in and out of the lamplight like shadow puppets: two cats arching their backs as they square up for a fight; a dog scavenging for food; two men, arm in arm, weaving home unsteadily after a visit to the toddy tavern.

Arjun picks up the schoolbook and turns to Neleni's favourite poem, 'The Lady of Shalott'. Unconsciously, his hand caresses the page as his thoughts stray back to an image of Neleni, caught earlier that afternoon on the bridge at Sigiriya as she watched the dragonfly, her lips parted, her skin glowing in the sunlight, as warm and radiant as one of the Maidens. He regrets calling one of them 'Queen Mother'. It was stupid, the sort of remark only a boy would make. That portrait was Neleni's favourite and, with his clumsy attempt at humour, Arjun risked offending her.

But why did she identify so strongly with the least attractive of the Maidens? Could it be that Neleni regards herself as ageing and unattractive? Nothing could be further from the truth. She is beautiful. Surely she can see it? Any man would be proud to have her. All except her husband.

"That man is a fool," thinks Arjun, angrily. Only a fool, or a drunkard, could fail to appreciate her.

Back there, at Sigiriya, she brushed against him as the old woman passed them on the stairs. Briefly, her hand grazed his shirt. He felt the light, warm imprint of her fingers through the fabric. Then, with a rush of excitement, he felt the warmth of her body, smelt the jasmine in her hair. He can smell her still, if he closes his eyes. He breathes deeply, willing her to come to him. His head fills with a sweet fragrance. But it is only the temple tree. Not Neleni.

He opens his eyes. This will not do. He must beat down these stirrings of attraction, stamp them out like the embers of a fire. She is a married woman: adultery, a mortal sin. He must resist with all his strength. And yet, every time he thinks of her ... No. He must reject these thoughts. He cannot love her. Inexplicably, he feels bereaved.

I will be her friend. There can be no harm in that.

A compromise. Or, so he hopes. For, if they are friends, he can buy her a gift.

***

That night, Raj makes love to his wife. As usual, it is a perfunctory affair. But with her imagination fired by Sigiriya and imagining that her lover is Kasyapa who, in her mind, strongly resembles Arjun, Neleni escapes into her thoughts and does not experience the dull, repugnance that the act usually arouses in her. But, when it is over, and with it her fantasy, her loneliness is unbearable.

Raj has turned his back to her and she can tell from his breathing that he is already asleep. He gasps, then snores loudly. It is always this way. No words, no tenderness, just the coupling of two animals. Lying on her side, with her back to her husband, Neleni feels something creeping across her cheek. Thinking it is an insect, she tries to brush it away and is surprised to discover a tear.

Part 3: 1956
Neleni awakens

Neleni's eyelids flicker open. Lying on her side, she stares blankly at the shuttered window trying, as she does every morning, to remember where she is, parting reluctantly from her dreams. Raj is no longer at her side. She does not have to look to know that he is not there. His weight, greater than hers, always draws her towards him in the bed with the result that they occupy the same narrow strip in the centre. Often, in the night, she wakes up with the feeling that she is going to be smothered. But now, he is gone, leaving a well in the mattress where he lay.

She is alone, with a few minutes in which to think her own thoughts. She feels curiously light-hearted and, as she drifts towards consciousness, lazily, dreamily, she remembers what happened the other day. Such excitement. She still cannot believe it.

Reaching under the bed, she searches the floor, patting it like a blind woman, her fingers encountering various objects that she has stowed away and forgotten; and then, she has it. Gently, she slides the parcel out from under the bed, clasping it tightly in her hand then clutching it to her chest, as if it had wings and might fly away. For a moment she holds it close then, raising herself on one elbow, she reads the letters, printed in dark ink on the brown paper wrapping. *Neleni*. It is the first time he has used her name; the first sign of intimacy: that, and the gift that lies within the wrapping.

Carefully, she removes the paper. She has already wrapped and unwrapped it a hundred times. Following the original folds, which are already becoming soft and worn, she folds the paper back to reveal a shiny metal box, navy blue with a curled rim around the lid. It is a box of paints. Water colours. The very best.

There is only one shop that sells these; Cargills, Ceylon's equivalent of London's Army and Navy store. There is nothing that it does not sell. For a price. She remembers wandering in there, trying not to feel conspicuous in the company of wealthy women in heavy silk saris and European planters with their leathery, sunburnt skin.

She used to stand for many minutes before the glass and mahogany cabinet in which art materials were displayed, wishing that she had the money, and time, to indulge her passion. However, her enthusiasm gradually diminished and she ceased to visit the store, or even to think of painting. But now, her interest has been re-kindled.

She will start today, using the large block of artist's paper that accompanied the paints. She must start with something simple, a single flower, perhaps. Trying to think of a suitable subject, she closes her eyes and, as she does so, a sweet perfume wafts in from the window. Yes, that is it. A flower from the temple tree that stands outside the house. He will understand the significance of that. And, when the picture is finished, she will give it to him.

The house reeks of turpentine. Ella, the new maid, is mixing floor polish under Sunny's supervision.

"Now, do as I tell you," the old woman croaks, testily. "Add five spoonfuls of red wax to one measure of turpentine. Put it all in this tin can, then mix it with the stick until it becomes runny. You can't put red wax straight onto the floor. It's too thick, and you'll never get it off again."

The old lady resents the new maid who arrives every morning at 6 a.m., depriving Sunny of her time alone in the backyard and her opportunity to converse with her dead husband. Her spiritual monologue has been replaced by a practical one in which she gives instruction on how to clean the floors, wash up, put the pans away, store the food, fold the ironing, polish the brass and dust the surfaces. For the first week of Ella's employment, Sunny has been unrelentingly crotchety; for, somehow, the task of instructing the new maid has fallen to her, not Neleni.

Intuitively, Sunny links the arrival of the new maid to the parcel which Arjun gave to Neleni the other day. There was no mistaking the joy on Neleni's face, or Arjun's sheepish embarrassment. They must have thought that they were alone, or they would not have been so open with their feelings. Sunny, who had been peeping through a crack in the kitchen door, was shocked. And then, the day after, the new maid had appeared. No doubt, that was his idea, too.

Sunny is determined not to make the girl's life easy. That way, she will soon become demoralized and leave. She is a scrawny creature with large, flapping feet like a water-bird and does not look as if she has eaten in a week. At first, Sunny doubted if she even had the energy to do a day's work.

***

Ella, the maid, is about twenty years old, although there is no record of her birth and she does not know her exact age. Whippet thin, she has large, irregular teeth and a skin blackened by working in the sugar plantation. This job is an opportunity, better pay for easier work. Even a few extra rupees are a powerful incentive to travel the long distance to work.

For Ella must earn enough to support her family. Her husband, a plantation worker, has recently fallen sick. A violent fever has left him so weak that he is hardly able to rise from his bed. Any movement induces a persistent, bubbling cough. Every spasm lasts several minutes. Often, he spits up blood and, every day, he becomes thinner and more pale.

Sometimes, Ella believes she can see the life literally draining out of him but, still, she has not given up hope of his recovery. If she can earn a little more, she may be able to pay for a doctor, or better food. Either way, her husband will be restored to health. Like most poor people, Ella believes that money itself has therapeutic properties. There are few ills that it cannot cure.

So, every morning, she rises at 4.30, makes herself a little tea, eats some cold rice left over from last night's meal and packs her tiffin box. Then, after kissing her children goodbye, she leaves them in the care of her elderly mother and starts the long journey to work before it is light.

Ella does not have the money for the train journey into town so she waits at a certain point on the track where the trains slow down in the hope of leaping aboard. If she is lucky, she will find a step on which to sit; if not, she must cling on like a human spider, flattening herself against the outer wall of the train as it whistles through black, soot-filled tunnels. But this is luxury compared to the alternative: an energy-sapping tramp of two and half hours along the track.

She does not possess an umbrella to shield herself from the sun and has only the protection of her skin, baked black from working in the fields. She is not a vain woman but she knows that her darkness marks her out as low caste. It is as much a sign of her status as the red potu that she wears on her forehead; the sign that she is a Tamil.

By the time she is thirty, Ella will be grandmother to a new generation of ragged children. Old and unable to sustain the punishing routine of travelling into town, she will be forced back to the fields to face an early death from snake bite, disease or exhaustion.

It is not a happy prospect but Ella, who knows that her lot is unchangeable, accepts it. And, for the present, she revels in the fact that she does not have to work for hours in the blistering heat. Anything is better than that.

Ella is Tamil, a sufficient recommendation for Neleni and Arjun; but she is also Hindu, which provides Sunny with further grounds for objection.

"Couldn't you have given the job to a good, Catholic girl?" she grumbles.

At this, Neleni had simply raised an eyebrow and walked away. Sunny's own grandmother was Hindu, a fact she conveniently overlooks when objecting to the employment of 'a heathen'.

***

Today, Ella is learning to wax the floors. First, she must apply the turpentine mixture to the concrete with a large clump of rag, then she must remove the excess wax using a large broom, its head wrapped in a towel. However, despite applying the whole of her meagre weight to the brush, Ella makes little progress. The brush skims over the wax without removing it.

"Push down harder," Sunny snaps.

But it is no good. Ella makes no impression on the slick of oily polish. She might as well try to empty a lake with a thimble. With tears in her eyes, Ella looks pleadingly at Sunny. If she fails in this, her employers will have good reason to send her away. And then, what will happen to her family?

Ella's fear is palpable. It arcs out of her, like electricity, streaking out and up, a flare of lightning that earths itself in Sunny. Finally, the old lady relents. She too has known sleepless nights, wracked with anxiety, tormented by visions of her own, starving child. Anyone who has not had that experience will never understand it.

Those who were in a position to help, did not; those who wanted to, could not. With bitterness, Sunny remembers how Edward's wealthy family turned their back on her. They had never approved of the marriage and, after Edward's death, they had vented their spite by simply ignoring his wife and child. She had vowed never to behave like that.

For a few seconds, the two women stare at each other, communicating without words, joined by their common experience of hardship. Then Sunny notices Saro who is playing under the table.

The little girl crept out of bed early when she heard her grandmother rise, following her into the kitchen. To keep her amused, Sunny has allowed Saro to set up shop: a pair of old scales, a paper bag and some saucers of dried beans and lentils. Saro is busy playing the part of both shopkeeper and customer.

"Hello Mrs Vishnapathy. What can I do for you today?"

"My children are sick. What can I give them?" whimpers the customer, also played by Saro.

"Feed them beans and lentils then three spoons of my special medicine," bellows the shopkeeper.

Saro offers her imaginary customer an invisible bottle. She is a maker of potions, just like her grandmother. For, whenever one of the family falls sick, Sunny concocts a herbal remedy. Handfuls of leaves are added to a great iron pot on the stove and left to stew for hours and, every now and then, Sunny will lift the lid, squinting through the steam, adding a pinch of some nameless ingredient: a piece of root or bark, a spice. Once she even added eggshells. Inevitably, the result is a foul-tasting brew that is insinuated into your mouth with a teaspoon while Sunny holds your nose. The very thought of it is potent enough to make Saro wrinkle her nose in disgust.

"Saro, come here. Come and play with Nanna."

Obediently, Saro crawls from The Shop Under The Table.

"Saro, Ella needs your help."

Coyly, Saro clings to her grandmother's legs, burying her face in the old woman's skirts. But Sunny will have none of it. Firmly, she unfurls the child's fists which are fixed like clams to the folds of her sari.

"Saro, listen to me. This is a new game. You stand on the broom and Ella will give you a ride. If you are very good, I will give you some jaggery."

That clinches it. The thought of a fat brown sugar crystal makes Saro's mouth water. Jaggery is a special treat, usually reserved for Sundays.

With the help of the two women, Saro positions herself on the brush, facing Ella, her hands clasped around the handle. Ella pushes. The heavy broom presses hard into the greasy surface, gliding forward, travelling under its own momentum as it gathers speed. Ella simply needs to guide it.

Saro squeals with delight. Ella laughs and kisses her. They have established a routine which will last until Saro gets too big to climb on the brush. However, by that time, Ella will have established herself in Sunny's affections, her presence having become as necessary to the old lady's happiness as that of the detestable cat.

1956: Egg hoppers

Arjun awakes slowly, his mouth thick and tacky from the lack of air. He has slept fitfully, waking at intervals then lapsing into dreams in which, once again, he has heard the voices of a man and a woman arguing. He could not see the man's face, but Arjun recognized the woman as the Sigiriya Maiden, the one that he so admired. He cannot recall exactly what they said, but he knows that they were fighting over him. The woman was screaming; flinging words, like daggers, at her opponent. Then, she had turned to stare at Arjun.

Twisted with rage, her face had lost its serenity. She was fearsome; a harpy; an ancient Eve. Rising from the ground, she had hovered for a second, considering him. The man had shouted, tried to catch her, but she had darted away, high up, out of reach, still watching Arjun. Then, she had dived towards him, scudding through the air, her silken scarves streaming behind her. Terrified, he had tried to run, but his legs were frozen. He felt a strange heat, like flame, licking over his skin. His only escape was to wake up, but he could not. Something restrained him. Hunger. She was nearly upon him, reaching out her arms, her fingers within an inch of his face. Then, quite suddenly, she was gone.

"Ugh," he groans.

His eyelids part, sticky with heat. He is panting for breath. Despite the open window, the air is hot and suffocating and the sun is shining directly on his face.

"That accounts for it," he thinks, with relief.

Heaving his legs over the side of the bed, he rubs his scalp and yawns. He pushes back the folds of mosquito netting that stick to his damp body like a vaporous dream then, stepping into his sarong, he secures it around his waist and reaches for his watch.

"Seven thirty. My god, I'm late. And this, of all days."

Struggling to his feet, he blunders about the room, searching for a clean shirt. He must wear his best. This is an important day. He has been seconded, at the last minute, to stand in for the Government Agent and check the progress of an important road-building project. It will be a test of his initiative and ability. He has got off to an inauspicious start by oversleeping.

At last, he finds what he is looking for; a brown paper parcel of clothes, washed and ironed by the dhobi woman. Cutting the string with his pen-knife, he spills the clothes over the bed, searching frantically for his best shirt. There it is, neatly folded and freshly starched. He shakes out the creases and hangs it over the back of a chair.

Checking his watch again, he upbraids himself for his stupidity. There is only time for a strip wash at the basin, using water that is still warm and soapy from last night. Dropping his sarong to the floor, he lathers himself, then rinses with the stagnant water that leaves his skin feeling slimy.

He has just started to shave, when a knock at the door startles him and he nicks his skin. Cursing under his breath, he pulls up his sarong and hurries to the door. Rani is standing outside, holding a large mug of tea. It is the daily chore which she prizes most highly, because she gets to see Uncle Arjun before anyone else and this task is usually rewarded with a sweet; a Bluebird toffee in a shiny wrapper. But today, there is no prize to carry off to the tin that she keeps under her bed. In fact, Uncle Arjun looks unusually annoyed. Wordlessly, she holds out the tea with both hands.

"Thank you."

He takes the tea and closes the door, leaving her outside, wondering wistfully what she has done to irritate him.

***

Neleni is in the kitchen, awaiting Arjun's arrival for breakfast. Meal-times give her an excuse to speak to him. She enjoys his conversation, laughing at his stories of recalcitrant overseers, eager to hear of the projects that he has been working on: new bridges, roads and irrigation systems. He is an important man, shaping the face of her country; while, she, on the other hand, is as insignificant as a speck of dust.

Breakfast and supper are now the main focus of Neleni's day and she has taken over responsibility for their preparation, demoting Sunny from chief cook to kitchen help. Stung by her loss of authority, the old lady regards it as a betrayal. It does little to endear Arjun to her for, as she rightly guesses, he is the reason for Neleni's renewed interest in domestic affairs.

Neleni, however, is oblivious to her mother's discontent. Their lodger gives her purpose, a means to straighten the meandering course of her life. She makes it her task to predict his needs and provide for his comfort.

Today, she will cook him egg hoppers. His favourite. She heats a small metal bowl over the stove, then tips in a measure of thin batter, swirling it around until it begins to set in the shape of the bowl. As it finishes cooking, she cracks an egg into the bowl to form the heart of the pancake.

The crisp batter and warm, melting egg yolk are irresistible. She eats the first one herself, pulling the hopper apart with her fingers, folding the outside around the yolk in an attempt to stop it running. She bites deep, closing her eyes. A skein of orange yolk, the colour of marigolds, trickles across her palm. She licks it. It is a good hopper.

"Ai," Sunny hisses in disgust. "You behave like a goonda!"

Neleni smiles benignly, then spots Rani in the doorway. With feet crossed and arms stretched across the door-frame, the child is rocking from side to side. It is what she does to while away the long hours of childhood.

"What is wrong with you?"

"Nothing."

When Rani says nothing in that voice, her mother knows that it is something. But she knows better than to question Rani in one of these moods. The girl often withdraws into her own world, a place firmly closed to outsiders.

"Go and do your homework," she orders with a trace of annoyance.

"I haven't got any."

"Then find some."

In a dream-like torpor, Rani hears her mother's voice as if from a great distance. It takes several seconds for Neleni's words to penetrate her thoughts and she responds slowly, looking fixedly at her mother without seeing her. Then, on a sudden impulse, she stirs, turns and drifts away along the passage.

"Sometimes, I wonder if she's all there," thinks Neleni to herself, not for the first time.

***

Rani intends to return to her room and count her store of sweets, the ones given to her by Uncle Arjun. She has amassed quite a collection which she keeps in an old, tartan shortbread tin. She never eats the sweets, preferring to gloat over them in private as if they are jewels. They are certainly jewel-coloured, wrapped in pink, green and blue foil; and they are more precious to her than any gem, because Uncle has given them to her. Each sweet is a sign of his special favour. His approval is important to her, and on the rare occasions that he shows displeasure, she feels it keenly. Like this morning. She still does not know what she did wrong and, in her ignorance, she grieves.

She is about to enter her room, when she sees him coming along the corridor. He looks so handsome. Like a prince. Rani stands, open-mouthed, watching him, her eyes as big as humbugs, so large they nearly swallow her face. Arjun rushes past but, as he does so, he pats her absent-mindedly on the head. Whatever it was she did, she is forgiven. Her heart sings. Counting her sweets can wait. She trots after him, suddenly hungry.

***

Breathless, Arjun bursts into the kitchen.

"Here you are. I've made some egg hoppers."

Neleni has already pulled out a chair for him.

"I'm sorry. Can't stop. I'm late already. Has my car arrived?"

"Car?"

There is a loud hoot from the street. The Government Agent's car has arrived to take Arjun to work.

"Oh. That's a shame."

Neleni is flustered.

"Here. I'll put some hoppers in a bowl. You can eat them in the car. You can't go without breakfast."

Despite Arjun's protests, Neleni busies herself packing his breakfast, folding the hoppers gently in greaseproof paper, then placing them in an enamel bowl, one that will be large enough to catch any drips of egg yolk if he holds it close to his face while eating. From a corner of the kitchen, Sunny glowers at all the commotion.

"Where's my briefcase?"

"Here Uncle Arjun."

Rani is standing behind him in the hallway, the case cradled in her arms.

"Thank you, darling."

Rani looks smug.

"And here's your hat."

Neleni offers him the battered panama.

"I'll bring your food to the car. Wait while I fetch it. I'll only be a minute."

She whisks back into the kitchen, then emerges, the bowl in her hands, darting after Arjun as he runs down the steps to the car. As she sees the vehicle, she catches her breath. It is larger than the one that took them to Sigiriya. Much larger. A great, black panther of a car: a purring Humber, with shiny chrome fittings. An ambassador's car.

"Oh my!"

"Splendid, isn't it?" says Arjun with a hint of pride.

"Oh yes. Splendid."

The chauffeur holds the door open for Arjun as he slips into the passenger seat. Neleni is suddenly embarrassed by the bowlful of hoppers. It does not seem right to eat in a car like this.

"Here, give them to me," says Arjun, reading her thoughts. "I'll save them for later".

And, taking the bowl, he places it discreetly on the floor beside him.

With a powerful rumble, the car pulls away, leaving Neleni and Rani on the steps, watching awestruck as the object of their fascination disappears.

1956: Asoka's meditation

Asoka has not slept well. In fact, he has not slept properly since the meeting at Hooniyam's shrine. He has woken at least three times already and this is the fourth. The hut is stifling. And it stinks. His own breath returns to him foetid and foul-tasting. Desperate for clean air, he hauls himself to his feet.

His legs feel as if they are covered with a hundred hot pin-pricks, confirming his suspicions that the filthy mattress on which he has slept is infested with bed bugs. Wrapping his blue sarong around him and pulling on a dirty, dust-stained vest, he lets himself out and walks softly down the steps.

The early morning air is clear and sweet, scented with the sap of forest trees. He lives here alone, but he likes it. He has found a peace here that he never knew in the monastery and it has become his custom, when troubled, to walk in the forest.

It is about half-past five and the men will begin to arrive at six, drifting in reluctantly like morning mist. He wonders how much longer he can hold them to their promise. They have not been paid for many months so he has turned a blind eye to their pilfering, but even the few things they are able to take will not feed their families for long. The men only remain out of loyalty to him. It is his gift, this ability to draw people after him on whatever quest he chooses. But now he must bring this venture to a conclusion, if not for his sake, then for theirs.

He should have done it last week. Soon it will be too late. The men are getting restless and his fellow conspirator, Anil, is beginning to question his judgement, if not his commitment. Perhaps he has reason. Asoka is mystified by his own inability to act. The plan is seamless, perfect. So why is he dithering?

As he walks around the clearing, he marvels at the profusion of plant-life. It scrambles from the soil, thrusting itself outwards and upwards with an aggression peculiar even for this fertile land. Huge arum lilies glow eerily under the trees, their pale cups as large as chalices; ferns and grasses grow waist-high; creepers and vines scramble up trees with unrestrained vigour, clutching their victims in a deadly embrace.

Asoka pauses, listening, watching. Moths with velvet bodies whir past his face, drunk on the nectar of nocturnal flowers. A harmonious discord fills the air: a chirping, squawking, humming chorus of animal life. Up here, he never feels alone. He is at one, not at odds, with the world around him.

The place breathes enchantment. He must resist. He is in danger of being distracted. He forces himself to walk on, across the clearing, away from the sights, smells and sounds that entice him away from his own thoughts. Determinedly, he marches down the track, away from the trees, until he finds a place where he can think, uninterrupted.

Climbing onto the verge, he seats himself on the grass and looks across the valley where tiny lights are still twinkling like fireflies. The villagers are starting their long day, lighting lamps and fires, boiling water, cooking food, milking cattle. By mid-day, there will be no trace of their existence, their hamlets invisible among the trees. Then, a stranger looking into the wooded ravine might assume that the area was deserted. Only at night and early morning, can one get a true picture of human habitation here.

Asoka prefers to keep people at a distance. It makes his job easier. He views them with detachment, as objects, in much the same way as he views the villages across the valley. Sometimes, he has even questioned whether other people really exist, or whether they are just a figment of his imagination, a delusion.

It is a theory supported by learning. He studied Buddhist scripture for many years. Since the age of eight, in fact, when his devout parents dedicated their younger son to the monastery. After an initial period of homesickness, he quickly adapted to the life of a monk; praying, chanting, processing through town with his begging bowl, and studying for hours in the library.

He has spent years, relentlessly pursuing knowledge, hungrily absorbing books on politics, philosophy and religion. He even studied for a while at the great monastery of Kelaniya where he imbibed new doctrines of political Buddhism. Having returned to his old monastery, he taught these theories to the younger monks. But there was still one question to which he could find no answer. *If, as the Scriptures imply, all life is an illusion, then how do I know that I exist?*

The application of logic to this premise, led to a devastating conclusion. *If I do not exist, then my faith is also an illusion.* Such was the reasoning that led him to despair; a chasm of unknowing that defied reason, a darkness so immense that it threatened to swallow him whole. Without faith, there was nothing.

It was a devastating loss. To the consternation of the other monks, Asoka fell sick with a mysterious illness, being unable to raise himself from his bed, eat or drink and, for days, lay in a darkened cell, his eyes fixed on the ceiling, apparently unable to see or hear. Then, quite suddenly, he rose up one morning and walked out of the monastery gates, never to return.

After that, he made a living wherever he could; portering, cleaning, running errands, living in the poorest part of town and spending his money on whatever books he could afford. He re-read Marx then, having purchased a book on Trotsky, acquainted himself with the theory of Permanent Revolution. Over and over again, he read it, feverishly turning its pages. Suddenly, ideas that formerly seemed as insubstantial as air, acquired meaning.

Living in a shanty, where rain and sun hammered alternately on the corrugated iron roof, rats swam in the open sewer, and his neighbours succumbed daily to death and disease, Asoka also discovered anger. It gave him strength and a new reason to live.

Truth, he decided, was found through action, not prayer. Then, gradually, step by logical step, he found a new belief and a determination to reform his country. His faith is politics and nationalism, his creed. He wants change and has already gone some way to achieving it; teaching and recruiting new followers and planning attacks on those he views as enemies of the under-privileged Sinhalese.

It is not that he hates Tamils as such; it is just that they happen to be wealthy, well-educated and powerful, while the majority of Sinhalese lack similar advantages. Tamils are, therefore, oppressors of the Sinhalese. For many months now, Asoka has dedicated himself to redressing the balance.

Now he has the chance to translate his beliefs into action but, suddenly, he has begun to waver. What is wrong? He cannot understand it. His commitment is as strong as ever. Why is he so reluctant to act? It is a question that has tormented him, ever since the meeting at Hooniyam's shrine.

Of course, that is it. It is not his own motives that worry Asoka, but those of his fellow conspirators. The Assistant Superintendent of Police is an opportunist, a man motivated by greed and even darker urges. He has a sadistic look in his eye, something suggesting that he takes pleasure in others' pain. He is impure, self-seeking, not the sort with which Asoka wishes to associate.

And, then, there is Anil. What has happened to him? In the monastery, Anil was Asoka's most dedicated pupil. His devotion to his teacher was so great that, shortly after Asoka disappeared, Anil, too, left the monastery in order to search for his master. Eventually, he found Asoka and begged to live with him.

But Asoka, unready for disciples and averse to company, had sent him away. Nonetheless, Anil returned from time to time, bringing parcels of food. He still wore monkish robes, so Asoka assumed that he had returned to the monastery. He did not realise until later that Anil had found shelter elsewhere, sweeping floors in Hooniyam's shrine.

Hooniyam: not exactly a conspirator, but another unwelcome element in Asoka's plan. From childhood, Asoka has known of Hooniyam's reputation for sorcery. It is common knowledge and Hooniyam's name is part of common speech, a word used to describe the kind of home-made witchcraft employed by the ignorant to curse their neighbours. Even children threaten their schoolmates with his name. *I will Hooniyam you.*

Although Hooniyam's status has recently been enhanced and his shrine dignified by important people, such as the Bandaranaikes, Asoka believes that the worship of such a god signifies ignorance and superstition. Those, like Anil, who have had the benefit of many years' education, are taking a backward step when they indulge in such beliefs.

How could Anil, a student of Buddhist scripture, have lowered himself to this level? Although Asoka has rejected the Buddhist faith, he still respects its teaching, its structure and discipline. For it is both a philosophy and, for many people, a means to spiritual enlightenment. But Hooniyam offers neither, only a view into the dark recesses of the human spirit; places that are best forgotten.

Asoka fears that he has lost control. For it was Anil, not Asoka, who arranged to meet in Hooniyam's shrine: Anil who invited the policeman. Asoka's former pupil has forgotten his place and the deference due to his master. In fact, now he thinks of it, Asoka cannot remember exactly how it was that Anil became so closely involved in his plans.

After he left the monastery, Asoka began to make a name for himself in underground political movements. Unbidden, Anil also attended the meetings. He was always there, at Asoka's elbow, winning a place at his side through sheer persistence. Then, one day, in an unguarded moment, Asoka had told Anil of his plans for direct action; assuming, wrongly, that Anil had no-one with whom to share the information. Anil, however, had befriended the Assistant Superintendent of Police, a regular visitor to the shrine. Without consulting Asoka, he enlisted the policeman's help.

Lost in thought, Asoka has walked a long way from the clearing. He now has a clear view across the valley and the blue-shrouded mountains beyond. Somewhere close by, he can hear the rushing torrent of a waterfall. Yet even here, surrounded by all this beauty, he cannot shake off his feeling of unease.

He turns and walks back along the track, silently cursing Anil for his stupidity. Anil should have known better than to go tittle-tattling to that policeman. Asoka has been compromised; his plan exposed. By involving the policeman, a fervent nationalist, Anil has committed Asoka to a course of action from which he cannot escape. There can be no second thoughts, no going back.

"Why on earth did he tell that man? And why, of all places, did he organise a meeting in that godforsaken shrine?" mutters Asoka, angrily. "Hooniyam, indeed!"

At that moment, there is a violent disturbance in the undergrowth. Asoka turns quickly, fearing that he has been followed, betrayed.

"Who's there?"

The clearing is filled with a breathless stillness. Nothing moves. No birds sing. Not even a leaf quivers. Yet Asoka is uneasy. Convinced that he is being spied on, he stoops swiftly, picks up a stone and flings it into the bushes, hoping to flush out any intruder concealed there. But the silence is undisturbed.

"Must have been a monkey," thinks Asoka.

He waits for a few seconds, watching for any further movement, but nothing stirs.

***

Asoka walks slowly across the clearing, occasionally stopping to glance over his shoulder, still unconvinced that he is alone. On the steps to the hut, he pauses again for one last look, before disappearing inside.

Once Asoka is out of sight, a new disturbance breaks out in the undergrowth; bushes shake violently as if moved by an invisible tremor, small spouts of soil are thrown in the air, then Hooniyam appears, groaning and rubbing his forehead as he examines the stone that Asoka hurled at him, and which found its mark in the centre of his brow. It required divine self-control not to cry out when the missile struck home. As the pain abates, Hooniyam swears to pay back the unbeliever who has shown him such disrespect.

1956: Tea

Leaving the main causeway, the sleek black Humber turns onto a road that becomes progressively narrower as it snakes back and forth across the face of the mountains in a relentless series of switchbacks. As the car climbs up from the plain, Arjun looks down at the little town spread out below; its houses, small lozenges of red and green, scattered along a brown ribbon of road.

He bites into an egg hopper. Still warm, the egg yolk seeps over his tongue, sensuous and creamy, with a flavour faintly redolent of grain. He has never tasted such eggs in the city. Out here, near the country, everything has more flavour, more colour, or, perhaps, it is simply that his senses have become more finely-tuned. There are certainly less distractions here: less noise, less filth, fewer people; and there is more time to think, an opportunity to savour new sensations.

Reaching for another pancake, he realizes, to his surprise, that he has already eaten three and there is only one left. He offers it to his driver Walter who, to Arjun's relief, refuses. As he folds the hopper in his fingers, one hand cupped below the other to catch any trickles of yolk, he wonders, idly, what Neleni is doing.

She was delighted with the paints that he gave her; although she accepted shyly, trying to conceal her pleasure. He wonders if she has found time to use them yet. He pictures her, sitting at her table, opening the box, running her fingers over the bright colours as she decides what to paint. Perhaps, as she does so, she will think of him. The thought ignites a spark of guilty pleasure. He tries to stamp it out. The paint box was a gift given in friendship. Nothing more. But, somehow, this argument lacks conviction.

***

They are travelling "up country". The air is cool, almost chilly, and the sloping contour of every hill is lined with rows of hedges. Tea. A member of the camellia family, the tea bush is unremarkable in appearance. It is famous only for its leaves. These, it is said, fell by accident into a Chinese Emperor's cup, scenting the water and starting the passion for tea-drinking. Since then, the leaves themselves have been treated with the reverence due to royalty. Only the bud and top two leaves of each twig are plucked, a process requiring such delicacy that picking is always done by hand, not machine.

In the 18th and 19th centuries, tea was introduced by the British into India and Ceylon where it was grown on a commercial scale. Because the high altitude gives the finest crop, vast acreages of highland territory were cleared to create plantations managed by British planters and worked by armies of native labourers. The cultivation of the humble tea-bush became an industry worth millions of rupees and spurred some startling demographic changes.

Tea has put Ceylon on the map or, at least, on the breakfast table. Originally the drink of Emperors, it is now the national beverage of a rain-swept country in the northern hemisphere. While Britons may be somewhat hazy as to Ceylon's longitude and latitude, there are some facts which they can all identify with certainty: firstly, Ceylon is synonymous with tea production, both in the general sense and regarding a specific variety to which the Island has lent its name: secondly, if a tea-picker were suddenly to materialize in the middle of an English high street, she would be instantly recognised.

This is because tea is an essential part of the daily curriculum, influencing both the popular timetable and vocabulary. Images of sari-clad women with baskets strapped to their heads appear at the breakfast table, smiling benignly at diners from the sides of metal tea-caddies and cardboard packets; tea-breaks have become the inalienable right of every worker and tea-time is the third meal of the day. 'High-tea' describes a regime of sumptuous cakes and thinly-sliced cucumber sandwiches, while the word "tea-leaf" has entered Cockney rhyming slang as a term for "thief".

But the British are not alone in their love of tea. The Ceylonese are also great tea drinkers having developed a variety of preparations, both recreational and medicinal. These include: light tea, made by adding just a dash of tea to a glass of hot milk; black tea; creamy tea made with milk powder; tea mixed with lime and sugar to treat stomach ailments; tea boiled in kettles with milk and spices, and tea prepared the western way in china pots.

However, everything comes at a price and tea, a cornerstone of the Ceylonese economy, is no exception. While it has brought wealth to the Island, its cultivation has led to political instability.

***

In the 19th century, the British imported thousands of labourers from southern India to work on Ceylonese tea plantations. To distinguish them from the Island's indigenous Tamils, these relative newcomers were referred to as 'Indian' Tamils.

But the growing influence of this immigrant community played on a deep-rooted fear: that of foreign invasion. A source of riches, Ceylon had frequently attracted the attention of Indian rulers. Separated from the mainland by only 20 miles of open sea, it was a tempting prize, easily accessible to adventurers from the mainland.

Working on the tea plantations, with status little better than slaves, the Indian Tamils should have remained safely out of the public eye. However, they possessed one thing of value. The vote. By itself, this was not a problem. However, combined with their rapidly increasing numbers, it transformed the Indian Tamils into a political force. In 1947, they returned seven MPs to Parliament. To add insult to injury, these elections took place in the historic Sinhalese heartland of Kandy.

The growing influence of the Indian Tamils posed a threat to factions hungry for change. With help from Buddhist scholars, Sinhalese nationalists re-constructed history, arguing that this gave them an inalienable right to the Island: a right established by the legendary prince Vijaya and confirmed by Buddha himself.

In their view, there was no room for interlopers and the relatively recent arrival of the Indian Tamils, encouraged by the British, proved a particular irritant; an itch that must be scratched. And the Sinhalese nationalists scratched to great effect. Soon after Independence, they passed laws disenfranchising the Indian Tamils. Without a vote, the Indian Tamils had no voice. Politically, they ceased to exist.

***

It is a cautionary tale. *If it could happen to them, it can happen to us.* This gloomy prediction is bandied about by armchair philosophers and politicians, indigenous Tamils of Raj's age and outlook. The young and upwardly mobile have not yet been infected by its pessimism, preferring to dismiss it as the maundering of disappointed old men.

Like his peers, Arjun is relatively unconcerned. He has many Sinhalese friends, but has had little contact with Indian Tamils. They may speak the same language, but they inhabit a different social stratum. While indigenous Tamils are mostly affluent, well-educated and middle class, Indian Tamils are usually illiterate, poor and of peasant stock. In fact, many indigenous Tamils regard their Indian counterparts as foreigners; 'coolies' working the fields whose lives have little bearing on their own. A few, like Arjun's previous boss Pius, positively disown them.

"Even the bloody Moslems here speak Tamil. It doesn't mean we are all tarred with the same brush."

It was one of Pius's favourite maxims, stated frequently, regardless of whether his audience was Tamil or Sinhalese.

As the car winds its way through the tea plantations, it passes a group of tea-pickers. They are all female: the large wicker baskets on their backs secured by a strap around the forehead sitting just above the potu, the dot of paint affected by Tamil women. Even by Island standards, the women are small, the result of generations of malnutrition. But they are cheerful and talk incessantly as they work. Their teeth, too large for their small faces, are as yellow as old ivory, contrasting with the sun-blackened hue of their skins.

It is painstaking work and many of the women look older than they really are. As the car passes, one looks up and smiles at Arjun, her face wrinkled and leathery. She waves at her friend, saying something as she points at the car. Arjun catches a few words, but not enough to make sense. The women laugh, a harsh, coughing sound like the cawing of crows. Arjun blushes, suspecting that he is the butt of their humour.

To cover his embarrassment, he pulls a file from his brief case and re-reads the case notes relating to the site that he is to visit. From the surname, he sees that the overseer is Tamil.

"What do you know of this man, Mennan Rasanayagam?"

"Never met him, sir."

In the rear-view mirror, Arjun can see that Walter, the driver, is frowning. Something in the tone of his voice alerts Arjun to the fact that Walter knows more. Anyone with a reputation will be known to someone on the Island and a man in Walter's position hears many things. Walter squints at the mirror, indicating that what he knows is not good, but he is reluctant to speak.

"Is he taking bribes?"

"I can't say for sure, sir."

Walter hesitates, then adds: "There are rumours."

Slowly, Arjun turns the pages of the file which contain copies of the site's accounts, submitted by the overseer. Accompanied by invoices and receipts for large amounts of building materials, they seem to tally. Then, at the back of the file, he finds a piece of paper, torn from a lined exercise book. It contains what appears to be a statement, written in pencil and unsigned.

"I work for the company that supplies materials to the road-building project managed by Mennan Rasanayagam. The company delivers many barrels of tar to the project site every week but, several days later, many of those barrels are returned to the company's yard. They are full and unused."

Frowning, Arjun flicks back to the front of the file. He re-examines the receipts and delivery notes. It appears that, over the last eighteen months, supplies worth thousands of lakhs of rupees have been trucked onto the site. A phenomenal amount. However, this in itself is not surprising. The building of this road, some thirty miles long, represents a major project. Arjun turns back to the site's accounts. There is no record of materials being returned to the supplier or any re-imbursement being made. Someone is lying.

***

They enter a thick belt of forest. The road dwindles into a cart-track and the car bounces and lunges as it encounters potholes and stones. They are close to their destination now, but this track neither feels, nor looks, like a new highway. Around the next corner, the track leads into a forest clearing which serves as a delivery point for supplies. To one side, under the trees, is a rickety-looking hut.

"Stop here, Walter. I want to have a look around before meeting the overseer."

The car ambles to a halt and, letting himself out, Arjun walks swiftly across the clearing. Three or four men are squatting around a fire from which a thin stream of wood-smoke rises in a straight column. They stop talking as he approaches.

"I'm from the Government Agent's office. I've come to view the site."

Without a word, one of the men stretches his arm, pointing to a track through the trees. The man's face is expressionless although his amber eyes are unnerving. As he walks away, Arjun can feel those eyes watching him, following him along the shadowy path into the forest.

***

Arjun's heart is beating fast. There is something strange about this place. The men at the camp-fire were wary, hostile, as if they wished to be neither seen nor heard. His arrival caught them unawares and, for a second, they looked guilty, as if they were hiding something. Arjun wonders what they were discussing. Whatever it was, his presence is unwelcome. And now he is walking alone, unaccompanied on a narrow track through the trees.

"What a fool I am. I don't even know where this path leads."

A few feet away, something moves in the undergrowth. Arjun starts. He is sure that he saw a human figure flitting between the trees.

"My god, they're following me."

Thoughts of ambush and murder spring to mind.

The trees tower over him like sentinels and he is surrounded by an oppressive gloom. His legs feel suddenly weak and, for a second, he is frozen to the spot, like a frightened animal, expecting the worst: a blow to the back of the head, perhaps, or a sharp, stabbing pain in the ribs. Whatever it is, he hopes it will be quick. But the moment passes, the air freshens and, as he begins to breathe more easily, his fears are dispelled. There, in front of him. He can hear them now. Faintly, just ahead of him: human voices. They are shouting to each other; the loud, unintelligible barks of working men.

Emerging from the trees, Arjun blinks in the sunlight. In front of him is a broad track along which two columns of men pass each other in opposite directions. One line of labourers heads downhill, carrying large baskets of rubble on their backs, while the other line ascends with empty baskets which they fill from a mountainous heap of broken stone, using their bare hands as shovels. This human chain consists of some two hundred men. But the accounts in Arjun's file clearly state that at least five hundred labourers are working on site. They even list the wages paid to each man. Where are they all?

Arjun's view is obscured by a sharp bend in the track so he decides to follow the men downhill to see where they are going. On the way, he passes a young boy, not more than ten years old, whose baggy shorts are held up by a length of coarse twine tied at the waist. Handed down by an older brother, the shorts have been moulded around the contours of an adult body. They wallow and sag around the boy's slender form, describing a shape that is not his, as if they are seeking the body of their former owner. The cloth from which they are made is stained and full of holes, their original khaki-colour replaced by a camouflage of squalor. The legs have been rolled up high over the child's bony knees for ease of movement. His chest is smeared with dust and his eyes look red-rimmed and sore. But it is the singular appearance of the boy's features that attracts Arjun's attention.

"A Vadda," thinks Arjun, noting the child's prominent cheekbones and mop of unruly hair. Although he has heard stories of the Island's aboriginals, he has never seen one before. For most Ceylonese, they exist only in legend.

Picking his way through the sweating gangs of men, Arjun finally rounds the corner. What he sees leaves him breathless. After widening into a circular space, the track runs abruptly into a rock wall. As the labourers empty their baskets, a few men with rakes push the rubble into heaps on the verge. However, there is not enough space for new deliveries and the mountain-side is streaked with long ribbons of red sandstone where previous piles of material have collapsed and spilled downhill. The road that was started over eighteen months ago has progressed less than half a mile.

Temporarily stunned by what he sees, Arjun does not notice a rangy man in a blue Kandyan sarong approaching him down the track.

"What do you want?"

Arjun starts. The fellow is inches away from him, staring straight into his eyes, challenging him.

"Are you the overseer?"

The man laughs, scornfully, as if Arjun has just insulted him.

"No. But I can take you to him."

"Who are you?"

"Does it matter?"

Although insolent, the fellow speaks with authority. He is dressed like a labourer but, from his manner, Arjun can tell that he is educated.

"No. It doesn't matter."

Arjun concurs, not wishing to provoke a confrontation. The workmen have stopped to listen. They eye Arjun suspiciously, looking him up and down. He feels conspicuous in his suit and tie. The odd one out. A stranger with no business to be here. Some of the men put down their baskets and move closer. There is a strong current of hostility and Arjun feels vulnerable. One push and he could fall to his death. The other man steps closer, his eyes are dark, deep-set and intelligent and they scan Arjun's face, trying to decide whether he is friend or foe.

"It's all right. Get back to work."

The man speaks softly over his shoulder. The labourers pick up their baskets and trudge away. Arjun can feel the sweat pricking his forehead.

"Follow me!"

The man leads Arjun back up the hill, along the forest path and back into the clearing where he indicates a ramshackle cabin. A temporary site-office, it has an inherent air of dereliction, being fashioned from ill-assorted planks of wood salvaged from other projects. Being raised on stilts to avoid inundation by the monsoon rain, the cabin is approached by a flight of narrow wooden stairs. With its heavy, thatched roof and single dark window, it has a forbidding aspect.

"You'll find him in there."

The man jerks a thumb in the direction of the building then, without another word, he is gone.

The fragrant aroma of tea fills the clearing. A rough tripod, made from sticks, has been erected over the camp-fire and from it a kettle hangs from a loop of coarse twine. The men do not see Arjun at first. They are leaning towards the fire with their heads together, talking urgently. Arjun steps on a twig. There is a sharp snap and the heads swivel around, as if on one neck. Once again, the men fall silent. They stare at Arjun as he emerges from the trees, their hostility almost tangible. But it is the man with the amber eyes that disturbs him most. He has the unblinking expression of a snake; watching, ready to strike. Those eyes follow Arjun as he mounts the steps to the overseer's office, then bangs loudly on the door.

"What is it?" demands a voice, irritable and slightly slurred, as if its owner has just woken up.

"My name is Arjun Kumaran, assistant to the Government Agent. I want to speak to you."

There are sounds of shuffling inside the hut. A chair scrapes across the floor. Papers rustle. A metal drawer clangs shut. A key rattles in a lock. Footsteps, quick and fussy, clicking across the wooden boards. The door opens to reveal a small, plump man in immaculate white clothes. His hair, parted at the side, has been drawn across his balding crown and stuck in place with Brylcreem. His shoes, which match his belt, are of expensive leather. Smelling strongly of cologne, he dabs at his face with a white linen handkerchief the size of a serviette. On his little finger, he wears an onyx signet ring, carved with elaborate initials. His watch-strap is made of fine gold links.

Arjun can hardly contain his surprise. He had expected crudeness and aggression or, perhaps, an arrogant, overbearing sloth like Pius, but not this popinjay.

"I wasn't expecting … I mean, I was not prepared for your visit. So sorry. I am the overseer, Mennan Rasanayagam."

The man holds out a podgy hand. Arjun forces himself to shake it. The palm is soft and slightly damp.

"Come in, come in."

The overseer's tone is completely different from the one with which he initially greeted his visitor. Pushing the door wide, he affects a kind of mock bow and, with a sweeping gesture of his arm, beckons Arjun into the hut. Inside, the air is stale, tainted with creosote and something else unpleasant. Several fat blow-flies bounce against the window-pane, dazed by the heat. In front of the window are two chairs and a table covered with scraps of paper, an overflowing ashtray and two empty beer bottles. At the back of the hut is a bench covered with grimy sheets and a pillow. A crate of beer lies half-concealed underneath. At the back, the door to a small storeroom has fallen off its hinges and been propped cross-wise across the frame.

"Please, please sit down."

Perhaps it is a sign of nervousness, but the overseer repeats himself constantly, laughing without cause. His agitation is palpable. There is a sudden thud from the room next door. The overseer starts and turns pale. Visibly shaken, he mops at his face with the white handkerchief then takes a deep breath, trying to regain his composure.

"Of course," he mutters to himself, "I had forgotten. Silly of me. Silly."

In a twinkle of highly-polished shoes, the overseer crosses the hut with amazing speed, stopping just outside the broken door.

"Hey, you," he barks. "Get us some tea. And mind you wash the cups properly this time."

A small, wild figure appears from the gloom. It is the Vadda boy. Climbing silently over the broken door, he slinks past the overseer, casting him a look of undisguised hatred.

"Hmph," snorts Mennan when the child has gone. "One tries to find servants up here, but it's useless. They're no better than monkeys."

But Arjun ignores the remark. He is wondering how the child got back here so quickly. Was he sent to warn the overseer of Arjun's arrival? That might account for the sound of papers being locked away as he stood outside the door. Settling on one of the greasy chairs, Arjun opens his briefcase.

The blowflies are flinging themselves at the window in a frenzy. Their fat bodies tap against the glass. The unpleasant smell has grown stronger. It seems to rise from the floorboards. An animal has crawled in there to die. A rat or mouse, perhaps. Maybe something bigger. Arjun tries to block out these unpleasant thoughts and focus on his work. Taking the case-file from his brief-case, he lays it on the table in front of him.

"I want to ask you some questions about the road you are building."

"Of course, of course. Anything. What can I tell you?"

The overseer, who began to shuffle uncomfortably as soon as Arjun produced his papers, is now hopping from foot to foot: backwards, forwards, sideways, in a dance of awkwardness.

"Sit down, please," says Arjun, a little more sharply than he intended. At present, he feels an equal measure of pity and contempt for the overdressed little man.

"Yes, yes," the overseer mutters, distractedly. "Thank you," he adds, quite unnecessarily.

Without thinking, he pulls out the chair that is closest to the window. The light shines full on his face, revealing every twitch, every sweating pore. Now that he is sitting, his feet are still, but his hands take up the dance, crossing and uncrossing, the fingers jigging and drumming on the table. One of his eyelids begins to flicker uncontrollably.

Arjun feels a twinge of sympathy. It is like pulling the legs off a frog. He must put compassion aside, but it is more difficult than he thought. His throat and eyes are sticky with the heat. He coughs, covering his mouth with his hand and turning his head away. It is an affectation worthy of a maiden aunt but, instinctively, he knows that it will impress Mennan. The overseer is a man susceptible to charm and the outward display of good-breeding. Perfect manners are more likely to win his respect than bullying.

"This project began eighteen months ago. I have a list of all the materials that have been delivered to the site. Here."

Opening the file at the accounts section, Arjun pushes it across the table to the overseer. The man leans over it, his arms on the table, pretending to read, but his hands are shaking. A large bead of sweat drops from his brow onto the paper, leaving a greasy stain. The overseer mops frantically at his face.

1956: Drinking tea

Outside, the wooden step creaks. The Vadda boy re-appears at the door carrying two mugs of tea. He has been given strict instructions by the man at the camp-fire, the one with the amber eyes: the blue mug is for the visitor; the white one, for the overseer. If he gets it wrong, the man with the amber eyes will want to know why. Terrified, the child has sworn to get it right.

He fears the man with the amber eyes because he is accompanied by a powerful spirit. The child has seen it often: a creature in the form of a man with long tusks, matted hair and a living girdle of snakes. Although he does not know its name, the boy knows that it is a demon. There are many of them, living here in the forest, skulking behind trees and bushes, always ready to stir up trouble. They have been here for ages, almost as long as the Vaddas. Most of them are relatively harmless, but some have left the forest and become strong by dabbling in the affairs of men.

This man's spirit is more powerful than any the boy has ever seen. He is afraid and wishes that he had one of his mother's charms. But one does not always carry such things; especially not to work. Other people, who are not Vadda, would not understand.

Without protection, the boy must rely on his memory. He has walked across the clearing, carefully repeating to himself: white for the overseer, blue for the visitor. But by the time he reaches the hut, he is no longer sure. Was it blue for the overseer and white for the visitor? He cannot remember. The harder he tries, the worse it becomes. He can feel the amber eyes watching him as he mounts the steps. His hand shakes and he spills a little of the tea.

"Put it here," says the overseer gruffly.

Awkwardly, the child reaches across the table, spilling tea onto the open file. Mennan flings him a furious glance.

"Get out!" he orders.

The child stares at him with impenetrable, coal-black eyes, then creeps from the room.

***

Arjun's hand hovers over the mugs. He is not sure which to take because the child has placed them side-by-side in the middle of the table. He is about to take the white mug, when he notices a tea-stained chip in its rim. It looks unclean. Changing his mind, he takes the blue mug and sips the tea. It has a bitter taste. He wonders how long it has been stewing in the workmen's kettle.

Mennan crouches over the file, as if studying an exam paper. He licks his finger, flicks over a page, then pushes the file away.

"That all seems in order."

The overseer tries to look cheerful but his hands continue to dance over the table.

"Those are the materials that have been delivered? You are sure?"

"Ha, well, I couldn't say exactly. Not off-hand. I'd have to check."

Mennan is flustered, floundering. His eyelid flickers even more furiously and the sweat stands out on his brow. Sitting in the full light of the window, there is nowhere for him to hide. Every twitch, every flinch is visible. He opens his handkerchief and buries his face in it.

"Surely you have some idea. You've been on site for 18 months?"

"Ye-e-s. Sixteen, eighteen. Something like that."

"Yet not even half a mile of the road has been completed."

"What?"

Raising his head from the handkerchief, Mennan stares at Arjun in alarm.

"You went there? Without telling me? You should not have done that."

"Why? Was there something you didn't want me to see?"

Mennan raises his hands in denial, but it is useless. Arjun presses his advantage.

"I have seen it all for myself. The track leads around a corner to a dead-end. A rock face, to be exact. And the rubble that should be used for the road is simply being pushed off the cliff."

Arjun's throat is burning. It is hot in the room. He drains the tea. Mennan is bleating an excuse. The drone of his voice blends with the buzzing of the flies in the window.

"You have to understand. It's not my fault. At least, not all."

"Whose is it then?"

Momentarily, Arjun's vision becomes blurred. He tries to focus on one of the flies. Tap, tap, tap. It bangs against the glass. He blinks and rubs his eyes. Mennan is still speaking.

"It is the fault of the labourers. These men are not like us. Not educated. They are savages. Come and go as they please. Sometimes they feel like working, sometimes not. If they don't show up, there's nothing I can do."

"Perhaps you should pay them," suggests Arjun, dryly. It is a wild, but lucky, guess. Mennan's mouth flaps open like a fish gulping for air.

"I have promised to pay them. As soon as I get the money. Soon. Soon."

Mennan stumbles from his chair and starts to pace about the hut, wringing his hands.

"The dynamite went missing. That was none of my fault."

"Dynamite?"

Incredulous, Arjun raises his voice.

"The dynamite for blasting the rock. It was stolen."

"When? How much?"

"All of it. Months ago," whines the overseer, miserably.

"And you told no-one!"

"I couldn't."

"Why not?"

The overseer opens his arms and shrugs. If he had reported the theft of the dynamite, there would have been an investigation and his own profiteering would have been revealed.

"Please, help me," Mennan, paws Arjun's elbow. "We can come to an arrangement. People like us should stick together."

"Just because I am Tamil, does not mean that I will protect you!"

Arjun is astounded by this assumption. He tries to ignore the queasy feeling in his stomach.

"What about the other supplies? Were they stolen too?"

"No. We had nowhere to store them, so I sent them back."

"You sent them back, or you sold them back?"

"Oh, please … You don't understand. I have a wife. Look!"

Reaching into a drawer, Mennan produces the framed photograph of a woman. He waves it in Arjun's face, clutching at his arm. For a second, Arjun is distracted. The woman in the picture is outstandingly beautiful, far younger than her husband. Arjun thinks he has seen her before. Where? An image of Sigiriya flashes through his mind: standing in the gallery, looking out over the water gardens and the forest; Neleni beside him; the sound of faint laughter.

A dull thump beneath the floor of the hut startles him out of his reverie, recalling him to present business. It is followed by a dry, slithering sound.

"A snake," explains the overseer, glumly. "They shelter under the office when it is hot."

Defeated, Mennan appears to sag visibly, his distorted shape melting into the objects around him.

"I must go," murmurs Arjun, trying to focus on the table. The file changes shape, evading his fingers. It has come to life. He sweeps it awkwardly into the briefcase, shutting the catch with fingers that fumble and feel as thick as bananas.

Mennan is still talking, but the sound of his voice is muffled and indistinct. Pushing his way past the overseer, Arjun walks unevenly out of the hut. At the top of the steps, he pauses to get his breath. He is panting, his heart racing, although he has only taken a few steps. At least the air is fresher out here than inside the dank, unwholesome cabin. He climbs down a couple of steps but, looking up at the canopy of trees, he becomes dizzy. Leaves and branches begin to whirl above his head, faster and faster in a sickening kaleidoscope of colour.

Closing his eyes, Arjun clutches the rail for support then sinks down, half-sitting, half-lying on the steps. A twig snaps nearby. He recalls that a snake lives beneath the cabin. He can almost see it, a huge snake with amber eyes, raising its head, ready to strike. He tries to get up, but his limbs do not respond. Seized with panic, he tries to call out, but his tongue cleaves to the roof of his mouth.

Crack! The sharp retort of another twig snapping. Somewhere behind him, he hears a soft movement in the dust. His heart beats wildly inside his helpless body. In his head, he screams, but silence issues from his mouth.

"Mr Kumaran?"

A figure appears in front of him. Bending over, it takes him by the shoulder, gently shaking him. He cannot see the face, his vision is too blurred, but he knows the voice. Walter.

1956: Collapse

After Arjun had left him, Walter ventured out of the car to stretch his legs, intending to walk around the clearing; but, as soon as he stepped out of the door, he was aware of being watched. The further he strayed from the car, the stronger the feeling became and yet, with the exception of the men around the camp-fire, he could see no-one. Every bird call, every rustle of leaves, every snapping twig startled him. Filled with invisible life and inexplicable sounds, the empty space around him was suffocating. He longed for the city, the anonymous companionship of crowds.

Having made a few circuits of the car, he got back in, thankful for its protective shell. One of the men at the camp-fire was looking at him. Even from this distance, Walter was struck by the unusual lightness of the fellow's eyes. There was something about that cool stare, steady and unblinking, that unnerved him.

"I hope that Mr. Kumaran is all right," he thought, wondering if he should follow him. But Arjun had not invited Walter to accompany him. Fearing that his presence might prove an embarrassment, Walter decided to wait.

Even the shade under the trees was stifling. Walter began to doze. Every so often, he would surface: brief seconds of consciousness in which his eyes opened; a few snapshot images between bouts of sleep. Arjun crossing the clearing. A child with wild hair. Men around a camp-fire. A rangy fellow in a blue sarong. A man with amber eyes. A demon. Men making tea. Something being slipped into a cup. The child walking back to the hut. Then Walter drifted down into the peaceful depths of a deep sleep. Alone. At peace.

He awoke suddenly, gasping, like a freshly-landed fish. Voices, loud and argumentative, were coming from the hut; Arjun's and that of another man. Walter could hear them across the clearing. So could the men at the camp-fire, listening intently, their faces turned in the direction of the noise. Several words leapt out of the angry torrent. One in particular. Dynamite.

***

Arjun emerges from the cabin, hesitant, staggering, a strange expression on his face. Suddenly, he collapses on the steps, eyes open, his face frozen in fear.

Walter is running, as fast as he can. Now, he is at Arjun's side, yelling for help. A couple of men drift over from the camp-fire, prompted more by curiosity than a desire to assist. The overseer is standing in the doorway, wringing his hands, his white shirt stained with sweat.

"Oh, my God. Oh, my God!"

Ignoring the overseer, Walter leans over Arjun.

"Mr Kumaran, what is the matter? Are you ill?"

But Arjun's tongue is locked. His attempts to speak produce only a strangled groan.

"Can you hear me?"

Arjun tries to nod his head, but his body is as rigid as iron.

***

"You! What have you done?"

Arjun can hear Walter shouting, accusing someone. A plank creaks behind him. Thud, thud. Feet. Just behind his head.

"Me? It was not me. I don't know what is wrong with him."

Mennan. Making more excuses.

"Hah!"

Walter. Irritable, frightened. Not in the mood to listen.

"Help me get him to the car!"

"You must understand. I did nothing to hurt him."

Mennan, still pleading. His voice, faltering, near to tears.

"Hurry up!"

Walter again, urgent and angry.

***

Arms grip him tightly around the waist. They try to set him on his feet, but his knees buckle beneath him. He is a dead weight and he can hear the other men grunting with the strain as they try to keep him upright. They pause for breath, discussing what to do. Then, they drape his arms over their shoulders and half-carry, half-drag him across the clearing. He is aware of his shoes scraping and scuffing along the ground. He can hear the noise they make, but he cannot feel his feet. Or his legs, for that matter.

There is a smell of scorched metal. They are passing the camp-fire where the kettle has boiled dry. If no-one removes it, the kettle will melt, dropping globules of metal into the flames. But there is no-one to attend it. Sensing trouble, the men have disappeared.

Arjun's breath comes in short snatches. His limbs feel numb. As they bundle him into the car, he begins to shiver uncontrollably, seized by a deadly cold, despite the cloying, airless heat. Weeping, the overseer grasps Arjun's hand.

"Please, Mr Kumaran, believe me. I had nothing to do with this. And the dynamite. I promise you, it was stolen."

"He is sick. We must go," says Walter, tersely, pushing Mennan aside as he closes the door.

"But you do believe me?" pleads Mennan.

Arjun's tongue rolls back in his mouth. He makes a strange gurgling noise.

"Oh, my God." Mennan buries his head in his hands.

The man is pitiful, his desperation genuine. He stands alone in the middle of the clearing, weeping. In other circumstances, Walter would have tried to comfort him, but there is no time. Arjun's condition is serious. He needs help. Even now, it might be too late.

Walter slides into the driver's seat and turns the key. When the engine rumbles into life, he almost cries with relief. An ancient potency governs this place, a primeval force malevolent to outsiders. They must escape or be destroyed. As the car turns, Walter thinks he sees a shadow moving stealthily between the trees; a moving patch of darkness in the gloom.

When Arjun collapsed, Anil watched, smiling. When he saw that look of satisfaction, Asoka knew. It was no accident, no sudden illness. But before he could question him, Anil had disappeared into the trees.

Now Asoka is running after him, along a narrow path to a clearing; a place known only to them, where they meet secretly to discuss plans and matters of urgency. It is also the place where Anil comes to pray, sitting cross-legged on the ground, quietly chanting to his serpent god. It is the only part of the forest that holds any fear for Asoka: for he can feel its power; an ancient malevolence, older than time, full of dark secrets.

Angrily, Asoka confronts the man who professes to be his disciple.

"What have you done?"

"More than you, it would seem."

Asoka clenches his fist. But Anil stands his ground. His impenetrable amber eyes stare deep into Asoka's soul. It is as if someone, or something, else is reading his thoughts. Everything is laid bare: his hopes, fears, weaknesses, things he did not even know about himself. Suddenly, Asoka is no longer sure of himself; or what he is doing here. He begins to pace the clearing; up and down, up and down. He needs to think, but confusion has filled his head like black smoke. Nothing is clear.

Anil has changed in the time that he has been here. No longer content to be Asoka's subordinate, he has started to meddle on his own account, befriending the labourers, winning them over, feeding them ideas that are inimical to Asoka. The People's Army, that's what he calls them. Hungry, poor and desperate, they will do whatever he wants. He rouses them with his talk, but it is all of revenge: he promises them power, but only to destroy. It has become clear to Asoka that they are travelling along separate paths.

First, there was the matter of the dynamite, dozens of cases of it, stolen from the site and stashed god knows where. Asoka did not sanction that, did not even known about it until recently, until Anil let something slip in the conversation. It was then Asoka realized that he had lost control. Anil was making the decisions, although he still paid lip-service to his mentor. Although he does not bother to do that any more.

"Don't worry," Anil says, eyes still closed. "Everything is going to plan."

"To plan? It wasn't in my plan to poison a government official. Or anyone else for that matter. It was you, wasn't it? I've seen your handiwork before. If he dies – and even if he doesn't – the authorities will be down on our necks. They'll be here in hours and they won't stop until they find us. Even your friend, the policeman, won't be able to help us."

"We'll be long gone before they get here. And, anyway, who's to say that those two will ever get back. Accidents can happen on these roads. Cars slip into ravines and are never found. It happens all the time."

"My god, you're planning to kill the driver, too."

Astounded, Asoka is unable to speak.

"Getting cold feet?"

Anil sneers, disdainfully. Once he revered Asoka, but now he has a new god. One who has promised him power.

"Those men have nothing to do with this."

Asoka is pleading, the expression in his eyes softer and kinder than anything Anil has seen before. Momentarily, Anil wishes that he had been the one to inspire such warmth. But then, disgusted with himself, he hardens his heart. It has room for only one passion now; one which has nothing to do with Asoka.

"They have everything to do with this," retorts Anil, coldly. "That civil servant was a Tamil."

"His driver was Sinhalese."

"Then he is a traitor."

"Oh, for god's sake!" Asoka throws up his hands in despair.

"That's right," says Anil. "It is for God's sake. It is for our religion, our country, our language."

He steps closer, so close that his face almost touches Asoka.

"Those are your words, Asoka. Have you forgotten them?"

Anil's voice is so soft that it is little more than a breath. Asoka imagines the other man's tongue flickering like that of a serpent as the words drip into his ear. His own words. Anil is right. But they are poison to him now.

"We must get away from here. Leave now."

Asoka is desperate. He paces the clearing like a caged animal. But Anil is unmoved.

"There's plenty of time yet. It will be hours before anyone reaches the site. No-one will travel in darkness on those roads. And anyway, we can't abandon our plan. 'Teach by example. Give them a lesson. Injustice will not be tolerated'."

His own words come back to taunt Asoka. He is breathing heavily, gasping for air.

"Plans can always be changed."

"Not this one. Not now."

"Why not?"

"Because our target knows too much. Or, at least, he suspects. You heard him yourself, telling that civil servant about the dynamite."

"The dynamite was nothing to do with me."

"Perhaps not. But it's too late now."

Frantically, Asoka looks around him, seeking a way out. But the trees seem to rise up, encircling him like the bars of a cage. He is trapped. Defeated. The hunt is over. He hangs his head and sighs, running his hands through his hair.

"All right. Meet me after dark. Exactly as planned."

The trees shrink and part, revealing the path that leads back to the camp. It is the only way open to him now. With a sinking heart, Asoka plunges into the deep, arboreal gloom, watched by his vanquisher. Anil smiles quietly to himself. Power is better than love. And now he controls Asoka.

***

In the middle of the clearing is a circle of bare earth with Anil at its centre. Like a man at the bottom of a well, he cranes his neck and looks up. Far above him, branches and leaves form a dark tracery against the brighter blue of the sky. Closing his eyes, he inhales slowly, breathing in the smell of warm, red earth and the resinous scent of pine. Silently, he offers a prayer of thanks to Hooniyam. At the edge of the clearing, ferns begin to sway gently, shaking their fronds, as if agitated by a gentle breeze. Yet the air is still.

"God is with me," murmurs Anil as he thinks of the dynamite, now safely hidden in a cave. Before long, it will be put to better use than building a road. Smiling to himself, he contemplates the divine chaos to come: the first step towards perfect order.

1956: The flight

The car wheels round in a tight circle, throwing up a cloud of dust and stones. The overseer still stands in the clearing, his arms hanging helplessly by his sides. A man whose luck has finally run out.

"God help him," thinks Walter, distracted by the man's image in his mirror.

The car is half-way across the clearing, when Walter notices a group of men, hanging around the entrance to the track. He thinks nothing of it at first but, as the car approaches, the men cluster together: a human barrier blocking escape.

Instinctively, Walter presses down hard on the accelerator. The car shoots forward, scattering the men like leaves, bouncing one off the fender. Walter slows and looks in his mirror. The fellow is sitting on the ground, clutching his leg. At least he is still alive.

Thud! The car's metal skin reverberates. Thud! There it is again. A hail of rocks flies from the trees. The rear windscreen shatters under the impact of a stone, cracks snaking across the glass like fingers of frost. Gripping the wheel tightly, Walter presses his foot down. Although sleek, the car is elderly. It growls in protest. Walter tries not to think of what will happen if it stalls.

Thud! Another rock hits the back of the car. Walter hears muffled shouts but can see nothing through the damaged rear window. The car bounces and flounders, unable to build up speed on a surface littered with holes and obstacles. Then, thankfully, after skidding around a corner, the car is back on a narrow, but level track. Walter presses his foot down on the accelerator, and the car leaps forward. He keeps his foot down, ignoring the deep ravine to his right, slewing around hairpin bends, driving as fast as he can until he is sure that they are no longer pursued. He has been so preoccupied that he has almost forgotten his passenger.

"All right, sir?"

Walter checks the mirror. What he sees makes his heart stop. Arjun's eyes are closed and his lips have a dark, bluish tinge. Pulling over to the side of the road, Walter gets out and runs to the back of the car. Wrenching open the passenger door, he leans inside. Arjun's head is thrown back and small trickle of bile is oozing from the corner of his mouth.

Pulling Arjun from the car, Walter lays him on the ground, rolling him over onto his side. He thumps Arjun hard on the back, but when nothing happens, Walter sticks his fingers down the other man's throat as far as they will go. It triggers an instant reaction. Arjun vomits, coughing and gurgling, wracked by spasms, each attack lasting so long that he gasps for breath. It seems he will never stop. The smell is terrible. Not just the clinging stench of sick, but an overpowering odour of putrefaction, like rotten rice or jackfruit.

After a few minutes, Arjun coughs weakly, spitting to rid his mouth of the foul taste, but he has stopped vomiting. His clothes are stained with yellow fluid and they stink. Walter notices thankfully that the paralysis that seized him earlier appears to be wearing off.

"I've got a clean sarong in the car," says Walter. "You can wear that."

Gently laying Arjun on the ground, Walter goes to the back of the car where he retrieves the sarong from the boot. Although Arjun can move a little, he is still too weak to help himself. So, propping him up against the wheel hub, Walter undresses him, peeling off his dirty clothes until he is naked, then pouring water over him from a plastic container that he keeps in the back of the car. After cleaning him as best he can, Walter wraps Arjun in the sarong and helps him back into his seat. Although the air is still warm, Arjun shivers violently.

"At least he's still alive," thinks Walter with relief.

Carefully wrapping the soiled clothes in an old piece of rag, he places them gingerly in the boot hoping, a little selfishly, that they will not taint the car. After setting off, they are forced to stop several times for Arjun to be sick. Subject, in turn, to raging heat, then unnatural cold, he sleeps fitfully for a few minutes, then wakes wide-eyed. He begins to talk excitedly, his speech a confused and feverish babble.

The journey home takes twice as long as the outward trip. Walter drives slowly, trying not to cause his passenger any discomfort. He also makes frequent stops in order to check on Arjun's condition, mopping his sticky face with a damp cloth and trying to relieve his thirst by drizzling water into his mouth, a few drops at a time. Too little and he will become dehydrated, too much and he is likely to be sick.

The setting sun plunges towards the horizon, sucking light away from the valleys and hollow places and leaving them in darkness. Heaven is painted with a last, glorious blaze. Fiery corals and reds light the sky, then darken to indigo as the sun quivers and sinks.

The darkness which follows is sudden and complete. Night replaces day with the immediacy common to the Tropics. The darkness slows their progress. Even headlights are of limited use on the unfamiliar track which twists and turns with serpentine unpredictability. To one side is a cliff face, to the other a vertiginous drop of hundreds of feet. One mistake will be fatal.

At last, the lights of the town appear, twinkling in the darkness below. Walter, a child of the city, is filled with inexpressible relief. He craves lights, buildings, the company of other drivers who are his friends.

As the car cruises into the suburbs, Walter notices election posters at the side of the road, some lit by harsh electric lights. His mind wanders back to the overseer. Mennan is rumoured to have the favour of a politician. It is not an uncommon occurrence; all aspiring criminals seek political patronage. Many get it, in return for a cut of their profits or a valuable service, such as the one which reminds voters where to place their cross on the ballot paper.

"Whole damn place has gone to the dogs," thinks Walter.

Then, he passes another poster. "VOTE BANDARANAIKE" proclaim large black letters under the photograph of a clever-looking man with glasses. This man is intelligent, well-educated, an aristocrat. Walter's spirits begin to lift. Perhaps there is hope, after all.

1956: Mennan's cabin

Mennan stands in the clearing, staring down the road which leads back to town, considering his options. The enquiry into his misdoings is gathering momentum. If he returns home, he will probably be arrested. If he stays here, he can buy a little time, plan his next move. He could send a message to his protector, the politician; he will know what to do. He must write the man a letter and get one of the labourers to deliver it.

The politician is sure to help him. Mennan is certain of it. They went to school together. The man found Mennan his current position and, in return, Mennan has given his patron a generous percentage of the proceeds. Both have profited handsomely, each protecting the other. Surely their arrangement still holds good? The politician cannot abandon him now. If he tries to, Mennan will take him down too: for he knows things that would damage the politician's career irreversibly if they came to light. The politician will be implicated, as surely as Mennan, in the misuse of public money.

The sun is sinking. Mennan shivers, feeling a chill unrelated to the diminishing heat. As he turns to walk back to the hut, he becomes aware of many eyes, watching him. As usual, the men have gathered under the trees to smoke before returning home; but, tonight, there is no gentle hum of conversation, no chatter or laughter. Leaning against trees, gathered in groups or squatting, singly, on the ground, the men are silent and attentive, as if waiting for something, or someone. Each has his eyes fixed on Mennan.

As he walks past them, Mennan feels himself stripped and exposed. It is as if those eyes have pierced him to the bone, discovering every lie he has ever told, every pretence he has ever practised. Under such intense scrutiny, he feels the protective coating of falsehood, in which he has wrapped himself for so long, beginning to dissolve, melting like wax: a modern Icarus, bereft of plumage; his beautiful wings exposed; a sham of borrowed feathers and string. With every step, Mennan is diminished.

His feet stick to the soil, his breathing is laboured and he gasps with the exertion of walking. An icy sweat prickles his skin. He longs for the safety of the cabin: to be hidden, forgotten, of no account.

Holding on to the rail, he drags himself up the steps, pausing at the top to catch his breath. A crow hops sideways across the verandah, ragged black wings outstretched. It starts pecking between the boards, stabbing mercilessly at insects and crumbs of food. Mennan flicks his hand. The bird pauses, its wings quivering, primed to fly; or attack. With ravenous bill half open, the crow cocks its head, inspects Mennan then, having dismissed him, continues its search, hopping about defiantly, scavenging within inches of his feet.

With relief, Mennan enters the hut and tries to close the door. But it resists him. He pulls at it frantically, until the thin planks quiver, threatening to fall apart. There is an obstruction beneath it: a stone, or some grit. He kicks it hard, then pulls again. The door grinds across the swollen, dirty floorboards and he drags it shut, leaning with his back against it for a while, eyes closed. The malodorous gloom offers sanctuary from prying eyes. At last, he is invisible.

He pulls a bottle of arrack from a hiding place in the derelict cupboard. On the table is a dirty glass with stains around its rim. After pouring a few drops of liquor into the glass, Mennan swills it around, tips the contents through a hole in the floorboards, then refills the glass with a large measure of arrack. He drains the glass, then pours himself another.

"Gaagh!"

It is the noise, part groan, part gasp, made by one who finds relief in alcohol. Although the arrack burns his throat, it makes him feel stronger. Taking in a deep draught of the warm air, he holds it in his lungs, puffing out his chest.

"Ahhh!" He releases the air with a sigh, almost of satisfaction.

At the back of the hut is the foreman's locker. Mennan rummages through the contents until he has found what he wants. A packet of cigarettes. They are made of coarse, cheap tobacco, the sort favoured by workmen. Mennan inspects the label and winces. He would prefer a cigar, but has brought none with him. He lights a cigarette and inhales, wincing as he picks a shred of loose tobacco from his tongue. The cigarette, little larger than a hand-rolled bidi, is soon gone. After lighting another, he settles at the table by the window, filling the unlit room with smoke as he considers what to do.

He must write to the politician. Reaching behind him, Mennan opens the drawer of a battered filing cabinet and pulls out a sheet of yellowed paper and the stub of a pencil. The paper has been damp at some stage because it is wrinkled and one corner bears spots of mildew. The pencil is blunt and writes badly, but Mennan has neither the inclination, nor the energy to sharpen it.

He writes a few, desultory lines then, stopping mid-sentence, he puts the pencil down and gazes out of the grimy window at the darkening forest. The crow is still tap-tapping on the verandah and the air is rich with nocturnal sound; crickets; frogs; owls; the yelps and squeaks of predators and their victims.

Mennan thinks of his wife. What if he were to go to her, tell her everything? Perhaps she would help him. But, in his heart, he knows that she would not. He has committed a mortal sin. He has been discovered. His disgrace will jeopardise the life to which she has become accustomed, and which is a condition of their union.

The sharing of ignominy was not part of their marriage contract. Neither was poverty or loss of status. Having made her position clear from the start, she has taken care to reinforce it at regular intervals. Her loyalty comes at a price. She must be cosseted, spoiled and protected. He must continue to prove his devotion with costly offerings, or lose her. In return, she offers nothing, except her continued presence under his roof.

Mennan returns to the letter, adding another few lines:

"… *and, as we have both profited from mutual co-operation in the past, I am counting on your continued goodwill…*"

He re-reads it. It is wrong, the tone insufficiently deferential. It sounds as if he were addressing a supplier, not someone on whom his life depends. *Goodwill*. That is wrong, too. It is too distant, too commercial. He crosses it out, replacing it with *favour*. He rubs his neck. His skin is sticky and his head aching. He pours himself another arrack and, as he drinks it, his thoughts return to his wife, Leela.

What did he get in return for marriage? What has dishonesty bought him? The envy of other men? The gratification that comes from parading a beautiful woman around town? Leela does not love him, he knows that. She will only stay as long as he provides the things she wants. It is her greed that has pushed him into criminality. Or so he has told himself. Now he is in a bind and it is all her fault. Damn her!

111

He bangs his fist on the table. The glass jumps and a few drops of arrack leap out; they fall onto the letter, further staining the yellowed paper and lending it a strong odour of alcohol. Resting his elbow on the table, with his chin on his hand, Mennan stares through the filthy pane of glass. It will soon be night and, when the light has drained from the world, he will be left alone in a darkened room. He should light a candle. He will do it in a minute. But the darkness is strangely comforting. He can hide within its folds, become invisible, unseen. That is all he wants now.

And yet, after a few minutes, something urges him to continue with the letter. He still has the will to save himself. He rubs his eyes and moans a little, like a small, reluctant child. It is an indulgence, but the sound of his voice reminds him of his own existence, even if others have forgotten it.

Outside, something moves in the undergrowth. His heart beats faster. Who knows what lives out there? Night no longer offers safety, but a threat. He must have light. Pulling out the drawer of the table, he scrabbles inside. He is sure he has seen a candle and matches in there. Desperately, he feels around with his hand. Nothing. A sob of fear rises in his throat. Wrenching open the drawers of the filing cabinet, he checks there too, frantically tapping inside with his fingers; but the search is fruitless.

Overwhelmed by despair, he sits alone in darkness. It is too late to finish the letter. The paper glows white and tantalizing on the table. In a sudden fit of anger, he closes his hand on it, crunches it, twists it, then tears it apart, scattering the fragments on the floor where they gleam like petals. An image comes to mind: a temple tree. He shudders. Is it a premonition?

"Fool. You are thinking like a fool."

He speaks aloud, hoping that the sound of his voice will frighten the shadows, but it sounds hollow, muffled, like a drowning man coming up for air. He pours himself another glass of arrack and downs it in a gulp. Its caustic warmth scorches his throat but he welcomes the numbness that follows. He pours himself another and settles down to finish the bottle. Hope returns, encircling him like vapour.

"I must disappear," thinks Mennan.

He could fake his own death. Suicide by drowning. That would do. He could leave a pile of his clothes on the beach with a note explaining the reasons for his death. He could admit everything, wipe the slate clean, then begin again.

His cousin has a buffalo farm in a remote part of the Island. He could live there, work as a farm-hand. All he requires is food and a place to sleep. Life would be simple, uncomplicated. No need to chase wealth or position. He would be without care … or his wife. That is the sticking point. He cannot contemplate life without her.

Hope cools and Mennan gently descends, spiralling like a feather into the abyss. What would she think if she heard of his death? Would she grieve? Would she miss him? Or, after a brief space of mourning, would she remarry? He knows that the latter is most likely and yet he cannot bear to think of her as another man's wife. It would be a living death. Yet he knows that his only chance of survival is to disappear without trace.

He pours the dregs from the bottle. He will leave decision-making until morning. Nothing can be done tonight and, perhaps, the new day will bring another plan, a change of luck. He will wait. He drains his glass then, resting his head on his arms, falls asleep at the table.

It is dark, but not silent. The forest reverberates with the sound of insects. The throb of crickets is deafening. Spots of light, like fireflies, dart between the trees. They dance before Mennan's eyes which are heavy with drink and sleep. He dozes for a few more minutes and, when he opens his eyes, the fireflies appear to have grown.

Then, above the insect chorus, there is another sound. A murmur of voices. Harsh laughter. Figures emerging slowly from the darkness, some carrying burning brands, limbs and faces distorted in the guttering light. Demons. Rigid with fear, Mennan recalls stories of spirits abducting their prey, carelessly shucking the souls from their victims like peas from a pod. One tale, told by his grandmother, taught him the true meaning of fear. It told of a washer-girl plucked from her work, tormented, tortured, her mutilated remains scattered along the river bank, tangled up with her discarded and bloody linen. It haunted his childhood.

His grandmother had told him the story to illustrate what happens to those without faith or, at least, those without what she considered to be the right faith. One didn't have to be inherently bad to incur the wrath of hell, just non-Catholic or, even worse, one who had lapsed.

Mennan tries to recall the last time he attended Mass. He cannot remember. He has never had much time for religion. He has always been too busy attending to his business interests and, of course, his wife. Leela is his faith; a religion without promise of salvation.

The figures outside have gathered into a dense knot at the edge of the clearing. One detaches itself and moves towards the hut, its outline flickering in the torchlight. Almost bursting with terror, Mennan's heart ricochets against his ribs.

He tries to recite a Hail Mary but the words falter on his lips. It needs faith to make them work. When they catch him, the demons will make him pray backwards and, sinner that he is, he will be eternally damned.

The creature has reached the top of the steps. Mennan can hear its feet, shuffling on the rough wood of the verandah. With a crash, the door bursts open and the incubus falls upon him. In a single rapid movement, it reaches forward, grasps him roughly by the shirt and pulls him from the hut. Gripped tightly by the neck, he is propelled into the clearing.

"Who ... who are you?" he stammers.

Laughter. Many voices. A torch is raised to illuminate the carrier's face. It is Asoka the foreman. Mennan is wild with joy. He has never liked the man but now he is relieved to see him.

"I thought you were a demon".

Mennan chortles at his own foolishness. The other men join in. He recognises them now, labourers from the site.

"I'm so glad to see you".

He is so overcome that he grabs Asoka's hand and shakes it. The general mirth increases.

"Really?"

The foreman's tone is ironic.

"Perhaps you should wait until you hear what we have to say."

Mennan ceases laughing. There is menace in Asoka's voice. His eyes gleam in the torchlight, hard and pitiless. The circle of men has contracted around them. Mennan needs air, space, but, by now, he is so tightly hemmed in that he cannot move. He feels the men's breath, hot on his cheek and he smells the sweat of many bodies. Knuckles are digging into his back.

Asoka exerts an authority over the other men far in excess of his age or status. That is why Mennan employed him, but his own relationship with the foreman has soured. Mennan's profiteering has seen to that. The men received less and less money, so that the fittest among them soon left to find work elsewhere while those who remained were required to work longer hours for little or no pay. But they did it, because Asoka asked them to. At first, Mennan had regarded the foreman as his ally but recently he has begun to suspect his motives.

"Damn Communist," thinks Mennan, but he has become too reliant on Asoka to sack him.

In the last few weeks, factions have broken out at the site. Asoka has led increasingly vociferous demands for pay. There have been loud, abusive arguments between himself and Mennan.

"I'll sack you," shouted Mennan, but the foreman had just smiled and walked away.

Then Asoka was joined by another man: Anil, a Sinhalese who spends most of his time at the camp-fire, stirring tea; that is, when he is not holding meetings with the men. Mennan caught him at it once. He could not hear what the fellow was saying, but he knows he was stirring up trouble. The man has mesmeric, amber eyes. They seem to watch Mennan wherever he goes. Mennan suspects that the man has been spying on him, reporting every move back to Asoka. Since Anil's arrival, the other men have become open in their lack of respect for Mennan.

"What do you want?" stammers Mennan.

"What do you think?" sneers a familiar voice.

Pressed tightly between the other men, Mennan can only turn his head. Anil is standing next to him.

"I don't have the money."

"No," hisses Anil. "Wives like yours cost a lot to keep."

"Yes, yes. You have no idea. Really, it wasn't for me …"

"Save your breath," snaps Anil. "No-one wants to hear why it is more important for your wife to have jewellery than it is for their children to have food."

"And we all know what she gets up to behind your back," quips Anil, "although you probably don't!"

"What do you mean?"

There are ripples of laughter. Some of the men make lewd gestures, leaving Mennan in no doubt as to what they mean.

"Your wife has many visitors while you're away. Most of them young men. A couple are quite good-looking by all accounts."

"Liar. I don't believe you."

His face contorted with rage, Mennan lunges at Anil, trying to strike him with his pudgy fists. The man steps sideways, avoiding the blow. Mennan is grasped by many hands and restrained.

"Be careful who you call a liar!" Anil spits the words in Mennan's face. "You of all people."

Despite his desperate situation, Mennan's heart is wrung. Tears prick his eyes.

"Oh look, he's crying," mocks one man, digging Mennan sharply in the ribs. A storm of taunts and ribald remarks follows.

"Enough," says Asoka. "That is not what we came here for. Follow me."

Mennan is shoved forward, parcelled and pushed from hand to hand until, his shirt torn and his arms bruised, he is manhandled across the clearing. The comforting warmth of the arrack has deserted him. He is tired and scared. The men press around him in a tight circle, guiding him towards a chair under the trees. It looks strangely out of place. Mennan lowers himself, as if to sit down. There are shrieks of raucous laughter.

"No. That's not it. Show him boys."

Rough hands grab Mennan's arms and push him forward. Something brushes against his cheek. He turns and, realizing what has touched his face, he screams.

***

When Mennan sees the noose, he struggles wildly, trying to fight free of the circle that encloses him. But his arms are wrenched behind his back. Someone is tying his hands. He kicks out and hits a man on the shin. The fellow swears, then paralyses Mennan with a powerful punch to the stomach. While Mennan is still gasping for breath, the noose is lowered over his head. The men try to lift him onto the chair but he squirms and, being a heavy man, makes their task impossible.

"Forget the chair."

Anil's eyes are burning, fanatical. He points to several men at the edge of the crowd.

"You. Pull him up."

Mennan shrieks with terror until his breath is cut short by the pressure of the rope. With feet flailing, he is slowly winched into the air by his neck. The searing pain in his throat is matched only by that in his lungs. In an agony of fear, his bowels become water and he loses control. Howls of disgust and laughter follow as he soils himself.

Mennan is off the ground, hanging by the neck, his spine still intact. He can neither scream nor breathe. The men at the end of the rope continue to pull, jerking him upwards until he is fifteen feet above ground.

Momentarily liberated by this act of violence, each man forgets himself, existing only as part of the group. Fear is translated into fury and Mennan's torment arouses frenzied excitement. He is pelted with stones and clods of earth. The men run around beneath him, spitting, screaming and leaping in the air, their faces distorted by rage. Like demons.

Still conscious, Mennan searches for a prayer but sees only his wife's face. She has betrayed him many times, but no matter. It is her right. He forgives her as he has always done. Leela. His goddess.

The screaming of the men becomes fainter. The tendons in Mennan's neck burn, torn by the impossible weight of his body. A rushing sound fills his ears, roaring like the sea, then darkness swallows him like a wave.

1956: Nunc dimittis

Mennan is dead. It is obvious from the stillness of his body: the limbs have ceased twitching, the swollen tongue blocks his mouth, the eyeballs have rolled upwards under their lids. And yet, the screaming and taunting does not abate.

Mennan is dead. But the men continue to attack him, pelting his corpse with stones, clods of earth and any missiles that come to hand. They jeer at him, yelling curses, voicing the unspeakable acts that they will visit upon his wife, she-devil and harlot, if ever they find her. By tomorrow, those awful threats will be forgotten; but they will lie dormant in the minds of those who made them, ready to be repeated when the time comes.

All the while, Asoka has been watching, his heart frozen and his mind numb. The frenzied display reminds him of one of the exorcism ceremonies in which dancers, wearing devil masks, enact elaborate rituals to cast out demons. But the expression on the faces of these men is more terrifying than any mask: their features are contorted by hatred. It is difficult to believe that they are human.

Anil acts as ring-master, a macabre director of ceremonies, his amber eyes flaming with hatred and excitement as he inspires the men to further excess. He has acquired a taste for power and there will never be enough to satisfy his craving.

**

From the shadows, Hooniyam laughs softly as he caresses his favourite serpent. Head stretched forward and eyes narrowed, the snake hisses contentedly as it is tickled under the chin. Proudly, Hooniyam points to Anil.

"Look at him. He is truly my disciple, a fitting brother for you. I wonder if he realizes that this is the site of my old home. He has even stored dynamite in my cave. And, now, he has offered his first sacrifice. Wonderful. He is a king of cobras, unlike that other pathetic creature."

Hooniyam nods briefly towards Asoka.

"Ughh," says the god in disgust, "he thinks too much. That policeman was right about him. He's no use to us. We need men like Anil, driven by pure instinct. And today, he has discovered a lust for power and bloodshed that will carry him forward with the power of fifty elephants. He will be impervious to pain, fatigue, or hunger. Superhuman, in fact. I tell you, my friend, he has all the qualities of a true demon."

The snake hisses softly, but whether this indicates agreement, pleasure or, even, a little jealousy, not even Hooniyam can tell. The thoughts of serpents are obscure. Even to gods.

**

In the clearing, the men begin to tire. The ecstasy which inspired their fervour has begun to pale. They are weary, exhausted and spent. One by one, they drift away into the forest, back to their huts and cabins, where they can immerse themselves in the comforting rituals of home – eating, drinking, making love – until the events of this night merge into their dreams. By the time they awake in the morning, they will have only the faintest recollection of what happened here.

Paralysed, Asoka gazes at Mennan's battered corpse. Set in motion by the prolonged assault, the body is moving, twisting this way and that, the rope creaking under its weight. The air is filled with the smell of violence: human sweat, bruised foliage, the stench of the body's secretions.

"Was this ever a man?" thinks Asoka, as he scrutinizes Mennan's face.

At first, he feels no more than the passing interest of a scientist examining a speck under a microscope. It is all so distant and unreal. But then, as he stares at the ravaged face, a strange thing happens. Something leaks from one of the eyes. It trickles slowly down the cheek, then stops: a single, frozen tear.

"My God!"

Asoka laughs. His voice is harsh and unnatural. Inhuman. But he cannot take his eyes from that face. It grows in his mind, imprinting itself, branding every thought. That hideous face redeemed by a solitary, human tear. Suddenly, a wave of shock passes through him. He is seized by revulsion; not at the ghastly sight hanging above him, but at himself.

"He was a man," says a voice in his head. "Like you!"

"Oh God, what have I done," murmurs Asoka.

"Hurry up. It's time to go."

A voice breathes in his ear. Anil. But Asoka does not answer, cannot move. He is stuck fast, frozen with vertiginous fear.

"Hurry up!"

Anil grabs him roughly by the arm, propelling him towards the trees. But Asoka's eyes are still focused on Mennan's corpse.

"Move," urges Anil, angrily. "There isn't much time. We must run, hide. We need to get away. As far as possible. Come on!"

Stumbling, hardly knowing which foot to place in front of the other, Asoka is dragged into the forest. They pause. Anil leans forward, his hands on his knees, trying to get his breath. Asoka stares back at the clearing. Most of the flaming torches have gone, taken by the men to light their way home. But a few remain, casting an eerie glow over the trunks of the trees and the limp body dangling above the ground like a fly hanging from a spider's thread.

Asoka is gripped by another surge of horror. This time, it has a form and a face. The face is that of the dead man who whispers: *murderer, murderer, murderer*. The word seeps into Asoka's ear like poison, infecting his brain with madness. Suddenly, he bounds forward and takes to his heels, running he knows not where, it does not matter. He must get away from the leering eyes and the mouth whose blackened tongue accuses him: *murderer, murderer, murderer*.

"Hey! Where are you going?"

Anil tries to block his path, but Asoka is too quick. He leaps into the darkness and is gone, leaving Anil clutching at the air. Deeper and deeper, he runs into the forest, not knowing where he is going, pursued by a memory of evil that grows stronger with every step, goaded by the words of his victim: *murderer, murderer, murderer*. On and on he runs, hounded by guilt until, stumbling on a tree root, he crashes forwards and, lying with his face in the dirt, weeps, sinking ever deeper in misery until he reaches oblivion.

The doctor steps into the corridor, closing the door quietly behind him. He is perplexed and has to confess, if only to himself, that in all his years of practice he has never seen anything like this. His patient, now drifting in and out of consciousness, is covered in an unusual, mottled rash and his lips have a bluish tinge. He has not vomited for at least half an hour, a good sign although probably due to the fact that his stomach is empty; but he is running a dangerous fever.

"What has he eaten?"

"Egg hoppers," suggests a young woman with a frightened, pale face. "I made him egg hoppers this morning. He took them in the car with him. But I ate some, too. I was all right."

"Hmmm. Unlikely to be that," says the doctor, thinking that the young woman would be pretty but for her pallor. Her hands fidget with her scarf, threading it back and forth through her fingers, then wringing it tightly as if it were wet.

Nervous type, thinks the doctor, who prefers women to have their feet on the ground. He, himself, is married to a nurse; a woman he met at the hospital although, with his salary, she no longer has the need to work. It was an unusual match for a country where families still prefer to have a hand in the marriage of their relatives.

"Tea?" suggests a man with a broad, moon face. Unlike the woman, he smiles.

"Thank you."

The doctor takes the tea and stirs it thoughtfully as he stares down the corridor at the man who claims to be the patient's driver. He is leaning against the wall, gazing dejectedly at his feet. He says his passenger fell ill when visiting a remote site in the mountains. And something else. He says he thinks the young man has been poisoned, but he does not know how. The driver is Sinhalese.

Probably not significant, thinks the doctor. However, one must consider all possibilities. The doctor, himself a Tamil, is aware of increasing hostility to his profession from the nationalists; particularly Sinhalese Ayurvedic practitioners who resent what they regard as the stranglehold exerted by western medicine and the Tamils.

As the doctor raises the cup to his lips, the driver becomes agitated. An image has flashed through his mind: something which seemed significant at the time for a reason that he could not explain: a man dropping something into a teacup with his fingers.

"I know what it was," the driver says, excitedly. "I know."

The doctor does not speak, but waits, encouraging the man with his silence.

"That's it. At the site. I saw someone put something in his tea. I didn't really think about it at the time, but even workmen would use a spoon for sugar. This fellow was using his fingers. It was as if he was grinding something between them before dropping it in the cup."

The doctor raises his eyebrows, then pushes out his lower lip and squints, an affectation indicating deep thought. Poison could well explain the unusual symptoms displayed by this patient, none of which are consistent with disease, bad food or even snake bite. The more he thinks about it, the more attractive this theory becomes, but first, he must be sure.

"You think that one of the men at the site put something in Mr Kumaran's tea with the intention of making him ill?"

"Yes."

"You're sure?"

Walter recalls the malevolent amber eyes.

"I have no doubt."

The young woman gasps and puts her hand to her mouth. Her eyes fill with tears. The doctor hopes she won't cry.

"The police must be told. I believe you work for the Government Agent?"

"Yes, sir."

"Then you must contact him immediately. The police will be more inclined to act quickly if he speaks to them."

The doctor gives Walter a meaningful glance. Walter understands. The local police are notorious for their inefficiency. A misdemeanour in a remote place, even if it were attempted murder, is unlikely to guarantee a speedy response. Only prompting from a higher authority will ensure that.

The doctor makes ready to leave. The young woman, now attended by an old lady, is leaning against the wall, her face buried in her scarf. By the motion of her shoulders, the doctor can see that she is weeping, albeit silently.

"No need for tears, my dear," he murmurs. But she does not seem to hear him. The doctor frowns. He cannot account for the change, but young women these days seem prone to hysteria, less accepting than they used to be when he was a young man. Perhaps that is it. He is getting old. He walks along the corridor, accompanied by an old lady who appears to be the young woman's mother. Unlike her daughter, the old woman remains quiet and sensible, untroubled by the drama that is unfolding.

As he makes his way to the door, the doctor is struck by the number of old photographs strung along the walls. Their subjects eye him as he passes, giving him the impression that he is being scrutinised and assessed. The overall impression is one of disapproval and hostility.

They must all be dead by now, thinks the doctor, wondering why anyone would wish to display such depressing pictures.

Rather like a mausoleum, he thinks with distaste, an opinion confirmed by the statue of the Madonna in the hallway, lit by an everlasting flame.

Although his parents were Hindus, the doctor was educated in a Presbyterian college where he learned to distrust religious images. They carry a whiff of idolatry and arouse in him feelings of deep disquiet.

With relief, he steps out of the front door onto the porch and is on the point of leaving when a thought occurs to him. It might be appropriate for the old lady to convey a few words of comfort to her daughter.

"Tell your daughter not to worry. Her husband will be all right."

The old lady's reaction takes him by surprise. Her face aflame with anger, she grunts a farewell and shuts the door in his face.

119

1956: Walter's journey

The car whisks along night-blackened roads. Speed helps Walter to think. Two audiences will require an account of today's events: the Government Agent and the drivers with whom Walter spends his free time. Muttering to himself, he sketches out what he will say, occasionally taking his hand off the wheel to emphasise a point. The Agent will require a concise report. He is a busy man who has no time for irrelevant detail. The drivers, however, will expect a theatrical narrative, for they love a good story and Walter is a gifted raconteur.

He should have been a journalist but, lacking the education, he conveys his news by word of mouth, rather than the written page. He has a sixth sense for a good story and, in its absence, can hack an interesting angle from the most unpromising material. His tales, usually derived from the small doings of daily life, require the skill of a miniaturist to shape their flat landscape.

Despite his anxiety for Arjun, Walter is excited. Never has he uncovered a story of such dramatic potential. Now he can paint a broad canvas. With bold brushstrokes and brilliant colours, he will depict deceit, betrayal, falsehood, fear and attempted murder. In the downtown bars, where the drivers meet after work, Walter's account of today's events will establish his pre-eminence as a story-teller. His rivals will be vanquished, particularly that young upstart Thaha who has tried to seduce Walter's audience with racy yarns from the city.

"They are not even his own stories," thinks Walter indignantly. For he has heard them from other mouths prior to Thaha's re-telling. On one occasion, when Thaha was relaying a borrowed tale, Walter was tempted to interject and deliver the ending himself, just to expose the other man as an imposter.

However, he had resisted the urge. Such action might be interpreted as jealousy – Walter, the aging champion, unable to oppose a youthful contender, striking out in the bitterness of loss. No, he will not accept the mantle of embittered loser. He will bide his time, use cunning to mount a counter-offensive. If he defeats his opponent, it will be with skill, not savagery.

Walter presses down on the accelerator. The car races through unlit lanes. Caught in the main beam, eyes wink and gleam in the darkness. Most belong to pye-dogs, vagabonds drawn to the highway who cause more deaths than snake bite. All have a fine disregard for the principles of road safety. In day-time, they stretch out on the hot tarmac, scratching languidly: at night, they are simply pairs of eyes. Walter is forced to brake suddenly as a bitch and her pups scamper across the road.

The headlights reveal other, fleeting images: a buffalo grazing on the verge, raises its head, stretching its neck and rolling its eyes; a large cat emerges from the gloom before sauntering off to pursue its prey; then, a man, steps out of nowhere, into the road. He stops, momentarily, staring wild-eyed at the car, then runs off, back into the darkness. He looks familiar. Yes, Walter is sure he has seen him before. It is someone he has seen recently. But his memory fails him.

He shakes his head. He must have been mistaken. And, anyway, the fellow looked crazy. He was filthy and dishevelled and the upper part of his body was covered with bloody scratches, as if he had been forcing his way through thorns. And yet … there was something about his face. Walter sighs. It has been a tiring day. He has neither eaten nor slept for many hours and he is getting light-headed. It is as if he has entered a dream world. Nothing seems quite real.

"Better concentrate," he tells himself, staring fixedly at the road ahead of him.

If he were to look in the rear-view mirror, Walter would see another figure, emerging from the darkness. A man with amber eyes has stepped into the road. He stares around him, as if searching for something, or someone. Then, setting off at a run, he, too, disappears into the darkness.

***

An hour or so later, Walter reaches the outskirts of the city. He guides the car through narrow streets, past shops whose wares, displayed on racks outside are lit by the harsh brilliance of naked light bulbs. Even at this time of night, the streets are filled with the clamour of people: shoppers, friends, people going to work on the late shift, those returning home from offices and bars. Shopkeepers stand in their doorways and chat to neighbours or each other.

The air is filled with the warm scent of humanity, fruit, flowers, hair oil, hoppers and incense. The butcher's stall has already closed but the assistant, a devout young man, prompted by the teaching of religious faith and his own, innate generosity, is feeding pye-dogs and cats from a bag of scraps, the off-cuts and sweepings from his trade that not even the poorest can eat. The cats and dogs have already begun to gather, prowling the shadows, waiting for the food to be thrown to them, snarling and squabbling over any thread of fat or skin that comes their way.

It is people now, rather than animals, that stray in front of the car, crossing the road without looking, their heads turned away from the flow of traffic. It is as if they trust divine will, rather than their own senses, to guide them.

Walter's pulse begins to race. He loves people and needs to be surrounded by them. That is why he seeks the company of other drivers, all men, like himself, who have no permanent home and, because of work, rarely see their families. They have no status, no hierarchy, except for that which they create themselves. Their exclusive community is the only one in which Walter feels truly at home.

A horn blasts loudly. Startled, Walter slams on the brakes. It is a junction and he has drifted into the cross-flow of traffic, narrowly missing a lorry, garishly painted and decorated with tassels and streamers.

"Must stay awake."

He is tired now and the urge to close his eyes is getting stronger. Thankfully, it is only a few minutes to the Agent's residence.

***

The compound is brightly lit, comprising a large bungalow and a number of whitewashed out-buildings, encircled by a high metal fence. Walter identifies himself to the gatekeeper and drives around to the back of the house. He rings a bell at the servants' door and is met by Godfrey, head servant and an old friend.

Godfrey is the protecting spirit of the residence. Without him, it might simply crumble and fall into disuse, like the shrine of an ancient god. He has been here so long, that no-one can remember where he came from. It seems that he sprang out of the ground along with the bricks and mortar. He is now so old, that he is ageless, beyond the reach of time.

He wears native costume: a spotless white tunic and floor-length sarong under which his bare feet, just visible, are as gnarled as old tree roots. While a tracery of wrinkles has crept about his eyes, the mounds of his cheeks are as plump and smooth as apricots. His perfect teeth, a gift from benevolent gods, will outlast him to his grave where they will grin benignly from his skull.

Inside the residence, Godfrey's word is law and none dare oppose him, including the Government Agent. Yet his regime is a benign one. He governs the servants with fairness and impartiality and his displeasure, like his favour, must be earned.

"Hello, Machan. What brings you here at this hour?"

"Godfrey, I must speak to the Government Agent. It's urgent. It cannot wait until morning."

Although Walter tries to pre-empt delay, Godfrey requires an explanation. In this house, time ticks to his regime.

***

In the kitchen, shining white tiles and sinks create a clinical atmosphere which is reinforced by the smell of disinfectant. Walter sits at a wooden table whose surface is bleached white with much scrubbing and pitted where careless knives have missed the chopping board. It is where roti-dough is kneaded and stories exchanged; the focus of frenzied activity before mealtimes and a place of relaxation afterwards; an altar to domestic ritual.

Rapidly, Walter recounts the day's events. As he does so, strange sensations come spinning out of the darkness. Pure and unadulterated, he can taste and smell them: excitement, as hot and invigorating as chillies; fear, as acrid and choking as smoke. Shock has confused his senses. He begins to shiver uncontrollably. He presses his palms against the rough surface of the table. Holding on. Just holding on.

Godfrey offers him milk, a roti, cold rice, a little curry. But Walter refuses.

"I must speak to the Government Agent, Godfrey. There is no time."

The old man nods his head. He expected as much.

Godfrey leads Walter through a maze of passages to a study at the front of the house. The room is in darkness except for a small lamp which concentrates a pool of light on the desk, illuminating pens, an elaborate inkstand and a leather-bound book with gold lettering on its spine. Beyond, at the edges of the room, black shapes loom in the shadow.

Walter is offered a seat in a deep, leather armchair. Studded with small buttons, it is hard and unyielding, the back of the seat slightly raised so that it tilts forward, making it impossible to rest on the slippery surface. Walter must shift and squirm continually in order to remain seated and avoid sliding onto the floor. He waits, uncomfortable and uneasy in the dark.

A voice from the doorway alerts him to the Government Agent's arrival.

"Hullo, Walter. Don't get up."

The shape of a large man strides through the gloom, skirting around the furniture until he arrives at the other side of the desk. The chair is pulled back, the figure sits down, pulls the chair forward and Nash Tharmalingam enters the halo of light thrown by the desk-lamp. Dressed in pyjamas and a silk dressing-gown, he is a tall, angular man with deep-set eyes and powerful hands.

"Godfrey tells me that you have something momentous to report."

Kindly but patrician, there is a note of humour in the Government Agent's voice when he addresses Walter and he seems to gaze down from a great height, the streaks of white in his grey hair giving him the stately appearance of a heron.

Diminished in this man's presence, Walter has an overwhelming sense of his own smallness. He loses his composure, his tongue flailing like a bell clapper, clanging out a single, discordant message: alarm, alarm.

Gone is his beautifully worded narrative, concise yet devastating. Instead, he can hear himself babbling like a peasant, the kind of high-pitched chatter used by any illiterate to get attention.

However, his words take effect. While Walter speaks, Nash listens attentively, his hands placed before him on the blotter. It is those hands, rather than his face, that express Nash's thoughts. As the story unfolds, the fingers tense, their tips pressing hard against the desk. When Walter digresses, the fingers start to beat impatiently on the blotter. When he reaches the climax of the story, the account of Arjun's poisoning, the hands clench convulsively, their knuckles gleaming white in the lamplight.

***

Nash leans forward into the light so that Walter can see his face clearly. All trace of humour is extinguished and the generous mouth is compressed into a thin, hard line. The fingers of both hands are tightly laced together and he rests on his elbows, like a man praying, his eyes fixed on the desk as he weighs up the facts. Then, with a sudden movement he seizes the telephone, dials, then speaks rapidly into the receiver.

It is like a rock fall. A small explosion of energy at the top of a mountain, a pebble shifting, a few stones being dislodged, then more, until a landslide is roaring down the slope, sweeping away everything in its path. No-one's life will be the same after this. Words, once spoken, cannot be retracted. A story, once told, cannot be changed.

For the first time, the events of that day seem real to Walter and he is struck by their enormity. He can no longer distance himself from them. They are facts, not the stuff of legend to be woven into some elaborate tale. Bereft of their dream-like quality, they appear crude, ugly, appalling. His face is misted with sweat and, feeling suddenly nauseous, he grips the arm of the chair to stop himself from fainting.

Nash does not notice. He is all decision and energy. He summons Inspector de Silva, the regional chief of police and Mr. Arumagam, the local judge. Within an hour, the Residence is pulsating with light and activity. Sleepy-eyed servants, roused from their beds are set to work, preparing food, tea and coffee. Nash's wife hovers at the bedroom door, anxious and a little bemused. It is unusual for her husband to be roused from his bed at such a late hour. It can only be bad news.

Two black cars draw up at the front door where Godfrey, inscrutable and immaculate, is waiting to greet the guests. He shows them into the Government Agent's study where they sit, grim-faced, awaiting further details. It is something that they have feared for many weeks: an attack on a Tamil by Sinhalese.

Nash introduces them to Walter, instructing the driver to repeat his story. Walter pats his face with his handkerchief, dabbing the corners of his mouth which feel strangely wet and sticky. Hoping that he will not shame himself by being sick, he takes a deep breath and begins to speak. His fears are unfounded. This time, he is word-perfect: his delivery, polished; his account full but entertaining; his audience engaged. Walter's heart pounds. But this time it does not pump with fear, but a giddy mixture of pride and pleasure.

A brief silence follows his oration. The policeman taps his foot. The judge gazes up at the ceiling, lost in thought. Walter's tale contains a particularly disturbing fact. This was no bar-room brawl, no spontaneous outburst of violence. However vague the details, it is clear that there was an element of calculation. The man was poisoned. No matter that he is a junior civil servant; he is a Tamil, representing a public office, also headed by a Tamil. The poisoner was, almost certainly, Sinhalese. Race is the issue here.

"It is a delicate matter."

The judge is the first to speak.

"We should proceed carefully."

The policeman interjects.

"We need to act quickly. Catch the wrongdoers. Make an example of them."

"Yes, yes," says the judge testily. "But if we are too heavy-handed, it could spark a riot."

The inspector represses a sigh. There are times when the police and judiciary do not see eye to eye. Sometimes, he even wonders if they are on the same side.

"What I propose," says Nash, addressing them both, "is that we first make sure of the facts. I suggest we visit the young man who was poisoned and that you question him yourselves in order to confirm Walter's story. Once we have heard Arjun's version of events, we will have a better idea of how to proceed."

"Exactly."

The judge nods in agreement. The policeman concedes that he will have to wait a little longer.

"Walter will come with us although, in view of his ordeal, I will not ask him to drive. There is another fellow who can do that."

Hearing himself spoken of in the third person, Walter flushes. He feels insulted, as if his word alone is not good enough, that he cannot be trusted to tell the truth. Then he panics. He is tired, has not slept nor hardly eaten for eighteen hours. At times, he has been unsure whether he was asleep or awake. Perhaps he has mistaken some of the facts, confused dream with reality. Has he got it wrong? The more he tries to remember, pinpointing specific events, the more illusory they become. An error of this magnitude could have severe consequences. He will be branded a liar, lose his job, even go to prison.

"It's all right."

A hand rests on his shoulder. Nash speaks to Walter in the same voice that he uses to soothe his pet spaniel.

"I don't doubt you, Walter. If this man has done what you think, he must be arrested and brought to trial. But we must be certain of the facts. Any mistake on our part could have far-reaching consequences. Possibly a riot. Do you see?"

Nash pats him on the back. A kindly gesture, meant to comfort and reassure but, somehow, it has the opposite effect. He feels small, insignificant and helpless; a pebble caught up in a landslide.

1956: A disordered house

The four men set off in the Government Agent's car, driven by Nash's junior housekeeper, a man of many skills who secretly covets Walter's job. Seated in the back next to the judge, Walter tries to make himself invisible. Withdrawing into the smallest possible space, he minimises every breath and movement, while staring out of the window at impenetrable blackness so as not to discomfort his illustrious companion. Not a word passes between them. Head erect, the judge stares before him, randomly tapping a finger against his bony knee, his mind elsewhere.

Meanwhile, Nash and his new driver are conducting an amiable conversation, their profiles outlined as they turn their heads to speak: the Agent's, strong and square-boned, giving an impression of power, even at this oblique angle; the driver's, round and chubby, with a baby's high-domed forehead.

They speak in low voices, too soft to distinguish words. However, their animated repartee is frequently broken by soft, whispering chuckles. Walter is piqued, pricked by jealousy, envious of the other driver's easy manner with his master. The position of driver to the Government Agent is a prestigious one, much sought after. Yet drivers, like servants, are easily replaced.

If Arjun's version of the story contradicts his own, then Walter will be discredited. Even worse, if these important men have been dragged out of their beds on the word of an unreliable servant, then Walter will lose his job. The Agent will have no choice. Then this new driver, who is currently doing his best to ingratiate himself, will take Walter's place. And all because he was unlucky enough to be picked for a trip to that stupid road project. It should have been this fellow, not him.

Walter's blood bubbles in his veins. His head throbs. It is as if he has been placed over a simmering heat. He feels a rush of anger against Arjun. Silly young fool. If only he had not confronted the overseer, not drunk the tea. He walked right into it. Serve him right if he was ill!

Then guilt takes the edge off his heat. Poor fellow, he nearly died. It is still not certain that he will recover. Sickened by his own self-interest, Walter curls up in the corner, fearful that the judge may have read his thoughts.

***

Finally, they arrive at Arjun's lodging. The Government Agent squints through the glass, beyond the steps and the porch to the front door. Strange. He never pictured his assistant in a place like this. There is no plan to this house, no geometry. It sprawls unevenly, being higher on one side than the other, as if rooms have been added piecemeal whenever required or money allowed. That is the way most houses are built on the Island. This one is obviously no exception. All the same, it does not fit Nash's image of Arjun and he feels mildly surprised that this is where his assistant should choose to live.

"Must have a word with him when he's better," thinks Nash. "Find him somewhere more suitable."

As he leaves the car, Walter catches a fragrant whiff of frangipani. A delicate, yellow bloom whirls softly to his feet. An omen. Walter shudders. Like most Islanders, he knows it by another name. The Temple Tree. It thrives in the precincts of sacred buildings where its flowers are used in rites for the dead, often being made into garlands for the corpse.

Neleni opens the door, her face pale, framed by fugitive strands of hair. The three men file past her into the hall, the Inspector's shiny boots clicking smartly over the cold concrete as if he were on parade.

"We need to speak to Arjun," says Nash gently. "Is he conscious?"

"Yes."

She can barely whisper. In the uncertain light, her eyes look watery and red-rimmed. Walter wonders if she has been crying, or if she is simply tired. She leads them across the hallway and down the corridor, past the many rows of photographs whose faces people the wall like ghosts: spirits trapped in celluloid who can only watch and wait. Then, Neleni herself seems to wilt into the shadows as they reach the bedroom door.

Pert as a jungle fowl, Sunny sits at the head of Arjun's bed, guarding her patient. But from what, or from whom, Walter cannot tell. The room is lit with candles, rather than the electric lamp. Sunny explains that it is easier on Arjun's eyes. They hurt him and he complains of violent headaches that have caused him to cry out in pain. In the candle-light, the thick lenses of her glasses reflect the three men standing in the doorway.

"He is waking, I think."

She is as bright and lively as one half her age. If he were to be uncharitable, Walter would say that the old lady was actually enjoying herself. Some people thrive on crises and many an Islander loves a good drama, as Walter knows. The old lady is as fresh as one newly woken from sleep.

"Unlike her daughter," thinks Walter.

As the men enter the room, the figure of Neleni drifts into the doorway where she watches them, silently. Like a hungry ghost. Walter cannot remember where he heard that expression, but it fits her perfectly.

***

Arjun stirs, aware that other people have entered the room. Slowly, opening his eyes, he sees Nash and Walter standing beside him. Then, he frowns, bemused. In the twilight, he can see two other figures, standing at the foot of the bed. The judge and the policeman.

Pulling up a chair, Nash sits down and leaning over the bed speaks softly to Arjun who nods and murmurs. The Government Agent then asks the women to leave.

"We will not be long. Just a few questions."

Mumbling, Sunny shuffles out of the room, reluctant to leave her patient. Neleni follows her to the end of the passage, then sinks to the floor. Her head, enfolded by her arms, rests on her knees, her face hidden so that none should catch her weeping. Unchecked, tears splash onto her sari, darkening the cloth like grease stains. Dirty, shameful tears.

It is the first, painful acknowledgment of something illicit. But she will not call it love. Rather, it is an oppressive truth which, at a stroke, has destroyed the delicate balance of her life, revealing the true extent of her confinement, the hopelessness of her situation, the lack of a solution. Locked in a stillborn marriage, becalmed in a rural backwater, her life is stagnant and rotten; Arjun, the only light in this dark place, a breath of freedom, a hope that must be denied.

She weeps, then falls into the trance-like state that follows grief and weariness. Her skin is tight and drawn, her eyes empty hollows. She is a thousand years old, so tired she can barely move.

"Neleni."

Someone touches her shoulder. Sunny is at her side.

"Come child. You cannot sleep here."

The kindly tone of Sunny's voice encourages a fresh surge of tears. This time, they spring not from despair, but a more congenial ailment: self-pity; childish abandon in sympathetic company; pain handed over to one better able to cope. Holding her mother's hand, Neleni allows herself to be led to her room, undressed and put to bed, the old lady stroking her forehead to soothe her.

The strangers have gone. The house is quiet. Everyone is in bed. Except Raj who keeps a solitary vigil in the kitchen. It is late. But he cannot sleep. It has been an extraordinary day. He must work it over in his mind. Make sense of it. What happened to Arjun has disrupted the whole family.

And yet, no-one has thought to explain anything to Raj. Earlier this evening, he heard Neleni and her mother, arguing in the hallway. It was nothing really. Neleni wanted to sit with Arjun. For some reason, Sunny would not let her. There had been a flurry of tears and sobs. Someone ran along the corridor. A door had slammed.

After that, Sunny had put the children to bed, then served Raj's meal, offering only the briefest explanation for his wife's absence. Neleni, it seemed, had shut herself in the bedroom, pleading a headache. However, when Raj approached the door with the idea of offering help, he heard the sound of muffled crying. When he asked Sunny what was happening, she just shrugged. *Women's things*. She always says that when they have had an argument. It is her way of keeping him out.

In order to relieve his own sense of uselessness, Raj offered to sit with Arjun. But Sunny warned him off.

"Not good. He is delirious. Saying things that make no sense. You should not hear it. It would shame him."

A few minutes later, Raj saw Sunny trotting off to Arjun's bedroom with an armful of towels and candles. So he followed. Only to have the door firmly closed in his face. It seems there are many places in Raj's house where he cannot go.

Frustrated and perplexed, Raj took himself off to the toddy tavern where he stayed all evening; not, as usual, in the company of friends, but drinking alone. He returned home late, carrying a fresh bottle of arrack, to be greeted by Sunny and told that he had just missed the Agent.

"Hmph!"

She seemed excited, ready to speak; but he was no longer interested. Gauging his mood, Sunny shuffled off to Arjun's room, where she is now dozing in a chair.

"Sometimes," thinks Raj, as he pours himself an arrack, "I think I am the only sane bugger in the whole family. Women!"

Although tired, and a little the worse for drink, his head is still relatively clear. It is a particularly warm night and he keeps the kitchen door and windows open in the forlorn hope that a draft might ease the heat. Something catches his eye.

There is a swift movement outside the window; a fleeting shadow, like a human figure, flits by. Raj starts to his feet, unsteady, heart pounding. Blood curdling howls are followed by the crashing of mops and pails. A commotion of cats. Several night-time prowlers have slipped over the fence and are fighting for sovereignty of the yard.

"Damn, bloody animals," mutters Raj, his heart resuming its normal pace. "If Aunty doesn't kill that cat, then I will."

Opening the door, he hurls one of his slippers into the dark. Demonic shrieks are followed by mutinous growls, then silence. His wits shaken, Raj returns to his seat and takes another drink, assuring himself that it is for medicinal purposes. Although he is a man of limited imagination, Raj is sure that there was something else out there, in the dark. He has a distinct premonition of evil, as if a dark and malevolent star is passing overhead.

"Poppycock," he says, banging the door as if to shut out whatever is lurking outside.

"I'm going to bed," he announces over his shoulder.

As he switches off the lights and leaves the room, a tusked face presses against the window.

1956: The convoy

Dawn is breaking as the convoy sweeps through town. Sunny is on her way to the kitchen when she hears a rumble of engines, unusual for this time of day. Shuffling into the living room, she looks out of the window, her view of the street framed by the temple tree. Four green lorries thunder past, followed by an open-topped jeep. Their passage causes a small tremor, shaking blossom from the tree and rattling the panes in the windows.

Sunny's sharp eyes spot two passengers in the back of the jeep; one, a man in uniform, the other a civilian, big-boned and handsome with greying hair. Recognising the police inspector and the Government Agent, she wonders if Walter is travelling with them, perhaps, in one of the trucks. She has taken a liking to the Sinhalese driver.

But once the convoy has passed, Sunny's thoughts return to her patient. The last time she checked, Arjun was sleeping peacefully. At least that crisis has passed; although, remembering her daughter's tears last night, Sunny has a sense of foreboding. It is clear that Neleni's feelings for their lodger run even deeper than her mother suspected.

With a new heaviness of heart, Sunny makes her way to the kitchen, intent on a few quiet moments with her pipe. Opening the door, she discovers Raj, his head on the table, one hand loosely cupped around a glass and, next to him, an empty bottle lying on its side.

Rocking from side to side in the truck, Walter dozes fitfully. Surfacing briefly from a deep sleep, he opens his eyes. He is seated in the back of the lorry with ten other men, two police sergeants, a number of young recruits and another man, more high-ranking than the others, who is seated on the bench next to him. An Assistant Superintendent of Police. He is an important man to be travelling with the lower ranks but, before Walter can consider the question further, he is lulled back to sleep by the murmur of conversation: someone is reading a letter from his wife; others are comparing the latest cricket score; two are discussing their next trip into town.

Walter awakes to a light tap on his face and the sound of muffled laughter. While asleep, his head has lolled back and his snores have attracted the attention of two young recruits. Finding the journey tedious, they have distracted themselves by rolling pieces of roti into pellets and flicking them at his open mouth. It was one of these that hit Walter on the cheek. Startled, he awoke with a loud snort. The boys nudge each other, wheezing with suppressed amusement.

"That's enough," rasps the man sitting next to Walter. "If I catch you doing that again you'll be confined to barracks."

The boys blanch and mutter their apologies.

"I am sorry," says the man, turning his pock-marked face to Walter. "They're village boys. Peasants."

He scowls menacingly at the boys who shrink back into their seats, their heads lowered.

"You're the Government Agent's driver, aren't you?" says the man, abruptly.

"Yes."

Walter senses that the man's presence in the lorry is no coincidence.

"Walter Madurasinghe. A Sinhalese from Kandy."

The man laughs, trying to sound jovial, but the effect is unpleasant. Now alert, Walter is on his guard. The two recruits, now fully recovered from their admonition, are eyeing him slyly, as if they know something that he does not.

"Times are changing," opines the policeman. "Take this man running the road project, Mennan Rasanayagam. Our country no longer needs people like him. They are like ticks on the back of an ox, draining it of blood."

Walter feels uncomfortable. This is not idle conversation. It is leading somewhere.

"All criminals should be punished for their crimes," mumbles Walter.

"It's not just criminals that I was thinking of."

The man leans closer, lowering his voice.

"There are plenty of other parasites in this country: people in positions of authority, who will resist change, who want power only for themselves. That is bad for Ceylon. Bad for the Sinhalese."

Walter is beginning to sweat. The policeman's words have a hidden meaning, intended for him. His tongue cleaves to the roof of his mouth. The lorry is grinding over the last leg of the mountain track, bouncing and lurching through potholes. The air is thick with exhaust fumes. Clinging to a metal bar, Walter tries to ignore the sick feeling in his stomach.

"This is our opportunity. The Sinhalese nation has been reborn. We need to know where our loyalties lie, who we can trust."

The man leans even closer and whispers.

132

"Whose side are you on, Walter? Where do your loyalties lie?"

The lorry halts abruptly, swinging its passengers forward, bunching them together. Cursing, the policeman rises heavily to his feet, pausing to brush the creases from his uniform. Then, before climbing out of the lorry, he claps Walter on the shoulder.

"Come and see me when you are next in Kandy."

He smiles but his words contain a threat. He has issued an order, not an invitation.

The men stand in a semi-circle, staring up at the corpse that hangs over them like an incubus.

"Cut it down."

A rasping order from the Assistant Superintendent of Police galvanizes the spellbound men. One, as agile as a toddyman, shins up the tree and starts to hack at the rope. Responding to the motion, the body begins to twirl gently. The other men gather beneath, ready to ease it down. Suddenly the cord snaps, catching the men unawares. The body thuds to the ground, where it lies with its arms and legs twisted at right angles: a swastika, the ancient sign for good luck. It is an irony noted by the Government Agent.

One of the younger men sniggers, trying to cover his fear. Others simply stare at the corpse which exerts a horrible fascination over them. Death is not a new experience. All have seen the dead bodies of family members or friends: for, in this country, it is traditional for the dead to lie in state in the family home before the funeral and there is a strong bond between the living and the newly-deceased. Tradition demands that coffins should be left open, so that those who remain in this world can pay their respects to the departed. Whole families may even gather around the corpse for a last photograph before the lid is nailed to the coffin.

But nothing has prepared the soldiers for what they find in the clearing. This body has not been groomed for viewing. It has not been washed and dressed in clean clothes; its hair has not been combed and its features have not been arranged to suggest a state of somnolent tranquillity. Rather, the moment at which a terrified and unwilling victim was torn from life has been preserved. Here, death sits in majesty.

The corpse's clothes are torn and bloody, the pants soiled. To the stench of faeces is added that of rotting flesh. Swarms of flies are gathering, attracted by the smell. But, worst of all, is the face: the eyes, now white and filmy, bulge from their sockets; the tongue, black and swollen, pokes from the mouth in a last, lewd gesture, mocking the world from which its owner has departed.

The soldiers shuffle about, elbowing each other out of the way, trying to get a better view of the corpse. Once the initial shock is past, the body begins to exert a strange attraction. The soldiers gaze down at it, open-mouthed. Already, this memento of Mennan's final torment is being transformed from an object of horror to one of morbid curiosity; a fairground entertainment.

"Cover him up," orders Nash, angrily.

One of the soldiers runs back to the lorry and climbs into the cab. After a few seconds, he emerges, staggering under the weight of a heavy, green tarpaulin. Another man goes to help him and, carrying the bundle between them, they trudge back to where the others are waiting. The men unfold the tarpaulin then, laying it on the ground, roll Mennan's body in the sheet, until he resembles a great, green cocoon. Four young recruits are then nominated by the Assistant Superintendent of Police to carry the corpse back to the lorry. They look at each other uncertainly, unwilling to approach the horrific object lying at their feet.

"Get on with it!" barks the senior policeman.

Reluctantly, the young men stoop to lift the bundle. The stiffness of the tarpaulin and the weight of the body within make it difficult to get a grip and the men soon discover that the only way to carry their burden is to cradle it in their arms. Each wears a look of quiet revulsion, as he shuffles forward, sometimes tripping, trying to match his steps to those of his colleagues.

***

Walter is still sitting in the back of the lorry. The soldiers have all gone about their business and Walter welcomes the opportunity to think, disturbed, as he is, by the policeman's words. There was some hidden meaning in what the man said. And a threat.

"He wants something," thinks Walter.

But, for the life of him, he cannot think what.

The air in the lorry is stifling, over-breathed and foul from the sweat of so many bodies. Outside, Walter can hear voices shouting. But they are faint and, anyway, that is the nature of soldiers, always to shout. In need of air, Walter descends from the back of the lorry, where he leans against the tail-gate looking wistfully across the valley at a waterfall sheering down the granite face of the mountain. He can hear its soft whisper from here although, even as the crow flies, it must be at least a mile away. There is more shouting from the soldiers, then silence.

"Thank god," thinks Walter.

His view of the clearing is obscured by the high sides of the vehicle and he has no inclination to look. He saw enough of the place yesterday. He has no need to be reminded. He is unaware that the soldiers have discovered Mennan's body.

"What a business," he mutters to himself. "I don't know why they brought me here. I hope they find the bugger soon and arrest him. Then we can all go home."

Fatigue makes Walter crotchety. He is hungry and has not slept in thirty-six hours. He is indulging in a reverie of food and a soft bed, when he hears the sound of heavy boots scuffing over dry earth. Someone swears quietly.

"Stop a minute. Don't go so fast at the front. I'm losing my grip."

"Just hurry up," snaps another voice. "I can't stand this stench much longer. It's turning my stomach."

Walter peers around the corner of the lorry. Four sweating recruits are carrying what appears to be a long roll of green cloth. They have stopped for the man at the rear to adjust his grip. He is smaller than the others and, as a result, has been burdened with a greater proportion of the weight.

Idly, Walter wonders what is in the bundle. Then, on the clear morning air, a faint whiff of something noisome reaches him. It grows stronger as the men approach: a stench like every form of rottenness mixed together. Trying to hold his nose, Walter looks up. The Government Agent is hurrying across the clearing towards him.

"Wait," says the Government Agent to the recruits. "Put him down a minute!"

Then, turning to Walter, he beckons him forward.

"I'm sorry, Walter. I hadn't expected this. I brought you here because I wanted to be sure we were arresting the right man. Now I need you to identify a body."

He signals the recruits to open the tarpaulin. As they do so, the unpleasant odour blossoms into a foul-smelling miasma.

"Oh, my God!"

Walter pulls out his handkerchief and holds it to his face, as much to protect himself from the sight, as from the smell, of the corpse.

135

"Is this Mennan Rasanayagam, the overseer?"

Walter looks into the blind eyes that seem to be staring at something over his shoulder. Is this really the man he met yesterday? The features, now hideously distorted, have been transformed. It is difficult to imagine how this carrion could ever have been human; how it walked, talked, ate, lived and loved. How could this rotting lump of flesh have held a man's soul?

"Walter ..." Nash prompts him gently. "Is this him?"

With a trembling hand, Walter removes the handkerchief from his mouth.

"Yes, sir. It is."

"Thank you."

Nash motions the recruits to cover the body. Side by side, he and Walter watch it being loaded into the lorry.

"How did he die?"

"We found him hanging from a tree. We don't yet know if it was suicide, or something else."

But Nash already knows the answer. The undergrowth near the place of hanging has been trampled and bruised, witness to the presence of many feet.

"There will have to be an inquest before any conclusion is reached."

The Agent's tone is matter-of-fact but, inwardly, he is troubled. Disturbing rumours are circulating, ugly stories of tension between Tamils and Sinhalese all, as yet, without substance: suspicious attacks, threats of reprisal, nothing specific but all inflamed by political campaigners who are active about the country and whose speeches feed the febrile imagination of the populace. Elections are always a dirty business and this one promises to be no different. At times like this, it is impossible to separate truth from fiction.

Relieved of their burden, three of the soldiers take the opportunity to walk around and stretch their aching arms. One lights a cigarette and passes it around. The smallest of them, to the amusement of the others, is being noisily sick behind a tree.

"Now that's what I call a stinking Tamil," says one of them, jerking his thumb at the lorry where Mennan's body lies wrapped in the tarpaulin. The others laugh, not realizing or, perhaps, not caring that the man with greying hair who stands nearby is, himself, a Tamil. Walter blushes at their rudeness. Nash pretends not to notice.

"Come with me, Walter," he says, putting a hand on the driver's shoulder. "We'll be travelling back together."

1956: An old man remembers

Bicycles, taxis and lorries career along the road, jostling for position with rickshaws and pedestrians. The old monk can hear their noisy clamour, although from his window, he sees only the temple's roofs stepping up to heaven, their red-tiled slopes stacked neatly, one above the other.

They remind him of sun-soaked terraces where rice and vegetables grew on narrow ribbons carved from the hillside; where the soil, if left to dry, baked in the heat, turning the same colour as the temple roofs; memories of childhood, so distant they seem more like a dream.

For he escaped life in the fields to become a monk. He is now abbot of a small monastery where the only intrusion from the outside world is the distant rumble of traffic, passing on a road that winds back and forth through the city, coiling itself about the monastery like a great, sleepless serpent.

The world is a beast whose hungry whispering keeps the abbot awake at night. For years, he has kept it at bay, fending off its restless aspirations, protecting the tranquillity of this quiet place. So far, the monastery has been undisturbed by temporal concerns, although the battle to preserve its peace becomes a little harder each day. From the tone of its roar, the old abbot can tell that the beast at the gate is becoming restless. Change is coming. But will it be for the better?

***

Until recently, Ceylonese Buddhism existed in a state of torpor, worn down by centuries of colonial rule. Monasteries and temples, neglected by successive waves of Christian rulers, became so impoverished that even the greatest fell into disrepair: including the royal monastery of Kelaniya.

But now, Buddhism is entering a new era. The monasteries have regained their wealth and power: politicians seek the advice of their scholars and the monastic vocation is so popular that record numbers of young men are seeking admission to monastic orders. Buddhism is stronger than it has been for centuries. One only has to see the fervour with which the anniversary of Buddha's death, the parinibbana, is being celebrated. Indirectly, it will be responsible for toppling the incumbent prime minister.

Once more, Buddhism is in the ascendant. Yet, although recovery is welcome, there are some who have misgivings; some who, like the old monk, detect a current of self-interest amid the renewed professions of faith. The old man's study overlooks a courtyard. His window faces inwards, not out. That is the way he likes it, for he wants no dealings with the world of men.

***

The boundary between religion and politics is dissolving faster than mountain snow. Soon, the two currents will run together and rush forward in a single torrent. The abbot sighs as he looks down at the hands, clasped in his lap. They are the weak, gnarled hands of an old man who no longer has the power to resist.

"Ahem!"

Someone coughs, rousing the old man from his reverie. A young man steps out of the shadows and approaches the abbot's desk: a visitor, bringing news of the turbulent world beyond the monastery walls. Despite his policeman's uniform, the other man is awkward and diffident in his manner: an unlikely herald of change. But, nonetheless, that is what he is.

Licking his thumb, the policeman opens his notebook and flicks rapidly through the pages. Then, tapping his lip with the end of his pencil, he pretends to consult his notes although, as yet, every sheet in the notebook is blank. The old man waits for him to speak.

"Erm, we're making enquiries about a man called Asoka Rajaguru. Do you know him?"

The abbot nods his head.

"What can you tell me about him?"

What indeed? The difficulty is knowing where to start.

"Asoka was my brightest student."

The old man sighs and stares at his hands. There will never be another like Asoka. At least, not in his lifetime.

"And ..." the policeman urges, pencil at the ready.

"He was brilliant. Exceptional."

"And," thinks the old monk, "I allowed myself to be blinded by that brilliance."

But he cannot admit to this flaw in his judgement. Not to the young man standing in front of him who holds his pencil so clumsily and who uses it to carve, rather than write, letters on the page. He would not understand.

If the abbot tried to explain how he was seduced by the intelligence of his student, this policeman would interpret it as some form of physical infatuation. People like him will never understand the love of intellect. For the love of a mind is a pure love, devoid of sexual motive. Such brilliance draws others towards it, like moths to a flame, blinding them with its bright light and singeing their wings.

The young policeman shuffles his feet. He is getting impatient.

"What more can you tell me about him?"

What indeed? The old monk considers his words carefully. He will tell the policeman enough, but not too much. Although Asoka abandoned the monastic life some time ago, the abbot still feels responsible for his former student. To give too much information would feel like betrayal and the abbot still has much on his conscience. He sent Asoka away when he should have kept him close.

"He was restless."

The policeman raises his eyebrows. Further explanation is needed.

"I doubted his aptitude for the religious life."

"But you said he was brilliant."

"The two do not necessarily go together. Spirituality and intellect are separate things."

The policeman looks puzzled.

"No," thinks the abbot, "I would not expect you to understand."

"His interests began to stray beyond scripture," says the monk, aloud.

The policeman gives the abbot a knowing look, one often shared by young men, the facial shorthand for 'girls'.

"He became interested in politics," corrects the monk.

"Oh."

"I sent him away, thinking it would be in his best interests."

"And it was the worst mistake of my life," thinks the monk. "I sent him away when I should have kept him here. Why did I not see the danger?"

The old man looks sad. He stares out of the window to where a great bird, no more than a black outline, is circling the sky.

"Poor old fellow," thinks the policeman. "I'll bet he sits here for hours every day, just staring out of the window like that. What a life!"

The policeman has no sympathy for the deprivations of monastic life. He has a new girlfriend. A Hindu girl. A Tamil. And an Indian one, at that. His parents, devout Sinhalese Buddhists, would go mad if they knew. So would hers, most likely. But it is worth the risk. The very thought of her makes his head swim.

"I sent him to another monastery."

The policeman starts, his mind having wandered to more pleasant thoughts of his girlfriend.

"I'm sorry?"

"I thought, if Asoka were to go somewhere with better resources – a bigger library, a greater collection of texts, better teachers – he might become less restless, more focused on his studies."

"So where did he go?"

"To the monastery at Kelaniya."

"Kelaniya!"

The policeman whistles through his teeth. Even he has heard of Kelaniya, a vast and powerful monastery once favoured by Sinhalese kings.

"That's Buddharakkita Thera's place, isn't it?"

"Yes."

The old man smiles. He wouldn't have put it quite like that. No monastery is the property of one man. But people like Buddharakkita Thera, the abbot of Kelaniya, are challenging the traditional view of monasticism. Everyone has heard of Buddharakkita. Even this worldly young policeman.

That abbot's name is on everyone's lips. He is as active outside the monastery as he is within it, pursuing lawsuits, brokering commercial deals, dabbling in politics. These days he is less of a monk, more a man of the world. He has become heavily involved in political campaigns, sponsoring candidates like Mrs Vimala Wijewardene with whom he has a close association. When he visits her at home, he exchanges his monastic robes for a suit and hat. Their friendship has been the subject of lewd speculation in a number of anonymous pamphlets.

But the old abbot knew none of this when he sent Asoka to Kelaniya. It was only afterwards that he realized his mistake. For, within Kelaniya's walls, Buddhism and politics are synonymous. Instead of being discouraged, Asoka's new interest was nurtured until it became an obsession.

"He was very different when he returned."

The monk's voice has dropped to a whisper. He seems almost to wince with pain at the memory.

"Yes ..." prompts the policeman.

"Tell him," thinks the monk. "Why not? What harm can it do now?"

Gazing out of the window, his eyes averted, he begins to speak slowly:

"Asoka returned from Kelaniya in a state of suppressed frenzy. Every night, he would shut himself in the library, reading by the light of an oil lamp, hardly sleeping. Then, he began to encourage political discussion amongst the other monks. I often saw them, in small groups, talking together in quiet corners of the library or the cloisters. I never heard what was said, but I noticed a change."

"What sort of change?"

The abbot shrugs. How can one explain a thing like that? New ideas trickling into the monastery like the first rivulets of a spring tide. The delicate equilibrium between the monastery and the world outside being upset. The restless concerns of the material world creeping in under the gates and taking root like weeds.

The younger monks have started to express an interest in politics, seeing themselves, not as separate from the world outside, but as an integral part of it. Buddhism, they say, has been compromised by western colonization. Now that Independence has been achieved, it is time for the Sinhalese to reclaim their Buddhist heritage.

Of course, the abbot cannot argue with that. But what troubles him is the way in which those views are expressed. With such force, such aggression. Buddhism is being invigorated, and that is a good thing, but revival has brought with it a new militancy, a political awareness that does not reflect the abbot's view of spirituality. If he were asked his opinion, he would express his disapproval. But no-one asks what he thinks. Not any more.

The old man lapses into a reverie. The policeman taps his notebook with his pencil, eager to be gone.

"Is there anything else?"

"No. I don't think so."

The policeman signs his notes with a flourish, then excuses himself and takes his leave, shutting the door with such force that the books rattle on their shelves.

***

Still staring up at the sky, the abbot contemplates an eagle, wheeling over the city and he prays: *Asoka, my son, may you find peace.*

Suddenly, chaos breaks out beneath the abbot's window. The courtyard reverberates with an insistent bellowing. A young elephant is calling for its mother. His keeper is walking him around in gentle circuits, putting him through his paces in preparation for the annual perahera when holy relics will be paraded through the city, accompanied by temple elephants, dancers and drummers. Perahera always attracts thousands of pilgrims, but this year there will be even more. Buddhists across the world will be celebrating the 2,500th anniversary of Buddha's parinibbana. Yet, on the Island, there will be tension as well as festivity.

Fearing that his support is dwindling, the Prime Minister has called elections early, bringing them forward a year. The Buddhist monks' party, of which Buddharakkita Thera is secretary, has condemned the decision. But it will also exploit it. The government, so desperate to cling to power, has ensured its own demise.

"It was not always like this," reflects the old monk, sadly.

Such things would not have happened under Prime Minister D. S. Senanayake. He was a true leader. After negotiating Independence with the British, he ensured a peaceful transition, so unlike the bloodbath in India. There was space for everyone in his Ceylon. But he had died, too soon, taking his vision of a pluralist nation with him.

Now, ten years after Independence, the country is beginning to fragment. Marxists, Communists, left-wingers, Sinhalese nationalists, Tamils, all going their separate ways, all jockeying for position, like the traffic outside. A constant hum of discontent that has now seeped into the monastery.

Down in the courtyard, the young elephant trumpets wildly, tossing its head, trying to slip its halter. Two monks run to the aid of its handler. All three take hold of the rope but, despite their combined efforts, are dragged across the courtyard, their bare feet slipping over the sand-strewn concrete.

"That little elephant is the real symbol of our country. That is what we should put on our flag," thinks the old man as he pulls down the blind.

1956: An inquest

The fan whirs, clicks, falls silent, its flails taking shape as it loses speed, then stops. All eyes are anxiously turned upwards. Everyone hopes that, by some miracle, the fan will come back to life. Not that its feeble efforts have cooled them – the Coroner's Court is like an overheated cauldron – but the noise of the fan reminds those crammed into this airless room of what it is like to feel air wafting over hot, perspiring skin. As the courtroom grows hotter, the smell of hair oil gets stronger, mingling with the scent of soap, perfume and, occasionally, the rank odour of sweat.

Strangers strike up conversations with their neighbours. Chairs scrape against the parquet floor; some people cough, others hand around sweets which are noisily unwrapped. There is an air of suspense, a mingling of excitement and fear, the sort that precedes a religious spectacle, a devil dance or an exorcism.

Despite Independence, the law courts still affect the trappings of colonial power. Imperial ephemera are a protective charm against disorder. Half wood-panelling, half regulation green paint, this courtroom belongs to another age.

With a portentous creak, a door at the front of the room opens and two men emerge: one, in black robes, leading the other.

"The Court will rise!"

Chairs scrape across the floor and there is a general sound of scrabbling as everyone scrambles to their feet. They all want to see the Coroner; a man renowned for his singular appearance. Tall and emaciated with long, fleshless limbs, he is the living embodiment of death: an impression strengthened by his hollow cheeks and deep-set eyes. Who better to unravel the mysteries of mortality than one who, himself, appears to be on the point of departing life?

The Coroner lowers himself into his seat so slowly that some fancy they can hear the creaking of his joints.

"Sit!" shouts the man in black robes.

More rumbling and scraping as the audience resume their seats. Tightly packed, like peas, those in the public gallery jostle together, positioning themselves for the best view. Necks are craned and shorter visitors curse themselves for not having secured a better seat. For this is an occasion not to be missed: the hearing into the overseer's mysterious death. Everywhere, there has been gossip and speculation. Was it murder or suicide? Today, the court will give its verdict.

Several of the spectators nudge each other. Like children on a school outing, they can hardly contain their excitement. But their levity is not shared by all. Seated in the front row, Nash anxiously anticipates the outcome of the hearing. All around the country, election fever is running high. Society is polarizing with alarming speed. New factions appear every day.

Speakers with soap-boxes spring up at every street corner. Some have the ability to attract huge crowds. So far, the rallies have been peaceful, but the tone of the speeches is more virulent than usual and, in some places, there have been scuffles and fist fights. The country is holding its breath, waiting to see what will happen next. If the cause of Mennan's death is shown to have been a racial attack, then trouble may ensue. The finding of this inquest will be crucial.

Unhurried and in silence, the Coroner deals his papers like a pack of cards, shuffling them, rotating them, knocking the edges against the desk until he has a neat stack, then arranging them in front of him in three piles of equal height with exactly a hand's width between them. Next, to the left of the bundles, he lays out a pen and two pencils, always in the same sequence, then pours himself a glass of water.

The liquid in the jug is viscous and tepid. It has a dead fly floating in it and a bubble at the rim. With predictable negligence, the clerk has forgotten to change the water between hearings. In fact, the same jug has been here for several days; the Coroner recognizes the chip in the spout. But it doesn't matter. He never drinks the water. It is the pouring of it into the glass that counts, part of the ritual that helps to focus his mind.

The Coroner addresses the court, speaking in a slow, deliberate voice as he recounts the facts: Mennan's name, age, occupation, where and when his body was found. The muscles in Arjun's stomach tighten. Pulling a handkerchief from his pocket, he holds it to his mouth, knowing that Nash, sitting next to him, is watching from the corner of his eye.

"Are you all right, old man?" Nash murmurs, discreetly.

Arjun nods, trying to swallow the bile in his throat. He feels sick. He has never given evidence before.

"Before we proceed" drones the Coroner, "I should like the Court to note that two individuals, whose evidence may have proved conclusive, will not appear as witnesses. Those individuals are: Asoka Rajaguru, a foreman, and Anil Galla, a labourer, both of whom worked at the site with the deceased.

"Both of these men have disappeared. The exact time of their disappearance is in doubt although it is generally agreed that they were still on site on the day on which Mr Rasanayagam died. To date, this Court has received no information as to their whereabouts which is, to say the least, unfortunate."

Pausing, the Coroner slowly turns his head to stare pointedly at the Assistant Superintendent of Police who is sitting in the front row. The policeman glares back. The Coroner, impassive, turns his attention to the usher.

"Call the first witness," he says, in a hollow undertone.

"Mr Arjun Kumaran," bawls the man in black robes. A woman in the front row presses her fingers to her ears.

Still weak from his illness, Arjun stumbles as he crosses the room and is gathered up by the usher who herds him to his seat. With everyone's attention focused on him, Arjun remembers an excursion, long ago, into the country. A rare treat, in his uncle's car, driving along narrow roads at night. A mongoose had run out and stopped dead in the road, mesmerised by the oncoming headlights. The car had swerved and the creature had escaped. Here, in the witness box, Arjun knows what compelled the animal to freeze in its tracks.

"Mr Kumaran. Please tell us who you are and when you last saw Mr Rasanayagam."

Falteringly, Arjun starts to give evidence. Listeners at the back of the courtroom cannot hear him and begin to get restless. A woman clucks at her neighbour, a man well-padded with fat who sits with his legs wide and has inadvertently dug her in the ribs while shifting about in his seat. Without the fan, the room has grown even hotter. Tempers are fraying.

"Speak up please, Mr Kumaran."

Arjun coughs, takes a breath and tries to raise his voice. His words echo in his head and it sounds to him as if he is shouting, but the courtroom settles instantly. He has their attention. He describes what he saw at the work-site in the forest; the unfinished road; the men at the camp-fire, one of whom is suspected of poisoning him, and his meeting with Mennan. His listeners are riveted. Arjun is describing his confrontation with Mennan in the hut, when he is distracted by a movement in the front row.

A woman in a green sari. He recognizes her instantly. Mennan's wife. And Mennan's voice in his ear: "Beautiful isn't she?" He remembers how Mennan's photograph worked on his memory, reminding him of something he could not recall. He has it now. Sigiriya. The painting of a Maiden in the rock gallery. The one that he admired. This woman is her living image.

"Mr. Kumaran?" The Coroner leans towards him. Suddenly, in mid-sentence, Arjun has stopped speaking.

"Mr Kumaran, please continue."

But Arjun's thoughts continue to drift. Back to Sigiriya where, for a few hours, an ancient world came to life and captured him with its magic.

"Would you like some water?"

The Coroner offers his glass to Arjun.

"No, thank you."

Arjun can hear gentle, mocking laughter. He looks at the overseer's wife, but she is dabbing her eyes with a handkerchief. Both thought and speech elude him. The last part of his evidence has to be painstakingly teased out by the Coroner who, after a few more minutes, declares Arjun's ordeal over, allowing him to leave the stand. Without warning, the fan overhead clicks back into life.

As Arjun resumes his seat, Nash leans over to speak to him.

"Are you all right?"

"Yes ... I think so."

"What happened?"

"I thought I saw a face. From the past."

"Someone you know?"

"No. I've never met her before."

"Then how ..."

"A photograph ... a painting. The same face but hundreds of years apart. Tell me," Arjun, his eyes suddenly wild, grips the Agent's sleeve, "is it possible for the past to come to life?"

"No. Of course not."

Arjun sinks back into his seat, his eyes fixed on the revolving sails of the fan, his face pale and haunted. Nash frowns, trying to hide his concern. Arjun is still weak from his illness. He is muddle-headed and confused. A little delusional. Better keep an eye on him. Nash gives Arjun a reassuring pat on the knee.

"Next witness!"

It is Nash's turn to take the stand. Brief and to the point, his evidence is delivered with professional aplomb. The Coroner nods, approvingly. All too often, witnesses stray from the subject, guided by prejudice or their own opinion. But this man is different. There is no superfluity, no embellishment. At the end of Nash's statement, the Coroner proffers a rare compliment.

"Well done!"

To show that his gratitude is genuine, the Coroner attempts a smile and, as he does so, the skin tightens over the contours of his face, increasing its likeness to a skull. Nash returns to his seat and sets himself down with the quiet concentration of a large man filling a small space.

The next witnesses are dispatched in a few minutes. Two labourers. One with wide, terrified eyes responds to questions with monosyllabic replies. The other, an old man with few teeth, can barely be understood. Neither has anything of interest to offer.

Then, comes the Vadda boy. He speaks of omens: snakes and the shadowy figure of a man; strange configurations of leaves and stones; magic, sorcery and enchantment. He describes the overseer on the last day of his life, walking around in a trance, his face like that of a drowned man, cold and expressionless.

"For days, he had been followed by a demon."

There are gasps of horror. A woman crosses herself. Another, of a nervous disposition, nestles close to her husband. Thrilled by the prospect of witchcraft, the crowd begins to whisper until the courtroom is filled by a confused babble.

"That boy is right. I have heard of such things before."

"You remember that old story of the nail? If it is driven through the head, you can turn a man into a slave."

"No, no. This is different. It was a curse. My aunty told me of such a one in Galle. A man hanged himself and, under his doorstep, they found a broken egg with his name written on the shell."

The court is in uproar.

"Quiet, please. That's enough!"

The Coroner's voice booms above the chatter. He waits for the excitement to die down before inviting the boy to continue.

"Go on."

"A demon had been following the overseer."

The Coroner looks thoughtfully at his papers.

"A demon, you say?"

"Yes."

"Not a man?"

"No."

The boy is adamant.

"How do you know it was a demon?"

"My people often see them. They have lived in the forest for centuries."

"And this demon? What did he look like?"

"Not like a man."

Quietly attentive, the Coroner has been taking notes. But, in the margin, he writes: *Inadmissible*.

"Very good. That is all. You may go."

A disappointed murmur reverberates around the courtroom. The spectators had hoped for more. But the Coroner has no time for fantasy, only fact.

The boy climbs down from the stand, nervously walking back to his seat past rows of people who all stare at him and whisper as he passes. He is unused to city-dwellers. They look and smell peculiar, not like people at all. The boy thinks that he would rather face an army of demons than live among these strange folk.

By now, the room has heated to an intolerable level. Women and men are fanning themselves with oddments of paper or, for want of anything else, their hands. Mennan's wife cools herself with a fan, its delicate ivory panels laced together with silk ribbon. Arjun is mesmerized by the movement of her hand; the long, slender fingers, the elegant wrist. A dancer's hand: one that can paint the air with beautiful shapes, or express a thought with a single eloquent movement. The air of Sigiriya blows sweetly across his face.

The remaining witnesses give their evidence: two young policemen who discovered the body and the Assistant Superintendent of Police whose statement initially describes his own involvement in the matter. Then, suddenly, he changes tack. He begins to describe Mennan's character, although he never met him, and the views of his workmen, although only a couple of them were interviewed. It is clear that he is trying to influence the outcome of the hearing. His testimony points to murder. The cause? Racial tension between the overseer, a Tamil, and his workforce who were all Sinhalese. He glowers at the courtroom as he speaks, daring anyone to challenge him. Unperturbed, the Coroner repeatedly interjects, often before the policeman has finished a sentence.

"As a senior police officer you, of all people, should know that a court is only interested in ascertainable facts. Not unsubstantiated opinions and hearsay."

The Coroner makes no attempt to hide his dislike of this witness. Nor does the policeman, infused with rage, try to conceal his hatred of the Coroner. Having finished his statement, the Assistant Superintendent of Police stumps back to his seat in an ill-humour while the Coroner quietly consults his notes.

"From the post mortem report, it is clear that Mennan Rasanayagam died a violent and unnatural death by hanging. When the body was discovered, it was hanging some considerable height above ground. This, and the lack of any ladder which may have been used by the victim, are cause for concern.

"It is not inconceivable that Mr Rasanayagam climbed the tree and lowered himself from its branches, although this seems unlikely, particularly in view of the amount of alcohol that he appears to have consumed. Alternatively, he may have used a ladder which was later removed by a person or persons unknown. This is, perhaps, more feasible. However, I would not describe it as a distinct possibility, even less a probability."

The Assistant Superintendent of Police lifts his head, listening intently. A verdict of unlawful killing could tip the balance, destroy the delicate equilibrium on which peace depends. There will be outrage, retaliation, reprisals. A short spell of controlled anarchy could alter the course of these elections. At least, that is what his political masters have told him. It would be worth the price if it secures a change in government. The future of the Sinhalese nation would be assured.

Nash leans forward, head down, hands clenched on his knees.

The Coroner continues in a monotone:

"The evidence that I have heard today is largely circumstantial. As we have heard from the Government Agent, Mennan Rasanayagam had recently learned that his business operations were under official investigation, with the potential of very severe consequences for his future career. No doubt he was extremely distressed. Certainly, the post mortem shows that he had been drinking heavily. Upon this evidence alone, it would be tempting to return a verdict of suicide."

The members of the court-room ready themselves to leave. It is over.

"However ..."

The Coroner's voice rises above the various rustlings and scratchings of the courtroom. The audience freezes. He has not finished.

"… fragments of a letter, dated from the day of this incident and found in Mennan Rasanayagam's office, show that he was hoping to strike some sort of a deal with someone he thought might help him. This is not the sort of behaviour normally associated with suicide. Indeed, it indicates that, only a short while before his death, Mennan Rasanayagam still entertained hopes of resolving his difficulties. I feel, therefore, that there is insufficient evidence on which to base a finding of suicide."

With an audible hiss, the Assistant Superintendent of Police sucks air through his teeth. His eyes glitter wickedly as a slow smile spreads across his face. Looking up, the Coroner addresses the next words directly to the senior police officer. There is no mistaking his meaning.

"Had the missing witnesses, Asoka Rajaguru and Anil Galla, been found and required to attend, this court might have arrived at a more satisfactory conclusion. I would therefore recommend that the police continue to search for these men and make every effort to apprehend them."

A slight pause. The atmosphere is electric. No-one moves. For the first time, the court-room is completely silent except for the hypnotic whirr of the fan overhead.

The Coroner laces his fingers together, his knuckles glowing white through the skin.

"As it is, there is only one verdict available to me."

The courtroom braces itself.

"An open verdict."

Furious, the Assistant Superintendent of Police rises from his chair, knocking it over. He opens his mouth, ready to remonstrate but is stayed by a flinty glance from the Coroner. The policeman glowers back, then storms out, elbowing people out of his way. Nash runs his hands through his hair. The finding has been neutral, neither offending, nor pleasing any faction. Disaster has been averted. Justice, of a kind, has been done.

**

As they file out of the court room, Nash and Arjun draw level with Mennan's widow. Despite the handkerchief applied to her face throughout the hearing, her eyes betray no trace of redness.

"Oh, Mr Tharmalingam," she says, addressing Nash while glancing at Arjun. "My husband's funeral is on Thursday. Eleven a.m. at St Michael's church. There will also be a reception at my house. So that people can pay their respects. I should be honoured if you would attend."

Caught off guard, Nash has no option but to accept.

"And please bring your assistant," she adds.

Arjun stammers a reply. As the widow disappears into the crowd, he hears once more the sound of faint laughter.

1956: Requiescat in pace

A moist gloom presses around the worshippers as they enter the church. Like new arrivals in the underworld, they blink in the unnatural darkness then fumble for places among the pews, tripping and knocking prayer books to the floor as they shuffle, purblind, to their seats. Then, as they adjust to the dim light, their eyes are drawn to the coffin, a rich carapace of mahogany, shining darkly like a beetle's back, wreathed in garlands of temple tree flowers.

Even after the service has begun, people continue to arrive, silhouetted in the bright arc of the door. The priest makes a series of slow circuits around the coffin, swinging the gold incense burner from side to side. The long chain of the thurible rattles rhythmically as perfumed smoke streams from its vents. Round and round the priest walks, swinging the thurible like a pendulum, until the coffin is veiled in white mist. With swift-moving lips, the priest intones the prayers for the dead. He crosses himself, and the congregation follow; he kneels, and so do they. He bids them sit or stand, and they obey. A ritual performed for countless souls; yet, this is no ordinary funeral.

To Arjun, himself a Catholic, it is unlike any service that he has ever attended. Less of a mass than a pagan sacrifice. An offering to appease the gods and ward off a nameless evil. Fear and uncertainty overshadow them all.

Was Mennan murdered? If so, by whom? Despite the Coroner's verdict, rumour still stalks the community. There are tales of conspiracy and assassins. Speculation is rife. Was it significant that Mennan was Tamil? Or was he the victim of a vendetta? And what about the letter reputed to have been found in his possession? It named names, or so it is said. The politician of whose patronage Mennan boasted so often, is absent today, claiming a pressing engagement elsewhere. But what could be more pressing than a funeral, especially this one?

Draped in white, the traditional colour of mourning, Mennan's widow stands in the front pew, her sari, pulled tight across her hips. At one point, she reaches around to adjust a pleat at her waist, her scarlet nails contrasting with the white cloth like a spray of red petals.

The service has finished. The coffin is raised onto the shoulders of six attendants then carried slowly down the aisle. As it approaches, Arjun is stricken with guilt. Did he have a hand in this? Was he somehow responsible for Mennan's death? He will never know. The thought torments him. The casket is now within a foot of his face, floating silently past. Soon it will slip beneath the earth, leaving Mennan's remains to rest in obscurity. But his memory will haunt them all.

***

The cortege files along the narrow path to the cemetery, a parched brown field where the remaining tufts of grass have turned to straw and the earth is baked so hard that it is often necessary to soften it with buckets of water before digging a grave. A railway runs along one side of the plot and graveside services are often interrupted by the harsh whistle of passing trains. Beyond the track are rows of shanty dwellings, tiny cubicles of corrugated iron separated by dirt paths and open drains.

148

There is no shade in the cemetery, only a single, dead thorn tree that stands at the boundary: a lonely memorial to the departed. Across the railway track, someone is cooking onions in the shanty on an open air stove. The smell wafts across the graveyard, a reminder to some that they have not eaten for hours.

"I hope that priest gets on with it. I'm hungry," mutters one man to his wife.

"Shh!" She puts her finger to her lips, warning him to be silent.

The mourners unfurl their umbrellas against the searing heat of the sun, clustering like a colony of black mushrooms around the open grave. Mennan's widow is motionless, her head cast down, as the priest completes the prayers for interment. Then, grasping a handful of earth she scatters it over the coffin, her rings glittering in the sunlight as she opens her fingers. Her palm, stained red by the soil, resembles the hennaed hand of a bride.

To Arjun, she is majestic, a figure from the ancient world; a queen or an empress, contemplating death on her husband's funeral pyre; a royal widow whose last act will be to leave her palm-print in wet clay before leaping into the flames.

"What will happen to her?" he murmurs.

"She'll remarry," says Nash, abruptly.

"How do you know?"

"Women like her don't stay single for long."

Shocked by Nash's callousness, Arjun falls silent. Mennan's body has just been committed to the ground. The circumstances of his death were shocking. Surely, his widow needs time to grieve? Even the thought of remarriage at a time like this seems like sacrilege. How can Nash say such things?

Standing a little apart from the other mourners, Mennan's widow is staring into the grave. She seems lonely and bereft; the postscript to a tragedy. Arjun wishes he could help her. After all, he played a part in her loss. He was one of the last people to see Mennan alive and, if his presence at the site did not actually contribute to the overseer's death, at least he might have prevented it. His proximity, both in time and place, to the death of a man he hardly knew has somehow made him a party to that terrible event. It is a conviction that took root even before the inquest and has grown stronger every day.

The mourners start to drift away. The younger ones chastened and a little depressed while the elderly seem curiously untouched. Their mood is governed by the law of diminishing returns, the less you have, the more grateful you are for it. In fact, the older mourners seem strangely light-hearted, exulting in their own survival. By their age, the edge has rubbed off tragedy and death wields a blunt axe. Each new day is a triumph and time spent in regret is time wasted.

At last the widow draws near, surrounded by a covey of supporters and well-wishers, most of them men. She seems pensive, serious, until she glances at Arjun and a look of surprise animates her face. His eyes are moist. Unlike hers. Her scarf slips back from her shoulders to reveal a voluptuous bosom. Gold and gems gleam at her neck, ears and wrists, catching the light as she moves, emitting rainbow-coloured sparks that contrast with the purity of her white sari. She is dazzling. A goddess. Arjun averts his eyes.

"Mr Tharmalingam".

Without taking her eyes from Arjun, she addresses Nash.

"Thank you for coming. I am honoured."

There is a hint of irony in her voice.

"Of course, you will come back for some refreshment?"

Nash opens his mouth to refuse but, against his inclination, finds that he has accepted. Even a woman, like this, is entitled to some courtesy on the day of her husband's funeral.

"Good. I'll see you back at the house, then. You know the way?"

"I know where it is," replies Nash, curtly.

She stares at him for a second, unsure of herself, a little afraid. Then, modestly, she lowers her eyes and pulls her scarf up to cover her shoulders. She starts to move away but cannot resist a second glance over her shoulder. There is a hint of flirtation in her smile. But it is not directed at Nash.

The road to Mennan's house leads across town through one of the poorer districts where open drains run along the side of the street. In some places, an attempt has been made to cover the gullies with paving slabs but, in others, small boys wade ankle deep, hunting the guppies that breed in dirty water and capturing them in jam-jars. A group of children has gathered on the pavement to compare the morning's catch.

"I'm the winner. I'm the winner!"

Holding up a jam-jar that contains a quantity of cloudy water and ten brightly-coloured fish, the smallest of their number declares himself the champion. There is a dispute. A fight breaks out. Small fists throw knuckle-hard punches. Jam-jars are tipped over, their live contents left flipping and gasping on the oven-hot concrete as their owners engage in a fierce contest.

"I won. I won," insists the small boy as another, larger contestant, sets about him, slapping and thumping, until he lands a blow on the child's nose.

"I'm the winner!" sobs the child, still unwilling to concede his title, despite the blood and snot running down his lip.

There are jeers and shouts from the onlookers. The small boy continues to fight furiously for his title, his feet and fists a blur as he assails his rival with a flurry of punches and kicks. But his opponent is too big for him. With one vicious shove, he pushes the small boy over. The child rolls onto his back, his feet in the air. There is a roar of laughter.

"Yah! Tamil brat. Run home to Amma. We don't want you here."

Nah. Run home. Tamil brat! The victor has his followers, a small clique of boys who swagger along in his wake, mimicking his speech. They begin to taunt the boy in the gutter, hoping for recognition and further encouragement from their leader. But he has lost interest. Another boy has taken his eye, a weedy child with glasses. Soon, another drubbing is underway. More insults are thrown.

"Squinty eyes. Squinty eyes. School swat. Teacher's pet."

The bully and his followers have moved on. The spectacle is over. The other boys jump back into the gully and, scooping up water in their hands, fling it at each other. There are shrieks and giggles as they scamper up and down the drain, kicking and stamping, spraying each other with water. The small boy on the pavement is forgotten. With tears streaming down his face, he crawls around on his knees, trying to gather up the dead occupants of his jam-jar. One day he will get his own back. He swears it. Such oaths, made in childhood, are not forgotten.

***

The Government car rolls past the children in the gutter, its driver cautiously navigating around potholes filled with rubble and cows that amble across the street. At the end of the road, the vehicle crosses a railway track then, a little further on, a narrow, filthy-looking canal, its oily black water dividing the shanty from the new developments on the outskirts of town.

Next, comes a turning along an unmade road that leads away from the slum. Until recently, this was undeveloped land with only a few, small homes shaded by cashew trees and drifts of scrubby vegetation. Now, it is being cleared to build homes for the newly-affluent: people unused to money who can only enjoy their riches if they remain in close proximity to their origins: but, whether this is due to a desire to flaunt their good fortune or to the fact that they feel uncomfortable around those who, unlike themselves, are accustomed to wealth, is a matter of conjecture.

The land has been cleared and laid out in plots. White stakes with strings stretched between them indicate the position of new foundations. Some houses are already rising from the dust, great eyeless mansions whose bare brick will soon be covered with a layer of immaculate white plaster in homage to imperial style. Yet pye-dogs and urchins in hand-me-down rags still roam the area, peering through the gates at great houses where shiny new cars sit gleaming on the drive.

Set on a slight rise in the land, Mennan's house overlooks all the neighbouring homes, presenting them with a vista of bowling-green lawns, extensive flower beds and ornamental ponds filled with carp. There are few who do not admire its grounds, or envy its owner.

Smothered in pink and yellow bougainvillea, Mennan's house is approached by sweeping steps which fan out onto a wide verandah. Tradesmen and others, whose arrival or departure must be kept secret, are obliged to use the small door at the back which leads directly into the kitchen. But today, the French doors at the top of the verandah have been thrown open. Mourners are required to make a public entrance, queuing to be greeted by the widow, now wearing a white sari trimmed with gold. The road outside the house is lined with locals, not invited to the wake, but hoping for a view of proceedings over the fence.

On the steps, Arjun and Nash quietly await their turn. Discreetly, Nash draws a handkerchief from his pocket and wipes his brow. They are standing in the full sun and Mennan's widow is taking her time, talking to every guest at length, playing the hostess to perfection. Even in the absence of her husband, she knows how to throw a party.

With disgust, Nash compares her to his beloved Chitra. He wonders how his wife would deal with his death. He has always supposed that he would go first. Men generally do. But, when the time comes, he is sure that Chitra will act with more decorum. She has dignity. It is an inherent quality, not something that can be affected or acquired.

Death. He has thought about it a lot recently. His own, in particular. But he doesn't know why. He is still in the prime of life and he and Chitra are both fit. So why these morbid thoughts? They began at the time of Mennan's death, creeping up on him like a black tide, reminding him of his own mortality.

He did not want to come today. He did not want to be reminded of the thought that darkens his waking hours, or to see this woman, with her artificial smile and her finery, whose show of grief is so patently false. No doubt her selfish demands contributed to Mennan's dishonesty. And his demise. Now she has it all, without the encumbrance of the man she despised.

"Mistress of all she purveys," thinks Nash, with grim humour.

"She's very brave, isn't she?" Arjun is staring at her, mesmerised.

"Mmm."

Nash cannot bring himself to agree, even for appearance's sake; but he cannot express his views openly, either. It would seem churlish, especially today, and anyway, Arjun would not understand. He is naïve, like all clever young men who have been cloistered for too long, their minds exercised only by long hours of study. He would have made a good priest, thinks Nash. For Arjun has just the right blend of innocence and humanity. A good man, but vulnerable.

Another guest is speaking to the widow. The line shuffles forward. Arjun and Nash climb a few steps. They can hear her voice now, soft and charming but, to Nash's mind, starved of sincerity. He looks at the garden, the flowers, the fish; a small square of Surrey grafted onto the skin of his country. Like a velvet spot on a courtesan's face, an affectation that hides a mark of shame.

Nash appreciates western culture and has received an English education, but he loves his country, too. He has never felt the need, as this woman and her husband have done, to disguise his origins, pretend to be something he is not. He supposes that he should feel sorry for her but, instead, he feels angry. They may all be Tamils, but he feels no kinship with people such as these.

A man with a paunch and a fat, overfed face is speaking to her now, kneading her hand in his hot paw. He has a thick crop of greying hair that grows low over his ears and which, when he laughs, gives him the aspect of an ageing monkey. She leans forward and whispers something in his ear. He roars with laughter. Nash is sickened.

Patting her guest on the arm, the widow gently pushes him through the French windows towards the press of guests that can be dimly seen, hovering inside the room, like souls in limbo. Now it is their turn. She greets Nash politely, lowering her eyes to give an appearance of modesty then, holding out her hand to Arjun, boldly raises her eyes to his face. She gives him a slow, hungry smile. He stammers a few nervous pleasantries.

He is holding her hand in his. He can feel the tapered fingers, cool even in this heat, their soft, smooth skin contrasting with the unyielding rings that press into his palm. Is it his imagination, or does her thumb, for a brief second, stroke the back of his hand? She is laughing at him. He can see it in her eyes. She keeps hold of his hand, gripping his fingers with surprising firmness. It is a game of power. And he is helpless.

"We mustn't detain you. You have other guests to greet."

Placing his arm around Arjun's shoulder, Nash gently draws the young man away. She is forced to relinquish her hold; reluctantly and with bad grace. For, although she smiles graciously, there is a flash of anger, a spark deep in her eyes. It is visible only to an experienced reader of faces. Like Nash.

Impatiently, Nash herds Arjun to safety, through the door into the living room. People are squeezed together, with hardly enough space to raise drinks or cigarettes; girls carrying platters of food ease their way between guests who must shout to make themselves heard. Grasping Arjun's arm, Nash propels him through the crush, over to the other side of the room where they find a corner in which it is at least possible to breathe unhindered.

"My god, what a circus!" groans Nash.

"I think it's very kind of her, considering what she's suffered."

There is a sharp edge to Arjun's voice; a note of criticism. Nash dismisses it. The boy is overwrought from the funeral and has not yet fully recovered from his illness. One must be patient with him. Nash accepts a drink from one of the servants and lights a cigarette. By now, the guests have all arrived and Leela, the widow, is circulating among them.

In the middle of the room, a group of men, settled in easy chairs, is laying siege to a bottle of whisky. The 12 year-old single malt meets with their approval and is rapidly consumed.

"I'll say this for old Mennan," says one, approvingly. "He always bought the best. Must have had this specially imported, the cunning old devil. Hi Leela! This bottle's almost empty. Have you got any more?"

"I'll find out."

Tilting her head coquettishly, their hostess disappears into the kitchen, returning after a couple of minutes with another bottle. Prising off the cap, she bends forward to refill her guests' glasses, revealing a glimpse of cleavage. Awkward as schoolboys, they cast appreciative eyes over her figure as she turns away.

"Anyone who thinks Mennan committed suicide needs to see her," one mutters. They all laugh, thinking that Mennan's widow is out of earshot. But Nash sees her smile secretly. Despicable woman.

***

Arjun has heard the other men's comments and is incensed. These are exactly the sort of fellows who bully helpless women. He wonders if he should say anything but decides, on reflection, that it would be better to keep quiet. He is a stranger here and these men were probably friends of Mennan.

Nash is now talking eagerly to a colleague, a fellow civil servant that he has not seen for years. Feeling awkward and out of place, Arjun makes his way to the kitchen in search of a glass of water.

He is confronted by a group of women, who circle the kitchen like humming tops, all talking, none listening nor looking where they are going and yet, true to an obscure law of physics, avoiding collision. Baskets and bags, piled in one corner, are being constantly churned as raids are made for hairpins, handkerchiefs and other necessities.

Orbiting the other women like a couple of stately satellites, two old dames pass by on a circuit of the room. Cheerful and talkative, they revel in the fact that they have outlived their host, a man much younger than themselves.

"I always said he would come to no good," says one to the other. "My son was always 'Mennan this, Mennan that', every time the man got a new car or house. But I used to say, anyone who makes money like that will come to a bad end. Now look what's happened."

Her companion, equally old and probably deaf, appears not to hear the last sentence. Determined that her words of wisdom should not be lost, the speaker adds a coda.

"And I was right!" she screeches in her friend's ear.

The other old lady starts in alarm. Heads turn. But the two old women shuffle forward, oblivious to the attention they have attracted.

At the far end of the room, a plump woman with a heavily powdered face is washing crockery at the sink. Fussily swiping and plunging with the dish mop, she relentlessly stacks up plates, despite the lack of anyone to dry them. Having finished her task and transferred half the watery contents of the sink onto the floor, she absent-mindedly wanders off in search of her friends, leaving piles of china teetering on the draining board. As she departs, the servants, whom she previously ordered aside, quietly resume their tasks, restoring order to the chaos that she has created.

At the back door, a human chain has formed, passing saucepans, bowls, boxes and plates to the helpers in the kitchen. There is much scurrying and bustling as cupboards are opened and inspected in the search for suitable containers. The stove is lit and curry and rice are re-heated over a fierce flame. Vast slabs of butter-cake are cut into slices and snacks of fried fish and goat arranged on plates.

There are not enough servants to deal with this welter of food, so younger daughters, cousins and nieces are lined up, handed plates and told to circulate amongst the guests. Young and skittish as colts, they giggle and roll their eyes behind the matrons' backs. No thought of the funeral dampens their exuberance. This is a party and there are men present, mostly influential, many wealthy and some, widowers.

One of the girls brushes past Arjun, pouting prettily. She stares into his eyes, flutters her eyelashes, then minces off towards the living room where, together with her companions, she will glide through the company, hopeful of being noticed and admired. The funerary feast is about to commence.

Arjun wonders what relevance all of this has to Mennan. Is it callousness or simply an attempt to re-affirm life after a terrible death? At a wake, the guests are encouraged to indulge so that the dead host may enjoy himself, vicariously, through them. But there is a note of hysteria underlying these revels. It is as if everyone is trying too hard. The aim is not to remember Mennan, but to forget him. Food, drink and laughter are being employed to chase away the shadows, especially his.

"Are you looking for someone?"

She is at his elbow, the soft folds of her sari stroking his arm. The suddenness of her arrival has caught him unprepared.

"I just wanted some water," he stammers.

"Of course."

The other women lower their voices and simper at her as she crosses the kitchen. She opens a large cupboard with a glass-front and, reaching up with one elegant arm, removes a glass from the shelf. Arjun is staring at her. She can see his reflection in the glass pane of the door as she shuts the cupboard. The other women coo with envy as she opens the large American fridge and pours water into the glass from a large jug. There is frost inside the fridge, even in this heat. The other women resolve to explore it once Leela has left the kitchen.

"Here."

She offers him the water, her fingertips leaving a print in the fine mist of condensation that has formed on the outside of the glass.

"Thank you."

He takes a mouthful of water. It is enough. But, although he is no longer thirsty, he drains the glass. He must do something to hide his confusion. She is waiting for him to speak. Tongue-tied, he casts around for something to say.

"I'm truly sorry about your husband."

Oddly, any mention of Mennan seems like a solecism.

Still, she waits, cool and impassive, drawing him out with her silence.

"We had an argument. On the day that he died. I feel, well, sort of responsible. I hope ... I hope you will forgive me."

The seed of guilt, that he has carried for so long, blooms into a dark and terrible flower. Soon, it will consume him. He is seeking absolution. A cure. From her. For only she can give it. Secretly, she exults. She has the power to save or destroy. He is hers. To sacrifice or enjoy.

She hesitates, considering her response. And, with every second, his weakness grows. She does not need him. She has other men. Plenty of them. But, unlike them, he offers her complete power. He has put his life, no, his soul, in her care. It is a divine right only accorded by one other man. And now he is gone.

"You are no more to blame than anyone else."

She neither damns, nor absolves him. By this means, she will keep him hanging in the balance, teetering on the edge of an abyss, dependent on her mercy. By the use of one word, she has sent him a message. Blame. It is with blame that she will punish him if he does not obey. Blame will tip him over the edge, into perpetual darkness and the everlasting torment of guilt.

Downcast, he stands before her, a condemned man with his head bowed and his mind in shadow. She waits a little longer, until she is sure of her position, then offers him a grudging reprieve, a small salve for his pain.

"Actually, the greatest blame lies with the Government Agent."

"The Agent? Why?"

"He persecuted my husband for years."

"What?"

She whispers, her breath caressing his ear.

"Jealousy."

Arjun is stunned.

"But, the road project … there was proof. I saw it."

"What proof?" she retorts angrily. "What do you really know? Nothing! Only what you were told. My husband had many powerful friends and they all betrayed him."

"I'm sorry. I don't see what that has to do with the Agent."

"No? I suppose not."

She sighs wistfully, raising her hand to her long neck. A lonely and vulnerable woman.

"What does he say of me?"

"Nothing, really."

The Agent has clear views on this subject, but Arjun thinks it better not to repeat them. The widow laughs sadly, as if she knows what he is thinking.

"Have you met his wife?"

"Yes. She seems very nice."

"Mmm. No doubt. But I believe she was his second choice. Rumour has it there was someone else."

She has a persuasive, knowing smile. Eve in the Garden.

"It's not that I'm vindictive," she says, softly.

Her sari brushes his leg and he can smell the delicate scent of her perfume.

"I just need help. Mennan was a clever man. I never understood his work but he left a lot of papers. I may need someone to take a look. Someone I can trust. A friend."

She lifts her beautiful face, her neck as lithe as a swan, her arms floating up through the air, the hands held out, pleading. A dancer's body. A maiden of Sigiriya.

"A little kindness. That's all. I think I deserve that, don't you?"

Like wine, she goes to his head. His mind reels like a drunkard. She is about to speak again when something catches her eye. Someone else has entered the kitchen.

"Mr Tharmalingam."

She greets him with a smile; sweet, courteous, yet defiant.

"Are you looking for someone?"

***

They take their leave: the Agent with his hand on Arjun's elbow, directing him towards the door. By now, the living-room is crammed with people drinking, talking and eating. The air is heavy with cigarette smoke which hangs below the ceiling in a thick, curling layer. Just in front of the French windows is a large, noisy group of people, all laughing and shouting, who block the exit onto the terrace.

The Agent leads Arjun out of the living-room and they head towards the hallway, in search of another door. On the way, they pass a small passage. There is a cough and a rustle of silk. In the darkened archway, two figures separate, extricating themselves from a hurried embrace.

Guiltily, they stare out of the shadows. The man tugs at his zip as the girl pushes her skirt down. It is the monkey-faced man and the girl who eyed Arjun in the kitchen. She stares defiantly at the passers-by, her mouth pulled down, angry and insolent. The man turns his head, as if by looking away, he will become invisible.

"Dear god," mutters Nash. "It's like the fall of Rome."

***

In the car, neither speaks. The effects of his recent illness are still apparent in Arjun's face. He looks pale and exhausted. He sits with his head resting on the back of the seat, looking out of the window. His eyelids flicker occasionally and the Agent wishes that he would sleep because there is a strange look in his eyes, something that Nash has never seen before.

"That damn woman," he thinks. "What did she say to him?"

He revisits the events of that afternoon, acknowledging that he felt uneasy when he saw Arjun speaking to the widow, although he resisted the urge to intervene for fear of humiliating his assistant. It was obvious that she was attracted to Arjun, but Nash had doubted her ability to do much harm in such a public place.

Yet now, he believes he misread the situation. He underestimated her. Arjun was only with her for a few minutes in the kitchen, but something happened. Afterwards, he seemed unusually distant, unsettled. He still has that same, strange look in his eyes. All is not well.

What was it she said? *Your support has been a great comfort. I hope we shall meet again.*

Words aimed at Arjun, not the Agent. Arjun had looked at her, imploringly and, in return, she had patted his arm, carelessly, as one might treat a child. Then, she had turned to Nash, her eyes glittering with cold laughter and, for some inexplicable reason, he had wanted to strangle her.

As Nash and Arjun had criss-crossed Mennan's living-room, navigating the maze of people in search of a way out, they had passed Leela, entertaining a group of male guests. The men lowered their voices as Nash and Arjun approached but, after they had passed, there was a ripple of suppressed laughter. Bitch! He should never have taken the boy to that place.

158

It is late and they are in their room making the last preparations before sleep: he, on the bed, surrounded by sheaves of official papers; she, in front of the mirror, unpinning coils of hair which she brushes around her hand. Although careful, she always manages to litter the floor with hairpins. She bends to pick one up, dropping it into a small glass dish on the dressing-table. Then, with her head tilted to one side, she resumes the ritual brushing of her hair; long slow strokes, twenty for each hank. Four, five, six. She counts under her breath, her lips moving in the mirror.

Behind her, she can see Nash sitting on the bed, pretending to read. But she knows he is not because, every so often, he raises his head, gazes around the room and then, willing his attention back to the book, he stares at the page as if he had never seen it before. He must have read the same paragraph at least three times, scanning the words without absorbing their content.

"Hah!" Sighing, he flings the book across the bed, looking at her image in the mirror.

"What's the matter?"

"That woman."

"Mennan's wife?"

"Hmm."

Reaching across the bed, he retrieves the book and flicks idly through its pages. He always behaves like this when something is troubling him. Chitra has learned to wait, not to expect an immediate response to her questions. He will speak of the thing that disturbs him when he is ready. Sometimes, not until the next day. Sometimes, not at all. He is a man who likes to find his own solutions.

He snaps the book shut and stares at her, calmed by the rhythmic movement of her hand. There is such wisdom in her face, such sweetness. A warmth flows through him.

"I know something about that woman's history. Things that I'm not sure even Mennan knew. I've never told anyone. I didn't think it fair. But now, I wonder if I should."

"Why?"

"I found them together."

"Who?"

"Arjun and Mennan's wife."

Chitra raises her eyebrows.

"No, no. Nothing like that. They were just talking. Or, rather, she was."

"What's wrong with that?"

"Nothing, except that it looked like I had surprised them. They looked guilty. At least, he did."

"But she was doing the talking?"

"Yes. I think she must have been saying something about me. I don't know what she can have said, but it definitely wasn't good."

"Are you sure you're not imagining things?"

"No. I asked myself that at first, but when I drove home with Arjun, he seemed distant, even hostile."

"Why would she do such a thing?"

Chitra lowers the brush, holding it with both hands in her lap as she turns to look at her husband.

"I think she has designs on Arjun."

"And you think it would help to tell him what you know of her?"

"I don't know. But I am concerned for him. Arjun is a clever young man, but he's unworldly. His illness and Mennan's death have made him vulnerable."

Chitra tilts her head back, shaking her hair free of her shoulders. Reaching to her waist, it is as long and beautiful as when she was a girl. She winds a skein around her hand, inspecting it for threads of grey.

"Women like her will always deceive handsome young men with stories. And innocent boys like your assistant will always listen, until they discover the truth for themselves."

"You don't think I should speak to him?"

"What good would it do? Better to let nature take its course."

Swinging his long legs over the side of the bed, Nash walks over to where she is sitting and puts his arms around her. For a few seconds, they stare at themselves in the mirror, a handsome couple, whose contentment with each other deepens daily. Tenderly, he kisses her glossy head, inhaling the faint scent of jasmine and noting, with a pang, a streak of silver in her hair.

"I miss our boys." A confession he has never made before.

"You wanted them to go."

"Yes, but England is so far away. Sometimes I think I will never see them again."

"What are you saying?" She is alarmed. "Don't you feel well?"

"No, no." He waves his hand. "Nothing like that."

"What then?"

She puts down the brush and turns to look at him.

"I can't say exactly. But ever since the death of Mennan Rasanayagam, I've felt uneasy. It was murder, there's no doubt in my mind about that. And not just by one or two people. The grass where we found him had been trampled by many feet. He'd been lynched."

"You mean, by a gang?"

"Yes."

"But why?"

"I can think of several reasons. But one in particular worries me. Mennan was a Tamil and his work-force was Sinhalese, including the two men who disappeared. I'm afraid that this could be the beginning of something else."

Raising her hands, Chitra cups them around her husband's face. She used to do the same for her children, to quieten them after a nightmare, or a fall.

"You've been to a funeral today. You're depressed. It's all been an awful business but I'm sure it's just an isolated case. You'll feel better in the morning."

But as Nash lies awake that night, the anxiety that has haunted him, returns; hovering overhead, like a familiar.

1956: A walk in the hills

Neleni is searching for the large black umbrella that serves as a parasol. She is kneeling on the floor, inching her arm into the space between the wall and the back of a murderous old coat-stand which resembles a cupboard with the front and sides cut off. In fact, that is probably what it is.

Such pieces of furniture are common to Ceylonese homes. Relics of colonial occupation abandoned by their previous owners, they have been salvaged from overgrown gardens, out-houses or pedlars' carts, then carved up, cannibalised and adapted to a new purpose. They have a dreary sadness about them, like a poor relative who has been taken in and tolerated for the sake of charity.

Neleni hates the coat-stand. She loathes the convex mirror that winks at her like a wicked eye as she passes, distorting everything it sees into a grotesque reflection. But she detests the back of the coat-stand even more than the front; for it is rough and unvarnished, prickling with sharp splinters and covered with fleecy cobwebs.

The coat-stand is too heavy to move and the space behind it is narrow and impossible to clean. Unaccountably, this is always where the umbrella is found, although no-one can ever remember putting it there.

She taps the floor with her fingers. Something tickles the back of her hand. She gasps. A scorpion or a spider? She waits for the creeping pressure of insect feet on her skin, wondering what to do. But it was nothing more than a floating shroud of cobweb. Cautiously, she resumes her search. She needs the umbrella for she is planning a long walk today.

Her friend Nirmala lives a couple of miles away, high up on a slope overlooking the town. The path is exposed and, as morning progresses, the sun will strike down with relentless heat. That is why Neleni needs the umbrella and also why she rose before dark, making tea for herself and swallowing a little cold rice and curry before her mother appeared in the kitchen.

Sunny is out there now, clattering about, standing on tiptoe as she reaches up for her tobacco jar. They have spoken, but only briefly, Neleni hurrying out of the kitchen as soon as her mother entered. Relations between them have been cool for several days.

There has been another argument. About Arjun. And the paint-box. Somehow, Sunny discovered that it was a gift from him. Bitter accusations have been made and sharp words exchanged. This was not one of their usual tiffs. Wounds have been inflicted which will take time to heal.

The truth has been spoken, at least by Sunny, although Neleni denies it, even to herself. She cannot accept that what she calls friendship is really love. But whatever it is, she is determined to do something about it. Driven by pride, she will prove to her mother that she is not the feeble creature of Sunny's imagining. But, first, she must speak to Nirmala.

Her arm is at full stretch, immersed in the dark space behind the coat-stand. Her fingers trawl through the layer of dust that has collected on the floor and which is so thick that it feels like felt. There it is! She can feel the rubber feral, added to the spoke by her father as a precaution against lightning; although who would ever walk out in a tropical storm with an umbrella for protection, she cannot imagine.

It is months since she last used the umbrella. It is supposed to stand upright against the wall but somehow it has been knocked over and pushed deep into the darkness, possibly by Ella's enthusiastic manoeuvres with the mop. Neleni walks her fingers up the metal spoke then, hooking her nails into a fold of the harsh silky material, she pulls the umbrella towards her. Eventually it emerges, covered in dust. There is a red weal on her arm where she has pressed against the corner of the coat-stand.

The umbrella is filthy and she will hold it at arm's length until she is outside on the verandah where she means to give it a good shake, opening and shutting it rapidly so that it flaps like the wing of a great black crow. She collects her bag and is half-way across the hall when Arjun appears from the passage.

He is dressed for work in a crisp white shirt and pale, cotton trousers. Since his illness, he has lost weight and his clothes look a little large on him. It is possible to see where he used to fasten his belt, because the hole is loose and worn around the edges but it is vacant now and the buckle is always fixed two or three holes tighter. His face is leaner, too, and some of the smooth, boyish curves have disappeared. But it is not unbecoming. He looks more like a man.

"Where are you going?"

"To see a friend."

Her reply is unusually curt. He is stung. He has risen early, as he does every morning, in the hope of talking to her at breakfast. But she clearly wants to avoid him. Umbrella in hand, she slips past him, her head lowered, avoiding his eyes. Her sandals tap over the cold floor as she passes beneath the plaster statue of the Madonna with its flickering perpetual flame.

Sliding back the bolts, she pulls open the heavy front door and is momentarily framed in a rectangle of light. As she turns to close the door behind her, she catches a glimpse of his face: a child, hurt and bewildered, punished for a mischief that it does not understand. She will remember that expression for many years and, every time she thinks of it, it will stab at her heart.

She tries to smile but all he sees is a cold and artificial twisting of the lips. An empty courtesy. The kind of smile a landlady gives her lodger. She slams the door and hurries down the steps. She is at the end of the street before she remembers that she has not cleaned the umbrella. It hangs over her arm, still furled and furred with dust. She shakes it angrily.

Her pulse is racing. She tries to tell herself that it is the result of a brisk walk, but she knows that it is not true. She had hoped that, by not engaging Arjun in conversation, she would be more in control of herself. But even the briefest word, the merest sight of him, disarms her. She is a woman made of wax, melting from within.

***

After forty minutes' walking, Neleni has reached the edge of town and is beginning to climb the steep cinder track that leads to Nirmala's house. Despite its strengthening rays, the sun has not yet banished the night chill. It is an invigorating, optimistic time of day whose newness courses through the veins and sets the pulse racing.

162

Neleni has told her mother that she wants some clothes altered and has packed a bag with a few items to give her story credibility. For her friend, Nirmala is a professional seamstress, earning a living by catering to the needs of the townswomen. But this is not the real reason for Neleni's visit. She is coming to Nirmala for advice.

They first learned to share their secrets at school: two little girls in white skirts and blouses, their long plaits tied up with ribbon, reading poetry to each other in the playground, sharing plans for their future. Neleni was going to be an artist and Nirmala, a writer. Both would marry rich and important men. Their children would grow up together, fall in love and marry.

"And look what happened," thinks Neleni.

As she walks, her sari brushes the verge, stirring insects into momentary activity. A grasshopper springs into the air, then lands on the path in front of her, momentarily basking on a small stone before it hops back into the undergrowth. Butterflies rise from the ground in a brief flutter of iridescence – red, blue, green – then perching on flowers or swinging blades of grass, they close their wings, hiding their brilliant colours and displaying only muted tones of dun or black.

The road gets steeper and the heavy umbrella is making her arm ache. Neleni decides to rest for a few minutes, seating herself on a milestone at the edge of the road. From her vantage point, she has a sweeping view of the valley, from the craggy heights of the mountains to the gentle, scalloped terraces on the lower slopes.

Breathing in long draughts of air as cool as spring water, Neleni listens carefully, counting the many sounds that float up to her. She hears the rush of streams that will eventually be channelled into the fields of rice, leeks and carrots. Then, somewhere, a dog barks to the accompaniment of clanking pails. There is the chugging of an engine, the hollow clang of a cattle-bell, the lowing of buffalo, people shouting, even a child crying. Yet behind it all, is the low, discordant rumble of traffic rising from the town which she has just left.

Shading her eyes with her hand, she stares down into the valley, at the thin line of traffic worming its way between houses and shops. She can see her home from here, distinguished from all the other, insignificant rectangles by the temple tree growing against the front porch. Covered in yellow blossom, it is the finest tree of its kind in the whole town. It was planted by her father. It is the tree that killed him. Yet, no-one thought to cut it down. Over the years, it has flourished, a memorial to one man's folly, its beauty contrasting with the dark, lop-sided house.

At one stroke, that tree re-defined Neleni's life. She should hate it. Yet, rather, she feels that her fate and that of the tree are entwined. It is, after all, the last link with her father. She would not wish to lose it and, yet, the sight of it is painful. She turns her eyes away.

Beyond the valley, is a high, granite ridge. Its peaks crowd together, cramped and austere with planes of napped stone, sheer and forbidding, where nothing grows. Further down, the sharp angles of the rock-face resolve into softer curves where fields and gardens are stacked against the hillside and where farmers have worked the terraces for generations. Men are working there now: flicking their oxen with switches as they plough the narrow strips of land.

Neleni envies their tranquillity; the quiet continuity of lives mapped out according to the requirements of crops and seasons. Sowing, planting, weeding, harvesting: routines that are pre-ordained, passed down from father to son over generations and followed without question. Perhaps, if she could accept her lot, as they do, she would be at peace. If her life were as simple as theirs, she too might find contentment.

But it is her nature to aspire to impossible goals and to suffer from her failure to achieve them. To find peace, she must relinquish her dreams, the childish ambition that knows no boundaries, the voice in her head that tells her that happiness is still possible. She tells herself that it is time. She must change, learn to think like others, embrace each day with quiet acceptance and not look beyond.

And yet, a question remains. Is she really prepared to stifle hope? Can she live without it altogether? She remembers the sunny days at school when she and Nirmala talked with their heads together; whispering, planning, forever looking forward; always optimistic and excited. What happened? She stares down at the town and the dingy little house where the temple tree sheds its flowers on the pavement. That's what happened. A shadow steals over her heart. Peace, like happiness, is ephemeral.

A tiny black dot appears in the sky. Far above, she hears the faint, haunting cry of an eagle; a poignant reminder of Sigiriya; and Arjun. Neleni springs to her feet. She cannot allow herself to sit and think any longer. Thinking or, perhaps, remembering, is a dangerous pursuit. It can lead to despair.

She sets off along the hill road, her black parasol propped against her shoulder, her wrist hooked over the handle. The sun is strong and, under the deep canopy of the umbrella, the air is warm and humid. Neleni is becoming breathless. The track winds steeply upwards, doubling back on itself as it loops and curves around the rocky hillside.

Around the next bend, she has her first sight of Nirmala's house. It is a deserted spot, but there is a reason for Nirmala's isolation. There is a secret; something in the past that gives her an insight into matters of the heart. That is why Neleni is coming to see her. She will understand.

A simple, single storey construction, Nirmala's house stands slantwise to the road on a south-facing terrace. A verandah, shaded by a porch, runs along the front of the house while, at the back, there is a garden planted with vegetables.

Alongside the neat rows of leeks, carrots, spinach and potatoes, squats a shed made from panels of corrugated iron. Its rusting walls are submerged in a dense cloud of Morning Glory whose purple-striped flowers are as large as teacups. It is a weed, but a beautiful one and Nirmala encourages its growth with dregs of cold tea.

On the roof of the shed, clothes are laid out to dry. Sheets, towels and two saris, one yellow and one green, have been weighted down with large stones from the garden. From a distance, the roof has the appearance of a patchwork quilt.

In a corner of the garden is a small patch in which Nirmala grows spices for her kitchen: garlic, fennel, lemongrass, chillies, coriander and fenugreek. On this sunny, well-drained slope they grow in profusion. Neleni would like to stop and admire them, but a hornet, as large as her finger, is hovering over the plants. Fierce flashes of sunlight rebound from its wings. She hurries past.

Near to the back door is a short, stubby tree to which a goat is tethered. Kneeling on its front legs, the goat is grazing a strip of grass at the edge of the path. It pauses at Neleni's approach, then raises itself up to stare at her with flinty eyes, grass hanging from its frozen mouth as if it has suddenly forgotten to chew.

"Bahh," it bleats hoarsely, stamping its foot to warn off the intruder.

"It's all right, Milly. It's me".

Neleni holds out her hand, palm up in a gesture of peace as she skirts around the animal. She does not trust it. It tried to charge her once and sent her sprinting up the steps – much to Raj's amusement. Yet Nirmala loves it. The goat is her pet, not intended for the table.

In the safety of the back porch, Neleni smiles to herself. Just a few minutes ago, she had been fantasising about life in the countryside. But she had forgotten how many stinging, biting, butting creatures it accommodates.

At home, she cannot abide even a fly in the house but here there are armies of insects multiplying on the earth's decay: rotting vegetation, cattle dung and stagnant water. No doubt there are snakes also, sheltering under the verandah or under the cool green leaves of Nirmala's melon patch. She shudders. It is not the place for her.

She taps lightly on the back door. It has a scabrous appearance. Blistered by the sun, the dark brown paint is cracked and peeling and, in places, small flakes have chipped away to reveal an undercoat of dark green. With her hands cupped around her eyes, Neleni peers through the frosted glass window. A flash of kingfisher blue emerges from the gloom, taking shape as it approaches the door.

There is a clunk. A bolt is slid back and the door swings open to reveal a woman of about thirty. She has a full-lipped, vivacious smile, an olive skin and a halo of black hair. Her unconventional beauty exerts a powerful attraction which has often resulted in attention from unwanted admirers. It is one of the reasons for her reclusiveness. However, she still dresses up for her own amusement and today she wears one of her best saris and a new, red lipstick.

"Neleni! How lovely to see you."

Nirmala sings when she speaks. Her voice has always had that peculiar lilt, as sweet and clear as a bell. Taking Neleni's hand, she leads her through the kitchen and into the living-room that doubles as a workshop.

The table is littered with the paraphernalia of her profession: a black Singer sewing machine decorated with flourishes of gold and worked by a treadle; pinking shears; bright cottons; tailor's chalk and pins. Half-finished clothes are spread over the chairs and a long length of silk lies on the floor with pattern pieces pinned to it, ready for cutting out.

Turning to Neleni, Nirmala embraces her and, as she lifts up her arms, her scarf gently brushes her friend's cheek. Its touch resembles a kiss. To the surprise of them both, Neleni begins to cry.

"Darling, what's the matter?"

Nirmala grasps Neleni's shoulders, now shaking with sobs, and looks questioningly into her eyes, but Neleni turns her head away. Seeing that her friend is unwilling to speak, Nirmala presses Neleni's head to her shoulder and strokes her hair.

"There, there," she coos, soothingly. It is the voice that adults use for a child with a grazed knee; one intended to give comfort and win trust.

"What's the matter? Tell me."

"It's nothing."

Neleni extricates herself from Nirmala's embrace and searches for the handkerchief that she keeps, tucked in the front of her blouse. Unable to find it, she wipes her face with her hand. But it is useless. The tears continue to flow. She is unable to stop herself. It is as if an underground spring, long hidden, has suddenly found its way to the surface. She is merely its channel.

"Neleni!"

Through the curtain of misery, she hears Nirmala's voice, kind and encouraging. She sinks back into her friend's arms, indulging her need for comfort.

"All these tears and you say it's nothing! Come on, Neleni. We're like sisters. You can tell me anything."

Neleni struggles to speak, but cannot find the words. They must be teased out of her. Nirmala whispers, creating that sense of secrecy so necessary to confession.

"It's Raj, isn't it?"

"Yes ... no. I don't know."

Suddenly, Neleni panics. Once she has spoken, there will be no going back, no denying her feelings, no more pretence. The truth is like a genie in a bottle. Once released, it can no longer be contained. It will follow its own course and she does not know where it will lead. She feels like a hunted animal, searching for cover, with Nirmala in pursuit. Soon, she will be chased into the open and forced to confess the truth. She should not have come here today. She is not ready.

"I must go. I must go."

Frantically, she tries to push Nirmala away, escape from that suffocating embrace. But Nirmala grips her firmly by the wrists.

"Tell me, Neleni. There's no shame. It's Raj, isn't it?"

Nirmala persists. She never approved of Neleni's marriage and actively tried to dissuade her friend from what she viewed as an ill-advised match: one arranged by her mother at a time of grief and despair.

"There is more to life than security," Nirmala had warned.

But, whatever girls of their generation desired, whatever ideals of emancipation and independence they professed, they always obeyed tradition. A parent's wishes were sacrosanct. And so Neleni had married Raj.

They had not spoken for a while after that. Having made a decision based on instinct rather than reason, Neleni could brook no challenge. It was as if she feared that the slightest whisper of doubt would blow down the delicate structure of her marriage and reduce its straw walls to chaff.

But that was in the early days. As she came to accept her lot, Neleni developed a protective shell, impervious to thought or criticism. With this in place, she was able to resume her friendship with Nirmala on the implicit understanding that the subject of her marriage to Raj was never to be discussed.

Yet Nirmala knew that it could not last. No-one can bury their true self forever. No matter how hard they try. And Neleni always had such spirit. Nirmala has waited a long time for this day and, when it eventually came, she knew that Neleni would need her. That is why she holds on to Neleni's wrists although her friend is squirming and fighting to free herself.

The truth is coming. Neleni fights it back, but it can no longer be suppressed. It is struggling out, towards daylight; a pale and thwarted creature that has grown in the dark. Neleni must not be left to face it on her own. There is no telling what she may do if she does. That is why Nirmala must keep her here.

"It's Raj, isn't it? Does he hit you? Has he been unfaithful?"

"No!"

In a fever of despair, Neleni twists and writhes trying to free herself. Her sari is stained with tears. Her hair, loosed from its pins, has fallen over her face covering her eyes and, as she twists her head from side to side, she has the aspect of a madwoman, of someone possessed by a demon. The harder she pulls, the tighter Nirmala grasps her wrists. It has gone too far. She must not let go.

The thing is nearly out. Neleni's eyes glare out from under her tangle of wild hair. They glow with a strange pale light and she seems neither to recognise Nirmala nor her surroundings. One final push. She screams, throwing her arms up, trying to break Nirmala's hold. Taken by surprise, Nirmala lets go of one wrist and is caught a glancing blow by Neleni's flailing hand.

"Ow!"

Wincing with pain, Nirmala puts her hand up to her mouth where blood is running from her lip. Blood the same colour as her bright, red lipstick. She drops Neleni's other wrist, but Neleni makes no attempt to escape. She is mesmerised by the trickle of blood that runs from Nirmala's mouth.

"Oh god," she murmurs. "What have I done?"

"Don't worry. It's nothing."

Nirmala dabs at her lip with a scrap of white cotton, an off-cut of the stuff she uses to make patterns for blouses.

"Nirmala, I'm so sorry. Please forgive me. Please. You're the only friend I've got."

Neleni reaches out, tentatively, as if to touch Nirmala but pauses, her hand frozen in mid-air; too ashamed to offer comfort.

"Please say you forgive me. Please."

She is clutching her sari, wringing it between her hands, her eyes brimming with tears. But the storm has passed. Nirmala, still dabbing her mouth, raises her hand.

"It's fine. Really. Just a scratch."

Neleni's shoulders sag. She looks exhausted, miserable. A single tear creeps from the corner of her eye. Taking a clean piece of lint from her workbox, Nirmala gently mops her friend's face, pushing back the dishevelled wisps of hair from her forehead, wiping away the tear that languishes on her cheek.

"I'm sorry."

Neleni's voice is less than a whisper. It is only because she stands so close that Nirmala can distinguish the words. If she had been a few inches further away, it would have sounded like a sigh. She presses her fingers to Neleni's cheek. It is cold and pale as if the blood had been drained out of her. There will be no more resistance. It is time for confession.

Taking her friend's hand, Nirmala leads Neleni along a dark echoing passage, out onto the verandah where she makes her comfortable on an old wicker sofa, arranging cushions around her back and lifting her feet up so that she can rest properly.

"I'll be back in a minute. I'm just going to make some tea."

Neleni nods and tries to smile but, already, her eyes are half shut. In a few seconds, she will be asleep. Nirmala tiptoes from the verandah, trying not to disturb her. She does not want Neleni to follow. She needs time alone to think. In all the years that she has known Neleni, Nirmala has never seen such an outburst.

"Not that I didn't expect it," Nirmala tells herself, as she stands at the stone sink. But, even so, she is disturbed by what she has just witnessed. She turns on the tap, then waits until she can hear water rumbling in the pipes outside. A few seconds later, it gushes into the sink, bearing with it a cloud of rusty iron specks.

She lets the tap run for a few seconds, then holds the kettle under the stream of water, filling it through the spout, listening to the roiling sound as it fills. Distorted with age, the kettle lid is loose, given to spinning and rattling in its enclosure although it cannot be removed. Suddenly, it pops up, water streaming from its vents.

Distracted by her thoughts, Nirmala has overfilled the kettle. Cursing under her breath, she pours the excess water into a jug, making a mental note to use it for her plants. The kettle clanks as she places it on the hob. The trivet is loose and ill-fitting, borrowed from another appliance that she found rusting in the shed.

No-one knows how Nirmala manages up here. No-one cares sufficiently to ask. If they did, they would discover a life of hardship in which just getting by tests resourcefulness to the limit. Nirmala lives on her own: a rare thing for a woman in this country. And if people do not know the reason, then they can guess.

A woman of her age should be married with children. If her husband dies, a young woman marries again. If she does not, then there is something wrong. Women, whatever their status, do not choose to remain unmarried or live alone, far away from their families. Not without good reason.

The match refuses to strike. She discards it, tries another then, after that, another. Either the box has become damp or the tinder strip along its side too worn. At last, leaning over the stove, she manages to ignite the kerosene. The flame is low and weak. The kettle will take several minutes to boil. She has more time to think.

Whatever Raj has done, his shortcomings alone cannot account for Neleni's outburst. For theirs is a marriage based on passionless acceptance. No, it is Neleni herself. Nirmala casts her mind back to their childhood. From the age of nine, they attended convent together and were as close as sisters.

She knows the depth of Neleni's affection, the strength of her loyalty, her romantic nature: yet she has never been in love. That is why Nirmala advised Neleni against the marriage with Raj. It was wrong, against nature that someone capable of such passion should settle for a lifetime of shallow affection. For, Nirmala is sure, that that is the most that Neleni has ever felt for Raj.

The flame sputters angrily under the kettle. The kerosene is getting low. She must order some more. Money has been short in the last month with fewer orders coming in. She has had an argument over a bill with a customer, an influential woman with an evil tongue who never expects to pay the full price for anything. The gossips have been at work, steadily unpicking her life. Just as they did before. She bites her lip. It was ten years ago but the pain is still raw.

She succumbed to illicit passion and was discovered. Both her husband and lover rejected her. She returned home to her mother, in shame, giving birth to a stillborn child in a dingy back-room. Her grief was unutterable, her humiliation complete. For months, the gossips circled like vultures until it felt as if her bones had been picked clean.

Acquaintances avoided her, even her mother was out of patience, so she grieved alone, in quiet corners where she could not be discovered or disturbed. Had it not been for the generosity of an aunt, who provided her with this place of refuge, she would have been forced to remain at home, drowning slowly in a mire of contempt.

And so it is that she has given up all idea of meeting a man and dresses only for herself. It is not so bad, really. Not once you get used to it. But she would not wish it on anyone else. A solitary life can be torment for those used to the company of family and friends.

The water is boiling. She turns off the heat and waits a second before grasping the kettle's metal handle, which is tightly bound with string for insulation. The water gushes from the beaked spout into the teapot, filling the kitchen with a sweet vapour.

She does not often make tea this way but, on the rare occasions when a friend comes to visit, she likes to use the china tea-service; another gift from her aunt. The cups are translucent, covered with swags of pink roses and touches of gilt, with handles so small that they must be held with the tips of the fingers. Only women can use them with ease.

It is another man. The thought comes to her as she is arranging slices of butter cake on a plate. That would account for Neleni's excess of grief. Nirmala pauses, her hand hovering over the teapot. She cannot tell which is uppermost in her mind: anger, because her own suffering has failed to act as an example to her friend; or pity, for that friend's predicament. Still, nothing has yet been said. She may be wrong. She hopes so.

She piles saucers, cups, milk-jug, teapot and cake onto a tray, then walks briskly back to the verandah where Neleni, lying with her head against a pillow, is looking thoughtfully across the valley towards a trail of smoke. A train, as small as a child's toy, is steaming along the mountain track, shards of sunlight glancing off its steel fenders.

Quietly placing the tray on a table, Nirmala settles herself in a chair by Neleni. They sit together, in silence, for a few minutes, before Nirmala takes her friend's hand.

"Tell me," she says. "No-one can hear us up here."

Leaning her head back on the sofa, Neleni stares up at the underside of the porch. For some reason, it has been painted bright blue; a bad choice, for the pale colour exposes an intricate netting of cobwebs. Some of the inhabitants are busily spinning, while others, tucked into crevices are waiting, as patient as fishermen, for the first quiver of a line. Still staring at the ceiling, Neleni begins to speak.

It is a strange confession; on the verandah of the dressmaker's house. As she listens, Nirmala's heart fills with dread. Neleni is treading a dangerous path. She has fallen in love with a man who lives under the same roof as her family. She is not even sure if the depth of her affection is returned. He is a friend, perhaps he will never be more, but she cleaves to him with a terrifying desperation.

Across the valley, the little train climbs even higher. Now it is almost level with the ridge, its funnel puffing out small clouds of white steam. It is incredible to think of men laying a track across such hostile terrain. But sometimes it is easier to shape a mountain than to curb one's heart. The human spirit is a curious thing.

"What shall I do?"

It is the question that Nirmala fears most. Her own experiences with men have been bitter, her mistakes have led to disaster. She is virtually an outcast; hardly the sort of person to give advice on such matters.

"Does he feel anything for you?"

"I don't know. He's very kind. He gave me a beautiful paint-box and we've talked a lot. About poetry and art. He listens to me."

Nirmala squeezes Neleni's hand.

"And this man is living in your house? Neleni, would it not be better for him to leave?"

"No. No. You must not say that."

"But one day, Neleni, he may want to go. He's young and single. You told me yourself that he already has an important position in the civil service. One day, his employers may want to move him somewhere else, just as they moved him here. He won't have a choice. What then?"

"No. I could not bear it. I thought I'd lost him once, when he was ill. That's when I realised. I love him, Nirmala. As I have never loved any man. If he leaves, I truly think I shall die."

Once again, her tears flow unchecked, spattering the wooden floor of the verandah. She seems so distraught that, for a moment, Nirmala wonders if she is quite sane. She strokes Neleni's arm, trying to soothe her.

"Shh. There, now. I was only asking what you would do. How you will manage to live from day to day with this man in your home."

"I will go on as before," murmurs Neleni. "We can be friends. There's no harm in that, is there?"

"No, of course not."

But Nirmala's reply lacks conviction.

1956: Portrait of a marriage

Leela pours herself a whisky from the cut-glass decanter. It is not her habit to drink in the mornings but she is bored. Since the funeral and post mortem, the excitement over Mennan's death has died down. Leela's friends, who kept her company in the first days of her widowhood, have turned their attention elsewhere. Life, for them, at least, has returned to normal. Each week, she receives fewer visitors. In fact, in the last few days, no-one has come to see her at all. Not even her lover who has become preoccupied with his own affairs.

She downs the whisky. Pours herself another. Its warmth runs through her, lulling her fear, a salve for loneliness. She wanders around the house, through each empty room, across the marble floors that echo with her footsteps. There is nothing so lonely, or silent, as a place built for pleasure that has fallen into disuse. She is like a child in an abandoned fairground.

She runs her fingers along a windowsill. Not a speck of dust. But no sign of human habitation either. It is as if no-one ever lived here. The bleached whiteness of the walls reminds her of a mausoleum. She never noticed it before when the house, full of people, rang with laughter and the sound of many voices.

Then, its starkness acted as a foil for the kaleidoscope of faces and bright colours constantly passing through. But now, it is like a stage without actors, an empty theatre whose nocturnal grandeur, exposed to the light of day, is revealed as a tawdry sham; a few pieces of tarnished gilt and moth-eaten velvet. The magic has gone. The house is dead.

When she first received the news of Mennan's death, she was neither grief-stricken, nor sad. On the contrary. She was relieved. She had become tired of him long before he died: his fawning was grotesque; his constant whining for sympathy, a bore; his attempts to please her, clumsy. His adoration was sickening and treated with the contempt it deserved.

Only with gifts, large and expensive, could he buy her favour. Only then, did she smile on him, for a brief moment, laughing to herself at his foolish display of affection, dismissing it as sentimentality. But now, even Mennan's company would be welcome.

Sipping from her glass, she contemplates the large portrait photograph that hangs in the hallway. It was taken by a professional photographer in a studio. She remembers that day well because she threw a tantrum. But, for once, Mennan had insisted, demanding, with all the firmness he could muster, that they should have their photograph taken together. And, for a brief moment, she had almost respected him. She had, at least, conceded to his wishes.

And there they remain, recorded for posterity, caged inside a gilt frame: a fat little man in a white suit and his beautiful wife. At least the photographer had done her justice. He was intoxicated by her. She had seen it in his eyes. A young man, nothing special, neither good looking, nor exciting, but whose devotion to her made him interesting. It had been exciting at first, pursuing their affair in the studio, surrounded by photographer's props, in the knowledge that the couch on which they were making love would soon accommodate the family of four, the university graduate, or the elderly couple, patiently awaiting their appointment in the room next door.

But she had soon tired of him. He began to talk incessantly of his love for her, how she was driving him mad, how his life would be nothing without her. In fact, he started to sound much like Mennan. The glitter wore off their affair. The studio lost its allure. It became what it had always been; a place of make-believe, full of gaudy vases, cheap scenery and artificial flowers. Angrily, Leela had ended their liaison and left the photographer weeping on his couch.

She drinks another mouthful and winces. The whisky tastes sour. It always does, after the first edifying rush. Leela leaves the glass next to a bowl of flowers. Who cares? No-one else will see it and the maid will clear it away later when she cleans the house. She glances angrily at Mennan as she passes the photograph on her way up the stairs. This is all his fault.

On the landing, she opens the door that leads into his study. She turns on the light and sits in the large swivel chair. It is a foreign place; more foreign and strange than anywhere else in the house. It is where Mennan ran his affairs, made his telephone calls, plotted the complicated course of his business.

She opens a drawer, sifts haphazardly through the contents and, with a sharp intake of breath, discovers an old black-and-white photograph of Mennan. He was slimmer then, his thick oiled hair, slicked over to one side. He is looking her straight in the eye and smiling: not a smile of triumph or disdain, but the smile of a friend; kind, welcoming; the sort that says he is glad to see you; that he wishes you well, that he would help you if he could.

"Oh!"

Her hand is clamped over her mouth as if to stop any other sound escaping. For that one, involuntary gasp sounded like an admission. She misses him. Hastily, she wipes away a tear, uncertain whether she has shed it for herself, or her dead husband. She lifts a letter from one of the piles of paper on the desk and examines it. It is a bill for ten thousand rupees. She turns over another, then another. They are all bills. For huge sums of money. She had no idea.

In desperation, she searches drawers, pulls files off shelves, pores over books and bank statements, invoices and bills. None of it makes any sense. She finds an invoice for a sapphire necklace, the last present Mennan gave her before he died. She turns out drawers and boxes looking for cheque stubs, then compares them to the bills. Nothing has been paid for. Not even the necklace.

"You bastard!"

Her hands are shaking. It is worse, much worse, than she imagined. Of course, she always knew that Mennan's business methods were unorthodox, questionable even, but she never thought she would be the victim of his dishonesty. She is stung by his betrayal. It is as if she had discovered him having an affair. Any question of her own probity in such matters eludes her; she fails to appreciate the fine irony of her situation.

"How could you?"

She bangs her fist on the desk. Some of the papers slip to the floor. They are the older ones, yellow and dry, like the scales of some monstrous lizard that has sloughed its skin. By sticking them all together, one would get the measure of the beast. It is huge. She is terrified, alone, quivering with anger and fear.

Her beauty will not be sufficient to charm the creditors. There is only so much that a man will do for a pretty smile and there is no favour she can offer that equals cash in the bank. Only a magician could make these papers disappear; someone practised in deception and sleight of hand; someone capable of juggling figures to create an illusion of wealth when, in fact, he is as poor as a beggar. Only a great artist, like Mennan, could perform such tricks. But he is gone. For the first time, she is aware of her loss.

"What can I do?"

She grips the arm of the chair to stop herself from fainting then begins to weep in earnest. For a terrible moment, she has a vision of her old life: the one from which Mennan rescued her; the one she never speaks of; the one that may reclaim her. It must not happen.

She dries her tears and tries to think. She needs money. Fast. Mennan had a secret fund, stashed away in various bank accounts. But where? She will never find it on her own, does not know how. She needs help. Who?

She could ask her boyfriend to help – he is an accountant for an international company – but recently, their relationship has become strained. Since Mennan's death, her lover has become more demanding, pestering her to marry him despite the fact that he is engaged to another girl.

Leela has seen his fiancée, pretty enough, with the complexion of a milk jelly and half the animation. Not the sort of girl to keep her lover interested for long. Not suitable at all. He knows it. He has even begged Leela to save him from a disastrous marriage.

But when he said this, she just laughed. Some men will go to any lengths to get what they want, say anything. In any case, she refused him. Leela has had enough of marriage for a while and requires a spell of freedom, doing as she wants without answering to anyone. But the obstacle to her independence is money.

She leaves the study, locking the door behind her as if this will contain the beast within. Slowly, she wanders back downstairs, collecting the whisky glass from where she left it on the table in the hall. As she passes the photograph in its great gilt frame, it seems to her that Mennan is looking at her, not so much with adoration, but amusement.

Furious, she flings the glass at his face. It bounces against the canvas, falls to the floor and smashes. Dribbles of whisky run down Mennan's face like amber tears. But, still, he smiles at her: the magician, who disappeared in a puff of smoke, leaving his assistant to face a baying crowd.

Turning her back on him, she walks swiftly across the hall. But she still has the uncomfortable impression that he is watching her. Laughing. In the living-room, she pours herself another whisky, then pauses to look at herself in a large, full-length mirror. It is a compulsion, a ritual repeated many times a day. The sight of her beautiful face usually cheers her: from the delicate arch of her eyebrow, to the curve of her chin, it is perfect. But today, it gives her no comfort.

No-one has visited her in days. Not even the lover that she has rejected. When Mennan was alive, she lacked for nothing. She was queen in her own court. Everything was done at her command.

But now, her followers have deserted her. She has the disconcerting feeling that she has either fallen out favour or gone out of fashion. Perhaps, the most chilling realisation of all is that she no longer matters. To anyone. She sheds another tear. Despite his faults, she has no doubt that Mennan loved her.

Delicately, she wipes her eye with the tip of her finger, careful not to smear the thick line of kohl which encircles her lid, telling herself that even grief must be kept in its place. Then, she lies on the couch, reclining on one arm as she plays with the gold fringe trimming. Covered in cream and gold brocade, this sofa was specially imported from abroad. Its opulence makes her nostalgic for the old days and she sheds another tear.

Then, she remembers; an idea which occurred to her at Mennan's funeral; a request made and accepted by one who felt unable to refuse. Someone with potential.

Rising to her feet, she crosses the room to the telephone. It sits on a walnut-veneered sideboard which, like the sofa, was imported from France: an expensive replica of an 18th century original. Next to the telephone is a notepad and, attached to that by an elaborate brocade ribbon, a pencil. No messages have been taken for many days. Picking up the pencil, she uses it to turn the dial, protecting her manicured nails.

"Hello, operator? Please put me through to the Government Agent's office. It's a matter of urgency."

A door slams. Two men, approaching from opposite ends of the corridor greet each other noisily then stop to exchange views on the latest cricket score. Scraps of their conversation drift into a room where a man is sitting at a desk covered with files. More files are arranged around the walls in racks which reach to the ceiling.

A smell of ageing paper pervades the room: not the pleasant, bookish odour of a library, but the smell of paper that has passed through many hands to be signed, certificated, stamped and scrutinised. It is a smell more akin to that of a very old rupee note that has become yellow and greasy with much handling.

If you spend too much time in this room, its odour will sink into your clothes like an invisible stain. Civil servants who have worked for many years in this building all smell the same, tainted by its unique aroma. For every room has its store of files.

While some offices are large, accommodating several people, this one is little more than a cubicle, dedicated to the use of a single individual. Ironically, its cramped surroundings signify the elevated status of its occupant. Superior to the general office staff, he must be separated from them, kept apart and nurtured, like a royal egg in a beehive, until his potential has been realised. However, at present, he is merely a leader in embryo, untried and unproven, insufficiently important to warrant a more commodious room. Until his talent has matured, he will continue to suffer the double disadvantage of isolation and discomfort.

The window in the tiny room has been opened in the hope of encouraging a breeze. Even the merest draught would be a relief. But the air inside is stubborn, refusing to circulate. It has been here for many years, filling the lungs of civil servants, bathing each office in its sullen warmth. Still and stagnant, it is as old as the building, as fixed and immovable as the clock on the wall.

Putting down his pen, Arjun massages his forehead with the tips of his fingers, pressing hard, willing himself to concentrate. Normally, the men chattering outside would have provided a diversion but, today, they are a distraction. Arjun tries to concentrate on the papers in front of him; but it is useless. He has already spent two fruitless hours trying to extract sense from a single document.

"Tea, sir?" Sarath, the chief clerk insinuates his head around the door.

"No thank you."

It is as much as Arjun can do to be polite. He has only been here a few months but he has already formed a strong dislike for Sarath. The man always appears when he isn't wanted, usually when Arjun is speaking to the Agent although, when his services are required, Sarath is nowhere to be found.

The thin, sinewy neck contracts and Sarath's head withdraws behind the door, reminding Arjun of a tortoise returning to its shell. He listens for the chief clerk's footsteps, until he is sure that he has gone. The two men discussing cricket have also gone about their business, no doubt through fear of the chief clerk.

The corridor is deserted, the silence oppressive. Arjun tries to focus on his work but, once again, his mind turns to Neleni. He is perplexed, not to say hurt, by the remoteness of her manner. After Sigiriya, he felt assured of her friendship; but recently, she has distanced herself from him. Even friendship seems out of the question now. She is cold, aloof, neither looking at him when they meet, nor speaking to him of anything other than mundane necessities such as food, washing, or a change of linen.

He cannot think why her attitude to him has changed so drastically. Although he secretly wishes for more than friendship, his demeanour towards her has been blameless. He treats her with kindness and consideration; he is friendly, but never over-familiar.

Someone has said something. His experience of office life has taught him that spiteful tongues can do irreparable damage. Her mother. That must be it. Sunny never liked him. Wherever he is in the house, he always feels her watching him, like one of those damn photographs on the wall.

"Old witch," he thinks, with uncharacteristic savagery.

Such thoughts come to him frequently these days, flashes of anger or fear, triggered by the smallest event or, sometimes, nothing at all. He is suspicious of everyone because everyone seems to suspect him. When he sees people talking in the corridor, he is sure that they are discussing him. He feels their eyes on him as he passes and he is reminded of the amber eyes that followed him at the camp-site, watchful and malevolent: the eyes of a murderer, a man who wished to kill him, although he did not know him.

If hatred can spontaneously infect one stranger, why not others? Is Arjun deluded, or has the attitude of other people changed towards him? Are they plotting his destruction? Sunny, for instance? The chief clerk? He cannot tell, but what he knows for sure is that his life changed irrevocably after Mennan's death. Nothing will ever be the same. And now, Neleni, his only friend, has turned against him.

Listlessly, he runs his finger over the telephone on his desk; a mark of prestige of which he should be proud, but which fails to touch him, as most things do these days. Nonetheless, he admires it, appreciates its sturdiness, the smoothness of the shining black bakolite, the chrome dial, even the black cord that connects the earpiece to the stand. Solid and reliable, it represents modernity, something created by science, not superstition. He takes comfort from that.

A gust of air passes through the office, causing the blind to clang against the window-frame then, with a suddenness that makes his heart leap, the phone begins to ring. As if his thoughts had brought it to life. Perhaps it is Neleni. He has recently had a telephone installed at her house, ostensibly for work, but in the forlorn hope that she may pick it up one day and speak to him. The telephone jangles brazenly. He lets it ring for a few more seconds, before picking up the receiver and holding it to his ear.

"Hello."

His greeting is guarded, cautious. However many times he uses it, the telephone is still a thing of mystery. He imagines his words, dropping into a great black void, like stones falling down a well.

"Is that Mr Kumaran?"

A woman's voice. But it is not Neleni. Disappointed, he grieves, inwardly.

"Yes. This is Arjun Kumaran. Can I help you?"

"I hope so."

There is an archness to this voice. It is familiar, but he cannot place it.

"Who am I speaking to?"

"Leela Rasanayagam. Mennan's widow."

"Oh."

His heart squeezes, flutters. A quickening of his spirits. Like panic. Only more pleasurable.

"I need your help."

177

The bus rumbles to a halt outside the office and a welter of people, who have been milling about at the stop, surge towards it. The vehicle is already crowded, its passengers as tightly packed as fish in a tin, their ribs so tightly compressed that, if one man breathes in, his neighbour is forced to breathe out.

Women in saris and diaphanous scarves cling to straps, rails, the backs of seats and one another. Their faces, already pained, assume a look of quiet martyrdom as the bus lurches around corners and more people are crammed in at every stop. They are reluctant to relinquish their anchorage but the pressure from new passengers forces them to let go, pushing them further down the bus. They cast around anxiously, looking for fresh support, but it is not necessary.

There are so many people on the bus now that the women are held upright by the sheer pressure of bodies. There is no danger of them falling or being thrown over although such overcrowded buses have other hazards. There are men, not all of them honourable, who may take advantage of such close and unavoidable proximity. Many things may be hazarded and, later, denied, blamed on the teeming conditions of the bus. The women roll their eyes, agitated but unable to move, like cattle corralled in a pen.

The bus is now so full, that young men are hanging from the rails at the back with barely a toe-hold on the running board. Their hair is lustrous and thickly-oiled, glinting blue in the hot light of the sun. For the most part, they are clerks and low-paid office workers, drinkers of cheap beer and smokers of bidis although many regard themselves as too refined to chew betel. They chatter and giggle like a troupe of excitable monkeys, enjoying the motion of the bus and the air that fills their loose white shirts and caresses their skinny chests.

If there is a pretty girl on the bus, their chatter will become louder as they stare at her through the window; their faces ranged one above the other, like a totem. Although flattered by these attentions, few of the pretty girls return them. The best the boys can expect is a tiny, crimped smile before the object of their adoration turns away or, if she cannot move, raises her eyes to the ceiling where she appears to have spotted an object of absorbing interest.

Sometimes, one of the braver members of the troupe will attempt some extraordinary antic in order to get the girl's attention. He will swing from the rail with one hand and walk his feet up the side of the bus or flatten his face against the window, grimacing and contorting his features. It is usually the older women who are amused by this, nudging each other and giggling softly, while the middle-aged men "tut" and shake their heads in disapproval.

Even the bus conductor's high-pitched threats, shouted down from the top deck, prove no disincentive to this behaviour. The boys just laugh and mimic his reedy voice. They probably knew him at school: a boy whose aspirations were fulfilled by the gift of a uniform and a ticket-machine. Truth to tell, they pity him, but he is also an object of fun. Unlike them, he does not know how to enjoy himself: never had a girl, probably never will.

The boys yell and whoop. Life is good, to be enjoyed, but it is often short. The daring young outriders of the omnibus are often the victims of gruesome accidents, either falling into the path of oncoming traffic or colliding with some passing object.

Bones are fractured, skulls crushed, deaths frequent but such incidents are simply regarded as a process of natural selection. When one of the troupe goes missing, his space is quickly filled. There is always room for one more.

***

Arjun, carried forward by the crowd, is almost at the door of the bus, when he changes his mind. With difficulty, he turns and forces his way back through the crush to the pavement. He will walk a couple of miles then pick up a bus on the outskirts of town. His mind is racing and he needs to think.

An hour ago, he received a telephone call. Heart pounding, he had picked up the receiver, hoping to hear Neleni. But it was Leela, weeping and barely audible. He had to ask her to repeat herself several times so that he could make sense of what she said and, all the while, he knew that the chief clerk was on the other side of the door, listening.

He could hear the man coughing quietly, see the flicker of a shadow in the corridor, a shadow that neither came nor went but moved slightly as an accompaniment to the coughing. And, after the coughing, there came the silence that proclaims, louder than anything else, that someone is listening and does not wish to be discovered.

In desperation, Arjun had asked Leela to call him back. At home. And he had given her the number of Neleni's telephone. He knew it was wrong. But what was he to do? Sarath was spying on him.

Life has changed during the run-up to elections. Previously, Arjun would simply have ignored Sarath, but now he fears him. Sarath often talks of his political connections. He is vague about what they are, but he talks warmly of Sinhalese nationalism. Previously, he would not have dared to air his opinions so openly, particularly in front of those, like Arjun, who he knows to be Tamil.

While Sarath is still careful not to express these views to the Government Agent, he makes sure that Arjun overhears him speaking to his colleagues. The atmosphere in the office is beginning to sour and polarise. Even those with no political views are being drawn into Sarath's camp, more through fear than conviction.

Sarath is everywhere, snooping into files, lurking within earshot, listening in to conversations. Arjun is sure that he is being singled out for the chief clerk's particular attention and, although innocent, fear makes him act as if he has something to hide.

Even speaking on the telephone to Leela has made him feel uncomfortable. While he was still alive, Mennan's reputation was tainted by corruption. Now, despite his awful death, the case against him is not closed. Investigations are still proceeding into the overseer's financial dealings. Accountants are searching for records of his transactions. Any money that he is found to have embezzled will be sequestered and returned to the State. Any contact with Mennan's widow, however innocent, could compromise Arjun's position. Sarath will make sure of that.

Walking fast, Arjun turns off the main street into a narrow road filled with sweet shops and cheap eateries. Having walked two miles already, he is thirsty. He stops to buy sweet tea at a street stall. He is hungry and would like to eat. The thought of string hoppers bathed in an aromatic sauce is tempting, but he must get home. If Leela rings, he does not want Neleni to answer the phone. He does not want anyone to know who is calling him.

He finishes the tea and hands the glass back to the vendor. The street, edged by tall, thin houses, is shaded from the sun, offering a welcome relief from the heat. Arjun hurries on.

At Mennan's funeral, he offered to help Leela. Now she is holding him to his promise. Today, between tears and incoherent sobs, she asked once more for his advice. Would he come and see her? There are things she must ask him. Only he can help her.

He has to admit, he was flattered. He did not expect her to remember him and she is a beautiful woman. But he is also afraid. He suspects that Nash would disapprove of his involvement, however innocent, with Mennan's widow. And yet, since the funeral, Arjun's sense of complicity in Mennan's death has increased, rather than diminished.

What was it Leela said to him? He cannot remember, but the poison is still working within him. His sense of guilt now outweighs his professional loyalty and the greater that guilt becomes, the closer he is bound to Leela. If she asks for help, he must give it.

He thinks guiltily of Neleni feeling that, in some way, he has betrayed her. But that is ridiculous. How can he betray a woman who is already married to someone else? And anyway, nothing has happened between them: nothing of which either can be ashamed. He should be grateful. He tries to laugh at himself, but is filled with bitterness, disappointment mingled with anger.

He thinks of Neleni's recent treatment of him; her coldness. It is she who has betrayed him. The sweetness of the tea has turned sour in his mouth. He is dogged by misfortune. He aims straight, but the arrow always goes awry; his good intentions are always misplaced.

He passes the church, then the tailor's shop where the owner is sitting cross-legged in the window, intent on hemming the sleeve of a shirt. Not for the first time, Arjun wishes that he could exchange places with someone else. He bites his lip and his eyes dim. He loves her and there is no hope. It is time that he admitted it. She does not care for him.

He steps sideways to let a woman pass him and almost falls over a bundle of rags propped against a wall. The rags moan and quake. A beggar raises his head from where he was sleeping and holds out his hand. He is toothless and old, his eyes milky and almost blind. Arjun drops a few rupees into the outstretched hand. There are some things, at least, for which he can be grateful. There are always others who are worse off.

And yet, he cannot overcome his pain. Whatever it is that he feels for Neleni, cannot be buried. It has taken root and cannot easily be eradicated. He has tried already. It is useless. After Sigiriya, he lived in hope of her affection. At first, he thought it was returned, but recently she has held herself aloof from him. The early flowering of their friendship has withered.

Perhaps, he was mistaken. Perhaps, she only needed someone to talk to and, that day, on the outing, he had provided a convenient ear in which to pour the pain of her thwarted ambition. Perhaps …

Time and again, he has convinced himself that she has no interest in him. Then, a look in her eye has set his heart racing and given him fresh hope. But he cannot play this game forever. He cannot live without hope. He cannot love without return. It is draining him. His life is beginning to unravel.

The more he thinks of her, the quicker he walks. Soon, he will break into a run. He passes monumental government offices, crosses a park whose flower beds are filled with red and yellow canna lilies, then enters another street whose shops sell saris, jewellery and sandals and whose cramped restaurants emit smells of fried onion and spices.

A sharp turn into a passageway where a pye-dog is worrying a pile of rubbish; another turn, another street; past houses crammed together where washing lines are strung across the road and shrill voices, mingled with the smell of cooking, issue from windows and doors.

On the pavement, small boys are fighting for possession of a cricket bat. *It's my turn, my turn, my turn.* Their voices pursue him, around the corner, along the alley and onto the main street where a bus is waiting by the kerb.

1956: The visitors

A small black car turns into Neleni's street, its chassis hanging uncomfortably low over its back wheels. It is a Morris Minor; a new one. In a country where the possession of any car, even an old one, is a symbol of affluence, two conclusions may be drawn about the owner of this Morris: firstly, he is a man (women rarely own, let alone drive, cars); secondly, he is a man of some substance (indicated by the newness of the car).

Such a car is a mark of status for middle-grade civil servants, senior bank clerks and those rising through the ranks of foreign corporations. It is either the car of a young man on his way up, as yet unmarried with sufficient capital to indulge himself or of an older, embittered man whose aspirations have ossified and who must provide for the needs of a large and demanding family. In many cases, one often leads to the other.

**

Having lurched to a halt outside Neleni's house, the little car bobs and sways like a small boat at anchor. Voices float out through the window, one in particular, loud and strident, that of a woman giving orders.

"No. No! Not like that. You are hurting me. You are stepping on my scarf. Stop it! You stupid man."

In between her shrieks and recriminations, another voice can be heard, softly apologising. It is difficult to tell from outside, whether it is the voice of a man or a woman.

The driver's door flies open. A young man, so tall that he must have been collapsed like a telescope, eases himself out, unfolding first one leg, then the other. Having extracted himself, he stands with his back to the car, stretching his arms, his expression one of studied ennui. Nothing, it seems, can excite him, not even the drama unfolding in the back seat of his car where his future mother-in-law is attempting to extricate herself from the seat, the door-handle, her husband and any other encumbrance worthy of blame.

"Ow. Ow! You silly man. Now look what you've done!"

The car sways violently.

"For god's sake," murmurs the young man. "Think of the suspension."

But he dares not speak aloud. Sighing, he walks around the car and opens the back door.

"Here, Aunty. Let me help you!"

He bends forward, offering his arm to a large woman dressed in a sari so tight, that she resembles a bun covered in pink icing. A fat arm issues from the car and plump fingers are clamped around the driver's arm. A good deal of tugging and pulling ensues and the car yaws and lunges even more violently. But no-one emerges.

"Push!"

The young man mouths a suggestion to someone sitting behind the woman when she is not looking. However, the woman is so large that she obscures the view from within. The other occupant, sitting on the far side of her, is very small. Only the muffled whisper of a voice indicates that there is anyone there at all.

"Push. Uncle. Push. It is the only way."

182

With her hands placed either side of the door, the woman tries to ease herself out. Following a sudden impetus from behind, she lurches forward. The car rocks even more violently. With her knees pressed up against her chest, the woman is now firmly wedged in the door. She is changing colour. Her cheeks darken to a dangerous puce. It seems to the young man that, if she took one good breath, the car would probably explode. He imagines the boot flying open and the doors spinning off in all directions.

"Ow!" the woman complains. Her face is now the colour of a ripe aubergine. If she is left in this position any longer, something terrible will happen.

"Uncle. Get out and help me!" the young man orders.

The passenger door on the far side of the car slowly opens and someone with white hair gets out. However, he is so small that only the top of his head can be seen over the roof of the car. A few seconds later, a small, crumpled man appears. Resembling an inflatable toy that has lost its air, he is somewhat flat and wrinkled; partly due, no doubt, to sharing the back-seat with someone of his wife's ample proportions. But it is also a measure of his character.

"Here, Uncle. You take one hand, I will take the other. Then, you must pull. On the count of three Aunty, you must push."

As he takes hold of one of the fat, bejewelled hands, the little man strokes the fingers affectionately. Seeing this, the young man has to suppress a smile. Such passion for such an unbecoming subject is hard to imagine: for there is no doubt, the little man adores his wife.

"One, two, three!" The young man has to resist the temptation to follow this with the word "Heave".

All three pull and push to varying degrees but, despite their efforts, the woman remains stuck in the car. She sinks back into the seat, exhausted. Puffing out her cheeks, she takes deep breaths, expanding into every available space and looking, to the young man's eye, like an explosion of pink marshmallow.

"It's all right, Uncle. Let me try!"

Fearful of hurting his wife, the little man was unable to exert sufficient force to extract her from the car. Overcome by affection, he stands on the pavement, ogling her with watery eyes and nervously wringing his hands.

"Stand aside, Uncle."

Grasping the little fellow by the shoulders, the young man propels him towards the steps where he stands, still wringing his hands and muttering.

"Oh dear. Don't hurt her, will you!"

"No, of course not."

But there is something of the crocodile about the young man's smile which the husband does not find reassuring.

"Come on, Aunty. Give me your hands!"

Obediently, the woman holds out her fat arms in front of her, her wrists encased in gold bracelets which are so tightly bound to her flesh that they cannot be removed and never jangle like those of other women. She simpers, girlishly, as the young man takes her hands.

"Now, when I tell you, push. Really hard. Understand?"

The woman nods meekly.

"Go!"

The young man pulls hard, leaning back on his heels, using his weight as a counterbalance. Suddenly, the woman pops out of the car, like a cork from a bottle, taking the young man by surprise.

"Oh, Michael," she giggles girlishly, as she plunges into his arms.

But Michael is filled with revulsion. The amplitude of that great bosom, pressed against his chest, has quite winded him. With disgust, he notices the rolls of fat around her neck, stacked up like rubber rings; the loose, wrinkly skin around her bosom; the whiff of her perfume that reminds him of an elderly aunt, a combination of talcum powder, flower water and old age.

"Jesus!"

"What was that?" retorts the woman sharply, her head swivelling upwards on its tyres of fat.

"Nothing. I sneezed."

The young man flashes his best, film-star smile. He must hide his disgust. He is not brave enough to confront this gorgon directly. Few are. Like everyone else, he humours her.

"A cold?" All thought of flirtation has disappeared.

"Well, don't give it to Dalia. We have more visits next week. Important family members. No-one wants to see your fiancée with a runny nose."

The man nods in agreement. In fact, he wonders if he wants a fiancée at all. The mother's repulsive embrace has stirred up doubts about the daughter. Will Dalia resemble her mother in twenty years? Will Michael resemble the father, whose life has been slowly sucked out of him, like marrow from a bone?

Michael looks anxiously towards the car where the passenger door has opened a few inches to reveal a small delicate foot whose brightly-painted toenails resemble polished rubies. Encased in a tiny gold sandal, the foot is lowering itself tentatively towards the pavement. It is followed by another foot of equal perfection.

The door opens wider and is grasped by a pale hand with long fingers and shapely nails. A girl emerges, moving with such delicacy that the little car which, up to now has been swinging and bouncing on its springs, remains quite still. Even the air around her seems undisturbed. She stands up and, with a barely perceptible movement – the slightest shimmer – her hair and clothes tremble into place.

The girl's pale skin and green eyes hint at an interesting quirk of ancestry – Portuguese or Dutch perhaps – although her mother fervently denies it.

"We are Tamil, through and through," she insists to anyone with the temerity to suggest otherwise.

"Dalia is just fair, like my grandmother. Very lucky. Not black like some of those up-country folk."

It is a cultural irony that, while pale skin is desirable, mixed blood is not.

Leaving the door open behind her, the girl floats, rather than walks from the car, like a spirit from another world, undisturbed by the recent commotion if, in fact, she noticed it at all. With head held high, she glides up the steps to the front door where, tilting her head to one side, she admires her reflection in the window.

"Dalia," the mother croons. "Wait for me, darling. I'm just coming."

And, lifting her sari with one plump hand, she lumbers up the steps.

1956: Long lost enemies

Lakshmi is busy, fussing with her daughter's hair, first combing it forward so that it cascades over both shoulders, then pushing it back to reveal her heart-shaped face, each time standing back, examining the girl from every angle, admiring her handiwork.

"Pretty as a picture," coos her mother. The girl smirks.

But the hair is still not right. Winding the long, silky skeins around her hand, Lakshmi arranges it first over one shoulder, then the other. All the time, the girl remains immobile, as passive as a tailor's dummy, rolling her eyes occasionally to express her infinite boredom; a gesture that is repeated many times a day.

"That's it. Beautiful. Don't you think she is beautiful, Michael? Aren't you lucky to have such a lovely bride?"

"Yes, beautiful," comes the mechanical reply. But Michael is not looking at Dalia or her mother. He is assessing the house, calculating its overall worth. From his expression, it is clear that he is not impressed. He has seen better. His mistress's house, for example. Now that is truly a home fit for a man of his standing.

Thoughts of her home lead to thoughts of his mistress and he wonders why he has not heard from her. Usually they speak at least once a week, but he has been busy recently with wedding preparations and the endless round of family visits that precede the ceremony. He has taken care to explain all of this to her. She seemed to understand at the time. But, all the same, she has not been in touch. Michael makes a mental calculation. It is now ten days since they last spoke.

He is not usually given to nervousness or self-doubt, but he experiences a brief pang of anxiety. Not that he doubts his attractiveness or his prowess as a lover, but his mistress has a reputation for fickleness. Perhaps she is sulking. He explores this line of logic. It is a good one. If she is sulking, it means that she misses him and, by inference, that her affection for him is undimmed. In this case, silence is definitely a good sign. The thought pleases him and he smiles.

"You see, Dalia. How happy you are making your future husband."

Lakshmi beams at him. Michael tries to arrange his face into an appropriate expression but his smile becomes set and rigid, something between a snarl and a grimace. But Lakshmi does not notice. She has turned her back on him and is attacking the front door, hammering on it with her fist, her gold bangles glinting in the sunlight. Lakshmi stands back, tapping her foot impatiently then, after an interval of only a few seconds, pounds on the door again.

"What is taking them so long?" she demands shrilly. "Don't they know it is rude to keep people waiting?"

Her husband emerges briefly from the background to whisper something inaudible, then sinks back against the wall.

"I'm coming. I'm coming," calls a muffled voice.

The door swings open and Raj's beaming face appears.

"Lakshmi, Niran, welcome."

His mouth twitches at the edges. His grin is a little too wide, his smile placatory. Lakshmi, his cousin, has terrified him from childhood. He makes a deferential gesture resembling a bow and stands aside to admit his guests. Affecting a haughty, disinterested expression, Dalia glides in first, leaving her parents and fiancé to follow in her wake.

"Dalia. Wonderful to see you darling," babbles Raj, effusively. He tries to grasp her in one of the affectionate bear-hugs that he reserves for younger members of the family; but she slips past him without a word, her pale eyes flashing a warning, like a cat about to have its tail pulled.

Michael enters last, his temper having turned to one of acute irritability. No-one has bothered to introduce him. His future mother-in-law is in full flow, blethering about the wedding, how much has been spent and how beautiful her daughter will look. She has quite forgotten about Michael. He is not even an afterthought. Raj coughs and tries to direct Lakshmi's attention to the tall, young man who stands glowering on the step.

"Oh, Michael, there you are. Raj, I don't think you have met Dalia's fiancé. Come here Michael. Meet my cousin Raj."

With an imperious wave of her hand, Lakshmi summons Michael to her. He obeys with a bad grace. He has not slaved to become senior accountant of an international insurance company to be treated as a lap-dog by this woman. Unsmiling, he thrusts out his hand to Raj.

"Pleased to meet you."

With horror, Michael notes the change in his own voice. Suddenly shrill and deprived of its manly tone, it sounds to him like the yapping of a poodle.

"Yes, yes. Very pleased."

Raj bobs and bows, patting the young man's hand. But he is at a loss for anything to say. The young man appears to be tongue-tied. Lakshmi has this effect on everyone. There is an uncomfortable silence.

"Dalia, how you've grown," says Raj, attempting to make conversation.

The girl's eyes flash green sparks. Raj continues, regardless.

"Such a long time since we've seen you."

"I know, I know," says Lakshmi. "Can't be helped. Such busy lives."

Lakshmi swats the air with her hand, as if Raj's comment was a troublesome mosquito. The real reason that she has not seen Raj for so long is due less to the frenetic pace of her life than to her dislike of his wife, of whom she is bitterly jealous.

Many years ago, Lakshmi's parents had considered a marriage between their daughter and her second cousin, Raj. It was a plan much favoured by Lakshmi. But, ultimately, it came to nothing. Lakshmi secretly grieved for her lost marriage to Raj and, when Neleni captured his heart, Lakshmi was unable to forgive her beauty and good fortune.

Subsequently, Lakshmi had married Niran whom she regards as a weak and spineless little man, a poor substitute for her manly cousin. Unable to appreciate the strength of Niran's affection, she punishes his devotion with a regime of ceaseless nagging, wearing him down until he has finally collapsed into two dimensions, a flat image of his former self to be toted around without complaint and neatly folded away when no longer required: a perfect handbag of a husband.

"Dalia will make a beautiful bride."

At last, Raj says something with which they can all agree. His niece rewards him with a pert smile. She thinks so, too.

"Look, look, Dalia. See these pictures here."

Squealing with hilarity, Lakshmi waddles across the passage to where Neleni's photographs begin their solemn procession along the wall.

"See, here. Such funny old photographs. So stilted. Look at this one. So buttoned up in his starched collar. Fair, too. Must be of mixed race. A burgher, perhaps."

Lakshmi is pointing at a picture of Neleni's father. She seems not to have seen Neleni, who has appeared at the kitchen door, but her remarks strike home. Particularly the one about the burgher. Those of mixed blood are regarded as not quite belonging to any group; not Tamil, Sinhalese, or European. Mortified, Neleni shoots a furious glance at Raj, who pretends not to see her. An argument between the two women would be more than he could bear.

"Ah, Neleni," coos Lakshmi, noticing her hostess for the first time.

"We were just admiring your photographs, weren't we Dalia?"

The pale girl smiles, slyly.

"Such a fine collection," continues Lakshmi, unabashed. "Where did you get them?"

"My father took them," says Neleni. Her smile has frozen and she has to force the words out between her teeth.

"Of course, I had forgotten," says Lakshmi, who obviously had not. "Such an unfortunate accident that he had. Fell out of a tree, didn't he?"

She smiles at Neleni, feigning sympathy, but there is a hint of irony in her voice. Her small eyes, buried deep in the fleshy folds of her face, glitter wickedly. Behind her, Dalia makes a small gasping noise which may be a suppressed sneeze, or a giggle. Raj holds his breath and prays. Neleni has just opened her mouth to reply when she is interrupted by a commotion from the kitchen.

"Damn you!" screeches a high, reedy voice. "Damn you!"

Lakshmi presses a hand to her vast cleavage, her mouth forming a tight little "O" of shock.

"My mother hates cats," says Neleni, enigmatically.

They pass into the sitting-room where food is laid out for the guests on the table at which Neleni usually paints. Raj lingers behind in the hallway. Crossing himself, he offers a prayer of thanks to the plaster Virgin for having averted disaster. Flickering at her feet in its red glass cup, the eternal flame bathes her pale skin with a rosy glow. The Virgin smiles serenely and, to Raj's mind, looks almost like a living woman.

"It's going to be a long afternoon," he confides.

The visit is not going well. Neleni, sitting a little apart from the company has, so far, failed to say a word. Every line of her face spells antipathy, from the pallor of her cheek (always a sign of anger), to her tightly-pursed lips. Sunny remains in the kitchen where she continues to declaim loudly and rattle pans, while the girls make a fleeting appearance during which Rani declares war on her aunt.

Lakshmi insists on kissing both children and, although Saro submits meekly, Rani resists, standing stiff as a board, her face screwed up in disgust. Encompassed by two great arms, she is pressed to a hot, fleshy bosom that smells unpleasantly of Parma violets. With horrible fascination, Rani notices beads of sweat bubbling through the thick layer of powder which Lakshmi has plastered over her face. However, even this cannot conceal the fringe of dark hair over her lip.

Thick scarlet lips plant a rubbery kiss on Rani's cheek, leaving a sticky, wet imprint. Scowling, Rani rubs her face. It is an act of open defiance. Lakshmi would not tolerate such insubordination from her own daughter, let alone the brat of her cousin's detested wife. Gripping the child tightly to prevent her struggling, she pulls her close and kisses her determinedly on the other cheek. A hair, sprouting from a mole near Lakshmi's mouth, pricks Rani's skin.

"Ow," exclaims Rani loudly, jumping back.

"What's the matter, darling?" says Lakshmi in a voice as treacly and malignant as hot tar. Seeing the glint in her aunt's eye, Rani glares back.

"What's the matter?" persists Lakshmi, her moon-face looming closer, until it is only an inch from Rani's nose. The child notices that her aunt has no eyebrows, only thin arches of brown pencil that do not move with the rest of her face. They are grotesque but nothing is as nauseating as Aunty's mouth. Smeared with a greasy slick of lipstick, Aunty's lips look permanently wet like someone who has forgotten to wipe the sauce from their mouth after a meal.

"I don't like being kissed," mutters Rani.

"But darling, why not?"

Her aunt's face is so close that the air expelled from her great, red mouth blows hot on Rani's cheek. She is a dragon with lungs like bellows and a mouth like a furnace. Rani can almost feel her hair frizzling in the heat. She looks urgently to her parents, hoping for rescue, but none comes. She must defend herself from the hot blast of that awful mouth and the torment of another kiss.

"You've got a hairy face," she blurts. "It prickles my skin."

"Oh," Lakshmi falls back in her chair, her face contorted with shock. She looks so comical that Rani begins to giggle.

"Bad girl!"

Raj is out of his chair, shaking Rani by the elbow.

"Apologise to Aunty. Give her a kiss and say sorry."

"No!" Rani stamps her foot. "No, no, no!!!"

"Rani! Child!"

Raj is mortified. He doesn't know whether to smack the child or plead with her. He tightens his grip on her arm, hoping she will realise the embarrassment she is causing her father and relent. But it only makes her worse.

"No," she screams. "I won't kiss her. She's an ugly old witch!"

A perilous silence falls over the room, the sort that precedes a storm. Lakshmi, her face purple with rage, is on the point of either exploding or suffering a seizure. The volume of noise depends on whether her anger is projected outwards or inwards. Everyone holds their breath.

Niran, her tired little husband, cowers in his chair, his hands jerking and twitching nervously. Standing behind his future mother-in-law, Michael smirks, enjoying the vicarious pleasure of hearing his own thoughts spoken aloud by someone else. Only Dalia remains untouched, as cold and expressionless as the stone carving of a goddess.

Suddenly, Lakshmi rocks herself forward, her finger raised in the air. Her eyes glitter wickedly in the fleshy depths of her face. They are fixed on Rani. An eruption is imminent. Rising quickly from her seat, Neleni seizes Rani by the shoulders and guides her out of the living-room.

Cheated of her prey, Lakshmi suddenly finds herself becalmed, frozen on the cusp of an indignant outburst. Deprived of her target, she must quickly change tack or lose her advantage. The transition is effected with consummate skill. Clasping her throat, she rolls her eyes then falls back in a dead faint.

***

In the kitchen, Rani is sitting at the table, trembling yet defiant, still refusing to apologise. Her mother stands over her, her grandmother watches from a corner by the cupboard. Rani sits hunched, her hands in her lap, waiting for the inevitable slap. But it does not come. Cautiously, she raises her eyes and sees the two women exchanging a look. Her mother's face is not terrible, as expected, but seems to conceal a smile. She is amused rather than angry.

Rani risks a furtive glance at her grandmother. The old lady is beaming and, most unusually, she is holding the cat, nursing it like a baby. She only does that when she is especially happy and, usually, when no-one is looking. Rani raises her head for a better look and, quite suddenly, the smile disappears from her grandmother's face. It is not something to be shared with a child.

The old lady mutters and throws the cat to the floor. Yowling with indignation, the animal looks at her accusingly, then stalks out into the yard, its tail held high. Rani looks up at her mother. Neleni's face is expressionless. No trace remains of the smile that Rani saw just a moment ago. Perhaps there will be no reprieve as Rani hoped. She hangs her head.

There is a movement at her elbow and, to her surprise, a large glass of lemonade is placed on the table beside her. Rani is confused. Lemonade is usually a reward for good behaviour, particularly a glass this big. She hesitates.

"Go on, child, drink," her grandmother urges.

"Don't you want it?"

Neleni is smiling now; a mother's smile; the sort that Rani understands. She reaches for the glass and quietly sips the tangy, sweet liquid. As she drinks, it occurs to her that both her mother and grandmother tacitly approve of her actions; although they cannot say so. Perhaps she is not the only one to dislike Aunty Lakshmi.

***

In the sitting room, Raj is promising a remedy; six of the very best to punish Rani for her bad manners. However, even this tempting offer fails to revive Lakshmi who has slumped back in her chair, her eyes closed, in what appears to be a dead faint while her husband fusses about ineffectually, fanning her with a minuscule white handkerchief. From time to time, Lakshmi emits a faint moan while pressing a large, be-ringed hand to her bosom.

"It's her heart," says the little man, frantically flapping the handkerchief in her face.

"We need something to revive her. A little whisky, perhaps?"

Lakshmi moans louder as if to reinforce this suggestion.

Raj, overawed by the thought of causing his cousin's death, is persuaded to part with a bottle of premium Scotch which he has been hoarding for a special occasion. As soon as the cap is off the bottle, Lakshmi's eyelids begin to flicker. A small glass of restorative is then wafted under her nose and she is coaxed into taking a small sip, followed by two large gulps. The effect is miraculous. Her eyes open wide and she gazes around the room with the dazed expression of Lazarus, newly-awakened from the dead.

"Where am I?" she murmurs weakly, her eyes fixed on the bottle in Raj's hand.

A further glass of whisky is swiftly applied to aid her memory. This pantomime might be prolonged for the best part of the afternoon and Raj's bottle of whisky completely emptied, were it not for an unexpected diversion. The figure of a young man is quietly stepping past the open door.

The car outside has already alerted Arjun to the fact that the family has guests. Not very welcome ones, judging by the conversation in the kitchen this morning. At the same time as she was serving Arjun his breakfast, Neleni was carrying on a shrill discussion with her mother, raising her voice to compensate for the old lady's deafness.

However, for once they appeared to be in agreement. Receiving these visitors would be more of a painful duty than a pleasure. The two women had discussed the matter openly, as if Arjun had not been there and, although he tried not to listen, it had been impossible not to get a flavour of their dislike for Raj's cousin.

Remembering this, he has let himself in quietly through the front door, hoping to take refuge in his room. His mind is still reeling from events earlier in the day. The telephone call from Leela has thrown him into confusion. He does not know what to do. He tried to see Nash before leaving the office, hoping to seek his advice, but the Agent had been called away on urgent business.

On his walk home, Arjun decided to consult Neleni instead. More than ever, he feels the need of her friendship, that intimacy briefly experienced at Sigiriya which still eludes him. He has made up his mind to speak to her. One last try. Depending on her reaction, he will either continue to hope or give up altogether.

Having eased the front door open with his knee, he has closed it quietly behind him and is stealthily crossing the hallway. He can hear agitated snatches of conversation from the living-room. A crisis is unfolding. However, according to what Neleni said this morning, it is to be expected. What was it she said? Always some drama, always something to capture the attention. It would appear that Raj's cousin has an exaggerated sense of theatre.

The hall, as usual, is dark and gloomy, filled only by the somnolent ticking of the clock. In her niche on the wall, the Virgin appears to smile at some private joke. Perhaps she is thinking of Raj's earlier comment or perhaps it is a trick of the eternal flame which is flickering feebly in its glass vase, burning low because Sunny has forgotten to top up the oil.

Arjun approaches the door. Inside, he can see Raj and another man bending over a chair that contains a large woman in a pink sari. So that is her. Although he does not wish to be seen, Arjun pauses to look, fascinated by the woman whose vast girth spills over the sides of the chair and who appears either to be sleeping or to have fainted. Having absorbed this strange little scene, Arjun is about to turn away when the woman's eyelids flash open.

"Who is that?" she barks.

All eyes turn to the newcomer who has the guilty aspect of a burglar caught in the act. Transfixed, Arjun stands in the doorway, nervously feeding the rim of his hat back and forth through his fingers. The woman in the pink sari smiles a welcome. Her expression is evidently meant to be sweet; the scarlet lips pucker coyly and the hint of a dimple appears in one fat cheek; but the tiny black eyes remind Arjun of a conger eel watching for prey. There is no escape, no Neleni, just a roomful of strangers and Raj who seems overjoyed to see his lodger.

"Arjun, come in my boy."

Raj cannot hide his relief. Arjun's arrival is the answer to his prayers. Perhaps Lakshmi will forget about the earlier, embarrassing incident with Rani.

Taking a deep breath, Arjun steps into the living-room and delivers himself up for inspection, gratefully accepting the drink offered to him by Raj. For once, it is welcome.

***

Lakshmi has recovered. Even in the kitchen, there is no escape. Her voice soars above the crashing of pots and pans.

"I tell you, Raj, there is no place like Colombo. There is so much life, so many opportunities. Not like this out-of-the-way place. You should come and live there, then we could be a family again."

This little barb arrows its way towards Neleni's sensitive ear. Despite her mother's more than usually loud commotion, she cannot help but hear. It is meant for her and it strikes home. Unusually, for a traditional marriage, Raj moved to his wife's home town. Normally, it is the other way around, but Raj was besotted with his new wife and Neleni had insisted. It is something which rankles with Lakshmi who, against all expectations, spent the first years of married life in her mother-in-law's home. It is another facet of her jealousy and another dart in her quiver of vengeful remarks.

"She would make me feel guilty for breathing if she could," thinks Neleni.

It is ironic that Lakshmi should envy a marriage which Neleni regards as a penance. She pours Rani another glass of lemonade and gives her four milk biscuits arranged on a china plate. The child, sensing that she is in favour, leans her head against her mother's arm. Absent-mindedly, Neleni strokes Rani's hair while trying to catch the rest of the conversation.

"A man of your talent is wasted here," croons Lakshmi.

"O, o, o." For some reason, Raj adopts the Sinhalese affirmative. Neleni thinks she detects a note of self-pity in his voice. There is a gentle tap on her arm. Looking up into her daughter's face, Sunny's eyes loom large behind her thick-lensed glasses.

"Are you going to let her get away with it?"

Neleni hesitates. Raj seems to be coping without her and she feels betrayed by the way in which he encourages his cousin's sympathy. But, suddenly, the conversation changes direction.

"Tell me exactly what it is you do?"

Outside the window, the temple tree shakes, shedding its blooms. The wind is blowing in another direction. The conversation has changed course. Lakshmi has found a new object for her attention. But who can it be? Neleni is perplexed. She was outside in the yard, comforting the cat with a few scraps, when Arjun returned home.

She does not know of his ambush by Lakshmi and Raj or she would have gone to his rescue. On hearing his voice, her heart leaps. In reply to Lakshmi's question, he tells her that he is something in the civil service. Neleni admires his modesty, but it fails to impress Lakshmi who, without waiting for him to finish, rudely interrupts with another question for Raj.

"And why do you continue to live in this old place? It's only fit for termites. You should come to Colombo, buy a new place like ours."

This is not to be borne. Scooping up a plate of butter cake, Neleni hurries towards the living-room but, as she crosses the hall, the telephone rings. Although she will not admit it, Neleni is still nervous of the strange contraption which sits in a dark angle of the hallway on an old card-table. It has been installed at Arjun's insistence and, although he says that it is for the family's use, Neleni feels that she has no right to touch it. It continues to jangle irritably. She stands, looking at it, unsure of what to do.

In the living-room, Lakshmi has turned her attention to Arjun, grilling him about his background, his parents, where he came from, every conceivable question designed to weed out any weakness and expose him as a pauper or a fraud. Neleni is torn. She wants to run in, stop Lakshmi in her tracks, but the telephone continues to ring, demanding attention. Cautiously, with the plate of cake still in one hand, Neleni picks up the receiver.

"Hello."

There is a pause. Then a silky voice asks:

"Is this 651?"

"Yes."

"Is this the residence of Arjun Kumaran?"

"Yes."

It is not a real conversation, just questions and answers, an interrogation like the one being performed in her living-room. Not knowing what else to say, Neleni waits.

"May I speak with him?"

Although courteous, there is a touch of insolence about this voice. It seems to imply that Neleni is stupid; yet, despite its haughtiness, it betrays something that is not in keeping with its studied languor. It is not an educated voice. Neleni hesitates.

"Can you hear me?"

The tone is imperious, irritable.

"Yes."

Neleni would like to bang the telephone back onto its receiver. Without an invitation, without even being physically present, this caller has insinuated her way into Neleni's home with the sole intention, it seems, of insulting her. And yet, with the receiver clamped to her ear, she continues to listen, spellbound.

"Well, is he there?"

Neleni can imagine the other woman, tapping her foot with impatience.

"I'm not sure. I've been outside," Neleni replies, evasively.

This time, the caller sighs audibly.

"Can't you go and look?"

"Yes. I suppose so."

Again, Neleni hesitates. She does not want Arjun to speak to this woman. She does not like the sound of that voice, anonymous, yet mocking her from a distance.

"Well, is he there?"

The voice is sharp, inquisitive. Neleni can imagine it addressing a hapless shop assistant or servant. She is on the point of saying *No*, when she sees Arjun standing in the doorway.

"Yes," she replies, miserably.

But the woman cannot wait.

"Tell him that I am sending a car. It will be there in a few minutes."

"Who ... who...?"

But before she can ask the caller's name, the line has gone dead.

"Was that for me?"

Having slipped out of the living-room, Arjun is watching her, anxiously. He looks almost guilty. He was evidently expecting that call. Neleni experiences a stab of envy.

"Yes. The caller wouldn't leave her name."

"Oh."

He looks awkward, embarrassed. Plunging his hands in his pockets, he stares at the floor, scuffing at an imaginary spot of dirt with the toe of his shoe. Then, quite suddenly, he seems to make up his mind to speak. Walking swiftly over to where she is standing, he starts to explain.

"Listen ... I ..."

But he is interrupted by the loud bleat of a horn. A car is waiting outside.

"That's for you. She said it would be here in a few minutes."

"Oh."

His face registers surprise, shock; but, to Neleni's relief, no pleasure. He looks around him, agitated, as if seeking a means of escape. But the horn blares again. Three times.

"I'd better go."

He smiles apologetically and lightly touches her arm. Her heart soars. Her resolution is broken. She must tell him what she really feels. But he is gone. His jacket slung over one shoulder, he is running down the steps towards the large shiny car waiting at the kerb. Neleni can hear its engine throbbing from where she stands. She runs after him to the door, hoping that he will see her, waving discreetly.

The living-room has fallen silent. The tableau of guests is being re-arranged. By nature mistrustful and always alert to suspicious behaviour in others, Lakshmi feels a renewed interest in Neleni's lodger. First a mysterious telephone call, then the arrival of a car followed by a hurried departure. Something is going on.

Following whispered instructions from his mother-in-law, Michael strolls across the room, casual, hands in pockets, his expression a mixture of boredom and disdain. But, just as he reaches the window, he allows himself to become distracted. Picking up a small picture from the table, he pretends to admire it. It is a watercolour of a flower. Hand-painted.

"Not bad."

He holds it up for Lakshmi to see, knowing that this will annoy her. He is right. She is changing colour. Her cheeks are a deep pink and she is making a discreet gesture with her hand, so as not to be seen by Raj who is busy mixing drinks in a corner of the room.

"Go on," she mouths. "Hurry up!"

Swathed in her pink sari, she looks, for all the world, like an over-boiled lobster. Her small black eyes glitter fiercely and she mouths again: *Hurry up*!

Michael strolls past Dalia who is staring vacantly at the wall. Having finished the bird's portion of food on her plate, she rests her elbow on the arm of the sofa and, rubbing her fingers together, rids them of the remaining crumbs which fall onto the polished surface of the floor.

Michael regards her with distaste. Despite her beauty, she is vacuous and vain. They are not yet married and already he is bored with her. He turns towards the window. Even a view of the street is preferable to the sight of his bride and her overpowering mother.

But he is not prepared for what he sees. The shock is like a punch in the ribs, so painful that he winces.

"I know that car," he mutters.

Withdrawing his hands from his pockets, he leans against the window, his face pressed to the glass.

"What is it?"

Lakshmi edges forward on her seat.

"Nothing."

He withdraws from the window, hands thrust deep in his pockets, his face expressionless but unusually wan. His mother-in-law must not find out. But Lakshmi is on the scent, her suspicions aroused. Although Raj is present, she cannot contain her curiosity.

"Tell me. What did you see?"

Michael shrugs.

"Nothing. Just a big shiny car."

"What sort?"

"I don't know," he shrugs. "An expensive one. A Humber or a Jaguar, I think."

But his attempt at nonchalance fails to convince Lakshmi. She glowers at him from her armchair. He knows something and, sooner or later, she will have the truth. But Michael no longer cares. Turning his back to her, he gazes out of the window, along the street to where the chrome bumper of the car is disappearing around the corner. He remembers a time when that same car came to collect him.

There is a quiet click, imperceptible to all but Lakshmi. The front door has closed. Neleni appears, a plate of butter-cake in her hand. Lakshmi eyes her suspiciously. Why would anyone go to the door with a plate of cake in their hand? Neleni seems distracted. Her thoughts are, evidently, elsewhere. Perhaps she, too, has something to hide.

"Neleni, dear. You've been away from us for so long. Are you all right?" Lakshmi croons.

"Yes, yes. Quite …" She does not finish the sentence.

"You must be so busy. What with your lodger coming and going and the telephone ringing the whole time."

"Yes," says Raj, eager to show off to his cousin. "Who was that on the telephone, Neleni?"

"I don't know. It wasn't for us. It was a call for Arjun."

Lakshmi notes how Neleni uses his first name.

"For Arjun? Who?"

"I don't know. She didn't say."

Neleni is beginning to get irritable. She wishes Raj would change the subject; but, without meaning to, she has revealed a precious detail.

"She? You said she?"

"Yes. It was a woman."

"And she wouldn't give you her name?"

"I didn't ask."

"Oh ho!"

Raj taps the end of his nose with his finger and winks at Lakshmi.

"I think our lodger has a girlfriend. What do you think, cousin?"

"Almost certainly."

Lakshmi smiles a fat smile, contented and cruel, like a cat who has trapped a small bird under its paw. And, all the while, her eyes never leave Neleni's face. She is waiting, watching for any sign of change, the slightest quiver of emotion. But Neleni's face is as expressionless as a mask.

"Have some cake, Lakshmi? You must be hungry after your long journey."

Although she has been eating continuously for the last hour, Lakshmi fails to grasp the irony of this remark. Without acknowledging Neleni, she sweeps two slices of cake onto her tea-plate then, breaking off a large chunk, squashes it into her mouth.

"Did you know that our lodger is assistant to the Government Agent?"

There is a sharp intake of breath. Lakshmi begins to choke. She gasps and wheezes, her face turning purple. Raj rushes to her rescue, patting her on the back, holding her hand, mopping her powder-streaked brow. Lakshmi's husband has unfolded himself from his seat on the sofa and is standing behind her, paler than the paint on the walls, wringing his hands and emitting small moans of dismay.

As frantic efforts are made to revive Lakshmi, Neleni notices Michael, standing a little apart, smiling to himself. It is the first time that he has betrayed any hint of amusement. But it is a cruel smile; revenge for past torment. Lakshmi is spluttering into another glass of whisky, administered by Raj. Finally, after several large gulps, she is restored.

"That cake," she grumbles, "too dry."

"I'm sorry."

Neleni affects a contrition that she does not feel.

"Serve her right," she thinks and sees her thoughts mirrored in Michael's face.

***

The conversation turns to Dalia's wedding, her trousseau, her new house, her hair, her guests, her clothes. Michael, now sitting by the window, makes no attempt to participate in this conversation.

It has been an hour since Arjun's departure and Neleni has done her best to make herself invisible, running backwards and forwards to the kitchen to replenish tea-cups and plates and, when she can no longer find a reason to absent herself, seeking obscurity in a corner of the room.

By now, having consumed a substantial amount of whisky, Lakshmi has become strident in praise of her family.

"Of course, Dalia and Michael are having a new house built. From scratch. All mod cons."

Perched uncomfortably on the edge of the sofa, Dalia does her best to minimise contact with its tired covers. Despite frequent washing, age and use have given them an earthy odour. They smell of hardship. Trusting it is not infectious, she folds her hands delicately in her lap, her left hand uppermost so as to display her engagement ring.

As his mother-in-law continues to extol the wonders of the new house, Michael gazes around the sitting room, making a mental inventory of its contents. He seems particularly amused by the table whose battered surface is concealed by a heavy chenille cloth. There are hundreds of such tables in homes all over the country, each bearing a venerable aspidistra in a brass pot.

Neleni burns with shame. The room of which she is so proud suddenly seems tawdry and old-fashioned. She hates it for letting her down. She wishes Arjun were here to rescue her and wonders what called him away so urgently. As if echoing her thoughts, Raj dives into the conversation, like a cat charging a group of pigeons.

"I'll bet it's a woman."

"What?"

"Arjun. I'll bet he's got a girlfriend."

All thoughts of the new home, wedding and trousseau are scattered.

"Why do you say that?" Neleni's pale cheeks are unnaturally flushed.

"Why not? He's a handsome young fellow. Unattached. He's probably taken the fancy of some rich widow."

There is a sharp clang as Michael's tea-plate hits the floor. It spins for a few seconds then comes to rest, upside down. Michael stoops to pick it up then briskly dusts the crumbs from his trousers. Although she cannot see his face clearly, Neleni can tell that he is angry. His mood increases her own anxiety.

"Don't be so ridiculous, Raj," she snaps.

"Why ridiculous?" retorts Lakshmi, seizing an opportunity to irritate her cousin's wife.

"Because he has more sense."

"Who?" asks Lakshmi, archly.

But Neleni does not answer. Gathering up empty tea-plates, including the one discarded by Michael, she retreats into the kitchen where she dumps the crockery in the sink.

"Careful!" squawks her mother who has been feeding scraps of food to the cat. "What's the matter?"

"Nothing. I just need some air."

Neleni darts through the strings of coloured beads that form a curtain over the door, out into the yard which has been quietly baking in the sun. Freed from the inner gloom of the house, she is almost blinded by the intense light and has to shield her eyes with her hand. But both heat and light are welcome.

She takes deep breaths and, closing her eyes, lets the sun beat down on her face. At least out here she can escape the sense of suffocation that threatens to overwhelm her indoors. The fear that gripped her subsides. Rocking back on her heels, she folds her arms around her waist, hugging herself and listening to the faint sounds that float down the passage from the street.

***

In the living-room, Lakshmi quietly congratulates herself as she sips her drink. Now she is certain. There is definitely something going on between Neleni and her lodger. She knew it. She will discover their secret and, when she does, she will tell Raj. And then …

She pauses for a second. What if she finds no proof? Well, never mind, in that case she will just tell him of her suspicions. That should be enough. As she sinks back into the cushions, Lakshmi's red lips part in a smirk of satisfaction. Altogether, it has been a very successful visit.

The car creeps up to the front of the house and halts at the steps. Climbing out from the warm, leather-clad interior, Arjun stands alone on the drive, watching the great, gleaming vehicle as it rolls away, around the side of the house to the garage. He has never ridden in such a car before and is still tingling with childish excitement. As it glides past, he can feel his body vibrating with the motion of its engine and his lungs are filled with the intoxicating aroma of hot metal and oil. For the first time, he experiences the seductive power of wealth and, for one guilty second, he understands why Mennan acted as he did.

The car is gone. The house, looming over him at the top of the steps, looks empty. A house filled with ghosts: memories of money, parties and people; laughter, eating and drinking. But now it is silent. It is a silence so imposing that it can be heard: no birds sing in the branches; there is no servants' chatter, no clash of plates from the kitchen, no sound of men working in the garden.

In fact the grass, previously so neatly manicured, has begun to grow long in the shadow of the trees; its cool, green depths now shelter snakes. The fishponds are green and overgrown with weed and the nets that used to protect the pools' occupants lie discarded in a flower-bed. Many of the carp that gracefully swam around the shallows have disappeared, victims, no doubt, of a heron or egret.

Arjun remembers the day of the funeral, when the house was teeming with people. Now, it looks mournful and neglected. Weeds are sprouting from the gaps between the steps and, in places, the paving stones have come loose. A green stain has appeared in the white plaster below the roof where rainwater has leaked from a blocked gutter and, immediately below, the overflow has washed away the gravel on the path, leaving a small pit and exposing the rough cinder track beneath.

As he climbs the steps to the front door, Arjun feels as if he is being watched by a host of invisible eyes. Several times, he stops to look around him, but he can see no-one. With the exception of a dog barking in the distance, this district is remarkably quiet. Although the sky is perfectly clear, it feels as if a storm is brewing. The atmosphere is oppressive and the humidity so high that the air seems dense and heavy. Arjun's shirt is sticking to his back. As he nears the top of the steps, he has second thoughts. Even now, it is not too late to change his mind. He could catch a bus home, or hail a rickshaw. He is on the point of turning away when the door opens.

She has been waiting for him. She heard the car arrive and, opening the door a fraction, has spied on him through the chink, watching him drag his feet up the steps, then stop to take in the ruin of her home. She sees him hesitate and turn to leave. But she will not let him escape. She flings the door wide.

"So kind of you to come."

She walks out to meet him as he reaches the top step. Startled by her sudden appearance, he loses his footing and stumbles. She reaches out to steady him, her cool fingers brushing the back of his hand. He shudders, but it is a pleasant kind of fear, the sort experienced on fairground rides, hurtling through the air at unnatural speed, excitement heightened by the risk of disaster.

"Come in."

She does not wait for him to speak but turns, beckoning him to follow, a shawl tightly wrapped around her in spite of the heat.

He enters the hallway where he is confronted by the giant portrait of Mennan and his wife. The overseer smiles down at him, enjoying a secret joke, an ironic twinkle in his eye. *Soon you will know. Then you will understand.* The portrait does not move, but Arjun can hear Mennan's voice, whispering in his ear. Memories of that terrible day crowd back. The man's fear. His own lack of compassion. His sickness. Mennan's death. Reports of the terrible, swollen-faced corpse.

"Follow me."

Leela's voice breaks in on his thoughts like the tinkling of bells. Meekly, he obeys. The marble floors echo with the sound of their footsteps and the tapping of Leela's sandals has the pleasant effect of cool water dripping on stone. The horrific memories subside. He finds himself in a place as cool as an underground cavern: somewhere private, protected from the heat and screened from the sight of prying eyes. So unlike the office or his lodgings. A refuge.

Leading him into the sitting room, Leela guides him to a chair, plumping up the cushions and making him comfortable before sinking onto a couch where she reclines, her head resting on one hand, her scarf drifting from her arm like a diaphanous wing, as fragile as a butterfly resting on a flower.

She stares at him for a few seconds, and he notices that there are flecks of green in her honey-coloured eyes. He is in limbo, awaiting judgement. He remembers the day of the funeral, when she held his fate in her hands and his happiness or torment depended on her mercy. Has she forgiven him for his part in Mennan's death?

She tilts her head back and, closing her eyes, breathes deeply, so that he can see the swell of her breasts under her thin, silk blouse; then, breathing out slowly, she opens her eyes and gazes into his face. Her lips tremble as if she is about to speak but, instead, she leans forward and lifting up a bell from a small table by her couch, rings it three times.

Before the bell has stopped ringing, a servant in white pyjamas and a black waistcoat appears, as swiftly and silently as a genie from a bottle. He is one of the few to remain in her service.

"Something to drink? What would you like?"

Her voice has a slight coarseness that jars with her beauty.

"Whisky?"

Arjun is still in a reverie. She does not wait for his decision.

"Bring us a bottle with ice and two glasses."

The servant fetches a tray, opens a bottle, fills glasses with whisky and ice and, after serving his mistress and her guest, disappears with alacrity. All the time, Leela continues to watch Arjun without speaking.

"Chin, chin," she says, when the servant has gone. Over the rim of her glass, she watches as Arjun drinks.

Unlike Raj's harsh grog, the refined liquor trickles smoothly down Arjun's throat. Unnerved by the strangeness of this situation, he takes another sip, then another. Soon his glass is empty. Leela re-fills it herself, her fingers drifting over his hand as she passes it back to him. A tingle of electricity passes through him, but without pleasure this time. Perhaps the whisky has dulled his senses or, perhaps, it is the moment of clarity before drunkenness sets in. He thinks of Neleni with longing. He is not so drunk as to forget her.

"Have some more."

Leela scatters his thoughts, disarranging them like a child kicking a pile of leaves. She tries to re-fill his glass but he cups his hand over it. She pouts playfully and pours some whisky into her own glass. She takes a sip then, placing the glass down, reaches for a cigarette box. It is made of polished wood with a pewter plaque in the centre of the lid. There is no writing on the plaque which still awaits an inscription: a name or initials.

Leela opens the box and offers it to Arjun. When he refuses, she seems amused. She takes a cigarette and taps it on the lid of the box, casually looking around for a lighter. There is one on the table. Made of polished granite, it would look more at home in a gentlemen's club. Neither ornament nor useful artefact, it is too heavy to lift and Leela has to bend over it to light her cigarette. She straightens up, turns to face Arjun and, with the cigarette elegantly poised between her fingers, closes her eyes for a second as she savours the first draught.

"Of course, everything changed when my husband died."

Ghastly images are rekindled. Guilt is revived. Never far from the surface, it seeps back into his consciousness like a black stain.

"It's strange how quickly friends forget you," Leela continues. "Many have disappeared altogether. I think they're embarrassed."

"Embarrassed! Why?"

"Because they think I might ask them for money."

"But ..."

Arjun looks around him. The house is sumptuous. Leela does not appear to lack for anything. Then he remembers the view from the steps: the overgrown garden, the broken gutter, the neglected fishpond. She seems to read his thoughts.

"I can't afford to keep this place going. I've already dismissed half my servants."

"But didn't your husband provide for you?" Arjun is incredulous.

"He didn't expect to die."

There is sharpness and a note of accusation in Leela's tone that is intended for Arjun. It is clear that she holds him responsible, at least in part, for her predicament.

"Don't you have any money?"

"No. At least ... not enough. Soon, I'll be bankrupt."

Having exhaled a thin column of smoke, Leela is watching it drift towards the ceiling. She seems almost bored by her plight, too tired to fight any longer; a widow who must share the fate of her husband or face a life of penury and humiliation.

"She means to kill herself," whispers a voice in Arjun's ear. "Only you can save her."

"Surely something can be done?"

"Perhaps. Perhaps not. I'm not sure I care any longer."

She inhales, slowly. It is intriguing and slightly shocking. With the exception of Sunny, Arjun does not know any other woman who smokes. It is not approved of in traditional circles.

"I know nothing about my husband's business. He had a lot of interests, knew a lot of people. He left a lot of papers. They are a mystery to me. But perhaps they may contain something of use."

She exhales, her lips pouting as if she were blowing him a kiss then, closing her eyes, she stretches her head back, exposing her beautiful, long neck. Silence creates a tension between them, forcing him to speak.

"Perhaps I could take a look at your husband's papers. That is, if you don't mind."

Slowly raising her head to look at him, Leela smiles.

"Why, that would be very kind."

She feigns surprise but it is what she has been waiting for. He is trapped. He had not meant to make this offer. Indeed, if he had any idea at all, it was to persuade her to hand her husband's papers over to the authorities. But pity and guilt have created a force as ineluctable as gravity and, between them, have drawn the words out of him.

With one short breath, Leela expels the smoke from her lungs and disposes of the cigarette in a crystal ash-tray. Then, reaching her arms behind her head, she catches her hair with both hands, twists it in a skein, then shakes it loose; like a cat preening itself after a good meal. All the time her eyes are fixed on Arjun.

**

Swiftly, she rises from her chair. There must be no time for second thoughts.

"My husband's papers are in the study. Would you like to see them?"

She sounds as if she is doing him a favour. Perhaps she is. Perhaps it is a means of assuaging his guilt, freeing himself from an overburdened conscience. She is offering him a means of escape. He should be grateful. Obediently, Arjun follows her across the hallway, past Mennan's smiling portrait and up the stairs to a door that looks as if it opens into a cupboard. Leela produces a key, although he did not see her pick it up. She must have been carrying it with her. He wonders if she knew all along that he would offer to help. But it is too late for conjecture.

She turns the key and opens the door onto a small airless room, lit by a single lamp. There is no window, only a filing cabinet and a desk covered in sheaves of paper. There is no clock on the blank wall and it is impossible to tell whether it is night or day. The room is little bigger than a prison cell. Arjun imagines Mennan sitting in the leather swivel-chair, poring over his accounts, concealing his duplicity in columns of figures, sweating over the mounting pile of invoices.

Leela gestures towards the filing cabinet: its top stacked with files, its drawers crammed with paper. Then, she points to the desk, burdened with yellowing sheaves of paper shovelled together in untidy heaps.

"I don't know where to start. I don't understand any of this."

Her lip trembles and she brushes a hand over her eyes. Instinctively, Arjun puts out a hand to comfort her, touching her shoulder.

"Don't worry. I'm sure there's a solution."

She raises her eyes, now meek and submissive. Her future, if she has one, is in his hands. She is at his mercy.

"Call me if you need anything. I'll be close by."

Quietly, she leaves him to assault the mass of paperwork left by her unconscionable husband. Bills, both paid and unpaid, have been crammed into the same files. There seems to be little order to any of it and Arjun wonders how Mennan ever kept track of his affairs. In the last months, it is obvious that he did not even try. On the desk is a stack of unopened mail. Judging by the date stamps, Mennan did not open the post for several weeks before he died.

Arjun sifts through files and tears open envelopes, organising their contents into various piles; debtors in one; creditors in another; one for statements of account and another, the largest, for miscellaneous correspondence. However, when it comes to deciphering Mennan's book of accounts, he is defeated. They are almost certainly incomplete, and the figures shown are probably artificial, a foil for Mennan's real activities, intended to fool any authorities who inquired into his affairs.

Arjun notes that no entries were made for several months before the overseer's death. Towards the end, Mennan had abandoned any pretence of recording his dealings, either through complacency or because his fraud had become too blatant to conceal. The blank pages mark the point at which the fiction of Mennan's life began to unravel, becoming credible no longer, even to its author.

Closing the book, he places it on top of the miscellaneous pile. He has done his best but it amounts to little. He has grieved over Mennan's death and his own guilty part in it, but now, surrounded by the chaos of the man's misdealing, he is angry. How could Mennan have left his wife to deal with this? How could he have been so thoughtless? His whole existence was just an elaborate pretence, without basis or substance.

He must tell her that he has found nothing. There is no hope. He must break the awful news. Better sooner than later. Sighing, Arjun rubs his eyes then pushes his chair back, a little too violently. The sudden movement starts a landslide. Papers slither from the various piles into which they have been sorted. They slide over the desk, spill over the floor and softly shuffle together, re-arranging themselves into a fresh state of disorder.

Sighing, Arjun kneels on the floor and patiently begins to gather up the scattered documents. Then, a letter catches his eye. It is hand-written in the sloping scrawl which he now recognises as Mennan's hand. The text is interspersed with strings of numbers which look like bank accounts. On closer inspection, this assumption proves correct although there are no references to these particular accounts in any other correspondence. Providing the names and addresses of two banks in Switzerland, the letter gives instructions as to how the accounts are to be managed in the event of Mennan's imprisonment, illness or death.

However, the letter is not addressed to Leela, but to a Mr Michael Kandiah. Arjun thinks that he has heard the name before but, at present, he cannot remember where. Mr Kandiah, it seems, was nominated by Mennan to act on his behalf in connection with these accounts. However, the letter is unsigned and Arjun cannot make out whether it is simply a copy or the original itself. Has Mr Kandiah already received his instructions, or did Mennan change his mind before sending the letter?

The question is: what should Arjun do with it? Its value to Leela may be limited but it would certainly advance the official investigations into Mennan's affairs. In official circles, it is believed that, despite his heavy spending, Mennan retained a large proportion of the money which he had fraudulently obtained. This letter could be the clue to its whereabouts.

"What is that?"

Leela has silently entered the room, catching Arjun unawares. There is no opportunity to hide the letter, or even to lie about its contents for, with her usual, keen instinct, Leela senses its relevance to herself. She snatches it from Arjun's hand. As she reads it, she becomes increasingly agitated, pacing the room and murmuring to herself although Arjun cannot hear what she says. Having finished, she turns on him, her mouth rigid with fury.

"Where did you find this?"

She approaches, brandishing the letter. For a moment, Arjun thinks she might hit him. He points guiltily at the desk.

"Here. In this pile of letters."

"And there was nothing for me? No copy? No other letter?"

"No. Not that I could see. Of course, I might have missed something."

"Bastard! Bastard!"

Crumpling the letter in her hand, she runs from the study. A door slams. She has shut herself in her room, but he can hear the sound of her weeping through the walls. It is an eerie sound in this echoing, deserted house. At the bottom of the stairs, Mennan's portrait smiles serenely.

1956: The legacy

Leela has flung herself on the bed where she lies with her face buried in the pillow, trying to stifle her screams, almost mad with fury. Her husband has connived with her lover to deny her access to the money which she so desperately needs. In order to escape poverty, she must bind herself to a man that she no longer loves. She had already begun to tire of him before her husband's death and had been on the point of ending their affair when Mennan died. But this letter changes everything.

"Damn you, Mennan. Damn you!" she weeps.

She used to despise her husband for his pathetic devotion, but since his death, she has begun to hate him, principally, for his failure to provide for her. Now, it seems, there may be another option, but one almost as inimical as destitution. Solvency can only be achieved at the price of her freedom. She sobs hysterically, beating the pillow with her fists.

Now she curses Mennan, for providing her with the means to live. The letter reveals how he has conspired with her lover, giving him access to hidden accounts of which she, his wife, has been kept ignorant. It is spite. It must be. Despite all her careful concealment, Mennan must have discovered her affair. Now he has taken his revenge.

She cries and sobs until she is exhausted. Then, propping herself up on the pillow, she wipes her tear-stained face and smoothes out the letter on the bedspread. It is wrinkled and soft from where she clutched it in her hand. She has half a mind to tear it up but, always pragmatic, she decides to read it once more. Gloomily, she scans each line until she reaches a postscript on the back page; something which she missed in her first reading. It is a note from her husband to her lover.

I ask this of you because you have been a good friend to my wife and me. Also, I know that you are discreet and have a good head for business. If anything should happen to me, I do not want my wife to have the added worry of dealing with matters which she does not understand, nor of becoming implicated in issues which may involve the authorities. That is why I am asking you, dear friend, to accept responsibility for these matters and look after her.

"Ha!"

Leela begins to laugh. She cannot help it. What irony! She clamps first one hand, then the other to her mouth, trying to smother the giggles that follow, one after the other, in quick succession. She is shaking with mirth. No. She is trembling. It is too much. She is laughing and crying at the same time. So Mennan never knew of her love affair. For some reason which she cannot quite explain, she is relieved.

* * *

Arjun sits motionless at the desk, listening to the sound of Leela's cries. If he had known her a little better, he would have followed and tried to comfort her. But he is a stranger. He cannot intrude. So he waits, staring blankly at the papers ranged in front of him. But he does not touch them. Coming here was a mistake. He has unearthed secrets that should have lain hidden. Not only has the suffering of Mennan's widow been increased, but his own position has been compromised beyond repair. Knowledge, once gained, cannot be recalled, nor can it be unlearned or forgotten. It can only be concealed; the effect on its bearer becoming more corrosive as time passes. He must tell Nash.

The sobbing subsides, followed by silence.

Arjun loathes himself. Everything he does, every well-intentioned act, increases the suffering of others. He wants to leave, immediately, forget he was ever here, but courtesy prevents him from acting on impulse. He cannot go without saying goodbye. So he waits, his head bowed, his hands in his lap, reduced to helpless inactivity by his own guilt.

Time passes in that windowless room without being measured. There is no ticking clock to mark the minutes or hours, no way of knowing whether it is night or morning. He breathes the same air that he breathed minutes or hours ago and the atmosphere thickens. Starved of oxygen, he becomes sleepy.

Mennan has stepped out of the portrait and is slowly climbing the stairs. He is bringing a message. The heels of his custom-made, leather shoes click on the marble steps. He is coming closer. Arjun tries to run, but he cannot move. He is paralysed, bound by invisible threads to the chair. His breath comes in great, lurching gasps, but he cannot call for help. He must wait. Mennan's hand is on the door. It creaks open.

But is it not Mennan from the portrait that stands there, but his corpse with its leering face and soiled clothes. The lips are working, trying to form words, but the mouth, blocked by the blackened, swollen tongue, cannot speak. Only the eyes convey a message. Sad and accusing, they are fixed on Arjun, drawing him into their depths. He cannot look away. Mennan approaches and, reaching out a hand, touches Arjun's sleeve.

"Oh god!"

His head jerks back. He is awake. Staring wildly ahead of him. Into Leela's face.

"I have such dreams, too."

It is a lucky guess.

"Do you?"

"Yes. All the time."

She is stroking his hand. For comfort.

"Oh."

He is looking at her with the same pleading vulnerability that she saw in court and, later, at Mennan's wake. He is seeking absolution. From her. She has him.

***

Taking him by the hand, she leads him gently back downstairs and feels him shudder as he passes the portrait of Mennan. Guilt is a powerful toxin; one that she has used to great effect in the past.

"You are tired. You must eat."

He does not answer, nor resist, but lets her lead him to the dining-room where two places have already been set. The servant brings an assortment of small delicacies: egg hoppers, sini sambal and devilled beef, dishes calculated to tempt even the most jaded appetite. But Arjun pushes the food around his plate without eating.

"What is it?"

"That letter. I will have to tell the Agent."

"What?"

For a second, her fury returns. He can see it, boiling up within her. But, then, she looks away, lowers her head. He cannot see what she is thinking. When she raises her eyes, they are filled with tears.

"If you do that, you will ruin me."

"But ... how? The letter does not mention you."

"Yes, it does."

She takes a gamble. Perhaps he did not read the postscript on the back of the letter.

"There is a note on the back of the letter. It names me. Anyone reading it will assume that I knew everything, that I was involved. I knew nothing of Mennan's intentions. I promise you."

Reaching across the table, she grasps his wrist. That look of desperation undoes him, convinces him that she is telling the truth. Still, he hesitates.

"And there is something else…"

She looks at him slantwise, from the corner of her eye.

"The Agent will want to know how you found that letter. How will you explain that?"

He sighs, running his fingers through his hair. He had not thought of that.

"I'm sure there is nothing to worry about," she reassures him. "That letter was never sent. It is just a draft. The man that it was addressed to has said nothing to me. It is obvious that he knows nothing of it. I don't believe those bank accounts even exist. Even if they do, the money is almost certainly gone. Otherwise Mennan would have used it to pay off his debts. He must have spent it all before he died. That's why he never sent the letter."

She persists, wearing him down with her logic. And, as she does so, she pours wine into his glass, encouraging him to drink. The rich, dark wine laps over his tongue, reminding him of things he had forgotten: spices and fruit cake; warm happy days; the comfort of friends. As he relaxes, his fears evaporate. If he only does what she says, everything will be all right.

Leela is an attentive hostess, allowing neither Arjun's plate nor glass to empty. It is impossible to keep track of how much he has drunk. He is quite sure that he has had only a couple of glasses, but already she is opening a second bottle.

"Please, no more."

"Don't be silly!"

There is no arguing with her. He accepts more wine while resolving not to drink it and yet, when he looks again, his glass is empty. She quizzes him politely about his family, his upbringing, his work and his aspirations. Soon, she knows everything about him, while revealing nothing of herself. It feels more like a confession than a conversation. She is understanding and thoughtful but there is one thing he does not tell her: his feelings for Neleni.

Neleni! He must get home. By now, Leela has sunk into a reverie, her eyes fixed on an invisible point in the air. Surreptitiously, Arjun looks at his watch. But she sees him. He is planning his escape. She waits, observing him with a kind of nocturnal watchfulness; a hunter stalking its prey.

"What time is it?" she asks, innocently.

"Ten thirty. I should be going home."

"Of course," she tries to hide her disappointment. "I'll fetch the driver."

She disappears, walking to the servants' passage at the end of the hall where she waits, just out of sight, around the corner. She must make her story convincing. It would not do to reappear too soon. After a few minutes, she walks slowly back to the dining-room, practising a face of contrition. Arjun looks at her hopefully. His eagerness to be gone is irksome. It gives her pleasure to disappoint him.

"I'm very sorry. I cannot find the driver. The servants do as they please these days. I expect the lazy fellow has gone home."

"Then I must find a taxi."

"There are none in this area. I would drive you myself, but I don't know how."

"Oh."

She waits, watching his panic rise like mercury in a glass, before she offers a suggestion.

"I have a guest room. You are very welcome to stay."

"No, really. That's very kind, but I couldn't. Perhaps your driver will return?"

"Perhaps."

She sounds uncertain, unwilling to commit herself. There is no alternative. He must wait. Meekly, Arjun allows himself to be led into the sitting-room where Leela pours him a large glass of whisky.

***

He checks his watch for the fifth time. It is nearly midnight. There is still no sign of the driver, although Leela has obligingly gone to look for him. Impatiently, Arjun paces the room, sipping his whisky. The molten heat courses through his body then rises to his brain, like fume in an alembic. He is not used to alcohol, or the darkness it brings.

Alone with his thoughts, he broods on the guilt that this trip has awoken. It has been an unpleasant reminder of the part he has played in ruining two lives. By coming here, he had hoped to make amends but he has only made matters worse. He imagines Mennan, swinging at the end of a rope, his tongue blackened and his eyes protruding. And here he is, drinking the man's whisky.

***

Although the windows are open, the heat of the day has not dispersed. The air hangs heavy and still. A storm is brewing. Leela has returned. Without the driver. She encourages Arjun to sit in a chair with soft cushions. No point in being uncomfortable. She refills his glass and, under her watchful eye, he drains it. He tries to stay awake but, he is drowsy from alcohol and the lateness of the hour. His eyelids shut as tight as clams and he is soon asleep. He awakes with a start. Leela is standing in front of him.

"The driver will not return now. You must stay here. You can go home in the morning."

He looks at his watch. 1.30 a.m. Any doubts about the propriety of his situation are overridden by his need for sleep.

Leela leads him to a pale green room with an inviting bed, informing him quietly that her own room is across the corridor. It is not an invitation, just a detail, a small dose of comfort for one who may wake alone in a strange bed. She yawns, delicately. She says she is tired and must go to bed although, after she has left his room, her shadow hovers in the strip of light at the bottom of the door. Too weary to notice, Arjun sheds his clothes and climbs naked into bed, gratefully surrendering to sleep.

***

Two hours later, the storm breaks. The air quivers, rocked by thunder. Flares of lightning probe the sky. Arjun drifts towards wakefulness, his senses quickened by the storm. A vivid flash illuminates the room and he sees Neleni standing in the doorway, a silhouette surrounded by a halo of white light. Slowly, she approaches the bed and bends to kiss him, murmuring his name in a voice that he does not recognise. It is a dream in which familiar attributes are stolen from their owners and matched together in an incongruous coupling.

Her soft hands run lightly over his body, rousing it to pleasure. The bed yields under her weight and he can feel her body, imprinted on his skin as she covers him in kisses, moving down, until her mouth envelopes his aching member and he is consumed with longing.

Now, she is on him, straddling his body, initiating him into the mystery of her sex, forcing him into the moist cleft between her legs where he grows large within her. The darkness is so complete that he senses, rather than sees, the violent thrust of her breasts, feels their rhythmic lapping as she works him.

Lightning shoots across the sky, piercing the window and, with dream-filled eyes, he sees the face, not of Neleni, but Leela. Impaled on his body, she rides him, howling like a demon as her nails dig into his flesh. He raises a hand to dispel the succubus but instead, explodes inside it with such force that the very essence of his being seems to flow from him.

With an exultant shriek, she throws back her head then drops, spent, to his side. For a while, they lie as still as corpses, wrapped in shadow, neither speaking nor acknowledging the other. Then, without a word, she rises and leaves him. He hears the soft click of the door as it shuts behind her.

Her perfume lingers to remind him that he has not been dreaming: a feral scent of musk, not the sweet jasmine of Neleni. He can smell it on his skin like the trace of a wild animal. He wants to wash, scrub his body until it bleeds, but he remains inert; drained of volition, paralysed by conscience.

Night enfolds him with the dense blackness of a cave in which the only movement is the solitary beating of his heart. Otherwise, he is dead: betrayed by the body that has acted against his will. Only instinct remains: dread of the morning and the shame that light will bring.

***

The thin muslin curtains are flung about by the wind. Somewhere, a door is banging. One of the French windows has flown open. Rain is lashing against the house and, tomorrow, the marble floors will be drenched with water. Lightning crackles across the sky, filling the room with livid colour.

Alone in bed, Leela smiles to herself. She got Arjun by trickery, although she feels no remorse. Guilt is not an emotion that troubles her, although she is seasoned in applying it to others. Arjun will grow to love her. Eventually. She is sure of it.

As for her old lover, she must be clever. Like her, he enjoys deceit for its own sake. She used to tease him about it. It was his game, telling audacious lies to friends, including Mennan, just to see if he would be discovered. He never was. She had laughed then. But now she wonders if he also lied to her. Does he know about Mennan's letter? Has he already helped himself to the money? She must find out. Betrayal is something she will not forgive.

***

A face peers in at the window, watching Leela as she sleeps.

"Well done, my sister."

Pressing her fingers to her lips, Yaani blows Leela a kiss. In the form of a small, glittering cloud, the kiss floats through the open window and comes to rest over Leela's head where it shimmers like a nimbus before bursting in a shower of silvery sparks.

"Very clever!"

Yaani, who is standing on tiptoe, spins around, the jewels in her headdress flashing as another streak of lightning illuminates the sky. A man in silver armour is standing behind her. His arms are crossed over his gleaming breast-plate and he is scowling, his face as thunderous as the elements battling overhead.

"Kasyapa! What are you doing here?"

"You must think I'm stupid."

Yaani shrugs insolently. Of course she does. But how did he discover her plan?

"I suppose the Queen Mother's been blabbing again?"

"It doesn't matter who told me. I'm ordering you to stop."

"Too late!"

Yaani raises her chin defiantly, her eyes flashing.

"I'm telling you, Yaani. Put a stop to this. Now!"

"I can't. I told you. It's too late. Your little favourite has been pushed aside by mine. Hardly surprising, really. Mine is a copy of me. No-one can resist her."

"She used trickery. He didn't have a chance to resist."

"Mmm." Yaani inspects her nails, a faint smile parting her lips.

"You've gone too far this time. I'm tempted to give you a good beating."

"Ha!" Yaani laughs and sways her hips, but she is afraid. Kasyapa might be a memory, an insubstantial wraith, but he still has the power to hurt her. And he knows it.

"Come here!"

"No!"

Yaani shrieks as the king grabs her arm and drags her away from the earth, up into the rain-split air and into a storm-cloud where her screams are drowned by rolling cracks of thunder.

1956: A preacher

The mynah bird pauses. Cocking its head on one side, it eyes the strangers walking along the path, hoping that they may throw it a few crumbs like its friends, the village children. But as the men approach, the bird decides that caution is the better strategy. With a few listless flaps, it flies up into the trees to continue its vigil from a low branch. The men are within a few feet of it. The bird squawks. It sounds like *hello*, a word that the village children have been trying to teach it for months. One of the men stops, looks up, then stooping, picks up a stone and flings it at the bird. With an angry cluck, the mynah flutters to a higher perch, out of reach.

"Why did you do that, brother?" asks the man's companion who, despite his height and rangy limbs, is little more than a boy.

The man who threw the stone just laughs: a sound without humour.

"Why not?"

The boy looks perplexed. Words are forming on his lips. He wants to say something, but thinks better of it. One glance from his companion is enough to silence him.

From its hiding place in the tree, the bird watches as the two men enter the village and knock at the headman's door.

***

The two monks are seated on rush mats in the shade of a Bo tree. Centuries ago, Buddha would have chosen such a place for meditation. However, these monks do not seek enlightenment. They have a different message.

The headman has summoned his people to the square of beaten earth in front of the Bo tree where all village matters are discussed. The villagers drift in from all directions: women from their vegetable plots carrying hoes; others from home balancing babies on their hips; men returning from the fields with scythes and spades: old people, young people, some beautiful like the headman's daughter, some plain, some with lop-sided faces distorted by disease and untreated ailments. They are a motley, ill-assorted group, ignorant, badly-educated and mostly unprepossessing.

"What did he see in them?" muses the older monk.

He wonders why the late Prime Minister, D.S. Senanayake, felt such an affinity for these ignorant country folk, placing them at the forefront of his plans for regeneration of the country. They were the ones who would help Ceylon to become self-sufficient. They would colonise the uninhabited dry zone, make it fertile and, by their efforts, wean the country off its dependency on foreign food imports.

Of course, his plans failed. But Mr. Senanayake had been right about one thing. The peasantry is a great untapped resource. The trick is knowing how to use it. Now another great man has appeared: a spiritual leader who is also a politician. This holy man is also a businessman, a monk with a head for figures. He understands the power of numbers and having realised the potential of the rural masses, he intends to exploit it.

Buddharakkita Thera, abbot of Kelaniya, has urged thousands of Buddhist monks to travel out into the countryside on a preaching mission. Their aim? To galvanize support for Mr Bandaranaike, the opposition leader who is heading a coalition of political parties in the forthcoming elections.

"I'd be surprised if any of these fools can even write his name," thinks the monk in disgust.

Then, unbidden, comes an answering thought: "They don't need to write. Just put their cross in the right place on the ballot paper. Sometimes ignorance is an advantage. Stops them asking silly questions. Thought is not something you want to encourage in your followers. Just blind faith."

It is the voice of Hooniyam. The monk offers a prayer of gratitude. He hears the god's voice regularly these days. Sometimes, they even converse. And today, Hooniyam has blessed his mission.

Gathering his robe about him, Anil prepares to address the crowd.

1956: The pursuit

Asoka has lost track of time. He has wandered for miles, through forest and coconut groves, along forgotten paths, hiding if he hears people. Crouched behind a tree or in a hollow, he hears snatches of conversation, but he is now so unaccustomed to the sound of human voices that they sound strange and foreign. He lives in a twilight world, fearful of being seen.

Occasionally, he creeps into villages at dusk, hopeful of finding a little food, usually the scraps thrown out for animals. Eggs are a rare luxury. He eats them raw, cracking them into his mouth and letting the yolk slide down his throat. His mouth is often parched but he can only visit the wells at night and, even then, he has to avoid the keen eyes of the village dogs. There is always one that greets his approach with a low growl and he has to be quick, scooping up food or water, before the barking of a single dog turns into a crescendo of howls.

Sometimes, he does not eat for days and, as he gets weaker, so it becomes more difficult to forage. Constantly faint and dizzy, he often wakes up on the ground, realising that he has blacked out, but not knowing for how long. Yet none of this is what frightens him – oblivion and anonymity are welcome – it is the growing certainty that he is being watched.

From the corner of his eye, he sees a shape, human in outline although it is not a man. It wears a belt of writhing snakes but, unlike the statue in Hooniyam's shrine, it is not gaudy or comical, but sinister, moving swiftly and silently through the shadows like dark vapour. Initially, Asoka tried to confront his pursuer. He would turn swiftly and without warning, but every time he did so, it disappeared. Eventually, he gave up. He is being hunted. All he can do is run.

***

Seated in a tree, Hooniyam is looking down at where Asoka is lying on the ground, asleep. Tearing a handful of leaves from a branch, the demon god drops them so that they patter down on Asoka's face. He wakes with a start, looking around him, expecting to see someone. What a fool! One cannot see what one does not believe in unless a god appears of his own volition. And, just now, Hooniyam is taking a break.

Asoka is up on his feet, running this way and that, his eyes starting from his head like those of a madman. Cupping his hands around his mouth, Hooniyam grunts and snorts. A herd of wild pigs on the rampage. Asoka has heard these sounds before. They pursue him through the forest. Each time, they get closer. He must move on. Without looking for a path, he charges blindly through the undergrowth. He neither knows where he is, nor where he is going.

In a few minutes, Hooniyam will follow him. He has been following Asoka for days, hovering on the perimeter of his vision, appearing as a shadowy figure, a man defined in smoke. It is working. Asoka is already half-mad. Soon, he will lose his wits completely. Only a miracle can save him now.

***

Hooniyam leans back on his branch, shaded by the canopy of leaves. An unsuspecting parrot lands next to him. He swipes it with one hand and stuffs it, protesting, into his mouth. Wiping the green feathers from his lips, he belches and smiles. He is content. At last, his plan is taking shape. Soon, he will get his own back for the centuries of neglect in which the gods abandoned him. He will pay them out in good measure. Then, the demons will have their day and reclaim what is rightfully theirs.

But, first, there is another score to settle. With Asoka. Hooniyam has not forgotten the insult in his own shrine, nor the stone thrown by Asoka which hit him on the forehead. He still bears the scar. Such wounds can only be inflicted by unbelievers. It is an outrage, an offence to a god's dignity. And, having ascended to dizzy heights of popularity, Hooniyam is increasingly concerned about his appearance.

Like his political protégé Mr Bandaranaike, who has discarded western dress in favour of a traditional tunic and sarong, Hooniyam must pay proper attention to his image in order to gratify his audience. He has even begun to comb his hair, or at least to backcomb it, so that its wild appearance is more sculpted. For, unlike other gods, Hooniyam tries to keep abreast of popular culture.

There is a fashion, it seems, for bad boys. Although that is not what they are called. The new name is anti-hero. Hooniyam likes it. It sounds, well, more heroic. In this extraordinary age of the atom bomb, it is actually good to be bad. It is a fashion that appeals to Hooniyam who is an aficionado of anti-heroes: James Dean, Marlon Brando and his favourite, Elvis Presley.

The singer's face is everywhere: on posters, in magazines, on television. Hooniyam has even spotted a picture postcard of Elvis sticking out of a worshipper's back pocket. He should be jealous, but he is not. Even gods need their idols and, while the Brylcreemed quiff is not in keeping with Hooniyam's style, he has taken a lesson from the rising star of rock'n'roll. To become a truly successful icon, you must present yourself accordingly. Appearance, these days, is everything.

The god belches again. A cobra that was sleeping in the crook of his arm opens one eye disapprovingly.

"I never do it in public," Hooniyam excuses himself.

But another large belch is on the way. This time he coughs up claws and a beak.

"Ugh! Must have been an old one!"

Wakened from their afternoon nap, the serpents begin to hiss and whisper amongst themselves. Writhing and wriggling, they coil and uncoil, twisting themselves around the god's limbs until they pinch him.

"Ow! Stop that!"

But the snakes squeeze tighter.

"Oh, all right. I suppose we'd better be going. He can't be too far away."

With his hands above his head, Hooniyam soars upwards, through the canopy of leaves, hovering over the forest until he catches sight of Asoka.

"There he is. What form should I take this time?"

Elvis's voice rings in his ears:

"*…you ain't nothin' but a …*"

Hooniyam turns a somersault, for sheer pleasure, then dives down through the trees, baying like a pack of hounds.

1956: A discovery

Bang!

The forest reverberates with the sound of explosions and the night sky is aflame. Asoka wakes with a start. Something is happening. Heart beating fast, he pushes himself up into a sitting position. But even the slightest exertion makes him pant. He tries to stand. He barely has the energy, but he manages it somehow, clinging onto a tree, pulling himself up slowly. Once upright, he can see a little better and his dulled brain begins to clear.

Bang! Bang! Bang!

Firecrackers. They are often used to scare elephants away from crops. He must be near to a village. Perhaps it is the same one from which he stole food a few days ago. Perhaps a different one. It makes little difference. Wherever he goes, he will not be welcome. Yet, even so, he is curious to see what is happening, drawn towards the light like a pye-dog to a fire.

He takes a few steps, then staggers forward, his heart pounding erratically. He knows he is being followed, but he no longer has the strength to run. Soon it will catch him, the dark shape that has hunted him for days. He has seen it many times from the corner of his eye. Lingering at the margin of his vision, it watches him from the trees, wild-maned and bloody-tusked, the image of a man, yet not human, closing in, getting closer, waiting. For what? At first, he did not dare to imagine, but now, he no longer cares.

The fizzes and cracks grow louder. He is getting close. A rocket whooshes into the air, then explodes in a shower of stars. This is no exercise to scare elephants. It is a celebration. Can it be New Year already? He does not think so, although he lost track of time long ago. What then? He takes a few more steps then his legs buckle beneath him. He falls to the ground like a discarded sack, the thundering of his heart resounding in his ears, the world around him faint and blurred.

Crack!

Not a firework this time, but the snapping of a twig. Asoka strains to see through the mist that veils his eyes, his mind racing with images of demons, murderous, mad-eyed, baying for blood as they leap up and down in a dance of death. Then he sees it. A shape emerging from the trees, approaching him sideways, stepping one foot over the other, a great knife in its outstretched hand. It has come for him.

***

Cautious as a cat, the figure inches towards him then stops a few feet away. Petrified, his body numb, Asoka can only wait. The creature approaches, a few steps at a time, then leans over, a dark shape in the gloom.

"So you're the one who has been stealing my eggs."

The voice is surprisingly human.

"Starving," it muses. "When did you last eat?"

Asoka realises that this is not a demon, but a man, and tries to mumble a reply. But the words coagulate. He groans, feebly.

"You'd better come with me."

A lean arm is hooked under his shoulders and he is hauled to his feet. After a few, staggering steps, he finds that he can walk if the other man supports him although their progress is slow. Asoka frequently has to stop for breath and he often trips, either due to some unseen obstacle or sheer weakness.

Another battery of fireworks explodes overhead. The air is filled with thick smoke and the acrid smell of gunpowder. Disoriented, Asoka halts, afraid to go on.

"It's all right," says the other man. "They're celebrating. Bandaranaike has won the election."

Bandaranaike. The name sounds familiar although Asoka cannot remember the face; even less, the man or his politics. It was all so long ago. The significance of the election is lost on him. They walk on in silence.

After a few minutes, they reach a clearing with a cluster of low, wooden huts, each with a small cultivated area at the back. At a slight distance from the others, set in a yard, is a larger building, its window lit by the dim glow of an oil lamp. Figures are moving about inside; silhouetted against a square of light, like shadow puppets.

Although he has few memories of childhood before the monastery, the sight of those figures reminds Asoka of his grandfather: the old man, twisting his fingers in front of a lantern, projecting shadows onto a wall; parrots, rabbits, monsters; all for the entertainment of the small boy who sat on his knee, sipping tea from a saucer.

Somehow, the sight of those shapes, dancing across the lighted window eases Asoka's fear. It is as if he is coming home.

***

A volley of rockets explodes over the water. Showers of sparks twinkle overhead and are reflected in the oily stillness of the paddy field. Running up and down the banks, young men are setting off more rockets. They yell, half with fear, half with delight, as the fireworks whoosh from their hands, leaving their palms tingling from the friction and heat.

As they caper about, one detaches himself from the rest and, climbing to the highest point of the bank, peers into the gloom. He thought he saw something. He waits for the next round of fireworks to light up the sky. Yes, there it is again. A strange misshapen shadow with multiple arms and legs has emerged from the forest. The boy's heart beats fast. The creature is skirting the far side of the paddy field, making for the path that leads back through the trees to the village.

Without a word to his companions, the boy leaps down the bank and runs towards the trees. The other boys shout after him.

"Hey, Tissa, where are you going?"

He does not reply and they begin to jeer.

"Gone to find that girl of yours? Going to propose? Better hurry up or someone will beat you to it."

Their hilarity is increased with the help of a large bottle of toddy that is passed from hand to hand. Soon, their friend is forgotten as the boys turn their attention to the serious task of lighting fireworks.

***

Tissa runs fast, unafraid of tripping in the dark. He has lived all his life in the village and knows every termite heap, tuft of grass and rabbit hole, every path, track and shortcut. He is sure that he can head the creature off or, at least, reach the village at the same time. He is unsure what he will do when he gets there but at least he can protect Sriya. Instinct warns him that the creature has come for her.

Driven by fear, he races over the open ground and through the trees, careless of the branches that scratch his legs and arms. He is close now, the path is just ahead. He scrambles down a bank onto the open track which is rutted with cart wheels and covered with sharp stones. For a few seconds, he pauses, getting his breath, looking back along the path to the forest, but he sees nothing. He has miscalculated. The creature must have reached the village already.

He is close. He can see the lights of the houses. He dashes along the track and enters the clearing dominated by a Bo tree under which two monks recently came to preach about the elections. He looks wildly about him, but can see nothing. Never mind. He will go to Sriya, make sure that she is safe.

The headman's house is at the other end of the village and, within seconds, Tissa is hammering on the door. It is opened by a lean, elderly man.

"What is it, my son?"

The man looks tired, unusually so for someone of his undoubted energy.

"Prema, I have seen a creature. It had legs and arms, many of them. It came from the forest and was heading towards the village. I followed but it disappeared. I was afraid for Sriya. For everyone."

He corrects himself. Too late. The other man smiles, amused. There is a knowing look in his eye.

"Have you been drinking, Tissa?"

"No, well, only a little."

"Go home, boy, and sleep it off."

"Can I see Sriya?"

"No, my son. She has gone to bed. You can see her tomorrow. Goodnight."

Politely, but firmly, the man shuts the door, leaving Tissa alone on the step. Feeling dejected, he turns to leave, then hears a voice. It is her. The house is built on a mound of earth and the windows are too high for him to see through, but he can hear her talking, somewhere at the back of the house. Pressing himself against the wooden walls, he strains to listen at the open window.

Sriya and her father are talking, but not to each other, nor to Sriya's mother, he would recognise her voice. Tissa cannot hear what they say, but Prema appears to be questioning someone and Sriya to be gently cajoling. Occasionally, but not always, there is a reply. Monosyllabic. A man's voice.

Angrily, Tissa makes his way home. Prema has lied to him. Why? He will see Sriya tomorrow and get the truth out of her.

1956: A taste of oranges

Mr Bandaranaike is sitting in his study, taking a break from the celebrations. The coalition that he founded has won the election with a landslide victory, ejecting the United National Party that had clung onto power for nearly a decade. *Prime Minister Bandaranaike.* He repeats the words to himself, savouring them. He has dreamed of this moment but, now that it is here, he can hardly believe it.

He has not failed the expectations of his family, nor the jubilant colleagues who have nicknamed him Lokka, the Boss. So much for all the doubting Thomases who said that he could not hold a candle to his father. Even his father would be proud of him now.

A powerful man, both in stature and status, the Prime Minister's father, Sir Solomon Dias Bandaranaike, had been knighted for his service to the Empire by King George, having acted as Maha Mudaliyar, or chief interpreter and adviser, to one of the Island's provincial governors. He was a legend in his lifetime and a man to whom grand gestures were second nature. Stories of his generosity are still recounted with affection long after his death.

Only the other day, a neighbour told Mr Bandaranaike how once she had been standing at her garden gate when she saw his father out riding. Sir Solomon had stopped and asked after her family. She had told him that one of her children was sick. Nothing much, just a fever. Sir Solomon had listened sympathetically then ridden off, returning half an hour later with a large bag of sweet Moroccan oranges, a rare delicacy in a country where the native variety is green and sour.

"A knight in shining armour," the neighbour had quipped.

But Mr Bandaranaike could tell that she meant it. He grew up in the shadow of that shining knight. A skinny, myopic child who preferred books to sport, he could always sense his father's disappointment in him. It was not something ever expressed in words but he felt it, nevertheless, weighing down on him like a great burden.

His dissimilarity to his father even gave rise to jokes that he was a changeling child, a cuckoo in the nest. One story, in particular, riles him. Some say that when his mother was pregnant, an astrologer had predicted that when her child was born, its father would die. It is rumoured that, a few days after Mr Bandaranaike's birth, one of the gardeners dropped dead.

All his life, he has been tormented by others' perception of him, by comparisons with his father. He has been belittled, ridiculed and dismissed as the runt of the litter. Now, all those who used to make fun of him will be made to eat their words. Now they will taste bitterness, the sort one gets from biting into a Ceylonese orange.

***

A shivering breeze approaches. Hooniyam is stalking the streets of the city. The celebrations of his protégé's election victory have put him in a bad humour. Earlier this evening, he peered through the window of Mr Bandaranaike's study and saw the Prime Minister sitting at his desk, a satisfied smile on his face. However, although the Prime Minister was staring out of the window, at exactly the spot where Hooniyam was standing, he had looked right through him.

"The true sign of an unbeliever," mutters Hooniyam to himself. "Otherwise he would have seen me."

There is nothing so belittling, especially for a god, as simply not being seen. Being rejected or ignored are different matters. For, insulting as these may be to the divine ego, they spring from an initial acknowledgement of one's existence. But invisibility. Now that's a different matter.

"I should have looked into his background more closely," grumbles Hooniyam.

For, since pledging to help the Prime Minister, he has discovered that Mr Bandaranaike was brought up as a Christian, only converting to Buddhism in adulthood. In fact, Hooniyam suspects that the radical change in Mr Bandaranaike's religious beliefs may have been dictated by political ambition.

"It's all for show," he growls. "All done to impress the voters. Not that I care. After all, I'm a god. Why should I?"

But, although he would never admit it, Hooniyam is stung. His divine dignity has been affronted by the politician's ability to forget him now that he has got what he wants.

"He'd better watch out," warns Hooniyam, shaking a finger at the empty air. "You can't just turn your back on your friends like that."

But there is no-one to hear him. They are all out celebrating. Even the gods that decorate the roofs of the Hindu temple are swaying in time to music from the streets below. It seems that the whole island is overjoyed at Mr Bandaranaike's victory. All except Hooniyam.

"Hmph! Another bloody firecracker."

The god aims a bad-tempered kick at a stray firework, sending it skittering down a dark alley where it hits a dustbin, raising a commotion of yowls from a group of plundering cats.

Down-hearted, Hooniyam climbs the steps into his shrine and squats on the floor facing his own image. He has to admit, it is quite imposing. It portrays him in a traditional pose (his favourite) seated on a great white horse with a fire-lamp in one hand and, in the other, a sword: the Sword of State, one that can raise a man to power, then cut him down.

The Sword of State.

Hooniyam chuckles to himself.

The stranger is sleeping, lying between sacks of rice and beans in the store-room. Earlier, he all but collapsed as Prema helped him into the house. The women encouraged him to eat some broth which revived him a little although, disoriented and mentally adrift, he was only able to answer a few of their questions. His name, he said, was Asoka, but they discovered little more about him, or why he had been living rough in the forest.

"And you think it is this man who has been stealing our eggs?"

Prema's wife turns startled eyes on her husband. She was striking in her youth, although her hair is now shot with grey. Although the wife of a headman has an easier life than some, this is not a rich village and years of work in the fields have taken their toll.

"I'm sure of it. The question is: what do we do with him?"

A girl appears, bringing tea from the lean-to kitchen at the back of the house. Silently, she serves her parents, then sits with them on the floor. Sometimes, when Prema looks at her, he thinks he sees his wife again, as she was in her youth. The girl has the same eyes, the same gentle expression and yet, there is something else, a streak of obstinacy, a wilfulness that sometimes reveals itself.

"I suppose I should hand him over to the police."

"No."

Prema assumes a stern face for his daughter. It is not usual for children, especially girls, to question their parents' decisions. But Sriya is different. Of course, it is all his own fault. His wife warned him long ago that arguments and disobedience are all that one can expect from an educated girl.

"No?"

He tries to look angry but, when he looks at her, his heart melts.

"Please, Thaatha. Please don't. At least not yet. He's sick. You know what the police are like. They may beat him. He may die."

She is wringing her hands, pleading, an artful routine that she adopted in childhood when she wanted something badly. It always works. She knows how to get round him. But, just to punish her impudence, he will make her wait.

"Hmmm."

Prema pretends to consider his options. Sriya holds her breath. Literally. She always does that when waiting for an answer. It is her way of winning an argument.

"I shall have to think about it."

But it is no good. If he keeps her waiting any longer, the stupid child will faint. Prema concedes.

"Well, I suppose if he were to die, it would be a waste of the eggs that he stole. I don't feed my hens to keep thieves alive, but there is no sense in feeding a corpse. He can stay here until he's better."

"Thank you, Thaatha."

Sriya flings her arms around her father's neck.

"Prema!" his wife exclaims, shocked.

But there is nothing he can do. He lost the battle with Sriya long ago.

***

A cock crows, voices mingle in the kitchen outside, a pail clatters under the window. Lying between the sacks of grain and dried pulses, Asoka breathes deeply, savouring the sounds of domesticity before opening his eyes. As it seeps between his lids, the sunlight burns away the remnants of a dream, melting it like morning mist.

Every time he sleeps, the same nightmare pursues him, a shapeless horror, always at his heels, on the point of taking him just before he wakes. In the forest, he often lay, shivering with fear, too terrified to move, waiting for the touch of icy fingers. During that period of solitude, neither wakefulness nor daylight was sufficient to defeat his terror. It just receded into a corner of his consciousness. But today, it has gone.

Cautiously, he sits up and, running a hand over his face, encounters the matted growth of his beard. His hair is in the same state; having grown almost to his shoulders, it is filthy and knotted, with small twigs and bits of forest detritus embedded in its tangles. Although he has not washed or shaved for weeks, it has not troubled him. Until now. He is suddenly conscious of his unkempt appearance, and his odour, a rancid accumulation of dirt and fear.

In the next room, someone has begun to sweep the floor with swift, energetic strokes. It brings back memories: the swishing of brushes over cool stone in the cloisters as the novices performed their daily chores. He had forgotten that comforting, hypnotic sound and, in hearing it again, he experiences a moment of peace.

Peering through a crack in the door, he sees Sriya, brushing the floor with rhythmic strokes. A shaft of sunlight flows in from the open front door where chickens are pecking about the step in the hope of finding scraps mixed in with the sweepings. As she crosses the room, Sriya enters the beam of light and is transformed, the warm colour of her cheeks replaced by a glowing pallor, her hair crowned with a blue patina. The image of a goddess.

As he watches her, Asoka catches his breath, momentarily forgetting his troubles. Like a man in remission, not yet certain of his cure, he feels a tentative joy.

Sensing that she is not alone, Sriya looks up and smiles in his direction, as if she can see through the door. Instantly, his happiness dissipates. He feels doubly ashamed; both on account of his appearance and for spying on her. He moves clumsily into the doorway, stubbing his toe on the lintel.

"Are you feeling better?" she asks, gently.

"Yes."

Words crowd into his throat, but he cannot say more. He just stands there, staring at her, his arms hanging at his sides.

"Perhaps you would like ...," she falters, afraid of appearing rude or too forward. She tries again.

"I can show you where to wash. Then, perhaps, you would like to eat."

Asoka's mouth forms the word "Yes".

"Good."

She speaks with the eagerness of a schoolgirl sharing a confidence.

"You can borrow some of my father's clothes while I wash yours. And I've left scissors and a comb on the wash-stand. A razor too. Is that all right?"

Looking into her hopeful face, he feels that his heart will burst; but whether from joy or pain, he cannot tell.

***

She leads him into a yard at the back of the house. In a shady corner, discreetly hidden from view, is a washstand with a bowl of clean water, a yellow bar of soap and an old, frayed cloth which serves as a towel. Lying on the earth, neatly folded, are a clean sarong and shirt.

From a string, attached to a hook on the washstand, hangs a mirror from which much of the silvering has disappeared, leaving an archipelago of dark patches. Leaning forward, Asoka takes a look at himself and recoils in shock.

The face that stares out at him is not one that he recognises. Beneath the matted mane of hair, his eyes, red-rimmed and bloodshot, shine wildly from darkened sockets. He looks like a madman. Or a demon.

He is overwhelmed by hopelessness. What is the point in trying to improve his appearance? How can he rejoin any community after all that has happened, after all that he has done? The nightmare, which was so recently vanquished, creeps back to keep him company. He can never rest. He must always run, not just from others, but also from himself. He has murdered a man. Not a good man, but one who deserved his pity.

He realises that his slowness to perform Mennan's execution was not due to external factors, but his reluctance to perform an act inimical to his own humanity. His nature rebelled against such cruelty, but he persisted, smothering his conscience and perverting his innate sense of justice. He had thought himself capable of stopping up compassion, but such feelings do not die, they only remain dormant.

Looking into the mirror, he tries to discover the face that he once recognised as his own, but all he sees are the tears glistening in his eyes.

"Too late," he murmurs.

"Are you all right?"

Her voice drifts out from the window of the lean-to kitchen.

"Yes," he calls back.

He has lived in silence for so long that his voice is like that of a stranger. Yet it reconnects him to himself, a channel to the person that he once was. As he discards his dirty clothes, he remembers pieces of verse, things he learned as a monk. He begins to recite them under his breath, just for the pleasure of hearing them:

... fruit weighs heavy on the bough ...

He hacks at his hair, cutting away the tangles and knots. When he has finished, he brushes the clippings from his shoulders and looks down at his feet, surprised to see so much hair on the ground. He begins to wash, damping his skin with water from the bowl then rubbing himself with the sticky bar of yellow soap. The harsh, carbolic smell is invigorating. Perhaps, one day, he will bathe in the tank with the villagers, immersing himself in its waters, soaping himself under his sarong as he exchanges gossip with the other men.

He pours water over his arms, watching it run in rivulets to his hands, letting it drip from his elbows as he tries to shave with the blunt razor, manipulating the contours of his face with his fingers to catch every hair, scraping at the obdurate stubble until his skin feels raw.

... while trees are still in bloom ...

Asoka continues to recite half-remembered verses as chickens peck the earth around his feet, gently clucking as they scratch for insects. Somewhere nearby, pigs grunt contentedly as they root in the undergrowth.

From the kitchen comes the rhythmic thump of a pestle. Sriya and her mother are grinding spices which they will blend into different mixtures for meat or fish. Each household has its own recipes which, jealously guarded, are handed down from one generation to the next. There is a mouth-watering smell as hints of the secret formula waft into the yard: the menthol aroma of cardamom; a strong note of aniseed; dill. But it is the quantities and other, unidentifiable ingredients that make each recipe unique.

Thud, thud! The pestle beats a laborious rhythm. In the background, Asoka can distinguish another noise; a soft sizzling and popping. The next batch of spices, most likely cumin, fenugreek and mustard seeds, are being dry-roasted in a flat pan, the small seeds leaping in the air as they explode in the heat.

The preparation of spice mixture can take many hours, especially if several days' supply is prepared in advance. Children, too young to work in the fields, often help to grind the spices, holding their mothers' hands as they grip the heavy granite pestle. Even Asoka can remember such kitchen chores, although he always ran off to play, leaving his mother patiently pounding and crushing until the hard brown seeds and twigs had been reduced to an aromatic powder.

He wonders how she is, where she is. He has not spoken to her for so long; cutting himself off to pursue an end that he believed was greater than any family consideration. It stings him to think how he must have hurt her. How much more grief would it cause if she knew what he had done? Perhaps she believes him to be dead. He hopes so. He could not live with her pain as well as his own.

***

"What's he doing out there?" mutters Chandra to her daughter.

"Washing, Amma."

Her mother snorts.

"Filthy as he is, it cannot take that long to wash."

"Shall I call him?"

"You'd better. His food is getting cold. If he doesn't come soon, I shall throw it to the pigs."

Sriya calls from the window.

"Hello?"

"Hello."

Although pleasant, there is a note of uncertainty in his voice. And it is husky. She noticed that last night, putting it down to exhaustion. But now she thinks there may be another reason. It is as if he has not spoken to anyone for a long time.

"Are you all right?"

"Yes."

Another monosyllabic reply.

"Your food is ready. I'm putting it on a plate. You should come and eat."

He listens, savouring every word.

***

As she watches him eat, Sriya wonders who this stranger really is. Despite his former wild appearance, he is no peasant. She can tell that by the way he eats. By the look of him, he has starved for weeks, and yet he takes his time, forming a small ball of food with his fingers, scooping it into his mouth, chewing, savouring it. If he drops the occasional grain of rice, he is careful to pick it up and place it on the edge of his bowl, uneaten. A hungry peasant would shovel the food into his mouth until his cheeks bulged and he could hardly swallow, staining his clothes with sauce and liberally scattering the floor with scraps. He would not eat like this man.

He has hardly spoken, and yet she knows that he is educated. There is something about the dark eyes, ringed with shadow and set in deep sockets; a quickness, an intelligence. He may not talk much, but he listens. He already knows more about her family than they know about him. So far, all they have discovered is his first name; Asoka. He has offered no second name, the one that he would have inherited from his father. He is a man without identity or family, shipwrecked and alone. Like Robinson Crusoe. Or Prince Vijaya.

Most of the village is related to Sriya by blood or marriage. She has countless cousins, aunts and uncles. They often visit her father's house and she visits theirs. There is always noise, company, friendship. Arguments are few and never serious. All branches of the family gather together for births, weddings and funerals offering their help and support. No widow is left to grieve on her own. Sriya cannot imagine what it would be like to be without family; alone and unconnected. It must be like being invisible with people all around you going about their business, completely unaware of your existence.

"Would you like some more water?"

"Yes, please."

She takes his glass into the kitchen where she ladles boiled water into it from an earthenware pitcher. He must be very thirsty. He has drunk three glasses already. She wonders how he survived in the forest without clean water. She supposes that he must have drunk from the tank, like a wild animal. She returns to where he is eating and gives him the glass. He drains it.

"Ai," she laughs. "If you drink so much, your stomach will have no room for food."

She smiles at him. Seeing pity in her eyes, he looks away, ashamed.

1956: Tissa

Tissa is loitering by the Bo tree in the middle of the clearing. After a heavy drinking bout last night, his father returned home in a bad mood, his homecoming marked by the sounds of shrieks and slaps from his mother's room. Tissa lay awake, listening to her crying softly, the sound of her muffled sobs audible through the thin plank wall that separates their rooms. He longed to put his arms around her, comfort her. She was so close, only inches away, but he could neither touch nor see her. Only listen. And vow revenge.

Things are bad for his family. The farm is in decline, but every year the landlord raises the rent. While this may account for his father's drunkenness and violence, it is no excuse. Someone still has to work the farm, scrape a living from the fields. And it is Tissa. His brother and sisters do little to help him, either claiming physical weakness, or some other, imagined incapacity. And, without a father's firm hand, no-one can force them. Sometimes, Tissa considers running away to the city, but he has no trade or education, no-one to give him shelter. Besides, he cannot leave his mother. Or Sriya.

But sometimes he finds it hard to bear. When he left the house this morning, his father was still sleeping, snoring loudly as if he did not have a care in the world, while his mother crept around the house, trying not to wake him, keeping his breakfast fresh between two plates. As soon as he wakes, his father will demand food, shovelling rice into his mouth like a beggar, carelessly scattering it down him, the grains of rice clinging to the hair on his stomach, like maggots.

By the time his father wakes, the sun will be high and the other farmers will have been working for hours. Normally, Tissa would be in the fields, too; working on his own, trying to ignore the good-humoured jibes from the other men. *Father still asleep? Good night out? All right for some!* They would laugh and he would try to make light of it but, inwardly, he would be trembling with rage.

Sometimes, the other men lend him a hand but, at busy times of year, they need all their energy for their own plots and Tissa is left with the impossible task of ploughing, planting or reaping on his own. Sometimes, when they cannot see him, he weeps.

The late Prime Minister D.S. Senanayake loved the peasants. He often said so. He encouraged their cultivation of the land and their production of rice, restoring the ancient irrigation tanks established by the Sinhalese kings. In his socialist utopia, the rural classes would make the country self-sufficient, freeing it from its dependency on overseas imports. According to Mr Senanayake, peasants were the backbone of the nation. Its future. But he had not met Tissa's father.

How can you restore dignity to a man who never had any? Tissa's father is a laughing stock, tolerated with humour by the community which nurtured him. If life is difficult here, it would be impossible elsewhere. There is no hope, no future. Only a relentless progression towards ruin.

Then what? More charity from the village? Tissa knows that he should be grateful, but he is not. He wants respect, not sympathy. He longs to be someone in his own right, not the pitiful reflection of his father's misfortunes. Who would want to marry into such a family? Who would ever look at him?

His thoughts turn to Sriya and he is seized by agitation of another kind. Who was it that Prema was helping into the house last night? Who was it that he did not want Tissa to see? In the light of day, Tissa can laugh at last night's fear; the dread that forced him to run helter-skelter through darkened fields, heedless of snakes and scorpions, convinced that a demon had emerged from the forest to abduct Sriya. Of course, all of that was nonsense, but he still has a lingering sense of threat.

He hesitates. He should be working the fields. But the screams and slaps of last night still ring in his ears. Why should he help the man who brutalises his mother? They have all protected him for too long. Tissa makes up his mind. Defiantly, he sets off up the road towards Prema's house.

***

As he opens the gate and approaches the headman's home, Tissa experiences a pang of jealousy. Two fat pigs grunt contentedly from their pen in a corner of the yard, a clutch of plump hens scratch in the dirt under a thin sapling and a small, white goat bleats for attention, straining against the tether which holds it to the fence. From behind the house, comes the lowing of oxen. They, too, are sleek and well-fed, their eyes bright and their velvet-brown hides smooth and free from parasites. The yard, recently swept, exudes an atmosphere of orderliness and well-being. It only serves to heighten his frustration, providing a stark contrast to the ramshackle untidiness of his own home.

He strides up to the open door, then hovers, uncertainly. As he prepares to knock, a man appears from the kitchen; a thin fellow with ragged hair and wild-eyes who looks as if he is wearing borrowed clothes. Tissa recognises the sarong as one of Prema's. The two men stare at each other, unable to break the silence that divides them.

"What are you doing here so late in the morning? Shouldn't you be helping your father?"

A heavy hand slaps Tissa on the back. Prema is standing behind him, holding a pail of milk.

"He is not feeling well."

Tissa looks away as he speaks and Prema raises an eyebrow. He knows of these illnesses and what causes them. But, as he reminds himself, it is not the lad's fault. He likes Tissa. The boy is a hard worker and Prema would have liked a son like him. He would certainly have treated him better.

"Why aren't you working?"

"Oh," Tissa hesitates. "I wanted to see if everything was all right with you. After last night, I mean."

Prema stares at him steadily.

"Who was that?"

The other man has disappeared into the back of the house. Tissa nods towards the space where he was standing.

"A visitor. His name is Asoka. He, too, has been unwell."

"How long is he staying?"

"Until he is better."

"But how long will that be?"

227

Tissa's curiosity makes him rude. A figure of respect, the headman is never held to account in this way, particularly with regard to his personal affairs. Such behaviour is not to be tolerated, particularly from younger members of the village; even one with a special claim to the old man's affection. Prema's face darkens. He repeats his reply.

"Until he is better."

The answer is stern. Realising that he has outworn his welcome, Tissa turns abruptly on his heel and runs off down the path.

1956: Recovery

It is several weeks since Asoka was brought to Prema's house. Since then, he has been fed, clothed and his wounds regularly dressed and tended to. The sores on his feet and legs have healed and he can now walk without pain. Altogether, he is feeling stronger.

As a monk, he was used to receiving gifts from lay people. Alms, usually in the form of food, were regularly provided by devoted Buddhists in order to acquire spiritual merit. If sufficient merit is acquired, the alms-giver may be assured of an easier time in the next life. For, unless a believer emulates Buddha and achieves nirvana, he will not break the cycle of rebirth that ties him to this world. He, or she, will be reborn many times, repeating the cycle of earthly trial and suffering for generations. Even gods, who have exhausted their spiritual merit, may be reborn.

To enable the faithful to gain spiritual merit it is, therefore, a monk's duty to receive alms and, like most of his brethren, Asoka did it unquestioningly, never asking himself what sacrifices donors had had to make in order to feed him. But Asoka is no longer a monk. Having read Marx, his unquestioning faith dissolved like rice paper in rain. He no longer regards it as his right to take from others, even when those gifts are freely given.

During his convalescence, he has watched Sriya and her mother at work. Rising early, they roll out dough for rotis that are cooked on a flat griddle. Breakfast is first served to Prema who departs early for the fields, carrying his tools wrapped in a cloth over his shoulder or, sometimes, taking the ox-cart if there are heavier things to transport. After he has gone, the women sit and eat quietly together, enjoying a few peaceful moments before the long day ahead.

Once work starts, there will be little chance to sit down. Rice must be sifted to rid it of impurities, dough mixed and left to ferment, spices ground and curry cooked. Water must be drawn from the well, poured into large pitchers and carried back to the house where that used for drinking must be boiled. The house must be swept and cleaned and clothes, often stained and filthy from manual work, must be soaped, scrubbed and rinsed at the tank, then spread out to dry on flat stones.

There are also chores to perform around the small-holding: eggs must be collected and cattle or goats milked. The yard must be swept and manure from the animals collected and dried into flat cakes for fuel or thrown onto the midden to make compost for the vegetable garden. This, also, requires attention.

Garden tools must be carried to a clearing in the forest which must be weeded, seeded and hoed. Plants must be regularly checked and pests, such as caterpillars, removed from their leaves. Bird-scarers made from tin cans attached to lengths of string must be made and strung across the vegetable patches in order to deter parrots who regularly plunder the garden and, if the soil looks dry, then a round trip must be made to the well to collect water for the plants.

In addition to these tasks, there are often children or sick relatives to attend to. The only rest an active village woman gets are the few hours she spends asleep on the floor at night. Even then, a husband's requirements must be put before her own.

In the first days following his arrival, Asoka was too weak to do more than sit on the porch, watching the women as they worked. But by observing, he has learned much. Having entered the monastery at the age of eight, he has had little contact with women. He knows them only as worshippers or alms-givers, but he knows nothing of their lives. In fact, he has never given the matter much thought. He knows that they are wives and mothers but his recollection of his own mother is too sketchy for him to understand what that entails.

As his strength returns, he has asked to help with the chores, but they refuse. In their world, the tasks of men and women are clearly delineated. To get a man to do a woman's work is to humiliate him in the eyes of others.

"But I want to help," Asoka has insisted several times.

"When you are better," is the only answer he gets.

Finally, he understands. It is not woman's work, but man's work that he must do. He must wait until he is strong enough.

***

Prema is sitting on the porch after his evening meal, watching the last streaks of sun through the trees. His back and legs are aching after a long day in the fields. He is getting older and he has no son to succeed him. It is a lack that nags at him increasingly, like a dog worrying a bone. There have been sons, but none of them lived longer than a few days. Extraordinary that out of so many boys, only a girl should survive. From inside the house, he hears her laugh. Prema smiles. He loves her more than any boy, but Sriya cannot work the farm. .

Although he owns only four acres of paddy, Prema is a wealthy man compared to his neighbours, many of whom are sharecroppers; some of whom, like Tissa's family, are being bled white by their landlords. Mr Bandaranaike's government has plans to redress the balance between farmers and greedy landlords. In two years' time, an Act will be introduced which will limit the landlord's entitlement to a fixed percentage of produce from the farmer's land.

It is a plan concocted by left-wing politicians, intended to ease injustice but, ultimately, it will have the reverse effect. Landowners will circumvent the regulations by using wage labourers and small farmers will be chased off the land altogether. But this is all in the future. At present, the Paddy Lands Bill has not even been drafted. And it will not help Prema who owns his land and whose chief concern is how to keep it in the family.

He sighs and leans his head against the rough wood of the porch. What has it all been for? All those years of back-breaking toil. Sometimes, the fields have yielded hardly enough grain to feed the family, let alone enough to sell. But the land is sacred. Inherited through his family for generations, it must be kept intact and passed on. But how?

A board creaks. Asoka is standing in the doorway, looking at the sun. He is already different from the wild, starved creature that came to their house a few weeks ago. He still speaks little of himself, but is willing to be drawn into conversation on neutral matters, showing genuine interest in the affairs of the village.

"May I sit with you?"

Prema motions to a spot on the ground. Asoka sits like a village man, with his legs drawn up in front of him, his feet placed flat on the ground, leaning against the warm wooden wall of the house. Men have gathered under the Bo tree to smoke. The smell of cheap tobacco floats across to where Prema and Asoka sit, side by side.

"Let me help you," says Asoka, his face still turned towards the sun.

"How?"

"In the fields."

At first, Prema is inclined to laugh. How could this man with his thin arms and stooping back be any help? But, being a wise man, Prema thinks before he speaks. What is the harm in letting him try? So far, there has been no return on the food he has eaten. Not even an animal would be kept on those terms.

"All right," says Prema, simply. "You can start tomorrow."

***

Long after Asoka has gone to bed, Prema remains on the porch, listening to the chorus of night-insects. Thinking. His request for work has finally brought Asoka into focus. Prema now views him, not as a burden on the family, but as the answer to a prayer.

It is the beginning of a busy season and he would normally have counted on Tissa for help but, this year, all the boy's energies will be expended on his own family's farm. And he will be working alone. The boy's father has not been seen about the village for many days, although there have been rumours that he has been seen at a toddy tavern on the road into town. Everyone knows the nature of his malady, and they pity Tissa, but they can do little for him. These days, subsistence and ruin are separated by the narrowest of margins.

In recent years, the economy has slumped and there is talk of repealing the rice subsidy to farmers. So far, D.S. Senanayake's vision of rural regeneration remains little more than a fantasy. Of course, the politicians do not see it like that. As a measure of its success in the countryside, the Government refers to its programme for peasant colonisation of the hinterland. This includes the inhospitable dry zone, in which thousands have died from malaria and other areas, such as Gal Oya, in the east.

But even these projects are not without their problems. As the population expands and natural barriers are eroded, various factions, who previously lived in contented isolation, have been brought into sudden contact with each other. Incursions into the dry zone have introduced Sinhalese peasants into the resident community of Tamils in the north; while Gal Oya, another area of Sinhalese colonisation, is situated in what Tamils regard as their traditional heartland. Sinhalese and Tamils are being forced together at breakneck speed, like a reluctant bride and groom.

Prema has heard reports from cousins who joined the colonisation programme, people whose own farms had failed and who joined the programme in desperation. They had hoped for a new life, a new beginning. But all is not well. There is friction with the Tamils and, in some areas, there have been minor incidents of violence; mainly scuffles and abuse.

Prema wonders how he would feel if the forest nearby were chopped down and the land given to Tamil settlers. It is an uncomfortable thought: one which he dismisses. It is not healthy to dwell on the imponderable. He has enough real problems to occupy him.

Even if Asoka turns out to be a good worker – and he may not – there is no guarantee that he will remain beyond the end of the season. He may have family to return to. A wife, even. And, if he leaves, Prema's position will not have changed. He will be left with land that he finds increasingly hard to manage and no-one to leave it to.

The next day, Asoka and Prema rise before dawn and, after they have eaten, Prema leads Asoka to an enclosure behind the house where two buffaloes are tethered to a tree. The animals have sleek, brown hides and long horns. When the men approach, the buffaloes snort a little, but in recognition, not alarm. Prema pats one of them, scratching its back, inviting Asoka to do the same. Warm to the touch, the animal's warm flank is still damp with morning dew. Savouring the stillness of the new day, the buffaloes champ contentedly, churning the food around their mouths with their great pink tongues.

"Mother and daughter," says Prema proudly, slapping one on the rump. "The best in the village."

Asoka pats one of the beasts, admiring the sinewy strength of its neck and shoulders. He runs his hand down its back, marvelling at its massive vertebrae and the powerful build of its hindquarters. A little unsure of the stranger, the creature tosses its head and lows, calling to its companion, its breath as sweet as hay.

"Don't be silly."

Prema reassures the animal, patting it on the rump. The buffalo snorts then, raising its tail, ejects a stream of manure that narrowly misses Asoka's feet. He steps back in surprise.

"You'll have to get used to that. Learn to move fast."

Prema's eyes twinkle with amusement.

With Asoka's help, Prema drags a wooden cart from a shelter under the trees and hitches it to the older animal.

"Mother leads, child will follow," mutters Prema enigmatically, indicating a pile of sacks and tools in a corner of the shelter.

Together, they load the cart with an old wooden plough, two harnesses, sowing baskets and several sacks of seed paddy. Then, after tying the young buffalo's tether to the back of the cart, they climb aboard. Prema taps the rump of the lead animal with his cane and the cart lurches forward, wobbling precariously on its two huge wheels as it rumbles out of the gate and onto the track that leads to the paddy fields.

It is a pleasant ride through coconut groves and forest tracks, the sun occasionally piercing the leafy canopy overhead to create a fretwork of light on the dry soil floor. Occasionally, coarse palm fronds rattle together like dry sticks, disturbed by the movement of air or birds. A small grey wagtail lands on the road in front of them.

"Pitta bird." Prema points a gnarled finger at the bird. "Do you know it?"

"No. I've never seen it before. Is it important?"

"Of course. Pitta bird arrives with the monsoon winds. It is the sign to start planting rice."

Prema is surprised at Asoka's ignorance. But then, he is a city boy. One only has to look at his hands to know that: the skin of his palms is as unblemished and soft as a child's. Prema must start at the beginning.

"There are two growing seasons each year: Maha and Yala. Maha is the most important because that is when we get the most rain. It lasts for six months, from September to March, and gives us the best rice crops. Yala lasts from May to August and produces less rice because there is only enough rain to cultivate half the fields."

"Ah."

The knowledge being offered is practical, not metaphysical, and Asoka finds it surprisingly difficult to absorb without reference to a written script. Yet he is thrilled and fascinated by what Prema has to teach. To his shame, he realises that he has always thought of peasants as stupid, in need of liberation. But from what? They have their own culture, their own way of life and a fund of knowledge that has never found its way into books.

Having gained the boy's attention, Prema racks his brain for further interesting titbits, feeding them to Asoka, grain by grain, as one might tame a wild pigeon with pinches of corn.

"Do you know how many types of rice there are?"

Asoka has never thought about it. Until recently, his food was prepared for him by monastery kitchens or alms-givers. He simply ate it, obediently and without question. There is white rice and red rice, wild rice and the parboiled rice that is set out on the road to dry and which has an unmistakeably pungent aroma when cooked.

"I don't know. Four, five?"

"Ha ha!" Prema chortles. "More like three hundred."

The old man recites a litany of rice. Different types are grown depending on the season, the location and whether the soil is wet, dry or muddy. Each variety has its own distinctive characteristics, name and purpose: Mawee nourishes Buddhist monks who fast daily from noon until the following day; Heenati sustains breast-feeding mothers, while Kanni Murunga is ideal for field-workers.

From the corner of his eye, the wily old farmer can see that Asoka is listening intently. It is the first time he has seen the boy take an interest in anything except, perhaps, Sriya; but all young men are interested in her. Most of the time, Asoka has been distracted, restless, as if there is a great weight on his mind. It is not Prema's business to enquire after the cause but, now that he has accepted this stranger into his home, he feels that he has a duty to help him. A diversion from one's worries is sometimes the best cure.

"Have a look in that sack."

Asoka reaches into the musty smelling bag and withdraws a handful of seedlings.

"It's already sprouting," he says, rolling the green-tipped grain between his fingertips.

"That's right. Only sprouted rice is sown in wet fields. We germinate it at home before sowing. When the rains come, this seed will come up four days earlier than unsprouted seed. If there is little rain, it means that the crop gets off to a good start. It can mean the difference between a successful harvest or a failed one; whether we eat or go hungry."

Prema continues with his lesson, his words keeping pace with the cartwheels grinding over the red earth; a slow, rhythmic chant of initiation. Asoka is being absorbed into a new order; the peasantry, whose knowledge comes, not from books, but from the soil itself.

***

Emerging from the trees, they are struck by a flare of heat. Although the air under the palms was warm and stifling, there was plenty of shade. But here, in the open, there is no shelter from the sun which glares down upon the watery surface of the fields, turning it into quicksilver. Almost blinded by the light, Asoka shields his eyes with his hands. Already, the sun is boring into his scalp.

"Ow!"

"If you don't cover your head, your brain will catch fire."

From the back of the cart, Prema passes him a length of cloth which has the appearance of a patchwork quilt. It is made from old pieces of sarong, roughly stitched together to make a square one metre wide. Prema shows him how to tie it, knotting two ends together behind his head so that it fits snugly around his crown while the remaining length hangs free, protecting his neck and shoulders from the sun.

As they climb out of the cart, they are met by a saffron-robed priest who exchanges a few words with Prema.

"He has come to bless the crop," Prema explains. "Each season, I visit the astrologer. He tells me which day will be most auspicious to begin sowing. Then I ask the priest to come and bless the fields before we start."

As his eyes become accustomed to the searing light, Asoka sees that the banks around the fields are lined with other workers, men, women and children, all wearing similar head-dresses to himself, the older people dark and leathery-skinned from years of working the land. There is a sense of expectancy and excitement, the kind of tension that runners experience before a race. Everyone is eager to get started. This crop will determine the narrow margin between survival or ruin, who remains on the land, and who will be forced off it. The fate of the village depends on Maha.

People continue to chatter as the priest intones a prayer, his voice rising and falling, sometimes louder, sometimes softer, carried back and forth by the wind. As the prayer ebbs and flows, egrets stalk the margins of the fields, stabbing the water with their beaks in search of food and a pair of ducks fly overhead, their soft, throaty quacking mingling with the words of the priest. Asoka pays no more attention to the prayers than anyone else. It is a ritual to be performed, without change, year after year; its power, like that of the seasons, lying in repetition and immutability.

Some of the younger boys, already bored, nudge each other and giggle while two others, engaged in silent combat, elbow and knee each other until one dislodges his opponent who, losing his footing, slithers down the bank into the water. The sound of a sharp slap, administered by the boy's mother, echoes across the field. Chastened, the child stands close to his mother, restrained by her hand, which has closed on his arm like a vice.

After what seems an age, the priest finishes his prayers. After sharing a few words with Prema and the other farmers, the priest collects his payment and picking up his staff, walks delicately along the track that leads through the village to the small roadside temple where he is the incumbent.

Now work starts in earnest. Carts are unloaded, tools laid out on the bank, sacks opened and children clamber up and down the bank as their parents wade into the water. As they fill pan-shaped baskets with paddy seed from the sacks, Prema whispers to Asoka.

"Be careful. These people may not know how to read but they're sharper than you think. Don't say anything you don't want everyone to know. News travels fast in the village."

"What shall I tell them?"

"That you are my guest. A distant cousin from the city, recovering from an illness. I have told them that much, but nothing more. They are already asking what you do. It's obvious that you are an educated man."

Asoka thinks for a moment. "I will tell them that I am a teacher. Will they believe that?"

"Yes. They will believe that. Now follow me, we are ready to start sowing."

234

Prema scrambles down the bank, plunging into the water up to his knees.

"Walk alongside me and copy what I do; only you must cast seed to the right as I throw to the left."

Scooping seed from the basket, he throws handfuls in a wide arc as he pushes forwards, mud and water roiling about his calves as he walks. Asoka follows, stumbling occasionally where the ground is uneven, his feet stirring up clouds of sediment. Warm mud seeps between his toes and he feels something squirm beneath his foot. He prays that it is a fish or a frog and not a water-snake. Every year, hundreds of Ceylonese, mostly agricultural workers, die from snake-bite. It is an unavoidable hazard.

In a neighbouring field, an entire family is at work, from the oldest, an elderly woman in her sixties, to the youngest, a child of about four. They pause to greet Prema, straightening their backs, staring at the farmer and his guest, openly inquisitive. Prema croaks a brief greeting, jerking his thumb at Asoka.

"My cousin, the teacher."

Their curiosity satisfied, the family nod and smile at Asoka before resuming their work, as methodical and unhurried in their movements as oxen, impervious to the sun that beats down relentlessly on their backs.

Asoka marvels at their resilience. After only ten minutes, he is drained of energy, the sweat constantly running into his eyes and stinging them with its saltiness. His arm aches with the action of sowing and his mouth is parched. But Prema is a hard taskmaster. There is no break for rest until half the sacks have been emptied. Only then, is Asoka permitted to stop for a few minutes and take a swig of cold tea from a tin flask.

As he rests, he sees two men approaching along the bank; one of them he recognises as Tissa, the boy who he met the day after his arrival at Prema's house. Although they did not speak on that occasion, he saw hostility in Tissa's face. For some reason, the boy dislikes him. No good can come of this conversation, but he cannot escape. The men are too close and trying to avoid them will look suspicious. Asoka looks around for Prema, but the old man is still sowing, far away at the other end of the field with his back turned.

"Hello, brother!" says the man that he does not recognise. "How is it going?"

"Well."

But Asoka's voice quavers. He sounds uncertain. The other man looks at him quizzically.

"You're new here, aren't you?"

"Yes."

"I am Bandula. I live in the next village. Tissa, here, is my nephew. I think you have met already."

Asoka nods cautiously. Tissa glowers at him from over his uncle's shoulder.

"So, where do you come from?"

"The city."

"The city, eh? Big difference. You must find it very dull out here."

"No, not at all."

"No?"

The man laughs jovially, but his eyes never leave Asoka's face. It is as if he is waiting for something, a sign of weakness. Sweat trickles down Asoka's spine.

"Hello, Bandula. Busy as usual?"

Prema sloshes towards them and scrambles up the bank, rivulets of muddy water running down his calves.

"Of course!"

Bandula bridles at the irony in Prema's voice. Unperturbed, Prema continues with his inquiry, determined to give Bandula a dose of his own medicine.

"Because if you were not busy, I was going to suggest that you give this lad a hand. His father is ill again and the boy is on his own. At times like these, families should pull together."

Bandula looks as if he were roasting over a hot fire: his cheeks flame and his lips bubble together, mumbling something incoherent.

"Too busy. Goodbye," are the only words which Asoka can distinguish as the man turns away, retreating quickly along the track, trailed by his nephew.

"Father's brother," mutters Prema. "Suffers from the same disease. Thought of work makes him ill."

For the first time, Asoka roars with laughter.

As a child, Sriya hated the track through the forest, claiming that she saw faces in the trees. Her mother tried reasoning with her but then, when this did not work, resorted to a remedy of sharp slaps. However, nothing could be done to cure Sriya's fear and, whenever possible, she avoids the forest. So it comes as a surprise when Sriya suddenly expresses a desire to visit her father in the fields, a trip which will take her along the forest track.

"I will take Thaatha his tiffin today."

Sriya's mother raises her eyebrows. Although diligent in most things, Sriya has always refused to take her father his tiffin box and it is one of the few causes of friction between the two women.

"Why today?" asks her mother, bemused.

"Why not?" replies her daughter.

Shaking her head, Chandra disappears into the kitchen, a dark, lean-to shed made of corrugated iron with a window in one end and a door in the other. The floor has no covering but consists simply of earth, beaten down and compacted to make it hard. Bunches of onions and garlic hang from nails on the wall along with cooking utensils, mostly ladles, spoons and pans.

Chandra wishes that the shed was more open, like some of the other village kitchens which consist only of supporting beams and a roof; but Prema reasons, rightly, that animals will get in and steal the food. *We do not grow it for them to eat*, he says. And there, all argument ends.

Selecting a large onion, Chandra severs it from the string of plaited shoots by which a number of onions are bound together for storage. She then quarters the onion with a kitchen knife, dropping the skin into a bucket of vegetable peelings which will later be fed to the chickens. The onion is then diced into smaller and smaller pieces as Chandra considers the enigma of Sriya's request.

"Why has she suddenly offered to do this after refusing for so many years?" Chandra muses.

She turns the question over and over in her head, examining it from every angle. She takes another onion, skins it, quarters it, chops furiously for a few seconds, then stops, looking ahead of her at the blank face of the wall. She has already dismissed sickness and fever. Sriya is in good health and, apart from this odd request, appears perfectly rational. There must be another reason. Start again. At the beginning. She selects another onion.

Prema already has plenty of food. He took it with him this morning but, she supposes, there is no harm in sending more. There are two hungry men to feed now that Asoka is helping. She wonders how he is getting on and if he has proved to be a help or a hindrance. Of course, that is it! Momentarily distracted, Chandra cuts herself.

Sucking her finger, she places the knife on the table next to the pile of chopped onion and walks out of the lean-to kitchen into the yard. Fresh air is always more conducive to thought. Is it a desire to see their guest, rather than her father, that has persuaded Sriya to overcome her fear? Chandra is in a quandary.

She circles the yard, past the pecking, clucking hens, dizzy at the prospect of her only daughter falling in love. Should she give in to Sriya's request, knowing what prompted it? What harm can it do? The girl's honour is not at risk. She could as easily meet the man here, as in the fields and there, at least, she will be chaperoned by her father.

Allowing her to go will also help Sriya to overcome her fear of the forest. Those tales of faces in the trees have always disturbed Chandra. One cannot live in this place and be haunted by such fears. The forest is as much part of village life as the fields. It must be tolerated, if not loved. Yes, on the whole, it would be best to let her go. Chandra's other concerns can wait. She will discuss them later with Prema.

Stepping back through the door into the kitchen, Chandra is careful not to catch her sari on the rusty nail that sticks out from the doorframe. There are many jobs around the home for a man to do but they never get done because Prema has no help on the farm. Formerly, he could rely on Tissa, that is, when the boy's father was sober enough to work his own land. But there is not much chance of that these days.

There was a time when Chandra and Prema had considered Tissa as a future husband for Sriya. But no-one would yoke their daughter to a family facing ruin. Apart from that, Tissa can barely write his name. Asoka, at least, is educated. And Prema needs help on the farm. He hides it well but Chandra knows that he is exhausted. He cannot continue for much longer on his own. In times of need, one cannot be fussy. Asoka is a stranger, a man without property or connection. But, at least, he is unencumbered by a string of hungry mouths. Moreover, he is fit and willing to work.

Chandra considers the possibilities as she works, weighing up the advantages and disadvantages of such a union. To her surprise, she concludes that, if not positively in favour, she is not absolutely against it.

"I'm getting ahead of myself," she says to herself, aloud. "All of this just because Sriya asked to take a tiffin box to the fields. I've probably got it all wrong."

But something tells her that her instinct is correct. However, she needs to be sure before she says anything to her husband. She must observe Sriya and Asoka together before coming to any conclusion.

"Sriya, come here!"

For the moment, practical considerations must come first. If Sriya wants to take the tiffin boxes to the fields, then she must help to prepare the food.

***

Sriya has crossed the square and is standing at the entrance to the forest track. Tall trees arch over it, their branches touching, like the entrance to a tunnel. She hesitates. Her mother is watching her from the doorway of the house.

"I must go on," she urges herself.

But it is pride, rather than courage, that speaks to her now. She insisted on performing this task. She will look stupid if she turns back now. She steps forward into the gloom, one foot at a time, like a bather testing the water. The forest draws her in. She walks a little way, then stops, surrounded by the eeriness of trees.

Close to the village, the forest floor is bare and dry, stamped down by the passage of many feet. Pigs, brought here by their owners to forage for roots and berries, have left scrapes at the bottom of tree trunks, while goats have stripped the lower branches of their leaves.

"Uh!" Sriya catches her breath.

But it is only the cackling of a hen that has escaped from its pen. She can see it now, happily clucking as it scratches at the soil in search of insects. Village chickens are closely related to jungle fowl. They are almost wild and, to them, the prospect of finding food in the forest is far more attractive than squabbling over a few scraps in a yard. They are always escaping, obliging their owners to recapture them on a regular basis.

Something disturbs the hen and it scampers away, squawking as it zigzags crazily through the trees. Sounds from the village become faint: no longer distinct and recognisable, they merge into a hum, then gradually fade into silence. The forest floor is no longer bare, as if it had been swept, but is covered with dead vegetation. The trees are thicker here and there are fewer patches of sunlight peppering the ground.

Sriya hurries forward, straining her eyes and ears for any threat. But she sees no faces and the only sounds she hears are those of insects and the birds, high above, in the branches of the trees. And then, quite suddenly, she feels it. As if something has slipped away. Her fear has gone.

She now walks slowly, deliberately, without trepidation, looking around her, admiring the twisted limbs of the trees, the strange shadows made by their branches. A butterfly, as large as her hand, flaps lazily in front of her. It alights on a tree-trunk, turns a half circle, then comes to rest. Stepping carefully over the dead leaf litter, Sriya gets as close as she can without frightening the creature. Its outstretched wings, set against the silvery bark of the tree, are thrown into relief: their scalloped edges and long, trailing lobes look as if they have been carefully cut out with scissors.

Unable to resist, she puts out a hand to touch it. Before she can blink, the butterfly has gone. Never before has she lingered in the forest to look at a butterfly. Never has she walked here alone. She feels liberated, almost light-headed. Anything is possible.

The trees thin out and, in some places, there are clearings, bright patches of sunlight where flowers grow. Sriya leaves the track and, finding a narrow path, follows it into an open space. Although she is no longer afraid of the forest, it is good to feel the sun on her face.

The clearing is covered with a layer of low vegetation which almost conceals the stumps of trees that have been chopped down for firewood. Next year, this area may be converted to chena, the gardens in which village folk grow their vegetables for two or three seasons, before allowing the forest to reclaim them.

"But it is a long way from the village," she murmurs, thinking of the work entailed in carrying water, tools and produce to and from the village. "Perhaps they will not use it after all."

At the side of the clearing, a hibiscus bush is in full bloom. There is a flash of colour and a bird, no bigger than a large butterfly, hovers over one of the flowers: a humming bird, probing for nectar with its long beak, its wings beating so fast that they buzz like an insect. The bird travels from flower to flower then flits off, whizzing through the air like a tiny meteor.

The flowers are dazzling, scarlet with long stamens that project beyond the trumpet and explode in a delicate puff. A firework of a flower. Determined to have one, Sriya strides through the tangle of weeds that twine around her ankles. She selects a flower so perfect that it must have opened that morning and, snapping its stem, twists it from the branch and tucks it behind her ear. It is a long time since she wore flowers in her hair. But today, for some reason, it seems appropriate.

She is bending over to pick up the tiffin boxes, which she placed on the ground beside her, when a twig snaps, as loud as a rifle shot. Startled, she turns suddenly, to see a shadow flitting between the trees. The old, familiar sense of being watched floods back and her heart pounds in her throat. She runs back to the forest track. She must get out of here. Quickly. The trees are watching her.

She stumbles forward, impeded by a terror that sucks the breath from her lungs and turns her feet to lead. Sobbing with fright, she bolts along the track, turns a corner and almost collides with Tissa who is returning with his uncle from the fields.

"Tissa. Oh, thank god it's you!"

"Sriya! What's the matter?"

He puts a hand on her shoulder to steady her. His expression is tender, but the trembling of her flesh excites him. Her fear gratifies him more than her affectionate greeting.

"There, in the trees. Didn't you see it?"

Screwing up his eyes, he takes a few steps towards the trees, turning his head from side to side, pretending to scrutinise the inky gloom.

"I can't see anything."

"But there was. I saw it. Over there."

She waves a hand, still clutching the tiffin box, towards the forest.

"There's nothing. Really. Would you like me to walk with you?"

He shoots a meaningful glance at his uncle.

"Would you?"

Her eyes are large and frightened, like a hunted deer. Her terror is strangely exhilarating. It arouses him. He wants to hold her, so tight that she cannot escape, squeeze the breath out of her. And then … and then …

"Of course."

He is hoarse. The words curdle in his throat. Bandula gives him a knowing look.

"I'll be off then. Aunty expecting me home, you know."

Bandula disappears towards the village. Tissa relieves Sriya of one of the tiffin boxes, although she will not allow him to carry both.

"I'm sure I saw something," she murmurs, peering back over her shoulder into the trees.

"You should not walk here alone," he admonishes her, sounding quite the man.

"I have no choice."

"But you do."

"How?"

"If you had someone, a husband, you would not be alone."

"Mmm."

She considers the idea and her face brightens. Reading this as encouragement, Tissa tries his luck and tentatively curls an arm around her shoulder.

"What are you doing?"

She springs back, a cat with its back arched, ready to fight, her transition from terror to fury so sudden that Tissa is knocked off balance.

"I'm sorry, I'm sorry," he stammers. "I didn't mean anything."

"Give me that!"

Snatching the tiffin box from him, she runs off along the track.

Tissa begins to follow, but gives up. Sitting down, in the middle of the road, he draws his knees up to his chest. Not so long ago putting his arm around Sriya's shoulder would not have offended her. They have been friends from childhood, constantly in each others' company, in and out of each others' houses. Everyone has predicted that they will marry, even the astrologer, but making the transition from friend to lover is not as easy as Tissa supposed.

He sees little of Sriya these days. She does not seek him out as she used to and, when they meet, she is always in a hurry to be gone. He suspects that she is avoiding him. There is no chance to press his suit and he is becoming impatient. His love, thwarted and frustrated, is beginning to run through darker channels.

Something has happened to change her. But what? He rocks back and forth as he always does when thinking. Then, a thought presents itself with such force that he can almost hear it, an insinuating whisper in his ear. She is going to meet someone. With a flower in her hair. Why else would she be walking here alone? Normally, nothing can induce her to take this path. She hates the forest. No, she is going to meet a man. Who?

A voice whispers in his ear: "Asoka, the stranger. It is him."

A dove plunges through the trees, landing clumsily on a branch overhanging the track where it coos softly. Feeling over the ground for a stone, Tissa flings one at the bird, laughing bitterly as it flaps away in alarm, wishing that he had killed it.

1956: A toddy tavern

The man in the striped T-shirt sweeps the dirty glasses from the bar, dunks them in a bowl of grey water, wipes them on the same tea-towel that he has just used to clean the counter, then re-fills them for the new arrivals. Business at the toddy tavern is brisk, and customers are always waiting.

The shop itself is little more than a tin shack with a large open window at the front. A narrow wooden plank, which runs along the bottom of the window, serves as the bar. Few formalities are observed here. People come, they pay, they drink and, most nights, they find their way home.

Occasionally, one customer may become so drunk that he can no longer walk unaided, relying on friends to carry him. If he has no friends, he will wake in the morning, propped against the metal wall of the cabin or lying in the gutter. Eventually, after rubbing his head, which feels like a bruised water-melon, he will feel in his pockets and curse, realizing that he has been relieved of his money by pick-pockets; but then, he reminds himself, it is only money that he has lost. He is still alive.

This is the philosophy of the toddy tavern. A unique repository of practical wisdom, it has many disciples who return every night, eager to increase their learning. The toddy tavern owner knows most of them and, at one time or another, has heard confession from them all.

Their secrets and sins have all been laid bare, although not their aspirations. They have none. Nagging wives, debts, no money, lack of work: all can drive a man to the toddy tavern. But, although the reasons are various, all customers suffer from a common ailment: despair. At the toddy tavern, they find solace in the company of fellow sufferers.

The barman can generally tell a man's character by the cast of his face and his financial means by the state of his clothes: clean and shabby, in work; unwashed and shabby, out of it. But tonight there is one who perplexes him. The little round man in the neatly-pressed shirt is unlike the usual clientele, the most affluent of whom are casual labourers. This man has a regular job and, by their standards, a good one. As he passes the man a glass, the barman looks into his eyes and sees something different: fear. The toddy-man can smell it; a bitter odour, like unrefined liquor.

He watches as the man takes the drink and seats himself a little away from the others on one of the upturned crates that serve as seats. Even there, hidden in the shadows, the man is nervous, constantly glancing over his shoulder, as if he expected to see someone.

One of the other customers tries to strike up a conversation, but the little man leaps in the air, his eyes popping open like those of a startled rabbit. The other man shrugs and walks away, attaching himself to another, more communicative group of drinkers. Soon, they are deep in conversation and the stranger is forgotten.

Then, another man arrives. A second stranger. And in that man's eyes, the barman sees something different, too, although he cannot put a name to it. Whatever it is, it makes him shudder. The man stands with both hands on the bar, palms down, a fifty-rupee note sticking out between two fingers. The barman pushes a glass towards the man, snatches the note, then flings the change back across the counter. Then, pretending to wipe a glass with his tea-towel, he watches furtively as the stranger walks over to where the other man is sitting.

Walter turns the glass in his hand. It has a misty quality which intensifies at the bottom, where the toddy-seller's thumbnail cannot penetrate awkward angles. But Walter does not notice. Now and again, he takes a sip of the liquor, wincing at the sour taste, yet glad of its warmth. It takes the edge off his fear. It is not a fear he has experienced before. It is unspecific, cold, like an invisible vapour which infects every corner of his life, allowing no respite, even in sleep. It all started with that journey in the lorry. And that policeman.

He cannot remember exactly what was said, only the feeling of menace that the man evoked in him. And the invitation, which was not an invitation, but a threat. *Come and see me.* The terror that he felt at those words was underlined soon after by the sight of Mennan's body. But it is not the face of that sad, swollen corpse that haunts his dreams but the pock-marked face of the policeman. Every night, it leers out of the darkness, repeating the same message. *Come and see me.*

He wonders if he is sick. Perhaps he should see a doctor. But then, they might think he was mad and he would lose his job. He could not afford that. Too many people at home depend on him. He even wonders if he has been possessed by an evil spirit. The cure for that is exorcism, no questions asked. But he doubts its efficacy and, anyway, such rituals are expensive.

At first, he tried to drive out the phantom by seeking the company of his fellow drivers. And, for a while, it had worked. Thoughts of the policeman began to fade and he felt more optimistic. He convinced himself that he had just been going through a bad patch, a reaction to the shock of Mennan's murder.

But, after a couple of weeks, the drivers were joined by a newcomer, a youngish man called Cyril who soon made himself popular with his quick wit and friendly disposition. Walter liked him. He seemed to like Walter, too, and had quickly attached himself to the older man, seeking his advice on any number of matters. Walter was flattered. Then a change took place.

Cyril's conversation turned to politics. Like all the other drivers, he was Sinhalese, but he had some radical views. He certainly did not approve of Bandaranaike whom he termed a time-server and a coward. At first, Walter suspected that his new friend was a Marxist – they have recently become active in the cities, especially among the railway unions, and are busily organizing hartals, or strikes, which threaten to bring the country to a standstill. But then Walter realized that Cyril's interests lay elsewhere.

He was obsessed with a new Bill introduced by the Prime Minister. The Official Language Bill, also known as the Sinhala Only Bill, proposes that Sinhalese should replace both English and Tamil as the language of the administration. Its introduction has caused bitter rivalry between opposing groups.

The well-educated, wealthy Tamils are threatened with the loss of their influential positions in government. They will no longer be able to take public exams in English. To appease them, the Prime Minister has proposed that the changes regarding the Tamil language should not be introduced for another decade. This, in turn, has met with violent opposition from Sinhalese nationalists.

"Those bastards have the country by the throat," said Cyril one night, banging his fist on the table. "It's time we showed them who's boss. It's time to choose sides."

Walter pretended that he had not heard, but Cyril's speech recalled the policeman's words.

"It's up to all of us to do something. Even you, Walter."

There was no mistaking his meaning then. Walter felt as if the earth was spinning on its head.

"What do you mean?"

He asked, but he did not want to hear the answer. He knew it already.

"You work for an important man. You could be useful to us."

At that moment, there had been uproar among the drivers. A fortuitous argument. Walter had taken advantage of the distraction to slip away. He had avoided all contact with the drivers after that, subjecting himself to voluntary exile, clinging to the compound where he lives with the Agent's staff, rarely venturing out. Except for tonight when, desperate for conversation which does not involve the petty rivalries of servants, he has sought anonymity in a group of strangers.

'Hello, brother.'

A stocky man is staring down at him. Walter did not hear him approach. He mutters a greeting and looks away, hoping to discourage the man but, instead, the stranger sits down next to him. Walter shifts to the end of the crate, trying to put as much distance as he can between himself and the stranger without actually moving away. That would seem rude. And, anyway, the man might follow him.

"Haven't seen you here before," the man begins, conversationally.

"No."

Walter tries not to look at the man. There is something about his joviality, his refusal to be put off, that he does not trust.

"Don't talk much, do you?"

Walter does not reply.

"I know someone who would like to talk to you. Can you guess?"

Walter freezes. Despite the presence of the other men around him, he feels exposed. The man leans over. As he does so, he presses against Walter, almost pushing him off his seat. Walter can feel the hard muscularity of his arm, like coils of iron.

"The Assistant Superintendent of Police."

The man whispers in Walter's ear. He seems to think it a great joke. Then, sitting back, his hands on his knees, he stares into Walter's face.

The sweat from Walter's fingers mingles with the grease on the surface of his glass. It becomes slippery and he clutches it tightly, fearing he will drop it. The laughter of the other drinkers sounds distant, tinny and artificial like something relayed through a loud-speaker. He is alone. With a demon.

"Lost for words?"

The man nudges him hard in the ribs and chuckles.

"Never mind. We know where to find you."

And with that, he rises and disappears into the darkness, the only reminder of his presence being the empty glass that he has left on the crate.

1956: Sergeant Gunasekera

Sergeant Gunasekera has a penchant for detective novels. It is his custom, in the quieter moments of his watch, to hold a book out of sight under the desk, furtively turning the pages as he immerses himself in the plot. Thrillers are so much more exciting than real life. The same characters appear in every edition, but Gunasekera loves them: the punks with their Brylcreemed hair, two-toned shoes and Italian names, Martini, Rossi, Bianco, which sound like the elegant drinks consumed by their mistresses who are predictably blonde and voluptuous. Sergeant Gunasekera likes the blondes: women of easy virtue and few brains who can be persuaded to cheat on their lovers on the slightest pretext.

He thinks of his tight-lipped wife and wishes that she was blonde. She might sleep with him then or, at least, cheat on him, giving him a chance to get rid of her. He sighs. There is little chance of her doing either. He has married a woman as icy and foreign as Himalayan melt-water and yet she only came from a neighbouring village. Sergeant Gunasekera wonders if it would be worth reading science fiction to gain an insight into alien behaviour. Then he might understand her better. But he soon dismisses the idea. His life is determined by his wife's constant nagging. Reading is his only means of escape. He will not allow her to dictate his literary interests.

Putting these distractions aside, Sergeant Gunasekera returns to his novel, one of his favourites. He has read it many times. The cheap, soft paper has turned yellow with age and some of the pages are coming loose. He has tried to fix them with sticky tape but they persist in playing truant. He found one this morning, wedged under the leg of his chair. He has no idea how it got there. Like fledgling birds, the pages of the book are trying to escape their covers. He will have to take more care of them.

He skips a couple of pages to one of his favourite scenes. The blonde is trying to seduce the detective, a rough-spoken gumshoe whose tawdry clothes belie the brilliance of his mind. Gunasekera admires the man who, lacking a college education, still manages to outshine his superiors and get the blonde. He wonders what he, himself, could have been with a college education. A civil engineer, a doctor? Anything but a desk sergeant with a nagging village girl for a wife.

These thoughts are followed by the usual twinge of bitterness, the sense of having been cheated of something that was his due. Life is easy for the rich and so difficult for the poor. He, himself, was one of ten children. Considering his background, he has done pretty well for himself; but he knows he could have done better and the thought rankles.

Still, there is one cheering thought. His children, if he ever has any, should have a brighter future than their father. Since Bandaranaike's election, there has been much talk about the Sinhalese getting a better deal. Parliament is currently considering a bill that would make Sinhalese the official language of government, ousting English and Tamil from their current positions of pre-eminence. That would even things up a bit.

The Tamils have dominated the administration for too long. Not that Gunasekera has anything against them. Some of his colleagues are Tamil and they get along well. Even his wife is Tamil. Enough said.

Still, like that monk Buddharakkita Thera says, it is time to restore Buddhism and the Sinhalese to their rightful place. After all, the Sinhalese are the majority and they were here before the Tamils. At least that is what the scriptures say. Gunasekera heard monks preaching before the election. According to them, ancient texts like the Mahavamsa confirm that the Sinhalese have a prior claim to the country. Gunasekera has never read the scriptures for himself. But it all makes sense.

A shadow falls across the page. With a sense of foreboding, Gunasekera raises his eyes. The Assistant Superintendent of Police is leaning over the desk. Gunasekera can smell the garlic on his breath.

"Give that to me," growls the senior policeman.

Reluctantly, Gunasekara hands over the book. The Assistant Superintendent turns it over in his large hands, grunting with amusement at the lurid cover.

"So that's where you learn your police work, is it?"

"N-no, sir," Gunasekera falters.

"Good, because if I see you reading on duty again, you'll be demoted. Understand?"

"Y-yes, sir," stammers the desk sergeant. He can feel the sweat prickling under his armpits. Like most of his colleagues, he is terrified of his superior and always tries to keep out of his way. He feels like a helpless ant who, having fallen into a trap, is being eyed up by a praying mantis.

"Hm!"

The senior policeman drops the book into a waste-bin and strides heavily towards his office. Gunasekera waits until the door has closed before crawling beneath the counter to retrieve his novel.

The Assistant Superintendent paces his office, stopping every so often to stare out of the window at the bleak courtyard, an arid expanse of bleached earth unrelieved by plants or shade. The day has begun badly, putting him into an ill-temper. Over the past months, he has sent various plain clothes officers to spy on the Government Agent's driver, even using one to infiltrate the man's close-knit band of colleagues, but, so far, all attempts to suborn the driver have failed.

Having realised that he is the subject of surveillance, the man has become as wary as a cat, hiding away in the government compound where the Government Agent lives with his servants. Last night was a bonus. The driver visited a toddy tavern and was approached by one of the Assistant Superintendent's officers, but the policeman's report was disappointing.

Sure, the driver had been frightened but, if anything, that will work to their disadvantage. He will just make himself more inaccessible, bolting like a frightened rabbit every time he senses a threat. The Assistant Superintendent has no more time for such games. He must find an alternative.

Despite the overhead fan and the fact that the office is on the shady side of the building, the air is stifling. He needs to think. He will go for a walk. Taking a back route past the cells and the room which he uses for interrogation, he lets himself out of a side door and crosses the street. Another few minutes walking and he finds himself in front of the temple where the outer courtyard has been transformed into a maze of stalls.

Trailed by beggars, pilgrims flock to the flower stalls where they buy paper trays of sweet-smelling jasmine, pink water lilies and lotus to place on the altars. As egrets ride oxen, relieving them of ticks, so the beggars relieve the pilgrims of their coins.

Beside a stall, a young fellow is strapping an arm up behind his back so that his hand flaps out of the neck of his collar. Having done this in full view of everyone, the boy then approaches an elderly woman who drops a couple of rupees into his extended hand. The policeman guffaws. Helping himself to a tray of blue hyacinths, he offers a few pice to the stall-holder who, noting his uniform, wisely refuses payment.

As he makes his way through the stalls, the Assistant Superintendent spies a small boy with a blank, buck-toothed face, slipping his hand into the bag of an unwary pilgrim. Dropping his flowers, the policeman lunges forward and seizes the boy by the scruff of the neck. There are some crimes that even the Assistant Superintendent will not tolerate.

"Got you, you little shit!"

With a terrified squeal, the child flails his legs and arms, catching the policeman a glancing blow on the shin. The Assistant Superintendent winces and tightens his grip, lifting the child off his feet. He is an unpromising specimen, goggle-eyed and skinny, but he has plenty of spirit.

"You're coming with me."

Clutching the child around the waist, the man drags him back to the police station, past the now-watchful eye of Sergeant Gunasekara.

"Can I help, sir?" offers the sergeant, hoping to redeem himself.

"No," snarls the Assistant Superintendent. "I'll deal with this."

The child is shrieking and kicking but a heavy slap across the head puts a stop to his noise. Gunasekera, who hates violence, at least in real-life, buries his head in his book. He does not care if his superior sees him. He has to do something to stop his hands from shaking. He has seen people carried off to the cells before. Sometimes, they do not come out for hours; sometimes, not at all.

***

The Assistant Superintendent chooses the cell at the farthest end of the corridor, the one from which least noise will escape. He throws the child down so hard that he sprawls on the floor then, closing the door, he locks it and pockets the key.

"What is your name?"

Hands on hips, the policeman casts an imposing shadow.

The child gathers his legs up under him, turns round then, to the utter surprise of his captor, launches himself into the air, clutching and clawing with his small hands. Caught off guard, the policeman grabs the child around the chest, only to have a set of sharp teeth close on his knuckles. It is the Assistant Superintendent's turn to yell.

"You little bastard!"

The child is a screaming, squawling ball of fury. Extricating his hand from the boy's mouth, the policeman holds him up with one hand, while striking him squarely across the back of the legs with the other.

"Stop screaming, you little sod, or I'll leave you here all night with no food and water. In the dark. If you shut up, I'll make sure you're fed."

It works. The child goes as limp as an old sock. The Assistant Superintendent puts him down. He feels a grudging admiration for the boy. Despite his size, he fights with the desperation of a feral cat. He has courage, unlike many of his betters. The Assistant Superintendent has no time for cowards. Particularly, liberal-minded politicians: those paralysed by fear of causing offence.

"What's your name?"

"Ranu."

When he speaks, the boy reveals a set of unevenly-spaced, jagged teeth. His voice is nasal and his expression so blank that he might even be retarded. But the policeman suspects otherwise.

"How old are you?"

"Thirteen."

He is the size of an eight-year old.

"Where do you live?"

The boy shrugs. He has no home. The policeman rubs his chin thoughtfully.

"I can charge you with attempted theft. You are sure to go to prison. Or, you can do something for me."

The boy says nothing, but there is a lively twinkle in his eye.

"You'll be fed and, if you work really hard, you'll be paid."

The boy nods eagerly.

1956: The abbot's dilemma

A car pulls out of the grounds of the vast monastery at Kelaniya.

"Where to, my lord," asks the driver.

"Mrs Wijewardene's residence."

Buddharakkita Thera, abbot of Kelaniya, sinks back against the soft leather seats of the Opel saloon. The car and its driver were presented to the abbot by a devoted supporter. His well-cut, western-style suit was a gift from the woman he is going to visit. She has also sent him a hat, a black Fedora, which he often uses in public to disguise his monkish baldness.

It is not always convenient to be recognized. Especially when the abbot is visiting Vimala Wijewardene. True, she owes her political career to him, but so does Mr Bandaranaike. Unlike the Prime Minister, however, Mrs Wijewardene does not forget her friends.

Buddharakkita muses on how Mrs Wijewardene's family history has become interwoven with his own, the two strands now so tightly knit that they form a single thread. Like her late husband, she is a vociferous champion of Sinhalese rights. A stalwart supporter of Buddharakkita. Now, despite their friendship or, perhaps because of it, Buddharakkita needs a favour.

Over the past decade, the abbot has backed two attempts by Mrs Wijewardene to get elected. It has caused him considerable expense. And then, there was the general election.

A committed nationalist, Buddharakkita dedicated substantial resources to getting Mr Bandaranaike into office. The abbot directed the United Monks' Front, the powerful monastic organisation of which he is a founder, to lead the campaign for Mr Bandaranaike's election. Thousands of monks were sent out into the countryside, galvanizing the peasantry with their preaching, encouraging them to vote.

Buddharakkita is delighted with the result. Not only did Mr Bandaranaike win the election but Vimala, also, has been returned to Parliament, one of only four women MPs. And there is a bonus. In recognition of Buddharakkita's help, the Prime Minister has appointed Vimala to his Cabinet. She is now Minister of Health.

However, while Buddharakkita is flattered, he is not deceived. Vimala's appointment cost Bandaranaike nothing, while he, Buddharakkita, has poured rivers of money into the election. Vimala's campaign alone cost him 100,000 rupees. And there are still debts, huge ones. Buddharakkita is having trouble balancing the books. In order to win the election, he has spent money that he does not have.

Creditors are becoming troublesome and those who previously backed the abbot's political stratagems are not only weary of his incessant demands for money, but are also less willing to extend their generosity now that victory has been attained.

One actually said: "You've won the election, what more do you want?"

The fool. That is the trouble with this country. How can shopkeepers and sellers of saris ever understand politics? It is one thing to achieve power; quite another to keep it. It requires money. Lots of it. A never-ending supply. And that is why Buddharakkita is coming to see Vimala today.

The relationship between the Wijewardene family and the powerful Kelaniya monastery, of which Buddharakkita is abbot, is more than a matter of personal friendship. It dates back to the previous generation when Helena Wijewardene, Vimala's mother-in-law, raised the ancient monastery from a crumbling ruin to its present position of pre-eminence.

Centuries ago, Kelaniya was a powerful institution, enjoying royal patronage but, in the 19th century, it fell from grace. Colonial rulers, staunchly Christian, had not appreciated either its beauty or its significance to their Buddhist subjects.

But, under the influence of Helena Wijewardene, Kelaniya's fabric, both moral and physical, was repaired; its stonework re-crafted, its frescoes re-painted, and its influence restored. Even in death, Helena remembered the monastery, bequeathing it 250 acres of prime paddy land. However, the administration of this valuable legacy was entrusted, not to the abbot, but to Helena's sons, one of whom married Vimala.

By law, neither the abbot nor the monastery can own property. Helena's legacy is run by trustees. But Buddharakkita has plans to overcome that obstacle. With Vimala's tacit support, he has challenged the bequest in court, arguing that, as abbot, he should be sole trustee. If he wins, he will be able to direct the money wherever he wishes. With Vimala's help, he can present a formidable case.

As he nears his destination, Buddharakkita stares out of the car window. He has been too distracted until now, to notice anything outside. They are approaching the Hindu temple in Bambalapitya. From the bottom of the tapering edifice to its pinnacle, every surface is smothered with row upon row of gods and demons. All are engaged in some form of strenuous activity, legs raised, arms waving, fingers pointing, limbs inter-locked with those of their neighbours. To Buddharakkita, it looks as if these figures are engaged in a well-orchestrated brawl, each trying to push his fellow out of the way in order to reach the top.

Buddharakkita smiles. So like humanity. So unlike the pale stone saints in Christian churches whose rigid, unsmiling images remind him of corpses. One can almost imagine that the temple's gods and demons are alive. In fact …
Buddharakkita starts. An image with black matted hair and tusks has caught his eye. Hooniyam, isn't it?

Anyway, by some trick of the light, he thought it moved. Leaning out of the window, Buddharakkita tries to get a better look, but the car has pulled away and the small image disappears into the scrambling mass of figures with which it shares the temple walls. All the same, he could have sworn it winked at him. Ridiculous. He must have been dreaming. Even a god would not show Buddharakkita such disrespect.

The car rounds the corner into Glen Aber Place and Buddharakkita spots a girl standing at the entrance to one of the houses. She is young, not more than fifteen, but tall for her age and striking. He smiles at her, hoping to catch her eye. She looks at him, then bolts back into the house. *Pity*, he thinks. She was handsome and it would have pleased him if she had returned his smile. Monastic vows do not prevent him from appreciating feminine beauty.

The car pulls into a drive and stops before a shallow flight of steps leading into a large, colonial-style house. Putting on his hat, Buddharakkita eases himself out of the back seat and adjusts his suit. A woman appears at the front door and stands waiting for him at the top of the steps.

"Hello, Vimala."

This time his smile is returned. With a light heart, the abbot climbs the steps to greet the Minister with whom he enjoys an intimate friendship: one rumoured to be inappropriate to his calling.

The morning sun filters through the branches of the Bo tree casting dappled shadows on the courtyard. Several novices are sweeping the flag stones while one, taking a break from his duties, is feeding the resident monkeys with slices of mango. The monkeys normally inhabit the tiled roof of the monastery where they spend most of the day sleeping, grooming or suckling their young. However, the young novice has encouraged several of them to climb down into the courtyard and take fruit from his hand.

"Look, brother. See how friendly they are."

Anil is on his way to the cloister. He ignores the boy, wondering why the old abbot encourages such foolishness in the younger members of the monastery. In Anil's view, they should work to greater purpose. As he has done.

It is a good time of day for meditation and, as he enters the relative coolness of the cloister, Anil reflects on the progress made in the last few months. With help from his friend, the Assistant Superintendent of Police, he has returned to the monastery where he grew up with Asoka. The abbot is elderly and cowed by the visits he received from the police following Mennan's death. Their questions concerned Asoka and the old man felt that he was somehow to blame for the terrible crime in which his former pupil is implicated. He was eager to make amends.

It required only one visit from the Assistant Superintendent to convince the old man that he should take Anil back. Pacing the abbot's room, the policeman voiced his private thoughts on the matter. It was clear to him that the abbot's decision to send his brightest pupil to Kelaniya had determined Asoka's regrettable fall from grace.

Having planted this seed, the policeman allowed the abbot a little time to reflect. It worked. The thought of his own complicity in Asoka's downfall tormented the abbot. However, the policeman offered a salve for his conscience. The abbot could save another monk, Anil, from sharing Asoka's fate and prevent further damage to the monastery's reputation. All he had to do was receive the errant monk back into the community where he would be protected from worldly distractions. The abbot had agreed wholeheartedly.

Anil was welcomed back without protest. The abbot's fears that the police might wish to question him further in connection with Asoka's disappearance were dispelled. No further visits were made to the monastery and no-one, either within the community or outside it, expressed any further interest in Asoka or his whereabouts. Everyone was preoccupied with the elections.

***

But Anil has not forgotten. He still wants to find Asoka. Of all the people involved in Mennan's execution, Asoka is the only one that causes Anil any anxiety. He trusts everyone else to keep their mouths shut. They all know that retribution awaits anyone who speaks out. But Asoka is a different matter. That night, he took leave of his senses. Everything he had preached to Anil about direct action, everything he had lived for, was reversed in a matter of moments. Anil saw it for himself. The man was mad, or worse, a coward. Either way, he betrayed his cause. And his most loyal disciple.

That is the other reason for finding Asoka. Revenge. Asoka's word was law and Anil had obeyed, blinded by devotion. Or was it desire? He has never had a lover, but Anil loved Asoka more than his own flesh, worshipped him like a god. But, in an instant, he saw his idol fall. The foundation of his world collapsed. He even contemplated suicide. He will never forgive Asoka.

Anil circles the cloister, remembering the dark eternity that followed Mennan's execution. He had run after Asoka for many hours, trying to find him, calling his name until, finally, lost and exhausted, he was forced to accept that Asoka was gone. Alone in the darkness, he had wept for his loss. It was like mourning a death, only worse, because instead of sweet memories, he had only bitter ones.

Deserted by Asoka, Anil had returned to the shrine where he had offered himself to Hooniyam, prostrating himself in the dust, weeping, begging, abasing himself before the other worshippers. He was alone, without direction, lost. Then, finally, a miracle. Salvation. Hooniyam had answered his prayers and, in his divine mercy, sent another guide. Buddharakkita Thera.

Anil heard Buddharakkita preach for the first time at a public meeting and fell under his spell. He had listened enthralled to Buddharakkita's proposals: Sinhalese would become the official language; Buddhism would be restored to its rightful place; Ayurvedic medicine would be promoted. The foreign cultures to which the Sinhalese had been subjugated for so long would be cut out like a cancer and cast aside. A new nation would arise.

Along with thousands of other supporters, Anil had shouted and cheered until he was hoarse. And then, he had wept. On that day, he had been re-born. Soon after, he had returned to his old monastery and, without any interference from the elderly abbot, had devoted himself wholeheartedly to Buddharakkita's cause. He had joined the Monks' United Front, campaigning in rural areas, arguing, preaching, winning votes for Bandaranaike. And they had won.

Bandaranaike might be Prime Minister but the election had been won by Buddharakkita's monks. What a triumph for the sangha! But that was just the beginning. There is more work to be done. Much more.

"Brother." A voice, light and childish in its softness, disturbs him.

"What is it?" Anil rouses himself from his thoughts, angry to have been disturbed.

"Forgive me, brother, but there is someone to see you."

The novice who feeds the monkeys is bowing to him, his hands pressed together as if in prayer. The boy has still not lost the large round eyes common to all the Island's children. Dark as liquorice, they are fixed on Anil with an expression of innocent devotion. Something within Anil stirs as he remembers how he, too, stared at Asoka in that way, watching his master as he studied or slept.

Even now, he can recall Asoka drinking water from his tin mug with slow calmness. He would meditate, even when eating, paying less attention to the rice in his bowl than the wonders in his head. And, without waiting to be asked, Anil would refill his mug, grateful for any opportunity to be in Asoka's company.

Anil, who struggled at his studies, marvelled at his master's ability to draw wisdom from the dry ink of books. He basked in his teacher's brilliance, never taking offence when Asoka, exasperated at his pupil's slowness, called him names. *Ignorant cockroach. Lazy dung beetle.* But Anil did not care. He had loved Asoka more than his own mother and father. He had loved him more than anything.

"Brother."

The boy touches him lightly on the arm, trying to rouse him from his thoughts and get his attention. Whether it is the gentleness with which he is addressed, or the look on the child's face that reminds him of his old self, Anil feels a surge of anger so strong that he wants to slap him. The only deterrent is the presence of other novices.

"Brother," the boy persists, oblivious to Anil's rage. "A boy called Ranu is at the gate. He says he wants to see you. What shall I tell him?"

"I will go myself," says Anil, pushing the boy aside and striding towards the outer gate.

***

A few minutes later, Anil returns to the narrow cell in which he sleeps. Closing the door behind him, he prostrates himself before a small image of Hooniyam and gives thanks. The god is truly a worker of miracles. *To the Buddha for refuge, to the gods for help*. An ancient saying full of wisdom.

For several weeks now, Anil has been working on a new plan. Something that will underpin Buddharakkita's manifesto. Something that will tell everyone that this country belongs exclusively to the Sinhalese and that outsiders, whoever they may be, have no place in the new regime. No competing claims will be tolerated.

Of course, he tried it once and failed. Mennan's execution was a fiasco. Badly timed and planned, it had been dismissed by the Coroner with an open verdict. No message was sent to the wider world and none received. Even those who suspected that it was murder had assumed it to be the result of a petty squabble; the sort of thing that happens every day in this country. Arguments over a boundary, unpaid wages, or adultery with another man's wife: such disputes often result in shootings, stabbings or beatings. Most investigations are cursory and few perpetrators are ever caught.

The choice of Mennan was a mistake. Asoka's mistake. Inspired by idealism, he had wanted to show that injustice would be punished in the new order. It was Mennan's dishonesty, not the fact that he was Tamil, that had really prompted Asoka to choose him as a victim. True, the hanging had been unusual, headline-grabbing in its brutality, but who really cared about the death of an obscure overseer? The country is full of corrupt officials. As soon as one disappears, another takes his place. There was no lesson to be drawn from Mennan's death. An execution must send an unequivocal message. Now Anil has a better target. Strangely enough, one suggested by Asoka himself. But, so far, Anil has lacked the knowledge to set his trap.

Hunters stalk their quarry for days, following their movements, learning where they eat, drink and sleep, in order to plan the perfect ambush. For weeks, Anil has sought the same information but, even with the Assistant Superintendent's help, all efforts have proved fruitless. An appropriate hunter was required. Someone unremarkable, who could blend into his surroundings and track his prey for hours at a stretch. Now, the perfect tracker has appeared. With the help of a street urchin, Anil may get what he needs.

As he presses his head to the floor, Anil feels small grains of sand grating against his skin. They have drifted in under the door from the courtyard as a result of the novices' sweeping. Anil presses down even harder, grinding the sand into his forehead, salting his prayers with pain, giving thanks to Hooniyam.

The forest is unusually quiet. The nocturnal shrieking, squeaking, squawling cacophony of its inhabitants has been replaced by a fearful, trembling silence. Night has fallen as thick as a cloud of soot, a darkness so tangible that it fills the mouth and muffles the ears. The only illumination is a faint, luminous glow that shivers in a clearing beyond the trees. Yet none of the forest creatures approach. Except one.

A moth, newly-hatched, flutters dizzily across the clearing, its wings damp with newness. It circles and spins, frantically seeking the source of light until its trajectory is interrupted. A hairy hand with long yellow nails closes around the insect.

Hooniyam licks the moth's remains from his palm, noting with pleasure how the phosphorescent scales of its wings have stuck to his fingers. Having never reached adulthood in human company, he still retains a childish, if warped, sense of wonder.

A breeze shakes the trees and several small green flames ignite spontaneously in the earth around the clearing. Dark columns of smoke rise from the flames, twisting and spiralling, knitting themselves together until twelve demonic shapes stand around the clearing.

"Father," says one, kneeling before Hooniyam and touching his feet in greeting.

"Arise, my son and let me look at you."

Standing, the demon draws himself up to his full height, a towering nine feet. Hooniyam roars with pleasure, a sound that rocks the forest and sends its inhabitants scurrying for cover.

"Behold, my mighty brood. Our time approaches."

In his long years of exile, Hooniyam has not been idle. He has fathered a clutch of sons by many mothers, some human, some demonic, but the existence of all has been kept secret from the gods. Hooniyam has concealed his offspring, some in caves or cracks in the rock, others in forests where they live in trees and burrows. But now the time for secrecy is nearly over. Hooniyam's plan is nearing fruition.

"What do you want us to do, father?" asks the youngest and smallest demon.

"Together we will overturn the gods and take our rightful place at the pinnacle of heaven. This island, its temples and shrines, will be ours and all the deities will bow before us – even Kali and Vishnu. As for the churches, mosques and synagogues, they will be razed to the earth and all foreign gods sent packing.

"Come to think of it," muses Hooniyam, "Kali and Vishnu are foreigners."

"But," ventures the smallest demon, "aren't you, I mean, didn't you come from over the Water yourself? A bit like Prince Vijaya?"

Hooniyam spins on his heel, serpents hissing at his girdle, and the small demon cowers, not daring to look his father in the eye.

"Insolent child," he booms. "How dare you link my name to that slayer of demons. Vijaya, indeed! You forget. I have feasted on the blood of this country for centuries. It runs in my veins. The Island is mine. No-one, god or demon, has a greater claim to it than me."

"S-s-sorry, father," stammers the demon, his coarse black mane quivering with fear.

"Your plan is a good one, father."

The huge demon steps hurriedly between Hooniyam and his youngest son. It is not unknown for demons to eat their offspring when displeased. The best strategy, in such cases, is to distract the angered party.

"We have lived in hiding for too long," continues Hooniyam's eldest son. "I grow three inches every day and soon I will have to move out of my cave. Soon, I will be unable to stay hidden and the gods will discover our secret. We must act quickly. What is your plan?"

"I have already set it in motion," says Hooniyam, smugly. "It just needs a little help from you. We must create a diversion, focus the gods' attention elsewhere. Already those silly humans are at each others' throats, squabbling over which language they should speak. The fire is set. We simply need to fan the flames."

He roars with laughter and claps his hands, his serpents hissing and writhing as he breaks into a triumphal dance, joined by his sabre-toothed, shaggy-haired sons.

1956: The chena

Sriya is hoeing the chena, the rectangular patch on which her family grows vegetables. When the land becomes exhausted, the chena will be abandoned and another created. When cultivation ceases, the forest moves back. First weeds smother the soil, then ferns and bushes spring up, followed by saplings which magically appear, thrusting towards the patch of sky that has been temporarily cut into the tree canopy. No trace of the old garden is left.

The sound of Sriya's hoe rings through the trees as it occasionally hits a pebble. She is working her way between rows of maize, attacking her task with more vigour than usual. She always comes here when she wants to think. The garden in the forest is relatively quiet compared to the village or her parents' house and today, her head is bursting.

For some time, an attraction has been growing between her and Asoka. Now that she thinks of it, she must have loved him from the first time she saw him, the bedraggled vagrant that her father brought home from the forest. She must have loved him even then, or why else would she have begged her father to let him stay? And he loves her too. She has seen it in his eyes, growing daily as he has learned to trust her.

Asoka is teaching her to read Sinhalese. She traces the letters with her finger and, as they follow the text together, their heads draw so close that their faces nearly touch. Study has become an excuse for intimacy and the exchange of small gifts – a bird's egg, a flower, a smooth stone turned up by the plough – commonplace objects of uncommon significance.

Sriya has learned to read stories from scraps of old newspaper, but they are all sad tales of cholera deaths, robberies and murder. She prefers the stories that Asoka tells in the evenings when they sit on the edge of the paddy field, watching the moon; tales from the ancient scripts of the Mahavamsa about the great kings, Vijaya who founded the Sinhalese race and Dutugemunu who conquered the Tamil king Elara. Asoka says they are only myths but those heroic exploits seem more real to Sriya than the dreary items in newspapers.

Of course, she knows the legends from childhood, but they have acquired greater currency these days. Even the Buddhist monks who visited the village before the election had repeated them but, unlike Asoka, they had assured the villagers that these tales were indisputable fact: a true representation of Sinhalese history. According to them, the tales of the great kings Dutugemunu and Vijaya prove that the Sinhalese have a prior claim to the country. The Island is theirs.

Sriya remembers one monk in particular, a man with cold, staring eyes. He had frightened her, but Tissa was greatly taken with him. She had seen them talking under the Bo tree in the village after the monk had addressed a crowd. Ever since, Tissa has been as restive as a colt. The elections have come and gone, but Tissa still speaks of that meeting as if it was yesterday. After his awkward encounter with Sriya in the forest, Tissa has begun to speak about the monk with renewed enthusiasm. Only a few days ago, he stopped Sriya on her way to the well and began to talk excitedly, hardly stopping to draw breath.

"He asked me to join him, you know. He said I could follow him to the city. Live with him in a monastery until I find work. I think I might."

And his eyes had shone with a wild light as he contemplated his escape.

"What about your parents?" Sriya had asked, quietly.

"They don't know. And you're not to tell them."

He had pointed a finger in her face, warning her off, his face contorted with rage. She had stepped back quickly, fearing that he might hit her. All she had done was to remind him of his duty, one that every eldest son assumes at his coming of age.

"But the farm …"

"Damn the farm! Anyway, what do you care?"

"Of course, I care. I'm your friend."

She had put out a hand to calm him, but he had pushed it away.

"We can't be friends. Not now."

"But nothing has changed."

"Exactly," he had laughed bitterly. "Nothing ever changes. Not here. Not with you."

"I'm sorry."

He had looked so miserable that she had reached out to touch him, trying to comfort him. But he had misunderstood, as he always did. Grabbing her arms, he had pulled her to him.

"Marry me, Sriya!"

"No."

"Marry me! Or I will leave."

"Stop it!"

She had tried to wrest herself free, but his grip was too tight. His fingers had dug into her flesh.

"Hey. What's happening here?"

Prema had appeared from the trees, a mattock slung over one shoulder. Tissa had looked from one to the other, then pushed Sriya away.

"Damn you!" he had shouted, before stalking off angrily in the direction of his farm.

***

Sriya has not seen Tissa since. It worries her, but there is nothing she can do. Ever since childhood, Tissa has been prone to swings of passion, great joy, great anger, great sorrow. She used to be able to tease him out of it but a change has come about. Tissa has issued an ultimatum. Unable to comply, Sriya can only hope that time will restore him to his senses. She grieves for their friendship, but not too much. Someone else now occupies her thoughts. Asoka.

Last night, Asoka told her. About himself. Something terrible. Remembering that conversation, Sriya lunges angrily with the hoe. It slides forward, further than she had anticipated, chopping clean through the stem of a maize plant.

"Oh no."

She kneels to pick it up. She has nurtured these plants from seed, pricking them out as seedlings then re-planting them in six, straight rows. It took the best part of a day to perform that last task and now, morning and evening, she must fetch water to keep them alive. Chena gardens never have the advantage of a well. Sriya curses herself when she thinks of all the energy she has expended on growing these plants: the hoeing, the back-breaking journey with two full pails of water, three trips for each of the two watering sessions. And she curses Asoka. It is his fault. After what he said last night.

She flings the plant into the nearby trees and, dropping the hoe, walks to the edge of the garden where two full buckets of water stand in the shade. Cupping her hands, she reaches into one and splashes water over her face. The sudden coolness restores her and she sits down, her feet resting on the freshly-turned earth.

Her thoughts return to last evening's conversation, when she experienced greater extremes of joy and horror than she had ever thought possible. However, she now knows that the two are sometimes companions, as inextricably linked as the twins, once born to a woman in the village.

Sriya saw the children a few minutes after birth. What nature had intended to be two separate entities had been fused into one. The babies had been joined from the shoulder to the hip. Neither could exist without the other and, when one died, the other's fate was sealed.

It is strange that Sriya should remember them now. But, in a way, that memory reflects the dilemma that she faces. Sometimes, opposing feelings are as inseparable as those children. One cannot have one without the other. One must accept both, or neither.

***

Yesterday evening, she had been sitting with Asoka on the wall of the tank, watching the reflection of the moon in the dark, oily water. It was a clear night, unpolluted by the lights of human habitation and the moon, hanging low and full, had cast a pale gleam over the landscape. To please her, Asoka had narrated a tale of love and self-sacrifice: the story of Buddha and the hare.

He knew that it was her favourite and, as he spoke, his voice had cracked with emotion. She had turned to look at him and been surprised to see a tear running down his cheek, like a drop of silver ink. But she had pretended not to notice and concentrated instead on tracing the shape of the hare on the moon's face. Although Asoka had stopped speaking, his words were still warm in her ear.

"After a long fast, Buddha had become weak and was in danger of dying. Hopping through the undergrowth, a hare had spied him and taken pity. "Eat, Lord, and live," said the hare and had promptly leapt into the fire. Gratefully, Buddha ate the hare and, when he had revived, he cast around for some means of showing his gratitude.

"In those days, the moon's face was free of any blemish presenting, as it were, a blank canvas. With his finger, Buddha traced the outline of the hare on the moon's face, so that no-one should ever forget the sacrifice of that humble animal."

Sriya had leant back, stretching her neck to get a better view of the moon and, in doing so, her hand had come to rest against Asoka's fingers. For a second, their hands had lain together, touching lightly, but then Asoka had drawn away.

In the darkness, she had blushed. He must think her very forward. A vulgar peasant girl. True, she had wished him to take her hand, but she had not meant to touch him. It had been an accident. She was so lost in her own confusion that she did not realise that he had started to speak again.

"Sriya, there is something I want to ask you."

Her heart had leapt as she held her breath.

"I have wanted to ask you for a long time, but there is something that you must know, also. Then, and only then, you must give me your answer."

"Ask me first, ask me first."

She could no longer contain her excitement.

"Sriya, please. This is difficult. You know what it is. Of course, you do. You know my feelings for you. I want, no, I wanted, to ask you to marry me."

"Oh."

She had clapped her hands, then hugged herself, nearly bursting with happiness.

"Yes, my answer is yes."

"No, no, it cannot be. Not yet. Perhaps never."

He had got to his feet and was pacing up and down.

"First, you must hear what I have to say. You must know what sort of man I am. Then you may not be so quick to accept."

And then, walking up and down, he had unfolded the terrible account of his part in Mennan's death. By the time he had finished, Sriya felt as if her heart had been ripped open: the joy of his love eclipsed by horror at his complicity in another man's murder.

"Oh, god."

She had put her head in her hands, covering her eyes.

Asoka had put out a hand to comfort her but, thinking better of it, had pulled away, unable to bridge the chasm that now divided them. Instead, he had positioned himself some feet away, looking at the moon as he spoke.

"If you wish, I will give myself up to the police. I have been thinking about it for some time. Punishment is what I deserve. I know that. But…" and his voice had dropped to a low murmur, "since coming here, I had begun to hope for forgiveness. I don't know why. There can be none for what I have done."

Finally, he had heard it from his own mouth. Passed sentence on himself. He was a murderer. There could be no mercy for him. Or those associated with him. He must retract his offer.

"Of course, marriage is impossible. I would never bring such shame on you or your family. You have all been so kind to me, more generous than I ever deserved. I only wanted to let you know what I would have done, had I had the opportunity.

"I wanted you to know how I felt about you. I could think of no greater happiness than being your husband. But, of course, it's too late for that. In a few days, when I have finished helping your father, I promise you, I will be gone. All I ask is this: forgive me."

She had run home, leaving him there, staring at the moon, his face reflecting its pale rays, like a drowned man. With the excuse of a headache, she had shut herself in her room and wept for long hours until she had soaked her pillow and her cheeks were swollen and red, sore from the brine that streamed from her eyes. With only the pale gleam of the moon to lighten the darkness, she had felt as if the whole weight of the ocean lay above her.

When she could cry no more, she had turned her salt-stung eyes to the window where the moon was in full view. For a while, she had lain there, perfectly still, staring at the sky then, like a creature that stirs on the sea-bed, pulled by a tide many fathoms above, she had risen from the floor and, pushing the darkness aside with her arms, waded to the window. For many hours she had stood, staring at the image of the hare etched on the moon's shining face, until the sun sprang into the sky and the vision faded.

**

Now, sitting alone in the chena garden, Sriya realises that the hare has a message for her. Last night, she felt as if it was trying to tell her something. Covering her face with her hands, she closes her eyes, trying to recapture the familiar image. There. She can see it now. Breathing deeply, she tries to hold it in her mind and, as she does so, she can hear Asoka's voice recounting the story that she loves.

It is late in the afternoon and all the other men have gone home, returning to eat meals that have been cooked over wood fires, before gathering beneath the cool shade of the Bo tree to smoke and talk. But Asoka lingers in the paddy field where, last night, he made his confession to Sriya. Since then, he has plunged into the blackest despair. Finally, it seems, he has received punishment for his great sin. The murderer has ripped out his own heart.

He gazes out over the watery meadow to where an egret steps delicately through the green shoots of rice. From somewhere nearby, there is a loud splash. A toad, perhaps, or a water bird, launching itself from the bank into the water. But such rural tranquillity does little to lift his mood.

Sriya loves him, that is clear. Or, at least, she did before he told her the truth. What she feels now, he can only guess. But the fleeting joy that he felt when she said she would marry him, has only increased his pain. His hope of love was short-lived, extinguished by the look of horror on her face when he told her of Mennan and his part in the overseer's death. He was scrupulous in sparing her no details. Was it his desire for punishment that prompted him to tell her everything, or supreme arrogance? Did he really expect her to love him after that? No-one has a right to such love. Especially him.

He had intended to wait for her answer. But there is no point. He had it last night. He must leave the village. Once he has repaid his debt to Prema, he will go. But where? He neither knows, nor cares; for, wherever it is, he will be tormented by the thought of what he has lost and what he so nearly gained. Her love. Without it, there is no hope of redemption. He is simply a man living out his punishment, waiting to die. And the end, when it comes, will be a relief.

Sriya. The memory of her stricken face burns his heart. He had no right to speak of marriage until he had told her what he had done. By doing so, he only increased her pain. For that alone, he deserves this torment. No. She will be well rid of him.

A flock of black-headed ibis fly overhead in a V-shaped formation. They are returning home to roost. In the morning, they will fly the other way, to the tank where they spend their day trawling the shallows for food. Asoka has come to recognise all the birds in this area, each with its different routine. Although she will be his greatest loss, it is not just Sriya that he will miss.

***

When Asoka first arrived here, he was friendless, a stranger even to himself; stranded, like the victim of a shipwreck who, washed up on some foreign shore, finds that his compass has been smashed and that the stars, from which he previously took his bearings, have changed their aspect. In this environment, his years of learning proved useless. He was an illiterate among sages whose lore had been formed before ink ever appeared on paper or thoughts were recorded on parchment.

But, gradually, he has learned to plot a new course. The seasons, which meant little to him in the monastery except as periods of wet or dry weather, have drawn him into their cycle.

He has begun to understand, with his heart as well as his head, the vital importance of rain to the success of crops and the delicate mechanism of their relationship. Water does not simply fall from the sky and cause rice to grow; it must come at the right time and in the right quantity. Too little, and the rice shoots will wither; too much, and they will rot.

Passed down by word of mouth from one generation to another, the lore of rice cultivation is more ancient than the oldest religious texts, and it, too, requires a lifetime of study. Humbled by this knowledge, Asoka has developed a profound respect for the peasant community which has given him shelter.

Yet, despite his affection for the villagers, nothing compares with what he feels for Sriya. She is his lodestar; her compassion and sweetness, his path to redemption. And yet it looks as if that road is closed to him. He wishes he could reverse time to undo the evil that he has committed but, failing that, he must seek another cure. At present, he has a vague notion that it will consist either of forgetfulness or forgiveness. But how he will achieve either now is a mystery. Without Sriya, he finds himself, once again, in a foreign land without a guide.

Rising from his seat, he pauses for one last look at the paddy field before walking sadly back to the village where a group of children awaits him.

**

Until recently, there were few Buddhist-run schools and those were poor, most of the available resources being diverted into Christian missionary schools. This has been one of the main grievances of the Buddhist reformers who helped Mr. Bandaranaike to power.

Partly in return for the kindness shown to him by her family, partly as an excuse to spend more time with her, Asoka has been teaching Sriya to read and write in Sinhalese. Under his guidance, she has made rapid progress, but it has been somewhat hampered by the lack of learning material.

There are few, if any, books in the village so they have to improvise with whatever comes to hand: instructions on packets of soap, the occasional political pamphlet or odd pages torn from old newspapers that have been used to wrap goods bought in the market. Sometimes, there is a bonus: a whole newspaper, several days out of date, retrieved from a passing bus.

At Sriya's suggestion, Asoka has also begun to teach some of the village children their letters. Having started with one or two children, the class has expanded rapidly, so great is the hunger for learning. Asoka is now obliged to hold two sessions a day; one in the morning for the smaller children, and one at night for the older ones, returning from the fields. The evening sessions are his favourite. Seated on the dry earth under the Bo tree, he instructs his weary pupils to recognise, then write, a few basic words.

Quite apart from the mental rigors of learning, pupils must also contend with physical discomfort. As the sun sets, Asoka lights a large kerosene lamp. The glow attracts many insects, especially mosquitoes, and the chanting of the class is interspersed with the sound of sharp slaps as the pupils try to beat off their attackers.

Despite these irritations, enthusiasm remains high and everyone stays until the end of the lesson when, as a treat, Asoka recites a story from one of the ancient texts. Sometimes a small head nods prematurely, the sleeper being roused with a prod in the ribs when it is time to go home.

This evening, Asoka takes his class as usual, sitting under the Bo tree surrounded by a group of children. The open-air school has proved so popular that now it attracts pupils, not just from the village, but also from outlying areas. They are all ages, from ten to late teens, but all starting from a position of ignorance.

Looking at the expectant faces of his pupils, Asoka experiences a painful twist of conscience. Some have walked miles through the forest, braving snakes and an even greater fear of the supernatural. As every child knows, evil things lurk in dark places. Others have come direct from the fields where they have spent long hours, labouring in the full heat of the sun. All are exhausted. The few letters and sums that they learn are a poor return for their efforts. Yet still their numbers increase.

With a sharpened stick, Asoka scratches a letter in the earth. The children watch, fascinated, as an elegant, curving script flows from the end of the stick. It is like watching a spell emerge from a magician's wand. They are transfixed by a magic whose meaning they can only guess.

The stick rasps as it scores the earth, dislodging the odd pebble. *Sri*. A symbol used by Sinhalese that, in coming years, will acquire increasing significance. The stick stops writing. The children try to guess what the word will be. The stick starts to write again, swiftly sketching letters to finish the word. The brightest pupil, whose hand is always ready to shoot in the air, looks perplexed. He scratches his ear.

Sri – ya. A woman's name. Some of the more forward pupils begin to giggle, nudging each other and raising their eyebrows, but their humour quickly dies away. Asoka is staring at the letters with a stricken face. Bending down, he reaches forward as he usually does when he wants to erase a word, but his hand seems to freeze as it hovers above her name. An uncomfortable silence falls over the class.

"Sriya".

A voice, soft as a breeze, whispers in his ear. He thinks he has imagined it.

"Look," says a child. "It's magic. He's summoned her with his letters."

There are giggles and an awed, intake of breath. Asoka raises himself and turns around. She is standing at his shoulder, smiling, wearing her best sari, her hair dressed with jasmine.

1956: The lovers

Set against a deep black sky, the moon is as round and white as a communion wafer. After dismissing his class, Asoka has accompanied Sriya to their usual place beside the paddy field, where they sit on the bank, listening to the call of a brown hawk owl: *koo-ook, koo-ook.*

"What made you change your mind?"

Laughing softly, Sriya leans back and looks up at the moon, her face white with reflected pallor, her hair tinged with blue light. She points at the shadow of the hare.

"That story. You often recite it to your class, just as my parents used to tell it to me. But sometimes, if you hear a thing many times, you listen to the words without thinking. But today, I heard the message behind the words."

"And what was that?"

"Love, forgiveness ..."

She hesitates.

"... and self-sacrifice?"

He finishes her sentence, his brow furrowed with deep lines.

"Sriya, you cannot sacrifice yourself for me".

"The sacrifice is mine to make and I do it willingly."

Turning her head, she gazes directly into his face, her chin raised in a display of obstinacy, well known to her father, but rarely shown to others.

"I am afraid for you. Have you thought what could happen if I stay?"

"Have you thought what would happen to me if you leave?"

"You would soon get over me."

"I would be married to Tissa and he would beat me as his father beats his mother."

"He's not so bad."

"He's changed."

"How do you mean?"

Asoka pulls up some blades of grass and begins to twist them around his fingers. The thought of Sriya marrying someone else torments him but he must be sure that she is not acting on a whim.

"You don't know him as I do," continues Sriya, softly. "We played together as children. I loved him like a brother, but now it's as if someone else is looking through his eyes. I see something in him that I never saw before."

"What do you see?"

"Cruelty. A desire to cause pain."

"And what makes you think I am any better?"

"Even good men do bad things."

He leans towards her, grasping her hand, squeezing it so tightly that she winces.

"Sriya, I am a murderer. I knew what I was doing was wrong. I just chose to ignore my conscience."

Tears prick his eyes and he tilts his head back to prevent them spilling down his cheeks.

"It wasn't your fault. You were ..." she struggles to find a word. "Possessed."

"What?"

Despite himself, Asoka begins to laugh.

"Sriya. There is no such thing as possession by spirits."

She swallows hard and bites her lip. Realising that he has wounded her, he strokes her hand.

"Forgive me. I didn't mean to hurt you."

Her lip quivers as she speaks.

"I am just an ignorant village girl. Are you sure I am good enough for you?"

"Of course."

"Then what is there to discuss?"

Realising that he has lost the debate, Asoka surrenders himself to happiness.

***

At supper, the lovers can barely contain their excitement, laughing and smiling at inconsequential remarks and exchanging glances in the belief that no-one can see them.

"Something's up," thinks Prema. "That rascal has his eye on her."

He falls prey to a fit of paternal jealousy; a protective father required to share the affection of his only child with someone else.

"I should send him packing," he thinks angrily. Then, speaking aloud, Prema addresses his wife.

"Which rice did you use tonight?"

Chandra is perplexed. Her husband rarely meddles in household matters unless something is worrying him.

"The rice from the brown bin."

"Foolish woman. That is new rice. You should use the two-year old rice first. You will ruin us with your wastefulness."

Startled, Chandra opens her mouth to reply, then thinks better of it. Years of experience have taught her to deal with Prema's tirades. Contradicting her husband would only make him more argumentative and, anyway, the cause of such fretful moods is never the topic under discussion but something entirely different.

She has an inkling of what it might be and lowers her head submissively, fearful of revealing her own secret. She has known for some time of the mutual attraction between Sriya and Asoka and, in her own way, she has quietly conspired to bring them together.

Sriya shifts uncomfortably, looking first at her mother, then Asoka. Both look awkward and uncertain. Thinking to placate her father with more food, Sriya reaches forward but, as she is about to take his bowl, he dabs at the back of her hand, shooing her away.

Sriya jerks her hand back as if stung. Her father is not usually given to such unreasonable behaviour. She catches Asoka's eye and gives him what she thinks is a secret look, an imperceptible nod of the head in the direction of the door. But she is intercepted by Prema.

"What? What? I suppose you two want to go for a walk. Go on, get out of my sight!" Prema splutters angrily.

Exchanging looks of alarm, Asoka and Sriya rise to their feet and try to take their leave. They murmur a few words to Prema but he waves them away and they depart silently, one following the other, through the front door into the darkened yard. After collecting the empty bowls, Chandra quietly slips away into the kitchen. Prema is left alone, seated in the middle of the floor.

A large beetle flies into the room. Wings whirring, it sails drunkenly into the kerosene lamp, then thuds to the floor where it lies, capsized, legs flailing in the air. Prema flicks it expertly with his finger and, now upright, the beetle totters off to a dark corner, its oil-coloured carapace like a blob of petrol running across the floor.

Deep in thought, Prema taps the ground with his horny fingernails.

"What am I to do?" he muses. "It has always been understood between our families that Sriya would marry Tissa."

But then, Sriya shows no inclination for the match. It is clear where her interests lie. What is he to do? If he gives her to Tissa, then Asoka may leave and Prema has come to depend on the stranger who provides invaluable help on the farm. There is also another, more disturbing consideration.

If Sriya is disappointed in her hopes, Prema will be responsible for a lifetime of unhappiness, especially if Tissa turns out like his father. What if Tissa beats her? Prema's blood boils at the thought. But once she is married, he will be unable to intervene. The thought of trying to console a weeping daughter is an unpleasant one.

"Hmph! Women's tears. If it rained as often as they cry we could grow rice all year round."

Rising to his feet, Prema stumps out into the yard. As he crosses the dark space to where the cattle are tethered, he can hear soft voices talking urgently in the kitchen.

"That will be Sriya and her mother," he thinks, convinced that the whole family is plotting against him.

Angrily, he sets about cleaning the animals' water trough, a task normally performed in daylight.

Rumour spreads quickly, wafting from house to house like smoke. The schoolmaster is in love with the headman's daughter. The story of Sriya's visit to the class is swiftly embellished: sick with love, Asoka had conjured her image by magic and she had appeared before him, dressed as a bride, taunting him with her beauty. If she does not marry him, he will surely fall sick and die, then they will all be cursed. The village holds its breath, willing Prema to agree the match: all except one.

Having heard the rumours, Tissa has decided to visit Prema at his home where he finds the old man beating at the tines of a fork with his hammer. The new chena patch has proved unusually hard and stony and the fork has been bent out of shape.

"Is it true?"

Prema looks up in surprise. Absorbed by his work, he did not hear Tissa arrive. The directness of the boy's question perplexes him.

"Is what true?"

"There is a rumour that Sriya will marry Asoka."

"Then it is only a rumour."

Prema bends over the fork, running his soil-grained fingers along the tines. His efforts have achieved only partial success. One of the tines is still crooked. The thought of buying a new fork puts him in a bad humour. He only bought this one a few months ago and he has a peasant's hatred of waste. If an implement does not last a lifetime, then he knows he has been cheated. It is a scandal for a good fork to break within months. He was assured that it was stainless steel, but now he wonders if he has been sold a cheap imitation. When he next goes to market, he will take it back to the trader and give the fellow a piece of his mind.

"Will you speak to her? Surely she will listen to you."

The boy is pacing feverishly up and down, like an animal in a cage.

"What about?"

"You know. About me. As a husband."

Prema puts the fork to one side.

"I will think about it."

"But you will not promise?"

"She already knows what you think of her. Once she has made up her mind, nothing I can say will change it."

"But you are her father!"

"Yes, and she is my only child."

Prema wishes he could do more for the boy but, all his life, he has spoken the truth. He cannot lie to salve someone's pain, especially when he knows such a lie would raise hopes that may never be realised. Nonetheless, the sight of Tissa's agonised face wrings his heart. He steps forward, meaning to place a hand on the boy's shoulder, to reassure him of their friendship, but Tissa springs away. The look of angry malevolence in those eyes is something Prema will never forget.

Turning swiftly, so that Prema should not see his tears, Tissa runs into the forest.

***

Full of misgiving, Prema watches until Tissa has disappeared. It felt unnatural, rejecting the boy in that way. For years, Prema has treated him almost as his own son and he now suspects that his informal adoption of the boy has overstepped the boundary of wisdom. He has trusted too much to luck and to the friendship of the two children, assuming this would transform into mutual love as they grew up. But it has not and he is now placed in an awkward position.

Prema walks a little way up the dirt track, hoping to find Tissa so they may talk rationally. But Tissa is nowhere to be seen and, after a few minutes, Prema turns back, shuffling slowly, a small wizened man dwarfed by the trees. More than ever, he is aware of approaching old age, like a weight bearing down on him.

"It is no use," he murmurs. "I cannot alter fate."

Sadly, he trudges home, in a silence broken only by the shrieking of a parrot.

***

Tissa's mother, Manju, is squatting by a fire over which she is cooking the evening meal. Beside the fire is a large panful of rice, although there is little meat to go with it. Money is short and curry in Tissa's home now consists of vegetables in a thin gravy. Even eggs are a rarity and the chickens eat far more than they produce.

Roused by the clack of the gate, Tissa's mother looks up but her son strides past without giving his usual greeting. After walking for several miles, his anger has temporarily abated, but he is in a dark and sullen mood. Sensing there is something amiss, Manju quietly places a lid over the pan and follows her son.

Indoors, Tissa's younger brother Nihal is playing carrom with one of his three sisters. Nihal is a great favourite with the girls and is frequently called upon to braid their hair or amuse them with snippets of gossip that he has picked up from the village.

Some time ago, Nihal expressed a desire to become a dancer. Then, one day Tissa had surprised him, dressed in one of his sister's saris, posturing in front of a mirror. Tissa had torn the clothes off him and beaten him soundly with a bamboo switch, but it made no difference. Nihal simply took his revenge by appointing himself Tissa's tormentor. Gifted with a sharp tongue and ready wit, Nihal directs his verbal barbs with such deadly accuracy that any lingering friendship between the brothers has been extinguished. Tissa generally deals with Nihal's stinging comments as an ox deals with flies, but occasionally they penetrate his defences.

With his usual purposeful stride, Tissa walks swiftly into the house. Yet, once inside, he looks about him with the puzzled air of a messenger who finds himself at the wrong address. He has not washed for many hours and smells strongly of stale sweat. His clothes are filthy and, when he runs his hands through his hair, it stands out from his head, stiff with dirt.

"Ooh. Look what the cat dragged in!"

Nihal rises lightly to his feet and circles his brother, making an exaggerated inspection of his appearance. Two sisters, who have been squabbling in the kitchen, peer around the door.

"Hm, what can it be?"

Nihal adopts the pose of a dandy: one leg planted in front of the other, knee slightly bent, head on one side, chin resting in his hand as he contemplates his brother. The girls snicker despite their mother's frantic gestures for silence.

"Nihal be quiet!"

But he ignores her. Like a small stinging insect, he never misses an opportunity to needle his brother.

"Let me think."

He taps his cheek with one finger.

"Mmm. Bird's nest for hair, ragged shirt, dirty legs and, oh," he sniffs, "essence of armpit! It's a scarecrow. Irresistible!"

Throwing his arms above his head, he rolls his eyes at the girls in mock ecstasy. They shriek with laughter. Encouraged by his brother's silence, Nihal probes deeper, his taunts becoming increasingly outrageous as he works himself up to an act of sacrilege.

"No wonder Sriya loves someone else. Ha! Ha! Ha!"

Drunk with his own daring, he swaggers about the room, as if challenging the sky to fall on his head, his enjoyment heightened by the shock on his mother's face.

Suddenly, the room erupts: the carrom board flies into the air scattering the counters across the room; the younger sister, who had been playing with Nihal, screams and holds her hands over her head, and Nihal is thrown to the floor.

"Stop him, Amma. Stop him, stop him."

Tissa is sitting on his brother's chest, his hands around the boy's throat, banging his head on the ground.

"I'll kill you. I'll kill you!"

The two sisters run in from the kitchen and try to pull the boys apart but Tissa's fingers are locked around his brother's throat. They scream at Tissa and slap him but he neither hears nor feels them.

"He's possessed, Amma, he's possessed!"

And it really seems as if he is. As he squeezes his brother's throat, Tissa's lips part in a hideous grin and he grinds his teeth, as if relishing some demonic pleasure.

Thwacckk! The girls' screams are submerged in a howl of pain and a string of curses. Tissa rolls off his brother and lies face down on the floor, clutching his head as his mother beats him frenziedly with a broom.

"Bastard! Devil!"

She strikes him repeatedly across the back as she rails at him. Crack! The broom snaps in two. She continues to beat him with the stump that remains in her hands, wielding it like a baton, striking him over the head, forcing him to curl into a defensive ball, knees drawn up to his chest, arms over his head. At last, worn out with her exertion, she throws the stick into a corner.

"Get out of my sight. Go on, get out!"

Grasping his ear and twisting it until he grimaces, she forces Tissa to his feet and pushes him out of the door into the yard. Then, returning to where Nihal is still huddled on the floor, she kneels to inspect the bruises on his neck, ten dark and angry blotches, the colour of egg plants. He moans when she touches them, partly from pain, partly to extract more sympathy from his audience. Obediently, the girls fuss around him, clucking like worried hens.

"You'll live," says his mother, matter-of-factly.

"But mother," pleads Nihal, desperate to prolong his claim to attention, "he attacked me."

"Are you surprised?" his mother enquires cuttingly, as she rises to her feet.

"You know how he feels about Sriya. You brought it on yourself. Now clear up the mess you've made and let me rest."

She stands up wearily, pressing her palms against her ribs, aching from her chastisement of Tissa. She is too old for this. They should all be too old for this but age does not seem to have instilled sense into her sons. She wonders what the future holds for any of them.

***

Two days after the fight with his brother, Tissa is sweeping the yard as the village children straggle home from their class. Two, more lively than the rest, skip past the fence.

"Sriya loves Asoka. Sriya loves Asoka."

They chant the phrase over and over, occasionally stopping mid-sentence for short gulps of air, before starting again. Tissa can hear their piping voices even after they have rounded the corner of the building and disappeared from sight.

"Sriya loves Asoka. Sriya loves Asoka."

Tissa clutches the handle of the broom tightly, locking his fingers around the rough wooden stake as he continues to sweep, stabbing the earth with short, vicious strokes, snapping the twigs of the broom-head.

Inside, his mother moves slowly about the house, weakened by a beating that she received last night from her drunken husband. Under loose-fitting clothes, her body is covered in ugly black bruises that will gradually fade to purple, then red, then a greenish-yellow, only to be replaced by fresh ones.

Tissa loves his mother but he can no longer help her. He cannot stay here. Not with his heart torn out. A chicken runs stupidly between his legs, chased by another. He hates the yard fowl. Their cackling and squabbling remind him of the village gossips, always pecking spitefully at each others' wounds. Two more hens chase past, wings spread, beaks open, cackling with fear, squawking the usual false alarm. *Murder, murder!* Quietly, Tissa puts the broom down and follows them.

When his mother comes to find him a few minutes later, the yard is empty, except for a broom lying on the ground and the bloody remains of her chickens.

1956: A sleepless night

Rumour has come full circle and the account of Sriya's miraculous appearance at Asoka's class has reached Prema. *As if by magic*, whisper the villagers with a knowing wink or a nod. It is time for Prema to make his choice. Indecision will only make matters worse.

On the flat straw-filled mattress that they share, Chandra is kept awake by her husband's restless tossing and turning. Thoughts of the wrong choice torment Prema. Either way, the consequences could be disastrous. First, he favours one candidate, then the other, then neither. There is no easy solution to his dilemma.

In the countryside, betrothals still follow a traditional pattern: conditional promises, made between families when the prospective bride and groom are a few years old, are followed by prolonged negotiations regarding the bride's dowry as the wedding approaches.

Marriage is primarily a contract designed to strengthen family alliances and prevent the fierce squabbles that frequently break out over even the smallest portion of land. It is not uncommon in these communities for violent disputes to erupt over the positioning of a fence, sometimes resulting in murder and vendettas between neighbours that last for generations.

***

Asoka, also, lies awake, racked by self-doubt. An outcast, hunted by the police, he has had the temerity to propose to Sriya. He cannot live without her, but how will he support her? What future can he offer? A life on the run, if word gets out, or the shame of being married to a convicted murderer? His actions have been prompted by selfishness. He has not thought of her at all. Better to leave her with her own people where she belongs. She will soon get over him.

The random whine of a mosquito distracts him. Scrabbling for matches beside the bed, he lights a candle. The wavering flame reveals a host of insects swarming over the ceiling; winged creatures of such variety that only an expert could hope to name them all. He tries to count them and, briefly, drifts into a fitful sleep until he is awoken again by the high-pitched drone of a mosquito, close to his ear. Once more fully alert, he passes the night calculating the effect of his actions.

***

With open eyes, Sriya stares into darkness, contemplating the exchange that must soon take place between Asoka and her father. The whole village now knows of her love for Asoka. It is common knowledge, openly discussed. There is no more time for prevarication. Tomorrow, Asoka must ask for her father's consent.

One minute, she is sure of success, the next, tortured by the thought of what will happen if Asoka is refused. Reveries of marriage and a blissful life together are interspersed with ghastly images of a future with Tissa. She makes up her mind. If she cannot have Asoka, she will have no-one. She will grow old alone, taunted by the children of the village.

"Please Thaatha, please. Say yes," she murmurs, chanting the words over and over, projecting her thoughts at her father's unconscious mind, hoping to influence his choice.

If Asoka is refused, he cannot continue to live with them. He will have to leave. She will be deprived even of his companionship. Her broken heart will be a lifeless thing, her breast hollowed out by grief. Tears sting her eyes as she imagines her pain.

Then, clenching her fists, she rises from her thin mattress and walks to the window where she can see the moon. Beneath its delicate sheen is the dark shape which has captivated her since childhood. The hare. Her heart leaps. It is a sign. The Lord remembers those who love him; those who are prepared to sacrifice themselves.

"Lord Buddha, help me," she whispers, as she stares unblinking at the crouching image.

"Bless my family and bless Asoka. Bless my father and let him approve our marriage."

She remains at the window, staring at the sky, perhaps for minutes, perhaps for hours. She cannot tell. But eventually, overtaken by exhaustion, she returns to bed, sleeping deep and dreamless until dawn.

1956: Daybreak

Sriya rises early, roused by the old cockerel strutting about the yard, performing his rounds and crowing brazenly. She dresses hurriedly, yawning as she ties her lunghi. Dizzy with sleeplessness, she trips over her feet. There is work to do: a fire to light and food to cook. Her mother has agreed to let her make something special today – pittu and goat curry – her father's favourite, something to sweeten his mood before Asoka asks his blessing.

From the living area of the house, she enters the kitchen. It is really a storage area for pots and food, where rice and flour are kept in jars and meat in a small cupboard with a metal grille to protect it from cats and flies. Cooking and the preparation of ingredients often take place in the open air unless, of course, it is monsoon season when roads become rivers and the yard outside is turned into a vast puddle of mud.

It is still barely light when Sriya enters the yard. With trepidation, she approaches the woodpile, collecting sticks and twigs from its outer edges, careful not to dig her hand in too deep or disturb any snakes that might be sleeping within. Carrying an armful of kindling to the centre of the yard, she arranges it inside the clay pot which serves as an outdoor oven. After lighting a few of the driest sticks, she bends down on hands and knees, blowing gently until a thin stream of smoke emerges. Once the fuel has begun to smoulder and burn, she turns her attention to preparing the food.

Having selected her vegetables, some freshly gathered from the garden behind the house, Sriya lays them out on the table in the yard. They are almost too beautiful to touch: purple aubergines, shiny and supple-skinned; rough, green gourds; plump red tomatoes; carrots with feathery crowns. She can still smell the dirt on those that she lifted from the soil last night. Expertly, she chops and dices, dropping the peelings into a bucket for the chicken.

Her mother then brings her the meat, purchased from a neighbour who yesterday slaughtered a goat. This task is less to Sriya's taste. She hates the slippery feel of the flesh and the faint smell of blood as it dries on her fingers. Once it has been hacked into chunks, the meat is then rolled in chilli powder and spices to thicken the gravy.

Sriya places the meat and vegetables in a clay pot, pouring in just enough water to cover the contents then, clamping on the lid, she carries the pot to the fire where it will be left to simmer for several hours before more spices are added.

Next she prepares pittu, a staple like rice which accompanies curries, bulking out the meat and soaking up the sauce. She grates fresh coconut into a dish then, in a separate bowl, mixes rice flour to a paste with a little salted water. The two ingredients are then layered in a hollowed bamboo cane, the base of the tube being wrapped in a cloth to prevent water penetrating as the pittu is steamed over a pot of water. When it is cooked, a long rod will be inserted into one end of the cane and, pushed out of the other end, the pittu will appear as a long, brown and white roll, which will be cut into slices.

As she works, Sriya can hear the men moving about indoors. Someone yawns long and loud – her father she thinks – protesting at the start of another day's labour. He appears briefly at the door, one hand scratching under his vest, a look of puzzlement on his face at seeing her out here so early. He looks as if he might say something, but thinks better of it, turning back into the shadows of the house.

Asoka eats inside the house then leaves for the fields without speaking to her. For once, she is grateful for his absence. Her heart is too full to speak. No doubt he feels the same. She is out of the way in the yard, able to collect her thoughts in solitude.

Later in the morning, when the food is ready, she will bathe, rinsing the smell of wood-smoke from her hair and putting on her second-best sari while her mother makes tight packages of rice and curry wrapped in fresh banana leaves. Then, she will make her way to the fields to learn her father's decision.

***

Something is about to happen. Prema senses it. He has been observing the two young people closely, noting their attempts to avoid each other with bitter amusement. Each behaves as if the other were invisible; a denial that betrays their excitement. When she thinks he is not looking, Sriya scrutinises her father's face, as if looking for a sign. Although more subtle, Asoka does the same, glancing away if Prema turns to look at him. Convinced that Asoka is about to ask for his consent to their marriage, Prema decides to seek his wife's opinion.

"What do you think?" he asks playfully, when they have a moment alone. "What are they up to?"

Chandra shrugs, bending over the plates that she is washing, scraping at an invisible speck of dirt with her finger. Lacking the capacity to lie, she cannot dissimulate and the closest she ever gets to an untruth is either to pretend that she has not heard or does not understand. This morning, she succeeds in neither. She is obviously part of the conspiracy and Prema will have to seek an answer elsewhere. Angered at being excluded from the secret, Prema resolves to take his revenge.

First, having told Asoka that he intends to clear some new chena, Prema instructs him to load the cart with the axes, machetes and kerosene necessary to clear a fresh patch for cultivation. However, once this task is complete, Prema then changes his mind, considering the need to protect the rice crop to be more pressing.

Consequently, Asoka is obliged to unload the cart and start again, fetching bags of coconut husk that have been stacked against the back of the house. Leaning against a tree while Asoka works, Prema rolls a few strings of tobacco into a thin cigarette.

"That'll teach him," he thinks, drawing slowly on the bidi. "Shouldn't count his chickens before they've hatched."

The sacks are heavy and Asoka begins to sweat as he hoists each one onto his back, carries it across the yard then swings it over his shoulder into the cart. With silent approval, Prema notes the muscles that have developed in Asoka's back.

"Skinny as an old hen when he first arrived. Now look at him. Not scared of hard work, either, although he's come to it late."

As he watches Asoka work, Prema, once again, weighs the advantages of having him as a son-in-law. By favouring Asoka, he would insult Tissa's family. By not honouring an implicit promise, he would risk losing face among his neighbours. Such damage to village relationships can have many repercussions and take years to repair.

And what will he get in return? An educated pauper. Tissa, at least, has been brought up on the land. On the other hand, Asoka is devoted to Sriya. There would be no question of the beatings and harshness that are sometimes the lot of a village wife, nor would the toddy shop take its toll of Asoka's energy, robbing his family of its precarious income.

Asoka stops momentarily to wipe the sweat from his eyes before climbing into the cart and adjusting the sacks so that the weight is evenly distributed.

"He works hard, but will he stay out of trouble?" Prema wonders.

274

For there is another consideration. The old man has guessed the reason for Asoka's mysterious appearance in the village. Soon after Asoka's arrival, Prema made a trip into town, a four-hour journey by bus in which he had mixed with people from other villages, exchanging gossip and news.

It was here that he heard stories about the murder of an overseer, a man whose reputation for dishonesty was known even in these remote parts. It was said that the police were seeking the overseer's foreman, a man of education, whose age and physical description closely matched those of Asoka.

Since then, Prema has avoided making trips into town whenever possible. Once or twice, he has been on the point of asking Asoka outright whether he is the fugitive being sought by the police, but then he has changed his mind. The past is the past. An admission would change nothing or, perhaps, it would change everything. For Asoka has become close to Prema, replacing Tissa as the son for which he always longed. Prema will never abandon him. But should he let him marry Sriya? That is a different matter. It is not just a question of right and wrong, life is never that simple, but the balancing of risk against survival.

Still, he cannot make up his mind.

The day grows hot as the two men ride the cart to the fields. Neither speaks. Prema applies his switch to the oxen with unusual severity. Nodding their heads, the animals strain at the yoke, swishing their tails to ward off the persistent attack of flies, their skin flinching under the whisk of Prema's cane. Asoka's excitement gives way to apprehension.

Once at the fields, Asoka unloads the cart under the strict eye and even sharper tongue of his employer. Some of the villagers, who are also preparing for a day's work, walk over to greet them. Many, whose children attend the school, have a warm smile for Asoka. Prema just grunts irritably and busies himself about the cart, unhitching the oxen and leading them to a place in the shade where they can graze and drink from a shallow pond.

Several of Asoka's pupils are already at work in the fields, dragging long ropes behind them as they patrol the paddies. Soaked in Jak fruit extract, the ropes' sticky fibres trap insects that would otherwise attack the tender rice shoots.

Paddy fields are never left to fend for themselves. They must be constantly tended to ward off pests. When young rice is at its most vulnerable, cactus milk is poured into the irrigation channels to protect the crop from waterborne invaders, while monks' saffron robes provide an effective deterrent against airborne assailants. Converted into torches, the cast-off garments emit a brilliant flame and pungent odour repellent to flying insects. Protecting the rice crop requires endless vigilance and imagination.

"Time for me to deal with pests," snaps Prema.

The skin on Asoka's neck prickles and burns; his discomfort caused, not by the effects of the sun, but by the undisguised irony of Prema's remarks. He is desperate to broach the subject of marriage but can neither make, nor find, an opportunity as, every time he begins to speak, Prema ambushes the conversation, diverting it into other channels.

An occasional twinkle in Prema's eye implies amusement at this game of verbal hide-and-seek but, at other times, he is gruff and preoccupied. It is impossible to gauge his mood. There are also other obstacles to contend with.

Thinking that, at last, he has found the right moment, Asoka has just begun to speak when he is spotted by one of his pupils. The boy waves and shouts to attract his schoolmaster's attention then begins to wade through the paddy to where Asoka and Prema are working. Prema looks irritable and turns his back. Asoka groans to himself.

"Sir, sir. How are you today, sir?

The boy is tall for his twelve years and a fringe of hair shadows his upper lip. He is a quick learner, one of Asoka's brightest pupils, but once he has come of age he will be expected to work full-time on the farm which will leave little opportunity, if any, for continuing his studies.

"Will there be a lesson tonight, sir?"

The boy's eagerness cuts Asoka to the quick.

"Yes, Govinda. At the usual time."

"And will you teach us more letters, sir?"

The boy's questions are getting uncomfortably close.

"Yes, yes," says Asoka, hurriedly. Although Prema's back is turned, Asoka is sure that he is listening.

"It was very funny the other night, sir, when you spelt Miss Sriya's name and she appeared straight away. Some of the little fellows think it was magic."

"Yes, well, it was just coincidence." Asoka laughs awkwardly, wishing the boy would leave.

"Some of the others are saying that you will marry Miss Sriya, sir. Is that true?"

"No, no. Not, at least … no."

Asoka is more perplexed than ever. He dare not look at Prema who has given up any pretence of working and has turned to listen to the conversation. Unperturbed, the boy continues with his interrogation.

"Will you tell us a story tonight, sir? You always end the lesson with a story, but the other night, when Miss Sriya came, you forgot. The little ones were very disappointed."

"Yes, yes, I will tell you a story."

"Of Prince Vijaya?"

"Perhaps."

"That would be very fine, sir. I will tell the others."

"Good. Now run along. I have work to do."

Lifting his muddy feet in a circular movement, Govinda affects the delicate gait of a wading bird as he picks his way across the paddy field. Having reached dry land, he bounds off to join the other children who, grouped together at the top of the bank, are awaiting his return. In small communities, news is a precious commodity.

The children gather around Govinda, some of the smaller ones standing on tiptoe, others hopping from foot to foot, anxious not to miss a word. They bunch up, heads together, listening carefully to what he has to say then, as one, they turn towards Asoka, waving heartily, each sunburnt face creased in a white smile. He waves back. More excitement. The children whisper to each other, hands over their mouths, giggling.

"So, that is what you are teaching in your lessons! You are making my daughter a laughing stock."

"No, it's not like that. My intentions are honourable. I have been trying to ask you, but …"

"No time for that now," says Prema gruffly, stooping so that his face is hidden. "We must work quickly if we are to protect the crop. We will talk more of this later."

Motioning for Asoka to follow him, Prema stumps off to the cart where they unload several sacks bulging with crushed coconut husks. The coconut waste will be spread around the fields to attract the seven sisters bird, a member of the greedy starling family. As it gorges, the bird will devour the worms that attack vulnerable young plants.

As he bends under the weight of his sack, Asoka thinks miserably of the forthcoming conversation with Prema. Govinda's revelations will, no doubt, prove fatal to his chances of getting Prema's consent. What a fool he was to have entertained the possibility of marrying Sriya. What has he to offer her? Nothing. No home, no future. Prema is right; he has turned the woman he loves into a figure of fun. The whole village is now waiting for an event that will never take place. Prema is sure to refuse. How will he break the news to Sriya?

Of course, he will have to leave the village and find somewhere else to live: a place where he will find neither redemption nor enlightenment. Without hope of either, he may even drift back to the old life, become again the man that he has tried to reject: angry and pitiless, pursuing a goal that, despite the bloody sacrifices made to achieve it, will not last a generation.

What gift will he leave to posterity? A memory, perhaps, enduring briefly in the minds of others. But nothing to be proud of. While a few extremists may regard him as a hero, most will only remember him as a murderer. And what of Sriya? How will she remember him? As a man who made promises that he could not keep? The man who ran away and broke her heart? He does not wish for that kind of immortality. He would rather choose oblivion.

Rolling the sack off his shoulder, Asoka lowers it to the ground and, untying the string that loosely binds its neck, plunges both hands into the pungent darkness within. Once he has scooped out half the contents, the sack will be light enough to lift, allowing him to shake the husks directly onto the ground.

There are at least sixteen sacks and Prema wants them all emptied by mid-day. Asoka cannot understand the reason for such haste and would have proposed finishing the task in the afternoon, but, in his present mood, Prema is not amenable to suggestions.

After shaking the last sack free of its contents, Asoka stretches, pressing his palms into the small of his back, trying to loosen the knots in his muscles. Aching and tired, he longs to rest but there is no respite without Prema's permission. He is a hard taskmaster, but a good farmer, and Asoka respects him. In fact, he loves the old man.

A white egret lands in the paddy and, after pacing slowly up and down, adopts its customary hunting pose, standing motionless, its spear-like bill poised for attack. Even now, despite the gloomy prospect that faces him, Asoka can still take pleasure in his work. He notices with satisfaction that some seven sisters birds are already attacking the coconut waste. For the time being, at least, the crop is safe.

"Well, are you coming to eat? That useless daughter of mine is bringing food."

Sriya is walking towards them. Her sari is blue, the sort favoured by Kandyan women; as bright as a kingfisher's wing, iridescent in the shimmering heat. Prema, who has already climbed the bank to meet her, is looking down at Asoka with a forbidding expression. Reluctantly, Asoka climbs up to meet him.

**

Prema has enjoyed his morning. He has punished his young protégé for plotting behind his back and, now, here is the other conspirator, Sriya, approaching in her new sari. He has half made up his mind to inflict some milder form of torment on her when he notices the look of consternation on her face. Running up, she kisses him then hands over the packets of food.

"Have you heard? Tissa has run away!"

"What? When?"

"Last night. They're saying he's gone mad. He killed all the chickens. With his hands. Just tore them to pieces. Feathers and blood scattered all over the yard."

"Who told you this?"

"Bandula, his cousin. He says Tissa's mother is distraught."

"No doubt."

Prema stares out over the shimmering paddy. This is an interesting turn of events. He wonders if Tissa's madness is related in some way to Sriya and Asoka. Still, mad or not, by leaving the village, Tissa has abandoned his suit for his daughter.

"Go, girl. I need to think."

Sriya hesitates, exchanging anxious glances with Asoka.

"Go!" her father orders sharply.

"Yes, Thaatha."

She runs off along the path into the forest, pausing once to look back at Asoka.

***

Prema motions Asoka to sit by him in a hollow of the bank. It is where Prema always sits to eat his food and there is just enough room for two people. At first, he does not speak, preferring to eat in silence, his hand moving mechanically back and forth from the food to his mouth while his eyes remain fixed on the horizon.

The package of curry and rice lies unopened in Asoka's hand. He has no appetite. In Sriya's eyes, he saw hope, then disappointment when she realised that he had not yet spoken to her father. As she walked back along the path to the trees, she had stopped to look back at him. His heart had flinched. More than anything, he fears to hurt her.

He watched until she was swallowed by the darkness of the forest and, even now, he searches for her. As he stares into the black shadow under the trees, he sees a flash of kingfisher blue. She is watching, waiting to see what will happen.

"So, you have taught these peasants to write my daughter's name in the dirt."

Prema speaks so suddenly that he catches Asoka off guard. The old man continues, still looking ahead, his eyes fixed on a point in the distance.

"And then, when asked if you intend to marry her, you say no. In return for our kindness, you have made my daughter a laughing stock."

"No, that's not right. Please, I only wanted to …"

"There is only one thing for you to do now. I think you know what it is."

His face knitted in a leathery scowl, Prema still does not look at Asoka. His displeasure is obvious.

"But, you must listen to me. I love your daughter. I want …"

"It has nothing to do with what you want. I am thinking of her."

"So am I!"

Asoka responds with unusual ferocity. The old man jerks his head around and stares deep into the young man's eyes.

"Then, if you really care about her, you know what to do."

The meaning of the old man's words is plain. No argument will sway him. Asoka lowers his head, waiting for the final blow.

"You want me to leave."

"No. I want you to marry her."

An eternity passes before the meaning of those words becomes plain to Asoka. Then, thinking that he has misheard, he looks up to see Prema convulsed with silent laughter.

"Young scamp! Did you think I could not see what was happening?"

He laughs uproariously then, just as suddenly, becomes serious.

"I cannot say that it has not worried me. She was promised to Tissa but, now that he has gone, I can see no objection to you marrying her. What do you say?"

"Yes. Yes."

Asoka grasps the old man's hand, holding it tightly between his own.

"Then go and tell her. I do not have to have eyes in the back of my head to know that she is waiting over there."

He jerks his head towards the trees.

***

Asoka stumbles down the slope into the paddy, toiling through the muddy water to the road, mindless of the snakes that he feared on his first visit to the fields. Scrambling up the bank, he runs, heedless of the burning track and the sharp stones which assault his feet, waving his arms, shouting at the place where he knows she is waiting.

Within seconds, Sriya emerges from the darkness of the coconut grove, a distant speck of turquoise moving swiftly along the dry brown path, gliding across a frozen landscape in which all other life has been suspended. Stopping in the middle of the road, Asoka holds his breath, knowing that this scene will remain with him forever. A glimpse of heaven.

Her scarf fluttering behind her, Sriya runs like the wind, the brilliant colour of her sari flashing like the plumage of a tropical bird. Her hair, so carefully arranged, escapes its pins and falls about her shoulders. She does not care. She cannot wait patiently in the dark shallows of the trees. She must know. She wishes her legs would move faster. Surely the news will be good, but Asoka's face is still unclear. Why has he stopped? Why is he not running to meet her?

"Oh, oh please," she murmurs. "Please, please."

Finally, she reaches him, unable to speak, out of breath. But Sriya needs no words to learn her fate. Reaching out, she takes Asoka's hand. At her touch, Time, which had temporarily halted in its tracks, returns to its normal pace.

Sound and movement pour back into the landscape, seeping in from the edges, filling the stillness that had separated them from the world. Slender egrets bob for fish, distant oxen bellow, men shout instructions and children shriek as they chase each other up and down the banks, slithering into the water and pelting each other with lumps of mud.

"Sriya, Sriya." His only words.

Where once there was only intemperate anger, a new light burns in Asoka's eyes. Suddenly, he begins to weep: not with sorrow, but inconsolable joy. Gently, Sriya reaches up, and wipes away his tears with her scarf.

It is a week since her son's disappearance and Manju searches the forest once, twice, three times a day: often more. She has lost count. She hardly eats or sleeps, convinced that, if she relaxes her watchfulness, a terrible fate will overtake Tissa. She has searched the overgrown chena and the unfamiliar coconut groves beyond the paddy; she has asked at the shrine and questioned the driver of the local bus; she has trudged wearily through the heat to neighbouring villages, seeking news of her son from headmen and housewives; she has even approached the men who fish the tank, steeling herself to ask the unthinkable question: have they seen a body? They have all listened patiently, offering kindness and sympathy, but no-one has heard or seen anything of Tissa. Now, she avoids the company of other people, preferring to wander through the forest alone.

Today, she sets out in the early afternoon. The village is quiet with most of its active residents away in the fields and those, too old or too young to work, asleep in their homes. As she crosses the clearing, a pye-dog resting in the shade of the Bo tree, raises its head inquisitively and thumps its tail on the ground. She ignores it and the dog lowers its head back onto its paws, its lids drooping over milky eyes.

Despite the heat, she walks swiftly, following paths into the forest known only to villagers, striking at clumps of undergrowth with a long stick, in case the lush greenery conceals some sign of her son. She slashes angrily at ferns and creepers until her thin arms are covered with a film of sweat and her hair, hanging in damp strings, falls in her eyes and makes them sting. As she thinks of her family, her anger increases. Secretly, she blames Nihal for their ills.

Her husband rejected the boy long ago. Declaring that Nihal "should have been a girl," he has developed such an aversion to the child that he is unable even to sit at meals with him. Manju has often wondered if this is what initially encouraged her husband to spend more of his time at the toddy tavern than at home. Whatever the reason, he has dissociated himself from the workings of the family, abdicating all practical responsibility for its management, leaving his wife with the burden of raising their five children.

Using her stick as a scythe, Manju swipes at a tall arum lily, severing its head from the stem. She does not have the luxury of choosing between her children, indulging her whims as to which she finds acceptable and which not, abandoning one and favouring another. By her efforts alone, the family has stayed together. Until now.

Leaning on the stick, she tries to regain her breath, staring at the arum flower lying at her feet, still fresh and immaculate, its purity belying the deadly poison of its fruit. Whatever his faults, she has to admit her husband was right about one thing. Whenever there is trouble, Nihal is always close by, protesting his innocence.

For his own amusement, the boy starts disputes between his siblings and, when he can no longer control the passions that he has aroused, he accuses the others of bullying him. It has been his ploy since childhood and yet, often, he becomes the victim of his own provocative nature. His tongue is so wounding that, on occasion, even his peace-loving sisters are goaded into acts of violence. One girl, the sweetest-tempered of them all, once kicked him for an ill-judged remark about the colour of her skin. Yet every time, he pleads innocence.

Whatever his intentions, Nihal's influence has skewed the domestic hierarchy. His father having abdicated his duties, Tissa became head of the family. He was his mother's help and confidante and his sisters' protector. From early childhood, he umpired sibling disputes, dividing them when they fought, soothing their cuts and grazes and dealing out punishment and advice with a neutral hand. As he grew older, he intervened in the frequent, vicious exchanges between his parents. Eventually, even his father had grudgingly accepted his authority. The only one to deny it was Nihal.

With the tip of her stick, Manju flicks the arum flower into the undergrowth. Tissa has been her consolation and support through many troubled times: shortage of money, lack of food, crop failure and his father's feckless behaviour.

Always, when she was near to despair, Tissa would seek her out, put his arms around her and assure her that things would get better. And generally they did – just a little, just enough for them to survive the crisis, leaving the rest of the family unaware of how close they had come to disaster. But they always knew, she and Tissa.

She has confronted catastrophe so many times that it has taken shape in her dreams; an apocalyptic cloud of fire and ash, rolling inexorably towards her, always stopping just short of where she stands, but always a little closer than before, so close that she can taste its acrid fumes on her tongue, feel its burning breath on her cheek. It consumes all that lies in its path and she knows that, one day, there will be no exit from its roiling, black depths. And yet, with Tissa beside her, the cloud could not take her. With him, there was always a means of escape.

The marriage that she planned for her son would have provided for his parents in their old age. It was an ideal arrangement: both families knew each other; the children had been friends from childhood. Prema had only his daughter to whom he could pass his inheritance and that inheritance, although not large, was substantial by village standards.

Both sets of parents would be able to give up the hard labour of the fields when time crabbed their joints and weakened their bones. Manju's tasks would be light and pleasurable. When aching from work or the bruises inflicted by her husband, she has often consoled herself with thoughts of contented old age: sitting in the shade of the trees, peeling vegetables and exchanging leisurely gossip with Chandra; watching their grandchildren play.

But Tissa has gone and her dreams are less than a handful of dust. There will be no security, no rest in old age, no time to reflect, no dignity before death. Without hope of respite, she will continue her battle with the land until she dies; planting, harvesting, digging, hoeing, carrying heavy sacks and pails of water. Her body will bend under a ceaseless round of chores until she can no longer stand straight and sleep no longer cures her weariness. Only death will relieve her exhaustion. She will work until she drops, a worn-out husk, reclaimed by the soil that has grudged her a living.

Eventually, Manju's path leads her back to the place where she nursed Tissa as a baby, a small patch of dry earth under a banyan tree. Here she held him to her, seated between the sprawling roots at the base of the trunk, watching chains of ants issuing from powdery holes in the ground as birds fluttered and quibbled in the foliage overhead. Drowsy moments spent in intimacy with the one she loved most in the world.

Leaning against the trunk, Manju lowers herself to the ground, her palms sliding over the coarse bark of the tree. From Tissa's early years, this place has been their secret. Once, when he was little, perhaps five or six years old, she discovered him here, whispering to the tree.

"Promise not to blab if I tell you a secret. Promise."

Blab! Where had he learned that word? From Sriya, no doubt, his confidante and alter ego.

Intrigued, Manju had hidden so that she could eavesdrop on his childish confession. In a small, mumbling voice, Tissa had told the tree of a trick that he had played on his grandmother, moving her glasses, letting her find them, then moving them again until the poor old lady thought she was going mad.

Manju smiles at the memory. It was not the only time that he returned to this place when in trouble. She has often found him here after family arguments. Perhaps he will return. She closes her eyes, digging her fingers into the soft, sand-like soil.

What has happened to her son? Opening her eyes, she stares up at the tree canopy. As the branches sway in the breeze, rays of light pierce the gloom, playing over the bare floor of the forest. Suddenly, an arrow of light pierces her eye, almost blinding her. She squints. A branch moves and the light is extinguished.

As if cold, she folds her arms around her, although the sun still strikes hot through the leaves. Light and shadow play together like flickering images on a screen. Manju watches them, remembering scenes from the past: small battles, triumphs and tragedies. But she cannot distract herself for long. She knows that she must face the question that has dogged her since Tissa's fight with Nihal; a question that she has tried to avoid, although it has pursued her with increasing persistence until it fills every waking moment of her day.

Would Tissa have killed Nihal if she had not intervened? Yes. Tearfully, she admits the truth which, to her loving heart, is tantamount to treachery. Her gentle boy has been transformed. Grief enfolds her like a soft, black cloth.

Who, or what, raised a demon in her child? For Manju is sure of one thing. Tissa is possessed. Nothing else can explain the startling change in him, the reversal of his nature. But how did it come about?

She thinks of Tissa's betrothal to Sriya, which she had planned for so long, and her own disappointment, sharp as a scorpion's sting. How much worse must it be for her son? He had accepted his mother's plans without question, allowing her to plot his future. In doing so, the urgency of Manju's own need was transferred to her child. She had persuaded him to believe that something, if greatly desired, would become reality. He was convinced that he would get Sriya simply because he wanted her, and his mother had colluded with him in that belief, leading him up to a dizzy pinnacle of faith from which he has been pushed with devastating force.

She accepts that much of the fault is hers; but not all of it. The dreams she wove proved insubstantial, a nebulous support for Tissa's desire; and yet, if fortune had taken another turn, his hope might have been realised. If it had not been for an unforeseen event: the chance arrival of a stranger who took up residence in Prema's home and stole her son's intended bride. The more she thinks about it, the more she is convinced of an evil perversion of fate. Something unnatural has surfaced in their lives; an invisible malevolence has poisoned their future.

A recent visit to the astrologer has confirmed these fears. He said that Manju's family had fallen under the shadow of a malignant star. Each stage of its trajectory would herald a worsening of their fortunes: crop failure, sickness among their animals; events not reflected in the lives of their neighbours. Manju perceives its influence in every aspect of her life, and she feels it now, more strongly than ever. One cannot alter the stars, but surely something can be done to neutralise their effect.

"What to do?" she ponders. "What to do?"

Then, an idea gradually forms. Her son is sick in his soul and it requires a particular kind of medicine to cure him. She will consult the local priest.

Some weeks after the announcement of Asoka's engagement to Sriya, Prema is alone in the yard, treating one of his oxen for an injury to its leg. Despite many years of treating animal ailments, this wound perplexes him. It is not the sort of scratch or tear normally inflicted by barbed wire or undergrowth. It is neither a cut from a stone, being too high up the leg, nor has it been inflicted by the teeth of another animal. Instead, the injury is clean and deep, as if inflicted by a sharp instrument. If the wound had been a fraction of a centimetre to one side, it would have severed the animal's hamstring, disabling it for some considerable time, or even requiring its destruction.

Prema bathes the wound carefully, disinfecting it with powdered turmeric. Then, having anaesthetised it with a home-made concoction, he begins to pull the gash together with a sharp needle and some thread. Everyone knows the pride he takes in his animals; they are almost as dear to him as his own child. Has someone deliberately inflicted these wounds? He holds the animal's foot up as he stitches, cradling it against his own leg. It is a sign of the trust between Prema and his oxen that they will allow him to perform such operations on them with so little protest. The animal's hide shrinks from the needle and its tail flicks vigorously to one side, just missing Prema's ear, but it continues to munch on its hay, largely unperturbed by the pin-pricks to its leg.

Prema has just finished stitching up the wound when he becomes aware of someone watching him. It is Tissa. No-one has seen him for weeks.

"What are you doing here?"

Taken by surprise, Prema speaks more sharply than he had intended.

"I wanted to speak to you about Sriya."

"Oh."

Securing the cotton with a knot, Prema bends down and bites off the loose end.

"I wanted to marry her."

"I know."

Prema sighs heavily. Standing up, he stretches and rubs his back. He is getting too old for this type of work.

"You promised me."

Tissa fixes Prema with a baleful stare. The ox snorts and tries to turn its head, tugging at its tether and becoming suddenly agitated.

"I didn't promise you. Nothing was said."

"But it was understood."

It is true. Prema has to admit it. A long time ago, there had been an unspoken agreement between the parents. But things were different then. Tissa's father, a young and vigorous man, had worked night and day on his plot, setting an example to everyone in the village. He was intelligent and a skilled farmer. It was only later that an inherent vice had surfaced. There was no apparent reason for his decline and yet it was swift. He abandoned his family for the toddy tavern, leaving them to shift for themselves. Tissa was only fourteen at the time. Prema had helped him, guided him and become his mentor and the boy had regarded him as a surrogate father.

"My son ..."

Words fail him.

A green pigeon flutters noisily through the branches overhead. Prema's thoughts fly to his daughter, his most precious possession, dearer to him than any land.

"It was Sriya's choice."

"But that is not the way we do things. You know it. No girl chooses her husband."

Tissa is almost crying with rage.

"My daughter is not an animal to be traded."

Tissa is tense, like an animal ready to spring. Prema sees two pinpricks of red light in the eyes which he was once able to read but whose secrets are now closed to him. The ox, which has been shuffling restlessly since Tissa's appearance, now bellows and with one sideways jerk of its powerful head, pulls out the stake to which it was tethered to the ground. Bending forward to grasp the halter, Prema's eyes fall on the wound that he has just stitched; an injury inflicted deliberately, with a knife.

"Did you do this?" he asks, pointing to the animal's leg.

Tissa does not reply, but smiles, secretively. A cold shiver passes up Prema's spine, setting the hair on his neck on end. The boy is mad – or evil.

"If I don't marry Sriya, you will regret it. All of you."

Tissa's voice has dropped to a whisper.

"And I swear that, old as I am, if you harm my daughter in any way, I will take my revenge."

Tissa laughs. Old fool. He will teach him.

"Don't worry. I'm going. But when I return, I will take your daughter, married or not."

"Get out of here. Get off my land!"

Prema shakes his fist at Tissa, ready to strike him, but both know that he would be no match for the younger man. Tissa saunters away, laughing, stopping every so often to turn and stare at Prema with a look in his eyes that will trouble the old man for a long time.

A wild creature leaping over tree roots and ducking branches, Tissa flees through the forest. Thorns tear his skin and stones score his feet but still he runs, pressed by the urgency of his despair, his lungs wrenching painfully as he gasps for breath. He tires, unable any longer to push away the leaves and branches which slap him in the face. His arms hang at his side. He moves with an awkward, loping gait, half man, half animal. The deeper he penetrates into the forest, the easier it becomes to slough his humanity. Abandoning thought eases his pain. No reason, no hope, no despair.

Charging through a curtain of undergrowth, he stumbles into a clearing. Inside, the air is still, as undisturbed as water in a well. Above him, the trees have joined their branches, filtering the sun through their leaves so that the space beneath is filled with a pale, green light. Exhausted, Tissa falls to the ground where he lies face down in the dirt, his mind steeped in darkness.

***

"Will he do, father?"

The air shimmers like heat haze then resolves itself into the shape of a gigantic demon, Hooniyam's eldest child.

"Yes, my son. He will do very well."

Hooniyam steps from the trees, the serpents at his waist writhing like flames. His eyes are bloodshot, his mane of coarse black hair unusually tangled, studded with leaves and twigs. He has been sleeping rough and smells unusually bad, even to his children. Away from the perfumed air of the temple, deprived of his audience, Hooniyam neglects to wash. His breath stinks with the foetid smell of stale blood. He has broken his oath to Vishnu. Blood sacrifices are essential to a demon.

He has tried it their way. Done what the gods asked him. But it has only made him weak. And what use has he for divinity? The best jobs are already taken: Kali, Vishnu, Hanuman. There is no space for him in the magic circle. He is simply a cipher among the millions of minor gods in the Hindu pantheon. The only way to get what he really wants is to launch a coup, a palace revolution; and for that, he needs demonic strength and cunning.

Hooniyam picks a shred of flesh from his tusk then licks his finger thoughtfully as he contemplates the sleeping figure. He is still hungry and, for a second, he is tempted by the thought of fresh meat, but then he reproaches himself. He must resist the short-term, instinctive behaviour of his demonic nature. This boy is part of his plan. Bending on one knee, Hooniyam prods Tissa with a yellow-clawed finger. The boy does not move. Then, turning him over, Hooniyam props Tissa in a sitting position and, cradling him in one arm, he lifts the boy's eyelids and stares into the vacant orbs beneath.

"Good," he murmurs. "All light has gone out. It's as black as night in there. You've done a good job, my son."

"It took a while, father. I have chased him hard for many weeks. I prised him away from his family and forced him to live in the forest like an animal. But his conversion has proved difficult. Something still holds him back. His attachment to that girl is still strong."

"Hmmm." Hooniyam sniffs Tissa's ear. "Still a slight trace of her. Never mind, I'll soon get rid of that."

Holding Tissa close to him, he begins to murmur in his ear, a long incantation, the chant of demons from the time of chaos, before light or time were created, when all was darkness and hunger the only thought. He sings to Tissa until the boy's blood reverses through his veins, flowing backwards, plunging him back through aeons, until his heart stops and his arteries freeze and he is as pale and cold as a corpse. Then, opening the boy's mouth, Hooniyam breathes into his lungs, filling Tissa with his own demonic life. With a jolt, Tissa's heart begins to beat again and the air rasps in and out of his mouth. Lifting Tissa carefully, Hooniyam passes him to his son.

"He is ready. Take him to Gal Oya. He will know what to do."

Cradling Tissa in his arms, Hooniyam's son melts into air, leaving only a slight haze to show where he has been. Hooniyam caresses his snakes affectionately, allowing them to lick the last traces of blood from his fingers.

"It has started," he says. "Ceylon will soon be mine."

1956: A marriage

For days, Prema's home has been in turmoil. The yard has been swept and cleared, the chickens penned in, the cattle moved to the back of the house and the local carpenter called in. From early in the morning until late in the evening, the village has echoed with the sound of hammer blows and the wheezy rasp of a saw. Now, the preparations are complete and, today, Sriya and Asoka will be married.

Woken early by her mother, Sriya has been bathed at an auspicious time, dictated by the local astrologer. Village women, female friends and relations have gathered around the house, prompted by curiosity to peer through doors and windows, hoping for a glimpse of the bride. They giggle and gossip, becoming so engrossed in their own stories and memories that they almost forget what occasion brought them here. Some have even inveigled themselves into the room where Sriya is being washed and dressed. But no-one is turned away. Such interest is usual in a village where everything is shared.

During the preparations, Sriya is treated like one of the goddesses whose images adorn the local temple: an object to be bathed and perfumed, dressed in fine clothes and paraded through the village. As still as a statue, she listens impassively to the other women's tales of ribaldry, childbirth and, inevitably, death. Deaths of husbands, children and young mothers are mixed in with bawdy tales of illicit love affairs, comparisons of this or that man's sexual attributes and what are referred to as his 'appetites'.

There is much shrieking and giggling from the watchers at the window as Sriya's hair is brushed many times and scented with oil until it forms a long, lissom coil that slides between the hands like a skein of silk. The hair is then tugged back brutally and Sriya winces as pins, securing it in place, are jabbed into her scalp. When her head-dress is in place, large sprays of scented jasmine will be fixed to the back of her gleaming, blue-black hair.

Once she has stepped into her undergarments, which include a long, waist-length petticoat tied with a cord, the bridal sari is wound around her. It is white, the traditional colour for Sinhalese Buddhist weddings and, being heavily brocaded with gold thread, smells faintly of tarnished metal. The sari, over eighteen feet long, weighs several pounds. It is hot, heavy and stifling and, due to its weight, each tuck must be secured with pins.

Finally, Sriya is adorned with wedding jewellery which includes seven gold chains, like those worn by the goddess Paththini. Heavy gold earrings are hooked through her ear-lobes, while her wrists are encased in gold bangles and an armlet is fixed around her upper arm. Then, her mother attaches the head-dress to her hair, with ornaments representing the sun on the right and the moon on the left.

Cocooned in her heavy sari, the bride waits silently in the stifling heat, under the watchful eye of the village women. She can only leave the house at the precise minute dictated by the astrologer. It is an anxious time. The make-up which has been applied to her face feels sticky and uncomfortable. The lipstick, which she has never worn before, is unpleasant. It feels as if her lips have been smeared with goose-fat and her cheeks daubed with plaster. Sriya begged her mother to spare her this additional discomfort, but Chandra was implacable.

"It is traditional," she replied: the usual, irrefutable answer to all argument.

It is time. Weighed down by her finery, Sriya can barely walk. Led by her mother, she shuffles slowly out of the house where she is joined by her relatives who accompany her to the area in which a wedding canopy, or Poruwe, has been erected. A curtain of scented jasmine has been strung from the awning and lamps burn brightly in each corner.

Sriya catches her breath. She has never seen anything so beautiful. It is too much. She thinks that she will cry, or faint. But then a hand takes her arm. Just the lightest touch of fingers on her elbow. To steady her. It is Asoka. He looks as he always does, yet different. There is a light in his eyes. Something wonderful. And he is smiling. At her. With one look, he leaps through her eyes, into her heart, pouring his soul into her, filling her up with his love. They are already one.

"My love," she whispers. And he smiles.

***

Greeted by the eerie bellowing of conch shells, the couple tread slowly along a white cloth to the Poruwe where Prema escorts them onto the dais. Having already welcomed Asoka into the family by washing his feet, Prema will also perform the ceremonial rites: for priests play no part in Buddhist weddings and only officiate at funerals.

His heart beating wildly, Asoka is enthralled by his bride. In her white brocade sari, she is a consort worthy of any king. By turns, he wants to laugh and weep, nothing having prepared him for the excess of joy that he now feels. He is like a pauper who finds himself suddenly elevated to a position of power and wealth. He cannot believe it. The real world cannot hold such wonders. He is like a dreamer who dreads the end of sleep. For, when he wakes, reality will dawn, spreading its cool greyness over his life, dimming the sun with its shadow and dissolving this vision of heaven.

Sriya, her head modestly lowered, listens intently to the chanting of Pirith, Buddhist verses performed at weddings by professional singers. Despite her mother's insistence, she has not eaten for many hours and this, combined with the heavy scent of jasmine from the many garlands draped around her neck, make her dizzy. The weight of her shawl makes it difficult to turn her head but she knows that Asoka is watching her and, suddenly, she feels shy of the man who has been sharing her home for many months: her teacher and her friend who will now become her lover.

Theirs will be a Binna marriage in which the husband lives with the wife's family. Life will, therefore, be the much same after their wedding as before, but it will also be different. Sriya will be a wife and, soon perhaps, a mother. She lowers her head even further, hoping to hide her blushes and the secretive smile that she has seen on the faces of other brides. Now she understands their meaning.

As the chanting continues, Prema pours water over the couple's hands, joined together by the golden thread that binds their little fingers. They exchange rings, gazing into each other's eyes. From the quiver of his lip and the moistness of his eye, it is easy to read Asoka's thoughts. It is a touching sign of vulnerability in the man that Sriya still regards as her superior, as far above her in intellect and learning as the gods are from Man. It makes her proud.

She is his weakness and also his strength. Asoka, the scholar and leader who, through mistaken belief committed a terrible crime: he, who was cast down by guilt, rejected by society and who lost everything, has now been restored by his love for her. With his former life obliterated, Sriya has become his future. All bearings of the compass now point to her.

***

Sriya's hand wanders up to her throat. Her fingers explore the gold chain that Asoka has just placed around her neck. The new gold band around her finger feels large and heavy. Until now, the only ring she wore was a fragile trinket, no thicker than wire, given to her when she came of age. She rubs the inside of the wedding ring with her thumb. It is slightly too big and slips around her finger. Yet despite its awkwardness, she is proud of it. She is Asoka's wife.

It is time for the ritual exchange of sweetmeats when bride and groom feed each other with rice cakes, known as kaun. As he watches Asoka break off a piece of cake and gently place it in his daughter's mouth, Prema knows that he has made the right decision; a thought that brings him relief but does not entirely salve his conscience. When Sriya came to the fields, bearing the news of Tissa's sudden departure, he had felt relief. He has not told anyone of his subsequent meeting with Tissa. No-one else has seen the boy since he first disappeared and Prema thinks it better kept that way.

Even so, his conscience sometimes troubles him and he wonders, briefly, what sort of farmer Tissa would have made. He used to think that the boy showed promise and he berates himself for having raised Tissa's hopes. But, even before Asoka's arrival, doubt had set in. What if Tissa had become like his father, a drunkard and spendthrift? In the hands of such a man, the farm that Prema has spent years cultivating would soon be ruined. No-one who is not born to the soil can understand the deep attachment felt by one who is. Prema would prefer a slow and painful death rather than see his family inheritance destroyed. No. He was not wrong to choose Asoka.

Sriya and Asoka have now left their seats and must circle the Poruwe three times. Encumbered by the stiff folds of her sari, Sriya trips. But she does not fall. Asoka has caught her. Their eyes meet. She giggles. He waits until she is steady then, holding her hand, gently leads her around the canopy.

Having completed their circuits, the couple arrange offerings of betel around the Poruwe to pacify the gods. Asoka guides Sriya's hands, tenderly stroking her fingers when he thinks no-one is looking. But Prema sees, his eyes a little misty. He tells himself that it must be due to heat or old age, but he knows that it is not. All his dreams have been realised. His daughter is happy, married to the man who has become not only his son, but his heir.

The fierce protectiveness that Prema feels for his land extends to Sriya and Asoka. He vows never to tell them of the incident with Tissa or the fear that now torments him. For Tissa, he is sure, has the capacity to do great evil. He tries to take comfort from the fact that, now married to Asoka, Sriya will have a younger, stronger man than her father to protect her. He hopes that his anxiety is unfounded. Perhaps, he tells himself, Tissa has disappeared for good and will leave them all in peace, and yet, a nagging doubt remains.

***

That night, lying beside Sriya, Asoka watches her as she sleeps, curled peacefully at his side. Drawing up his knees, he wraps himself around her as the flesh of a fruit protects its precious seed. The act of love has performed its mysterious union. Having offered himself, a willing sacrifice, he was accepted with all his frailty, or perhaps because of it. Plunged in bliss, he was carried along by its dizzying waters, then immersed body and soul until, finally, he emerged: resurrected, born to a new life, free from the past, free from sin. He has known ecstasy. For the first time.

Light from the waxing moon floods the room. In a few days, when the moon is full, it will be a Poya day and Sriya will go to the shrine to make a special offering: a lamp filled with coconut oil and a fresh linen wick will be lit and placed before the statue of Buddha while prayers will be said to ward off demons.

Asoka does not know if he will accompany her. It has been a long time since he was in a place of worship and, then, his faltering attempts at prayer were accompanied by vivid recollections of Mennan's suffering. When he tried to meditate, he was presented with an image of the overseer's distorted face with its bulging eyes and blackened tongue. Emerging from the darkness, it invaded his head, blocking out all hope and filling him with fear. For that reason, Asoka ceased to pray.

The lack of spiritual practice left him empty and desolate. But, now, he has acquired a new focus for worship. Sriya is the object of his meditation and the awe, inspired in him by nature, has become his prayer. He has learned to surrender himself to both, to put their well-being before his own and, with that sacrifice, comes peace.

Sriya sighs in her sleep and brushes her hand across her face: a fleeting dream, like a cloud passing the moon. From the other room, come the rhythmic sounds of Prema's snoring and, outside the house, a mouse scratches at the walls, searching for a way in. The night no longer holds terror for Asoka but, rather, a feeling of calmness, of being at one with the unconscious world.

1956: The demon's disciple

Tissa lies on his back, neither sleeping, nor waking, his unblinking eyes fixed on the stars. A pale face, like the moon, appears above him, only, unlike the moon, it has amber eyes.

"Come, my son. Follow me. There is work to be done."

Tissa recognises the face, but cannot remember where he has seen it. A hand fastens itself around his arm and pulls him up, only then does he realise that the face is attached to a body; a man wrapped in saffron robes, a monk.

The man leads him along a dirt track to a great tank where, by the light of the moon, Tissa catches sight of himself in the water. His face is streaked with dirt and tears, his hair tousled, his clothes torn and filthy. He hardly looks human. A deep and aching void has opened within him like a wound and his skin is merely a shell for unfathomable emptiness. He has a fleeting memory of the terrible pain that consumed him, piece by piece, destroying his former self. Nothing now remains.

He cannot remember who he is or where he came from. In fact, he has wandered many miles, filled with madness, swiping at the air, flinging stones at anything that moved, howling like a lost and lonely animal until, finally, the roaring fire in his brain diminished to a smouldering agony; a hot ember, dormant, yet ready to burst into flame if stirred.

"Drink," says the monk, holding out a tin mug which he has filled with water from the tank.

Taking the cup in both hands, Tissa throws his head back, drinking so fast that water streams from his mouth and down his chin. The monk re-fills the cup and Tissa drinks again. The blackened space, formerly occupied by his heart begins to pulse. Cool liquid pumps through the fiery veins of his body, although it never reaches his head, in which the ember continues to glow.

"That is enough," says the monk, taking the cup. He leads Tissa along the road to the outskirts of a village, where a group of other men are waiting, armed with clubs and knives. The men are expecting them.

"This is your leader," says the monk. "You must follow wherever he goes and do as he tells you."

Then, pointing to the village, he whispers in Tissa's ear.

"The people in that village took your woman."

At these words, fire engulfs Tissa's brain. Shrieking in agony, he stamps his feet and shakes his mane of knotted hair then, darting forward, he snatches a knife from one of the men and, brandishing it above his head, runs screaming into the village. Taking this as their signal, the men race after him.

***

Yogendran has returned home late from a visit to his girlfriend. It is not an auspicious arrangement. Yogendran is Tamil and his woman is Sinhalese. She also has a husband. Still, this does not worry Yogendran who shuns the dull predictability of commitment, the tears, the tantrums and the nagging, favouring, instead, the excitement of illicit romance.

"And why not?" he thinks. "I am still young."

Like most nineteen year-olds, he regards time as his servant. It is in plentiful supply and he can squander it as he wishes. When he feels that time is running out, then he will consider marriage, but not before. Just now, he intends to enjoy himself.

After seeing his girlfriend, he ambled back to his parents' house where, still invigorated by his nocturnal escapade, he is too wakeful for sleep. Instead, he helps himself to a ripe mango from the wire-safe at the back of the house and pulling away its soft peel, he bites into its sweet flesh as he walks up and down the road, taking deep breaths of the scented night air and listening to the distant baying of a dog.

"Strange," he thinks, as another dog, much closer, begins to bark wildly.

Stopping to listen, he hears shouts and a muffled explosion. Whoompf! The thatched roof of a house at the end of the street bursts into flame. Yogendran starts to run towards it but is knocked off his feet by what feels like a cannonball hurtling through the air. Lying on his back, winded, he realises that a man is sitting on his chest. He can feel his ribs bending under the pressure of the man's knees as the air is squeezed from his lungs.

A piece of mango has lodged in his throat and he begins to choke, but he can neither cough nor draw breath. The man's hands are around his neck, the thumbs pressing into his windpipe with such intensity that he can feel the nails piercing his skin. Panicking, he tries to struggle free but his upper body is paralysed by the weight of his attacker. Only his legs are free, his feet drumming frantically on the ground as he tries to get some leverage by digging his heels into the earth.

His vision becomes blurred and the sound of soft thudding becomes louder. It is the blood in his head, pounding against his skull, seeking release. Soon, it will burst from his ears and run to the ground in two black streams. The pressure on his throat intensifies. Two thumbs are digging into his neck with murderous determination. Two thumbs, like those of any labourer, with ragged yellow nails and deep whorls cut into the rough skin.

Thwack! The creature howls and falls sideways, its head caved in by the shaft of a spade. Painfully, Yogendran rolls over and chokes up the mango, followed by a stream of bile. He tries to sit up but the effort is too great and he rolls onto his back, coughing feebly, snatching short, wheezy breaths. His rescuer, a man of about fifty who lives three doors away, is now grappling with another man. His opponent is much younger, wild in appearance, with black matted hair and skin dusted with earth. His lips, parted over his teeth in a snarl, are wet and red, the colour of blood. Suddenly, there is a flash of silver. With a single, quiet groan, Yogendran's neighbour slumps to the ground and lies still. Leaping up and down, the other man shrieks. A terrible blood-curdling cry of victory. As he waves his arms in the air, Yogendran can see that he holds a knife smeared with blood.

Lacking the strength to get up and run, Yogendran closes his eyes and holds his breath, hoping the other man will think he is dead. After a minute, he opens his eyes a squint. The wild creature has gone and been replaced by others. Everywhere, there are people running up and down the street. Women's feet pass, bangles clanking around their ankles. From the ground, their heads appear as small as pins and their skirts balloon as they run this way and that.

There are screams of terror, shouts and the sound of babies crying. There are also other sounds, indescribably ugly, snarling and grunting, voices screaming hatred and obscenities. It is as if all the demons in hell have gathered on the streets of this quiet village to perform a terrible blood rite.

Yogendran closes his eyes tightly and prays for dawn.

1956: A flame in the dark

Sitting at his desk, Mr Bandaranaike stares at the candle which he often lights when working late at night. It helps him to concentrate. A breeze enters the window, and the candle starts to gutter sending up thin spirals of dark smoke. There is something ominous about the twisting, wraith-like fumes, dark images emerging from the light.

At Oxford, everything had seemed possible. Within the protected confines of academe, it was possible to believe in the superior power of the human intellect. There was no problem that could not be solved by the application of rational thought. He had believed that implicitly, but now his faith has been shaken.

He stares deep into the flame, watching the blackened wick curl in the heat. Lucifer: the word means bringer of light. Before falling from grace, God's sworn opponent had been an angel. But what if light is actually the creation of darkness? What if his beliefs have been mistaken? What if those he trusts are not as they seem?

Mr Bandaranaike holds out a finger to the flame until its lambent heat singes his skin. That monk is becoming a problem. True, he helped Mr Bandaranaike to victory in the election and, in acknowledgement of this, Mr Bandaranaike appointed the abbot's protégée to his Cabinet. But that was not enough for Buddharakkita who seems to think that he is entitled to a share of Mr Bandaranaike's newly-won power. He is beginning to meddle in matters that do not concern him.

***

The day after the election, the Prime Minister received delegations from the Moslem and Tamil communities at his home, hoping to strike a deal with them over the introduction of the Sinhala Only Act. The discussion had opened on a promising note. In return for some conciliatory measures, his visitors had agreed to lend him their support, but Buddharakkita, who was also present, had intervened.

"Are you telling us what to do?" he had demanded, angrily. "The people elected us. We cannot betray their trust. Sinhalese must be the language of this country."

Fuming at Buddharakkita's interference, Mr Bandaranaike had reminded the abbot that the delegates belonged to his own party and had a right to speak. But the moment had been lost, along with the delegates' faith in their new Prime Minister. Mr Bandaranaike saw it in their faces as he showed them out afterwards, leading them across the well-kept lawn to the gate.

Apart from a few pleasantries, few words had been spoken and they had avoided his eye as they took their leave. He could see that they no longer trusted him and he had gazed after them with the same regret that one feels when watching a ship departing from the dock, knowing that it will never return.

As they walked away, he noted the set of their shoulders, slightly hunched, reflecting their disappointment. It sickened him to think that their faith in him had been rewarded by ingratitude. He wanted to run after them. Explain. *It was not me. That is not what I think.* But it was too late.

He had raised his hand to wave; a last gesture of friendship. But neither of the men looked back. Each was too wrapped up in his own thoughts, considering what to say to those expecting news of a compromise. Without the prospect of hope, one cannot preach patience.

Since then, things have gone from bad to worse. In an attempt to mollify minority interests, it was initially envisaged that the Sinhala Only Bill would include provisions for the reasonable use of Tamil. Such measures would have permitted Tamils to take civil service exams and run local councils in their own language.

But it was not to be. Stirred up by Buddharakkita, prominent Sinhalese citizens demonstrated against the provisions; one leading academic even threatened to starve himself until the conditions favouring Tamils were removed.

In turn, the Tamils tried to stage a satyagraha, the kind of peaceful protest espoused by Gandhi. But when they took up their positions on the green facing Parliament they were set upon by a band of Sinhalese thugs. Heads were split open and bones broken. Mr Bandaranaike's old class-mate, Chelvanayakam, a decent fellow, was thrown into a lake and publicly humiliated. Mortified, the Prime Minister had apologized personally to Mr. Chelvanayakam who had shaken his hand in sporting fashion. Yet worse was to come.

And here it is, sitting on the table in front of him, a carefully folded, typewritten report from the police chief at Gal Oya. Mr Bandaranaike picks it up and re-reads it for the hundredth time. It was brought to him only an hour ago by an ashen-faced clerk. The Prime Minister had already been warned of trouble, having received a phone call in advance of the letter. The telephone line had crackled and the details had been garbled, although he had heard enough to know that peasants in the eastern district had come to blows over the Sinhala Only Bill. Yet nothing had prepared him for this.

Holding the sheet of paper up to the candle, he can see where the old typewriter ribbon, faint with age, has been replaced. Pale, indistinct words have been typed over with a line of dark crosses, then re-written. If only one could re-write history so easily. The candle flame glows faintly through the paper, its flickering light illuminating the figures: "Estimated: 100 – 200 dead".

Carefully re-folding the paper, Mr Bandaranaike slips it in a drawer.

Centuries ago, the great Emperor Ashoka, weary of the bloody massacres by which he had conquered vast swathes of India, converted to Buddhism and consequently secured, not only peace of mind, but a new, more subtle means of domination. Prompted by his new-found faith, Ashoka sent his son and daughter as missionaries to the little island of Ceylon.

They bore a gift. In keeping with their shaven heads and rough-woven robes, the gift was modest, even daring, in its simplicity. It consisted of neither gold, nor jewels, silks, nor perfume, but a shoot of the Bo tree under which Buddha had received enlightenment.

At first, this offering was received with astonishment, then rapture, for with it came the promise of release from worldly suffering. In Anuradhapura, the ancient capital of Ceylon, the sapling was planted in the courtyard of the first temple of the new religion. It flourished and, soon, cuttings from that tree were being taken to other cities in the Island where they also took root alongside new temples.

It was as if the very stones of the Island were putting forth shoots. Soon, a profusion of temples, dagobas and monasteries flourished alongside the royal palaces built for Buddhist rulers.

Yet not all invasions from Ceylon's neighbour were so peaceful. One after the other, the fate of the Island's capital cities was decided by the violent incursions of Indian raiders. After 1,400 years of pre-eminence, the great metropolis of Anuradhapura was the first to fall. Situated on the north-western edge of the Island, it was within easy striking distance of the Indian mainland and, after suffering repeated depredations, it finally succumbed to a cataclysmic attack by the Tamil ruler, Rajarajah, in the tenth century.

Several decades later, having defeated the south Indian invaders, the Sinhalese king Vijayabahu chose Polonnaruwa as his seat of power. Situated on the south-eastern side of the Island, the city had the advantage of being less accessible to Indian attack from the mainland. Ceylon's new capital thrived and, like its predecessor, blossomed with beautiful buildings and wonders sculpted in stone: immense statues of Buddha, moonstones with delicate traceries of elephants and flowers and an exquisite bathing pool, its layers of concentric steps carved in the shape of a lotus.

Two generations later, Polonnaruwa reached its apogee under king Parakramabahu whose promotion of agriculture and irrigation projects set a precedent for his twentieth century successor, Prime Minister D.S. Senanayake. Parakramabahu's greatest achievement was the construction of an artificial reservoir, or tank, over eight miles long and forty feet deep. The Parakrama Samudra, or Sea of Parakramabahu, encircled the city, simultaneously providing a defence, drinking water and irrigation for the surrounding fields.

In Parakramabahu's time, the city of Polonnaruwa was entirely self-sufficient. And yet, after his death, his successors slipped into a cycle of internecine squabbling and alliances with south Indian rulers that inevitably led to a further, catastrophic invasion from the mainland and the decline of the city.

The glories of Anuradhapura and Polonnaruwa have now passed; their only monuments, the ruins of buildings and sculptures that litter the ground like frangipani blossom; a fleeting vision of beauty, destined to rot into the ground. Yet one thing remains. The original Bo tree, brought by Ashoka's children, still flourishes in the temple courtyard at Anuradhapura.

A memory of greatness lingers, particularly in the minds of those trying to invent a Sinhalese state. And with it comes bitterness. And blame. Fragments of history bolster fresh grievances. Tamils are now perceived as destroyers of a great civilisation, a fifth column, the invisible arm of India governing the State from within. They are the worm in the bud that must be cut out if the tree is to bear fruit.

It is time for the morning walk. A door onto the verandah flies open and the Government Agent steps into the garden followed by his spaniel, Skipper. The dog is eager for exercise. He races around the lawn then, finding a spot at the centre, he yaps and leaps in the air, hoping for a game. But Nash is preoccupied. Hands behind his back, he walks slowly, lost in contemplation, trying to make sense of his country's complexity and its many contradictions.

He lives in Polonnaruwa, the second of the country's ancient capital cities, where images of the past are still imprinted on the landscape in brick and stone. There is a palace by the lake, reputed to have had one thousand rooms, where Nash often sits on a crumbling wall, listening for voices from the past. But the ghosts of those places are silent or, at least, they do not speak to him.

Nash has often considered writing a history of Ceylon. However, these days, the prospect seems less appealing. Here he is, a Tamil, in a position of influence in a largely Sinhalese city. It is a situation which, until recently, never struck him as ironic.

There is a commotion in the kitchen. The cook is berating the housemaid in Sinhalese.

"These pans are filthy. Do them again."

"It wasn't me!"

"Don't argue, cheeky girl. Just do as I say."

Their shrill voices float out to the garden. The housemaid begins to cry. Nash sighs. He has followed every word of their conversation, being as fluent in Sinhalese as Tamil, although his first language is English. Like most influential men of his generation, he attended one of the Island's English-style public schools, then travelled abroad to study at an English university. He speaks his native languages perfectly, but his accent is English.

In the kitchen, the cook threatens to strike the housemaid. The sound of crying gets louder. Nash pauses, listening anxiously. He tries not to interfere in the affairs of servants but he will not tolerate violence. The crying stops. Silence. No sound of a slap. Good. He will not be required to intervene on this occasion. But he will speak to Godfrey. Tell him to keep an eye on the cook, who is efficient but a bully.

"Skipper, heel!"

Nash is distracted by the dog that is energetically digging holes in the flower bed. Nash's wife, Chitra, a keen gardener, will forgive neither the dog nor her husband for any damage to her precious plants. Feigning deafness, Skipper ignores his master, earth spurting from his paws as he paddles furiously in search of treasure.

"Wretched animal," mutters Nash, striding over the lawn to the border where Skipper's activities have already resulted in a large hole. Grasping the dog by its collar, Nash drags it, reluctant and whining, from its excavations.

"Now, sit," orders Nash sternly, pointing to a spot at the foot of a garden seat where the two of them often sit in companionable silence. The dog whines and growls, turning a few restless circles before settling down and quietly licking his paws.

"I don't know what's got into you," murmurs Nash, taking up his usual position on the seat then bending over to scratch the dog affectionately behind the ears.

"Chitra will be angry. With both of us."

Stretching his long legs in front of him, he folds his arms behind his head and inhales the sweet scent of the temple tree which overshadows the seat. His thoughts turn once more to his wife. Chitra. Like him, she seems to come from another age. In common with most other middle-class Tamils, her father rose to prominence under British rule.

While Ceylonese were not allowed to act as judges, some made a profitable living from translating for the courts. Chitra's father had been one of those translators. His money had bought him a large house with many servants, a carriage drawn by two fine horses and a place for his daughter at an exclusive convent where she had been the first Ceylonese girl to study alongside the daughters of English civil servants and planters.

Like Nash, Chitra regards English as her first language. How like him she is. And how out of step they both seem with the changes taking place in their country; one that is rapidly being re-invented.

"Like two old dinosaurs," thinks Nash, bleakly.

The world they knew is collapsing around them. Daily, the impression that he is a foreigner in his own land grows stronger. He does not discuss it with Chitra, but he knows she feels the same. There is a sadness about her these days which, although indefinable, reflects his mood. Ordinary things have acquired a poignancy for her. She talks of them, looks at them, as if saying goodbye. Like him, she rarely speaks of the future, instinctively avoiding it.

Of necessity, Chitra lives in the present, but she prefers the past, frequently reminiscing, travelling back to a world that was safe and predictable. Sometimes Nash catches her, looking out of the window, staring at something he cannot see, and he wonders what she is thinking. He guesses, but he does not ask. Naming a fear makes it real.

But not everyone has been left behind. Mr Bandaranaike, a man only a few years Nash's junior, from a similar background and education, has been successfully assimilated into the new order, many viewing him as its creator. Of course, he has the advantage of Sinhalese birth. However, he was brought up in the Christian faith, only espousing Buddhism in adulthood.

The motive for the Prime Minister's conversion is not particularly suspect. Many families only converted to Christianity in the last couple of generations. It is not surprising, in a largely Buddhist society, that a number should drift back to their roots. However, Mr Bandaranaike has made another statement. He has abandoned western clothes in favour of national dress. Among the middle classes, this is more a cause for amusement than alarm. But it has won him votes among the rural electorate. A smart move, if a little cynical.

What really worries Nash is not the Prime Minister's dress or religion, but his choice of allies: Buddharakkita Thera, in particular. It is evident, even from snippets of news in the Government-run press, that the abbot wields considerable influence behind the scenes.

It is inevitable that in return for his support during the election, Buddharakkita should expect some form of reward. But surely this did not have to include appointing his protégée to the Cabinet. One cannot treat offices of State as if they were sweets, doling them out to appease one's favourites. There will simply not be enough to go around.

And there is another problem. How can the Prime Minister ever hope to cement a coalition representing such a wide diversity of views? At one end of the spectrum is Mrs Wijewardene, an extremist proponent of Sinhalese nationalism; at the other, Philip Gunawardane, leader of one of the Island's Marxist parties. It is impossible. Sooner or later, the coalition party will crumble and one faction will emerge victorious. It is not difficult to predict which that will be.

Skipper whines, pawing at Nash's foot. There is a tacit understanding between them that the dog should sit quietly beside the garden bench while, seated on it, his master takes advantage of the early morning calm to plan his day. However, in Skipper's opinion, Nash has taken an unconscionably long time to collect his thoughts and Skipper's reward, always the culmination of their morning sessions, is now overdue.

"All right, all right. I'm coming."

Nash strokes Skipper's silky head, noting as he does so how a few white hairs have appeared around the dog's muzzle. It is a small, touching reminder of the passing of time and it increases Nash's melancholy mood. He pats the dog on the back, receiving, in return, an affectionate lick on the hand.

"Come on, old boy. A walk would do us both good."

Searching in the flower bed, Nash finds an abandoned stick, once used to train a climbing plant and, picking it up, flings it far across the lawn, watching as the dog bounds and capers after it. Skipper leaps and catches the stick in mid-air. Then, dropping the stick, he crouches over it, a paw over either end, growling to prove his mastery, before trotting back to Nash, his prize firmly clenched between his teeth.

"Good boy. Good boy."

Nash pats the dog, remembering how he bought him as a puppy from a British planter. The man was selling up, returning to the cold wet island that he called home and yet, as he placed the small, wriggling creature in the hands of its new owner, Nash had sensed his reluctance to leave.

That is the Island's secret magic. The power to entrap and enthral. The ancient Greeks understood that quality, portraying it as a woman; the witch Circe who, along with her sirens, enticed sailors onto land, never allowing them to escape. This island exerts the same fascination for all strangers; once they have seen it, they never wish to leave, desiring only to possess it for themselves.

For centuries, Ceylon has been fought over as bitterly as a beautiful woman, and its soil has absorbed the blood of many suitors. Like a sorceress who constantly changes her shape, the Island has had many identities, one of the oldest, Serendipity, has found its way into the English language as a synonym for "happy chance".

No doubt that word expressed the relief of ancient sailors, adrift on the high seas, who made a sudden and unexpected landfall. According to one ancient chronicle, it was in exactly this way that the founder of the Sinhalese race, Prince Vijaya, discovered the Island. And yet Ceylon always extracts a price for its bounty. It is no mistake, thinks Nash, that it is shaped like a teardrop. It is a warning for all who care to see but, of course, no-one does.

"Perhaps I shall still write that book," he thinks as he extracts the stick, now wet, from Skipper's mouth and flings it across the garden. But it could not be a history book, at least not one of the rigidly factual works favoured by western authors.

Bare facts and dates could never encompass the Island's personality. It requires a history written in the manner of the ancient Greeks: part Iliad, part Odyssey, in which mythology is used to explain reality. How else could one explain the extraordinary influences that have shaped Ceylon?

"We are all strangers in this land," thinks Nash, remembering the planter whose skin, stretched tight over his cheeks, had crinkled about the man's eyes, the way that westerners' skin always does after it has been exposed to the tropical sun for a few years. The man was like one of Circe's sailors, neither a native of his own land, nor of Ceylon. Nash wonders where he is and if he has adapted to the aching chill of the British climate.

From his student years at Oxford, Nash remembers how the cold ate into his bones, numbing his brain as well as his body. His college lodgings had been heated by a tiny stove which was not proof against the drafts that whistled in through cracks around the door and windows. As soon as Nash had sealed up one entrance with pieces of rolled-up newspaper, the wind would find another. Even the keyhole had provided a channel for blasts of icy air.

Having graduated, he had been thankful to return home, eager for warmth and the constant brilliancy of sunlight. His appreciation of what he had formerly taken for granted, doubled. He cannot deride Mr Bandaranaike's wholehearted espousal of the culture which both had once disdained. Perhaps, Mr Bandaranaike is the wiser of the two. For, there is no place for Nash in the culture and society that are now emerging. Soon, like the planter, he will be abandoned by the island that he once regarded as home. But unlike the planter, he has nowhere else to go.

Changes are taking place, faster and with more violence than anyone could have anticipated except, perhaps, Buddharakkita Thera. The political squabbles over the Sinhala Only Act are now being played out in the public arena.

Sinhalese peasants who have recently colonised the eastern lands around Gal Oya have clashed with their Tamil neighbours. The result has been bloodshed on a shocking scale. Of course, the Island has had its fair share of riots and hartals, but nothing like this. At least, not in Nash's life-time. Even peaceful demonstrators against the Act have been set upon and brutally beaten by their opponents.

Everyone is on edge: even Sinhalese like Walter who have no reason, as far as Nash can see, for any anxiety. And yet the driver, who has been part of his household for years, seems nervous and fearful of leaving the residence, except in the car. His young assistant is also giving Nash cause for concern. Arjun is not as punctual in his timekeeping or as diligent in his work as he used to be and, much of the time, he seems distracted, like a sleepwalker.

Yet, Nash suspects that whatever dream Arjun has fallen into is not a happy one. The boy looks pale, his skin has a greyish tint and there are dark rings around his eyes. However, the deterioration in his physical appearance is counterpoised by a distinct, sartorial improvement. He wears new and expensive suits, silk ties and his old panama hat with the hole in the crown has been replaced by a new one: all luxuries that he cannot afford on an assistant's salary.

Making a mental note to speak to both Walter and Arjun in the next few days, Nash throws the stick for Skipper. It sails through the air and lands in the gravel drive, pursued by the dog who, despite his enthusiasm, is beginning to tire. As Nash retrieves the stick, preparing for a last throw, he becomes aware of a commotion at the gate.

Damasiri, the gatekeeper, is remonstrating loudly with a small boy.

"Go! Get away! You are here every day. Just hanging around like a bad smell. What do you want?"

The question is rhetorical, the man shooing violently at the child with outstretched arms.

"What is the matter?"

"This boy. He is here every day. Just looking through the bars. He is no good."

"What is his name?"

"No good," repeats Damasiri. That seems as good a name as any.

"Here," says Nash, reaching in his pocket for some change. "Take this and run along."

Without a word, the buck-toothed child accepts the coins. Cupping them in one hand, he sorts through them with one finger, making a careful inventory of his haul.

"Retarded," thinks Nash, turning away to discuss his plans for the week with Damasiri.

He does not see the shiny new bicycle propped against the outer wall of the residence or he might wonder how such a ragged child had acquired such a valuable possession. Nor does he notice the intelligent gleam in the boy's eye as, hovering about the gate, he listens to Nash explaining his usual routine for attending the office and at which hours Damasiri should expect to open and close the gates.

Traders are touting their wares along the kerb. Cheap aluminium pans are ranged according to size, largest at the back, smallest at the front; rush baskets hold sardines, freshly-caught and packed in sand, a little of which is added by unscrupulous traders to make extra weight on the scales; chickens in wooden crates are piled, one on top of another, in precarious towers that mimic the teetering edifices of the shanty quarter.

Sarath, the chief clerk, pushes his way through the crowds to the Moslem hotel on the street corner. Above the door is a sign whose bold green lettering proclaims in four languages – Arabic, Sinhalese, Tamil and English – that the establishment specialises in halal products. Being Buddhist, Sarath has no particular requirement for halal food, but the Moslem hotel is conveniently close to the office and it is part of his daily routine to drop in mid-morning to buy lunch.

This convenient break from work is based on the pretext of picking up lunch for his colleagues. With faultless logic, Sarath has argued convincingly that half an hour of one man's time, put to good use in collecting the lunch of six of his colleagues, can save three hours' working time in the office. The more lunches he collects, the more time he saves his employer.

This charitable act also allows Sarath to walk around the office, giving the impression of being busy while, actually doing very little. He is omnipresent, appearing unannounced at his colleagues' desks, looking over their shoulders or, if they are absent, through their papers. But, as long as everyone gets their lunch and no-one goes hungry, they have no cause for complaint. On this point alone, Sarath is scrupulous.

Sarath's altruism has paid dividends. His own lunch-break has been extended to two or, sometimes, three hours. This can be managed by making frequent trips to and from the Moslem hotel with breaks for coffee in between.

***

The Moslem hotel is not a guest-house in the western sense. It provides no overnight lodging, being closer in function to an old-fashioned hostelry, although it serves no alcohol. The door, loosened on its hinges through much use, wobbles as it opens, striking a metal bell which is mounted on a spring on the inner side of the lintel. However, the announcement of a new arrival is unnecessary as the counter is always manned by at least two members of the family who run the hotel.

"Hello, brother. What can we do for you today?"

The owner, a man with fat, gleaming cheeks and a black, bushy beard, leans across the counter to shout his usual welcome.

"The usual."

"Very good. Will you take a coffee while you wait? And a cake, perhaps?"

Pointing his chubby finger at a glass case, the owner indicates a display of assorted pastries, some triangular, others oblong, some resembling nests of the finest vermicelli, others consisting of wafer-thin layers, crisp, golden brown and saturated in honey. Sarath eyes them greedily, then selects three for himself. Unable to curb his appetite for sweet things, he already has several teeth that are black and rotten.

The cakes are arranged on a white plate and brought to him with a small cup of sweet black coffee. Having taken up his usual position at the counter, he settles down to savour his treat and listen to the lively gossip exchanged by the other customers. He rarely takes part in these conversations, but he listens.

Sarath's frequent visits have rendered him invisible, as familiar and innocuous as a chair or table. Consequently, the restaurant's clients speak freely in his presence. Their acceptance of him enables Sarath to glean snippets of useful information which, together with secrets from the office, are supplied to his patron, a Buddhist monk, in return for money or favours.

Long ago, the monk told him that there would be a new order, one in which the Sinhalese would finally gain control. Now, his prophecies have been fulfilled. Within months of the election, the Sinhala Only Act – so strongly opposed by Tamils – was passed with a simple majority vote. The Bill, so hotly contested, is now law.

Sarath licks his fingers. The monk has promised him promotion. He has influence, he says, with certain politicians and when the new regime takes effect there will be a place within it for loyal supporters such as Sarath. The thought is as sweet as honey.

Sarath wipes a finger around the plate, marshalling the last drops of syrupy nectar. He already has a position in mind. He has mentioned it to the monk who implied that he would do his best. That is as good as a promise. Of course, the post is currently occupied by someone else but, with the information that he has recently obtained, Sarath feels that his promotion is assured. Soon, his rival will be displaced and, sweetest of all, humiliated.

Considering that a celebration would not be premature, Sarath orders three more cakes.

From his window, Arjun stares into the street, following the ebb and flow of the crowd as it swirls first around one stall, then another, until his eyes come to rest on the green and white sign of the Moslem hotel. It has been half an hour since Sarath left on the pretext of buying lunch and, no doubt, he is still in there, gorging on sweet cakes paid for with the change that should be returned to his colleagues. But no-one complains. It is worth the loss of a few rupees to secure Sarath's absence. The longer he stays there, the less time he has for spying on his workmates.

Arjun returns to his desk, hoping to summon sufficient concentration for work without the distraction of Sarath's presence and the footsteps that pass and re-pass his door, stopping abruptly whenever he is in conversation with the Government Agent or on the telephone.

Pulling a stack of files towards him, Arjun takes the top one and opens it. Having scanned the correspondence and columns of figures, he begins jotting a few notes on a pad but then the sharp tip of his pencil breaks and, finding no replacements in his desk drawer, he has to get up in search of another. He passes the window and finds himself again staring at the door of the Moslem hotel, praying that Sarath will not emerge.

Since his affair with Leela began, Arjun has fallen prey to fancies of persecution. Any insignificant noise, every fleeting shadow presages a spy or malevolent intruder. Any comment directed at him, however slight or uncritical, represents a plot to undermine his position. Sarath is the embodiment of his paranoia.

But it is not just in the office that Arjun feels pursued. Outside, the menace is more vague, but just as persistent. At Leela's house, where he presents himself more as a sacrifice than a lover, he senses that he is being watched. One night, hearing a noise outside, he ran out onto the lawn where he stood in the blackness, quite naked, until Leela herself was forced to come out and lead him back into the house. He is sure that, on at least one occasion, he has glimpsed Mennan looking back at him from the mirror although, when he leant closer to inspect it, the image had instantly resolved itself into a faithful reflection of his own face.

His fearful notions are confirmed by stories in the newspapers. The country, whose unity he has hitherto taken for granted, is fragmenting. Races that have co-existed for hundreds of years are squabbling over which language to speak. The world has gone mad. Or is it him?

Sarath's familiar silhouette appears beyond the frosted glass pane of the door. Arjun's heart leaps. He did not even hear him arrive. How long has he been there? What has he heard, or observed?

"Come in," shouts Arjun, although no-one has knocked. The shadow disappears. He contemplates opening the door and looking into the corridor, but he already knows what he will see. Nothing. He is going mad. He knows it.

Sitting back at the desk, he loosens his collar and straightens his back, trying to encourage the air into his lungs, but he can only breathe in short, shallow puffs. Droplets of sweat appear on his forehead and trickle down his back. He gasps like a drowning man bobbing up to the surface for a second before being submerged by a mighty wave.

There is a sharp rap on the door and the Agent saunters in.

"That fellow Sarath was lurking outside your door again. Ran off when he saw me coming. Are you all right? You look as if you've been running."

"Yes, fine. Thank you."

So, he is not mad after all. Sarath really was listening at the door. The news induces a perverse sense of relief so powerful that it deprives Arjun's legs of all strength. He usually stands when the Agent enters the room, but this time he cannot. He wonders if he should apologise but Nash, who is rummaging through papers on top of the filing cabinet, seems not to notice.

"I was looking for a copy of today's newspaper," he mutters by way of explanation. "Ah, here we are."

Noisily shaking the creases out of the newspaper, he spreads it out on a low table, leaning forward to read it from a standing position with both hands firmly planted on the work surface. This is the usual prelude to discussion of an unrelated matter. Arjun waits anxiously.

"Hmm," muses the Agent. "That fellow Buddharakkita seems to be everywhere these days. Here's a picture of him with the Prime Minister and here's a short item on his legal battle with the temple trustees. He won't be content until he's got his hands on all Kelaniya's wealth."

"Why do you think he wants it?" asks Arjun, not really concentrating on what the Agent has said.

Looking up from the paper, Nash fixes Arjun with a comical scowl.

"Why do you think? Money is power, especially for a man with his aspirations. Political influence doesn't come cheap."

"No, I suppose not."

His arm on the desk and his head supported by one hand, Arjun is doodling on a notepad.

"Is anything the matter?"

"No, no. Just seem to have some difficulty concentrating these days."

Arjun tries to smile, but his attempt to look carefree has the opposite effect. He looks sad, distracted, like a man labouring under a great weight.

"I'll leave you alone, then," Nash says gently, folding the paper.

Looking closely at Arjun as he passes the desk, he notices the cut of his clothes, all new and expensive. He has heard the rumours about Arjun and Mennan's widow that Sarath has been putting about the office. At first, he dismissed them – Sarath is always jealous of someone – but now he wonders if they bear any truth.

Nash has an uncomfortable feeling in the pit of his stomach. If the stories are true, Arjun could well be compromising investigations into Mennan's fraud; he will also have compromised his own reputation. Nash wants to warn him but struggles to find the right words. He clears his throat.

"You know, people like us have to be especially careful these days."

"What do you mean?" Arjun's head jerks up.

Did the Agent imagine it or was there a flash of youthful anger in that response?

"You only have to read the papers to see what I mean," replies Nash sternly. "We're both Tamils, Arjun. We can't afford to make mistakes. Either at work or in our personal lives. Take care when choosing your friends."

For a moment, he holds Arjun's eyes with his own, willing the boy to understand him. There is a scuffling sound in the corridor and Sarath, after knocking loudly on the open door, insinuates himself into the room, his head bent low in deference to his superiors.

"Lunch, sir."

Reaching into a small basket that he carries on his arm, he places a package on Arjun's desk.

"I wonder how long he's been outside that door," thinks the Agent.

At that moment, the telephone rings. Arjun hesitates, unwilling to pick up the receiver. Sensing Arjun's discomfort, Nash herds Sarath out of the room and along the corridor out of earshot. Nevertheless, he cannot help wondering who has called Arjun and why it was that his assistant seemed so reluctant to speak in front of him.

With the other men out of the room, Arjun stares at the phone, letting it ring. His attention wanders to the objects on his desk. The file is still open, but he cannot concentrate. His lunch has been delivered, but he is not hungry and, even if he had been, the package looks unappetising. Oil has seeped from the food, staining the paper in which it is wrapped with shiny, sweat-like marks.

The phone continues to ring. Insistent. Unrelenting. Arjun rises from his chair and, on his way out of the room, he picks up the greasy package from his desk and drops it in the bin.

The sound of the telephone pursues him along the corridor. Let it ring. Every day she calls him. Most days she summons him, with a promise or, more often, a threat. The Agent knows of their liaison, he is sure of it. But what is he to do? He has been manoeuvred into a relationship that he does not want. Admittedly, Leela excites him, but he does not love her. The more she pursues him, the further she pushes him away.

As often happens when one is distanced from something familiar, a person or a place, the true depth of one's feelings for the missing object is revealed. Arjun's relationship with Leela has distanced him from Neleni and now, having put himself beyond the pale of her affection, he has discovered how deeply he loves her. Conversely, the more idealised that love becomes, the further he sinks in his own self-esteem and the less able he is to resist Leela's demands. He despises himself.

Legend tells how the Island's shamans would drive a nail through the forehead of a slave to secure total submission. The victim became docile and biddable, no longer able to function under his own volition. When growing up, Arjun listened to these tales with fascination then, as he grew older, disbelief; but now he wonders if they contained some truth. Is there some magic by which one human being can render another powerless? For he, too, feels as if an invisible nail has been driven into his brain, hindering its natural function, parting him from his conscience. He knows that what he is doing is wrong, but he is unable to stop. He has become the creature, the slave, of a stronger entity.

Stepping into the street, he finds temporary relief amidst the crowd. Plunging into the centre, he allows himself to be carried along by the current, as anonymous as a ghost in smoke.

"So I told him, if your mother is a better cook, you go and live with her."

A woman is directing a shrill monologue at a stall-holder who nods sympathetically while his assistant loads sardines, accompanied by generous dollops of sand, onto the scales.

"Hey, not so much of that!" shouts the woman, who must have a third eye in the side of her head.

"No wonder my husband complains about my cooking if all you give me is sand. Take it out!"

The stall-holder wrings his hands apologetically, then slaps the assistant around the head; a little scene, nicely rehearsed, that is re-enacted most days.

The crowd whirls along, groups of individuals breaking away and re-forming around the stalls, as water eddies around rocks. Immersed in the welter of warmth and noise, Arjun's senses come to life. Colour and sound seem to explode in every quarter until his eyes smart and his ears ring. The smell of people, frying fish, tea, perfume, hair oil, fruit and flowers assault his nose until he can no longer breathe. Forcing his way out of the crowd, he steps up onto the pavement, leaning against a wall for a few seconds with his eyes closed. The clang of a nearby bell, crack-mouthed and urgent, startles him. He is standing against the wall of a church. The bell is summoning worshippers to Mass.

Arjun allows himself to be swept along with the crowd; up the steps of the church, into the porch, through the heavy door with its polished brass handle, into the darkened interior where the air is heavy with the smell of incense and tallow and the flames of votary candles flicker like tiny stars before the images of saints. Passing the holy water stoop, he moistens the tips of his fingers and crosses himself before moving into the aisle where he genuflects before the huge wooden crucifix that hangs over the altar.

Slipping into an empty pew at the back of the church, he tries to fill his mind with prayer but the words that issue from his mouth fail to engage his brain. He wants to exorcise Leela. He prays that she will leave him or that he will find the strength to renounce her but, as his mouth utters the responses, one thought occupies his mind: *I am too weak, I am too weak.*

The priest, a young Irishman of similar age to Arjun, climbs into the pulpit and begins to preach a short sermon, his eyes shining with the enthusiasm of untried innocence. He speaks of love, hope and simplicity, all of which make Arjun feel unutterably old. His mind wanders back to school and the fiery sermons of its spiritual director, Father Ignatius.

Rejecting kindly promises of redemption as being unsuitable for degenerate boys, the elderly Jesuit had preferred, instead, to dwell on the torments of eternal damnation. Every sermon reeked with fear and some of the more imaginative boys swore that they caught a whiff of sulphur as the old man preached. One boy, an asthmatic, even fainted during a particularly vivid description of the demonic torture awaiting sinners.

After finishing his sermon, the young priest bounds down the steps of the pulpit, as eager as a puppy. Full of optimism, he is untainted by guilt. It suddenly occurs to Arjun that, for all his fire and brimstone preaching, Father Ignatius had a more complete understanding of the human soul than this young man.

Father Ignatius may not have sympathised with Arjun's dilemma, but he would have recognised the torment that he now suffers as something real and tangible; not a vapour to be wafted away with fine words, but something attacking the core of his soul that needs to be excised.

The service is drawing to a close and Arjun feels as out of place in this congregation as a stowaway on a ship.

"Would you like to make confession?"

The young priest is standing at his elbow, smiling in an encouraging sort of way.

"No, thank you, Father."

The priest persists.

"We all have something to confess."

Arjun wavers. It is tempting to unburden himself. The priest raises himself on his toes, then bounces back lightly on his heels, a boyish habit which he has not outgrown and for which he has been reprimanded many times. He has the irrepressible light-heartedness that springs from naivety, a levity which throws Arjun's mood into sharp relief, highlighting the dark contours of his guilt, underscoring the loss of his own innocence.

"Another time, perhaps."

"Oh!"

The priest looks disappointed. His green eyes are as round as buttons, his pale skin peppered with ginger freckles that match his tight, curly hair.

"I'm sorry, Father. I'm not ready."

"Of course. Don't worry."

311

The priest raises his arms in a gesture intended to be comforting but which signifies helplessness.

"I'm always here, you know. The door is always open."

"Thank you, Father. I'll remember that."

Picking up his hat, Arjun walks swiftly towards the door, trying to contain the tears that prick his eyes.

Rani is playing jacks on the porch. Scattering her handful of star-shaped counters, she bounces the small red ball as high as she can, scooping up all five jacks before catching it again. It is the third time in a day that she has achieved a full score and she is beginning to tire of her success.

"I need more jacks," she thinks to herself. "Another packet, then I can double my score. Perhaps play with two balls. I wonder if anyone has ever done that. I must ask Uncle."

Most questions of this sort are referred to Arjun, not only for his opinion, but also in the hope that he might indulge her request for further toys which would otherwise be refused by her parents. When asked for a favour, Uncle Arjun automatically complies, a generous feature which makes him a great favourite with his landlady's daughters and which sometimes earns him a gentle scolding from their mother.

The ball bounces and Rani scoops all five jacks in one go. Bored with the game, Rani tries to find another use for the jacks, interlocking their arms to build a tower, shaking them together in her cupped hands like a rattle, laying them out in patterns. She wishes Uncle Arjun would come. He is late. She knows because she always waits for him, here on the porch. In some ways, she looks forward to seeing him more than her own father.

Most days, after his return from work, she takes a gift to Arjun's room: a flower, an interesting pebble, or perhaps a picture or poem that she has composed. On special occasions, she might give him one of the sweets, wrapped in brightly-coloured foil, from the special collection kept in a biscuit tin under her bed.

The sweets are not meant to be eaten, being quite old and sometimes soft, but they are shared tokens of esteem, having been given to her, previously, by Uncle Arjun himself. When she gives him the sweets, he smiles and thanks her. But she knows that, when she is at school, he will replace the sweets in her tin so that she can give them to him again on another occasion.

Anxiously, Rani looks down the street. Here he comes, walking more slowly than usual. He looks tired. There is something about the way he hangs his head. Is he ill? Rani leaps down the steps and runs to meet him. Grabbing his hand, she prances about, chattering all the time, leading him up the steps into the hall.

He takes off his hat and wearily hangs it on a hook on the hat-stand. She notices that his eyes, usually so bright, are red. He does not look at her. In fact, he has hardly spoken since she met him in the street.

"Uncle, are you all right?"

"Yes."

His voice sounds far off.

"Can I read to you?"

Sometimes she reads to him from one of the poetry books on his shelf: Hiawatha or The Lady of Shalott. She likes poems that tell a story. Long ones that spill over the page and run away in a torrent of words.

"No, no."

He repels her with unusual urgency. He does not want her anywhere near him. She can hear it in his voice. She struggles not to cry as he walks past, nodding briefly to her mother who is standing in the kitchen door and whose face seems to reflect her own distress.

Rani pads across the hall, her bare feet making a soft, sticky sound as they cross the red-painted concrete. Quietly letting herself out of the front door, she tiptoes across the hot wooden boards of the porch and down the burning steps to the forecourt where the temple tree leans against the wall. Despite its sturdy-looking branches, the tree would provide a treacherous support for those foolish enough to climb it, resulting in broken limbs or, as in the case of Rani's grandfather, a broken neck.

Having been warned many times, Rani treats the old tree with respect and never climbs it – at least, not when anyone is looking. Today, she only ventures a few inches off the ground, clinging to the smooth trunk with her knees while waving one hand overhead in an attempt to knock some flowers to the ground.

After several fruitless attempts, she gives up and, jumping down, shakes the tree vigorously until several blossoms have been dislodged. She watches, fascinated, as they spin slowly earthwards; then she scoops them up, with other recent windfalls, until she has a sizeable handful.

Cradling the flowers gently in both hands, she creeps back into the house and places the blossoms in a glass of water. Bending over them, she breathes in several times until their scent makes her dizzy. Voices from the kitchen echo through the house. Fat hisses and spits in a pan. The smell of onions wafts into the hallway. Neleni is preparing the evening meal with Saro for company.

"We like cooking, don't we? Yes, we like to help Amma. Here, give me that!"
The tone of Neleni's voice suddenly changes.
"Bad girl. Never play with knives. How did you get hold of that?"
The short tirade is followed by a low, whimpering moan. Saro never cedes anything without a struggle, even if she knows her cause is hopeless. That streak of stubbornness often leads to fights with her sister, who is generally blamed for starting the trouble because she is the eldest and expected to know better. Rani grits her teeth, thinking how unfair her mother can be. It is no secret that she favours Saro.

Quietly crossing the hallway, Rani holds her breath as she passes the kitchen. If she is seen, she will be challenged and probably stopped from visiting Arjun. Her mother is always telling her not to be a nuisance, although Uncle Arjun doesn't seem to mind her company. In fact, he seems to welcome it, especially as he does not speak much to her mother these days. With remarkable insight, Rani wonders if this is why Amma is so cross.

Passing the kitchen, Rani tiptoes along the passage to Arjun's room. The door, as usual is slightly ajar and she peeps cautiously through the opening. Inside, the room is hushed and still. She can see his jacket hanging over the back of the chair. It is new, made of pure white linen, not yellowing and threadbare at the cuffs like the old one. His shoes and socks have been discarded close by, but she cannot see him. Usually, she can hear him moving around, humming a tune as he busies himself with books or papers, but today, the room is so silent that she wonders if he is there.

Taking a step forward, she peeps around the door. He is lying on the bed, covered by a sheet, his arm hanging limply over the side. The sheet rises and falls rhythmically and she can hear him breathing. Creeping closer, she places the flowers on the table and peers into his face which is turned towards her. The eyes are shut and the lips slightly parted.

He must have been reading something before he fell asleep, because a sheet of paper is lying on the floor below his outstretched hand. Reaching out, she draws the letter towards her. She cannot make out all the words, but she knows it is from a woman called Leela. Although she does not understand its contents, she knows instinctively that that letter is trouble.

The rattle of a teacup and saucer warns her of her mother's imminent arrival. Scuttling across the floor on her hands and knees, Rani hides behind the cupboard. There is a light knock on the door.

"Can I come in? I've brought your tea."

Having waited for an answer, her mother peers around the door, then steps inside. Walking up to the bed, she gazes at the sleeping figure and her cheeks flush pink. Quietly, she places the teacup beside the flowers and has just turned to leave when she spots the letter. She bends to pick it up, presumably with the intention of placing it on the table but, unable to resist, she begins to read it.

From her hiding place, Rani can see the change in her mother's face. Neleni's hand flies up to her mouth and she makes a choking noise. It seems to Rani, as her mother runs from the room, that she is crying.

1956: A bedtime story

This evening, the mood around the table is subdued. Pleading illness, Arjun has kept to his room while Neleni, red-eyed and silent, pushes food around her plate in a listless attempt to eat. The food is noticeably below standard. The vegetables have been boiled to a pulp, the meat is tough, having been cooked too quickly on a fierce heat, and chilli has been applied so liberally to everything that copious amounts of water are required to wash it down.

The elastic quality of the meat guarantees a minimum of conversation and encourages a thoughtful silence. Owl-like in glasses that dwarf her small face, Sunny peers at Neleni, trying to divine the cause of her malaise. The old lady's mouth works vigorously as she chews but, her dentures not being equal to the task, she finally gives up, removing a half-masticated ball of flesh from her mouth which she places on the side of the plate.

Eyeing her grandmother's plate with fascination, Rani calculates her chances of success if she adopts the same stratagem. However, she concludes that failure is inevitable. On account of age, her grandmother enjoys concessions that are not available to younger members of the family. Abandoning inedible food is one of them.

As she bites determinedly into a large piece of gristle, Rani's attention wanders to her mother. Not a scrap of food has passed Neleni's lips since the beginning of the meal and Rani is just about to raise her voice in protest when something terrible happens. A single tear courses down Neleni's cheek.

Rani gasps and, carried back by her sharp intake of breath, the piece of meat that she has been chewing, lodges in her throat. She coughs, then chokes, her eyes streaming while Raj slaps her on the back until, finally, a pellet of meat shoots out of her mouth and lands on the table.

"Drink some water, child," urges Sunny.

Giving her his own glass to drink from, her father watches attentively as Rani gulps down the contents. As she raises the glass, Rani's eyes meet those of her mother. Her coughing fit has diverted attention from Neleni's distress. Only Rani saw her mother's silent tear and only she guesses the cause.

It has to be the letter that she found in Arjun's room. Rani did not understand its contents, but she knows instinctively that it exerts a malevolent power. Whether she sensed this from the words on the page or from the expression on Arjun's sleeping face, she cannot tell, but she knows she is right. Who would believe that a single sheet of paper could cause so much misery? Its author must be a witch.

Rani peers guiltily at her mother. She knew that that letter would cause trouble. Why had she not hidden it? If she had re-folded it and placed it on the bed next to Arjun, her mother would not have touched it. It was almost as if, through some perverse desire of her own, she had left it on display, hoping that it would be found. By acting as she did, she has become the creature of an invisible force: a witch's familiar. She has heard of such things from the young Jesuit priest who teaches RE at school. She can already feel a change taking place in herself. She begins to shiver and sob.

"Why, whatever is the matter?"

Torn from her own preoccupation, Neleni reaches across the table and takes Rani's hand; a gesture whose kindness stings sharper than any slap. Rani only cries harder.

"The child has eaten too much chilli. She's overheated," opines Sunny, pressing her hand to Rani's brow. "Get a jug of water and make her drink it all."

Susceptible to the sympathetic magic of tears, Saro also begins to whimper.

"Stop now, girls, and I will tell you a story – a very naughty one," says Raj with one of his rare flashes of brilliance. Saro quietens immediately while Rani's curiosity gradually gets the better of her. When the mood is upon him, Raj has the power to enthral his children.

"But I will only start when you have finished crying."

Rani catches a sob in her throat and Raj begins his story.

"I went to Moorthy's shop today. That fellow is having such a time with his neighbours. Their children behave like criminals, always stealing from the counter when he isn't looking. So he thought he would teach them a lesson.

"They particularly like fudge. So he got his wife to make some – beautifully sweet and thick with cashews – but, as the mixture cooled, he sprinkled it with laxative pills that he had ground to a powder.

"He put them out on the counter, at the time of day when the children usually come into the shop. Just as he had finished arranging them, another neighbour, an old man, came in and demanded to buy all of the sweets."

"What did he do?" asks Rani, intrigued by the shopkeeper's dilemma.

"Well, he tried to interest the old man in something else but no, he wanted those sweets. When Moorthy tried to reason with him, the old man flew into a rage and threatened to call the police.

"Why have you got these sweets for sale when you won't let me have them? Is there something wrong with them?" said the old man.

"Moorthy assured him that they were freshly made that day. He didn't lie. And he was afraid that, if the old man called the police, they might find out about his little trick. So he sold them to the old man, warning him to eat only one a day as they were medicinal. He said that, if taken in the right quantities, they would make him feel like a new man!"

"So what happened?" Rani is spellbound by her father's tale, not sure whether to believe him or not.

"The old man snorted and said: "Whoever heard of medicinal sweets? You're off your head. I'm going to eat as many as I like, when I like." And with that, he took a bagful and disappeared. That was three days ago and Moorthy hasn't seen him since. He's worried he might have poisoned him but he's too afraid to enquire after his health in case he draws attention to himself.

"I told him not to worry. The old man probably ate them all at once and hasn't been able to leave the toilet. Serves him right for being so greedy. It'll certainly make a new man of him!" He chortles to himself.

"You want to take care, girls. If you eat too many sweets, you'll end up like the old man, shitting from dawn till dusk!"

"Raj!" Neleni is scandalised.

Rani giggles, eyes sparkling with amusement at her father's risqué, and highly improbable, story. Not to be outdone, Saro giggles too.

At that moment, there is a sharp rapping on the front door.

"Who can that be?"

Rising from the table, Raj disappears into the hall. The rest of the family listens attentively but, as Raj is conducting his conversation out of earshot on the porch, they learn nothing apart from the fact that the visitor is a man.

"All right, all right. I'll go and get him," says Raj, whose footsteps can be heard passing down the passage that leads to Arjun's room. A few minutes later, two sets of footsteps return, one making its way out of the front door and down the steps to the street. The door snicks shut and Raj returns.

"Well, well," says Raj. "It's that car again. The same one that we saw when Lakshmi was here. A Jaguar. I'm sure now. Definitely positive. Our boy has got himself a rich girlfriend. I asked him. Outright. He didn't deny it."

He has hardly finished speaking when there is a resounding crash from the kitchen.

"What is happening out there?" he shouts.

There is no reply.

***

Leela is angry with Arjun for not answering her telephone calls: her note, which was waiting for him on his return from work, said as much. Fearing what she might do, that she might even be waiting outside in the car, Arjun has left the house in a hurry, running from his room without washing or dressing properly and now, seated in the Jaguar, he realises that he is still holding her letter in his hand. He reads it again. Among the lurid expressions of affection, passion, and professions of love, is a threat so subtle that it would be imperceptible to anyone but him.

"Give my regards to the Agent."

He knows what that means. One word to the Agent about their affair would destroy him. He is lost. Her creature. Slowly, methodically, he tears the letter into pieces, careful to retrieve the tiny fragments that fall to the floor, then, holding his arm out of the window, he allows the air to whisk the shreds of paper from his fingers. As the remains of the letter stream from his hand, Arjun takes comfort from one thought. No-one else has read its shameful contents.

The kitchen is in turmoil. Neleni has fainted. Raj found her, lying on the floor with the shattered remains of plates and bowls scattered around her.

"Put your head between your knees. That's it. Lean forward."

The voices buzz around Neleni like hornets as she slowly regains consciousness. Hands, placed under her shoulders, have pulled her upright and bent her forward. She can see feet: Raj's sandals, half a size too big; the girls' bare feet, soft and round; Sunny's wizened toes peeping from the hem of her sari, and her own feet at a different angle from the others, resting on their heels, their painted toes pointing towards the ceiling.

"What …?"

She puts a hand to her head. There is a small, pulsing pain at the base of her skull and her temples are throbbing. Seen from a different angle, familiar objects adopt an unfamiliar aspect. She can see the metal flanges that attach the kitchen table top to the horizontal panels beneath; the battered legs of the table, scarred by many collisions, and scored with a knife point – that must have been one of the girls; the dark recess beneath the kitchen cupboard where something shiny lies on the floor, possibly a coin or bottle top.

"You fainted," says Raj and, with unusual tenderness, he picks her up and carries her to bed, laying her down as gently as a child.

She stays there for what seems like hours, mute with grief, staring at the ceiling until Raj comes to bed and turns out the light. Soon, he is asleep, but still she lies awake, staring at the ceiling which, faintly gleaming in the darkened room, resembles the surface of the moon.

"Why?" she murmurs, soundlessly. "Why?"

Casting her mind back to when she first saw Arjun walking up the street, she knows that she has always loved him. At Sigiriya, she first became aware of an attachment, winding its way around her heart, like a vine. But it is a vine with thorns. The harder one tries to rip it out, the more deeply embedded it becomes and the more it hurts. She has tried, God knows, but the pain was too great, so she simply tried to ignore it, denying her feelings, pretending.

She should have listened to Nirmala, rooted it out, destroyed it. For, like all wild plants, this vine thrives on neglect. In adversity, it simply becomes stronger, pushing out fresh shoots, strengthening its grip. And now Arjun has twisted the vine even tighter, squeezing her heart until she thinks it will burst. How can one live with such unbearable pain?

She closes her eyes and prays to die and yet, when the sun peeps through the blinds next morning, she is still alive despite her agony. Now, she feels anger, gathering force like a great wave, racing in from the horizon across miles of watery waste, bringing with it havoc and devastation. Soon earth and water will collide.

Only a god could contain this primordial fury; Shiva who holds the violence of the universe in check. Encircled by flames, he performs an eternal dance, taming the opposing forces of creation and destruction. Surrounded by cosmic chaos, he holds the balance, one foot planted on the earth, the other delicately raised in the air. It is said that if Shiva stamps his foot, the universe will shatter.

But Neleni is no god. The opposing passions of love and hatred are at war within her, their fury so great that if she moves, even an inch, they will tear her apart. They rage inside her, seeking an outlet. Afraid of her own, uncontrollable wrath, Neleni fears to get out of bed for, if her foot touches the ground, the world may explode.

So she remains where she is, speechless and immobile for another day and a night until, the next morning, Raj enters the room with a tray.

"I … we thought it might help if you did something. I've brought you your paints and that picture of a temple tree you were working on. It's really beautiful. I think you should finish it."

As his wife shows no sign of moving, Raj raises her up and places the tray on her knees.

"I'll leave you alone for a while. See if you can't paint a little."

He leaves the room and resumes his place outside the door in the chair in which Sunny and he take turns to keep watch. At first there is silence but then he hears a movement. Peering through the door he sees Neleni, standing at the window, the picture of the temple tree crushed in her hand.

Raj is sweeping the backyard watched by the stray cat. Every time he pauses in his sweeping, the cat leaps off the upturned bucket on which it is seated to wrap itself lovingly around his legs, mewing tenderly in the hope of food. Sunny has been less generous of late and the cat is on the look-out for a new benefactor.

"Get away," says Raj.

The cat is now on its hind legs, the claws of its front paws firmly fixed into his sarong. If he moves, its feet will leave the ground altogether. Raj has no option but to pick the creature up. As he does so, it begins to purr with a raucous whirring that threatens to split its ribcage.

Raj does not normally like cats but today he finds comfort in the animal's company. It looks at him with great saucer-like eyes and almost seems to smile. No matter that its adoration is shallow and self-serving. Tomorrow, it may find another master, but its devotion at this moment is simple and unquestioning.

Raj carries the cat into the kitchen where he finds it some scraps of meat and a saucer of milk. As soon as it sees the food, the cat leaps from his arms, all thought of companionship forgotten. It nuzzles the bacon rind, sniffing delicately before holding one end down with a paw and tearing at the other with needle-sharp teeth. Raj quietly returns to the yard, leaving the cat chewing noisily on a piece of skin too big to swallow.

Outside, Raj turns his attention to some withered brown stems, given to him by a friend, which he had potted up in the hope that they would flower. He was told that they were orchids although they look more like slender rolls of parchment. As he tends the unpromising plants, it occurs to Raj that his family has gone mad.

It has been several days since Neleni collapsed in the kitchen and, since then, she has wandered the house like a ghost, showing little interest in the children and responding with a look of such fury to the simplest question that it is generally thought best to leave her alone.

She avoids meal-times, instead, shutting herself in her room where she lies on the bed with her eyes open, staring fixedly at the wall. Raj has taken her food on a tray which several hours later, remains untouched. When he suggests that she joins the family at the table, she simply rolls over on her side, with her back to him. She treats him with latent hostility and the children with indifference. Even Sunny does not have the power to rouse her.

As he arranges the orchid pots in a neat row on top of the wall, a thought suddenly occurs to Raj.

"She's pregnant!"

Reaching inside his shirt, he scratches his chest reflectively. Of course, that must be the reason for Neleni's extraordinary behaviour. And then, a pleasant thought occurs to him. Perhaps, this time, she will have a boy. He will put up with anything if she gives him a son.

Raj begins to hum a tune to himself as he goes about his work, convinced that he has solved the mystery of his wife's strange mood. Women! There is no accounting for their behaviour. Like the phases of the moon, or the turning of the tides, they are governed by unseen forces of nature whose mysteries are beyond the reckoning of ordinary men like him.

Best not to interfere. Just let them get on with it. That, at least, is Raj's philosophy and, so far, it seems to have been successful. Their marriage is not passionate, but neither is it particularly subject to spite or animosity. On the whole, their relationship has been amicable. One cannot ask more than that.

The pink plaster covering the wall has come loose in several places, exposing the brick beneath. Sweeping up several fragments, Raj empties the dustpan over the wall into the alley beyond. A gate leads from their yard into the passage but Neleni has stopped the girls from playing there, fearful that snakes or scorpions might be hiding in the overgrown grass and weeds. Abandoned by humans, the alley has become the domain of feral cats that meet, mate and litter there. Occasionally, there are noisy fights between the cats and stray dogs that are equally attracted to the alley's sunless squalor. But the cats always win.

As he continues with his chores, Raj's thoughts turn from Neleni to other members of his household. Several of them have been acting strangely as well. Rani has become secretive and distant, a fact which Raj ascribes to the onset of womanhood. She is nearing the time of her first period when she will come of age. That, too, will be an occasion for family celebration. In recognition of her adult status, uncles and aunts will each send her a gold coin and she will receive a special gold bangle from her parents.

But it appears that it is not only the women of the house who are subject to the mysterious workings of nature, but Arjun also. He is absent, more often than not, often for several nights at a time. Indeed, he has not re-appeared since the evening when he was fetched away in the sleek limousine.

But Raj is not worried. Arjun is simply indulging the needs of a young man. No doubt, he will soon move out of their home altogether, now that he has a rich woman to look after him. Raj feels a slight pang at the thought. He likes Arjun and it has been good to have the company of another man in this house full of women. Still, as Raj often says to himself, one cannot stand in the way of progress.

"Ai, what are you doing? See what a mess you have made!"

Raj steps into the kitchen where Sunny, leaning with one hand on the table, is bending over the cat. However, her voice lacks its usual note of protest and she lets herself down heavily on a chair, her thin chest rising and falling rapidly with the effort.

"Are you well, Aunty?"

"Why shouldn't I be?"

It is their usual exchange but, deprived of its pepperiness, Sunny's response sounds flat. She waves feebly at the cat in an attempt to drive it from the kitchen.

"Shoo!" bellows Raj.

Raising its head, the cat stares at him, outraged at this betrayal by its new friend.

"Shoo!" Raj claps his hands.

The cat pelts from the kitchen, runs helter-skelter across the yard and scrambles over the wall. There is an ominous crash. Peering from the door, Raj sees that several of his flower pots have been dislodged and are now lying in broken heaps at the foot of the wall.

Turning the great chrome taps, Leela steps into the shower and, eyes closed, holds her face up to meet the oncoming rush of water. She always immerses herself like this, when her mind is racing, imagining herself under a waterfall until her thoughts run at a steady pace.

She takes a pink soap from the dish and, still with her eyes closed, runs it over her arms, filling the shower with the scent of roses. Her mind flies back to Nuwara Eliya, an upcountry metropolis, a corner of England perched on a tropical plateau. Complete with Victorian villas, Anglo-Saxon churches, department store, golf and race courses, Nuwara Eliya is the epitome of an English county town, perfect in every detail.

Leela has never been to England, but she knows how it would look because Mennan once took her to Nuwara Eliya. She fell in love with it instantly and has aspired, ever since, to join its smart Anglo set.

She has even been introduced to the mayor, Mr Seneviratne, a charming Sinhalese with courtly manners. On meeting her, he kissed her hand – a daring, European gesture, far removed from the gauche, prudishness of traditional manners. He also invited her to his house, but Mennan had been reluctant to go, making an excuse to return home early. His real motive had been jealousy, but he had tried to cover it up with stories of how Seneviratne could not be trusted. There were rumours: some said he was a ladies' man, others that he had been involved in shady dealings. That was rich, coming from Mennan!

In any case, Mr Seneviratne appeared to have as many enemies as admirers, but that only made him more intriguing. Leela has not forgotten him and treasures her memories of Nuwara Eliya. She dreams of living there and visiting the exclusive Hill Club.

A refuge for tea planters and local dignitaries, the Hill Club is a model of Home Counties style: an imposing, red-brick clubhouse, whose lawns require an army of servants to water, cut, trim and feed them and whose frowning, low-arched door is as difficult to enter as the gate of heaven. If one is poor, one might as well pass through the eye of a needle as that door: for, contrary to the parable which recounts the rich man's difficulty in entering heaven, only the wealthy can enter the Hill Club.

Once, with Mennan, she was allowed, for a few minutes, to stand within the entrance hall. Her view of the interior revealed an old-fashioned luxury to which she still aspires: the heavy, dark furniture; the highly-polished parquet floors, the white-jacketed valets.

Every year, the Hill Club gardens produce a fragrant crop of roses which win the Nuwara Eliya gardening trophy with predictable regularity. The scent of those roses is one that Leela will never forget; a cool, sharp greenness so unlike the musky sweetness of tropical flowers. She has tried to grow roses in her own garden; but at low altitude, they languish in the heat. Perhaps, one day, she will live in Nuwara Eliya with a rose garden of her own.

Opening her eyes, she leans against the shower wall, looking through the curtain of water at the room beyond, the white tiles and chrome fittings, as sterile as a hospital theatre. She can no longer take refuge in dreams. Her money is running out and there is an added complication. She has fallen in love.

She turns off the tap and wrings out her hair, listening to the last drops of water tamping on the floor of the shower. There was a time when she courted the admiration of many men, and received it, in full measure. Sometimes, she rewarded them, fascinated by her own ability to manipulate and control; at other times, she listened to them beg with tears in their eyes, only to send them away, unsatisfied. Mistress of all, she wanted none: but, since meeting Arjun, she has fallen victim to her own desire. The absolute power which she previously enjoyed has deserted her.

She used Arjun's naivety to trap him but, try as she might, she cannot possess him. He comes when she calls, but only in response to coercion, never of his own volition. Always, there remains a part of him that is withheld, concealed; a longing, perhaps, for something, or someone, else. This elusiveness infuriates her, igniting the passion that now consumes her.

She has done everything in her power to bind him to her, resorting alternately to threats and blandishments, buying him gifts and clothes. Yet, despite the expensive labels on the suits and silk ties, it is evident that he wears them more from courtesy than pleasure. There is something mechanical in the way that he accepts her presents, dutiful acknowledgment without the real spark of gratitude that she so desires. She wants to touch him, reach that part of him that is hidden from her, but the harder she tries, the more distant he becomes.

Not knowing what else to do, she spends more money, buys more gifts in the hope that eventually, she will wring a drop of pure joy from his heart: but her only achievement is to fall deeper into debt. Shopkeepers no longer bother with the niceties when writing to her with their final demands and she has become so terrified of opening the post that, as soon as it arrives, she hides it in a drawer.

Soon, the bailiffs will come. Then she will lose everything: she will be destitute, she may even be sent to prison but, worst of all, she will lose Arjun. To survive and retain her tenuous hold over him, she must have money. Belatedly, she begins to envy Mennan's financial wizardry. Like a magician, he had the ability to produce money out of thin air and, had he still been alive, he would have saved her from this desperate situation. Sometimes, she misses him.

There is, of course, one other person who could help her: a former lover who was Mennan's confidante and adviser. Ever since learning of Mennan's letter, she has planned to confront Michael. Yet the time has never been right. She needs his help but is afraid of what he might demand in return. It is a dilemma. Her passion for Arjun has made her unusually monogamous. Faithfulness is a novel experience for her. She rather likes it and wants to continue the experiment, see where it leads her, without being compromised by necessity or financial considerations.

Pressing her cheek against the cool, white tiles, she shivers. Her thoughts are interrupted by a violent hammering at the door.

"Madam, madam."

It is one the young Sinhalese maids; her voice, although muffled by the door, full of intense excitement.

"What is it?"

You have a visitor."

"Who?"

Her heart races. Perhaps Arjun has come to see her, uninvited, of his own accord.

"Mr Michael."

Leela catches her breath. He is the last person she wants to see. She must think quickly.

"Tell him I'm out. And don't let him in if he wants to wait."

"Very good, madam."

Stepping quickly out of the shower, Leela wraps herself in a towel and walks stealthily to the window. She can hear him talking to the maid, remonstrating with her – he can be very persuasive, even intimidating, when he wants to be – but the girl holds her ground. With relief, Leela hears the door close followed by the sound of footsteps on the gravel.

There he is. She can see him now, stalking back down the drive, his head lowered and the fingers of one hand flexing and clenching in agitation. Instinctively, she ducks down just as he turns to stare back at the house. He does not believe the maid's excuse, that is clear, and expects to catch a glimpse of Leela watching him from her window. How well he knows her. Better than Arjun, in many ways. It is irritating that a man she does not want should understand her so well.

Sitting on the floor, she draws the towel tightly around her and, with one hand, reaches up to a packet of cigarettes lying on the dressing-table. She does not dare to stand up, for fear that he might return and catch sight of her. Then, she will have to see him, and she fears what might happen if they meet. Lighting a cigarette, she notices that her hands are shaking.

Preparations for the wedding of Dalia and Michael are in full swing and Lakshmi is in an ecstasy of busy preoccupation: arguing with caterers, receiving well-wishers, opening parcels and directing operations with the same verve and urgency as a general in the field. Although she tries to cultivate a calm and charming manner, this is frequently punctuated by bouts of shrieking apoplexy, usually directed at those around her and prompted by what she perceives as their shortcomings. The result is that both servants and family have become adept at making themselves invisible when Lakshmi flies into one of her moods.

Tonight, as a respite from her duties, Lakshmi has invited various friends and members of her family to a small, informal party. The table has been set with her best cutlery, a present from her own wedding, little used but much prized. Each implement bears the motto "EPNS" and further inspection reveals the words "Birmingham, England" stamped in tiny letters on the back of the handle. Lakshmi thinks of it as her family silver, an heirloom to be passed down to her daughter and grandchildren.

She sighs with satisfaction as she stands back to admire the table, her hands resting on her ample hips, Niran hovering at her side. Secretly, he thinks the party is an unnecessary expense, given the amount that they have already spent on Dalia's wedding. Lakshmi might like to tell everyone that Michael has paid for the matrimonial home, newly-built on its own plot of land, but it has been built largely with Niran's money.

There are also saris to be paid for, a trousseau, furniture, and the wedding party itself to which at least three hundred people have been invited. And the party is not going to be held in someone's home or a community hall. Oh no, only the best will do for Dalia. There were tears and sulks from his daughter and threats from his wife until Niran finally agreed to a wedding party at the Grand Oriental Hotel. Tonight's affair is a trifle in comparison, a tick-bite on the hide of a buffalo but, all the same, it is extra expense and Niran worries about where it will all end.

Ostensibly, Lakshmi's party will be a homely affair, an opportunity to catch up with people she has not seen for some time. However, it is really a preliminary to the wedding, allowing Lakshmi to flaunt the happy couple prior to the main event, rather like a theatrical preview. With great open-handedness, she has invited everyone who lives within the vicinity of her home, even those that she does not like.

It is with great relief that she has received Neleni and Raj's apologetic refusal. One of their children has a minor fever, nothing serious, but she cannot be left. Lakshmi smiled when she read the note and dashed off an effusive letter in reply, expressing her sympathy and heartfelt desire for the sick child's speedy recovery; although she secretly hoped that the patient was the elder daughter, the one who had insulted her, and that the little monster's suffering would be prolonged and painful.

"I hope she has leprosy and it attacks her poisonous little tongue. That would be justice!" Lakshmi had thought as she added a final flourish to her signature.

In the absence of Neleni, whose very presence is a challenge to her own pre-eminence, Lakshmi will be free to direct proceedings without constraint.

1956: Lakshmi's party

The evening starts well. After being greeted by their hostess, new arrivals are led to where Dalia, perfectly groomed and manicured, is enthroned on a large red couch. Lakshmi's heart swells with pride as she watches her guests paying homage to her daughter who looks just like a princess. She positively basks in the reflected warmth of their praise.

The only flaw, if one could call it that, is Michael's absence. Where can the boy have got to? Never mind, he is probably slaving away in his office, providing a secure – and Lakshmi hopes – an affluent future for her daughter. Dalia deserves nothing less. Look at her. Sitting there, smiling graciously. She looks almost royal. In fact, Lakshmi has always suspected that aristocratic blood flows in her veins. Never mind her humble upbringing, every family has its lean time. No, somewhere, hundreds of years ago, her family was related to princes, if not kings. She is sure of it.

"May I go out on your verandah? It's a little warm."

A hand touches Lakshmi's arm, breaking her train of thought. It is Cousin Mary. She was quite a beauty in her day but time and six children have weathered her looks. Her hair, scraped back in a bun is dyed black, although it shows white at the parting. Even worse, it is thinning!

Lakshmi shudders, praying that age will be more merciful to Dalia. It is essential that Michael looks after her, cherishes her as her own mother has done. Lakshmi has convinced herself that he will. She and Michael understand each other. He is a good boy. The best. Unlike Cousin Mary's husband who burdened her with all those children then had the temerity to die young. Poor woman, living off the charity of relatives. Thank God that will never happen to Dalia.

"Of course, dear. Have another drink."

Cousin Mary accepts gratefully, then weaving through the other guests, slips out through the French windows onto the verandah. She moves so quietly that the couple who are already out there do not hear her. Unaware that they are no longer alone, they continue their conversation.

"Honestly, have you ever seen anything like it? It's quite sickening. And where is the groom? That's what I'd like to know."

The woman pauses to sip her drink before continuing.

"Really, I wouldn't mind, but Lakshmi is such a damn snob. We all know where she came from, so why all these airs and graces? And that stupid daughter of hers! God, I want to slap her. Simpering and smirking, smirking and simpering. As if she hadn't got a brain in her head."

"Perhaps she hasn't," suggests the husband.

"Oh, Peter, you are awful!"

The woman taps her husband's elbow affectionately and they both laugh. As she turns to look at him, her profile is illuminated by the light from the room, revealing an elderly woman with a large hooked nose and an uncompromising mouth that, although it turns down at the corners in repose, splits into a wide crescent when she laughs.

"Oh, Mary, I didn't see you there. So sorry."

The woman who has been talking looks abashed and, for a second, there is an awkward silence.

"I've only just arrived," says Cousin Mary, diplomatically.

The other woman, whose name is Agnes, looks relieved. She and Mary are distantly related, as are most people in the room, but they do not know each other that well and one cannot always trust relations to keep their mouths shut.

"How is your family?" asks Agnes's husband, a round, jolly man with large horn-rimmed glasses and white hair.

"Oh, they are very well," replies Mary meekly. "Two are already practising as doctors and another has just qualified as a dentist."

"Really?" Agnes cannot hide her surprise. According to Lakshmi, Mary is practically destitute, a charity case.

"Yes. My husband, God rest him, left a lot of money when he died. He came from a wealthy family. I have been able to send all the children to good schools."

"That, at least, is fortunate."

"It is. I am very lucky. I want for nothing. And, when I get old, I will stay with one or other of my children. There are plenty of them to look after me."

"That is good. You know, Mary, you really must come and visit us some time."

Agnes puts her arm around her smaller cousin's frail shoulder. It amuses her to think of Lakshmi's face when she discovers that 'the charity case' is not only independently wealthy, but blessed with a clutch of intelligent children, at least three of them successful professionals. Lakshmi will simply die with envy. Agnes must find a way of telling her.

***

In the dining room, Lakshmi is extolling Michael's virtues.

"He is so clever, such an eye for business. Everything he touches turns to gold. He works for a foreign insurance company. Oh, how silly! Its name escapes me. You know … that big new building in the centre of town? Its headquarters are in New York, or is it Washington? I forget. Anyway, it has offices in London, Ottawa and some German place I can't pronounce. Stutt.., Stutt…"

"Stuttgart?" suggests one of the relations.

"Yes. That's it. German names! So hard to pronounce. Anyway, Michael is a senior accountant at our national office. One of their top executives."

An executive. She savours the word.

"Before that, he used to have his own clients and there was so much paperwork, he had to carry it around in a briefcase."

One of the relations, who knows Michael by sight, thinks he used to see the 'executive' with his briefcase, selling policies door-to-door in their neighbourhood. However, he thoughtfully refrains from mentioning this and contents himself with a meaningful wink at his wife who stifles a giggle. She shares the joke, having once rejected Michael's attempts to sell her "Life Insurance at best possible premium".

"An executive," purrs Lakshmi, her huge bosom rising and falling in contentment. "You will see, very soon he will be running the whole shooting match. And he has built a new home, brand new. You should see it."

Niran, who has been appointed barman, clinks the glasses loudly, although this mild protest goes unnoticed.

The woman, who rejected Michael's commercial advances, is now coughing vigorously into her handkerchief. Yes, she has seen the new home. In fact, she and her husband made a point of driving past it on the way here.

True, it looks nice enough. But the location! Only a stone's throw away from the shanties with a railway track on one side and a cemetery on the other. Not the sort of place she would want her daughter to live. But, as she reminds herself, beggars cannot be choosers and Lakshmi is only a generation away from the slum dwellings of Araliya Flats. Hiding her face in her handkerchief, the wife wipes her streaming eyes.

"Oh dear!" Lakshmi exudes concern. "Niran, get some water."

Lakshmi directs her husband with the same peremptory wave that she uses for servants. Meekly, he obeys, disappearing into the kitchen in search of water.

"Goodness, eight 'o' clock already."

With an ostentatious flourish of her wrist, Lakshmi inspects her watch. It is her best: gold-plated, its face surrounded by fake diamonds and set with tiny black numerals that gleam with a pleasing blue-grey sheen.

"I think we should eat now. I don't know where Michael has got to."

She laughs, as if she has only just noticed his absence although she has spent most of the evening eulogising him. Niran re-appears, cradling a full glass of water in his hands. As he passes her, Lakshmi hisses audibly.

"Where is he?"

"Who?"

"Michael!"

"I don't know," Niran mumbles, flattening himself into two dimensions so that he appears to melt into the wall. A tantrum is brewing.

With a rush, Lakshmi's good humour runs out, like the last grains of sand in an egg-timer. She hates being made to look stupid. Where is Michael? He should have been here an hour ago. What has kept him? What could be more important than an evening with his family? And Dalia looks so pretty tonight!

One of the servants, instructed by Lakshmi, strikes a dinner gong in the hall. The guests shuffle to the table, allowing themselves to be directed and, in some cases, propelled by Lakshmi, who lines them up like pieces on a giant chess board.

"No, no, not there, Aunty. Sit here next to Uncle Joseph. That's better!"

She shunts her guests back and forth until, finally content, she gives the sign for them to sit down. To most, her behaviour is perplexing, if not a little insulting. Family gatherings, however large, are normally informal affairs, with adult guests sitting where they wish and children, of which there is a marked absence tonight, allowed to run about the room unchecked. Lakshmi's party, however, is modelled on the starchy gatherings of colonials.

As they take their seats, Lakshmi's guests note with dismay that each place has a full complement of cutlery. The meal is to be eaten in the western manner, with food delivered to the mouth on metal instruments: a procedure reminiscent of a clinical operation, it has unpleasant associations with visits to the dentist. The metal feels hard and cold in the mouth and, often, it has a peculiar flavour of its own. For Islanders, used to eating with their fingers, food eaten with cutlery acquires an unpleasant tang. Moreover, taste is not the only sense to be compromised by this manner of eating, but also that of touch; the tactile quality of food is as important to its enjoyment as its aroma and flavour.

"Not even silver," whispers Agnes to her husband, as she examines her fork. "EPNS. It's only plated. Who does she think she is?"

"Shhh!" whispers her husband, afraid that Lakshmi will hear: but their hostess, deaf to all criticism, has launched into another exposition of Michael's merits.

"Michael may be young but he has such a good mind. He makes twice as much money as other fellows his age. Did I tell you, he already has a car?"

Everyone listens obediently, occasionally wagging their heads in agreement. All except one, a snub-nosed cousin who is a journalist on the Island's daily newspaper. He and his wife are an unprepossessing couple; he with his round snout and snorting laugh and she, a quiet ruminant, peacefully munching her food without comment, a picture of bovine complacency. To those who do not know them, they appear to be, not so much man and wife, as cow and pig, but the depth of their mutual devotion is fathomless and often underestimated by those who do not know them.

Lakshmi invited them tonight simply to make up the numbers. However, her lack of interest in these guests is apparent from her embarrassing inability to remember their names. It is a mistake that she is soon to regret.

"And, em ..." Lakshmi struggles to remember the cousin's name.

"David ..." prompts the cousin, his patience wearing thin. It is, after all, the third such instance of Lakshmi's absentmindedness.

"Yes, David," she corrects herself and turns on a beaming smile. "Are any of your children married yet?"

An awkward silence descends over the table broken only by the squeal of a spoon on a plate. Looking up from her food, the cow-like wife stares sadly at her husband, her huge brown eyes glistening. Reaching under the table, he squeezes her hand.

"We don't have any children," says the cousin in a strangled voice.

"Oh no. Of course not. I had forgotten. So unfortunate."

Flushing with embarrassment, Lakshmi simpers and flutters her eyes, but the cousin has not finished with her.

"So, where is that fine fellow, Michael, that you have been telling us about? I am dying to meet him. Where is he?"

Unaware of the irony in her cousin's voice, Lakshmi grasps the opportunity to recover from her gaffe by talking about her family.

"Of course, Michael has been held up at the office. He often works late, you see. Very dutiful."

"Really," remarks the cousin, jovially. "If I were him, I'd be making the most of my freedom, you know, goodbye to all that: saying farewell to all my friends, especially the female ones!"

Rendered speechless by the sudden shock of this onslaught, Lakshmi turns puce. Meeting no resistance, the cousin continues.

"Ha, ha!" He pokes a stubby finger at Dalia. "Don't you worry, my girl. The novelty will soon wear off, you'll want him out of the house. Just like my wife, always asking me why I don't find a girlfriend. Says she'd be happy to have some time to herself. David, she says, it's a pity you're not a Moslem, then you could have a different wife for every day of the week and I'd have six days off!"

The other guests roar with laughter. The cow-like wife rolls her eyes and helps herself to another spoonful of rice. Expecting Niran to intervene, Lakshmi shoots a murderous glance in his direction, but he has already disappeared into the kitchen. Leaning forward on the table, the cousin wags a finger in the air.

"You know, Lakshmi, I know a thing or two about the insurance business. A salesman's position is a precarious one. Do you remember Shoba's son?"

Some of the other guests shift uncomfortably. Lakshmi, who has never heard of Shoba, is unable to gauge the drift of the conversation, although instinct warns her to be on her guard.

"Shoba's son made a fortune selling insurance. New house by the beach, fast car, expensive clothes. But he hadn't got the brain for business, only selling, that was all he was good at. Anyway, he decided to start a business of his own and – hey presto!" the cousin snaps his fingers, "he lost the lot. He and his wife are struggling to make ends meet now. He is a shop assistant and she works in a factory."

Leaning back in his chair, the cousin dabs his mouth with a serviette while suppressing a belch.

"No," he shakes his head ruefully. "Once a salesman, always a salesman. You can't go changing the colour of your coat. Although, I expect Michael has many coats, hey! Ha ha!"

Laughing uproariously, the cousin thumps his pudgy fist on the table with such force that the plates rattle. The other guests hold their breath. There is the same, still tension in the air as there is before a storm breaks. Dalia, already mortified by Michael's absence, looks to her mother for support. At the sight of her daughter's ashen face, Lakshmi feels something tighten around her heart. Puffing up like an angry cobra, she primes herself to spit venom.

"Michael … is … not … a … salesman. He … is … an … EXECUTIVE."

"Hello. What's that? Talking about me!"

Michael is standing in the doorway. He looks unusually dishevelled, as if he has been running, his tie loose and off-centre, strands of Brylcreemed hair hanging over his forehead. The cultivated elegance of Clark Gable has been exchanged for the look of another matinee idol, a James Dean or a Marlon Brando. Few of the guests doubt that Michael's appearance is anything but calculated. Strolling into the room, with the kind of feline arrogance that defies challenge, he kisses his fuming mother-in-law, then saunters over to the sideboard where he pours himself a whisky.

"Ha! Return of the wanderer," announces the pug-faced cousin triumphantly.

"No," counters Michael, calmly. "Just working late."

1956: Dulce domum

Pleading an early start in the morning, Michael has escaped from Lakshmi's party. When he announced his departure, Dalia pouted and Lakshmi glared, but there was little else they could do for fear of losing face in front of their guests. Even so, it took him a good half hour to effect his release; kissing all the hideous old aunts, shaking the uncles by the hand, listening to their gushing compliments and hints that Lakshmi is looking forward to being a grandmother. Michael is tired. He has heard it all before. A hundred times. He wishes the wedding was over; or, even better, that it could be avoided altogether.

Driving through the narrow streets, past the shanties where men idle in groups or lean against the tin walls of their shacks smoking bidis, Michael feels a sense of apprehension. He will have to make this journey twice a day, past the open sewers, the lines strung with washing, the dogs and cats worrying piles of rubbish. This is not how he saw his future. A narrow little house, a sulking wife, a screaming baby. And Lakshmi. No doubt she will take up residence on a semi-permanent basis, especially if there is a child.

"Surely," thinks Michael, swerving as a pye-dog lurches into the road, "surely there is more to life than this."

And he thinks once more of his mistress.

***

The little car draws up outside the house and Michael waits for a minute, steeling himself, although he knows no-one is there. Every time he returns here, he has a strange feeling, like a prisoner viewing his gaol for the first time. He must stay here every night to guard the house, but it feels as if it is guarding him.

The house is nearing completion, increasing the risk of occupation by squatters. It is a problem throughout the Island. The recent population explosion has created a hunger for land that cannot be satisfied by lawful means. While the Government hopes to satisfy demand by colonising areas of low population, it cannot stem the tide of petty incursions that frequently result in violence.

Everywhere boundaries are being eroded, perimeters re-drawn and land appropriated by trickery or force. It is common practice for neighbours to re-position shared fences without reference to each other. The courts are awash with territorial disputes, many of which remain unresolved for years.

Those unwilling, or unable, to engage in legal proceedings, often employ more direct means of breaking the deadlock. Small acts of hostility, such as the laming of a neighbour's cattle or the theft of his chickens, often escalate into campaigns of terror, with friends and family being called in for support. Violent clashes ensue and, while these usually consist of harmless brawls, they sometimes lead to serious injury.

Occasionally, frustrated at his inability to obtain justice, one neighbour will simply murder another. There will then be a trial and an appeal against the inevitable death sentence to the Privy Council in England.

Although Michael's new house stands in its own ground surrounded by a barbed wire fence, it is not far from the shanty where new developments, constructed of corrugated iron and railway sleepers, spring up in hours with no regard for the niceties of urban planning.

Permission is not a concept that troubles homeless people drifting in from the countryside in search of work. With small children in tow, their only imperative is shelter. The only way to protect one's property is to live in it; even if it is unfinished.

With Lakshmi's hoarse laughter still ringing in his ears, Michael lets himself into the darkened house. It smells of sand and cement, especially in the lower half where the plaster on newly-rendered walls has not yet dried. As he walks across the hallway, his footsteps echo on the concrete which, as yet unpainted, is still ridged and rough. In daylight, one can still see pebbles embedded in the floor.

Michael presses the light switch. It clicks, but nothing happens and the interior remains obscure. The electricity, like the plumbing, has not yet been connected. The house is a shell, a pretence of a house, not real. He senses it, mocking him, its emptiness a reflection of his own life.

The only relief from the darkness comes from the light of a street-lamp outside. Once his eyes have become accustomed to the gloom, Michael makes his way to the kitchen where, with a curse, he stumbles up a step in the doorway, a device of Lakshmi's which, for some reason, she insisted should be included in the design.

Although no meals have yet been cooked on the gas stove, the kitchen reeks of burned milk. Two days ago, Lakshmi insisted on performing the new-house ritual of cooking milk in a pan and allowing it to boil over. It has taken many attempts to scrub away the brown rime baked onto the shining new hob. In fact, having run into various crevices, the burnt milk can never be entirely removed. The whole house stinks of Lakshmi's interference.

Opening one of the empty cupboards, Michael withdraws an arrack bottle. There are no glasses, but that does not trouble him. Unscrewing the cap, he lifts the bottle to his lips and takes a long draft. He is drinking more these days, much more. At least, here, there is no-one to see him.

Walking unsteadily into the living-room, he sits on the floor in a pool of pale light cast by the street-lamp. He lied tonight. He had not been at the office, but hiding from the police. Moodily, he contemplates the events that nearly led to his arrest. An act of stupidity that could have ruined him.

A few hours before Lakshmi's party, Michael tried to see his mistress. Once again, he was told that she was out. Not that he believed it. So he waited in his car around the corner until he saw the sleek black Jaguar slip out of the drive. He could see her, quite plainly, in the passenger seat, looking at herself in a small mirror, the sort that women carry in their handbags.

Keeping a discreet distance, he had followed the Jaguar into town, where it had stopped outside Cargill's store. Leela had got out, given the driver her instructions, then disappeared into the dark interior of the shop. Parked on the opposite kerb, Michael had waited until, at least an hour later, she had emerged, carrying several bags, no doubt full of luxuries that she could no longer afford.

It had all happened so quickly. In a few long strides, Michael had crossed the road and placed himself between Leela and her waiting car, cutting off her escape. This time she would have to speak to him.

"Leela. Why won't you see me?"

She was unprepared for this encounter. Her eyes flamed with anger, the fury of a trapped animal. She tried to step around him, but he moved quickly, blocking her way.

"Tell me who he is?"

"What are you talking about?"

At the point of contact, her eyes darted away. He already knew the truth, but he needed to hear it from her.

"You've got someone else."

"There's always someone else," she taunted him.

"Not to the exclusion of me," he hissed.

Momentarily, another expression passed over her face. Guilt or pity, perhaps? Michael could not be sure. She made another move to pass him. He grabbed her arm.

"Let me go!"

"No. Not until you tell me who it is."

"I'm busy!"

She writhed, trying to free herself. He tightened his grip.

"You were never too busy to see me – even when your husband was alive."

"You helped to pass the time. Now things are different," she snarled; a tiger, ready to rip and claw.

"So tell me it's over."

She hesitated, unable to deliver the coup de grâce.

"Tell me it's over," he persisted.

Still struggling to free herself, she looked frantically at the little crowd that was beginning to grow around them.

"Tell me! It's that boy who works for the Government Agent, isn't it?"

A flash of her eyes. Confirmation. But, still, he needed to hear it.

"Tell me, Leela!"

He shook her in desperation. It was a mistake.

"Help. Police!" she yelled.

A young man detached himself from the onlookers and loped off down the street.

"Leela. Tell me, please!"

"No. You don't own me."

"Leela …"

In his anguish, he grasped her so tightly that she winced with pain. Fear increased her panic and she screamed, almost hysterical.

"Help, help!"

Men in the crowd were shuffling restlessly, uncertain as to whether they should intervene. One, more courageous than the rest, stepped forward.

"Listen, brother. Let the lady go."

He looked like a shopkeeper, a man of about fifty, greying at the temples, slightly heavy around the jowls. He put his hand on Michael's arm. Nothing violent, just a gentle restraint. But, fired with anger, Michael struck out, hitting the man on the jaw, sending him spinning backwards into the crowd. At that moment, the young man who had run off earlier reappeared, followed by a police officer wielding a baton.

Fearing arrest, Michael had darted down a side street inhabited by pye-dogs and urchins. Having lost himself in the maze of derelict alleys, he had hidden for a couple of hours until he judged it safe to emerge. He had then slipped back to his car and driven off at a furious pace, first returning home and draining half a bottle of arrack, before presenting himself at Lakshmi's party.

***

Sitting on the floor of his empty house, Michael swallows the last of the arrack, reflecting bitterly on how Leela has betrayed him. Enough. He must sleep. Crawling onto his knees, he rises unsteadily to his feet, then staggers along the passage which leads to the bedroom. On his way, he passes an empty room, bathed in blue light and his heart stops. The figure of a man, suspended by the neck, is outlined against the window.

"Oh God!"

His skin tingling with icy sweat, Michael puts out a hand to steady himself against the wall then, summoning a spark of courage, he enters the room and approaches the hanging figure. As he gets nearer, he notices that its legs and arms are stiffly akimbo, unlike the limp appearance that he would have expected from a dead body. He carefully reaches up and tugs at the sleeve. With a slithering sound, the rope unhitches itself and the body falls to the ground in a shower of straw. It is a dummy, the sort put up by workmen to ward off evil spirits when building a new house.

Weak with relief, Michael sinks to the floor, where he lies with his head on the dummy's chest.

"A man of straw," he murmurs, "in an empty house."

He laughs bitterly before falling asleep.

***

Michael awakes, his head still propped on the dummy's chest, his mouth as dry as parchment. He panics and, trying to remember where he is, runs his fingers over the rough surface of the concrete floor. Remembering, he rests a little longer, watching small blades of light play on the ceiling, listening to sounds from the street, trying to guess what time it is.

"Maalu! Maalu!"

It is a fish-seller who travels the streets on foot, a basket suspended at either end of a long pole which he carries over his shoulder. The baskets are filled with a variety of fish, bought directly from the small boats that put out to sea every day and whose owners, the fishermen, live in huts only yards from the sea-shore. When the fish-seller starts on his rounds, the pole over his shoulder is heavy, weighed down by the full baskets and, as he walks, it bounces up and down.

First, he visits the wealthier areas in the hope of selling the more expensive items: seer fish or parrot fish, which only the rich can afford. Next, he circulates the neighbourhoods where, although there is less demand for luxury, housewives will nevertheless pay handsomely for wholesome specimens. After that, if anything is left, he travels to the poorer, less accessible areas, where he offers the remaining sprats and prawns at a discounted price, hoping to shift them before they go off. Fish rots quickly in this heat, sometimes becoming too tainted even for the undiscriminating palates of the poor. The fish-seller must sell all of his stock by the end of the day and, for this reason, he will walk many miles.

"Maalu! Maalu!"

The fish-seller has stopped outside. Michael can hear him conversing with a woman, arguing over the price of a few sardines. From his position on the floor, Michael can see the top of the man's battered straw hat. It has a large hole in the crown and the brim is frayed. There is a chink of coins. Money is changing hands. The voices outside the window murmur pleasantly, the heat of their debate forgotten now a price has been agreed.

"Maalu! Maalu!"

The thought of fish turns Michael's stomach. He prefers meat. His stomach rumbles and he longs for pittu and curry, but the house is empty. Even the arrack has gone. Painfully, he raises himself into a sitting position. His body is stiff and his head is throbbing, as if his brain is knocking to get out.

"Ohh!"

Leaning forward, he rubs his temples with the heel of his palms. The pain disappears temporarily but, as soon as he stops rubbing, it comes back. Rising unsteadily to his feet, he staggers to the door and lets himself out, skulking along the street like a pye-dog in search of food.

Leela's day starts badly. She has tried to phone Arjun at his office but, each time, has been told that he is unavailable. Slamming down the receiver, she flies into a rage and screams at the housekeeper who is hovering by the door.

"Angela, what are you doing there?"

"Nothing, Madam."

"Are you spying on me?"

"No!"

The housekeeper's eyes, as round as boiled sweets, always give her a look of surprise. Leela did not think it possible for those eyes to become any bigger but they widen into saucers at the sharpness of her accusation. In the midst of her fury, Leela almost laughs, the woman looks so funny, her face dwarfed by huge eyes, like those of a lemur.

"Get away from me!"

Needing no excuse, the housekeeper runs to the back of the house where she hides in the scullery, vowing revenge. Mr Michael will hear of this. He will understand. And, as usual, he will pay for her gossip about the mistress's new boyfriend.

***

Opening the French windows, Leela steps into the garden, her heart still beating wildly after her confrontation with the housekeeper. She is angry. Everyone has let her down. Those she needs, desert her; those she does not want, will not leave her alone.

The unplanned meeting with Michael has unsettled her. Why did she not put an end to it all, there in the street, when he asked her to? It is not that she wants Michael but, perversely, she cannot let him go. She wants to be free of the past, to start again, but something is holding her back. Money. He is the only one who can help her.

Kneeling beside the fish pond, she dabbles at the surface of the water. A large carp with silver scales emerges from the weed where it has been grazing, gaping its large mouth in the hope of something more substantial. Leela lets it suck the tips of her fingers, enjoying the soft pinch of its bony lips. Her hand looks pale under the water, like that of a corpse. She shudders and withdraws, shaking drops of water from her hand. The fish sinks back into the shallows.

From the house, she can hear the shrill voice of the housekeeper. She is reciting a litany of complaints against her mistress. Formerly, such behaviour would not have been tolerated, but Leela is no longer in a position to object. Anyway, she has more to worry about than the trivial concerns of servants.

She wanders round to the other side of the house, where it is quieter and there is more shade. Sitting beneath a tamarind tree, she rests her head against the trunk. A small bird hops through the branches, pausing occasionally to pipe a cadence of bubbling notes. Idly, Leela pulls up blades of grass, winding them around her fingers, then threading them into knots. What was it that attracted her to Michael?

They first met when he came to advise Mennan on his financial affairs. Even then, Michael must have known that the source of Mennan's wealth was irregular, even unlawful. But that had not deterred him. Rather, it seemed to draw him in. He liked to take risks. There was an edginess about him which she found exciting.

Does she still find him exciting? Is that why she was unable to dismiss him completely; even when he gave her the opportunity? She shakes her head, remembering the awful embarrassment of that scene in the street yesterday. No. It is unthinkable. Michael has no attraction for her now. She was simply caught off guard.

But, still, she needs him. Without Michael, she faces ruin. She must reconcile herself to the truth, however unpleasant. Examining her fingers, she discovers that they have been stained. In disgust, she flings the broken blades of grass away. The bird has stopped singing. Momentarily, the garden is plunged into silence. But it is enough to convince Leela of her own, dangerous solitude.

She cannot continue to avoid Michael. Mennan's arrangement has seen to that. Still, after yesterday, she is sure that she has the advantage. She must meet him, explain, come to an arrangement that will not compromise her interests. Or her freedom.

The bird resumes its song.

It is too late to go to work. After eating, Michael wanders aimlessly back to the house. Everywhere around him there is a buzz of activity: women scurrying past with baskets balanced on their heads; traders, laden with wares, travelling on foot or by bicycle; rickshaws; cars; a cow, ambling wearily across the road; the anxious hooting of horns. Everyone is busy, but him. Everyone has somewhere to go.

Despite drinking several cups of sweet tea, Michael's head still aches. The noise and energy around him make it worse. Gratefully re-entering the house, which is as cool as a cave, he goes to the darkest corner he can find and sits down, his back and head resting against the newly-plastered wall. It has a strange, but not unpleasant smell; slightly salty. In fact, the whole house has a faint tang of seaweed as if it has been washed by the tide. Michael almost expects to see a crab scuttling across the floor or an encrustation of winkles and sea anemones around the base of the wall. He shuts his eyes and dozes.

A sharp trill awakes him and he thinks, for one moment, that a bird has got into the house; but it is a couple of geckos, chirruping as they chase each other. They move like lightning, two little flashes of pink darting over the smooth surface of the walls. Their presence is somehow comforting. They inhabit every home, rich or poor, even Leela's.

Michael remembers their first encounter. Mennan had invited him to a party at his house where Michael entertained a group of guests with an account of his latest conquest. His jokes could sometimes offend but, on this occasion, he knew that he would not be judged harshly: the other guests were like him; he could tell by their demeanour, the way they held a glass or smoked a cigarette. They listened attentively with furrowed brows and laughed in all the right places but what they really wanted was to be seen and the best way to be seen, for those of mediocre talent, was to join a set like Mennan's, currently the smartest in town.

Mennan's guests adored Michael who had just the kind of humour they admired: harsh, uncompromising and usually practised at someone else's expense. They had roared with laughter at his jokes. Glowing with success, Michael had paused to sip his Martini and, over the rim of the glass, he had caught sight of Leela, standing just beyond the ring of guests that surrounded him, her hand cupped over her mouth to hide her giggles, her eyes sparkling like polished jet.

After that, whenever he visited Mennan, Leela was always present, artfully drawing Michael into conversation, until he spent longer with her than her husband. Then, one afternoon, he had gone to the house for a meeting, only to find that Mennan had been called away on business. Apologising for the inconvenience, Leela had detained Michael on the pretext of asking his advice.

However, when it became obvious that Mennan would not return, their conversation had strayed from business to the discussion of more pleasurable subjects. This, in turn, led to a more intimate exchange; one of a physical, rather than verbal, nature. In Michael, Leela discovered an excellent subject on which to practice her artistry; the perfect partner, unhindered by conscience or shame who, like her, delighted in novelty.

For two years, Leela and Michael were lovers, enjoying a relationship entirely dedicated to pleasure, free from responsibility. But, somehow, Mennan's death had changed all that. While Mennan was alive, Michael had sometimes been troubled by a vague fear of discovery, although never by remorse. Guilt was simply not in his nature. However, after Mennan's death, Michael actually regretted his passing. It did not offer him the freedom that he had supposed, rather, the opposite.

While she was Mennan's wife, there was no question of Leela tying herself to someone else. True, she had had other lovers, but none of them serious enough to be of real concern and yet, from the moment Mennan was laid to rest, Michael knew that he had lost her. She was free and could marry again, but it would not be Michael that she chose. He had known it as surely as if she had told him herself, even before she started the affair with Arjun.

A pulse of anger begins to throb in his head. How could she abandon him for that office-clerk? They are two of a kind, Michael and Leela. She has always been capricious – he accepts that, it is part of her charm – but now she is behaving like a half-wit. What possible future can there be in a relationship with an inexperienced boy? Michael knows the type: half man, half youth; one who combines the freshness of a schoolboy with the innocence of a seminarian. Why do these men exert such power over women?

He remembers convent girls who casually gave up their virginity to any local boy. Unresisting and bored, they behaved with the same tired acceptance as women twice their age: yet those same girls practically fainted with pleasure if the young priest stopped to speak to them after Mass. Standing in little groups, they would blush and giggle, following him hungrily with their eyes.

Is it the knowledge that innocence can never be possessed that makes it so attractive? For, once touched, it dies, like a flower blasted by the wind. It is a mystery to Michael who has never prized virginity over experience. Trying to instruct a novice in the art of lovemaking is not only tedious, it is grotesque. He tried it once, laughing until he was nearly sick and the girl was in tears. Unresponsive and clumsy, she had kept her eyes closed throughout.

Doubting if Dalia will be any better, he succumbs to a wave of revulsion. It will be like making love to a corpse. In her case, experience will never lead to improvement: she is too self-regarding to think of her partner's pleasure. No doubt she will recount every detail of her experience to her mother. He feels sick at the prospect. After Leela's exquisite skills, how can he ever settle for less?

No doubt, when the novelty has worn off, Leela will tire of Arjun. Then she will want Michael back but, by then, his circumstances will have changed. He must do something before it is too late. He must try, once again, to reason with her.

***

As hamlets and coconut groves skim past the car, Michael considers the irony of his situation. The advice he gave to Mennan has put the overseer's money beyond the reach of his pursuers and there is enough to keep Leela in luxury for the rest of her life: but, first, she has to find it and the only person who can help her is Michael. For Michael has a letter. Not a draft, but a final copy, signed by Mennan. Leela does not know of its existence. He is sure of that.

Again and again, he has tried to see her, arriving at the house unannounced, only to be turned away. Unable to meet her, he once managed to surprise her on the telephone, but their conversation was like a fencing match, verbal thrusts then a parrying of words in which she bested him with evasive answers.

The car bounces and jolts. The rural roads are rough and uneven. A small girl is leading a sleepy buffalo by its tether. When the animal stops to graze the verge, the child flicks its hindquarters with a switch to get it moving. As the car passes, she stands aside and smiles at Michael, waving her hand. If he stops, she will probably ask him for money.

"Bloody peasants!" he mutters.

Michael detests the countryside. He fears it: the ignorance, the lack of sanitation, the stupid-looking people. He can never understand why anyone praises its space and openness. He feels suffocated here, as if his oxygen had been cut off. The town is the only place in which he can breathe and he cannot wait to return to it.

One after the other, bitter memories flick through Michael's head. He tries to block them out but, like an observer at an execution, he is forced to witness them, each more painful than the last. He punches the steering wheel and howls like a wounded animal.

Worst of all was his humiliation when he confronted Leela in the street. It all went so wrong. Now he fears a visit from the police. If they come knocking on his door, everything will be lost – even the prospect of a respectable, but tawdry, marriage to Dalia.

A woman chases a fugitive chicken into the road. Michael swerves, missing her by inches, momentarily losing control of the car.

"Bitch," he shouts, as the car screeches to a halt.

With the bird now safely tucked under her arm, the woman stands in the middle of the road, uncomprehending, mutely staring at the car.

"Stupid bitch!"

Leaning forward, Michael rests his head on his hands which are still tightly clenched around the wheel.

"Stupid bitch," he murmurs to himself.

The peasant woman is shouting, complaining to a group of villagers, waving her arm in the air, pointing at the car. Stolid and silent, they stare in Michael's direction. The woman yells, her voice shrill, touched with a note of hysteria. Something stirs in the pit of Michael's stomach. Fear. He gazes at the villagers' faces, reflected in his mirror. As intractable as cattle, they have the same capacity to charge without warning. Jamming the car into gear, he drives off at speed, a cloud of dust from the back wheels obscuring his view of the villagers.

Michael is sweating. He reeks of panic: a sour, unpleasant odour. He wonders if people, like animals, can interpret that smell. Can they scent a man's weakness? Leela must not think him weak. She must believe that he is stronger than her.

When he meets her today – and he is convinced that he will – he must not repeat the mistakes of yesterday's meeting outside Cargill's. He must remain calm. He holds a single, indisputable ace: he, alone, can provide her with money. And she needs it. It is already rumoured that she has sold much of her jewellery. Today, he will test her love for Arjun by giving her a choice.

***

The road leads across a railway line and the car bounces as Michael guides it over the rails. On either side of him, people are walking along the tracks, sheltering from the sun under black umbrellas. Some of the umbrellas are old: in places their spines have broken, poking out awkwardly and giving the umbrella a lop-sided appearance; in others the fabric has been pierced, creating small pinholes of light; but, with careful manipulation, owners can position umbrellas to counter these weaknesses. In expert hands, even the most battered brolly affords protection from the sun.

The light that falls on the railway tracks is dusty and heat-ridden, giving everything a faded aspect. The view along the track is always the same: people trudging barefoot, some laden with baskets or parcels, women in saris, men with their sarongs hitched up over their knees. Every so often, they stand to one side as a train approaches, shading their eyes as it rattles by, watching the passengers crammed into airless carriages. Then, once the train has passed, the walkers step back onto the tracks and continue their toilsome journey. It is a scene of weariness and desolation.

For that very reason, Michael hates the railway tracks. One passes by his new home, much too close. Although he had not wanted to build a house there, he had little choice in the matter. The money which has paid for the house is not his. Neither is it Lakshmi's for that matter but, as usual, she has had the last word. The site of the house was her choice, a narrow ribbon of land with a railway track on one side and a cemetery inhabited by pye-dogs on the other. Even Niran had tried to reason with her, but she simply would not listen. No. Dalia's house must be built on that particular spot: its special attraction lying, not in its aspect, but in the fact that it is the closest available plot to Lakshmi's home.

No matter that the married couple will be kept awake at night by the howling of dogs rutting between the gravestones or the shunting of heavy goods trains. Lakshmi must be close to her daughter. It is a choice that anticipates future interference. Michael has been condemned to live in a place that he dislikes, with a girl for whom he has no affection and whose mother he hates.

Why did he ever agree to it? Respectability. That was it. He needed a wife to make him credible. He cannot live off his wits forever. It is time to settle down. At least, that is what his own family told him and, in a moment of weakness, he had believed them. They had introduced him to Dalia and, temporarily blinded by her beauty, he had agreed to the marriage. He even consulted Leela about it. She had laughed and said it seemed the perfect arrangement. Under the cloak of respectability, they could continue their affair uninterrupted. Like a fool, he had believed her, too.

***

The car bounds along a rough dirt track, stones flying from its wheels. Then, rounding a corner, Michael slows to cross a bridge whose planks rattle under the vehicle's weight. From below, a foul stench rises from the stagnant canal whose slimy green surface bubbles with gas. It is one of the poorer quarters whose residents, nonetheless, count themselves superior to the shanty-dwellers because their homes are made of breeze blocks and plaster, not tin.

Children with dusty bare feet and clothes that are either too large or too small for them are playing in the street. When the car slows at a bend, some of them run after it, their hands stretched out, hoping for a few coins or sweets. Pressing his foot down hard, Michael slews around the corner. The wheels scream and throw up a cloud of dust, obscuring the view from the rear window. There are so many things that can contaminate you in this country. The only remedies are distance and speed. Michael urges the car forward, his foot pressed down to the floor.

Civilisation, at last. Michael turns into the road that passes Leela's house and which is covered, for only a few hundred yards, with tarmacadam. Mennan obviously had some influence with the authorities or perhaps he had simply diverted resources from a Government project to create his own private road. Good old Mennan! That would have been just like him. He had been, as Michael likes to put it, 'a wily old bird full of guile'. It has never struck Michael as contradictory that, while cuckolding Mennan, he should still have regarded him as his friend and mentor.

"One day," he used to think, "I shall be as wealthy as Mennan, with a fine house and many servants."

He wonders now if his own decision to marry was not prompted by Mennan's example. A man can go far with a beautiful wife. But Dalia is no Leela. She does not have Leela's wit or magnetism, or that slight air of mystery that keeps one guessing as to what she will do next. No, Dalia is totally predictable. There is nothing behind that beautiful face, except a pettish nature and a desire to be spoiled. Michael is bored with her already.

Passing Leela's house, Michael follows the road around a corner to where the tarmac finishes abruptly and is replaced by a dirt track. Parking the car on the verge, he walks back along the road.

"Like a damn thief," he mutters irritably, noting the dust that has dulled the patina on his shoes.

Circling around the garden with its tall clumps of red and yellow canna lilies, he peers through the metal palings to check for visitors' cars on the drive. There are none. Only the Jaguar, parked crossways at the bottom of the steps.

He approaches cautiously, skirting the car then treading stealthily up the stone steps to the front door, the pulse in his head pounding like a hammer. He knocks, then listens for the sound of feet. The house is silent. After a few minutes, he knocks again, his temper rising. Waiting on the doorstep makes him feel like a tradesman. It underlines his fall from grace, increasing his humiliation.

The panel behind the grille slides back.

"Who is it, please?"

He recognises the soft voice of the housekeeper.

"It's me, Angela. Michael."

"Oh."

The woman seems hesitant. Tetchily, Michael flicks an insect from his sleeve.

"I don't think ..."

There is a murmur of voices from behind the door.

"Come in, Michael."

The heavy teak door swings wide. Leela is standing there, her smile both welcoming and mocking. As he brushes past, he can smell her perfume, sandalwood, contrasting with the natural musk of his own body. It has been hot in the car and, although he washed before coming out, the smell of sweat now overrides that of aftershave.

She regards him with quiet amusement. A little disdain.

"This way."

She leads him to a door at the end of the passage, into a room which was used by Mennan to entertain his friends. At one end is a bar with high stools. The wall behind is faced with mirrors and glass shelves. In the middle of the room is a huge billiard table made of heavy, lacquered oak. A hint of cigar smoke still lingers in the air, although the room has not been used since Mennan's death. Michael wonders why Leela has brought him here.

"Drink?"

Playfully, she waves a bottle of whisky at him. His heart trips, with a little pain, a little nostalgia. It is the bottle that she kept exclusively for him, the one that only they drank from at illicit meetings. He nods, unable to speak.

Having poured a generous measure into a tumbler, she turns to seek the other ingredients, bending so that the stuff of her sari stretches tight across the gentle curve of her buttocks. His throat constricts. He feels that he may choke. A terrible hunger, like fire, kindles within him.

Ice cubes clink as Leela swirls the contents of the glass, her waist swaying gently, in time with the movement of her hand. She selects a soda siphon – there are three – and presses the handle. There is a short, gasping sound as water gushes into the glass. Just a dash, the way he likes it. She has not forgotten. Tilting her head coquettishly, she holds out the drink and, when their fingers meet, she does not remove her hand at once.

Walking around the bar, she seats herself on one of the high stools next to him. Briefly, her thigh grazes his. She seems not to notice. After such a long absence, he finds her presence unnerving. His wits desert him and he struggles to speak. After a few seconds, she comes to his rescue.

"Well. How are you?"

"OK."

He does not look at her but stares hard into his glass. This is proving harder than he thought. He had not expected to be so tongue-tied.

"I'm sorry."

"What about?"

"Yesterday. In the street."

"Oh."

She shrugs as if it were nothing. The conversation falters and they both fall silent. Leela runs a finger around the rim of her glass, teasing it into a high-pitched whine. He knows that gesture. It is something she does when bored. She wants him to go.

"You've treated me badly."

A pathetic comment, not what he meant to say. The whining of a petulant child.

"You knew it wouldn't last."

Without looking at him, she languidly waves her hand, as if sweeping a cobweb from her face.

"We could have come to an arrangement. You could have spoken to me. Given me a chance."

"Ahhh."

She sighs wearily, tilting her head to one side, exposing the delicate angle of her jaw, the soft curve of her neck. He hates and desires her in equal measure. The fire within him burns hotter, scalding his heart. Rejection and pain whet his desire.

"I came to help you but it looks like I'm wasting my time."

"What do you mean?"

At last, a flicker of interest.

"You might live like a queen but you don't have the money to pay for it"

"How dare you!"

She flushes with anger, a slight tremor in her voice. Michael has found her weak spot. Angry and humiliated, he wants to hurt her, torment her as she has tormented him, watch her squirm.

"I know where Mennan hid his money."

The silence of boredom is replaced by shock: a crackling static of anticipation.

"You know about the letter? You've seen it?"

He examines the whisky in his glass, takes a sip, looks around the room.

"You can help me?"

She places a manicured hand on his arm, grasping it so tightly that he can feel the red nails digging into his flesh. Reflected in the mirror, her profile stares at him, intense and hungry, the lips slightly parted. He can see the rapid pulse in her neck.

Slowly, he drains his glass, savouring every mouthful, aware that she is watching him; anxious, wary, hungry. But he does not return her gaze. To look into her eyes would be fatal.

"Why should I help you?"

He watches in the mirror as she struggles to master her rage, torn between pride and fear. He pours himself another glass, drinks it slowly and waits while desperation takes effect and quietly wears her down. It is like watching a fish at the end of a line. He sips his drink, taking pleasure in her anguish.

"What do you want?"

She is pale and breathless, her voice a mere whisper. For once, she has been outwitted. Michael laughs inwardly. He was right. Her need for money is stronger than desire. After the briefest of struggles, she has lost to her own cupidity. It has undermined her resistance, crumbled her defences, reduced her will to dust. Now, from the rubble of her independence, Michael will raise her up to be his creature. Lifting her off the stool, he carries her to the billiard table where he pulls up her skirts and roughly closes their bargain. She does not even struggle.

When he has done, he gazes on her dispassionately. On her back, hair strung across her face and clothes dishevelled, she is no longer the society lady who shared her favours with admirers, but a whore who opens her legs for money. But he takes no pleasure in this conquest. Rather, he is filled with revulsion. Somewhere, deep down, he experiences a flicker of conscience. A small part of him grieves for what he has destroyed and loathes what he has created. Absolute power will be his only consolation. It is an empty victory.

Leaning over, he brings his face within an inch of hers.

"If you behave, I'll let you keep your toy. What's his name? Arjun. You'll soon tire of him anyway. But be sure to make some time for me each week. As long as our arrangement continues, you'll be sure of an income."

"And what if it doesn't?"

"Then you'll be a beggar."

"You bastard!"

He catches her wrist as she tries to strike him, pushing her away. She falls back on the table, her arm over her face, a tumbled mess of clothes and hair. It reminds him of the straw doll, lying inert on the floor of his empty house.

"That is all we are," he thinks. There is comfort in the thought that life is meaningless.

Leela moans faintly but the sound is as remote as an echo from the seashore. It does not touch him. Calmly, he walks over to the bar and pours himself another whisky. As he drains it, a hundred faces stare back at him from the mirror-tiles lining the wall.

I am all of those yet none in particular.

The thought amuses him. Putting the glass down, he smoothes his hair with both hands, watching the multiple reflections copy him, like a gallery of imps. Then, tucking his shirt back into his trousers, he checks his zip to see that it is closed, and saunters out of the room without acknowledging Leela, as if he has already forgotten her.

1956: Regret

The sweet-smelling soap no longer evokes memories of rose-scented gardens but of corruption and decay: lilies past their prime, temple flowers, hair oil, the concentrated odours of a funeral parlour.

With startling keenness, the smells associated with Mennan's funeral are brought back to Leela. When she viewed his body in its silk-lined coffin, she had felt only relief; but now, months after his death, her regret at his passing is as sharp and painful as if he had just died. It is not always love that prompts remembrance, but a longing for the past.

For all his faults, Mennan had been both tolerant and kind. He had always shown her respect, despite her treatment of him. Of course, he had probably suspected her infidelity, but had chosen to ignore it. His indulgence of her whims had turned her into a spoilt child; she could always get what she wanted by a stamp of her foot, or a tantrum. But now, she is nothing. The tap-water running down her face mingles with her tears.

Rubbing the soap over her skin, she washes herself for the third time. A livid bruise is blossoming on her inner thigh. She winces as she touches it. Despite the steam that curls around her, she shivers. Her liberty has been compromised.

In the past, it would not have concerned her to sleep with a man for gain. She never required love, only the power to choose; but, today, the choice was not hers. Lack of money has forced her to take back a discarded lover. The memory of her violent coupling with Michael sickens her. It was like rape because, deep in her heart, she had resisted him. Her conscience, dormant through years of reckless betrayal, has suddenly murmured its disapproval.

If he were to find out, she doubts if Arjun would be as tolerant as Mennan. Her power over him is already tenuous, incomplete for a reason that she does not fully understand. Added to that, he has a scrupulousness that both fascinates and frightens her. So far, she has forced him to compromise but there are boundaries in his nature that cannot be crossed. If he discovers that she is seeing another man, whatever the reason, he may leave her. Once that happens, no amount of threats or cajoling will persuade him to return. She fears his loss almost more than destitution. He must not find out.

Without covering herself, she steps out of the shower and walks into the bedroom, leaving a trail of wet footprints. She sits naked in front of the French dressing table, its three mirrors contained within an elaborate frame of gilt roses and angels. By moving the side mirrors, she can view herself from different angles, see a side of herself that she has not seen before. For that reason, she generally keeps the three mirrors in the same plane, flat and facing outwards.

Today, she manipulates the mirrors so that she can see what other people see, what is otherwise hidden from her. From every angle, strands of wet hair snake down her neck like streams of black ink. Her life is being unwritten, like words on a page left in the rain. Soon, she will not recognise herself. The three other women who lean forward with her to look in the mirror see uncertainty in her eyes. Like her, they are angered by their fear.

All this is Mennan's fault. If her husband were still alive, Michael would have no power over her and she would not be grieving over her betrayal of Arjun. She would still be a queen, subject to no-one. But Mennan, God damn him, created this mess and has left her to deal with it.

"Damn you! Damn you!" scream the three weeping women in the mirror.

***

In the hallway, the portrait of Mennan smiles into the distance, his hand planted firmly on his wife's shoulder.

Neleni is rummaging in a cupboard under the sink, searching for saucepan lids. It is several weeks after her collapse, for which there has been no explanation, although Raj has told everyone that she is pregnant. She is happy with that. It precludes further enquiry as to the cause of her unhappiness or her unpredictable moods.

She feels around in the darkness with her hands, moving cautiously, fearing to touch mouse droppings or cockroaches. Despite these concerns, there is something comforting about the black space under the sink. It smells pleasantly of washing-powder, polish and domesticity.

A curtain wire, with a small hook at either end, has been strung across the top of the cupboard space and from it hangs a length of red and white gingham. It is a perfect hiding place and Saro is often to be found curled up in here. Sometimes, she is so quiet that Neleni is unaware of her presence until a small hand reaches out and touches her ankle as she stands at the sink, startling her and making her jump. Such daring often results in a smack.

Unable to find what she is looking for, Neleni inserts her head into the cupboard. She is afraid of spiders and wonders if, when she emerges, her hair will be covered with sticky strands of cobweb. She sweeps at the air in front of her then, finding no sign of spiders, becomes bolder and pushes herself further forward until her shoulders also disappear into the space under the sink. She has always feared this dark hole; but now she wishes that it was big enough to hold her. Like Saro, she would like to crawl in and hide, pulling the curtain across so that no-one could find her. In such a place, she could be alone with her thoughts.

Raj is standing behind her. He often does that, as she is working, just watching her. She rankles at the unwelcome attention. Why can he not leave her alone, not even for one minute? Knowing that his eyes follow every movement, she can almost feel the heat of their gaze, as if two beams of light are being projected onto her back, burning through her clothes and into her skin, increasing her desire to hide and become invisible. She can hear him shuffling, drumming his fingers on the table in that annoying way that he has, clearing his throat, as he often does, before opening the conversation.

"I've just bumped into our boy. He looks unhappy."

Neleni grits her teeth. Raj often refers to Arjun as 'our boy'. As if he was their son. As if she was too old to be desirable. As if her life was over. Rattling some pans together, she pretends not to have heard him, hoping that he will drop the subject. But Raj persists.

"I'm worried about Arjun."

Neleni does not reply although Raj thinks he hears a faint moan, a single low note, without inflection, accompanied by a sigh. But he could be wrong. Communicating with his wife, partly-hidden in the cupboard, is like consulting a spirit at a shrine; the likelihood of a response just as unpredictable. Sometimes she ignores him, even though she is looking straight at him. At times like that, he feels invisible, as lonely as a ghost in a roomful of people; so, he has developed a strategy. You just have to keep talking, in the hope that, at some point, she will reply.

"Arjun. I just saw him in the hall. Going out. He looks terrible."

Neleni says something that Raj cannot hear. Her voice is muffled, subterranean, accompanied by a clatter of pans like the clash of small cymbals. She inches backwards on her knees, keeping her head down in order to avoid hitting it on the lintel of the cupboard. Clutching a selection of saucepan lids to her chest, progress is slow as she cannot use her hands to push herself out of the cupboard or loosen the sari which has wound itself tightly around her knees. She becomes hot and angry.

Raj ought to help her but he is preoccupied by his recent encounter with Arjun. Ignoring the fact that his wife is still crouched on the floor, her head only partly visible, Raj launches into a detailed narrative. He tells her how, on his return from work, he was winding the grandfather clock when Arjun hurtled out of the corridor. He had not seen Raj, obscured by shadow, and, racing across the hallway, had nearly knocked him over. Raj had teetered backwards but had just managed to right himself and catch Arjun before they had both lost their balance.

"Well held, eh?" Raj had chuckled. "Where are you off to in such a hurry?"

"A friend," Arjun had mumbled.

This evasive reply and Arjun's apparent embarrassment had aroused Raj's suspicions. He noticed that Arjun smelt of cologne and that his hair, neatly slicked down, was still wet from a hurried wash. He was carrying a leather hold-all, embossed with gold initials. Raj could not read it all, but the initials were definitely not Arjun's.

"'M' something. I'm not sure about the second letter," Raj ponders. "Could have been a 'G' or maybe an 'R'. I wonder who that could be. Still, it was a very nice bag. Very expensive."

Neleni has her own ideas about whose initials they might be and where the bag has come from. She has been listening intently, despite herself. At this moment, she does not know who she hates most: her husband, for his incessant chatter; Arjun, for his perceived faithlessness; or herself, for being such a fool.

Raj drones on, recounting how he saw the black Jaguar parked in the street on his return from work. Although the car was stationary, its engine was idling, a low rumble, like a hungry animal. As he passed it, the powerful purr of the engine had reverberated through his chest.

"Quite wonderful," muses Raj.

Then he recounts how he watched from the window as Arjun ran down the steps. On the pavement, Arjun had paused and checked his watch, as if he was late for an appointment, then he had run over to the car where the chauffeur was holding the back door open. Before climbing in, Arjun had looked up and seen Raj, watching him. They had stared at each other for a few seconds and Raj had been struck by the boy's strange expression.

"Not happy," says Raj cryptically, although he cannot find the words to describe exactly what he saw. Despair or fear might be nearer the mark.

"But why should he feel like that?"

There is no reply.

Raj sinks back into thought.

For a second, he had considered running after Arjun and making some excuse to get him back into the house but, by then, it was too late: Arjun had disappeared into the car, as if he had been sucked in and swallowed whole. Unable to see Arjun, Raj could not tell if he was still looking but, nonetheless, he had raised his hand to wave; a friendly, but useless, gesture of goodwill.

"Do you think it's that woman?"

"Hmmph!"

351

Neleni has emerged from the cupboard and is now bending over the sink. She is examining the inside of an ancient saucepan, scratching with her nail at a patch of charcoal. Someone has burnt food and hidden the evidence under the sink. Sunny is probably the culprit. She has been getting forgetful lately and the bitter smell of scorched food often seeps from the kitchen when it is her turn to cook. A few days ago, Neleni found the old lady asleep at the kitchen table while three pans were boiling over on the stove. Yet, despite her failing powers, Sunny obstinately refuses all offers of help.

Neleni attacks the saucepan with a knife, jabbing savagely at its blackened interior. She is angry with her mother for burning the saucepan, for being so forgetful and, above all, for getting old. Sometimes, when she looks into her mother's eyes, Neleni sees blankness, as if Sunny has momentarily forgotten who she is. She is quietly slipping out of reach and the distance between them grows wider every day. They rarely argue now. It is a bad sign.

The thought of losing her mother fills Neleni with despair for, despite their constant bickering, Sunny is her one true friend. Without her, Neleni will have no-one: no-one to turn to, no-one to talk to, no-one who understands her. When Sunny dies, Neleni will be completely alone. For a while, she dared to hope that Arjun would be her comfort, a companion to assuage the pain of her mother's loss: but when she entered his room that day and found the letter from Leela, describing the intimate details of their liaison, she realised the extent of her foolishness and the falseness of her hope.

No. There will be no-one for her when Sunny dies. She will be left alone to face the vacuum of her own, empty life. As she digs angrily at the charred saucepan, her eyes fill with tears.

"I wonder if something's wrong."

Raj's mind is still fixed on the same subject. Like a dog worrying a rag, he refuses to let it rest.

"Who cares?"

"I thought you might," Raj ventures timidly.

"Why should I?"

Neleni narrowly misses cutting her finger with the knife. The blade hits the bottom of the pan and squeals against the metal. Raj winces. Neleni leans over the sink, trying to hide the tears that course down her face. She prays for Raj to leave her alone, but he never takes the hint.

"I thought you liked him."

"Why should I care what he does? He's not family."

"Because," says Raj, struggling to explain, "he looks unhappy. He nearly knocked me over a few minutes ago, racing out like there were demons after him. He looked, well, I don't know ... If you'd been there, you'd know what I mean."

He ends weakly, struggling for words to describe the things he senses but cannot comprehend. He is perplexed by his wife's indifference. Not so long ago, she would have pricked up her ears at the mention of Arjun's name. Now she cannot bear to speak of him. The novelty has obviously worn off. Although he could never imagine his wife being unfaithful, Raj has to confess he is relieved. There is something unseemly about a grown woman having a schoolgirl crush, however innocent.

"Anyway, I don't suppose we'll see him until tomorrow night," Raj muses.

"Why not?"

"I told you. He was carrying an overnight bag."

Neleni, who has paused to look out of the window, now resumes her frenzied attack on the pan, stabbing and scraping with such vigour that the knife scores the soft aluminium with deep scratches. Her slender shoulders are shaking, apparently with the effort of her labour.

"Anyway," says Raj. "I suppose you're right. It's none of our business."

Then, they are silent, Raj staring out of the window into the narrow yard and Neleni continuing to scrape the pan. Occasionally, she pauses to dab her face with the back of her hand which she wipes quickly on her apron so that Raj should not see the wetness of her tears.

"Poor Neleni," thinks Raj, "she thinks I cannot see her. It is always thus with pregnant women: laughter one minute, tears the next".

So, out of consideration, he pretends to ignore her distress at the very moment when an arm, tenderly placed around her shoulder, might win her heart.

After a few minutes, Neleni has recovered and begins to busy herself about the kitchen, noisily stacking pots, carrying them from one end of the room to the other, then re-arranging them in cupboards. Raj can neither get her attention nor make himself heard above the clamour with which she surrounds herself. Finally, sensing that she would rather be alone, he drifts out of the kitchen into the yard.

1956: Dead flowers

Despite Raj's careful attention, the orchid cuttings have failed to thrive and now resemble withered dry sticks. The sight of them depresses him. In their native country, where the plants thrive naturally in almost any condition, he cannot manage to rear them in pots. The shrivelled cuttings are a symbol of his ineptitude. It does not occur to him that one cannot revive what is already dead.

He picks up the pots and, one by one, tips their contents over the wall into the alley. It is pleasant at this time of day: the sun having moved round, the yard now lies in shadow, a little well of coolness in the heat. Sunny often appears at this hour, her face crinkling with pleasure as she takes the air. After standing for a few minutes on the step, she will make her way down into the yard where Raj has placed a chair for her. Then they will talk.

In fact, Raj often has the impression that he discusses more with his mother-in-law than his wife. Although Sunny does not share Raj's enthusiasm for politics and he cannot match her religious conviction, they share a common view of the world. It is as if, starting from separate points on the map, their paths converge at the same destination.

There is little about his past life that Raj has not told Sunny, although he feels self-conscious when confiding in his wife, believing her intellect and tastes to be superior to his own. Without meaning to, he often offends her. Her expression sometimes implies that she finds him crude and uneducated and he is frequently aware of causing offence where none is intended. His own belief that he is not good enough for her causes Raj to keep his distance when, in fact, he would like to shower her with affection: but she is too delicate for him. As a giant might regard a flower in the palm of his hand, Raj is afraid that his clumsiness will crush her.

Sunny, however, is a different matter. A poor girl who married into a wealthy family, she, too, has been the focus of bitter disappointment. Although her husband tried to shield her, his family made no attempt to hide the fact that they found her unacceptable; and, after Edward's death, she experienced the full force of their displeasure. She was ruthlessly cut off. With a teenage daughter, and without a rupee to support either of them, marriage afforded the only solution. Raj was their salvation. At least Sunny appreciates that.

Having emptied the last pot over the wall, Raj looks back into the yard. Sunny has usually appeared by this time, but there is no sign of her. Apart from the quiet clink of pots from the kitchen, where Neleni is still tidying up, there is no other sound. Having stacked the empty flower pots in a corner, Raj crosses the yard and pokes his head around the kitchen door.

"Where's Aunty?"

"Sleeping."

"Will she come out in the yard?"

"Not while she's sleeping."

He knows that tone of voice. Neleni is being deliberately obtuse. Knowing better than to question her further, Raj retreats into the yard where he busies himself with a broom. It is difficult living with a wife who is pregnant; but, if she has a son, he will forgive her anything.

***

354

When Raj narrates stories of his childhood, Sunny's eyes become moist. This perplexes him. He does not feel sorry for himself. But he never shows emotion either. If someone tells Raj a sad story, he is more likely to laugh than weep. For long ago, he learned that emotion makes you weak. It is something to be kept hidden, stifled.

Yet he is not unfeeling. Raj loves his wife passionately. He is just unable to show it. Sunny understands that, even if Neleni does not.

As he trundles around the yard, sweeping up the earth scattered from the flowerpots, Raj remembers how Sunny encouraged his courtship of her daughter, although Neleni's friend, Nirmala, had openly expressed her disapproval. When Raj told Sunny that Nirmala thought he and Neleni were mismatched, Sunny had responded with fury.

"Pah! What would a woman like her know about it? A fine mess she's made of her own life!"

Sunny had curtly dismissed his misgivings although, sometimes, his doubts resurface, especially when he catches Neleni staring wistfully out of the window. Then, he experiences a pang of uncertainty, an irrational fear that her desire for something else will spirit her away, leaving him stranded and helpless. That fear has returned today. He badly wants to talk to Sunny; but she has kept to her room.

Sunny sleeps often these days and is slowly withdrawing from family life. The thought of losing his mentor fills Raj with sadness, made more acute because he cannot give it expression. He simply does as he has always done: he endures. Perhaps, thinks Raj, as he sits in Sunny's seat, things might be different if he had a son.

Raj grew up in Araliya Flats, a crumbling, overcrowded tenement in the poorest part of town. A good-natured tearaway, he belonged to a small gang of boys with whom he roamed the streets looking for excitement and often getting into trouble. Despite the poverty, they were happy times which Raj remembers with nostalgia. There were boyish scraps, pranks, minor acts of vandalism, impromptu games of cricket and tag played in alleyways filled with rubbish.

Many of those boys are still Raj's friends, not that Neleni approves of them much. They bear the indelible marks of their upbringing: coarse manners; poor education; a tendency to get drunk, talk loudly and brawl. What Raj can never explain to her is their loyalty and the goodness in their hearts.

But Raj loves them, their friendship having been forged in the shanties, a jumble of derelict buildings where families paid extortionate rents for a single, damp room in which rottenness seeped from the plaster. Poor sanitation and lack of food were a part of life, inevitably accompanied by sickness and mortality. If the shanties bred a philosophy for existence, it consisted, not in aspiring to improve one's lot, but in accepting it.

Although she now denies it, Raj's cousin Lakshmi also grew up in Araliya Flats. She was a different person then, full of fun and daring, not caring what anyone thought of her. In fact, she had the same adventurous spirit, without the imagination, of her niece Rani. It is strange that the two of them, who have so much in common, should dislike each other so much; but, of course, Lakshmi has changed.

Raj is not sure when that change came about, perhaps it was on her marriage, or even earlier, on her betrothal; but, whenever it was, Lakshmi had abruptly turned her back on the past, devoting herself single-mindedly to the pursuit of social status. In fact, the only link to Araliya Flats that she continues to acknowledge is her cousin, Raj.

***

While Lakshmi was a childhood friend, it was her brother Madhan who had the greatest influence on Raj, casting a long shadow over his early life. Some six or seven years older than his cousin, Madhan led a gang of tearaways who terrorised their fellow tenants. At first, their exploits were performed only for their own amusement but, soon, they discovered that a profitable living was to be made extracting money from residents who wished to be left in peace.

Anyone using the communal, urine-stained staircase or walking alone through the rat-infested alleyways around the tenement ran the risk of a beating from the members of the Araliya Flats gang. It was worth a few rupees to be spared a bruised and bloody face – or worse. The gang even varied their tariff according to their victims' means, Madhan making it his business to know just how much anyone was worth.

Madhan himself was powerfully-built. Stocky yet strong, he was barrel-chested with long arms and legs slightly bowed from a youthful attack of rickets: all of which gave him the appearance of a large and powerful monkey.

His head was as square as a block of wood, with a wide forehead, a flat boxer's nose and a deceptively charming smile. Anyone who knew him feared that smile. It appeared like a crescent moon as he approached a victim, widening to a grin when he had finished his work. It was the smile that he wore when he discovered one of his sisters in the arms of his lieutenant. He was still smiling when the boy's body was discovered a few days later, lying on waste ground with a slit throat, partly-eaten by pye-dogs.

Even family ties were no protection against Madhan's sadism. Having witnessed his eight-year old cousin being soundly beaten in a schoolboy scrap, Madhan thrashed Raj with his belt until his face was lathered in sweat and blood ran down the boy's back.

As a result of this salutary lesson, Raj became expert with his fists, learning to hit harder, dodge quicker and take blows without a whimper: but the ultimate test of his courage came when Madhan swaggered in late on Saturday nights, followed by several of his cronies.

"Hello, Aunty. Where's Raj? I want to talk to him."

Madhan would push his way into the flat, staggering a little after a session at the arrack shop. Ignoring his aunt's protests, he would pull his sleepy-eyed cousin out of bed and drag him up to the roof, sitting the boy on a low parapet with his back to the road.

Then, in a gravelly, liquor-steeped voice, Madhan would recount endless yarns until Raj, overcome with weariness, began to doze. At this point, Madhan would lunge forward, grab the boy by the ankles and tip him backwards, suspending him, headfirst, over the street.

"Wake up, you bastard. I'll teach you to sleep while I'm talking."

Then, encouraged by his jeering friends, Madhan would perform a feat of strength, holding his cousin in one hand and swinging him from side to side.

"Go on, you little shit, cry for mummy!"

But Raj never did, even on the occasion when Madhan nearly passed out and Raj could feel his ankle slipping through his cousin's sweaty palm. Even Madhan had looked worried then, but he was soon smiling again. In fact, Madhan smiled a lot on these occasions. Other people's fear gave him pleasure, even when those people were his own kin.

Enjoying Madhan's joke could save your life. So Raj trained himself to laugh. Even hanging upside down with the meagre contents of his stomach sliding up his throat, he could emit a falsetto giggle. This won him credit with Madhan's gang. But it was not the only lesson he learned: these nightmarish experiences also improved his mental arithmetic.

Hanging by his ankles, forty feet above the pavement, Raj tried to distract himself. Tormented by thoughts of what would happen if Madhan dropped him, he resorted to complex games of calculation. Initially, he would count all the objects in a single category: six dogs, three cats, five piles of rubbish, two drunks, one pickpocket.

However, simple addition soon lost its power to divert him and he was again beset by images of the ground rushing up to meet him and his head cracking on the pavement like an eggshell. In order to defeat these thoughts, Raj resorted to more complex computation. The result was a series of mathematical conundrums of extraordinary complexity.

He trained himself to add, subtract and multiply to the power of seven, then reverse the whole process so that he ended up where he had started. This was to prove invaluable in later life when, due to his numerical fluency, Raj was able to secure a responsible position at the municipal post office. This, in turn, enabled him to leave Araliya Flats and move to a more respectable part of town.

Quod erat demonstrandum: Madhan helped Raj to hone his mathematical talent and raise his social status thus enabling him to marry Neleni. This was reason enough for Raj to remember Madhan with gratitude.

Madhan, however, did not share his cousin's good fortune. In fact, his life was cut short by a stroke of fate so ironic that, had it been his own invention, he would have smiled for days.

***

Madhan's many business interests included working as a debt-collector for one of the shanty landlords. It was a lucrative pursuit that afforded much amusement, allowing Madhan to indulge his sense of humour at the expense of those who were unable to retaliate. Or so he thought.

Late one evening, after several hours of drinking cheap arrack, Madhan became bored and, for the purposes of entertainment, decided to visit a tenant facing eviction. The man, a tailor with one leg shorter than the other, lived in one room with his elderly mother. The old lady had recently fallen sick and, having paid for her medicine, the tailor had fallen behind with the rent. He pleaded and promised, all to no avail. Madhan smilingly told him that he must be out at the end of the week.

The man wept like a baby. Wearing a wide grin, Madhan paused to enjoy the scene before leaving: the tailor, sitting on his mother's bed while the old lady tried to comfort him, her skinny arms clasped around her son's shoulders. That made Madhan laugh. In fact, he laughed so much that he was almost sorry to see the man go. Still, money was money. The landlord had made that quite clear. If he did not get paid, then neither did Madhan. There was no arguing with that kind of logic.

The tailor was due to leave the next day. Madhan pictured him, pushing his few possessions on a handcart. He would probably have to put his mother on the handcart, too. That made Madhan smile. With their departure, a rich vein of entertainment would be exhausted. Madhan felt almost nostalgic and, for that reason, he decided to pay the man one last visit. For old time's sake.

Stumbling up the tenement steps, Madhan relieved himself in a corner of the stairwell before hammering on the tailor's door. When it opened, he pushed his way in, swaggering around the gloomy room, helping himself to a few meagre trinkets before crossing to the bed where the old lady was sleeping. He bent over her, his breath stale with drink.

"Make the most of it, old witch. You'll soon be out on the street."

Then, just so she got the message, he kicked the bed. The old lady opened her eyes, moaning in terror. The tailor hobbled to Madhan's side, anxiously wringing his hands.

"Please sir, I will pay you. I have some money. It is up on the roof. I keep it hidden up there. Come. I will show you."

Madhan's delight increased and he laughed out loud. He would take the man's money and evict him anyway. It would be the tailor's word against his. He knew who the landlord would believe. Following the tailor upstairs, he became impatient, abusing the man for his slowness. The tailor apologised, limping painfully up the stairs, clinging onto the rail. Madhan felt like pushing him but, for once, exercised self-restraint as he did not know where the money was hidden.

And then an idea came to Madhan. Once he had the money, he would lead the tailor back to the top of the stairs then shove him hard from behind. That would avoid any awkward arguments about whether or not he had received the rent. Madhan smiled.

Once on the roof, the tailor led Madhan to a corner, politely asking him to take a seat while he found the money. There was no seat, so Madhan sat on the parapet, leaning back on his hands and closing his eyes, his face turned up to the stars.

Then, suddenly, the world turned upside down and the sky was replaced with a view of the street that magnified with alarming speed. Madhan hit the pavement before he realised what was happening or could remember the tight grip of hands around his ankles that had preceded his fall.

Death was instantaneous so he did not see the tailor peering over the parapet at him, nor the smile that lit the man's wan face as he pushed back the limp strands of hair sticking to his forehead. A tailor may have weak legs but he has strong hands. Agile fingers that dart after a needle or cut cloth with shears are also capable of grasping ankles in a single, deft movement.

So it was that Madhan died from the very act practised on his cousin. It was a pity that he could not appreciate the irony of his own demise. No doubt, it would have appealed to his sense of humour.

His body was found the next day, his face gashed and gory, his skull caved in. As he had consumed a large amount of alcohol (enough to kill a buffalo, according to the Coroner), there was no reason to suspect foul play. The case was closed without further investigation and the tailor, having found the money to pay his arrears, got a reprieve from the new debt-collector who, fortunately for the tenants, did not have Madhan's sense of humour.

Always soft-hearted, Raj had mourned his uncle in a manner befitting their relationship. He had even managed to laugh a little.

Neleni is lying on the bed after lunch. Raj and the girls have gone out and the house is quiet, brimming with the stillness of heat. The only sound comes from Sunny, snoring in the room next door. She is having what Neleni refers to as "a tired day".

Yesterday, Sunny was as active as ever, shuffling about the house, giving her orders to Neleni or the servant girl, Ella, without distinguishing between them. She had smoked her pipe at the usual hour, chopped vegetables, pottered around the yard, chatted to Raj, and played games with Saro. But, today, she has energy neither to eat, nor even wake up. While trifling ailments have the power to lay her low, this is not the reason for her lassitude. It is the fatigue that comes with age, the slowing down of a life as it nears its end, like a top that ceases to spin.

On Sunny's 'tired days', Neleni takes her mother trays of food, only to bring them away untouched. If she cannot hear anything, she tiptoes into the room to check that her mother is still breathing, as one does with a small baby. Then, she stands beside the bed, stroking the old lady's hand as she sleeps, watching the small face, unprotected by its thick glasses, the skin like parchment, the hollow cheeks and the thin mouth, curled over gums that have long been empty of teeth.

At times like this, Neleni feels that what she is witnessing is not reality, but a premonition of death. It makes her heart ache and, before leaving the room, she has to clear her throat and brush away a few tears. On these occasions, Sunny's snoring comes as a relief. Silence is worse.

Neleni rolls over on the bed. Beyond the window, she can see a branch of the temple tree, shedding its elegant flowers. It reminds her of Arjun and the painting of frangipani flowers that she destroyed on learning of his affair. She has not painted anything since and has hidden the box of watercolours he gave her although, unable to part with it completely, she has concealed it at the back of a cupboard which she rarely visits. Her sense of loss for a man who has never been hers is acute becoming, if anything, more painful by the day.

Yet, she nurtures that pain, because it is the only way of being close to him. She examines it tenderly, as a surgeon examines a tumour, assessing its extent and malignance, comforting herself with the thought that she will never recover. At times like this, the thought of her own mortality is attractive.

Like the Lady of Shalott, death offers grandeur, a noble end to a wasted life. Her thoughts often stray to suicide although she dismisses it as a possibility. Sometimes, the promise of a journey provides a better escape than the journey itself; a prospect that is appealing because it is remote, like a tree on a distant hill-top.

Perversely, now that life means nothing to her, she is able to enjoy its small pleasures. She reads voraciously, late at night when Raj is asleep or, at times like this, when she is alone. Packed into a small orange box, her books and magazines are kept under the bed, always within reach. It is a varied collection, old hardbacks with colour plates, cheap paperbacks with lurid covers, magazines and a few old schoolbooks. Out of this eclectic selection, she has three favourites.

The first is a book of Chinese watercolours with the picture of a camellia so artfully drawn that, if she runs her fingers across the page, she can imagine the satiny texture of its petals. To re-create nature with a few strokes of the brush is the height of genius: one slip of the hand and the work is ruined. There can be no concealment with additional layers of paint. Chinese art is transparent and honest. As a child, she longed to paint like this.

Art should provide an escape from daily life; a means of meditation, raising the viewer's thoughts to a more spiritual plane. For years, Neleni has calmed herself by gazing at the flower paintings in her book. But it contains a picture of frangipani which reminds her of Arjun and so, like the paints, this book has been abandoned.

The second of her favourite books is an Oxford anthology of verse: a school prize. A label, carefully printed in purple ink, has been pasted inside the cover: "To Neleni Jansz, Class 3a, Form Prize for Literature". The book's covering of green, waxy cloth has become frayed at the corners and the gold lettering of the title has been partially rubbed away. The pages inside, made of thick, soft paper, have browned to a gentle sepia, dotted with occasional, mildewy blotches and, when opened, the book releases a pleasant, musty fragrance. Yet, containing many love poems, it no longer provides her with a refuge.

By default, Neleni is restricted to her third favourite; an American fashion magazine, presented to her by a tourist that she met on a train. The woman was a school-teacher. Travelling alone, she represented independence; a state to which Neleni aspired. In the short space of an hour, they had discussed families, love, marriage, poetry, art and, for a brief moment, a window had opened in Neleni's closed world through which she saw another place, full of light, opportunity and freedom.

It was a brief view of Paradise; her longing for it increased by the fact that it was unattainable. The woman had looked sad when Neleni told her of her own life, her schooling that had come to an abrupt end with her father's death, her unfulfilled dreams of becoming a painter. When she reached her destination, the teacher had patted Neleni's hand kindly and given her the magazine, a token of their friendship.

Neleni often thinks of her friend in America. The magazine revives pleasant memories and a brief glimpse of another life. The photographs show skyscrapers and shiny cars. There is even a picture of the statue of Liberty, silhouetted against a bright orange sky, streaked with purple clouds. Men wearing suits stride along the streets, their hats pulled down over their eyes while women, heads held high, pose for the camera with elegant self-assurance.

One picture, in particular, draws Neleni back. Jets of water gush from a fire hydrant and, by some trick of the camera, each cascading droplet contains a tiny spark of sunlight. Neleni dreams of bathing in that fountain, fully-dressed in the middle of the street, just like the children in the photograph.

The magazine is her choice this afternoon. As she turns the pages, she wonders how it would feel to wear full, pinch-waisted skirts and high heels. What if she tried it? What if she did something to liberate herself? There will be a family wedding in a couple of weeks and she is invited. It will make a change to wear Western clothes rather than the traditional sari. A seed of courage begins to grow. Who cares if no-one likes it? If she changes the way she looks, perhaps she will feel different inside. It will be a statement of intent, if only to herself.

Her friend Nirmala might be able to make a pattern based on the photographs in the magazine. She will visit her tomorrow. Folding down the corners of the pages that interest her, Neleni reverently tucks the magazine into the orange box and slides it back under the bed.

Nirmala is bending over, weeding the vegetable patch with a hoe. There has been no rain and the ground is dry and stony. She wipes the sweat from her face with the back of her hand and re-positions the battered straw hat that protects her neck from the sun. Freed from its tether, the goat is roaming up and down the path, tearing at patches of grass and, when Nirmala is not looking, a few herbs. It bleats loudly when it sees Neleni.

"Stupid animal," she thinks, crossly.

Dropping her hoe, Nirmala stands up, shading her eyes with her hand.

"Neleni!"

She runs towards her friend, holding out her arms, ready to embrace her, until she remembers that she is sticky, her hands covered with soil which has worked its way under the nails. Gloves are a luxury which she cannot afford.

"Don't worry about that!" exclaims Neleni, catching the look of hesitation on Nirmala's face.

Flinging her arms around Nirmala, she hugs her friend, breathing in the earthy warmness of her skin. Nirmala's cheek is damp, her neck wet and glistening, the short strands of hair at the nape forming tight curls.

"Neleni, I can't breathe!"

Laughing, Nirmala pushes her away.

"What a pleasure. Come inside. Would you like to eat? I have some rice and vegetables. Enough for two."

Grabbing Neleni's hand, she pulls her towards the house. The clasp of that firm, dirt-stained hand comforts Neleni, reminding her of how they had been as girls, running to school, hand-in-hand, their hair tightly plaited and secured with red ribbons, their schoolbooks held together with a leather strap, the sun glancing off their immaculate white pinafores.

She clutches Nirmala's hand tightly, as she used to, and allows herself to be led, up the cinder track, around the vegetable garden where curry plants and fennel throb with bees, past the goat that nips at her sari, its soft mouth briefly working the silk until it is pulled away. They mount the creaking wooden steps through which tall blades of grass are growing and dive into the shady depths of the house, giggling stupidly, like two silly girls.

Neleni leans against the table, trying to get her breath, while Nirmala lights the gas on the small stove.

"Tea, first. Would you like to eat as well?"

"No, really."

"But you should. I saw Raj in the town the other day. He told me."

"Told you what?"

Neleni's mood suddenly changes. She can feel herself getting irritable. Nirmala looks confused.

"That you were pregnant."

Unable to meet Nirmala's eyes, Neleni picks compulsively at the embroidery on her scarf, pulling at a loose thread.

"Well, aren't you?"

"Raj is a fool."

"I don't understand."

"It's my fault. I passed out and Raj assumed it was because I was pregnant. I should have denied it, but I couldn't. He seemed so excited."

"But why? I still don't understand."

"I fainted because …"

She is unsure how to continue.

"It doesn't matter. I'll tell Raj soon. He'll understand. It'll be all right."

She pulls the thread tight, puckering the fine material of her scarf. Diplomatically, Nirmala changes the subject.

"So what brings you here today?"

"This."

Neleni's mood has changed; her brief spell of vivacity has evaporated and she seems unsure of herself. Timidly, she holds out the rolled-up magazine that she has been carrying under her arm. Nirmala takes it.

"An American magazine?"

With her head tilted to one side, Nirmala looks at Neleni enquiringly, sensing that something interesting is about to happen.

"I want some new clothes. For Dalia's wedding. Look. Here."

Neleni speaks rapidly, not looking at her friend, fearing she may laugh at her but, as she turns the pages, Nirmala makes a small cooing sound of admiration.

"These are beautiful. Look at that one!"

Neleni becomes excited. Without knowing it, Nirmala is pointing to the outfit that she has chosen for herself.

"That's it. That's the one. Do you think it will suit me? Can you do it?"

Nirmala smiles, a little bemused.

"It's lovely. Quite daring … for a wedding. Are you sure?"

"Yes."

Neleni is breathless with excitement.

"All right. I'll measure you up for a pattern. Now, where are my things?"

Leading Neleni into the room which she uses for fittings, Nirmala takes her measurements then, placing her in front of a mirror, holds swatches of material up to her face to help her pick the right colour. Eventually, they decide on a cherry-red skirt, with a pink blouse and gold belt.

"That will go nicely with your bangles," says Nirmala. "Now, what are you going to wear on your head?"

"My head?"

"It's a church wedding, isn't it?"

"Yes, of course. I hadn't thought about that."

"What about this?"

Nirmala drapes a length of chiffon around Neleni's head and shoulders. Neleni stares in the mirror and sighs.

"It's no good, Nirmala. It just looks too traditional, too old-fashioned. It won't look right with those clothes."

"Mmm. The woman in the photograph has short hair."

Nirmala makes the comment without thinking. Neleni's reaction takes her by surprise.

"That's it, Nirmala. You're so clever. It's not the scarf, it's my hair. It needs to be short. Here, we can do it now."

"What?"

Nirmala stares at Neleni in disbelief. Her friend has grabbed the dress-making shears and is already unwinding the tight bun at the back of her head.

"No, Neleni, wait!"

"Too late. There. I've done it."

Neleni has sliced off a long hank of hair. Holding it up in her fingers, she examines it for a minute, then lets it fall to the floor.

"I feel better already."

"No, please. Let me do it."

Grasping Neleni's wrist, Nirmala prises the scissors out of her hand. Her friend's eyes are sparkling and she is suddenly animated. With some concern, Nirmala remembers the sudden mood swings of her previous visit. Is she still grieving for that boy? Does she know that he has a mistress? Nirmala wonders if she should tell her but, judging this not to be the right moment, occupies herself with more practical matters.

"You should really go to someone who knows how to cut hair."

"No." Neleni is adamant. "I don't want anyone else. It must be you."

Nirmala sighs. She does not want to cut Neleni's hair but there is no option. If she refuses, Neleni will do the job herself, probably with disastrous consequences.

"All right. Let's take our tea and sit out on the porch while we do it. I need some air. It's hot in here."

They make their way to the front porch where Neleni sits on an old, high-backed chair while Nirmala snips delicately at her hair. Across the valley, a small green train steams along the mountain track to Nuwara Eliya and a dog barks, its distant yapping floating up from a farm, far below.

Soon, Neleni is sitting in a pool of her own hair. She watches with satisfaction as the pool grows larger. A weight is literally being lifted from her and, with it, comes a sense of release, so strong that she feels almost light-headed. Closing her eyes, she smiles and takes a deep breath of the scented air.

"It's so peaceful up here. I'm so happy."

Nirmala appears not to have heard. At least, she does not answer.

It is the day before the wedding and excitement has kept Lakshmi awake most of the night. Now, she is giving vent to it in her usual manner: rage. She storms into the kitchen, waving a letter in the air and shrieking until her cheeks turn purple.

"How dare she! How dare she!" she screams at the servants, who shrink back in terror.

"Monster! Whore!" Lakshmi shrieks.

The housemaid opens her mouth to speak but is silenced by one of the older servants who, by holding his finger to his lips, warns her to be silent. It does not pay to cross the mistress when she is in one of her tempers. Although the servants rarely discover the cause of Lakshmi's outbursts, they are usually the first to witness the full force of her fury because the kitchen is generally where it starts. After delivering her first tirade, she will then storm into the living room, with the servants cowering in her wake.

If she finds no-one in the living-room, Lakshmi will search the house, shouting at the top of her voice until she finds whatever hiding place her husband has chosen for that day. Once discovered, he will greet her sheepishly and try to explain why he happened to be in the broom cupboard with the door closed or at the back of the larder, hidden behind the vegetable racks. Today, he is in the garden, crouching under the verandah wall on the pretext of inspecting the plants, although he is no gardener and cannot tell a weed from its cultivated cousin.

Without actually seeing Lakshmi, Niran knows that she is standing behind him: there is a sudden coolness on his back where the sun was shining and a dark shadow slants across the grass in front of him. Despite her girth, she can move silently when she chooses, and she usually does so in order to trap him. Hunter and huntress: it is a game they often play, his excitement refined by terror. For Niran loves his wife as much as he fears her.

"Hello, dear," he murmurs, waiting for the onslaught.

Lakshmi takes a deep breath. Niran can hear the sharp passage of air as she sucks it into her lungs, priming herself for the final diatribe. He closes his eyes. This time, unlike her previous, victimless raids, this attack will have a target.

"It's all your fault," she screams. "I can't trust you to do anything right!"

"Why, dear, what's happened?"

Niran is still kneeling, with his head bowed. It is always best at such times. In the past, he has caught not only the full force of Lakshmi's fury, but also a missile. It is always advisable to wait until the first paroxysm of anger has passed before venturing to stand up and, only then, when the absence of projectiles has been confirmed.

"It's that niece of yours!"

"Which one, dear?"

"Vidya."

Niran does not think it wise, at this point, to remind his wife that Vidya is related to her side of the family. Still, what does it matter? In this country of extended families, a niece on one side of the family is almost certain to have a blood tie with the other. Thus, Niran concludes, Lakshmi may have a point.

"What has she done?"

"It's the wedding tomorrow and now, at the last minute, she is refusing to come. Here, read for yourself."

The sound of rustling paper indicates to Niran that Lakshmi has a letter that she wants him to read. It also implies that it is safe for him to rise from his crouching position, a small mercy for which he is duly grateful. He unfolds himself, painfully straightening his back and legs, like a contortionist exiting a conjuror's box.

"Spoilt little madam," hisses Lakshmi now that she has her husband's full attention. "One day before the wedding, she writes to tell us that she is pregnant, that she can't come because she is feeling sick. Who does she think she is?"

Niran shrugs, helplessly.

"Thinks she's a cut above us because she married a doctor. Thinks she can do what she likes. And her mother! No better. All her conversation is "my daughter who married the doctor," "my son-in-law the doctor." No doubt, she even recites it in her sleep. Well, I grew up with Vidya's mother. I'll bet that snooty little madam, Vidya, doesn't know what her mother got up to before she married, but I do, I do!"

She jabs a red-painted talon at her breast, drawing her husband's attention to a vast bosom that heaves and rolls like an ocean swell. As he considers the depths of that unfathomable cleavage, Lakshmi's words fade away, becoming distant, like the cry of a sea-bird in a storm.

"Are you listening to me?"

He is summoned from his reverie. Dutifully, he takes the letter and reads it, now and again peering furtively over the top to check on the progress of his wife's mood. She seems to be calming slightly.

"Well, I can't really see anything wrong in this."

"Nothing wrong!" Lakshmi screams in a paroxysm of rage. "Nothing wrong!"

For a second, she looks as if she will explode then, quite suddenly, anger yields to tears and she starts sobbing like a small child. It is the moment that Niran has been waiting for.

"There, there, dear," he soothes, wrapping his arms around his wife's ample waist.

For reasons of health (he is not sure whose), Niran has been banned from the matrimonial bed and these occasions offer the only opportunity to re-acquaint himself with the quivering expanse of his wife's body.

"Fool," she whimpers.

"Yes, dear," he agrees, smiling as he lays his head on her breast.

Neleni is at the house of her friend Nirmala, the dressmaker. The next day is Dalia's wedding and Neleni has come to collect her wedding outfit. Having stripped to her underwear, she steps into the new clothes with a great deal of trepidation and is now having second thoughts about whether or not she should wear anything so daring.

Kneeling on the floor, Nirmala adjusts the hem of the skirt which needs to be made even shorter to ensure the correct degree of flounce. She has perfected the dressmaker's art of talking while holding pins between her lips, removing them one by one as she secures the hem, leaning back every so often to check that it is even.

Assuming that Neleni has conquered her infatuation for Arjun, Nirmala begins to relay some gossip passed on to her by one of Leela's servants. Leela, also, uses Nirmala's services but frequently sends her housekeeper, Angela, to collect the finished items rather than coming herself. As a result, Nirmala has become quite friendly with the housekeeper, whose visits have turned into a social event.

On these occasions, after their business is concluded, the two women often drink tea on the verandah and, while they follow the progress of the tiny train puffing along the hill track across the valley, they exchange a few interesting items of news or, rather, Angela will give a full account of her mistress's private life.

Professing to be scandalised at what she has witnessed, the housekeeper passes on every detail of what she has seen and heard: the young man who is brought to the house in Leela's car, once or twice a week; how her mistress dotes on him; the strange look in his eyes, as if he were sleepwalking (she suspects her mistress has used magic); their noisy – and sometimes public – love-making (she saw them naked on the living-room floor and Leela was on top, shrieking like a thing possessed).

The housekeeper knows this man as Arjun and thinks he works for the Government Agent. So there is no doubt. Neleni's lodger has become the lover of Mennan's widow.

"It's just as well that nothing happened between you two," says Nirmala, taking the last pin out of her mouth and jabbing it firmly into the material.

"Fancy having an affair with that woman. A man in his position! He's mad. Or maybe he's just greedy. She's supposed to have a lot of money. Perhaps he's hoping to marry her. At least, if he does, he'll move out. That would make life easier, wouldn't it?"

Neleni winces.

"Oh, sorry. Did that go in you? This material is so stiff. Just stand still."

Absorbed by her work, Nirmala does not pause to look up at Neleni's face. If she did, she would realise the effect that this news is having on her friend. However, interpreting Neleni's silence as a cue for more gossip, Nirmala chatters on, giving as many details as she can remember of the housekeeper's tale, hoping that this will dispel any lingering regret for Arjun, not understanding that each new revelation is like a needle stuck into Neleni's flesh.

Captive in her new clothes, Neleni is unable to move for fear of scratching herself against the rogue pins still lurking in the seams of her bodice. With arms outstretched and head bent dolefully to one side, she is the parody of a martyr, a female Saint Sebastian, pierced with many darts, or Saint Theresa, patiently awaiting the spear that will be plunged into her heart. But there was ecstasy in their pain. There is none in hers. Just a sense of aching loss.

Without realising that her words are making a slow incision around Neleni's heart, Nirmala continues.

"But Arjun isn't the only one. There's another man, as well. Angela, the housekeeper, doesn't think they know about each other. She says this other man is a tall, handsome fellow, a bit like Clark Gable. He's good to Angela, often gives her money. She likes him better than the other one. Anyway, she says he's getting married soon, but not to Leela. I'll bet his future wife doesn't know. Men are such bastards!"

"Yes."

Neleni has to agree.

***

That night, pain takes possession of Neleni's dreams. Normally, sleep provides an escape from the agony of her waking hours. In her dreams, she defies the laws of science. Soaring above the earth, she circles the planets and then, her skin dusted with ice crystals, she flies through the star-speckled night, diving down from the icy depths of space to skim an ocean where salt spray flecks her skin and the wind twists her hair. She is, at once, a bird and a mermaid, a comet and a fish. In sleep, her freedom is complete. But not tonight.

Tonight, her unconscious mind is racked with anger; her dreams splattered with blood and the terror of death. An alien spirit has entered her body and is directing her thoughts. She imagines herself cracking bones, clawing flesh, drinking blood. She will tear the earth asunder, plunging it into primeval darkness. She has become a demon.

A shaft of light pierces the blinds, falling across Neleni's face as she sleeps. Brushing a hand across her eyes, she tries to push the light away, but it continues to seep under her lids, warning her that she must soon get up. Her breathing becomes more rapid then, with a deep sigh, her lungs fill with thick, warm air.

She moans, resisting wakefulness. She cannot remember what day it is, but she knows that it is significant; and there is something else, something unpleasant, that she does not wish to recall. Her thoughts whirl in front of her, tiny motes glinting in the sunlight; but she cannot lay hold of them, does not want to. Curling an arm over her face, she drifts back to sleep, unwilling to join the waking world for, with it, comes remembrance.

But sleep brings no comfort either, only darkness filled with screams and the sound of drumming; the kind of drumming that accompanies demon dances, the drumming used at temples to exorcise evil spirits. The drumming comes closer, louder and there is a sudden shriek. Neleni gasps and opens her eyes, her hand reaching across the bed for Raj; but he is gone.

"Naughty child. Come here! It's time for you to wash."

Sunny's voice penetrates the room, shrill and piercing. It is answered by a giggle and the sound of running feet – the drumming sound of Neleni's dreams. Saro, as usual, is resisting her bath.

Neleni's eyes follow the flickering blades of light on the ceiling, tracing them down the walls to the wardrobe where something is hanging from the door: her new clothes, collected the day before from Nirmala. With news that was painful.

It is the day of the wedding. She must get ready, but her limbs are leaden and unwilling. The sight of those clothes fills her with sadness, reminding her of Nirmala's account of Arjun's affair. Of course, she has known that there is another woman since finding that letter in his room but somehow, being told by someone else, makes that relationship a reality.

She can no longer lie to herself and pretend that she has not seen the letter or has somehow mistaken its content, nor can she tell herself any longer that he loves her secretly and that it is only her marriage that keeps them apart. No. It is clear to her now that she means nothing to him. Everyone knows about his affair with Leela. Nirmala even mentioned marriage. Neleni's hopes have been stifled in her sleep.

And now, she remembers something else that is almost as painful. She has argued with Nirmala. Over something trifling, she cannot remember what, but it was a pretext for revenge. Nirmala had chattered on incessantly, not sparing her feelings. Neleni had felt hurt and betrayed. Wrongly, perhaps. Quite suddenly, she had retaliated, lashing out, determined to repay Nirmala for her insensitivity, although she had regretted it immediately.

Kneeling on the floor, Nirmala had looked up at her with eyes filled with tears and, in that face, Neleni had seen a reflection of her own pain. They had parted soon after, quietly and with few words and, as she walked home with the clothes bundled over her arm, Neleni knew that she had alienated her friend.

Now, rising reluctantly from bed, she walks across the room to where the clothes are hanging: the skirt, vivid scarlet; the petticoat made from layers of netting; the pink silk top, more like the blouse worn under a sari than the one in her magazine, but pretty nonetheless. They are intended to celebrate her new life, her liberation from desire; but she realises now that it will take more than this to free herself from Arjun.

Perhaps, she must learn to live with pain: the loss of Arjun; her estrangement from Nirmala. She feels much older than her years, deserted by those she loves, alone like an old widow in a white sari. Her wedding clothes are not white, but they are, nonetheless, a sign of mourning, a symbol of her bereavement.

Running her hand over the smooth satin skirt, Neleni wonders whether she should simply abandon this idea and wear her best sari; but a streak of stubbornness bars retreat. She thinks of Lakshmi, gushing over her guests: huge, powdered and sari-bound, her crimson lipstick sticking to her teeth, affecting a baseless grandeur: and Dalia, assuming the airs of a queen as she binds herself to an office worker.

No. Neleni will not concede defeat: she will not succumb to ordinariness, like all the rest of them. That would be the end of her. Her new clothes make a statement. She is different.

Lifting her knee, Padmini the kitchen-maid balances the tray on her leg, steadying it with one hand as she taps gently on the door with the other. There is no reply. The girl's leg begins to quiver under the weight of the tray which is loaded with a heavy teapot, a plate of curry, a dish of pittu, chapattis wrapped in a cloth, a bowl of curds with kitul treacle and a large, ripe mango. The leg on which the girl is standing begins to wobble and the teapot slips across the tray. Fearing an accident, the girl grasps the tray with both hands, lowers her leg and, applying the corner of the tray to the door, gently pushes it open.

Many of the other servants have left so the kitchen-maid's duties have been extended. She has never been to this part of the house before and, when she enters the room, she gasps. She is unaccustomed to such luxury. Her home consists of two rooms: one in which her parents and grandparents sleep and another which she shares with her eight brothers and sisters. She has often fantasised about having a room to herself but she can never quite picture it, being unable to imagine what that amount of space would feel like. It is inconceivable.

Open-mouthed, she looks around her, her eyes hovering over every detail like a bee sipping nectar: the wooden wardrobe with its tiny silver key, the book-case, the dressing table, the bed for one person. There is even a window that looks out onto a small garden where red anthuriums grow in the shade of a cashew tree. Spellbound by this opulence, she is hardly aware of Leela, coolly staring at her reflection in the mirror.

"I don't remember telling you to come in. You should have knocked first."

Leela's lips are compressed into a thin line. This is not the maid who usually brings her breakfast. Leela supposes that yet another member of her staff has left. Loyalty counts for nothing these days. Only money. Despite her promises, not even the servants are prepared to wait for payment. The only ones left are those who are too old, or young, to find work elsewhere.

"Where is Angela?"

"Don't know," mumbles the girl.

"Have you seen her today?"

"Mmm."

"If you see her, tell her I want to speak to her."

The girl nods, mutely. She displays all the awkwardness of pubescence without any of its vitality, like a butterfly too tired to emerge from its chrysalis. Leela wonders how anyone so young could look so old, so careworn. The girl has lost the roundness of childhood if, indeed, there has ever been any softness to the sharp contours of those thin arms and legs. Her thin fingers have large, knobbly knuckles, her elbows are sharp, almost pointed and her front teeth, too big for her mouth, jut out beyond her lower lip. She is ugly and probably stupid. Leela shudders.

"Put it on the bed," she says, sharply, watching the girl's terrified face in the mirror.

Creeping across the room on long bare feet, the girl hardly dares to let her heels touch the floor. Nervously, she places the tray next to Leela who irritably dismisses the maid with a wave of her hand. Her heart beating furiously, the girl has just reached the door when she is summoned back.

"How do you expect me to cut a mango without a knife?"

372

Leela is holding the mango up in one hand, as if to demonstrate the impossibility of the task.

"In fact, why am I expected to cut this at all? That's cook's job. Take it back."

The girl runs back across the room, half stooping, apologetic, holding out cupped hands into which Dalia negligently drops the mango.

"Go on. Get out. Just leave the tea."

Leela is too bored to be really angry but, all the same, one cannot be soft with servants.

**

The girl darts from the room, clutching the mango to her skinny breast. On the way to the servants' quarters, she passes Angela, the housekeeper, but forgets to give her the mistress's message. It does not matter. Angela already knows. She was listening at the door. It was her idea that the maid should bring Leela's breakfast. As housekeeper, she believes such tasks to be beneath her dignity. When she first joined as a humble housemaid, it was Angela's job to bring Leela her morning tea.

Angela loathes that tea-set. Fine bone china, covered with pink roses, the words 'Made in England' printed on the underside. She can picture it with her eyes closed: the gold line around the rim of the cup; the dainty curlicue handle; the place where the bowl of the cup meets the stand, nipped in like a tiny waist.

Every day, she used to walk the long passage from the kitchen to her mistress's bedroom, bringing her tea; and, every day, the delicate cup rattled in its saucer. It never mattered which one she used; they all did it. To spite her. By the time she reached the bedroom door, her heart would be thumping.

She would wait outside while her mistress drank her tea then, when the cup was empty, she would take it back to the kitchen where she would wash it by hand in soapy water, careful not to rub off the gold paint or the pink roses as she scrubbed at the tea stains that ringed the bowl.

She always knew that, if she broke one of those cups or saucers, she would lose her job. That is why Angela has given the job to the kitchen-maid. Someone else can walk that particular tight-rope.

Angela tiptoes past her mistress's door. She will work in another part of the house today. Somewhere she cannot be found. She is expert at making herself invisible when she is needed.

In the hallway, she dusts the mahogany table with her apron, still musing on those cups and saucers. Her mistress was excessively fond of that tea-set and has become even more attached to it after the death of her husband. Angela thinks this strange, considering the way the mistress treated her husband while he was alive. Unable to comprehend this behaviour, Angela wonders if it is somehow due to witchcraft. She already believes this house to be cursed. Look what happened to the man who built it.

He was a strange man; not unkind, but distant and, at the end, troubled. Angela often saw him, sitting in the cupboard that he called a study, the room without a window in which he kept his ledgers. She used to pass him as she carried tea to her mistress, but he was not working, just sitting there with his head in his hands. She had felt sorry for him. Everyone knew how he doted on her mistress and how, when his back was turned, she entertained other men.

It was as if her master had been under a spell, his senses dead to all news of her mistress's wrongdoing. He was just another servant, bringing her the things that she craved and others that she did not require, allowing himself to be consumed by her greed until he became a shadow.

Now the mistress has a new victim; a young man, beautiful, but with the same dead expression in his eyes that her master had. It is definitely witchcraft. The maid has heard stories of the nail that can be driven through a victim's head to control them. The mistress has driven an invisible nail through the heads of both her husband and her new man. But there is one who resists her. The man called Michael who looks a little like Clark Gable or, perhaps, the Indian actor, Raj Kumar.

Angela would consider herself lucky if such a man even looked at her; but the mistress cheats on him, too. Angela likes Michael. He is kind to her and gives her money. She is saving it up to pay for an exorcism, a sacred cleansing that will rid her of the curse that has made her barren. She has tried for seven years to conceive, yet still she has no child. Definitely witchcraft. Probably through contact with this evil house.

When Michael questions Angela about her mistress, she tells him everything. It is the least she can do in return for his kindness. She also tells her friend, the dressmaker, sparing no details, knowing that they will be passed on; but she feels no guilt. People have a right to know. To be warned about what happens here. A house filled with the devil's work.

***

In the kitchen, the maid cries softly over the sink. The cook, a kindly lad of eighteen, puts his arm around her.

"Don't cry, Padmini. It won't always be like this. My brother works for the railway. They've got a union. He says that the Communists have got plans. Things will change soon. You'll see."

The girl wipes her eyes and, under the cook's supervision, cuts the mango, slicing off the cheeks and scoring the flesh so that the skin can be turned inside out and the soft fruit extracted without being pulped. As she works, she begins to dream; not of her own space and a bedroom to herself, but of joining a trade union.

Carefully, Leela lifts the cup and saucer then takes a sip of tea. Her attachment to this china is irrational but it reminds her of something that she now recognises as happiness; circumstances in which she never had to think about her own security, or the future, because it was all done for her. She did not love Mennan, but she misses him.

She remembers, as she always does at this time of day, how he brought the tea-service home with him from a trip to England. How excited he was when showing it to her; how he had unpacked the crate himself and laid all the cups and saucers on the table.

"Only the best for my angel," he had said.

His expression had been like that of a dog hoping for a reward after fetching a stick. Perversely, she had feigned disinterest, considering that he had no right to expect anything of her. She regrets it now, having since learned that the affection of others is not so easily bought: Arjun's, for instance.

With belated compassion for Mennan, she remembers how, on that occasion, she had stormed around the house, screaming at him. She had wanted clothes and jewellery, not a stupid tea-set. She had had half a mind to smash it but, before she could do so, he had prudently hidden it away. Then, a few months later, she had changed her mind. The society women that she had invited to tea raved about the delicate rose-covered china, besieging Cargill's in search of copies. After that, Leela had been acclaimed as a woman of taste and fashion, someone to be watched and emulated.

After that, she became reconciled to the tea-set and will drink from nothing else, insisting that it should be used to serve her tea every morning. It is a ritual that brings her comfort; especially now, in the dark days after Mennan's mysterious death, when the truth of his dealings has begun to seep out. The society women avoid her now, fearing that contact with her tainted reputation will infect them, too. The tea-set is a reminder of better times.

"But what am I thinking? Things are better now."

She puts down the cup and looks across the room to where her reflection is staring back at her from the mirror.

"Things are better now," she repeats to herself.

But the image in the mirror does not agree as wholeheartedly as she expected. It looks uncertain, as if it needs convincing. Indeed, it seems to question her.

What does she really feel? Shame, guilt? Not particularly. Mennan chose his own path. Remorse? Sometimes. Joy. That was what she felt at first. Joy at being free. Joy because she had Arjun. Staring at the mirror, she sees something she had not expected; a face that she no longer recognises as her own, as blank and passionless as a painting.

She tries to reason with it, addressing her words to the mirror.

"I should be happy. I am happy."

But the image remains unchanged, its expression cold and uncompromising, a little haughty, as if it no longer recognises her as its owner. Leela remembers the unsettling experiences of childhood when, seeing herself in a mirror and unable to identify with the reflection in the glass, she sometimes wondered who she really was. She even wondered if the face that stared out at her had a separate existence from her own. Then, gradually, this sense of duality disappeared. Content to see herself through the eyes of others, she had adopted their image of her; a spoilt and beautiful woman with an inherent right to do as she pleased.

Yet, now, looking at herself in the mirror, she revisits the uncertainty of childhood. As long as there is praise, she is secure, but there has not been much praise recently. Her possession of Arjun is incomplete and even Michael, who she regards more as a convenience than an object of affection, is asserting his independence. She is no longer essential to anyone's existence, as she was to Mennan, and her power over her remaining admirers is no longer absolute. Why?

A shadow passes across the blinds, on the other side of the window. It is probably the gardener or a servant but, in the coolness of that shadow, Leela feels afraid, alone. One day she will lose her beauty. What then? Old age. Death. A void. Who will care for her then? Or now, for that matter?

Gripped by panic, she leans towards the mirror and examines herself closely, searching for wrinkles and white hair. She finds none. She is still beautiful, her skin as flawless and smooth as a peach. Then, as quickly as it descended, her mood passes like the lifting of a black veil, and she rallies. She smiles at the mirror. Obediently, her image smiles back. The two faces move in harmony, reflecting each other's mood. Leela sighs, relieved to be in command of herself.

Now satisfied with what she sees, she gazes in the mirror, remembering how Mennan had often likened her to a precious gem, calling her his ruby, his sapphire, his diamond, depending on his mood. He was right. Everything about her is jewel-like, from the amber of her eyes to the pearl-like perfection of her teeth. She shakes her head and, as her hair glistens in the light, she fancies that she can see a heavy emerald drop hanging from each ear. It is a waking dream that often comes to her as she sits in front of the mirror. Ever since childhood, she has pictured herself as a queen from the ancient world.

Raising her arms above her head, she entwines her wrists, closing her palms in an inverted prayer, a posture both provocative and beautiful, like that of a dancer, a seductress of kings. In another age, she would have been the consort of an emperor. Dropping her hands in her lap, she imagines a crown on her head, intricate tiers of gold, scattered with gems, at least two feet high. And a ruby in her navel.

Her reflection stares at her proudly. *You are a match for any man*, it seems to say. *Do not be afraid*. It smiles back at her, joyful, confident, as it should be. She laughs at herself. Today is Michael's wedding day; a day which she has been awaiting with greater eagerness than the groom himself. She has found it difficult to keep Michael's twice-weekly visits a secret from Arjun and lives in constant fear of discovery.

Surely, with marriage, Michael's grip on her will loosen. He will not be free to visit her whenever he chooses. How would he explain such absences to his wife? And, perhaps, with marriage, he will also become kinder and give her access to Mennan's funds without requiring anything in return.

In anticipation of her freedom from Michael's attentions, Leela has planned a celebration of her own. Having persuaded Arjun to take a day's leave, she has planned a trip to the hill country. She has booked a room in a rest-house, although they will not be staying the night. Perched on a hillside near Nuwara Eliya, the hotel offers spectacular views over the surrounding countryside. It is a pity they cannot spend the night together and watch the dawn rising over the mountains, the valleys below filled with early morning mist. But it cannot be helped. Arjun has to be back at work the next day.

Still, they will have a whole day together, undisturbed: an early lunch, followed by a long afternoon. Leela has booked one of the best rooms and it gives her pleasure to think that, indirectly, Michael will be paying for it, although not with his own money.

Contemplating pleasures to come, another more daring thought occurs to her. Perhaps they should abandon the room altogether and drive to some deserted place where they can make love outdoors – under a waterfall, against a tree. She could even satisfy him in the back-seat of a car like a whore from the city, skirts around her waist, blouse torn open to reveal her breasts. She feels a pulse between her legs. The idea excites her.

There is a knock at the door but, before Leela can answer, the kitchen-maid scuffles into the room, carrying the mango, now peeled and sliced, on a plate. She places it clumsily on the dressing-table, tipping it up so that the soft, pulpy fruit slides dangerously close to the rim of the plate.

"Careful, silly!"

Leela does not usually speak to the servants so harshly but she is tense, filled with apprehension and longing. The girl's incompetence grates on her nerves.

"You can take that cup. I've finished with it."

Bowing her head, the maid scurries from the room, the cup rattling dangerously in the saucer.

"Ninny!" murmurs Leela.

Alone again, she turns back to the mirror and tries to imagine how she will look in ten or twenty years. Still, what does it matter? She is beautiful now. And the present is all that matters. She cannot hinder time but she can gorge on life until it is torn from her. Today, she will feast on Arjun.

Before turning her back on the mirror, Leela smiles coyly at her reflection. Then, picking up her robe, she walks into the bathroom where she will take a leisurely shower.

The mirror gleams, dull and empty, in Leela's absence. Suddenly, its surface shimmers, like the surface of a pool touched by the evening breeze; then, after a few seconds' disturbance, it clears and the face of Yaani, Maiden of Sigiriya, appears in the glass. She wears a tall, gold headdress and, as she moves, the emerald drops hanging from her ears flicker with light.

Yaani uses mirrors to check on the progress of her various reincarnations and, as they are usually vain, she can be sure of regular contact. Leela is simply the latest embodiment of a long line of which Yaani was the first. Peering from the glass, Yaani tries to get a good look at Leela's room. Staring from the flat plane of the mirror, she cannot see around corners, but what she sees is enough. She clicks her tongue in disgust.

"Is this what I've come to? Is this what they call wealth nowadays? Just look at this tiny place. No paintings. No peacocks. No warriors. And her jewellery! Tinsel! I'm glad it's hers and not mine."

Lovingly, she strokes one of her earrings, a large, pear-shaped emerald. As a window onto Leela's world, the mirror is limited, but interesting. And it is the means by which Yaani communicates with her alter ego. By a simple process of suggestion, she has persuaded Leela that the image of herself wearing a crown is a daydream, a figment of her imagination, not an echo of her former self. It would never do for Leela to know the truth for, if she did, she would instantly go mad.

Of course, visiting one's future incarnation is strictly forbidden by the gods but, centuries ago, Yaani taught herself the art of necromancy.

***

It all started quite innocently. To fill the hours of boredom when Kasyapa was away fighting battles or indulging his latest fancy for a serving girl, she had taught herself to read. Well, not quite. She had needed a little help and, conveniently, among Kasyapa's many captives, there had been a scholar from one of the rival kingdoms.

Without Kasyapa's knowledge, Yaani had the man brought to her under cover of darkness. In return for reading lessons, she promised him freedom. He accepted willingly. She was an able pupil and soon graduated from simple texts to more complex works.

Kasyapa had a well-stocked library with many manuscripts, some pilfered from other kingdoms, some written by his own scribes. In fact, he had so many scrolls and texts and parchments that he never knew exactly what he had got and, as there was no index of these works, he did not miss a few now and again.

In the king's absence, Yaani became an avid reader. One day, she discovered a set of manuscripts hidden away in a camphor-wood box. The lid of the box was inlaid with brass symbols which Yaani could not decipher, so she showed it to the scholar.

When he saw it, the man blanched and told her to destroy the box and its contents immediately. They were evil, he said, the work of demons and they would bring much bad luck. Yaani had laughed at this superstitious talk and declared her intention of reading the manuscripts. In a frenzy of panic, her teacher threatened to tell the king.

Of course, she could not allow him to do that. Kasyapa forgave her most things but even he drew the line at witchcraft. So, a small accident was arranged in which the scholar, while being led back to his cell by a circuitous route, fell from the battlements to his death.

When told the news, Kasyapa was mystified. He asked how a man who was supposed to have been incarcerated in a dungeon at the foot of the fortress had apparently fallen from its highest parapet but, although he suspected Yaani's involvement, he never unearthed the truth. For her part, Yaani felt no remorse. She had promised her teacher freedom and he had got it – in the next world.

After that, Yaani had been free to study the black arts without any hindrance. Starting with simple poisons, she soon progressed to mind control through the device of a nail inserted into a victim's skull. Fortunately for her, there was no shortage of human material for her experiments. After every campaign, the king's jail was crammed with captives of every age, size and description.

Formerly, Kasyapa had regarded captives as a reflection of his dignity: the more he had, the more invincible he appeared; but these prisoners, whose numbers were constantly increasing, had begun to drain the royal coffers, sitting around all day, waiting to be fed without doing anything to earn their keep. They were one of the invisible costs of war; or so Kasyapa complained to Yaani in a moment of unusual frankness.

Taking the king at his word, Yaani realised that she could perform a valuable service, relieving pressure on the royal purse while, at the same time, perfecting her illicit skills. With the connivance of the head jailer, she gained a key to the prison and a small annex in which to perform her experiments. For the price of a few extra coins, she could also buy a little brute force from the other jailers who were happy to help whenever a victim became feisty.

The wardens respected her privacy and, despite the odd ghastly scream from a subject, no-one ever came to investigate. Of course, Kasyapa never found out and, even if he had, would probably not have cared about the torture of a few innocent souls. Like all ancient kings, he was in the fortunate position of being able to conduct his affairs unhindered by conscience or other modern concepts of humanity.

Having learned the basic principles of her art, Yaani wished to graduate to more complicated tasks but, first, she needed expert advice. Initially, this presented something of an obstacle until she had the bright idea of summoning supernatural aid. To her delight, she discovered that there were plenty of demons, desperate for a human advocate with access to the king's ear. Through her, they could direct the workings of human history; through them, she could survive both death and reincarnation.

Of course, she did not wish to be alone in her eternal life, so she enlisted the companionship, if not the consent, of her fellow concubines and her royal lover. Thus, Kasyapa and the other Maidens of Sigiriya fell prey to her magic and were forced to endure the centuries as shadows of themselves, neither living, nor dead. It was not something for which Yaani earned their thanks although, over the years, they have grudgingly learned to accept their fate. Although he would never admit it, Kasyapa even derives a perverse pleasure from his attenuated half-life.

When the Maidens' bickering gets too much to bear, he takes himself off into the garden to stalk whatever beautiful visitor he can find, returning to extol her virtues to his companions and watching the expression on their faces. This is something that Yaani had not bargained on. With the loss of Kasyapa's physical body, she had hoped to secure his undying affection. But she was wrong. After all this time, his faithlessness still hurts and, it is in order to pay him back, that she is now directing Leela.

From Leela's bathroom comes the sound of water, drumming against the hard surface of the shower. Yaani frowns. It is a sound that perplexes her. She cannot imagine what is happening in there. She would like to step into the room, walk around and take a look but, despite her art, she cannot bend all the laws of science. She is constrained to observe from the mirror.

A slender wisp of steam issues from the bathroom, carrying with it the scent of rose soap. Yaani sniffs. She likes that smell. Perhaps this reincarnation is not entirely lacking in good taste. Unlike some of her predecessors who are best forgotten.

In fact, Yaani is quite proud of this one, considering her to be the truest representation of herself for a long time. That being said, Leela has recently displayed some alarming glimmers of conscience. Or is it just weakness? It is too early to tell.

Nonetheless, Leela gave Yaani cause for alarm a few minutes ago when she seemed to be experiencing a crisis of confidence. Yaani, who never suffered from such heart-searching, will not tolerate it in her followers. Having been alerted to this dangerous state of mind, she was forced to make an unscheduled appearance. Being forced to act on such short notice is particularly draining. And annoying. She was in the middle of a chess match with Kasyapa which she was winning. Still, it was worth the sacrifice. Leela has recovered and Yaani's plan is back on course.

Through Leela, Kasyapa will be taught a lesson. By securing her hold over Arjun, Leela will defeat her rival, Neleni, the woman that Kasyapa has had the temerity to stalk at Sigiriya; the one that he still talks about in his sleep although that first sighting was months ago. And he has visited her since, Yaani is sure of that.

Since that day, there have been many unexplained absences on the part of her royal lord. Of course, he's always been a sly dog but, recently, he has been more than usually secretive about his whereabouts. He is up to something. After many years – centuries in fact – Yaani understands Kasyapa's ways. She knows him too well to believe in any innocent motive for his actions. She bites her lip to prevent it from quivering.

***

In the bathroom, someone is singing. Leela is happy, unwittingly inspired by her other self. Yaani laughs and holds up her chin, defiantly.

Yes, today will be the day. With that troublesome fellow Michael out of the way, Leela's victory will be complete. Kasyapa's little fancy, Neleni, will have her nose rubbed in the dirt. That will pay him out! And her, too!

Clapping her hands with pleasure, Yaani disappears into the shimmering surface of the mirror.

A gull screeches as it wheels over the harbour, stretching its wings to take advantage of the warm air rising from the sea. Dipping suddenly, the bird dives like an arrow into the water. A fishing boat is returning to port and, having cleaned their catch, the men are emptying fish entrails over the side. Bobbing along in the wake of the boat, the bird pecks furiously at the water, gorging itself before its fellow gulls descend in a feeding frenzy.

Having swallowed its fill, the gull slowly flaps its wings, beating the water and pushing itself up into the air, its scaly legs and paddle-feet trailing beneath it. It soars, higher and higher, over the harbour and the busy road that runs beside it, up to the parapet of the great white building and the nest where three hungry chicks are waiting with open beaks.

Above the nest, a large banner runs along the top of the building, announcing the 2,500th anniversary of Buddha's parinibbana. Such posters are common in this year of celebration, but it strikes a discordant note with some of the guests gathering at the entrance below. Dalia's wedding party is arriving at the Grand Oriental Hotel. All are Tamil and Catholic. All regard the hotel as a symbol of their colonial past. It is therefore strange and somewhat disconcerting to see it so blatantly associated with one of the underlying strands of Sinhalese nationalism; a new and, to some, worrying development in the Island's politics.

Originally built to house British officers, the Grand Oriental Hotel still retains a hint of its former military grandeur. Echoing the confidence of a distant age and another race, its stolid façade and colonnades would not be out of place among the Government buildings of London's Whitehall. Yet now, even the Grand Oriental seems uncertain of its identity, adorned with a slogan that would have mystified its builders.

The whole country is on the cusp of change and its hierarchy, both political and social, is under threat. In recent months, the Communists have organised a series of devastating strikes, undermining the national infrastructure. Strikers have clashed with the police in bloody riots and the newly-elected Government is already in a state of crisis. Buddhist nationalists, inspired by their success at the polls, are pressing the Government to bring the Sinhala Only Act into force as soon as possible. This, too, has led to violence.

In rural areas, the rapid rise in population and increasing cultivation of virgin land has removed the physical barriers that previously separated communities of Tamil and Sinhalese peasants and each now fear incursions by the other. At every level, the status quo is being challenged. The infiltration of modern ideas and the resurgence of ancient beliefs are combining to form a poisonous leaven. The future seems uncertain and some, particularly among the Tamils, are beginning to fear the worst.

Perhaps, for this reason, Dalia's guests, having noted the Buddhist banner fluttering above the hotel, are more subdued than is usual for a wedding party. Marriage is normally an excuse for hilarity and prolonged celebrations but, on this occasion, there is a marked absence of humour, high jinks or even enthusiasm. People seem unsure of how to conduct themselves, or even, what to say. It is an uncertainty that springs from the general mood of the country, but it has been augmented by the bridegroom himself.

***

Michael arrived late for his own wedding, forcing Dalia to wait a full twenty minutes at the church door. Just as the guests were beginning to murmur their concern, he had turned up, breathless and dishevelled, muttering some excuse about the traffic and an overturned ox cart. To make matters worse, he hesitated when making his vows and, when the priest asked if there were any objections to the couple's union, Michael had looked back over his shoulder, towards the door, his face expressing hope rather than anxiety. After the wedding, the couple had posed on the church steps for their picture to be taken but there was little sign of happiness on Michael's face. His expression, captured for posterity, was one of deepest gloom.

The groom's obvious reluctance has jarred the guests, unnerving them and, now they file quietly into the Hotel with the feeling that they are mourning the loss of something indefinable. As they enter, they are directed along a series of corridors, until they reach one of the smaller ballrooms at the back of the building where Lakshmi, heading the family line-up, is waiting to greet them, her arms held out in promise of a fleshy embrace. As they approach her, the guests suck in their breath, as swimmers do when anticipating a dive into icy water.

The handshakes, kisses and congratulations are something to be endured, not enjoyed. At the end of this ordeal, everyone sighs with relief, taking comfort in the prospect of companionable conversation with other, like-minded sufferers. There is, at least, no shortage of food and drink.

The wedding breakfast is drawing to a close. Speeches, which will continue for many hours, are being delivered over a faulty PA system that either buzzes like an irritated bee or keeps cutting out, so that the message is lost. No matter. No-one ever listens to speeches at a family reunion. They are simply a backdrop to conversation; a meaningless ritual, generally ignored, but whose absence, once noticed, would be cause for complaint.

By now, everyone is talking at the top of their voice, each trying to be heard over the prevailing hubbub. At a table on the far side of the room, Raj is vigorously expounding his political views to two elderly aunts.

"I tell you, Martha Aunty, it will all end in tears. If they try to bring in Sinhalese as the main language, there will be violence."

"Do you really think so?" The old lady looks terrified. "Did you hear that, Agnes?" She turns to her sister. "Raj says there will be violence if they bring in the Sinhala Only Act."

"There has already been bloodshed, Martha Aunty. Look at Gal Oya and what happened there. Almost two hundred killed in riots."

"But they were peasants," observes Agnes Aunty who is of a more sanguine disposition than her sister.

"Anyway," she continues, "we've had worse riots before and they never led to anything. This sort of thing happens everywhere from time to time. It's just human nature."

Stout and companionable, Agnes Aunty always takes what she calls 'the commonsense approach'. It will take more than a squabble between peasants in a remote part of the Island to convince her that the country is facing disaster.

"Well, if you ask me, it's just the beginning," retorts Raj, nonplussed at having his judgement questioned.

"Peasants, monks, nationalists! All troublemakers. All the bloody same. Not to mention the Communists! There's a strike every other day, or so it seems. This country's going to the bloody dogs!"

An old gentleman, husband to Agnes Aunty, thumps his fist on the table. Wine glasses quake and wobble, unsettled by the tremor.

"Ha, ha! Peter gets so angry. Always thumping the table. Hit it so hard the other day that he smashed one of my plates," Agnes Aunty chuckles.

Stealing a glance at Peter, Martha Aunty concludes that he has not heard his wife's comment and giggles. In fact, Peter heard Agnes's remark quite clearly. He is just observing a protocol of their marriage: she knows he heard but, to avoid any unpleasantness, they both pretend otherwise.

"Anyway," says Agnes Aunty, quickly taking control of the conversation as her husband opens his mouth, ready to launch into another diatribe, "where are the drinks? My glass is empty. So is yours Martha, and yours Raj. Go on, Peter, see what has happened."

With a murmur of discontent, Peter pushes out his chair and shuffles off between the tables to the bar at the other end of the room.

"Good," says Agnes. "Now he's gone, we can talk about him. Or, at least, his brother."

This subversive remark is met by a peal of laughter from her sister. The two old ladies chortle and nudge each other. Weddings are a wonderful excuse for gossip and a little discreet misbehaviour.

"Did you know that Peter's brother, Anthony, has joined an evangelical sect? Abstinence in all things."

Raj is agog. "No! Him! A teetotaller!"

"Yes. Unbelievable isn't it? It's that daughter-in-law of his. A typical village girl. Completely uncultured but a real zealot. She has a lot of influence in that family. Did you know that they won't accept any medical treatment whatsoever?"

"Ah hah! You remember Judge Joseph? A really nice man. He used to live near you."

Agnes screws up her eyes as she tries to recall the name.

"Ah yes, I know. What about him?"

"He was a Pentecostalist. His whole family converted. Then, a year or so later, he got some minor illness. Could have been treated but he refused. He died, you know."

"Ahh, no!" Placing her hand on her bosom, Agnes registers exactly the kind of surprise required by news of such scintillating horror. "When was this? I didn't know."

Raj obligingly supplies the details.

"Well," says Agnes, her face unusually animated by the shock of this unexpected revelation, "it makes you glad to be Catholic. I certainly shan't convert. Wouldn't do for us, would it Martha. A gin a day keeps the doctor away!"

The two old ladies hoot with laughter, revealing soft, plump midriffs rising like dough over the waistline of their saris.

"Religion has a lot to answer for," declares Raj, ominously.

Draining his glass, he places it back on the table and stares bleakly into its empty depths. It is difficult to tell whether his darkening humour is due to contemplating the excesses of religion or the current lack of alcohol. At that point, Peter re-appears bearing a full bottle of whisky and the remainder of a bottle of gin.

"All I could find," he apologises.

The mood around the table lightens instantly. Raj cracks a joke and the loud guffaws of the old ladies draw a disapproving glance from Lakshmi who rises from her seat at the top table to scowl at the source of this uproarious behaviour. Unabashed, the old ladies rock from side to side, gently bumping against each other, like two small boats at anchor, gently bobbing up and down on the tide.

Still cackling, Agnes removes her glasses, wiping the lenses with the end of her sari. No longer magnified, her eyes appear small and rheumy, the skin around them creased and wrinkled like those of a tortoise. Without her glasses, she is a frail old lady in whose face the workings of age are clearly visible.

***

Sitting quietly beside Raj, Neleni has not taken part in any of the conversation. Politics do not interest her much so she has nothing to contribute. Besides, any comment of hers would be drowned by the loud voices of Raj, Peter and Agnes. Instead, she observes. Watching Agnes remove her glasses, she is shocked at how vulnerable her aunt appears, as if a protective layer has been peeled away. Neleni has always regarded Agnes as being invincible, immune to the effects of time.

"I suppose we are all fighting the inevitable," thinks Neleni.

She fidgets uncomfortably, trying to smooth down her skirt which is constantly being pushed up by the fullness of its petticoat. The layers of net are coarse and scratch her legs and the blouse is too tight under the arms. Her new outfit has been a mistake. It makes her feel self-conscious. She should have worn a sari, like everyone else. She has done her best to carry it off but her confidence has withered under Lakshmi's disapproving eye. The new clothes have simply provided a new target for her hostess's venom.

As her companions continue to laugh and joke, Neleni relives the awful moment when it was her turn to greet the bridal party, all of whom were lined up at the ballroom entrance like a set of tribal totems. After giving Neleni's clothes a sly, sideways glance, Dalia allowed the glimmer of a smile to pass over her lips. Lakshmi was more forward with her compliments.

"Darling," she crooned, her eyes gleaming with malevolent pleasure. "What a wonderful outfit. Tell me. What is it meant to be?"

"It's an American pattern. From a fashion magazine," whispered Neleni, her courage deserting her. "I had it made."

"So I see," said Lakshmi, coiling her arms around Neleni, like a giant python embracing its victim.

Helplessly, Neleni allowed herself to be crushed against her cousin's vindictive bosom where, overpowered by the smell of cheap scent and face-powder, she felt dizzy and a little sick. Then, as she lifted her face to kiss Lakshmi's cheek, she saw Michael smiling at her, rakishly, unnoticed by either his bride or her mother.

Unnerved, Neleni insisted on clutching Raj's arm in an unusual display of affection. Once they had found their places at the dining table, she nestled down in her seat and tried to make herself as inconspicuous as possible. Her new clothes were a disaster. Making her feel cheap and awkward, they had attracted the wrong kind of attention.

***

Raj laughs loudly, recalling Neleni from her unpleasant daydream. Grateful for this interruption, she tries to catch up with the conversation which has meandered through considerations of politics and religion to family affairs. Agnes is talking about her eldest son, Ramesh, who, having followed his father's example and joined the Services, is currently a captain in the Navy.

"You must come and see us when Ramesh is next on leave. He brings us real rum. From Jamaica."

"Yes, real rum," echoes Martha Aunty. "Not dishwater like the usual stuff."

"And how is Ramesh?" asks Neleni, returning to the principal topic.

"He tells me he's all right, but I'm not sure, really," says Agnes, suddenly serious.

"He was in line for promotion but something has happened. We've heard no more about it and, every time I ask, he clams up. Doesn't want to talk about it. Or can't."

"He's a Tamil," mutters Peter. "What do you expect? We're in for trouble and no mistake."

"Peter, not now."

Agnes tries to intercept the forthcoming monologue but, as usual, her husband ignores her.

"Those politician fellows of ours had better do something bloody quick if they are to avoid trouble. All the signs are there. Everyone keeps saying that civil war can't happen here. But it can.

"Just because we're an island, there's no reason to be complacent. India is on our doorstep. And look what happened there during Partition. Millions dead. Ordinary people uprooted and forced to move hundreds of miles away from the villages in which their families had lived for generations. Hundreds of people slaughtered on trains just because they happened to have a different faith.

"None of this new generation of politicians has seen war. I have. I fought with the British in Europe. At Monte Casino. In Italy. You can't imagine the carnage. Not until you've seen it. It's terrible."

Agnes cuts in quickly before Peter can elaborate.

"Partition was over ten years ago. And this is not India. That was all to do with the Moslems and Hindus. Pakistan. There is no Mohammed Ali Djinna here. No-one is demanding a separate state."

"No," says Peter, crossly. "We just have Bandaranaike; a man who wants to be all things to all men. His coalition is full of extremists. Once they get control, Ceylon will have its own Partition."

"I don't agree. It couldn't happen here. We're too sensible. No-one cares that much."

But Agnes speaks without conviction. Suddenly, everyone becomes thoughtful and, for the first time, the conversation falters. Although Neleni has no particular opinion regarding politics, like many others, she has recently begun to experience a feeling of unease.

The violence at Gal Oya has unsettled everyone, Sinhalese and Tamil alike. For a brief moment, it raised the spectre of civil war. Whatever Agnes says, the cataclysmic violence following Independence in India is still fresh in everyone's mind. They have all seen the newsreels showing streets lined with hundreds of dead bodies.

The atmosphere has become oppressive and Neleni decides that this would be a good moment to go and find the children who are playing outside with their friends. She longs for fresh air and the opportunity to be on her own. Quietly excusing herself, she threads her way through the tables to the door. Nobody notices Michael quietly slipping out behind her.

1956: The looking-glass

As she walks along the corridor, Neleni's heels click against the marble floor. It is a pleasant sound, unlike the soft patter of the sandals that she usually wears, but the shoes, lent to her by Nirmala, are closed at the toe and uncomfortable in the heat. Supporting herself with one hand against the wall, Neleni bends over and fiddles with the strap at the back of one shoe. It has become too tight and is digging into her flesh. Unable to undo the tiny buckle, she finally slips the shoe off. The strap has dug so deeply into her heel that it has left its impression in her flesh.

Straightening up, she puts her shoeless foot to the floor. The marble is as cool as water. Taking off her other shoe, she stands for a moment with her eyes closed, enjoying a moment's respite from the heat. She must find the girls but, first, she must wash her face and hands. Running cold water over her arms will provide relief from the withering heat. Her hair is sticking to her face and her clothes are hot and uncomfortable. Perhaps, in the privacy of the rest-room, she can remove her blouse for a few minutes.

She hurries forwards, into the foyer where arrangements of bridal flowers – orchids, lilies and orange blossom – are already wilting in the heat. Without asking directions, she turns into the first corridor that presents itself, sure that it leads in the direction of the rest-rooms; but, after a couple of minutes, she realises that she has taken a wrong turning. Seemingly endless, the corridor snakes left, then right, becoming narrower and darker, leading to parts of the building seldom seen by guests.

An open door allows a glimpse of a room with furniture covered in dust-sheets. Intrigued, Neleni steps inside. The air smells stale as if it has not been disturbed for years, a faint but musty combination of cigar-smoke and polish. Situated in a lightless angle of the building, the room never catches the sun and, despite several large windows, reaching from floor to ceiling, it has a gloomy aspect.

Chairs, stacked against the walls, are covered in white sheets which have developed a bloom of grey dust and, although the patina of the parquet floor indicates regular polishing, its age is apparent from a number of blackened grooves: deep scratches and indentations which have been filled with successive layers of lacquer.

A piano, swathed in green baize, has been pushed into one corner and the only piece of furniture left uncovered is a curious old dresser, topped by a device like the headboard of a bed into which has been set a convex mirror. The entire ballroom is drawn into its unblinking lens which stares like a single, cyclopian eye.

Fascinated by the distorted image of the room returned by the mirror, Neleni approaches the dresser. When standing directly in front of the mirror, her face looms out of the reflective surface, the largest object in a distorted panorama in which every object is miniaturised, its scale reduced according to its distance from the mirror.

She runs her finger along the top of the dresser. It is similar to the hat-stand in her hall, but this mirror returns a kinder reflection. The tiny image of her face stares back at her from a great distance, trapped, as it were, in a different dimension. Wide-eyed and slightly distorted, she has the appearance of an alien visitor: a face transported from a great distance, like a signal flashed from another planet, light years away. However much she tries, standing on tiptoe or moving from side to side, she cannot look directly into the tiny face which seems to be staring up at something which she cannot see.

Neleni imagines the reflected room full of people. Men and women from a different age, pale-skinned and pale-eyed, in dinner jackets and long dresses, talking, laughing, dancing. Does the mirror hold memories of the past? When no-one is looking, do those images still float across its silver face?

"Lost?"

The figure of a man appears behind her in the mirror.

"No. Not really."

Michael is watching her from the doorway. He is drunk; she can tell by the way he is standing, one hand against the wall to balance himself, the other holding a glass of Scotch, his shirt collar open and tie pulled loose with the knot to one side.

He saunters towards her, across the empty dance floor, his feet occasionally crossing in an exaggerated manner as he tries to steady himself. And all the time his eyes are on her. She feels something lurch in her stomach, something instinctive, a warning. His presence makes her nervous. Drunkenness scares her, even Raj's, and she does not like to be alone with other men, except, of course, for Arjun. He is different. Or, at least, he was. The sudden memory of her loss is painful and she turns her head away, pretending to look in the mirror.

"So this is where you've been hiding."

Michael is standing close to her, too close; she can smell the whisky on his breath.

"I wondered where you'd got to."

She does not respond.

"Pretty outfit. Very seductive."

He runs a finger up her forearm then grasps her tightly, just above the elbow. She can see his face in the mirror, leaning towards her miniature image, trying to kiss it. She tries to move away but, sliding an arm around her waist, he pulls her towards him while his other hand releases her arm and, brushing her breast, wanders to the buttons on her blouse

"Stop it! What are you doing?"

She tries to push him away but he tightens his grasp, pulling her close so that their faces touch. Then, he begins to speak, spitting the words in her face, mouthing them so that she will understand and, although his voice drops to a whisper, speaking with such deadly clarity that she misses nothing. Every word hits her like an arrow.

"I went to my girlfriend's house today. I wanted to see her before I got married. That's why I was late for my wedding. But guess what? She's spending the day at a rest-house with your lodger. What do you think they're doing there, eh?"

"I don't know. What's it got to do with me?"

"He's your lodger. He's taken my woman, so I want something in return. You'll do. Don't complain. It's the best offer you're likely to get."

He pushes her backwards, pinning her against the wall in order to free his hands. Dazed by the speed of his attack, she cannot think of what to do. It is as if it is all happening to someone else. His hands are clawing at her skirt, trying to pull it up, reaching into the layers of net. She feels his fingers on her leg, following the line of her thigh, sliding upwards.

Looking up, she catches sight of herself in the mirror, an image projected from another time; a helpless victim, a sacrifice, compensation for someone else's mistake. She will never be able to tell anyone of this terrible secret for she will be blamed. A woman is always guilty, like Eve, or Nirmala. Whether it is her clothes, or the fact that she has wandered off on her own, they will find some reason for her guilt and, after a while, even she will be convinced that, although innocent, she asked for it.

"You bastard!"

Galvanised by fear, she jerks her leg up and, by chance, finds her mark. Michael doubles over, nursing his crotch. Pushing him aside, Neleni runs as fast as she can. As she races across the slippery dance floor, the mirror reflects her retreating image as it shrinks to a pinpoint, then vanishes altogether.

Neleni runs all the way back to the dining-room where the guests, having finished eating, have re-arranged themselves into little groups, changing tables to sit with friends or relatives they have not seen recently and where, having pushed the chairs back, they are all talking at once. Arms and legs are stretched out in the leisurely attitude that follows a good lunch and hands, resting on the white table linen, hold cigarettes propped between their fingers from which columns of smoke rise lazily to the ceiling.

They seem not to hear or see Neleni, who has to push her way across the room, through the fog of cigarette smoke and conversation, squeezing between chairs and their animated occupants and stepping over children who suddenly appear between her feet as they crawl from hiding places behind chairs and under tables.

She can still feel the imprint of Michael's hands on her body, burning her skin. She feels sick. She wants to wash, scrub herself until she bleeds, rid herself of his dirty fingers which still seem to play over her leg, inching their way up her thigh. Clamping her hand to her mouth, she struggles against the desire to vomit.

Then, with relief, she sees Raj who is sitting with his profile to her, his head tilted back, his eyes crinkled with laughter. Amidst this Babel, she can distinguish his voice and it brings her comfort. He will protect and comfort her. He will be outraged on her behalf, understand what she feels. She just needs to tell him.

"Raj," she pulls anxiously at his sleeve. "Please, I want to go home."

But Raj is enjoying himself too much to listen. He hardly seems to hear her.

"Please, Raj, please. Listen to me."

"What?"

He jerks his head around, irritated and indignant. He has been drinking heavily. His face is flushed and his skin damp with perspiration. He screws up his eyes and frowns at her, pretending to listen. But he is too far gone to understand. She may as well be a visitor from Mars, speaking a foreign language.

"I want to go home."

She repeats her request with increased urgency. She can hear the tone of her own voice, how it must sound to others, demanding, like a petulant child.

"We can't," snaps Raj. "Too rude. Only just got here".

It is always like this. He likes a crowd, conversation, heated discussion. Sometimes, he seems more intoxicated by company than drink. Either way, it makes him aggressive and obstinate. He never wants to leave.

"Please, Raj," she pleads. "Please."

"No."

Turning his back on her, Raj starts talking loudly to Peter, obviously hoping that, if he ignores her, she will either shut up or go away. Neleni always has a way of spoiling his fun and, today, he will not let her. He will make a stand as any man should when his wife gets too demanding.

Neleni stands behind him, in her red skirt and pink blouse, her arms hanging at her sides, her head drooping, like a wilted flower. Tears are streaming down her cheeks.

"What is it, dear?" Martha Aunty grips Neleni's limp hand and squeezes it. "Don't you feel well?"

Neleni shakes her head. Let them think what they like. She will make any excuse to get away. It doesn't matter. She must get home, away from Michael and the memory of what he has done. Back home, where it is safe. But Raj isn't listening. Can he not see her distress? Does he not care? He is her husband. He is supposed to protect her but, instead, he ignores her. As he has always done. To her mind, he is as guilty as Michael.

"Go on, dear. You go home. We'll look after Raj and the children."

Pushing her chair back, Martha has started to get up but, being a large woman in a confined space, she is making something of a commotion and attracting attention from neighbouring tables. The thought of other people staring at her only increases Neleni's sense of shame and, fearing that Martha will offer to accompany her home, she swiftly murmurs her thanks and withdraws. Martha is left with her mouth open, her face frozen in surprise.

As she pushes her way through the roaring, heaving groups of guests, Neleni passes Lakshmi who raises an eyebrow in studied disapproval.

"Just let her ask me where I'm going. And why," thinks Neleni. "I'll tell her. Here. In front of everyone."

For once, Lakshmi has the sense to keep quiet. Seeing danger in Neleni's eye, she wisely holds her tongue, swallowing the biting remark that she was about to deliver and thereby saving them both from embarrassment.

Ducking around a waiter with a full tray of drinks, Neleni hurries down the passage to the hallway, where Michael is leaning against the desk, smoking a cigarette. As soon as he sees her, he affects an awkward smile.

"Hey, Neleni …"

"Go to hell!"

"Neleni, come back. I didn't mean it. Let me buy you a drink. Neleni!"

He steps forward, as if to greet her, but she runs past him at full tilt, knocking into one of the plaster columns with its vase of wilted wedding flowers. The arrangement tilts dangerously, ready to topple, but she does not stop. On she runs, across the marble floor, through the swing door and down the steps; out to the street where she can smell the salty sea air, laced with tar and diesel smoke and the fumes from the cars and lorries that speed along the road.

She stops for a second, trying to catch her breath, taking strength from the familiar, bustling street where strangers press around her, brushing her arms, tugging at the flounces of her skirt as they push past; and, in their careless touch, she finds comfort, because it is done without intent. No-one cares. She is anonymous and nothing is required of her. No-one even sees her. She feels strangely liberated, as grateful for this bath of noise, sound and colour as a prisoner, newly released.

"Neleni!"

Faint but distinct, Michael's voice rises above the hum of the street. He is standing on the steps of the hotel, trying to attract her attention. Without turning to look, she runs into the oncoming traffic and hails a taxi, waving her arms, forcing it to stop. The brakes squeal and the driver swears.

"Do you want to get killed?"

Offering no apology, Neleni steps into the taxi, ordering the driver to take her home as she settles herself on the hard seat with its gashed upholstery.

***

391

The taxi sways dizzily through the traffic, its driver ignoring the hoots from other vehicles as he lurches from one lane to another. Hunched in the corner of the vehicle, her arms wrapped around her waist, her head pressed against the door, Neleni is lost in a mayhem of thought hardly less chaotic than the traffic that surrounds her.

Suddenly and without warning, in a place where she felt safe, she became the victim of attack. The shock is only just beginning to sink in. She has been molested by a man who, if given a chance, would have raped her. He was neither a criminal nor a stranger, but someone she knew, someone who is now related to her by marriage. And the attack did not take place in a dark and deserted alleyway, far from help, but in a room close to where other people were celebrating, laughing, joking and drinking, in total ignorance of what was happening next door. It was both awful and banal, like drowning within a few feet of people eating a picnic.

Her thoughts convert into images. She remembers a picture once seen in an art book. Called 'Icarus', it seemed, at first, to be a study of two farm-workers; one ploughing, the other tending sheep. But, on closer inspection, one could see a pair of tiny legs, sticking out of the sea. Insignificant, almost comical, a man had fallen to his death, unobserved. The horror of a man, plummeting to earth on melted wings, had passed without remark. Unacknowledged, the victim suffered alone, condemned to experience a reality unreal to everyone else.

"Like me," thinks Neleni.

The taxi lurches clumsily as a stray cow wanders into its path. Fearing that she might be pitched out of the vehicle, Neleni grabs the back of the driver's seat. He smiles at her in the mirror; a long, appraising smile. She is suddenly conscious of how different she looks from most of the women in the street, dressed in her brash, western clothes. She releases the back of the seat and huddles back in her corner, holding her skirt firmly down around her knees. She feels conspicuous, vulnerable; a wounded bird in the middle of a field.

Where is Raj? Why did he not protect her? The stupid man did not realise that anything was wrong, even though she begged him to come home. Even when she cried, he chose to ignore her distress. All for the sake of a good time and a few more drinks. Men. They fall into two categories. They are either wicked, like Michael, or weak, like Raj. She hates them all.

With one foot curled up under him on the seat, the other free to control the pedals, the driver has affected an attitude of nonchalance, steering the taxi with one hand. Despite the traffic hurtling past, he has turned in his seat to look at her.

"What do you think you're looking at?"

She has never spoken to a stranger like this before, always hiding her anger under a veil of timidity. Shaken by her ferocity, the driver turns away, muttering curses in Sinhalese. She misses most of what he says, although she picks out the words "Tamil bitch" and, for some perverse reason, it pleases her.

"That's right," she thinks. "I'm a bitch. Just say it again. Then you'll see how much of a bitch I can be."

She wills him to speak, staring intently at the back of his head, noting idly, that the comb marks are still apparent, like small furrows, in his thickly-oiled hair. She longs for confrontation, a chance to vent her fury, but the driver says nothing. She glares at him, like a cat waiting to strike, disappointed that he does not give her the opportunity.

***

392

He has already said too much. It perplexes him. After years of dealing with difficult customers, the driver has learned to hide his feelings but, today, aroused by this woman in her short skirt, he has looked at her with longing, as a man sometimes looks at a woman. And she saw him. It was not so much her response that shocked him, but his own. Infuriated by his own embarrassment, he has insulted her, pointedly referring to her race, something he has never done before.

Antipathy towards the Tamils. Until this moment, he has never felt it or, at least, never openly acknowledged it. He has Tamil neighbours. They are all right. He likes them well enough. But they are different. Like many Sinhalese, who do not regard themselves as being particularly political, his perception of racial difference has been sharpened by recent events. There are two groups of Tamils in this island: those, like his neighbours, who get on quietly with life and the others, the troublemakers. Tamils in the North and East are agitating for recognition of their language and are threatening satyagraha, a massive peaceful demonstration, if they do not get it.

Sour grapes, that is what he calls it. They are bad losers, these Tamils. They do not want to share power, even though they are in the minority. They are like spoilt children, having a tantrum when they cannot get their own way. Like this woman in the back seat. Fast and flashy, looking down on people like him, always acting like they are better. In his head, he rehearses a popular slogan: *Ceylon for the Sinhalese*. It sounds good. Calms him. He repeats it, like a mantra, all the way to the woman's home. Bitch. Tamil bitch. He won't forget her in a hurry.

Having paid the driver, who sullenly refuses to look at her, Neleni runs up the steps into the house, anxious to be alone. Sunny is away, staying with a cousin. The old lady tires quickly these days, wincing with pain when she walks the few steps into the yard, nodding off at the meal table, every day sleeping more and waking less. She was too weak to attend the wedding and Neleni would not leave her alone, fearing what might happen in her absence. So Sunny has gone to stay with cousin Ana.

As she opens the door, Neleni is struck by the silence of the house. It is a silence that impresses itself on the ear. It is absolute, complete, as if the house itself has died for lack of human company. This barren stillness suits Neleni's mood. For the first time in her life, she feels that she is alone when she most needs to be.

The anger within her is so great that she fears she might vent it on the first person she sees. It is uncontrollable, welling up within her and finally bursting the barriers which have restrained it for years. Anger at her father, her mother and Raj. Fury at Michael, hatred of her relations, disgust at herself: especially herself; her lack of courage and conviction, her acceptance of what she knew to be wrong in order to be safe.

She knows she should never have married Raj. Nirmala tried to warn her, but she was scared of the unknown. She has offered herself up, like a blank page, allowing other people to write their history over her while writing none of her own. By trading fear for certainty, she has enslaved herself.

Her statement of individuality has come too late. How could she ever have imagined that a change of clothes would reverse the nullity of her life? It was a pathetic gesture, one that emphasised her weakness and made her vulnerable. Disgusted by her foolishness and consumed with self-hatred, she begins to tear at the clothes, not bothering with buttons or fastenings, but ripping them apart, venting her fury against them.

Weeping, she pulls and rips and tears until, finally, she is naked, surrounded by tattered remnants of silk and netting. As she looks down at herself, another wave of shock breaks over her and, once again, she can feel Michael's fingers probing her body.

She scrabbles at herself with her nails, inflicting scratches and bleeding weals as she tears at the imprint of his hands. She would tear the flesh from her bones if she could, but his touch cannot be erased. He did not rape her but, nonetheless, she feels violated. His actions only confirm what she has long feared: she has no mastery over herself, but is merely a thing to be possessed.

Then, as suddenly as it appeared, the shock vanishes and she feels nothing. Becalmed, surrounded by stillness and silence, she returns to the level flatness of normality, without movement or direction. She is sticky and hot, her legs and arms smeared with blood, the skin on her face salty and tight with dried tears. For now, the storm is over. Exhausted, she walks slowly to the bathroom where she turns on the bath tap, watching, mesmerised, as cold water gushes into the tub carrying with it small, hard fragments of rust that settle in the bottom of the bath.

Turning off the tap, she stirs the red sediment with her finger. Fragments of rust swirl up lazily, then sink back to their original position. They will feel hard and gritty against her skin, but she does not care, has not the energy to drain the water and start again. Lowering herself into the bath, she immerses herself completely, allowing the water to close over her face like a shroud.

***

Her skin is cool, the water having absorbed the heat of her body. She wishes it would do the same for her thoughts but, at the back of her mind, a storm cloud is gathering. All the anger and disappointment, stealthily growing over many years, are merging into a single, explosive mass.

She must dispel the shadow in her head before it overwhelms her. She rises from the bath, wraps herself in a towel, and steps into the corridor. Warm, airless and without light, it is filled with watchful gloom. From the wall, the ghostly faces of her family look down from their sepia photographs.

Her heart jolts. What she has created is not a living album, as she had supposed, but a memorial, a faded catacomb in which pictures of dead people are categorised by date and arranged in rows, one above the other. Everywhere she is surrounded by death, the house reeks of it; dead people, dead hopes, dead dreams.

She is a captive to the past because her future was stillborn, necessity having propelled her into a convenient marriage without any notion of love. Those photographs, so neatly arranged, are not a celebration of her family but her way of mourning what she could not have. She has sealed herself into a mausoleum of her own making.

Her temples ache. Her head feels as if it will burst. The storm has returned and is about to break. She runs from the pictures, along the corridor, into the hallway where she finds Arjun, stooping over the discarded remnants of her clothes, gathering them up in his arms.

"What happened? Are you all right?"

He looks concerned. He has no right to be. Her anger gathers itself up, then surges forth, carrying with it the detritus of pain and disappointment; a screaming tide that breaks over his head like a wave.

"You bastard. How dare you?"

He wants to ask her what she means but, stunned by this sudden onslaught, the words lie frozen on his tongue. He just stares at her, open-mouthed, stupid with shock.

"How dare you ask if I am all right? After what you have done. Sleeping with that woman. Because of you, her boyfriend tried to rape me today."

"No."

"Is that all you can say?" she screams.

He looks so stupid, standing there, still clutching the shreds of netting and silk as if he were making her an offering. She hates him. She hates all the men who have suffocated and tortured her. He represents them all. That stupid, innocent look on his face, so boyish and pleading. He is worse than all the rest because he has breached the wall around her heart, creating a window through which, for a moment, she saw daylight and breathed the air of life, only to have it snatched away again.

She hates him and now he will know how much. Quickened by fury, she flings herself at him, slapping him hard across the face, then pummelling him with her fists. He does not resist, just stands there with tears running down his face, so she hits him harder, digging her nails into his skin. She wants to tear him apart. Furiously, she strikes him on the face, the chest, the arms, anywhere she can. Then, as if roused from a dream, he catches her wrists. Like Michael. That's what he did. She begins to scream.

"Shh, Neleni. It's all right."

He tries to put his arms around her, to comfort her, but she sees, not Arjun, but Michael. Maddened with fear, she fights him off.

"No, no!"

As she struggles, the towel in which she is swathed works itself loose and falls to the ground. He releases her wrists and she stands in front of him, naked, gasping for breath. Neither of them moves, waiting to see what the other will do. Then, suddenly, it happens, without warning.

They are kissing, as hungry as two flames: flickering, burning brighter than the whitest light, melting with the intensity of their own heat. Writhing, caressing, tearing at each other's flesh, a roiling mix of tenderness and violence, they fall to the floor. And he is inside her. Pushing. Harder and harder. She screams. Her legs apart, the soles of her feet pressed against the cool, stone floor. Then, in a glorious release of energy, she comes and the last drop of her pain is released.

Afterwards, he rests his head on her arm as she kisses the tears from his face. They do not talk, do not need to, because they can read the thoughts in each other's eyes. Then, after kissing with lazy passion, they sleep: she on her back, her head pillowed on his shoulder, their bodies entwined on the cool, blood-red floor.

Part 4: 1957
A prayer

Last night, Sriya and Asoka took their usual walk beside the paddy and, for many minutes, stared in silence at the shadow of the hare on the moon's face. Then, standing on tiptoe, Sriya whispered something in Asoka's ear. He laughed and tenderly kissed her face, wrapping one arm around her waist and cradling her head with the other, as if to protect her from a cold wind. He laughed a lot after that and, when they went to bed, he kissed her again, stroking her hair as one does a child. Whatever she told him made him both fearful and proud.

***

It is a Poya day: the full-moon time of the month when devout Buddhists everywhere cease their ordinary business and go to the temple to pray. In years to come, Poya days will be the cause of further tension between the Island's nationalists and its non-Buddhist community.

Every month, by order of the Government, all Islanders, whether Buddhist or not, will be obliged to respect Poya days. Shops will close, all trading will cease and offices will shut. For non-Buddhists, it will be impossible to do business, either locally or with customers from abroad. Like the Sinhalese language, Poya days will be transformed into symbols of political mastery. However, at present, Poya days are simply occasions for religious observance, a welcome respite from the hard labour of tending the fields.

Sriya has risen early in order to accompany her mother to the temple. After washing, they dress in clean white saris, like those worn by widows. Sriya's father, who rose even earlier, has returned from the tank with a basketful of blue water hyacinths which he has placed outside in the shade in a bucket of river water to keep them fresh. Once they have dressed, Sriya and her mother clean the flowers carefully, washing them in purified water then, after cutting off the longer stems, they arrange the blooms on two paper trays. These are offerings for the Buddha.

The temple is only a few minutes' walk from the village along a track shaded by coconut palms. As she walks beside her mother, Sriya savours the cool morning air. A flock of green parrots rise from the branches as they pass, screeching and chattering with excitement. The sun glints overhead, its rays scattered, lighting whatever falls within their narrow scope: the hairy trunk of a palm; a patch of red earth; a wasp hovering between the trees, its wings streaming gold.

The women turn a corner. The temple appears before them; its walls and stupas searingly white against the dark mantle of the forest. Sriya and her mother mount the steps with crowds of other worshippers arriving to celebrate Poya day. Although it is still early, they have to queue to make their offering. The crowd squirms and squeezes, carrying the women forward until, eventually, they are pushed before the altar where they place their flowers on a mounting layer of lotus blossom, water hyacinth, jasmine and frangipani. The scent is so overpowering that Sriya becomes dizzy. Concentrating on the flame of a candle, she steadies herself, and, clasping her hands together, quietly recites the prayer that accompanies flower offerings.

Then she offers a prayer of her own, for the safety of the child that is now growing within her, so small that it sleeps, curled up in her womb like a lotus bud. Worshippers are still arriving and those at the altars are being jostled and crushed by the pressure of the queue. Sriya stumbles and, for a second, the world around her becomes dark. Her mother catches her arm before she falls and, assisted by other pilgrims, they are helped to the door where, sitting on the base of a pillar, Sriya begins to revive.

"What is the matter, child? Are you ill?"

"No, Amma."

Sriya blushes and looks away. Her mother smiles and pats her shoulder. She needs no further explanation.

"Come, let us make an offering at the Bo tree, then you can go home."

Making their way through the crowds, the two women queue at a stall selling votary lamps. Each lamp has a wick made of pure white linen and most are filled with coconut oil; not the sort used for cooking, but a special, purified oil used for offerings. These are made in the courtyard where a wall, with recesses for the lamps, has been built around the base of the temple's sacred Bo tree. The wall is already hot with the heat from many flames and, fearing that this might cause her daughter to faint, Chandra leads her to a place where fewer lights are burning. Together, they offer up the prayers for light offerings.

Camphor is burning in ceremonial lamps and, now and again, Sriya catches the scent of its fragrant smoke, wafted out by the constant movement of pilgrims. All around them, worshippers are softly chanting their prayers, making offerings in the hope of gaining merit so that, after death, they may be released from the toils of this world.

Sriya had hoped that Asoka would accompany her to the temple today but, when she made the suggestion, he had seemed unwilling, almost nervous. She did not pursue the matter, supposing that his reluctance has something to do with his past life.

Chandra now leads her daughter towards the entrance, holding her arm and gently steering her through the crowd of worshippers. They descend the steps, brushing past a steady stream of pilgrims passing in the opposite direction. For a second, they are engulfed by a gentle press of warm flesh, a murmur of prayers, the combined scent of hair oil and flowers. Then, quite suddenly, they are released onto the pavement. Crossing the street into the shade, they walk slowly back to the village, wrapped up in their own thoughts, companionable and happy. Having passed the bend in the road, they see a familiar figure walking towards them, its shoulders bowed as if by a great weight.

Since Tissa's disappearance, Sriya has only seen his mother a couple of times and then, only from a distance. She waved and called on both occasions but, on receiving no response, had assumed that Manju did not see her.

They draw close to the stooping figure and, as they pass within a few feet of each other, Sriya turns to speak, but the greeting dies on her lips. With a look of disgust, Manju turns her head away, pulling her scarf over her face as if to shield herself from sight.

Sriya hesitates, stops, then makes a move towards Manju, intending to cross the street and talk to her, but her mother pulls her back.

"No," she hisses. "Let her go. She does not want to speak to you."

"Why? Surely, she doesn't blame me?"

It has never occurred to Sriya that she might be blamed for Tissa's disappearance. He took a different path long before she agreed to marry Asoka. He changed and became unrecognisable as the boy she grew up with. She saw it on that day returning from the paddy field and has assumed that others saw it, too. Obviously not. Parents are blind, none more so than those who are desperate.

Sriya looks back over her shoulder. Further down the road, Tissa's mother has turned and is staring at her with a look of undisguised venom. Stunned, Sriya clings to her mother's arm, like a child seeking protection.

"She hates me," she whispers, her eyes brimming with tears.

"Just ignore her."

"But why?"

"She's half mad. Probably always was. I always thought, when she married that man ... Well, never mind."

"Have I done that to her? Is it my fault?"

"No, of course not. People always have to blame someone else for their misfortunes. Don't worry. Tissa will come home soon and then she'll forget all about it. Besides, you have something far more important to think about. Am I right?"

She squeezes her daughter's arm affectionately.

"Yes, Amma. You're right."

Smiling, Sriya rests her head on her mother's shoulder. Folding her arms protectively around her daughter, Chandra prays that Sriya will not hear the other gossip that is circulating in the village.

***

Without moving, Manju continues to watch Chandra and Sriya as they embrace, then walk slowly away along the road, in the direction of the village. For a second, as she held her daughter in her arms, Chandra stared defiantly at Tissa's mother, as if to say: "What are you looking at? It's not my fault. It's not my fault that your son has left you and your life is in ruins."

After her son's disappearance, Manju's heart was consumed with rage, a burning hot flame that has left only ashes and a bitter stain in the space once occupied by love. Summoning the anger that now fills the hollow pit of her heart, she directs it at Sriya and her mother, hurling it at their backs, infecting them with her hatred. Of course, they feel nothing. One never feels the full force of a curse at the moment of its making: only later, when it has taken root, strangling hope with its poisonous tendrils.

Having momentarily expelled her venom, Manju feels cleansed, but she knows this relief is only temporary. Soon, the corrosive anger will seep back, filling her up with its bile.

To the side of her, just out of sight, something slides through the undergrowth, rustling the dead leaves that lie in its path. She listens, her pulse throbbing. A snake. She grew up fearing them, but now something inside her calls to them. She longs to touch them, caress them, to slough off her human skin and join them; then she would be free, of care, of love, of pain, answering only to her serpentine nature and the god she worships. But, first, there is something she must do.

Pulling her scarf tightly about her face, she begins to walk in the direction of the temple. Villagers, returning from their prayers, greet her, but she only replies with a nod of the head, not wishing to be drawn into conversation.

It is not difficult to avoid talking these days; in fact, other people seem relieved by her unwillingness to communicate. Words are little comfort to one whose life consists only of tragedy. There is a limit to the amount of sympathy that can be given, or received, and words of commiseration become mechanical and insincere. But soon, that will change. Sympathy will be needed in another quarter.

Manju bows her head as she passes the temple, not from respect, but from a desire not to be seen. She will make an offering today, but not here. Nestling in her hand, wrapped in a soft white cloth, she can feel the smooth outline of a chicken's egg. Afraid of dropping it, she clutches it to her. There are still several miles to go before she reaches her destination.

From a vantage point in the hills, the cave-temple can be seen from miles away, a tiny speck in the forest, gleaming white in the sun, its courtyard shaded by a sacred Bo tree, its smooth, plastered walls contrasting with the rough face of the cliff into which it is set. Tiled roofs and colonnades are the façade for a series of caves, some natural, some carved from the rock many centuries ago.

Huge images of the Buddha have been carved into the cliff, their faces worn away with age and blackened with lichen, yet the shrine overlays a more ancient site of worship, one that has never been eradicated, although it has been submerged, and which is now forcing its way back up to the light, like a hardy plant covered by a flagstone.

From the courtyard, a set of broad stone steps descends to the entrance of the temple; two gigantic wooden doors, studded with iron, with a great rusting latch and a keyhole the size of a child's hand. To step inside is like entering a well: the glaring sun is blotted out and weary feet meet the coolness of stone. On painted floors, deer and hare leap over a carpet of lotus while, overhead, a bed of lilies floats across the ceiling.

The natural hollows and swellings of the oldest chambers have been incorporated in the painted canopy: religious symmetry imposed on nature's irregularity. In red, white, yellow and black, geometrical patterns cover every inch of the ceiling.

Recesses, carved from the rock, house effigies of the Buddha; some sitting, some reclining, their skin of gold-leaf reflecting the light from scores of votive lamps. Offerings of fresh flowers are piled before them; blue lotus, sweet jasmine, handfuls of pink and yellow frangipani which lie alongside everlasting lotus blossom stitched together from patches of coloured cotton.

Yet, in the oldest chamber, there is a different image: that of Hooniyam, god of sorcery, a flaming brand in one hand, a sword in the other, a serpent clasped between his lips. Two figures stand before the god: a woman, her face thin and lined with grief, and an elderly priest, deaf and half blind.

"What is the name?"

The woman mutters something which the priest does not hear.

"Say it again," he commands, tetchily.

"Asoka."

The woman looks fierce.

"Ah."

The priest is holding an egg in one hand. He writes a word in pencil on the shell.

"And the other name?"

"Rajaguru".

At the mention of the second name, there is a slight movement in the doorway. Unseen by the worshippers, a figure has slipped into the chamber and, from a hiding place in the shadows, is observing the ritual with interest.

The priest scratches another word on the egg while the woman looks on, her face contorted with fury. Taking the woman's right hand, the priest places the egg in her palm and gently folds her fingers over it so that it should not fall to the floor. Then, still holding her hand, he begins to intone a prayer in a loud voice.

Oh Lord Hooniyam, god and king of demons,
Avenge this woman's son, Tissa.

Punish the man who stole his woman and took for himself the marriage that was
promised.
Seek out the thief and make him suffer.
Afflict him with disease,
Cut out his heart,
Scorch him with fire,
Let his name be wiped from memory.
Restore this woman's son by visiting justice on the evil-doer.

As the old man finishes the prayer, a sudden gust of cool air blows through the chamber, momentarily causing the lamps to gutter. The woman shudders, thinking she has heard something; the faint hissing of a snake. Every sinew stiffens as she listens, trying to recapture the sound but, deep in the heart of the cliff, there is only silence. It was probably air, sucked through a fissure in the rock. Caves as old as these are full of drafts and thermals. They have a life and a climate of their own.

The priest holds the woman's hand aloft, then releases it.

"Now," he whispers.

With all her force, the woman flings the egg at the base of Hooniyam's statue, where it shatters in a mess of yolk and shell. Somewhere in her head, a voice shouts triumphantly: her son will be avenged. Bowing her head, the woman allows herself to be led out of the chamber by the old priest.

***

After the priest and the woman have left, the figure of a man steps silently from the shadows. Hooniyam releases the hand that has been firmly clamped around the head of his favourite serpent, keeping its jaws tightly closed.

"You nearly gave the game away there. Hissing like a damned kettle. What's wrong with you?"

Raising its head, the snake nuzzles Hooniyam's cheek, its tongue flickering in and out of its mouth, as if whispering in his ear.

"Exciting," murmurs the god. "You're right there. It's very exciting. Until now that unbeliever has been protected by his wife's prayers. I couldn't touch him. But now, I've had a direct request to intervene. No god can be blamed for responding to a prayer for help. What luck! And what a coincidence! That woman is the mother of our new recruit, the young fellow who led the fighting at Gal Oya."

Sensing the onset of a monologue, the snake acts quickly. Its tongue flickers as it nudges Hooniyam's cheek, then points its flat head at the statue.

"Oh, all right. Just this once. I haven't got much taste for the stuff myself, especially after it's been on the floor. Off you go!"

Lifting the serpent from his girdle, Hooniyam lowers it gently to the ground where it slithers across to the base of the statue and laps contentedly at the broken egg.

"That old priest was quite good. Funny! He seems familiar."

Hooniyam scratches his matted head as he tries to remember where he saw the old man before. In fact, he is the same old priest that Hooniyam nearly cursed at the city shrine a few months ago. If the snake had eyebrows, it would raise them in disbelief. It is amazing how forgetful gods can be! Suddenly, the creature seems to have trouble swallowing: its throat vibrates rapidly and it makes a strange choking sound. Fortunately for the snake, Hooniyam does not realise that his pet has mastered the art of laughter.

402

He has done it. Mr Bandaranaike watches as the man in the pale suit climbs into the back of his chauffeur-driven car and, as he does so, the Prime Minister notes how the back of the man's jacket is crumpled and stained with perspiration. It looks as if he has lived in that jacket for a week although it looked quite fresh when he arrived a few hours ago for their meeting. And what a meeting it has been, conducted with the utmost secrecy, with almost the thrill of a romantic assignation but with much greater significance.

Not even Mr Bandaranaike's Cabinet knew of the meeting and he found it peculiarly exciting to act on his own initiative, unhindered by the constant bickering of his ministers. He wonders how they will react when he tells them what he has done. He has a sudden stab of unease in the pit of his stomach, especially when he thinks of Vimala Wijewardene and her sponsor, Buddharakkita Thera.

Buddharakkita has also been Mr Bandaranaike's patron, helping to organise the campaign that won him the election: a fact that he is never allowed to forget. But he is Prime Minister now, he has to put personal loyalties behind him and act for the good of the country. Surely, Buddharakkita will understand that. But something in his heart tells him that he will not.

The car drives slowly past and the man inside waves discreetly, not wishing to draw attention to himself, but he is smiling, the Prime Minister can see that. A smile of triumph. He has achieved everything he wanted and the members of his party will receive him as a hero.

Mr Bandaranaike wonders what the members of his own party will say when they find out. It is unlikely that they will receive the news with much enthusiasm. Of course, the extremists will grumble, they always do, but the moderates will accept it – in time.

The Prime Minister waves back at the man in the car thinking how strange it is that, after all this time, there is an imperceptible bond between them. They were acquaintances at school and, all these years later, despite the fact that they have gone their separate ways, they still speak the same language, not Tamil or Sinhalese, but the language used by people who share a common background, one determined by education, social status and wealth.

Extraordinary. They come from different races and are at opposite ends of the political spectrum but Mr Bandaranaike can still communicate more openly with his friend, Mr. Chelvanayakam, than many of the people in his own party. It has proved to be a blessing.

***

The Tamils in the North and East are becoming increasingly vociferous. Disillusioned by their exclusion from government and frustrated by the passing of the Sinhala Only Act which threatens to impose Sinhalese as the official language of the State, the Tamils have begun to organise themselves, demanding recognition of their own language as well as control of local government in areas where they are in the majority. For their spokesman, they have chosen the leader of the Federal Party, Mr Chelvanayakam who, by sheer serendipity, is also an old school friend of the Prime Minister.

When the Tamils threatened satyagraha if their needs were not met, Mr Bandaranaike knew that he must do something. Only a few years ago, Gandhi ousted the British from India by employing the same tactic. Although peaceful, these mass protests can bring a country to its knees. Unless Mr Bandaranaike deflects the Tamils from their intended action, he will face humiliation and, ultimately, loss of power. So, he has employed a strategy which has served him well in the past: appeasement. And Chelvanayakam has become his ally.

Several secret meetings have taken place. The two politicians have discussed and argued, sometimes hotly; but always in a good-natured, gentlemanly way, much in the manner of a school debate. Eventually, they drafted an agreement. Tamil would remain the official language of the administration in the north and east where Tamils would continue to govern their own affairs through regional councils. The Government would also promise to preserve the Tamil majority in these regions by not introducing Sinhalese colonists into areas of new development.

Like all gentlemen's agreements, the deal has been finalised over a glass of whisky and a cigar. It is a pact that will seal the fate of the country, although not in the way that its makers expect.

**

Mr Bandaranaike whistles softly on his way back to the house. It has all been remarkably easy. The Tamils will be happy, there will be no satyagraha and both his position and the country will be safe. All in all, a good day's work. As he walks, Mr Bandaranaike stretches out his arms and takes a deep breath of evening air and, as he does so, he catches the faint scent of a temple tree.

The abbot of Kelaniya is pacing the room which he refers to as his study. In truth, there is little about it of monastic austerity and it bears more of a resemblance to a luxurious sitting-room than a monk's cell. There are paintings on the walls, large comfortable chairs, a sideboard containing a soda siphon, crystal tumblers and several bottles of premium malt whisky and, in front of the window, a huge oak desk, highly polished with a leather-bound blotter and a black bakolite telephone.

Without knowing to whom the room belongs, anyone entering here would guess its occupant to be a man of status and influence, a businessman, perhaps, or a politician and they would be right on both counts. For, although he is a man of religion, Buddharakkita is also a man of the world. Today, he views that world with a cynical eye, as a businessman whose affairs have entered the doldrums.

Up and down, up and down, he paces the room for the hundredth time, like a caged tiger that has not eaten for several days. A newspaper is lying on a chair where he has thrown it in disgust. The sight of the front page makes him curse. It purports to announce some historic news: the Bandaranaike-Chelvanayakam pact.

Snatching up the paper, Buddharakkita re-reads the story, if it can be called that, for all the newspapers are Government-controlled and publish only what they are told; but it does not matter in this case. In fact, it actually confirms the truth of the story. The Prime Minister has done a deal with the Tamils without telling anyone, not even his Cabinet because, if he had, Buddharakkita would have known about it. His friend and protégée, Vimala Wijewardene, the Minister of Health, would have seen to that, calling him discreetly from her home, talking to him over the big black telephone on his desk. He does not doubt her integrity. She has always been loyal to him, showing her gratitude for all he has done. Unlike the Prime Minister.

Now he comes to think of it, he has never trusted Bandaranaike whose reasons for converting to Buddhism have always seemed suspect to a man of Buddharakkita's instinctive perception. There has always been an uneasiness about their alliance that the abbot has never been quite able to explain. Their dealings with each other have always been marked by a certain cautiousness, each treading warily around the other, careful not to give too much away.

Yet, it was Bandaranaike who approached the abbot for help. Back in the days when no-one would support his cause and he had no hope of winning the election, it was Buddharakkita he turned to. And with what results! Together, they were invincible but, of late, Buddharakkita has found it increasingly difficult to get an audience with the Prime Minister. He cannot even reach him on his private telephone. Now he knows why. Mr Bandaranaike has been forging a new alliance, one that, if he had known about it, Buddharakkita would have done everything in his power to prevent.

Buddharakkita crushes the paper between his hands, as if to squeeze the offending words from the front page, then he hurls it at the wall. All along, that little weasel has been planning to betray him. Having promoted Vimala to the Cabinet in order to repay his debt to the abbot, the Prime Minister thinks he is now free to do as he pleases, without consulting anyone, especially his old ally Buddharakkita. Well, he is wrong.

Walking over to the window which overlooks the monastery grounds, the abbot pauses for a moment. Below, novice monks are tending the garden and sweeping the paths in readiness for the daily influx of the faithful. He feels a surge of pride. Long before its power ebbed under the missionary influence of the Europeans, Kelaniya played an important role in affairs of state: founded by kings, its abbots had been mentors to royalty. Now, following a period of decline, the monastery has been restored to its former grandeur, largely due to the patronage of Vimala's family and, while the last abbot oversaw the restoration of its fabric, Buddharakkita has pledged himself to rebuild its influence.

But Bandaranaike's Government, the one that he, Buddharakkita, helped to power, is obstructing his progress. The pact with the Tamils is only the latest in a series of setbacks. Just as lethal to Buddharakkita's ambitions is a Bill currently being discussed by Parliament. Presented by another of the Prime Minister's favourites, a left-wing MP called Philip Gunawardane, the Paddy Lands Bill seeks to increase the rights of tenant farmers at the expense of landowners.

Thanks to the generosity of Vimala's mother-in-law, Kelaniya has a substantial acreage of paddy land. With a view to increasing his income, the abbot is already engaged in a legal tussle in order to get direct control of this land and, more importantly, its revenue. Buddharakkita is no supporter of the Paddy Lands Bill.

Pausing in his reflections, the abbot glances at a letter which lies open on his desk. He stares at it thoughtfully, picks it up, then reads it for the fifth time. Mr Jayawardene, leader of the Opposition party, wishes to meet the abbot. *At your earliest convenience*, the letter says. Of course, Mr Jayawardene is a Buddhist politician so there is nothing extraordinary in this request, except for the fact that everyone knows the abbot to be an outspoken supporter of the ruling party and its leader, Mr Bandaranaike. In theory, the abbot and Mr Jayawardene are from opposing sides.

With the letter in his hand, the abbot returns to the window, staring across the gardens to where a steady stream of pilgrims is already beginning to trickle through the gates. He can command their loyalty, in their hundreds and thousands. If he can put a weakling like Bandaranaike into power then why not someone else, or even himself? He smiles, musing on what it would be like to be the first Buddhist monk to lead a nation.

But, of course, it would be ridiculous. His brother abbots would have something to say about that. Eyebrows have already been raised at the level of his involvement with the ruling party. It is not so much that they mind him being involved in politics, they all are to some extent, it is the fact that he does it so conspicuously. Monks should play a passive role. It is perfectly acceptable for them to give advice when it is asked for, but not so seemly for that advice to be given when it is not. By openly dabbling in politics, Buddharakkita has crossed an invisible line.

As one old abbot tried to warn him: "The Sword of State has two sharp edges, one pointing at your enemy and one at yourself."

Buddharakkita had laughed, congratulating the old man on his wit as he patted him on the back, but the old monk had turned away, muttering to himself: "Buddharakkita is a fool."

To some extent, the old man was right. The Sword of State is something to be feared. But, in truth, it is the lesser danger. The real peril lies in the one who wields it. Several shrines now bear the image of a new god, hideous in appearance with bloody tusks and matted hair. Girded with serpents, it is he who holds the Sword of State in his hands. That god is Hooniyam.

1957: Stone, paper, scissors

Among the novice monks, carefully sweeping the paths of Kelaniya's gardens, are two new arrivals: one, a man with a lean, feline face; the other, a boy with wild eyes whose nervous, jerky movements are out of keeping with the calm of the monastery. He is constantly looking over his shoulder as if expecting someone to creep up stealthily behind him. If surprised, he will become angry and clench his fists, as if resisting the desire to strike out. It is obvious to everyone that he is disturbed and, probably, capable of violence. Some of the monks have dared to question the presence of these two men in the monastery, but they have been told that the abbot wills it. That is reason enough.

"Brother Anil!"

A young boy in saffron robes, no older than twelve or thirteen, is running down the path towards the two newcomers.

"Brother Anil. The abbot wishes to see you immediately."

Straightening his back, the man leans on his broom and gazes steadily at the boy. The man's amber eyes make the child shudder. He did not want this task. With youthful intuition, he fears these two men, but one does not make excuses to the abbot and there was no-one else to deliver the message.

With quiet deliberation, the man lays down his broom and addresses his companion.

"Stay here."

Then, leaning closer so that the child cannot hear, he adds:

"Stay out of trouble."

Mumbling, the younger man nods and lowers his head but not before shooting a glance at the child that convinces the latter that he is in the presence of a madman: such staring, bloodshot eyes, almost bolting from their sockets. In all his sheltered life, the boy has never seen anyone like this. Instinctively, he knows that this man is capable of sudden, irrational moods and must be avoided; but it is the other one he really fears: the man with the cool, calculating eyes.

Dutifully leading the way, the boy scuttles a few feet in front of Anil, all the way back to the building. As they step inside, Anil puts a firm hand on the boy's shoulder and pushes him aside.

"I know the way."

The child pauses a second, then runs off, eager to escape the quiet menace that has accompanied him from the garden. Crossing the hallway, Anil threads his way through a maze of corridors until he reaches a new extension to the building which houses the abbot's apartment. Softly climbing the stairs, he raps on the abbot's door.

"Come in."

Anil enters, quietly shutting the door behind him. The abbot is staring out of the window, a letter in one hand, a glass of whisky in the other.

"Brother Anil."

Buddharakkita Thera turns to greet his guest. Anil notes that the abbot is wearing a dark suit, not saffron robes; indicating a visit, incognito, to a female friend.

"My lord."

Anil bows, his hands pressed together; a greeting that resembles prayer.

"I wish to ask your advice on a certain matter."

The abbot smiles. He is a large man with a jovial face, but his eyes are shrewd.

"My lord, I am a simple monk. I have little knowledge of the world."

Buddharakkita snorts.

"Don't fool with me, man. I know your history. Why do you think I had you transferred here from that other, sleepy monastery – a place fit for old men but not someone with your ability? You may be posing as a novice but we both know what you are."

The abbot's smile has disappeared. His eyes glitter like flint. Anil knows better than to anger a man as powerful as Buddharakkita. He bows low, in submission.

"Forgive me, lord. I meant no disrespect."

"Hmmm."

The abbot gives him an appraising look. He is one of the few men not to feel the menace of those amber eyes.

"How can I help, lord?"

"You know of my support for the Prime Minister?"

"There are few who do not."

"And you have heard the news of his pact with the Tamils?"

Anil does not speak, but his face becomes pale and angry.

"I see you have. I also see that you feel as I do."

For a moment, there is silence between them, then the abbot takes a sip of whisky and turns back to the window. He seems to consider his words for a minute then, turning back to face Anil, he brandishes the letter in his hand.

"Today, I received a letter from the leader of the Opposition, Mr Jayawardene, requesting a meeting. The letter says no more than that. Why do you suppose that the leader of the Opposition would seek a meeting with me, the Prime Minister's staunch supporter?"

Anil chooses his words carefully.

"Mr Jayawardene used to be the Member of Parliament for this district, for Kelaniya, until he was unseated at the last election by your candidate. Perhaps he has an eye on re-election and wishes to ingratiate himself. You have proved yourself to be a powerful patron, my lord."

"You mean he wishes to pay a courtesy call?"

"That is one possibility, lord."

"Is there another?"

Anil hesitates. The abbot knows much about him, probably sympathises with his views, but they have never openly discussed politics before. As he looks around the room, Anil spots the crumpled newspaper lying on the floor. He knows what story occupies the front page. He has read it himself. The sight of that paper, crushed in rage, then discarded, encourages him to speak freely.

"Perhaps, lord, Mr Jayawardene feels as you do about the Prime Minister's pact with the Tamils."

"And what of his request to see me?"

"It is a meeting, lord. What harm can it do?"

"And if he asks for my help? What then?"

"The interests of the nation come first. Not those of a single man. Or his personal interests."

The meaning of Anil's last words is not lost on the abbot, who stares at the monk through eyelids that have narrowed to slits.

"Do those words refer to me?"

"They refer to every man who would see this country run by the Sinhalese," replies Anil, boldly.

Despite his earlier irritation, the abbot laughs.

"You answer well, brother. And, for the most part, you are right. Now leave me. I wish to think."

Anil bows, then melts from the room like a shadow, leaving Buddharakkita Thera staring thoughtfully at the letter in his hand. He reads it again, then again, trying to extract meaning from every word, willing it to speak to him, reveal its intent. Surely there are hidden messages here, if only one knew how to decipher them.

The abbot re-reads the letter, turning it around in his hand, even holding it up to the light. But, apart from the written words, the paper is blank. There is no code, no invisible writing. The message is short and simple. Mr Jayawardene, leader of the Opposition, requests an audience with the abbot. No more than that.

The abbot paces up and down the room, past the crumpled newspaper. He gives it a contemptuous kick, then stoops to pick it up. He hurries to the desk where he flattens the paper out with fleshy, eager hands. He remembers reading something. Where was it? A single line. A quote. From Mr Jayawardene who, it seems, is fervently opposed to the Prime Minister's pact with the Tamils. Yes. Here it is. He was not dreaming.

Frantically, he searches the waste-bin for the envelope which bore the letter. There is no date-stamp. It was delivered this morning. By hand. This is the sign for which he was seeking. A letter that was delivered, in a hurry, on the same day that news of the Pact was announced to the nation. Mr Jayawardene is not interested in courtesy calls. He has other, more pressing matters to discuss with the abbot.

Buddharakkita drains his glass and pours himself another whisky. Is it a trick? Mr Jayawardene has reason to dislike the abbot. He has not only been unseated by Buddharakkita's candidate, but he is also the nephew of Vimala Wijewardene and he has made it clear, on several occasions, that he disapproves of her friendship with the abbot. Leaning his elbows on the desk, Buddharakkita kneads his temples, trying to remember everything he has heard or read about Mr Jayawardene.

***

Mr Jayawardene's upbringing has not been dissimilar to that of his opponent, Mr Bandaranaike. Both the Jayawardene and Bandaranaike families rose to positions of prominence through close association with the British. Both men were raised as Christians and, in adulthood, converted to Buddhism. Both trained as lawyers and are well-connected: Mr Jayawardene, having married an heiress, now lives in the most exclusive part of Colombo in a house quaintly named 'Braemar'.

Coming from such a privileged background, neither man, initially, had popular appeal. Nonetheless, Mr Bandaranaike has won the country's heart, winning votes from the most underprivileged parts of society. It is a lesson which Mr Jayawardene hopes to emulate. He must simply find a trigger, a hook by which he can latch onto the masses.

And there is something else. Something that the abbot and Mr Jayawardene have in common. A strange coincidence. Rice, the staple of the Ceylonese diet, has played a significant role in the destiny of both men: Buddharakkita's fortunes depend on gaining direct control of the paddy land left to the monastery by old Mrs Wijewardene and, more importantly, the revenue from the rice crop; while Mr Jayawardene's career has been so severely compromised over the subject of rice that, at one point, it looked as if he would have to retire from politics altogether.

As Finance Minister for the previous Government, Mr Jayawardene was under pressure to curb its mounting expenditure. What better way than to cut the rice subsidies. Millions of rupees could be saved at a stroke. But this plan only served to emphasise the gulf between Junius R. Jayawardene, lawyer and son of a judge, and the country's poor whose livelihood depended on Government rice subsidies. In 1953, Mr Jayawardene's radical proposals caused near revolt. A hartal, or general strike, was called, forcing the country to its knees and Mr Jayawardene to reverse his policy.

It was a shattering blow followed, three years later, by the overwhelming election victory of Mr Bandaranaike's rival party. After that, it seemed as if Mr Jayawardene would be consigned to political obscurity. His career was becalmed, apparently beyond resurrection. But Mr Jayawardene is a fighter, the sort Buddharakkita admires.

***

Standing at the open window, the abbot closes his eyes for a minute and lets the warm breeze play across his face. There is a murmur of voices from the path below. As they approach, they grow louder, then softer, passing into the distance. Two novices discussing lessons. The abbot recognises each by his voice. The warm air carries a faint whiff of curry leaves, pungent and aromatic. Someone is tending the vegetable garden. The abbot often catches the scent of herbs from his window.

Buddharakkita lets his mind wander then, opening his eyes, holds the letter up to the window and inspects the writing. The text has been battered out on a typewriter but Mr Jayawardene has signed his name in ink. Large, powerful letters slope across the page.

What does this letter say about the man?

Certainly, he is bold. The fact that he has approached Buddharakkita, a stalwart sworn supporter of the Prime Minister, shows a certain kind of courage. It indicates a man prepared to chance rejection, even humiliation, on the off-chance of gaining a political advantage. He is prepared to take risks. It indicates either ruthless bravado or desperation.

But what would be the advantage to the abbot in this meeting? Buddharakkita thinks hard. Mr Jayawardene still has influence. He is a committed Buddhist and, if his quote in the newspaper is correct, someone who will not be afraid to openly defy the Government and oppose the pact with the Tamils. He might, therefore, be a useful opponent to the Prime Minister's favourite, Philip Gunawardane.

So far, the abbot has had little luck in his struggle to wrest control of the monastery's paddy lands from its trustees and Philip Gunawardane's new Bill makes his ownership of that land seem even more remote. The abbot has tried to elicit the Prime Minister's support but, so far, has been met with stony silence. He needs a new ally and Mr Jayawardene might be just the man. Through bitter experience, the ex-Minister of Finance understands the value of rice.

Buddharakkita smiles as he watches worshippers flowing in through the monastery's gates. With their help, he has put a Prime Minister into office. With their support, he can oust him from power. The abbot begins to wonder if, perhaps, it is time for a change.

Closing the window, he walks around the desk and, lifting the telephone from its cradle, dials the number written on Mr Jayawardene's letter.

1957: Old news

In a jungle village so small that its name is known only to its inhabitants, Sriya and Asoka are seated in the shade. She is reading to him from a newspaper. She has progressed well in the last few months and can read Sinhalese fluently although she is still slow and hesitates over a few of the longer words. Nevertheless, he is proud of her as only a husband can be when the woman that he loves has flourished under his care. The newspaper is a week old and its pages have turned crisp and yellow from where they have been left in the sun.

Asoka found the paper this morning, on the seat of a bus returning from town. Well-thumbed by many hands, it has been turned inside out, so that the front page is somewhere near the middle and several pages are missing, but he has still brought it home for his wife to read. The columns of advertisements on the matchmaking pages provide her with endless amusement, partly because they allow her to feel smug, her own future having been secured, partly because they afford a small insight into other people's lives.

For Sriya has an agility of imagination that surprises even her husband, allowing her to construct the most intricate stories on the basis of a few, sparse facts. He hopes that one day, in between the requirements of daily life and household chores, she will find the time to write, even if it should only be a few lines in a journal. She laughed at him when he first suggested it, looking at him with that steady peasant gaze that told him, even before she spoke, that she considered the idea frivolous.

"What should I write?" she asked. "Who would wish to read anything of my life?"

"That's not the point," he remonstrated. He then tried to explain how the experience of every life was unique, but she just laughed, shaking her head. He now keeps these ideas to himself, waiting for a time when she might prove more receptive.

"Asoka, Asoka!"

Her voice breaks in on his thoughts and he realises that he has not been listening to her reading.

"I'm sorry. What is it?"

"There's a story here. I think it might be important, but I'm not sure."

While he has been dreaming, she has re-arranged the pages of the newspaper and has discovered the article on the front page. Asoka leans closer. It is an excuse to slip his arm around her waist which is already beginning to lose its girl-like slimness, to stroke her belly with his hand, to feel its roundness and know that, within, his child is growing. He kisses her small brown ear, smells her hair, nuzzles her cheek. Her skin is soft and scented.

"What do you think?" she says, pointing anxiously to the article.

Still dazed with love, he peers over her shoulder. He can see a few words but nothing to catch his attention.

"Read it to me."

She sighs. Being a relatively slow reader, she hoped that he would read the article to her. He is so much quicker and, from the few sentences that she has already deciphered, she knows that this story is important. But Asoka does not relent. She reads the headline, then stumbles through the first paragraph. It is enough. Asoka gently prises the paper out of her hands and pores over it.

"My god!" he murmurs.

"Read it to me!" Sriya urges, tugging at his arm.

"All right."

He reads aloud, paraphrasing some of the article to cover it more quickly. The story is continued somewhere on the inside of the paper but, when Asoka turns to find the page, it is missing. Sighing with frustration, he closes the paper and returns to the front page. He re-reads it, incredulous.

"What does the man think he is doing?"

It is the first that they have heard of the pact made by the Prime Minister with the Tamil leader, Mr Chelvanayakam.

"What does it mean for us? Is it good or bad?"

"I'm not sure."

But he knows how he would have reacted a few months ago, before he met Sriya. And there are plenty of others who still think like that. It scares him.

"In principle, I think that this agreement could be good, but I also think that there are a lot of people who will see it as bad. They will be angry and afraid. That is the danger."

Then, seeing the anxiety on his wife's face, he pats her hand.

"It's all right. It's the sort of thing that politicians do, always making and unmaking alliances. They would tie themselves in knots if they could. Nothing for us to worry about."

She smiles, relieved and, taking the paper from him, turns back to the match-making pages, her mouth crinkling with amusement. But Asoka cannot so easily dismiss thoughts of this news. The more he thinks of it, the greater the danger becomes. The Prime Minister is walking a tight-rope. There are many extremists in his coalition. Surely they did not consent to this pact. And, if not? Asoka tries not to pursue thoughts of what may happen.

He rises from where he has been sitting next to Sriya and paces about the hard earth floor of the yard. He has finished most of his chores and there is little that needs doing at the moment, but he feels suddenly restless, disquieted by memories of the past.

"I am going to the fields," he announces.

"To do what?"

"To check the crops."

"Didn't you do that this morning?"

"Yes. But I want to check the perimeters. For pests."

Secretly, he hopes that Prema and some of the other men will be there and that, by conversing with them, ordinary concerns will drive away his anxiety. Sriya laughs, shaking her head. He's a strange one, but she knows better than to question him in one of these moods. He has less of them these days but, when he does, she leaves him alone. There are some demons that even she cannot challenge.

Asoka walks up and down once more, as if trying to make up his mind.

"I'm going," he says, softly, looking out across the yard towards the tops of the trees.

She smiles, but does not reply. He stoops to kiss her brow and feels love glowing within him.

1957: A private audience

It is now several months after news of the Prime Minister's pact with the Tamils first broke. So far, nothing has happened. The pact with the Tamils remains in place; at least in theory. For while it has not been revoked, neither has it been implemented. On the surface, everything is as calm as a paddy-pond. But, beneath, where the eye cannot penetrate, the political water is teeming with microscopic activity. Secret discussions are taking place, new relationships are being forged, former allies are changing sides. As yet undetected, there is a new undercurrent. The tide is beginning to run against the Prime Minister.

On the surface, Buddharakkita's support for Mr Bandaranaike appears solid. Yet he, too, has been seeking new alliances. Under his direction, diverse elements of the opposition have begun to coalesce, like drops of steady rain that first form puddles, then ponds, then rushing streams. But, all the time, Buddharakkita remains out of sight, covering his traces, using others to carry out his plans.

***

Anil has been called to the abbot's study. Buddharakkita is sitting at the desk with his back to the light dressed, this time, not in western clothes, but in the traditional saffron robes of a monk. They have not spoken more than a few words since their last meeting when Buddharakkita asked Anil what he thought about Mr Jayawardene's request for a meeting. Because he has heard nothing more, Anil assumes that the meeting did not take place. The conversation starts awkwardly.

"Are you happy here, my son?"

"Yes, my lord. Very happy."

Anil answers cautiously. Better not to say too much until he knows why the abbot has summoned him. One cannot be too careful what one says to Buddharakkita. He has a phenomenal memory and can remember the smallest details of a conversation months later, often to the detriment of the speaker. He would have made a good lawyer.

"Hmm."

The abbot has picked up a paper knife and is toying with it, balancing it between the fingers of both hands. He turns it this way and that, inspecting every detail of the delicately carved handle as he fires questions at Anil. Is it true that his father was an Ayurvedic doctor? What does he think of Western medicine? How do the two compare? Is his father still alive? Is he homesick? Anil replies, briefly, not knowing where this is leading, wondering if, indeed, any of it is relevant.

Then, the questions stop and the abbot, deep in thought, places the paper knife on the blotter, staring at it intently as he drums his fingers on the polished surface of the desk. The silence is so prolonged that Anil wonders if Buddharakkita has forgotten about him. Then, quite suddenly, the abbot looks up, his eyes narrowed into crafty slits, fixing Anil with a look of undisguised cunning.

"Mr Jayawardene is planning a pilgrimage to the Temple of the Tooth."

Anil frowns, unsure of the abbot's meaning. Buddharakkita leans forward, his elbows resting on the table, his hands raised with the fingers pressed together so that the lower half of his face is obscured. Only his eyes, twinkling under lowered lids, reveal his excitement. He speaks quietly, in the measured tone usually reserved for instructing students.

413

"As you know, the Temple has great significance for our people. It is the symbol of our religion, the beating heart of the Sinhalese nation. Like you, Mr Jayawardene has strong views on the pact with the Tamils. Like you, he believes that our people have been betrayed. He thinks that a pilgrimage to the Temple will help other people to express their opinions and that, perhaps, the Government will be persuaded to revise its policy."

Anil says nothing, although his heart is beating fast. The abbot's eyes do not leave him for a second.

"Of course, I do not say that I agree with Mr Jayawardene but, as this is a matter touching on religion, I believe that our monastery should send observers and I have chosen you for this task."

He speaks as if it was a minor event of no importance, but Anil knows that this is the beginning of something significant. After all the empty words and gestures, the political twists and turns, the passing of the Sinhala Only Act that has still not been enforced, the promises, the betrayals, the pact with the Tamils; now, at last, something will be done. The tide is turning. He bows, trying to conceal his elation.

"Good. Of course, you may take someone else with you. That other novice. The one who helps you in the garden. What is his name?"

"Brother Tissa, my lord."

"Yes. Take him. Now, I must get on. Leave me."

The audience is at an end. The abbot waves peremptorily at Anil, dismissing him, then busies himself with the papers on his desk, as if to attend to more pressing matters.

Speaking into a megaphone, Mr Jayawardene addresses the crowds from his open-topped car, repeating the themes that he has adopted over the last few months and which have made him so popular. Catchphrases such as 'betrayal of the Sinhalese' are a cue for rapturous applause. His audience has heard it all before but, the more they hear it, they more they like it. The crowd adores him.

Having finished his address, he closes his hands and bows his head, as if in prayer, invoking the aid of the gods. Then, looking up, he holds out his arms and, above the roar of the crowd, the clapping and stamping, rises the chanting of monks.

"He is a great man, is he not?" whispers Tissa to Anil, his eyes shining.

"Yes, indeed."

Except for a slight twitch of the mouth, which might be interpreted as a smile, Anil betrays no emotion, yet his pulse is racing wildly. At last, he thinks. We have found our leader.

He has listened intently to Mr Jayawardene condemning the Prime Minister's betrayal of his people and has felt his own heart glow within him like a red-hot coal, fired with anger and hatred. This will be the day when the tide turns. The Government will be brought down. Just one good push is all that it will take to topple that gimcrack edifice; a mirage of hope and unkept promises, based on a spent coalition.

All talk of national unity is an illusion. One must have reality, results: Mr Jayawardene, so in tune with Sinhalese aspirations, is the man to deliver them. Of course, Anil felt the same about Bandaranaike at one time – everyone did – but now, in hindsight, he sees that he was wrong. Bandaranaike is just a play-actor, a fraud, saying whatever is expedient, spinning a web of lies and deceit just to keep himself in power. Anil clenches his fist. If anyone deserves to die, it is that traitor, Bandaranaike. Anil licks his lips and tastes the saltiness of his own sweat.

Slowly, the crowd forms itself into a procession with Mr Jayawardene at the head, Tissa and Anil chanting prayers with the other monks. For the first time in months, Sinhalese nationalists have a sense of direction. Expectations run high as the chanting, cheering, sweating crowd rolls towards its destination.

***

From the window of his apartment, Buddharakkita can see the road beyond the monastery gates. It is lined with people, four or five deep, all standing on tiptoe to get a better look over their neighbours' shoulders, all waiting, expectantly. There is an air of excited anticipation and an atmosphere of carnival, the sort associated with great religious festivals, such as the perahera in Kandy, when dancers, drummers, priests and elephants parade through the streets.

But today is different. This is not a religious event, although it is fuelled by religious devotion. Lay people, monks and politicians have gathered for a day's march from Colombo to the Sri Dalada Maligawa, the Great Temple at Kandy where, lying at the heart of a nest of caskets, is the holiest relic of all – a fragment of the Buddha's tooth.

Over the centuries, the Tooth has been coveted by rulers both within the Island and outside it. The influence that it exerts over the minds of the faithful is so great that some of Ceylon's early kings even attached the prefix Datha, or Tooth, to their own royal title to emphasise their authority. To the Sinhalese, the Tooth is symbolic of both religious and temporal power which is why, with extraordinary astuteness, Mr Jayawardene has chosen this shrine as the focus of what is, essentially, a political rally. His protest march will take the form of a religious procession. Its purpose? The invocation of divine aid against the unholy pact with the Tamils.

As Buddharakkita watches from his window, he notes with satisfaction that many of the crowd below are dressed in saffron robes. On his journey, Mr Jayawardene will be made fully aware of the strength of monastic support for his cause. He is learning quickly, turning to the allies who brought Mr Bandaranaike to power, speaking to ordinary people in terms which they understand, addressing their fears and, of course, playing on them.

It occurs to Buddharakkita that, if Mr Bandaranaike should be removed from office for any reason, a suitable replacement will be waiting in the wings. Someone who has a longer memory than the present incumbent, one who might not be inclined to forget his friends as quickly. And, of course, Mr Jayawardene understands the value of rice.

The crowd lining the road is now ten people deep and still growing. Men carrying baskets or billy-cans swinging from yokes across their shoulders are sauntering up and down the road touting for business; sellers of garlands, rotis and tea who frequent any gathering where there is hope of scratching a living.

Suddenly, the crowd parts and all heads turn to look down the road. A large, open-topped car cruises slowly down the centre of the street. Mr Jayawardene, garlanded with temple flowers, stands at the front of the car, steadying himself against the windscreen as he waves to the crowd. Also with him in the car are three monks, chanting pirith, texts from ancient Pali scriptures to ensure success and protection from evil.

As the procession draws level with the monastery, Mr Jayawardene looks up and, seeing the dark outline of the abbot at the window, presses his hands together and bows his head. Buddharakkita smiles and returns the greeting, then, as the car is about to sweep out of sight, he leans out of the window, trying to get a better view. Surely, for a second, he saw a fifth figure in the car, the same figure that he thought he saw a while ago on a temple roof in Colombo. The one that seemed to move and wink at him. Hooniyam.

Buddharakkita rubs his eyes and looks again, but the car has disappeared. The crowds close together in its wake and surge forward, the monks in their midst, taking up the chant of pirith.

***

Seated in the back of Mr Jayawardene's car, Hooniyam is enjoying himself immensely, waving at the cheering onlookers, although he is visible only to a select few. Flinging his head back, he laughs out loud as he flourishes the Sword of State above his head. It is a gift, presented to him by the gods in recognition of his following among politicians.

It is a double-edged sword, with both the power to protect and destroy, and Hooniyam has already put it to good use. Today, he will present a future Prime Minister to the gods. For this, surely, he will receive pride of place in the divine pantheon and be worshipped as the equal of Vishnu and Kali. His chest swelling with pride, Hooniyam blows a kiss to the crowds.

1957: The pilgrims' progress

From Colombo, the procession winds its way slowly through Gampaha district. It is the home of the celebrated Ayurvedic doctor, Wickremaachi, founder of a school of medicine whose practitioners are to be found all over the Island. Being mainly Sinhalese speakers, the Ayurvedic doctors resent the way in which they have been pushed aside by western medicine and its English-speaking practitioners. Under colonial rule, they were relegated to the status of rustic herbalists, little better than witch doctors and, for decades, they have been victims of cultural ignorance. For this reason, Ayurvedic practitioners are staunch supporters of Sinhalese nationalism and many have come to swell the crowds marching with Mr Jayawardene to Kandy.

Anil's father was an Ayurvedic doctor and, as he trudges along the road, near to the place where his father studied, Anil thinks bitterly of the disillusioned old man whose practice was destroyed by the arrival of a new western-style surgery with its young, arrogant GP: an English-speaking Tamil whose wealthy family had sent him to study in England. As his practice declined, Anil's father had visited the young doctor to plead with him, hoping that they could work together.

Anil accompanied his father on that occasion. He will never forget the young doctor, dressed in a fine, hand-stitched suit of English cut, his thick hair neatly slicked back over his ears, his white collar starched to bone-white crispness. He had listened impatiently to the old man's entreaties, then laughed in his face with the same whinnying cackle used by all British administrators to dismiss troublesome natives.

Even now, when he thinks of it, Anil still burns with the anger he felt at his father's humiliation. He had wanted to kill the doctor. He would have done so but, sensing his son's fury, the old man had put a restraining hand on his shoulder and marched him out of the surgery. That night, Anil had sworn revenge, an oath that he repeated, six months later, as he watched his father's body burn on its funeral pyre.

Yet, as he marches through Gampaha, chanting pirith, Anil's spirits lift. The sight of so many people, all from different backgrounds but with one aim, gives him hope. And, this time, they have found a leader who will not be diverted from his purpose. Junius Jayawardene will lead them to victory.

***

The crowd is approaching Imbulgoda, renowned for its road-side pineapple sellers. Rough wooden booths, open on three sides with sloping roofs of corrugated iron, are built on both sides of the road. Along the sides of each booth, wooden poles have been strapped to form racks from which pineapples, as large as a man's head, are strung by their stalks.

The pineapple-sellers, young attractive women, are leaning on the shelves of their booths, watching the crowd with interest. One, a beautiful girl in a pink lunghi and short-sleeved, striped shirt, draws the particular attention of passers-by. She is about sixteen years old with thick, wavy hair drawn back from her face and an expression whose promise of a smile lends her an air of mystery.

As they pass her, several members of the crowd discover an unquenchable thirst. The tea-sellers have long since disappeared and many of the marchers have not drunk anything for hours. There is a minor stampede to the girl's booth where, watched by a withered old crone who sits unseen at the back of the shelter, the beautiful pineapple-seller is slicing fruit with a machete.

"Ahh! The pineapples of Imbulgoda are sweet," sighs one man as he passes the booth.

"Not as sweet as those who sell them," whispers another, digging him in the ribs. They laugh, light-heartedly.

Having arrived at Imbulgoda Pass, the procession grinds to a halt.

"What is happening?" people ask, craning their heads to get a better view.

Not realising that the procession has halted, the marchers at the back are trying to push forward. The result is an unpleasant crush, especially distressing for those caught in the middle. Anil and Tissa, who are close to the front, manage to push their way out of the press. Mr Jayawardene's car has stopped and he is remonstrating with someone in the road. The three monks who accompany him have stopped their chanting and are looking anxiously at each other. There is a sound of shouting and jeering coming from further down the road.

Having shoved their way through the crowd, Anil and Tissa are within a few feet of Mr Jayawardene's car. Now they can see the cause of the trouble. Another large car has been parked across the road as a blockade and, beyond it, is a crowd of protesters, shouting political slogans. Led by a local MP, they are supporters of Mr Bandaranaike.

Some of Mr Jayawardene's protesters start to shout back and, at the front line, several scuffles break out. Something flies through the air, narrowly missing Tissa's head. There is a thud and a scream. A man with blood pouring from his forehead is carried, semi-conscious, to the roadside. There is more shouting and yelling and some of the marchers, incensed at what has happened to their comrade, rush forward to take on his attackers.

Mr Jayawardene tries to climb down from the car, but is held back by the monks. He starts shouting through his megaphone, but no-one listens. The arena is set for a violent affray when, as if from nowhere, a group of armed policemen appear. Their leader, a large man with a pock-marked face, walks over to Mr Jayawardene and, bowing deferentially, speaks to him in a low voice. Protesters on both sides fall silent, watching with bated breath.

"What is he doing here?" murmurs Anil.

"Who?"

Following Anil's gaze, Tissa stares at the policeman then turns to his master in anticipation of a reply. But Anil is praying to Hooniyam, rapidly, urgently, begging for deliverance.

After a few minutes, Mr Jayawardene nods his head. He looks grey and tired. The policeman bows, then withdraws to where his men, now three ranks deep have formed a human cordon across the road. Mr Jayawardene has a hurried conversation with the monks in the car. They all seem to be in agreement with him, although one is openly weeping. Then, tapping his driver on the shoulder, Mr Jayawardene signals with his hand, ordering the man to turn the car around.

As the car cruises past, Tissa sees Mr Jayawardene, straightening his clothes and sucking in his breath, the nervous gestures of a politician readying himself for a difficult speech. With one hand resting on the windscreen, Mr Jayawardene lifts the megaphone to his lips with the other and, for a fraction of a second, hesitates.

"My friends, I have been informed by the police that our march has been cancelled. You must all go home. Do not regard this as a defeat, but a victory. What we have done has struck fear into the hearts of those who would betray the Sinhalese. Go home and pray."

Silent and crestfallen, the crowds open to let the car pass. There is an atmosphere of deflation and angry disappointment. Some begin openly to question whether Jayawardene is the man he claims to be. Perhaps he is simply another false prophet. Sadly, angrily, the crowd begins to disperse.

Anil remains standing in the road, as if frozen, watching the retreating car.

"Come, Master, come back with me to the monastery. You must speak to the abbot. He'll know what to do."

Tissa paws gently at Anil's arm and, looking up into the other man's face, realises that he is weeping.

***

Four days later, after being turned back at Imbulgoda Pass, Mr Jayawardene completes his pilgrimage to the Temple of the Tooth. In a motor car. There are speeches from the influential abbots of Malwatte and Asgirya. There are also a few haphazard scuffles between supporters of the march and protesters, but these are quickly stifled by police who are well-prepared to deal with any trouble. It is a Pyrrhic victory for Mr Jayawardene.

1957: Asoka's nightmare

Grasping the newspaper tightly in one hand, Asoka runs from the porch, across the clearing and along the path into the jungle. Then, looking around him to make sure that he is alone, he re-opens the paper to examine the photograph. For a second, the page is illuminated by the light of the setting sun. Now, he is sure. Among the pilgrims attending Mr Jayawardene's rally are two monks: Anil and Tissa. The two faces, staring from the newspaper, seem to fix him with their eyes. Asoka's heart lurches with fear. His past has returned; seeking him out with soft black tentacles, reaching for him in the dark.

***

Again, in his dreams, Asoka revisits the scene of Mennan's death. Alone in the middle of the clearing, he is surrounded by a great clamour, although he can see no-one. A hunt is taking place. He can hear undergrowth being beaten with sticks and the shouts and screams of pursuers, now close, now far-off.

Then, he is projected into the forest. Lush ferns part before him and thorns tear at his flesh. He can hear the wild beating of a drum: it becomes louder and louder, until it reverberates in his throat and pounds in his head. Then he realises: it is the beating of his own heart and he is the creature being pursued.

He finds himself in the clearing, unable to move or see his tormentors. At the periphery of his vision, where open ground meets forest and the light grows dim, he senses something moving, a dark shadow slipping in and out of the trees. He has seen it before, when wandering through the forest, out of his wits after Mennan's murder. Although he wishes to look away, his eyes are drawn towards it.

The creature is man-shaped but not human. It begins to leap about in wild abandon, performing an obscene parody of a dance, flinging out its arms and flapping its hands, kicking its legs high into the air, jumping, jerking, bending low and shaking its shaggy head so that its matted locks fly out behind it.

Then, as the shadow strikes a pose, lifting up one knee and flexing its foot as if to strike the earth with its heel, Asoka sees that it is accompanied by other creatures. He realises that what he first believed to be shadowy, black flames are, in fact, serpents, attached to the waist of the man-shape, writhing and hissing, their forked tongues flickering about their mouths.

"Who are you?"

Without speaking, Asoka challenges the figure to speak.

The shadow flits between the trees then, stands still, its hands cupped together in front of its breast. Then, quite suddenly, it flings its arms forward, hurling something into the air. A black shape wheels skyward on silent wings, then swoops down and, as it approaches, Asoka sees the livid face of Mennan, his black tongue poking from his mouth, his putrid lips parted in a hideous grin. Asoka screams and tries to beat the thing away with his arms but it whirls about his head, veering away, then diving down as the figure in the trees, its arms held above its head, makes small, precise movements with its hands, as if guiding the strings of a kite.

Asoka screams again and fights madly as something brushes his face.

"Shh, my love. Wake up. You're dreaming."

He opens his eyes and sees Sriya, leaning over him, her hand stroking his forehead.

"Has it gone?"

He sits up and looks wildly around the room.

"Yes."

His mouth is dry with fear. His tongue cleaves to his palate.

"It was just a dream, my love. Lie down and go to sleep."

Asoka wipes his face with a corner of his sarong. He is drenched with sweat, his hair stuck to his forehead. He peers into the darkness, examining familiar corners of the room as if he has seen them for the first time, his mind still lost in the shadow of dreams.

Finally, yielding to the pressure of Sriya's hand and the coaxing of her gentle voice, he lies down beside her but, as his wife drifts back to sleep, so Asoka regains consciousness. For many hours, he lies awake in the darkness; his arm wrapped around Sriya's sleeping form, his hand resting on the contented swell of her belly. The soft, feathery touch of her hair against his cheek and the warm, bed-odour of her body comfort him and, yet, even her gentle presence cannot dispel his fear.

***

Light floods through the small window. The sky has switched from night to day in a few, brief seconds. A tropical dawn. Leaning on his elbow, Asoka watches Sriya as she sleeps, lying on her side with one hand cushioning her head. Normally, he draws strength from the purity of that sleeping face, so peaceful and innocent but, today, it sends a knife through his heart. Fear has begun to taint his paradise. Gently, he strokes Sriya's hair. She murmurs in her sleep and smiles.

"Asoka."

He even inhabits her dreams. He wipes a hand over his eyes, dismissing the tears that well up whenever he thinks of her suffering. The dangers of childbirth already torment him – the thought of losing her is intolerable – but, at least, that is a natural hazard of life. The source of his new fear is not. It is a peril, caused by his own stupidity.

He is forced to acknowledge a bitter truth. One's past cannot be separated from the present or future, as he had hoped. They are all one, each directing the course of the other, and that which exerts the strongest influence is the past. For, unlike the present and future, the past is concrete, complete; something that has been realised in its entirety. Beyond alteration or redemption, the past is without hope.

He had sought to contain it by severing all ties with his old life, but time is a continuous stream whose flow cannot be interrupted. With a sinking heart, Asoka concedes that, at some point, the past will dictate his future and, more importantly, that of Sriya. It is inescapable.

His heart weighs heavy in his chest. He rises slowly from the floor and, tying his sarong tightly about his waist, walks quietly from the room. In the kitchen, he helps himself to a glass of boiled water, still tepid from the night heat, and half a stale roti then, without bothering to wash, he leaves the house.

He crosses the yard where one of the buffalo is lying by the fence, its forelegs folded under it, gently rolling its tongue around a mouthful of hay. The animal looks at him in a disinterested manner then blows through its nose as if to dismiss the inexplicable behaviour of humans. Asoka quietly unlatches the gate and lets himself into the clearing where a mangy rooster, too old and weary to crow, is scratching at an ant heap.

Revived by the purity of morning, Asoka feels his spirits rise. He strides across the clearing, swinging his arms, determined that the new day will put his fear to rest. He does not see the face of Tissa's mother, pale as a rising moon, staring at him from the corner of her window.

Manju watches Asoka disappear under the shadow of the great waving palms that line the track to the paddy field. Every day, since Sriya passed her on the way to the temple, she has quietly crept out of the house and into the forest where, in the place where she nursed Tissa as a baby, she repeats the curse; scratching Asoka's name on an egg and calling Hooniyam to her aid as she hurls it to the ground. So far, she has received no reply and her tormentor has continued to prosper. Asoka is safe and well, his wife pregnant and his father-in-law's farm more productive than ever; while Manju's son, Tissa, his heart broken, has run away, his mind corrupted by pain.

Manju continues to stare from the window, at the spot where Asoka left the village, clenching her fists so tightly that the nails bite into her skin. Since Tissa's disappearance, she has become thin and wasted, surviving only on hatred. Many of the villagers now regard her as a pariah, someone so infected with grief that the slightest contact with her is to risk the spreading of contagion. It was not always so. In the early days after Tissa's disappearance, they tried to help her, even Prema and his wife, but she rejected all their attempts at comfort, sneering at their sympathy, despising their pity.

Fools! She feels stronger now than she has ever felt before. Her anger is so great that she no longer fears even her husband's beatings and he, sensing that she no longer fears him, has ceased to beat her.

She shudders. Sensing a change in the air, she pulls her scarf around her bony shoulders. Her husband is snoring loudly in the next room. He returned home late last night and will sleep for most of the morning. By the time he gets to the fields, if he ever does, he will be in no fit state to work and there will be insufficient time before sundown to do all that is required. Nor will there be help from anyone else. The men of the village despise her husband almost as much as she does and her children, despairing of any improvement at home, have drifted away from their parents' house, one by one, hoping for a new start and a better chance in the city.

They are on their own now, Manju and her husband, facing ruin together. Still, she prefers it that way. Without other people to worry about, she can concentrate all her efforts on Tissa. She will find him and restore him to health. He will return to live with her and, working together, they will revive the family's fortunes. Her husband can go or stay as he pleases but, if he stays, it will be on her terms.

Then, when everything is in order and Tissa has taken his rightful place as head of the family, they will take their revenge. She smiles. That will heal her wounds all right. Bowls of curry and small sacks of rice, handouts from the village, cannot assuage her pain; only vengeance can cure that.

She withdraws from the window and, as she passes through the squalid, lean-to kitchen, she picks up a small cloth pouch from the table. Slipping out of the house, she crosses the clearing to make her way along the same forest track taken by Asoka a few minutes earlier. The darkness under the trees reassures her. It is better to be alone, safe from the prying eyes of neighbours, protected from their idle interest and contempt.

She has no fear of the forest, or what it holds, indeed, she feels closer to it every day, becoming attuned to its sounds and smells. She feels more at home here than she does in her own, ramshackle house. This is where she brought Tissa as a baby and held him to her breast. This is where he disappeared and, she feels sure, this is where she will find him.

After a few minutes, she abandons the main track and slips through the trees along a narrow path. All around her, she is aware of a strange stillness. The forest is silent, undisturbed by the screeching of parakeets or the shrill squabbling of monkeys. There is no breath of air to rattle the palm fronds overhead.

As she nears the clearing, the atmosphere becomes hotter and more intense in its stillness, as if waiting for something. It is the silent heaviness that precedes a storm, so thick that it is tangible. It fills her ears, her mouth, her nostrils. It sinks into her lungs and presses against her with its unutterable weight and yet, her heart feels light, expectant.

In the middle of the clearing, she opens the bag and draws out a chicken's egg which she has already marked with Asoka's name. She holds it in front of her, cupped in her skinny hands while, with eyes closed, she repeats the incantation to Hooniyam, summoning the god of sorcerers to punish Asoka.

Let him suffer! Let him suffer! Let him suffer! She hears the voice of her heart repeating over and over as she whispers the words of the curse. Then, when she has finished, she raises her hand above her head and dashes the egg against the root of the old banyan tree, the place where she nursed her son.

She waits for a few seconds, her senses as receptive as the string of a spider's web, twitching, waiting. But nothing happens. With a sinking heart, Manju tucks the cloth pouch into the waist of her sari and, lowering her head, closes her eyes and prays to Hooniyam with thanks, as she always does.

Then, she hears a soft sound: the rustle of a leaf. Something is moving softly across the earth floor of the clearing. Manju's heart begins to beat wildly. She opens her eyes but fears to look up. Something brushes her foot, something dry and smooth, then she hears it move away in the direction of the old banyan tree. Gradually, not daring to breath, Manju raises her eyes. There, at the base of the tree, lapping at the yolk of the broken egg is a young cobra, its lustrous scales shining like flakes of black jet.

Softly, Manju drops to her knees then, bending forward, her forearms resting on the ground, she presses her hands together in an attitude of prayer and lowers her forehead to touch the earth. The snake finishes its meal in a leisurely manner then, without seeming to notice Manju, slips silently away into the undergrowth where its master is waiting.

Sriya hacks at the vegetables with an old rusty knife. A piece of carrot springs from the chopping board and falls to the ground. Within seconds a gang of chickens are squabbling over it. Sriya shoos them away bad-temperedly. It makes little difference. The chickens continue to fight until one, larger and more aggressive than the rest, emerges the victor and, with the carrot firmly wedged in its beak, bounds off to a corner of the yard to enjoy its prize.

Straightening up, Sriya kneads the base of her back with her fingertips. Already, the weight of the child that she is carrying pulls at her spine, making her weary. Leaning forwards over the table, she continues with her work, peeling, chopping and slicing. Normally, she takes pleasure in the preparation of food, but today it is a chore. Simple household tasks no longer have the power to calm her thoughts and her mind is unsteady.

Recently, Asoka has woken her with his tormented sleep. He writhes and shouts, murmuring words that she cannot hear, holding his arms out in front of him, as if to protect himself from a terrible, unseen enemy. Last night, he even wept in his sleep, murmuring her name: Sriya, Sriya. But he never wakes from these terrible dreams and Sriya has to shake him hard before he can even open his eyes. Then, while the dream is still in his head, she can see the true depth of his terror.

Once awake, he does not return to sleep but lies on his back, still and silent as a corpse, looking into the darkness, as if waiting for something, or someone. Then, early in the morning, when he thinks she is asleep, he gets up quietly and leaves the house, making straight for the fields. She will not see him again until the evening when he returns, almost too exhausted to eat. Then, after exchanging only a few words with her, he goes to bed and the whole process begins again.

It all started when a neighbour brought them a new paper. The old one, carrying the story of Mr Bandaranaike's pact with the Tamils, had dropped to pieces and Sriya had read it so many times that she could almost recite the articles word for word. She had mentioned it, laughingly, to their neighbour Nirudaka, then thought no more of it.

A couple of days later, the man had shyly presented Asoka with a new paper. One that he had bought in town. Wrapped in a brown paper bag, its folds were as crisp as the day it had left the printers. The pages were flat and clean; untouched – as previous papers had been – by numerous hands. It was Nirudaka's way of showing his gratitude; for Asoka is teaching his boy to read. One day, Nirudaka hopes that his son will read to him from the newspapers, as Sriya now reads to Asoka.

Sriya had blushed when Asoka told her of the gift, but embarrassment had not stemmed her hunger for news. As Asoka carefully unfolded the paper, she had peered over his shoulder. On the front page, there was a headline in large, black type: '*Protesters turned back at Imbulgoda.*'

"What is that about?" she had enquired, craning her neck for a better look.

"Mr Jayawardene, an opposition MP, has tried to organise a protest against the pact with the Tamils," mumbled Asoka, as he scanned the article.

Sriya had leant forward, craning her neck but even then, she could not see clearly. There was a large photograph of a man standing in a car, surrounded by people, many of them monks. Asoka scowled, bending over the photograph to get a better look. Then, with a sharp intake of breath, he hurriedly closed the paper and folded it so that she could no longer see the front page.

"Hey! Let me see!"

Playfully, she had tried to grab the paper from him. But Asoka was in no mood for games. Grim and unsmiling, he had simply walked off, without a word, towards the track leading to the fields, taking the newspaper with him. She never saw it again.

Ever since, she has wondered what it was that he did not wish her to see. Every time she tries to question him, he evades her, often making an excuse to leave the house: the fields must be checked, the oxen need tending.

***

Determined to get to the truth, she waited for him this morning and, as he got up, she asked him again. He had given her a look, warning her to be silent, but she had persisted, following him into the kitchen and out into the yard, a thin lunghi tied around her body and another around her shoulders.

"Please, please, tell me what is wrong?"

She had tried to grab his hand, to hold him back so that he would have to answer her, but he just shook her off, running towards the track into the forest, knowing that she could not follow him. She watched him go with a sinking heart, barely able to restrain her tears then, as she turned to go back to the house, she saw a pale face, watching her from a window: a face so gaunt and thin that it looked like a death's head. Manju.

The sight of that face has poisoned her day. She knows that Manju witnessed her distress and took pleasure in it. As she chops the vegetables, narrowly missing the tip of her finger with the rusty blade, Sriya thinks of all the stories she heard as a child. Tales of demons and slaves, spells and curses. They frightened her then but, as she grew up, she dismissed most of them as superstitious fancy. But, having seen that face at the window, with its thin, evil smile delighting in her pain, she begins to wonder whether there is any truth in the old stories. They may account for Asoka's strange behaviour.

***

Asoka. She loves him with every thread of her being. Until now, they have shared everything. She knows all his secrets, even the darkest. He has confessed everything to her. He killed a man. What could be worse than that? So why can he not talk to her now? There can be only one reason. He does not love her any more.

Wiping her eyes with the back of her hand, Sriya tries to resume her task, but the piles of vegetables have blurred into a swirl of colour. The world melts before her eyes. She puts down the knife and, resting the tips of her fingers on the table, she weeps silently.

"What is it, child?"

A firm, gnarled hand takes her by the shoulder. Prema has been watching for some minutes from the shadow of the lean-to kitchen. Over the last couple of days, he, too, has noticed that all is not well between his daughter and her husband. While parental instinct urged him to intervene, his commonsense told him to leave well alone – and he did – but he cannot ignore his daughter's distress.

"Oh, Appa, I am losing him."

Resting her head against her father's shoulder, Sriya sobs uncontrollably.

So that is it, thinks Prema. Asoka has found another woman. That is why he is out so early every morning. He is meeting her in the fields. Well, I will catch them. Together.

Furious, he leaves Sriya in the yard, weeping and wringing her hands, murmuring something inconsequential about a newspaper story and Tissa's mother having cursed her. Poor girl! She is almost mad with grief. He will teach Asoka a lesson he will never forget.

Grabbing a spade from the yard, Prema swings it over his shoulder. With murder in his eye, he stalks off along the forest track, towards the paddy fields. Asoka has made his daughter cry and Prema will have an explanation, or revenge.

The forest is alive with sound – the screeching of parrots, the angry chattering of monkeys, even the faint clattering of dry palm fronds agitated by the breeze – but nothing can distract him from the image of Sriya's face, its calm beauty distorted by weeping. Anyone who does that to her is his enemy; even the man he regards as his own son. The more he thinks of it, the more his heart boils with rage. He has often said, half joking, that he would die for his daughter, but he now knows that he would kill for her, too.

Emerging from the trees, he sees Asoka, knee-deep in the paddy, bending to check the progress of the tender young shoots. Prema marches towards him, his hand tightening its grip on the spade, ready to strike. One blow to the back of the head is all it will take.

Drawing level with the place where Asoka is working, Prema walks half-way down the bank. Asoka's head is now in line with the spade. It would be easy to strike from here.

"Hey!" Prema barks.

Asoka straightens up and turns a weary, grey face towards his father-in-law. Prema is shocked. The boy has aged overnight. A thin crack appears in the crust of anger that has closed about Prema's heart. Asoka's face is lined with suffering. But suffering for what? An affair with another woman can cause a man to suffer, even though he is the wrongdoer, but that kind of suffering will not elicit Prema's sympathy, or excuse Asoka from punishment. Better not to be too sympathetic until he has discovered the cause.

"Come and speak to me, my son. I have something to ask you."

Prema's voice is less harsh than he intended. It is not in his nature to be cruel. If Asoka is guilty, Prema wonders if he will have the strength to mete out the punishment that his son-in-law deserves.

Wearily, Asoka wades through the water and is about to climb the bank but Prema holds up his hand, warning him to stay back.

"No. That's far enough."

Asoka looks up enquiringly at his father-in-law. The old man's mouth is set in a tight line, his wrinkled face contracted as if to squeeze out any softness of expression and his eyes, usually twinkling with humour, now glitter with suppressed rage. Asoka notes how tightly the gnarled fingers clasp the handle of the spade as if in readiness to swing it at his head. It seems to him that Prema has been transformed from saviour and friend to judge and executioner. *He has come to kill me*, he thinks, and feels a strange calmness, a kind of relief.

428

"What's the matter?" he asks, his voice as steady as if they were discussing a sack of grain or a problem with one of the animals.

"That's what I have come to ask you. I found my daughter crying this morning. I asked her what was wrong. At first, she did not want to tell me, but then she said she thought she was losing you. I have come to ask if you have found yourself another woman."

"What?"

Asoka is incredulous. Prema's accusation is so ridiculous, so far from the truth, that he begins to laugh. Incensed, the old man steps towards him and, as he does so, he raises the spade, ready to strike.

"Have you been unfaithful to my daughter?"

"No, of course not."

"Then why is she crying? You must tell me the truth. Now."

Asoka sighs and, before he speaks, he turns to look across the paddy. In the distance, a few other farmers are bent over their work, their heads protected from the sun by ragged pieces of cloth; white egrets stalk the waters nearby, pecking for insects disturbed by the labourers' feet, and everywhere, the surface of the water is broken by rows of green shoots. Ever since he saw the photograph in the newspaper, this has been Asoka's refuge, the only place where he can find peace; but he can hide no longer. He has committed a crime and its ghost is determined to haunt him.

"Very well. Let me sit here and I will tell you. Then, you can do as you wish. I will not oppose you."

Prema nods and allows Asoka to climb the bank to a dry spot where he can sit comfortably, then he himself sits down a few paces away, a little higher up, the spade beside him, gripped tightly in one hand. Just in case.

Asoka speaks slowly, looking not at his father-in-law but at the scene in front of him, almost caressing it with his eyes as he recounts his part in Mennan's death, his flight into the forest, his love for Sriya and how he tried to leave her, but could not.

"She knows everything. It is not an excuse but at least I told her the truth. I never lied to her."

"But you never told me!"

The old man sounds bitter, hurt, although he guessed the truth long ago.

"No. I never told you," Asoka murmurs. "I am sorry for that."

He stares out across the paddy, to the palm trees that encircle it and beyond, to a distant ridge of mountains and the faint outline of Sigiriya; the fortress of Kasyapa who murdered his own father to steal a kingdom. He shakes his head and sighs. Our past always catches up with us, wherever we try to hide.

"Foolish children!" Prema breaks the silence. "You both deserve to be punished. But, if Sriya knew of your past and accepted it, you have still not explained what has happened recently to upset her. She said something about a newspaper. Something you would not show her."

"I saw a photograph of Tissa, dressed as a monk, in the company of the other man who murdered Mennan."

"Ahh."

The old man thinks for a minute, taking in the news.

"And what does that mean for us?"

"They were staring out of the photograph, straight at me, as if they could see me. I had a bad feeling. A premonition, you might call it. A sense of evil. The peace that I have found here, even my love for Sriya, all felt like an illusion."

"Is that all?"

It is Prema's turn to be amused. He waves his hand, dismissively.

"You sound like an ignorant peasant. This morning, Sriya told me that someone had put you under a spell and now you are telling me that you are afraid of a photograph in a newspaper. If you were not adults, I would beat you both soundly for such stupidity."

"So, you think it is all nonsense."

Asoka looks enquiringly at Prema like a child seeking reassurance.

"Yes, my son. It is all nonsense."

Squeezing the young man's shoulder, Prema is surprised at how thin he has become.

"You have not been eating?"

"No. Not much."

"Weakness of body leads to weakness of mind. Come home with me and eat. Forget all this foolishness."

"Then you forgive me?"

"You are the husband of my daughter. Only if you betray her will I not forgive you."

Asoka smiles and takes the old man's outstretched hand, allowing Prema to help him up the bank. At the top, he pauses, using handfuls of grass to wipe the mud from his legs and feet. He feels relieved, absolved, as if a shadow has lifted. He can go home to Sriya without a care. Prema is right. He has been foolish, allowing himself to fall victim to superstition. He has become closer to this community than he ever thought possible. He is even beginning to think like them. Before walking back, he takes a last look at the paddy and wonders how he could ever have entertained such unquiet thoughts in this tranquil place. Breathing deeply, he lets its peace invade him.

As they walk home, Asoka chatters like a boy. It is good to see him so happy but Prema has a new concern. Tissa is still alive. Although he will only admit it to himself, Prema had secretly hoped that he had disappeared for good. The boy's wits have been turned by madness and anger and Prema fears what he might do if he ever returns to the village.

1957: A sergeant's daydream

Things look bad for the wasp-waisted blonde. Her husband, the millionaire Augustus T. Hofmeier, has been found dead on the golf course, his skull caved in with one of his favourite clubs and all clues point in the direction of his voluptuous wife. When a woman in her twenties marries a man in his seventies, one has to ask why. No doubt about it, Mrs Hofmeier is heading for the electric chair. Unless ...

Surreptitiously, Sergeant Gunasekera licks his thumb and turns the page, wondering if all white women are as seductive as Mrs Hofmeier. He cannot yet tell whether she is the heroine or the villainess of the story but he knows that Detective Joe Baci will eventually uncover her secrets. All of them. Even the most intimate.

Sergeant Gunasekera squirms slightly on his seat as he entertains lascivious thoughts of his gumshoe detective undressing the beautiful, pampered widow. Of course, the details of their love-making are only hinted at but Sergeant Gunasekera thinks the story is all the better for that because the reader is allowed to use his own imagination. He thinks how much more enjoyable it would be to make love to a woman like that, even if she were a murderess, than to his own tight-lipped wife with whom coupling is a mere duty, something to be done and endured in the dark, like a guilty secret. Although Hindu, Sergeant Gunasekera's wife was brought up by nuns. He blames them for her frigidity.

Sergeant Gunasekera's unhappy marriage has affected his outlook on life. A Buddhist by upbringing, he has, for many years, been agnostic and, yet, recently religion has begun to play an increasing part in his political beliefs. For even people like Gunasekera, mild-tempered and, for the most part, passive, are being won over by the teaching of the Sinhalese nationalist movement. Just the other day, he was spellbound by a monk preaching on a street corner about the iniquities of Christianity.

According to this preacher, Christianity underpinned foreign domination of the Island: a cunning stratagem, introduced by colonists, for the subjugation of the native population. By this means, foreigners subverted the Island's ancient culture and stole its wealth. As part of the colonial policy of divide-and-rule, the Island's education system was entrusted to missionaries. Only Islanders who either professed Christianity or, who at least tacitly accepted it, had access to a decent education, as all the best schools were run by missionaries. Christian schools were the only ones to get Government funding. Sinhalese, who were mostly Buddhist, received an inferior education, that is, if they got one at all.

These words struck a chord with Sergeant Gunasekera whose own inadequate upbringing has condemned him to the role of desk sergeant and marriage to a woman who regards conjugal relations as a form of martyrdom. Instead of moving the preacher on, as he was supposed to do, he stopped to listen.

When the preacher spoke of downtrodden, second-class Sinhalese, Sergeant Gunasekera knew he was addressing him. His heart warmed when he heard the man speak of Ceylon for the Sinhalese and he nodded approvingly when the monk berated the Government for its betrayal of the people: the Sinhalese people.

The monk looked him straight in the eye as he preached and Sergeant Gunasekera was rooted to the spot by the man's strange, mesmerising eyes, at one time green, at another amber. His taut, high-cheekboned face hinted at a subtle intelligence, although the same could not be said of his companion who, although dressed in the saffron robes of a monk, had the look of a rough, untutored country boy: a little mad, too, judging by the glint in his eye and the way in which he turned his head, restlessly looking this way and that, as if expecting to see something over his shoulder.

Had it not been for the monk, Sergeant Gunasekera might have been tempted to arrest that boy. He has enough of a policeman's instinct to know a villain when he sees one.

Hoping to see the preacher again, Gunasekera has made a point of passing the same street corner whenever he can, but the monk and his companion have disappeared. However, the preacher's words have had the desired effect, burrowing deep into Gunasekera's head like a worm biting into an apple, worrying his thoughts and sharpening his innate sense of disappointment. He now regards the dull routine of his life as drudgery and his disappointing marriage as slavery but, in the absence of any solution, the only way to staunch his discontent is to lose himself in cheap detective novels. At present, the only man with the answers is Detective Joe Baci.

The small boy pushes his way through the crowds. With his long front teeth and wide eyes, he has the startled face of a rabbit and, yet, that gormless, buck-toothed expression has proved an advantage in a line of work where the cunning features of Hanuman, the monkey god, would have been a positive drawback. Judging the boy to be witless, adults indulge him, lowering their voices when they speak, helping him with directions, accepting his presence where they would be inclined to question that of a child of greater apparent intelligence.

When he hangs around the doorways of Government buildings or the gates leading to great houses, doormen and guards are less inclined to see him off with a sharp cuff around the ear. Instead, many have befriended him, sometimes sending him on small errands to buy them packets of cigarettes from the bidi seller and rewarding him with small pieces of amber-coloured jaggery. Then, if he continues to loiter, as he often does, they engage him in a one-sided conversation, proudly boasting of their encounters with the great men whose homes and offices they guard.

Without appearing to, the child listens attentively then, when he has learned what he wants, he reports back to his patron: the man who feeds and clothes him; the man who has found him somewhere to sleep, safer and more comfortable than his old haunts of the pavement and shop doorways; the man who has given him a bicycle with a leather saddle and chrome handlebars. He is proud of that bicycle.

He wheels it now, through the crowds, past the street vendors, across the road to the police station where he leans it carefully against the wall by the entrance. No-one will dare to steal it from here.

***

The electric fans are humming overhead although their great paddles make little difference to the sultry air which is tainted with the masculine smell of sweat and hair oil. In the back office, clerks move between the desks, talking in low voices, pulling files from the wooden shelves that line the walls. Reaching from floor to ceiling, the shelves are lacquered with shiny brown paint that is chipped in places from much use, showing the white undercoat beneath. The files consist of fat sheaves of paper, crisp with age, stuffed loose into soft manilla folders. They, too, have their own smell, a faint tincture of mustiness, hinting at decay.

A fat, lazy fly drones through the stagnant air to settle on Sergeant Gunasekera's book. He flicks it away, irritable with the heat and the drowsiness that is beginning to roll over him. His eyelids flicker. He longs to sleep. He is brought to his senses by the sound of someone rapping on the desk. How long has he been dozing? He hopes that it looks as if he has been working, not sleeping. He prays that it is not the Assistant Superintendent of Police. Cautiously raising his eyes over the edge of his folder, he stares across the counter. A small fist is rapping impatiently on the polished wooden surface and a pair of round, stupid-looking eyes is staring at him from the other side.

"Oh, it's you," snaps the sergeant, crossly.

He detests the child, partly because he fears him. He does not trust that vacant face as some of the other officers do. Sometimes, Sergeant Gunasekera displays the insight of a good detective.

"I suppose you want to see him?"

It is a rhetorical question. There is only one reason for the boy's presence in the police station. Closing his sheaf of papers around the novel, Sergeant Gunasekera is careful to place it out of sight under the desk. The suspicion that the child knows about his reading habits prevents Gunasekera from treating the urchin to the sharp edge of his tongue: that, and the fact that the boy has the ear of the Assistant Superintendent. It is a relationship that Gunasekera cannot explain and does not want to. He just wants to move the boy away from his desk as quickly as possible.

"Come with me," he grunts, lifting the counter to let the child in.

Ranu stoops slightly, as if fearing that the Sergeant will drop the heavy counter lid on his head. Admittedly, it has crossed Gunasekera's mind on some occasions but he is not the sort of man to stoop to cruelty, even when he dislikes someone as much as Ranu.

With one hand on the boy's shoulder, he propels him forward, holding him away from him like something foul-smelling he has picked out of the gutter. Sergeant Gunasekera always makes sure the boy walks in front, where he can see him.

"Wait here," he says, pointing to an empty corner where he can keep an eye on the boy and where, more importantly, there is nothing to steal. The child obeys, staring dully at the sergeant, his lips parted around his protuberant teeth in a permanent smile.

"Ugh. He gives me the creeps!" thinks Gunasekara, adopting a term used by Detective Joe Baci. The detective's snappy American jargon acts like a charm against fear. Sergeant Gunasekera often resorts to a phrase or two, running them around his head, as he summons the courage to address the Assistant Superintendent.

He taps deferentially on the door.

"What is it?"

The man's booming voice has a curious effect on Gunasekera's entrails, turning them to water.

"It's the boy, sir."

"Send him in."

At the mention of his guest, the Assistant Superintendent's voice instantly softens. Gunasekera shudders. He motions to the child who is leaning against the wall, his arms crossed, one foot resting on top of the other, his head slightly to one side as he looks sidelong at the sergeant: the attitude adopted by all street kids who are up to no good, just waiting for an opportunity.

"Go on," hisses Gunasekera.

Ranu shuffles forward, casual and unhurried and the sergeant detects a certain, sly arrogance in his lack of speed. Opening the door to the Assistant Superintendent's office, Gunasekera all but pushes the boy in. He closes the door as quickly as he can but not before catching the expression of satisfaction spreading over the senior policeman's face, like a toad that has just swallowed a fly.

***

Ranu enters the room, positioning himself at a respectful distance from the policeman's desk. The man does not look up at once. It is his custom to make the boy wait. Balancing on one foot, Ranu watches the top of the man's balding head, shiny with sweat, as he bends over a letter, pretending to be engrossed in its contents.

This charade does not worry Ranu; in fact, he has frequently turned it to his advantage. Standing as motionless as a flagpole, Ranu lets his eyes wander about the room. At first sight, there is little of interest, but you never know, there is always a market for pens, pencils and small items of office stationery: if he cannot trade them for money, he will certainly be able to exchange them for food or sweets.

His eyes alight on a metal pencil sharpener, a small box of paperclips and, best of all, two small notebooks, unused. The items are perched on the corner of a neighbouring desk, one which never appears to have an occupant. Checking to see if the policeman is watching, Ranu fidgets, then moves a couple of steps closer to the desk while looking fixedly in the opposite direction. The policeman is still reading.

Ranu slides sideways, his bare feet passing silently over the polished red floor. The policeman jerks up one arm ... and rubs his nose. Frozen in his progress for a couple of seconds, Ranu resumes his sinuous journey towards the desk. Once there, he quietly closes his hand over the desired items, as if to stop them screaming, then slips them into the pocket of his baggy shorts.

The Assistant Superintendent laughs to himself, wondering when the boy will realise that this is a game, that he has selected the items and left them, just out of reach, for the pleasure of seeing the boy steal them.

"He gets better all the time," thinks the policeman.

He can always find work for a boy like Ranu.

At the precise moment when Ranu has pocketed the items and before he can take anything of greater value, the policeman puts aside the letter and looks up, feigning the short-sightedness of older people who must allow themselves a few seconds to re-focus on a distant object after they have been reading.

"What is it?" he says, scowling at the boy and looking pointedly at his pocket.

Ranu stares back at him steadily, without flinching or changing colour. Silently, he reaches into his other pocket and draws out a small notebook, similar to the ones that he has just taken, but filled with a series of strange symbols. He still cannot tell the time from the cheap chrome-plated watch strapped to his wrist, a gift from the Assistant Superintendent, but he can copy the position of the hands on its face, using a different coloured crayon according to whether it is morning or evening. The book is filled with these symbols, giving a detailed account of the movements of one person. The Government Agent.

Ranu hands the book to the policeman who flicks through its contents and grunts with satisfaction.

"Good. Very good. You have done well."

Still, Ranu's face betrays no flicker of emotion. It is as if he did not hear. His eyelids droop lazily over the protuberant eyes, giving him the appearance of someone about to fall asleep. He stares at the Assistant Superintendent, his long neck craned backwards, one leg crossed in front of the other.

"I think that deserves something extra."

The policeman reaches into his pocket and flicks a coin at the boy. It curves through the air in a glittering arc until it is stopped abruptly in its trajectory by Ranu's hand. The coin disappears, whisked away with the same rapidity as a fly on a chameleon's tongue.

Wordlessly, Ranu resumes his previous position and continues to stare at the policeman. Normally, the gift of a coin would be the sign for him to leave but today he has another message to deliver. Something the Assistant Superintendent does not expect.

Experience has taught Ranu never to initiate conversation with the policeman. He made that mistake. Once. The result was a severe beating and ejection into the yard where he was made to wait in the burning sun, without water or any place to sit, until the policeman was ready to hear him.

He does not know how long he waited in the searing heat, but it seemed like hours. Lack of shade and water made him so weak that, when he was eventually summoned, he had to be dragged to the Assistant Superintendent's office with Sergeant Gunasekera's arm firmly wedged under his armpit to support him. When the sergeant was ordered to withdraw, Ranu nearly collapsed, only managing to remain standing by pressing his bony knees together. With a mouth as dry as parchment, he had croaked out his message and was rewarded with 50 rupees. A generous gift.

And so, through reward and punishment, he has been taught to respect rules without logic; rules which only serve the obscure design of their maker. He has learned only to speak when spoken to. So, today, even though he has another message to deliver, he waits for the Assistant Superintendent to question him.

"What is it, boy?"

The policeman is becoming impatient. The boy's silence can sometimes prove unnerving. Without speaking, Ranu pulls an envelope from his pocket and, having handed it over, swiftly withdraws to his former position, a few feet away from the Assistant Superintendent's desk.

Squinting, the policeman bends his oily, pock-marked face over the note. His thinning hair forms black streaks across his glistening scalp. Dark patches of sweat have formed in the armpits of his shirt. Strong-smelling cologne does not quite mask the man's own, rank odour. But it is not the smell of someone who does not wash. Indeed, the cologne is overlaid by a harsh note of carbolic. Rather, it is an odour secreted from within: a faint smell of rottenness like that which rises from a stagnant pond stirred by a stick.

"Is this everything?" asks the Assistant Superintendent gruffly.

"O".

It never does to say too much. Yes and no are usually all that is called for. Ranu has learned that. He does not move, unsure of whether or not he has been dismissed. Best to be on the safe side and not make an untimely departure. To leave too early could lead to a beating and the Assistant Superintendent is agitated, he can tell by the tone of his voice.

So, Ranu remains where he is, swaying slightly, like a reed, feet crossed, hands in his pockets, his eyes fixed on the top of the man's head as he re-reads the letter. There is obviously something out of the ordinary in that note. Usually, messages from the monastery consist simply of a few numbers written on a scrap of folded paper. A time and date, or so he guesses. He knows this, because whenever he is given a note, he always stops in a side street to inspect it, turning it over and over in his hands, tracing the numbers with his finger.

But this note is different. Although Ranu cannot decipher the script, he can tell, simply by the amount of writing, that it is important. The characters look like a piece of elastic that has been stretched too far and then released, bunching up to form a series of wild loops and curves that almost seem to fall over each other as they race across the page. They even spill over onto the back of the letter.

The policeman reads, then re-reads the note, holding it in his thick fingers. He seems to have forgotten that Ranu is still present. The boy shuffles his feet, his toes tingling from lack of circulation.

436

"Still here," grunts the Assistant Superintendent, raising his small, blood-shot eyes to look at the child.

"Here. Take this and go."

Tearing a sheet from a notebook, he writes something in reply then, folding the paper, he adds a few more coins from his pocket, and offers them to the boy who holds out his hand. The man lets his heavy fist rest in the child's palm for several seconds before releasing the money. It is not a sign of affection, or even attraction, but control.

Ranu retreats softly from the room, pulling the door quietly to behind him until he hears the snick of its catch. He feels a lightness of heart as he pads back to the entrance, past the men at their desks, sweating under fans like ships' propellers, churning the hot air. Gunasekera is still at his desk, immersed in the novel that he always hides in a sheaf of papers. He does not even notice the boy, who melts past like a vapour.

Once outside, Ranu crouches in a corner, fingering the coins in his cupped hand. Another 50 rupees! This message must be important. Congratulating himself on his good fortune, he wheels his bike out of the precinct and sets off for the monastery, weaving his way through dark streets and narrow alleys on a route known only to himself.

1957: Despair

The protest failed. There will be no rising of the Sinhalese nationalists. At least, not yet. Every minute of the day and, during frequent wakeful moments of the night, those words torment the abbot of Kelaniya. It is Anil's account of how Mr Jayawardene's supporters were turned back by the police at Imbulgoda. At the time, Buddharakkita had absorbed the details without comment, grim-faced, in absolute silence. For once, he had said nothing, although anger seared his heart.

Having absorbed every painful detail reported by Anil, Buddharakkita had swivelled on his chair to look out over the grounds of Kelaniya where clusters of canna lilies blazed like red flames in the sunlight. Buddharakkita had slapped the arm of his chair, then gripped it tightly as if trying to crush it between his fingers. Then, still with his back to Anil, he had waved his other hand, dismissing the monk. Anil had bowed and walked stiffly from the room, rage and desolation competing for the black hollow of his heart.

Since then, Buddharakkita has locked himself away in his apartment, refusing to see anyone, brooding in isolation on what he deems a personal defeat. Despair has settled over the monastery, mantling it with dark wings. One monk says that he has heard the abbot shouting at the top of his voice although, to his certain knowledge, there was no-one with him in his study.

Amongst the more gullible brethren, fearful rumours have begun to circulate that the abbot is possessed. Those of a more sanguine nature dismiss these suggestions. After all, the abbot has a telephone in his study. He is probably speaking to his powerful friends in Government. And yet, whatever the explanation, nothing can dispel the deep sense of gloom that seems to grip the whole community. A new silence has descended, not the tranquillity of a holy place, but rather the brooding silence which precedes a storm.

***

Anil and Tissa are at work in the vegetable garden. The two men labour in silence, each moving in time to the rhythm of his hoe. A heavy downpour of rain has blighted the tomato plants and the patch is being cleared for a fresh crop of sweetcorn. The sun glints on the blade of the hoe as Tissa slices through the base of the rotting plants, watching with satisfaction as they keel over. The strong, green smell of tomatoes rises from the bruised flesh and the juice which spatters his feet dries into a pungent, yellow stain.

Wiping the sweat from his face with the back of his hand, Tissa leans on his hoe. The sun is burning his neck with its relentless heat and, although he is a farmer's son, it has been a long time since he laboured in the fields. For want of something better to do, he breaks the silence.

"So, it was all for nothing?"

Anil does not reply. He has been like this for days. Frustrated by the failure of Mr Jayawardene's pilgrimage, he initially gave vent to his anger in the bitterest terms, swearing vengeance and death to his enemies: but, after that, he fell silent, walled up in his thoughts. Tissa cannot tell what he is thinking. He never can. But this time it is different. Somehow, he knows that Anil's anger is turning inwards, devouring the man's mind. He has not eaten for days. He is becoming thin and sunken-cheeked and has a wild-eyed look, the sort that comes from hunger fed by despair.

During the day, Anil labours in self-imposed silence but, at night, he howls in his sleep; long, low moans that sound like the lost spirit of a ghost. Those sounds are worse than his silence and Tissa often lies awake at night, his scalp prickling, his skin covered in goose bumps, listening to Anil's wordless litany of despair. One night, he crept quietly to Anil's bedside and shook him gently by the arm but, on opening his eyes, the monk did not recognise Tissa and glared at him with such hatred that Tissa has not attempted to wake him again.

The change, so rapidly taking place in his friend, makes Tissa fearful for the other man's sanity, even his life; yet he dares not ask for help. He does not know any of the other monks as Anil has deliberately kept him away from them and, anyway, he is only living in the monastery on sufferance, dependent upon the goodwill of the abbot who has, also, disappeared from sight, no doubt wrapped up in his own misery.

Tissa now has to make decisions for both himself and Anil, leading his friend around much as one guides a blind man. Taking him gently by the arm, he leads him into prayers where, instead of chanting, Anil stares blankly in front of him. Then, at meal times, Tissa takes Anil to the refectory where, seated on a long bench with the other monks, he stares at the bowl of rice in front of him, leaving it cold and untouched.

Secretly, Tissa is beginning to panic. He has no monastic training himself and saffron robes are no camouflage for his ignorance. Anil, in his right mind, provided cover for them both but now they are exposed and Tissa has already noticed questioning looks from some of the other monks.

He welcomed the opportunity to bring Anil into the garden, away from inquisitive eyes. Here, at least, Tissa can engage in an activity which he understands and he puts all his energy into hoeing the garden, rooting up the diseased plants and hacking up the soil.

Sweat trickles into his eyes, stinging them with its saltiness. He stops again and wipes his face on his robe. As he does so, seemingly blind, he swings the hoe at the earth and nearly slices through his own foot. Tissa gasps, but Anil seems not to notice. It is then, in desperation, that Tissa knows he must do something. Without thinking, he wishes for help, so urgently that his wish becomes a prayer. But nothing happens. Anil continues to thrash the soil with his hoe and Tissa notices that the man's cheeks are streaked with tears.

"Oh god. Oh my god," murmurs Tissa.

Anil's hoe slashes into a curry bush, releasing a pungent, spicy smell and disturbing a large hornet that was basking on the leaves. It is the biggest hornet that Tissa has ever seen, easily as long as his thumb. It hovers unsteadily then, buzzing angrily, darts towards Tissa. He is sure it is going to sting him. Having worked for many years in the fields, he has had his fair share of insect bites and stings and has learned to accept the resulting discomfort without fuss, but a sting from a creature like this is unbearably painful. The hornet is now hovering in front of Tissa's face as if it is deciding whether or not to attack.

"My god," whispers Tissa again.

It is an invocation, a prayer for help. He can see the hornet's eyes, shiny black domes on the side of its head, looking straight at him, or so it seems. The insect's wings beat the air so fast that they look like streaks of gold. The back of the black abdomen curls slightly beneath the great body, revealing the point of its sting. Tissa is mesmerised. Unable to control himself, he starts to talk, babbling at first, an unintelligible rush of words, guaranteed to irritate his master. Yet, Anil does not notice and continues his blind harrying of the soil.

Through fear, Tissa's tongue unlocks and he begins to talk freely of himself, something he has never done, describing his background, where he came from and, finally, his love for Sriya. Then, before he can stop himself, he begins to talk of his rival: how and when he arrived in the village, how he speaks, what he looks like, how he stole that which was most precious to him. How he hates him. As he speaks, he feels the anger rushing through him like a wave but, instead of engulfing him, as it so often does, it bears him up, gives him strength. He has tamed his hatred, like a wild horse. Now he can control and direct it. For the first time, he can think and speak of Asoka with a clear head. His cure, as far as he can tell, is complete.

Tissa is so taken up with these thoughts that he does not notice that Anil has stopped working and is now listening intently. Something in what Tissa said has caught his attention.

***

When Tissa first began to speak in his soft, droning voice, it was an irritant to Anil, like the buzzing of a hornet.

"How stupid he looks. Like an ox," thought Anil and it occurred to him that Tissa's head was filled with clay, as heavy and inert as the stuff on which he was working. Anil even considered hitting the boy to shut him up but something, not linked to his own will, had deterred him. Tissa babbled on, trying to lift his master's mood, offering words of encouragement, timeworn saws of peasant wisdom that sounded as empty to Anil as a clanging bucket.

It was drivel, mostly, about how one should bear up in the face of adversity and how hope never died, peppered with examples from Tissa's own, limited experience. Anil had hardly bothered to listen, so, it was with some surprise that, while mechanically following the movement of his hoe, something that Tissa said shot through him, a revelation that that hit him like an arrow. The context for the remark was trivial, the emotions banal: Tissa's heartbreak at the loss of the girl he should have married. Anil had tried to block out the buzzing in his ears, but then came the casual remark that he nearly missed.

Tissa's usurper was an outsider, an educated man who could read and write. Nothing extraordinary in that, except for the fact that the man's past was a mystery and that he had appeared about the time that Mennan had died. According to Tissa, the man had been found wandering in the jungle, filthy and deranged and been taken in by the girl's family.

***

It is like a clear voice calling to him from the end of a dark tunnel. For the first time in days, Anil speaks.

"What was the man's name?"

Tissa thrusts out his lower lip and becomes suddenly sullen, as sulky as a child bent on misbehaviour. For a minute, Anil fears he will not reply. If he does not, Anil will have to beat it out of him. His hands tighten on the handle of the hoe.

"Don't know. At least, not his last name."

Tissa kicks savagely at a lump of earth. It shatters, sending out a shower of small pellets that patter against the surrounding plants with a noise like rain.

"Everyone just called him Asoka."

Anil's heart lurches and he catches his breath. He bends swiftly to his work, hiding his face so as not to betray his feelings. How had he known? Why had he asked that question? What had persuaded him to listen to Tissa despite his own disinclination?

Anil detects a divine hand guiding him back to Asoka. He is meant to meet again with the man that he once revered as his master and who he now despises as a coward. Asoka still has a part to play, that is clear, but what that will be is still a mystery to Anil. He must have time to reflect. He must not act hastily but bide his time and wait for the right opportunity. Nothing must be hurried.

"Is anything the matter?"

Tissa is stooping, trying to look into Anil's face. The boy's concern is almost touching, but he must not suspect anything. Not yet. Suddenly, the silence is disturbed by the loud purr of an engine. A shining limousine sweeps past with a passenger in the back. The abbot's profile is clearly outlined. He is wearing a black trilby and a dark suit.

"I wonder where he's going?" whispers Tissa, awestruck.

Anil shrugs and resumes his work, feigning ignorance although he knows that the abbot is on his way to the home of Vimala Wijewardene. It is his custom to wear western dress on such occasions.

The appearance of the abbot, after such a marked absence, is encouraging. Perhaps he has found a way out of his despair. Perhaps, thinks Anil, the game is not yet over.

1957: A pair of slippers

The pedestrian traffic of early morning is enlivened by groups of schoolchildren. Chattering and giggling, playing tag and comparing homework, they contrast with their adult counterparts, most of whom are solemn-faced and soberly-dressed. The girls, dressed in white skirts and blouses, have their long hair tightly bound in plaits which, secured in a loop on either side of the head, are tied with scarlet ribbons. The boys also wear white; neatly-pressed trousers and starched shirts, the poorer families using rice water, rather than shop-bought products, to stiffen collars and cuffs.

Although immaculately dressed, few of the children wear shoes, some from preference, others from necessity. In either case, the lack of shoes causes no hardship. The soles of Island children are tougher than elephant hide, seasoned by playing barefoot in the streets, running over stony tracks, hunting in scrubland or fishing in open drains. In a country often afflicted by extremes of heat or wet, shoes are no protection against the elements and are generally regarded as an encumbrance, rather than protection for the feet. There is no shame in going barefoot; rather it is the state to which every Islander aspires. Fathers returning from work kick off their shoes and lift their sarongs over their ankles, allowing the air to play around their toes, while housewives pad barefoot around the house, savouring the coolness of their polished red floors.

Rani wears slippers; not from choice, but to satisfy her mother's fastidious taste. Rani hates her slippers. Made of rubber, they chafe between her toes and their soles stick to her feet and make them hot. She longs to take her sandals off but, having done so once and been caught by her mother, she fears a terrible retribution if she does so again. So Rani drags her feet, scuffing dust over the hated slippers, hoping they will break, thinking evil thoughts about her mother.

She kicks bad-temperedly at a pebble. It spins away from her foot and hits the kerb opposite, startling a child with a pale, nervous face; the sort that cries easily. The boy pauses and stares at Rani, his lip quivering, his eyes brimming, his expression both petulant and fearful. An only child, thinks Rani, savagely, as she kicks another stone towards the boy. The pebble hits the kerb with a thwack and the boy literally jumps in the air.

Spoilt brat, thinks Rani, imagining the boy being fawned over by adoring parents. The thought makes her angrier than ever and she kicks another stone directly at the boy. It misses him by a couple of inches, but this time, he just stands there, with his mouth open, a willing target. Rani contemplates sending another stone. She cannot miss. They stand, staring at each other, the boy in terrified anticipation, Rani considering her next move.

If I do it again, he'll wet his pants. She giggles. Seizing his opportunity, the boy whimpers and darts off, seeking refuge among the groups of bigger girls and boys. Pity, thinks Rani, with a certain sense of loss. She needs an object on which to vent her anger.

Rani is approaching the time when girls become women. At the first sign of menstrual blood, the whole family will be informed and aunts and uncles will congratulate her parents and send Rani gold coins. At least, that's what her friends tell her. Most girls look forward to the event but the approaching loss of childhood fills Rani with dread. She does not wish to grow up, fearing the complexities of adulthood.

Rani has never been as close to her mother as Saro but, recently, Neleni seems to have had little time for either of them, wandering about the house in a happy, preoccupied state. She often mixes the girls' names up and, having asked them a question, never waits for the response. Her mind is always somewhere else.

However, although Neleni is happy most of the time, there was a strange little episode a couple of weeks ago. The family were seated at the table, having just finished dinner, and Rani was helping her mother clear away the plates. Having attained the state of pleasant mellowness that follows a good meal and three glasses of arrack, Raj had been chatting to Arjun when Neleni reached past him for his plate.

"Look at my beautiful wife," said Raj, proudly.

And, indeed, Neleni had looked very beautiful that night, her short hair pinned back and decorated with fresh sprigs of jasmine. She had smiled at the compliment, blushing slightly, but then, the good humour around the table had been suddenly dispelled. Sliding his arm around his wife's waist, Raj had tried to kiss her.

Neleni had pulled away sharply, pushing him back with her hand. Reading this as a bit of coquetry, Raj had pushed his chair back and, laughing, tried to clutch Neleni and pull her towards him. She dodged again and darted around the table with Raj in pursuit. The girls had thought it a huge joke, clapping their hands and shouting: "Kiss chase, kiss chase." Meanwhile, Uncle Arjun had sat at the table, his face pale and set like stone.

Excited and a little bit frightened, the girls had shrieked, urging their father on. Laughing, he had grabbed Neleni by the arms and tried to pull her towards him and kiss her. She had tried to turn her head away with a look of disgust but Raj had persisted and succeeded in landing a large, wet kiss on her mouth. Arjun had risen in his chair, his expression a mixture of outrage and anger. The girls had held their breath, not understanding what was happening, but sensing an unusual tension between the adults. Then, Raj had let Neleni go, giving her a friendly pat on the bottom.

"Just a game," he had said, trying to repress a belch. "Don't be angry, wifey."

But Neleni was looking at the empty seat where Arjun had been sitting a few minutes before.

"Where's he gone?" said Raj, his voice a little slurred and querulous, like a child.

Without a word, Neleni had swept the cloth from the table, rolled it up, then carried it out into the kitchen to shake the crumbs out of the back door. Raj and the girls were left in silence, stunned, not knowing what to expect next, not understanding what had happened. Raj had then taken a few steps towards the kitchen, as if he meant to follow Neleni but, thinking better of it, he had poured himself another glass of arrack and settled himself down beside the radio to listen to the day's news.

Creeping into the kitchen after her mother, Rani found Neleni with her head bowed over the sink. Most of the jasmine had fallen from her hair but one piece was hanging over her ear. She seemed not to notice.

"Amma?" Rani had whispered. "Are you crying?"

"No."

But Rani knew that she was.

Rani thinks of that evening as she scuffs along the road to school. For several days afterwards, her mother's mood had changed, from silent happiness to one of brooding disquiet. She became taciturn, sometimes hostile, especially when the girls became boisterous or noisy. It was as if she hated everyone, except Uncle Arjun who seemed distant and sad. She could not do enough for him, even relieving Rani of taking his tea to him in the morning. Rani had protested. It was her favourite household duty. Uncle Arjun always greeted her with a smile and, in return for his tea, always gave her a piece of bull-toe toffee or a chunk of jaggery. However, Rani's resistance was no match for her mother's determination. To her disgust, she was dismissed and relieved of all tea-carrying duties.

Rani kicks at another pebble. Stupid slippers! It is all her mother's fault; but the sandals and the loss of her tea duties are not the only grievances she has against Neleni. There is something darker and more terrible preying on her mind: new knowledge, imperfectly understood which, nevertheless, she knows she should not have. A secret.

Last night, she was silently padding around the house on bare feet, searching for a place to read, away from Saro's attentions. It was late and she should have been in bed, but she had nearly reached the end of her book and she wanted to finish it.

She decided to go to the other end of the house, where Uncle Arjun has his bedroom. There is a linen cupboard nearby with just enough room for her to curl up with a torch. Passing the kitchen where her father was asleep with his head on the table, she crept along the dark passage, past rows of photographs with the faces of dead relatives, solemn and humourless. She can never understand why her mother keeps such a grim collection. For some reason, they remind Rani of hunters' trophies.

As she tip-toed past the pictures, she felt the hair rising on the back of her neck. It was as if the dead were watching her. She turned quickly, looking behind her, almost expecting them to have materialised from their frames and to be following her along the corridor. Suddenly, her idea did not seem such a good one but, being stubborn, she was determined to persevere and, then, it happened. She heard a long, low moan, like a sigh.

Rani clapped her hand to her mouth to stop herself from screaming. For a few seconds, she stood still, wondering whether to retreat or advance but, where most children would have run shrieking to their mothers, Rani's intrepid nature drew her on. Terrified as she was, she was also inquisitive.

Clutching her book to her thumping heart, she walked warily down the dark passage, stopping at the place where it turned a corner. Here there were no pictures and she leant against the wall which felt cold and clammy against her hot skin, like the hand of a ghost. She shivered. Then, taking a deep breath, she peeped around the angle of the wall. The passage was in darkness except for a thin beam of light shining from under Uncle Arjun's door. That, in itself, was unusual because Uncle Arjun usually keeps his door open. Why had he shut it?

Urged on by her own curiosity, Rani stepped carefully along the corridor as if to avoid invisible traps. Then, she heard it again. A moan. A sigh. A soul in torment. Uncle Arjun. She must rescue him. Softly, she approached the door. Then she heard voices. One was his; the other, her mother's. The door, which has never closed properly, was slightly ajar and peeping through the crack, Rani saw them, together, on the bed. She gasped, then bit her finger hard to stop herself from crying out. They did not see her and continued as before, her mother whispering Arjun's name with increasing urgency.

A large, painful lump swelled up in Rani's throat and tears seemed to push themselves, unbidden, into her eyes. Frozen by shock, she was unable to move and the tears lay heavy on her eyelids, blurring her vision. Then, she blinked and two hot streams ran down her cheeks; but the lump in her throat remained, a huge stillborn sob. She turned and ran, back along the passage to the kitchen where her father was sleeping, his arm curled around his head, his hand clutching an empty glass.

"Appa," she whispered.

"Mmnh, nngh," he grunted in his sleep.

His thick hair was ruffled and untidy. Gently, she stroked his head.

"Ugh!" he raised a hand and swatted her away, like a troublesome fly.

Bending over, Rani looked into his sleeping face. He looked vulnerable, like a baby, his mouth half-open. She did not know exactly what she had witnessed in Uncle Arjun's room, but she knew, somehow, that it was wrong and her first impulse was to run and tell her father, but she could not rouse him. For a couple of minutes, she watched over him as he slept and saw his brow wrinkle into a frown as he muttered something. A name. He was calling in his sleep for her mother.

Rani backed silently out of the kitchen, on tiptoe, so as not to wake him then softly pattered back to her room, the bare soles of her feet sticking to the surface of the polished floor. She heard voices behind her, murmuring softly and concealing herself in the darkened hallway, she peeped around the corner to see her mother and Arjun standing close together at the other end of the passage. She could not tell if they were kissing but she could clearly see Uncle Arjun's hand raised to her mother's face as if stroking her cheek. She could hear them laughing softly, could see the soft gleam of her mother's white teeth as she smiled, the glint of gold along the border of her sari.

Biting her lip, Rani had flattened herself against the wall, tears coursing hotly down her cheeks. At that moment, the hallway seemed the bleakest place on earth, filled with dark shadows and the towering mass of the grandfather clock. The only light came from the tiny flame, flickering in its red glass pot before the image of the Virgin. It threw an eerie light over the blue-cloaked figure, illuminating the whiteness of the praying hands, the plaster face and the eyes, upturned to heaven. Suddenly, everything that was familiar had become strange and treacherous.

Rani crept back into the room that she shared with her sister. Saro was asleep on her side, her face framed by black curls, her fist curled up on the pillow, the thumb which she had been sucking, still resting on her lower lip. While Rani had previously envied Saro for being her mother's favourite, she was now jealous of her ignorance, her lack of knowledge, her peace. Tonight, Rani had been brutally ejected from the innocent world of children, where the ugliness of adult life could not intrude on the world of make-believe. She could never again pretend that Uncle Arjun was her prince. Her mother had seen to that.

Hearing the soft clatter of her mother's sandals approaching along the passage, Rani climbed into bed and pretended to be asleep. Her mother came in, as usual, first bending over the cot to kiss Saro, then leaning over to kiss Rani's cheek. At the touch of those lips, Rani wanted to scream. Her stomach leapt in revolt and she thought she would be sick.

"Please, please, make her go," she prayed, trying to visualise the white face of the Virgin's statue, but she could not make it appear. Everything was blotted out by the touch of that burning kiss.

"Good night, my darling," whispered Neleni, stroking her daughter's hair. Then, to Rani's relief, she quietly left the room.

Rani felt as if her body was alight. She imagined small flames licking at her skin.

"She's going to hell," she thought. "Serve her right!"

But the thought brought little consolation, particularly when she realised that Uncle Arjun would probably be joining her mother there. With bitter tears, Rani cried herself to sleep.

That terrible secret follows Rani to school, squatting on her shoulder like an incubus. She will never forget what she saw last night. She picks off one of her hated slippers and, imagining her mother's face on it, hurls it over the parapet of the bridge, watching as it falls into the shallow water below. The stream carries it a little way, but then it gets lodged between two rocks. She can see it, stuck there, like an accusation, a reminder of her guilt. Who cares? She takes the other one off and throws that in, too.

A washer-woman, squatting on the flat rocks by the bank, looks up at her and shouts. A small naked child runs up to the woman. Rani feels guilty. The woman is berating her for throwing things into the river, polluting the clean water, throwing away shoes which she herself could not afford. Terrified, Rani scampers across the bridge.

"Hey," shouts a voice behind her. "Hey! What do you mean, throwing stones at my brother?"

She turns and there is the small boy that she victimised earlier, holding the hand of a much bigger boy, pointing at her. Although her heart is pounding with fear, Rani shrugs, drawing her mouth down as if to say "So what if I did?" The boy marches towards her, dragging his small brother behind him. He jabs a warning finger at her face.

"Don't you ever do that again, you hear. Or I'll give you a beating."

Then, for good measure, he pokes her in the middle of her flat chest. Other children begin to gather round, watching silently, waiting to see what will happen. Rani's cheeks burn and her eyes fill with tears. After last night, this humiliation is too much to bear. The boy is much bigger than her but she doesn't care. Suddenly, she springs forward and with fists and feet flailing, she attacks him. Taken by surprise, the boy falls backwards with Rani on top of him, shrieking and scratching like a banshee.

"Ai, ai. Get her off me!"

They roll in the dust, their white clothes turning the colour of parchment. The boy delivers a well-aimed punch to Rani's stomach. The pain is excruciating and she is momentarily winded but, within seconds, she has renewed the attack, kicking and punching, biting and spitting, carried along by the joyous release of her anger.

The boy whimpers as Rani sinks her teeth into his arm, she wants to bite right through his shirt, make him bleed. She can feel the sinew between her clenched teeth. Then, all of sudden, fingers pinch her nose and she is forced to release her grip and gasp for air through her mouth.

"Rani Chelvam, what do you think you are doing?"

Several sharp slaps are delivered to the back of her legs, then a pair of strong hands lifts her onto her feet. White hands, like those of the Virgin, only much bigger and covered in ginger freckles. The hands grasp Rani's shoulders, spinning her round to face a flame-haired young man in a black soutane; the young Irish priest who teaches history at school.

"We're going straight to see Mother Superior," he snaps.

There is a low cackle as Rani's opponent, now sitting up, winks at his friends. As if he was the victor.

"And you needn't look so cocky, Edward Darsan. Yes, I know your name. Father Benedict will be hearing about this. Let's see what he thinks about you picking on girls half your size."

Blushing, the boy lowers his head and pushes himself onto his feet. Sheepishly, he goes to pick up his satchel which is lying in the gutter, the strap having been broken in the scuffle. With grim pleasure, Rani notices that he is rubbing the place on his arm where she bit him.

Sunny shuffles along the street, on her way to cousin Ana.

"Come, child, hurry up. Don't dawdle."

Squatting down, her chubby hands resting on her knees, Saro has stopped to admire something in the gutter. Something shiny. A piece of tin, or is it a coin? Lowering herself onto her knees, she tentatively reaches out a hand, one finger extended, ready to perform a preliminary examination of the object, which glitters from a bed of roadside debris; mango skins sucked clean of their contents and betel nut, chewed to a pulp by former owners.

"No!" shrieks Sunny who, forgetting her age and the limitations of her joints, totters forward and grabs the child by the wrist, dragging her back from the kerb just as a rickshaw hurtles by, its bell tinkling wildly.

"Bad ... bad child," Sunny wheezes, the ribs in her concave chest pressing against her lungs, preventing her from drawing breath. Passers-by look at her quizzically as she stands gasping in the middle of the pavement, one hand kneading the painful stitch in her side, the other firmly holding onto the child who, whining and pointing to the gutter, is trying to pull away.

"Are you all right, Aunty?" asks a young man, a Moslem wearing a white, crocheted skull-cap. He speaks in Tamil.

"Yes, my son. I am all right now."

The boy looks uncertain, unsure as to whether he should leave her, but Sunny nods her head reassuringly and waves him away. Reluctantly, he leaves them, and is swallowed by the streams of people hurrying to work or school, although Sunny can still see his skull-cap, weaving in and out of the crowds. Then, he disappears and Sunny is left alone, like an island in the middle of a fast-flowing stream. Instead of lessening, the pain in her side has attained a knife-like intensity, making it difficult to breathe.

"Come on," she says, none too gently, yanking Saro by the wrist and, together, they shuffle forward, the child chattering and twisting Sunny's arm as she stops suddenly to gaze at some new attraction.

The journey to Ana's is not a long one, she lives only a few streets away but, at this speed, it will take some time; half an hour or forty minutes, where it could normally be done in five. Sunny knows that she should not have undertaken this journey. Both Raj and Neleni offered to take Saro, but Sunny insisted. Despite her physical frailty, she wanted to escape the oppressive atmosphere in the house. Like Rani, she noticed Arjun's sullen departure from the dinner table the other night, when Raj had playfully kissed his wife and Neleni's distress, when she glanced at the seat where Arjun had been sitting and realised it was empty. It was a good thing Raj had been drinking that night, or he might have noticed, too.

And there have been other things, small things, that do not mean much in isolation but, when added together, form an unsettling pattern: the change in her daughter's expression when Arjun enters the room; how her fingers tremble when she brushes against him and how, when they speak, their eyes seem to lock together in wordless understanding.

Sunny also noticed how, the day after that incident with Raj, Neleni had insisted on relieving Rani of her duty of delivering Arjun's morning tea. The girl had looked stricken and her eyes had filled with tears, but Neleni had dismissed her objections with a callousness that seemed almost deliberate. Sunny rages inwardly, but says nothing. She has no proof, although she has good reason to suspect Neleni's infidelity. How long before Raj comes to the same conclusion? Although not a quick thinker, he is not as stupid as many suppose. What then?

"Oh!"

A sharp pain stabs Sunny in her side, causing her to catch her breath, or what remains of it. She gasps at the air like a fish, trying to suck it in through her mouth. Even so, she can only draw shallow draughts and is beginning to feel light-headed. Tottering across the pavement, she leans against a wall.

"Aunty, this is no good. I came back to find you."

A hand touches her lightly on the elbow and she sees, with relief, the young Moslem standing beside her.

"Here, let me get you a taxi. Where are you going?"

Too tired to protest, she tells him. Striding across the pavement, the boy raises a hand in the air to hail a passing taxi. Sunny notices how the sunlight, flowing through the full white sleeve of his tunic, reveals a slender, child-like arm.

A black Morris Minor judders to a halt at the kerb. Each door is decorated with a row of chrome studs in the shape of skulls-and-crossbones, like the memento mori found on the carved memorial tablets in Christian churches. Sunny shudders. A cold shadow passes over her, brushing her cheek with its wing.

"Aunty, take my hand."

The boy addresses her in a no-nonsense tone of voice, taking her frail hand in his and helping her into the taxi. Once she is settled, he lifts Saro, who beams into the stranger's face with the sudden insight that sometimes illuminates the hidden thoughts of children. Putting her hand up to his face, she strokes the thin fringe of beard that frames his jaw line. He laughs, amused and a little embarrassed by her lack of inhibition.

"Here you are. Sit with Aunty."

Leaning into the taxi, he places Saro on the back seat then, after repeating the destination to the driver, the boy pats him on the shoulder to let him know that his passengers are ready to leave. As the taxi pulls away from the kerb, the boy shouts and waves.

"Salaam uh-leikum, Aunty."

And then, in Tamil:

"God be with you."

"And with you, my son," murmurs Sunny, responding to a universal blessing.

As the taxi picks up speed, Sunny catches a last glimpse of the boy, his arm raised in the air, his voluminous white clothes fluttering in the breeze from the traffic. Angels, she thinks, take many forms.

Leela is sitting at her desk, trying to compose a letter.

"My darling ..."

She stares at the blank page, twirling the pen between her fingers, a gold fountain pen that Mennan gave her for her birthday. She berated him at the time, calling him a cheapskate. Why had he not given her jewellery? He always gave her jewellery? Did he not love her? She can see his face now, anxious and afraid, as he pleaded with her, telling her that it was a very expensive pen: it had cost him twice as much as any diamond necklace; it would be the envy of all her friends.

It was and she had, eventually, forgiven him. But those were happier times, when men who loved her did her bidding. They are not so biddable now. She has not seen Arjun for weeks and her heart aches. He has simply disappeared without a goodbye or an explanation and, now, it is proving impossible to contact him. She has written many letters, all addressed to his home. He has responded to none of them. What has happened? Has she offended him? The slight to her dignity, to what she considers her irresistible charm, has shaken her confidence.

She tries to think of suitable words, something that will force him to respond but she can only think of one thing: blackmail. She can threaten to tell Arjun's boss of their affair. The Government Agent would probably fire him, bringing the young clerk's promising career to an abrupt end. She taps her lower lip with the end of her pen as she considers this possibility.

Of course, the discovery of their relationship could also have negative consequences for Leela. The enquiry into Mennan's financial dealings is still continuing. So far, she has managed to avoid the unwelcome attention of the investigators, successfully pleading ignorance of her late husband's affairs. In one respect, that is true. She never understood the minutiae of his dealings or his two sets of ledgers, one recording false accounts, the other revealing the true state of his finances. Yet, she has never doubted that his wealth was gained dishonestly. Anyone with half a brain could see that; but, so far, she has managed to convince the enquiry that she is innocent; just a silly, pretty woman who spent the money her husband earned without asking where it came from.

So far, she has managed to deflect attention from herself, but the revelation of an affair with someone closely involved with the enquiry would change all that. People might start to draw their own conclusions as to her motives. They might think that she initiated the affair simply to protect her own position and her innocence would be compromised. She might become the subject of investigation herself. She might even face a jail sentence. Who knows what the outcome might be? No, the threat of exposure is not something she can safely employ.

"My darling ..."

Leela stares at the words on the page. They seem to speak back, mocking her. Why is it she cannot write what she really feels? In all, she has written thirty letters, none of them longer than a couple of lines, just asking Arjun to meet her: all hinting at a good time, but none telling him what she really thinks, how his absence hurts her, how she pines for him. Why can she not write those things? Songs are full of such sentiments, written by people who probably do not feel them. Stories of broken hearts and lost love are available from every shop and market stall, inscribed on vinyl discs or crammed between the covers of cheap novellas. So why can she not speak of her own feelings?

Looking up from the desk, Leela gazes across the room and catches her own reflection, staring back at her from the mirror and she hears a voice in her head, as if her own image is speaking to her across a distance of centuries.

Do not let him see your pain.

Pride. That is it. She is too proud ever to tell any man that she loves him. While happy to exhibit her body in all its lovely nakedness, she can never expose what lies in her soul. She would die, lonely and unloved, rather than bare her feelings.

Putting down the pen, she crumples up the sheet of writing paper without looking at the two words she has written. Even they reveal too much of her affection. Dropping the ball of paper into the waste basket, she picks up the telephone. Using a pencil, an affectation learned from an American movie, she carefully dials the number of Arjun's office, then watches as the chrome dial turns, clicking back into place after each number, like an astrologer's wheel.

"Hello. Office of the Government Agent. Can I help you?"

The girl's voice has a nasal tone. She sounds stupid.

"I want to speak to Mr Kumaran."

"He's not in," replies the girl, abruptly.

It is the same response that Leela received two days ago.

"I suppose you're going to tell me he's in a meeting," she snaps.

"No. It's his day off. He's at home, madam."

The girl puts the emphasis on the last word. She has perfected the civil service trick, acquired from the British, of using courtesy as an insult.

Furious, Leela slams down the receiver.

"Angela, Angela," she shrieks through the open door.

"Yes, madam."

The housekeeper appears almost immediately, out of breath, her face full of expectant terror. Her mistress is looking at herself in the mirror and the housekeeper notices how, when she speaks, she seems almost to be speaking to herself.

"Tell Rammale to get the car. I'm going out."

Since she first made love to Arjun, Neleni has been in a state of nervous euphoria. The enclosed atmosphere of the house, the constraints imposed by its other occupants and the need for secrecy only serve to increase the lovers' passion. It is all-consuming and in Neleni's case, undiluted by work or the cares of the outside world, obsessive. An innocent manoeuvre – the passing of a plate or dish at supper or meeting in the narrow passage by the kitchen – may result in Arjun brushing her hand. At such times, Neleni feels such ecstasy that she nearly faints.

Sometimes they take risks – Sunny is always somewhere in the house. Last week, Neleni visited Arjun in his room and they made love, fully clothed, Neleni sitting on the school desk, her feet locked around his back. Another time, he pushed her into a corridor and they made love standing against the wall, Neleni's skirts bunched up around her waist, her naked buttocks pressed against the cool plaster of the wall while he penetrated her. She had to swallow her moans of ecstasy, try not to let anyone hear her rapid breathing. And three nights ago, on his bed, with the door ajar. The sheer opportunism of these encounters heightens the pleasure, but it is risky. The fear of getting caught only makes the experience more intense.

The fact that they cannot give full rein to their feelings, the need for secrecy and the risk of being discovered, only serve to increase their passion. Like a jungle orchid, rooted in the bark of an old tree, their love flourishes within the humble confines of the home.

However, the hot-house atmosphere in which their affection thrives, also gives rise to other, less pleasurable sensations. The inability to communicate freely leads to uncertainty and a heightened anxiety about the thoughts or feelings of the other. Such concerns, if not dealt with swiftly, can easily ignite, fanning the flames of jealousy, urging the lovers to greater acts of recklessness simply to quiet their mental torment.

Neleni cannot forget what happened two weeks ago when Raj kissed her at the dinner table. Turning her face away, she had tried to dissuade Raj but he had exhibited the amorous persistence that often follows a bottle of arrack. She had tried to push him away, wincing when he kissed her; but her show of unwillingness was lost on her husband and, more importantly, on Arjun for, having freed herself from Raj's clutches and the possibility of another wet, lascivious kiss, Neleni realised that the young man's chair was empty. Swiftly, quietly, Arjun had left the room.

She can only guess what he felt. She had wanted to run after him, but knew she could not. Her mother's face, with its quizzical expression, was turned towards her and, although the old lady's eyes are weak and milky behind their out-sized spectacle frames and thick lenses, they miss nothing.

Further pain and indignity was to follow. Aroused by his daring kiss at supper, Raj visited his desire upon Neleni that night. She could not refuse. He was, after all, her husband, but never before had the feel of his skin, his smell or the weight of his body on top of her, filled her with such intense loathing. Previously, she had been able to accept his attentions with detached neutrality but, during that perfunctory coupling, she had to bite her lip to stop herself from screaming. Holding tight to the metal bedpost to stop it thumping against the wall, she had prayed that Arjun would not hear.

His work done, Raj had rolled off her and turned on his side, falling into a deep, stertorous sleep. Lying awake with the sheet pulled up to her chin, Neleni had been racked with guilt and fear. Just a glimpse of Arjun's face that evening, when Raj had kissed her, had been enough to tell her that he felt angry and betrayed. What would he think if he knew what she had just done? Would he hate her? She felt sick with fear. She wanted to go to him. Immediately. Explain. *It is not easy for a woman in my position.* But she could not. No-one must suspect their affair.

While increasing her desire, the uncertainty and fear also make her irrational. One minute she pities Arjun, the next she is angry with him. How dare he judge her? She is the one protecting them both. It is she who is making sacrifices, sleeping with a man who disgusts her. Arjun can just go back to his room, sleep soundly and in peace. On his own. That is a privilege she has not enjoyed for years.

At other times, she wonders how long he will be able to bear the pain of sharing her, however unwilling she may be, with another man. If she was in his place, could she do it? She thinks not.

He will tire of me, I know it. And then he will find someone else.

Often, in the middle of the night, she feels as if she is being stifled. She wants to get up. Pace the room. Burn off the fumes of her poisonous anger, fear and anxiety, but she cannot. If she does, she might wake Raj, then he will want to know what is wrong. No. She must lie here. In the dark. Alone with her fear.

***

Joy. Arjun has announced that he will spend the next day at home, studying for exams. If he obtains a good grade, his future success will be assured. He may, in time, become a Government Agent himself.

But Neleni is not concerned with his prospects. She only lives for the present and the opportunity to be with him. Alone. And there is something that she must ask him. Thinking of it dulls her pleasure but she can no longer contain her curiosity or the jealousy that it feeds.

For weeks now, almost since the beginning of their affair, he has been receiving letters: expensive cream envelopes, faintly scented with jasmine, with his name written in a hand that she recognises. The letters come from the author of the love letter that she found on his floor that day, many months ago. Is he still seeing Mennan's widow? Does he regret his involvement with Neleni? She has no way of telling. The only way to find out is to ask him and, yet, she fears the truth. How can she compete with a woman like that?

Once again, Neleni lies awake all night.

The next day, Arjun takes his breakfast early and returns to his room without speaking. He wears an expression of intense concentration, one that defies interruption or distraction. Even Rani senses that he does not want to be spoken to and leaves the house without giving him her customary greeting, hanging on her father's hand as he leads her to school. The nuns have forbidden her to make the journey unaccompanied since her unfortunate squabble in the street. She must be escorted for a whole month or face expulsion. Her father does not speak on these journeys, letting her feel the quiet force of his anger.

Shortly after Rani's departure with her father, Sunny also leaves the house, accompanied by Saro. Once again, they are to visit cousin Ana. Sunny is puzzled by the suddenness of this arrangement. Neleni only announced the plan this morning, rising early to seek out her mother, disturbing her peace as she smoked her pipe in the yard. Sunny was not pleased. She does not welcome another journey in the heat, however short. She even asked why Neleni was not going herself, but received an evasive reply. However, Sunny suspects that it has something to do with Arjun's presence in the house today.

She wonders if she should say something; warn her daughter against folly, tell Raj to come home early, but she is too tired. Young people must be allowed to make their own mistakes. She no longer has the energy to intervene. Even the journey to Ana's, a few streets away, will tax her strength. She cannot face the argument that will result if she tries to refuse, so she has resigned herself to the inevitable. The trip will do her good and she can always count on a warm welcome at Ana's house. There, she is treated as a guest, rather than the ghost that she has become in her own home.

With Saro skipping in front of her, Sunny descends the creaking wooden steps that lead from the front door to the street. Saro is waiting for her on the pavement, one cheek swollen with a large sweet that her mother popped into her mouth as she kissed her goodbye. Locking hands, Sunny and Saro begin their journey, walking at the old lady's shuffling pace, stopping at the corner to wave.

***

Neleni watches from the window as her mother and younger daughter disappear. Then, she waits another five minutes, in case they return. They do not and, suddenly, she feels as if a weight has been lifted from her. She has not spoken to Arjun for several days. There has been no opportunity. Or is it that he has not made one? Is he avoiding her?

These days, anxieties crowd around her, like fish nibbling a piece of bread. Eventually, they will wear her away. She must do something. Make an opportunity to speak to him. He will not thank her for distracting him while he works, but there must be something she can do. Of course. She will cook a meal. Something special. She runs to the kitchen and collects the large wicker basket that she always uses when visiting the market. She likes shopping for food and the fresh air will do her good.

Closing the front door quietly behind her, she descends the steps, pausing briefly to admire the temple tree. It is covered with delicate, lemony blossom and its sweet fragrance catches in her throat. It is sad and wonderful, bitter and sweet. She sees everything now with the heightened perception of love. Nothing is ugly, not even the pain that she is sometimes caused by Arjun. Even that is beautiful.

She steps into the street and crosses the busy road to the place where the market begins, immersing herself in the crowds, revelling in the intense colours and smells that surround her. Vegetable stalls are piled high with produce: shiny purple aubergines; fat peppers, yellow, green and red; carrots with hair-like roots, their leaves resembling bunches of fern; leeks; potatoes and, at the neighbouring stall, piles of dry spices: yellow turmeric, hot red chilli powder, star anise, coriander and cumin.

Neleni selects some fresh chillis. She is careful to choose the ones known as Kashmiri chillis: although fiery red, they are milder than they look, especially if the seeds are removed. Then she buys fresh coriander, garlic and onions with a pearly pink skin. She has enough dry spice mix at home, having made a large batch only a few days ago.

At the meat stall, she buys pork. Pigs are allowed to root freely through jungle and pasture and the meat is dark pink and flavoursome, covered with a layer of thick, fragrant fat. Neleni likes pork. It is her favourite.

She wanders past stalls selling cheap shoes, bags and saris until she reaches the end of the street. As she turns to walk back, a voice hails her.

"Some sweets, Madam. Freshly made!"

The young man is a Moslem, dressed in flowing white robes and a white skull cap. He speaks in Tamil, the language used by most of his race, although they owe their ancestry to Arab traders rather than the inhabitants of southern India. Neleni is easily identified as Tamil from the potu on her forehead. She smiles.

"Too many sweets will rot my teeth."

"But Madam," he remonstrates, "these are special. Try one."

Before she can get away, he takes a pair of tongs and, selecting a piece of fudge, holds it out to her. The sweet is cream-coloured, speckled with slivers of nut. She tries it and cannot conceal her pleasure. It is sweet, combining the flavour of coconut and cashew. It is also soft, which means that it is fresh, without the sugary staleness that so often spoils factory-made sweets.

"Fresh this morning," says the young man, reading her thoughts. "I made it myself."

He grins, proudly. No older than sixteen, he still has the trusting warmth of a child. He has not yet encountered disappointment and his expansive innocence reflects Neleni's own happiness. She laughs.

"How can I refuse? I will take ten pieces."

It costs more than she expected, but it is worth it. The boy is overjoyed and she will have something special to end her meal with Arjun. Expertly, the boy rolls a length of brown paper into a cone and drops the sweets inside, folding the top over to seal the packet. As she takes the small parcel, he smiles at her happily and it strikes Neleni that there is something other-worldly about this boy; a radiance, uncontaminated by care. Thanking him, she promises to return, then makes her way back along the crowded street.

She is on the corner, about to cross the road, when she notices a large car that has pulled up outside her house. It cannot have been there long, because the driver is helping a woman out: a beautiful woman with expensive jewellery that glints in the sun, showering the space around her with glints of red and green. Her sari is also the colour of gemstones, emerald and ruby, shot with lavish amounts of gold thread. She shimmers as she stands in front of the car, smoothing her hair with one hand as she looks up at the house.

Neleni's heart lurches and her throat tightens as she watches the woman mount the steps. Neleni notes the elegance of her figure, a tiny waist flowering into shapely hips that sway as she moves. She is almost regal, a consort fit for a king.

The woman pauses at the front door, examining it for some means of announcing her arrival. There is neither bell, nor door-knocker. The visitor makes a face, a small pout of displeasure, or is it disgust. Neleni cannot tell. She is too far away.

The woman makes a dainty fist and raps the door with her knuckles, wiping her hand on her sari afterwards as if it has become soiled. She waits, then knocks again. After a few minutes, the door opens and Arjun appears. He looks surprised. Without waiting, the woman walks inside and, in full view of the street, kisses Arjun on the mouth; not a peck, but a long lingering kiss. Then, the door closes.

Neleni feels as if she has been thrown onto a fire, for her skin is aflame, burning from head to foot. She is jealous, desperate and bitterly aware of her own inadequacy. She is hot from the crowds and dressed in an old sari. Her hair is out of place and she is ageing, ageing, so much older than Arjun. What hope can she have of keeping his affection now that she has seen her opponent; for she knows, instinctively, that the woman who has just entered her house is the author of the letters.

Never mind, whispers a voice in her ear, *it is still your home and she has no right to be there.*

Neleni crosses the street, darting between buses and lorries, cows and bicycles. She must know the truth, however painful. As she mounts the steps, she catches a faint whiff of jasmine.

***

The door clicks softly as she shuts it behind her. Neleni blinks, unable to see in the darkness of the hallway. Alert, yet completely motionless, she listens, like a shy animal hiding in the undergrowth that senses danger nearby. Voices, softly murmuring in the living room. She cannot hear what they are saying but recognises one as Arjun's. The other is that of the woman: soft and mellifluous, it wheedles and cajoles.

Quietly laying her basket on a chair, Neleni creeps across the hallway, keeping to the shadows, until she is close enough to hear a few words.

"Why have you not answered my letters? What have I done?"

There is a movement, as if someone is rising from a chair and walking across the room, although Neleni cannot tell in which direction. Is it Arjun? Is he comforting the woman? Has he put his arms around her?

Neleni's heart is beating so fast that it becomes hard to breathe, or even swallow, and her throat is dry and taut. The smell of jasmine grows suddenly stronger. The woman is pacing the room. It is she, not Arjun, who has risen from the chair. Neleni can hear the rustle of her sari as she walks; the stiff swish of heavy brocade; an expensive sari that women like Neleni only wear once in their life, at their wedding, if they are lucky. No doubt this woman has a wardrobe full of such clothes. Neleni can hear the click of the woman's heel as she steps off the rush mat, onto the hard concrete surface of the floor. Neleni is momentarily overcome by a feeling of shame.

The woman is still talking; haranguing Arjun for his ingratitude although her voice has become slightly less clear and Neleni can no longer smell the jasmine. The visitor must have resumed her seat.

"I love you, you stupid boy. That's why I came here. To tell you. I couldn't put it in a letter. I had to tell you myself."

Still, Arjun says nothing. The woman continues, undaunted.

"I'm a widow. Free to marry again. You need never worry about money. Or those silly exams you're taking. You say they are the reason you have not contacted me. I don't believe you! Tell me the truth."

Arjun coughs, awkwardly, and murmurs a reply which Neleni cannot hear. The tone of the woman's voice softens.

"Come back to me, my love. We could be happy."

There is a movement, a soft rustling. Are they kissing? Neleni can bear it no longer. Gently, she presses her hand against the door so that it swings open, gradually revealing the room beyond. With dreadful anticipation, her eyes seek the unfamiliar in a room, so well-known to her that she can summon its exact image with her eyes closed: the ancient padded sofa with its threadbare covers and antimacassar, the aspidistra in a brass pot, the large sepia portrait of her grandparents in their wedding finery, the side-table with its bowl of highly-polished fruit, the grandmother clock hanging from the wall that fills the room with its dolorous ticking.

First, she sees Arjun seated on a high-backed wooden chair. He is leaning forward, his elbows on his knees, his chin propped on his hands, staring fixedly at the floor. His white shirt is open at the neck; the sleeves rolled back, the cuffs unbuttoned and hanging open. The sight of him sends a thrill shuddering through her: the tension of his forearms; the blue gleam of his dark hair; the curve of his nose; the fullness of his lips; his elegant wrists and long-fingered hands. The careless beauty of a boy on the threshold of manhood.

Then, she sees the woman, her rival, seated on the sofa, arms flung back. Her slender fingers are loaded with rings, her wrists with gold bangles, an emerald necklace adorns her neck and long pendant ear-rings hang from her ears. As she moves, her jewels glint with many colours, like dewdrops caught in a spider's web. Although her face is beautiful, there is something raw and cruel about Leela's expression, like a predator eyeing its kill. She holds Arjun in a hungry gaze, willing him to give the answers she desires.

The door creaks on its hinges. Cheated of her prey, Leela turns a look of fury on the intruder. When he sees Neleni, Arjun's first reaction is one of pleasure until, remembering his circumstances, it turns to one of guilty confusion. Looking from Arjun to Neleni, Leela realises the motive for her lover's absence. She has been abandoned for another woman. This woman. She is both angry and incredulous.

"I see," she says, softly, rising to her feet. "I see."

Walking across the room, she stops a few inches in front of Neleni then slowly and deliberately runs her eyes over her rival, lingering every so often over what she considers to be an imperfection. She raises her arm so that the long drape of her scarf slips effortlessly onto her shoulder, then takes a step back, as if to give Neleni a final appraisal.

"You have chosen well, my love!"

She turns to Arjun with a smile of forbearance as if humouring a schoolboy; one who has just repeated an outdated fact in the belief that it is something new and interesting. Arjun blushes. Shaking her head in disbelief, Leela laughs pityingly; a laugh of ancient malice.

"Still, you know where to find me ... when you get tired."

Then, winding her scarf around her wrist, she drifts past Neleni and out of the door, like a malevolent breeze.

A sudden draft of air shakes the temple tree, covering the pavement in a shower of blossom. Dead to the muffled sound of the street outside, Neleni and Arjun stare at each other, caught in a dreadful silence.

Neleni waits, holding her breath as the grandmother clock on the wall measures out the seconds, its laborious ticking spreading across the room like invisible ripples. Her heart is frozen, her head too, she can neither think, nor speak.

Arjun takes a breath, looks down at the floor and clenches his fists. Neleni can see his knuckles turning white. He is summoning the courage to speak. She knows what he will say. She saw him blush just now. He is ashamed of her. For all her fury, that woman has seen with the clear sight of an outsider: their liaison is ridiculous. With quiet venom and a few well-chosen words, she has dissolved their illusion of happiness. How could Arjun love someone like Neleni? Why should he when he could have the beautiful, wealthy widow? He has been fooling himself. They both have.

Neleni can no longer look at him. Lowering her head, she waits for the words of ending: the faltering explanation; the clumsy attempt to soften the blow; the dismissal of her love as a thing of no meaning, a mistake, a wrong turning, a stillborn connection. And, as she waits, tears run thickly down her cheeks as if her very soul is bleeding salt water. With those tears, it seems to Neleni as if the pure essence of her life is streaming out of her. She is dying. Soon there will be nothing left: just an empty husk, another ghost to keep her mother company and take its place among the rows of dead faces along the walls.

"Neleni."

The voice which she both loves and fears, to which she thrills, while praying that it will never speak to her again, for it can only bring her pain.

"Neleni, look at me!"

With gentle fingers, he lifts her chin, his face so close that she can feel the warm breath that seems to write the words on her skin as he speaks, tantalising and torturing her, filling her with a hunger that will never be satisfied and which, in time, will devour her.

"Neleni ..."

The final blow is imminent. She can no longer look at him but lifts her eyes to the window, to where the temple tree stands, as still as death, filling the room with its sweet fragrance. She never dreamed of such exquisite pain.

Still, he does not speak. She knows that he is waiting for her to look at him. He cannot say what he wants if she looks away. If only she can avoid his eyes, she can avert disaster, but she knows it is impossible. Slowly, she turns her head to look at him, her heart quite still, like a bird lying dead in its cage.

"Neleni, please forgive me!"

"What?"

She hears his words but, her wits, dulled by pain, cannot interpret their meaning.

"I love you, Neleni."

"Ahh."

She sighs: relief beyond words. The air enters her lungs in tiny gasps and her heart, suddenly revived, flutters wildly.

***

A small green lizard emerges from its home in the shadow of the step and crawls up the wall of the house to bask in the sun. The white plaster is cracked with the heat and as hot as coals but the lizard's veins are touched with ice and it feels no discomfort, only a primitive yearning for warmth. Finding its habitual spot just below the window, the lizard freezes into position and waits, scenting the air for small flies and insects with the tip of its flickering tongue.

In the room, on the other side of the window, are two people, their arms wound about each other, like statues, impervious to the passing of time or the changing of seasons. Neleni and Arjun cannot tell how long they have stood together, her head resting against his shoulder. It may have been minutes, or centuries.

Caught by the wind, a blossom from the temple tree flies from its branch and hits the shutter, startling the lizard and the figures inside. Neleni raises her head and looks at Arjun.

Softly, without a word, their lips meet in a delicate kiss. They part, smiling, exploring each other's faces with their fingers. Then, they kiss again, bolder this time, engaging their tongues. Arjun loosens Neleni's blouse. She feels his hand slip inside to cup her breast, his fingers caressing her nipple which rises and hardens in eager response. A pulse begins to throb between her legs, at once so delicious and agonising that she thinks it will kill her. His hand slips under the folds of her skirt, skimming the tender reach of her thigh until it finds that secret place, now damp and eager to receive him. He lifts her onto the couch where, fully clothed, they make love.

Afterwards, he smiles at her dreamily, then lies with his head on her breast while she strokes his hair. As she looks around her, Neleni discovers that the room, with all its familiar angles and spaces, has taken on a different aspect, as if her surroundings have altered, reflecting her mood with a new perspective. Simple objects, that never merited a second glance, now assume a new and interesting form: the carved beading on the chairs, delightful in its rustic imperfection; the silvered face of the grandmother clock with its elegant Roman numerals; the green chenille cloth on the table; the blue jug filled with pink hibiscus, their petals slightly crinkled, like paper that has been crumpled then smoothed out; the sheen on the polished red floor; even the shifting arabesques, etched on the wall by sunlight seeping through the shutters.

Where there was formerly only dullness and sterility, she now sees vibrant, living colour: rich hues of plum and aubergine, crimson and carmine, gold and emerald; colours redolent of luxury, of wine, silk and gems. She has fallen into a poem that she read in one of Arjun's books and admired, but regarded as fantastical, something to be imagined but not experienced. It is an account of ships and their cargoes: the Quinquireme of Nineveh, sailing home to Palestine with ivory, and apes and peacocks, sandalwood, cedarwood, and sweet white wine. She used to wonder how anyone could write with such vividness, painting with words, drawing perfume from the page. But now she understands. She is seeing it, feeling it for herself, with all her senses.

***

461

The rest of the day passes in bliss. They bathe together, limbs entangled in the great white bath, then Neleni cooks the meal with Arjun at her side, fondling her neck, playing with her hair, feeding her the sweets that she bought from the market. Once the food is ready, they discover that they no longer have the desire to eat. Unable to part from each other for longer than a few seconds, they return to the bedroom where in the lazy heat of afternoon, they make love; the old, soft mattress wallowing beneath them like a wave while the iron bedsprings grate a rhythmic response to their sighs.

Afterwards, they lie, fingers entwined, staring at the ceiling as if it were a sky filled with stars. Neleni knows that she is bound to him for life.

"You must end it with her."

"It's over anyway. She just didn't realise. Until today."

He falls silent, prey to a small, stinging memory, the sort that will return many times, unbidden, to taint his pleasure. At Leela's insistence, they had driven up into the hills, to spend the day at a rest-house while Neleni attended Michael's wedding. It had all been Leela's idea, an attempt to claim for herself that part of him that she had never possessed, that secret thing that he had always kept from her and that he now recognises as his love for Neleni. It was the last time that they had tried to make love and she had almost smothered him with her desperation.

Unable to elicit a response from his unwilling body, Leela had stormed around the room, angrily berating him for his lack of masculinity. He had wondered then, if this was how she had treated Mennan, thinking it fitting that he should be subjected to the same punishment.

Leela's persistent demands, her rage and her tantrums had finally killed his desire for her. Over many months, she had drained him of all feeling. It was as if his soul had been slowly and painfully extracted through a hole no bigger than a pinprick like the contents of an egg being drawn from its shell. Finally, at the rest-house, she had extracted the last drop. On the outside, he had remained intact, but he was empty within. Emptier even than Mennan who, although reduced to a shadow, had continued to love his tormentor.

Hers is a hunger that devours everything around it. She must feed off others or consume herself. Only one who controls her with the utmost savagery will be proof against her destructive tendencies. She will never be the equal of any mate, only his superior, or his slave. Like a demon that must be contained.

"You must tell her that it is over," Neleni's voice breaks in on Arjun's thoughts. "You must explain. Once and for all. So that she understands."

She speaks in short, breathless sentences and, having rolled onto her side, is staring at him. Her body has become taut and his hand, lying on her breast, can feel her heart beating wildly. Her eyes are wide, fixed on him with an implacable intensity, afraid, threatened by a love that has never existed.

"I don't trust her and … I can't share you. It would kill me."

He kisses the lobe of her ear.

"You have nothing to worry about."

Holding her to him, he rocks her in his arms, kissing her forehead.

"It will be all right. I promise."

Comforted, Neleni places her head on his shoulder and is soon asleep. Yet, as he strokes his lover's hair and stares into her peaceful face, Arjun questions the future. Will Leela be content to let him go without a fight, or, even worse, revenge? He has never doubted her potential to become vindictive when crossed. She has a man's pride and his rejection of her is an assault on her honour. It will not go unpunished. She will let it be known that she has had an affair with the Government Agent's assistant. Word will get around and news of Arjun's transgression will soon reach the Agent's ear. And then? Arjun's career will end abruptly. With luck, he might be kept on in the civil service as a minor clerk.

He feels a stab of regret in the pit of his stomach: a short-lived grief for his unrealised potential, for all that he might have become. And yet, it is soon over and, when it is, he feels an extraordinary lightness of spirit. The future holds certainty, which is preferable to the unknown, even if it is only certainty of something bad. Ever since Mennan's death, Arjun has been haunted by a vague but impending sense of retribution. Leela not only saw his fear but identified its source, using it to control him, increasing it by subtly nurturing his sense of guilt. He has been her creature, not her lover. And now he is free.

Tenderly, Arjun kisses Neleni's sleeping face, pressing his lips to her smooth forehead. Her lips part and a small, sweet note escapes from her throat which is neither a sigh, nor a word, but something like a note at the beginning of a song. She presses into him, burying her face in the warm place at the base of his neck. He folds his arms around her tightly, holding her in a protective embrace. They have each other. What else matters?

Crack! Creak! Arjun holds his breath, his nerves taut, his heart pounding with the fear of discovery. But it is only the house, shifting in the afternoon heat, making itself comfortable as the sun beats down on the roof. He sighs and tightens his grip around Neleni's waist then, resting his head on his hand, Arjun falls asleep.

Thud! Neleni awakes. Somewhere in the house, someone is moving. Neleni holds her breath, listening. A chair scrapes across the floor. There is a clashing of plates and a clinking of pots. Sunny has returned and is at work in the kitchen. The old lady has just returned from cousin Ana's and has not yet realised that anyone else is in the house. If she had, she would have come in search of them, shuffling along the passage, calling in her reedy voice.

"Quick. Wake up!"

Neleni shakes Arjun who pulls her towards him as she struggles to leave the bed.

"Stay with me."

"No, Arjun. You don't understand. My mother has returned."

He opens his eyes. Slowly, her message permeates the mists of sleep. Drawing the first, deep breath of consciousness, he stretches and sits up. By now, she is sitting on the edge of the bed, pulling on her blouse. Reluctant to let her go, he strokes her hair, winding it round his hand as he kisses her neck. Laying his head on her shoulder, he moans contentedly.

"Shh! She'll hear you."

"I thought she was deaf."

"All the same ..."

She seems irritated, a little afraid, her movements no longer languorous, but quick and furtive. Small tremors pass through the bed as she dresses, perched on the edge of the mattress. He lets her go. She springs to her feet and, with remarkable swiftness, arranges her sari, pleating and tucking, folding with one hand, gathering with the other, winding the material around her waist, layer over layer. Finally, flinging the loose end of the sari over her shoulder, she hurries to the door, pausing at the threshold to smile at him. Then she is gone.

Darting into the bathroom, she scoops up the clothes lying on the floor. The dhobi woman who does the family's washing is due later today, so it will not seem strange for her to appear in the kitchen, carrying a bundle of washing; Arjun's and her own. However, if her clothes are left lying next to Arjun's in the bathroom, it might look suspicious.

Swiftly, she gathers up the garments, realising that this is the way life will always be. She will always have to think ahead, guessing how others might interpret her actions. Or Arjun's. The merest sight or sound, the slightest departure from daily routine, could give them away. Like the clothes in the bathroom. Her freedom to do what she wants without thinking has gone. But it is a small price to pay.

The sun, trapped by a fault in the window, casts jewelled lights on the wall. Neleni reaches out her hand. The light plays over her fingers, covering them with flickering gems. She is filled with joy. Overwhelmed. Yet it is a poignant beauty, tinged with pain because it cannot be shared. She cannot simply call him to her. *Come and see what I have found.* As she would another member of the family. For that very reason, the experience is all the more intense. Like her love for him.

1957: A bitter tongue

In the kitchen, Sunny is feeling irritable. She often feels tired these days, but today has been worse than ever. Saro was unusually truculent and screamed when Sunny tried to bring her home. For that reason and, possibly because she sensed Sunny's fatigue, cousin Ana agreed to keep the child a little longer and bring her back in the evening.

Stubbornly, Sunny refused the offer of a taxi, even though Ana had offered to pay for it herself. The old lady insisted that the exercise would do her good. But the walk has exhausted her. The route seemed twice as long as usual and the sun pierced her dry, papery skin with cruel persistence. Her limbs ached and her joints grated against each other as she moved. Her bones are turning to chalk and her flesh into parchment. Her step is less sure and sometimes she trips over small objects, or nothing at all. Age has got her in its grip and there is no escape. All that remains is dogged resistance. So, on her return to the house, she declines rest, although there is no-one to see her.

The kitchen is in a mess. That lazy servant, Ella. It doesn't matter how many times you tell her, she always puts things away in the wrong place. Sunny, usually sympathetic to the girl's frailties, is out of patience.

"She just makes more work," mutters the old lady, as she pulls pots and pans out of the cupboards and re-arranges them on the shelves.

Once finished, she leans against the stone sink, catching her breath. She has a sharp pain in her side. A stitch, she thinks, pressing her hand against it as she drags herself across the kitchen in search of somewhere to sit. She tugs a chair from the table and sits down, slowly and painfully. She is as light as a leaf but her limbs feel like lead, her bones like rusting iron. Closing her eyes, she breathes heavily, her heart clattering against her ribs like a spoon in an old tin can. She opens her eyes and, for a few seconds, sees only blackness. She puts her hand up to her face, runs her shaking fingers over her lids. Yes. Her eyes are open. But she cannot see.

Keep calm, she tells herself. It will pass. Leaning back against the chair, she closes her eyes again, concentrates on her breathing then, slowly raises her lids. This time she can see, although her vision is blurred at first, the kitchen slowly becoming clearer, like the view one gets through the lens of a camera as it is being adjusted. Edward showed her how to do that. Edward. She tries to picture him, here beside her, but the room feels empty. Not even her imagination can fill it.

As her eyes adjust, the kitchen gradually comes into focus. The first objects to confront her are two glasses, part-filled with water. Next to these are two spoons, as if two people, not one, have been tasting the contents of the pan sitting on the stove. There is also a paper bag, its side torn open, spilling a few sweet crumbs of fudge onto the table.

"Oh, oh".

Sunny is affronted. Other people's slackness means more work for her and she is already tired. Slowly and painfully, she rises to her feet intending to clear the table when Neleni appears at the door, her arms filled with washing which she deposits in a corner.

"Neleni. I didn't know you were here."

"Hello, Amma. I was just collecting the laundry. I heard you in the kitchen."

"That maid. She has left the place in a state again."

Sunny indulges in one of her favourite complaints. The other concerns the cat.

"Do you want us to get rid of her?" Neleni asks, innocently.

"No, of course not," Sunny snaps.

It is tiring talking to young people. They are obtuse, never understanding the difference between the things that should be changed and those that should be left unaltered. Ella, the maid, falls into the latter category. She provides a constant source of irritation and, therefore, amusement for the old lady. Without her, Sunny's days would be endlessly long and dull. Anyway, Ella isn't that bad and she has a family to feed. How could Neleni suggest sacking her? Sunny shakes her head in dismay at her daughter's heartlessness.

Neleni tries not to laugh. She usually knows how to defuse the old lady's anger. However, owing to her tiredness and a strange, nagging feeling inspired by the two glasses and spoons sitting companionably on the table, Sunny is more irritable than usual. Something is wrong. She will not allow her ire to be drawn, nor her attention deflected.

"What are those?"

She points accusingly at the glasses.

Neleni blushes, her heart beating fast. She needs an excuse but, unable to think of one, she shrugs her shoulders, raising her eyebrows, her lips pursed as if to suppress a giggle. Her attempt at humour looks more like insolence, a joke at the old lady's expense.

"Who has been cooking?" persists the old lady.

"I bought some fish from the market. I thought I would cook myself some lunch, but then I didn't want it."

"But there are two spoons here!"

"Yes, well. You always said I was messy around the kitchen."

Bending over to try and hide her embarrassment, Neleni pretends to sort the washing. But Sunny persists.

"There are two glasses also," she says, in a tone of quiet accusation.

"Amma, I told you. It's nothing."

A shadow flickers past the kitchen door and is gone.

"What was that?" demands the old lady, her eyes bright and suspicious behind their thick lenses.

"What was what?"

"I saw something. In the passage. There is someone here."

"I keep telling you Amma. There is no-one here. Just me."

Neleni is becoming exasperated; her tone more shrill than intended. Whether from anger, or weakness, Sunny's hands, resting on the table in front of her, begin to quiver.

"You always think you know best. Never listen to anyone. Like those clothes you wore to Dalia's wedding. You should have worn a sari. I tried to tell you but you wouldn't listen. You insisted on wearing something different and made yourself look foolish."

"I did not look foolish!"

Neleni glares at her mother. Sunny's words are unduly harsh, but they are also true. She cannot deny it. Sunny continues, unperturbed.

"I know other people. Show them the slightest weakness and they'll attack you. Not everyone is as tolerant as Raj. Or as blind."

The old lady stares at her daughter steadily. Unable to hold her mother's gaze, Neleni turns away, her face burning, as if guilt were branded all over it.

"I must get on," she says briskly, hoping to change the subject. "The dhobi woman will be here soon and I need to sort the washing and count it. Some things went missing last time."

"And whose fault was that?"

The old lady's voice is shrill.

"Not yours."

Nothing is ever your fault, thinks Neleni. *Like my marriage.*

"You always blame me."

It is as if the old lady can read her thoughts. Neleni sighs, inwardly, suddenly too tired for anger. They have reached the usual place at which all arguments end; or, perhaps, where they really begin. The subject of Neleni's marriage.

"It's not my fault!"

The old lady's voice is tremulous, partly defiant, partly pleading.

Neleni bites her lip, feeling her eyes swell with tears.

"Go and lie down, Amma."

"It's not my fault ..." insists Sunny.

"I know."

The words almost choke her. She does blame her mother. She does. But she can never say it directly: *You ruined my life.* Because, despite her anger, she loves her mother and she knows the depth of a mother's guilt. Some things must never be said, even if they are true. So, once again, she finds herself forced into submission by her mother's vulnerability. She wipes her eyes with the back of her hand, hoping that Sunny will not notice and, as she does so, realises that the cat is winding itself around her ankles, purring contentedly, having taken advantage of their argument to slip unseen through the back door.

"Go and lie down, Amma. You're tired. I'll bring you some tea."

"Well, if you insist ..."

"I do."

Unable to accept outright defeat, Sunny welcomes this excuse to end the debate, although her lips quiver, still petulant. With the intention of guiding Sunny to the door, Neleni places her hand on the old lady's back and, feeling the bony shoulder beneath the slackening skin, is shocked by a sudden sense of her mother's mortality. Sunny's physical frailty, normally masked by her peppery spirit, is exposed, as if her clothing had been ripped away. Neleni's anger is defused. She kisses the old lady's head.

"Go and rest, Amma. I will follow soon."

The old lady shuffles to her room, followed by her bent and weary shadow and the cat, which winds its way lovingly around her ankles, hoping for a place beside her on the bed. Sadly, Neleni watches her go, then sets herself half-heartedly to work, thoughts skittering through her head like scraps of paper on a windy day. She tidies the table and counts the clothes then, remembering that she has left her scarf in the bedroom, she leaves the kitchen and walks along the passage, passing the place where Arjun is waiting for her, concealed in shadow.

Grasping her around the waist, he presses her against the wall, kissing her fervently. Consumed by fire, she holds him to her, guiding his hands, feeling the exquisite warmth of his flesh. Life for her is not yet over, and she will take all that it offers before the end.

1957: Sunny's garden

Early in the morning, when the shadows are still cool and the sun is still rising in the sky, Sunny sits in the yard on the chair that Raj has left for her. It is an old chair, no longer suitable for use indoors. The sun has melted the glue from its joints and burned its varnish until it has blistered and peeled away; the wood has weathered and cracked, turning grey with mildew in the sultry heat and the legs have warped and become uneven, wobbling precariously without provocation, creaking and groaning under the weight of Sunny's bird-light frame.

Perched on the seat, her frail hands folded in her lap, her eyes closed, she sits with her face up to the morning sun, hoping to absorb some of its gentle heat. She longs for her pipe but has been forced to give it up. Instead of bringing her consolation, the smoke now clogs her lungs, choking her every time she tries to inhale, increasing the breathlessness that now torments her. These days, she often feels that she is gasping for air, like a fish, as if the terrestrial medium that she has inhabited all her life has suddenly turned hostile and is rejecting her.

Without her pipe, few pleasures remain. She spends much of her time in this chair, allowing Neleni to move her to the shadow when the sun moves around. It is Neleni's decision, not hers. Now that her blood runs thin and cold, she does not find the sun too hot. Even at its height. Only its brilliance troubles her, so she sits most of the time with her eyes closed, allowing the light to shine with pink radiance through the thin transparency of her eyelids.

She prefers it outside. She can breathe more easily and can close her mind to what is happening indoors. Despite her failing senses, she is neither deaf, nor stupid. Every day, she sits here and listens to sounds floating out from the house. In the morning, Raj is always the first to stir. He coughs as he enters the kitchen. The tap squeals as he turns it on; too hard, because the water gushes out and splatters him with cold droplets. He swears and closes the tap a little, allowing water to race into the saucepan, to which he adds milk and three spoons of tea, boiling it all up together on the stove until he has a strong brew.

Raj always remembers his mother-in-law, calling softly from the kitchen door: "Tea, Aunty?"

The answer is always the same.

"Yes, please, son. Don't forget. Two sugars. I like it sweet."

"OK, Aunty."

They never tire of this exchange, regarding it as one of the small rituals that must be performed if the day is to start properly. It is as essential to them as brushing their teeth or washing their faces.

Having given Sunny her tea, Raj then sits on the step and, in companionable silence, they watch the sun as it rises steadily up the sky.

Next, Neleni arrives and busies herself about the kitchen preparing breakfast for the family. There is often a brief exchange with Raj, some small point about which she nags him and to which he replies with a good-humoured grunt. Sunny never doubts the goodness of his intentions although she increasingly questions those of her daughter.

Sitting in the yard, listening to what goes on in the house, she has learned to interpret the tone of a person's voice. Each pause and inflection holds a subtle nuance. Words alone are not always a true indication of what someone feels. But the voice, especially its tone, is the true guide. When talking to Raj, or even the girls, Neleni's voice is often shrill, brittle, like thin glass ready to snap; but when she speaks to Arjun, it is sweet and melodious. Sunny wonders whether the others have noticed. Sometimes, she wishes that she did not. Such knowledge is a burden.

The house empties: Raj taking the girls with him, accompanying Rani to school, leaving Saro at cousin Ana's where she spends an increasing amount of time these days. It is only a few weeks since Sunny made her last journey to Ana's house, but her legs are now so weak that she has difficulty just walking around the house.

It grieves Sunny that she can no longer look after Saro as she once did, but she wonders if this is the only motive for the child's frequent absences; for Sunny has noticed that these seem to coincide with days when Arjun is working from home. On these days, he shuts himself up in his room on the pretext of studying or he takes Neleni out in the small car that he has recently bought; a little black Austin with red leather seats. To his credit, he always invites Sunny; but she always refuses, partly because of her frailty, partly out of loyalty to Raj. She can always sense Neleni's relief on these occasions.

Today, Arjun will be working at home. Lacking its noisier members, the house is quiet but, somewhere inside, Sunny can hear her daughter laughing.

1957: Rani's loss

On the way home from school, Rani scuffs through the cart tracks, watching with satisfaction as a thick layer of dust coats her toes, turning them grey. One of the bright red ribbons that ties up her plaits has come undone and is hanging loose in two long tails which flutter behind her when she runs. It is quiet along this stretch of road. There is no-one about.

Stretching out her arms on either side, Rani races along as fast as she can, imagining herself to be a kite. For a second, she closes her eyes and pretends that she is high up in the air, floating miles above the ground, looking down on everyone.

She dips and soars, imagining herself to be a bird-shaped kite; a swift with paper wings and a forked tail, like the one she saw at the New Year festival. Uncle Arjun promised to buy her such a kite, but he has forgotten. He forgets a lot of things lately.

Rani halts in the middle of the road, panting, her arms still outstretched. The ribbons hang limply from her hair, sticking to her damp neck. One of her plaits has come undone. She does not care. Neleni ties them so tightly that they give her a headache. Rani wishes she could have short hair, like a boy. Then she would not have to bother with stupid plaits and ribbons. But every day, she is becoming less like a boy.

Her breasts are beginning to swell and, last month, she bled for the first time. Everyone made a terrific fuss. Relations congratulated her and sent her money. Even the girls at school expressed their envy. But, for Rani, the first signs of womanhood have brought disappointment and a sense of loss. It is not something she can describe exactly. Just a feeling that she can no longer visit her old, imaginary haunts. It is like trying to get into clothes that you wear every day and suddenly finding that you have outgrown them.

A bird sings sweetly from the top of a palm tree. She does not recognise it and steps closer to get a look. A taxi putters past in a cloud of dust, carrying an overweight woman and a skinny boy with innumerable parcels and brown paper bags balanced on their laps. Rani watches as the car disappears up the road, listing dangerously on the woman's side, its luggage flap open to accommodate two large suitcases.

Rani wishes that she could go on a journey. Far away. It does not matter where. She no longer feels happy at home and her friendship with Uncle Arjun has waned. Replaced by her mother as the carrier of tea and letters to his room, Rani has fewer opportunities to speak to him now and the source of foil-wrapped sweets, comics and stories has dried up; but it is not the loss of presents and gewgaws that dismays her so much as the loss of her trusted confidante. Uncle Arjun was her friend and now she has been supplanted in his affections by her mother. With a twinge of guilt, Rani realises that she hates her mother.

Irritably, she kicks at a pebble which conceals a piece of sharp metal embedded in the road. Blood pours from Rani's big toe. She bites her lip and tries not to cry although the pain is intense. Dark spots form in the dust where the blood drips from her toe. Sitting on the grass verge, she spits into her handkerchief and tries to clean the wound. The small piece of linen is soon soaked with blood. Then, she realises. It is the handkerchief that Uncle Arjun gave her for her birthday. Ruined. Hugging her knees, she weeps quietly.

It is a sultry, airless afternoon. The mercury has soared to over a hundred degrees and there is no respite from the merciless heat, even in the deep shade of the house. Yet, despite the heat, Neleni cannot be still: wandering about the kitchen, she needlessly re-arranges its contents, fussing over the knife drawer, stacking pans that are already tidy, opening doors to cupboards, then shutting them again, unable to set her mind to any task.

"She is late again," she thinks, angrily.

Since the lifting of the restrictions which required Rani to be escorted both to and from school by her father, she has been allowed to walk home on her own, unaccompanied by Raj. Neleni is not happy with this arrangement, but Raj assures her it is for the best.

"She is a young woman now," he had said one day, as if that explained everything, as if some magic talisman would shield their daughter from harm.

"But she has come of age," Neleni had retorted. "She is in more need of protection than ever."

Raj had given her a strange sideways look.

"Then she will have to learn to behave herself," he had said.

He had then shaken out the newspaper and held it up in front of him so that Neleni could not see his face. She had stormed out of the room and, hiding herself in a dark angle of the hallway, wept silently, her muffled sobs accompanied by the slow ticking of the grandfather clock.

Every day, Rani is late home. When Neleni asks her where she has been, she looks away and mutters some excuse. The words are barely audible but it does not matter, Neleni knows she is lying. She no longer recognises her daughter in this surly, furtive child who, until recently, sought Neleni's affection but who now avoids her gaze, preferring to look at her feet, rather than her mother, as she speaks.

***

"Ten minutes," thinks Neleni, looking at her watch. "She should have been here ten minutes ago."

She paces the room, getting angrier every second. This should be her time. When Sunny and Saro are taking their afternoon nap, when everyone else is out, this is the time that she keeps for herself, the time in which she tries to paint, arranging a few flowers in a vase, dipping her brush into the jam jar, watching it bleed streaks of paint into the clear water. It is something that feeds her soul. Like prayer. But that time has been stolen from her by a selfish child.

Neleni fumes as she paces around the hot kitchen. She looks again at her watch. Twenty minutes late. Where is she? It is unfair of Rani to occupy her mother's time with worry. Unfair of Raj not to fetch her from school. Neleni bites back tears of frustration. She hisses at the cat which is attempting to insinuate itself through the back door. The animal freezes, stares at her with wide green eyes, then turns and scampers across the yard where it crouches behind a bucket, waiting for Sunny to appear and a chance of more congenial company.

Neleni leans against the sink, grasping the edge with both hands, feeling the cool enamel against her palms. She struggles to turn the creaking handle of the tap around which Raj has tied a piece of string to stop it leaking. It has not worked. She will have to call a plumber. She lets the water gush into the basin and holds her hands under it, cooling her wrists, trying to restore some calmness to her thoughts. The water gurgles pleasantly as it swirls around the sink. As she stands there, she notices how the enamel has become pitted and brown in places where heavy pans have been dropped, chipping the surface.

It is an old sink. She remembers standing here as a child, next to her mother as she peeled vegetables. Sunny was young then, her face beautiful, her hair black and her spine straight. She used to wear a green apron which had become soft and faded through much washing. It had a pleasant smell that always made Neleni think of baking, although she could not think why. She wonders if she was difficult as a child. Like Rani. Had her mother worried about her in the same way? If she had, she has never said so. It all seems so long ago.

Neleni turns off the tap and, instead of drying her hands on a cloth, she holds them in front of her, letting the water drain off her fingers into the sink. There is another reason for her anger with Rani; one which she has tried to ignore. Often, when she tries to steal a few moments alone with Arjun, she will open a door to find Rani behind it, or she will see her disappearing around a corner.

Neleni has begun to suspect her daughter of spying on her. What does she know? Surely Neleni has given no-one any reason to suspect her? At night, she often lies awake, revisiting the day in her head. What has she done? What has she said? Who has been listening? Sometimes, she lies awake all night, rigid with fear, wondering what will happen if they are caught. Yet she never considers giving him up. Only death can separate them now.

Across the yard, the cat peers out from behind the bucket, considering whether to chance another visit to the kitchen. Carefully, it ventures a paw into the open, then another. Neleni watches as it creeps across the yard, its back straight and low, ears alert for any sign of danger. Then, just as it reaches the back step, it hears something inaudible to the human ear and, taking fright, darts off across the yard, clearing the wall with one bound and narrowly missing the flower pots that Raj has re-planted.

Neleni checks her watch again. Forty minutes. Where is she? Sharpened by fear, her anger returns. Rani is never where she should be. Now, she should be home and she is not. Yet she is always there, hanging around, when not required. It makes it difficult, sometimes impossible, for Neleni to speak to Arjun privately. And there is a new matter about which she needs to consult him. Urgently. She has tried, several times, to get his undivided attention, to speak in private, but each time, Rani has interrupted. It has been several days now and Neleni has still not had the opportunity to speak to her lover alone. The suspense is unbearable. She can neither sleep, nor eat. She must speak to him. Soon.

Creeping up the front steps, Rani quietly lets herself into the house, grateful that the front door has been left on the latch. She can enjoy a few seconds of peace before confronting her mother. The hallway is cool and welcoming, the cold concrete balm to her aching feet. Ella must have worked here today because she can smell polish. She loves the warm waxy scent which is always accompanied by the pungent tang of turpentine. Instructed by Sunny, Ella has diluted the polish: the old lady always insisting that everything should be made to "go further".

The hallway is Rani's favourite room. Her mother hates it, complaining of its darkness but, for Rani, it has an atmosphere of church-like tranquillity. The tiny candle, in its red glass container, flickers before the image of the Virgin making shadows dance in the corners, while the grandfather clock marks time with its laborious ticking. It is a place in which peace can be found, from the bright and bustling street outside and from the tensions that seem to occupy the rest of the house. It is a room, but not a room; within the house, yet not quite part of it; a place of neutrality, like a chapel.

Breathing deeply, Rani closes her eyes, saying a quick and hopeful prayer to the Virgin. A prayer for protection.

***

Leaving her school bag in the hallway, Rani tiptoes towards the kitchen, hoping that her mother will be out. Of course, she is not. Amma is always in the kitchen. Unless, of course, she is with Uncle Arjun, in which case she is always where you never expect to find her. Rani flushes angrily and clutches the bloody handkerchief tight.

"Amma."

Rani's voice is querulous, fearing trouble. She does what she always does when she feels awkward. Propping herself against the doorpost, she stands on one leg, like a crane, one foot held up behind her, the wounded one, out of sight, cradled in her hand. Neleni does not speak or turn around. Rani thinks she has not heard.

"Amma. Can I have a glass of water?"

Neleni's heart lurches when she sees her daughter. Rani is standing in the doorway, a waif-like figure, her hair hanging in her eyes, the buttons of her blouse undone, her legs spattered with blood and a blood-soaked cloth in her hand. Immediately, Neleni assumes the worst. She wants to run to her daughter, cling to her, but she is frozen with fear.

"What has happened?" she whispers.

"Nothing, Amma."

"What do you mean nothing?"

"Nothing."

Rani glares at her mother defiantly.

"But you're covered in blood. And what is that you've got in your hand?"

Neleni reaches for the blood-soaked handkerchief but Rani swipes it away. She is hostile, challenging, first glaring at her mother in silence, then looking away when Neleni questions her. Cheated of an outlet, Neleni's fear turns to anger.

"What have you been doing? Tell me."

"Nothing."

"Nothing? Look at you. I have been out of my mind with worry. You are nearly an hour late. Where have you been?"

Rani does not answer but looks furtively about the room as if she has not heard.

"Rani, I am speaking to you!"

"Can I have some water?"

She avoids her mother's questions with a determination that borders on insolence. Neleni clenches her fists and digs her elbows into her sides, feeling the rage boil within her.

"You know where the tap is."

Rani tiptoes across the kitchen, leaving a trail of blood spots on the floor. Cautiously, she helps herself to a glass from the cupboard, then fills it from the tap. She tries to be careful, but the glass is overfull and, as she turns from the sink, a few drops of water slop onto the floor. Afterwards, she will wonder why such a small thing could have provoked such anger. With a speed that seems to give her wings, Neleni crosses the kitchen. Grabbing her daughter by the shoulders, she shakes her hard.

"Look what you've done. Look."

"It's only water Amma." The child looks scared. "I'll clear it up."

"No, No. You've done enough. Leave it. Leave me. Get out."

Rani begins to cry. Her look of bewilderment and hurt is more than Neleni can bear.

"Stop crying."

Rani struggles to control herself, but she is trembling, afraid. The tears continue to flow.

"Stop crying or I will give you something to cry about."

Desperate for her mother's affection, Rani howls. Unable to cope with the pain that she herself has inflicted, Neleni finally loses her temper. Then she does something that will haunt her for the rest of her life, something that will form a secret but unbridgeable chasm between them. She slaps Rani. A resounding smack across the face that carries the child backwards across the kitchen. She is only saved from a fall by the kitchen table which meets her squarely in the small of her back. The glass is jolted from her hand arcing through the air like a meteor with a watery trail, tiny drops of water frozen in its wake until it hits the floor, exploding in a fountain of crystals.

Shocked at her callous behaviour, Neleni runs towards Rani, to comfort her. But mistaking her mother's intentions, the child yelps and runs from the kitchen.

Tap, tap, tap! Sunny opens her eyes. She was asleep, dreaming that she was young again, that Edward held her in his arms. She feels the same sharp disappointment that she always feels on waking these days. Sleep is preferable to consciousness: it anaesthetizes the pain of her aching body, relieves her of problems that she cannot solve and introduces her to a world in which she is once again mobile, light-hearted and young.

Sunny's mouth is dry, filled with the rancid flavour of sleep. She moans as she pushes herself upright. It takes all her energy these days to raise herself from the bed. As she moves, she can feel her bones slipping in and out of place like beads on a loosely-strung necklace.

Tap, tap, tap! There it is again. She looks towards the window and thinks, by some miracle, that it is snowing until she realises that it is the wind, shaking the branches of the frangipani tree and blowing a blizzard of blossom across the yard. One long twig, like a jointed finger, is tapping against the glass.

"Hmph".

She laughs, wryly, then reaches a toe to the floor. The concrete feels unusually cold, like ice, which is impossible for this country. Sunny knows that the change in climate is happening within her. Her body obeys different rhythms to the rest of the world. It inhabits another place.

As she sits on the edge of the bed, gasping for breath, Sunny hears another sound. Someone is weeping softly outside her door. Placing both feet on the floor, she steadies herself against the side of the bed and, holding onto it for support, drags herself across the room to the door. Outside, Rani is sitting in the passage, legs drawn up, head resting on her knees. Her hair is in disarray: one plait, completely undone; the other, a rope of wispy strings to which a red ribbon still clings limply.

"What is it, child?" asks Sunny, stroking the girl's hair.

Raising her head, Rani reveals eyes puffy with weeping. She tries to speak, but each word is transformed into a sob.

"What have you done to your foot?"

Sunny has noticed Rani's toe which, despite a thick rime of congealed blood around the nail, is still leaking liberally onto the floor.

"Huk ... I ... huk ... hit it," Rani gulps.

"Come with me."

Sunny motions the child into the bedroom. Obediently, Rani rises to her feet and follows her grandmother, her red ribbon hanging like a single, defeated streamer from just a few threads of hair.

After sitting the child on the bed, Sunny wets a flannel in her wash-bowl and bathes the wound. She then binds it with lint and a bandage which she keeps with other emergency supplies in her dressing table.

"It's not so bad," she says. "Is this why you were crying?"

Rani's eyes fill with tears and she bites her lower lip, trying to stifle a sob.

"Is there a problem with Amma?"

"Mmm."

Rani nods her head as two large tears course down her cheeks.

"What happened?"

"She hit me."

"Why?"

"I was late from school. My foot was bleeding. I spilled some water. She hit me."

Reliving the scene in the kitchen, Rani sobs uncontrollably. Sunny sits beside her, rigid, staring out of the window at the temple tree, its flowers being torn from the branches in even greater numbers by the quickening breeze.

"Is that all?"

"She's always angry with me these days."

"Why? What makes her angry?"

"When she's with Uncle Arjun. Sometimes I walk into a room and find them together. She gets really angry with me then."

"Ahh."

Sunny sounds weary, although not surprised, as if she already knew the answer to her question. She strokes the child's cheek with her finger following the track of her tears. The girl's skin is still young and soft, like a baby's, with a haze of dark down just in front of her ear where the hairline meets her cheek. She is developing the heavy jowl of her paternal grandmother which, in later life, will lead to a double chin. Although she will not have her mother's beauty, she has inherited her pale complexion. She will be 'fair' as the Islanders call it, always an advantage when a girl reaches marriageable age. It will not be long, thinks Sunny, as she casts an appraising eye over her grand-daughter whose breasts are already pressing against her blouse.

"Am I very bad?"

Rani has become calmer and is able to speak without sobbing. Her tears flow more slowly, squeezed out by her eyelids when she blinks.

"What do you mean, child?"

"Amma is always cross with me. I sometimes think she hates me. I must have done something to upset her, but I don't know what. Perhaps I'm just wicked. I fought with that boy and ... and wicked people don't always know they are wicked, do they? Am I wicked without knowing it? Will I go to hell?"

Her questions are tinged with panic, a child's terror of a strange and inhospitable place, a dark and empty room, or adulthood. Sunny's eyes mist over behind her heavy glasses. Wrapping her fragile arms around Rani's shoulders, she holds her against her bony chest and strokes the girl's hair with the slow clumsy movements of someone whose fingers are bent with age.

"Hush, hush," the old lady croons. "I don't know who has put such ideas into your head but God loves all little children, including you. And if you can't think of what you have done wrong, then that probably means that you haven't done anything. Hush, my love."

Sunny's heart is pounding, fired with anger and distress. With her head pressed to the old lady's ribs, Rani can hear it. Thud, thud, thud. Like the ticking of the grandfather clock, only quicker. The sound is strangely soothing and, soon, Rani's eyelids begin to flicker and become heavy. She tries to stay awake – there is something else that she wishes to tell her grandmother – but she is unable to resist the desire to sleep. Her eyes close and her breathing becomes soft and regular. With care and great effort, Sunny lays her grand-daughter down on the bed, arranging her ungainly limbs as best she can so that the child will sleep comfortably.

Gently, the old lady sweeps the wet mesh of hair from the girl's face. In sleep, Rani loses the nascent traces of womanhood. She is a child again, lost and lonely. Sunny's lip trembles, not with sadness this time, but with fury; righteous anger aroused by the torment of an innocent victim. She has tried to stifle the murmuring of her own conscience, dismissing it as the warped imagining of an old woman. Yet now, she knows that she was right. Rani's words have confirmed her suspicions. Neleni and Arjun are lovers.

Sunny sighs. She had wished to be spared this. She is too old and weary to bother with other people's intrigue and yet, now, she has no choice. Neleni's wrongdoing has spilled over and is slowly poisoning her family. Knowledge, Sunny reflects, can be a great burden. It can ensnare as well as liberate. She remembers Christ at Gethsemane. *Lord, let this cup pass from me.* But, like him, she knows it will not.

Rani's lips part in her sleep and her tongue makes a soft clicking noise as it did when she was a baby, when Sunny held her in her arms and silently declared that she would be her favourite grandchild.

"Sleep tight, my treasure," whispers the old lady, as she did to the baby.

Tap, tap, tap. The temple tree beats at the window, a small but persistent drum-beat that echoes in her head.

Painfully, Sunny eases herself off the bed. Her heart is pounding and she has to steady herself for a minute to catch her breath. Her vision is more clouded than usual, a result, no doubt, of the tears that she has been forced to swallow and she staggers a little as she moves away from the bed. But this is no time to consider her own weakness. She must speak her mind. Slowly, she makes her way across the room, holding onto the furniture then, out into the passage towards the kitchen where she knows she will find Neleni.

1957: Conscience and a cat

I must befriend Rani. I must win her back. Neleni is standing at the kitchen sink, her wrists resting on its cool sill. Outside, the cat is playfully batting the air, its front paws boxing furiously as it teeters a few steps on its hind legs. It is fighting an imaginary butterfly, or an insect too small to see. Its awkward, dainty tottering reminds her of the girls when she used to let them try on her old shoes. They would wobble and scream, giggling as they walked on tiptoe, dragging the shoes so that the high heels rasped against the floor. Neleni smiles, remembering happier times when they were all friends.

The cat prances, first forward, then back, working itself up into a frenzy of playfulness. It crouches, wiggling its behind, then springs, back legs outstretched, front paws clawing the air, mouth open to reveal needle-sharp teeth. It swipes at the air, misses and lands with a soft thud. Then, crouching with its back arched, it looks furtively over its shoulder to see if anyone has witnessed its moment of madness. It spots Neleni, staring out of the window and, after flinging her a dark look, the cat slinks off to a corner of the yard where it sits hunched and sulky, its tail curled around its feet, the tip flicking angrily.

As unpredictable in its moods as a teenage girl, the cat reminds Neleni of her daughter. Rani has always been an enigma, retreating into her imaginary world, playing out small dramas to herself in quiet corners of the house, whispering to invisible friends, telling herself stories, getting angry when adults attempt to pry into her secret thoughts.

They are not so different: Rani and her mother. Neleni is painfully aware that, with Arjun, she has entered her own secret world, one into which she resents the intrusion of other people, including her own children. It would be untrue to say that she does not feel guilt, but it is outweighed by her love which is as irresistible as a spring tide. At night and, in the quiet moments of the day, she is troubled by her conscience but she can never tell Arjun. For admissions of guilt are forbidden to lovers. At best, they diminish joy; at worst, they provide an excuse to end the affair.

Neleni accepts that she must live with her guilt but, by some strange quirk of reasoning, she regards Rani as its cause. The child is always nearby when Neleni wants to be alone with her lover. When they are together, Rani always seems to be there, just around a corner, behind a door, disappearing along the passage: watching, listening, spying. At times, Neleni feels as if she hates her daughter; a feeling that she suspects is mutual. When Rani comes across Neleni and Arjun together, her face sours with resentment.

Rani is like a rival, competing for Arjun's affection; not her own daughter. Sometimes Neleni cannot contain her anger and speaks sharply to the child. Once Arjun heard her and took Rani's part, upbraiding Neleni for her harshness. This led to a bitter exchange after which they did not speak for several days. During that period, tormented by her fear of losing him, Neleni could not bear to look at her daughter.

Eventually, life returned to normal and, relieved at having made peace with her lover, Neleni smothered Rani with affection, liberally rewarding her with pieces of jaggery on the slightest pretext. But such spontaneous displays of affection only confuse Rani, making her more resentful than ever. It is clear that she no longer trusts her mother.

And, today, when Neleni had a perfect excuse to show maternal affection, she had ruined the opportunity, slapping Rani when she ached to hold her, shouting in anger when all she had wanted to do was tell her how much she loved her.

"What is wrong with me?" she asks herself as she watches the cat stalking a lizard in the yard.

Sunny's journey from her bedroom to the kitchen is agonisingly slow. She has to stop many times on the way, supporting herself against the wall to regain her breath, drawing thin streams of air into her thirsty lungs. She pictures those organs as a pair of leaky bellows, wheezing and pumping, their leathery sinews stiff and cracked. It takes a great deal of effort to make them work but, however hard she tries, she cannot fill them.

She creeps around the edge of the hallway, steadying herself against the furniture where, for a few seconds, she rests against the grandfather clock, her ear against the dark walnut casing, listening to the dark beating of its heart. The plaster statue of the Virgin smiles enigmatically, eyes cast modestly down under their lids, the light of the eternal flame flickering over her blue mantle.

Crossing herself, Sunny murmurs a prayer before passing on to the kitchen, but it does nothing to calm her anger, exacerbated by shortness of breath and the heavy pounding in her head. The sight of her daughter causes further agitation. Lost in thought, Neleni is staring from the window. She does not hear her mother enter the kitchen and is only startled from her reverie when the old lady coughs. Then, she turns to see who is watching her.

But, before Neleni can speak, Sunny attacks.

"Why are you treating her like this?"

Stupid with surprise, Neleni falters.

"What do you mean?"

"You know what I mean. Your daughter. Rani. Or has your interest in your lodger caused you to forget her name?"

Neleni gasps. In the darkness of her pupil, a spark of anger flashes, like a comet.

"What has she been saying to you?"

"Enough for me to know that you are making her unhappy."

Run away. Don't answer. But Neleni knows there will be no avoiding her mother's questions, only postponement. Sunny will pursue the subject relentlessly until she gets her answer. Neleni feels as if she has been dragged to a precipice and forced to look down it. She clasps her hands together to try and stop them quivering.

"How have I made Rani unhappy?"

She tries to challenge her mother with calm effrontery, but her voice carries a false note. It holds no conviction. Sunny is undaunted.

"You must finish your affair with that man. It is destroying your family. Send him away."

"No, no. It's not true."

"Don't pretend! Ever since that man came to this house, you've run after him like a lovesick schoolgirl. And now … now I don't know what you are. I didn't bring you up to behave like this. I'm ashamed of you, Neleni. Thank God Appa isn't alive to see it."

"How dare you. You spiteful old woman!"

Neleni is trembling. She has been pushed over the edge, into a chasm; a tiny, diminishing speck, spiralling downwards in hopeless descent. In desperation, she lashes out.

"If Rani is unhappy, it is your fault," she shouts.

"How so?" croaks the old woman.

"You forced me to marry a man I did not love."

The old accusation never loses its sting. Sunny shrinks, as if she has received a blow to the chest.

"It was the only choice."

"For whom?"

Neleni is weeping uncontrollably; her beautiful mouth, now raw and cavernous, releasing her agony like a dying scream.

"You ... you ... married the man you loved. Why couldn't I?"

The pain of her child passes through Sunny like an arrow. It always does but, today, the old argument, so frequently rehearsed, has a new aspect. It no longer resembles the skirmishing of mother and daughter, a mild irritation that is soon healed, but a deadly dispute between adversaries. Neleni speaks with unaccustomed bitterness. For the first time, Sunny detects hatred in her daughter's voice.

There is logic in Neleni's argument. She has been treated unfairly, but she has been a victim of circumstance, not spite and, while Sunny accepts her part in Neleni's fate, she had always hoped that Neleni would understand. It is clear that she does not. Sunny has lost the battle for her daughter's forgiveness.

Without a word, the old lady turns and shuffles away, her back bent so low that her chin touches her chest.

"Amma ... Amma ..."

Neleni calls to her mother, first shrieking and angry, then pleading but Sunny, her heart wrung with anguish, ignores her. There is nothing more to say.

Tap, tap, tap! The temple tree beats insistently against the window. Its rhythmic drumming echoes in Sunny's head and is answered by the heavy pounding of her temples. The argument with Neleni and the long, slow struggle back to her room have exhausted her. No. It is more than that. Her body feels like an outsize suit of clothes, limp and heavy, dragging her down with its weight. She leans against the bed, too tired to pull herself onto it and closes her eyes, willing her head to stop throbbing. She breathes slowly, trying to pull the air into her lungs, listening to the rackety pounding of her heart. Tap, tap, tap. It keeps time with the tree. Tappety-tap. It races ahead. Silence. It misses a beat.

For five minutes, she stands still as her heart continues to race then, finally it slows and her breath comes more easily. She hoists herself onto the bed, digging her claw-like fingers into the mattress to get some purchase on her own, frail weight. Then, her heart and head pounding again, she lies next to Rani. The child is turned away from her, deep in sleep, her knees drawn up to her chest, her hands folded into her stomach, like a small, hibernating creature which, in a colder climate, would curl up to protect itself from frost.

Poor Rani! With a feeble hand, the old lady strokes her grand-daughter's head noting, as she does so, the small ringlets that fringe the nape of her neck. Just like Neleni.

"They are too alike ever to be friends," thinks Sunny.

Disturbed by the touch of Sunny's hand, Rani sighs and not quite awake, turns over to face her grandmother. She holds out a hand and Sunny takes it in her own, squeezing it tight. Over Rani's shoulder, she can see the photograph of Edward, still young and handsome in his suit. Edward, whose daughter has inherited his pale skin and whose half-European family rejected his wife. But do past slights have a bearing on the present? They were painful at the time but now, when she tries to remember what it was like, it is like looking at someone else, infinitely small and remote, an insect at the bottom of a glass.

Yet, in a way, the past unkindness of Edward's family has had a bearing on the present. It was Sunny's pride that stopped her asking for help when Edward died. In her grief, she could not face the added sorrow of their scorn, the 'I told you so' look in their eyes as they counted out their money then grudgingly handed it over. Alms to a poor woman. How they would have enjoyed that! She had vowed not to give them the satisfaction. She would not sell herself to them. Instead, she had sold her daughter.

She has never thought of it like that before, but Neleni's angry words have brought it home to her. What was it she said? *You married the man you loved. Why couldn't I?* In one, terrible instant, Sunny realises that it was her own pride, not Edward's death, that compromised Neleni's future.

"Oh my daughter. I have betrayed you. Forgive me."

Sunny's lips tremble with the weakness of old age and two heavy tears, thick as syrup, run from her eyes into the pillow.

"Nanna, are you all right?"

Rani speaks without opening her eyes. She is dreaming, rather than waking, her face plump and smooth, sleekened by sleep.

Sunny murmurs a response. Instinctively, Rani snuggles up to her, wrapping an arm around the old lady's shoulders. Sunny kisses her grand-daughter's forehead, then raises her head so that she can see the picture of Edward. Her sight, previously misty, clears a little and she feels, as she looks at him, that he is smiling at her. He is telling her that she is forgiven, that she must not worry.

Sleep now.

She lays her head on the pillow and, for the first time, realises that the pounding in her head has stopped. She feels Edward reaching out for her and she senses something that she has missed over the last months: his presence, close by. A shadow passes over her face; whether it is the tree at the window, or something else, she cannot tell, but she is sure that something brushed her cheek. Edward used to stroke her face when she was upset. Curious. She no longer feels any pain, only a strange lightness in her head that seems to spread outwards, relieving her body of its weight.

Sunny closes her eyes.

1957: The call

Gentle hands are pulling her off the bed, picking her up, carrying her away. Rani smells her father's hair oil and the slight tang of sweat which follows a day's work. Her head lolls against his shoulder as he cradles her in his arms. Drowsily, she peeps through her eyelids, still sticky with sleep, and sees Sunny lying on her side, peaceful, her eyes closed, the arm that previously enfolded her granddaughter, now resting on the bed. Neleni is sitting next to her mother, ashen-faced, like death, holding the old lady's hand. She looks ill.

As she is borne away, Rani thinks she sees another person in the room. A man in a dark suit, standing next to her mother.

"Who is that man?" she mumbles.

"Which man?"

Her father's voice, strangely taut, but not unkind. Humouring her.

"The man beside Amma."

"It's the doctor."

"Why? Is Amma ill?"

"No. Amma is not ill."

They are outside the room now, passing the rows of sepia photographs on the wall. Raj gulps noisily, as if he is trying to swallow something. Rani can hear it, gurgling in his throat. She tries to look at him, but he avoids her eyes. He is looking straight ahead, concentrating, his mouth clamped tightly together, fearing something might escape his lips.

It reminds Rani of the game she plays with Saro. You stare into your opponent's eyes, trying to make them laugh while not laughing yourself. The way to win is to focus your concentration on something far away, so that you do not really see your opponent, although you are looking straight at them. It is difficult, suppressing laughter, feeling it push against your lips, like water against a dam. Sometimes, the pressure is so great that it makes your mouth twitch and your eyes crinkle.

Her father is making that sort of face now, but something tells her that it is not laughter that he is trying to control. When adults try to hide their feelings in this way, it is usually a sign of something bad.

The pictures of the dead people on the walls stare back at Rani, fixing her with frozen smiles. She has a sudden sense of foreboding.

"Appa, what's the matter?"

Raj clutches her to him so tightly that she can hardly breathe. And then it comes. A great rending sob. Tears, hot and salty, splash onto her shoulder. Unable to see, Raj raises his arm, trying to dry his tears on his shirt sleeve. As his grasp loosens, Rani slips to the floor and, in a second, is racing back down the passage to her grandmother's room.

"Rani. Come back. Don't go in there!"

Raj tries to catch her, but she is too fast for him, ducking through his outstretched hands. She is running fast, faster than she has ever run before and yet it seems to take years to cover the few yards to Sunny's room. She is running in slow motion to the faded amusement of onlookers. It is as if the people in the photographs have gathered together for a purpose. An occasion. She arrives at the doorway, panting and terrified.

In front of her, she sees a frozen tableau: Sunny, Neleni and the strange man, all mute and impassive. It reminds her of something. A picture she has seen at convent. The Assumption. Why does it remind her of that?

She looks at her grandmother, lying quietly on the bed. She is still not moving. Rani can hear her father lumbering after her along the passage, calling her name. He must not catch her. She must get to Sunny. She must speak to her.

Bounding across the room, she reaches the bed before anyone realises she is there. Putting her face close to Sunny's ear, she whispers: "Nanna."

There is no movement, no flicker of the sunken eyelids.

"Nanna," she howls, as the realisation breaks that Sunny will not wake up. Her friend, her only friend, has left her. Gone without a word.

"Nanna, Nanna, Nanna," she wails. As if, by repeating her name, she can call her back.

Then, another voice joins hers, moaning softly. Rani looks up and sees her mother's face, twisted with grief. Still holding Sunny's hand, Neleni is rocking to and fro, mouthing, rather than speaking, the same words, over and over.

"I'm sorry. I'm sorry."

Outside, the temple tree shakes violently and a shower of blossom patters against the window.

1957: A missing friend

Like a tremor, news of Sunny's death passes through the neighbourhood. Everyone knew her and her advice has been sought by many people on many matters, from remedies for stomach-ache to the marriageable prospects of their children. Without seeking it, she assumed the role of local wise woman and her loss is a cause of widespread grief. With her passing, an era has ended when common sense, rather than doctrine or politics, could be relied upon to solve the small problems of daily life. Everyone feels that something important has disappeared even if they cannot say exactly what.

Sunny's family are surprised at the degree of respect which she commanded in the wider community and which has only become apparent on her death. That those of her own age should miss her is to be expected. Death is rapidly thinning their circle and each loss of a friend or acquaintance is an unpleasant reminder that their own end is approaching. But she is equally missed by the younger members of the community, people for whom she performed small acts of kindness which went unnoticed by her own family.

Even those, of whom Sunny was critical, mourn her passing. Ella, the maid, is inconsolable. She howled and wrung her hands when the news was first broken to her and, since then, has performed her work to the accompaniment of quiet sobbing. The cat, ever the target of Sunny's threats, has been skulking in the yard, crouched behind a pile of broken flower pots. For days, it has neither eaten nor slept, waiting patiently for its tormentor. In a few days, when Sunny has still not appeared, the cat will slink away to resume its former life: a homeless wanderer scavenging food from waste-bins and tips; a nameless creature, unworthy of insult.

On the day before Sunny's funeral, there are many visitors to Neleni's house. Large men with fat bellies and sweating faces hug Raj enthusiastically and speak in ill-concealed whispers.

"Sorry about the old lady, Machan. Come for a drink with us when it is all over."

Raj weeps as he embraces them but takes comfort from their presence. Friends from his childhood and the arrack shop, they remind him that death, unless it is one's own, is a transient affair and that, after the funerary arrangements have been completed, life will continue as normal.

Neleni, pale and worn, has been left to deal with the other visitors. Helped by cousin Ana, she escorts them into the front room where Sunny's coffin lies on a trestle table. The coffin has a patina of dark, lustrous varnish which reflects the flickering image of four church candles. Specially purchased for the occasion, they sit in brass candle-holders at each corner of the table. As they burn, the odour of their thick yellow wax mingles with the scent of flowers which Neleni has placed in vases around the room. Marigolds and frangipani: the flowers of death.

Sunny, dressed in a white cotton sari, seems almost lost in a coffin that was intended for someone much bigger than her. A recent outbreak of cholera has carried off many of the neighbourhood's children, causing a shortage of smaller coffins. The coffin-maker also caught the disease and, although recovering, is still weak from his illness. He has been unable to work for several weeks and the families of those who have died in the interim have had to make their choice from his existing stock, however unsuitable.

"So tiny," whispers one old lady to her grandson as she leans over the coffin to get a better look at her friend. "I can't believe that she managed to live for so long."

She squeezes his arm, indicating that she wishes to be led out. As she takes a last look at Sunny, the old lady thinks with some satisfaction how, at the same age, she is much less frail than Sunny was. A good few years in me yet, she thinks, comforted by the fact that she has survived another friend. This makes three since the beginning of the year. Tomorrow, she will scan the paper for the obituary which she will cut out and add to the others which she keeps in the top drawer of her dressing table, along with her scarves and handkerchiefs.

Outside the house, many of the visitors greet each other cheerfully, momentarily forgetting the reason for their visit in their pleasure at meeting old friends; but, on entering the house where Sunny lies in her coffin, all light-heartedness is extinguished.

Many emerge from the front room dabbing their eyes or weeping audibly. The sight of death descends like a chill, dampening their spirits.

***

"What can you see?"

Saro tugs impatiently at Rani's elbow. The two girls are crouched down behind the kitchen door and, having opened it a crack, are peeping at the visitors in the hallway. Her height and seniority give Rani the better view, a fact much resented by her sister.

"Shh! Be quiet. If Amma finds us she'll send us to our room and we won't see anything. Look, I'll tell you if I see something exciting."

This seems to appease Saro and, for several minutes, the girls continue their silent vigil behind the door. Many of the visitors are strangers to Rani, although she recognises some, such as Lakshmi Aunty. She winces when she sees her arrive, noticing how Lakshmi pauses on the doorstep, turning her head this way and that, trying to identify anyone she knows, deciding whether they are worth speaking to or not. As she stands there, large and beaming with the light behind her, she reminds Rani of a malevolent rain cloud, an impression reinforced by her dark purple sari.

Lakshmi Aunty is followed by her frail little husband, who looks more terrified than usual, and then by her daughter, Dalia, who Rani thought so beautiful on her wedding day. However, whether it is due to early pregnancy or a strange trick of the light, Rani now thinks how like her mother Dalia looks. Her mouth has an ironic twist at the corner, as if she thinks no-one else is quite good enough for her.

The last member of the party is Dalia's husband, Michael. He trails in, several feet behind his wife and, with a strange flash of childish insight, it occurs to Rani that he should be holding his wife's arm. He has the same air of disinterest today as he had at the wedding. Rani does not like him much, although she has to admit that he looks handsome, albeit in a contrived sort of way. As he passes through the hallway, she notices how he casts a quick, sideways glance at the mirror on the dresser, then runs his hand over his hair. Rani is sure that he has a comb concealed in that hand. She thinks him a cold-hearted peacock, so unlike Uncle Arjun who is both handsome and kind.

Uncle Arjun left early for work this morning, taking his breakfast before Rani was awake. She did not even have chance to wave goodbye from the steps as she often does. She misses him acutely and wishes that he would return. His presence might soothe the loneliness that has followed her grandmother's death. At the thought of Sunny, a large lump like an indigestible toffee sticks in her throat and she is overwhelmed by sadness. Amma has promised that, when the visitors are gone, she will take Rani and Saro to see their grandmother. For the last time. Rani's eyes become hot with tears and her lip quivers.

"Don't cry!"

Two small arms are entwined around her neck and she feels the plumpness of a soft cheek pressed against her own. Rani clutches her sister to her and, burying her face in Saro's hair, weeps softly.

Impervious to sorrow – at least, to that of others – Lakshmi's family leave the front-room where Sunny lies, much as they entered it; all except Michael who, with head bowed, seems preoccupied with picking lint off his sleeve. Clutching a glass of sweet sherry, Lakshmi is scouring the hallway for somewhere to sit. Unable to resist her gimlet gaze, two guests rise to leave. Propelling Dalia towards the two vacant chairs, Lakshmi forces a path through the mourners then, spying an old acquaintance, she pauses, to make an announcement.

"Only six months after their marriage and my Dalia has fallen pregnant. Wonderful isn't it?"

Lakshmi rolls her eyes as if offering thanks to heaven. The woman to whom she is speaking has three daughters, none of whom has yet succeeded in producing a child although each has been married for several years. The companion purses her lips and looks sour then, with some effort, murmurs her congratulations, squeezing the words out between her teeth like the remains of toothpaste from a tube. Lakshmi beams with pleasure. Nothing sweetens one's own success so much as other people's failure.

"Ahhhmm!"

Standing across the room from Lakshmi, Michael yawns audibly, raising a long hand to cover his mouth. Lakshmi's bragging bores him. He averts his eyes, looking away from her, avoiding the inevitable dart of anger that he knows has been sent in his direction. His relationship with his mother-in-law has rapidly deteriorated since his marriage, possibly prompted by his frequent absences from home. He has already tired of his insipid, simpering wife. He is bored and every day that boredom becomes a little worse until he thinks he might eventually die of it. It is a depressing thought.

He tries to distract himself by making a casual inventory of the hall's contents. It is something he learned to do as a salesman and it is a habit that he has been unable to break even though, due to subsequent promotion, he is no longer required to sell insurance policies at the doorstep.

With one glance, he scans the room, pausing at the grandfather clock, then passing on to the plaster image of the Virgin which, for some reason, causes his mouth to twitch in amusement. He breathes out sharply, trying to expel the smell of warm candle wax from his nostrils. The place is like a morgue, even without a cadaver. Nothing worth insuring. Still, he will mention it to one of his salesmen, get him to visit Raj. One should never pass up an opportunity to make money, however small.

"She is a truly beautiful girl, a gem. I am blessed."

Lakshmi's shrill cadenza rises above the general hum of conversation. By now, displeasure has concentrated her companion's face into a collection of puckers and wrinkles, like the mouth of a purse when the drawstring is pulled tight. The unfortunate woman has made several attempts to escape but each time has been restrained by Lakshmi's friendly arm, which, slipped through her own, now holds her with a vice-like grip.

Clinging in her turn to Michael's arm, Dalia has been sufficiently impressed by the gravity of the occasion to make a rare alteration to her appearance, exchanging her usual expression of smug radiance for one of bored hostility. She resents coming here and being forced to view the corpse of a wizened old lady. The experience has turned her delicate stomach.

Unusually superstitious, due to her condition, she wonders if it is bad luck for pregnant mothers to view a dead body. She will ask her mother when she gets home and then, perhaps, cry a little. She needs to be petted and reassured. Michael has been less attentive to her recently, possibly due to the fact that business calls him away from home for a couple of nights every week. At least, that is what he tells her and, confident in her own undeniable charm, she has no reason to disbelieve him.

She sniffs a little and dabs her nose with a tiny, delicate handkerchief, a gift from her wedding day. She still warms to the memory of it, although she feels a little hollow now that the excitement is past and she is no longer the centre of attention. She thinks she feels a genuine tear making its way into her eye and dabs at it with the corner of her handkerchief. The world is a sorry place and she is far too young to view a corpse. It is really too much. Raising herself on tiptoe and leaning heavily on Michael's arm so that he is forced to bend towards her, she whimpers in his ear.

"I'm tired. I want to sit down. I don't feel well."

Michael is forced to switch his attention from thoughts of business to the mewing of his wife. As he does so, he thinks how much of a dead weight she has become, no longer a light and pretty ornament, smiling and silent, but the equivalent of a human ball and chain, always clinging to him, always pulling him down.

He is about to respond with a short, but cutting remark, the sort that would amuse Leela, when he sees that his mother-in-law is watching. Although they are separated by some distance and a low hubbub of conversation, Lakshmi knows instinctively that her child is in distress. Releasing her companion, who scuttles off to a remote corner, Lakshmi cranes her neck, peering over the heads of the intervening mourners. Her tiny eyes, buried in the folds of her face, glitter like coals as she pierces Michael with her gaze.

Suspended by those two pinpoints of malevolent light, Michael is forced to swallow his response to Dalia. It lies in his throat, as hard and indigestible as a pebble, while he tries to produce an alternative: words dripping with treacly sympathy. They rasp over his tongue, clinging to his palate until he is forced to cough them out. As he does so, he raises his hand to his mouth concerned that, if Lakshmi sees his lips, she will detect his insincerity. Despite his need to appease her, he fights an irresistible desire to laugh hysterically. As he speaks, his voice wavers.

"It's all right, darling. We'll go straight home."

Dalia purrs and rubs her face against Michael's shoulder. She likes to think of herself as a sleek little cat, affectionate and contented but, as she winds herself even more tightly around his arm, all Michael can think of is a snake, a boa constrictor that will eventually crush the life out of him. She is holding him now just as her mother was holding onto her companion a few minutes ago. Michael saw the look of desperation on the other woman's face and thought it funny then. But now he is filled with incipient terror.

Lakshmi gives him an approving smile, the corners of her mouth disappearing into her fat cheeks. Michael feels his stomach heave. His thoughts turn to the tiny foetus growing in Dalia's belly. Soon, there will be three of them, Dalia, her mother and the baby; all watching him, all making demands, all telling him what to do; surrounding him like a human wall; complaining, crying, nagging, whining. He is losing himself. They will drink him dry and leave him, a wizened old husk like the one in the next room.

Confronted with death, he tried to affect a worldly disdain but the sight of the old woman, lying in her coffin, has shaken him. It sounds ridiculous but what affected him most was the fact that she looked so tired; not peaceful, as one is supposed to look in death, but careworn, as if life had been drawn out of her, drop by drop, over the years. A slow, joyless journey that ended in exhaustion, not rest. He noted how the hands, crossed on her breast, seemed to clutch desperately at the rosary entwined between their fingers. The coffin, purchased ready-made from the coffin-maker down the road, was two or three sizes too big, emphasising the smallness and frailty of her corpse.

Although, previously, he never gave it much thought, it is not the end that Michael wishes for himself. And yet, the demands of his new family are piling up, like earth being heaped over his head. He feels the inexorable pull of gravity and imagines himself, slowly being pulled down by the ankles, lower and lower, until the world around him disappears and he is surrounded by suffocating darkness. Buried alive.

The odour of warm wax, from the candles around the coffin, permeates the house and fills his nostrils. It mingles with the smell of hair oil, released by the heat of many bodies, and the sweet pervasive scent of frangipani garlands. Beads of sweat prick Michael's brow and a strand of neatly-combed hair flops into his eye. Panic grips him. Unexpectedly, in this house of mourning, he sees the spectre of his own death.

"Let's go," he murmurs and, putting an arm around Dalia, he herds her towards the door.

Lakshmi smiles approvingly and, clicking her fingers at her husband, who is quietly sipping a glass of water, she trips nimbly after the newly-weds, beaming a fond goodbye to her fellow mourners.

That evening, the family bids farewell to Sunny. Saro, in her mother's arms, reaches out to the old lady.

"No, Saro, you cannot touch her."

Neleni feels a strange revulsion for the cold flesh of the corpse, thinking that it will be somehow sacrilegious for it to come into contact with the warm hand of a child. Saro is reaching out a plump hand to the figure in the coffin.

"No, don't touch!" says Neleni, grasping the small fingers in her own.

"Grandma!" Saro calls softly, squirming in her mother's arms.

"She will not wake, Saro. She has left us. You must say goodbye now."

Saro is still of an age where death and long journeys are beyond comprehension. Bemused, she waves at the figure in the coffin: a tentative, hand-flapping wave; the sort given by children to strangers when they think the occasion, or their parents, require it. Then she yawns, revealing two rows of perfect little milk teeth. Her eyelids flutter and, nestling her head into the crook of her mother's neck, she falls asleep.

"I must put her to bed. Will you stay here with Amma?"

Neleni's face gleams in the candlelight. She is tired and yet, despite her sadness and her pallor, Raj thinks how beautiful she looks. He reaches out to touch her, but she has already turned away. Opening the door into the hallway, she passes through, as silent as mist. Raj cannot tell whether his sorrow is due to Sunny's death or the fact that his wife seems always to be beyond his reach. Whatever the cause, he weeps silently, one hand stroking the coffin whose lacquered surface shimmers in the dim light of the candles.

The door opens slowly and Rani creeps in, walking on tiptoe, a bunch of temple-tree flowers clutched in her hand. She has picked them from the tree outside the house and, to keep them fresh, has wrapped their stems in a twist of damp tissue. She approaches the coffin and, taking a deep breath for courage, peers in.

It is only a few hours after Sunny's death but, already, her face has changed. Without the expression that animated it in life, it looks not so much like her grandmother as a mask, an effigy of what she once was. Rani feels a sharp pang of disappointment. She has come to say goodbye but her grandmother has already gone. That thought, rather than the sight of the body, increases her loss.

Reaching into the coffin, Rani places the posy beside her grandmother's head. In doing so, her finger touches Sunny's ear. Despite the warmth of the room, it is cold. Rani recoils yet, at the same time, she longs to kiss the wrinkled old face.

"Goodbye, Nanna," she whispers, knowing that her words no longer have any meaning for the little figure draped in the white sari. No sound can pierce the impenetrable silence of death. Sunny is beyond her reach.

"Grandma," she sobs, overwhelmed by the agony of loss.

A hand feels clumsily for her shoulder, turning her away from the coffin. Raj, also weeping, holds his daughter to him. They remain, clinging to each other, like survivors of a shipwreck, until Neleni returns.

"You can go now," she murmurs to Raj, placing her hand on his arm and speaking with a softness of tone that she rarely uses to him.

"Put Rani to bed. I will stay with Amma now."

"But, you are tired?"

"No, Raj. Go now. I want to be on my own."

Her voice sharpens, warning Raj not to challenge her. Meekly, he kisses her on the cheek, hoping for a response, but she continues to stare ahead of her, gazing into the guttering flame of a candle.

"I am going," Raj says, unnecessarily and, taking Rani by the hand, he leads her slowly out of the room. In the doorway, Rani suddenly twists around, trying to get a last glimpse of her grandmother, but Raj restrains her.

"Come, child. It is enough. You have said goodbye."

Sitting in the same seat that Raj recently occupied, Neleni listens to the sound of Rani sobbing as she is led away along the passage. She wants to cry too but the pain and guilt are too deep and the tears will not come. One of the candles goes out, releasing a stream of thick black smoke that winds upwards to the ceiling.

Neleni rises from the chair and walks heavily to the sideboard to fetch another candle. Lighting it from one of the other flames, she pushes it down into the soft, squashy wax left by its predecessor. Standing beside the coffin, she gazes into the closed face of her mother.

Was it my fault? Did she die because of me? These are questions which have haunted her since Sunny's death and from which she can find no relief.

Reaching into the coffin, she strokes the cold hand clutching the rosary.

"We had our differences, but I always loved you, Amma. You knew that, didn't you?"

But now she questions whether her mother really knew the depth of her feelings. They always seemed to be arguing. It was not the most obvious way to express her affection. She wonders if she could have done more and, if so, what that should have been. She was always too preoccupied with bitterness at her own fate to give it much thought. Perhaps she should have done so. And yet part of her, a small part, is unrepentant. Arjun: the only real subject of disagreement between them. The only point which Neleni could never concede to her mother, living or dead. That is why she cannot cry.

Arjun has been working late at the office, the only one to remain at his desk long after everyone else has left, sifting papers, writing letters, staring for long, blank minutes out of the window into the darkness where bats swoop silently over the street, hunting their prey.

Before sunset, his door opened a few inches, pushing back several piles of files that lay against it. There was just enough room for Nash to insert his head and part of one broad shoulder. He had craned his neck around the door, trying to discover the impediment that stopped him from entering. On seeing the files, he was amused and slightly bewildered.

"Couldn't it wait?"

Arjun had no answer. Of course it could. Nash had hesitated, on the point of saying something. However, he had thought better of it.

"OK. Just don't work too late."

***

Arjun agreed that he would not and Nash had gone home. That was an hour ago. It was light then. It is dark now and he has had to switch on his desk lamp. The heat from the electric light is making the room hot and he is becoming drowsy. Outside, a group of friends are greeting each other noisily outside the Moslem hotel: workmen and labourers meeting for a meal, exchanging gossip, enjoying the soft night air as they stand on the pavement, embracing each other with brotherly affection, their white robes and skull caps giving them the appearance of ghosts when they stray out of the lamp-light.

Arjun closes the window and tidies his desk, arranging his pens, straightening the blotter, discovering a dozen little tasks that must be completed before he leaves. Then, reluctantly, he switches off the desk lamp and makes his way out of the building, down long silent corridors to the side entrance.

It is not so much that he does not wish to return home; rather that he feels he does not belong there. An impenetrable wall of grief now separates him from Neleni and her family. He feels out of place, an outsider without purpose or function.

He crosses the street and enters the Moslem hotel. After ordering a meal of curry and pittu, he sits in a corner by the window where he can see people passing in the street. It is good to be surrounded by conversation, yet not to be involved in it. Tonight, he simply wants to listen, observe.

The cook emerges from the kitchen, carrying two plates and trailing an aura of steam. He is a fat man with a thick black beard and cheeks like two full moons. A large white cloth, smeared with gravy, is tied around his ample stomach and his face gleams with sweat. He places one of the plates in front of Arjun and grins. His front teeth are missing.

"Enjoy your food, brother," he growls.

Then, turning expertly on the ball of one foot and, carrying the other plate aloft, he weaves his way through the tight clusters of people to the other side of the crowded room.

Arjun eats so slowly that, by the time he has reached the last mouthful, the food has gone cold. He orders tea and a sweetmeat, which he does not really want. The tea also turns cold before he finishes it. Then, with no further reason to continue his stay, he pays up and takes the long route back.

**

It is late and the street is deserted, except for a couple of pye-dogs pawing at a pile of rubbish. Occasionally, one of them finds something that smells interesting, a piece of fat or stale roti, an empty can or bottle still containing a trace of its contents. Excavations are instantly suspended. The dog pauses to explore its treasure and its companion, alerted to the prospect of a meal, sidles up, hoping for a share of the find, a move which results in much growling and snapping. Eventually, the interloper is forced to slink back into the shadows where it crouches, jealously watching as the other dog consumes its trophy. Then, the search begins again.

Giving the dogs a wide berth, Arjun walks along the other side of the street until he is level with Neleni's house. Before crossing the road, he stands for a moment on the edge of the pavement, watching the house as it sleeps. The pale blossom of the frangipani glows in the dark and fallen blooms have gathered around its base in a luminous pool.

With the exception of one window, in which three points of light flicker dimly, the house is in darkness. Arjun knows that the illuminated window is the room in which Sunny lies. He will have to pass that room as he crosses the hall and, for some reason, it fills him with dread.

"You're being silly," he tells himself and, stepping smartly into the road, he crosses over to the house. The steps to the front door creak beneath his feet although he treads as quietly as he can. The front door has been left unlocked; pushing it open, he steps into the deathly stillness of the hallway where the convex mirror and the face of the clock gleam like two opposing moons.

The door into the living-room is ajar and, beyond it, is a faint glow. Despite himself, Arjun is drawn towards that room and, softly crossing the hall, he presses the door open with his fingertips. At first, he sees only the uncovered coffin in the shimmering light of the candles. The room is hot, filled with the pungent smell of burnt wax. Arjun approaches the coffin, unable to take his eyes off its occupant.

Of course, he has seen death before but, on previous occasions, the deceased was a family member, someone dear to him, someone he would miss. In such circumstances, he knew what was expected of him. Grief and regret came easily. He cried and was comforted and, as he grew older, he learned to return that comfort. Yet none of that enables him to deal with what has happened here.

He always knew that Sunny disliked him and he suspects that she said as much to Neleni. Sunny often muttered when looking in his direction and, in fanciful moments, he even wondered if she was casting a spell on him. He did not hate her, but he feared her. It is difficult to mourn the passing of someone who was so unremittingly hostile. Indeed, if he feels anything, it is relief. Overcome with guilt, he blushes as he looks at the tiny face, grey in the dim light and wizened as a walnut.

Would she have liked me if I had been in Raj's place? It is a question he cannot answer. In fact, he never allows himself to think of what it would be like to be Neleni's husband. When the chance of something happening is so remote, speculation is painful. Too painful. You grieve for what you can never have, spoiling all that you possess. No, he will never contemplate that possibility.

A rustle and a sigh. Someone is in the room with him. Arjun looks up and sees Neleni, asleep in a chair in the corner. She looks pale and, even in this light, Arjun can see that dark rings have formed under her eyes. Neleni asleep, keeping company with the dead. The thought makes him shiver. Kneeling by the chair, he touches her hand.

"Neleni, what are you doing here?"

"Mmm."

She stirs but cannot rouse herself.

"You must go to bed."

Gently, Arjun gathers her up in his arms and carries her across the room. Suddenly, she is awake.

"No, no. I must stay with her. She must not be on her own."

"I will stay with her. She will not be alone. You must rest."

"Mmm."

Her head rolls against his shoulder. He carries her past the kitchen, vibrant with the sound of loud snores. Raj is asleep at the kitchen table. Arjun can just see his form, outlined by the moonlight, an empty glass clutched in his hand.

"All on your own," he murmurs. "He left you all on your own."

He kisses Neleni gently on her forehead. She wraps her arm around his neck. In the bedroom, he places her gently on the bed, sitting beside her and cradling her in his arms for a while. She stirs, half asleep.

"Arjun ..."

"Yes."

"Must tell you."

"What?"

With her lips to his ear, she whispers something. But Arjun cannot hear. It was probably nothing important. He holds her to him, his hand cradling her head, his face next to hers. She drifts back to sleep. He holds her for a few more minutes, rocking her gently, unwilling to leave her, but he has made a promise, one that should not be broken. Laying Neleni on the bed, he strokes the hair from her face then, after kissing her gently on the forehead, he returns to the front room to keep his vigil by Sunny.

The next morning, more visitors arrive. Close family this time: Ana, her sister and brother and their spouses. They disappear silently into the living-room where Neleni is sitting, wan-faced, at the head of the coffin. The door clicks softly shut behind them but soon the sound of muffled sobs drifts through the house.

Rani and Saro are in the kitchen, occasionally joined by their father who seems glad of an opportunity to leave the oppressive atmosphere of the mourning room. Each time, he enters the kitchen, red-eyed and flushed, wiping tears away with his stubby fingers. He then pats the girls on the head with a heavy hand, a gesture of affection that Rani has come to dread, then squeezes them tight, pressing their little faces into the soft sides of his belly.

"Have you drunk your milk?"

"Yes, Appa."

"Good girls."

Contented with their reply, he returns to the living-room. As he opens the door, the sound of weeping floods out, piercing and anguished, momentarily amplified until the door closes again and muffles the sound, like putting a stopper in a jar. It reminds Rani of the time she tried to keep a cricket in a bottle. She had amused herself for hours, sitting on the porch step with the bottle to her ear, lifting the lid, then closing it, listening to the chirping of the cricket, first loud, then soft. But that was a happy sound, one that reminds her of good things. She will have no good memories of today, although she will never forget it. An icy cold slips over her, frosting her skin and squeezing her heart, filling her with a great fear, although of what, she cannot say.

"Hello, girls."

Arjun is standing in the doorway, holding a huge bouquet of flowers; white orchids, anthuriums, lilies and the flamboyant orange and purple spikes known as Crabs Claws.

Rani launches herself from her chair and flings her arms around Arjun's waist. He kisses her cheek.

"Hello, Rani dear."

She clings to him, tightly, as one might cling to a life-raft. He kisses her cheek, stroking her hair affectionately with one hand while he struggles to keep the flowers upright with the other. In the heat of the room, they begin to release their scent, stephanotis and jasmine, sweet and uplifting.

"Are they for Granma?"

"No," he looks embarrassed. "They are for your mother. Let go of me now, dear. I must put them in water."

Applying a gentle pressure to her shoulder, he pushes her away from him and goes to the sink where he runs the tap to make a bath for the flowers. With a sudden rush of jealousy, Rani begins to cry; softly, so that Arjun, who has his back to her, will not hear. Saro, who has been quiet for many minutes, slips off her chair and runs to her sister. Leaning against her, as one might lean against a tree, she puts her arms around her. Rani clutches her sister tightly.

Rat-tat! There is a sharp knock at the front door. Aroused from his occupation at the sink, Arjun walks across the room, then pauses at the kitchen door, staring across the hallway.

"Should I go?" he says, uncertain as to what to do.

The problem is resolved by Ana who hurries from the living-room, her scarf held up to her face, blotchy with weeping. She opens the door; a murmured conversation takes place, then four men step into the hallway. The undertakers. Two of them follow Ana into the living-room and soon the house echoes to the sound of hammer blows. The weeping stops, as if everyone is holding their breath.

"What is happening?" whispers Saro, her eyes wide with terror.

"They are nailing the lid down on Granma's coffin."

Rani's legs feel weak and, for a second, she thinks she might be sick. In the doorway, Arjun is turned to stone. Rani cannot see his face, but she knows his eyes are fixed on the living-room door. Instinctively, she knows he is thinking of her mother.

The hammers fall silent. The two other men, who have been waiting in the hallway, walk quietly into the front room and, for a few seconds, there is a sound of shuffling. Then, the door is opened wide. The family comes out first, each couple arm-in-arm, the men supporting their wives. They line the hallway, standing close to the walls, waiting in expectant silence. Then, slowly the coffin emerges, borne on the shoulders of the undertakers. As it passes, Neleni, shaken by sobs, puts her fingers to her lips, then presses her hand against the side of the coffin.

"Amma," she cries. "Amma."

Rani thinks that Neleni sounds like a small, lost child, calling for its mother and she, too, begins to sob aloud.

The family follows the coffin out of the house, the women staying behind on the porch while the men follow it down the steps and into the street where it is loaded onto the back of the undertaker's cart. Then, with one man pulling on the long handles at the front of the cart and the others pushing from the side, the procession makes its way along the street to the sound of wailing and the rattling of wooden wheels.

A few passers-by stop to pay their respects, crossing themselves and murmuring a prayer, but the cart is soon absorbed into the general commotion of the street, surrounded by taxis and pedlars, bicycles, shoppers and workmen. At the corner of the street, it passes the young Moslem sweet-seller who, busy with bagging up salted nuts and sweetmeats, is oblivious to the fact that the coffin holds the old lady who considered him an angel.

From the porch, Neleni and her cousins watch the coffin disappear. It is their last view of it as only the men will attend the funeral; an old-fashioned custom still observed by some families, a remnant of colonial practice.

In the hallway, Rani and Saro stand with their arms around each other, watching the women on the porch. Neleni's grief is terrible and she has to be supported by Ana. Then, Rani is aware of someone passing her. Quietly, Arjun walks up to Neleni and stands beside her. Rani observes how, behind her mother's back, Neleni's hand seeks that of Arjun and how their fingers become entwined, unseen by any of their companions.

Feeling lonelier than she has ever felt in her life, Rani weeps: not for her grandmother, this time, but for herself.

Part 5: 1968
The patient

Seated on the edge of the bed, the man holds the woman's hand. The skin is still smooth and soft, not wrinkled or speckled with age; the hand of a woman who, were it not for a terrible illness, would have many years to live. Her fingers are long and straight. Even now, they have a firm grip, as if all her remaining energy has been concentrated in one hand. A painter's hand. The man strokes the fingers tenderly, then looks away, swallowing the tears that he cannot allow himself to shed. Not here. Not in front of her.

Somewhere at the front of the house, music is still playing on the gramophone. They thought it would soothe her, revive memories of the past. It was his idea, although he has taken no credit for it, letting the others think it was their idea. But he chose the music. Each song conveys a message, something that only she can understand, because it represents a memory, something shared: soft words, a view of the stars, a stolen kiss. A dream unfulfilled.

But someone else has chosen the music today. A song, not one selected by him, has been placed on the gramophone. He knows, almost by instinct, although he cannot hear it clearly. He bows his head, listening intently.

"… *A certain smile* …"

Johnny Mathis. A song without meaning, either for him or the woman lying beside him. The woman stirs slightly in the bed and licks her lips as if they are dry, although her eyes remain closed.

"Neleni?"

He speaks softly, knowing that he should not wake her, because wakefulness means a renewal of her pain. Yet, he wants her to acknowledge him. Just a flutter of her eyelids or a squeeze of his hand. That would be enough. He wants to know that the connection between them has not been broken, that he has not been forgotten. Selfish, perhaps, but even at this advanced stage, the thought of losing her is unbearable. As long as she remembers, that part of him that is his true self will stay alive. Everything else is a facade.

"Mmm."

A sound so soft that it is not even a sigh. At this stage, even the merest breath has meaning.

"Neleni," he whispers again, straining to hear in case she speaks, but her lips do not move. She is sleeping. She will not wake. Bending forward, he kisses her softly on the forehead and eases himself off the bed, trying not to disturb her.

"Goodnight, my darling."

He bends over her, looking carefully into her face. Is that the trace of a smile? He cannot tell. The light is fading fast and her face is in shadow.

"I will leave the door open, so that you can hear the music."

He still feels the need to speak, to tell her things, although she cannot hear. The morphine has raised a wall of silence between them. Reluctantly, he leaves, turning once he has reached the lighted passage to look back into the darkened room.

Light and dark: the contrast, between where he stands and where she lies; he, in the world of the living; she, on the threshold of death. He will bring her some night-lights. She must not spend her last hours in darkness. It will not be long now. She will probably die in her sleep, but whether it will be minutes or days, no-one can tell. She has entered the last, unpredictable stage before death.

He hesitates in the doorway, unwilling to return to the brightly-lit kitchen for, every time he leaves her, he wonders if it will be the last time. Part of him prays for her to die, to get it over with, while another part of him wills her to live, wildly hoping that she will recover, against all the odds, the doctors' predictions and the evidence of his own eyes.

Sadly, he walks back along the echoing passage, past the sepia photographs on the walls. They watch him as he passes. He knows. He can feel their eyes upon him. He turns his head suddenly, trying to catch them out, but they stare glassily ahead, at a view that he cannot see. Perhaps it is a trick of his imagination, or the effect of many sleepless nights, but he feels that they are waiting. For something. Or, someone.

***

An old song. The imprint of lips on her forehead. For hours, it seems, she has toiled back up from the darkness to find him. Only now, he is gone. She is alone in the dark. But it does not frighten her. She abhors bright light. In her weakened state, even daylight is too strong for her. She wonders if it would have been better to have died young – even younger than she is now – for some cause, taking a bullet to the back of the head or the heart, as many have done while still in the peak of health. A quick death. One that would have avoided the horror of a slow, draining sickness.

No. Even now, she does not wish for that, for she would not have known him. He has been here. Recently. She can smell his cologne. Expensive. Something French. Only he smells like that. And he has been holding her hand. She can tell, can still feel the soft touch of his fingers. Usually, she squeezes his hand, just to let him know that she knows he is there. But, today, she could not wake in time. She wishes he would return, but has not the strength to call him. She must wait. She will listen to the music, waiting for his message.

"… *A certain smile* …"

It is not music chosen by him. Yet it has memories. 1958. That is when she first heard it. It was popular then. You could not pass a bar or a tea-shop without hearing it. And, for some reason, it has happy memories; perhaps because it came from that period which she now regards as the calm before the storm, when people still had hope and no-one knew of the horrors to come.

Neleni drifts on her bed and lets the music wash over her.

Part 6: 1958
The Prime Minister

Mr Bandaranaike emerges from the Parliament building looking smug. If he were an athletic man, a tall equestrian type like his father, he would throw out his chest and breathe deeply, ready to stride out and meet the day. As it is, he is thin and angular, with pebble glasses and a sickly disposition. However, such physical shortcomings do nothing to allay his pleasure on this bright morning.

He sniffs the air delicately, like a cat, turning his head this way and that, scenting success in every direction. At last, he is in control. The pact with the Tamil leader, Mr Chelvaniyakam, has been in place for several months and the Prime Minister is now considering how to implement its terms. The Tamils in the North and East will soon enjoy a considerable degree of regional autonomy.

So far, all attempts to oppose conciliation with the Tamils have failed miserably. The most notable of these defeats was the disruption of Mr Jayawardene's protest march to the Temple of the Tooth. Intercepted by the police at Imbulgoda Pass, the march was successfully defused.

"A totally damp squib," thinks Mr Bandaranaike, hugging himself.

The honking of horns and tinkling of bicycle bells float on the breeze. Mr Bandaranaike watches the coil of traffic which winds around the Government buildings like a giant snake. In the midst of the pandemonium, he thinks he sees a familiar face peering out of a shiny sedan. He cannot be sure, but he thinks it is Buddharakkita. He cranes his neck for a better view, but his eyesight is weak. He removes his glasses, wiping them swiftly on his sarong but, by the time he has replaced them on his nose, the car has turned a corner, obscuring its passenger from view.

"Never mind," thinks Mr Bandaranaike, "he won't be showing his face here again for a while."

He smiles to himself as he remembers their meeting last week.

***

After repeated telephone calls to his office, the Prime Minister had eventually been persuaded to hold an audience with the abbot. In desperation, the abbot had admitted to the Prime Minister that he was in dire financial straits. He had overspent on the election campaign, bargaining on funds from his wealthy monastery to make up the difference.

However, due to a quirk of law (introduced by the British), Kelaniya's assets are controlled, not by its abbot but by a panel of trustees. With his usual optimism, Buddharakkita had counted on the trustees' support for his political schemes. However, when he approached them to explain his difficulties, the trustees had proved less than sympathetic. In fact, they had refused to grant him a single rupee.

In addition, Buddharakkita's attempts to win control of the paddy lands, donated to the monastery by Vimala Wijewardene's mother-in-law, have made little progress, despite the fact that legal proceedings have been in motion for at least two years. In short, the abbot is bankrupt: an unusual position for a man supposed to have no possessions.

"You will understand, my friend, how necessary it is to pay off my debts?"

Buddharakkita, dressed in monastic saffron, had mopped his round face with a large white handkerchief, as he pleaded with Mr Bandaranaike. Amid panelled oak and dark veneer furnishings, standing in front of the Prime Minister's large, shiny desk with his bare toes sinking into the Axminster carpet, the abbot had looked strangely out of place.

"A fish out of water," Mr Bandaranaike had thought to himself.

Despite his own traditional dress of sarong and short-sleeved shirt, these were surroundings in which Mr Bandaranaike was at home. They had a stuffy, collegiate feel, rather like a barrister's chambers and felt pleasantly familiar to the English-trained lawyer. His adversary, on the other hand, was distinctly ill at ease.

"How can I help?" the Prime Minister had asked, playing the abbot like a fish on the end of a line, before reeling him in.

"There is a Government contract for the transportation of rice … I have interests in a shipping line."

The Prime Minister looked puzzled although he had already worked out the equation for himself. He had shaken his head in an enquiring sort of way, encouraging the abbot to spell out his request.

"If I could secure the rice contract … if you would grant it to me … the shipping line would pay me a share of the profit. I would have independent means, enough to cover my debts."

Rising from his chair, Mr Bandaranaike had wandered about the room in a thoughtful sort of way, head down, hands behind his back. Back and forth he had paced until his perambulation had brought him to within a few inches of the abbot. Then, he had stopped and, orchestrating his features in what he had thought to be a look of sincere sympathy, he had delivered the coup de grâce.

"My friend, do not think that I have forgotten your kindness to me but the thing that you ask is not in my gift."

"Not …!" The abbot had begun to quake, as if shaken by an internal tremor.

"No," said Mr Bandaranaike, turning sadly towards the window in order to suppress a smile. "Perhaps you have not heard. My ministers are reviewing our shipping lines with a view to nationalisation. Philip Gunawardane is working on this." And then, as an afterthought: "I can arrange for you to speak to him, if you like."

The abbot was now trembling violently and, for a second, the Prime Minister wondered if he was going to fall down in a fit. Droplets of sweat ran down his face and he seemed on the point of swallowing his tongue, so difficult was it for him to speak. Finally, he screamed:

"Philip Gunawardane! That Troskyite? That disbelieving heretic? You expect me to speak to him?"

Mr Bandaranaike had raised his hands in a gesture of hopelessness. There was nothing he could do. With a roar like a lion, the abbot had taken a step towards the Prime Minister, his eyes filled with a deep and unrelenting hatred.

"You … you traitor!"

Even Mr Bandaranaike had been taken aback by that and had been on the point of summoning one of the armed guards posted outside his office, but there had been no need. Like a furious whirlwind, the abbot had spun on his heel and, his loose robes flapping about his legs, had stormed out of the office. Shaken, but triumphant, the Prime Minister had dropped back in his chair and laughed.

That was a week ago and since then, there have been no further communications from Buddharakkita.

Standing in the protective shadow of Parliament, Mr Bandaranaike feels invincible. Pushing back his shoulders, he takes a delicate sip of air and coughs.

Built by the British in neoclassical style, the Parliament building is a geometric confection of columns, pilasters, porches and white limestone. Although it would not have looked out of place among the architectural remnants of ancient Greece, it is, in fact, only a few years old, having been officially opened by Governor Sir Herbert Stanley in 1930. Supported on all sides by free-standing Ionic columns, it is approached by a set of imposing stone stairs which lead up to a massive porch, surmounted by a triangular pediment.

Reclining on that pediment, Hooniyam has been watching the Prime Minister, gloomily reading his thoughts. Mr Bandaranaike is exuding an aura of confidence that surrounds him like a fiery halo.

"Upstart," mutters Hooniyam as the Prime Minister struts to and fro beneath him.

"Ingrate! He wouldn't be here if it wasn't for me, but he hasn't visited my shrine for months. Not once."

Moodily, he runs a long black fingernail along the sill of the porch, dislodging a pile of pigeon droppings that narrowly miss the Prime Minister's head. Mr Bandaranaike's halo shines more brightly, sending vivid flashes up into the sky as he flexes his arms and tries to thrust out his concave chest.

"Ha, ha!" Hooniyam roars. "Look at that puny human! Ha, ha, ha!"

Hooniyam laughs so loudly that he scares a flock of pigeons. Panic-stricken, they flap up into the air, quitting the roosting places where they have been pursuing their amorous interests. However, the god's laughter goes unnoticed by the Prime Minister who simply mistakes it for the roar of traffic. With a self-satisfied sigh, Mr Bandaranaike rolls his head back, stares happily into the clear blue sky then, adopting a business-like air, walks briskly back into the building.

"Who do you think you are?" Hooniyam shouts after him.

"Mr Prime Minister Bandaranaike," he sneers under his breath. "What a fancy title for a little man! What a sham. Pretending to be something you are not. Like this building."

Sitting up, Hooniyam dangles his legs over the sill. Beneath him, politicians come and go, bustling up the stairs, self-important with briefcases and bundles of papers, sometimes gathering in small clutches to discuss their plans. Hooniyam reads all their thoughts.

"Not one good idea between them!" he concludes in disgust.

He had forgotten how dreary it is to look into the minds of politicians. It depresses him. He left Colombo several months ago, just before the conclusion of the Prime Minister's pact with the Tamils. But now, he realises that that was a mistake. The politicians and priests that he trusted to protect his interests have failed him. Neither Jayawardene nor Buddharakkita are a match for the Prime Minister. The government of the country is spiralling out of Hooniyam's control.

Launching himself into the air, Hooniyam hovers over the Parliament building, piercing its limestone casing with his divine gaze. For a few seconds, he considers its contents: corridors with people scurrying past each other like ants; ante-chambers stacked with files; the Chamber of Representatives where MPs are gathering for a debate; and, finally, the ceremonial mace and Speaker's chair, gifts from the British House of Commons.

"Bah! Foreign imports!"

Hooniyam spits viciously, watching with satisfaction as his venomous green spittle burns a hole in the roof. Then, with a rare stroke of philosophical insight, he thinks how strange it is that the Island's matters of state should be decided within an edifice built by the British in the style of ancient Greece.

"Barbarians," he hisses, savouring the word which he learned, centuries ago, from one of his worshippers who had served as an emissary to Rome. It occurs to him that, perhaps the Romans encountered similar problems to those that he is currently witnessing. Only, in this case, it is Tamils and Indians, not Goths and Vandals, who threaten the Sinhalese civilization.

"I must do something. Quickly. Or we will be overrun."

Hooniyam speeds through the air: skimming the golden roofs of temples; scudding over traffic and trains; passing towns, villages and paddy fields until he reaches the clearing in the forest, where he will hold his own parliament – an assembly of his kin with whom he will plot the next stage of his campaign.

1958: Letters and signs

Who would have thought that the number-plate on a bus could cause civil unrest? Yet, the characters on that humble plaque symbolise the bitter struggle between two races, each competing for power.

The trouble starts when the National Transport Board sends new buses to the Tamil heartland in the north of the country. Each bus has a smart new number-plate, bearing the Sinhalese character for "Sri". Tamil activists, who have been promised that their own language will be used in regional government, regard this as an affront. So, they busily get to work with their paint pots, replacing the Sinhalese characters with Tamil letters.

This, in turn, is regarded by Sinhalese activists as a challenge to their authority. Retaliation is swift in the south of the country and, within twenty-four hours, groups of Sinhalese defacers, some led by monks, are patrolling the streets of the capital, painting over Tamil lettering wherever they find it. Not even the Prime Minister's official car escapes their attention: the Tamil section of a three-language sign reading "left-hand drive" being neatly painted over.

Of course, moderates on both sides dismiss these events as the silly posturing of a few hotheads and, if they are not exactly amused by it, they are not particularly worried either. Yet, there are some troubling signs which, when considered in hindsight, are like the boils that herald a plague.

A journalist, working in Colombo, recalls the rough thuggery of the gangs of defacers. He also witnesses an extraordinary scene in which several men, equipped with a pot of tar and a paintbrush, attempt to smear over a Tamil advertisement on a kiosk.

One of the gang urges his friend to daub a Sinhalese 'Sri' sign on the door of the cabin. But the man wielding the paintbrush looks baffled. Being illiterate, he has to pass his brush to someone else so that the job can be completed. It is a terrible irony that this dispute, over a language that many can neither read nor write, should have such disastrous consequences.

1958: The speech

Mr Bandaranaike is at his desk, sifting through a sheaf of police reports. The setting sun shoots several brilliant rays through the window which, momentarily, bathe the room in amber light. The polished surfaces glint, the silver in the cabinet twinkles and even the dark wood panelling glows as if it has come to life. Mr Bandaranaike winces and, pushing a finger under his glasses, rubs the corner of one, rheumy eye.

The reports make tedious reading. Nothing bores the Prime Minister more than these accounts of mindless vandalism: the blacking out of signs that have led to tit-for-tat reprisals across the country. He yawns, patting a pale hand politely over his mouth. The sun drops below the horizon and the room darkens. For a few minutes, Mr Bandaranaike sits in the gloom, resting his eyes before switching on the desk-lamp. The papers now lie before him in a pool of yellow light. Illuminated. Demanding his attention.

Running a hand over his hair, Mr Bandaranaike leans forward on his elbows. As a lawyer, he is used to making sense of complex documents but these paltry pieces of paper, some crumpled, others smattered with bad grammar and crossings-out, hardly seem worth his attention. He flicks through them without enthusiasm.

His wife, Sirimavo, has invited guests over tonight. Family friends. It should be a pleasant evening, but Mr Bandaranaike's work will not be done when he leaves the office. After entertaining his guests, he will have to work into the night, drafting a speech for his Party's annual conference. Every word of that address will be relayed to the nation through the medium of Government-owned newspapers. It is essential to get the message right and, this year, his task will be a difficult one.

For many months, he has tried to breathe life into his pact with the Tamils. Of course, he has the backing of his old schoolmate Chelvanayakam, leader of the Tamil Federal Party, and a few of the more liberal Sinhalese politicians. But, beyond the narrow confines of their support, he is unable to gauge the general mood. Even in his own Cabinet, there are still pockets of resistance. Mrs Wijewardene, Minister of Health, is a renowned proponent of the nationalist viewpoint. Privately, Mr Bandaranaike thinks her a bigot.

Although he has ridden to power on the back of the nationalist vote, Mr Bandaranaike's real desire is to represent a moderate majority. He has little sympathy for the likes of Mrs Wijewardene, or her patron, the abbot of Kelaniya. The trouble is that Buddharakkita has also been the Prime Minister's patron. It is an uncomfortable truth. Such thoughts cause the Prime Minister's stomach to flutter uncontrollably.

Is he really a traitor, as Buddharakkita suggested? His gracious upbringing has taught Mr Bandaranaike to despise ingratitude. It is certainly not the mark of a gentleman. He wonders what his father would have said.

He picks up a pencil and sketches a few words on a notepad. "Moderate, moderate," he mutters to himself. The trick is to explain this concept to a country with little experience of democracy and whose political parties can suddenly change their hue with the dexterity of a chameleon.

"I need a middle way," he says, speaking aloud to the shadowy room. The words reverberate, gathering force, until they seem to echo in his head. *The middle way. The middle way.*

"Of course!"

He flings his pencil across the room in delight. Maddiyama Prathipadawa, the Buddhist concept of the Middle Path. By adopting it as a political principle, he will be able to speak to the majority in a language that they understand.

Frantically, he scrabbles around for another pencil and, having found one, quickly roughs out a sentence: *I am not merely a Prime Minister but a Buddhist Prime Minister.*

That will get them on board. What next? He must make the connection between his leadership and the idea he is trying to put across: the Middle Way. He sucks the end of the pencil for a second, then hurriedly scratches out a few more words, tiny pegs on which to hang his argument.

"Good, good," he murmurs, jotting down a new idea. He will describe how his faith is not just a label, but a profound conviction, one which dictates his political decisions. His pencil flies across the page, then stops. He tries to finish the sentence, yet stumbles over the last words.

In describing his agreement with the Tamils, he must avoid the word "pact". It is too emotive, too sinister, too redolent of underhand dealings. He taps his lip with the end of the pencil, trying to think of a lawyerly phrase. *These discussions.* That will do. He completes the sentence, re-reads it, then adds a conclusion which implies that his agreement with the Tamils is the result of divine intervention.

With renewed optimism, the Prime Minister tears the page from the notepad, stuffs it in his briefcase, then hurries from the office, leaving behind the unread pile of police reports.

The corridor is dark and hot, filled with jostling bodies that push and shove past each other, frothing and simmering like a stream of boiling sugar. In an attempt to avoid the flow, two men have stepped aside into the recess of a doorway. One is considerably older than the other. He has thick grey hair, a portly belly and a cynical gleam in his eye. Years of experience have inclined him to mistrust even his closest colleagues and there is little that they, or anyone else, can do to shock or surprise him.

"What did you think of it?" he says to his younger companion, who is obviously nervous at being marooned with this overbearing figure.

"Of what?" stutters his neighbour, his eyes darting this way and that, eagerly seeking a means of escape. A wrong answer given to a man like the Minister could mean the end of his career.

"The Prime Minister's speech, of course," snaps the older man.

"Oh, well, um, very persuasive," murmurs the colleague, his brow furrowed as if trying to find the right answer to a particularly tricky exam question.

"You think so?"

The Minister raises his eyebrows in an attempt to feign genuine surprise. It simply makes him look more menacing.

"Well, er, of course, I'm not very experienced in such things," stammers his companion.

"Pooh, you civil servants are all the same. Yes, sir. No, sir. Three bags very, very full, sir. Always giving the answers you think people want. Never saying what you think. You've got no more brains than a bunch of tea-sellers!"

The younger man flushes. *A description that also fits politicians*, he thinks savagely, although he does not dare to voice his opinion.

"Well, I know what I thought of it," growls the Minister, his eyebrows bristling.

The younger man gives him an enquiring look, although he does not say anything. Just a few feet away, a bottleneck has formed in the corridor. Suddenly, under the pressure of massed bodies, pushing from either direction, it gives way and a large group of argumentative men push past. The two men in the doorway hold their breath, trying not to get swept up with the crowd. Neither says a word and the civil servant guesses that the Minister is waiting until the men are out of earshot before he speaks again.

"You were saying, Minister?" prompts the younger man with a hint of sarcasm.

"I think that the Lokka has lost his way. No-one supports this pact with the Tamils. Not even his own supporters. Especially not after that business with the bus number plates. It was the Tamils that started that. They can't be trusted. And now, even the Prime Minister is dithering.

"If he really believed in compromise with the Tamils, he would have pushed ahead with legislation for the establishment of regional councils in Tamil areas and the reasonable use of Tamil. But here we are, months later, and nothing has been done. *It's still in the hands of the legal draughtsmen*. That's his excuse.

"He's having second thoughts. It's obvious. Especially when he makes speeches like the one this morning. *Buddhist Prime Minister*, indeed. *The Middle Way*. Pooh! No-one's going to fall for that."

"And will you tell him what you think?" asks the civil servant with an obsequious smile.

"Are you mad? It would be political suicide. No, I'm just going to sit tight and see what happens. Like all the rest of them."

The Minister jerks his head, indicating groups of men who, now that the flux of traffic is over, have gathered in every doorway. They look anxious and, with heads nearly touching, are talking in low voices. The corridor has been transformed from a busy highway to a long, whispering gallery.

"You see," says the Minister, "they all think the same. The conference that was supposed to have united our Party has only served to fragment it."

There is a sudden flurry of movement in one of the doorways and the corridor falls silent. Surrounded by a gaggle of well-wishers, Mr Bandaranaike issues from the conference room and strides energetically down the corridor. The men lining the corridor smile and bow deferentially as he passes. As he draws level with the Minister and the civil servant, he addresses one of his supporters.

"I think it went very well, don't you. They seemed to like my speech."

"Oh yes, sir. Very much. A great success, if I may say so. One of your best yet."

The Prime Minister beams and sails down the corridor.

"Well," says the Minister quietly. "You've heard the story of the Emperor's New Clothes. Now you've seen it in practice. The Prime Minister stripped naked and exposed as a fool. It can only get worse after this."

"What do you suggest?" The civil servant is visibly shaken.

The Minister laughs grimly.

"Do what civil servants do best. Say nothing and keep your head down."

And with that, the Minister stumps away, thinking that this will be an appropriate time to renew his acquaintance with Mr Jayawardene, leader of the Opposition. In fact, as he walks along the hot, airless corridor, he resolves to call on his friend this very afternoon.

1958: A morning walk

Mrs Thambiah is an early riser. Today is no exception. At half past five precisely, she opens her eyes and raises herself slowly from her bed, sitting for a few minutes on the edge of the mattress while she collects her thoughts; sifting, sorting and arranging them like seeds in a tray.

Her husband, who remains motionless in the bed, will sleep on for another hour or two. No need to disturb him. In fact, she tries not to, hoarding the precious early morning for herself.

Stretching out a chubby foot, she sticks out her big toe and pulls a slipper towards her. It makes a soft rasping sound as it slides across the floor. After insinuating the thong between her fat toes, Mrs Thambiah reaches for the other slipper, pauses a minute to catch her breath then, with a soft groan, rises to her feet.

"Never mind," she thinks, as she shuffles towards the bathroom. "A bit of housework will get me going."

Not even the grumbling of her joints can alloy Mrs Thambiah's early morning optimism. After washing and dressing, she treats herself to a cup of fragrant tea, the very best, sent to her by a cousin from his own plantation, high in the mountains near Nuwara Eliya. Closing her eyes, Mrs Thambiah sniffs the delicate scent, imagining herself on the green slope of a mountain, surrounded by tea bushes. The first cup of tea is the best of the day but, like all good things, it is over too quickly.

Regretfully, Mrs Thambiah rinses her empty cup and sets to work. She likes to start early, frying onions and grinding spices while the day is still cool. Then, when her chores are done, she will tour the garden, watering the orchids and sniffing the white gardenia while taking sips of her second cup of tea, which tastes almost as good as the first.

These early morning perambulations inevitably lead to a little area at the bottom of the garden where Mrs Thambiah raises her seeds and cuttings. Here, pots, tins and even old breakfast bowls are put to use, arranged on shelves constructed of rough wooden planks supported by bricks. It is an invention of which Mrs Thambiah feels duly proud, taking credit for the originality of her design although it was largely the creation of her gardener, Thomas.

A source of both anxiety and pride, Mrs Thambiah's plant nursery receives a daily visit from its patroness who performs a careful inspection of all the pots, bending over them so that her eyeball is nearly level with the soil. Mrs Thambiah fears incursions of weeds which, if left unattended, will inveigle themselves into the pots and strangle the legitimate inhabitants. So, each morning, armed with a cup of tea and the blade of an old kitchen knife, Mrs Thambiah marches to the end of her garden, ready to do battle and deter intruders.

Cuckoo in the nest, she thinks as she savagely digs out a green sprout with the tip of her knife. It is a morning in early April and, so far, everything except the contents of her pots seems to be in order. Mrs Thambiah spends nearly half an hour bending over her plants until a twinge of rheumatism makes her gasp and she stands up to rub her back. As she does so, something unusual catches her eye.

Beyond the pot-bound shelves is a tall fence of living bamboo which, through various natural cracks and crevices, affords a good view of the broad avenue beyond. A flash of saffron, as bright as the plumage of a tropical bird, flits past, followed by another, then another.

Intrigued, Mrs Thambiah gathers up her sari and, stepping carefully over a pile of empty pots so as not to disturb any resident scorpions, selects a gap in the bamboo fence and, putting her eye to it, peers through.

Shaded by the trees, a group of saffron-robed monks is quietly passing along the avenue. Ten. Twenty. No, she counts fifty at least. Mrs Thambiah rubs her eyes. She must be dreaming. Monks usually travel in couples or, perhaps, in small groups, but she has only seen this many on holy days and there is no festival, nor even a temple nearby, to account for the presence of so many in this district. Cinnamon Gardens is an exclusive, residential area, the refuge of wealthy civil servants and politicians, not holy men.

Where can they be going? wonders Mrs Thambiah, absent-mindedly picking up a watering-can and tilting it over her plants. Once again, she applies her eye to the gap in the fence. She has not been dreaming. More monks are filing by. Pressing her cheek against the bamboo and holding her head at an angle, Mrs Thambiah tries to get a view along the avenue. As far as her myopic eye can see, the road is filled with monks, passing along in an endless stream.

They are chanting now. She can hear them. And some are carrying hand-painted banners with messages written in Sinhalese. Mrs Thambiah squints, trying to read what they say, but she has left her glasses indoors and, anyway, her view is now obscured by increasing numbers of passers-by, crowds of lay-people who appear to be accompanying the monks, walking alongside them. There are so many of these additional supporters that there is hardly any room for them on the pavement and some brush against Mrs Thambiah's fence so that, from time to time, her only view is that of someone's ear or the back of a sleek, oiled head.

Due to her excitement, Mrs Thambiah has been holding her breath and, now, she realises that her lungs are aching. Standing back from the fence, she rubs her cheek which now bears a long scar-like weal where it has been pressed against the joint of the bamboo. Mrs Thambiah's feet also feel unusually damp. Looking down, she realises that instead of watering her plants, she has been sprinkling her toes with the watering can and that the hem of her sari is sodden and sticking uncomfortably to her ankles.

"I should go and change," she murmurs but, unable to tear herself away from the spy-hole in the fence, she resumes her observations. The crowds on the pavement have thinned a little now and she has a clearer view of some of the banners. Being an English-speaking Tamil, Mrs Thambiah has some difficulty in deciphering all of the Sinhalese characters; but she can make out the word 'Swabhasa', meaning 'Mother Tongue'.

This gives Mrs Thambiah a fluttering, uneasy feeling in her stomach. It brings to mind the events of recent months, when groups of thugs took to the streets with tar-pots, scrawling signs in Sinhalese on the walls of Tamil shops and homes.

Some of the graffiti were obscene, but they were not the worst. The worst were those which, in their simplicity, conveyed the purest hatred of the Tamils. One such was daubed on the wall of her own house. She had it re-painted directly, but such signs can still be seen around town, especially in the commercial quarters: huge black letters depicting the Sinhalese 'Sri' sign on the side of Tamil shops and merchants' booths.

While the sign-painting can be explained as the work of a few, ignorant goondas, Mrs Thambiah has not found it so easy to dismiss other, related incidents. Although uneducated and, therefore, supposedly ill-informed, the sign-writers managed to identify the homes of Tamil politicians with extraordinary efficiency. This included the home of Mr Thambiah who is, himself, a retired MP and a staunch supporter of the Tamil Federal Party. Then, as if the incursion of hooligans into the leafy avenues of Cinnamon Gardens was not bad enough, the police had simply stood by and watched as they ran amok and defaced the Thambiah home.

From subsequent discussions with her friends, Mrs Thambiah has discovered that she was not the only one to suffer from the indifference of the authorities. All over Colombo, the activities of the Sri sign-writers have gone unchecked. Even the Prime Minister's car has been vandalised.

"I don't know what the country's coming to," huffs Mrs Thambiah as she peers into the street. The crowds have thinned considerably and now consist of only a few stragglers: five or six monks and as many supporters.

A cluster of leaves, piled against the bamboo fence, shifts ominously. Momentarily distracted, Mrs Thambiah holds her breath, her eyes fixed on the ground, waiting to see if a snake will emerge. Although her sight is poor, her hearing is sharp and she listens, carefully. The leaves remain quiet and undisturbed. However, by now, Mrs Thambiah's finely-tuned ears have picked up something else. Two men are speaking quietly on the other side of the fence.

"What will happen?"

"We will force the traitor to submit."

"Then what?"

"We must seek out another traitor and make him finish what he started."

"Who? Who is this man?"

"Someone known to both of us."

"Tell me."

Mrs Thambiah strains to hear, but the men are whispering. Standing on tiptoe, she presses her eye to the spy-hole. To her surprise, she sees two monks, standing in the shade of a tree, directly in front of her.

The younger of the two is restive and his constant movement, verging on agitation, seems out of character for someone of a spiritual calling. First, he sways to and fro, then rubs his ear with such vigour that he reminds her of a dog scratching a tick. His hands are unusually large and strong for his size, the fingers coarse and thick with blackened, broken nails. A labourer's hands ingrained with soil, not the soft, uncalloused hands of a holy man.

Despite his robes, there is something about him that is wild and unpredictable, much like the goondas who painted Mrs Thambiah's wall. Ignorance can be read in a face and Mrs Thambiah doubts if this young monk can even spell his name. With extraordinary insight, she suspects that he is quick to anger and, when roused, is irrational to the point of madness, unrelenting in his ferocity.

But it is the other monk who really frightens her. Where his companion is governed by instinct, this man is calculating and implacable, his stillness emphasising the atmosphere of silent menace that seems to surround him. He has pale eyes and the lean, hungry features of a feral cat.

Fascinated, Mrs Thambiah tries to change her position, hoping for a better view. As she moves, a twig catches under her toe and snaps. With a slow, deliberate movement, the monk turns around and, seeing Mrs Thambiah's eye twinkling at him through the fence, puts his hands together and bows.

Mrs Thambiah's heart patters in her plump little breast. *I must fetch Thambiah*, says a small voice in her head; but, she remains rooted to the spot, like one of her seedlings; a small, pumpkin-shaped woman dressed in a green sari, her mouth gaping in amazement.

The monk seems untroubled by her presence.

"Come, brother," he says, taking the other by his elbow, "we must move on."

Realising that they are being watched, the younger man glowers at the spy-hole and makes a move, as if to strike the fence, his face twisted with a dark and ignorant fury. But the other man restrains him and, with a vigorous shove in the back, pushes him away. Then, turning back to the spy-hole he gives what passes for a smile although, to Mrs Thambiah, it resembles a sneer of ineffable malice.

"Ugh," she shudders, stepping back quickly from the spy-hole. A cold tingle of goosebumps speeds over her flesh and she rubs her arms with her hands, trying to warm herself.

When she looks again, the man has disappeared. Yet, a sense of menace remains, casting a long shadow over Mrs Thambiah's day.

The arrival of hundreds of monks is met with mild surprise by the residents of Cinnamon Gardens. Some come out to watch, shading themselves from the sun with large umbrellas, while others phone friends, or the police, to find out what is happening. However, in one particular household, the event generates consternation bordering on panic.

At about 8 a.m., the police telephone the Prime Minister's home in Rosmead Place to warn that a demonstration will take place that morning. But Mr Bandaranaike has already left for work.

With little more than an hour's warning, his wife, Sirimavo, and the household staff are left to deal with the situation as best they can. The gates to the Bandaranaike compound are firmly barred and barbed-wire erected at the boundary.

"Do you think it will be enough?" whispers the head servant to his mistress.

"Of course."

Her reply is crisp. But the servant notices how Mrs Bandaranaike's lips clamp tight as soon as she has spoken; a sign of resolve, to prevent her real thoughts from escaping.

The old man follows his mistress's gaze through the window to where a few armed policemen, summoned at short notice from the local constabulary, are patrolling the grounds. Every so often, they cross the lawn to confer and, inevitably, one of them looks over to the house with the hopeless expression of a novice contemplating Everest.

Having lived for decades among politicians, the old servant has learned that the truth is to be found, not in the spoken word, but in the speaker's face. The twitch of an eyebrow, a frown, or the curve of a mouth can tell him much more than the most eloquent speech. He checks the signs: first, the stern but ashen-face of his mistress; then the young policeman, staring up at the house from the garden, his face impassive but his eyes glimmering with fear, his rifle clutched tightly to his chest.

"So it is hopeless," concludes the old servant. "We shall be at their mercy."

For a second, he is gripped by violent fear, but it is a servant's lot to accept his fate and, after offering up a silent prayer, the old man regains his composure. Turning an expressionless face to his mistress, he asks with stony calmness if there is anything else she requires.

"No, you may go."

Her voice, renowned for its gruff, masculine depth, is unusually soft.

Bowing, the old man withdraws. Mrs Bandaranaike does not look at him but remains where she is, staring out of the window to where the first flecks of saffron are gathering beyond the fence. Instinctively, the Prime Minister's wife checks her watch. It is 9 a.m., the precise time at which the police predicted the arrival of the demonstration.

1958: Satyagraha

Finding the gates of the Prime Minister's residence barred, the protesters settle in the street outside. Initially, there are two hundred bhikkus accompanied by three hundred lay people but, soon, the crowds are swelled by onlookers bringing with them the inevitable pedlars of sustenance and carnival frippery. At first, the monks chant and pray, asking for the Buddha's blessing then, the real work of the day begins. For the next few hours, a succession of speakers addresses the crowd, denouncing the Prime Minister's pact with the Tamils.

***

It is mid-day and the sun is at its height, beating down relentlessly on the heads of the crowd. Faithful supporters of the monks have brought dhana, the gift of alms which traditionally takes the form of food. Each monk has brought his own bowl, carried within the folds of his robe and all sit cross-legged, waiting patiently while the alms-givers dole out rice and a watery soup of vegetables. Rotis are then handed out from large baskets.

As a meal it is simple but adequate; but, for Tissa, who has the fresh-air appetite of a farm boy, it is not enough. Wiping his finger around the inside of his bowl, he tries to capture the last grains of rice. His suffering will be compounded by the fact that, after this meal, monastic custom requires him to fast until dawn.

"I bet Buddharakkita doesn't go along with all this nonsense," thinks Tissa.

Amongst other things, it is said that the abbot rarely observes the daily fast, visiting the homes of lay friends in the evening where he eats and drinks, sometimes to excess. It is also rumoured that, on these occasions, he refuses to cover his chair with a white cloth, a practice required of all monks.

Tissa looks around him, in the forlorn hope of receiving a second helping of food. He knows that Anil is watching him closely and that he will disapprove of such un-monkish behaviour; but Tissa is still hungry and, despite the rice and roti that he has just eaten, his stomach is rumbling loudly.

Together with all the other monks, they are seated in the road and all around them is a great press of people. Some are faithful members of the laity who hope to gain merit by providing the monks with gifts of food and drink. Others are political supporters, including many members of Mr Jayawardene's party, who have less interest in religion than the annulment of the pact with the Tamils.

The rally has also brought with it the usual rag, tag and bob-tail of camp-followers: traders and spectators who have drifted along in the hope of profit or the satisfaction of idle curiosity. Even the sound of the monks' chanting cannot entirely suppress the excited chatter from this section of the crowd.

Tissa's eye is drawn to a young couple who are sharing a bowl of curry and rice, bought from one of the street-traders who has set up his kitchen on the kerb. They eat with their heads close together, scooping up rice with their fingers. The boy has prominent cheek-bones and affects a moustache which hangs above his lip like a scrawny centipede. He has thin arms and bony elbows, his youthful flesh worn away by too much work and too little food; a labourer, already old before his time who will die before his thirty-fifth birthday, a martyr to ignorance and poverty.

The girl, however, is pretty. She has a sweet, warm face and puts her hand up to her mouth to cover her giggles as the boy whispers something in her ear. Light-hearted and coquettish, there is something about her that reminds Tissa of Sriya. His heart twists in his chest at the pain of her memory. Neither madness, bloodshed, nor removal to another place has yet provided Tissa with a cure. At this moment, he would trade his life to see her. He envies the young man. Hard labour and a short life are a small price to pay for a few years of happiness.

"Look!"

Anil pokes him sharply in the ribs.

"What?" retorts Tissa, angrily.

"Over there. She's about to speak."

He points over the heads of the crowd to where a woman, clutching her sari, is being helped up onto a tea crate. She shuffles about, first making sure of her footing, then arranging her skirts and ensuring that her head is appropriately covered by her scarf. A loud-hailer is handed to her by a monk at the front of the crowd.

"Who is that woman?" whispers Tissa.

"The abbot's friend," replies Anil, the irony in his voice, unmistakeable.

***

For some time, rumours have been circulating among the monks about the abbot's double life. Everyone knows that he leaves the monastery most days in a chauffeur-driven car, dressed in a dark western-style suit and a Homburg hat, looking more like a gangster than a holy man. Initially, no-one knew where he went, although it was assumed that he was visiting political allies or business associates.

Discipline is strict in the monastery and the older monks try to prevent their younger brethren from gossiping, taking the view that it distracts them from more spiritual pursuits. Few newspapers find their way in from the outside and, anyway, as these are largely Government-run and nationalist in outlook, they are unlikely to contain any criticism of one as influential as Buddharakkita.

However, despite these strictures, a number of scurrilous pamphlets have found their way into the monastery. Some have even been pinned to its gates. They claim that the abbot has a mistress: a high-ranking Sinhalese woman from a staunchly nationalist family. The alleged 'mistress' is a Member of Parliament who owes her position to the abbot's patronage. The pamphlets also claim that she is a Cabinet minister. There is only one woman to hold this rank: Mrs Vimala Wijewardene.

***

Mrs Wijewardene is a beautiful widow in her middle years. Her elegant house is located in Bambalapitya, a wealthy district of Colombo, and her neighbours are judges, politicians and businessmen. One end of the road in which she lives leads to the seafront: the other offers a view of the largest Hindu temple in the city, a construction whose roof, shaped like a pyramid, is crammed with brightly-coloured images of the gods, neatly arranged in ascending order of importance. In fact, it was from this very roof that Hooniyam once appeared to Buddharakkita.

While Mrs Wijewardene's home provides a sanctuary from the rigours of monastic life, it is not the only attraction that Mrs Wijewardene has to offer Buddharakkita. She has inherited the mantle of her husband's family who, in the newly-created Sinhalese state, are prominent supporters of the Buddhist cause.

In fact, it was Vimala's late husband, Don Charles, who first welcomed Buddharakkita into the Wijewardene home where the young monk was introduced, not only to Vimala, but also to a unique brand of religious nationalism. According to Don Charles, the fate of Kelaniya was inextricably linked to that of the nation. He even wrote a popular tract, promoting the active involvement of Buddhist monks in secular politics. In his words: '*When Kelaniya fell, Lanka fell; when Kelaniya rose, Lanka rose.*'

However, it was Vimala's mother-in-law, Helena, who provided material support to the Buddhist cause. Prior to Buddharakkita's incumbency, she spent many lakhs of rupees, restoring Kelaniya monastery to its former glory. From a dilapidated and neglected state, its walls have been raised and its glorious frescoes restored. By the beginning of Buddharakkita's abbacy, its renaissance was complete and it was, once again, a monastery fit for kings.

Having naturally assumed the role of monarch, Buddharakkita has found a fitting consort in Vimala Wijewardene. Although convention prevents them from founding a dynasty, it does nothing to curb their political aspirations. In Vimala, the abbot has discovered an ally and soul-mate whose bigotry and hunger for power exactly match his own. Through her, he reaches deep into the heart of the Government, thwarting the liberal tendencies of the Prime Minister, undermining his policies and subverting other members of his Cabinet.

Now, their plans have reached fruition. They are at the peak of their power and ready to challenge Mr Bandaranaike.

Hooniyam is enjoying himself immensely. Sauntering through the Parliament building, he passes from room to room, waving his arms as if conducting an orchestra. The serpents at his waist writhe and twist, their eyes glinting, cold as wet pebbles.

Everywhere, groups of people are huddled together, whispering and murmuring until the whole building simmers with the sound of voices. All are discussing the crisis. Those gathered around Mr Jayawardene express grim satisfaction. A few months ago, their protest march to Kandy was intercepted by the police at Imbulgoda Pass. On that occasion, the authorities, notified in advance, had plenty of time to prepare their response.

But the opposition has learned a vital lesson from that humiliating defeat. This time, no word of the monks' protest got out until it was too late. The march has been master-minded by Buddharakkita and other members of the monkish political party, the Eksath Bhikku Peramuna, of which he is a founder. Although several trusted politicians knew of their plans, preparations for the march were made within the impenetrable sanctum of the monasteries, far beyond the reach of police informers.

Hooniyam pauses, listening, not to members of Mr Jayawardene's immediate entourage, whose opinions are predictable, but to those who form the outer circle: those most likely to change sides in a crisis; the waverers and doubters.

A small man, with the sharp face of a shrew, is fumbling nervously with a pocket-watch.

"What do you think?" he whispers to his neighbour. "Will there be bloodshed?"

The other man narrows his eyes, taking a moment to consider.

"No-o-o, not this time."

The man speaks slowly. He has thick, beetling eyebrows which, when he frowns, join together in a continuous line, shading his deep-set eyes.

"What then? What do you think will happen?" squeaks the small man as he rubs his pocket-watch on his shirt, a ritual act of cleaning that he performs when excited. His neighbour takes a deep, portentous breath.

"Who knows?"

"What do you mean who knows? Someone must know. Jayawardene must have an idea. I'll bet he was in on this from the beginning. Look at him. He must have known what the monks were planning, but he never told us. Why do you think he didn't tell us?"

"Perhaps," says the other man, frowning, "he doesn't trust everybody."

"Not trust, not trust …" the little man twiddles the chain of his pocket-watch furiously as he hops from foot to foot. "That's outrageous."

Hooniyam rubs his hands in satisfaction while his serpents nod approvingly. Mr Jayawardene has learned his lesson. He trusts no-one, not even the members of his own party. The opposition is shaping up nicely.

Hooniyam passes on, stalking the corridors and ante-rooms of Parliament, peering into corners, pressing his ear against doors and listening at keyholes. The place is in turmoil. Some openly support the monks' protest, talking feverishly, exchanging gleeful comments and wagging their heads knowingly. Others prefer to stay silent, sitting on the fence and awaiting the outcome when they will swiftly align themselves with the winning side, loudly telling everyone that this was what they had always predicted.

Bored with eavesdropping, Hooniyam makes for the meeting room where Mr Bandaranaike is in council with his Ministers. Stepping through the wall, as if it were a mere veil of mist, the god finds himself in a room redolent with Victorian grandeur. Dark and oak-panelled, it has an affluent but gloomy aspect. Pictures of former prime ministers hang about the walls, foremost among them a portrait of D.S. Senanayake.

Reformer, friend of the rural poor and darling of the nation, Mr Senanayake's picture hangs just above where the Prime Minister is sitting. The irony of this juxtaposition is not lost on the Cabinet, most of whom are drawing unfavourable comparisons between the two premiers. The crowning irony, of course, is that Mr Bandaranaike is completely unaware of all this. Hooniyam is delighted. Hooting with laughter, he turns a somersault in mid-air.

The Prime Minister has just broken the news of the protest at his residence and a glum silence has descended over the room. Philip Gunawardane, the Minister for Food, is first to speak.

"Get the police to disperse them."

Mr Bandaranaike sighs and removes his glasses, carefully wiping the lenses on his handkerchief. Then, placing the glasses back on his nose, he leans backwards and, with his eyes on the ceiling, begins to speak slowly, as if explaining a point of grammar to a classroom of recalcitrant schoolboys.

"You don't understand. At least five hundred protesters, many of them monks, have laid siege to my home. They have camped in the street. They are attracting others, scores, perhaps hundreds, and the numbers are growing as we speak."

"I don't see the problem," persists Gunawardane, stubbornly.

Like a schoolmaster, exasperated by the obtuseness of his pupils, Mr Bandaranaike shakes his head.

"Forcibly removing monks may result in injury, or even death. Even worse, it will turn public opinion against us. It is sacrilege to lay hands on a monk. You forget. I am a Buddhist Prime Minister. It was the Buddhist vote that got me into power."

"And it is the Buddhists who will destroy you," snaps Gunawardane, ferociously.

A murmur of disapproval ripples around the table.

"You see, Philip," says the Prime Minister, holding out his hands to indicate the other members of the Cabinet. "Your ideas are too radical, even for the people in this room. You are a Marxist, but the majority of people in this country are Buddhist."

"This is a democracy. Religion has no part to play in politics."

Peering over his spectacles, Mr Bandaranaike glowers at his friend.

"Democracy depends on consensus. That is why you, a Marxist, have a seat in this Cabinet."

Duly reprimanded, Philip Gunawardane slumps back in his seat, crossing his arms. He wants to remind the Prime Minister of how his Buddhist policy of the Middle Way has been rejected by his co-religionists who resent any compromise with the Tamils. Buddhist monks are now openly preaching against the Prime Minister in his own constituency. Even the members of his own Cabinet are deserting him.

"We are living in the Dark Ages," thinks Mr Gunawardane, gloomily.

In an attempt to break the awkward silence, another Minister poses what he considers to be an innocuous question.

"Where is Mrs Wijewardene? Surely she should be here by now?"

Mr Bandaranaike flushes. He struggles to speak and, momentarily, gives the impression that he is about to suffer a fit. The members of the Cabinet hold their breath. Someone passes Mr Bandaranaike a glass of water and he drinks it quickly. As he does so, they notice that his hand is shaking. At last, he speaks.

"Mrs Wijewardene will not be joining us."

There is an expectant silence. An explanation is required. The Prime Minister clears his throat.

"Mrs Wijewardene will not be joining us because she is attending the rally at Rosmead Place."

"What?" Philip Gunawardane starts from his chair, pushing it back so violently that it topples over.

"Do you mean that she has gone as an observer?" ventures another Minister.

"No," snaps the Prime Minister. "She has gone to support the protesters. Together, they are demanding the annulment of the pact with the Tamils."

"And what if you don't agree?" asks another Minister.

"It seems that the protesters will not disperse until I do," says the Prime Minister quietly, looking down at the table.

"Then you must comply with their demands," says one Minister.

"Rubbish," retorts Philip Gunawardane. "If you give in to them, you might as well step down and call an election. You cannot agree to this. It is against everything you believe in."

"This pact was made without the consent, or even the knowledge, of this Cabinet," shouts another Minister. "You, Philip Gunawardane, who preach to us about democracy, should understand that it is unacceptable for any Prime Minister to act in this way. The pact with the Tamils is illegal. It should be done away with. Now!"

This spirited speech is followed by cheering, then more shouting and the sound of fists being slammed on the table. A small fissure, created by Mrs Wijewardene's defection, is spreading through the Cabinet, splitting it into rival factions. At the top of the table, Mr Bandaranaike sits with his head in his hands as the consensus, upon which he created his government, fragments.

***

There follows a vociferous, blustery session. Personal enmities, shaken loose by the disturbance, begin to surface. Finally exposed, it will be impossible either to conceal or submerge them again. It is clear that the majority of Mr Bandaranaike's Cabinet wish him to annul the pact with his old schoolmate, Chelvaniyakam; but, even at this juncture, he is unwilling to abandon his plan for conciliation with the Tamils.

Mr Bandaranaike was a late convert to Buddhism: a move prompted more by political considerations than religious conviction. However, the more he promotes himself as a Buddhist Prime Minister, the more Mr Bandaranaike begins to think of himself as a Buddhist. The religious precepts, initially adopted as political tenets, have filtered into his soul by a process of divine osmosis. Now, as a matter of conscience, he finds it impossible to renounce the Middle Way.

521

Rubbing his temples with his hands, he raises his head and stares at the men around the table. He has not spoken for several minutes and they are now squabbling so fiercely that they seem to have forgotten him altogether. Philip Gunawardane is on his feet, leaning across the table and jabbing his finger at one of his right-wing opponents, a colleague of Mrs Wijewardene.

"The only reason she got a place in this Cabinet is because of that bloody monk. Now he's using his puppet to stir up trouble."

"His puppet?"

"You don't like that word? Then I've a better one."

A lewd reference is made to Mrs Wijewardene's relationship with the abbot. The table erupts. Ministers leap from their chairs and all start shouting at once. Instinctively, Philip Gunawardane rolls up his sleeves. He is used to the rough-and-tumble of politics and is equally comfortable addressing workers in the docks or politicians in Parliament. But there are times when his blunt speech offends his colleagues, men who share the same class and upbringing, if not the same ideas.

"Quiet!"

Mr Bandaranaike roars at his Ministers, surprising them into silence. In other circumstances, he might even have found it amusing to see the expressions frozen on their faces, their hands raised in the air, caught in gestures of hostility or exasperation. He has never shouted at them before, preferring to rely on the sharpness of his tongue, but it has the desired effect.

He coughs to clear his throat, then primly adjusts his glasses before speaking. He must play for time. There is still hope for the pact as long as his own Cabinet does not force him into a precocious decision. If he can negotiate with the protesters, there is still a chance to save the agreement.

"It is obvious that we cannot agree."

He raises a hand to stop any unwanted interjection.

"I therefore propose to go and meet these people to discuss their grievances. Face to face. And I will take six of you with me."

A gasp of shock rises from the table. Philip Gunawardane smiles to himself. The 'Boss' is back in control.

"Philip, you will not be coming."

"What?"

Philip Gunawardane, staunch ally of the Prime Minister, is dismayed.

"And neither will you," announces Mr Bandaranaike, indicating Mrs Wijewardene's right-wing colleague.

Philip Gunawardane and his opponent glare at each other across the table with unconcealed hatred as the Prime Minister makes his selection: six middle-of-the-road parliamentarians; unremarkable men whose pragmatism outweighs their political convictions.

As usual, Mr Bandaranaike's choice contains an inherent conflict. On the one hand, he hopes that men of such confirmed blandness will be unlikely either to antagonise or encourage the protesters. On the other, he hopes to be able to convince them of his preferred Middle Way and the inviolable nature of the pact.

A glimmer of an idea has formed in his mind. He will mount a counter-coup, starting with his own Cabinet.

A couple of hours later, the Prime Minister peers gloomily out of his window at the crowds in the street. On the journey here, his car had to ease its way through them. Hands were pressed against the windows and faces leered at him, goblin-like, or so it had seemed, full of hostility and mistrust. It is a far cry from the euphoria that greeted him, two years ago, after winning the election. Then, the people had wanted to carry him on their shoulders; but, judging by their faces today, it seems that they would prefer to lynch him.

The ministers who accompanied him to his home emerged, pale and shaking, from their cars. One clutched at his heart, while another rolled his eyes like a terrified animal. In normal circumstances, Mr Bandaranaike might have felt sorry for them but, on this occasion, he only feels anger. They were supposed to support him, stand firm, give advice. Instead, they have been reduced to six piles of quivering jelly. The only one that he can rely on is Sirimavo, his wife, who, undaunted by the events of the day, is bustling about, ordering servants to bring tea, water and glasses of whisky to steady the nerves of the ministers.

Mr Bandaranaike is now alone in his study, having made the excuse that he wishes to make some important telephone calls. But what he really wants is time to think. His brain is so stewed with discussion and debate that it has begun to throb, pressing uncomfortably against his skull as if about to explode.

Taking off his glasses, he massages his temples with the tips of his long fingers. At least, he can no longer see the crowds, their heads bobbing up and down beyond the fence like so many fishing floats. But he can still hear them; chanting, cheering and shouting and, above the general hubbub, the sound of a single voice, whichever speaker it might be, addressing them over a loud-hailer, denouncing the Government, especially the Prime Minister, who has so scandalously betrayed their trust.

While Mr Bandaranaike cannot hear the speaker's exact words, he knows their drift. Upon his arrival, he went straight to the perimeter fence to try and engage with the crowd, to reason with them. But they were unreceptive to his brand of logic, receiving his protestations of good faith in sullen silence. Then, one fellow at the back shouted: *He's a liar.* This was met by a murmur of consent, then others took up the chant, until the whole street resounded to the words: *He's a liar. He's a liar.*

Mr Bandaranaike was forced to withdraw, outwardly composed, but inwardly furious. And shaken. His Magic Wand – his own term for what he believes to be his infallible power of persuasion – lies broken and useless. His silver tongue is tarnished. No-one wants to listen to him. No-one cares. They are resolutely determined to get their own way, regardless of reason, sense, or fairness.

"Break the pact. Break the pact. Break the pact!" they chanted as he walked back to the house. He can still hear them chanting as he stares with myopic eyes, out of the window across the green blur of the lawn.

He wishes now that he had brought along his old ally, Philip Gunawardane. Unlike the other men, who have quiveringly submitted themselves to Sirimavo's ministrations in the front room, allowing themselves to be plied with tea and other, stronger substances, Philip would be pacing up and down, hatching a plan, or down at the front-line, sleeves rolled up, arguing with the protesters. Philip may sometimes be a hot-head; but, at least, he is a courageous one.

Mr Bandaranaike's hand strays towards the telephone. Perhaps he should call Philip, ask his opinion. Good, honest Philip who always speaks his mind. The only man he can trust – or would, if only he was not a Marxist. A highly-educated man from aristocratic stock, the Prime Minister has an innate mistrust of the ignorant masses. He does not have D.S. Senanayake's love or understanding of the common man, nor Philip's desire to empower him.

He is suspicious of Philip's motives with regard to the trade unions and fears that he may even wish to re-enfranchise the Indian Tamils, an ignorant mob if ever there was one. Living like animals on the tea plantations, they can neither read nor write, and yet their numbers alone (over one million) could swing the left-wing vote in Parliament. The country would then be run by radicals. And Mr Bandaranaike, committed to moderation and the Middle Way, sees this as the route to disaster.

No, on second thoughts, he will not call Philip Gunawardane. He cannot afford to.

Outside, the crowd falls silent. Another speaker takes the stand. A woman's voice. One well known to the Prime Minister. Mrs Vimala Wijewardene. She speaks for a few minutes. The Prime Minister strains to hear, catching only one word in three. It makes little sense but, when she stops speaking, the crowd erupts with chants. *Ceylon for the Sinhalese. Ceylon for the Sinhalese.* There is no doubting the content of her speech. She is openly rallying support. Against the Prime Minister.

He has already spoken with her once today. There was a barely-concealed gleam in her eye. She is winning and scents victory. Mr Bandaranaike fumes, hating the Minister for her betrayal of him and yet, he is forced to be grateful for her presence, for she is his only means of negotiating with the mob. And who raised this rabble? He knows only too well. When he approached the perimeter fence, he recognised many monks from Kelaniya. They were organising the crowds, the speakers and the chanting.

"Aagh!" Mr Bandaranaike gives an agonised cry and bangs his fist on the desk in frustration. He is caught, like a fly in a web, his hands and feet firmly bound. And the spider? Who other than Buddharakkita. All day, there has been neither sight nor sound of the abbot. Keeping a discreet distance from the trouble, he has closeted himself in his monastery, like a medieval king in his fortress, but his influence is everywhere.

Mr Bandaranaike wonders if he should telephone the abbot and speak to him directly; but pride prevents him. No doubt, Buddharakkita will try to wring further concessions from the Government in return for any favours. And, anyway, he would do nothing to save the pact. He has always been fiercely opposed to any compromise with the Tamils. Whatever happens, Mr Bandaranaike is determined to prevent Buddharakkita emerging from this episode with any increase in his credit. He will not speak to the abbot.

"Are you all right?"

Sirimavo bustles into the room. She has been alerted by the guard to a suspicious noise in her husband's study. The guard heard Mr Bandaranaike groan but could not bring himself to look into the room. Being fearful of either disturbing the Prime Minister or of being blamed for any catastrophe that had befallen him, he had considered it more prudent to summon Mrs Bandaranaike.

"What shall I do?"

A staunch nationalist and devoted Buddhist, Sirimavo can see only one answer.

"What can you do? Tear up the pact and send these monks home."

"Tear up the pact?" the Prime Minister murmurs, turning his glasses over in his hands.

"Of course. They won't go home until you do. If you stick to the pact, you only have one choice. Use violence to disperse the monks. If you do that, you will be out of government within a week."

Sirimavo is a pragmatist. One day, she will be Prime Minister herself.

Mr Bandaranaike sighs. He tries to imagine the Middle Way as a real road with tarmac and cars; but it is closed to him, barricaded by a pile of ancient handcarts.

"You really think that this is the only option?"

"Yes."

As usual, her answer is succinct. Sirimavo has many great qualities but, above all, her husband loves her for her common sense. Her logic is infallible and, her advice, usually sound. The Prime Minister's heart sinks.

"Leave me for a while. I need to think."

The Prime Minister sits alone at his desk, praying for enlightenment; but he receives no answer to the terrible dilemma that confronts him.

Seated in a comfortable chair in the Prime Minister's study, Hooniyam has had a ringside view of the day's happenings. He has watched, dispassionate and amused, as Mr Bandaranaike has descended through every infernal ring of despair. He has noted the small, but telling, gestures of impotence: the removal of the spectacles; the head resting in the hands; the writing of notes which were instantly torn up and thrown at the wastepaper bin which is now overflowing; the hand resting on the telephone, the fingers occasionally tightening around the receiver, as if in readiness to make a call, then straying to the dial, idly tracing numbers. But no note has been sent, nor any call made.

With calm detachment, he has watched Mr Bandaranaike, his faith in his own powers exhausted, praying for divine aid: first to Buddha, then to Shiva, then, in desperation, to the Christian god of his childhood. In fact, he has prayed to anyone who would listen. There was even a prayer to Hooniyam who derived a deal of spiteful satisfaction in not replying.

Indeed, the only person who can be bothered to speak to the Prime Minister at present is Mrs Wijewardene. With great interest, Hooniyam has observed the energy flowing between them, like an electrical current. At first, in the fullness of his confidence, Mr Bandaranaike exhibited a powerful aura, like that surrounding a planet; but, as the day has worn on, that power has passed steadily to his opponent until the Prime Minister has finally been dwarfed by her field of energy.

"Excellent. Excellent," chuckles Hooniyam as he passes through the door without bothering to open it.

Here, in the ante-room to the Prime Minister's study, sit the six ministers. Having canvassed their opinion earlier and received replies so contradictory as to be devoid of sense, the Prime Minister has temporarily abandoned them.

The ministers now sit, ranged around a large teak table like so many stuffed dummies. Conversation between them is restricted as they are not practised in the formation of ideas. In fact, as the day's events have shown, any expression of opinion by them only leads to discord. Their only strength lies in agreeing with other people's opinions, in which case, their unanimous agreement can always be counted on.

"What do you think will happen?" asks one, hardly daring to raise his voice above a whisper.

This question meets with silence. One shrugs his shoulders and another shakes his head but, apart from this, no-one ventures an answer. The Prime Minister is in the room next door and, even now, might be crouching with his ear to the keyhole, listening to their conversation. None of the six wishes to betray himself by speaking aloud.

The chanting from outside becomes louder. They can hear it clearly now and each of them shudders. It is like listening to the approach of a juggernaut, slowly rolling towards them, inexorable in its progress. It is not so much their personal safety that they fear for, as their political future. They left the Parliament building, puffed up with pride at being selected by the Prime Minister as his companions. Now they curse him for his choice.

It is clear that the Prime Minister has only two options: tear up the pact or set the police on the bhikkus. Either way he is finished. Whatever he does, he cannot exit with either his honour or integrity intact and anyone closely associated with him will be tainted forever.

"What can we do?" they all think as one.

Hooniyam cackles. Such thoughts, in the presence of a god, count as a prayer and, if he wishes, Hooniyam is at liberty to respond.

"Fools. I will tell you what to do."

Hooniyam breathes over the six ministers. A thick green smoke issues from his mouth and hovers about their heads.

"I know," says one, suddenly inspired. "We must advise the Prime Minister to abandon the pact. That is, if he asks us."

The others all nod sagely. Here is a solution. They will support the bhikkus and tacitly change sides. Later that afternoon, when Mr Bandaranaike again asks his ministers for an opinion, he receives a unanimous reply.

***

And so it ends. Mrs Wijewardene and several of the leading protesters are summoned to speak with the Prime Minister. Then, a few minutes later, they accompany him onto his verandah where, in full view of the crowd, he tears up the pact with the Tamils. This is met with furious cheering.

Mr Bandaranaike's humiliation is complete. The weapon of satyagraha, or peaceful protest, first employed by Mr Gandhi to drive the British out of India, has now been turned, with devastating effect, upon a Prime Minister by his own people.

Raj pushes back his chair and shouts at the wireless.

"Bastards! Liars!"

The family has gathered for the evening meal. However, as is customary, the food will not be served until Raj has listened to the evening news. He has been sitting close to the shelf; a small cheese-shaped plank of wood, wedged into an angle of the wall and specially constructed, years ago, to house the wooden-fronted wireless.

The radio is nearing the end of its useful life and broadcasts are frequently interrupted by a series of crackles and ghostly moans. When this happens, Raj sits with his ear to the set, frantically twiddling the dials in both directions, hoping, at least, to catch the gist of what is being said. But there is no mistaking the message tonight.

"Two-faced bastards!" Raj yells, grabbing the wireless in both hands and shaking it furiously.

"Stop, Raj. Stop! You'll break it."

Running from the kitchen, Neleni grabs Raj's arm and tries to restrain him. In his anger and grief, he pushes her away. Reaching out to steady herself, Neleni hits her hand on the edge of the table and winces with pain. Arjun, who has been standing nearby makes a move towards Raj but, with a slight motion of her hand, Neleni warns him away.

Arjun retreats into the hallway. At times like these, he is reduced to an onlooker, witness to a domestic fracas in which he is unable to intervene. His frustration and anger drive him almost to madness. Sometimes, he feels that there is nothing that he would not do to protect Neleni. In his darkest moments, he has even considered killing Raj. But, afterwards, he is overcome with shame: this and his guilt inspire him to acts of exquisite generosity. There is nothing he will not do, or buy, to make up for the wrong that he has done. Nothing. Except give up Neleni.

Tonight, he paces up and down in the darkness of the hallway, a feral animal stalking the shadows, clenching his fists, unable to act, but staying within earshot in case he is needed. In the living room, Raj has slumped back in his chair and is sitting with his head in his hands, every now and again muttering "Bastards, bastards."

With unusual clarity, the wireless has announced the annulment of the pact with the Tamils, the Prime Minister blaming its failure on recent Tamil opposition to the Sinhalese character 'Sri' on bus number-plates.

"Lying bastard!"

Angrily, Raj brushes his eyes with the back of his hand. Saro and Rani are sitting at the table, staring at him, terrified by this display of adult grief. They exchange anxious glances with their mother, but it is Arjun, returning from the hall, who takes the initiative.

"Come along. I'll read you a story."

He holds out his hand and eager to escape, they slide from their chairs and follow him out of the room.

Neleni rubs the hollow of her back then, moving slowly to the table, pours some liquor into a glass and offers it to Raj. He gulps it down noisily, holds the empty glass out for a refill and, after having drunk that, puts his arms around his wife's waist. Sighing, he rests his cheek against her belly, taking comfort from the determined kicking of the child inside.

"My son," he murmurs. "My son."

1958: A Maiden bound

High up, on the sheer rock face of King Kasyapa's fort, the Maidens of Sigiriya are taking their ease. The last sightseer has left them and is now descending the narrow iron steps leading from the creaking platform of the gallery from which he has just viewed the Maidens. Although impressed by their beauty, this visitor has no head for heights and his thoughts are now solely occupied with his safe return to earth rather than the wonders of ancient art.

Finally alone, the Maidens stare out at the sunset, protected from its rays by the overhanging rock. At this time of day, unseen by humans, they are allowed a few minutes of freedom in which to move and speak. All except Yaani, who remains frozen in the attitude of her painted image.

As punishment for her disobedience, Kasyapa has used one of Yaani's own spells to bind her to the rock. At first, she was mute as well but, after much persistent pleading by the other Maidens, Kasyapa has reluctantly agreed to loosen her tongue. Just for a few minutes and on condition that she makes no trouble. It is a miserable existence.

"It's not fair," she moans.

"It is perfectly fair," replies the one that Yaani calls 'the Queen Mother'.

"Kasyapa has been merciful to you. You interfered with his new darling, Neleni, and his alter ego, Arjun. You tried to thwart his plans, just as you did in life. You're lucky he didn't have you erased. He could have done, you know. A freak storm or an accident and your image would have been wiped from the face of the Rock forever."

"He'd never do that," spits Yaani.

The other Maidens titter behind their hands.

"He's just being spiteful!"

Shocked, the other Maidens look away, pretending that they have not heard. If Kasyapa hears this, he will stop Yaani's mouth forever. But she continues, undeterred, pouring out her venom and her anguish.

"What more can you expect from someone who killed his own father?"

Silence descends. A terrible hush falls over the gallery. If Yaani carries on like this, they may all be punished. The Maidens pretend not to have heard her.

"And what about my latest incarnation? That's what I'd like to know. Poor Leela. I've followed her since she was a little girl, watched her grow into a beautiful woman. What will she do without me?"

"She will find her way, as all the others do," says the Queen Mother gently.

"It was only by your black arts, Yaani, that you were able to view your incarnation. And you did it in the full knowledge that it was forbidden. No-one but a king is allowed to influence future generations or keep a presence in the mortal world. It is a gift for kings, not serving girls."

"What! You call me a serving girl. You ... you old woman!"

The Queen Mother smiles benignly. She finds it is easier to tolerate Yaani's sharp tongue now that her body is immobile. Deprived of the power of movement, her beautiful limbs have lost their seductive power. She is merely a graven image, a beautiful but impotent memory of the past.

"Sticks and stones," says the Queen Mother, smiling, but with a hint of callousness. It is a mild reprisal: one that she has earned, having endured Yaani's cruelty and scheming for centuries. Now she is free. Even better, Kasyapa has returned to her. For the present.

"Poor Leela," moans Yaani. But nobody listens.

Half-asleep, Leela reaches a slender arm over to the bedside table to where her morning cup of tea should be waiting. It is always in the same place at the same time and she can find it by touch alone, raising it to her lips without opening her eyes. But this morning, the cup is not in its accustomed place.

Without opening her eyes, she reaches a little further. Delicately tapping the table-top, she dislodges a necklace, which clatters to the floor. But she cannot find the cup. Leela opens her eyes. It is not there: the cup with its tracery of roses and forget-me-nots, its saucer as lustrous and delicate as a sea-shell; the cup she always drinks from in the morning. No day is complete unless she drinks tea from that cup.

With a seed of ill-humour growing fast within her, Leela reaches for her watch, a dainty thing with a mother-of-pearl face and tiny black numbers, so small that you have to squint to read them. A present from Mennan. Leela calls it her diamond watch although the fittings are really marcasite. It has acquired a particular significance since Mennan's death and she wears it every day although she rarely uses it to tell the time. Holding the watch up to the light, Leela screws up her eyes, still lazy from sleep.

Nine-thirty! She must have overslept. The maid usually brings her tea at eight.

"Padmini!" Leela calls for the kitchen-maid. Usually the girl is hovering outside the door and appears within a few seconds of being summoned.

"Padmini!!" Leela raises her voice, ensuring that it conveys just the right note of irritation. If she ignores it this time, the girl will know that she is in trouble. Still, no-one appears.

Lazy creature, thinks Leela. *I should give her the sack*. But she knows that she will not because no-one else would agree to work for so little while, at the same time, coping with Leela's capricious temper.

Before covering her nakedness, Leela admires herself in the mirror. This little ritual, performed every morning after drinking her tea, is usually a source of comfort. But, today, it proves the opposite. For the first time, Leela finds fault with herself. Although, still undeniably beautiful, her breasts seem a little heavy, her stomach a fraction slacker and there is a greyness to the skin around her eyes. Like a thief, age has stolen in during the night.

The mirror is no longer her friend. She looks in it and sees nothing. The image, which she has always regarded as her companion, has deserted her. Now, all she can see is the reflection of a beautiful, but ageing, woman: Leela, alone, with herself.

"Damn that girl!"

Pulling on her negligée, Leela runs out of the room in search of the maid.

***

At first, she was just angry but, as she runs from room to room, Leela becomes increasingly frantic. She checks the bedrooms, the bathrooms, the hallway, the living room, the kitchen, the pantry, even the cupboards; but all are deserted. The house is silent. The only sound is her voice, echoing through the empty rooms. She is all alone. Widowed and unwanted, touched by age. Friendless.

In one terrible moment, she realises that no-one will love her again as Mennan loved her. There is no-one to protect her or make her life easy. No-one will ever make excuses for her, or forgive her, as he did. The house, with its polished marble floors, is like a mausoleum. Her tomb. Soon, it will enclose her.

Unable to breathe, she runs outside where the gardener is poking at the border with a fork. Grateful even for his company, she races up to him.

"Where is Padmini?" she demands.

Embarrassed by his mistress's lack of clothing, the old man averts his eyes.

"Where is she? Tell me. Now."

Leela grabs his arm and shakes him. The old man, insulted by her behaviour, finds the courage to speak.

"She's gone."

"Where?"

"She hasn't been paid for more than a month. Neither have I."

Ignoring this useless piece of information, Leela continues her questioning.

"Where has she gone?"

"She's gone with cook. To join the Communists."

Stunned, Leela lets go of the old man's arm. Seeing that he has the advantage, the gardener throws down his fork.

"What's more, I'm leaving, too. I might be old, but I don't work for no pay. Or the whore of Babylon."

And, with this last cryptic remark, the old man stumps off.

Michael awakens to the shrill cry of the fish-seller.

"Maalu! Maalu!"

For several minutes, Michael lies with his eyes closed, convinced that he is still lying in darkness on the concrete floor of his unfinished house as he did for so many weeks. Then, an elbow pokes him in the ribs. He awakes suddenly, shuddering, almost sick with certainty. He is no longer alone. The house is no longer empty. In fact, it is stuffed full: of things and people; servants, sofas, chairs, tables, pictures, a wife, and now, above all, her mother.

At the first news of Dalia's pregnancy – a fact revealed to her mother before anyone else – Lakshmi had moved in: to help, as she explained to Michael with an ominous smile, daring him to disagree. She arrived, unannounced while he was at work and, by the time he got home, a full cargo of Lakshmi's necessities had been unloaded from a cart and distributed about the house by Michael's terrified servants.

"She threatened to sack us," explained an elderly servant, wringing his hands.

"Yes, but is she your mistress? Who pays you?" remonstrated Michael, fuming.

"She threatened to put us out onto the street," said the old man, shrugging, as if this was sufficient rebuttal to Michael's argument.

Michael had capitulated. It was no good arguing. The deed was done. Lakshmi was firmly installed and not to be dislodged. From that moment, mastery of the house and its affairs passed into her hands. From dawn to dusk, she can be heard shouting orders to the servants, berating them for their laziness, chastising them when they fail to follow her instructions and, even, when they do. Every crevice and corner of the house is filled with her things: suitcases, clothes and workboxes. She has even brought her own pots and pans.

From the luxury of space and silence, Michael has been pitched into a suffocating hell of high-pitched shrieking and obstacles that slide, unseen from corners, into his path. The continuous din and the fact that he is obliged to climb, rather than walk, from one side of the room to the other make him feel as if he is being relentlessly buffeted and battered.

It is as if he has been flung into a giant cauldron and is being stirred around while all the elements of his life that he previously regarded as constant, fly by in a whirl of colour and sound. By the end of the day, he is exhausted but, when he climbs into bed, he is greeted by the monotonous whine of Dalia's voice. She is miserable. The house is too small – her mother says so. If he really loves her, he will get a bigger house.

If he tells her that his funds are already overstretched and that he cannot afford another house so soon, she whimpers and snuffles and, the next day, when he returns from work, Lakshmi will be waiting for him. He is then subjected to a furious tirade on the obligations of a husband. He should give thanks for having such a beautiful wife and he should provide: abundantly. This shrill harangue continues until Michael is mentally wrestled into submission. He has quickly learned that the best policy on these occasions is to hang his head and humbly ask his mother-in-law's forgiveness, even if he feels no contrition which, usually, he does not.

Worst of all, is the change that Lakshmi's attentions have wrought in Dalia.

Although only a few weeks pregnant when Lakshmi first took up residence, Dalia has been persuaded that any exertion will have a detrimental effect on the baby. She must take three hearty meals a day (enough for two) and must rest constantly. Indeed, the less contact her feet have with the floor, the better. She must keep them raised whenever possible.

Reclining on a couch while her mother fans her, Dalia dutifully eats every scrap of the vast meals set before her, sleeps like a contented cat and only exerts herself in response to the most urgent necessities. As a result, she has swollen as rapidly as a well-watered pumpkin. Overnight, the delicate arc of her cheek has been erased, her chin has slackened and her figure, once so lithe, has become distended. With disgust, Michael notes that his wife is developing a startling resemblance to her mother.

Lakshmi is now mistress of the household. In a voice calculated to penetrate neighbouring homes, she shouts at the servants and, each day chooses a new victim, materialising, unheralded, at his or her elbow. This behaviour so unnerves the servants that crockery frequently leaps from their fingers and flings itself to the floor. In Lakshmi's presence, even inanimate objects acquire a suicidal will of their own, dashing themselves to pieces in a show of spontaneous destruction. Within the space of a few weeks, two entire dinner sets have been destroyed, not to mention tea-pots, tumblers, jugs and ornaments.

"Moron," she screams in the servant's ear, before the item in question has even hit the ground, "that will come out of your wages. Michael, where did you find this half-wit? If he was my servant, I would sack him. I would sack them all."

The servants creep about the house with long faces. It soon becomes clear that Lakshmi has no respect, either for their feelings or their religious beliefs. Being Buddhist, they are forbidden to break eggs, the symbol of life, on a full moon day. In the past, this problem has been resolved by Michael who has consented to crack any eggs required for the kitchen.

However, Lakshmi does not share his accommodating nature. Soon after her arrival, the cook asked her to break eggs for him on a Poya day; a request that was vehemently rejected.

"Hypocrite! You don't want to sin yourself so, instead, you ask me to sin for you! What do we pay you for? Crack the eggs yourself."

Thus, with the hypocrisy of surrogate egg-breaking being sternly proscribed by the new mistress of the house, custards, cakes and anything made from eggs have consequently slipped off the menu on Poya days. By this subtle means, the servants take their revenge.

Michael seethes inwardly. However, he draws some comfort from the fact that Lakshmi's religious intolerance does not extend to the Moslem butcher. To offend him would mean foregoing delivery to the door of the choicest cuts of meat. This service, provided for only a few extra cents, saves a daily trip to the market where the meat on offer is of only average quality. Moreover, to lose one butcher would be to lose them all, for most butchers on the Island are Moslems. Lakshmi therefore reserves her religious intolerance for Buddhists and Presbyterians.

Over past weeks, her influence within the household has been so deleterious that Michael might have lost all his servants, had it not been for the resourcefulness of the cook; a father of six, whose need to provide for his children has sharpened his wits beyond their normal acuity.

Of all the servants, it is for the cook that Lakshmi reserves her most offensive conduct. Entering the kitchen with a flourish, she regularly pushes him aside, announcing that today she will take charge of Dalia's meal, because, as she puts it, only a mother knows what her daughter needs at a time like this.

She then sets about preparing the desired delicacy, chopping, slicing, peeling and wielding her knife with great verve, until the ingredients have been sculpted into minute cubes and the floor is littered with vegetable peelings and scraps of fat. This anarchy is increased by the addition of pots, pans, basins, bowls and cutlery, some clean, some dirty, all mixed together and scattered about the surfaces until the room, covered in a chaotic mixture of debris, resembles the scene of an earthquake.

***

"I cannot stand it any more, master," the cook declared one day, pulling off his apron and flinging it over a chair. "Missus is driving me mad. Quite mad!"

Holding his hands up to his head, he had rolled his eyes in an unusual display of histrionics, more suited to a Parisian hotel than a small house overlooking a railway cutting next to the shanty. The maid, a girl of ten, had looked sombrely on.

"Please," Michael begged, keeping his voice low. "It won't be for much longer. I promise you. Here, what if I give you a pay-rise? Will you stay then?"

"Hmmm."

Casting Michael a shrewd look from the corner of his eye, the cook had made a small, encouraging noise but refused to commit himself until he knew the terms.

"How about 20 rupees? Per month, of course."

Cook raised an eyebrow.

"And for the little one?" he enquired, indicating the maid with a jerk of his head.

"Half again for her."

Smiling, the cook had picked up his apron and tied the frayed strings around his waist.

"To work," he said to the girl, indicating the flotsam and jetsam that lay around the kitchen, the high-water mark of Lakshmi's latest culinary exploit.

Michael was so grateful that he felt quite weak with relief. Of course, he had offered too much but it would be impossible to find, or keep, new servants, once the old ones had left. News travels fast in the servant community and he felt sure that his house had already acquired an undesirable reputation. Only the most desperate and, therefore, the least trustworthy or efficient, would be willing to work here.

***

And so the routine for future negotiations has been set. Every time Lakshmi upsets the servants, they first consult the cook, then lobby Michael, threatening to leave unless he offers them a sufficient bribe to stay. With servile cunning, they ask neither for too much, nor too little. In this manner, they achieve a small, but steady, increase in pay, keep their jobs and are forced to agree that life with Lakshmi, if not good, is at least bearable.

In fact, the only person without any hope of redress is Michael. Every day, he finds Lakshmi's tone more hectoring and her presence more intrusive. She has begun to follow him around the house, scolding him at every opportunity and offering advice for which he has no need. In the mornings, when he gets up, she is waiting with his breakfast. She reads over his shoulder as he opens his mail and greets each letter with comments such as: *You have paid too much for that*, or *Who is that from?*

There is no privacy in which to conduct his affairs and no peace in which to collect his thoughts. Even if he tries to slip outside for a cigarette, she follows him, taking the opportunity, now that they are alone, to recount the intimate details of Dalia's health and lecture him on the duties of a good husband.

The effect of all this is that Michael's tolerance of his mother-in-law is rapidly dwindling while, inversely, his loathing for her has increased to such an extent that it infects everything, even turning the affectionate neutrality, with which he previously regarded his wife, into a smouldering hatred.

***

This morning, as he surfaces from sleep, Michael pinches himself, hoping to wake from this horrible nightmare and find everything changed. But, on opening his eyes, he sees that Dalia is still beside him. The muffled screams emanating from the kitchen tell him that Lakshmi is still in residence. He sighs.

Once, he felt like a man. Now, he is no more than a human purse, to be mined and exploited; never thanked, only abused for his lack of generosity. However much he gives, it will never be enough. He rises, listlessly, and trudges past the end of the bed where Dalia is still sleeping, bloated and pale after days of gorging, like the queen of a fractious hive.

"Is there no escape?" he asks himself.

The shrieking gets louder. Lakshmi is on her rounds. Summoning all his patience, Michael prepares to meet her.

Sriya and Asoka are alone in the chena garden. Asoka, his head protected with a winding of rags and his sarong hitched up above his knees, is working his hoe between the lines of carrots, leeks and beans, pausing every so often to wipe the stinging sweat from his eyes.

"Let me help you."

Sriya touches his elbow, offering a glass of tea. Patting his face with the end of the rag tied around his head, Asoka takes the tea and drains the glass. Then, wiping his mouth on the back of his hand, he eyes her mischievously.

"And what would you do, fat little wife?"

As she opens her mouth to speak, he kisses her, his hand resting on the round swell of her belly. Her time is near, only a few weeks at most, and the child is getting restless.

"Look. You are now so fat that you are good for nothing, only sitting in the shade."

She pretends to pout playfully, but is soon laughing as he tickles her.

"Oh stop, stop," she giggles, breathlessly. "I cannot – oh I have a stitch!"

Wincing, she puts her hand to her side. Putting his arm around her waist, Asoka leads her gently towards the shade.

"Come, let us make a bed for Queen Sriya," he mocks, flattening a patch of short grass and checking that it hides no poisonous insects before gently lowering her to the ground.

"Now she must eat, but not too much or I will never get her back on her feet. She will have to stay here all night and sleep under the stars."

"Horrible man. You would leave me alone in the forest?"

She patters her small hands against his shoulders in pretence of beating him.

"No. Never. I will never leave you. Either of you."

Suddenly, he becomes serious and Sriya thinks that she detects something fearful in his manner. Even now, after so many months, his past life still haunts him. Although he knows greater joy than he ever thought possible, Asoka's pleasure is often fleeting, always chased by fear. Moments of frivolity are followed by brooding solemnity, as if any lightness of heart must be counterbalanced by darkness of the soul. It is as if one mistake, one single terrible act, has inverted the natural order of his life. Sriya grieves for her husband.

She looks up at his face, now in shadow, and knows that his thoughts have wandered away to that dark place in the forest where a man was murdered. On his orders.

"Sit with me!" She grasps his hand and pulls him down towards her.

"I should work. There is much to do."

He looks anxiously over his shoulder to the square patch of ground, hacked from the forest wilderness, now colonised by rows of vegetables.

"It is mid-day. Look at the sun. It is foolish to work now. You must eat and rest."

She squeezes his hand, threatening a pettish show of tears if he does not obey. It is the only way to break his mood, distract him from his inner self. She pulls at his hand, impatiently. Asoka sinks to his knees, then settles beside her, as she pours more tea from the battered kettle that serves as a flask and presents him with a bundle of curry and rice wrapped in a banana leaf secured with a splinter of wood. She watches him eat and the mood passes.

"Shall I read to you?"

He smiles. It is a rhetorical question as she has already produced a sheet of newspaper from the fold of her sari. It was gleaned from the bus that passes through the village. Side by side, they lean against each other, Asoka silently following the text as she reads aloud, ready to correct any mistakes.

"It says here that there have been many Communist demonstrations in Colombo, that the employers are refusing to give in to the protesters' demands and that the troops have been called out. That's bad, isn't it?"

Anxiously, she looks to her husband for reassurance.

"Colombo is many miles away. Anyway, you mustn't believe everything you read. All the newspapers are controlled by the Government. They only give one side of the story."

He strokes her hair and kisses her.

"Lie down. You should sleep."

She lies on her side, resting the weight of her belly against the earth. It is difficult to find a comfortable position these days but she closes her eyes, listening to the sounds of the forest: the whittling of insects; the quarrelsome chatter of birds; the sound of feet, softly picking their way over the forest floor. Lazily, she opens her eyes and realises that Asoka is alert and watchful, staring into the forest.

"What is it?"

"I'm not sure. I thought I heard something. Someone."

"Who?"

"I don't know. It's probably nothing. A deer, perhaps. Or a rabbit."

Although she does not question it, Sriya dismisses this explanation. She knows that Asoka does not believe it either. He is trying to protect her. But from what? She strokes his arm.

"Perhaps we should go back to the village. I can rest better in the house."

"Yes. Yes, of course."

He grasps eagerly at this excuse. Gathering up the empty kettle, he places the glasses inside it, and helps her to her feet. As they follow the path back to the village, Sriya notes that her husband seems unusually agitated.

"As if," she thinks, "he has seen a ghost."

***

Asoka is not sure what he saw, back there in the chena garden. He is not even sure if he saw anything. He might have been dozing and fallen prey to a dark dream or the mid-day sun might have dazzled him, tricking his eyes into seeing what was not there.

Yet, he feels sure that, for a second, he saw something move in the shadow of the forest. A dark figure had appeared from behind a tree. It was too far away, too lost in darkness, for him to distinguish anything other than its shape: a man. He had blinked and the image had transformed into a demon with long hair. He had blinked again and it had turned into Mennan, head tilted awkwardly to one side, feet dangling, suspended above the ground. On blinking a third time, the image had gone.

Asoka does not believe in witchcraft or magic and often used to berate Anil for his devotion to Hooniyam; a new divinity who, until recently, was a demon and patron of sorcerers. While Buddhist faith encompasses Hindu deities, Asoka cannot accept its tolerance of such a malevolent entity. Faith should strive for enlightenment and truth, not debase itself with the practice of magic. At least, that is what he believed when he still had faith. Strange to think, now, that although his Buddhist faith has faltered, he can almost believe that he saw the image of a demon. Back there. In the trees.

He holds Sriya close to him, careful that she should not stumble as he leads her along the narrow path to the village. The grass is high on either side and the ground is pitted with sharp stones. For a second, he forgets his own fears, and is consumed by anxiety for her. They are now passing through the narrow strip of forest that skirts the village like a protective girdle. A green parrot screeches suddenly, giving Asoka such a start that his heart seems to stop.

"We are nearly there."

Sriya's voice reaches him, faint and distant as if muffled by water. Her fingers stroke his hand. Asoka has stopped walking and is standing in the middle of the path, rigid with fear. While Sriya's voice is remote, Asoka's hearing is otherwise remarkably acute. Even the smallest sound dins in his ears. Butterflies are flitting about the tree canopy, birds are squabbling in the branches, cackling or clucking affectionately, palm fronds are rubbing together, creaking and rattling, insects are running up and down the tree trunks, snakes are slithering across the dry forest floor, seeking refuge in piles of bark and leaves and thousands of termites are busily chewing wood to build their nests.

All around him is a deafening profusion of life and, in the midst of all this, Asoka perceives his own smallness. He is no bigger than a grain of sand, insignificant. He does not matter. Strangely, the thought brings him comfort and his heart begins to beat again with a calm and regular pulse.

"Asoka!"

He can hear her clearly now. He is a man again, not a panting, terrified animal. She puts her arms around his neck and, cupping himself over the curve of her stomach, he kisses her on the mouth.

1958: The watchers

Within the forest, two figures stir: human shadows; creatures muffled in darkness, only distinguishable from the trees by their movement and the gleam of their eyes.

"You fool! He saw you. Why did you show yourself?"

One speaks, his voice cold and icy; like the hissing of mountain water as it passes over a bed of granite. The other man remains silent, still, as dumb as a rock, or one who is spellbound.

"Answer me! I am talking to you."

The voice grows louder. Full of sibilant menace, it no longer resembles the sound of water but the whispering of an angry snake. If that voice had a shape, it would be a serpent. Relentlessly, it winds itself around the other man, words dripping into his ears like poison, squeezing him tighter, constricting his heart until he is forced to speak.

"It was her," murmurs the other man, in a voice haunted by dreams.

"I did not expect to see her. And …," the words catch in his throat, "she is expecting his child."

"What did you expect? They are married. They sleep together every night," hisses the serpent voice.

The other man howls and puts his hands over his ears as if, by shutting out the words, he can also shut out the thoughts that accompany them.

"No. No."

"Yes. She is his whore. She is nothing to you now. Forget her."

"I cannot."

"You must."

Covering his face with his hands, the other man begins to sob.

"Stop this. Stop it, I tell you. Look at me!"

Grabbing his wrists, Anil pulls Tissa's hands away from his eyes.

"Listen to me! When he is dead, you may have her. Then you can do as you wish. But first, he must perform a service. For me. He must make amends for his betrayal. I will have justice. And, until I have it, you will do as I say."

Anil presses his finger against Tissa's forehead, leaning against it with such force that it feels as if it is drilling into Tissa's head. Like a nail. The sorcerer's nail, driven through the skull, that reduces a man to slavery. Amber eyes burn fiercely, holding Tissa in their gaze. He can feel them, piercing to his core, turning him to their will. Gradually, those eyes burn into his soul, dulling the pain of Sriya's loss until, after a while, he feels nothing; until his heart is cauterised and replaced by a black and arid void.

Anil pulls Tissa towards him, pressing the boy's head into his shoulder, tenderly stroking his head where the smooth monkish baldness is already being replaced by a stubbly growth. Soon, he will be ready to fulfil the mission that Anil has assigned him; a virulent entity, launched on an unsuspecting world; a demon, created within the confines of a monastery.

***

Now deserted, the chena garden basks in the brittle heat. The sun bears down on the neat rows of vegetables, bathing them in its light and feeding them with invisible goodness. Nothing stirs: neither the stems of maize with their silken-whiskered fruit; nor the broad-bladed leeks; nor even the feather-topped carrots.

Few animals brave the sun. Birds seek the shade of trees, while insects crawl into the cool shelter of leaves or burrow deep into the flesh of fruit. Even the lizards, basking on stones and tree trunks, are still, merely exercising their tongues in pursuit of food. Only scorpions, clad in protective armour, rattle about in the open, unconcerned.

Yet, within the forest, a sudden breeze rises, whisking the dust from the forest floor and shaking the branches. With a cough and a splutter, Hooniyam appears and hovers over the spot where the figures of two men are laid out in the shade. One is asleep, his tear-stained face resting on his arm; but the other is awake, looking straight up into Hooniyam's face. Although Anil cannot see the demon-god, he has summoned him through prayer. At this moment, his deepest thoughts are laid bare.

"Good, good," says the demon-god, rubbing his hands. "He's done well. Can't be easy with that fool tagging along."

He pokes the sleeping figure with his toe. Tissa groans in his sleep and turns over. Hooniyam has just raised his foot over the boy's head, ready to crush his skull, when a renewed prayer from Anil reminds him of why he has come.

"He's praying for guidance. Of course. I was getting distracted. Now, my son. Close your eyes and I'll tell you what to do next."

Instantly, Anil falls asleep, allowing Hooniyam to appear to him in a dream and explain the next stage of his demonic plan.

1958: The rally

Even for Colombo, the streets are busy, crammed with people who are all heading in the same direction. A thin girl, with huge eyes and long feet, is pushing her way through the crowd, trying to keep up with a young man who seems to know where he is going. Leela's kitchen-maid, Padmini, has to run to keep up with the cook. Although stockily built with a broad chest, he is surprisingly quick on his feet. As she tries to follow him, the girl's eyes grow wider and more protuberant, giving her the look of someone who has just received a terrible shock.

Having sworn undying allegiance to her companion, as only a girl of fourteen can, she now pursues him doggedly through the crowds of people that are streaming along the road like a human swarm on its way to a vast hive.

"Where are we going?" she calls after the cook but, walking a few feet ahead, he does not hear her.

She is breathless now and being buffeted from all sides as the crowd becomes thicker. People are pouring into the main street from all directions, issuing from cramped alleys and thoroughfares, flowing together like tributaries joining a river. There are so many of them that she cannot see the beggars sitting on the pavement or the brightly-coloured shop windows, only the spidery black lines of telegraph wires overhead or the signs pasted on the sides of buildings, mostly advertising Players Navy Cut or Singer sewing machines.

"Anton, wait for me!"

She cannot see him at all now. What if they become separated and she cannot find him? She does not know where she is, will not be able to find her way back. She has only been staying with his family for a week and the district is unfamiliar to her. She will end up on the street. A beggar. Or worse. Her stomach lurches with fear.

"Anton, Anton!"

Alone and bewildered, she bleats like a child that has lost its parent. Her eyes grow even wider, appearing almost to bolt from her head, increasing her look of shock. Tears of panic cloud her vision. He has abandoned her.

"So that's where you've got to!"

Anton pops up beside her, surfacing unexpectedly from the crowd. His round, smiling face has been scrubbed and his thick hair, combed back from his face, has been secured with a liberal application of Brylcreem. Altogether, he has the gleaming sleekness of a well-oiled seal.

"Here, take my hand!"

Anton holds out his hand. It is solid and comfortable with a square, padded palm and straight, well-formed fingers. The little maid is captivated by its beauty, but hesitant.

"What's the matter?"

"It wouldn't be right. We're not engaged. And, even if we were, it still wouldn't be right."

"Don't be ridiculous."

They are being pulled apart by the crowd and Anton has to wield his powerful arms in order to stay beside her. It gives him the appearance of someone swimming against the tide.

"Come on. Don't be so silly. Everything has changed. It's different now. We're Communists. No-one here knows us. And, anyway, I'm not going to take advantage of you. It's just for your safety."

The kitchen-maid feels re-assured, but also, for some unaccountable reason, a little disappointed. Cautiously, she places her hand in that of Anton. His solid fingers close around her thin ones with comforting strength. She feels safe.

Anton has already proved to be a kind and considerate friend. A few days ago, he found the maid in a corner, crying quietly into her apron; the victim, yet again, of Leela's furious tongue.

"Come on," he had said, tearing off his apron and throwing it on the floor. "I've had enough. Let's go!"

And without a word, or any thought of where they were to go, the maid had followed him, out of the silent house with its floors of cold marble, laid out in black and white squares like a chessboard, and into the warmth of the sun. It was like rising from the tomb and being re-born. Closing her eyes, she had let the sun warm her face, thinking all the time of the story she had once been taught by a priest of Lazarus returning from the dead.

Anton had taken her home with him, introduced her to his mother and arranged for her to sleep in a room with his three sisters. She was accepted without question and treated with kindness. From that day, she has literally become a new person: someone with friends, deserving respect and, even, possibly love; a change from the lonely slave that she had been, subject to Leela's capricious temper, obliged to accept all her insults and yet, at the same time, to be grateful because Leela provided her with food and somewhere safe to sleep.

Despite her modesty, the maid squeezes Anton's hand. He turns his fresh, honest face towards her and laughs. She laughs, too, just a little, before lowering her eyes. She is proud and happy, filled with a strange emotion. It is not love that she feels for him – not yet, that will come later – but ferocious loyalty, coupled with the desire to prove her gratitude. If Anton expressed a wish to make stew, then she would gladly leap into a cauldron of boiling water to provide him with meat. Like Buddha's hare, she would give her own life, just to ease his.

The crowd thickens, curdling like milk before it becomes cheese. There is no running, or even walking now, just a slow shuffle towards the end of the street. They are all ages, mostly men but a considerable number of women as well. Some are trying to hand out leaflets, although the press makes it difficult to move. A slip of yellow paper is stuffed into the maid's hand. She does not see who gave it to her. It is cheap paper, so thin that, if she were able to hold it up to the light, she could see through it. It is covered in printed black letters, some of them blotted and fuzzy because the ink has run. But it does not matter to her because she cannot read. Letting her hand fall to her side, she quietly drops the leaflet.

She is becoming uncomfortable. The crowd has coalesced to form a machine of elbows and knees, slowly grinding its way forward. She is constantly receiving blows to her ribs and arms and, several times, someone has trodden on her feet. The crowd presses together, closer and closer, until everyone stops and the maid finds herself caught in an excruciating bottleneck. Then, after several minutes, the crowd surges forward and people flood into an open space at the end of the street.

At last! Padmini feels as if she can breathe again, although she is sure she is covered in bruises.

"What is this place, Anton?" she asks, addressing him boldly, like a comrade.

"It's called Hyde Park, after the one in London. The Communists – that's us – are meeting with the Trotskyites. The employers are still refusing to listen to us. They've put notices in the papers claiming the strike is illegal, but we've got them on the run. The Prime Minister has threatened to nationalise companies whose bosses don't negotiate."

"Is that good?"

"It's more than good. It's excellent. Soon, this country will be a different place. Much fairer. Especially for people like us."

They are propelled forwards in the direction of a hastily-erected platform where speakers are addressing the crowd. Although she understands little of what they say, the maid is infected by their enthusiasm. Images of a glorious future are presented and she imagines herself, one day, in her own home, answerable to no master or mistress.

Looking sideways at Anton, she studies his upturned face. He is smiling and he seems to glow, as if lit up from within. There is a great cheer and he raises his fist in the air. She raises hers, too. There is more shouting, all good-humoured, then some singing, a refrain that she later recognises as the 'Red Flag'. Then, suddenly, there are several loud cracks, like gunshots.

The crowd screams and runs for cover. The change in mood is so sudden that many of those on the outskirts are taken by surprise and knocked over. The maid is lifted off her feet and only saved by the sturdy arm of Anton wrapped around her waist. Pulling her towards him, he points to a gap in the crowd.

"Through there. Quickly."

Clinging tightly to his arm, the maid follows Anton through people running and pushing in all directions. The rally, previously so orderly, turns into mayhem.

"Bastards! They're firing on us."

The maid looks around, expecting to see police or troops, but she sees neither. Anton pulls her into a shop doorway and for a few seconds they simply stand, catching their breath and watching the crowd.

"Where are the police? Who fired those shots?"

"I don't know."

He looks bemused.

The fear, which set people running in all directions, now turns to anger and the crowd begins to re-group, forming a single, malevolent entity.

"Bastards! Get them. Teach them a lesson!"

Get who? she is about to ask Anton, but the answer comes from an unexpected direction. A large stone hurtles past her ear and hits the shop window. With an ear-splitting crack, the glass shivers into a thousand fragments that fly through the air like deadly darts. Anton yells. Stunned, the maid puts her hand up to her head. When she withdraws it, her fingers are covered with blood, lacerated by the tiny splinters of glass that glitter in her hair.

"Anton!"

His face is running with blood and a jagged shard of glass is embedded in his cheek. Winding her scarf around her hand, she makes him stand still while she tries to extricate the glass from his flesh. It has gone in deep, almost to the bone, and he moans as she pulls it out, but at least it missed his eye. Having removed the glass, she tenderly wipes his face.

"Here," she says, removing her scarf. "Press this against the wound. You must try to stop the bleeding."

Bewildered, they cling to each other. A crashing, screeching mayhem surrounds them. A hail of stones and bottles flies through the air. Windows explode in sparkling showers of glass. Across the park, a thin column of smoke rises from a tea kiosk.

Now hysterical, the crowd picks its targets indiscriminately. Any vehicle that moves is stoned: those that are stationary are set alight. Dense smoke fills the square. Flames erupt spontaneously. The air shudders momentarily as a petrol tank explodes. The tea-kiosk now burns like a beacon. As the rally turns into a riot, new leaders emerge to direct its activities.

"Europeans," yells a voice above the others.

"Europeans. Find them! Kill them!"

The cry is taken up by a hundred other mouths until the mob, galvanised by hatred, hurtles off in search of new prey.

Anton and Padmini huddle in the doorway, too terrified to move; he, holding her close to him, determined to protect her from harm. Hardly daring to breathe, they pray that they will remain unnoticed, hoping to escape the attention of the mob that roars and bays around them like a demonic whirlwind.

Then, finally, the police arrive and, laying about them with truncheons and lathis, restore order with no less violence than that displayed by the mob. Gradually, the crowds disperse, limping home, aggrieved, to nurse their bloody wounds and hurt pride.

"I had no idea," murmurs Anton, staring out from the shop doorway at the wreckage in the street. "I swear. I had no idea. It wasn't meant to be like this."

His face is pale, a snapshot of horror, expressing the terror that they have both experienced.

"Hold on to me," the maid soothes, lifting Anton's arm over her shoulder so that he can lean on her.

"Here I am," she thinks proudly, "supporting Anton. Helping him. It used to be the other way around."

And, with Anton leaning on her arm, broken in spirit, if not in body, the little maid guides him home, through narrow streets where pye-dogs nose through rubbish in the gutters and laundry hangs from lines between the houses, past shops emitting the smell of baking bread or curry and open windows where the occupants can be heard, but not seen, chattering noisily, usually to the accompaniment of crying babies.

To the little maid, it all seems uncommonly beautiful, especially when Anton, groaning with pain, stops to lay his head on her shoulder. She stops then and speaks to him in a gentle voice as she tries to smooth his hair, now matted with blood.

"I am truly a woman now," she thinks, with pride, unperturbed by the blood, still oozing from Anton's wound, that has stained her dress.

Looking back, many years later, she believes that it was on that day that she first fell in love with the man who was to become her husband and she keeps the scarf, soaked with his blood, in a little box, a memento that will always evoke tender memories of her first happiness as a free woman. For it is a strange irony, that the event which destroyed Anton's faith in Communism, also marked the beginning of Padmini's new life.

1958: Caesar at bay

Mr Bandaranaike walks alone down the long corridor to his office in the Parliament building, past doors that quietly close as he approaches, falling unnaturally silent, although he is sure that, once he has passed, he can hear the soft murmuring of voices. Even the corridor itself seems to echo with the sound of whispering.

Once or twice, he passes people that he knows: men, formerly regarded as allies, who now meet him with downcast eyes. Each mumbles a cursory greeting, before scurrying away to find sanctuary in the maze of passages that encircles the heart of the building.

His pulse is racing. It will soon be Prime Minister's question-time, when he will be required to answer for his actions, or lack of them.

***

Since the annulment of his pact with the Tamils, the country has descended into chaos. First one, then another, group of extremists has stirred up trouble, encouraging strikes, bringing the nation to its knees. First, workers in the public services went on strike then, as soon as the Government had dealt with that problem, it was confronted with a general strike in the private sector. Despite pressure from the Prime Minister to capitulate to their workers' demands, the employers refused to give in. Infuriated by their intransigence, Mr Bandaranaike threatened to nationalise all the relevant companies.

Yet, when firmness is most needed, the Government hesitates, dithering between one option, then another, unable to pursue a single course of action. Troops, sent out to establish peace, have been suddenly re-called to their barracks. Police, patrolling the streets, have been mysteriously withdrawn. All without explanation. At the rally in Hyde Park, a riot was provoked, not by a round of bullets as the protesters supposed, but by a firecracker thrown into the crowd by an agent provocateur. Although his identity is known, he has neither been charged nor prosecuted.

There are now so many different elements at work that it is difficult to know where any of them begins or ends or, more importantly, who is on your side. Although he will never accept it and, certainly no-one near him would dare to suggest as much, Mr Bandaranaike's Government is fatally wounded. Consequently, all the conflicting interests that were previously kept in check are now emerging to circle around the dying Government like vultures around a corpse.

***

But Mr Bandaranaike sees it differently. He blames the current state of affairs, not on his own vacillations and inconsistencies, but on the actions of a few hundred monks. In particular, he blames Buddharakkita.

"He needn't look to me for favours in the future," thinks the Prime Minister, crossly.

"In fact, I'm going to make sure he doesn't get another penny. That'll stop him interfering in matters of State."

Turning the corner into yet another corridor, he imagines he hears a door click shut just in front of him. The muscles in his back tighten and he walks stiffly and slowly, his ears alert for any noise. The building is unnaturally quiet.

Is this how Julius Caesar felt on his way to the Senate, just before his friends plunged their daggers into him? *Et tu Brute*. It is a hackneyed phrase, bandied about by schoolboys – at least, those with the kind of education enjoyed by Mr Bandaranaike – but, for the first time, he grasps its meaning. It was not so much the knives that wounded Caesar, as his betrayal by the people he trusted. Mr Bandaranaike feels a profound sympathy for the hapless Emperor. He thinks of Caesar as a brother-in-suffering; another man of vision whose good intentions were misunderstood by an ignorant populace.

"It was always thus," he thinks, philosophically, while stealing a glance over his shoulder just to check that no-one is either creeping up on him or about to leap out from behind a pillar.

And yet, he is far from giving up. As far as Mr Bandaranaike is concerned, the Government is simply experiencing 'a bit of a bad patch', the sort of thing that follows the honeymoon period after an election. Although dampened, his optimism is far from being doused. The doubting Thomases may wag their heads and point their fingers and, no doubt, he will have a difficult time in Parliament. For a while. But all problems have a solution. He just needs to find the right one.

It comes in a flash. An idea so stunning in its simplicity that it stops Mr Bandaranaike in his tracks, or rather, outside his office with his hand grasping the doorknob. A diversion. That is what he needs. Something to take people's minds off the present troubles and unite them in the face of another, greater challenge. Of course, war is the usual resort for leaders in his predicament; but the only possible opponent, at present, is India, and that is hardly an option.

"Hmmm," Mr Bandaranaike chews his lip thoughtfully as he lets himself into his office.

The room smells musty, full of old cigarette smoke, the hallmark of interminable meetings with his ministers. A half-eaten sandwich lies on a plate on his desk. It has been there since last night. Obviously, some public service workers do not realise that their strike is over. With distaste, Mr Bandaranaike empties the plate into his waste-paper bin, then settles himself behind his desk. Pressing his fingertips together, he rests his head against the chair, trying to remember something that Philip Gunawardane said the other day.

Although a Marxist, it was Gunawardane who wanted to employ troops to disperse the protesting public service workers. He was furious when the order was given to withdraw the troops. Philip Gunawardane is a forthright liberal, a man of action, the sort of politician the Prime Minister admires because he is so different from himself. And yet, if he had taken Philip's advice, perhaps he would have been able to defuse the protest that resulted in the abrogation of the pact with the Tamils. Perhaps he should pay more attention to Philip's advice. What was it he said again? He had dismissed it then as nonsense but, given the present circumstances, perhaps it was not so stupid.

Mr Bandaranaike rubs his temples, trying to remember. His head is aching. He has not slept for hours. Or is it days? He cannot remember. Ah, that is it. He has it now. The other day, Gunawardane suggested that the Government should find a scapegoat. The Government should blame the Tamils for the strikes.

547

Mr Bandaranaike thinks hard for a minute, then dismisses the idea. No. It won't do. He will have to wait for another opportunity to present itself; another crisis that he can turn to his advantage.

1958: Under the Bo tree

The men of the village have gathered under the village Bo tree: the old men squatting, their sarongs pulled tight around their haunches, their toes digging into the dust; the young ones standing, or leaning against the thick trunk of the tree, the smoke from their cigarettes winding up into its branches.

The task of rolling cigarettes is entrusted to one old man who has the knack of making the tobacco go further than anyone else. It is a delicate operation, requiring care and a steady hand. Taking a whole tobacco leaf from a small wooden box, he flattens it on his knee, lays a few strings of tobacco along its length then, having dampened the edge of the wrapping against his lip, he rolls it between the thumb and forefinger of one hand in a gesture so practised and smooth that the whole operation takes less than a second. In this way, the men of the village can enjoy a continuous supply of cigarettes, enabling them to talk and smoke without interruption.

"Here, Grandpa, roll one for me! And have one yourself."

A young fellow, with a thick mop of wavy hair, drops a pouch of green tobacco into the old man's lap. The old man mutters something inaudible and grins, revealing a few long teeth, as yellow as old ivory. In fact, from the whites of his eyes to the nails on his fingers, everything about him has a yellowish, tobacco-stained tinge. The only exceptions are a few strands of pure white hair on his head and the tips of his fingers which are blackened with tar.

Placing his hand on his neighbour's shoulder, the young man leans forward and lights his cigarette from the glowing stub that hangs from the other man's mouth. Then, puffing prodigiously, he enters the conversation, noisily commenting upon the local news until one of his elders warns him to quieten down. Clasping his hands behind his back, he lowers his head, nodding frequently to show he is listening, but really trying to hide his embarrassment. He is fourteen, already a man and tolerated at men's meetings, yet not considered old enough to offer an opinion.

"Look. Here she comes!"

The men draw together in a tight knot, their heads all turned in one direction. Tissa's mother has emerged from her house and is stepping furtively along the track into the forest, her scarf wrapped around her head and body, concealing a package cradled in her thin arms.

"Where do you suppose she's going?" whispers one of the men.

"Who knows. But she's off there every night at about this time."

"Always carrying that bundle, too," observes a man with a thin face.

"Kithulsiri says he's seen her, walking through the trees. He says she goes down one of the old tracks that leads deep into the forest. Isn't that right, Kithulsiri?"

Emboldened by this attention, Kithulsiri murmurs his agreement.

"Then why didn't you follow her?"

Looking around nervously, Kithulsiri rolls his eyes, then shakes his head.

"Our Kithulsiri's a bit of a coward," ribs one of his friends, hoping to goad him into conversation, but Kithulsiri simply shakes his head.

"Who can blame him?" offers a kindly voice. "Not after what Prema found the other week."

"What was that?"

All eyes turn towards the speaker, a round-bellied farmer in his fifties whose dark face and white hair give him the look of a wise old monkey. This, combined with his crafty wit, has earned him the nickname 'Hanuman'.

"It happened last Thursday," says the farmer, not answering the question directly. He waits for a second until he has their attention and all eyes are upon him.

"So, what happened?" enquires a voice anxiously.

"Prema's pig got loose and he chased it into the forest. It went deeper and deeper, until it stopped at a clearing. And what do you suppose he found there?"

The listeners hardly dare to breathe. The farmer lets them wait: just one agonising second; expertly heightening the tension before he delivers his revelation.

"What? What did he find?" breathes a voice.

The farmer looks around him, as if to check that they are not being overheard, then, leaning forward, he addresses his audience in a low, confidential voice.

"A pile of broken eggshells at the foot of a tree. With a name written on them."

There is a gasp of dismay, followed by a clamour of voices.

"Sorcery!" exclaims one.

"Whose name?" asks another.

"Yes, whose name?" demand the rest.

Again, the farmer looks around him carefully, then mouths, rather than speaks the answer.

"Asoka."

Before anyone can repeat the name, the farmer puts his finger to his lips.

"You mean, he doesn't know?"

"Of course not. What good would it do? Besides, his wife is pregnant. She might miscarry."

There is a general murmur of sympathy. Everyone silently undertakes not to mention this story to anyone, except, of course, their wives.

"Who is responsible?" whispers one.

"That's obvious, isn't it?" replies another.

All heads turn in the direction of Manju's house. Since Tissa's disappearance, all the other children have left; each hoping to start a new life away from their mother's pain and their father's drunkenness. The roof of the house, long-abandoned, has begun to sag and will probably collapse under the onslaught of the next monsoon. It exudes ruin and misfortune, but no-one feels inclined to help. As a herd turns away from a sick animal, so the village has begun to avoid Manju.

"And Prema, what does he think?"

"Well, it's obvious, isn't it?" says the farmer, contemptuously.

"He thinks she's put the evil eye on the whole family. Only the day after he found those eggs, Prema fell and sprained his ankle. Couldn't be worse. It's harvest-time. If he hadn't got Asoka to help him, the whole crop would be lost."

This observation is met by murmurs of agreement. Misfortune is always attributable to something, or someone. In this case, it is clear that the culprit is Manju.

***

Rumours sweep through the village; one displacing another until it, too, is supplanted. Observations, grounded in fact, are rapidly expanded upon and exaggerated until, bolstered by wild notions and hearsay, they surpass the bounds of science and can only be explained by supernatural intervention. All relate to strange happenings in the forest and, by implication, to Manju's activities there.

Some villagers claim to have seen ghosts or demons, while others remark on the unusual number of snakes. One even claims to have seen a great assembly of serpents, gathered at the base of the tree where the egg curse has been performed.

"As if they were meeting, just as we do under our tree," says the man, his eyes crazed with fear.

"I crept closer to get a better look but one of them saw me. Then, all the serpents turned and looked at me and their leader, a huge python, said 'Get him. Find him' and they began to chase me. And I ran, brothers, I ran so hard I thought that my lungs would burst. You found me, didn't you Nandana. Just as I was running out of the forest. You saw them chasing me, didn't you?"

Nandana wags his head, obligingly. He certainly saw his friend stumbling through the trees, screaming in terror. He obviously believed that something was after him. But as to an army of snakes? Well, Nandana cannot actually swear that he saw them himself. But there had definitely been something. No doubt of that. He had sensed it. Definitely. And his friend – such a sensible fellow – would not be scared out of his wits over nothing, now would he?

The fear of incipient evil, first experienced by Asoka in the chena garden, soon spreads to the whole village, mimicking the mood of the nation. No-one knows what it is, but they feel its presence. Both waking and sleeping, it haunts their thoughts and follows them, wherever they go, infecting them with suspicion and mistrust, encircling them until they huddle together like cattle, hemmed in by a nameless dread. Skimming between trees or crouching in shadow, its messengers watch and wait; their presence sensed, rather than seen. Something is coming. Something bad.

1958: A mysterious accident

In the shade of the porch, Asoka has constructed a makeshift couch, made of sacks and covered with soft rag, so that Prema can watch the comings and goings along the forest track. From this position, he also faces the paddy fields, which provides some comfort, even though he cannot see them.

As a result of his accident, Prema has sustained a number of serious injuries, not just a sprained ankle as his friend, Hanuman, initially reported to the village meeting. He had been taking a short cut, along a bank which runs alongside an abandoned paddy field, when the ground collapsed beneath him. Although they heard him calling for help, nobody witnessed the incident and none can explain why the bank, previously so sound, should have given way so suddenly.

Some say that it was due to rainfall, although there has been none for weeks: others, that the bank must have been undermined by some burrowing animal, although there was no sign of holes or workings of soft earth. Finally, in the absence of a more convincing explanation, the village has concluded that Prema's accident was due to an act of God – or something less benign.

A day or so after the accident, a series of livid bruises surfaced on Prema's left side, turning it black. He has fractured his wrist and, although he makes little fuss, the old man winces with pain at every movement, causing his family to suspect that he has also broken several ribs. Every morning, he needs to be lifted from bed, carried to the yard where he can wash himself, then carried back into the house where he must be settled for the rest of the day: tasks that only Asoka can perform and which delay his departure for the fields.

Yet, despite these difficulties, or perhaps because of them, Asoka feels that a fragment of himself, so stained by his part in Mennan's death, is being cleansed. Now, he, alone, is responsible for the family and essential to its survival. They are all dependent on him, none more so than his father-in-law, and through their increased intimacy, occasioned by Prema's injuries, the relationship between the two men has become as close as that of a father and his natural son.

"What would we do without you, my boy?"

It is an unusual remark for Prema, causing Asoka to look away as he lays the old man on the couch.

"Please, Thaatha, don't mention it."

Asoka struggles to keep his voice steady.

The old man, his face compressed in a series of leathery wrinkles, his eyes shining with tears, reaches up his good hand and pats Asoka on the back of the neck.

"My son," he murmurs as a tear trickles from his eye.

"Hush, father," whispers Asoka, kissing the old man's forehead.

A movement in the doorway distracts him. Unnoticed, Sriya has been observing their conversation. She is smiling, contented, one hand resting on her belly, the other, at her side, holding a tiffin box. Her face mischievous, she lifts her arm, holding the box out in front of her. It is the sign for Asoka to leave.

1958: The mango tree

Carrying a scythe, its blade wrapped in hessian to protect him from any chance cut, Asoka starts out on his journey. He is later than usual today and so travels alone, the other men having already made their way to the fields. As he enters the quiet, forest track, he realises how much he misses their banter. Having overcome their initial mistrust, the other farmers now treat him as a friend, forgiving his occasional ignorance of rural matters, although they never lose an opportunity to tease him. He is one of them now.

When news of Prema's accident got out, there was a procession of visitors to the house, all bearing small gifts of food or medicine, all offering help. But, although Asoka does not doubt the sincerity of their promises, he secretly questions their ability to perform them. Harvest is the busiest time of the year and whole families will be called on to deal with their own crops. In his case, there will no help from the family. Prema is temporarily disabled and Sriya so near her time that neither she nor her mother can be spared. True, Chandra has offered to help, but Asoka will not hear of it, insisting that she stay at home with her daughter.

Excited thoughts of his child now fill his head. What will it be: a boy or a girl? He has already told Sriya that he does not mind what it is, as long as it is healthy, although he secretly hopes for a boy. All men wish for a son to succeed them. He has seen the same wish in Prema's eyes as he carries him around the house, his gestures, the way in which he speaks to Asoka; all betray a secret longing, a disappointment which he has never dared to admit for he loves Sriya more than his own life. But still, he wished for a son. Recently, he has confided in Asoka that, before Sriya was born, his wife miscarried three sons. The old man wept at that point.

"If only," he said, "if only ..."

Words failed Prema at that point. He was too ashamed to express his thoughts openly. But Asoka knew, without being told, that the old man wished that Sriya had been a boy – and still does – although such regrets are only confessed in the weakness of his injuries.

"Forget what I said," Prema begged once his tears had dried. After that, his manner to Sriya had been particularly tender. But Asoka knows that the hidden pain of disappointment remains, although neither has spoken of the matter again. Secretly, Asoka has sworn that he will never entertain any regret over his child, whatever its condition. He will greet it with joy and lay down his life to protect it.

***

As Asoka walks along the quiet track, the sun glints, brilliant white, through the branches of the trees. He closes his eyes, feeling its warmth on his face, alternating with the coolness of the shade. Birds are screeching and chattering above him although there are many that he does not recognise. Prema, on the other hand, can recognise each one by its call. By whistling and clicking his tongue, he can even attract them to him. A trick, he has told Asoka, that he learned as a boy, luring them close enough to shoot with a catapult. Asoka made a poor effort at hiding his horror and the old man had laughed.

"Soft city-dweller," he teased, his eyes gleaming with merriment. And yet, he does not despise Asoka for his sentiment. It occurs to Asoka that this ability to accept other people's differences, without despising them, shows a largeness of heart: one which he, himself, has lacked. How is it that he, with all his education and religious training, failed to learn this lesson?

He conspired to murder a man and even managed to justify it to himself only learning, too late, what a terrible thing it is to bring about the death of a fellow creature. What makes it worse is that it was not a crime of passion but one based on the cool rationale of prejudice and political belief.

He stops for a moment, breathing deeply, fighting the darkness which rises up from his heart every time he thinks of this subject. No matter how great his happiness, this memory will always be there to eclipse it. He sighs. It is his lot, his punishment, and he must bear it alone. Even Sriya, with all her gentleness, cannot reach this pain, so deeply rooted inside him.

He digs his toes into the soft, red earth, as if contact with the soil will conduct the evil out of his body. It somehow makes him feel stronger to think that this is what he will be reduced to in the end. Just a handful of soil.

"And from that," he thinks, "some goodness may grow."

He walks on and, drawing level with a wild mango tree, spies a large ripe fruit hanging from its branches.

"I must have that for Sriya," he thinks and, stretching up, uses the tip of the scythe to dislodge the fruit. It comes away easily and he has to drop the scythe to catch it before it hits the ground. He strokes the smooth red leather of its skin, then, putting it to his nose, smells it, devouring its perfume. The thought of Sriya biting into its sweet, yellow flesh arouses him. Even now, when she is heavily pregnant, he desires her. Especially now.

He carefully places the mango into a bag slung over his shoulder in which he carries the tiffin box and other, small farm implements then, picking up the scythe, he continues towards the paddy fields. He has not been walking for long, when a movement overhead catches his eye. Looking up to see what has caused it, he does not see the figure of a man, stepping out of the trees in front of him. It stands waiting, in the middle of the path, the embodiment of his darkest thoughts.

"Hello, brother."

It greets him with soft cunning.

Asoka starts.

"Who is that?"

Partially blinded by the sun, he shades his eyes with his hand. The outline is familiar, but he still cannot see the face.

"Have you forgotten so soon?" mocks the voice.

"Anil?"

The figure steps out of the sunlight and into the shade where he can see it better. It is smiling: not a smile of friendship, or greeting, but a slow, gloating smile; the sort favoured by pagan kings, hot with victory, their faces streaked with the blood of their enemies.

"Yes, it is me," says the voice, soft and sinister.

It is Anil and yet not him. Although recognisable, there is something different about the face, making it difficult for Asoka to accept that this is his old friend. Sometimes illness, age or the onset of death can rob features of their familiar guise; but Anil looks healthy. In fact, he radiates energy: but of a destructive, ferocious kind, as if a speck of nature's fury has lodged inside him; a force, primitive and pitiless, that cannot be tamed or resisted, but which will communicate itself instantly and without words to others that possess it, leaping from one to another like a bolt of lightning, galvanizing them with its touch, propelling them to destruction. Asoka can feel it, seeking him out, as the pale, amber eyes stare into his.

"Hmm!" snorts Anil, unable to hide his disgust. "You've changed. Or perhaps," he says musingly, taking a step closer, "I now see you for what you really are. A coward."

"I am no coward, brother. What we did was wrong."

"Wrong!"

Fire leaps into the amber eyes. Anil clenches his fist, then stabs a finger at Asoka's heart.

"You dare to speak to me of what is wrong! When you had no home, I brought you food. When you had no-one, I was your friend, your family. I would have followed you anywhere. Done anything. For you."

"I never asked you to," says Asoka, gently. "You chose to do what you did."

"And the plans? The preaching? Ceylon for the Sinhalese? Was that all a mistake?"

Moving close, Anil breathes in Asoka's ear.

"You seduced me with your ideas. I would have died for you."

Asoka averts his eyes.

"Look at me!"

But Asoka looks steadily into the trees, back towards the village where Sriya is waiting. Quivering with rage, Anil lunges forward and grasping Asoka's jaw in his hand, forces his face around and kisses him savagely on the lips.

Pushing Anil away with disgust, Asoka swings the scythe up, intending to bring it down hard on the head of his attacker; but, as he reaches behind his head, ready to deliver the blow, a hand clenches his wrist, jerking it round so violently that he cries in pain and drops the scythe. His arm is then twisted up behind his back and another familiar face appears over his shoulder.

"Surprised to see me?" Tissa laughs through jagged teeth.

"Let me go!"

But, even as he speaks, Asoka thinks how stupid this sounds. Fear has crept into his voice making it reedy and thin. The more he pleads, the more they will torment him, so he struggles, in silence, until Tissa winds an arm around his throat, squeezing all breath from his windpipe.

"Stop it! Let him go," orders Anil.

"But he'll run. Raise the village."

"No, he won't."

Reaching into his robes, Anil draws out a revolver. It is old army issue, acquired at some time from the British, either by theft or bribery; since then it has changed hands many times making its way, through a tortuous route of crime and mishap, into the hands of the Assistant Superintendent of Police. He, in turn, gave it to Anil in order to carry out the new plan they have in mind. Cocking the trigger, Anil holds the gun to Asoka's head.

"If you run, I will kill you. Understand?"

Asoka nods, his throat still aching from the pressure of Tissa's arm.

"Tissa, take that bag from him. Check inside to see that he hasn't got a knife or something he can use as a weapon."

Tissa wrenches the canvas bag from Asoka's shoulder then, squatting down, empties its contents onto the road, holding up each item and grinning at Asoka, before flinging it into the undergrowth. He has lost his mop of tangled hair and his stubbly scalp still resembles the shaven head of a monk, although he has swapped his monastic robes for the blue-checked sarong favoured by peasants.

Crouched in the road, picking through the contents of the bag, Tissa looks more like a monkey than a man, wild-eyed and unpredictable, given to sudden fits of rage resolving into violence and spite; a creature, inquisitive and filled with hate, that hunts in packs, stalking country roads and lonely places, looking for prey that, once found, will be chased relentlessly, then dismembered, its limbs torn apart while it screams for mercy.

Tissa has found the tiffin box. He holds it in his hands for a few seconds, turning it this way and that, then his face clouds and, struck by the thought of what his life might have been, he dashes it against the hard surface of the road, smashing it. Meat curry and rice spill across the road filling the air with a pungent, spicy smell.

"What did you do that for, you fool?"

Anil glowers at his companion and Tissa crouches down, his head between his shoulders, like a dog expecting a kick. But none comes. Anil has no need to resort to violence in Tissa's case. A look is enough to ensure compliance.

"Finish what you are doing while I speak to our friend, here."

Tissa would like to say that Asoka is not his friend but, scared of causing Anil further displeasure, he quietly continues his search of the bag.

"You are coming with us," says Anil, his eyes glinting, although they reveal nothing.

"Why?"

"Because you must finish what you started."

Asoka does not speak, unwilling to provoke a reply.

"Remember your plan? Not the one concerning the overseer, but the other one. Well, I'm going to make sure you see it through. There will be no running away this time."

Asoka frowns. He cannot remember another plan. In the past, he discussed many things with Anil. It all seems so long ago. He has no wish to remember, no desire to be involved.

"No. Whatever it is, I won't do it!"

"Oh, you will."

Anil speaks with quiet assurance. Turning his back on Asoka for a second, as if daring him to run, he crosses the path in a single, athletic stride and springs onto the bank, where he crouches for a second, steadying himself as an animal might, his fingertips buried in the soft leaf litter. Then, in a single, sinuous movement, he straightens up and, grasping the trunk of a young sapling, swings himself around in an almost playful manner until he is facing Asoka again.

Their eyes meet and Asoka feels his gaze being searched with an intimacy that turns his stomach. Anil smiles, satisfied, as if he has found what he was looking for then, still clinging to the tree, he arches his back, like a cat stretching and tilts his head in the direction of the village. It is a speech without words but its meaning is clear. Asoka's heart squeezes itself into a tight fist.

"If you refuse, I will kill her."

Anil's words fall as soft as feathers, yet all the more menacing for the lightness with which he speaks. Tissa, who has been dutifully examining the contents of the bag, looks up, uneasy.

"Kill who?"

Anil ignores him.

"Kill who?" Tissa demands.

"Quiet!" Anil commands.

***

Tissa stares down at his feet. It does not pay to question Anil. He can get inside your head. Snap the strings of your sanity. Tissa knows. Anil is the only man he fears. And yet he loves him, too, with the blind obedience of a dog.

He continues to rummage in the bag. He has removed most of its contents by now. In fact, he is sure that he has emptied it but, to please his master, is making a final check when his fingers touch something cool and smooth, lodged deep in a corner of the sack. He cups his hand around its sensuous form with a curious excitement. It feels like a woman's breast.

Consumed with rage, he raises his eyes to where Asoka is standing in the road. He wants to hurl himself on his rival and tear his throat out with his teeth. But he cannot, for fear of Anil. He must be subtle. Like his master.

The mango still lies in his hand, concealed within the bag. He caresses its smooth skin with his thumb. Then, he realises, with sudden intuition. It is a gift. For her. Slowly, he withdraws his hand from the bag and, still squatting on the ground, he holds the mango up in front of him, as if admiring its beauty. This catches Asoka's eye. He stares, first at the mango, then at Tissa, quietly clenching his fists.

Tissa grins, then slowly runs his tongue around the edge of the mango until he reaches its point then, closing his lips around it, he makes a pretence of sucking it before sinking his teeth in, biting through the rosy skin and tearing at the soft flesh. Pulling the broken mango from his mouth, he grins, yellow shreds of flesh hanging from his teeth, juice dribbling down his chin.

Asoka makes a slight movement, no more than a twitch, but it betrays him. Tissa wills him to fight. He will finish him. Here. Now. But Anil, sensing the tension, steps between them, cooling their rage with menace.

"You are a pig. Wipe your face."

Anil slaps Tissa over the back of the head. Yet, despite this reprimand, his voice has a note of affection, the sort expressed to domestic animals. Tissa obediently wipes his face on the back of his hand, then hurls the mango into the trees.

Asoka turns away in disgust. He cannot bear to look at Tissa, his ragged, leering mouth and his grimy fingers, their nails blackened with dirt. He cannot bear to think of this dirty, degraded creature haunting his wife's footsteps, following her as she walks alone along the forest paths or as she bathes in the tank. The thought of those filthy hands touching her tortures him. The thought of what he might do. His stomach lurches and, for a moment, he thinks he might be sick. He will do anything, anything at all, to protect her. And Anil knows it. He is a captive.

"Come, we must be going."

Anil clicks his fingers at Tissa.

"Lead the way."

Scrambling to his feet, Tissa runs ahead of them, into the forest. Carefully secreting the gun in the folds of his robe, Anil signals Asoka to follow. With a leaden heart, Asoka steps off the path into the shadow of the trees. Every so often, Tissa pauses and looks back, the dappled light playing tricks with his form. Half in light, half in shade, he is the embodiment of a demon. Now Asoka realises what it was he saw in the chena garden.

It is evening and men, returning from the fields, notice fragments of a meal, lying in the road. Not much remains. While birds and other animals have feasted on the meat, ants have busied themselves with the rice, forming a chain to transport it, grain by grain, back to their earthy cellars. But the smell of spice lingers and there is a stain on the path where gravy, rich with ghee, has soaked into the dust.

"Someone went hungry today," laughs one, cheerfully, as his fellows gather around him to examine the spot.

"Wait. What's that?" exclaims another.

The youngest of their company, a sharp-eyed fellow, is pointing to something lying partly hidden in the undergrowth.

"Look at him," laughs one of the older men. "He is such a fellow. Always chasing after things."

His companions laugh indulgently and watch as the young man scrambles up the verge. Reaching into a clump of ferns, he holds the tiffin-box aloft.

"Look!"

"Very good. Now come along home, Jaya. We're all getting hungry."

"But why would anyone throw away a tiffin-box."

"Who knows? Perhaps it's broken."

"Or perhaps he meant to pick it up on his way home," suggests another. "No point in carrying an empty tiffin-box to the fields."

"But why hide it?"

"So that inquisitive fellows like you should not find it!"

They all laugh. The sun is sinking quickly and their limbs are aching after long hours in the fields. They still have some way to walk and all are anxious to return home. Even for those who have grown up beside it, the forest is not a place to go wandering at night. Stories of ghosts and demons haunt the village and recent sightings of strange creatures in the forest have unnerved them all.

Unwilling to wait any longer, some of the men detach themselves from the group and trudge slowly towards the village. Others, uncomfortable at the thought of deserting their friend, take out their tobacco and begin to roll thin cigarettes.

"Come on, Jaya," urges one. "We haven't got all night. My wife will be waiting for me with the broom-stick. Then she will mash my head!"

Waving his hand above his head, the man mimics the gestures of his wife, pulling his face into an angry grimace. The others laugh.

"Yes, Jaya. Come on. You can't get Sathi in trouble with his wife."

There is more chortling. A match is struck. The first cigarette is lit. With a deep sense of appreciation, the farmer sucks in the smoke. The match is passed around. Other cigarettes are lit, their tips glowing for a second, then several thin columns of smoke rise in the still evening air. Already, one half of the sun has disappeared below the horizon, while the other half quivers, like a great red jelly on a plate.

"Oh come on. Hurry up. It will soon be dark. We have waited long enough."

The men chivvy the boy.

"Wait a bit. There's something else here."

The young man crawls off into the undergrowth until nothing can be seen of him but a patch of blue sarong, stretched over his skinny rump.

"Watch out for snakes, you foolish boy," shouts one man, his patience wearing thin.

"Ugh!" exclaims the boy.

"What is it?" enquire the men, their interest aroused.

"A mango. Covered with ants. Black ones. Ow! One bit me."

"Serves you right," jeers a voice from the path. "Perhaps that will stop your foolish pranks."

"No. Wait. There's something else."

The boy has found Asoka's bag, loosely covered with leaves, and the scythe. Screwing up his eyes, he peers around him. In the bright shafts of the setting sun, other small objects, a cup, a knife, a roll of string, are illuminated, lying scattered over the forest floor, but invisible from the road.

"Come and look," the boy beckons to his friends.

In the hope that they will soon be able to leave, one man climbs the verge. At first, he is merely puzzled but, when he sees the scythe, he becomes alarmed. No-one would leave farm implements lying about the forest. They are far too valuable. Telling the boy to collect what he can and put it in the bag, he carries the scythe, still in its hessian binding, back to the men on the road.

"It was just lying there. And the other things, all scattered about. It looks as if someone tried to hide them, at least, from anyone passing on the road."

Solemnly drawing on their cigarettes, the other men examine the scythe, passing it from hand to hand.

"I recognise this," says one, holding his cigarette between his fingers as he turns the object over. "See, here. It has a nick in the handle. I borrowed it from Prema, last year. It is his. I am sure of it."

"But Prema cannot walk. He could not have brought those things."

"Asoka … did anyone see him today?"

The men shake their heads. Now they come to think of it, they have not seen Asoka since the day before.

"Better look again. See if he's still in there," ventures one, nodding towards the forest.

They all scramble up the bank, calling, searching as best they can now that the sun has plunged beneath the horizon, but it is useless without a light.

"We must take these things back to the village, then come back with torches," advises an elderly man.

Secretly glad to quit the gloomy depths of the forest, the others agree to this plan and set off with the boy leading the way. With the canvas bag wedged under his arm, Jaya pads along in the darkness, sucking the ant-bite on his wrist. Behind him, the men are talking softly. One mentions the egg curse but is quickly hushed by his neighbours. It is what they are all thinking but it does not do to talk of such things out here, beyond the safety of the village.

Jaya shudders and, tingling with horror, clutches the bag tightly to his ribs. And yet, he has an odd sense of satisfaction. It was his sharp eyes that spotted the tiffin-box, his determination that unearthed further evidence of a mystery. The discovery was his. Further revelations might follow: a robbery, perhaps; or a murder. Wide with anticipation, his eyes gleam in the moonlight.

News of Asoka's disappearance spreads rapidly through the village. A search is mounted instantly. Clumps of rag, dipped in kerosene, are tied to sticks and groups of men, lit by flaming torches, set off into the forest. Standing in their doorways, the women watch anxiously as husbands and sons disappear along the track that leads into the forest, as brightly-coloured sarongs merge into colourless shadow and figures, outlined by blue and yellow flame, eventually melt into darkness.

The lights divide, dispersing through the forest, shrinking to tiny pinpoints until they also disappear. Soon, the only trace of those engulfed by darkness is the sound of their voices, ringing faintly through the forest, like ghosts calling from the grave, repeating a single name: "Asoka. Asoka."

Patiently, the women wait, straining their eyes into the blackness, watching for their men, praying for their safe return. The forest is the keeper of dark secrets and nameless fears, unpredictable and untrustworthy. Although a giver of gifts, it is never wholly benign; a wild, untamed place, always waiting for the opportunity to take back what it has lost and, sometimes, to take revenge on those who have robbed it.

For centuries it has encircled the village, nurturing it with food, fuel and the necessities of life, but also sending out its scouts to probe the village defences. Unannounced, these interlopers unfurl above ground, raising small green heads like miniature periscopes, probing for weaknesses and the opportunity to mount a silent incursion. The villagers' response is swift and savage: digging, hacking and burning, they fight to reclaim their territory in a battle waged on a daily basis.

Each time, the forest retreats, but it is always there, always waiting, ready to claim another victim. Although they never speak of it, every family knows of someone who has disappeared: children enticed by curiosity; old people with feet led by wandering minds; disappointed lovers seeking solace; all have drifted into the dark maw of the forest, never to return.

And recently, there have been signs of unusual disturbance in the forest. By now, everyone has heard the story of the crushed egg-shells, bearing the traces of Asoka's name. A sacrifice. But to which god? It might be harmless, a request for blessings but, when questioned, Prema remains tight-lipped. Yes, he knows of it. No, he does not know what it means. But his eyes betray his fear. He begs anyone who asks him not to mention it to Sriya. She is in a delicate state, has been nervous and uneasy since her return from the chena garden recently. She saw something. Or, rather, Asoka did.

Then, one by one, other villagers report strange sightings in the forest: one, sometimes two, figures, dark and indistinct, slipping quietly between the trees, glimpsed only for a second; a view so fleeting that, if the observer blinks, it is gone and he is left wondering if he was dreaming. One man even claims that he was knocked over and his tiffin-box stolen but, as the fellow had been drinking toddy the night before, no-one pays his story much attention.

Another villager, of more sober habits, says that he saw Tissa's face, leering at him from the branches of a tree. He had picked up a stone and thrown it. He is a good shot. If there had been anything there, he would have hit it. But the stone had hurtled through the branches without impediment. There was no sound, no thwack as the stone hit flesh, no cry, no thud of a body hitting the ground. Just silence. The man had shuddered and run home to tell his wife.

A story begins to circulate that the forest is haunted by Tissa's ghost. The villagers have long believed Tissa to be dead. No-one who disappears for as long as he has ever returns alive.

And now Asoka is gone. The women wait for their men and pray.

***

It is dawn. The sun rises swiftly, floating up from the horizon like a gaudy yellow lantern, vaporising the night dew and shrouding the forest in early morning mist. Troupes of parakeets flash through the branches, screeching shrilly. In the distance, oxen low as they are led to drink at the tank.

The men return from the forest, scratched and dirty, their torches extinguished, speaking, if they speak at all, with muted voices. Their shoulders sag wearily and they keep their eyes lowered, unable to meet the enquiring gaze of their women. The search has revealed nothing.

As it travels up the sky, the sun begins to burn with a harsh light, its unrelenting brightness only increasing their gloom. Asoka has not been found. Someone will have to tell Prema.

The women lead their husbands to the food that they have prepared and the air is filled with the smell of warm bread as rotis are baked over the fire. They all watch as one of the elders walks stiffly by, his bones and joints aching from fatigue, his face set and grim, making his way slowly to Prema's door, across the square, past the great Bo tree, then up the narrow track to the house, past the pig, lazing on its side and the chicken, scouring the bald earth for grubs.

He disappears into the house and, a few seconds later, there is a terrible cry, the sound of unutterable loss, followed by the keening of a woman's voice.

The country lane is silent, except for the rackety passage of a cart, its thin, plaited sides shaking as the wheels trundle over stones and potholes. The driver dozes in the heat, his head propped against the side of the cart, the reins loosely held in one hand. In the other, he holds a cane, freshly cut that morning still bearing a number of green shoots at its tip. If the oxen falter or veer towards the verge, he corrects them with a smart flick of the switch, neither altering his position nor opening his eyes.

Hardly more than a track, where two vehicles cannot pass without one pulling to the side, the road is bathed in the dusty light of late afternoon. Palm fronds, nearly touching overhead, are tipped with gold while beneath, shadows cast by the forest begin to creep together from the verges, soaking the bright surface of the road with their fathomless ink. From the trees, a figure appears, peering out from the gloom, turning his head this way and that; a monk in saffron robes, waist high in the undergrowth, wading down to the road through a track in the trees.

He waits, silent and still, until the cart has rumbled out of sight, then turning back towards the forest, he motions with his hand. Two other figures appear: first, a thin man, his rough hair beginning to grey a little, his face gouged with fatigue; then, another, younger man, his head freshly-shaved, also wearing a monk's robes although his wild, darting eyes seem out of keeping with his calling.

"Quickly!" hisses the figure from the road.

The young monk prods the other man in the back, goading him forward as a herdsman drives a weary animal. The man in front stumbles. The monk pushes him again, appearing to enjoy his task.

"Hurry up!" urges the man in the road. "It's getting late. We have several miles to go yet."

The first of his companions stumbles down the verge into the road. Having fallen to his knees, the man is slowly pushing himself upright, when the younger monk, having landed on his feet, deals him a vicious kick which sends him sprawling, face-first in the dirt.

"Enough of that! We've no time for horse-play," snaps the other monk, testily. "Help him up!"

Sullenly, the young monk hooks his arm around that of the other man and pulls him to his feet. The other man coughs, his throat and eyes full of dust but, as he tries to brush his face clean, the monk gives him a sharp poke between the shoulders. The man stumbles forward, knowing that if he stops there will be another beating. He has already been subjected to two of these and his ribs are bruised and aching from kicks and punches, delivered by the young monk in a frenzy of rage. He has learned already that it takes nothing to provoke such violence and that the boy will act on the slightest pretext, welcoming the opportunity to punish his captive. A mere glance in his direction will trigger another attack.

Having wiped the dirt from his mouth, the man notices blood on his hand and realises that he has cut his lip. It must have happened when he fell in the road but there is so much pain elsewhere in his body that he did not notice. Running his tongue over his lip, he licks the blood. It tastes pleasantly salty with the savour of iron that blood always has. He is thirsty, but he does not dare to ask for water, although he knows that the monk carries a flask. He licks his lip again, hoping to draw a little of the moisture into his dry mouth. A hand nudges his arm, offering him a water bottle. It is the older monk.

"Here. Drink!"

Gratefully, the captive grasps the bottle and takes a long draft, the water burning at first as it touches his dry throat. He gulps the water down, trying to take as much as he can, not knowing when, or if, he will be allowed to drink again.

"That's enough!" The young monk tears the bottle from his hands and, pressing it to his own lips, drains it.

While his tormentor is preoccupied, the captive steals a glance at the older monk, searching his face for some sign of friendship or pity. But he sees none. As he stands in the sun, the monk's face glows, but as he steps into shadow, that brilliancy is extinguished, leaving only the pale, transparent gleam of his eyes. Without any show of emotion, he turns his back on his captive and walks ahead, leading the way.

"So that's the way it is," thinks the captive.

Overtaken by despair, he becomes rooted to the spot, until another sharp prod in the back reminds him to keep moving.

**

Night has descended, rapacious as ever, plunging the earth into darkness and obliterating every spark, except for the stars glimmering in their own light. Cold as ice crystals, they glitter overhead, mocking those less fortunate, like a woman wearing diamonds to a slum.

It has been dark for hours. Or, so it seems to Asoka who has no way of knowing how long they have walked, or where they are going. He can no longer think or reason, the limit of his senses reduced to bone-aching fatigue. He is a fit man, capable of labouring in the fields for many hours a day, but this enforced march, combined with his reluctance to leave the village, has sapped his strength. Every step is agony.

Eventually, he feels that he will collapse and must lie where he falls, whatever the consequences. His legs begin to quake beneath him, unwilling, or unable, to be driven any further. He is about to speak, for the first time in hours, an act of bravado that will inevitably end in a beating when, to his relief, Anil announces that it is time to rest.

As if he were waiting for the order, Tissa leads the way, diving eagerly into the gloom of the forest, like a dog down a burrow. Striking out with his arms, he pushes branches and ferns aside, almost appearing to swim through the undergrowth. After a few minutes, he brings them to a clearing which, judging by the bruised stems of the plants, was hacked out with a machete only a few days before. In the centre, a small pile of charcoal and ash indicates the remains of a camp-fire and Asoka wonders if his companions stayed here on their journey to the village. However, no fire is lit tonight for there is no food to be cooked, only a few drops of water, issued grudgingly to Asoka from Tissa's flask.

"Sleep," orders Tissa. "You don't have long."

Asoka rests his head on the ground and, as he does so, breathes in the earthy odour of soil. It reminds him of home, of the chena garden and Sriya. His heart aches to see her and, despite his exhaustion, he resists sleep, trying to picture her in his mind. But her image eludes him and he is able to conjure only isolated fragments from memory, a hand or a cheek, an arm or the curve of a shoulder. Closing his eyes, he tries to recall other details: how the wisps of hair at her neck curl when damp, how he wrote her name in the sand, how it felt when she kissed him. He feels a sudden glow and smiles to himself.

"What are you laughing at?"

Tissa kicks him viciously on the sole of his foot.

"Go to sleep."

Asoka rolls over, pulling his arm over his face so that it can no longer betray his thoughts. As long as he keeps his eyes closed, he can see her, feel her, and hope remains. Within seconds, he is asleep.

***

Squatting, locust-like, his shoulders hunched forward, his hands in his lap, Tissa watches Asoka as he sleeps, silently confronting the man who has stolen his future. He can no longer see the expression on the other man's face, but he wants to. He wants to know what it is like to sleep so peacefully, for the sound of gentle, steady breathing and the rhythm of Asoka's rib-cage as it moves up and down, shows that he is, indeed, asleep. He has been abducted, forcibly removed from all that he loves and forced to walk, non-stop, for thirty-six hours without food. How can he sleep like this? Is it just exhaustion, or something else?

Tissa's mind flies back to the moment when he saw Asoka smile. He had been lying there, helpless on the ground with his eyes closed, but he had smiled. Even here, in these circumstances, he can experience happiness. It is a feeling that Tissa has forgotten, perhaps never truly knew, but he desires it. He wants what Asoka has got. And that is Sriya.

He grits his teeth, grinding them together, his jaw working and twitching. The thought of Sriya with anyone else torments him. And here is the man who stole her, just inches away, asleep and defenceless. Tissa clasps his hands, clenching them together to prevent himself from committing an act that he has long considered. But the thought of it returns to him, as it does every night, bringing him comfort as he thinks of his fingers tightening around Asoka's neck, gouging his eyes, or tearing the beating heart from his chest. And now, he is here. Before him. Asleep and helpless.

What was he thinking of when he smiled? Was it her? A bitter pang of jealousy shakes Tissa. Clenching his fists, he clutches the folds of his robe, twisting them tighter and tighter, waiting for the madness to pass. In full flood, it rushes through his body, filling it with bile; a poisonous black quicksilver that swells every vein and rages about his heart, until, gradually abating, it creeps back to his infected brain.

Drenched in sweat and cooled by the night air, Tissa shudders and, looking down, sees that he has rent the front of his robe. He lowers himself to the ground, his back resting against a tree, his eyes fixed on Asoka, not daring to sleep for fear of what he might do. It is too soon for revenge. Anil has other plans, for the time being, although Tissa feels sure that his opportunity will come. Anil has promised.

Tilting his head back, Tissa tries to count the stars. He likes them much better than the moon. They are unobtrusive, disinterested. They do not trouble him as the moon does. By now, he has begun to breathe more easily although he feels weak, as if a dark shadow has drifted through him. He shivers. Old people would say that something had passed over his grave. He does not see the figure of a man, blacker than night, stooping over Anil's sleeping body to whisper in his ear.

1958: A village offering

After only a few hours' sleep, Tissa wakes Asoka, shaking him roughly with his foot. Rubbing his eyes sleepily, Asoka staggers to his feet, then stumbles forward through the undergrowth, following Tissa and Anil, back onto the road. Even here, beyond the trees, the world is bathed in inky blackness, as if all hope had left it.

Asoka shudders, rubbing his arms with his hands, although he is not cold. His brain, still clouded with sleep, plays tricks on him and he fancies that he sees figures in the trees from the corner of his eye. Once or twice, he turns his head quickly, trying to catch them, but they disappear. And yet, he still has the ticklish sensation of being watched.

"Anil," he murmurs. "Are you sure we are alone?"

Without slowing his stride, Anil turns to look at him, a pitying sneer on his lips. "Why do you ask?"

Already feeling stupid, Asoka mutters: "I thought I saw something. There. In the trees."

Anil laughs, softly.

"My friend, you are imagining things. Your life in the country has changed you. You used to say that irrational fear was the stamp of a primitive mind. Do you think differently now?"

"No, of course not."

But Asoka speaks without conviction. Although they have been walking briskly for several minutes, the feeling of coldness has not left him. The skin on his arms is covered with goose-bumps and the back of his neck is tingling. Something at the side of the road catches his eye.

Peering into the darkness, he sees that they are passing a funeral ground, its perimeter marked by strips of white linen hanging from wires, like ragged rows of washing. A funeral pyre has been lit recently. He can still smell the faint tang of wood-smoke, still see embers that look like two red eyes, glowing in the dark. The embers blink and go out.

Something is watching them. With a sudden lurch, Asoka's heart begins to pound with fear. He recalls stories, told by the villagers, of demons who inhabit cemeteries: terrible creatures with tusks who waylay unsuspecting travellers, hauling them into the shadows to feast on their flesh before carrying their souls off to hell.

"Oh God," he murmurs and, for the first time in many months, he finds himself praying.

***

The night lasts an eternity. By the time the first flickering light of dawn has appeared, Asoka is already weary. But there is to be no rest. Like two nocturnal creatures, Anil and Tissa head back into the forest; Tissa driving Asoka in front of him, thrashing him if he slows, with a switch of freshly-cut cane.

Every so often, Asoka thinks he is running into a cold mist, until he realises that it is his own sweat, suffusing his face with a clammy veil. Hot and cold by turns, but mostly cold, his body lapses into rebellion which he hopes is due to lack of food and sleep, rather than the onset of fever. The more they force him on, the more dream-like his state of mind, his thoughts arising at random, dissociated from each other, devoid of any logic or reason. He has lost control of himself.

Parakeets screech, rushing through the dim canopy of trees like emerald sparks. Somewhere, in the distance, a cockerel crows and is answered by the agitated barking of a dog. Now Asoka hears the clashing of pails and people shouting to each other.

They are nearing a village. He can smell the wood from the fires, sweet and pungent. For a few seconds, he is transported back to his own village. To Sriya. He sees her clearly now. She is smiling and talking. Then she looks at him and her face grows dark and melts into air, leaving him with an unbearable sense of loss. He aches for home and his wife. Unable to stop himself, he begins to weep.

"Ha. Look at him. Cry-baby!"

Crowing with satisfaction, Tissa taunts him with the cane, lightly tapping him on the head.

"Stop that!"

Anil glowers furiously at Tissa. With the cane still in his hand, Tissa's arm drops limply to his side and he stands with his mouth open, staring stupidly at his master.

"We are near a village. You are wearing monk's robes. What would they think if they saw you?"

Dumb with terror, Tissa makes a slight movement of his head.

"Fool!" spits Anil.

Tissa hangs his head.

"Get the bowls! We're going to the village. And you," says Anil, turning to Asoka, "stay here, or your wife will pay for your disobedience".

Mutely, Tissa produces two plain wooden bowls from a bag that he has been carrying over his shoulder. With his eyes lowered, he holds one out to Anil who snatches it away as a sign of his continuing displeasure. The two monks set off in the direction of the village; Tissa, submissive and eager to please, slinking at his master's heels. But before he disappears into the trees, he turns, furtive and cunning, to fling a last glance at his captive. It is a look of hatred, full of murderous intent, but it is lost on Asoka who, having slumped to the ground, has fallen asleep.

**

A couple of hours later, Asoka is woken again, roused from a dreamless void more akin to death than sleep, for it holds no memory but only an interminable blackness, unrelieved by the workings of the unconscious mind; a vast empty space, darker than night, unlit even by the cold light of stars.

"Wake up or you will go without."

Tissa is growling in his ear, shaking him roughly, as one might shake a sack.

"Wake up!"

Something thuds onto the ground beside his face. Asoka opens his eyes to see one of the bowls, filled with a little cold rice mixed with dhal and a few cold vegetables. Anil and Tissa have been to the village to beg for dhana, alms of food which, when given to a monk, buy spiritual merit for the donor. Whatever their means, villagers and townspeople alike are always glad to share their food with the monks, although dhana in the villages tends to be less substantial, reflecting the poverty of the donors.

But it is a monk's lot to accept what he is given and Asoka is so hungry that he is grateful for anything. He eats swiftly, scooping the food into his mouth with his hand, then wiping a finger around the bowl to extract the last drop of gravy.

He cannot remember when he last ate. Was it one or two days ago? He remembers the tiffin-box, lying abandoned in the road, its contents spilled negligently over the soil. Will someone find it? Will Sriya realise that he has not abandoned her? He aches to think of her suffering.

"Sriya, my love, I will return."

He speaks the words silently in his head, like a prayer, hoping that she will hear them. Then his thoughts are interrupted. A sharp kick in the kidneys.

"Get up! It's time to move on."

The bowl is torn from his hands. Someone has grabbed him by the hair and is forcing him to his feet: Tissa, full of relentless malice, pushing him forward, further and further away from home.

1958: Hooniyam's joke

In the village, the men have searched by day and night, but the forest has defeated them. In places it is dense and impenetrable, in others, criss-crossed by many tracks. Some paths lead deep into the forest, while others, after weaving a meandering course through the trees, end abruptly. The searchers have frequently lost their bearings and, despite many long, fatiguing hours, have covered only a small area, frequently doubling back without realising it and returning to the place from which they had started. Each time, they have returned home weary and disheartened.

Yet the men do not give up and, despite the pressing requirements of harvest, they abandon their work in the fields to look for Asoka. They search ditches and plumb wells, scour the undergrowth, walk the paddy fields and even send their best swimmers to search the tank, but there is no sign of Asoka: no body, no remnant of clothing, nothing to indicate what has happened to him or where he has gone. He has vanished, leaving behind only the objects that he was carrying on his way to the fields. It is as if he has been snatched from the air and carried off.

Ancient superstitions begin to surface and are fitted neatly around the evidence. When they meet to smoke under the Bo tree, the men repeat what their women have said around the fire, embellishing stories which will soon be accepted as fact. Several astute minds have linked the finding of broken eggshells bearing Asoka's name to the sightings of strange creatures in the forest. From here, it requires only a small step of logic to deduce that Manju has performed the egg curse, summoning demons to avenge her for the loss of her son and that it is demons who have abducted Asoka.

Terror grips the village. Children are forbidden to wander further than the yard or the path outside, where they can be kept in view while they play, and women abandon their lone visits to the chena garden to collect vegetables. In the village, it has always been rare, if not impossible, for anyone to do anything without company but now, the thought of being alone, holds a particular terror. It feels as if evil is stalking the hamlet, waiting to pick off the unwary.

Old stories are remembered of how demons used to carry off young girls as they washed their clothes at the tank. Adapted to fit the facts of Asoka's disappearance, these tales are now resurrected and repeated with spine-chilling effect. Starting with the elders, they are re-told at village meetings where they are picked up by the younger members of the group and then passed on to impressionable siblings. The children of the village, terrified by the potency of their own imagination, often wake up at night screaming and can only be soothed back to sleep by lying in their parents' arms.

Shamans are sought out and priests consulted. Visits to the local shrine are combined with requests for talismans to ward off the evil eye. Due to the steady stream of pilgrims, images of the Buddha appear to float on a perpetual lake of flowers, while shrines to other gods are illuminated by row upon row of tiny, votive lamps. An especial favourite is the patron of sorcery and exorcism: Hooniyam.

***

Reclining in a shady corner of the shrine, the god fans himself with a banana leaf, watching the worshippers prostrate themselves before his effigy as the old priest mumbles a series of incoherent prayers. Then, scratching his belly with a long, horny nail, Hooniyam chuckles to himself.

"What a delicious irony, my dears," he chortles to his serpents. "These stupid people are seeking protection from the same god who arranged the abduction of their friend. What do you think of that?"

Roused from their slumbers, the snakes hiss menacingly, then flicking their tongues at the incense-laden air, they blink wearily and go back to sleep.

The forest has thinned, yielding to cultivated plantations of coconut palm. Shielded from the sun by the corrugated fronds of the palms, the labourers work swiftly, the dappled light playing over their sweating limbs. Having first removed the outer covering of the nut, they split it with an axe and impale each half of the shell on a stake so that the long, rough fibres can be stripped from its surface. The denuded nut is discarded and the fibre flung onto a pile. Soon the piles are as high as the men, the heaps of red fibre resembling the rough, woolly hair of some monstrous creature.

At the end of the day, lorries arrive to transport both the men and the fruits of their labour to separate destinations. Tomorrow, the back-breaking process will begin again, continuing, as it has done, for centuries. Transported to factories, the coir will be transformed into doormats and string and few who work it, or buy the finished product, will have any idea of the primitive workings of the plantation.

As the men thrash at the shells with their axes, three small figures skirt the clearing, carefully stepping between the trees, following an ancient path that leads out towards the road. Filled with the dust from coconut shells, the air smells different here. It lacks the earthy pungency of the forest and the space between the trees is more open and airy. The soil, though it still bears its characteristic redness, is drier and, where it has been disturbed by animals or humans, Asoka feels it soft and almost sandy beneath his feet.

He is less tired now that they have left the forest and his thoughts seem more ordered although he has lost count of how many days they have been walking. After a particularly savage onslaught, Tissa was sharply reprimanded by Anil. Asoka's beatings stopped after that, although Tissa watches him constantly, his eyes shining in the gloom like baleful lanterns. But Asoka finds that he can cope with this, even learning to ignore it and, although still bruised, he is thankful for the absence of fresh physical torment.

***

They emerge from the coconut plantations, into flat, open terrain. Asoka senses his companions' nervousness now that they are in open country. By now they have travelled many miles and he wants to know where they are going, although he says nothing for fear of another beating. They are now on a wide road that skirts a tank, one of the great reservoirs built by the ancient kings. Ceylon once had many of these tanks which served both domestic and agricultural needs but, with the passing of time, neglect has reduced most to unusable sludge-filled pits while others have dried up altogether.

As proof of his devotion to the rural poor, the late Prime Minister D.S. Senanayake caused many of these tanks to be restored, thereby winning the gratitude – and votes – of the peasants. Since then, projects to advance the fortunes of the rural communities have proved less successful and have consisted mainly in colonising less fertile areas of the land, resulting either in thousands of deaths from malaria or, as at Gal Oya, violent conflict between the Tamil and Sinhalese communities. Nonetheless, the tanks remain; proof of at least one Prime Minister's commitment to those living outside the cities.

The tank extends for many acres: a mirror to the sky in which clouds scud and birds soar, their activities reflected in the flat, shining surface below. When the tank is deserted, without people bathing or fishing, sky and water are almost indistinguishable, except for the occasional stumps of drowned trees dotted about the lake's surface like sentinels.

However in monsoon, water and sky go to war. Pounded by heavy drops of water, the lake rebels and turns into a seething cauldron. Spitting and bubbling, it is converted from a looking-glass to a savage beast, with a life and beauty of its own. Then, excused from work in the fields, villagers and their children romp in the shallows, laughing and splashing, opening their mouths to catch the rain as their hair melts into black rills that trickle down their faces.

But that is many months away. Today, the road is hard and dry, the sun unremitting in its heat and the sky, of an infinite china blue, is reflected in the passive surface of the tank. Men are fishing in the lake from small, flat-bottomed boats and herons and wading birds stalk the shallow waters by the shore while, a few yards away, women wade up to their waists and soap themselves under their lunghis. After the primeval shade of the forest and the dappled light of the plantations, it is a relief to Asoka to come out into the open and feel the sun on his face, however hot.

On the opposite side of the road are paddy fields where labourers stoop to their work, ankle-deep in water, their sarongs hitched above their knees and their heads wound up in rags or shaded by broad-brimmed hats made from strips of dried reed. The sight of them recalls painful memories of home which are made more acute by the happy cries of children splashing in the water.

Asoka's heart feels like lead, weighing him down and slowing his steps as he thinks of Sriya, so near her time and again he finds himself praying: this time, for her safety. He vows to return to her as soon as possible, but first, he must find the opportunity and, even then, he must be sure that there will be no retaliation. A few hours with Anil has been enough to convince him that his former pupil is possessed by an implacable desire for revenge and, as he tramps along the road, he is also aware of Tissa, trudging behind him, always at his heels, a dull-witted but equally vengeful enemy.

Many people pass them on this road, some on bicycles, some walking, but all make a sign of respect to the two monks; Anil, erect, his back as straight as a cane, one hand folded across his stomach, holding the gun beneath his robe and Tissa, stumbling forward with the shuffling, stooping gait that he seems to have adopted since leaving the village.

Word of their progress has obviously passed ahead, because when they arrive at a village, women run out of their houses to offer them food. Then, the travellers rest for a while, sitting in whatever shade they can find, usually beneath the jutting roof of a shack or under a mango tree, but only long enough to finish their food before moving on.

After a mile or so, the road diverges: one half continuing through the paddy fields and leading to the main high road; the other, less frequented and following the contour of the lake, leading in the opposite direction. They take the latter and continue walking in silence for some distance. There are no villages here and no cultivated land to attract passing traffic.

The tank is deserted except for a lone fisherman standing at the water's edge, trying out a home-made rod and line with a safety pin bent into a hook and baited with the small red worms common to dung heaps. He turns as they pass and, propping the rod between his knees, presses his hands together and bows to the monks who return the gesture; somewhat awkwardly in Tissa's case, for he struggles to stop himself from grinning at what he still considers to be a huge joke. No-one ever showed him respect like this in the village but now strangers bow their heads and beg for his blessing.

"They would do anything," he thinks to himself, "anything I ask them."

He has even been tempted by some of the pretty village girls, after all, who would say no to a monk, but Anil is always close by, watching him like a hawk. He must wait for another opportunity, when Anil is not around. After all, he has the same needs as other men.

He wonders if Anil has ever felt anything for a woman. If he has, he has never mentioned it; but there again, Anil never speaks much about himself, only the Cause. The only thing he has ever told Tissa of a personal nature is that his father was an Ayurvedic doctor. It seems to make him angry, resentful of something, but Tissa has never discovered what because Anil refuses to say any more on the subject.

Still grinning at the fisherman, Tissa shambles after the others. A few months ago, he took a blow to the head during the attack at Gal Oya. He has never walked quite straight since then and has to stoop in order to keep his balance, always compensating for his feeling of lop-sidedness, as if something heavy is sitting on his shoulder.

Sometimes he has such intense pains in his head that he blacks out – he never knows for how long – and, for some time after such an episode, his thoughts become disordered. But it does not happen often and, anyway, it was worth it.

He can still remember how he felt when he looked back at the burning village, the sense of euphoria, the taste of charred wood and smoke in his mouth, the screams of the women, the outrage of the men, blood spurting into his face from their wounds. The pure eroticism of killing.

Tissa laughs out loud.

"What is it?"

Anil, who was walking in front, has stopped and is looking at him, his lips pressed together in a straight line, ready to show his displeasure.

"Nothing. I'm sorry."

Tissa hangs his head.

Batting a fly away with the back of his hand, Anil pauses for a moment and looks around him. Beyond the reach of the jungle, far in the distance, is a range of mountains, their jagged contours running along the horizon like the edge of a saw. Anil draws a deep breath. Without warning, he stops, looks around him then, climbing over a low wall, walks to the edge of the lake, beckoning the others to follow him. They are mystified. He has spoken little since leaving Asoka's village, but now he wants to talk – at least, to Tissa.

"Look before you," he says, pointing out over the glassy surface of the tank. "What do you see?"

Tissa fidgets, winding a fold of his robe around his fingers. He is not as quick as he used to be and he sometimes finds Anil's way of speaking confusing. Sometimes he appears to be asking questions when no answer is required. Tissa struggles to interpret the meaning of Anil's words and to understand exactly what is required of him. If he gets it wrong, Anil will make fun of him or subject him to a bitter tongue-lashing, worse than any beating: worse still, he will laugh at him.

"I ... I ... don't know, Master."

Tissa's lip droops stupidly and his mouth hangs open. He looks terrified. To his own surprise, Asoka finds that he pities him. Anil fixes the boy with his merciless, pale-eyes as a snake ensnares a rabbit with its gaze. He waits. Tissa's mouth works as if he is trying to form a word then, eventually, it stumbles out.

"W ... w ... water?"

Anil snorts with laughter, mirthless and sarcastic.

"Water, water! What you see before you is a monument. A reservoir built by the Sinhalese rulers to sustain their people. While the Europeans were still living in caves, we were cultivating the land, growing rice, trading. This tank was the symbol of a great civilisation, yet all you see is water. Pah!"

He turns away in disgust. Tissa stoops a little lower.

"Don't worry," says Asoka, sensing the boy's shame. "Anil always liked to speak in riddles."

"Shut up!" Tissa kicks him savagely. "Shut up! Shut up!"

Losing all control, Tissa throws himself upon Asoka, gouging at his face with his hands. Taken by surprise, Asoka staggers, tries to steady himself but, too late. He loses his balance and falls backwards with Tissa on top of him, gripping him by the throat, shaking him as a terrier shakes a rag, hitting his head against the hard mud and sharp stones of the lake shore.

"Stop!"

Anil's voice is like the crack of a whip. Instantly, Tissa rolls off Asoka and curls up on the ground, as limp and helpless as a bundle of rags. Anil speaks in a low and deadly voice.

"Never, never lay a finger on this man again. Not unless I tell you to. Do you understand?"

The bundle of clothes whimpers. A slight movement of the head shows that it acknowledges the command. Then, Anil speaks again, his voice low and deadly.

"If you disobey me, I will take you to Hooniyam's priest and get a nail driven through your head. Just here."

Crouching over the huddled figure, Anil presses hard on Tissa's forehead, indicating the point at which the nail will go in. Tissa lies still, not daring to move, his eyes unblinking and liquid with terror.

"If the nail is put in, you will have no life of your own. You will just be a slave. Until you die. Understand?"

Tissa nods, trying to swallow, but his tongue, parched with fear, seems to have swollen until it blocks his throat. It feels as if he is choking.

"He has put a spell on me," he thinks, his limbs quivering with panic.

"Drink this!"

Anil hands Tissa his water bottle. Still lying on the ground, Tissa holds it to his lips, not caring that water dribbles from his lip and down his cheek.

"Now get up and stand here. Next to me."

Obediently, Tissa gets to his feet, not daring to look at Asoka whose scalp and face are covered with bloody scratches.

"Look," says Anil, pointing across the tank.

But Tissa sees only the mirror images of lake and sky; earth and heaven reversed, like a conundrum, except for the drowned limbs of trees reaching up from the water. Despite its beauty, the place has an air of desolation.

"Look again," says Anil, directing Tissa's gaze. "Over there. Towards the mountains. Now tell me what you see."

His head having cleared a little, Tissa seems at last to grasp what Anil wants.

"I see the Rock of Sigiriya."

"Good," Anil smiles. "You are beginning to understand. It is another landmark in our history. Built centuries ago by the Sinhalese king, Kasyapa."

"Who murdered his father and was defeated by his brother with the help of an Indian army," adds Asoka.

"Who asked your opinion?" snarls Anil.

"Nevertheless, it is the truth," rejoins Asoka, quietly.

"Whatever Kasyapa did, at least he was not a coward! When his army deserted him on the battlefield, he chose a glorious death rather than a dishonourable life. Seated on his great war elephant, in full view of the enemy, he stabbed himself in the neck, then calmly re-sheathed his dagger before dying."

"Some would say that suicide is an act of cowardice," says Asoka.

"Not as cowardly as running away!"

Anil's voice quavers and an angry nerve twitches in his cheek as he struggles to retain his composure. Asoka turns away and, staring out over the lake, seems lost in thought.

"Anyway, none of what you say is to the point," retorts Anil, determined to justify his argument.

"Sigiriya, like this tank, is proof that the country is ours. They are our birthright, signs of our ownership, planted in the soil long ago by our rulers. This land belongs to us, the Sinhalese, and we will take it back."

Asoka makes no reply. The dark outline of Sigiriya is etched on the horizon, rising up in the distance like a great tablet of stone. Is it really what Anil claims or simply a work of nature, the retreat of a princeling whose only concern was to preserve his own guilty life, not to create a legacy for future generations?

Anil seems to read Asoka's thoughts.

"If you want other examples, there is that of Dutugemunu, the Sinhalese prince who overthrew Elara, the Tamil king. Or there is the story of Vijaya, founder of our race. Are these not proof of our right, as Sinhalese, to this country?"

With his face still turned to Sigiriya, Asoka quietly replies: "All it proves is that we cannot learn from the past."

The stones on the shallow beach clink. Anil is standing beside Asoka.

"You are not the man I once knew," he murmurs.

Then, grasping Tissa's robe, Anil drags the boy forward, indicating that they should start walking again. But it is also a gesture indicative of fear: a fear that Asoka's words might contaminate one too weak to know his own mind.

The mystery of Asoka's disappearance confers a special status on Sriya. Her already interesting condition, not uncommon in itself, is the topic of frequent discussion, each villager offering their opinion as to how the shock will affect the unborn child.

Some say that it is an ill omen and that the child will have a tragic life if, indeed, it survives at all. Others, of a more pragmatic nature, point to the example of other fatherless children and how their lives, admittedly a little sadder and a little harder, are essentially the same as those born to two parents.

All sympathise with the expectant mother and are keen to show their support by constant visits to her home. However, Sriya's attitude to her loss and to the concern of her neighbours does not conform to what is expected. She neither weeps openly, nor wails, nor pulls her hair. In fact, the few who catch her at home unawares, report that, if anything, she is unnaturally calm and reluctant to speak of her troubles.

This inexplicable behaviour only makes her more interesting and increases speculation about her state of mind. Then, for a few days, no-one sees her, giving rise to a rumour that she, too, has disappeared. The village holds its breath, anticipating news of her suicide, in some cases, with indecent eagerness.

However, both assumptions are far from the truth. After responding politely to kindly enquiries after her health, Sriya has begun to long for peace. She does not cry in public. She cannot, because she cries all night. Unable to sleep, she can hardly stay awake during the day. Shock and exhaustion numb her, while the double encumbrance of grief and late pregnancy require all her remaining energy. She may seem calm to those visitors who see her, but her parents have begun to fear for her health as the radiant bloom fades from her cheeks and she becomes increasingly wan and listless.

At first, they thought it would be sufficient to shield her from prying eyes. When visitors approach, she is led to a shady corner of the yard and left to sit in a cool place until it is safe to re-enter the house. But this simple subterfuge has done nothing to stem the constant stream of neighbours, aunts, uncles and cousins, all enquiring after Sriya.

There is no peace to be had anywhere in the village. Becoming paler and more silent by the day, Sriya has lost her appetite and stopped eating, picking only at a few grains of rice and sipping a little boiled water.

Then, one day, she disappears. In desperation, her mother searches for her; around the house, around the yard, running first along the track into the forest until, on impulse, she turns and heads back towards the chena garden where she finds Sriya, slumped beneath the tree where she recently watched Asoka hoeing between the rows, her eyes wide and unblinking, staring at something in the far distance, as tears course silently down her cheeks.

"Will he ever come back, Amma?" she whispers.

"Of course, my darling," says her mother, gently putting her arms around her.

"Where has he gone?"

"I don't know, my love."

And holding Sriya's head against her shoulder, her mother weeps, too.

That night, while the rest of the village is asleep, Prema yokes the oxen to the cart and drives the two women down the deserted, moonlit track to a neighbouring hamlet where they will stay with an elderly aunt, out of the sight of prying eyes.

No-one has seen Sriya. New stories begin to circulate. Rumours, like gossamer, are spun from thin air. Sriya has collapsed. A light has been seen, late at night, burning in her window. She has given birth. To a dead baby. To a live baby. To a monster. But when questioned, the woman who acts as village midwife knows nothing of it.

Unhindered by fact, the village gossips begin to weave more intricate yarns. The baby has been born, but with defects so horrible that Sriya can never show it in public. Alternatively, the baby was perfect but stillborn, its little hands shielding its face as if to express shock at its father's disappearance.

Women linger around their neighbour's cooking fires, hoping for news and tongues clack ceaselessly as pots are stirred and embers coaxed into flame. The most irritating thing is that Prema will say nothing, although his wife, too, has become invisible. Why does he stay silent? It is unnatural. No-one has secrets in the village. Secrecy is a simple, but unspoken, taboo. If someone has a secret, it means they have something to hide and, if something is hidden, that means it is bad.

Stirred up by the local gossips, the women become suspicious, then pass their concerns on to the men. Has Sriya, mad with grief, killed the baby, then herself? Why then should her mother disappear? Is she dead also? Darker tales begin to circulate, about murder and secret burials in the forest. Then Prema, also, becomes an object of suspicion.

Yet, during all of this, he remains silent, hobbling about the yard, going about his business as best he can, politely responding to enquiries after his health while ignoring hints about Sriya's whereabouts. All he will say is that she is away with her mother. And from such simple remarks, even greater mysteries are made.

It is, therefore, a surprise to everyone when, a week or so later, a small boy comes running, breathless, into the village to announce that he has seen Sriya and her mother on the road. Word leaps like fire from house to house and soon everyone who has not gone to work in the fields is outside, pretending to sweep the yard, feed the chicken or tend the children.

Soon, the ox-cart, led by Prema, rattles into sight and the villagers, giving up all pretence of work, stop what they are doing to watch it pass. There, in the back of the cart, huddled against her mother, is Sriya, a little pale but otherwise healthy, smiling at the baby in her arms as it gurgles happily and makes little, jerky movements with its fist.

It is dawn. The forest is steeped in mist but, as the sun rises above the impenetrable canopy of trees, it rests on Sigiriya. The smooth, polished surface of the Mirror Wall glints and, for a few minutes, the letters engraved on its surface are illuminated as the words of poets, dead for many centuries, are momentarily brought to life.

As the sun passes over the surface of the Rock, the letters shimmer briefly, then expire, puffed out like candles. They are a memory of forbidden love, an undying tribute to those long dead.

Forged from a vast pillar of granite, displaced by seismic revolt and thrust skywards, the Rock towers above its surroundings and casts a long shadow over the land below: the caves and gardens; the ancient stone seats; the rough stone walls pitted with mysterious hand-cut hollows, the size of a man's fist; the narrow paths and stairways, their flags worn down by the passing of many feet and the groves of trees in which monkeys sleep, their tails and limbs hanging carelessly from the branches.

From here, the royal gardens stretch for many acres, their swathes of emerald lawn segmented by irrigation channels whose waters, running over beds of hewn stone, are pleasing to the eye and ear. The ancient cunning of engineers and stonemasons ensures that the waters never dry out and that the soft, broad-bladed grass that they feed provides a permanent, cooling carpet for the weary feet of travellers.

From here, great armies set out to meet their enemies in battle; the king mounted on his great war elephant, watched by the women of his harem from their place of safety at the top of the Rock, the ropes and ladders used for its ascent withdrawn and wound up in coils at the summit, awaiting the return of the victor and his men. But all is quiet now.

There are no sentries, posted on precarious ledges, watching for the arrival of an enemy; no painted halls to welcome guests; no bakery, no ovens, no smell of warm bread; no armoury filled with the ringing of hammers on metal, no swords being sharpened at the stone; no chattering concubines making their way through narrow streets to the rectangular pool where, giggling and laughing, they undress and drape the steps with their silks before descending into the water to bathe.

Now, the great fortress of Sigiriya is silent, empty and decayed. No-one walks its streets or bathes in its pools, its halls have crumbled and its people have gone. Its splendours are no more than a memory, evoked by small fragments of stone and remnants of paint. The only visitors these days arrive in motorised vehicles that belch foul-smelling fumes. They trample through the royal gardens, caper over the rocks and sully the water channels with their hot feet. Such behaviour would not have been tolerated in Kasyapa's day and such people would only have gained entry as labourers or artisans. Soon, they will arrive: an army of children and hobbling aunties, equipped with tiffin boxes, flasks and picnic-baskets.

But for now, there is peace. It is close to dawn and the sightseers will not arrive until later. The gardens are empty and the grass unbruised by the passing of human feet. Lit by the early morning sun and encircled by forest, Sigiriya rests undisturbed.

Sheltering in an angle of the Rock, high above ground, the Maidens are asleep. Protected from the sun by a deep lintel of stone, they dream of their old existence, enlivened by intrigue and passion. Now, chained to posterity by the artful strokes of a painter's brush, they are mere images of their former selves, unable to act or move in the living world, permitted only to observe its workings from afar.

Even Yaani, who by the use of her black art gained a temporary freedom, has once again been confined to the flat surface of the rock by her master. Separated from Leela, her successor and protégée, she now shows little interest in the world of humans and sleeps for days, or even weeks, at a time. Unlike her royal lover.

At the summit of the Rock, outlined against the sky, is the figure of a man. His long black hair is whipped by the morning breeze and the sunlight glances from his metal breast-plate as he walks backwards and forwards, pacing the ancient ramparts that are now no more than piles of stone.

The man pauses. Placing one foot on the broken parapet, he leans forward, shading his eyes with one hand as he stares eagerly into the distance, over the gardens and beyond the dark encircling forest, to the cities of men beyond. And his heart is filled with an ancient longing, newly-awoken. For he has received news from an unexpected quarter. An army is coming.

Kasyapa's heart stirs. He remembers the days when sentries were posted around the Rock, day and night, watching for the approach of his brother, Mogallana. For days, weeks, months, they watched for the sign – a cloud of dust rising in the distance – that would announce the arrival of Mogallana with the army that he had raised in India. Mogallana, dispossessed by his brother, returning after years of absence to avenge the death of his father.

"Hmph!" Kasyapa snorts with derision when he thinks of it. Mogallana, too weak to stand his ground had run away, all the way to India, where he had toured the royal courts like a beggar, snivelling about his bad luck to anyone who would listen, grovelling for help. And, at last, he had found it. The ruler of a south Indian kingdom had loaned him an army.

The Sinhalese had reason to fear India. It was like a tiger, prowling around a village, always there, ever a threat. Only this Indian tiger had much bigger teeth and could swallow an island whole. What began as help for the Sinhalese, inevitably resulted in India helping itself. Mogallana, the fool, had invited a predator into the cattle-yard.

Yet, he had won. An unforeseen twist of fate had delivered the victory to Mogallana. The armies had joined in battle and Kasyapa had already felled many enemies when his elephant, charging towards a group of Indian mercenaries, sensed a hidden swamp and veered away. Seeing the royal elephant in retreat, Kasyapa's army turned, abandoning their king to the enemy. Determined not to be taken alive, Kasyapa drew his sword and slit his throat. And so, without courage or cunning, Mogallana had secured the throne.

Kasyapa picks up a stone and hurls it into the air. His defeat still rankles. But now there is one who might help him. Far below, the stone crashes into a tree. The branches quiver and several monkeys, roused from sleep, leap to the ground. They run about, hysterical with rage, protesting against their rude arousal then, mystified as to its cause, they quietly slope off to find another resting place.

Kasyapa resumes his post and stares into the distance. He is expecting a visitor.

1958: Kasyapa's throne

A small cloud of vapour rises above the forest but, unlike the morning mist, it does not disperse, but continues to rise seeming, if anything, to coalesce and become denser. Propelled by a mysterious thermal, it floats towards Kasyapa until it is hovering just above the ground a few feet from where he stands.

The centre of the cloud begins to glow with an intense green light then, suddenly, the surrounding vapour is sucked inwards until, curdling and thickening, it forms the shape of a man. Small threads of mist encircle his waist. They writhe and twist then, gradually, resolve themselves into several monstrous snakes. Stepping down from his cloudy platform, Hooniyam spreads his arms in greeting.

"My Lord."

Kasyapa bows, hoping to avoid an embrace which would, of necessity, involve contact with those squirming snakes. Of course, they cannot harm him now but, in life, he feared them and, even now, the sight of them fills him with loathing.

Hooniyam chuckles. He can read Kasyapa's mind. The king's gesture of obeisance is just a shield for his disgust. In ages past, Hooniyam was never welcome here. During the short but splendid years of Kasyapa's reign, Hooniyam was just a minor demon, worshipped only by peasants and, even then, despised as much as he was feared. Kasyapa was at the height of his power while Hooniyam was rootling about the forest floor, scratching up worms with his tusks, so hungry that sometimes he was forced to scavenge the village midden for scraps of food.

In those days, Kasyapa's court was the centre of refinement, of art and martial power. Only the beautiful or strong were accepted and Hooniyam was neither. And yet, there were times, in his great loneliness, when he crept out of the forest at night and, standing at the base of the Rock, looked upwards to the many bright lights burning at its summit.

In the days before he learned to hunt human prey, Hooniyam watched the sentries changing guard, climbing up and down narrow stairs cut into the sheer rock-face to the narrow ledges that served as look-outs. Occasionally, they would lose their footing, either through sleep or carelessness, and fall to their deaths.

On these occasions, Hooniyam would follow the changing expression on their faces as they plunged earthwards; first disbelief, then shock, then fear, before the sudden obliteration of life. Strange how leisurely it all seemed, until they hit the ground. Of course, such occurrences were fortuitous from Hooniyam's point of view: fresh meat providing a welcome change from his diet of bugs and beetles.

But there was also another reason for his nocturnal visits to the Rock. At that time, he was still more human than demon and, being of royal birth, he longed for the life of the court. From his hiding place in the trees, Hooniyam followed the lives of the Rock's inhabitants, with senses sharpened by animal instinct but interpreted by human understanding.

Although he could see little, the Rock provided a fascinating tapestry of sound: faint strains of music, lyres and flutes; trumpets announcing the king's arrival; drums beating the muster of the army; whispered assignations of lovers; raucous laughter of drunks; conversations between sentries, conducted in low voices, against orders.

And so, he learned much. Not just the homely memories of children and wives, recited by sentries trying to keep each other awake, nor the more interesting news of illicit lovers, but the plans and affairs of the king himself. And it was then, rejected and reviled by men, that Hooniyam first began to plot his revenge.

He discovered Mogallana, hiding in the wilderness and, at night, he crept alongside the sleeping prince and whispered a plan in his ear. Mogallana would never have thought of it himself, he was too naïve but, at Hooniyam's prompting, he set out to sea in a fisherman's boat and crossed the Palk Strait to India, reversing the journey that Vijaya, founder of the Sinhalese dynasty, had made so many centuries before.

And, with a little more coaxing from Hooniyam, India came to Mogallana's aid. The wily old Rajah had money to spare – and men. He could afford to lose a few. But, if Mogallana won, his investment would be returned a thousand-fold. So, Mogallana got his army. But that was only the beginning.

On the day of the battle, Hooniyam had hidden behind a rock, carefully following the progress of the armies and especially that of Kasyapa. What a splendid figure he had been, seated high on his war elephant, spear in hand, the sunlight glinting on its tip as he raised it above his head to direct his warriors into the fray.

The thunderous beating of drums that had led the armies into battle was replaced by the clash of steel and the cries of men as blades were driven deep into flesh and blood spurted in crimson fountains from deadly wounds. Hooniyam had licked his lips. He would feast tonight and for many nights to come. Then, he saw his chance.

In his battle-rage, Kasyapa had ridden ahead of his men and become separated from them. He was charging towards a group of enemy infantry, intending to trample them under the feet of his elephant. Seizing this opportunity, Hooniyam leapt out from behind the rock and into the path of the elephant. He danced about, shaking his crazy mane of hair, waving his arms, rolling his eyes, screaming demonic curses. Men could not see him. But the elephant could. The creature, already goaded and terrified beyond endurance, turned tail and ran, bearing his master away from the scene of battle. After that, the end came quickly.

Once again, concealed behind his rock, Hooniyam had watched as Kasyapa, in the despair of defeat, had slashed his throat with his own sword. Such was the man's valour that he had even re-sheathed the blade before falling dead from the elephant. Then, Hooniyam had watched the king's spirit as it rose from his body, shouting imprecations at the air, bewailing his bad fortune.

After that, Hooniyam had spread the story about the elephant sensing a hidden swamp and even Kasyapa never knew the true reason for his downfall. It was a great joke and Hooniyam has laughed about it ever since. It has all worked out just as he planned for here is Kasyapa, a mere shade, dependant on Hooniyam's intervention – as any subject should be.

It does not worry Hooniyam that the king secretly despises him. He abandoned the desire to be loved long ago. But to be needed. That is the thing. And Kasyapa needs Hooniyam for, far greater than his contempt for the demon-god, is his desire for power, undimmed after all these centuries of impotence. Hooniyam makes a courteous bow to the king, bending low to hide a smirk of satisfaction.

"Greetings, Lord Kasyapa. I trust I did not keep you waiting."

Hooniyam knows that Kasyapa has been expecting him for two days. The king opens his mouth to say something, then thinks better of it.

"Of course not. My Lord Hooniyam is welcome at any time."

Kasyapa's lips are compressed in a tight smile. Hooniyam chuckles to himself. In the days when Kasyapa was truly king, the likes of Hooniyam were barred from Sigiriya. He would not have been allowed as far as the ditch beyond the outer gate. But now he is the king's favoured guest. In fact, the only one that Kasyapa has entertained for centuries. For you cannot count the daily insurgence of trippers as guests. They are merely visitors. Sightseers do not come by invitation.

"Shall we?" says Hooniyam, gesturing towards the granite throne which, now unprotected by painted vaults and ceilings, lies open to the sky. Kasyapa nods his assent and the two walk over to the throne. Kasyapa is on the point of seating himself when he receives a rude reminder of his status.

"Ahhh!" Hooniyam stretches his arms and yawns. "I have travelled so far in the last few days. On our business. I am quite worn out."

"Forgive me. Please. Sit down."

With as much grace as he can muster, Kasyapa stands aside and indicates that Hooniyam should rest himself upon the only remaining seat in Sigiriya. And so it happens. Without thinking, Kasyapa cedes his throne to the demon-god.

"Draw near, my friend. We must discuss our strategy."

Hooniyam points to a block of masonry that might once have served as a footstool. The king obediently seats himself, although not without some awkwardness. It is difficult to squat so low when wearing armour. He removes his sword from the belt at his waist and lays it on the ground, at Hooniyam's feet. He seems not to realise the symbolism of this act, being distracted by what appears to be an unpleasant smell.

When touring outside the temple, it is not Hooniyam's practice to wash. He regards the performance of ablutions as purely ceremonial, not necessary or, in his case, even desirable. He has been travelling for many weeks. Trying to draw only shallow breaths, Kasyapa reaches inside his breast-plate and, drawing out a delicate silk handkerchief, presses it to his nose.

"A cold," he mumbles and, from the strange tinge of green in his face, one would almost believe him to be sick.

"Really? But the air is so clear up here. You must take one of my special preparations. I will get something made up for you."

"Thank you."

If anything, the king looks even greener than before. Hooniyam is enjoying this game immensely but time is pressing. They must get down to business. Bending forward, he begins to whisper in the king's ear. Miraculously, Kasyapa's biliousness passes and he removes the scented cloth from his nose. His eyes are lit with a fierce excitement.

"You are sure of this?"

"Certain."

"What must I do?"

"You must wait, then come when summoned. But only then. Understand?"

"Yes, yes, my lord."

Hooniyam is sure of Kasyapa's support. In fact, he never doubted it, but he decides to have one last piece of fun. He pretends to inspect his long nails which are filthy and broken, inlaid with moss and dirt.

"And you are sure you have nothing else to divert you? Some human interest, perhaps?"

"Pah! That is all over. It was a game. Something to pass the time. I no longer have time for such time-wasting pursuits. The mortals are of no real interest to me."

"Not even the young man who looks so like you? Arjun, I think you called him."

"Not even him. Although, strangely, he helped me to focus on my own problems. They have now been resolved."

Kasyapa looks grim. His thoughts wander to the image of the beautiful Maiden, now frozen to the wall of Sigiriya, deprived of her powers. A pity, because she was one his favourites, but he has ceased to grieve for her. Her intrigues were a distraction. Now that she is impotent, he is no longer tormented by the chattering anguish of the harem. The absence of tale-telling and tears is sufficient recompense for her loss. He can live without her. Just.

"Good. I'm glad to hear it. Now, I must be off."

Hooniyam gathers up his robes and his sudden movement awakens the serpents which have been dozing gently. Kasyapa is suddenly confronted by six pairs of cold, unblinking eyes. He is determined not to show his fear but he cannot suppress the cold tingle that skims up his spine. Hooniyam smiles indulgently.

"Farewell, my son. Look for my signal."

The demon-god clicks his fingers and dissolves into a cloud of green mist which hovers for a few seconds above the surface of the Rock, then whirls away, spinning like a small tornado. Kasyapa shades his eyes. Far in the distance, the cloud hovers over a thickly-wooded mountainside then, as if by force of gravity, it is sucked down into the trees and disappears.

"Why there?"

Kasyapa scratches his head. He remembers the place from the old days. It was Hooniyam's lair – one could hardly call it a shrine – and, as far as he knows, has long been abandoned. And yet he senses something; a busyness within the trees, like the stirring of ants, an energy that he has not felt for a long time. An army is gathering.

The car is motionless, yet Walter grips the steering wheel in both hands, tapping it softly with his middle finger. It is his habit while waiting. He peers sideways out of the window at the little, low house set back from the road, hiding behind its covered verandah, approached by a set of wooden stairs that creak with every step.

Like so many Island homes, this house looks grander than it really is: its true nature concealed by gimcrack frippery. But, underneath, it is like most other houses: the mortar, which glues its cement blocks, mixed with too much sand. Almost as soon as the brick was sandwiched together, the mortar began to crumble, creating little holes for the ants and other insects who, hidden from sight, gnaw and chew and scratch, always searching for a way in to what they imagine is the paradise beyond, a place of shade and plenty.

The paint on the brickwork is peeling and any varnish has long since disappeared from the woodwork, allowing the sun to crack and warp the timber. Walter doubts if those sash windows have ever opened and, with one glance, he knows that the boards of the verandah hold unseen hazards; long splinters that lie in wait, ready to drive themselves deep into a bare-soled foot.

Even the shining metal vases, filled with anthuriums and trailing plants, ranged artistically along the verandah, are not what they seem, having originally been designed to contain cheese, jam, or butter.

There is no shame for the owners of such a house. In fact, many would consider it a most desirable residence. Walter himself has no roof to call his own. But what puzzles the driver is why the Government Agent's young assistant should continue to live here. It is far from the office and he works long hours. It is not in the best part of town. There are better areas, closer to work and still affordable for someone of moderate means; places that are much better suited to the requirements of a young and ambitious civil servant.

So why here? It does not have a particularly welcoming aspect. Granted, the frangipani tree that shades the verandah is particularly beautiful. He can smell it from here and he knows from previous conversations with his young master that the tree overlooks his bedroom. In fact, Arjun has expressed a particular affection for it. But one does not stay in a house for the sake of a tree. And besides, these stiff-limbed trees with their whirling, scented blossom, have funereal connotations. Their flowers are used as garlands for the dead as well as the living.

Walter shakes his head. The house has something sombre about it, a joylessness that he cannot explain but which always seems to infect him when he looks at it for any length of time. What does Arjun find to keep him here?

As he watches, the front door opens a crack, emitting a faint echo of voices. Walter reaches for the catch on the door, ready to step out of the car and greet his master but, when the front door to the house opens, it is not Arjun, but a man and two girls who emerge. Walter knows the man to be Raj, the father of the house. He even knows the names of the daughters. How does he know this? They have never spoken, although Raj always acknowledges Walter with a cheery smile. It must be that Arjun speaks of them. In fact, now that he thinks of it, Arjun is always talking about the various individuals of this household: as if they were his daughters, as if it was his family.

Walter watches as Raj and the two children descend the steps. Raj is becoming stout and looks satisfied with himself. Leaving the children to play on the steps, he disappears around the side of the house and, after a few minutes emerges, pushing a battered old bicycle. The metal guard is loose and clangs against the front wheel and, as the pedals turn, the chain seems to slacken then, all of a sudden, pull tight. Walter wonders how Raj manages to ride that bike and watches with interest as Raj steadies the vehicle at the curb and, with a movement surprisingly graceful for a man of his stature, swings a leg over the saddle and mounts it.

Raj says something and the smaller girl runs towards him, her face alight with happiness. Bending over, he lifts her up and places her on the handlebars. She shrieks with pleasure. The other girl, carrying a school bag over one shoulder, seems sulky and diffident. Raj speaks to her, his tone a little sharper this time. She rises from her seat on the step and walks slowly towards him, dragging her feet but, when he holds out his hand, she runs forward and climbs onto the metal rack behind the saddle, her legs dangling to one side of the wheel. Then the little party starts on its way, Raj pedalling forward slowly, controlling the bicycle with extraordinary ease, like a circus performer. Walter smiles to himself and wonders how long it has taken Raj to perfect this art.

Walter gazes at the front door of the house, but it is closed and there is no sign of Arjun. He has the feeling that it will be a long wait. Not that he minds. Waiting is part of his job. It gives him time to think, to observe. But, today, he feels restless. He wants to stretch his legs and he is in need of company. Not the talkative company of friends, but the undemanding, jostling company of a crowd. There is a market across the street and, on the pretext of finding something to eat, he gets out of the car and strolls towards the stalls.

Soon, he is immersed in the crowd. Gently pummelled and pressed, he is passed along between shoppers whose flesh is as warm and soft as dough. All around him is an intoxicating aroma: the pungent odour of hair oil and sweat mingles with the delicate scent of flowers and freshly-cooked bread. It is like falling into a lullaby. He is rocked and comforted and close to falling asleep. He has not ventured out on his own for a long time. Not since that man approached him in the bar.

Relishing his freedom, Walter examines the wares displayed on the stalls as he listens to housewives haggling with the stall-keepers.

"Bull-toes, brother. ... toffee."

A smiling young face is looking up at him from the other side of the sweet stall. A Moslem boy, dressed in immaculate white clothes and a crocheted cap that glows white in the sun. Walter catches his breath. Perhaps it is a trick of the light, but the boy seems to shine from within and Walter, in his dream-like state, wonders if he is speaking to a vision. He blinks and looks again. The boy is still there. Flesh and blood. A child on the cusp of manhood with a thin fringe of hair on his upper lip and a wide, ingenuous smile.

"Sweets, brother? They are the very best. My father makes them. A family recipe. No-one can make sweets like him."

Walter laughs and points to a pile of cinder toffee. The boy measures out the toffee into a battered pair of scales then, swiftly rolling a square of paper into a cone, he tips the toffee into it and folds the loose end of the paper over to form a lid. Walter hands a few pice to the boy and has just taken the packet of sweets from him when a commotion breaks out at the far end of the market. With herd-like instinct, the crowd falls silent. All heads are turned towards the source of the trouble.

586

Two Sinhalese men are arguing with the owner of fish-stall, a Tamil. The trader is waving his arms, as if to shoo the men away, but one, leaning over the counter, is yelling, jabbing his finger into the man's face. The Tamil yells something at the top of his voice. There is a brief silence then, suddenly, both Sinhalese take hold of the stall and tip it over, scattering baskets of fish all over the pavement. Clutching his head, the man screams, then crouches and tries to gather up the fish, but no-one will want it now, dusted with filth from the street. The two men saunter off, laughing.

"That is not the first time," says the boy. His face no longer emits its radiant light, but is clouded with fear and sadness.

A sombre mood falls over the market and clutching his packet of sweets, Walter hurries back to the comparative safety of the car. Having locked himself in, he takes several deep breaths, trying to quiet the violent pounding of his heart. Why is it that such scenes disturb him so much these days? They are, after all, part of everyday life. And yet, he senses that something has changed. A delicate equilibrium has been thrown out of balance. The instances of anger that he witnesses in the streets are no longer random and isolated, but connected with each other.

Nervously, he looks in the rear mirror, to see if he is being watched. It is a feeling of which he can never quite rid himself. Ever since that man approached him in the bar. Opening the packet, he takes out a chunk of toffee and pushes it into his cheek, sucking on it urgently in an attempt to calm himself.

Gradually, the wild beating of his heart slows while, outside, the market returns to normal. Soon, it is as if nothing had happened; but the memory of that ugliness remains, like a small crack in a pane of glass. Walter looks nervously towards the front door of the house and wishes that Arjun would appear.

Finally, his prayers are answered. Arjun emerges, a large case in his hand, his eyes shaded by a panama hat of good quality but with a small hole in the crown. He is followed by a woman who Walter recognises as the landlady. She is a good ten years older than her lodger, but still beautiful and visibly pregnant. She says something and Arjun turns back, inclining his head towards her. For a moment, Walter thinks they will kiss but, possibly conscious that this is a public place, Arjun turns away and walks slowly down the steps. The woman's face is tense, contorted, as if she is holding back tears.

Walter helps Arjun to stow the case in the trunk then helps him into the back seat of the car. Inside the car, Arjun does not remove the hat that shades his eyes. This strikes Walter as unusual. As they pull away from the kerb, the woman, who is still standing on the steps, waves with one hand while pressing the other to her mouth, as if to stop herself from crying. Arjun does not look at her. Crestfallen, she turns and walks back up the steps, then merges into the darkness of the doorway.

As the car is about to turn the corner at the end of the street, Arjun suddenly turns his head, craning his neck as if trying to catch a last glimpse of her. But she is not there. He slumps back into the seat with a faint moan, his head down, his face hidden by the brim of his hat.

"There is a story to tell here," thinks Walter.

It is around three in the morning, the time at which the forest always seems a little quieter. The creakings, croakings and cries of its night-time inhabitants, having reached a crescendo, subside into a soft chorus; a gently throbbing murmur in which, except for an occasional yelp of fear or pain, no single voice can be distinguished from the rest.

Above the clearing, the moon is full and resplendent; the shadow of the hare sharply defined. No man has yet set foot on the moon and, for now, it remains undefiled, a thing of mystery, a sacred screen onto which man's aspirations are projected through legend and belief.

Tonight the moon is full so Asoka knows that it is a Poya day, although he does not know which day of the week it is and has almost forgotten the month. He is lying on his back, staring at the moon, hoping that neither of his companions will wake. This is his moment of peace.

For many days, he has not been able to think or act for himself, being driven like a beast of burden, stopping infrequently for food or water and short periods of rest, before being dragged back onto his feet and, when exhaustion makes him unwilling, being pushed and slapped until the physical pain incurred by standing still outweighs that of moving. Then, he cannot think. He does not have the energy.

But, at night, he finds tranquillity and has trained himself to wake when he knows the others will be sleeping. At this time, his thoughts are his own. And they are all of Sriya. As he stares at the moon, he wonders where she is, for the bearings of his compass have changed.

He has been blown onto another course; one not of his choosing which requires him to navigate new and hazardous waters. Sometimes, he thinks, it is not a matter of exercising control, but of simply holding on, letting fate lead him where it will. He has begun to pray again, regularly, as sailors do when lost at sea. These prayers are not just a plea for help, but an acknowledgement of his own weakness.

As he looks at the hare, he thinks of Sriya and prays for her safety. Several times since his abduction, he has had the terrible sense that she is unreal – a figment of his imagination – and the more he tries to conjure her image, the more she eludes him. It is at such times that his despair becomes greatest. It is then that he wishes to die. For Sriya is his life. Without her, there is nothing, only the black hollow of himself.

Then, even in the bright light of day, he is enveloped by nocturnal despair. Yet, when the darkness is deepest, he remembers. There will be a child. Their child. For this reason, he must endure. Survive. He must cling to the wreckage of his old life and see where it takes him. He can no longer direct his course. He can only wait. For what and for how long, he cannot tell. But he knows that he must endure, clinging to life like a dying man, happy to survive another day.

***

Asoka is startled by a loud, rattling snore. Uneasy in his sleep, Tissa claws at the air, then moans and rolls over. Misery has reduced him to a beast. Asoka pities him but he also fears Tissa for, as long as he lives, Tissa will not forget Sriya or the pain he has suffered on her account. As long as he carries that pain, Tissa will never be able to rest. But what is the cure? Asoka shudders. It can only be death. Or something worse.

He has seen enough of Tissa in the last few days to know that he has become a stranger to mercy. He is repellent. A brute compelled by primitive instinct. Asoka has caught the look in Tissa's eye when young girls pass him on the road. He often turns to look at them, his face full of indecent longing. Asoka forgets all pity when he sees what is written there.

His thoughts turn to Anil, who lies as motionless as the effigy on a tomb, his face white in the moonlight. In sleep, he has the majestic stillness of a dead pharaoh. It is enough, thinks Asoka, to convince one of reincarnation. Until now, he never realised the depth of Anil's strength. He has a relentless determination that Asoka never had, even at his most committed.

Asoka has experimented with many beliefs and found them wanting. Only his love of Sriya has awakened such single-minded devotion. Anil, however, has dedicated himself to a principle and, however wrong-headed he may be, Asoka admires his constancy. But he fears him also, for Anil's kind of zeal permits no argument or rational debate. It is fanaticism and to question it is blasphemy.

Something brushes against Asoka's foot. He jerks his leg away and sits up, but can see nothing. It is not the first time that he has imagined strange phantoms. The forest is full of whisperings and sometimes he thinks he sees things. He awoke the other night and thought he saw the shadow of a strange man bending over Anil, whispering in his ear as he slept. But, when Asoka rubbed his eyes, the man was gone.

And now he has been brought back to the scene of his crime. He is haunted by memories of this place and what happened here. They have stalked him since that awful day, even casting a shadow over his love for Sriya. And here he is again.

The clearing is somewhat overgrown, but still recognisable. There is the place in which the men brewed tea, the pathways through the trees. Apart from the lushness of the vegetation, it is as if nothing has changed. And yet, a terrible silence lingers here. There are no birds, not even the old crow that used to hunt for scraps.

But there are other things. Several times, out of the corner of his eye, Asoka has seen the figure of a man, dangling in the trees, its head hanging lop-sided on its shoulder, a hideous grin on its bloated face. Yet, each time he has turned to confront it, it has disappeared. He tells himself that he has become deranged due to lack of sleep and food. But these arguments cannot dispel his fear, or the image of the dead man.

The moon shines pale over the tree tops, tipping them with silver. It floods into the clearing, illuminating the tin roof and dull, grimy windows of Mennan's cabin. Unable to look at it, Asoka averts his eyes.

Many miles from where her husband is held captive, Sriya also gazes at the moon. Seated on the thin mattress which she shared with Asoka, she is nursing her child, feeling its tiny mouth crimp around her nipple, then the pull as it sucks. Its little round head is the size of a gourd, its stomach no bigger than a ripe cashew nut. It is frail and helpless and yet its tiny hands and toothless mouth exert a powerful grip far in excess of its size. If a man had such power in his hands, he would be able to crush stone with his fingers.

Sriya strokes the delicate wisps of hair that meet in a point on the child's forehead. They are smooth and fine, like strands of silk rather than hair. In a few months, the little head will be shaved. Babyhood will end and childhood begin. Will Asoka be there to see it? Will he ever come back?

She holds the baby close, covering it with her shawl so that only its face is visible. It is all that remains of Asoka, the only proof that he ever existed. He brought nothing with him and has left nothing behind. Only this child. She weeps quietly, as she often does when she is alone. At night.

Her parents are both sleeping or, at least, she supposes from the silence that they are. She envies all those who can close their eyes and rest peacefully until dawn. The baby's demands for frequent night-time feeds deny her this luxury. She is forced to waken while the world is still dark and empty and to confront her fears when they are most acute. Everyone has said that the child will be a compensation for her loss and, in some ways, it is; but this is a different love. It will never replace her love for her husband, nor assuage her longing for him.

Since the day of his disappearance, the men of the village have searched far and wide, but there is no sign of him and there has been no news from other villages of any sighting. She does not even know what route he took. And that, at least, would have been a comfort for then she would have known where to direct her thoughts. As it is, she can only address the one point which they have in common: the moon. Tonight, it is a full moon. She can see its lower quarter gleaming through a corner of the window as it floods the room with a pale light that washes the surfaces with silver but leaves crevices and corners in deepest darkness.

Softly, Sriya rises from her mattress and, clutching the child to her, walks to the window. There is the hare, emblazoned on the moon, the sign of mercy and compassion. Holding her child's tiny fist, Sriya traces the hare's outline with her finger while she murmurs a prayer for Asoka's safety, a ritual that she repeats whenever the hare is visible.

"Send him home safe. To me." Then, correcting herself: "To us."

Her prayer finished, she lowers her gaze and, as she does so, something catches her eye. A slight movement at the edge of the moonlit path leading into the forest. A figure, draped in loose folds of cloth, its head covered, is creeping back to the village. Manju. So the rumours are true.

By now, even Sriya has heard of Manju's nocturnal visits to the forest and of the broken eggshells, bearing Asoka's name, piled at the foot of the old tree. Instinctively, Sriya curls her hand around the baby's head, shielding it from the poison of despair that Manju seems to sow with every step.

The woman that Sriya once regarded almost as a mother is now a ruin of her former self; a cankered wreck of hopelessness whose only solace is to blame others for her pain. She tiptoes forward on feet so painfully thin that they appear to be little more than bone, held together by a frail membrane of skin. Then, sensing that she is being watched, she stops and looks around her. Sriya draws away from the window, holding her breath.

"Do not let her see me. Do not let her see me," she prays, although she has never believed in the evil eye. Until now. When she looks again, Manju is gone.

***

Neleni is also awake: with Raj, asleep, beside her. Stretched out on her back, like a corpse in a tomb, she wonders what it would be like to be dead. She might as well be. Arjun is leaving her. She knows it. The pale light of the moon bathes her face and highlights the contours of her body so that she glows with a pale aura. She places a hand on the gentle swell of her stomach as a tear, lit by the moonlight, runs slowly down her cheek.

1958: Dynamite

At daybreak, the deserted camp-site comes to life. Asoka, having finally drifted off to sleep a couple of hours ago, is awoken by the grunting of a large engine. The smell of diesel fumes fills his nostrils and he awakes to the shouting of men. Rolling onto one side, he wipes the dew off his face and pulls the old piece of sacking that serves as a blanket closer around him. Even in this hot country, nights are cold in the mountains.

Both Tissa and Anil have left their sleeping places. They are hurrying about the clearing, speaking to the newcomers. Anil addresses a man who appears to be their leader, while Tissa directs the other men to stow sacks on the lorry, swinging them backwards and forwards several times until there is enough momentum to heave them over the tailgate.

Asoka recognises several faces among the twenty or so men busying themselves about the lorry: old acquaintances; men who worked here with him on the road project; men who murdered Mennan. On his orders. He shudders and squeezes his eyes shut, trying to expel the image of the hanging body that has haunted him ever since his return to this cursed place. But it only becomes clearer: a memory set in crystal. The screaming and pleading, the pathos of a hunted animal facing death, the hopelessness in the man's eyes as he realised there was no escape. And what struck him most keenly: Mennan, whispering the name of his wife, over and over, like a prayer.

It had shocked Asoka that a man like that, a liar, a cheat and a thief, was capable of such intense love. Death, at the end, had stripped away all the evil and left only the good. A pure and selfless love that wanted nothing for itself. A philosopher, used to turning accepted principles on their heads, might argue that the purest expression of love is when a lover allows himself to be corrupted for the sake of his beloved. After all, he is sacrificing the most valuable part of himself: his soul. And Mennan did just that.

Painfully, Asoka raises himself on one elbow. The night-cold has turned his spine to stone and the bones in his back grind against each other like small pebbles.

"Hey, you. Come and help here!"

With a sweeping gesture of his arm, Anil indicates that Asoka should join the men at the lorry. Slowly, he rises to his feet and walks over to them. They are silent. Suspicious. Of course, they have all heard the rumours: that he ran away, betrayed them to the police, even killed himself; but no-one had expected to see him back here. Silent and watchful, they part to let him through. Asoka picks up a sack and, with a single swing, flings it over the tailgate of the lorry. It lands with a dull thud, perfectly upright.

"He's certainly got more muscles than before," says one man, a big, burly fellow with a hollow voice.

The others laugh, but it is a joke among themselves, not intended for Asoka to share. He neither smiles nor acknowledges their laughter but simply hauls another sack onto the lorry, then another. His work in the fields has taught him that beasts of burden have no feelings, at least, not any worth worrying about. In fact, it surprises him that comments which previously would have stung him, now make no impression. Seeing that he is impervious to their remarks, the other men return sullenly to their work. Soon, all the sacks are loaded, but there is still space in the back of the lorry.

"Now this," orders Anil, pointing to a pile of metal boxes lying in the deep shade under a tree.

Asoka awaits his turn as the men line up. The man at the front of the queue lifts the first box, grunting under the weight, then heaves it onto his shoulder. As he passes, Asoka gets a better look at the box. Painted dull green, it has a white skull and cross-bones painted on the side – the usual warning to illiterate labourers to exercise caution. Then, he sees black letters, painted along the side of the box in rough stencil: "DYNAMITE".

Leaving the queue, he runs over to where Anil is speaking to the leader of the gang.

"What are you doing? Are you mad?"

Taken off guard, Anil and the other man stare at Asoka, unable to understand the reason for the disturbance; then, recovering his wits, Anil strikes Asoka with the back of his hand, hitting him hard across the mouth. Tissa, who is only a few feet away from his master, bounds forward and, grabbing Asoka's arms, pulls them back and up behind his back, forcing him to his knees. Anil stares down at Asoka, his eyes alight with cold anger, but he cannot control the tremor in his voice.

"Put him over there," he motions towards Mennan's cabin. "And this time, secure him."

Twisting Asoka's arm until it feels as if it will part with its socket, Tissa half-drags, half-pushes his captive up the steps into the filthy den which was once Mennan's office. Pushing Asoka into a chair, he ties his ankles to the legs of the chair and his hands behind his back.

"You're lucky I don't gag you," he sneers, giving Asoka a kick as he passes. "Keep quiet, or I will."

As he leaves, Tissa pulls the door and tries to shut it, but it has warped and will not close. Asoka hears him cursing. The door quivers and shakes as Tissa yanks at the handle, but its swollen timbers are wedged firmly against the floor.

"Pah! Why am I bothering? You're not going anywhere."

Asoka listens, straining his ears. He hears Tissa, padding across the verandah, down the creaking steps and then, after a few seconds silence, he hears his voice, soft and distant, as he makes his report to Anil. After that, there is just a blur of noise: men shouting, Anil giving orders, the thud and scrape of metal boxes being loaded onto the lorry. Then, he smells smoke and, for one awful moment, he thinks that they have set light to the cabin. But it is the smell of a wood-fire.

Their work finished, the men are brewing tea and eating whatever meagre rations they have brought with them. Asoka even thinks that he can smell the aroma of rice. He has not eaten today and, although used to an inadequate and unreliable diet, his stomach begins to plague him with hunger.

Then, he smells another type of smoke; not wood-smoke this time, but the thin blue smoke of bidis; a smell that is accompanied by the gentle hum of voices. The men are standing around, under the shade of the trees as they used to, smoking and talking. It brings back memories of his former life, a past that he wants to forget.

It is as if he has always been confined within the walls of this foul-smelling cabin: like a genie in a lamp. He is incarcerated within the tawdry remains of another man's life. There is no escape. This cabin is both prison and torture chamber. He can smell the despair and the fear.

He sees the ringed stains of a whisky glass on the table, fragments of paper torn from letters that Mennan started then discarded, the pen that wrote them. He imagines Mennan, sitting at that table, looking out of the dull, fly-spotted window; alone and abandoned, praying for deliverance which, when it came, was dealt by a cruel and unforgiving god. And he, Asoka, had been that god's instrument although he had thought himself a non-believer.

As he stares at the table with its whisky stains and writing instruments, Asoka can almost see Mennan, staring out of the window into the darkness, a condemned man awaiting his executioner. He would not have shaved for many hours. The stubble covering his chin would have been flecked with grey; a contrast to the dyed hair on his head, of deepest black.

As he prepared to write, Mennan would have rolled up the sleeves of his immaculate white shirt – one of the ones that he always wore with tailor's stitching around the cuffs – only by now, it would have been stained with sweat. He would have drunk glass after glass of whisky as he stared out of that blank window, trying to compose letters, at least one of which would have been addressed to his wife.

What had he asked for? Help? Forgiveness? Whatever it was, the letters were never completed: the remains of some of them still lie scattered about the floor, some rolled into balls, others torn into shreds, all mildewing and forgotten.

Asoka experiences a sharp stab of pain, like a kick in the stomach. What if he were to die here? No-one would know where he was. His body might never be found. And Sriya would spend the rest of her life wondering why he had left her. He must get home. He must not die like Mennan. He must see Sriya again. Explain. Ask her forgiveness.

He struggles frantically in the chair, but it is useless. The more he tries to get free, the tighter the ropes become. Then, he remembers something that Sriya told him. Tissa had always been clever with knots. As a child, he had spent hours playing with a length of string, tying intricate loops and bows. No-one ever knew where he had learned to do it, but they had all marvelled at his ability.

How did Sriya know that? Why had she told him? Of course. Sriya and Tissa had been childhood friends. The village had expected them to marry. It was all settled. Until Asoka came along. Extraordinary. He had almost forgotten Sriya's previous connection with Tissa. His happiness with her has blotted out all pain; both his own and other people's. Love has made him selfish. But now, without her, he has time to reflect and his thoughts return to Mennan.

***

For months, Mennan has haunted him. Yet, until now, he has had only two guises: one, the repellent bloated figure, swinging at the end of a rope, more like the effigy of a man than the man himself; the other, a phantom that taunts Asoka from the shadows, haunting the uncertain margin where sight and perception meet, a demon of the lower orders sent back to torment his murderer.

But now, sitting in the same, dismal cabin in which Mennan lived out his last, miserable hours, Asoka realises that neither image is a true representation of the real man. Both are simply concoctions of his fear, manifestations of his guilt, the means by which his own conscience refuses to let him forget.

Only now, does he sense Mennan's real presence. The cigar stubs and accumulated ash under the table, the empty whisky bottle that rolled over the floor until it met the wall, even Mennan's jacket hanging from a peg. The authorities have overlooked that. It must have hung here ever since the night on which he died.

It seems pathetic now, the expensive linen jacket of which Mennan was so proud, its sleeves still wrinkled at the elbows, the seam at the back slightly stretched at the shoulders where it had moulded itself to Mennan's plump form. The inside of the collar darker, shiny with wear and sweat and, trapped within the broad weft of linen, relics of Mennan himself; a hair, a drop of aftershave, perhaps, even, the imprint of a cheek where Mennan's wife had laid her head against his shoulder. As Sriya used to.

Then Asoka remembers. By all accounts, Mennan's wife was not given to sentiment. She was beautiful, mercenary and faithless. She would not have performed any casual act of affection. Everything she gave was purchased from her, handed over at an allotted time and place. It was a relationship based on transaction. Once over, the service would not be repeated unless first negotiated and paid for.

Why did Mennan tolerate it? His marriage was little better than the arrangement between a prostitute and one of her customers. Yet Mennan had demeaned himself to keep her. He must have known he would be found out and yet he had continued, right up until the end, sacrificing himself and his own integrity.

Asoka sniffs and, with his heightened senses, catches a whiff of perfume. He remembers it as the floral, almost feminine aftershave worn by Mennan. Yes. There it is again. Surely, none of the men here would wear such perfume. Their preferences, if any, run only to the cheap, pungent oil which slicks their hair, an odour so sweet and cloying that it baffles the senses and masks other, less salubrious smells such as urine and sweat. No. Mennan is here. In this room. He can feel his presence.

Asoka closes his eyes and tries to picture that last day. Mennan was almost out of his wits after the visit of the Government Agent's young assistant. Asoka remembers, although many of the details are hazy. The young man had been carried to the car in some kind of fit and several of the men had thrown rocks at the car as it drove off. That was not part of the plan. Even then, Anil was following his own design. It no longer matters. They are both as guilty as each other.

Asoka concentrates, trying to think of Mennan, forcing himself to re-visit every painful detail of his agony. Asoka had despised Mennan that day. He had seen him simply as a greedy, dishonest little worm deserving punishment; which, in many ways, he was. But he was also something else.

Tormented, as no human being should be, he had been deprived of dignity or a last kindly word. And yet, stripped of pretension, reduced to a loathsome figure of fun, a helpless victim, he had been magnificent. For his last thought was not of himself, but of the wife who had betrayed him and who he continued to love and forgive with his dying breath.

A lump swells in Asoka's throat and tears well up in his eyes. Soon, they are running hot and fast down his cheeks and into his lap. More than any phantom of his imagination, the jacket hanging from its peg, speaks to him of the real man, as if it were waiting for him to return. It carries his shape and his smell, even part of his personality. Yes. Mennan was despicable in many ways, but he also carried a seed of greatness in his soul. But Asoka had stamped it out and denied it a chance to grow. Weeping, Asoka stares at the jacket.

"Forgive me," he murmurs.

The day wears on and Asoka's ear, having become attuned to the comings and goings of men, begins to track their movements: the clink of enamel mugs as they are filled, then gathered up; the swish of many feet, as soft as leaves, passing close to the door; grunts and dull thumps as men climb into the lorry, arranging themselves around its cargo; bolts rattling as the tailgate is secured; the bronchitic growl of the engine.

As the truck pulls away, one of the men shouts something in Sinhalese. It sounds like: 'Sinhala Hamudawa'. Then, the chant is taken up by the other men.

"Sinhala Hamudawa. Apey anduwa."

"We are the Sinhalese Army. It is our Government."

Asoka's stomach churns with fear. What is going on? What are they planning?

He cranes his neck, trying to get a view from the small crack in the door, but he can see nothing, only the dark penumbra of the forest. Suddenly, there is a flapping sound and something lands on the verandah of the hut. There is another sound, a hurried "tac, tac, tac," like a very small woman in high heels. It stops, then starts again. Then he sees it: a large black crow, hopping up and down outside the door, moving sideways, one leg trailing the other. With wings outstretched, it has the untidy, lop-sided appearance of a broken umbrella.

Arkk! He can see its tongue arch as it emits a harsh cry. Arkk! Arkk! Then, snapping its beak shut, the crow peers through the crack in the door, first one bright eye, then the other, training each one in turn on Asoka, sizing him up. It shuffles forward, its claws beating a sharp "tic, tac" against the wood. It stares him in the face, rolls its head slightly, lowers its gaze to his stomach, then his feet. Then, warily at first, it tries to insinuate its head through the gap in the door.

Asoka's heart begins to pound. He knows what crows do to helpless animals. The creature has already assessed his ability to resist and has judged him incapable of a fight. It will go for the eyes first. They always do. He once saw the body of a new-born calf, its eyes picked clean to the sockets. After that, while the victim is still alive, the crow will attack its entrails. He struggles, scraping the leg of the chair on the floor.

The crow hops back, but it does not retreat far, waiting by the door, one coal-black eye trained on Asoka, waiting for him to tire. Despite his repeated attempts to scare it off, the crow becomes more bold. Soon, the violent scraping of the chair has no power to deter it. With its head already through the door, it is trying to insinuate its body, collapsing the great black wings and folding them tight against its sides. Asoka is panting, his breath coming in short, rasping bursts.

"Get out!" he shouts.

But the bird simply cocks its head and looks at him knowingly. It has the better of him and it knows it.

"Get out. Get out!"

He rocks backwards and forwards on the chair. For a moment, the bird ceases its manoeuvres; eyeing him; inquisitorial. Then it starts again, craning its head around the door. It is so close he can see the coarse feathers around the base of its beak and the membrane that covers its eye.

"Aagh!" he shouts, as much in frustration as fear.

Arkk! the bird replies, taunting him. Then, suddenly it is whisked backwards. There is a coarse screech and a sound of frantic flapping. A man curses, then everything is silent. The door creaks open, grating against the floor and Tissa enters, blood streaming from a wound on his hand. Putting it to his mouth, he sucks it thoughtfully then, thinking better of it, he lets his hand drop to his side, still bleeding profusely. He gives Asoka a blood-stained smile.

"Bloody crows. I hate them."

Asoka nods. At least that is something on which they both agree. But the moment of camaraderie is gone. Walking around the back of the chair, Tissa squats down and loosens the ropes, dragging Asoka to his feet. But Asoka cannot walk immediately. He has been sitting for so long that it feels as if the blood has settled in his feet. He feels dizzy and his back is stiff. He tries to take a step forward and stumbles. Behind him, Tissa grunts with smug disapproval.

"Come on!" he snaps, pushing his captive in the back so hard that Asoka can feel the imprint of the other man's fingers.

Rubbing his wrists which have been chafed by the ropes, Asoka shuffles forwards, sliding his feet across the floor, the joints in his knees and ankles unwilling to respond. As he emerges from the cabin, he blinks. Even here, the dappled light of the clearing is blinding compared to the gloom within. He rubs his watering eyes, then shades them with one hand.

As he steps forward, his foot touches something wet and warm. He has stepped on a portion of the crow's body which lies, dismembered and bleeding, at his feet. Severed from the body, the wings and head have been scattered across the verandah. Asoka's foot has come into contact with the torso which has been pulled apart to reveal the ribs. The heart, lungs and entrails have been ripped out and draped over the railings.

"Oh god!"

He cannot help himself. He has no fear of blood, but the savage cruelty with which the creature has been butchered disgusts him.

"Squeamish?" whispers Tissa. "Just remember this if ever you feel like running off. Think of what your wife would look like. I'd do it, you know."

"I believe you," murmurs Asoka.

Something winds around his heart, slowly tightening until he finds it difficult to breathe. Paralysed by fear, he stands, staring at the bloody remains of the crow until Tissa pushes him again and he stumbles forward down the steps. Like an animal that is too terrified even to think, he lets Tissa drive him across the clearing to where Anil is sitting by the fire.

At first, Anil does not look at them. He is staring deep into the flames and his lips are moving soundlessly, as if he is speaking to someone, or praying. Eventually, he appears to rouse himself and becomes aware of their presence.

"Sit down," he says, almost amiably, as if welcoming visitors.

Seating himself beside Anil, Asoka begins to wonder how this all came about, how his former pupil turned into his captor.

"How did you find me?"

That should be obvious." Anil nods towards Tissa. "He told me of the mysterious stranger who had arrived in his village."

"But how did you know it was me?"

"It wasn't difficult: his description of you, the time of your appearance. It all added up."

"But it's all coincidence. You meeting Tissa, him telling you where to find me. I don't believe it. It's not possible."

Anil laughs. "Why not? Serendipity. Happy chance. The world took that word from us."

Asoka picks up a twig, snaps it in two and throws it into the fire, watching as the pieces flare and crackle.

"Everything in this country is left to chance. Even its politics."

"Not any more," snaps Anil. "The time is fast approaching when the Sinhalese will take control of their own destiny. It will no longer be a matter of chance."

"Ha! You mean the Sinhala Hamudawa. Your Sinhalese Army. A bunch of thugs with a few boxes of stolen dynamite. Is that your solution?"

"You don't know what you're talking about," replies Anil, angrily. "This is just the beginning. There will be uprisings all over this country and, sooner or later, we will drive the Tamils out."

"And replace them with what? People like him."

With a motion of his head, Asoka indicates Tissa who, standing some feet away, is regarding them sullenly, his arms crossed in front of him. Tissa makes a move, ready to pounce on Asoka, but Anil waves him away.

"Stop this, Anil," Asoka pleads. "It's not too late. We've already murdered one man. His death has been on my conscience ever since. I cannot watch other innocent people die."

"Innocent?" Anil snorts. "A liar and a fraud who cheated the poor out of their wages. Do you call that innocent?"

"He did not deserve to die."

"He did not deserve to live," retorts Anil, heatedly. Rising to his feet, he paces back and forth. Then, a thought occurs to him and he stops in front of Asoka, his mouth twisted into a cruel smile, the sort worn by torturers as they anticipate the tightening of thumbscrews.

"Anyway, the overseer was not the only one to die that day."

"What do you mean?" Asoka feels perspiration drift across his brow like a cold mist.

"Have you forgotten? The overseer had a visitor that day. The Government Agent's assistant. I poisoned his tea. Remember?"

"My god. I'd forgotten about that."

Once again, an image flashes across Asoka's mind of the young man wearing a white suit. Asoka had last seen him being lifted into his car, apparently suffering from the sudden onset of illness; not an unusual occurrence in the Tropics.

But now Asoka recollects, albeit faintly, that Anil admitted to poisoning him. With all that happened subsequently – Mennan's death and his own flight, starvation and sickness – Asoka had forgotten. Another death. He was involved with not one, but two murders.

Staring down at Asoka, Anil's face is a study in stony composure; a parody of the towering stone Buddhas that adorn the Island's sacred places, their faces so ancient and inscrutable that they seem more like a natural efflorescence of the rock than the creation of human hands.

"Why? Why did you do it?"

"Why not? That other fellow was also a Tamil. Instead of one, I had the chance to kill two. It was a gift. From god."

And with those words, the image of the Buddha that has formed in Asoka's mind, shatters, as if exploding from within, and the broken, swirling fragments re-form to create another image, that of the Hindu god Vishnu, who pledged himself to fight demons in order to protect Creation. Is that how Anil sees himself? As a just defender, like Vishnu, rather than a cruel and bloody aggressor? Does he regard Tamils, not as people, but as demons that must be purged before balance can be regained in his country?

"Anil, please, I beg you to think. What we did was wrong. It was murder, not justice. Please stop. Before it is too late."

But Asoka's attempt at reason meets with derision.

"When did you become a traitor?" says Anil, looking down at him with disgust.

"At the same time you became a fool," retorts Asoka.

"This is getting us nowhere."

Anil walks away, circling the fire, his head bowed as if deep in thought.

Asoka wonders if they will kill him now. He cannot see what possible use he could be. Anil's plans are reaching fruition and Asoka will only be an impediment. Why have they brought him here? He thinks of Mennan and tries to ready himself for death, telling himself it would be a fitting punishment for his crime. But he prays that it will not be in this place, not here where he abandoned his humanity, but in another place. Then, just like Mennan, he prays that he might see his wife again. Just once.

Turning to face Asoka, Anil reaches inside his robe. He is reaching for the gun. He must be. Hoping that it will be quick and that he will not die in agony, Asoka closes his eyes and tries to concentrate on the image of Sriya. He waits for what seems like centuries. But there is no noise. No click as the gun is cocked, no crack of gunfire, no bullet boring into his skull, shattering the bone and spraying the earth with blood and brains. Just a long, low laugh. He opens his eyes. Anil is standing before him with a small notebook in his hand.

"This will show you, Brother, that nothing I do is left to chance. Read it!"

He flings it in Asoka's lap. It is a cheap notebook, like the one kept by shopkeepers, its flimsy pages printed with blue lines, the ink slightly blurred, its outer covers made of thick cardboard covered with a thin film of red waxed cloth. The corners of the outer covers are already worn with much use and the cloth has frayed, revealing the layers of curling card beneath. Asoka turns the pages. It appears to be a diary, a list of arrivals and departures, but there are no words, just a series of crudely-drawn symbols that resemble clock faces.

"What is this?"

Anil smiles and turns to Tissa who seems to share the joke, grinning obsequiously at his master.

"It shows the daily movements of another man; one you yourself described as a 'much bigger fish' than Mennan. Remember?"

Something squirms in Asoka's stomach: a small, writhing knot of fear. He presses the book between his hands, as if to protect the life that it records. It is as if a beating heart were resting in his palm.

"What are you going to do?"

"Not me!" Anil seems amused. "You. As a punishment for your betrayal, you are going to kill this man. And Tissa and I will be there to make sure that you do."

"No. I won't do it!"

"Oh, but you must." Anil sneers, his mouth contorting itself into a smile. "Don't you care what happens to your wife? If you don't do this, we will have no use for you. We'll have to kill you. Then Tissa can return home. To his village. Who knows? He may even marry your widow."

"Oh god!" Asoka's head sinks onto his chest.

"What is your answer? I must know."

Anil's tone is harsh. He is not in the mood for postponement.

"All right. I'll do it."

Asoka can feel hot tears running down his face. They fall onto the book, dissolving the cheap red ink, until it looks as if the cover is oozing blood.

"Good. If you do this, we may even let you return to your wife."

Tissa raises his hand, as if to remonstrate, but Anil motions him to keep quiet. Tissa sinks back into sulky silence; his dark eyes, filled with murderous intent, fixed on Asoka's lowered head.

"When?" murmurs Asoka. "When must I do this thing?"

"Soon. First, Tissa has some work to do. When the lorry returns tomorrow, he will leave with it. He has a task to perform with the Sinhala Hamudawa. It should create a useful diversion. In a couple of days, we will meet up with him and, together, we will carry out the next stage of our plan. Then, Tissa and I will watch you perform your task. Are you not lucky to have friends who care so much for you?"

Asoka groans. If he had Anil's gun, he would put a bullet through his own brain. Death, of any sort, would be preferable to what he is required to do. But, if he dies, what will happen to Sriya? Again, his thoughts return to Mennan. Like him, Asoka will be obliged to compromise his integrity for the woman he loves. There is no alternative.

He wonders at his own arrogance in having dismissed Mennan simply as a cheat and a liar without questioning why he acted as he did. A wave of despair rolls over Asoka. It is as if his body has been hollowed out and filled with lead. He has lost his wife and, soon, he will lose what remains of himself.

Anil reaches down and, prising Asoka's hands apart, removes the notebook, placing it back in the folds of his robe, next to the revolver. He feels greater contentment, at this moment, than he will ever feel again. His plans are reaching fruition and the man who betrayed him is now in his power.

"Come, let us eat. Tissa, make up the fire and bring the food that our friends left us."

Anil's tone is almost jovial, but it is not matched by the mood of his companions. Asoka remains seated, as if frozen, staring at the ground, while Tissa, whose mood has changed inexplicably to one of surly taciturnity, seizes a broken branch and flings it on the fire. It crashes into the embers, sending up a shower of sparks. Neither Anil nor Asoka seems to notice. Grumbling to himself, Tissa slopes off to where the stores are kept. He returns, carrying several large tins under one arm, a burden which causes him to lean to one side, accentuating his lop-sided gait.

Anil, who has seated himself next to Asoka, speaks in an almost conspiratorial tone as he points at Tissa.

"He received a knock on the head. In the service of the Sinhala Hamudawa."

Asoka raises his head slightly and looks, sideways at Anil.

"How?"

"At Gal Oya. I'm sure you heard about it."

"I heard that many people were killed," says Asoka, dully.

"Oh, more than that, brother. It was a beginning. A small beginning, but a beginning nonetheless."

"If that is the beginning, then I fear what the end will be."

"The birth of the Sinhalese nation. What else?"

There is a note of asperity in Anil's tone, his good-humour having evaporated as suddenly as it appeared. He is impatient with Asoka. Until now, he had hoped to win him back, but it is clear that he will not. Rising to his feet, he walks across the clearing to the edge of the trees.

"Lord Hooniyam," he prays, "help me. I am alone, surrounded by fools and traitors. Do not let me fail."

Out in the darkness, beyond the range of human sight, there is a faint rustle as a breeze shuffles the leaves on the forest floor and, surrounded by a whirl of green mist, Hooniyam appears. He raises his hand in blessing towards Anil who, although he cannot see the god, senses his presence. Anil bows his head and, after a few minutes of silent prayer, returns to the clearing where he sits down to eat, in silence with his companions. True to his devoted follower, Hooniyam keeps watch in the shadows.

When the meal is finished, Asoka lays down to sleep, covering himself with the old sack that he found when he first arrived at the site. It affords little warmth and has an unpleasant, musty smell, but it protects him from the heavy night dew and, more importantly, offers him some slight shelter; privacy; an excuse, if he wishes, to hide his face; a space in which to think without his expression betraying his thoughts. Peering out from under the folds of the sack, he can observe Anil, unseen.

Reclining in front of the fire, his head resting on one arm, Anil is staring into the embers. Tiny images of flame flicker across his pupils and his eyes shine with red and yellow fire so that he seems to be lit from within. Asoka thinks again of Vishnu, ever watchful, the unsleeping god and, as he looks at Anil, he hears Vishnu's words, echoing in his head:

Now I am become Death, the destroyer of worlds.

Cramming the last handful of rice into his mouth, Tissa wipes his fingers on his robe and quietly gets to his feet. He roams aimlessly about the clearing, hoping that Anil will speak to him, offer him some word of comfort or explanation. But Anil remains motionless on his side, staring into the fire. Tissa's anxiety turns slowly into rage. And jealousy.

Although they are now enemies, the two men by the fire have more in common with each other than with him. He will always be an outsider: a faithful servant, a lackey, but never the confidante of the man he reveres almost as a god. Anil shows more regard for Asoka, a traitor, than he does for him. Tonight, he told Asoka that he could return home to his wife. That is not what he promised Tissa. He had told Tissa that he would have her. Sriya was to be his reward. His own master has betrayed him: casually, without a word of explanation.

Filled with rage, Tissa creeps into the forest. He is sick of the sight of men. Animals are more trustworthy. He thinks of the gentle oxen in the village: of leading them to the tank to drink, or following them at the plough; the slow and powerful churning of their legs as they trudge through the water-logged paddy; the swishing of their tails; their sweet hay-scented breath; the white egrets that ride their backs. The images fill him with longing: to return home, to regain what he has lost, to find Sriya. Why can things not be as they once were?

Concealed within the darkness of the forest, Tissa watches the two men as they lie, unprotected, in the pale ring of firelight. They neither know, nor care, where he is. An idea comes to him. He could kill them both. Now. Then Sriya would be his. He watches from the shadows, considering what to do. Then, he stoops, searching the black forest floor with his hands, patting the earth like a blind man, searching for a weapon. He does not see the figure looming over him, its face contorted with rage.

"You young scamp."

To a mortal ear, Hooniyam's voice sounds like the hissing of a serpent. Tissa looks up, alarmed, yet sees nothing although the god is standing in front of him.

"Murder your master, would you? We'll see about that."

Bending over, Hooniyam whispers into Tissa's ear. A few seconds later, Tissa shakes his head, mystified at his behaviour. How could he think of killing his master? He loves him. No. Anil has not betrayed him. He is simply playing a game with Asoka. It is Asoka he will betray. Once the deed is done.

"I must bide my time," Tissa murmurs to himself. "My opportunity will come soon enough."

Hooniyam rubs his hands in satisfaction as he watches Tissa return to the clearing where he sits, as usual, watching Asoka as he sleeps, plotting his revenge.

***

Asoka, drifting in and out of sleep, is startled to see a figure emerging from the trees. The glow from the dying fire highlights its stooping back and leering, loose-lipped mouth. *A demon*, he thinks, opening his eyes, only to realise that it is Tissa. He shivers and turns over, pulling the sack over his head.

Memories of Mennan lurk beneath the thin skin of his consciousness, always pressing against it, trying to break through. He fears sleep because then they will creep out and roam around his brain, reminding him of the thing he wishes most to forget.

Every tree, every leaf, even the soil in this place holds a memory of murder, sending out little echoes like ripples in a pond: a scream, a prayer, the sounds of a struggle; the taunting, jeering cries; the pounding of feet; then, worst of all, the silence. Asoka moans in his sleep.

***

The camp-site is quiet and the three men asleep when two small figures appear at the edge of the clearing. One carries a bow and a quiver of arrows, the other a home-made shotgun with a long muzzle: two members of the Vadda tribe, returning from a hunting trip, bemused by the sight of strangers.

They giggle softly, then one says something in a language unknown to most Islanders; a language of hunting and forests, with words for animals, birds, streams and plants but not for cars, buses and aeroplanes; a language that belongs to a time forgotten by the rest of the world; a time that pre-dates the arrival of Prince Vijaya and the Sinhalese.

Nudging his companion, the older of the two indicates that they should return to the forest. Silently, they withdraw, approaching the spot where Hooniyam is keeping watch. Drawing himself up to his full height, Hooniyam crosses his arms but the Vaddas continue on their way, passing right through his spectral presence. Throwing up his hands in disgust, Hooniyam sends two sharp curses spinning after them but, as soon as they touch the Vaddas' skin, the curses fizzle and pop like two damp squibs.

Laughing, the Vaddas turn and wave. They can see him but he has no power over them. The Vaddas are protected by a much older magic; gods and spirits that Hooniyam cannot even name. They regard him with amused detachment. He is simply another newcomer to the Island whose interests and ambitions have no relevance for them.

The jeep bounces and lunges along the unmade track. It is obvious that the driver has little experience, either of his vehicle or of the treacherous bends and potholes in the road. But there is little traffic on this road and, as Arjun has reasoned with Nash, it is the perfect place to practice his new skills. Walter has been teaching him to drive the jeep: half an hour, every day, after work for several weeks. It was Nash's idea. He says that the ability to drive this type of vehicle is an essential skill. Particularly if Arjun wants promotion.

Arjun humoured Nash, complying with his wishes. And now, he is grateful that he did. He loves the feeling of power that driving the jeep gives him: the freedom, the promise of escape inherent in the act of travelling. It has awoken a nomadic instinct that has lain dormant in his blood since birth; no doubt, the legacy of a seafaring ancestry. As the air rushes over his skin and the scenery melts into a palette of moving colour, he feels as if his troubles are slipping away and, as long as he can keep moving, they will never catch up.

As he passes a wide tract of scrubland, a hornbill dives headlong from a tree and, for a few seconds, keeps pace with him, flying low alongside the car, its great, heavy beak stretched out in front of it like the head of a lance. About half a mile away, deep in the scrub, some dark bushes appear to move. Wild elephants. He has never seen them before and, pulling the car over to the side of the road, he stops to get a better look. Until now, he has only seen domesticated elephants, driven by mahouts, trudging along the road carrying their heavy burden of logs or bales. In the distance, dark blurs of grey and brown move almost imperceptibly as the wild elephants browse the slender branches of kittul trees.

Arjun wishes he had a pair of binoculars to see them better. He would love to get closer, to get a better view. But even if there were a suitable road through the scrub, it would be too hazardous. Wild elephants are dangerous, particularly if the males are in 'musth' and, every year, the newspapers carry stories of people who have been killed by charging bulls. As human habitation encroaches further into the elephants' habitat, the problem will become so great that, eventually, bus shelters in rural areas will be built from reinforced concrete to provide protection for travellers.

Reluctantly, Arjun gets back into the car. He turns the key, eases the choke in and slowly takes his foot off the clutch. Just as Walter has taught him. The engine coughs, then stops abruptly. It is so unlike the small black Austin that he drives at home. Arjun experiences the incipient panic experienced by every novice who stalls a car. He looks around him. The road is empty in either direction. He tries again. The engine sputters, grunts, and dies.

"Damn!"

He clutches the wheel, wanting to shake it as he would shake another person by the shoulders. The brief pleasure of the trip is gone. He is alone; without any hope of help if he cannot get the jeep started. Why did he travel alone? Both Nash and Walter tried to dissuade him, but he insisted. Why? But he knows the reason. He needed to think. He turns the key again and, this time, the engine turns over, thudding like a reluctant heart.

"Thank god!"

His relief is intense, but the feeling of euphoria has deserted him. He remembers why he is here. A local agent has retired and the government bungalow that was his residence is now vacant. Nash has suggested that Arjun might like the job. Nash must have been considering this promotion for some time: hence the driving lessons. Today, Arjun has come to see for himself: to decide whether he will accept the post. It is tempting: more money, a step up the ladder, a place of his own. More than that, it will offer him an escape from the pain that is tearing him apart.

He steers the jeep back onto the road. It bumps and shudders, crunching and grinding as he changes gear. Never mind. There is no-one to see him: no Walter to nag him about his technique. He can drive all the way in third gear if he chooses.

The road begins to twist and turn, leading him from open scrubland into the dappled shade of coconut groves and rubber plantations, then out into the open again, past a huge tank where boys are fishing with home-made rods. Arjun consults a map which lies open on the passenger seat, but there is really no need: the road leads straight to the Government bungalow without any diversions. The only difficult part is the distance: a long drive, several hours from his current home. And Neleni.

He wonders if that is why Nash has suggested this move. Does he suspect something? Has something about Arjun's bearing or behaviour betrayed his unhappiness? It does not really matter. What matters is what he should do about it. He has pondered the question for weeks, even drafting a letter of resignation which he later tore up and threw in the bin. He is in an impossible situation, unable to move forwards or return to his previous life, caught in a trap of his own making.

The vehicle jolts as it runs over a large stone and his suitcase slides along the back seat, bumping against the door, then falling to the floor and lodging itself in the foot well. He hopes the lock has not broken. It has never been strong. It is the cardboard suitcase with which he first arrived at Neleni's house.

He remembers every detail of that meeting, how he mistook her reticence for coldness. He had thought her beautiful, but distant, as remote as a planet, a being that did not inhabit his world. But, at Sigiriya, he saw the real woman. And he has loved her ever since. He still loves her. More than ever. And that is why he must leave.

Neleni has changed since her mother's death. Arjun does not know the reason. She has become distant and almost prefers the company of Raj. Husband and wife have become openly affectionate, like old comrades and, the other day, when Raj put his arm around her waist, she did not object.

In fact, she appears to have become reconciled to her loveless marriage. Perhaps there is good reason. Neleni is pregnant. The baby is Raj's. It must be. A new responsibility has erased her love for Arjun.

She has tried to talk to Arjun on several occasions, but her nerve has failed her. She is trying to summon the courage to tell him something painful. He is convinced of it. But he will not let her speak, making an excuse to leave the room as soon as her face adopts that anxious expression. She wants to tell him that their affair is over. Of that, he is certain. But he will not let her do it.

She has betrayed him. Blinded by jealousy and rage, he can no longer bear to be near her. Every time he sees her, his heart bends and twists like a frail bridge in a storm. If she tells him to go, it will break. The cords that hold it together will snap, one by one, and he will be plunged into a place of darkness from which there will be no return. No. He must take this posting. Escape. Before his love for her kills him.

The tank and the small villages, strung along its shore, are now far behind and the road plunges into thick forest. The undergrowth is lush and green and colonies of arum lilies rise from the verge, each pale white cup furled around a yellow spindle. The lilies gleam, ghostly and pale, but their whiteness is not a whiteness bred of sunlight, but of darkness, a livid whiteness tinged with green. Arjun hates the lilies. They remind him of funerals.

He presses his foot down on the accelerator but the jeep will not go faster. It is still in third gear. He attempts a shift into fourth but misses. There is a terrible crunching and the car threatens to stall. He reduces his speed and returns to third. The forest gloom reflects his mood. Without Neleni, he can think only of death.

He is so preoccupied with his own misery, that he does not hear a lorry approaching. Suddenly, it rounds the bend and comes hurtling towards him. He wrenches the wheel and narrowly avoids a collision but the car slews off the road. He stamps on the brake and it lurches to a halt, almost flinging him over the low windscreen. He is thrown against the steering wheel. His ribs feel as if they will buckle, then he is flung back into the seat, the final gasp of air being forced out of his lungs.

He sits for a minute, trying to regain his breath. His hands, still gripping the wheel, are white and shaking. Then, he becomes aware of voices, shouting. He looks behind him. The lorry has stopped. It is full of men. They are drunk, full of alcoholic bravado. One flings an arrack bottle at him. Others follow.

The bottles fall short of the jeep. This seems to infuriate the men even more. One is waving excitedly. He has something in his hand. A machete. The man is urging the driver to turn around, pointing at Arjun. The other men join in, shouting and jeering. Then, suddenly, the lorry's engine starts and the driver, hanging out of the window, slowly turns the vehicle, until it is facing Arjun. Then, with a shunting of gears, the lorry begins to move forward. The men, inflamed by drink, are waving wildly. As they approach, Arjun can see that they are armed with clubs and knives.

The lorry lurches crazily towards him. It means to ram him. Then what? A quick and bloody mauling. Then it will be over. It is his chance to die. The thought passes. Desperately, Arjun tries to start the jeep. The lorry is approaching. Faster and faster. He can see the men's faces clearly in his mirror. They are screaming, fired with alcohol and hatred. The engine springs into life. Arjun slams the jeep into gear, praying that the wheels have not become embedded in the soft soil of the verge. The jeep lurches forward, onto the road. It begins to pick up speed but the lorry is so close it is practically touching the bumper.

Arjun presses his foot down hard on the accelerator and, for once, performs a perfect gear change. Up into fourth and a small space appears between the jeep and the lorry. But the lorry is still too close. A man could easily jump into the back of the jeep. He presses his foot down harder and the space widens, slowly at first, then with more speed.

Still, the lorry pursues him. They approach a sharp bend. Arjun is driving blind. If something is coming the other way, he will hit it. The vehicles screech around the corner. The lorry has to slow and Arjun increases his lead. But it is not enough. He must find some other way to evade his hunters.

He sees a narrow track, leading off to the right, rising steeply from the road. The lorry will not be able to pursue him there. Without braking, he swings the jeep onto the track and drives with his foot down hard on the pedal. Behind him, the lorry lurches to a halt. Several men leap out and make a pretence of running after him, but they know they cannot catch him. He laughs, strangely invigorated by his experience. He has beaten the odds.

The men's voices become faint and, in the mirror, he can see them turning away, giving up. Reluctantly, they walk back to their vehicle. There is a rusty churning as the lorry's engine fires up. Arjun holds his breath, wondering even now, if it will pursue him. Several minutes pass and he knows that he is safe. Suddenly, he is tired and his limbs feel slack and weak. Even the effort of driving is too much for him, but there is nowhere to stop on this narrow road and nowhere to turn. He must follow the route that he has chosen, even if it takes him miles out of his way.

The road rises steeply, twisting and turning, following the contours of the mountains. The track is bare, denuded of the usual covering of pines. Here, the rock is exposed, shot with the silver of freshwater springs. Across the valley, where the land is untouched, a mighty waterfall cuts a white gash through the forest. Arjun can hear its waters, murmuring in the stillness. If he was closer, he would be deafened by its roar. He would like to stop but is afraid that, if he does, he may not be able to start the jeep again. He has no faith in his mastery of the vehicle.

Briefly, he looks sideways, trying to check the map. But it is hopeless. He cannot see properly and, even if he could, he is unlikely to learn much. Judging by its worn and grubby edges, the map pre-dates the road on which he is travelling. He borrowed it from the office and it has been opened and re-folded so many times that there is a series of holes along the central crease.

Strange, he thinks, how he has placed his faith unquestioningly in an item of standard Government issue, however old or outdated it may be. Just like everyone else in this country. Even among the most radical, there is still a blind belief in the efficacy of all things colonial. It is like a talisman. Everywhere, there are symbols of order which, like the map, protect the bearer against the overwhelming forces of chaos. For beyond these small beacons of light, there is primordial darkness, always trying to push its way in. The Islanders regard order as a benign, but foreign, entity; something to be revered because it has never been fully understood. Perhaps, one day, it will acquire an image and join the Hindu pantheon. Arjun smiles. The thought amuses him. He has even thought of a name for this new deity: Civil Service.

Distracted by these thoughts, Arjun continues his journey, along the dirt track that twists and turns, its ruts and potholes filled with red mud. There is something familiar about it. Has he been here before? He cannot remember. He is tired and his concentration is failing. Then it comes to him. This road leads to the camp-site.

Suddenly, images flash through his mind, vivid and painful: the terrified overseer in his sweat-stained white suit; the man at the camp-fire brewing tea who followed Arjun with his eyes; the terrible pain of his illness; Neleni's tears. Even the thought of that place arouses painful memories. He does not want to go there, but the road is too narrow. He cannot turn around and he has come too far to drive backwards down the track with its hair-pin bends and the sheer precipice on one side. He must follow the road to its end.

This morning, after loading another lorry, Tissa left with the Sinhala Hamudawa. In a day or so, Asoka and Anil will set out to join him at a pre-arranged meeting place. Time passes slowly; a blank space of hours and minutes.

With nothing to do but wait, Asoka reflects gloomily on Mennan's death. For a while, his new life in the village had seemed to transport him so far from the past that he had hoped to escape it altogether. But now he realises that that hope was unfounded. Not even Sriya could part him from the consequences of his actions.

He has not, as he had hoped, been absolved by love. Coming back to this place has made him realise that. The guilt is still there. Last night, he thought he saw something beneath the trees, just as he was on the point of falling asleep. It reminded him of the image of Hooniyam in the temple.

"I am getting foolish," he says aloud, trying to banish his fears.

"What was that?"

Anil, who is sitting next to him, jerks his head around.

"I said …"

"No, not that. Listen."

Both men strain their ears. At first, Asoka can hear nothing but, then, he catches the faint chug of an engine. It is getting louder.

"Perhaps it is more of your Sinhala Hamudawa," he suggests with a trace of irony.

"That it is not the engine of a lorry," says Anil, his neck outstretched, his head still craned to one side. "I am not expecting anyone. We must hide."

Asoka is about to remonstrate, but when he sees Anil reaching inside his robe, he nods obediently and gets to his feet. They have been sitting on the edge of the clearing, under the shade of the trees. It is unlikely that anyone arriving from the road would see them, but that is not enough for Anil. He motions Asoka to walk deeper into the forest.

"Now stay here, out of sight," he whispers.

The noise of the engine becomes louder as the vehicle approaches. Anil motions Asoka to stay back while he creeps forward to get a better view of the road. A green jeep rounds the corner into the clearing. From where he stands, Asoka can see very little and is forced to deduce what he can from the reactions of his companion. Although Anil's face is obscured by shadow, his back stiffens, like a cat ready to spring.

Asoka cannot see the jeep at all now, but he hears the sudden sputtering of the engine as it stalls and a man's voice, cursing, as he tries to re-start the vehicle. Anil waits for a few seconds, watching intently, before stalking silently towards the clearing where he disappears from view.

Black fumes spurt from the exhaust pipe, fouling the air. The engine coughs, vibrates, then dies.

"Damn, damn, damn!"

Exasperated, Arjun beats the steering wheel with his fist.

"Why here? Of all places."

He stretches back in the seat, arching his back so that he is looking straight up at the sky. Its brightness seems remote from this dark place and, when birds fly across it, they appear only as a string of black dots. Despite its deserted appearance, the clearing still resonates with echoes of a violent past. Memories of that terrible day are probably embedded in the sap of every tree, as they are in Arjun's head. He has tried to rid himself of them but, like graveyard demons, they still creep back to haunt him in the night.

He turns the key in the ignition, but the car does not respond. Furious this time, Arjun gets out, angrily slamming the door behind him. He walks around the jeep a couple of times, trying to burn off his rage before trying again, when he spots something in the soft mud on the floor of the clearing. Walking forward, he bends down to inspect it. Fresh tyre tracks belonging to a large vehicle. A truck. And not just one. By the look of it, there have been several here. Arjun tests the tracks with his finger. They are still soft, like damp clay. He is intrigued.

Nash told him that the site had been abandoned following Mennan's death and that all work on the project had ceased. Surely he would have told Arjun if there had been plans to re-start it. It is not like Nash to forget something like that and why should he wish to withhold such information? Does the Agent not trust him? Or is it something to do with Leela? The hairs suddenly prickle on Arjun's neck. Has she told Nash of their liaison? A final act of spite, retaliation for Arjun's decision to end their affair?

He remembers her face when she visited Neleni's house: the realisation that she had lost Arjun to a rival and her ugly attempt to belittle Neleni. He had felt sorry for her, but also scared. Even with his lack of experience, he knew that the violence of her envy would need an outlet. Has she spoken to Nash? If so, the Government Agent has never mentioned it.

Arjun casts back for any sign of knowledge on Nash's part. But the Government Agent is too experienced a diplomat to betray his thoughts unintentionally. Is this what prompted him to suggest that Arjun should take up residence in the government bungalow, somewhere where he would be out of harm's way?

Rubbing the dirt from his fingers, Arjun rises to his feet.

"Don't be so ridiculous," he tells himself. "It's just this place. So eerie and dark."

He shudders. Walking forward, he examines the tracks of the lorries. In some places, untouched by the sun, the damp mud has been worked into a quagmire and the tiny pools of water left in the ruts have become an oasis for flies. Arjun kicks at them, watching as they rise in a black cloud, hover, then descend. Under a tree, he sees a large metal box, partially hidden by shadow. With his hands in his pockets, he walks over to get a better look.

The box is sturdy, painted green, a colour favoured by government departments. There is something written on the side, but the light is so bad that he cannot read it. However, he can just make out a warning sign; a white skull and crossbones. He has seen such boxes before on-site. He examines the lock and, finding that it is broken, he gently eases open the lid, whistling softly when he sees the contents. The box is filled with tightly-packed sticks of dynamite, the sort used for blasting on road projects.

"Surely this can't have been left here all this time," he thinks.

He runs his hand carefully over the contents. They are dry and show no sign of deterioration. A vague idea begins to form in his head. Could this box have anything to do with the lorries that have recently visited the site?

His mind flies back to the men who chased him off the highway. As the lorry passed him on the road, he thinks he caught a glimpse of another box, similar to this. He screws up his eyes, trying to remember but fear and desperation have jumbled his thoughts. He cannot decide whether he actually saw such a box, or whether it was simply his imagination. Anyway, he will report this to Nash when he gets back.

He is stooping, having just closed the lid of the box, when there is a sharp click in his left ear and something cold and hard is pressed into his neck.

"Turn around slowly. Don't make any sudden movements or I will shoot you."

Putting his hands up to his head, Arjun tries to move his feet, half an inch at a time. It is hard to turn in slow motion and he fears that he might lose his balance, giving the man a perfect excuse to kill him. He can feel a stone under his shoe, acting as a pivot and the sound of a faint breeze, soughing through the upper branches of the trees; or perhaps it is a waterfall, far off, in some remote place untouched by the troubles of men. He longs to be there: anywhere but here, a place haunted by Mennan's murder.

Somewhere in his head, he hears Leela laughing and he wonders if he has been brought back here for a purpose. Vengeance. Perhaps Mennan's ghost intends to punish his wife's lover. Then he hears a small voice, his own, trying to reason. *She was not unfaithful with me. She was a widow by then.* Yet why should an angry ghost listen to reason?

Arjun recognises his captor immediately, despite the monk's robes and shaven head. He will never forget those eyes. He remembers them: gleaming out of the darkness beyond the camp-fire, following his movements as he crossed the clearing towards Mennan's hut; cold and calculating as a cat's eyes as it crouches in the undergrowth, watching its prey. Then, quite suddenly, he recalls an image of this man squatting at a camp-fire, brewing tea.

"It was you!"

With a slight tilt of his head, Anil acknowledges the fact.

"Yes. The gods were kind to you. That day."

The emphasis is laid on the last two words. Arjun's skin tingles with a terrible coldness. The man's meaning is clear. Today, he will not make the same mistake. Arjun will not leave this site alive.

Neleni. My love. I will never see you again. The words murmur around his head, echoing, reverberating, growing louder and louder until they form a single, terrible shriek: like the cry of a dying man. Only now, it is too late. Tears start from his eyes and begin to run down his cheeks.

"Can I write a letter?"

"No."

There is a brief silence between them. An even greater silence beyond. Ring upon ring of silence, with them at the middle.

"Tell me what you saw today."

"Nothing."

"You're lying!"

Anil cocks the gun and holds it to Arjun's forehead. Arjun struggles to think of something to say, trying to win a reprieve, if only a few seconds.

"I just saw that box, lying under the trees. I thought it had been left. From before. When the overseer was here. But the contents are dry. They look new. I couldn't understand it."

"Anything else?"

"No. Just some men in a lorry on the highway. They were carrying clubs and machetes. They tried to follow me. That's why I'm here."

"Then you definitely know too much. It's a pity I didn't succeed the first time."

Arjun watches in horror as Anil's finger whitens, pressing slowly on the trigger. He hears the sound of the wind, rushing through the trees, gathering speed. Then, Anil is lifted off his feet and thrown sideways. There is a deafening 'Crack' as the gun fires, then a crackle of twigs as a bullet rushes through the trees before embedding itself in the soft bark of a pine. Dazed, Arjun looks about him, unable to understand what has happened.

A few feet away from him, he sees two men: Anil and another man, wrestling on the ground. They are fighting for control, of each other, of the gun. Each has a hand on the other's throat. Their teeth are bared, like dogs, as they stare into each other's eyes. Anil is trying to point the gun at his attacker, but the other man has him by the wrist. The gun is waving frantically in the air, first inwards towards the men, then up towards the sky. Anil squeezes the trigger, but the other man pushes his hand back just in time. The bullet scythes through the undergrowth.

Still too shocked to move, Arjun watches fascinated as the men struggle, writhing in the mud like two serpents, their bodies twisting and their legs kicking wildly in the air, each fighting for survival. You can see it in their eyes: desperation and fear, and, in Anil's case, a blazing purity of hatred that ripples through him like fire. He is no longer a man, but a supernatural being: the incarnation of an ancient will, without thought, conscience, or complexity; just a hunger for power and the need to win.

Crack! The gun fires a third time.

For a second, the men continue to struggle, then both lie still. Arjun holds his breath. Why have they stopped? Then, he sees Anil's face and it seems as if all the power that he emitted is being drawn inwards, rushing back through his eyes, funnelling down into the deepest part of him, where it finally disappears. His eyes are dull, empty; his mouth slack; his robes stained crimson.

Disengaging his legs and arms, the assailant rolls the body away, then falls back, his eyes closed, gasping for breath.

"Are you hurt?"

Having recovered his senses, Arjun kneels beside the survivor. The man opens his eyes and looks at him: deep, dark eyes, almost hidden in their sockets, but not angry like Anil's. Arjun can see relief there and, to his surprise, sorrow. The fellow is breathing heavily and the air rasps in his throat.

Remembering that he brought a flask of cold tea with him, Arjun runs back to the car to collect it. The man is still sitting where he left him when he returns. Without a word, he drinks from the flask then, wiping his mouth, he looks up at Arjun.

"Hadn't you better arrest me?"

Arjun stares at the other man, stupidly.

"Arrest you? Why?"

Either possessed of an ironic sense of humour or simply overcome by nervous relief, the other man begins to laugh.

"I've just killed a man. Two, in fact. You met my other victim, also."

The humour is gone. Without its smile, the face becomes taut and grim, the eyes a little wild. The man wipes his sweating forehead with the end of his sarong, as peasants do. Yet, although dressed like one, he is no peasant. He has an air of confidence, an educated cleverness that Arjun recognises. Perhaps that is why the fellow seems familiar although, if he has seen him before, Arjun cannot remember where.

"What do you mean?" prompts Arjun.

Against his better judgement, he is being drawn in, intrigued to know about the other victim. Yet, further knowledge of this man's crimes, will make it necessary to report him, even make a citizen's arrest. It seems ungrateful in view of the fact that he has just saved Arjun's life.

"The overseer of this site, Mennan Rasanayagam. You were here the day he died."

"You killed him?"

"Not with my own hands. I was too much of a coward for that. I got someone else to do it."

The man laughs bitterly, then points to the small gold cross that Arjun wears around his neck.

"As a Christian, what would you say was the greater sin: to kill a man yourself or to get another to do it for you?"

"I don't know," Arjun falters. "I suppose the crime would be less serious if you were an accomplice."

"Hah! I was no accomplice. I was their leader. I encouraged, incited and inspired. I told ignorant men what to think and they followed me like sheep. I manipulated their ignorance and instilled into them a sense of injustice. Then, using the principles of reason, I taught them how to hate. You have already seen an example of my handiwork."

"The men in the lorry?"

As if too ashamed to meet Arjun's eye, Asoka hangs his head and picks at a clump of grass.

"They are men who formerly worked at this site: hired-labourers whose survival depends on their ability to work. One day without work, means no food for them or their families. Two days without work means they lose their home. It is simple. I taught them to take back what I believed was theirs by right. To kill, if necessary."

He raises his head and looks Arjun squarely in the eye.

"No. I am guilty of more than the death of two men. That is why you must arrest me."

"You saved my life."

"And in doing so I killed another man. You cannot forget that."

"I will take it into account."

Arjun sounds like the perfect civil servant: disinterested, objective, calmly weighing up all the facts before he makes a decision; but inwardly, he hesitates. By handing this man over, he will send him to the gallows. He chafes at the rules which govern his life, requiring him to act against his will. And yet, there have been times when he has disobeyed those rules.

He thinks of Neleni: a beacon deep in the darkness of his mind. Then, with less pleasure, he remembers Leela. Disobedience in both cases, has led to guilt. And pain. From Neleni, heartache. From Leela, fear. Was it worth it? Would he not have done better to stick to the rules? To follow his head, rather than his heart?

He gazes at the blackness beyond the trees, towards the spot where Mennan was cut down from a tree: a bloated, stinking corpse that had once been a man. For an instant, Arjun glimpses himself as the overseer saw him: an officious, young clerk who applies rules with the arrogance of a Pharisee, reckless of other men's suffering. What makes him so different from the man sitting before him on the ground: a man who has the courage to admit to crimes for which he also demands punishment?

A large beetle flies discomfortingly close to Arjun's face. It rumbles past then, resisting gravity, hovers above the body of the dead man. For a second, it whirrs and spins, petrol-coloured wings scintillating in the forest light. Then, it plummets, dropping onto Anil's forehead with a soft 'pat'.

The beetle closes its wings, its body glinting green, then blue, as it turns to one side, then another, in a leisurely dance. It stalks casually down the dead man's face then, after a brief exploration, disappears into his mouth.

With horror, Arjun realises that the creature is laying claim to the cadaver. Soon others will follow: infesting the corpse, laying their eggs in its flesh, gorging on its rottenness, until it is stripped to the bone.

"The sun will set in a few minutes. You had better decide what to do."

Arjun looks across the clearing to Mennan's hut. The windows are dark and grimy and the door is hanging at an odd angle. One of the hinges has worked loose. He remembers the rustling under the steps when he was last here. The snake. He wonders if it is still there, curled up in the darkness.

"We cannot stay here," says the other man. "They will return for that dynamite."

"No. We cannot stay here." Arjun repeats mechanically.

The oppressiveness of this place is bearing down on his senses, making it difficult to think. But then, with a sudden flash of clarity, he remembers.

"I know of somewhere. Come with me."

Motioning Asoka to follow him, he runs across the clearing to the jeep.

1958: Neleni's kitchen

A curtain, made from strings of brightly-coloured beads, hangs over the door to keep the flies out: but it is a futile defence, as they cruise in through the open windows, attracted by the smell of cooking. Once inside, the flies circle close to the ceiling where tiny geckos lie in wait. Every so often, a long tongue flicks out and lands an unwary insect.

Today, there is good hunting for geckos although neither their hunting skills nor their appetite can match the numbers of flies attracted by the smell of food. As soon as one fly disappears, another takes its place, circling the ceiling, round and round, making the odd detour over the food cooking on the stove or, more frequently, to a wet patch on the kitchen table that still offers the tang of raw meat.

The bead strings of the curtain part with a faint clicking sound and a cat's head appears. The stray, both loved and hated by Sunny, has reappeared after a long absence. Neleni, who is stirring a pot at the stove, watches it from the corner of her eye. The darkness of her mood lightens a little. Unlike Sunny, she has always welcomed the cat. She now wonders if her own fondness for it was the cause of Sunny's antipathy. That would have been just like her mother whose beliefs, in later life, often seemed to result from a perverse reaction to those of other people.

If Neleni liked something, Sunny would make a point of disliking it. Like the cat. Like Arjun. Neleni tried to persuade her mother to like both, but Sunny had resisted with stubborn determination – although, in the cat's case, she had not been altogether successful. However, nothing ever persuaded her to change her mind about Arjun. Neleni's mood lowers. She would have liked her mother to have given just one sign of approval. But, of course, this would have run counter to Sunny's faith and her loyalty to Raj.

Tail erect, eyes squeezed shut with pleasure, the cat leans against Neleni's leg, purring. She smiles. The cat returned several days ago. Neleni was elated, but too eager in her welcome. When she tried to pick it up, the cat had leapt out of her arms with a strangled yelp and raced out into the yard, disappearing over the fence. Neleni had wept bitterly. Raj had comforted her, stroking her hair with the kind of protective kindness that he usually reserves for the girls.

"It will be back. You must be patient. Don't try so hard the next time."

Despite herself, she had clung to him. The sudden loss of the cat had awakened a bitter sense of loss. Without being told, Raj seemed to understand. Briefly, Neleni had felt a closeness to him; a warmth, not love exactly, but a companionable sense of comfort. Why could he not always have shown this side of his nature? If he had, would she have fallen in love with Arjun?

But, when she thinks about it, she knows that nothing will change how she feels. She loves Arjun and always will. She cannot simply transfer her affections to another man, even if he is her husband. It would feel like adultery.

The cat rubs against her leg. She forces herself to ignore it, continuing to stir the pot. She is heavily pregnant and her back is aching. She can hear the children playing in the hall, their voices increasingly raucous. Soon there will be an argument, followed by slaps and she will have to intervene. She wishes Raj would come home. They behave better with him.

Hungry for attention, the cat has raised itself on its back legs, clawing at her sari. Carefully, she lowers herself to the floor and, squatting beside it, strokes the animal's head, tickling it behind the ears. The cat licks her hand with its rough tongue. She can feel its ribs, sticking through its fur.

Raising herself up, she walks slowly across the kitchen to the table where she has wrapped a few scraps of fat in greaseproof paper. Opening the packet, she places it on the floor. After sniffing the contents, the cat crouches down and begins to gorge on the scraps. Still purring, it chews with one side of its mouth, making a wet, lapping sound as it eats.

There is a scream from the hallway.

"What are you doing?" shouts Neleni.

She is answered by muffled sobs. Wearily, she prepares to drag herself to the hall and discipline the wrongdoers. Then, she hears the key in the door.

"Hello. What's up?"

There are cheerful squeals as the girls greet their father, all thoughts of their disagreement temporarily forgotten. With a silent prayer of thanks, Neleni returns to the stove. Raj appears in the doorway.

"What's cooking?"

He comes over to the stove and, putting an arm around her, bends over to sniff the contents of the pot.

"Smells good."

He puts his arm around her and kisses her on the cheek. She acknowledges him with a smile but cannot bring herself to kiss him back. Suddenly, she finds his presence oppressive. Like the cat, it reminds her of someone else; someone she loves more and misses. Raj pats her on the back and goes into the dining room where she can hear him performing his usual ritual: pouring arrack into a glass, then turning on the radio to listen to the news.

The darkness of her mood returns. Arjun. She has tried so hard to put him out of her thoughts, but he is always there. In recent weeks, the distance between them has increased and now, she fears the worst. He is steeling himself to leave her, she knows it, and this trip is the precursor to a final move. She tried to ask him about it but he was unusually taciturn. That, in itself, is the answer to her question. She is losing him.

Having finished its food, the cat is now stretched out under the kitchen table, anticipating a long sleep. Such simple contentedness contrasts with Neleni's own unhappiness, throwing it into sharp relief. She wipes the tears away with her hand, quietly weeping as she continues to stir the pot.

In the next room, the radio crackles as Raj twiddles the dials, trying to tune it. Eventually, he finds the right station and the house resonates with the newsreader's voice. As usual, the volume is far too high. Yet, for once, it fails to irritate Neleni. In her grief, she pays little attention to the headlines.

"Members of the Tamil Federal Party are preparing for their annual convention at Vavuniya where they will consider a proposal for nationwide satyagraha, or peaceful protest."

The cat creeps into a pool of light, picking its way gingerly over the railway tracks. Something catches its eye and it crouches, softly placing one paw in front of the other as it crawls forward. Suddenly, it freezes, fixing its eyes on something in the darkness. After a moment's pause, it pounces, dabbling furiously at the ground with its front paws. But its prey escapes. Sitting in the middle of the track, the cat licks its paw, then tenderly wipes its face, pretending to wash.

A moth, temporarily blinded by its encounter with a lamp, dives into view, whirling around the cat's head. Distracted by the insect's blundering flight, the cat follows it with its eyes then, without warning, hurtles upwards at full stretch, swiping with its paws. On landing, the cat dances about on its back legs, still frantically boxing the air. But it has failed.

Disappointed, the cat drops back onto all fours and minces away along the track, hindquarters swinging jauntily, only the flick of its tail betraying its fury. The moth, too, resumes its journey, swinging out in a wide arc, then spinning upwards, into the nebula of light inhabited by a thousand tiny insects, all ceaselessly whirring and fluttering around the lamp, satellites of a miniature sun.

Relics of Edwardian England, the lamps would not look out of place along the banks of the Thames. As it is, they were shipped thousands of miles, to cast their chilly light over a railway station in what was once an ancient Ceylonese city. In the pale flare of their light, the elaborate swags and garlands, with which the lamps are decorated, writhe about like serpents. Beyond the pale glow of the station, the world is wrapped in a blackness as soft and enveloping as velvet, a consuming darkness that swallows light and muffles sound.

Pacing along the track in front of the station, the cat heads for the goods yard in the hope of better hunting. Its ears twitch as it catches an unfamiliar sound and it stops, one paw raised in mid-air, its head turned towards the station. At the centre of the platform, a group of men has gathered around a man in long, saffron robes. Other men are joining them, flooding in from the doors and gates until the platform is packed and the overflow spills backwards through the station office and the yard beyond.

Soon, some five hundred men have encircled the station. They wait, speaking in low murmurs that sound to the cat like the whispering of a breeze. Motionless, the cat stares at them with unblinking green eyes. Then, one of the men at the front of the platform raises his arm. Something flies from his hand, spins through the air and hits the ground, a few inches away from the cat. The cat leaps sideways, skittering off into the shadows where it seeks refuge under one of the goods wagons stationed at the side of the track.

"A fine shot, brother." The man who has spoken wraps a clumsy arm around the boy who has thrown the stone. "You will make a fine bowler."

There is a muffled snigger from the men on the platform.

"Quiet, you fools!"

Several heads turn to see who has spoken. Realising that it was the monk, they are silent, sheepishly hanging their heads or shuffling their feet. He is not like the other monk with the pale eyes. They have confidence in him. It seems natural to treat him as their master. But this one. He is little better than they are, a peasant boy in monk's clothes. Some even wonder if he is a monk at all.

It is rumoured that anyone wishing to assume the robes of a monk has only to present himself at one of the monasteries in Polonnaruwa to be ordained. In the next few days there will be an explosion in the number of such ordinations and everyone from taxi drivers to common labourers will be able to acquire a set of saffron robes. Wrongdoers are quick to appreciate the usefulness of a disguise that provides immunity from the law.

One of the men mutters something out of the side of his mouth. Two or three of the men beside him begin to snicker.

"What was that?"

The monk wheels around. His hearing is sharp enough despite his dull-witted face.

Who can trust a fellow whose mouth turns down at one corner and who stoops to one side when he walks? The man who has just spoken has said as much to his friends.

"Were you talking about me?"

Eyes blazing, Tissa pushes his way through the crowd to confront the man. The fellow looks embarrassed, cannot look him in the eye. It is him all right. Despite the cramped conditions on the platform, Tissa swings his fist, not caring who he hits. It lands on the other man's nose with a sickening crack. The fellow staggers, then his knees crumple beneath him like paper. He falls to the ground where he sits, knees tucked up to his chin, nursing his face. Soon, blood begins to drip copiously from the hand held over his nose. But it is not enough for Tissa.

"Bastard!" he screams and aims a kick at the fellow's head that lays him out cold. Tissa stoops over him, panting, his lips flecked with spittle.

"That's enough, brother. Save it for the Tamils."

A strong hand clasps Tissa by the shoulder, guiding him to the front of the platform. It is one of the land squatters that Tissa has befriended in recent weeks. He knows him only by his first name, Dasa, but the two have become firm friends. Dasa has taught Tissa a lot. He is more approachable than Anil, less terrifying, as well as being a man of peasant stock, like Tissa himself.

Dasa has told Tissa how, the year before, he and other Sinhalese militants resisted the Government's attempts to introduce Tamil settlers into Padaviya, an area which local Sinhalese have always regarded as their territory. The Tamils had formerly been workers in the eastern port of Trincomalee but, following the withdrawal of the British Royal Navy, they had been left without work.

The Government had planned to resettle these Tamils in Padaviya, allocating several hundred plots of land to them. But Sinhalese politicians had mobilised opposition, instructing their followers to resist any Tamil incursion. Under the leadership of a monk, Dasa and a group of wage-labourers had seized several plots intended for Tamils. After that, Sinhalese squatters had occupied the rest of the land, without any resistance from the Government. It was at Padaviya that the term 'Sinhala Hamudawa' was first coined.

The fear of invasion is imbibed by most Sinhalese with their mothers' milk. Not without reason. The country has been carved up and colonised by successive waves of invaders. Now, according to nationalist leaders, they are facing invasion from within and the events of recent months have done little to assuage their fears. Local politicians and political agitators, in search of suitable support, have found it in the loosely-formed Sinhala Hamudawa.

Now, Sinhalese activists have identified a new threat: the annual convention of the Tamil Federal Party at Vavuniya. Angered by the failure of the Bandaranaike-Chelvanayakam pact and mistrustful of the Prime Minister's intentions, some of the more vociferous Tamils are demanding a massive *satyagraha*. Vavuniya will give them a platform from which to promote a nationwide protest that could cripple the country.

***

Standing next to Dasa, Tissa regains his composure. He draws strength from Dasa's companionship and earthy confidence. Friendship and trust are not gifts conferred by Anil. Rather the reverse. Anil's relationship to Tissa is that of master to servant, defined by humiliation and abuse. But it never occurs to Tissa to question Anil's authority. That would be like questioning god, a form of blasphemy.

Although he sometimes feels betrayed by him, Tissa reveres Anil. He loves and fears him in equal measure, reserving for Anil a special, unquestioning devotion. In fact, on the occasions when he remembers to pray, it is Anil's face that appears before him, not the plaster image of a god. Surely, that is a sign of divinity.

"I will make him proud of me tonight," thinks Tissa, his heart racing.

All around him, men are packed onto the station: there must be at least five hundred of them, many recruited from the settlement at Padiviya. Yet, despite their numbers, the only sound to be heard is the distant clanking of goods trains. Occasionally someone coughs or murmurs but most wait in silence, tense with anticipation. Most are peasants or wage-labourers but, here and there, the flowing robes and shaven heads of monks can be seen, most of them recently ordained. A few yards away from Tissa, stand two muscular bhikkus who, if it were not for their robes, would be indistinguishable from their fellow peasants.

From its hiding place, the cat peers out from the wheel of a goods wagon where it has been hiding. It sniffs the air and ventures a paw onto the track. Its ears prick up. In the distance, it catches a sound as yet unheard by the men on the platform: the faint whistling of a train. The cat waits. The train whistles again, closer this time. The heads of the men on the platform all turn in one direction, looking into the darkness. Judging that it is safe to move, the cat creeps forward. It crouches, waiting to see if the men have noticed, its sensitive paws picking up the tremor of the approaching train. No-one pays the cat any attention. With one swift bound, the cat is off, running down the track, into the night.

620

Mr Pereira has had a long day. Two long days, in fact. The owner of a small factory on the outskirts of Vavuniya, he has just completed an unsuccessful sales trip to Colombo where none of the shopkeepers he approached were interested in his innovative ideas for children's toys.

The buyer for a major store, a slender young man with slicked back hair and an elegant pin-striped suit, had simply laughed at him. But he did not give up. Not him. That young man's arrogance had merely encouraged Mr Pereira to persevere.

Work hard and you will succeed. That was what his father used to say. In fact, that was his only legacy to his son when he died, weary and heartbroken, at the age of forty-seven. But Mr Pereira treasures those words, believing that they contain a profound truth.

Work hard and you will succeed. Mr Pereira had repeated that phrase to himself as he tramped doggedly through the streets, pushing his way through crowds, negotiating roads choked with traffic where you were as likely to be killed by a bicycle as a lorry. Each time, before speaking to a prospective buyer, he would find a quiet place on the pavement, usually in a doorway and, closing his eyes, repeat the words like a mantra. But it did not help.

The shopkeepers' politeness could not hide their indifference. They had all thanked him for coming and taken his phone number, promising to call once they had given the matter further thought. But he knew they would not. So, after two days of fruitless effort, Mr Pereira had packed his sample case and headed home. However, in order to delay breaking the news of his failed trip to his wife, he decided to break his journey at the eastern town of Batticaloa where he visited his sister.

Surrounded by nephews and nieces, fed and fussed over, Mr Pereira gained a few hours' respite from his cares. His flagging spirits were buoyed up by his brother-in-law, a Tamil businessman, who gave him some much-needed encouragement and offered to introduce him to a financier who, he said, could help to expand his business.

Mr Pereira had begun to feel much better. In the company of friends, he was able to relax, although he had to admit that it was strange to be surrounded by people who spoke Tamil as their first language; for Batticaloa is situated in the east which, together with the northern region centred around Jaffna, forms the Tamil heartland.

It was with some sadness that Mr Pereira had parted from his sister and her family and yet, his farewell was also tinged with relief. Already fatigued and suffering from lack of sleep, the strain of trying to communicate in Tamil had exhausted him. For, despite speaking it fluently, it is his second language. You can only be completely at home in your mother tongue, or Swabhasa, as it is commonly called. To speak in your own language is like arriving home and kicking off your shoes after a hard day at work. Mr Pereira thinks how good it will be to get home and speak to his own family in Sinhalese.

***

When Mr Pereira got to the station at Batticaloa, it was swarming with Tamils, all bound for the convention in Vavuniya. Cursing himself, Mr Pereira had joined the long queue for tickets. He had forgotten all about the conference. He would be lucky to get on the train, let alone get a seat. He berated himself for not having thought about this. After all, he had heard about it on the news. But for anyone who is not a Tamil and, more specifically, a member of the Tamil Federal Party, the Convention has little significance.

Most people are more concerned about the recent strikes, organised by Communists and Trotskyites, that have virtually brought the country to a standstill. At first the Ceylon Employers' Federation, of which Mr Pereira is a member, had thought the Government would support it; but, at the eleventh hour, Mr Bandaranaike had lost his nerve. Having initially declared the strike illegal, two weeks later he had ordered employers to reach agreement with their workers or face nationalization of their businesses. Forced to make concessions that he cannot afford, Mr Pereira is still fuming about what he regards as Mr Bandaranaike's betrayal.

"Good luck to them," Mr Pereira thought to himself as he watched a group of Tamils, greeting each other excitedly at the station. He had even begun to wonder what it would be like to live in a Tamil state.

"No worse than under this Government," he had concluded, grumpily.

Having bought his ticket at Batticaloa station, Mr Pereira had joined another queue for the train. Again, he was obliged to wait, hot and uncomfortable, his legs aching, unable to remove his jacket or even put his case down as he was pushed and buffeted by the crowd. The delegates were packed five deep on the platform and Mr Pereira had been at the back. Finally, after what seemed like hours, the train steamed sluggishly into the station. Officials shouted, whistles were blown and passengers surged forward.

Carried along with the flow, Mr Pereira had squeezed through the door with two other people, but everyone smiled good-naturedly, accepting that discomfort was inevitable. Although he had no seat, Mr Pereira counted himself lucky to get on the train at all. Latecomers were still flooding onto the platform, trying to board and, finding this impossible, some had clustered about the doors, sticking like limpets to the exterior of the train, finding a precarious toehold on the steps as they clung to open windows or passenger rails. Others were pushed back by the guards and Mr Pereira watched their disappointed faces with a sense of satisfaction as the train pulled slowly out of the station.

Wedged into a doorway, there was not even room for Mr Pereira to sit on the floor. However, the pressure from the bodies surrounding him was such that there was no possibility of falling over, so Mr Pereira allowed himself to doze, standing up with his head propped against the wooden doorjamb. It was uncomfortable but his exhaustion was so complete that he no longer cared.

He was still asleep, standing up, when the train pulled in to Welikande. For a second, Mr Pereira opened his eyes, checked the name of the station, then closed them again. Somewhere, far in the distance, an announcement was being made. There was a general stir amongst the people in the carriage then, as if triggered by the same switch, they began to swarm off the train. All of them.

"Aren't you coming?" asked the man who had been standing next to Mr Pereira.

"Where?" responded Mr Pereira sleepily. "This isn't my station."

"Aren't you going to the Convention?" asked the other fellow.

"No. I'm going home," mumbled Mr Pereira, lapsing into Sinhalese.

"Ah," said the man and, without any more explanation he, too, got off the train.

A seat! Mr Pereira could not believe his luck. In fact, he could have taken his pick of any of the seats because now, mysteriously, the train was empty. Drowsily, he pushed his aching legs forward and fell into the first available seat. Fatigued beyond the point of exhaustion, he was too tired to question why all the other passengers had left. He just hoped that the train would continue its journey. Just his luck if it terminated here.

But, a few minutes later, he heard the whistle blowing. The train jolted, grunted, then slowly pulled out of the station. Mr Pereira relaxed into a deep sleep, having first said a prayer of thanks for having found a seat.

The train lurches to a halt and Mr Pereira's eyes flicker open for a second. The lights are enough to tell him that he is at a station. Polonnaruwa. Some way to go yet. He can sleep a little longer. His eyes close, his head rolls back and his mouth falls open. Somewhere, in the distance, Mr Pereira dreams that he hears a crash, followed by the tinkling of glass.

Folding his arms over his stomach, Mr Pereira rolls over until he is sitting sideways on the seat, one cheek pressed against the head-rest, his knees curled up beneath him. He continues to doze, still vaguely aware of the sound of shattering glass. It seems to be coming closer. There is a thud as the door to the carriage is flung open, then the sound of feet as people board the train. There seem to be lots of them. A cool draft of air passes over Mr Pereira's cheek. He wishes the other passengers would hurry up and close the door.

"There he is." A man's voice, coarse and unpleasant.

There is a murmur and a shuffling of feet. Mr Pereira can feel the movement of air as people file past him. Then silence. For just a few seconds. A hand grabs his shoulder and Mr Pereira finds himself being roughly shaken. Startled, he opens his eyes.

A group of men, labourers by the look of them, are standing around him. Many are gaunt, unshaven, their cheeks covered with stubble. They wear cheap sarongs and old white shirts stained yellow with sweat. They have crowded around him so tightly that he can feel the heat from their bodies, smell their malodorous breath, stinking with the odour of garlic and onions. One of them belches, openly, not putting his hand to his mouth. Mr Pereira smells alcohol, too. A lot of it. Cheap grog, warm and rancid.

"What do you want?" he mutters, his brain so lazy with sleep that he thinks he might still be dreaming.

Like cattle, the men just stare at him. He must be dreaming. They are merely a figment of his imagination, images that neither move nor speak. Mr Pereira closes his eyes, trying to dismiss them but, when he opens his eyes again, they are still there, still staring at him.

"What do you want?"

Awake now, his voice clearer, Mr Pereira cannot conceal his alarm. It seems to be the signal the men are waiting for.

"Tamil bastard!" mutters a voice from the back.

"Yeah. Tamil scum!"

Soon they are all shouting and jeering, stamping their feet, waving their fists in his face.

"I'm Sinhalese. Like you!" stammers Mr Pereira.

But he cannot make himself heard above the voice of the mob.

Desperately, he looks around for a way out, but he is surrounded on all sides. The carriage is now packed with men, at least seventy by Mr Pereira's calculation. More have gathered on the track outside the carriage. He can see them from the window, all looking up at him. Then, to his horror, he realises that many are carrying clubs.

By now, the noise is deafening but, still, no-one has laid a finger on him. It is almost as if they are savouring him, postponing their moment of enjoyment in order to make it sweeter. Like children, thinks Mr Pereira, keeping the cherry on a cake until last. And then, he thinks of his own children. Of their birthday parties. Of his wife. Of the fact that he might never see them again and he begins to cry.

"Please, please," he begs. "I am Sinhalese. I can prove it. Here. Look. Here is my driving licence."

Fumbling inside his jacket, he finds the document then waves it in front of the men. One snatches it from him and holding it between his fingers, pretends to read, wagging his head from side to side as if following the words. A joker, obviously, because he is holding the document upside down. The other fellows laugh, snatch the paper, pass it around, tear it to shreds. They laugh and stamp and scream, passing around bottles of arrack wrapped in brown paper bags.

"Please," gasps Mr Pereira. "Please, let me go. I have a little money. You can have it all, if you like. Here. Take my wallet."

The wallet is seized and passed to the back of the crowd and, although they continue to taunt Mr Pereira, they still hang back. A spark of hope kindles.

"They will not hurt me," he thinks. "Not now. They've got what they want."

Then, the crowd parts and a man dressed in saffron robes pushes his way through from the back. A monk. *Thank God*, thinks Mr Pereira, although he does not like the look of the fellow. Shoving his way to the front, the monk pauses for a moment, taking in every detail of Mr Pereira's face, his western-style suit, his black leather, lace-up shoes. Mr Pereira gets the feeling that the man does not like him and that the source of that dislike is envy. Mr Pereira is a devout Buddhist but this fellow does not look like any monk that he has ever seen.

"Greetings, brother."

With his hands raised over his head in the prayer gesture, Mr Pereira bows to the monk but, as he does so, he catches the fellow's eye. He does not know exactly what happened but, in that moment, Mr Pereira feels the wheel of fortune turn against him.

"Tamil scum! You are all the same."

The monk spits in his face. Then, turning to his followers, he screams: "Show him how we deal with Tamils!"

Instantly galvanised, the mob surges forward. Punches and kicks rain down on Mr Pereira's head and he is beaten to the floor. But it is not enough. Only a few can reach him and the others, outside, are howling for blood. A man with huge, knotted hands grabs the merchant by his collar and drags him, screaming, through the crowd on the train to the door where he boots him onto the platform. Instantly, the others are on him like a pack of hounds: baying and yelling, clubbing him with sticks, kicking, punching and thrashing until vapour from their sweating bodies rises into the cool night air like smoke.

Then, a temple bell clangs. Once. Heads are raised at the back of the platform. *Police*. The word travels forward like an echo to the front of the platform where the furious beating has turned into a frenzy. *Police*. The crowd stirs. The men with clubs are pulled off the victim and, just as suddenly as it appeared, the crowd, now silent, disperses leaving what appears to be a bundle of clothes on the platform.

***

An anxious face appears at the station window. A railway clerk, who managed to conceal himself under his desk, has managed to call the police. Slipping out of a side door, he creeps stealthily along the side of the building, keeping to the shadows. Peering around the corner, he makes sure that the men have gone before running onto the platform. Stooping over the pile of clothes, he is shocked to discover that it is a man, his face bloodied and unrecognisable, the lids of his eyes so swollen and bruised that he can no longer see.

"Brother. Say something. Can you speak?"

Silence. Then, the man groans. His cracked and bleeding lips move slightly. He is trying to say something. Crouching over him, the clerk holds his ear to the man's lips.

"What is it, brother?"

"I am Sinhalese. Sinhalese."

Thick tears ooze from beneath the man's swollen lids.

Early next morning, Nash's wife draws his attention to a plume of smoke hanging over the town.

"What do you think it is, darling?"

"I don't know. Probably just a house fire."

Nash, his chin jutting out, continues to stare intently at the mirror as he grapples with a particularly slippery tie. Evading his grasp, the silk slithers around his fingers, like gossamer, reminding him why he banished it to the back of the wardrobe. But it was a present from Chitra and today, being their anniversary, he will wear it to please her.

"Damn!"

The tie has managed to knot itself too soon, leaving one end ridiculously short and the other, impossibly long. Chitra laughs.

"Here, let me."

For matters of this sort, Chitra employs a no-nonsense approach that defies resistance. Swiftly undoing Nash's crumpled knot, she re-adjusts the ends of the tie, pulling first one, then the other, until she is perfectly satisfied. Nash, who knows better than to move at such times, stands as still as a guardsman, his chin in the air. As he does so, he looks out of the window.

A great column of black, curdled smoke hangs over the town. Nash judges the source to be about two or three miles away, somewhere near the station. It is probably no more than a house fire. Still, it won't hurt to make enquiries. He makes a mental note to call the police station.

Chitra is still tugging at the tie. If he moves, she will scold him. Unable to move, he is forced to contemplate the vast pillar of smoke. It gives him a queasy feeling: not nausea, exactly, but a strange fluttering in the pit of his stomach. It happens often these days: that, and the uneasy dreams about death. He puts it down to age.

"Done!"

The mutinous tie has been mastered. A thing of perfection, the knot sits obediently between the lapels of Nash's shirt. Chitra stands back to admire her handiwork.

"That's a very nice tie. I don't know why you don't wear it more often."

Smiling to himself, Nash bends forward to kiss her; with one eye on the window and the billowing plume of smoke.

1958: A telephone call

Sergeant Gunasekera has been dozing quietly over his book. Although his shift only started an hour ago, Gunasekera is exhausted. His wife spent most of the previous evening screaming at him and, finally, he had retaliated, shouting back, calling her a 'crazy Tamil bitch'. Taken aback, she had turned pale, even staggered a little, as if she had been slapped. He had never called her that before. In fact, until now, he has never fought back, meekly taking whatever abuse she throws at him, seeking solace in his thrillers.

But his new-found aggression had an unexpected effect. Recovering from her shock, his wife followed him to bed, creeping meekly in beside him, then gently running her finger down his spine, she cooed a word that brought him instant arousal. *Sorry.* Its seductiveness lay in its novelty. She had never apologised before.

Last night, Sergeant Gunasekera rediscovered his marriage. And his wife. He did not timidly ask if she wished to be touched, as he usually does. He assumed it was his right and, to his surprise, his advances were eagerly welcomed. Finally, after years of sterile union, Gunasekera realised that his wife's shrewishness was the result of frustration. All this time, she simply wanted a man who was decisive, who could make up his own mind without constantly seeking her opinion. Gunasekera's diffidence had been his worst enemy.

This morning, he left their house, exhausted but happy, stumbling out over the front step as his wife kissed him tenderly on the cheek. Their apartment block fronts onto a dark alley, occupied by other Sinhalese families, most of whom live in overcrowded tenements.

As Gunasekera stepped into the street, he was greeted by a neighbour, a man who he knows is a Sinhalese nationalist, although has no idea of the man's activities and does not suspect him of fanaticism. Mumbling something, the man nodded at him with a knowing look. Gunasekera felt his cheeks flush. The walls of his house are thin and the other man had probably heard the sergeant shouting at his wife. With a sudden rush of protectiveness, Gunasekera regretted having referred to her as a Tamil. It is a sensitive issue, what with the recent coverage of the Vavuniya conference, and the Gunasekeras live in a fervently Sinhalese area.

The other man smiled with what Gunasekera will later think of as an 'I told you so' look. The Sergeant had wanted to challenge the man, tell him that his assumptions were wrong, but how could one broach such a subject. In a place like this, the workings of every family are the business of the neighbours and everyone is free to draw their own conclusions. Putting his uneasiness down to exhaustion, Gunasekera had continued on his way to work where, within five minutes of installing himself at his desk, he had fallen into a blissful doze.

***

Sergeant Gunasekera is woken by the shrill ringing of the telephone. Jumping to attention, he drops his book on the floor as he fumbles for the receiver.

"Hello. Police station."

His words are thick with sleep. Gunasekera rubs his eyes, trying to pay attention to the clipped voice at the other end of the line. His stomach lurches unpleasantly when the voice announces itself as the Government Agent.

"Yes, sir. No, sir."

Gunasekera could kick himself. His answers are mechanical, uninformed. In fact, it sounds as if he is repeating a nursery rhyme.

"What is that plume of smoke that I can see from my window?" demands the voice.

Raising himself from his chair, Gunasekera leans over the desk to get a glimpse through the door. He did not see any plume of smoke on his way to work but, there again, he had other things on his mind.

"Um, er. I don't know, sir."

"Then find out!"

"Yes, sir. Hold the line, please, sir."

Placing the receiver on the desk, Gunasekera scurries into the back office where another sergeant is quietly eating his breakfast from a tiffin-box.

"What is that smoke?"

The other man shrugs.

"Don't know. Something to do with the station. Probably a fire in a goods wagon."

Gunasekera hurries back to the phone.

"It's coming from the station, sir. A minor incident." Then, putting his own gloss on it: "All taken care of, sir. Nothing the police can't handle."

"Mm. Very well."

The voice at the end of the phone is clearly not satisfied with the answer. The line clicks and goes dead.

"Hmph!" says Gunasekera, looking with disgust at the receiver. "Too grand to say 'Goodbye'."

At the other end of the line, Nash has a similar reaction to the brusque curtailment of his call. He makes a note of the man's name and promises to have a word with the Assistant Superintendent of Police the next time he sees him.

Neither Nash nor Sergeant Gunasekera realises that the telephone wire has just been cut by a gang of the Sinhala Hamudawa.

Ella is late.

Yesterday, one of her children developed an alarming cough. Ella expected the worst. Coughs like that usually turn into a fever. So, she sat up all night, trying to give the child whatever home-made medication she could find, singing to it softly, trying to get it to sleep and stop its miserable crying, feeling its forehead for the first, tell-tale signs of fever. But, although warm, the child's skin never grew hot.

As dawn approached, the child drifted into contented sleep and Ella, still fully clothed, crawled onto her bed, a framework of split wood and woven palm fronds. The bed crackled under her weight and swayed a little, the bindings that held the wooden uprights to the frame having become loose. Her husband groaned and gave a deep rattling cough. But he did not wake.

Turning on her side, Ella tried to sleep but, although the source had been removed, her newly-awakened fear stayed with her. As soon as she closed her eyes, she became aware of the rapid beating of her heart. Opening them again, she stared into the gloom until, through the darkness she could distinguish several dark bundles lying on the floor.

She listened to her family as they slept: the soft murmur of the two younger children, both under five; the deeper breathing of the older boy, now eight and old enough to work in the fields; the feeble whistling of her elderly mother; the stertorous wheeze of her sick husband. At least, they were all here. Still alive. That was something to be thankful for.

Ella said two prayers of thanks: one to St Anthony; the other to Ganesha, the elephant-headed god. It did not worry her that one was a Catholic saint and the other, a Hindu deity. Her father had been a Christian, while her mother is a strict Hindu. Ella always felt that she was a bit of both and, with the Hindu ability to assimilate gods from other faiths, she frequently prays to Christian saints.

The terrified beating of her heart began to slow. Outside a cockerel crowed. Although it was still dark, Ella knew that dawn was approaching. Soon the village would come to life. First, she would hear the clanking of a bucket as a neighbour went to milk her buffalo. Next, she would smell the sweet odour of smoke as women lit fires which they fed with dried cakes of cattle dung.

Yawning loudly, men would stretch the stiffness from their limbs and chickens would run squawking from their feet as they strolled into the yard, taking deep breaths of cool air as they rubbed the sleep from their eyes. Children would run about, chattering, getting under their mothers' feet until they were scolded into good behaviour. A hundred domestic rituals would be performed in exactly the same sequence as they had been for the last hundred years. It was a comforting thought.

Without meaning to, Ella had fallen into a deep sleep.

***

"Are you not working today, child?"

Her mother is shaking her gently.

"Amma. Oh no. Have I slept late?"

"Not too late."

Ella swings her legs over the bed and rubs her face with her hands. It feels sticky and hot.

"Drink this."

Her mother places a cup of strong tea in her hand, making sure that Ella has a firm grip of the cup.

"I must wash."

"I have put clean water in the bowl and, next to it, some clean clothes."

Ella strokes the old lady's cheek.

"Where is Mahesh?"

"Your husband has taken Kuheswaran to the fields to find work."

"What? Will Mahesh work, too?"

"He says he feels better today."

The old lady looks away, not meeting Ella's eyes. They both know he lied.

"He must not. Amma, I must speak to him. Tell him to rest."

"No. You must work. I will go and tell him."

Ella kisses her mother then, still sipping the tea, has a perfunctory wash before hurriedly pulling the clean dress over her skinny frame. As she runs from the village to the railway line, she regrets not saying goodbye to her husband and eldest son.

**

Ella runs down the sun-baked track, flanked by fields of whispering sugar cane, oblivious to the sharp stones that dig into her feet. There is no time to pick her way carefully, as she usually does. She is late and must make up for lost time. From above, she looks like a slender child; her hair, still wet, streaming behind her; her frock, several sizes too big.

She cannot see through the densely-packed cane that towers above her on either side or she would see the lorry, approaching the village from the other direction. As it is, she can only hear the faint rumble of an engine in the distance. Nothing unusual. It is harvest-time and the planters often bring in labourers from neighbouring villages. Preoccupied with thoughts of losing her job, she gives it no thought.

Still running, she leaves the road, following a narrow track that leads through the cane-field, a short-cut used by the villagers which leads to the outskirts of town and, more importantly, the railway track. As Ella disappears into the cane, the lorry turns into the road which she has just left, heading towards the village.

1958: The journey to work

Ella regrets her choice of a short-cut. It has not been used for some time and the path is overgrown with coarse weeds that stick to her legs and tear at her skin. In places, the path has become so narrow that she has to squeeze through the cane. As she pushes the rigid stems apart, something large falls out of the waving fronds at the top of the plants, glancing off her shoulder. She screams. The cane harbours poisonous spiders. The thing lands behind her with a soft thud. She is sure it was a spider. But she does not look back.

Ella worries about her husband and son working in the fields. Although the labourers set light to the cane before harvesting it, this stratagem rarely succeeds in driving out all the venomous creatures that live there. If her sick husband is bitten by a spider, he will not survive. Every year, there are many such deaths: labourers, sweating and racked with pain, carried home on make-shift stretchers, watched by their helpless families as they lie dying in the sparse darkness of their huts.

Ella curses herself for oversleeping. If she had gone to work on time, her husband would not have dragged himself out to the fields, intent on finding work: and, although her son, aged eight, is old enough to cut cane, she would rather he had stayed at home and gone to school. But there is some consolation in the knowledge that all his schoolmates will be there with him. For poor families, short-term gains, however small, will always defeat long-term goals; an opportunity to earn a few rupees from working the land is always to be preferred to the advantages of education. The choice is stark. Eat or starve.

Not for the first time, Ella thinks with some nostalgia of the tea plantation where she grew up. Over a century ago, her great-grandparents had been brought with thousands of other labourers from Tamil Nadu in southern India. Little more than slaves, they had picked tea for the British as indentured workers. Yet, despite their hardship, there had been advantages to that life: security, a place to live, even schools and, sometimes, medical attention.

Fired by youthful optimism, Ella and her husband had abandoned the plantation to find what they regarded as freedom and a chance of bettering themselves. But it turned out to be a false hope. Working the cane fields has turned out to be harder and far more hazardous than picking tea. A kindly tea-planter might be prevailed upon to help in a time of hardship, but there is no-one to help you here. And it is hotter, far hotter, than the cool air of the hills. Ella often dreams of the fresh greenness of the tea plantations, such a contrast to the heat of the plains and the parchment pallor of the cane fronds.

She emerges from the path onto the side of the road where she dusts herself off, brushing her back and shoulders, vigorously shaking the full skirt of her dress in order to dislodge any insects. As she does so, she realises that her arms have been scratched in several places by the dry, rasping edge of the cane leaves. The short-cut was a mistake. She now feels dirtier than when she got up.

She wonders what Neleni will say when she sees her. Her mistress has been short-tempered of late and is not as sympathetic as her mother was. Ella has fond memories of the old lady. Unlike her daughter, who Ella regards as spoilt and wilful, Sunny appreciated how hard life could be for someone like her.

Ella was often angered by the way Neleni spoke to her mother but, being a maid, she could say nothing. Instead, she would pay particular attention to the old lady, listening to what everyone else regarded as her ramblings. They often used to laugh together and, despite being mistress and servant, had become firm friends. Ella misses her.

About half a mile along the road are the few houses and shops that pass for a town. Slung between the buildings is a cat's-cradle of ugly black cables which resemble the workings of a huge spider. Ella has never really known what they are for, although someone once told her that they were telephone lines.

Ella first saw a telephone through the window of the railway office where the station master, seated beneath a huge ceiling fan, was talking into something that he held to his ear. Ella had assumed rightly that this was a telephone. She had wanted a better look but, as she pressed her face to the window, the station-master had looked up and, on seeing her, had angrily waved her away. Terrified, Ella had run off. The station manager was an important man in the town; like god, almost. She had feared that, thinking her a vagrant or a thief, he might call the police. No-one wanted a visit from them.

Since then, Ella has been able to familiarise herself with the bakolite telephone in Neleni's house. She dusts it every day, although no-one seems to use it. The contraption sits on its table in the hall, displayed like an exhibit in a museum. Ella wonders why people need telephones at all. She gets all the news she needs from her neighbours and, as no-one in the village has a radio, she does not see the reason for that, either. Although the world is being rapidly transformed by new technology, it is not her world: that will continue as it always has, lit only by oil lamps, relying for its survival on manual labour and the use of a few primitive tools.

Because telephones do not form part of her world, Ella does not try to understand them. She does not, therefore, realise the significance of the wires, hanging loose and unattached, from the wooden telegraph poles that run alongside the road into town. If she were to stop for a moment to look through the window into the station-master's office, she might realise that something unusual is happening.

With the receiver pressed to his ear, the station-master dials a number, listens, presses the bar on top of the phone, then dials again, repeating the same process with a frown that expresses consternation, anger and disbelief. But, these days, Ella takes care to pass the station-master's office on the other side of the street; taking a less direct route to the railway track, down a lane that passes the town's only rest-house.

The lane is narrow, with high banks on either side and these, combined with frequent sharp bends, obscure the view in every direction. At last, after one final turn, the lane opens out onto a broad, flat road with a tall white building on one side, fronted by a broad swathe of short grass. Originally built as the home of a colonial official, this is now the town's rest-house, serving both as a cheap restaurant and a boarding-house for occasional travellers.

Ella is surprised to see a large number of men, at least a hundred, sprawled on the grass in front of the guest-house. As soon as she appears, all eyes are turned upon her. She feels uncomfortable, but it is too late to go back and, anyway, she has no time for detours. Taking a deep breath, she lowers her eyes and, trying to walk at an even pace, approaches the rest-house.

Before they saw her, the men were talking amongst themselves but, now, all are silent. They have been drinking. She can see a number of empty bottles scattered over the grass. Many, still wrapped in brown paper bags, she knows to be arrack bottles.

633

Although Ella tries to breathe deeply, the air does not seem to penetrate her throat. She feels dizzy and fears that she might faint. She is right in front of them now and still they are silent. But she can feel their eyes, taking in every detail: her dishevelled hair, her crumpled dress, the scratches on her arms. She keeps walking, her eyes focussed on the ground just in front of her feet. Now she can smell them: boozy breath; the sour smell of sweat and unwashed clothes; the sickly scent of cheap hair oil.

"Pigs," she thinks to herself.

They are wage-labourers, hardly better than vagrants. She knows the sort. Imported by the Government to work on road and irrigation projects, they travel the country, scratching a living where they can, often drinking more than they earn, getting into fights. They resent everyone but seem to reserve particular venom for poor people, like Ella, who lead a settled, village life: especially if they are Tamil.

Although she has no radio, Ella knows as well as anyone of the land-grab, a few months ago, at Padaviya, where land allocated to unemployed Tamil workers from Trincomalee, was seized by Sinhalese labourers. She has heard enough to know that the Government turned a blind eye and did nothing to evict the squatters. Men like these.

By now, she has almost passed the rest-house. As she begins to breathe more easily, she wonders why the men are there, why the owner of the rest-house has allowed them to loiter on the grass, littering it with their rubbish. She begins to feel angry.

"Tamil bitch!"

Ella freezes. The potu, the round red spot that every Tamil woman wears on her forehead, has given her away. Then, she remembers. She washed in such a hurry this morning that she had no time to apply it. There is no way they can know she is Tamil, is there? Without looking around, she continues to walk, slightly faster than before. She can see the next bend in the road, once around that, she will be out of sight and she will run, as fast as she can. It is not far to the rail-track. There should be other people there. She will be safe. She can hear voices behind her, arguing.

"She's no Tamil. No potu. You're drunk!"

"She is, I tell you. I know her. Seen her before. I remember that one."

"Fancy her, do you? Better go after her then!"

There is much raucous laughter, then the sound of running feet. Without looking around, Ella takes to her heels, ignoring the sharp stones that bite into her feet. Like the wind, she runs, her loose dress billowing out behind her. But she can still hear other feet. She does not know how many, but she has more than one pursuer. Still she runs, on towards the track. She can see it now. From this distance, it looks empty.

Then she sees something: a body, sprawled across the line, an old man with white hair, lying face down, his shirt gashed in many places, soaked in blood; then, further up the line, another body and, beyond that, another.

"Oh god!"

She almost stumbles but, quickly righting herself, she continues, aiming for the jungle that creeps up to the line on the other side of the track. At least there, she might have a chance to hide. Behind her, she can hear the sound of a man vomiting. Too much exercise for one so full of alcohol in this heat. She listens. She can still hear feet, but only one pair and they seem to be further away. Arms flung out to balance herself, she springs onto the track, crosses it in two long strides, then leaps onto the bank that leads down into the trees.

But she has misjudged the distance. She loses her footing and tumbles down the slope. At the bottom, she lies gasping, trying to regain her breath, crippled by a violent stitch in her side. After a few minutes, she listens again. Nothing. Painfully, she gets to her feet. Her ankle is throbbing. She must have twisted it in the fall. She tries to put her weight on it and winces with pain, biting her lip as she tries to prevent herself from crying out. There is still no noise from the other side of the track. They must have given up. Easing herself down into a sitting position, she rubs her ankle, wondering how she will ever get back home. Going to work now is out of the question.

Perhaps it is the pain in her ankle, or the effect of the fall, but she does not hear the soft rustle of leaves behind her. She only becomes aware of the man's presence when a heavy hand is placed on her shoulder and a voice, thick with alcohol, breathes in her ear.

"Got you!"

Following Ella's departure, her mother starts to tidy up; a process that never takes long due partly to the smallness of the house and partly to the lack of family possessions. Ella calls it a house but, in truth, it is little more than a hut with mud-brick walls and a thatched roof. Cattle have shelters made of the same materials which are often larger than the building occupied by Ella's family. Nonetheless, it is home.

Using a large broom made of twigs, Ella's mother sweeps the floor. Dust, leaves and stray grains of rice that fell to the ground during the last meal are gathered into a pile in the doorway then, with a deft flick of the broom, they are whisked out of the door in a grey cloud, a few particles of which blow back into the house causing the sick child to cough.

"You won't be coming with us, today," says the old woman as she tenderly strokes the child's head.

"Stay with me, Amma."

The child grasps the old woman's hand with frail fingers, her eyes shining brightly in the darkness, whether with fever or tears, the old woman cannot tell.

"I must go to the fields to find your father. I will take the others with me so that you can rest."

The child coughs feebly.

"But first, I will get you some water."

Turning, the old lady walks the few steps into the kitchen where water is kept in a large earthenware pot with a wooden lid. Although food is cooked outside, there is also a 'kitchen' inside the house where Ella's mother performs the more lengthy processes of food preparation, such as grinding spices or kneading bread, protected from the heat and the scorching rays of the sun.

Although it is just a corner of the single large room in which everyone eats and sleeps, this little kitchen has a character of its own which distinguishes it from the rest of the living space. It has low shelves made of mud brick, set against the wall, on which precious cooking implements are kept: a large metal mixing bowl, slightly dented; a stack of smaller bowls made from cheap, white metal; several brass pots containing spices; a long-handled spoon; two knives and a heavy pestle and mortar made of black stone. Every day, the mixing bowl is scoured until it shines then stood upright on the shelf where it serves as an ornament. One corner of this kitchen space serves as the larder, where two sacks, one of rice and one of flour, stand next to a jar of oil. Above these, hanging from nails fixed into the wall, are two strings of onions and several small net bags containing chillies, garlic and carrots.

Taking a ladle from the shelf, the old lady spoons water from the earthenware pot into a glass and takes it to the child who, supported by her grandmother, manages a few sips before sinking back exhausted. Like the others, the child sleeps on a reed mat, placed on the floor. The only bed in the house belongs to her parents and has been bought, at great expense, in the hope that it will improve her father's health. But, so far, there has been little improvement.

"I am going now," murmurs the grandmother, stooping to kiss her grand-daughter.

The child's eyelids flutter momentarily, but she says nothing. The old lady waits until the child's breathing is regular and her eyes firmly closed, then quietly withdraws.

Although hot outside, the air is fresh, a welcome change from the half-lit gloom of the house that seems always to carry a lingering smell of sickness. The old lady's heart is heavy when she thinks of her grand-daughter, lying inside. She fears, although she has said nothing to Ella, that the child has caught her father's illness. She has developed the same ivory pallor that makes her lips and eyes look unnaturally dark.

The grandmother sighs then, calling the other children to her, she leads them towards the fields, feeling her spirits rise with every step. It is not often that she has an excuse to walk outside, just for pleasure, and she is determined to make the most of it.

1958: The cane-cutters

Stones crackle under the lorry's tyres as it turns slowly into the road that skirts the cane fields. The gears clank once and the engine growls as the vehicle creeps forward, its flanks dusted with red earth. On either side of the track, the cane grows high, ten feet or more, concealing the lorry from the workers cutting cane further down the road. The driver turns the key, cutting off the engine.

Silently, the lorry heads down the slight incline, travelling forward under its own momentum for the last hundred yards, until it is level with the field in which the labourers are working. Finally, it rolls to a standstill. The tailgate drops and several men, bloated with drink, leap off to piss in the ditch, grunting with satisfaction as their bladders empty.

Peering from the cab window, their leader is staring at the field of sugar-cane where adults and children, protected by broad-brimmed hats, are harvesting the tall, yellow stems. The labourers have already cleared a third of the field and are working with their backs to the road, so none of them is aware of the lorry and the men watching them.

Opening the door, a man slides out of the cab. He wears the saffron robes of a monk and, although young, walks with a curious stoop. With one finger to his lips, indicating silence, he beckons the men to gather round him. There follows a hurried discussion which consists mainly of the young man giving instructions while the others listen, nodding their heads at intervals to show that they have understood. They go to the back of the lorry where a large sack is opened and knives and clubs handed out to those who have not already got them. Then, forming a silent line along the side of the road, the men quietly descend the bank into the field, advance a few feet and wait for their leader's signal.

With his hand raised in the air, the saffron-robed man senses a power, greater than himself, pulsing down from the air, through his fingertips and down his arm, like lightning, until it infuses his whole body. He is omnipotent. He pauses for a moment, wishing to prolong the sensation, seeking to fix a scene in his mind that he will never forget, like a bookmark.

Raising his eyes to the horizon, he scans the landscape, steadily shortening his focus: from a distant range of saw-toothed mountains to flat plains filled with ripe cane, a thin blue line that melts into a wide band of green; a vast expanse of sugar cane that gradually resolves itself into square plots as he lowers his gaze until, finally, his eyes come to rest on the field before him. For a moment, he stares at the labourers, as industrious as ants; but, although a peasant himself, he feels no bond with them, no interest in their lives. No pity. Just anger.

With slow deliberation, the man in saffron robes lowers his hand. At his signal, the other men move forward, slowly at first, then faster, until they are running, covering the short distance between themselves and the field-workers. One labourer, who has stopped to wipe the sweat from his face, turns and sees them. But he does not live long enough to give a warning.

***

Ella's husband and eldest son are working farthest from the road. By now, the exertion of heavy labour is beginning to take its toll. Every few seconds, the man stops, coughs uncontrollably, then wipes the spittle from his hand onto his sarong, along with traces of blood. His usual pallor has changed to a terrible greyness and his limbs feel heavy. He wonders how he will ever find the strength to walk home, let alone finish the day's work.

But then, he thinks of his family, particularly the sick child at home and, determined to put the last ounce of his strength to good effect, he begins again to slash at the cane with his scythe. Beside him, the boy is gathering up the fallen cane, tying it into a bundle which he will carry on his head to a wagon at the side of the field where it will be taken from him and laid neatly, on top of the other bundles, ready for transportation to the mill.

At first, they do not realise what is happening. Ella's husband does not hear the muffled screams. It is her son, stooping to pick up a bundle, who catches the first glimpse of the slaughter.

"Appa. Look. What's happening?"

Turning painfully, the man squints across the field. At first, he cannot believe what he is seeing. Armed men, dragging workers into the cane stubble, then setting about them with clubs and knives, hacking and bludgeoning. He can see their blood, spraying the air then, at last, he hears their screams, shrill and unearthly. As if waking from a dream, he turns to his son.

"Run, child. Into the cane. As deep as you can. Hide there."

"No, Appa. Not without you."

"I am coming. Go ahead. Find a place for me. Go. I am following."

The boy runs a few paces into the cane but then turns, waiting. They are being overtaken now by other labourers. The shrieks are hideous. Close by. They can hear people crashing through the cane, panting, running for their lives. And now, they can hear them being hacked down, their own scythes turned upon them as if they, themselves, had been stalks of cane.

The man pushes the boy ahead of him, motioning that the child should run, but the boy will not leave his father. Every so often, he runs a few paces ahead but, seeing that the man cannot keep up, he runs back and, taking his father's hand, pulls him forward, begging him to move faster. Together, they push deeper and deeper into the unyielding cane, regardless of spiders and snakes, filled with a greater fear, of humans pursuing their own kind in a deadly hunt.

At last, they stop, listening, hardly daring to breathe, the man trying to stifle the desire to cough although he can taste the blood in the back of his mouth, his one desire to get the child to safety. The screams are muffled, more distant and they are punctuated by longer periods of silence. Hopefully, other labourers have escaped to safety, deep within the cane, like themselves, and their pursuers are getting tired. This field alone stretches over many acres and, once hidden in the dense vegetation, it will be impossible to find the labourers. Perhaps, their attackers, whoever they are, will give up. Perhaps, they have gone already. Father and son crouch together, their arms around each other, listening intently.

For several minutes, they hear nothing. Hope returns. The men must have gone. Then, they hear a dry, crackling noise and there is a faint smell of burning, only too familiar to the man who has worked these fields for years. A thin twist of grey smoke insinuates itself through the cane, drifting past them. Then, all too quickly, it is followed by a dense cloud. The crackling becomes louder, the smell stronger and flames can now be seen flickering through the thick stems.

Fire! As they have driven spiders and snakes, so the workers are driven themselves. Coughing and choking they are forced from their hiding places; racing through the thickets of cane, desperately trying to beat the fire that pursues them as it engulfs the field in a wall of flame.

The child pulls at his father's arm, trying to support the man as he stumbles and coughs, blood and sputum now spilling unchecked from the corner of his mouth. They can feel the heat of the fire on their backs even though its source is a hundred yards away. Every so often there is a 'whoosh' as the flames leap forward, consuming scores of stems that roar and pop, exploding in the heat. Then the fire moves on, each time consuming a larger swathe, each time moving farther and faster than before.

With the fire at their heels, the man and boy push desperately through the last few feet of cane, blinded by smoke, their eyes streaming, their faces blackened by floating mites of charcoal that, having melded with the sweat on their skin, now run down their faces in inky streaks.

As they emerge into the open, coughing and gasping, they are grasped by strong hands and pulled apart. The boy, screaming and kicking, yells for his father. The man stretches out his arms, trying to reach the child but, as their fingers meet, he is felled by a lethal blow to the head. The child shrieks hysterically, kicking his attacker, who swears, then passes a hand swiftly across the boy's neck. There is a brief flash as the sun catches the edge of the blade, then a plume of crimson droplets flies into the air, pattering softly to the ground.

Still holding the boy, the man wipes his knife on his sarong. At the edge of the road, the man in saffron robes is signalling his men to return to the truck. They have more work to do and they must act fast before the police or army are alerted. With a careless gesture, the man flings the boy aside. By chance, the child's body comes to rest over that of his father, his small back arched over the man's torso, a look of terror frozen in his dead eyes, his throat torn open.

Enjoying her freedom from the house, the grandmother has decided to follow a longer route to the field, taking a footpath that leads from the back of the village to the side of the cane fields farthest from the road. She has tried to reason with herself, not very successfully, that this will save time in the long run. But it is an excuse and she knows it. A rare self-indulgence. But she will not be the only one to benefit. The two younger children are always begging to be taken along this path, for it passes a pond, usually forbidden to them, where the older children bathe and catch frogs.

The path hooks down behind the village, past tall fields of cane and down into a small hollow, so that anyone travelling along its narrow span is invisible from the main road. When they come to the pond, the grandmother allows the children to paddle but, when she tries to move them on, they prove reluctant.

Yielding to their plea for more time, the old lady settles herself on the bank with her feet in the water, watching as the children chase each other, splashing through the shallows as they try to catch damsel flies. It is so warm and pleasant by the water that, after a while, the grandmother begins to doze. She wakes only when one of the children begins to squeal.

"It's mine, Amma. He took it. Thief."

A fight has broken out. Raising herself unsteadily to her feet, the old lady orders the children out of the water. They come, slowly dragging their feet, full of tales and recriminations.

"I don't want to hear it!" says the old lady, holding up her hand. It is always the sign for her grandchildren to stop whatever they are doing, at least, where she can see them. But, when she turns away, many a silent pinch and punch are exchanged behind her back.

They continue on their way: the old lady walking briskly, refreshed by her sleep, the children dawdling, looking back longingly at the pond until, at last, it disappears from view. The path runs between two fields of sugar cane, a late planting that will be the last to be harvested. The tall green canes are fat and hard as iron, but they are hollow inside, full of sweet, spongy flesh. The children know because, occasionally, their father brings some home as a treat.

Then, they sit outside in the shade, contentedly sucking their pieces of cane for hours until long after the flavour has disappeared. Never have they tasted the end product of the milling process; large crystals of unrefined sugar, called jaggery, that have the colour of amber when held up to the light, a treat for rich children. In the short list of their childish desires, jaggery has first place.

"What is that?"

Shielding her eyes, the grandmother is looking above the forest of cane, to where a pillar of black smoke is coiling and twisting some hundred feet into the air. Something flies into her eye. Blinking, the old lady brushes her face. When she looks at her hand, it is covered with fine, black soot. It is not unusual for cane fires to get out of hand and, when they do, it is essential not to be down-wind as the flames can leap hundreds of yards in a few seconds, cutting off the unwary. The old lady studies the column of smoke. It is travelling to the right, in their direction.

"Quick. Follow me."

She takes them by another path which leads away from the fire and, further also from the village and the main road. The children begin to complain that they are getting tired.

"You must be patient," is their only comfort.

They plunge through the tall cane which towers above the children's heads like a green forest.

"Don't touch it!" warns their grandmother sternly and, if they stray from the path, she slaps both of them soundly, without offering an explanation. They whimper softly as they trundle along behind her, tired and hungry.

"Appa will have some food," she says encouragingly, relying on her son-in-law's lack of appetite. For once, she hopes that he has not eaten the contents of his tiffin-box.

It takes them an hour to skirt around the fire, the grandmother all the while keeping the smoke in view, checking to see if it has come any closer. Finally, they find themselves on a dirt track that leads to the end of the plantation where the father and eldest boy were working. Finding a vantage point on an old termite hill, the old lady squints into the distance. The plantation is now an inferno and the wind has swept round, pushing the flames back towards the main road.

"Appa!" squeals one of the children.

"It's all right. I'm sure he's back at the village by now. Let's go and find him."

Taking both children by the hand, the grandmother leads them back along the track, cursing herself for having dawdled by the pond. As they walk, she tells them stories and tries to reassure them, but without allaying her own disquiet. She has never seen such a large fire and, what is more alarming, no-one is trying to put it out.

Normally, when a cane-fire takes hold, there are crowds of labourers trying to contain it. Some would be using their machetes to cut fire-breaks while others would be forming chains passing buckets of water to dampen the flames and slow the fire's progress. Simply abandoning a whole plantation to burn is unheard of. It is their livelihood. Without the harvest, they will starve.

Every so often, the grandmother stops and listens to see if she can hear voices but the only sound is the crackling roar of the fire. What are they thinking of? If it is not contained, the fire might blow back towards the village and they will all lose their homes. The old lady feels sick with apprehension. Something is wrong.

When they get back to the pond, they see another plume of smoke, this time from the direction of the village.

"It must have travelled fast," thinks the old lady. "That's why I have heard no-one. They have all run away."

She needs time to think, so she sits down by the edge of the water. The fire is now behind them and to one side of them. Her main fear is that they will be cut off. She needs to get to higher ground, out of this hollow, to get a better view of what is happening. Judging the children to be safer where they are, at least for a few minutes, she tells them to wait by the pond with strict instructions not to go into the water. Hoping that, for once, they will obey her, she hurries forward, towards the main road.

Even from a distance, she can tell that it is not the cane-fire that has set light to the village. Plumes of smoke are rising from a number of homes, but the fires are random, dotted about the village, not consuming it systematically. She stops again and listens, but the only sound is the chugging engine of a lorry, fading into the distance.

The old lady creeps forward until she has reached the place where the footpath opens onto the road. Cautiously, she peers out, as wary as a cat, looking first one way, then the other, checking to see if anyone is approaching the village. But the road is empty and, apart from the crackling sound of fire, she can hear nothing.

Quietly, she tiptoes across the road, stooping into the high grass verge as soon as she reaches the other side. The village is only a few yards away, but she is approaching it from behind and can see little apart from the rough mud plaster of the houses. The smell of burning grows stronger as she approaches although she cannot make out which houses are alight.

What disturbs her most is the silence. Instinct tells her that, by now, she should have heard voices, seen people running about trying to put out the flames and yet, all around her, there is an unnatural stillness. Something is wrong. Creeping along the side of one of the houses, she emerges into the rough open space known as the 'square'. Then, the reason for the silence becomes clear.

Several bodies lie on the ground: some sprawling, face down in the dirt; some curled up on their side, their hands covering their faces; others, twisted into strange positions. Her hand held over her mouth, the grandmother walks across the square, examining the bodies to see if any are still alive, putting a name to each.

One woman lies on her back, her eyes open, her hand still clutching the handle of her milk pail. It is Geetha, wife of the headman who had been on her way to milk her buffalo. Another, an old woman, lies on her face, one hand raised above her head, the fingers sunk deep into the dirt. Most of the victims are women, some are children. The grandmother recognises two boys, twins, lying next to each other. Flies have already gathered to feast on the blood, black and treacly, that has congealed around deep wounds in their heads. As the old woman passes, the flies swarm up in a cloud, hover momentarily over the corpses, then settle again.

It is like stepping into a scene from hell. So removed is this from the village that she left this morning that the grandmother is temporarily unable to think. She just stands, her mouth open, the blood drained from her face, staring at the bodies, unable to comprehend what has happened. She would remain like this for hours were she not roused by a new sound: a low moan, so soft that it is barely audible.

Slowly, the old lady looks about her. One of the bodies moves its hand. Stepping carefully around the other bodies, the old lady approaches the figure of the young woman and kneels down beside her. The girl moans, twitching her fingers. Her clothes are torn and her body covered in blood and scratches. Her hair, matted and disarranged, hangs over her face, sticking to her cheeks and lips. Gently pulling the hair from the girl's face, the grandmother recognises her as Lalitha, a sixteen-year old, who is due to marry that season.

"Lalitha, what happened?"

Hearing her own name, the girl opens her eyes.

"Men. In a lorry. Bad men."

Her face crumples at the memory of what happened. The old lady strokes her face.

"Who were they?"

"Don't know. Not from here. Sinhalese."

The girl's eyes become cloudy. Her eyelids flicker.

"Lalitha, try to stay awake. It's important. Where are the others?"

The girl is drifting. Her eyelids close for several seconds, before flickering open again.

"Run away. All gone."

"And the men? Our men. Did they return from the fields?"

Her eyes close, the girl takes a long, rasping breath then releases it, in a low whisper.

"Nooo."

After flickering briefly, the eyelids are motionless, wide open; the blank eyes underneath having rolled up to expose the white and only the lower part of the iris.

"Lalitha!"

The old lady squeezes the girl's hand, then shakes her gently by the shoulder; but the girl's head rolls limply to one side.

"Surely not," murmurs the old lady. "She's only scratched and bruised."

But when she puts her hand on the girl's chest, it is still. Then, following the line of the girl's torn blouse, the old lady's gaze passes down, to a small gash in Lalitha's stomach. The old lady touches it gently with her fingers. It is not wide, but it is deep and she can see that it was made with a knife. Then, coming to her senses, the old lady remembers why she came. Her grand-daughter.

The square is now filled with choking smoke from four or five houses that are ablaze. Soon, the flames will leap to the neighbouring huts and the whole village will be alight. Getting to her feet, the old lady runs to her house. As she approaches, she can see that sparks have already settled in the thatch and are beginning to smoulder. Coughing, she runs into the gloom of the interior, calling softly for the child. When she sees the huddled bundle lying on the floor, her heart stops. Summoning all her courage, she hurries forward and bends over the child.

"Chick-pea, chick-pea!"

She calls the child by her nick-name. Blinded by tears, the grandmother moans the name in the dark, sure that the child is dead. But, a few seconds later, a small hand reaches up and tentatively touches her hand.

"Amma?"

"Chick-pea, my darling."

The old lady pulls the child towards her, holding her tight to her breast.

"Are you hurt? What happened?"

"I was asleep. I woke up. There was a lot of screaming. Then a man came. He was carrying a big knife. His face was black, covered in soot, and his hair was matted and standing on end. I thought he was a demon, come to take me. There was blood on the knife, Amma. It dripped on the floor."

The child points to several dark stains in the doorway.

"The man looked around the house. He went into the kitchen and took the cooking pots. He was on his way out when he saw me. He came and stood over me with the knife in his hand. I thought he was going to kill me. Then, he laughed and said "You remind me of her!" And, just like that, he turned and went. I was so scared, I just lay here, waiting for you to come home."

"It's all right, my darling. I'm here now."

The old lady rocks the child in her arms. Suddenly, there is a roaring sound from the roof.

"Quickly. We must go."

Pulling the child to her feet, the grandmother scoops her up in her arms and runs out of the house just as the blazing thatch caves in. What remains of their home is consumed in a cloud of smoke and flames. But the grandmother does not stay to watch. Clasping the child to her, she runs as fast as she can, away from the dead bodies and the burning buildings, across the road and back along the footpath to the pond where the other children are waiting.

1958: A night in the forest

Ella will never tell anyone what happened in the forest. The man assaulted her. That was shame enough. He tore her dress. Touched her in places that no man, other than one's husband, should touch a woman. But he did not rape her. She had a chance and she took it.

As he rolled on top of her, she felt his weight crushing her ribs as his thick fingers pushed roughly about inside her clothes. His smell sickened her. He was so drunk she wondered that he could have run this far. And then, just as suddenly as he had attacked her, he fell asleep, pinning her body to the forest floor. She only had a few moments grace, she knew that. She must make the most of it.

Taking a deep breath, she pushed, as hard as she could. He rolled over, waking, disorientated. But she was too quick for him. Digging her fingers into the dirt, she tore at a large stone, then as the man was raising himself up on his arms, she hit him: once, twice on the temple. He groaned and fell on his face, but still she hit him. Over and over, until she felt the bone of his skull shatter, until what was beneath it oozed through the wound in his skin, soft and pulpy. Until she was sure he was dead.

Then, rising unsteadily to her feet, she supported herself against a tree, trying to catch her breath. At first, she could not look at the man but, then, she made herself and, when she did, she felt nothing; only anger and the desire to hit him all over again. She wanted to grind him into pieces, pound him to dust like spices in a mortar, until there was nothing left. The impulse was so strong that she had to dig her nails into the rough bark of the tree to stop herself.

Then, as her rage subsided, her head began to swim and a thin film passed over her eyes clouding her vision. She started to tremble uncontrollably and her legs became so weak that she thought she would fall. All she wanted to do was to lie down and sleep. But not here. Not next to him.

Trying to keep the weight off her ankle, she tried to move, hopping and staggering to the next tree where she paused for several minutes, clinging to the branches until she had mustered enough energy to travel another few feet. It was slow progress but, after an hour, she felt that she had put sufficient distance between herself and the body to be able to rest. Sliding to the forest floor, she curled up on her side and fell into a deep sleep.

***

It is night when she wakes and the jungle has become a dark and forbidding place. Having been reared on the open slopes of the tea plantations, Ella is used to open skies and fresh mountain air. She has a deep mistrust of enclosed spaces: a feeling which grows initially from her dislike of the cane fields for, whenever she walks through it, the cane seems to close in around her, airless and suffocating. She feels the same about trees.

All around her, the jungle has come to life: a whirring, screeching, crashing cacophony of sound. Just behind her, Ella hears a swishing of branches, as if someone is pushing their way through the trees. Coming towards her. Her heart thudding in her chest, she sits, still as a stone, listening. It comes towards her, then stops a few feet away. What if those men are coming to find their friend? Even worse, perhaps they have already found him and are now looking for her, thirsty for revenge.

Straining her ears, Ella hears a soft thudding. Footsteps or is it her heart? She cannot tell. The rustling continues. Ella can see the undergrowth quivering a few feet away. Then, as she watches, hardly daring to breathe, a small deer steps into the moonlight, then rising on its back legs, begins to graze, stripping leaves from the lower branches of the trees. Ella gasps then, holding her hand to her mouth, begins to sob. The deer freezes, looking around it, scenting the air for a predator. Then, reassured, it continues to browse the foliage, so close now that Ella can hear the munching of its soft mouth.

Comforted by the deer's presence, Ella plans her route home. She will not return by the same route that she came. She does not want to run into those men again. Instead, she will travel under cover of the jungle, alongside the railway track until she reaches a village up-line. Then, avoiding the main roads, she will take a roundabout route that will eventually lead her home.

With her sprained ankle, she will not be able to travel far or fast but, with luck, she might complete the journey in daylight. Once back in the village, she will be safe. Taking strength from that thought, she dozes fitfully until dawn; her ears, now attuned to the sounds of the forest, still listening for human footsteps.

∗∗

Ella awakens to the sound of monkeys, chattering and screeching in the trees above her. She watches as they race through the branches, some with babies clinging to their backs, leaping from tree to tree with break-neck bravado. Sometimes, they venture into the open and she can see them, sitting in the branches, eating handfuls of fruit and flowers or grooming each other. At other times, they are so well hidden that she can only trace their movement by the violent trembling of branches and leaves.

Ella likes monkeys. They remind her of the cunning, monkey-faced god, Hanuman. But it is not to Hanuman that she prays at the outset of her journey, but Ganesha, the remover of obstacles. Everyone prays to him at the beginning of any difficult venture and it seems particularly appropriate to ask for his help today.

Struggling to her feet, she groans. Lifting up her skirt a little way, she stares at her legs which are covered in bruises and scratches. Overnight, the bruises have turned livid and black and the pain from her aching joints is excruciating. Still, she reminds herself, it could have been worse. She just hopes that she will not run into the man's friends on the road. She tests her ankle by putting her foot to the ground, but instantly yelps with pain. Not for the last time, she curses the man who attacked her. While remorse is something she may feel at leisure, her mind, at present, is filled with imperatives.

She must get home, find her family. She wonders how her husband has coped with his work in the fields, if her mother managed to persuade him to go home, whether the youngest child has recovered from her cough. It was a bad one, that cough. It sounded too much like the cough her husband had before he fell ill. Something clutches at Ella's heart. She must get home.

Searching around her on the jungle floor, she finds two large sticks of almost equal length which she can use as crutches. As she puts her weight on them, their rough ends sink into the soft flesh under her arms, but at least she is able to propel herself forward. She will just have to put up with the pain. It will be worth it to get home, see her family and forget what has happened.

1958: A changed landscape

Hours later, having skirted around the rest-house and the main town, Ella finds herself at the crossroads where the main road strikes off towards the cane plantation and her village. The route that she took to get here consisted mainly of footpaths, little used as they are winding and indirect, so she does not think it strange that she has not seen anyone all day.

She is thirsty and weak from exertion and hunger. Consequently, her senses are dulled. At first, she thinks she has taken the wrong turning. While she recognises the cross-roads, the view from this slightly elevated position is so different from normal, that she thinks she must be mistaken. Where, formerly, there was a tall forest of cane, its papery leaves a dark, purplish green at this season, there is now a flat expanse of smouldering charcoal where small clusters of flames still burn brightly. The air, thick with smoke and motes of soot, carries a heavy stench of burning.

"What has happened here?" Ella murmurs to herself.

Her stomach churns, not with hunger this time, but with fear. No ordinary cane fire would do this much damage. Sick with anxiety, Ella propels herself forward. This place, usually full of people, has become eerie, silent and abandoned. Nothing passes her on the road in either direction: no trucks or bicycles, no people carrying sacks or baskets, not even a pye-dog. High above her, two large birds wheel slowly, round and round, their black forms silhouetted against the blue sky, their huge wings outstretched as they cruise the thermals. Vultures. An omen of death.

As she draws level with the field in which her husband and son were working, Ella stops, shielding her eyes from the sun in order to get a better view. Here and there, strange bundles lie around the outer edges of the field, as blackened and charred as the surrounding stubble. One of them appears to move, fluttering in the breeze. Ella waves her arms.

With a harsh croak, the bundle separates. A crow flaps up from where it has been feeding. Under the bundle's black crust, there is raw meat. The crow hops sideways, its wings outstretched, its beak bloody, ready to see off any intruders. Across the field, Ella can now make out other crows, huddled over similar bundles. Every so often, a fight breaks out, with raucous squawking and pecking as the crows fight over a prize.

Ella squints, straining her eyes, but she cannot make out the shape of the corpses. Something terrible has happened, that is clear, but she is sure that the charred bodies are not human. Surely, once they had escaped the burning cane, people would have had the sense to keep running, not wait for the fire to catch up with them. The bodies must be those of animals; hares, deer, or possibly the stray calves of oxen. Comforted by this thought, she turns away from the field and heads towards the village.

A few minutes later, she is met by the same scene of devastation that greeted her mother the previous day although, by now, most of the houses have burned to the ground. Except for the ravages of crows and pye-dogs, however, the bodies scattered over the square have been left intact and the stench of rotting flesh combines with the acrid smell of fire. As she picks her way through the corpses, Ella's stomach heaves. Each one was known to her, a friend or a neighbour. Some she nursed in her arms as babies; others had nursed her. If she had eaten, she would vomit, but her stomach is so empty, she can only retch up bile.

Dragging herself across the square, she makes for her home where, for several seconds, she stands before the smoking remains, unable to comprehend the devastation, her shock so great that it blocks out grief.

"After the fields, they came here."

A young woman, wearing a faded red dress, has picked her way quietly across the square and is standing at Ella's side. Despite her numbness, Ella recognises the girl. Her name is Shakti, one of three sisters, each of whom has taken a turn as owner of the red dress. Being the youngest sister, Shakti was last to inherit it and the dress, by now much worn and mended, has lost most of its colour and all of its original buttons; replacements for the latter, consisting of an odd miscellany of mismatched shapes, sizes and colours, also account for Shakti's nickname; "Buttons".

Having married a few months ago, Shakti is now pregnant. The dress, always a little tight for her, can no longer be encouraged to fit over her swollen stomach, so she has opened the seams and let in gussets of whatever material she can find, further increasing the dress's piebald appearance. Shakti is what the villagers describe as 'happy-go-lucky'. Yet, today, there is no sign of her old cheerfulness. Her hair is streaked with dust, her face smeared with dirt and the dress, usually fresh and spotless, is stained and filthy.

Shocked, exhausted and hungry, Ella is unable to muster her thoughts. She stares first at the smouldering wreckage of the house, then at the girl, then back at the blackened earth.

"Come with me," says the girl, gently. "It's not safe here. I have a little food and some water. It's not far."

Ella seems unable to tear herself away from the smoking remains of her home, so hooking Ella's arm around her own, plump shoulders, the girl pulls her away, guiding her through the village and along a dirt track that leads into a palm grove. The air is filled with the musty odour of warm soil and, as Ella's eyes become accustomed to the dappled light, she thinks she sees another figure, moving quietly between the trees.

"It's my brother," says the girl. "He saw what was happening in the fields. He came to warn us, but not everyone got away."

"The fields?"

Ella's eyes shine like lamps in the gloom. Then, she remembers the crows, feasting on charred carrion. She begins to tremble. The girl lowers her gently onto the dry earth, then sits beside her, motioning the boy to join them.

"You have not yet heard?" the girl asks softly. Ella shakes her head.

"Mohan, tell her what you saw."

The boy begins to speak in a low monotone, like a reluctant schoolboy reciting a lesson.

"I had been working in the fields, but father sent me home to fetch some more food. We had started work early and had already eaten what was in our tiffin-boxes. I was returning to the fields from the village, when I saw a lorry arrive with a lot of men. They got out and some disappeared into the sugar cane. At first, I thought they were labourers, but then I heard screams. I hid at the side of the road in a place where I could see the field."

"I saw smoke rising from the cane, then people started running out. As they ran into the open, the other men attacked them with clubs and knives. When they had killed everyone, the men got back into the lorry and started driving towards the village. I ran as fast as I could. I managed to find Shakti and warn a few others. We all ran here. But not everyone got the message and others were too slow. The men came to the village in their lorry and killed everyone there. Then, they stole everything they could find and set light to the houses."

"My family. Did they escape? Has anyone seen them?"

Desperate for information, Ella grasps the boy's arm. Frightened, he looks to his sister for help. Shakti puts her arms around Ella.

"No-one escaped from the fields."

"But my husband and son. They were there. And my mother, she was going to the fields, later. Did you see her on the road? She would have had two of my children with her, the other was sick, she would have stayed at home."

Shakti shakes her head.

"We have not seen them."

"But, you say, some escaped from the village?"

"Yes, but we were all frightened, confused. I could not be sure who escaped and who did not. Perhaps they escaped by another route."

By introducing a degree of uncertainty, Shakti hopes to soften the blow but her brother, becoming suddenly voluble, discloses a detail that Shakti had hoped to keep from Ella, at least for the present.

"I saw a man go into your house."

"What man?"

"One of the men from the lorry. He went into your house and stole your cooking pots."

"And my daughter?"

Ella grasps the boy's hand, kneading his fingers as if to squeeze the information out of him. Alarmed by the expression on the woman's face, the boy begins to stutter.

"What happened to my daughter?"

"I don't know," the boy falters.

"Did you see her leave the house?"

Terrified by the woman's wide, unblinking eyes, the boy pulls away.

"Tell me, did you see her?"

Ella is rocking from side to side, restrained by Shakti's strong arms.

"Tell me," she implores. "Tell me."

"No. I didn't see her. She never came out."

Struggling to his feet, the boy runs deep into the trees where he throws himself onto the ground and weeps, his sobs echoed by the howls of the grieving woman.

1958: An abandoned house

In the darkness, a vehicle can be heard, grinding slowly over the rough stones of the track, its engine growling and sputtering. A leopard, caught unawares in the middle of the road, stares briefly at the jeep as it rounds the corner. For a second, the creature's eyes gleam in the headlights then, soft as a shadow, it slips into the undergrowth. The vehicle rumbles past, rattling over pot-holes, its occupants invisible in the black, lightless night, the moon having shrunk to a slender crescent, a mere slit in the sky.

Turning from the road, the jeep noses its way along an overgrown track, pushing through a dense tangle of grass and weeds that, being uprooted, twine themselves around the wheels and hang from the bumper like streamers. Finally, the jeep emerges from the undergrowth and comes to rest, its engine still chugging, on the forecourt of a darkened building.

For a minute or two, the occupants remain in the vehicle, waiting and listening for any sign of human occupation in the house. Then, from the passenger's side, a figure emerges, slipping silently to the ground, walking carefully, as if on needles, to the front of the jeep then darting across to the front of the bungalow, where it turns briefly and holds its hand up to the driver, signalling him to wait.

Stooping low, the dark form runs across the front of the house, disappearing into the gloom of the porch where its shadowy hands press the door and twist the handle. But the door is locked. Cursing under his breath, the man runs around to the back of the building, crouching against the wall. He disappears. There is silence. Crash! An explosion of breaking glass echoes through the darkness.

Attracted by the headlamps, moths are trapped within their span, twirling down the narrow funnels of light to the source where they bump and flutter helplessly against the glass. The driver, a dark presence behind the windscreen, waits, motionless. Then something catches his attention. A movement in the darkness.

He senses rather than sees anything; a disturbance within the deeper blackness at the side of the house, like the swirling of clear liquid. The driver's shadowy outline tautens, straining to see beyond the headlamps with their whirling mania of insects. A man steps into the light, shielding his eyes from the brightness.

"There's no-one here."

The vehicle's lights are extinguished, releasing the moths from their fatal grasp. The engine dies with a reluctant sputter. The driver, obscured by darkness, climbs from the jeep, switches on a torch, then walks towards the dark mass of the house where the other man is waiting. Together they walk around to the back of the house, treading carefully along the overgrown path which is sprinkled with glass.

"The doors are locked. You'll have to climb through the window."

The first man helps the other onto the ledge, watches him jump into the room beyond, then follows. By torchlight, they cross the empty room which echoes with every movement. Through a door opposite the broken window, they enter the hallway and are startled by their own reflections in a mirror which hangs from the wall in an elaborate gilt frame.

In the kitchen, after searching drawers and cupboards they are rewarded with several candle-stubs, a box of matches, and several tins of food together with a tin-opener; supplies, thoughtfully left in case of emergency, by the previous occupant.

Having softened the ends of the candles with a flame, they set them on the floor and light them then, realising, for the first time, that neither has eaten all day, they set to work with the can-opener and are soon spooning corned beef, cheese and peaches out of the tins, in no particular order, so hungry that they eat without speaking.

**

"That's better," Arjun places an empty can on the floor. It makes a hollow, metallic sound that echoes through the vacant building. With his legs stretched out in front of him, he rests his head against the cupboard, filled with a curious sensation of well-being.

Having lived for weeks off rations that consisted of little more than rice and water, Asoka continues to eat, savouring the food, feeling his strength return. Arjun watches him in silence, wondering at the curious turn of fate that has brought them together. He thinks that he recognises the man from his previous visit to Mennan's camp-site, although he cannot place him. It is the other one he remembers: the one with the pale staring eyes who now lies dead at the scene of Mennan's murder. A fitting irony, thinks Arjun.

Asoka finishes eating, wiping his mouth with his hand, a strangely rustic gesture for someone so refined.

"Who are you?" asks Arjun.

In the soft, uncertain light of the candles, Asoka sees himself reflected in the other man's eyes and senses that his character is being assessed. *What does he see?* he wonders. He knows what he thinks of himself and it is not good. But he will tell the other man anyway, everything, holding nothing back, the whole ugly truth of his mistakes and weakness, his crime and, most of all, his regret for what he has done. It seems that he talks for hours while Arjun listens, his face dispassionate and unsurprised. Like a priest.

At last, he has finished. To his surprise, Asoka has a sense of weightlessness, as if he is no longer anchored to the earth by the weight of his misdeeds, but emptied of all the shadows that have haunted him since Mennan's death. He waits for the other man to speak, to give his verdict. But Arjun seems to be dreaming, lost in thoughts of his own. Then, finally, he begins to speak, although not of Asoka and his wrongdoing, but of his own: an ill-judged affair with Mennan's widow and another, with a married woman.

Asoka listens carefully. It is clear that his companion is tormented: not only by his mistakes and the affront to his religion, but also by his profound love for the married woman. Strangely, he never mentions her name, as if is too precious to be shared. The woman is pregnant. Believing another man to be the father, he is thinking of leaving her, coming here to the Government bungalow, to the very place in which they have taken refuge. He has almost made up his mind, or so he says.

But it is clear to Asoka that Arjun is unsure of his decision. Every time he speaks of her, his eyes shine and his face becomes animated, as if he can see her in front of him. Asoka recognises that love. It is what he feels for his own wife and, from his recent experience, he knows that any separation from one so loved is tantamount to death.

"Perhaps," he ventures, "you should be sure."

"What do you mean?"

"Be sure of your actions. If you are uncertain, think again. It is doubt that protects us from error."

651

Arjun bites his thumb, pensively. One of the candles that they placed on the floor begins to gutter, its flame wobbling, circling around the wick as it sinks into a pool of hot wax. The tiny red ember glows hotly for a second, then dies, sending up a brief trail of smoke.

"Can you truly say that you have no doubt?"

Asoka is staring at him intently. Struggling to reply, Arjun realises that he is no longer sure; that, in fact, he never has been.

"No," he replies, softly. "I cannot say that. But I have wronged her husband."

"And by leaving, you may do your woman a greater evil. Your punishment, my friend, is not to have a choice between right and wrong. All you can do is to be sure of your motives. Are you running away for love of her, or from guilt?"

Arjun shakes his head. He cannot meet the other man's eyes for, to do so, would be an admission and he is not ready. Not yet.

"You cannot run from guilt. Sooner or later you must face it."

His voice, so low that it can hardly be heard, Asoka seems to be speaking to himself. The light is dim yet Arjun can just see the contours of his companion's face, haggard and etched with pain; but his suffering has not been physical. The haunted look in his eyes resonates deep within Arjun, churning up the dark secrets of his own soul. It is strange, he thinks, how two people from such different backgrounds should be bound by fate, their paths criss-crossing each other, brought into collision by a single event, each bearing his own burden of shame for Mennan's death.

If Asoka is a murderer, what is Arjun? An opportunist who, in his own way, has profited from Mennan's death and who contributed to the agony that preceded it: a jackal, a feeder on carrion. At least, he supposes, Asoka acted from some idealistic motive, but what was it that induced him into an affair with Mennan's widow: lust, fear, guilt? At least, his affair with Neleni has been motivated by something more pure. He did not need to be cajoled or seduced. It was a choice that he made for himself. Because he loved her.

Warmth floods his heart at the thought of her. Now, at a distance, he is able to discount all the petty jealousy that has soured his view of her. She has been trying to speak to him for weeks but he has avoided her, afraid of what she will say. He recalls the look in her eyes and, finally, understands. It was not the look of a woman about to dismiss her lover but one who feared that she, herself, might be rejected. How much she must have suffered. And all because of him. What a fool he has been. He realises now. The benefit of coming away was not to escape, but to be able to go back, sure in his own mind of what he feels. And now, there is no doubt whatever.

"Thank you," he murmurs.

Asoka nods, with a kind of soft, half-laugh. He smiles, but his eyes are sad.

"What of you?" ventures Arjun.

"My wife was expecting a child. They threatened to kill her if I did not join them."

The trauma of past weeks, augmented by hunger and fatigue, has deprived Asoka of a sense of time and reality. This, combined with the euphoria following his escape from captivity, has temporarily skewed his memory. Frustrated at his own stupidity, he strikes his forehead with his hand.

"My god! How could I have forgotten?"

"What's the matter?"

"There were two of them: Anil, the one who tried to kill you at the camp and another one, Tissa, a boy from my village. He was once in love with my wife. Still is, I think, but he also hates her for marrying me. His head was turned by Anil. He is dangerous, unpredictable. Before you came, Anil entrusted him with a task."

Something clutches at Arjun's stomach and the hairs on his neck rise. Instinctively, he knows that the news will be bad.

"What was this task?"

"To kill the Government Agent."

"My god. When?"

"I don't know. Soon, I think. Anil gave the boy a gun. It is to be used in some sort of ambush. That is all I know. Except …".

"What else?"

"Except that it was my idea."

"What?"

Asoka lowers his eyes, unable to look at his companion. He already feels a bond with the other man and to lose his goodwill will be painful.

"After Mennan's murder, I had plans for another. An assassination so bold that it could not be ignored, either by the Government or the Tamils. Something would have to change – or so I thought. It was madness and I am ashamed of my part in it. But, at that time, I saw things differently and I was foolish enough to tell Anil of my idea.

"As you know, our ways parted after Mennan's death. I forgot about what we had discussed, this other killing. After all, nothing had been agreed. There had been no plans. Just a few random thoughts. I assumed that Anil had forgotten it, too; but I underestimated him. He found others to help him.

"He showed me a book. It was a list of the Government Agent's activities: precise details of when he leaves his home for the office and when he returns. It is then, I think, that Anil planned to kill him. But I don't know for sure. Anil threatened to kill my wife unless I agreed to carry out the execution. Both Anil and Tissa were to be witnesses. Now Anil is dead, but Tissa knew of his plan. He may still try to carry it out. On his own."

"My god!"

Arjun looks as if he has been hit by a thunderbolt. Even in this, insipid light, Asoka can see that his face is drained of colour.

"I'm sorry."

The words sound ridiculous; a pathetic excuse for conceiving the death of another man. The lightness that filled him only a few minutes ago, drains away and is replaced by an inky cloud of despair. He has felt it before. After the death of Mennan. Then, it engulfed him. But this time, he resists.

"We must warn him."

"Yes."

Arjun gets to his feet and looks about him for the torch. It is a Government bungalow and, although remote, there should be a telephone. Followed by Asoka, he runs to the front of the house, along the passageway, opening doors as he goes: a broom-cupboard that smells of mildew; a living-room, echoingly empty; then, a small room with a desk – Government issue, of course – and, on it, a telephone, its chrome dial glittering in the torchlight. Arjun picks up the receiver, listens, dials the number, prods the hook, trying to get a connection, but the line is dead.

"It's been cut off."

He drops the receiver onto the hook, and thinks for a minute, running his hand through his hair.

"How long have we got?"

"I don't know. Tissa left with the other men in a lorry, but I think they were going somewhere else first. I don't know where. I only heard a few words, but I think it was somewhere out in the country."

"Then we've still got time?"

"Yes. A little."

"I must get back to town. Warn him."

"Do you know the way in the dark?"

"No."

"Then you must wait until dawn. It will not be long."

They sit in silence for a while: Arjun perched on the desk, one foot on the floor, the other raised in front of him, his foot swinging almost casually as he tries to think of what to do. He turns frequently, checking the window behind him for signs of dawn. Asoka squats on the floor, his knees drawn up to his chest.

"What do you think of me now?"

In the darkness, Arjun hears the voice of an outcast, without hope of acceptance. Being something with which he is familiar, it touches him.

"I think you are a lonely man."

Asoka smiles. It was not the answer he was expecting.

"Yes. I was. But with my wife, I am no longer lonely."

"No," says Arjun, turning to stare out of the window. "Not with her."

"What I was really asking was if you think I am a bad man?"

Arjun thinks for a minute.

"Had I known what you had done without meeting you, I would have thought you a very bad man. But, now that I have met you, you seem like a good man who has done bad things."

"And there is a difference?"

"Between the man and the action? Yes, I believe so."

Asoka laughs, gently.

"You are a philosopher, my friend, and a better one than ever I was."

"I was taught by Jesuits."

"But you do not think like them."

"How do you know?"

"I can tell. Your thoughts are your own. Free from prejudice. That is a rare thing these days."

"But my actions have been misguided." Arjun shudders as he thinks of Leela.

"Not all. There are some of us who have done much worse."

Asoka speaks with such sadness that Arjun is filled with a strange compassion. Surely, he thinks, such regret must absolve him from wrongdoing.

***

A flicker of red darts between the trees. The sun is beginning its rapid ascent. In minutes, dawn will turn into day.

"I must go," says Arjun. "It's getting light."

"Aren't you forgetting something?" asks Asoka, a quizzical look in his eye.

"What do you mean?"

"I am giving myself up. To you. You must deliver me to the authorities."

1958: Carpe diem

The morning air is sweet and damp. A gauze of mist lingers over the forest and the country is bathed in the brief stillness that follows dawn. The two men walk quietly around the side of the house towards the jeep. Before climbing in, they pause to look back at the bungalow. Last night it was a refuge, a place of safety and relative comfort. But now, it is desolate.

No light shines from its darkened windows, no spark of life animates its empty heart. Tendrils and vines sprout from the pathway and the plaster that covers the building is cracked and blackened with mildew. Paving stones are being lifted out of place by stray roots pressing up from below and the garden has become a tangled wilderness in which creeping figs are slowly strangling the fruit trees and weeds are choking the flowers. The jungle is returning. The house is slowly sinking out of sight. Soon, it will disappear altogether.

***

As the jeep pulls out of the driveway, Arjun knows that he will never return. He will politely decline the post and stay where he is. With Neleni. He will take Asoka's advice. For all his misdeeds, the man who is his prisoner has great wisdom and Arjun wishes that he could know him better.

He wonders how it is that someone who possesses such insight and humanity could ever bring himself to kill. What was it that led Asoka into violence? Was it one experience, or many? Frustration and a real sense of grievance, or misplaced idealism? In this case, Arjun thinks it must have been the latter.

Asoka was brought up in a monastery. Without his parents. Without the love of his own family. He suffered, not from an excessive experience of real life and its hardships, but too little. It is a strange irony that a life of relative comfort can often breed revolutionaries. But Asoka has learned from his mistakes. That is clear.

Arjun tries to think ahead. When he gets to the city, he will have to deliver Asoka to the authorities. Then what? A trial and execution. Asoka has no intention of defending his actions, rather, he has put himself in Arjun's hands. It will be Arjun's choice whether he lives or dies. This time, the conflict that faces him is not that between duty and desire, as it was with Leela, but between duty and conscience. It is a different choice, but no less hard.

In the passenger seat beside him, Asoka seems calm, at peace with himself, the deep lines around his mouth and eyes that made him look so haggard are beginning to disappear. Arjun can see that he is, in fact, a much younger man than he first supposed: not handsome, exactly, but with an arresting intelligence. He can see how less intelligent men would be won over by the reasoning of that powerful intellect and how, when Asoka changed his views, they might feel betrayed. Men like Anil, perhaps.

Then, suddenly, his mind switches to the Government Agent, whose life is in imminent danger, and he wonders how he would feel about Asoka if Nash were to be killed. He looks sideways at his companion, trying to catch the expression on his face without being seen. With the map open on his lap, Asoka is looking above the tree-line to where the flat-topped rock of Sigiriya rises above a row of craggy peaks.

"We are haunted by history," he murmurs.

Following Asoka's gaze, Arjun is reminded of the day at Sigiriya with Neleni, when speaking of art and unfulfilled dreams, she had touched his heart. It was the day when they fell in love, a memory that will bind him to her forever.

"We must not allow the past to dictate our future," says Asoka.

"Sometimes we have no choice," replies Arjun.

***

The last swathes of mist have evaporated from the tree-tops when they emerge onto the main road and, when they pass the turning to Mennan's work-site, both stare up the track and, for a moment, darkness seems to descend as they remember that forlorn and hateful place which, having so nearly claimed them, now holds the body of another victim.

Having rounded a wide bend in the road, they can no longer see the track and, with every mile, the power of that place, with its memories of violence and death, seems to diminish. They feel a powerful, almost euphoric sense of relief but, as they approach a small hamlet, the atmosphere changes. Even before they see the village, they smell the acrid odour of smoke. It hangs on the air, rank and ominous.

They pass a stilted hut, built into the slope at the side of the road. Its timbers, blackened and scorched, are still smoking and the roof has caved in. The door hangs open on its hinges and the meagre contents of the house have been strewn over the ground outside. They stop to look inside, but can see no-one.

A mile down the road, they come to two more houses, also destroyed, but here, the families are gathered in a huddle by the road, shivering with fear and shock, too traumatised to run when the jeep approaches, although Arjun can see the terror in their eyes.

A man, crouched on the ground, is cradling the body of a girl in his arms. One arm lies across her stomach, while the other hangs limply at her side. Her face has a pale, unearthly hue and her eyes, fringed with thick lashes, remain shut as if she were refusing to wake from a deep sleep. As they approach, Arjun can see that her skin is torn and cut in many places and that a deep crimson stain has seeped into her blouse, just above the waistline of her skirt.

Asoka jumps out of the car and kneels by the man.

"What happened here, brother?"

The man looks at him, uncomprehending.

"Is this your daughter?"

The man nods.

"What happened to her?"

In a thin, keening voice, the man speaks in broken sentences, his eyes wide with terror as if he were reliving the scenes that he describes.

"Men came ... in a lorry... attacked us...burnt our homes. We tried to run. Thought my daughter was behind me ... then heard her scream. Men had her ... carried her off into the trees... still screaming. One man ... a monk ... followed them. After a few minutes, the screaming stopped. They brought her back ... left her in the road. He stood over her ... the monk ... laughing. They laughed, too, the other men. Then they left. She is my only daughter."

The man holds her in his arms, gently stroking her hair, as if expecting her to wake. Asoka looks at the pale, dead face and feels as if his own heart had been ripped out. He puts his arm around the man's shoulders and, as he does so, the man begins to whimper, the sound made by lonely creatures that have been abandoned.

Seeing that he can do nothing, Asoka returns to the jeep. He brushes his hand across his face and Arjun can see that he is weeping. For a while, they drive on in silence.

"This is all my fault. I am responsible for their misery."

"No," says Arjun. "Each man is responsible for his actions. Yes. Those men chose to follow you in the beginning. But you admitted your mistake. You stopped, while they chose to continue. How can you be responsible for that?"

"Nevertheless, I started it," murmurs Asoka. "And when I knelt by that man, I felt as if I was looking at my own child. How can one survive such unbearable pain?"

Arjun shakes his head, lost for words. Then, a thought comes to him.

"That monk, the one who killed that girl, was that the man you were telling me about?"

"Tissa? Almost certainly. He has an unhealthy appetite for young girls. I have seen how he looks at them."

Arjun presses his foot on the brake, so hard that the jeep's wheels throw up a cloud of dust. Asoka turns to him in surprise.

"What are you doing?"

"Get out."

"What?"

"Get out and go home to your woman. That is what you told me to do. I am telling you to do the same."

Reaching across Asoka, Arjun releases the catch and flings open the door.

"Go. Before I change my mind."

After hesitating for a moment, Asoka lowers himself to the ground.

"Thank you, brother."

"No. It is I who should thank you."

Arjun drives off without looking back, but he can see Asoka in the mirror, standing in the road, watching him as the vehicle speeds out of sight.

1958: The gathering storm

The city is in turmoil. The violence is gathering pace and it is now clear that the initial attack was not just an isolated incident. The Sinhala Hamudawa has been busy. Following the first attack on a train at Polonnaruwa, another train on the east coast line has been assailed, resulting in two deaths and many injuries. Now, on the third day, a mob surges into Polonnaruwa station, its fury indiscriminate, vented on whatever lies in its path: people and property; passengers and railway staff; Tamils and Sinhalese. Brick, wood and glass are smashed and splintered as this human tornado sweeps through the station.

The city is burning. Shops have been wrecked and food is running short. Few are brave enough to attend work or venture out for fear of being attacked. To walk into the wrong street can result in a severe beating or, more likely, death. Schools have closed, transport has ceased to run and Tamils, terrified by the violence that is increasingly focused on them, abandon their homes and gather at government offices and police stations, clamouring for help.

Meanwhile, reports are beginning to filter in from the surrounding countryside: a sugar plantation has been set alight and the workers hacked to pieces as they tried to escape; a night-time attack on a Government farm has resulted in many deaths. All the latest victims are Tamil. The message is clear.

1958: At the gates

Nash has not slept for two nights – or is it three – he has lost count. Ordinary folk need protection in order to go about their daily business. There are also growing numbers of displaced people, from both town and country, in need of food and shelter. On the one hand, Nash must direct the police, making the best use of the limited numbers available to him; on the other, he must organise refugee camps.

Failure to act swiftly will result in more deaths, if not from violence, then from the secondary causes of starvation and disease. In this hot, humid climate, cholera and typhoid are the natural companions of disaster. Where deaths caused by human agents might be counted in hundreds, these assassins, swift and silent, can kill thousands.

Nash has been working ceaselessly, travelling between the office, the police station and the site designated for refugees; picking his way through streets crowded with people, huddled together on the ground, his ears filled with the sound of cries, pleas and weeping. Hungry and frightened, they cling to his hands and clutch at his clothes, trying to get his attention, sobbing and shouting, pleading for help.

There is no sanitation, no water with which to wash and the smell of excrement and filthy bodies is overpowering. Finding food for this growing number of hungry mouths is becoming impossible. Wholesalers and shopkeepers, intimidated by the Sinhala Hamudawa, are refusing to provide food to refugee camps and civil servants charged with finding supplies have, themselves, become targets for attack. Nash knows that if something is not done quickly, the situation, already critical, will result in disaster.

The telephone lines have been temporarily restored and Nash has spent hours arguing with officials, trying to get the ear of ministers in Colombo. But, whether by design or due to incompetence, the wheels of officialdom turn slowly. Nash's temper has begun to fray.

"For the hundredth time, why don't you listen? I must speak to the Minister. In person. Did he get my message – the one I left this morning? What do you mean, you don't know? Where is he? I must speak to him. Hello? Hello?"

The phone goes dead. With an unusual display of temper, Nash slams the receiver down and buries his head in his hands. The door opens and Skipper bounds in. Running over to his master, tail wagging earnestly, he rests his head on Nash's knee. Absent-mindedly, Nash runs his hand over the dog's smooth head, then fondles its long, silky ears.

Chitra enters, carrying a tray.

"I've brought you something to eat."

She places a plate of rice and curry on the desk.

"I can't. I must go into the office."

"But …"

"There's no time, my love."

He kisses her cheek, then leaves her staring wistfully after him. He hurries out to the front of the house where the car is parked; Walter, as usual, at the wheel, waiting for instructions.

"First the police station and then the office," snaps Nash.

659

As the car passes out of the gates, he fails to notice a young monk, sitting on the pavement, consulting a small exercise book. There has been such an increase in the number of monks recently, that one more, sitting outside the residence, is unexceptional.

Men in saffron robes are everywhere these days, walking in gangs along the streets, laughing together, hanging around outside tea shops, eating chicken curry in Moslem hotels. Most of all, they are to be found in the bazaar, preaching to the crowd or whispering to small clutches of people, who listen in awe, their mouths open and eyes wide, ready to believe anything. It is hardly the conduct to be expected from those committed to religious observance. But Nash has other, more pressing concerns.

Every day, increasing numbers of people gather at the gates of the residence, hoping for food, shelter and protection from the mob. As the gates open, they cluster round the car, pressing their faces to the window, begging and shouting. Nash tries to ignore them, because there is nothing else he can do. If something is not done soon, he knows that the imploring look on their faces will turn to anger. He does not blame them.

He just wishes that someone would answer his telephone calls, someone in Colombo with the power to make it stop. He has already suggested – no, begged – that a state of emergency should be declared and the army called out to settle the disturbances. But no-one in Colombo seems to care. Of course not. It does not affect them.

Nash wonders how previous prime ministers would have dealt with the situation. Surely D.S. Senanayake, the people's champion, or even the pugilistic John Kotelawela, would have done something to quell the violence?

But times have changed, giving rise to a new type of politics. Now, all that is required are a few articulate speeches, fair words and good intentions, signifying nothing. It is all very well for Mr Bandaranaike to speak feelingly of the Middle Way but, in reality, his political juggernaut is propelled by extremists. Now, it has thundered out of control.

The car pulls out of the gates, nosing through the importunate crowd. Nash tries not to meet their eyes. Their faith in him is misplaced. He has no answers for them and the help that he can offer is pitifully inadequate. As the car turns into the road, he looks down at his hands and realises that they are shaking.

Once the car has departed, the people at the gates fall silent, then begin to mill about, unsure of what to do next. Some elect to wait, while others, grumbling, melt away. Taking this opportunity, the young monk pushes through the shuffling crowd and secures a place on the kerb, next to the gates. Pulling the loose end of his robe over his head to protect himself from the sun, he settles down quietly, determined to wait.

When Sergeant Gunasekera begins his shift at 8 a.m., he realises that there will be no time for reading novels. The desk occupies a narrow space with barely enough room for two men to pass each other. The sergeant, who has just completed the night shift, looks up at Gunasekera with bloodshot eyes. "Thank goodness," is all he can say as he hurriedly stuffs his pen into his breast pocket and pushes the chair back, nearly crushing Gunasekera's toes as he squeezes past. Gunasekera notices that the other man's shirt has large sweat stains under the arms and he can hear his stomach gurgling.

"Haven't eaten in twelve hours," says the sergeant, by way of explanation, his breath foul from fatigue and lack of sustenance. Gunasekera's eyes wander to the desk, usually a model of pristine order. But today it is littered with sheets of paper: letter paper, business paper, scraps torn from notebooks, every sheet written in a different hand.

The departing sergeant nods towards the desk.

"Depositions. Five hundred of 'em. And there'll be more today. Lots more. Good luck."

He pats Gunasekara on the back, a gesture in which sympathy is mingled with a sense of relief at his own release. Raising the hinged counter-top, he hops out with uncharacteristic agility, then lowers it behind him, penning his colleague into the small, airless space behind the desk. Gunasekera feels more like a prisoner, than an officer in charge. Expecting the other officer to leave by the front entrance, he is surprised to see him heading towards a door that leads back into the police station.

"Where are you going?"

"Haven't you heard? We're on permanent stand-by until further notice. That means we stay here, even when we're off duty. There's a room at the back where you can sleep."

"But my wife. She's expecting me home tonight."

The other officer stares at him with raised eyebrows. Everyone knows about Gunasekera's marital problems.

"Well," says the officer, fishing for words, "you live in a Sinhalese district. She'll be safer than you are."

The man disappears with a swiftness that implies an end to their conversation. Lowering himself into his seat, Sergeant Gunasekera riffles through the untidy piles of paper, trying to put them into some sort of order, reading as he goes. Words leap out at him: looting, beating, stabbing, rape and, sometimes murder. These are not the crimes of his novelettes, homogenised and safe for all but the intended victims. These are random acts of savagery, breaking all the taboos of penny-dreadful crime because their victims are among the most defenceless: girls and schoolchildren, wives and mothers, old and young, even a deaf mute.

Gunasekera reads the last account, written by a local policeman, unable to raise his eyes from the page. Written in simple prose, devoid of adjectives, it is the most powerful piece of writing that he has ever read, terrible in its directness.

The deaf mute was a wandering labourer, apparently without home or relatives. Sometimes he worked, but more often he went hungry, begging scraps from villagers; a bowl of rice, a cup of water. A simple, harmless fellow, he had no friends but, more importantly, no-one to defend him. A gang of goondas had set upon him – kicking, punching and stamping – as his speechless mouth tried to form words that he had never learned. The policeman, who later interviewed an eyewitness, asked if there had been any reason for the assault. The witness had shrugged. *Not really.*

If the tale of the deaf mute was terrible, there is worse to come. In one place, the goondas set light to their victims and watched them burn; in another, they clubbed them to death. The dead include both Tamils and Sinhalese.

Gunasekera feels himself being drawn down into the horror of these accounts, until he can almost see it for himself. It is sickening, far from the erotic, carefully controlled mayhem of his novels. The macabre content of these reports introduces him to the brutal reality of violence; the stabbing and slitting, torture, pain, cruelty and humiliation.

"Ahem!"

Conscious that he is being watched, Gunasekera looks up to see an elderly gentleman peering at him over the counter. The man is dapper and well-dressed, with thin, gold-rimmed spectacles, the sort often worn by lawyers.

"Excuse me, officer, but we should like to make a report."

We? Raising himself up in his seat, Gunasekera peers over the counter. He is greeted by a crowd of pale, terrified faces: men, women, children, even a pet Labrador. And there is something else unusual. A terrible silence. Islanders are normally gregarious and even two or three can make as much noise as a colony of parrots. But these are silent, all looking at him expectantly as if they were waiting for something. Then, he notices the suitcases and bundles. As one woman re-arranges her scarf, Gunasekera notices that she is wearing six necklaces, one on top of another and to the necklaces are attached many pairs of ear-rings. She is wearing all her jewellery.

"What …?"

"We have been driven out of our homes," explains the elderly man, patiently. "In many cases, we have no homes at all. They have been burned and looted. We were lucky to escape with our lives."

"But you can't stay here?" blurts Gunasekera.

"We have nowhere else to go," says the man, with a flash of defiance.

It is a trigger. Everyone starts talking at once, all trying to be heard above their neighbours, all shouting accounts of beatings and assault, screaming about things that should only be whispered and then, only in the company of trusted family members. *My wife was gang-raped. My daughter was assaulted. Five men beat my father with clubs.*

"We are not going anywhere," shouts the elderly man, banging his fist down on the counter. "You are the police. You must protect us. Those goondas, who call themselves the Sinhala Hamudawa, are saying that the police will not confront them because they, too, are Sinhalese. Is it true?"

"No," shouts Gunasekera. "Of course not."

"Then protect us. There are more and more of these people, roaming the streets. There are hundreds of them by now. We have tried to speak to the Government Agent, but he is never at home. So we have come here. You must protect us."

"All right, all right."

Gunasekera stands up so that they can all see him, holding up his arms, trying to calm them.

"You can stay here. For now. Until we find you somewhere safe."

It is a grand promise, one that exceeds both his authority and his resources but, fresh from reading the depositions of other eye-witnesses, Gunasekera does not have the heart to turn them away. As he speaks, more and more people arrive until they are queuing on the steps, then along the street outside: some with handcarts, some with suitcases, some with nothing.

"Where is the Assistant Superintendent?" Gunasekera shouts into the office behind him.

"Don't know," says a voice. "Haven't seen him."

"What are we going to do about these people?"

"Take them to join the others."

"What do you mean?"

Getting up from his desk, the other man motions him to follow. They walk along a corridor and the other man flings open a door that leads into the quadrangle. There, sheltering themselves with scarves and umbrellas against the baking sun, are fifty other families.

By the end of the morning, not only the quadrangle, but the cells, corridors and even spaces between the desks will be filled with refugees. But that will not be the end of Sergeant Gunasekera's problems.

1958: Someone, somewhere

Hundreds of feet above ground, a red kite circles, wings outstretched, gliding the thermals. The long feathers at his wing-tips are momentarily agitated by a shift in current, but he is otherwise motionless. Balancing on a warm column of air, he looks down and sees what appear to be faint trails of smoke, rising from the city below.

The thermal sinks and the bird dips into pure, fresh air, as cold as crystal, dropping through layers of vapour that drench him with a sudden chill. He hears the rushing of the wind as he plummets towards the earth, before catching another uplift of air. He soars for a second then lets the shrinking current carry him gently downwards. On his slow descent, he turns his head this way and that, his gimlet eye trained on the world below.

Gently buffeted by thermals, he sees what appear to be tiny glowing embers at the base of the smoke trails and he catches the occasional whiff of smoke, dry and acrid. A crow passes, like a black shadow, then another, then more still. They wheel about beneath him then descend, one after the other, dropping into the streets like a sprinkling of black sand.

As the ground rushes towards him, the trails of smoke turn into thick, grey pillars, coiling and twisting like serpents. There is one quite close to him. He follows its course, down, down to the street where a house is burning. He is so close that he can hear the crackling of flames, feel the heat on his feathers. And now he can hear other things. Screams of terror from a house. Shouts and jeering from the street outside.

***

A group of men has gathered outside the house, about fifty of them, armed with clubs and knives. A door opens. A man runs out, choking, dazed, his hands held to his eyes, blinded by smoke. He is followed by a woman leading two children. The woman is holding a baby.

The men in the street gather round, watching as the man wipes the tears from his eyes and the woman and children, instinctively huddle around him for protection. He is a small man, not very old, a shopkeeper, more accustomed to using his brain than his muscles. He can add, multiply and subtract the most complicated figures, fractions and percentages in his head. But he has never wielded a hoe or a mattock. Unlike the men who now surround him.

Hair unkempt, eyes bloodshot, the men's teeth and lips are stained red with betel as if they had been drinking blood. Every so often, their eyes wander from the man to his wife. Hardly more than a girl, she glances around nervously, like a young horse ready to bolt. She looks first at her husband, then at the other men.

Both groups stare at each other for a few more seconds, each waiting for the other to make a move then, without warning, the blows rain down on the man. The woman runs towards him screaming, but is pulled away. A man tries to separate her from the baby. She screams and kicks him. He swears. Then a grotesque tug-of-war takes place, with the baby as its prize. It is torn away from her and thrown from hand to hand, screaming, its tiny hands and fists flailing as it flies through the air. The woman runs from man to man, trying to catch the baby then one man, holding it above his head, turns and smiles at her, before hurling the baby back through the door, into the flames.

The woman shrieks and runs towards the house, but is held back by rough arms tightly gripping her around the waist. She yells and kicks, her limbs flailing in the air, just like the baby a few minutes ago. She is screaming, distraught, her hair hanging in her face. Then, for a brief second, she gathers her wits. Catching the eye of the two older children, she mouths one word: *Run*. Then she starts screaming and kicking, louder than before. Her husband, lying in a pool of blood, has fallen silent.

The woman is passed around like a parcel, twirled about, and inspected, like an animal at market. The mob closes in and moves off, with her at the centre, towards an alleyway where no-one will interrupt what they have planned. The children cling to each other, watching in silent terror. The men have forgotten them. All except one. As he saunters away, he turns to smile at them, revealing a set of uneven yellow teeth, like those of a dog. He winks, as if to share the fun. It is a face they will never forget.

Having been relieved by the other desk sergeant, Sergeant Gunasekera is taking a break in the quadrangle where, seated in a shady place on a step, he has momentarily fallen asleep. He wakes with a cough.

"Uh, oh my god!"

The sun is hot and his throat dry. He tries to summon some saliva but his tongue sticks to the roof of his mouth. He dreamed during his brief rest: terrible images, influenced by his reading and the many depositions that he has taken that morning; scenes from hell, like those he once saw painted in a Catholic church.

"Must get some water," he thinks, pushing his way through the thick press of civilians that now occupies every space in the police station. But wherever he goes, there seem to be queues. As he approaches the lavatory, he hears uproar. A young police officer is besieged by a group of women, each holding a baby. They cluster round him; a clamorous, bad-tempered group.

"No, no. It is against regulations!" blusters the young man.

"What are you going to do? Shoot us?" one woman asks.

The others nod. Angrily, the woman pushes past the young officer, followed by the others. There is a rush and much jostling as each mother tries to secure a place at the sinks. Once successful, she will strip her child of its clothes and bathe it in the basin. A pile of discarded, stinking nappies soon forms in one corner because, as one woman patiently explains, there is nowhere else to put them.

Gunasekera, his stomach churning from the stench, makes his way back to the desk, offering to help the officer-in-charge for want of something to do.

"Go and take a look outside. See how many more there are," says the duty sergeant, indicating the queue of refugees packed tight in the waiting-room.

Gunasekera pushes his way through the sweating bodies, treading on toes, tripping over suitcases. The room has become humid with their heat and the combined odour of so many bodies is overpowering, for each has its own signature: perfume, sweat, food, stale tobacco, hair oil, chewing gum. At last, Gunasekera reaches the doorway where he gulps air like a drowning fish. But there is no more room here. The steps are crowded and a queue, hundreds strong, snakes along the street and around the corner of the building.

Then, from his vantage point, he sees something else. To his right, at the end of the street, a group of men is gathering. So far, there are about fifty of them, but their number is constantly being augmented by others, arriving in smaller groups, ten to twenty-strong. They wear the cheap, brightly-coloured sarongs, favoured by labourers which, in most cases, are hitched up above their knees. Even from here, Gunasekera can see that they are armed with clubs and katties. They are all looking in the direction of the police station. Gunasekera's mouth becomes dry with fear. Pushing his way back to the desk, he shouts over the heads of the waiting crowd.

"Get them inside, quickly!"

The desk sergeant, overwhelmed with paper and pleas for assistance, makes a face, showing that he does not understand. Unable to push his way through to the counter, Gunasekera is forced to shout.

"Goondas. There's a gang of them at the end of the street. I think they're coming this way."

Instantly, the crowd in the waiting-room is galvanized. With cries of terror, it surges forward, carrying Gunasekera with it. Children shriek as they are forced to release their parents' hands and the weakest are in danger of being crushed and trampled. Gunasekera feels as if his ribs will crack from the pressure as more people try to push their way in from outside.

"Open the doors," he yells. "For God's sake, open the doors and let them in."

Running around the back of the counter, the desk sergeant opens the doors into the administrative quarter of the police station. The crowd surges through the breach, like water escaping from a dam. But more are coming. Those outside the police station can see the goondas for themselves and, like terrified cattle, they push forward, desperate for a place of refuge.

Gunasekera, now behind the desk, can see that another stampede is imminent. Grabbing a set of keys from his colleague, he climbs up onto the counter.

"Stop! Listen to me!"

For a few seconds, the crowd continues to press forward. An old gentleman, close to the front, has his glasses pushed from his face and, reaching down for them is knocked to the floor. Diving into the sea of threshing legs, Gunasekera's colleague drags the old man back behind the counter where he lies moaning, more shocked than hurt.

"Stop or I shoot!"

Pulling his service pistol from its holster, Gunasekera takes aim at the crowd. After much jostling and shoving, they grind to an uneasy halt.

"No more of you can enter through here. There is not enough room."

There is a collective moan and a woman starts to cry. The crowd shifts angrily.

"Listen to me. There is another entrance at the back. I will go and open the door. It leads into a quadrangle. You will be safe there. But you must go back outside and follow the wall around to the left of the police station."

"Don't listen to him," says a voice. "He's trying to trick us. Once we're outside, they'll close the doors on us."

The crowd mutters, mutinously.

"All right," says Gunasekera. "I'll lead you there myself. Let me through."

With difficulty, he lets himself down from the counter, like someone sliding into a deep pool, feeling with his feet for the floor. Then, pushing his way to the door, he walks into the street and, hoping that the goondas are sufficiently far away not to hear him, repeats his instructions to the queue outside. They trundle after him, reluctant at first, fearing some kind of trick but, once the door into the quadrangle is open, they begin to flow through steadily, filling up every available space until there is hardly room to stand.

Confident that further refugees will be put off by the sight of the goondas at the end of the road, Gunasekera returns to the front of the building. To his dismay, he realises that the waiting mob has swelled to several hundred in just a few minutes. And more are arriving. Small gangs are gathering in front of the police station, taunting those who arrive or leave, especially if they wear uniform.

"Yah, look at him with his big gun!"

Slipping his hand down the front of his sarong, a goonda pokes the material out with his fingers, thrusting his hips forward suggestively. The others laugh and jeer. Gunasekera ignores them. As long as troublemakers engage in this kind of banter, they are unlikely to attack.

"Where is the Assistant Superintendent?" he asks the desk sergeant.

The other man stares at him, slightly awed. He has never seen this side of Gunasekera, who everyone treats as something of a joke, a dolt who spends his time day-dreaming and reading detective novels on the sly.

"Don't know. Try his office."

Gunasekera shoves and pushes his way to the Assistant Superintendent's office and, without bothering to knock, flings open the door. The senior policeman is sitting at his desk, his head in his hands.

"What are your orders, sir?" asks Gunasekera.

"Orders?" The man raises his head, looking at Gunasekera as if he has never seen him before.

"Yes, sir. We are overrun with refugees and there is a mob forming at the end of the street. It is my belief that they are planning to attack the police station."

The Assistant Superintendent groans, massaging his skull, pressing hard on his temples as if his head will fall apart if he lets go.

"Please, sir. What are we to do?"

"What do you mean?"

"Do we fire over their heads if they attack? Do we shoot them?"

"What? No! That would mean a Commission of Inquiry. Can't risk that."

"Then what?"

In his frustration, Gunasekera raises his voice, but the other policeman seems not to notice.

"It wasn't meant to be like this," he moans to himself.

"Look at him," thinks Gunasekera with contempt. "We could all be killed, but all he can think about is a Commission of Inquiry and his future career."

Furious, no longer caring what the Assistant Superintendent does or thinks, Gunasekera makes his way to the nearest telephone and dials the operator, asking her to put him through to the Government Agent's office.

Screams and shouts ring through the streets as the mob passes, deafening those who cower indoors, huddled together in dark corners of their homes, praying for the terror to pass. Stones and bricks are lobbed through windows; shop windows are smashed and their contents looted. Bottles are filled with petrol, lit with a burning rag and lobbed into houses. Cheers go up as buildings catch light.

Anyone who looks like a public official is set upon and viciously beaten. Those unfortunate enough to be travelling in cars are dragged out and questioned. They are frequently kicked and punched for sport, their unfortunate families standing by, helpless, watching in horror as they listen to the terrible sound of bones snapping under the onslaught. Wives and daughters are gang-raped as husbands and fathers are forced to watch. Grief-stricken mothers sit beside the road, nursing the bodies of their children.

Every so often, one gang merges with another group and, finding a fresh leader and a different purpose, it races back in the direction from which it came, diverted by some new tale of a traitor to the cause or a rich source of pickings. Looters emerge from houses and shops, staggering under heavy bundles of clothing, jewellery and household goods. Paintings and clocks, prized for their sophistication, but of little use in a labourer's hut, become a source of argument between the looters who, fired up with stolen liquor, set about each other with knives and fists, goaded on by their companions. Sometimes the fight is broken up by the leaders of the gang but, more often, after watching this spectacle for a few minutes, the audience tires and drifts away, leaving the contenders to themselves, as they roll on the ground, biting, spitting and stabbing.

This has been the pattern for many days. Householders do not dare to leave their homes for fear of running into one of the gangs and, without daily trips to the market, food is running short. Bodies lie in the streets, unattended and unburied, carrion for pye-dogs and crows, while the hospitals, now crowded with the injured, dead and dying, are little better than waiting-rooms for the morgue.

But, on the morning of the third day, a change takes place. Word passes round, from mouth to mouth, from gang to gang and, soon, all are converging on the police station; some inspired by political zeal, others simply following the direction of the crowd. Now, at last, the Sinhala Hamudawa feels like a real army. No longer groups of ruffians, capable only of random acts of violence, but a great band of men with a single purpose. Today, they are told, they will win a great victory and deliver their country from the Tamils and their supporters. For Tamils are not the only refugees at the police station. Many are Sinhalese civil servants who have been threatened and, often, cruelly beaten for trying to help Tamil civilians.

"Apey anduwa," shout the men at the front of the crowd as they march towards the police station. "It is our government." And their cry is taken up and repeated by the rank-and-file.

"Where are you going, brother?" a young man, who has appeared from a side street with two or three others, asks one of the passing crowd.

"We're going to teach those bastards at the police station a lesson," says the other fellow.

Signalling to his friends to keep up, the young man runs alongside his new companion.

"Will they not shoot at you?"

"No. Of course not. They wouldn't dare. The Government wouldn't allow it. They haven't lifted a finger before and they won't now. Because, secretly, they approve. We are doing what they dare not. We are reclaiming the country for the Sinhalese. Apey anduwa."

"Apey anduwa," shouts the young fellow in response, waving his fist in the air.

"Apey anduwa. Death to Tamils. Death to traitors. Death to the police."

"Apey anduwa," echoes a voice. "Let's kill them all!"

And so, the various gangs gradually coalesce, winding through the streets like a monstrous serpent, surrounding the police station on all sides until it is gripped in a single, deadly coil. Like an egg, waiting to be crushed.

Living in a Sinhalese district, the Gunasekeras and their neighbours have seen little of the mayhem that is sweeping through the centre of town and the Tamil quarters. Nevertheless, there is a change in the air; a sense of tension and nervousness combined with a certain mistrust of one's neighbours, especially if they are Tamil. Official means of communication, such as the radio or newspapers, carry little or no news of the current troubles, but word spreads quickly by mouth and, with the selfishness that afflicts all who are under threat, ordinary Sinhalese breathe a sigh of relief and congratulate themselves on not being Tamil.

However, other more menacing rumours are beginning to circulate. Sinhalese themselves are becoming targets of mob violence, particularly those regarded as 'Tamil lovers'. To acquire this dubious qualification, a shopkeeper has to do little more than sell a loaf to a Tamil and a civil servant merely to provide the service for which he is paid. This often results in a beating and damage to property. Bruised and humiliated, sometimes out of pocket, the victim will warn his friends to avoid contact with Tamils – exactly the result intended by the mob.

Special treatment is reserved for those who actively befriend Tamils or attempt to protect them. In a spirit of charitable kindliness, a number of Sinhalese have given shelter to Tamil friends or neighbours. But, somehow, news of this gets to one of the roving gangs which, although constituted largely of labourers from the countryside, seem to possess a considerable amount of local knowledge. An appropriate attack is then organised; punishment that will provide an example.

Both Tamils and the Sinhalese who protect them are dragged from their homes and beaten without mercy. Some survive with terrible injuries, unable to speak of what has happened. Others die where they fall, their blood and brains spattered over the pavement. Word soon gets around. To be named a 'Tamil lover' is to put your life and those of your family at risk. No-one knows how information gets to the gangs, but it is surprisingly accurate and now, they are finding their way into districts previously considered safe.

***

This morning, as Sergeant Gunasekera is poring over sheaves of witness statements, his wife is cleaning the house. Malika Gunasekera attended the same school as her husband, but it was not until they were seventeen, thrown together at a cricket match, that they had really spoken. Gunasekera had played for a team captained by Malika's brother. He was never considered much of a player but, with one cricketer having fallen sick at the last minute, he was the only choice. To everyone's surprise, he had surpassed all expectations, scoring a century before being caught out and Malika who, until then, had been her brother's faithful shadow, found a new hero to worship.

Sidling up to offer Gunasekera a cup of tea, she had made no attempt to hide her admiration. Gunasekera, a stranger to female attention, was enthralled. A year later, having overcome their families' initial resistance, they married. But, after a brief period of happiness, Malika became increasingly frustrated by Gunasekera's reticence. He had extraordinary qualities, she knew it, but he never tapped into them, never used them, always content to coast along, never making more effort than was necessary to get by. The same was true of their love-making. Until recently.

But now Malika has learned a valuable lesson. Nagging will never get her anywhere for, like most men, her husband has the knack of ignoring it. But temptation and treats, followed by a little gentle wheedling: now that is the trick. She has learned to coax, rather than goad, and it is working. He pays her attention, even helps around the house – a thing unheard of in a society where a man's role is to be waited on and a woman's is to serve. In short, Malika and her husband have become suddenly and unexpectedly happy.

She woke up this morning with a new recipe in her head, for she is not just a fine cook, but innovative also. In fact, she dreams of new dishes so often that she keeps a pencil and paper by the bed to record the ingredients. As she lets herself out of the house, she re-reads the list, standing on the step: goat, ginger, garlic, onions ... She does not see a movement behind the window of the house opposite.

Closing the door behind her, she pauses to check the plants, arranged in flower pots on either side of the steps, checking the soil in each pot to see if they need watering. The alley is narrow, flanked by tall tenement buildings and there is little light for plants; but Malika's collection of ferns seems to thrive in this dank, gloomy place, providing a small oasis for tenement dwellers who sit, talking on the steps, in the cool of the evening.

With her shopping basket over her arm, Malika steps lightly over the rough, rubble pavement, turning left at the corner towards the small, daily market in the main street. As she approaches, she notices that many of the stalls are missing; the iron frames, usually covered with awnings are bare and the wooden counters empty.

"Where is the greengrocer?" she asks the owner of the meat stall.

"No supplies. No-one can get in or out of the city. No-one wants to."

Speaking in a whisper, the man looks nervously over his shoulder. Malika has known him since she first moved with her husband to the tenement four years ago. The stall-holder is an amiable man who enjoys a joke with his customers and has always treated her with particular kindness. In fact, Malika believes he has something of a soft spot for her, as he often makes her a gift of a few, additional off-cuts, slipping them into the parcel of meat, waving away all her offers to pay. But today, he is different. He does not give her his usual, ready smile and seems anxious for her to be gone.

"Have you got any goat?"

"No."

"But, I can see it. There. In front of you."

She points at the tray of meat.

"It's promised to someone else."

It is obvious he is lying. Stunned and hurt, Malika turns to go.

"Wait," the stall-keeper hisses.

Swiftly tipping all of the goat-meat onto a sheet of paper, he wraps it and thrusts it at Malika.

"But that's too much!"

"It doesn't matter. Just take it and go."

"But ... I must pay."

"No, no. Just go. Quickly. And, please, don't come here again."

Dumbfounded, Malika stares at him. Seeing that she will not leave without an explanation, the man begins to gabble in a low voice, still looking this way and that over his shoulder.

"They have threatened me. If I serve any Tamils, they will beat me, burn my stall. I will never work again. I have a family to support. Now, please. Go!"

Disconcerted, Malika puts the meat in her basket and wanders around the few remaining stalls. There are no fresh vegetables to be had and what few remain are shrivelled and unappetising. As she approaches their counters, stall-holders pretend to busy themselves, turning their back on her as they re-arrange tidy piles of crates or count small amounts of change. It is obvious that none wants her custom and she returns home, disheartened.

Although she has noted a slight cooling of her neighbours' attitude to her in recent days, Malika believed her husband when he told her that this was just due to general unease. No-one trusts anyone else at the moment, he had said. It's nothing to do with being Tamil. But it is. She knows that now and it disturbs her.

As she turns into it, the small alleyway looks forbidding. It seems unusually dark and Malika does not experience the feeling of welcome that she usually has on returning home. It is with relief that she lets herself into the ground-floor apartment. She does not notice a movement behind the window in the house opposite. She is being watched.

Gunasekera waits nervously in the police station. The mob outside is growing by the minute, screaming obscenities and threats, often in response to a ring-leader, until the air resounds with their noise. Everyone inside the building can hear them, including the refugees in the quadrangle who, like penned cattle, are liable to stampede in any direction once panic takes hold.

Sitting at his desk, Gunasekera takes out his service pistol and lays it on the counter so that it is within easy reach. It will not be much use against a howling mob, but it gives him courage. He is not completely unprotected and, at least, he can give a good account of himself. Like that day at the cricket match when he first met Malika. For a few seconds, his thoughts return to a happier time.

There were bad times after that. Quite a lot of them. But most of that was due to their immaturity; his and Malika's. Neither had known how to bridge the gap when things went wrong. Their approach to problems was laughable: Malika adopted a billy-goat approach, continually butting her head against invisible walls, while her husband behaved like a hermit crab, retreating into his shell, scuttling away from problems whenever the opportunity arose. What a fine pair! But now they are through it. He smiles when he thinks of her these days, and he thinks of her often.

"The police are protecting the Tamils. What shall we do? Kill them!"

Gunasekera freezes. It would be ironic if he died now when his future with Malika looks so bright. They have even begun to talk of having children. For a moment, he is seized by a despairing sadness.

"A Tamil. A Tamil. Look at him run. After him, brothers."

There are shrieks from the road outside and a young police officer, who has been watching through a crack in the door, grimaces and turns his head away. Grabbing his gun, Gunasekera leaps over the counter and races to the door, pushing the other man out of the way to get a view of the street. Outside, a man is being bundled from hand to hand then, at intervals, a section of the crowd closes in, obscuring him from sight, laying into him with fists and feet. Then, he is hauled to his feet and passed back along the line, to another gang, where the process is repeated.

Every so often, there is a pause as the mob waits for a reaction from the police. When none comes, the beatings become more frequent, more brutal. By now, the man is nearly senseless, his arms and legs dangling drunkenly as he is passed about the crowd. Then, in an effort to revive him, they pour water over his face. He sits, staring up at them stupidly then, seeing his chance, scrambles for the steps of the police station, only to be hauled back and beaten again.

"Why are you not helping him?" Gunasekera shouts at the other officer.

The man shrugs.

"What can I do?"

"You have a gun."

"But we are under strict orders not to fire."

"Who said so?"

"The Assistant Superintendent."

"Damn the Assistant Superintendent," snaps Gunasekera.

Pushing the other man aside, he pulls the door open and runs down the steps.

"Leave him alone," he shouts.

"Or what?" jeers a man from the crowd.

"Or I shoot the next one who hits him."

There are laughs, more jeering.

"Go on, then."

Without hesitation, Gunasekera raises his pistol and points it at one of the mob. The man's eyes widen in fear. There is nowhere to run, he is too tightly packed in and Gunasekera's gun is aimed at his heart. Some rioters, further back in the crowd, begin to jeer but those at the front fall back, silent and uncertain, looking at each other nervously.

"Come here, friend."

Gunasekera addresses the man lying on the ground. There is no response. The fellow remains curled up, his hands protecting his head. Gunasekera prays for him to move. If he is unconscious, that will mean walking down into the mob. He cannot carry a man and protect himself at the same time. The goondas will then have two victims to play with.

"Come on, brother."

Gunasekera tries to steady his voice, but he can feel tension rising in the crowd. They are watching him intently, waiting for their chance to attack. A fellow at the front steps forward, makes an obscene gesture at Gunasekera, then looks back at his friends. A cheer goes up, slightly muted but offering encouragement nonetheless.

The mob is regaining its confidence, becoming restive. The front line begins to shift back and forth, testing Gunasekera's resolve. He holds his position, praying to all that is dear for the man on the ground to move. The man at whom he has taken aim begins to smile, cautiously at first, but with increasing awareness that Gunasekera is losing ground. Then, against all hope and to Gunasekera's intense relief, the victim hauls himself to his knees and slowly begins to drag himself up the steps.

"Come on, brother, only a few more feet. That's the way."

Gunasekera speaks softly, words of encouragement with which one might coax a stricken animal. Dropping his gaze briefly, he sees the man's face looking up at him, wincing with the pain of every movement, blood pouring into one eye from a gash on his forehead. Gunasekera wants to help, but he cannot trust the crowd. He must hold them back for a few more seconds.

"Hey," he shouts over his shoulder. "Get out here!"

He knows that the other officer is still watching from the doorway. *Damn coward*, he thinks.

"Officer Samaratunga, come out and help this man or I'll tell them where you live!"

Behind him, the door flies open and the other man emerges, swearing under his breath.

"Help this man into the station," orders Gunasekera. "Quickly!"

Dragging the wounded man to his feet, none too gently, the officer helps him up the steps, making sure to give Gunasekera one of his most dangerous looks as he passes. Gunasekera snorts. Once the other men are behind him, he backs slowly up the steps, still with his gun raised, aiming at the crowd. Finally, he is back at the entrance and ducks inside. None too soon for, as the heavy door closes behind him, it is hit by a volley of missiles that rattle against its thick panels like rain.

***

Panting, Gunasekera falls to the ground and, drawing up his legs, puts his head between his knees. The room begins to spin and he knows that if he tries to stand up, he will pass out. Pushing his way through the refugees crowding the waiting-room, Gunasekera's friend, the other desk sergeant, brings him a glass of water.

"It was a very brave thing that you did. Here. Drink this."

The glass is laced with something stronger than water. Gunasekera splutters.

"Assistant Superintendent's secret supply."

The sergeant grins.

"I know where he keeps it. Reckoned you had more need of it than him."

"Where is he?"

"Locked in his office. Hasn't come out for hours."

Gunasekera shakes his head in disbelief.

"Any news from the Government Agent?"

"Nothing. That's where I was when you were out front. I've left messages for him everywhere, that is, when I can get through. Many of the phone lines have been cut and those that are still working are constantly engaged. It doesn't look as if anyone is coming. We're on our own."

"Ah."

Gunasekera nods, trying to appear calm, but he has a sick feeling in the pit of his stomach.

Malika Gunasekera never locks the door to her home. She does not need to. There is little crime in this neighbourhood, largely because everyone knows everyone else's business. They all know who should be coming and going, who is a resident, who is a stranger and anything untoward is always challenged. People look out for each other here, so she feels safe, even leaving the door unlocked when she goes to market. Even now, with chaos raging elsewhere in the city, she does not feel threatened and sees no reason to change her habits.

Having prepared the goat and put it on to stew in a large pot, Malika is now scrubbing the floor, something she does at least twice a day. As she works, she thinks happily of how her marriage has been transformed. In one night. She is still not sure what happened to bring about this change. It has been like trying to tune a radio for a long time, then finally hitting the right waveband.

Like most women of her generation, Malika is unversed in the science of relationships. Unlike their western counterparts, Island women rarely speak of their emotions within marriage. Sex and babies, like rainfall and drought, are things that either happen or do not. While failure in either might lead to expressions of sympathy and commiseration from one's peers, such things are regarded as beyond human control, dependent solely upon a whim of Nature.

Because she does not understand how it is that she finally found the right wavelength with her husband, Malika is afraid of losing it. For her, the only means of securing future happiness comes, not through understanding, but through propitiation and prayer and this she has vowed to do at least twice a day, performing puja at her private shrine before a figure of the goddess, Devi, who, among her many forms, is a consort to the gods. In her role as celestial wife, Devi represents the shakti, or power, of her husband.

Scrubbing hard at the concrete floor, Malika vows that she will be her husband's shakti, just like Devi. She will be his strength and refuge. They will be happy. Forever. She pauses to wipe a strand of hair from her face and, as she does so, she becomes aware of someone standing behind her. She turns and sees the man from across the street, the one her husband has told her is a political agitator. Behind him are two other men.

"What do you want?" she says.

The man steps forward, smiling. Then, without a word, he grabs her hair, yanking her to her feet. She tries to scream but her voice betrays her. Mute with fear, she can only stare into his eyes, appealing for him not to hurt her. Still smiling, he deals her a crushing blow to the head which sends her sprawling across the floor. She blacks out for a few seconds because, when she comes to, the man is bending over her, his companions peering over his shoulders, one on either side. Pushing herself with her hands, she tries to scrabble away, crabwise.

He lets her go, smiling as she slithers on hands and knees across the wet floor, still stunned from the blow to her head then, as she reaches the shelter of the table, catching her ankle and pulling her back across the floor on her stomach. Wildly, she flings out her arms, grabbing at furniture, clutching the table leg, pulling down chairs on top of her, screaming at the top of her voice.

Calm and unhurried, he drags her into the next room where he rapes her before the image of Devi, watched by his companions. Even after he has finished, she continues to scream, shrieking and crying, calling for her neighbours to help. But, although they have all heard, no-one comes.

1958: The note

Having parted from Asoka, Arjun is heading towards the city. On the way, he stops at a country post office, attempting to warn Nash of the danger by telephone but, out in the country, the lines cut by the Sinhala Hamudawa have not yet been repaired. When he asks if there is any other means of communication, he is directed to the railway station. When asked for his help, the station master scratches his head, pushing his peaked cap to one side.

"You can send a message with the next train. I will give it to the driver. But I can't guarantee it will get there. Things are bad up there, you know."

Using the station-master's pen, Arjun drafts a note, sealing it in a brown envelope that somehow looks too banal to convey the urgency of the message inside.

"It is a matter of life and death," he says.

The station-master nods, wearily. Everything is these days.

With growing desperation, Arjun runs back to the jeep, firing up the engine and pulling away from the kerb with a screech of tyres, driving as fast as the pot-holed track will allow. But he is still sixty miles from the city.

1958: The siege

It is at least four hours since Sergeant Gunasekera first telephoned the Government Agent's office. He has tried many times since, but still, there is no response. Gunasekera and his friend, the desk sergeant, are manning the door, keeping an eye on the street.

"Where have they all come from?" asks the other man in dismay as he gazes out at the crowd now surrounding the police station on every side.

"Most are from the country," says Gunasekera although, as he speaks, it occurs to him that the numbers of the Sinhala Hamudawa are rapidly being swelled by recruits from the city. You can tell, just by looking at them.

"And how did they get hold of that?" breathes the other man, indicating a man at the front of the crowd.

"What?" says Gunasekera, trying to follow his friend's directions.

"That fellow in the blue shirt. Look at what he's got in his pocket."

"My God!"

Until now, Gunasekera has dismissed the stories of men carrying dynamite. To him, these are fables, generated by fear, the kind of rumours that often accompany civil disturbances.

"Do you think it's real?" asks Gunasekera.

"Shall we ask him?" retorts his friend and, despite their fear or, perhaps because of it, they both laugh.

"Tell me something," says Gunasekera, suddenly becoming serious. "Do you think that these riots have been organised?"

The other man sighs.

"I prefer not to think of such things. But, yes, now you come to mention it. This is not the work of a few, uneducated peasants. Look at them. How many would you say there were? Fifteen hundred? Two thousand?"

"More like three thousand," murmurs Gunasekera, scanning the crowd. "And more are coming. Look. Over there!"

He points to a junction, nearly half a mile away, where the road leading to the police station joins a main thoroughfare and where there is a disturbance at the outer edge of the crowd. They are jostling and pushing. He can hear shouts. They appear to be moving aside, letting something through.

"What is happening over there?"

Gunasekera points along the road, towards the junction. The other man shields his eyes with his hands, squinting in the bright light.

"I can't see. There are some trees there. Wait. I can see a lorry. No, two. They are coming this way."

The two men fall silent, praying that the vehicles are not bringing reinforcements for the Sinhala Hamudawa.

***

They wait, holding their breath, each knowing what the other is thinking but not daring to speak of their fear. If the rioters can get dynamite, they can get other things, too. His friend has just confirmed Gunasekera's suspicions. Someone with influence and power is directing the riots. Without direction, the Sinhala Hamudawa would be little more than a few roaming gangs of malcontents. But someone has brought these gangs together. And now they are here. In front of the police station. Ready to storm it at any moment.

Watching the two lorries, nudging their way through the crowds, Gunasekera feels sick. They must be bringing the ring-leaders and, probably more weapons. Once they are in place, the attack will start. What resistance can the police offer to so many? He thinks of the civilians, crammed in the quadrangle, as defenceless as chicken in a yard. They will run, screaming in all directions as soon as the goondas attack. Many will be crushed in the stampede, while the rest will be finished off by the rioters with clubs and katties. The carnage will be terrible and he can do nothing to stop it.

Momentarily, Gunasekera feels tears pricking his eyes. But he forces them back. The least he can do is act like a man, not cry like a baby. Taking deep breaths to steady his nerves, he plants himself in the doorway. They will have to get through him first. It is not over until the last ball is bowled. A stupid thought, but it cheers him. He has faced overwhelming odds before, even if it was only in a cricket match. At least he knows he has the courage to continue. Right to the end. Sometimes, that is all you can do. Just keep going and hope to wear your opponent down.

Slowly, the lorries push through the crowd, advancing a few feet at a time. So tightly is the crowd packed around the vehicles, that Gunasekera can only see the green canvas canopy covering the back of the vehicle and the outline of the driver in the cab. Many of the rioters have arrived in lorries such as these, transported many miles from remote areas of the countryside. It has to be organised. But by whom?

Although Tamils are the ostensible target, many Sinhalese have also been attacked. What is the purpose? Is the intention to drive the Tamils out or to use them as an excuse to bring the Government down? Who would unleash such apocalyptic violence in order to gain a political end? Such cynicism is unthinkable, at least to a simple man, like Gunasekera. Putting the thought out of his mind, he turns his attention to the street. The two lorries are inching closer.

"Wait a minute."

His friend has sharper eyes.

"Those lorries are not driven by rioters. It is the army."

***

Reluctantly, the mob parts to let the lorries through, cowed only by the fear that more will follow. They watch sullenly as the vehicles pull up outside the police station, forming a barricade in front of the steps. It may not be enough to prevent an attack, but it will give those inside more time to prepare themselves.

A tall man with grey hair climbs out of the cab of one of the lorries and, as he mounts the steps, one of the crowd begins to jeer.

"Look ! It's the Government Agent. He's a Tamil, too. Kill the bastard!"

Cautiously, the crowd begins to take up the chant, still anticipating more lorry-loads of soldiers. Nash climbs the steps slowly, with the deliberation of an old man, but he does not turn back to look at the crowd fearing that, if he does so, it will provoke an attack. Only when he is inside, will he stare out from the door, his heart momentarily failing him as he confronts the mass of hostile faces.

Having leapt nimbly out of the trucks, the soldiers are now struggling under the weight of heavy, canvas-covered bundles. Pausing for a moment, their sergeant looks around him, taking stock.

"Just here I think," he says, pointing to a spot on the steps with a clear aim at the mob. "Set it up here."

Swiftly, they unroll their bundles, revealing the components of a Bren gun, which they quickly assemble, and several boxes of ammunition.

A shout goes up from the crowd.

"Yah! They'll never shoot us. They wouldn't dare. We are Sinhalese."

Others join in but, for a short while, the mob's confidence stalls. Signalling to each other, the gang leaders get together, huddling just behind the front line, discussing what they should do.

"Excuse me, sir," Gunasekera addresses Nash who is standing beside him. "But when are the other soldiers coming."

"They're not," says Nash, still looking out of the door.

"But … there are only about twenty men. Twenty against so many!"

"It's all I could find," says Nash, abruptly.

The hope, so recently kindled, is extinguished. However, reasoning that hope is ephemeral and, therefore, of no practical use, Gunasekera wisely decides to do without it.

**

Beyond the steps, the gang leaders have come to a decision. The lorries, they argue, are only the forerunners of further reinforcements. They will have to act quickly, or not at all. Running back to their cronies, they tell them to spread the word.

Get ready!

A great bellow rises from the mob. One of the young recruits positioned on the steps looks nervously at the sergeant. The soldier manning the Bren gun massages his fingers, his face tense, his eyes fixed on the crowd. The sergeant runs up the steps to where Nash is watching the goondas. Reaching inside his shirt, the sergeant produces a piece of paper.

"Sign this, please, sir."

"What is it?"

"Even if the crowd charges, we have no order to fire. Here is the order. Please sign it, sir. I think they are about to attack."

Nash shakes his head, wondering at the bureaucratic stupidity that demands a signature on a piece of paper before innocent people can be defended.

"Here you are, Sergeant. There's your order."

"Thank you, sir."

The sergeant, it seems, sees no irony in the situation. Saluting smartly, he carefully folds the paper, tucks it back inside his shirt then runs back down the steps to the emplacement where, bending low, he whispers something in the gunner's ear. The soldier nods, not taking his eyes off the crowd, although he stops massaging his hands. Pulling himself closer to the gun, he takes up a firing position, patting the box of ammunition by his side, before placing his finger on the trigger.

Gunasekera, still standing beside Nash, can feel his heart thudding in his chest. The front line has been whipped into a frenzy. The ring-leaders, slightly ahead of the others, are goading them on. With sarongs lifted above their waists in a gesture of contempt, they scream insults at the soldiers. Heartened by this defiance, the front line advances, hands raised above their heads, waving clubs, knives and sticks of dynamite.

The sergeant makes a sign to the gunner, who fires a round into the air. But, instead of bringing the goondas to their senses, it only infuriates them. The ring-leaders scream and leap like demons, shrieking imprecations at their followers. The mob surges forward.

"Fire!"

The Bren gun judders. The crowd screams, swirling about, in a confusion of limbs, running and pushing, this way and that, trampling and shoving, a maelstrom of desperation and wild terror. Within minutes, they have fled, melting away into streets and alleyways, leaving behind only the dead and wounded.

1958: A message

Word of the siege at the police station spreads fast and soon, rumours of carnage and hundreds of casualties are circulating. Everyone is pre-occupied with the news, so no-one pays attention to a large fellow, pushing his way to the front of the group waiting outside the Government Agent's residence. Large and muscular, he looks like an out-of-towner, a day labourer who hires himself out for farm-work or road-building.

Workers like him can always be seen in town, wandering in from time to time to spend their wages in the slum quarters, drinking to excess and womanising before buying a few cheap trinkets in the market to take home. Such men usually die early, either of disease or exhaustion, mourned only by a few in villages that no town-dweller has ever heard of, their remains reduced to ash, consumed by jungle or paddy.

This fellow, remarkable only for his height, draws little attention from those absorbed by more immediate concerns, such as the loss of their homes and possessions. Passing among them, unobserved, he makes his way to the monk who is still sitting quietly on the kerb and whispers something in his ear.

"The Government Agent signed the order to fire."

Nodding grimly, the monk waves the other fellow away while he, himself, remains sitting on the kerb, his eyes now fixed on a spot at the end of the road, one hand resting inside his robe.

The train has come and gone, picking up Arjun's message but, unknown to him, it has been held up, outside the city, for the last three hours.

"What is happening?" shouts the engine driver to a railway worker walking back up the track.

"Riots in the city," shouts the other fellow. "Nothing is moving. No trains in. No trains out."

"For how long?"

The other man shrugs.

"Who knows?"

Enviously, the driver watches the maintenance man picking his way along the track, stepping lightly over the rails, avoiding the hot stones between the sleepers that, having baked all day in the sun, are now hot enough to fry an egg. As he steps into the shadow of a goods train, the fellow begins to whistle. He is going home. Fanning himself with the brown paper envelope that was handed to him at the last station, the engine driver settles down to wait. The cab is hot, but it is even hotter outside.

Putting the envelope down on the seat beside him, he opens his flask of tea and drains the last drop, crunching the granules of sugar that have not quite dissolved, thinking about supper and wondering when he will get home. He has no food and his stomach is beginning to rumble. The sun beats down relentlessly on the cab and he can feel the heat rising from the track. There is nothing more to drink and he is feeling faint. At least if you pull into a station, there is some shade and someone to bring you water, but he is stranded out here, mid-track, miles from anywhere. The heat closes around him like a thick, airless blanket and he begins to doze.

Ting! With his eyes still shut, the engine driver swipes at a fly that has landed on his nose. Ting! Ting! He opens his eyes a fraction, their lids flickering with the torpor of sleep. His mouth is dry and his lips are stuck to his teeth. Rubbing his eyes with the heel of his palm, the driver struggles to wake. The view from the window is blurred. He rubs his eyes again. The signal has turned from red to green.

"Time to go!" says the stoker, shaking the driver by the shoulder.

"Yes, yes."

Stumbling to his feet, the driver sets the engine in motion, enjoying the cool rush of air on his face. He does not notice the brown envelope, caught by the breeze, fluttering out of the open door.

1958: The city

After his brief stop at the railway station, Arjun has made good progress for several miles. Apart from a few bicycles and bullock carts, the roads are relatively deserted and he counts himself lucky to have had no further encounters with marauding bands of goondas in lorries, although the countryside bears the tell-tale signs of their progress. At his approach, mothers scoop up children from where they are playing in the road and swiftly bear them away, running into their huts or, more often, seeking the deeper cover of the jungle or the fields.

Standing in the shadow of their homes, those brave enough to remain, usually men, peer at him suspiciously, watching, waiting, to see if he will stop. If the jeep slows its pace, they tauten, shifting position so that both feet are planted firmly on the ground, their shoulders tense, their faces grim and unwelcoming. As he passes, he sees that many of them hold machetes, ready to defend themselves and their frugal belongings. The smiling faces that greeted him on his outward journey have changed in a few hours to expressions of fear and mistrust.

He has had the foresight to bring petrol cans with him, so he does not have to stop at villages to refill the tank. He knows that his presence is not welcome and he does not have time for long explanations of who he is or what he wants, provided of course, that they will listen. Some have already made their intentions plain by stoning the jeep, their line of defence being to treat all strangers as a potential threat. After what he has seen, Arjun cannot blame them. Even the open country is not safe from the depredations of the goondas. In the distance, columns of smoke billow skywards. Acres of crops have been put to the torch.

With the taste of desolation in his mouth, Arjun draws closer to the city. Now he notices small groups of people, travelling in the same direction as himself. Old people, young ones, parents with babies; men, women and children, some carrying cages of chicken, others pulling handcarts filled with possessions, while pigs, geese and oxen are driven ahead by children carrying switches; all trudging forward in the hope of refuge. Stepping onto the verge at his approach, they stand watching, shielding their eyes, some holding out their hands to beg, others staring mutely, dazed by the loss of homes or possessions, stunned by the violence that has struck with the suddenness of a biblical plague, disorientated by a journey of only a few miles that, to village people, feels like an exodus into a foreign land.

One mother holds up a baby, then points to her mouth. She is hungry. They are all hungry. The helpless longing in their eyes is almost too much to bear. But if he stops, they will all try to board the jeep. He cannot carry them all and would have to choose. But who? Worse still, fighting might break out. He can read it in their eyes, hungry with desperation. And he has to get to the city, quickly, in case his message fails, the one he left at the station. For someone is planning to kill Nash and instinct tells him that the attack is imminent.

***

After a few more miles, progress gets slower. Where, before, there were only isolated groups of people, whole communities now seem to be on the move. They fill the road with a slow, swirling chaos, unsure of their destination, their only idea to get away from wherever they have been. It is like trying to drive through the middle of a market.

The jeep slows to a crawl, sometimes stopping altogether and, frequently, he has to sound the horn just to make them move, pushing through the crowd, praying that no child or animal will fall under the wheels. All the time, his fear and frustration are growing. Will he be in time?

As the vehicle noses its way through the crowd, Arjun thinks he sees a familiar face. Braking sharply, he stands up in the seat to get a better look.

"Ella. Ella. Over here!"

He waves, trying to catch her attention. Pulling Ella by the elbow, a young woman, accompanied by a boy, forces her way over to the jeep.

"Ella. Are you all right? What has happened?"

Arjun climbs down to greet her, but gets no response. Ella does not recognise him.

"Our village was attacked, sir," the girl, Shakti, explains. "She lost her family."

"What? All killed?"

"We don't know. Two, at least, we think. Her husband and son. In the fields."

Arjun remembers the pall of smoke, hanging over the countryside.

"And the others?"

"Her mother and three other children have gone missing. One may have died in the village. She was left behind. All the houses were burnt down. The others? We don't know. They have disappeared. Perhaps we will find them."

"Get in the car," says Arjun. "Quickly!"

A crowd has already begun to press around the jeep, begging for food and help. The girl and her brother help Ella into the front seat, then climb in themselves. Arjun releases the hand-brake and the jeep begins to roll forward.

"What about us?" wails a voice behind him. "What shall we do?"

"I'll send help," shouts Arjun over his shoulder, praying that he can and that he has not lied.

***

On a narrow bridge at the outskirts of the city, the crowd slows to a shuffle. Refugees from the country, travelling towards town and, supposedly, safety, are joined by others: city-dwellers, also evicted from their homes, travelling in the opposite direction for the same reason. Members of the two groups, caught in the impasse, begin to question each other, exchanging tales of the atrocities that have forced them onto the road. The realisation that there is no safe haven, either in the country or in the city, leads first to despair, then panic.

"What are we to do?" wail the women, while the men, standing silently beside them, stare at each other with a kind of hopeless acceptance.

Those at the back of the crowd, not understanding the reason for the hold-up, continue to push forward, until those caught in the middle feel as if the whole weight of humanity is bearing down on them.

Women faint and have to be held up by their neighbours for fear of being crushed underfoot. Small children are whisked up into their parents' arms or seated on their fathers' shoulders where they are asked to give an account of what they can see. Some of the children, enjoying the game, laugh and chatter as if nothing had happened; others, disturbed by the weeping adults around them, begin to whimper, begging to be let down.

It is a strange sight: the rural poor mingling with the urban middle-classes, the only link between them, if there is one at all, being that of ethnicity, for many are Tamils. While those from the country are often Hindu and, at best, semi-literate; those from the town, are either Catholic, or at least educated to a high level by the brothers and sisters of various orders.

Shopkeepers, lawyers and civil servants rub shoulders with peasants whose work is governed by the seasons rather than by the ticking of a clock. Old and young, educated and ignorant, rich and poor, all now reduced to the same level: homeless and destitute, with only their lives in credit.

1958: The bicycle man

Having seen the main road thickening with people some miles back, Arjun decides to take a more circuitous route, through the back streets and poorer quarters of town. It is more risky, but he knows that he is under pressure of time. Nash's life is in danger, but only Arjun knows it. He begins to wonder whether he was wise to take on passengers because other people might mean delay; but the sight of Ella's stricken face and the suffering which has sucked the life from her eyes, now dull and listless, has moved him.

He wonders how he would feel if he ever lost Neleni. At the thought, a prickling sweat of fear dampens his forehead. He longs for her with a longing that resolves itself into a permanent, dull ache. It is always there, even when his mind is on other things and, when he does think of her, the pain is intense. How could he have ever considered leaving her? Any sacrifice, whatever it is, would be worth the price, just to stay near her.

They are now travelling through the slum quarter of town, through narrow streets strewn with rubbish, flanked by shanty buildings with roofs of corrugated iron which, if more than one storey high, look in imminent danger of collapse. Pye-dogs race in and out of alleyways, followed by ragged children; lean cats sidle along the streets then vanish into doorways or ease themselves through narrow holes under buildings, where they hunt rats beneath the floorboards while families eat and sleep above; and, at every street corner, are groups of men, smoking, idling, watching, their cheekbones sunken with hunger but with a new light in their eyes, hoping, that now, their time has come.

They shift as the jeep passes, murmuring to each other or just following it with their eyes, like famished strays. Some, the remnants of the mob that attacked the police station, are openly carrying weapons. One man peels away from the group. He breaks into a run and is joined by others. The men begin to chase the jeep, brandishing sticks.

The potu on Shakti's forehead marks her out as Tamil. In the back seat, she clings to her brother, shielding his head with her arm. Arjun presses his foot down hard on the accelerator, recklessly screeching around corners, weaving in and out of narrow streets, trying not to give the men an opportunity to stop them, praying that he will not turn, by mistake, into a blind alley.

Other men emerge from the side-streets. They fling themselves at the jeep, grabbing at the passengers, shouting obscenities at the women, promising what they will do if they catch them. Clutching her brother to her, the girl buries her head in his shoulder, trying to shut out the terror around her. But, all the while, Ella sits, quiet and hunched, staring ahead of her, seeing and hearing nothing.

A group of men gathers at the end of the street. Arjun presses his foot down to the floor and drives straight at them. They leap out of the way, yelping like dogs. Then, screaming imprecations, they join the chase, flinging bricks and stones and whatever missiles they can find. The insane flight continues. The jeep speeds around a corner, tilts, hits a low brick wall, then spinning around, slews across the street, finally coming to rest with its nose embedded in the side of an old warehouse.

Stunned, the passengers climb drunkenly onto the pavement. By now, the group of men that was following them has begun to catch up. They appear at the end of the alleyway, cutting off escape to the main road. They laugh and jeer, pointing at the women. Then, their leader approaches, sauntering towards them with the lazy strut of a victor.

"Come on, darling. Come to Daddy!"

He laughs, pointing at Shakti, singling her out, motioning to his comrades to follow. Stricken with terror, the girl clings to her brother, digging her fingers into his flesh.

"Look at this, darling!"

The man pulls up his sarong to reveal his genitals. The other men laugh and hoot, goading him on. The girl shivers and trembles.

Suddenly, the girl's brother tears himself from her grasp and, darting down the street, flings himself on the man, clawing at his face.

"You bastard!" he screams.

The man shrieks as the boy's fingers rip and gouge at his face.

"Get him off. Get him off!"

"Run!" yells the boy to his sister as the men close in around him.

"No!" she shrieks, preparing to follow him. But Arjun has her around the waist.

The boy is now surrounded. Invisible. Suddenly a hand, holding a stick is raised in the air, descending with a loud 'Thwack!' It is followed by others, striking many times until the narrow street echoes with a battery of thuds, like the sound of soft, heavy rain. Now, as each stick is raised, an arc of red drops flies into the air, spattering the walls like paint.

Shakti kicks and struggles, holding out her arms to her brother. But it is too late. Pulling her by one hand and Ella by the other, Arjun drags the women after him, forcing them to run; down the street, along an alley, then into another, snaking from left to right, hardly knowing what direction he is taking, hoping to evade the terror that will pursue them. He can hear it already. The sound of running feet.

"Which way?" shouts a voice.

"This way," answers another.

They are getting close.

"In here!"

Hands take hold of Arjun, Shakti and Ella, dragging them through a dark entrance.

"Into the corner. Cover yourselves!"

Too stunned to argue, they allow themselves to be manhandled into a dark, evil smelling space where crouching together, they are covered by an old tarpaulin. Outside, they can hear yelling.

"Hey!"

A voice shouts from the alleyway. It is close. Only a few feet away.

"Have you seen three people, a man and two women?"

"No."

Then, there is a muffled conversation. Two voices, maybe more, outside in the street. From their hiding place, Arjun and the girl strain to hear what is being said. He is still holding her hand. He can feel it trembling. Ella's, by comparison, is cold and lifeless. The girl tenses. She is about to speak. Arjun squeezes her hand hard to stop her. The dark, hot space beneath the tarpaulin is rank with fear. The voices stop and are followed by the sound of shuffling feet. Arjun closes his eyes. *They have betrayed us*, he thinks, as the tarpaulin is lifted from their heads.

"You are safe now. For a while."

Arjun opens his eyes and sees an elderly man and a younger woman standing over him.

"Who are you?" he whispers.

"Doesn't matter. Better you don't know my name. But this is my daughter and you are in my house."

Exhausted, Arjun rests his head against the leg of a wooden bench. His eyes are becoming accustomed to the dark and he realises that they are in a one-room, windowless shack, built of planks and iron panels. From hooks on the walls hang a variety of objects, jigsaws, hammers, screwdrivers, old bicycle wheels, handlebars, saddles, even circlets of inner tubing. The old man follows his gaze.

"I mend things. Mainly bicycles."

"Why?" says Arjun.

"Why do I mend bicycles?" There is a trace of amusement in the voice.

"No. Why did you help us?"

"Because I do not believe in violence."

"Are you Buddhist?"

"Does it matter?"

"No. I am grateful to you, whoever you are."

The old man waves his hand, as if risking his own life for three strangers was nothing. The daughter, who went outside a few minutes previously, now reappears carrying three mugs of tea on the lid of a biscuit tin. Arjun and the girl drink theirs gratefully, but Ella, clutching her mug, stares fixedly at the wall. Guiding Ella's hands, Shakti tries to make her drink.

"What is the matter with her?" asks the old man.

"She has lost her family."

"Missing or dead?" The old man has a blunt way with words.

"We don't know."

The old man sighs and scratches his head.

"The world has gone mad."

Arjun nods. The old man looks at him, up and down, inspecting every detail of his clothes, but with interest, not envy.

"You are an educated man?"

"A civil servant."

"Ah."

He nods his head knowingly and, squatting down next to Arjun, begins to speak in a low voice.

"You cannot stay here long. I told them that you had taken a different route, but it leads to a blind alley. When they find that you are not there, they will be back. As soon as you have finished your tea, you must leave."

"Of course. But what about you."

"What have they to gain from a silly old man? I have no possessions, nor am I a Tamil."

He gives Arjun a knowing look.

"While they have attacked Sinhalese, it is the Tamils they are really after."

"Yes."

Arjun wonders how far he will be able to travel with two women, one half out of her wits with terror, the other paralysed with grief. The old man seems to read his thoughts.

"There is a Catholic church. Not too far away. I have heard they are taking in refugees. I can give you directions."

"Thank you."

Arjun grasps the old man's hand and shakes it earnestly.

"Please, take this."

Arjun begins to unstrap the watch that his father gave him.

"No," says the old man. "I have no need of such things."

"Please," insists Arjun. "As a sign of friendship."

The old man draws a deep breath and reluctantly takes the watch.

"Very well. I will it give to my grandson – when he is older – as a token of better things."

"Thank you."

The old man pats Arjun on the shoulder.

A few minutes later, Arjun and the women emerge from the tin shack, having waited for the old man to signal that the street is clear. They part with few words, the old man seeming keen to get back into his house, possibly beginning to regret the rashness of his action, although Arjun hopes not. Somewhere, in this dirty soiled world, he hopes that some purity of purpose remains and, fleetingly, he thinks of Asoka, wondering where he is, hoping that he has fared better than himself.

Now, trying to remember the old man's instructions to the church, Arjun guides the women through the maze of backstreets. It is not easy. Shakti starts at every sound, shrinking into doorways, covering her head with her hands while Ella, if not directed, simply remains immobile. Holding their hands, one on either side of him, Arjun pulls and manipulates them along dark and dirty alleyways sure that, at any minute, the men will come back and find them. But, either due to the old man's wily misdirection or to the fact that they have found another victim, the men do not return.

Eventually, they find the church: a pretty stucco building, built by the Portuguese. Climbing the steps, Arjun hammers on the heavy teak door which, unusually for a place of worship, is firmly bolted. A pale face appears behind the grille, and pale blue eyes with sandy lashes inspect him.

"Can I help you?"

An Irish voice, soft but firm: the tone, that of a sweet-stall owner addressing unruly children.

"Yes. These women need shelter. They have lost their homes and families. They are hungry."

The pale forehead wrinkles under the crisp, white wimple. The nun peers through the bars, slowly inspecting each of them in turn. Then, with a clank, a bolt is pulled back and the door opens.

"Come in."

The nun is about fifty, her mouth tightly clamped, seemingly displeased at her own charity. Having shut the door, she smiles. A different face again. Arjun realises that she, too, is frightened.

"I'm sorry, but we've had people trying to trick their way in here. Bad people."

She gives him a look. He knows what she means.

"Sister, can you give these women a place to stay?"

"Of course. But they'll have to sleep on the floor with all the others."

Looking over the nun's shoulder, Arjun can see figures moving about in the jewel-lit gloom of the nave. The church is packed with refugees, whole families encamped in the space between the pews.

"They won't mind."

"And yourself?"

The nun looks at him, intently.

"I have to leave. I have an urgent message for the Government Agent."

She snorts.

"Like many others!"

Trying to stifle his sense of injustice at this remark, Arjun takes his leave of the two women; the girl now weeping softly into her hands, Ella sitting beside her, rigid and dazed. As he emerges from the church, a car sweeps by. A familiar profile appears briefly in the back window.

"Nash!"

Arjun runs after the car, shouting and waving his arms, trying to attract the driver's attention but the vehicle is travelling too fast, the gap between them widening every second until, rounding a corner, the car disappears. Desperately, Arjun looks around, hoping to persuade another car to stop and take him to the residence. He runs in front of one, trying to flag it down but the driver, a look of terror on his face, swerves, mounts the kerb then, having recovered, drives off at a furious pace.

Too many people have been stopped and dragged from their cars in recent days. Most have been beaten. Many who survive have sustained terrible injuries. Word has got around. *Don't stop for anyone.*

A cat appears from an alleyway where it has been resting in the shadows. It resembles Neleni's cat but, when Arjun calls to it, it eyes him suspiciously and slinks away. *What is happening to us?* thinks Arjun. Everything familiar has changed, or is it that unknown things now lurk beneath a cloak of familiarity? Perhaps they always did.

Standing alone in the middle of the road, Arjun senses the onset of madness, but whether it is within him or part of the world outside, he cannot tell. He cannot wait for the answer. It is better not to know. Instead, he starts running as fast as he can, after Nash's car.

When Walter arrived at the police station, the bodies of the would-be attackers were still lying in the street, their limbs splayed out awkwardly, as if they had fallen from a great height. The injured who could not walk, were also lying where they fell, groaning or unconscious, blood seeping from bullet wounds, forming small puddles on the tarmac or soaking into the grass. Pye-dogs, their hind quarters lowered, were already creeping into the street, tentatively sniffing the air, attracted by the smell of fresh blood.

Walter watched as Nash emerged from the police station, pausing to exchange a few words with a young police sergeant, before descending the steps, his gait unusually slow and stiff, the walk of an old man.

***

On the journey home, Nash contemplates the events of the last few hours, wondering where it will all end. He does not allow himself to dwell on the deaths and injuries sustained by the rioters. Regrets and soul-searching must be postponed until later, when he has the luxury of time. Now, he must direct his mind to priorities. Will there be further attacks? If so, when and where? And what is to be done about the refugees flooding into the city?

Nash closes his eyes for a moment. Exhaustion sweeps over him now that the immediate crisis has passed. He is asleep when the car passes the church, so he does not see Arjun emerging from its gloomy depths, stepping through the great teak door and blinking in the sunlight.

***

Checking the rear-view mirror, Walter sees a blurred figure running after the car. A man has appeared from nowhere, yelling and waving his arms. He is dishevelled, his clothes stained with dust and dirt, his hair hanging over his face. Walter sees only a stranger; a madman or a looter, racing after the car, possibly armed. So, without waking Nash, Walter accelerates, as fast as he can, until the man behind them is reduced to a tiny, helpless image in the mirror.

***

Nash is still asleep as they approach the residence. He awakes to voices, crying and pleading and the sound of hands, beating on the windows. The car has halted. Walter is leaning out of the window, shouting at the crowds to pull away from the entrance. The gatekeeper is signalling that he will not open the gates until the crowd has cleared for fear of them invading the grounds. They are desperate, panicked to the point of hysteria. Having heard of the siege at the police station, they believe that they will be next; unprotected, easy targets.

"Help us! Help us!"

Nash nods wearily, trying to wake up. His mouth is filled with a thick stickiness. His tongue cleaves to his palate. He has not drunk or eaten for hours. He considers whether he should stop and speak to the crowd. By now, Walter has got out of the car and, standing by the open door, is trying to communicate with the gatekeeper, telling him to get a few of the servants to help clear the crowd.

Neither Nash, nor Walter, notices a man, quietly getting to his feet and circling around the back of the car to where Walter is positioned by the open door. Suddenly, Walter is grabbed by the arm and flung to one side. He reels, loses his footing, and stumbles backwards.

Turning away from the window, Nash sees a monk, leaning into the car, leering at him over the driver's seat. He notes the loose-lipped grin, the expression of malice tinged with triumph and then, the revolver in the man's hand.

***

The sound of a gunshot echoes along the street. People run screaming in all directions. Walter, having recovered his balance, grapples the monk from the car as he is taking aim for a second shot. The gun fires and the bullet goes wide, thudding into the upholstery, ripping the leather open and sending up a puff of dust and tiny fabric hairs.

The gate opens. Two servants from the residence run out. Punching Walter hard in the chest, the monk winds him then, dropping the gun, takes to his heels, dashing down the street and off, around a corner, out of sight, where he slows his pace to a saunter, knowing that he will not be pursued.

With one hand to his ribs, Walter climbs painfully into the back of the car where Nash, slumped sideways over the seat, is lying in a pool of blood. He makes no sound and his eyes are closed. Holding his hand over the Agent's face, Walter tries to ascertain if he is breathing.

"Walter!"

The same dishevelled man, that he saw earlier, is banging on the back window of the car. Walter places a hand protectively over the Agent's head.

"It's me!"

"Mr Arjun?"

The young man is panting for breath, leaning against the back of the car. From where he is standing, he cannot see Nash.

"Where is he, Walter?"

Walter points to the open door of the car. Arjun leans in, then jerks back, his hand clamped over his mouth, fighting the urge to vomit. He tries to speak. His lips form silent words then, a fearful whisper.

"How is he?"

Walter's eyes fill with tears.

"He's dead, sir."

After a long shift, Sergeant Gunasekera is walking home. He is thinking about the momentous events of the day, not a little proud of the praise he has received from the Government Agent who has promised to recommend him for promotion. Suddenly, out of adversity, or perhaps because of it, Sergeant Gunasekera's future looks bright. The sergeant is now a hero, unlike his superior officer.

The Assistant Superintendent of Police remained locked in his office all day, except for a brief episode when he was persuaded to speak to the Government Agent. Gunasekera observed their meeting and noticed how shaken the Assistant Superintendent seemed when confronted by the elegant man with the manners and bearing of an aristocrat.

Stuttering, the senior policeman had tried to excuse himself when asked why he had done nothing, why it was not him, but his desk Sergeant, who had telephoned for help. Then, unable to provide a convincing explanation, he had tried to remonstrate with the Agent, becoming blustering and aggressive, trying to shift the blame.

Unperturbed, the Agent had swept into the office and closed the door. Gunasekera, who had remained outside, could hear raised voices. Angrily, the Government Agent had threatened to get the Assistant Superintendent dismissed. There had been some shouting, mainly from the policeman, then the Government Agent had emerged, as calm and dignified as before, followed by the Assistant Superintendent who leant against the door, his hand trembling as it clutched the handle, the knuckles white, sweat dripping from his greasy face. Like a pig on a spit, thought Gunasekera.

And, as he walks along the road, Gunasekera recalls the look on his superior's face after that argument with the Government Agent: not just anger, but terrible hatred and something else that Gunasekera could not understand: secret triumph. Only why the Assistant Superintendent should feel triumph after such a drubbing is a mystery. Gunasekera tries to apply all the detective skills learned from his many years of reading thrillers, but he finds no answer, arriving only at a single, unsatisfying conclusion: the Assistant Superintendent knew something that the Government Agent did not. But what that was, Gunasekera cannot guess.

***

Gunasekera is now leaving the administrative district and its colonial buildings with their grand facades. The streets are getting narrower and poorer. Pye-dogs are nosing through litter piled up at the kerb and there is a feeling of desolation. Windows are concealed behind shutters, doors are firmly locked. It is still daylight, but there is none of the usual friendly bustle on the streets. No traffic. No pedestrians. The whole district appears to be holding its breath. He passes through the market at the end of the road. The stall-holders have packed up early if, indeed, they worked at all today.

Gunasekera is filled with longing to see his wife, share everything with her. Now he is close, he cannot wait to be home. Turning into the dark alley, he runs to the apartment building, up the front steps, along the corridor lined with bicycles. He stops dead. The door to his home is open and, even from here, he can see his belongings, upturned, smashed and strewn over the floor. His heart lurches, seems to lodge itself in his throat. He cannot move. Just stare. Holding his breath.

It looks as if the building has been hit by an earthquake, although Gunasekera cannot recall feeling a tremor. Everything has been shaken from the walls: books, ornaments, even the clock which now lies on the floor with its face smashed. Then, he hears a low moan. It is unearthly. More animal than human, it freezes his flesh, raises the hair on his neck. Stepping inside, Gunasekera's boots crunch over shards of pottery. He follows the sound to the next room.

She is crouching in the corner of the room, arms hugging her knees, hair over her face. Rocking. He kneels beside her, tries to put his arm around her, but she shrinks away, her face to the wall.

"Malika, my love. What has happened?"

Curled up tight, she continues to rock, moaning to herself. Reaching into the curtain of hair, he tries to lift her face. She moans. This time, with pain. He withdraws his hand, sees it is covered with blood.

"Malika, look at me."

Gradually, she raises her head. He sweeps the hair back from her face, tucks it behind her ear. What he sees makes him gasp. Her eyelids are swollen and bruised so that she can hardly see, her face virtually beaten to a pulp. A trickle of blood is draining from her ear. She will be deaf on that side for the rest of her life. He looks around him and sees a tooth on the floor, then another. Weeping, he cradles her bruised and battered body in his arms.

"Who did this? Who did this?"

Her lips are so swollen that she cannot speak. The mumbled sounds she emits are incomprehensible.

"Show me."

She lifts her finger, pointing to the house of the nationalist.

"Him."

At last, one word that is unmistakeable. Rage consumes him. Yet, he thinks clearly, has one purpose. Revenge.

Kissing the top of his wife's head, Gunasekera covers her with a blanket, then makes his way into the kitchen where he arms himself with a large knife. Then, quietly, unhurried, he walks from the apartment and crosses to the house opposite.

After a few minutes, Gunasekera re-emerges without the knife. That lies embedded in the nationalist's heart. He is lying spread-eagled on the floor, a look of surprise on his face. He never expected this. Not from a Sinhalese. Not from the husband of that whining Tamil bitch. He had even supposed that the man would thank him. For teaching her a lesson. No, he had not bargained on this at all.

***

After re-entering his home, Gunasekera strips off his clothes. He carries Malika to the kitchen, where he washes them both at the kitchen sink. It is a grim baptism. Her blood, mingling with that of the nationalist, racing away with the cold water. He binds her as best he can, then dresses her in clean clothes. She shivers, whippet-like, and clings to him. He wonders if she will ever be herself again. Come to that, will he?

He lays her carefully on the bed as he gets dressed. Even in that small space, she cannot let him out of her sight, whimpering if he moves towards the door. He puts on a sarong and a clean white shirt then packs a suitcase.

He does not have to worry about valuables. They have not got any and what little jewellery Malika had has been stolen by her attackers. Fortunately, they did not find the bundle of notes, nailed to the back of the wardrobe: money, put aside for a child. Now their savings will be put to another use: escape.

Gunasekera divides the rupees into small bundles that he distributes around the bag, tucking some inside his belt. Then he packs clean underwear and clothes for them both. On the floor of the wardrobe, he finds a stack of paper-back thrillers. He wonders at his previous obsession. He has no heart for them now. Murder is so much more terrible in real life. And yet he feels no remorse. He wonders at that, too.

The bag is packed. He snaps the lock shut.

"Come," he says, gently.

Then, with the bag slung over one arm and Malika, still wrapped in a blanket, clinging to the other, he leads her to the door. Slowly, they walk out of the house, along the alley and out, onto the main road. For a few seconds, they pause on the corner, while Gunasekera lights a cigarette, but neither of them looks back. They resume their journey, heading away from the market and everything familiar.

1958: Rumour

Hooniyam and his sons have been busy, flying around the country whipping up a storm of hatred. Friends and neighbours have been reminded of long-forgotten injuries. Trifling hurts have been magnified and slights imagined. Everyone has been persuaded that they are a victim: a prey to prejudice, whether racial, social or religious.

Everywhere, Hooniyam whispers in people's ears, nurturing rumours that feed on fear. Some are of such unthinkable cruelty that they drive whole communities wild with terror. One such is the tale of the 'Tar baby' which relates the horrific death of an infant, plunged into a vat of boiling tar by thugs. Each side blames the other for this atrocity. Yet everyone accepts the story without question, because they were told by someone they trust. No-one tries to verify either the identity of the victim or the location of the crime.

So far the violence has focused on Polonnaruwa at the centre of the country. Elsewhere, pockets of discontent lie dormant, like piles of dry tinder, waiting to be ignited, connected only by rumour which runs between them like a fuse. Tales run back and forth and are embroidered in the re-telling. Overnight, myth becomes belief and acquires the currency of truth. No-one wants the facts because facts cannot express fear. And everyone is afraid.

In a country ready to catch light, all that is needed is a spark. And that will be provided by Mr Seneviratne.

Respected by some and envied by others, Mr Seneviratne is a man of considerable influence, albeit local. As a former Mayor of Nuwara Eliya, he has had dealings with some of the Indian Tamils who work on the surrounding tea plantations. However, being both Sinhalese and a planter, it is unlikely that he felt much sympathy for their cause.

For Nuwara Eliya lies within the ancient realm of Kandy, the last Sinhalese kingdom to resist foreign rule. More than any other, this region represents what it is to be Sinhalese. Yet it was nearly lost a few years ago. In 1947, the region's Indian Tamils elected seven MPs, threatening to wrest control from the Sinhalese. It was an unbearable insult, not to be borne. Under pressure from Sinhalese Kandyans, the Government legislated to disenfranchise the Indian Tamils.

By the time Mr Bandaranaike was elected, the Sinhalese had regained parliamentary supremacy while Indian Tamils had been wiped off the political map. These are facts with which Mr Seneviratne is familiar and, if he does not publicly rejoice at them, like most Sinhalese, he feels secret satisfaction. As far as he is concerned, the government of his country is now in safe hands.

While it is possible that Mr Seneviratne has offended some of the Indian Tamils, there is no evidence to support this. He may be a nationalist, but he is not considered radical. In fact, he is just as likely to have made enemies through his business or personal dealings as he is through politics. But that, too, is a mystery because Mr Seneviratne never talks openly of such things. In fact, no-one knows much about him.

If Mr Seneviratne's life is an enigma, his death will be a conundrum. The only certainties? Date and location. Nothing else.

***

Mr Seneviratne is planning a journey. It is not an auspicious time for travel. If consulted, an astrologer would advise Mr Seneviratne to stay at home. But Mr Seneviratne does not consult an astrologer, or anyone else for that matter, before climbing into his car to travel to the coastal town of Eravur.

Although he has heard something of events around Polonnawura, he does not attribute much importance to them, dismissing them as a 'flash in the pan'; a few drunken peasants running amok and terrorising the local community before returning to a life of anonymous drudgery. Every dog has his day. It has happened before.

Look at Gal Oya. Two days of hysteria, a few feathers ruffled in Colombo and an excuse for politicians to indulge in hours of fruitless debate. Then, as suddenly as it had started, the crisis was over. The goondas had gone home and the politicians had gone back to feathering their nests. No harm done. Or not much, at any rate.

***

What news there is has been severely restricted and, being Sinhalese, Mr Seneviratne has heard none of the rumours that now convulse the Tamil community. The Tamil version of events, amplified and distorted by fear, recounts a murderous attack on Tamils by the 'Sinhalese Army'. It is said that hundreds have been slaughtered. The train, attacked at Polonnawura, has disgorged corpses, riddled with bullets and slashed with bayonets. Even babies are amongst the dead. After reneging on the Chelvanayakam-Bandaranaike pact, the Government is finally showing its hand. It does not just want to contain the Tamils; it wants to purge them from the country. It is planning genocide.

Few make any distinction between the regular Sinhalese Army and the Sinhala Hamudawa. Rumour has fused them into a single entity. The Tamil-dominated eastern province, towards which Mr Seneviratne is headed, is seized by panic. Tamils reason that, having devastated Polonnaruwa only fifty miles away, the next and most obvious target for the 'Sinhalese army' will be the coastal towns. Attack is imminent. Some run to outhouses and cupboards to find makeshift weapons or ancient, army-issue revolvers. Others sink into quiet despair.

Mr Seneviratne knows nothing of this as he motors towards Eravur. As his car trundles along the long coastal road, sandwiched between the ocean on one side and salt-water lagoons on the other, he thinks longingly of Nuwara Eliya's cool air. The light sparkles and dances on the water and heat rises from the road which shimmers like a spirit lamp. The bone-white sand of the beaches adds to the brightness, nearly blinding drivers who are unused to it. The cool green expanse of the hill country would be a welcome relief to the eye.

Arriving in Eravur and, parched by the salty, dry heat, Mr Seneviratne stops at a roadside café for a thambili juice. He has been here before on his travels but today he receives an unusually cool welcome from the proprietor. No matter. The man has probably had an argument with his wife. He is moody at the best of times and she, by all accounts, is a dragon. Anyway, it is none of his business. Mr Seneviratne has other things on his mind. A meeting. A potentially unpleasant one.

Mr Seneviratne's business interests and his term as mayor have not made him universally popular. Some opposed his decisions, others were simply jealous of his success. He has made enemies. Sometimes it worries him. But he is not afraid. Just a little frustrated at his inability to talk everyone round to his point of view. He can be very persuasive. It is one of his strengths. But some people are intractable.

"Aahh," he thinks aloud, waving his hand as if to dismiss these minor irritants. Sometimes, other people remind him of flies, like those droning lazily around the counter. Full of noise and useless energy, but good for nothing. All they do is get in the way. But he does not let them stop him. He is cleverer than they are. That is why he became mayor. That is why his business has succeeded and theirs have failed.

Lost in thought, Mr Seneviratne does not notice the people outside looking suspiciously at the Sinhalese number plate on his car. Some show more than a passing interest. They seem to recognise it. One hurries off down a side-road. News is travelling fast today.

Several youths gather on the corner of the street, waiting to see what will happen. They too have seen the number-plate and have noted the excitement it has caused. Perhaps the other men plan to deface it, as other Tamils have defaced the Sinhalese number-plates on National Transport Board buses; as Sinhalese have defaced the Tamil lettering on the Prime Minister's official car and Tamil shops in southern towns. The atmosphere is taut with excitement.

702

Mr Seneviratne drains his glass. He would like another drink but time is getting on. Any further delay and he will be late for his meeting. It is not going to be easy. He had better pick his words carefully. Reluctantly, he pushes the chair back and, saluting the proprietor who hardly seems to acknowledge his presence, he returns to the car.

Not noticing the huddle of young men a few yards away, he walks around the car to the driver's side. He grasps the handle, then jerks his hand away, suppressing a curse. While he has been in the café, the sun has moved round, exposing the car to its blast-furnace heat. The door-handle is burning. Mr Seneviratne becomes increasingly irritated: with the car, with the heat, with the impending meeting. He reaches into the pocket of his shorts and draws out a handkerchief; Irish linen, a special order from Cargills. Wrapping the handkerchief tightly around his hand, he pulls the door open and is struck by a rush of heat from the interior.

"It's hot enough to fry a damned egg," he mutters, cursing himself for not having the forethought to select a shady parking place. This would not have happened normally. Normally, the car would have been driven by Lal, his driver but, for reasons of his own, Mr Seneviratne has decided to drive himself today.

He slides into the driver's seat. It is too hot to shut the door. He will have to wait for a few seconds. Mopping his forehead with the handkerchief, he gropes in his pocket, retrieves his bunch of keys, and plugs one into the ignition. Numbed by the heat, he leans back and closes his eyes. If he were to look in the mirror, he would notice a figure approaching from behind. But he does not.

Mr Seneviratne starts in surprise as someone reaches in through the door and leans over him. He thinks he recognises the face. Or does he?

Craccckk! A single shot. Mr Seneviratne slumps forward, his cheek slack against the wheel, eyes staring, his face frozen in surprise. The young men scatter. Set off by the pressure of Mr Seneviratne's body, the car horn blares ceaselessly, like a siren sounding an alarm.

1958: A distant view

A black dot appears over the horizon. As it approaches, the dot grows, takes shape: a small plane, flying high overhead, silhouetted against a clear blue sky, the loud roar of its engines disproportionate to its size. Inside the plane, the noise is almost deafening and the Minister for Lands, Mr C.P. de Silva has to shout to make himself heard.

"Go closer. I want a better look."

The steward nods and hurries to the cabin where he relays the message to the captain. The captain sighs. They are already late. But one cannot argue with a man of Mr de Silva's importance.

The plane banks a little too sharply, forcing Mr de Silva to hang onto his seat. He does not enjoy flying at the best of times. The captain knows that and Mr de Silva suspects that the present manoeuvre is in retaliation for his request. The plane rattles and shakes. Even the thin walls of its fuselage seem to quiver. It is like travelling in a cardboard box. But, for once, Mr de Silva forgets his fear. He is distracted by something on the ground.

Cupping his hands around his face, he tries to get a better view. The window is so small and the glass so thick that it is like looking through a goldfish bowl. But even up here, hundreds of feet above ground, the devastation below is unmistakeable. Acres of land that only days ago were full of sugar cane lie blackened and charred. Mr de Silva sucks in his breath. At this distance, all he can think of is the loss to the local economy. He has a particular relationship with this region, knows many of its landowners, for he is also MP for Polonnaruwa.

It is only minutes later, when the plane flies low over the Government farm of Hingurakgoda, that Mr de Silva gets his first sight of the human devastation. Last night, the goondas attacked the farm and bodies are still lying where they fell.

"Oh god!"

Mr de Silva claps a hand to his mouth.

"Oh my god!"

There are no words to express the shock at seeing so many dead. There are at least forty corpses. The attack came late at night and many of the inhabitants were taken by surprise, unprepared to flee or defend themselves. They included both women and children. Mr de Silva will learn later that on hearing of the attack, one woman threw herself down a well: her fear of the goondas so great that death by drowning was preferable to being taken alive.

Nothing has prepared Mr de Silva for this. No-one in Colombo took the reports of attacks on trains at Polonnaruwa station seriously. Not even Mr de Silva. Everyone believed the Prime Minister when he told them there was nothing to worry about. Reports of the violence, he said, were just an exaggeration. Give it a few days and it would all blow over. Despite increasingly panicky calls from local officials in various regions, everyone continued to believe him.

But for Mr de Silva it all changed this morning. The telephone in his office had not stopped ringing. He could no longer afford to ignore the reports of violence, streaming in from his constituency, especially when he was told that the police station in Polonnaruwa had been besieged. So, at last, reluctantly, he has come to find out for himself and the truth is worse than he thought.

As the plane comes in to land, Mr de Silva closes his eyes. He should have come sooner. He realises that now and he is astute enough to know that, if he does not appear to act quickly, his career may be forfeit. He is a politician. He must speak to people, show that he is listening. He will speak to the goondas.

He grits his teeth as the wheels make contact with the runway. The plane bounces and hops. The tyres squeal as the brakes are applied and Mr de Silva feels that he is losing contact with his stomach. He clutches the arm-rests, convinced that the plane will turn a somersault. Finally, to his infinite relief, it slows and taxis along the runway. Mr de Silva sighs, relaxes his grip and gives thanks for his deliverance.

***

Frowning, Mr Bandaranaike holds the telephone to his ear. The line is crackly, but the message is clear.

"Hello. Prime Minister? Can you hear me?"

"Yes," says Mr Bandaranaike, wearily rubbing his forehead with the tips of his fingers. "Yes, I can hear you."

It is the Minister for Lands, Mr de Silva, and he is in an excitable mood.

"Prime Minister, I am in Polonnaruwa. It is worse than we thought, worse than the violence at Gal Oya. Much worse."

Mr Bandaranaike has an odd fluttering sensation in his stomach.

"Are you sure that these people are not just exaggerating?"

"Prime Minister, I have seen for myself."

"Ah."

"Prime Minister, can you hear me?"

At the other end of the line, Mr de Silva thinks that he has been cut off.

"I am still here."

Whether, due to a fault on the line or some other cause, the Prime Minister's voice sounds particularly faint. But Mr de Silva continues, determined to get his message across.

"I spoke to some of the goondas today, the men who besieged the police station. And do you know what they said? *We did not vote you into office so that you could use the army to kill Sinhalese.*" They were angry at being fired on. They think the Government is protecting Tamils, rather than them. And they are not the only ones to have said it."

"Hmmm."

The Prime Minister is fiddling with his pencil. The lead has broken. He leans over, opens a drawer and searches inside for another.

"Prime Minister, you must do something. Please, for all our sakes."

Click. The line goes dead.

1958: Radio waves

Having quietly replaced the receiver, Mr Bandaranaike stares at the telephone for a minute. The modern improvement in communications is not necessarily a good thing. He longs for a simpler age when news was carried by word of mouth because that would allow a delay, a few more days, an excuse for inaction. Sometimes the best response to a crisis is to do nothing at all. But these days, one must act immediately. Everyone expects you to do something. Immediately. Waiting is no longer a solution.

Selecting a new pencil from the drawer, he inspects its tip then jots a few words in his notebook – Polonnaruwa, Tamils, Sinhalese, attacks on Government farms, initial estimate: 150 dead. Or was it 200? He forgets. Anyway, one cannot put one's faith in statistics – like everything else they are capable of manipulation. As a lawyer, he should know. The question is; how is he to explain his inaction for so many days?

He stares across the desk at the heavy glass paperweight that contains threads of blue and gold like petrified ink. Underneath the paperweight is a memorandum from his personal secretary, informing him that tomorrow he is to meet a delegation of important citizens who will urge him to announce a State of Emergency. They will not be the only ones to demand this course of action. He presses down hard with the pencil, so hard that the lead breaks. He flings the pencil at the bin and misses. The pencil clatters across the polished, parquet floor.

He gazes at it for a few seconds, drumming his fingers on the blotter. Then he raises his eyes to the portrait of Prime Minister D.S. Senanayake, champion of the people.

"What would you have done?" asks Mr Bandaranaike aloud.

The face in the portrait stares back at him, accusingly.

"Of course, it would never have happened to you, would it?"

Mr Bandaranaike feels a surge of bitterness against the man who, apparently, could do no wrong. Why is it that fate smiles on some people and not on others? But then, thinks Mr Bandaranaike, fate was not so kind to D.S. Senanayake's son and successor. In 1953, the outbreak of a bloody hartal forced Dudley Senanayake to declare a State of Emergency. But this only aggravated the crisis. Several demonstrators were killed: a catastrophe that ultimately led to the younger Senanayake's resignation.

The words of the goondas are still ringing in Mr Bandaranaike's ears. "*We did not vote you into office so that you could use the army to kill Sinhalese.*" It is a message that applies equally to the Prime Minister – and he knows it. He must avoid a State of Emergency at all costs. If he offends the nationalist elements that brought him to power, his Government will fail. Further use of the armed forces is not an option. He must find another way; appear to act, without actually doing anything. But how?

In despair, the Prime Minister leans on the desk with his head in his hands.

"God help me," he murmurs.

A few minutes later, Mr Bandaranaike is re-reading the words in his notebook. He cannot remember having written anything, nor having picked up the pencil that is now poised between his fingers, but a new name has been added to the list. He reads it carefully: Mr D.A. Seneviratne, former mayor of Nuwara Eliya.

***

706

Later that day, the Prime Minister addresses the nation with regard to what he calls "communal tension". However, instead of portraying Polonnaruwa as the origin of unrest, Mr Bandaranaike focuses on the Tamil-dominated coastal district where Mr Seneviratne met his untimely end.

While he refers to "some people" losing their lives, the Prime Minister specifies only one person by name: Mr Seneviratne, a Sinhalese. Crucially, he reverses the sequence of events, stating that the riots in Polonnaruwa were a response to Mr Seneviratne's killing, although they preceded it by several days.

Informed observers are baffled. Contrary to the facts, the Prime Minister's speech implies that Tamils are responsible for the outbreak of violence. It is a mistake that no-one with Mr Bandaranaike's intelligence and legal training should ever make. It is the act of a desperate man.

***

Mr Bandaranaike mops his forehead with a large, linen handkerchief then, looking across the room to the technician, motions at the large microphone on the desk in front of him. The technician nods, indicating that they are no longer on air. Mr Bandaranaike sighs.

"Well, what do you think?" he asks anxiously, addressing his question to the bevy of assistants, ranged around the edges of the room like a row of dominos.

"Excellent, sir," croons one.

"Yes, sir. A most inspiring speech," adds another.

Mr Bandaranaike smiles at them, gratefully, unable to remember their names. In need of moral support, he has invited these minor officials to witness his historic speech. Faceless and forgettable, they have proved to be an ideal audience, largely because they hold no opinions of their own. Unlike some members of the Cabinet.

Mr Bandaranaike shifts uncomfortably in his chair, wondering how his speech will be received by the likes of Mr Chelvanayakam. Nonetheless, it will probably be welcomed by extremists like Mrs Vimala Wijewardene and her patron, Buddharakkita Thera. In fact, recent events have caused Mr Bandaranaike to regret his harsh words to the abbot. Perhaps, he ponders, there might still be some way of accommodating him. It is a lonely time and he needs to ensure support within the Government.

For a second, the Prime Minister entertains the fear that everyone is deserting him. But then, he remembers Gal Oya. The massacre resulting in 150 deaths occurred only weeks after his election. He overcame that crisis. He will survive this.

***

Hooniyam, who was standing at the Prime Minister's elbow as he gave his speech, laughs uproariously. Everything is going to plan. His plan. The silly man has done just what he was told. By Hooniyam. In a dream. In the educated voice of a gentleman, the Prime Minister has performed a propaganda coup, convincing the nation that, far from being the victims of violence, the Tamils are the cause of it.

Clutching his sides, Hooniyam whirls about the room. This is too good. He must share the joke with his sons. Clicking his fingers, he is projected up, through the roof of the building and into the sky on a cloud of green vapour. As he races through the air towards his forest retreat, he catches the words and thoughts of humans below, rising on every side like huge, hot thermals. They have grown from an initial whisper to a chant and, then, from a chant to a roar, everywhere the same: *Avenge Seneviratne*.

Within hours of Mr Bandaranaike's speech, the trouble spreads south, leaping from one town to another until, at last, it reaches the capital, Colombo. Kiosks owned by Tamil traders are set alight and the shopping area of the Pettah ransacked. Smoke can be seen, rising from various quarters of the city, hanging in the airless sky like a banner. Doors and windows are barred and bolted while families huddle within, sweltering in the breathless heat, too scared to move, even in their own homes, for fear of attracting the attention of marauding goondas.

During the recent language protests, Sinhalese slogans were scrawled on Tamil homes and businesses. Those who did not have the foresight to remove them, now find themselves the target of more violent depredations. As tales of the Tar Baby gain a wider audience, so the real atrocities increase.

Frustrated by their inability to burn down a Hindu temple, the rioters set light to its priest instead, drinking and laughing as they watch him burn. Elsewhere, motorists are dragged from their cars and accused of being Tamil. One, a civil servant, insists that he is Sinhalese. As proof, the rioters demand that he recite a Buddhist verse: however, being Christian, the man is unable to comply. He is beaten mercilessly. Then, a terrible game of cat and mouse ensues.

Deprived of his glasses and partially blinded by blood pouring from the wounds to his head, the man is released. Sensing, rather than seeing, that he is free, he begins to run, staggering forward, his hands held out in front of him, stumbling into potholes, tripping over his own feet, bumping into cars and trees and weaving from side to side, unsure of the direction in which he is travelling, watched by the rioters who nudge each other, sharing the fun as they mock him, mimicking his rambling, uncoordinated progress that seems to be a reflection of their own, drunken antics. Until, eventually, they get bored.

Then, as a group, they watch him without laughing or speaking, silence transforming their mood from sullenness into brooding malice. The man trips and falls to his knees, grazing his hands on the sharp surface of the road. He groans then, sitting back on his heels, wipes his dirty palms on the front of his shirt. Although he makes no noise, they can tell that he is weeping by the trembling of his shoulders. At last, he gets back on his feet and begins again, that strange, irritating, half-walk, half-run, half-stumble, zigzagging from side to side, like a wasp that has gorged on fermenting fruit.

The goondas have become a single animal: a predator watching its weakening prey. With one pair of eyes, they follow him, waiting for the right moment. Without any word or sign they will strike. As one. It is time. A goonda raises his arm and a puff of smoke issues from the tips of his fingers. The man in the street jerks backwards, teeters, half turns, then falls on his face, stone dead, a bullet through his heart.

During all of this, nothing is done. Having made a speech inciting the goondas to further violence, the Prime Minister flatly refuses to declare a State of Emergency. To do so now, would not only be an admission of weakness, but also of guilt. For he has fanned the flames of chaos, causing it to spread across the country. Demoralised by the lack of leadership, the police stand by, watching helplessly as cities burn, unable or unwilling to act while the army, for want of an order, remains confined to barracks.

1958: Dalia's day

Reclining on a sofa in the living-room, Dalia is feeding herself with sweets from a small glass dish. Having placed a sugary bonbon in her mouth, she idly licks her fingers as a cat licks its paws, before turning the pages of a magazine. It is the sort of journal one might expect to find in a beauty salon, although not in the reception of a smart hotel. Smart hotels only have Vogue or Tatler. Dalia aspires to having her own subscription to those magazines one day. When Michael has enough money. For the time being, she will have to make do with lesser publications which, despite their inferior status, contain enough pictures of Hollywood stars and large, shiny Cadillacs, to make her envious.

Sometimes, she wonders if she has made the right choice in marrying Michael. Perhaps she should have waited for something better. A film star, perhaps. Someone like Raj Kumar. He is the Indian equivalent of Clark Gable and his affair with the actress Nargis is legendary. Dalia considers the woman very plain and wonders what it was that attracted Raj Kumar to her. Perhaps she used a potion. It is not unheard of. Anyway, Raj Kumar is getting on a bit these days – he is already in his thirties – and his position is under threat from younger actors; men who are equally handsome. And rich.

Dalia would have like to have married one of them. In fact, she is pretty enough to be an actress herself. Or she was until a few months ago. She looks sadly at the bump on her stomach then, holding the magazine up above her waist so that she cannot see the offending growth, stuffs another sweet in her mouth.

In the kitchen, Lakshmi is preparing a meal for her daughter; something to nurture both mother and child. The quantity that Dalia eats these days is amazing. Some, like Michael, might even call it alarming. But, to Lakshmi, it is just a healthy appetite.

"Only a few months pregnant and already she is SO fat!" she thinks with pride.

Some women try to conceal their swollen bellies, artfully folding their saris so that you cannot tell they are pregnant until they actually produce a baby. Lakshmi cannot see the point in that. If you are pregnant, everyone should know. It is something to be proud of: the more obvious one's condition, the better.

Lakshmi is a firm believer that mothers should eat for two, even when not pregnant. Because they have more need of energy after the baby is born, than before, she reasons. And Dalia is an excellent pupil, eating up every scrap of her food, even wiping her finger around the plate and always returning for second, or even third, helpings.

Lakshmi cannot understand why Michael does not share her enthusiasm for her daughter's condition. For instance, she caught him last night, giving her daughter a look which could only be described as disgust. It made Lakshmi very angry but, as Dalia did not notice, she has decided not to say anything, biding her time until it is safe to take her revenge. And she will, too. Lakshmi never forgets a slight, particularly if it is aimed at her dear Dalia.

"All right, my treasure?" she asks, peering through the kitchen door, her thick red lips spreading slowly across her face in a slick of contentment.

Dalia glowers at her mother, resenting the fact that she was encouraged to marry rather than try her luck as an actress. She blames her mother for everything: for her marriage which, after the excitement of the wedding, offers only moderate comfort in return for a great deal of boredom; for Michael, whose interest in her has waned since she announced her pregnancy; and, even for her pregnancy. She was told that it would transform her, make her radiant and, in the expectation that it would also make her the centre of attention, she made it her goal. But the reality is very different from the fantasy.

She has become fat and bloated, despite her periods of morning sickness. Her skin has lost its bloom, her figure has lost its shape and she is out of sorts with the world. Her only consolation is food, which she eats in copious amounts. Soon, she will be the same size as her mother. Dalia turns her head away, stuffs another sweet in her mouth, and pretends to read her magazine no longer able to countenance the sight of the fat, self-satisfied face beaming at her from the kitchen for, in a few years, she knows that it will be her face. She feels like crying but, instead, turns the page to a story about Cary Grant while cramming another three sweets into her already full mouth.

***

Lakshmi returns to the sink where she has been boning a large fish, not in the least discomfited by Dalia's failure to speak to her. Black looks and sullenness are all part of pregnancy. How well she remembers it. In fact, she proudly congratulates herself that Dalia is getting a bit more like her every day. There is no room for pretty, simpering ways in a marriage. Particularly, with a husband like Michael.

Lakshmi begins to brood. He is often absent from home in the evenings and her suspicions about his past life have been aroused. Still thinking of her son-in-law, she pulls the skin from the fish in one deft movement. As she hammers the fish with the flat of her knife, she wonders if he is seeing another woman. She rips the spine from the fish with unwarranted ferocity. Pieces of flesh are left hanging from the bone. She clicks her tongue in disapproval. Now, she will have to boil the bones for stock. A job she hates. And all because of her useless son-in-law.

At that moment, a dark object sails out of the sky. She can see it getting larger as it approaches. A rock. The window implodes, spraying her with shattered glass. She screams and has just enough wit to move away before another missile rushes past her head. Smashing against the wall, it explodes. She can feel the searing heat as it flares across the kitchen then watches, terrified as the wall turns to flame. Petrol runs across the floor, carrying fire with it. Towards her. She cannot move. Just watches, fascinated. Until a hand grips hers and pulls her away.

Dalia drags her mother from the kitchen, along the passage towards the back-door. Acting on instinct, she knows that they must leave the house immediately. As she pulls her mother along behind her, she can hear other windows breaking; the shattering of glass, followed by further explosions. More rocks. More petrol bombs.

"Come on, Amma! This way."

She can feel her mother's hand trembling in her own. She tightens her fingers, squeezing the soft, doughy flesh.

"Follow me. As quick as you can."

Lakshmi tries to muster some speed but something seems to detain her: a heavy weight of fear, squatting on her back like a great demon. She gasps and sobs.

"I can't. Oh, I can't."

"You must!"

Dalia, her brain no longer dulled by days of interminable eating and resting, understands the danger. Her mother, it seems, does not. She just stands there, panting, her face wobbling like a misshapen jelly. And suddenly it comes. A revelation. Dalia realises how much she despises her mother. No, hates her. And, with all the force that she can muster, she strikes her across the face. Lakshmi gasps, putting her hand to her cheek as if to reassure herself that she is not dreaming. Then, her face turns purple, contorted with rage.

"Insolent girl!" she breathes.

That's better. Back to your old self! thinks Dalia and, pulling remorselessly on her mother's arm, she drags her from the house and into the alley where, shoving and pushing, she manipulates Lakshmi along the narrow passage and out of danger. Fortunately, the goondas have not yet found their way to this side of the house but Dalia knows that it will not be long.

"Come on. I know where we can go."

Remorselessly, she pushes her mother ahead, directing her into a small lane, up a side street, then through a low gate and across a patch of earth overshadowed by cashew trees.

Later, Lakshmi will only recall unconnected fragments of their flight: a twig scratching her face; the smell of burning; the blue sky; the sound of men's voices, distant but threatening, and her own terrible, dry-mouthed fear. Unable to remember how she got there, Lakshmi finds herself at another house with Dalia hammering on the door. She will never forget the look on the woman's face as Dalia asks her to take them in.

The owner of the house is delicate, small-boned even for an Islander. And she is Sinhalese. Peering around the door, she listens nervously as Dalia tells their story, begging her to hide them. When Dalia tells her of the attack on their house, the woman looks so terrified that, for an instant, Lakshmi thinks that she will slam the door in their faces. Many Sinhalese now keep their doors locked, terrified that they, too, will become a target for goondas. But, as she listens, the woman's eyes fill with tears and she keeps glancing at Dalia's stomach. Then, quite suddenly, she seems to make up her mind.

"There is a room at the back. A cupboard, really. There is no window and I will keep it locked. No-one will see you and anyone who comes will not be able to get in. I will tell them I have lost the key. Are you willing?"

"Oh yes, thank you."

Gratefully, the two women step inside. As they do so, there is a muffled explosion behind them. Being built of the cheapest, untreated wood, the beams and joists of Dalia's house are burning like matchwood. The sound is that of the roof caving in.

1958: Michael's choice

Michael is returning from work. As usual, he drives slowly, putting off the moment when he will have to walk in through the front door to be met by Lakshmi's scowls and Dalia's indifference. He feels like a stranger in his own home, always having to make room for someone else: first, his mother-in-law, then, in a few months, a squawling baby.

Having commandeered the spare room and kitchen, Lakshmi now presides over every meal, watching Michael with her beady black eyes, taking note of every gesture that he makes, every word that he speaks, storing them away in that horrible Gorgon-head of hers, excuses for a terrible and swift retribution that will strike when he least expects it. Not wanting to give her more ammunition than is necessary, Michael censors himself, vetting everything he plans to do or say before he says or does it. For, once out in the open, no deed or word can be retracted and no apologies are ever sufficient to erase his mistakes.

At such times, he looks at Lakshmi and sees the scales tipping against him. Then, finally, the Day of Judgement arrives. Lakshmi will scream uncontrollably, only these days, the victim is Michael, not Lakshmi's husband. She often screams for hours, calling him all the awful things she can think of, bringing up all the evidence of his bad character that she has stored away and, caught in the foul blast of her rage, he is turned to stone, unable to defend himself. One day, he thinks, he may kill her.

In fact, he often comforts himself with this thought. At mealtimes, he sits facing her, doing and saying as little as possible, smiling into her fat, bloated face as he thinks of his hands tightening around her throat. Unfortunately, the thought of strangling his mother-in-law is now infinitely more exciting than that of making love to his wife. Not that that happens much any longer. In fact, since Dalia announced her pregnancy, he has not been allowed to touch her except, perhaps, for an occasional, chaste holding of hands.

Dalia becomes more sullen and disinterested by the day, burying her head in magazines and eating – always eating. It is obvious that she resents him, although he cannot fathom why. *I've given her everything she wanted, haven't I?* he asks himself and, however he looks at it, he can find no fault in his own actions. Except that he is still seeing Leela. But Dalia does not know about that – probably would not care if she did – and so far, although she suspects, Lakshmi has no firm proof.

No doubt she thinks he is seeing Leela in the evening when, in fact, he is working late in the office. For Michael has concocted a strategy. He visits Leela at odd hours of the day, making the excuse to his colleagues that he is visiting clients. Then, he returns to the office at night to catch up with the things that he should have done earlier. It works very well. So far, no-one at work suspects him, merely crediting him with a desire to work hard and get ahead.

Get ahead. He likes that term. It is so American. They understand the ethic of work and reward. Unlike the British who used to get people to work like slaves then took the reward for themselves. America. Land of the Free. He longs to go there. He knows he would be a success. He has got what the Americans call 'the right attitude'.

But there is no chance of going to America with Dalia. Not unless Lakshmi comes too. He sighs. The thought is too awful. Why was he not stronger? Why did he let himself be inveigled into marriage?

But he already knows the answer. Leela had found another lover. And Michael was not the sort to wait forever. Or, at least, that is what he thought at the time. With embarrassment, he remembers his advances to Neleni. He did not mean any harm. Anyway, he was drunk. But on his wedding day! What was he thinking? It is almost as if he was looking for an excuse to wreck his marriage to Dalia. Fortunately for him – or, unfortunately, if you look at it another way – Neleni has never breathed a word of that ill-judged encounter.

He sighs. It seemed logical at the time. Two people, broken-hearted by their loss, finding consolation in each other, taking revenge on those who had rejected them. But Neleni thought differently. He admires her for that. Perhaps, now, she has got what she wants. Leela has never actually said – not in so many words – but the affair with that young clerk from the Agent's office is over, has been for many months. There is hope again for Michael. Or there would be, if he hadn't got a wife.

Michael slows the car until it nearly stalls. A watermelon-seller has dragged his handcart into the road in front of Michael and shows no signs of moving over to let him pass. Normally, Michael would have cursed the fellow but, today, he feels only gratitude. It means a few more minutes' reprieve from the inevitable tedium of an evening with his wife and mother-in-law. He reflects sadly that he is now beset by two harpies.

As the car crawls along behind the watermelon-seller, Michael asks himself if he, like Neleni, has got what he wants. Leela now complies with all his wishes. Because she has to. She needs to get her hands on Mennan's money, and only Michael knows how to do it. He keeps her on a tight rein, only giving her enough to get by, no more. And she is pathetically grateful. Tame, almost. But, strangely, he regrets it. He misses the old Leela who never gave a damn about anyone. Her feisty recklessness used to enthral him. To be chosen by her, if only for a moment, was an honour; something to be remembered for the rest of one's life. It was dangerous and exciting, like courting a tigress. You never knew what would happen next.

But now, Leela has become predictable. The light in her eyes has died and their love-making is mechanical, like an encounter with a whore only less of an adventure. Yet, rather than despising her, he feels pain at her predicament and hates himself for destroying her spirit. It is one thing to have power over someone, quite another to be loved and that, he realises, is what he really wants.

The seller of watermelons pulls onto the kerb, allowing Michael to pass. Gloomily, Michael puts his foot on the accelerator. He is only a mile or so from home. Soon, his life will shrink to the narrow confines of that house, governed by the nagging of one woman and the silence of the other. Prison would be preferable.

As he skirts the shanty, he sees signs of a recent disturbance. Thin columns of smoke are rising from within the slum. One, two … he counts five at least. No ordinary fire, then.

So far this locality has escaped the violence, the rioters having focused their attention on the Pettah, the shopping area, which is miles away on the other side of town. That is understandable. People always attack commercial areas when they want to make a point. It would not surprise him if they had also attacked a few Government buildings. But what can be found in the shanty? He has heard that Tamils are often the target of attacks, but that is over a hundred miles away in Polonnaruwa.

"Surely," he thinks, "the army would not allow the violence to get out of hand here."

714

Driving through a set of red lights, as everyone does, he turns into the road which leads to his home. It is a winding road, with an assortment of tall warehouses and apartment blocks that obscure the view along the street. Shaded by trees, Michael's house sits back from the road in a gloomy little enclosure, invisible to anyone who is not directly in front of it. Tonight, Michael will do what he always does: park his car on a patch of ground across the road and wait for a few seconds, taking a few deep breaths or, perhaps, smoking a cigarette, until he has summoned sufficient courage to enter the house.

The car comes to rest in its usual place on the verge. Even now, Michael does not look at the house, although he can feel it, waiting for him: a dark and loathsome place; a demon's lair. He turns the key and the engine dies. Staring forward, along the road, he wishes he could just keep driving. Then, he turns to look and what he sees takes his breath away. The house, or what is left of it, is a smoking ruin.

From where he sits, he can see no sign of life. He considers whether he should get out and take a closer look but no-one, trapped under that pile of smoking debris, could still be alive. As he stares at the charred remains of the house, he feels no trace of sympathy for Dalia or her mother, no interest in their fate, only a strange sense of liberation. It flows through him like a draft of warming liquor. In the midst of disaster, he wants to shout his thanks to whatever god has freed him.

He knows, instantly, what he must do. It is not a sudden revelation, just something that he always knew he would do, sooner or later. Now, it is time. He turns the ignition key and, revving the engine, pulls away from the verge. Down the road he speeds, with the shanty on one side and the railway track on the other, through the centre of town past the devastation of the Pettah and the smashed kiosks daubed with Sinhalese slogans, out to the suburbs, where Leela lives.

1958: The scribe

On his trek home, Asoka tries to use country routes and tracks, avoiding towns and the main highways. But he frequently becomes lost and is obliged to ask labourers or villagers for directions to his village. Having heard of the horror in the towns and countryside in Polonnaruwa district, they regard him with suspicion. For all they know, he could be a spy for the rioters, a Tamil posing as a Sinhalese; for stories are now filtering out of the eastern districts about terrible reprisals, visited by Tamil goondas on innocent Sinhalese. So they hurriedly give him directions, pointing him in any direction that will take him away from their dwellings and families. And so, after many miles, he realises that he has walked in a huge circle and is no closer to home than he was before. And each day, he becomes weaker.

He tries to slake his thirst at waterfalls, to eat whatever fruit he can find growing wild, but it is not enough. Faint from hunger and thirst, he approaches a group of village women and asks them to draw him a draft from the well.

"Sisters, please, let me drink!"

He is wild in appearance: his hair unkempt and stiff with dirt, his skin filthy. From where they stand, several feet away, they can smell him, so rank is his odour. He staggers like a drunk, barely able to stand.

The women exchange nervous glances, then one, bolder than the rest, lowers her bucket into the well and drawing it up with a single sweep of her arm, allows him to drink and wash his face. Asoka is about to ask her for food, but someone shouts from the end of the lane.

"Your husband is coming!"

It is too late. The man, returning from the fields, sees his wife with the stranger. He flings himself on Asoka, beating him with his fists, knocking him down every time he tries to rise to his feet. He is forced to crawl in an attempt to get away. The man, who follows him for some distance, continues to hit him, aiming sharp kicks at his ribs and legs. Asoka groans but, digging his nails into the dirt, forces himself forward, slowly. When he is at the outskirts of the village, the man waits, watching to see what he will do. Asoka makes the mistake of pausing to catch his breath. Bending down, the man picks up a handful of stones and pelts him. Asoka crawls on, painfully.

The stones are sharp, thrown with precision. One glances off his ear, cutting the skin. Rising to his feet, he makes one last attempt, flinging himself forward, around a bend in the road where the man cannot take aim. He listens, can hear no sound of pursuit although many voices are shouting. The village has been roused, stirred up like an ants' nest, everyone running backwards and forwards, screaming murder, shouting threats. Then, one voice rises above the others. A woman shrieking. The sound of lashes. For her kindness at the well, the girl has earned herself a beating. She will think twice before helping a stranger in future.

Weak and exhausted, Asoka staggers a little further from the village, then collapses. Some time later, lying on the verge, he is found by two monks who, after reviving him with water from their flask, hoist his arms over their shoulders and help him to stagger to their monastery where he is bathed and his wounds dressed. After that he sleeps, too tired even to eat the bowl of rice that is placed beside him.

***

In the monastery, Asoka is given board and lodging in return for a few menial chores. He has time for reflection and even tries to pray a little, but his thoughts turn on a single subject: Sriya.

Late one afternoon, when he has finished sweeping the courtyard, he pauses to look at the sky. He is lost in thought for several minutes, before he notices that someone is standing beside him. It is one of the young monks who found him on the road. They have spoken many times since and a friendship has formed between them.

"You are worried," observes the young man.

"These days, there is much to worry about."

The young monk smiles and, not looking at Asoka directly, follows his gaze towards the sun which, at this time of day, no longer burns with a fierce white heat, but is beginning to turn a rich gold.

"I do not think that those are the things that concern you."

The monk smiles, his face smooth and hairless except for a shadow of soft hair on his upper lip. He is barely a man, yet he has wisdom far beyond his years. In a few months, he has achieved something that Asoka, for all his years of study, did not. The irony is painful. So many wasted years. When he could have been with Sriya. Asoka sighs heavily.

"No, brother. I am thinking of my wife. I have been away for a long time. At least, it seems that way. I have so much to tell her and yet …" he pauses, "I do not know how."

"Wait here!"

The monk scampers across the courtyard, disappearing into one of the cells that adjoin the shrine. A few minutes later, he returns, carrying what appears to be a box. Running lightly past Asoka, the boy places the box on the wall. It is a portable writing desk, the sort still used by men of letters with little money. Having opened the box's slanting lid, the monk produces a bottle of ink, a simple pen with a nib, like the ones used in elementary school, and a sheaf of paper.

"The abbot tells me that writing is another form of meditation."

Asoka smiles.

"He is a wise man."

"He is," agrees the monk, enthusiastically. Then, he offers the pen to Asoka.

"I think, brother, that if you write, your thoughts will become clear."

Hesitantly, Asoka takes the pen. It has been a long time since he wrote anything. How should he start? He taps his lip thoughtfully with the end of the pen then, tentatively, dips the nib in the ink. The monk withdraws, softly walking on his toes. At the door of his cell, he turns and looks back, then smiles to himself as Asoka begins to write.

"My beloved Sriya …"

He hardly knows how, or where, to start. It is not a normal letter. He will never post it, or entrust it to another messenger. He may not even give it to her himself. But, if he ever becomes lost for words, he will refer to it or, perhaps, let her read it. As he writes, he feels a strange calmness drifting over him. It is as if he is speaking to her directly.

Previous attempts to recall her features have resulted in only partial success. He may see her nose, but not her chin, her eyes, but not her mouth. However, as he writes, he sees her clearly: her head tilted to one side, the sweet smile that she always wears when she listens. At times, her presence is so strong that he thinks he can feel the touch of her hand, lightly brushing his arm. He wants to stop, look at her, gaze into her eyes but, he knows that if he tries, she will disappear. So, he continues to write, never lifting his eyes from the page, allowing her to sit beside him, holding her image in his mind.

He starts with the facts. Why he left the village so suddenly, his abduction by Anil and Tissa, how he struggled with Anil and killed him, the conversation he had with Arjun as they took refuge in the Government bungalow. How he comes to be writing a letter to her from a monastery. Then, once he has related the history of his disappearance, he strays onto more abstract subjects: his views, beliefs and fears; his hopes for the future; above all, what he feels for her, what she means to him. It is simple. She is his redemption.

He writes until sunset; until the light fades and he can no longer see; until the sun reddens and is about to drop from the sky like a ripe mango. During this time, he has not once raised his eyes from the paper and they feel sticky and sore. Putting down the pen, he closes his eyes and raises his face to the sun, bathing his face in its gentle rays. Bats whirl silently overhead, circling and swooping in search of insects and, as Asoka sits with his head up to the dying heat, he catches the faint, intoxicating fragrance of a temple tree.

The country is in turmoil. The attacks of Sinhalese goondas in Polonnaruwa district have left many Tamils homeless. Reprisals take place in the eastern district where Tamil goondas, eager to exact revenge, target innocent Sinhalese. Then, the violence moves south, consuming all the major towns and cities and most of the smaller ones.

Everywhere, those unfortunate enough to have lost their homes together with those too terrified to face the violence, are packing their possessions into handcarts, sacks and boxes and taking to the road in the hope of finding safety somewhere else. They have little food or water, trusting to luck and the generosity of villages and towns along the way.

At first, they are met with kindness and a good deal of sympathy but, soon, their numbers put an impossible strain on the resident communities. Those too poor to buy food, are forced to steal it and fights frequently break out. Sometimes, a deadly sickness, such as dengue fever, will strike a village and the residents, stricken with grief and fear, blame the stream of migrants passing through their community. Strangers, who were formerly greeted with friendly courtesy, are now treated with open hostility.

Yet still the migrants come, driven forward by desperation. Without shelter, they eat, sleep and perform their bodily functions in the open. Without privacy, they fall sick, give birth and die at the side of the road. The momentous events of family life, normally intimate and precious, are acted out in the middle of nowhere before an audience of disinterested strangers.

Like jackals, the goondas lie in wait, striking at will, picking off stragglers, forcing them to perform a rudimentary language test. But their victims are usually too terrified to speak. Even if they are of the same race, their background may preclude them from providing answers to the goondas' questions. Christians cannot recite Buddhist gathas and those wealthy enough to have had an English education often cannot read or understand passages from Sinhalese newspapers.

***

"Appa, where are we going?"
Everywhere, the same question, from every child.
"To a safe place."
The same answer, from every parent.
The child, weary from walking, hangs on its father's arm.
"Appa, I am tired."
"We cannot rest here. It is not safe."
"But Appa ..."
The child's lip quivers and tears fill its eyes. They have been walking since dawn. It is now nearly sunset. They abandoned their home in terror after a man ran into the village, breathless and sweating: *The goondas are coming this way!* So the father and mother took what they could, a few pots and pans, some food – mainly cold rice and curry, the scant remains of the evening meal – some clothes and what little money they possessed.

Each parent tied necessities in a bundle: the father's are wrapped in an old sarong, the mother's in a sheet. Then they left, with their three children and the woman's elderly mother; never looking back, pausing only to let the hens and the goat out of their pens, in the hope that they would be able to find their own food and that, somehow, the family might find them on their return. Even if they do not, it is better than leaving them to starve or, even worse, provide food for the goondas.

"Appa ...," the child implores, holding up its arms.

"I cannot carry you."

"Please ...," the child sobs, pitifully. "My feet hurt and I'm hungry."

The man turns his head away, swiftly dashing away his tears so the child will not see. Then, looking behind him, he sees his wife, her face grey and lined, carrying their two-year old, while her mother, slowly hobbling behind carries the baby.

"Where is your bundle?" asks her husband.

The woman stares at him, mute with exhaustion, but he understands. A child or worldly possessions? One cannot carry both.

"Wait, there," he tells the child and, struggling up the verge, he walks towards a clump of trees and, depositing his own bundle behind them, covers it with dead brushwood and grass. Perhaps, one day, he will return to claim it.

1958: A hurried goodbye

Arranged in haste, Nash's funeral is a dismal affair, performed by a priest unknown to the family in a church that is nearly empty. Nash's children, living abroad, have been unable to return in time and, such is the state of terror at home, that even relatives living on the Island cannot be persuaded to travel relatively short distances by road. Chitra, Nash's wife, has also made it plain that she does not want anyone from Nash's office to attend. Only Arjun.

They sit together, Chitra never taking her eyes from the coffin as the priest intones the prayers. Grief has diminished her. She looks smaller, older, her mature beauty withered, her hair almost white. Her white mourning sari, with its stark, heavy folds, appears too big and, rather than being worn, seems to enfold her, like a winding sheet. How different she looks from Leela at Mennan's funeral. She wears no jewellery, make-up or perfume. There is no theatricality at the graveside, no air of festivity at the wake. Just a quiet detachment and studied courtesy which conveys her sense of loss more forcibly than any words or extravagant gestures.

***

"What a fool I have been," thinks Arjun as he watches Chitra lingering beside the grave. He has witnessed enough real grief in recent days to be able to tell what is genuine and what is not. He recalls Leela, dropping a handful of soil onto Mennan's coffin, her jewelled fingers sparkling in the sunlight: a glittering phantasm, an image without substance, a woman in whom he had believed but who had never really existed. Then, just as quickly, his thoughts fly to Neleni. His need for her is like a physical hunger, gnawing incessantly at the pit of his stomach. But he cannot go to her. Not yet. Not while there is still work to do.

"Are you coming back to the house?"

Chitra looks up at him, hopefully. He had not wanted to. There is too much to do. Without an immediate replacement for Nash, he will have to perform the Government Agent's duties. He sighs inwardly. But he cannot disappoint her.

"Of course."

He offers Chitra his arm. They walk slowly back to the car.

"What is happening to this country?" she murmurs, softly.

He shakes his head, unable to answer.

1958: The house of refuge

After taking Chitra home, Arjun heads towards one of the refugee camps that have been set up outside town. Reports have reached him of dangerous overcrowding: the meagre resources of food and water are insufficient for the vast numbers of refugees, there is little or no sanitation and the first cases of disease have broken out. Added to that, the police have received reports that the goondas are planning to attack one of the camps, only they do not know when, or which camp it will be.

The small number of soldiers available cannot be stretched to protect all the camps, much less the ragged groups of refugees now clogging the roads. Further intelligence is needed, but neither the police nor the army have the resources nor, in some cases, the will, to provide it. The situation is critical and, yet, there is still no word from the Government in Colombo: no offer of help, no soldiers, no food and, above all, no declaration of a State of Emergency.

Arjun sighs as he looks out of the car window. They are passing along a familiar road that leads from the residence to the outskirts of town. The deserted streets are slowly filling with rubbish. Even the street-sweepers are too scared to work. Pye-dogs are furtively picking through piles of domestic refuse left in the gutter. Rats, too, are becoming a common sight, even in broad daylight. Despite the heat, Arjun winds up the window, trying to shut out the sickening stench of decay.

Every so often, between the rows of houses, there is a blackened ruin, its broken windows staring blankly onto the street where piles of charred timbers lie piled on the pavement. It is impossible to save houses torched by the goondas. The only solution is to pull down the smoking remains in an attempt to prevent the fire from spreading to neighbouring properties.

Arjun wonders what became of the people who lived in these houses. Did they escape? Or did they perish in the flames, too terrified to run out and face the fury of the goondas? Here and there, small objects are scattered over the pavement: a book, a broken plate, a child's toy, items discarded either by the family as they fled their home or by the goondas when they looted it.

The car speeds along the road. Walter has been told not to slow down or stop unless otherwise instructed as this would give the goondas a better opportunity for ambush. However, as it approaches a junction, the car slows. Across the road is a church, its steps crowded with people; sitting, standing, queuing, spilling onto the street, some carrying children, others carrying parcels. Arjun gazes at them, abstractedly, wondering where they have all come from, until memory comes flooding back.

"Walter, stop!"

Jumping out of the car, Arjun runs across the road and pushes his way up the steps, past families who look as if they have been camping here for days. At the top of the steps, he has to squeeze past more refugees who are blocking the doorway. Inside, the church is still dark and gloomy, but its usual coolness has been replaced by a warm, moist atmosphere. Everywhere, there are people, many of them standing, looking about with large, hopeless eyes. At the other end of the nave, two nuns are bending over a woman, one holding her hand, while the other encourages her to eat something from a bowl. The woman neither moves nor speaks.

Arjun recognises one of the nuns as the Irish woman to whom he entrusted Ella and her friend. To get to her, he has to step over people lying on the floor, many still asleep after an exhausting trek across country. In the pews, mothers suckle their babies, holding them tight if anyone approaches, their eyes betraying a fear that their child might be snatched away. Fathers herd the younger children together in protective groups, while older ones make impromptu friendships with their neighbours. Everywhere, there is the sound of voices and the smell of bodies.

"Hello, sister."

The nun stares at Arjun with a blank face. He blushes. Nuns have a way of making you feel stupid.

"We met the other day," he ventures.

"I've met a lot of people over the last few days," retorts the nun, shrewishly. She straightens up, massaging her side as she looks at Arjun appraisingly, twisting her mouth as she chews the inside of her cheek.

"No," she says. "I don't remember you."

"I came here with two women. You were kind enough to take them in. Two village women."

"Oh, yes. I remember now. I wouldn't normally forget a face like yours but, as you can see, we've been quite busy."

The nun smiles, almost flirtatiously. Her pale, blue eyes, piercing and steady, unnerve him. But, at least, she is friendly, making the effort although exhausted. He can tell that by the red rings around her eyes and the almost transparent pallor of her skin, a skin already so white that it appears never to have seen the sun.

"I've come to see how the women are."

"Well, there's only one now. The younger one. The other one left."

"Left? When?" Arjun cannot disguise his horror.

"I don't know. Yesterday, I think. I can't be sure."

"But she was sick."

"So are many of the people here. If one chooses to slip away, there's nothing we can do. There will be two or three more to take her place."

"I'm sorry ... I didn't mean ..."

"No, I know. We're all tired and bit short-tempered. At times like these, patience is definitely a virtue."

Arjun smiles politely, taking a deep breath before posing the next question.

"Do you know where she went?"

"No. Neither does her friend."

The last words carry an implicit warning: *Don't bother her.*

Arjun sighs, overwhelmed by a feeling of hopelessness.

"What will happen to her?"

"I don't know. At the moment, she has as good a chance as you or I."

Taking some rupee notes from his pocket, Arjun presses them into the nun's hand.

"For the refugees," he mumbles.

As he walks towards the door, he scans the church, looking for the girl. At last, he sees her, sitting towards the back, under a window, her dark head speckled with dots of red and violet light. He waves, trying to catch her attention. She turns dull eyes on him, raising her hand in a small gesture of recognition. Still under the watchful eye of the nun, he cannot reach her, hemmed in as she is by so many other people. So he mouths a question. *Ella? Where is Ella?*

The girl shrugs. *I don't know.*

1958: A taste of air

A child was crying. Ella's eyelids flew open. She always woke like that, jolted awake by the sound of distress. It passed through her like an electric shock, quickening her heart, forcing air into her lungs. Waking up quickly is what you do when you have small children and a sick husband.

"Chick pea!" she murmured, certain that her sick daughter was calling to her. Pushing herself up onto one elbow, she looked around her for the child. But she saw only the sleeping faces of strangers. Only one young mother was awake, stepping between the sleeping forms, balancing a small baby against her shoulder as she patted its back.

Ella remembered where she was and lay down again. But she could not sleep. Turning onto her back, she looked up at the heavy vaulted beams of the ceiling, like the rib cage of some great beast. Jonah and the whale. She listened to the sounds of the other sleepers, as she used to do with her own family at night: the murmuring breath of children, the heavy snores of men, the nasal whistling of old people. She wiped her hand across her forehead. It was damp with sweat. Even in the cool of the morning, the air in this place was hot and moist. Except for a few brief minutes the day before, Ella had not tasted fresh air. If you had a place in here, you had to make sure you kept it, or others would take it. Space was at a premium and soon occupied if left empty.

So, Ella and Shakti, the girl from her village, took turns outside. A few minutes, standing on the steps in the full heat of the sun, crushed and jostled by the other refugees who were always there, hoping for a chance to get inside.

"Are you leaving?" one had asked her yesterday.

The woman was poor. A village girl, like herself. Apart from a small child, clinging to her sari, she seemed to be alone. Her cheeks were hollow, her head constantly twisting this way and that, searching for opportunities with the keen-eyed madness of desperation. *No.* Ella had shaken her head, unable to look the woman in the eye. After that, she had stayed inside.

Conditions within the church were little better. Although her companion hardly spoke, she cried a lot, remembering her brother, reliving every moment of his awful death. In a strange way, Ella was jealous. She, herself, was unable to mourn. Not knowing for sure what had happened to her family, she carried the uncertainty with her: like a great iron ball, lodged in her chest, it became heavier every day, weighing her down, draining her strength. Sometimes, she felt unable to move at all, not even the tips of her fingers. It would be easier to lie here, forever, staring up at the vaulted ceiling, only she could not, because she was still alive. Only the dead had the privilege that she craved. Perhaps, if she knew the truth, she could make a decision. To live or die. Nothing could be worse than not knowing.

Early morning sun had pierced the windows, daubing the walls with jets of colour, red, purple and yellow. Like the festival of Holi, where Hindus sprayed each other with paint. She had seen it often. There had been many Hindus in her village. A memory of people laughing, of happiness; something she had forgotten. She clung to it, trying to remember individuals, their faces and expressions, what they wore, their peculiarities, their kindnesses and arguments and, just for a moment, she found herself in another place: not a limbo of uncertainty filled with strangers, but somewhere she belonged with people she knew. Surely, something must be left and, if not, she knew what to do. But first, she must find out.

Shakti was still asleep at her side, curled up like a child, her arms wrapped tightly around her, hugging herself for comfort. Ella felt guilty at leaving her but, steeped in sadness, the girl was too frail to make another journey. By now, Ella knew all the stages of grief. There was a time when you could look after yourself and a time when you could not. Shakti could not.

Quietly, Ella raised herself from the place where she had been lying, holding her breath in case she woke the girl. Then, raising her long bony feet high in front of her, she stepped over the sleeping bodies, slowly and deliberately, like a wading bird stalking through mud.

Once outside, she took a deep breath of air and, despite the stink of urine and rotting waste, she felt the weight in her chest lighten a little. The people on the steps were hunched together, the adults with their heads leaning on each other's shoulders, children cradled in their laps.

Picking her way delicately between them, Ella approached the woman who had spoken to her the day before. Shaking the woman gently by the shoulder, she put her finger to her lips, motioning her not to speak then, bending over, she whispered in the woman's ear.

"Third window from the back. On the left. There is a space."

The woman took Ella's hand and kissed it.

1958: Missing persons

Neleni is feeling irritable. It is mid-morning and Ella has still not arrived. In fact, she has not been to work for several days. In the late stages of pregnancy, Neleni is having to do all the housework and prepare the food unaided. The girls are shrieking and running about the house with the restless energy of children who are bored. Soon, their game of tag will turn into a fight, or something will get broken. More work.

Neleni is on her knees, trying to clean the floor, wiping at a dark, sticky stain with a damp cloth. Strangely, this position eases the dull ache in her back that has been troubling her for several hours. She feels tired, drained of all energy, but even lying down offers no relief because there is no comfortable position.

The baby is big, an alternative point of gravity, pulling her towards it, an invisible planet in her belly. A small universe has formed, deep within her, a place of mystery, dark and infinite that is, in reality, only a preparation for the world beyond. Sometimes, when she thinks of it, it scares her.

Sunny would have understood, but she is gone. Neleni bites her lip. Her throat tightens, the way it always does before she cries. Tilting her head back, she tries to stop the tears from rising to her eyes. Grief. It always catches her unawares, at times like this, when she is alone.

She sniffs, closes her eyes, takes a deep breath. She must not cry. If she starts, she knows that she will not stop. Not just grief for Sunny, but everything else. Small things, large things, her family, herself, the country. Arjun. Although due back several days ago, he has not returned and there has been no message.

On the morning of his departure, he had not been able to look her in the eye. He could have kissed her – there had been no-one to see – but, instead, he had hurried out of the door and down the steps without even a backward glance. He was leaving her. Or thinking of it. She was sure. At night, she lay awake, wondering if he would return, crying silently into her pillow.

Then, a day or two after Arjun's departure, there was a brief report on the news. Neleni never listens, but Raj had turned the volume up so high that it was impossible not to hear. There was trouble in Polonnaruwa. Riots. A train derailed. But, said the announcer in confident, clipped tones, it was over now. Just a few hooligans who were soon dispersed by the police. The next night, the same clipped voice announced that there had been other, sporadic violence, in the countryside around Polonnaruwa. But no details were given.

After that, the coverage had been intermittent. Reports of the violence that was contorting Polonnaruwa district were low-key, end-of-news items if, indeed, they merited a mention at all. Until the Prime Minister made his extraordinary speech, telling the country that Tamils had murdered a high-ranking Sinhalese in an eastern coastal town and that their misdeeds had sparked the terrible violence in Polonnaruwa district.

"Lying bastard!" Raj had yelled in response. Kicking his chair back, he had switched off the radio in disgust, before storming around the room, knocking over chairs, yelling at the top of his voice. Neleni had never seen him in such a rage. But it was no use telling him to keep quiet. She just told the girls to stay in their room until it was over and Appa was feeling better.

It is obvious that, whoever was responsible, the violence was much worse than had previously been reported. Rumours have begun to fly in the Tamil community. The Sinhalese have unleashed an army on unsuspecting Tamils. Stories are told of horrific crimes. And now, it seems, the violence is spreading.

For days, there has been no word from Arjun and Neleni has to admit what she dared not think before. Something has happened to him. If he was going to leave, surely he would have had the courage to tell her? Surely, he would have said goodbye? He would not simply disappear. Anyway, he has left most of his possessions in his room, small things that he values beyond price: his books, a photograph of his parents.

Ironically, the thought that he might have left her has been Neleni's only comfort. Although a personal disaster, it would be preferable to the image that she now has of him, lying dead or injured in some remote place, far away from those who love him. But, indirectly, Ella's disappearance has robbed her of the last crumb of hope. It is no coincidence that both the maid and Arjun should have disappeared within days of each other in the same part of the country.

"Damn her!" thinks Neleni, unreasonably.

As she scrubs vigorously at the stain on the floor, Neleni realises how little she really knows about her servant. Ella arrives at work every day, with her black umbrella furled under her arm, having travelled from where her family live in the plantations. The only mystery is how she manages to travel so far, so quickly. By walking alone, Ella could never get to Neleni's house. The distance is too great.

The only likely explanation is that Ella hitches an illegal ride on one of the overcrowded commuter trains, waiting for it to slow at a junction, then hopping onto the running-board and clinging onto the side. In this way, she could travel many miles, jumping off the train as it enters the goods-yard on the outskirts of town. But Neleni has never been sufficiently interested to ask and Ella has never told her.

Although she knows so little about Ella, there is one thing of which Neleni is sure. The maid would never quit her job without notice. Ella has formed a particular attachment for Neleni's family, especially Sunny who showed her great kindness. She was genuinely grief-stricken at the old lady's death, snuffling quietly to herself as she performed her chores around the house and, although Neleni sometimes does little to deserve it, she knows that Ella is as unswervingly loyal to her as she was to her mother.

Ella's continued absence points to some kind of disaster and, coupled with that of Arjun, there is only one likely explanation.

"Damn her!" murmurs Neleni.

But, far from dispelling her misery, the sting of her own meanness only increases it. In a fit of temper, she flings the damp cloth across the floor. Then, she begins to weep, resting on all fours, her head hanging down between her shoulders, the weight of her stomach dragging her down as tears drip from her nose, falling to the floor in a cluster of star-shaped splashes.

Pull yourself together! She can hear her mother's voice chiding her. She cannot tell how long she has been kneeling there, weeping, but her knees hurt and the dull ache in her back has grown, sickening in its intensity, as if the pain in her body is concentrated in one, small spot.

She tries to heave herself to her feet but finds that she cannot rise without assistance so, grasping the edge of the table, she places her weight on one knee as she slides the other foot flat on the floor, groaning as she hauls herself up, pulling against the weight in her belly. She is sweating with the effort, her hair sticks to her face, stinging her eyes, but she cannot brush it away. If she lets go of the table, she will fall. She takes a deep breath, places the other foot beneath her and pushes. Finally, she is back on her feet, panting for breath, shaking with the effort. Outside, she can hear the children playing. *I must not cry.*

Weak and exhausted, she lowers herself into a chair. She is alone. No-one to talk to. Not Sunny or Arjun, not even Ella or Raj. She bites her lip to stop it quivering. Raj is on one of his trips out of town, visiting a post office in a remote rural area. She does not know when he will return. Probably not until tomorrow. Secretly, she welcomed the news of his absence, happy to be left alone. She needed time to think and was glad of the peace, but now she wishes him back, if only for the company.

"Ow!"

The pain in her back permeates her body, draining her of energy.

***

The girls have had their lunch – cold lentils and rice. It is unlike the food that their mother usually prepares and Saro has complained, whining that she wanted it hot. Normally, her mother would have retaliated with a few sharp words and an even sharper smack, but today she seems not to care. So Rani, acting upon her mother's behalf, slapped Saro instead. A good resounding blow, right across the ear. She enjoyed that. But Saro did not. There was a good deal of squealing and tears.

Neleni, too big to sit Saro on her knee, has put an arm around her and is stroking her hair. Rani, consumed with jealousy, has taken herself off across the kitchen where she leans against the door, watching them sullenly as she kicks her heel against the skirting-board.

"Come here, Rani!"

Rani slinks over to the kitchen table, bracing herself for a smack. But it never comes. Instead, her mother takes her hand and looks steadily into her eyes.

"Rani. I want you to help me. I need to lie down, but I'd rather be in the front room. On the sofa. That way, I can hear you playing."

Rani nods, obediently. Taking her mother's outstretched arms, she helps to pull her to her feet. It is difficult. Her mother's legs seem stiff and she is unable to bend like normal people. She has to push herself right to the front of chair then lean forward, using the weight of the baby to lift herself from the seat. Then, Rani has to catch her, before she topples over. Neleni clutches at Rani, leaning with both hands on the girl's shoulders, before slowly straightening up. But, even then, she does not let go, keeping one arm around her daughter, holding on tightly. Rani feels herself pressing against the huge, distended belly. It feels hard, as if it contains a rock.

Slowly, she shuffles alongside her mother, leading her through the cool, gloomy hall and into the living-room where she helps her down onto the sofa. Leaning against the cushions that Rani has placed at her back, Neleni smiles at her daughter gratefully.

"You are a good girl, Rani."

Then, quite unexpectedly, she pulls Rani down and kisses her on the forehead. Rani feels a small shiver of pleasure passing through her.

"I love you, Amma."

"I love you, too."

Although she is pale and worn, Neleni's eyes shine with a special light. Rani thinks she has never seen her look so beautiful.

"Amma, Amma."

Saro is using her special baby-voice; the one that fools all the adults and makes Rani cringe.

"Amma, Amma."

She is trying to climb up on the sofa next to Neleni, but there is not enough room. Rani sees her mother wince.

"Stop it, Saro. You're hurting her. Stop it!"

Grabbing Saro roughly by her clothes, she pulls her off the sofa. Saro's face crumples, ready to cry but, first, she steals a glance at her mother.

"No!"

Neleni holds up her finger. It is a warning. Saro pouts, hangs her head, looks at her mother accusingly from under her long, fringed lashes, but makes no sound.

"Go with your sister. Do what she says and, if you are very good, I will give you a piece of jaggery. But I must first hear from Rani that you have been good. Understand?"

Saro nods, still pouting, her dark curls bobbing with the movement of her head.

***

The girls have gone. She can hear their voices as they play on the steps in front of the house or run up and down the verandah. Even though they are just outside, the house feels empty without them: a great echoing space of loneliness. Restlessly, Neleni rummages with the cushions, trying to get comfortable. She tried to eat at lunch-time, but it was no good. The baby is pressing against her stomach and even the smallest mouthful seems to stick in her throat. So she contents herself with sipping tea.

Rani, on one of her frequent mercy-visits, brings what remains in the pot, carrying it in carefully on a tray, the tip of her tongue pressed into the corner of her mouth, concentrating hard in case she drops anything. Thoughtfully, she pours her mother a cup of the strong black brew, topping it up with milk. As she drinks, Neleni tries not to look at the yellow globules of cream floating on top of the tea. Even the smell of milk makes her feel sick. But tea, even when luke-warm, is better than luke-warm water.

Reaching her arm down, she carefully places the cup on the floor beside the sofa. Sinking back onto the cushions, she lies looking up at the ceiling and the patterns of light that bounce and shimmer over the walls as a warm breeze gently agitates the blinds.

It is mid-afternoon. She closes her eyes and wishes Arjun would return.

Saro and Rani are playing tag on the front steps. They get hot and excited, chasing up and down the wooden verandah, Saro becoming increasingly frustrated at her elder sister's ability to evade capture while she herself proves an easy target. Breathless and giggling, Rani swoops and ducks, dodges behind a post then, in a daring move, leaps over the verandah fence and drops to the pavement where she crouches for a moment like a cat, gasping at her own audacity and waiting for Saro to catch up.

But Saro is beginning to tire; her laughter has a plaintive note that will soon turn into a whine. Frustrated by her inability to catch her sister, she plumps herself down on the top step, her favourite doll 'Mrs Chutti' clasped to her breast as she sucks her thumb.

"Baby," taunts Rani.

Lost in a pleasant daydream, Saro ignores her.

Keen to prolong the game, Rani tries to goad Saro back into action. Springing up the steps, she grabs 'Mrs Chutti', whirling the doll above her head as she performs a victory dance. Suspended by its feet, the doll is dangled just out of reach, its face buried in its inverted skirts while the naked shame of its pink rump is revealed to all. Shrieking in protest, Saro lunges for the doll, but Rani jerks it away.

"Mrs Chutti's got no drawers, Mrs Chutti's got no drawers," chants Rani, jigging the doll up and down in front of her sister, whose face is a comical mixture of rage and exasperation.

A passer-by looks up at the girls, smiling at their antics. Encouraged by this attention, Rani's behaviour becomes even more extreme. Grasping the doll's slender pink ankle between her thumb and forefinger, she dangles it over the railing, yelling at the top of her voice: "Look everybody, Mrs Chutti's got no drawers, Mrs Chutti's got no drawers!"

Unable to sustain these insults, Saro launches herself at her sister. Rani side-steps nimbly and her younger sister, clutching at the empty air, sprawls headlong. For a second there is a terrible silence then, with a moan like an approaching hurricane, Saro begins to yell.

"Ah, hah, aaaaaagh!"

Frozen in terror, Rani listens as her sister's screams rise two octaves in as many seconds.

"Saro, Saro," she holds out a hand as if to dampen the noise. "Come on. Don't cry. I'm sorry. Look, here's Mrs Chutti."

Reaching out a hand, Saro snatches the doll, but she refuses to get up or stop crying.

"Come on, Saro. Get up. Give me a cuddle."

For a second, Saro stops screaming then, deciding that she still has the advantage, she begins again, louder than ever. Rani holds out a hand to help her up. Pushing Rani's hand aside, Saro struggles to her feet. There is blood on her knee. That means trouble. With a sense of doom, Rani trundles after her sister as she runs, a little unsteady, to find her mother.

***

Rani is standing in a corner of the living-room; a punishment for her treatment of Saro. Arms crossed, she glowers at her mother as Neleni dabs Saro's knee with a piece of damp lint. While her mother is bending forward to examine the wound, Saro stretches her little neck and, unseen by Neleni, sticks out her tongue at her sister.

"You're a very naughty girl, Rani. I told you to look after her."

Saro sticks out her tongue even further. Rani retaliates, pulling a face. Then, suddenly, Neleni sits up. Caught off guard, the girls begin to giggle.

"Shh! What's that?"

Faintly, in the distance, they hear the sound of men shouting.

"Rani, did you shut the front door?"

"I don't know, Amma."

"Well, go and do it now. And lock it. Turn the key until you hear it click. Understand?"

"Yes, Amma."

"Go quickly. Then come back here and pull the blinds. Go."

Rani speeds from the room, pattering across the polished floor of the hallway on her bare feet. The door has been left ajar. She peers out. Some way down the street she sees a group of men. They are behaving strangely, roaring, yelling, waving bottles in the air. Then she notices. There are no other people in the street, no bicycles or cars, and all the houses opposite have their doors shut and blinds drawn. Even the hardware shop, usually open until late, is closed.

"Rani?"

Her mother's voice has lost its usual self-assurance. It is quavering, fearful. Rani closes the door and turns the key.

"Rani!"

She races back into the living-room and pulls the cord to close the blinds.

There is a sudden commotion in the street. Right outside their house. Laughter followed by shrill screams. Rani peers through a crack in the blinds. There is a man outside, a Tamil who owns one of the shops down the road. He is being driven along the street by a group of jeering youths armed with sticks. Trembling, the man turns and tries to plead with the youths. They laugh, then set upon him with the sticks. The man shrieks and runs, blood pouring from his ears and forehead and spattering his sarong. He stumbles along the street, pursued by his attackers. Some stragglers saunter along at the rear, looking for other likely victims. Rani thinks she recognises some of them, boys from school.

There is a crash from across the street, followed by the tinkling of broken glass. The gang is attacking the shop across the road, climbing in through the broken window to loot its contents. One man climbs out, holding a metal bath over his head.

"Get back," hisses Neleni. "Stay away from the window."

But Rani is transfixed. One of the gang is standing in the street, eyeing their house, deciding whether it is worthy of his attention. Rani holds her breath. He has summoned some of his friends. They are pointing at the window. Have they seen her? One runs up the steps and hangs over the railings, impudently peering through the window, his hand shading his eyes, but he is blinded by the sun reflected in the glass. Then he tries the handle of the door. Unable to open it, he gives it a bad-tempered kick, leaving the imprint of his sandal on the paint.

"Come on. We've got better things to do. You don't even know who lives here."

"Yes, I do. It's that Tamil whore. Her old man works at the Post Office."

"Yeah, yeah. We believe you. Last time we followed your advice, we attacked a Sinhalese home. Remember?"

But the boy persists.

"Come on out, bitch, I know you're in there."

Clutching Saro to her, Neleni feels a sharp pain in her belly. She bites her lip, trying not to make a noise.

The youth runs up and down the verandah, banging on the door and windows, shouting and cursing. *He's drunk*, thinks Neleni, although that is little consolation. Then, she hears his friends, a little way up the street.

"Come on, keep up. We've still got some unfinished business with the shopkeeper here."

They lose interest. Move on. With a last burst of fury, the boy throws himself at the door.

"Dirty bitch. I'll be back for you. We all know what you get up to when your old man's out. Filthy whore."

Then, he crashes down the steps and runs up the street, affecting the ragged gait of a drunk.

"Hey, wait for me. Don't kill him 'til I get there. I want to see the fun."

He is answered by faint laughter. They have gone.

1958: Treasure Island

They sit, huddled together on the sofa, Neleni leaning forward, listening, her face taut, like a terrified animal, not daring to move. Saro begins to whimper.

"Shh!" Neleni hisses. It is a strange sound. Like air escaping from a tyre. Harsh. Unlike her usual tone.

Suddenly, there is more shouting outside. Screams too, a woman shrieking in fear, then harsh laughter. Crashes, breaking glass, a flash, sudden and violent as a flare, then an explosion. Boom! The windows rattle in their frames. A fireball bathes the street in its orange glow. There is a fierce, crackling sound and sparks drift past the window. They can feel the heat through the glass. It must be a ferocious blaze.

Motioning the girls to stay where they are, Neleni pushes herself up from the sofa and makes her way to the window, clinging on to the arm of the sofa to steady herself. Her legs feel weak and the pain in her back is almost unbearable. But she has to look. Standing in the shadow beside the window, she parts the slats of the blinds with her fingers. Flames and black smoke are belching from a shop at the end of the street.

Although there is no immediate danger from that fire, the shop directly opposite has also been vandalised. The windows have been smashed and from where she stands, Neleni can see how everything inside has been upturned and scattered about. A trail of objects has spilled onto the street, items that the looters have dropped or discarded. Soon, they may return with petrol and matches. The street is not wide enough to protect Neleni's house from sparks born by the wind.

The other, greater fear is that rioters might target her house. It is obvious from their conversation that they know it is a Tamil home. Her only hope is that they become too distracted, or drunk, to return. What can she do? There is nowhere to run, no means of escape. Even if she had a car, it is doubtful she would get far with rioters roaming the streets. Anyway, her condition precludes travel. Even moving from room to room is an effort. She winces, pressing her hand into the small of her back.

All she can do is stay here, and hope. At least she can take the girls to the back of the house where they will be safe from prying eyes and missiles thrown at the windows. The kitchen. That would be the best place. There is food and water within easy reach and, if the house catches fire, there is a chance that they could shelter in the yard. Its high wall abuts a small back-alley. But she does not think that rioters will approach from that route, as it is narrow and overgrown with weeds. The residents warn their children not to play there for fear of snakes. Hopefully, the rioters will avoid it for the same reason.

Putting a finger to her lips and, motioning the girls to follow her, she leads them quietly out of the living-room. As they pass into the syrupy gloom of the hallway, a small hand slips into hers, squeezing her fingers.

"It'll be all right, Amma. I'll look after you."

Rani's eyes are wide in the darkness, her small mouth set in a firm, straight line. Her resemblance to Sunny is striking.

***

With one arm resting on Rani's shoulder, Neleni makes her way into the kitchen where she eases herself onto a chair. The air in the house is becoming thick, tainted with the smell of burning. Wisps of charcoal float in through the air channels under the roof then waft lazily to the floor. Saro tries to pick one up. It melts, covering her hand with fine, velvety dust. She licks her fingers and begins to cough.

"Don't!" scolds Neleni. But her real concern is that one of the strands of carbon might carry a living spark. So, she instructs Rani to dampen some tea-towels and keep watch for stray embers. It is not much. Not enough to prevent a fire which, in all likelihood will start in the roof. But it is better than nothing. Obediently, Rani sets to work, pouncing energetically on anything resembling a spark while Saro stares out of the window, mesmerised by the motes of soot drifting past. Some are quite large, their edges furled like black leaves while others seem to twist and turn, waving tiny black limbs.

"That one looks like a man. Look!"

Rani picks Saro up so that she can see more clearly. Saro giggles then, quite unexpectedly, plants a kiss on her sister's cheek. Rani pretends not to notice, but squeezes her sister tightly.

It is quiet outside. The shouting has died away and been replaced by silence. Apart from the muffled roar and pop of the burning shop, they hear nothing: none of the usual street sounds, no firemen or police. Just a terrible, eerie stillness. Perhaps everyone is doing the same as them, pretending to be somewhere else, trying not to attract attention. Or perhaps they have really gone, leaving them behind, the only remaining occupants of their street.

***

Later, when she considers it safe to move about the house, Neleni sends Rani to fetch linen and pillows from the bedrooms as well as the old chamber-pot which still lies hidden in the gloomy space under Sunny's bed. During these travels, Rani also takes the opportunity to collect her copy of 'Treasure Island', a gift from Uncle Arjun. It seems an appropriate book for the occasion. She cannot explain why, but she has a growing sense of excitement, the sort that accompanies a departure from normality. Sleeping in the kitchen will be a great adventure.

Back in the kitchen, Rani makes up three beds on the floor as her mother cooks a simple dish of rice and vegetables. Neleni's movements are slow and awkward. She finds it difficult to reach around the great bulge of her belly and she often sighs, pressing her hand into her back. Cooking seems to sap her strength and, afterwards, she sits in the chair, her eyes closed, fanning herself with a sheet of paper while the food steams in plates on the table.

"Amma, shall I help Saro."

Neleni nods, too exhausted to speak. Her own food lies untouched on the plate.

Suddenly, there is a crash in the yard. Neleni starts from her seat, her face pale and taut with terror. The cat appears at the window, pawing at the glass to be let in. In leaping over the wall, it has smashed another of Raj's flowerpots. Sighing, Neleni gets to her feet. She tugs at the sash-cord window which has swollen, once again, in the heat. The paint is peeling and, as she pulls at it, she can smell the faint rottenness of mildewed timber.

"Stupid thing," she exclaims. Finally, with a wrench, she forces the window up a few inches and the cat squeezes in. Picking its way daintily around the sink, it leaps to the floor, purring happily as it rubs around a table leg.

"Uh!" Something warm is trickling down her thighs, travelling down her legs to her ankles. Looking down, she sees a darkening stain on the front of her sari and, on the floor at her feet, a pool of liquid. Her waters have broken.

***

Neleni has had several violent contractions. The pain in her back is intense and her only relief is to lie down, so she makes the girls go to bed early. Lying together, they watch the sun set through a pall of smoke. After that, Neleni will not allow a lamp or overhead light to be lit but, as a reward for her help, she allows Rani to read under her sheet with a weak torch.

***

There is a clatter. Rani has fallen asleep and the torch has rolled from her hand. Reaching over her, Neleni turns it off, then lies on her back, watching the bright moon, tracing the shadowy outline of the hare as she remembers stories from childhood. Light is now shining directly through the window, casting a luminous glow over the kitchen, throwing everything into relief. She gazes down at the arc of her belly, pale and mysterious, like another small moon rising from the dark contour of her body.

***

Neleni sleeps fitfully, waking several times to an unusual noise, but unable to tell if it is real, or if she has been dreaming. There is a loud crash, like a house being demolished. For a while, she lies in the darkness, listening, but all she can hear is the steady breathing of the girls. With arms and legs akimbo, Saro lies on her back, purring like a wheezy kitten. Rani lies on her side, her legs drawn up, her arms folded around her, as if clutching a secret.

Neleni drifts back to sleep, only to awake suddenly to the sound of screams and cries. Tense and sweating, she listens, oppressed by the closeness of the room, its air thick with the stale breathe of sleep. There. Surely that was something. A faint cry. But she cannot tell if it was human or just the howl of an animal. Night is often disturbed by the yelping of pye-dogs, defending their scraps of food from fellow scavengers.

Neleni winces. Another contraction. She is panting. The curdled air presses down on her, but she cannot fill her lungs. Where is Raj? Why hasn't he come home? Why can she never rely on him?

The crisis passes. Her breathing becomes more regular. There is silence outside. She berates herself for her weakness. It is not Raj's business to help her. She has no right to expect anything of him. Yet, she does. Marriage has made her dependent on him. She will never be truly free, her own person – or Arjun's – until she stops relying on Raj's support. She loves Arjun, there is no doubt of that, but Raj has become a habit. One, that she now realises, will be difficult to break.

It is so unfair. Why didn't she meet Arjun earlier, or refuse to marry until she was sure she was in love? But her society does not sanction romance. Love is a practical matter and she complied with Sunny's wishes, convinced that doing what was expected would lead to happiness. And it did. Up to a point.

Married life entails a certain contentment, if only because it leaves deeper passions undisturbed. There has been love, of a kind; love of her children, love of her mother, even affection for Raj. But it has been safe. Love with its wings clipped.

Deeper, more complex emotions were sealed away. She recognised them only as formless shadows, like creatures locked in ice, as she skated over them. Then, with one event, one person that she might never have met, her life changed. But has she changed? She thinks not. Somewhere, at the back of her mind, doubt is growing. If she cannot alter her thinking to match her circumstances, she will never really be free and Arjun will never be hers. The turmoil, into which they have been thrown, will never be resolved. What is love without the freedom to enjoy it? But, perhaps, it no longer matters. She stares up at the moon, filled with the bitter conviction that he has already left her.

Rani opens her eyes, unsure if she is dreaming or awake, for she does not recognise her surroundings. Then, she remembers. They have slept in the kitchen. Shafts of morning sun are streaming through the window above the sink, making patterns on the wall and floors and a warm patch on her face. She rubs her eyes: shuts them again: the light on her face so bright that, from the inside, her closed lids glow pink. With a little effort, she thinks she might be able to see right through them. It is that kind of light. She concentrates hard, hoping, at least, to see a tracery of blood vessels. But she cannot.

She opens her eyes and notices that, despite the sunlight, the window looks misty. It is covered with a film of dust. Soot. Now she remembers. The man running up the street. The burning shop. The screams outside. She shivers. A cool stream of air is flowing through the grille over the door and drifting across the floor. It brings with it the smell of smoke, fainter now than it was last night, but still acrid with a vinegary tang that sticks in the back of the throat. Something touches her foot. She jumps. The cat is licking her toes. It has been sitting there, at the end of the table, silent and wide awake, watching the sleepers to see who will wake first, hoping for food. It watches her carefully, as she removes Saro's arm which has been lying across her chest and sits up.

The cat is rarely this friendly and Rani leans forward in an attempt to stroke it. As her hand approaches, the cat crouches, head down, looking wary. Rani waits, hoping the cat will come to her. Gingerly, it sniffs her fingers. She can feel the soft blow of its breath on her skin. Then, after licking her fingers, it nuzzles her hand, wiping the side of its head down both sides. Carefully, Rani moves her fingers, just a fraction at a time, tickling the cat behind the ears. It begins to purr, a soft throaty rumble of contentment.

"I love you," whispers Rani.

The cat purrs louder, stretching its head up, pushing against her hand. Stepping onto the blanket that is her make-shift mattress, it digs its claws in, kneading its paws up and down, its tail flicking, its eyes narrowed in ecstasy.

"Rani?"

Her mother is awake. She looks pale and sickly, her hair sticking to her face in limp strings. Rani, who has slept soundly, wonders why her mother looks so tired. She knows nothing of the fears and imaginings that have kept Neleni awake for most of the night.

"Can you bring me some water?"

Regretfully, Rani pushes the cat away and rises from her bed, stepping onto the red, polished floor which sticks slightly to the soles of her bare feet. Taking a glass from the cupboard, she pours her mother some of the boiled water that is always kept in a jug on the table. Usually, Neleni refreshes the water every few hours, covering the jug with a crocheted net, edged with coloured glass beads. But the water, unchanged since last night, is now warm and cloudy. Neleni forgot to cover it and a dead fly is floating on the surface. Intrigued, Rani notices that, if she looks at the fly through the side of the jug, its hairy legs are magnified by the glass. She wonders if she should say anything but, thinking better of it, she fishes the fly out with her finger, fills the glass and takes it to her mother. Hoisting herself up onto one elbow, Neleni takes a sip, wrinkling her nose in disgust. The water is warm and viscous.

"Have you heard anything?"

Rani looks puzzled.

"I mean, in the street. Have you heard any noises?"

"No, Amma. Should I?"

"No, no."

Her mother shakes her head, distracted, considering some thought that she does not wish to share. She finishes her water, then signals for Rani to help her up. It is difficult. She is heavy and unsteady. At one point, she stumbles and nearly loses her footing. Rani tries to hold her but she is too slight and, for a moment, it looks as if they will both fall over until, with an effort, Neleni manages to steady herself by catching the side of the table. She leans forward, both hands flat on the table, breathing deeply until she is able to right herself. Then, slowly and painfully, she struggles over to the window.

The pipes groan as she turns on the tap and a stream of rusty water splashes into the sink, spattering the front of her sari. After a few seconds, the water runs clear and cool. Neleni holds her arms and wrists under the tap then, cupping her hands, splashes water over her face. Dabbing herself dry with a tea-towel, she stares out into the yard. Sunny's chair, unused since her death, has been pulled into a corner, a broken flower-pot lies by the gate and the whitewashed wall is stained with mildew. A small square of desolation, full of bleak silence.

"I wish I knew where he was," she murmurs.

"I'm sure Appa's all right," Rani says, reassuringly.

But Neleni frowns, confused, as if she does not know who Rani is talking about.

Saro is being fed cold rice and curry by her mother. Obediently, the little girl opens her mouth to let Neleni drop the ball of food onto her tongue. Her sister's wide gape reminds Rani of a nestling. She has seen them. At Uncle Ivan's. She was staying with him, in his big house on the other side of town, with his wife and four children. One night, Uncle took her out into the garden to a bush that grew near the front door.

The bush was nothing special, just a rounded, low-growing shrub with no flowers. But, after Uncle had gently parted the leaves, Rani gasped in wonder. Inside, wedged between two branches, was a thrush's nest. The mother bird shuffled slightly in the light of Uncle's torch, cocking her head to look at them with a bright black eye. But she did not fly away, or even look alarmed. Uncle explained that that was because it was dark. Then, a little shame-faced, he told how, as a boy, he had taken birds from their nests at night. Next day, Rani waited until the mother had left the nest, then peeped in again. As she parted the twigs, three little mouths had opened, each of the chicks pushing its face up to the source of food. They were like Saro who knows exactly when to open her mouth when being fed. Just like a little bird.

"When can I see Uncle Ivan again?" she asks her mother.

Neleni frowns. It is an odd question. Especially, at a time like this. But children do not think the same way as adults.

"I don't know," she says, vaguely.

Disappointed, Rani wonders whether to pursue the subject, but her mother has the sort of expression that tells her not to ask.

Neleni's fingertips, clenched around another ball of rice like the beak of a bird, are pointing at Saro's mouth. Saro has just opened her mouth to take the food when Neleni, suddenly gripped by a violent contraction, jerks her hand away, scattering rice over the floor. She grimaces and leans forward, her hands pressed against her belly. She pushes back in the chair, her spine flexed, her legs stretched out in front of her, her feet pressed hard against the floor. Then, as the strange fit passes, she breathes out, a great sigh, like a moan. Large drops of perspiration have collected on her brow and her hands are shaking. The girls stare at her, silent and terrified.

"Rani. I'm going to lie down. I think the baby is coming."

"How soon, Amma?"

"I don't know."

Rani helps to lower her mother to the floor. Neleni's huge belly makes her unwieldy and she hardly has strength to support herself so, holding her mother's hands tightly, Rani pushes back on her heels, trying to compensate for the great weight that is pulling them both down. Finally, she is sitting on the floor. They are both panting and Rani's arms are trembling with the effort.

Pale and exhausted, Neleni lies back on the make-shift mattress, her black hair streaked across the pillow. Her labour started at least twelve hours ago. She knows it will be difficult. It always is. She just prays that there will be no complications. There is no chance of finding a mid-wife, much less of getting to hospital, in these conditions. She will have to take her chances. She wonders how many other women are in the same position as herself, imprisoned in their homes with no-one to help them.

In the past, there was no shortage of help and advice; from her mother, from aunts, even from neighbours. There was a steady stream of visitors in and out of the house, each with a self-appointed task, carrying water, providing towels or preparing food. Some just came for the company, settling themselves down in the kitchen for a chat with their neighbours.

Births are an occasion for socialising and, often, the conversation and hilarity provide such a distraction that the mother is temporarily forgotten, as she writhes on the bed, sweating and straining. Only her screams momentarily divert the women from their chatter. Suddenly, the house becomes quiet as everybody sits and listens. Informed by instinct and experience, they can quickly tell whether this is the real event or just a false start. If the latter, they quickly resume their banter at precisely the point at which they left off.

There were times, in the past, when Neleni wished for less of this company, but now she misses it. Giving birth is lonely and frightening, and the presence of the other women brought a feeling of normality to the whole terrifying process. But now, she is on her own, with the exception of two little girls for whose well-being she is responsible, despite her own incapacity. Suddenly, as acute as any physical pain, Neleni feels the loss of her mother.

***

Grief at Sunny's death has re-united Neleni with her eldest daughter. Their shared loss has resulted in a truce, healing the rift that had begun to develop between them. Now, Neleni's need for her convinces Rani to forget what she saw, or thought she saw, when she spied her mother and Arjun together in his room a few months ago. One should never entertain such wicked thoughts about one's mother. What if she were to die, suddenly, like Sunny? Then, it would be too late ever to say sorry.

Rani has learned her lesson. One does not question what happens within the family. One cannot hope to understand the ways of adults. For her part, Rani has resorted to the more pleasurable occupations of childhood. She is still not a woman, despite the machinations of her body, and she has no intention of becoming one if she can possibly help it. If she chooses to forget her suspicions, to put her antipathy aside, she can remain a child. And she can be what she always wished: her mother's favourite daughter. That is enough.

***

Dutifully, Rani clears up the rice that has been spilled on the floor then, filling a large glass with water, places it by her mother's head.

"Here, Amma. Try to drink."

But Neleni simply groans. She has not opened her eyes for several minutes and when she does, they do not focus on Rani who is bending over her, but seem to stare through and beyond her daughter. Saro whines and crawls up to her mother, hoping for attention, but Rani pulls her back.

"Leave her alone," Rani whispers. "She's not well. We've got to let her rest."

For once, Saro obeys her. Silently, they watch their mother as she drifts in and out of sleep, murmuring to herself in her dreams. Once or twice, Rani thinks she hears the name "Arjun". But she cannot be sure. It is difficult to know what Neleni is saying. Her head rolls restlessly from side to side and the words, when they come, are jumbled and indistinct. Then, in the grip of another contraction, she awakes suddenly, her face screwed up in pain as she weakens under the strain of protracted labour.

She is getting visibly weaker. On the few occasions that she opens her eyes, she seems unaware either of her daughters or her surroundings. Rani knows enough about illness to know that her mother is becoming feverish. She is sweating profusely and her speech is rambling. Rani tries to get her to drink, but Neleni pushes the glass away, looking at something – or someone – behind Rani's head. When Rani turns to look, there is nothing there.

"Amma is seeing spirits," thinks Rani, as she dabs her mother's brow with a tea-cloth. She is afraid and wishes that Sunny was here. She would know what to do. People always came to find Sunny when they were in trouble.

"I must get help," she thinks.

She whispers her plan to Saro. The child clutches her arm and, for a minute, Rani thinks her sister is going to cry. There is no time for one of Saro's bawling fits. Rani grabs her sister's arms and looks her in the eye.

"Listen, Saro. Amma's ill. I've got to find someone to help her."

"I want to come with you," pleads the child.

"No. You've got to stay here and look after Amma. She needs you. You must be brave. For her."

Saro nods wisely, her small face grave, old beyond its years, her mouth drawn down, her forehead crinkled, like a temple monkey. Rani nearly laughs but quickly brings herself under control. She must not sacrifice Saro's goodwill.

"Good girl. Sit here by Amma and give her anything she wants. Don't tell her where I've gone. I'll be back as soon as I can."

Saro wags her head, looking more like a monkey than ever. Resisting the desire to snigger, Rani lets herself quietly out of the back door and steals across the yard to the gate, which leads into the alley.

The bolt on the gate is rusty and will not budge. Rani tries to jiggle the bolt around in its setting but it refuses to move. *Beast*! She kicks the door hard so that its wooden panels rattle, but still the bolt sticks fast. What can she do? She has often seen her mother oiling locks in the house to stop them creaking. Perhaps that would work. She creeps back into the kitchen, motioning Saro to keep quiet. Too late.

"What are you doing?"

"Looking for oil. Now shush!"

Neleni moves restlessly and moans. Rani thinks she hears her murmur Uncle Arjun's name. Yes, there it is again. But people say a lot of strange things when they have fever and she does not have time to think about it now. She must get help. Inexperienced as she is, Rani knows that a combination of fever and childbirth could place her mother in mortal danger.

Beside the cooker, Rani finds a small amount of ghee sandwiched between two saucers. Her mother always improvises with containers, using whatever comes to hand rather than searching the top shelf of the cupboard where there are many dishes with lids. Whether through laziness, or fear of losing her balance as she stands on tiptoe on a wobbly chair, or perhaps for some other reason, Neleni avoids forays into the cupboard. Raj has often berated her for not using the items, all perfectly serviceable, which have been gathering dust on the top shelf since they were placed there the day after their wedding. Rani sometimes gets the impression that her mother does not want to be reminded of those presents.

Grabbing the saucers, Rani races out of the door, pursued by Saro, who has forgotten her promise to stay behind. An adventure is in the offing and she wants to be part of it.

Scooping some of the liquid fat from the dish, Rani slathers it over the bolt, trying to ease the grease under the retaining ring where the rusty metal has fused. Pressing against the gate with all her strength, she wriggles the bolt again. There is a slight movement. With relief, she realises that the bolt is not immoveable. But it is still extremely stiff. It needs someone with more strength than she possesses to move it. Unless … Rani looks about her. The yard is filled with a variety of objects, tools occasionally used by Raj for household necessities. In the corner, Rani spots what she needs. A hammer.

"Run and get me that hammer, Saro."

Eager to oblige, the little girl obeys. Grabbing the tool from her sister, Rani taps, first gently, then with more vigour, at the bolt. It shifts slightly but not enough. With one bad-tempered swing, Rani throws all her weight behind the next blow. It hits the bolt squarely on the head, separating both bolt and retaining ring from the gate. She is through!

For a second, she stands back, admiring her handiwork, hammer in hand, a warrior queen who has disposed of her enemy. Then, she feels Saro tugging at her skirt.

"Let's go!"

"No, you're not coming."

"Aaargh!"

Saro gives a blood-curdling scream, her eyes firmly fixed on Rani. Then she stops, draws breath, opening her mouth ready for the next scream but waiting to see what her sister will do. If she screams again, everyone for miles around will know where they are. Rani has no choice. She will have to take Saro with her.

"All right. You can come. But you must promise to keep quiet."

Saro nods her assent. Rani hopes she can trust her. Lifting the latch, she pulls the gate open. It groans on its hinges. She should have greased those too. Between them, she and Saro have made a great deal of noise, announcing their presence to the whole neighbourhood. She prays that there are no trouble-makers around to hear.

Beyond the gate is the alleyway, a wilderness of vegetation, broken boxes and other debris. Rani shudders. It is a perfect hiding place for snakes, full of shade and secluded corners in which they can shelter from the sun. She imagines them, coiled like springs, eyes glittering in the shadow, tongues flickering, tasting the air for a scent of prey or danger.

She hesitates. She must have a weapon and some protection. Searching the yard, she finds her grandmother's walking stick, tucked in a corner. Grasping the stick, Rani uses it to poke about behind some old boxes. Like all Islanders, she has been taught from an early age to identify hidden dangers. You never explore anything by touch without first using your eyes. You never insert your fingers into dark cracks or hollows, never climb woodpiles nor brush against vegetation for fear of attack from the many stinging, biting creatures that may lie hidden within. In her time, Sunny kept the yard meticulously clean, keeping it clear of such hiding places. But, in the last months of her pregnancy, Neleni has become dilatory in this respect, conserving her energy for only those tasks which she judges most important.

Prodding behind the boxes, Rani finds what she is looking for. A pair of large Wellingtons. More of a novelty than a necessity in this climate, they were given to her father by a friend on his return from England. Why he had returned with gum-boots, no-one could say, but he had presented them to her father as a kind of exotic novelty. *Excellent for monsoon*, he had insisted. Raj had thought otherwise, but had thanked his friend and duly admired the boots before consigning them to the nether region of the courtyard, where they have remained, unused and largely forgotten ever since.

Cautiously, Rani picks the boots up, one after the other, tipping them upside down to rid them of any inhabitants. A house-spider falls from one, while a scorpion is dislodged from the other. The spider scuttles off on spindly legs but the scorpion squares up to its attacker, intending to fight for its home. Arching its tail skywards, it prepares to attack. But, before it can strike, Rani whips off her slipper and whacks the scorpion to a pulp.

"Ooh!" Saro breathes, admiringly.

Rani slips her feet into the boots. They have a nasty, moist feel and they smell of mould. Taking up the stick, she motions to Saro to follow her. Together, they walk to the open gate and peer round the corner into the forbidden alley.

"All right," says Rani, taking a deep breath, "get on my back. I'll carry you. I don't want you getting bitten."

She squats down, allowing Saro to climb on her back.

"Ow! Don't squeeze my neck so hard," protests Rani, as she struggles for breath. In her excitement, Saro has clutched her around the windpipe. "Hold onto my shoulders and grip with your knees."

"Like an elephant?"

"Yes, I suppose so," Rani agrees, grudgingly.

They set off slowly, Rani struggling under the double handicap of the outsize boots and her sister, who squirms with glee, squeaking comments in a shrill voice as she points out objects of interest.

"Look, look. I can see into Mrs Jayasena's yard."

"I can't look, I'm too busy. And anyway, I couldn't see if I wanted to. You can only see because you're higher than I am," Rani grumbles. She is already dripping with perspiration from the effort of carrying Saro.

Swish! Something moves in the undergrowth. Close to the ground, the leaves of a small bush begin to tremble. Rani halts, holding her breath, her heart pounding in her throat, her eyes fixed on a point at the side of the path from which the noise came. The bush stops moving, but still she waits, watching every blade of grass.

Oblivious to the danger, Saro prattles on. "Look. Senaka's got a swing. I want a swing. Do you think Appa would get us one? Or maybe Uncle Arjun, if we asked him nicely."

"Oh, do shut up," snaps Rani crossly. The mention of Uncle Arjun grates on her nerves.

Saro begins to whine. "You're so horrible to me. I want to get down."

"Well, you can't. I think there's a snake in those bushes. And if you keep making that noise, he'll probably attack us. We'll both die and it'll all be your fault. So just shut up."

Gulping back her tears, Saro falls silent.

Gingerly, Rani pokes at the bushes with her stick. She thinks she sees something but the movement is so slight she cannot be sure. She waits again. The alley is silent, breathless.

"I suppose I must go on," she thinks. "Amma needs help. I must be brave."

She edges past the bush where she thinks the animal is lurking. If she is lucky, it might be a rat and not a snake. She has just passed the spot where she thinks danger is hidden and is drawing breath when a small arrow-shaped head darts from the undergrowth. In one, slow second, she sees the small blue-black head, the mouth gaping wide to expose two wicked fangs. A krait. The deadliest snake on the island.

Lunging forward, the animal sinks its fangs into the thick welt at the back of her boot. Rani feels the impact of its head against her leg. She screams in terror. Then, realising that the snake's fangs have not made contact with her skin, she whacks furiously at it with the stick. After receiving two or three sharp blows, the animal recoils and slithers away into a thick patch of weeds.

"Oh. Oh." Rani is panting with shock. A small hand parts the damp hair at the back of her head. A gentle kiss is planted on her neck. "I love you," whispers Saro.

"I love you too," says Rani as tears stream down her cheeks. She tightens her grip on Saro's legs. She knows that she must go on but her knees have become weak with fear. Only a few yards lie between her and the end of the alley, but it seems like miles. Bent under Saro's weight, she leans on the stick, contemplating the perilous journey before her. Like St Christopher. Then, an idea comes to her. If she pretends to be someone else, someone brave, perhaps she can overcome her fear. St Christopher would be a good choice. She even looks a bit like him with her stick and Saro on her back.

"Saro. Let's pretend I'm St Christopher and you're the baby Jesus. Just until we get to the end of the alley. Let's pretend that I'm carrying you over a river and that you can see lots of fish. Let's try to name as many as we can. Go!"

744

Rani pushes forward, hitching Saro higher onto her back as they recite the names of all the fish they can remember: parrot fish, conger eels, sharks, few of whom, if any, inhabit rivers. But it doesn't matter. It distracts Rani from the perils of their crossing.

Dear St Christopher, grant us safe passage – through the passage! A play on words. She likes that. She will tell mother or Uncle Arjun. They will appreciate it. They like words. They are always reading, just like her. She repeats the prayer with every step, like a mantra, filling her head with it so that there is no room left for fear. Over and over, she repeats it: *Grant us safe passage, through the passage. Grant us safe passage, through the passage* – until finally, they reach the end of the alleyway.

"Down you get Saro, we've reached dry land."

Saro slides down her sister's back, then waits, expectantly, her cheeks flushed with excitement. This presents Rani with another dilemma. She cannot take Saro with her. It is too dangerous. She must think of a game to keep her close to the house. She racks her brains. Then, she remembers the book she was reading last night. Treasure Island. Pirates!

Bending over Saro, she whispers in her ear. Their house is a ship and pirates are coming to take it. Real pirates. Saro shivers with excitement.

"You've got to stay in the crow's nest and keep watch," says Rani, pointing towards the verandah. "Only you can do this, Saro. Do it for Amma. All right?"

"Aye, aye, Captain."

Saro stands to attention, salutes, then follows Rani up the steps onto the porch where she hides in an angle of the verandah, clutching the Wellingtons and the walking stick, her eyes shining with excitement. In her own mind, she is a brave buccaneer. To Rani, she looks small and infinitely fragile. The sight of her sister, ready for adventure yet so vulnerable, wrings her heart. She regrets her earlier resentment and the murderous thoughts that crossed her mind.

Please look after her. A prayer forms silently in her head, rising upwards like a small paper kite. Then, taking a deep breath, Rani dives down the steps into the shark-infested waters of the street.

The road is deserted: no-one about; not even a pye-dog, panting in the shade. Tentatively, she takes a few steps, treading on tiptoe. Then, she freezes, a small human statue in the middle of the road; watching, waiting, listening, sniffing the air for strange and unfamiliar smells. No traffic, no people, no sound except for that of a loose shutter, banging in the wind and only the smell of burning. Everywhere, the thick, sick smell of smoke, so strong that it burns the throat and chokes the lungs.

Ssss! A dry, hissing wind. A brief current of air. A piece of paper rolling along the gutter. Ticca, ticca, ticca, ticca, ticca! A sound, normally lost in the daily hubbub of bells, horns and screeching tyres; an insignificant sound grown large to fill an empty space. All around her, a terrible, echoing solitude.

She takes a step forward. Then another. On impulse, she spins around. If any pirates were to creep up behind her, she would see them. But there is no-one. Only a cat, scratching in the debris of a burnt-out shop. It is Mr Albert's shop, the little man who she saw being chased up the road last night. She wonders what became of him. And his family. He has a son, about her age. They play together and, sometimes, she is asked to tea. That is a rare treat as she is given bought cake, out of a packet – something she never gets at home – and when she leaves, Mr Albert always lets her choose some sweets from the shop.

Something flutters in the doorway. Unable to contain her curiosity, Rani changes direction. She creeps up the street. As she approaches the shop, the acrid smell of burning fills her nose and mouth, although the fire has gone out long since. She stops opposite the place that once displayed fruit and eggs, sacks of rice, churns of milk and cans of cheese. The windows have been smashed and the interior is a blackened ruin. She now sees what attracted her attention. A piece of green gauze, part of a woman's sari, has been caught on the charred doorposts. She recognises it as one of the saris that Mrs Albert often wore in the shop.

The cat ventures inside where it prowls around the charred contents, delicately placing its paws, one in front of another as if, instinctively, sensing some danger. It finds something, sniffs, dabs with its paw, then stretches its head forward. She can see its pink tongue, lapping at something. Then, her eye following the cat around the shop, she sees something else. It looks like a hand.

At once fascinated and terrified, Rani starts to cross the road. She has just got to the middle, when there is a sharp 'rat tat'. She looks around. An elderly woman has appeared at a window in the house behind her. She is banging on the window, gesturing to Rani to come away from the shop. Rani takes a few steps towards her.

"Go home," the woman mouths through the window. "Go home!"

Rani walks towards the house. Perhaps this old woman could help her mother. But as she gets to the pavement, the blinds rattle down and the old woman disappears.

From behind her, comes a sound like a great yawn, as if a giant is waking from sleep. Heart beating, she turns, to see the roof of the shop collapse. She is caught in a great cloud of dust and debris and splints of charcoal spatter her skin and clothes, matting her hair.

Choking and spluttering, she runs back along the street then, out of breath, she stops, leaning forward, her hands on her knees, trying to expel the acrid stench from her lungs. Why did she come down here? She is supposed to be getting help for Amma.

Then, a terrible thought occurs to her. The strip of sari cloth, the outline of a hand. Was that Mrs Albert that she saw back there? If it was, she must be dead. And what about Sujan, her son? Rani shudders. She hopes she was mistaken. She cannot be sure about the hand. Perhaps she imagined it. Perhaps Mrs Albert tore her sari while running away. Maybe she is safe by now. But in her heart, Rani knows that Mrs Albert lies buried in the wreckage of her shop. Perhaps the screams they heard last night were her screams.

Rani begins to run up the street. Better to run than think. She must get help. She must look after Amma and Saro.

***

She runs and runs, until winded by heat and exertion, she is forced to stop and gasp for breath. A painful stitch in her side distracts her from all thoughts of the burnt-out shop and its grim contents. She kneads the stitch with her fingers, while she looks about her. Then, it strikes her. She has been running up the middle of the road. Something she could never do normally. On a normal day, the road would be a heaving mass of vehicles: bicycles, rickshaws, brightly-painted buses, lorries and cars. But today, there is no hooting-tinkling cacophony of traffic, no friendly human voices. Just silence.

"Perhaps the street is really full of people but I just can't see them. Or, perhaps, they can't see me. What if I'm dead? I don't remember dying. But would I know? Maybe it's only other people that know you're dead. Perhaps, I'm a ghost. But, if I'm dead, wouldn't I see other dead people?"

She looks behind her, half expecting to see the ghost of Mrs Albert drifting up the street in her torn sari. But she sees no-one.

She pinches herself hard. Her sharp little nails sink into the flesh, leaving crescent-shaped marks.

"Ow! That hurt. I can't be dead."

She sees a movement from the corner of her eye. Slowly, she turns her head, almost too scared to look. A boy is standing on the corner of the road, staring at her. His face is dirty and his hair matted. His clothes are torn and stained and there is a wild, vacant look in his eyes. But she recognises him instantly.

"Sujan!"

The boy continues to stare, his face blank and expressionless, as if he does not recognise his own name. Rani holds out her hand, moving slowly towards the boy, trying not to startle him. She knows, instinctively, that a sudden movement will frighten him and cause him to bolt in the opposite direction.

"Sujan. Where have you been? What happened?"

He does not reply but when she slips her hand into his, he grips it tightly, his eyes frozen in a look of mute horror, as if they hold the imprint of some terrible event.

"He knows I'm here, but he can't really see me," she thinks. "It's as if he's somewhere else, seeing something else. Something awful."

Her thoughts wander back to the fire-blackened shop – and what lies inside. Suddenly, the silence is broken by muffled shouts. The same sounds that she heard last night, only farther off.

"Uh!"

The boy tightens his grip on her hand. Rani winces. She can almost feel the bones being squeezed out of shape. The boy, now agitated, is staring about him, his head twisting wildly from side to side. He has passed from a bad dream into a nightmare. Reality and memory, past and present, fantasy and the physical world have merged into one hideous entity. He must hide, away from the demons that pursue him.

He wants to run, but something is holding him back. He turns in the direction of the shop.

"No, Sujan. Not that way. Come with me."

He is staring down the street to where the noise is getting louder. His eyes begin to focus. He can see the outline of men, running and swaggering.

"Hey, you!"

One of the men has seen him.

"Sujan. Quickly! This way."

She tugs frantically at his arm. Sujan looks as if he is trying to remember something. The sound of her voice. He cannot remember whose it is, but it sounds familiar; the voice of someone he trusts. After a moment's indecision, he allows her to guide him, stumbling along behind her, looking back over his shoulder at the end of the street, where the men have broken into a run.

"Come on. Faster!"

Desperately, Rani tugs at his arm, pulling him along behind her. She can hear the men behind them, shouting for them to come back. The voices are getting louder. The men are getting closer.

They draw level with the house.

"Saro, quick! The pirates are coming."

Having crept from her hiding place, Saro has been sitting on the steps.

"Quickly, get on."

Rani squats down to let Saro scramble onto her back. There is no time to put on the Wellingtons and, with Saro on her back and the boy's hand in hers, she cannot carry the stick. They must take their chances. Pulling Sujan behind her, Rani wades into the alley, into a dense thicket of weeds and roots that slap around her ankles and tickle her legs.

"Keep quiet now, and keep your heads down. We mustn't let them see us."

Saro crouches low, her arms clasped tightly around Rani's neck, her knees digging into Rani's side. Clinging to Rani's hand, Sujan has to be pulled along. Distracted by the approaching noise, he hesitates, turning frequently to look behind him.

"Keep up," she hisses.

The men are close but they are not yet sure where the children have gone. There are many small alleyways that lead from the backs of houses onto the street. The men are not sure which one they have taken. She can hear them, a little way down the road, crashing over dustbins, hammering on fences, like beaters trying to flush out small birds.

"Oh, quicker, quicker," she murmurs to herself.

Carefully, she pushes forward with her toes before putting her foot down. A few feet ahead, the bush moves and she hears a familiar slithering sound. Her heart batters wildly against the walls of her chest and her mouth is dry with fear. Saro is scared, too. She is clutching Rani so tightly around the neck that she can hardly breathe. Rani yanks viciously at Sujan's hand to make him speed up.

"Where are they?" says one voice, quite distinctly. He is only a few feet away from the entrance of the alley. A few more seconds and he will see them.

"They could be anywhere. Why are you bothering with them? They're only children."

"They are Tamil children," the voice corrects. "We got that kid's parents last night. Pity you missed the fun. We made the husband watch while we gave his old woman a good seeing to, then we left her to burn while we chased him up the street. Gave him the rubber necklace when we caught up with him. You should have seen him. Like a bloody human torch, running up the street screaming. The kid should have got the same but we couldn't catch him. But he saw everything. He'll remember us."

Rani shudders. She does not understand all that has been said but she knows that something terrible has happened. And she has seen the inside of the shop. The other man says something but his reply is indistinct. Perhaps he has disagreed, implied his disgust. She hopes he has. Then comes the sound of shared laughter. Sujan's hand trembles. She grips it tightly, trying to encourage him. Afraid that he might cry out, she digs her nails into his flesh.

At last, they are level with the gate. She pushes against it. The hinges groan. She squeezes through, pulling Sujan in after her. A split second after the children have entered the yard, a face appears at the end of the alley.

"I heard something. They've gone down this way. Come and look. I'm sure they're here."

Holding their breath, the children squat in an angle of the yard, next to the boxes that house scorpions and spiders.

"Don't be ridiculous. No-one's been down there for years. Look how overgrown it is."

"They're down here. I know it."

Plants swish and twigs snap as a man ploughs into the vegetation that chokes the passage. He is coming to get them. The two girls look at each other, eyes wide with fear. Rani puts a finger to her lips. Saro must not make a sound. Next to Rani, the boy is quivering, his eyes rolling wildly, powerless to escape the terror that pursues him.

Rani looks around for a weapon. There isn't much to hand, just a broom and a mop. They will have to do. This man isn't going to make an end of her – at least not without a fight. If nothing else, she can scratch and bite while the others run into the house. Perhaps they will be able to lock themselves in. Of course, they cannot stay in the kitchen. Perhaps they could run through to the front of the house and escape through the front door. Then she remembers her mother, lying helpless on the floor. She cannot run. It is hopeless. They are trapped.

The man has almost drawn level with the wall that separates them from the neighbour's yard. Soon he will be at the gate and he will see them, cowering in the corner. He swears. He has scratched his hand on one of the thorny plants growing out of the fence. He stops, sucks the wound, then kicks out, in temper, at the undergrowth.

There is a swish. Then a scream.

"Ai, ai! A krait! A krait!"

The quiet alley erupts as the man blunders about, banging into the fence as he struggles to turn and flee along the passage. The bushes tear at his clothes, the long grass winds around his ankles. He struggles, panicking, fearing the prick of poison-bearing fangs.

There is a thud. Another yell. The snake has broken cover and attacked, missing the man's ankle by a hair's breadth, dashing itself against the fence. Incensed, it gathers itself up to strike again. Shrieking, the man hurtles forward, stumbles, staggers to his feet, then sprints for the safety of the road.

"The snake," thinks Rani. "The snake saved us. The man disturbed it and the snake attacked him. Now he's gone. Thank you, snake. Thank you."

She allows the air to filter back into her lungs. Relief floods over her. Now that the immediate danger is over, she feels light-headed, drained of energy. No-one can enter the back of the house with the snake guarding the alley. For the moment, at least, they are safe.

She sits for a minute, her back against the wall and her face up to the sun, waiting for her legs to stop trembling. Then, motioning the others to follow her, she leads them into the kitchen and quietly bolts the door behind them.

Neleni's fever has increased. Droplets of sweat trickle from her brow and damp strings of hair stick to her face and neck. The movement of her head against the pillow has dislodged several hairpins and they lie, scattered around her on the floor, like the disjointed legs of insects. Occasionally, she opens her eyes to stare at the empty air, a look of terror on her face.

"What is wrong with Amma? What is she looking at?" whispers Saro.

"Nothing. She has a fever. That's all. That's what it's like when you have fever."

Neleni's face is suddenly contorted with pain. She shrieks and writhes on her make-shift bed. The violence of her contractions is increasing. Now they are only minutes apart.

Saro sobs, her small, screwed up face reflecting her mother's pain. The boy, whose hand she has been holding, since they huddled together in the yard, looks bewildered.

"Amma," she squeals. "Amma's going to die."

"Stop it," snaps Rani, biting back her own tears. "Stop it or I'll slap you. Just sit in the corner and keep quiet."

Rani knows she must do something. She thinks of Sunny. Her grandmother would have known what to do. A wave of longing sweeps over her. Tears well in her eyes. She swallows hard, determined not to cry. She must think. What would Sunny have done?

Rani remembers the old lady, sitting by her bedside, mopping her brow when she had a fever. Running to the sideboard, Rani opens a drawer and pulls out a tea-towel, one of the new ones, white with red checks. Never used, it feels coarser than the others and has a strange smell, like wood smoke. She runs it under the tap, squeezes the water from it, then, kneeling beside her mother, cautiously dabs her forehead. The coolness of the cloth seems to calm Neleni. After a while, she begins to breathe more deeply and her eyes no longer flicker frantically beneath their partly-closed lids.

However, her short respite from pain is soon wrecked by another violent contraction. Having taken her mother's hand, Rani winces as Neleni's grip tightens convulsively.

"Ow, Amma!" she breathes. But she does not take her hand away.

Perhaps prompted by the sound of her daughter's voice, Neleni opens her eyes. She struggles to raise herself but, after a feeble attempt, sinks back onto the cushions. She closes her eyes again and murmurs something.

"What is it, Amma? Speak up. I can't hear you."

Rani bends low over her mother, trying to catch what she says. Neleni's dry lips part, try to form a word, then release it in a sigh. *Ahhh.*

"Amma. What did you say?"

The lips move again. The voice becomes a little clearer.

"Come back."

"But I'm here. Beside you," whispers Rani.

Neleni smiles weakly, then opens her eyes. Her lips part, as if she is about to say something and she turns her head towards Rani. Then, as if she has seen her daughter for the first time, she stops, confused.

"I thought …," she murmurs.

"What, Amma?"

But Neleni has closed her eyes again. The moment of lucidity has passed. Her head rolls from side to side. She seems agitated, frowning, as if angry, murmuring, her hands restless, her heels working against the floor.

"I'll get you some water."

It is all Rani can think of, the only practical thing she can do. Neleni's grip tightens on her hand, unwilling to let her go.

"It's all right. I'm coming back."

Neleni moans. Perhaps it is agreement, perhaps not, but she relaxes her hold on Rani's hand. The girl withdraws, rubbing her fingers, which feel as if they have been caught in a vice. It awakens an unpleasant memory of the time she caught her hand in a mangle.

There is a shuffling noise in the corner. Saro has ceased her whimpering and is getting restless.

"We're hungry."

She pokes her chin out defiantly. Having assumed responsibility for the boy, she is now enjoying the sensation of being in charge. For the time being, at least, he has become her pet.

"Well, you'll have to wait. Either that, or you'll have to find something for yourselves. I'm looking after Amma."

"How can we find something for ourselves?"

"I don't know," sighs Rani exasperated. "Go and look in the store-cupboard."

"Really?"

Saro's eyes shine with excitement. The store-cupboard holds forbidden treasures.

"Just don't make yourselves sick. And keep out my way."

Rani's admonition ends with a histrionic flourish. It is the way Amma speaks when she is flustered, usually before dinner when the kitchen is full of steam and lids are jangling on the pots. At such times, Amma becomes a blur of colour as she flies backwards and forwards with dishes of vegetables and pans of hot water.

Saro scrambles to her feet, fear for her mother forgotten, superseded by the delightful anticipation of exploring the store-cupboard.

"Come on," she says, yanking the boy's hand.

Passively, he follows her to the cupboard, where his height and long arms will prove an invaluable asset. Having opened the door, the children disappear inside and soon, the only indication of their presence, is the rustling of paper and the muted clinking of glass jars as they examine the contents of the shelves.

Relieved that Saro and her companion are otherwise occupied, Rani pours another glass of water from the jug on the table, then hurries back to her mother who has lapsed into the exhausted, semi-conscious state that now alternates with periods of intense pain. Putting her hand under Neleni's head, Rani tries to raise it, but she cannot. Her mother is too weary to help herself.

"Amma, please try. You must drink," pleads Rani. But Neleni does not hear her.

"Please!" Rani speaks loudly, hoping to rouse her mother. It is no use. Neleni has drifted off into another world.

Saro emerges briefly from the cupboard and helps herself to two spoons from the cutlery drawer.

"Here, try this," she says to her companion as she re-joins him in the larder. There is a snap and a click, as if the lid has been prised from a pot of jam. At a loss, Rani stands gazing at the cutlery drawer which Saro has left open. She remembers how Sunny used to feed her medicine from a spoon when she was poorly, sweet-smelling concoctions which often tasted foul.

That is it! She races to the table, helps herself to a teaspoon from the drawer, then runs back to her mother, dropping to her knees beside the woman lying on the cushions.

Slipping her hand behind her mother's neck, Rani tilts Neleni's head forward. Neleni's eyes flicker open for a moment, then close. The girl dips the spoon into the glass of water and trickles a few drops between her mother's parched lips. How long is it since she last drank? It must have been hours. Dehydration will aggravate even the mildest fever. Rani learned that much from her grandmother. Tentatively, Neleni's tongue runs over her moistened lips.

"Here, Amma, try some more. That's it. Well done."

Rani whispers encouragement, as her mother has done to her when coaxing her to eat after a sickness. The words have a seductive power. Like a spell. She feels the muscles in her mother's neck tauten. She is trying, as hard as she can, to take down the water, swallowing in small, painful gulps. Then, when the glass is almost empty, she sinks back onto the pillows. But her eyes are fully open now, and they are brighter, more alert. Neleni looks at Rani, recognises her, and her mouth twists in a faint smile, although she is too frail to speak.

"Amma, are you feeling better?"

Her skin seems cooler, her smile stronger, but Neleni is still weak and she has yet to face the ordeal of childbirth. Rani kisses her mother gently on the forehead and strokes away the damp locks of hair. Holding her mother's hand, she warms with a quiet joy as she feels her own hand being squeezed in return. For now, she has complete possession of her mother's affection. Neleni's survival depends on her eldest daughter and, for a single, precious moment, Rani has become the most important person in her life. They are linked by a powerful bond, based on nurture, in which the dependence of child on mother has been reversed; a love, pure but ephemeral as a mayfly.

Caught up in her own happiness, Rani does not hear the sharp tap of footsteps on concrete. But Neleni does. She grips her daughter's hand even tighter, willing her to hear. Seeing the look of urgency on her mother's face, Rani listens. Her heart freezes. Someone is inside the house. There is a sound of furtive shuffling in the hallway. Unaware of the danger, Saro and the boy continue their assault upon the larder. The crackling of paper bags and the soft clink of spoons in jars will be audible to any ear pressed against the kitchen door.

Rani springs to her feet and runs on tiptoe to the store cupboard.

"Shh. Someone's coming."

Saro, reluctant to break off her illicit feast, turns a cross, jam-streaked face to her sister but her protests are silenced by Rani's hand which is swiftly clamped over her mouth.

"Be quiet," hisses Rani. "Someone's got into the house. They're in the hall."

Saro's eyes grow round with fear. Seeking shelter, she leans against her sister, her arms tightly wrapped around the older girl's waist. Rani feels the child's heart beating wildly through the thin cotton of her dress. Instinctively, the boy has blended into the shadows; squatting on his haunches in a corner, a jar still clutched in one hand, only the fearful oval of his face still visible between the sacks of rice and onions.

The footsteps become louder, advancing towards the kitchen, then stopping in the passage outside. Hardly daring to breathe, the girls peep around the larder door, watching with terrified fascination as the handle of the kitchen-door rattles in its socket, then turns slowly.

Five days after trouble first broke out in Polonnaruwa district, a State of Emergency is declared. But the violence does not end immediately. Rather like a badly-lanced boil, the infection merely spreads to other areas. South of Colombo, on the west coast, the manipulation of rumour by criminals convinces thousands of Tamils to flee. Their empty homes are then looted and torched.

Sinhalese, living on the eastern coast, fare little better. Their abandoned homes are razed to the ground and when the police and army finally come to the relief of refugees hiding in the jungle, they find many corpses.

In Colombo, the army and navy set to work, chasing the goondas from their strongholds but, as soon as one area is made safe and the military move on, the goondas return to reclaim their territory. Pitched battles take place on the streets. Rioters are shot and explosive devices are flung at both soldiers and civilians.

The day after the declaration of Emergency, Jaffna, the northern stronghold of the Tamils, erupts. As usual, the violence is sparked by rumour: stories of attacks on Tamils elsewhere – some verifiable, some not – but also the true account of a Hindu priest, burned alive in his shrine. Retaliation is swift and devastating. The remote Buddhist temple of Nagadipa, located on an island off the coast, is demolished by Tamil goondas. A bronze statue of Buddha, a gift from the Burmese government to celebrate the occasion of Buddha Jayanthi, is hacked to pieces and dumped in the sea.

The temple is one of Ceylon's most sacred shrines, having a direct connection with Lord Buddha who is reputed to have visited the island to resolve a quarrel between two kings. News of this outrage would have an even more far-reaching and disastrous effect than that of the murder of Mr Seneviratne. Violent reprisals against Tamils would spark even bloodier retaliation and, ultimately, a descent into civil war. Yet now, in the midst of chaos, something extraordinary happens, a miracle in a country contorted by violence and riddled with rumour. The destruction of the temple is kept secret. Moreover, it is entirely rebuilt in two months and the statue of Buddha replaced.

Elsewhere, other flash-points threaten to spark a conflagration. In North Central province, hundreds of labourers, with trucks full of weapons and stolen dynamite, march on the ancient city of Anuradhapura. With suicidal bravery, five policemen keep the mob at bay until the arrival of the army. Surrounded by soldiers, the goondas panic. In an attempt to break free, they charge in all directions, like terrified animals. They are trying to escape but perhaps, to the army, this vast surge looks like a charge. The soldiers open fire and several rioters are killed.

During this time, authority passes, almost by default, to the Governor-General Sir Oliver Goonetilleke. In fact, it was not the Prime Minister who declared the State of Emergency, but Sir Oliver in his role as nominal head of the Government. Eager to distance himself from responsibility for the current anarchy, particularly the violence sparked by his recent address to the nation, Mr Bandaranaike has temporarily withdrawn from the public arena. Sir Oliver now steps into the limelight, offering the Prime Minister a welcome reprieve.

The son of a postmaster, Sir Oliver has risen from relatively humble origins to become the first Ceylonese Governor-General. His official residence is a museum-like blend of colonial splendour and exotic archaism where male servants, dressed in magnificent traditional costumes, address the Governor as Rajjuruwo, or 'King'.

Like the Prime Minister, Sir Oliver is a wily, political survivor. However, unlike Mr Bandaranaike, he has not thrown his lot in with the nationalists, preferring to maintain firm links with the Island's former rulers. The possessor of several prestigious British titles, Sir Oliver will eventually make his home in London, having left the Island following an attempted military coup.

But, for now, he is enjoying a brief moment of glory. Unlike the Prime Minister, he is untainted by error and therefore able to take credit for resolving a situation that is not of his making. He is responsible, at least in part, for the secret reconstruction of the Nagadipa temple, having acquired a replacement for the original statue of Buddha from the Burmese authorities.

A measure of his extensive power is his ability to silence the press. Although outwardly affable, Sir Oliver reminds journalists of the Detention Laws which, during a time of Emergency, permit incarceration without trial, as well as the suspension of other legal rights such as bail and habeas corpus. The message is clear. Without Sir Oliver's prior approval, the press cannot make any reference to the civil disturbances.

A group of men sit in a woodland clearing, staring despondently into the flames of a small fire. Several miles from the nearest town, this is one of the places that they have used to store kerosene cans, petrol and stolen dynamite; an arms dump and a secret meeting place, allocated to them by their leader who, in turn, received instructions from one of his contacts. Having been emptied of its arsenal some time ago, the clearing has been abandoned for several weeks and now, partially reclaimed by rampant vegetation, is screened from the sight of inquisitive eyes by a thick curtain of creepers and undergrowth.

A billy can, filled with water, is bubbling furiously over the flames. A man in saffron robes picks up a stone and throws it at the fire. It glances against the can, tipping it off balance so that some of the water spills down the sides, steaming and spitting as it hits the fire. No-one speaks. They have been waiting for days. Still, there is no word from their leader.

Squatting by the fire, Tissa stares into the flames, unable to tell his men the truth. Anil's scheme misfired. Tissa pokes at the fire with a stick, watching the sparks fly as he relives every detail, trying to work out what happened.

Both Anil and Asoka were due to join Tissa outside the Government Agent's residence. But Asoka only knew half of the plan. For, he was not only to be the executioner, but also a victim of the plot. Anil had revealed this second element of the plan to Tissa just before they parted. Tissa had approved. It would assure him of his reward.

The plan had been for Asoka to kill the Government Agent and, simultaneously, for Anil to shoot Asoka. In the resulting confusion, no-one would notice an additional gunshot. A terrorist suicide. Not unheard of. Only later, if at all, would the police realise that the murderer had not shot himself with his own weapon. But where would that lead them? A dead end. Better to keep quiet. Case closed.

But, the plan that in theory had seemed so complete, had unravelled in practice. Despite waiting for several days outside the Government Agent's residence, Tissa had not been joined by Anil and Asoka. He had received no word, either of their whereabouts, or of any change to the plan. Hour after hour, he had waited patiently in the scorching sun: thirsty, hungry, buffeted by the desperate crowd of refugees waiting at the gates; watching the Government Agent's car come and go, each passing an opportunity lost.

Then, finally, his patience had run out. His friend, Dasa, had brought him news of the siege at the police station. The Sinhala Hamudawa had suffered a reversal of fortune. Hitherto unchecked, the rioters had been fired upon by the army. And Nash had signed the order.

When he heard the news, Tissa was consumed with rage. He no longer cared to wait for Anil and Asoka. He would do the job himself. The execution was carried out with extraordinary ease. Afterwards, he had congratulated himself on his success. But, as the euphoria wore off, he wondered what Anil would say. Perhaps he should have waited longer. But why had Anil sent no word?

On the run from the city, Tissa met up with other members of his gang who, having encountered unexpected resistance from the authorities, were making their way out of town to the lawless safety of the countryside. Tissa assumed control. Telling them to follow him, he led them to the clearing, hoping for news from Anil.

They have been waiting for a couple of days now. Without any word from Anil. Even worse, there has been no general uprising of the Sinhalese, no great wave of enthusiasm, as Anil had predicted, for the killing of a prominent Tamil. Rather, stories circulate of how the army and navy are using force to clear rioters from the streets, dispersing them like sewer rats. The support that the agitators had counted on has ebbed away. Added to this, the members of Tissa's own gang are getting restless.

Day-labourers and illegal squatters, they are men who live on the margins of society. Poor, ignorant and often exploited, they welcomed a chance to get even; against those wealthier and more privileged than themselves, against those that they hold responsible for their plight.

A lethal mix of fable, history and religion, has been poured down the throats of this gullible underclass, strengthening grudges against its supposed oppressors; the wealthy, the educated, non-Buddhists, Tamils and even those who, not being Tamil, speak their language; in short, anyone who is not one of them. However, those in whom they placed their trust have betrayed them. Instead of being hailed as saviours of the nation, they are now vilified as enemies of the State. The Government has declared a State of Emergency and the police, the army and the navy have opened fire on their comrades.

At first, Tissa's men followed wherever he led, looting, killing and raping, laying waste to villages and plantations, the viciousness of their actions inspiring terror in a much greater area than was actually affected. But now, their enthusiasm has begun to wane. This is no army, well-disciplined and deployed. It has no strategy except that of pure destruction and the wreaking of revenge. Without a real leader, they have nowhere to go, no purpose and no future.

Tissa's supporters have begun to melt away. The first to leave were those who played a lesser part in the violence, thieves and looters mainly, who watched from the sidelines while the real damage was done by others. Since the first departure, there has been a gradual attrition, until now only the hard core remains; those who believed that their service to the nation would be recognised. But now, even they are forced to acknowledge that political control, whoever wields it, will never be conceded to them. They will remain what they have always been: insignificant, deluded and powerless. A little violent enthusiasm might be tolerated now and again by those in authority, but sooner or later it must be reined in.

"Give me some tea," Tissa demands. One of the men obliges. All eyes turn towards him expectantly. He is their line of communication to Anil and now, in need of direction, they wait hopefully for news. Tissa takes the tin cup that is offered him, drains it quickly, then holds it out for more.

"Give me something to eat."

Rice and rotis are swiftly found and he falls upon them hungrily, shovelling the food into his mouth like a starving beggar. Once finished, he does not speak, but stares into the fire again, absorbed by its crackling flames.

"Have you heard from Anil?" one man ventures. "Has he sent a message yet?" "No."

Tissa continues to stare into the fire. The men exchange furtive glances.

"Do you know where he is?" the man persists.

Tissa shakes his head. The men begin to mutter amongst themselves.

"What are we supposed to do?" asks another man.

"Wait."

Raising his eyes from the fire, Tissa shoots the man a murderous look.

A young fellow, bolder than the rest, gets to his feet and slings his cup to the ground.

"You can all wait if you like, but I'm going home. We've already waited for three days. The food's run out and we can't live on thin air."

There are several nods of agreement.

"Is that all you can think about? Your bellies!"

Tissa rises, flinging his cup into the fire. There is a hiss as the dregs of liquid spill onto the flames.

The other men gaze sullenly at the ground; one begins to trace circles in the dust with his finger; another stares into the trees, apparently preoccupied by the scuffling of an animal. A few days ago, Tissa's words would have roused them, but now they are weary, glutted with violence, homesick for their families.

They are not soldiers or revolutionaries capable of sustaining a long campaign through discipline or conviction. They are day-labourers whose moods and instincts often reflect those of the village animals with whom they share their lives. Like bulls, stung to madness by the persistent pique of flies, they occasionally express their frustration in brief episodes of violence only to sink back into passive obscurity once the urge has been satisfied or the source of irritation removed.

"Pigs! Cattle!" Tissa yells.

Eyes bolting from his head, arms jerking wildly, he appears to dance before them, spittle flying from his mouth as he rages at their obstinacy; a banshee reduced to screaming impotence.

The men are unmoved. They sit at his feet, as stubbornly silent as a ring of stones. If a hundred Tamils were to jump out of the trees at this point, they would offer no resistance. The fighting talk which so recently incensed them, now inspires only apathy. The more Tissa insults them, the more they are inclined to inaction.

One man looks at another, catching his eye with a sideways glance. Silently, the message is transferred, like a charm passed from hand to hand in a children's game, until the circle is complete. Then the first man stands up and, without looking at Tissa, walks slowly away into the trees. In a few seconds, he is followed by another, then another, until all have drifted away into the shadows, as harmless and insubstantial as ghosts.

Furious, Tissa kicks at a tin cup, abandoned by one of the men. It goes spinning through the trees, landing in the undergrowth with a muffled clang. Looking back over his shoulder, one of the men laughs aloud. Inflamed, Tissa picks up a small rock and throws it at one of the retreating shadows. Missing its target, the stone falls to earth with a dull thud.

**

Tissa stares into the fire: watching as branches catch light, smoke, turn red then crumble apart, forming piles of embers; watching as the embers cool from blood red to orange, then turn to ash. He does not know how long he has been sitting here, nursing his rage now that the men have deserted him.

As the shadows creep closer to the fire, a speck of doubt enters his mind; a tiny germ, smaller than a pinprick. Swiftly, it takes root and begins to grow, poisonous, dark and deadly, insinuating itself into every channel of his brain, until only one thought remains. Anil has abandoned him.

He digs his fingers into the soil, clenching his fist. He has committed his soul to Anil, murdered, raped and tortured in his name. But what if Anil has betrayed him? He closes his eyes, lets the darkness consume him. He remembers the madness that took him after the loss of Sriya. Anil saved him. But, without Anil, madness will return. He is on the brink, a bottomless black pit yawning at his feet. He must find Anil. Discover the truth. Save himself.

Tissa heads back to Mennan's camp, the last place he saw Anil. Re-tracing his steps, he clings to the shadows like a lonely beast of prey, avoiding villages, careful, now that he is alone. He stalks through groves and fields, anger boiling within him, fuelled by fear. He eats little, drinking only from streams and springs, unwilling to risk visiting a well where he might be seen.

Tired and light-headed from hunger, he reaches the camp after a journey of three days. It is silent, long shafts of sunlight streaming down from the high canopy of trees, illuminating lush clumps of arum lilies. The bare soil of the clearing is now covered with a fuzz of green growth, grasses, creepers and vines. Thin green spikes are pushing through the cracks of the verandah outside Mennan's hut, its door hanging limply from one hinge. The steps are nearly submerged by plants, pushing their way up towards the sunlight: the railings, choked with bines of morning glory, are covered in a profusion of purple flowers.

Kark! On the balustrade, sits a great black crow, eyeing Tissa menacingly. It looks like the one he killed. Perhaps it is its mate. He will kill this one, too, if he gets a chance. Kark! Tipping its head to one side, the crow clicks its great black beak. Careful not to look at the bird, Tissa bends low, picks up a stone then, swift as lightning, hurls it at the crow. It misses, but only by inches, hitting the wood with a thwack and sending up a shower of mildew-softened splinters. The crow squawks, falls backwards in surprise, its wings outstretched, its legs held stiffly in front of it. It lands on the verandah, out of range, hidden by a screen of vegetation. But he can hear its long talons, clattering up and down the wooden planks.

Tissa hunts around. There are no signs of recent occupation. No ash from a camp-fire, no tracks, just a green box, jutting out of the gloom, a skull and crossbones still visible on its side. And something else. Lying just beyond. As his ears become attuned to the sounds of the clearing, he notices something else. A humming, hissing sound. He walks towards the box and, as he approaches, a black cloud lifts from the thing beyond. He turns his face away, retching, his nose and mouth filled with the stench of rotting meat. The black cloud hovers, expectantly, then breaks up as he nears, revealing its secret. A body, partially consumed by flies, the sockets of its eyes hollowed out, unrecognisable except for its yellow robes.

"Anil! Anil! My brother!"

Tissa's howls are swallowed by the forest.

***

He finds a spade, hanging on a nail in the hut, and buries the body. As he pulls the stinking, slippery mass into the grave, something falls to the ground. He pays it no attention at first, intent on covering the corpse, patting the soft soil down with the back of the spade. He would have liked to build a pyre, but cannot risk the plume of smoke, a visible sign of his presence. Burying Anil's body is the best he can do, better it should be eaten by worms than flies. Having finished his labour, he sits at the head of the grave, weeping, intoning Anil's name like a prayer, over and over, as if repetition will summon him from the grave.

Exhausted, he wipes his eyes and, putting out his hand, his fingers touch something hard and cold. Anil's gun. The one which he had kept to kill Asoka. Tissa turns it over in his hands. Idly, he flips it open and realises that three of the chambers are empty. Several bullets have been fired. For many minutes, he sits musing, staring at the gun, letting it speak to him. It is a message from Anil. Fallen from his robes. A gift. Tissa was meant to find it. He wonders what happened to the bullets. Anil's body was too badly decomposed to tell how he had died. Once more, he is overcome by loss. Holding the gun in his lap, he hangs his head and weeps, filled with a blank void of misery.

Like a drowning man, he surfaces, momentarily. In these few seconds of clarity, he knows that he must move, leave this place or sink, with his tears, into the soil. He rises heavily to his feet, the gun still in his hands. He looks at it, thinks for a while, then places it carefully within his robes. A memento. Perhaps something more. Raising his head, he looks up to the small tract of blue sky, immaculate beyond the dark outline of the trees. He cannot tell what time it is, or how long he has been here.

He stares ahead, at the dark mass of the forest, rising like an impenetrable wall at the edge of the clearing. Which way? He sobs, shaken by a sudden spasm of grief, as lost and lonely as an abandoned child. Then, he hears it. Anil's voice. Soft, barely audible, like a sigh. *This way*, it breathes. *This way*. Still blinded by tears, he follows it to the edge of the clearing where a narrow track opens up between the trees. *This way*. The voice seems louder now, urging him to follow. Tissa brushes his eyes with the back of his hand. He hesitates. The voice becomes fainter. He must not lose it. He plunges headlong into the forest, stumbling over tree roots, groping at branches with his hands to try and steady himself. As he follows, the voice becomes stronger.

"Anil," he murmurs.

This way, answers the voice, soft and soothing, soughing between the leaves like a breath of air. Sometimes, it is ahead of him, at others, to the side. If he hesitates, it grows fainter. If he halts, the darkness rushes him, threatening to swallow him up. He must keep moving, follow the serpentine trail that switches this way and that between the trees, twisting and turning, constantly changing direction like a living creature.

This way. This way, hisses the voice, encouraging, enticing, promising relief from his agony. Desperately, he tries to keep pace. He runs without seeing, frequently stumbles, is gouged by thorns, tripped by vines and scourged by unknown plants, their stems as rough as ground glass.

This way. Anil's voice. Calling him. Deeper and deeper, into the heart of the forest where, at last, he will be able to bury his grief in primeval darkness.

***

Hooniyam sits on a rock, his head resting on his chin, reflecting. Between his feet, lies the figure of a man, wrapped in what appears to be a ragged saffron cloth. The man is sleeping, curled up like a child, his knees drawn up to his chest, his arms folded around him. Hooniyam bends over to inspect him. From the head, once shaven, sprouts a wild mane of hair, filthy, black and matted, while, at either corner of the mouth, long, uneven teeth protrude over the lower lip. Hooniyam strokes the man's head, patting it affectionately as one might pet a dog.

"Anil," the man moans in his sleep.

"Shh! I am here."

761

Hooniyam speaks in Anil's voice. The man sighs and rolls back onto his side. Hooniyam sits back and smiles, admiring his handiwork. His skills as a god are limited, but he still has the power to convert a man into a demon. And Tissa is perfect material. For he is made of baser stuff than most. Being closer to clay, he is easier to turn. Like a pot, he can be shaped. But he will never rival his master.

At the thought of Anil, a shadow falls over Hooniyam's heart. It might be centuries before he finds another like him. He tried to catch Anil's soul as it left his body, but it was too quick for him, slipping through his fingers like quicksilver and disappearing with a sigh, carried off to the place where souls await rebirth. Who knows when that will be, or what form Anil will take. Whenever it is, Hooniyam knows that the gods will use the opportunity to spite him. For they have discovered his plan.

He sinks into gloomy reflection. He planned a civil war among men to distract the gods from his own scheme to seize power. He intended to make himself the supreme deity, using his demons to ensnare the gods and subject them to his will. But he has failed. The dissension sown by him has failed to bear fruit. There have been riots, violence and a lot of bad feeling, but nothing more. He cannot understand it. He was so sure of success. But the failure of his plan has led to discovery. Someone has talked. A lesser demon, probably, trying to save his miserable skin. And now the gods are looking for Hooniyam. It is only a matter of time before he is caught.

The man at his feet rolls over and groans. Hooniyam looks at him, thoughtfully. Perhaps, not everything is lost. There is still time to serve out those who betrayed him. One, in particular. *Tic, tac, tic.* Hooniyam drums his long nails on the rock. A new plan begins to form. Hooniyam chuckles. The thought of revenge always cheers him.

He leans forward and scratches the sleeping man behind the ears.

"I have work for you," he whispers in Anil's voice.

Tissa whines in his sleep, like a dog.

Ella has no idea where she is going, whether her family is alive or dead, or, if alive, where she will find them. So, for want of a better plan, she follows the stream of people leaving the city. Some carry bedrolls and bags; others, nothing at all. Many are Tamils, but there are also Sinhalese and Moslems, all headed they know not where in the slender hope of finding safety. Every day, they walk for many miles, without shelter from the sun and, often, without food or water.

Exhaustion and disease soon take their toll of the weakest. It is a familiar sight; small groups of relatives, huddled around a sick or dying person at the side of the road, murmuring to each other anxiously, suggesting remedies to which they have no access, holding hands, whispering encouragement, hoping that the worst will not happen then, when it does, sitting by the road, their heads on each other's shoulders, weeping and inconsolable. The travellers who pass these little groups, lower their heads and look away, trying to distance themselves from the infection of despair that travels quicker than any disease and kills just as certainly.

"Good morning, sister."

A man is picking at Ella's shawl with trembling, agitated fingers.

"Hello."

Her heart sinks, but she does not turn him away. He has been travelling with their group for several days, alone, speaking to anyone who will listen with nervous intensity. Another woman in the group, walking alongside, casts a sideways look at Ella, expressing a mixture of sympathy and relief. Ella notices that the woman has begun to distance herself, taking a few steps to the side, until she is walking at the edge of the group, as far from Ella and the man as she can get.

The man's name is Mahendran. They all know him. In civilian life, he was a doctor, well-to-do and middle class. His speech and manner still bear the mark of education and a good upbringing. He uses words that Ella has never heard. At first, she assumed that it was her ignorance that prevented her from understanding him. Until another of her companions told her Mahendran's history.

A Tamil from Polonnaruwa, his home was targeted by rioters. They had broken into the house, late one night, and Mahendran had been forced to watch as his wife and daughter were gang-raped, then burned alive by the goondas. With a flourish of sadistic logic, the attackers had then reasoned that the man's suffering would be increased if they left him alive. So, with a torturer's mercy, they spared him.

Having disposed of the charred remains of his wife and child, he took to the road, trying to escape the horrors constantly re-enacted in his head and the guilt of his own impotence. But the atrocities that he had witnessed pursued him, both waking and sleeping, like a horde of shrieking banshees. They drove him on, never allowing him to rest, until sanity finally parted with reason.

He is a philosopher, of a kind, trying to apply learning to his madness, trying to make sense of his incoherent train of thought. Speaking in Sanskrit, he quotes the scriptures, reciting the Bhagavad Gita for hours on end to anyone who will listen, always ending with Vishnu's words: *I am become death, the destroyer of worlds.* Like a fool in the court of a medieval king, he is a constant reminder of unpleasant truths. His presence is a burden, but no-one has the heart to turn him away, each taking turns to listen to the stream of nonsense that issues from his mouth.

"It has all been written. There is a reason. Listen. I will quote to you."

Tilting his head towards Ella, he begins to recite from the Bhagavad Gita, speaking with rapid desperation, pointing to the sky with one finger to emphasise passages of particular importance.

"Do you not see? Does it not make sense?"

His eyes shine with the wild light of one who has not slept for many days. At night, when they are all lying at the side of the road, looking up at the stars, shivering with their own loneliness, they can hear him, reciting everlasting verses.

"Do you agree, sister?"

He plucks at Ella's shawl.

"Yes, of course."

She smiles, reassuringly and, for a moment, he seems to take comfort, a misty look in his eyes as if he senses peace. But, in a second, it has passed and he is off again, gabbling in Sanskrit, Tamil and English, his eyes bright with insane zeal. He squeezes her arm as he points to the sky. Ella can almost smell his madness: the dirty, sweaty odour of a man driven by the relentless working of his mind.

For many weary miles, she listens to his ramblings, until she feels as if he will drag her down with him, down into a pit with unscaleable walls. His constant chatter wears her down, tiring her more completely than any physical exertion.

The sun is sinking and people are settling by the roadside: some, almost collapsing with exhaustion, sleeping where they fall; others, sharing what little food they have with their families. Ella has brought a little bread from the church, her own portion as well as that of the girl from the village, still sleeping at her side. She felt a twinge of guilt at the time, but not now. Shakti will get more food from the nuns but, once Ella's small ration runs out, there will be nothing between her and starvation unless she can reach a camp.

The man is sitting at her side, his head raised to the sky where the pale image of the moon shines like the face of a ghost. His upstretched neck is thin and scrawny with a tracery of thick veins and the outline of a large Adam's apple that quivers when he swallows. He is silent, staring at the moon, his cheeks wet with tears.

"Here," says Ella, gently nudging his elbow. "Eat this."

The man takes the bread she offers, but he does not eat it, just holds it in his hand, working it with his fingers. As Ella settles down to sleep, wrapping her thin shawl around her, she has a last image of the man, still staring at the moon, the bread in his hand.

**

Ella wakes, chilled by the night, her head thick from fatigue and lack of food. She hears voices, close by, like the angry murmur of bees. Sitting up, she rubs her eyes, then pulls herself onto her knees, squatting back on her heels as she looks around her. A little mound of white crumbs, the remains of the bread that she gave the man, is lying beside her. She sees a group of people, gathered round a tree, staring at something.

Unsteadily, she gets to her feet, rubbing her arms with her hands, trying to get a little warmth into her veins. Drawn by the crowd, she walks slowly towards it, yawning, pushing her hair back behind her ears. As she gets closer, she has a better view of the tree. Something white, like a bundle of cloth, seems to be suspended from the branches. Then, the crowd parts, and she sees that it is the man, her companion of the previous day.

"Hanged himself," says a woman from the group. "We found him this morning."

764

Already, they are turning away, returning to the places where they have spent the night, picking up their things, moving on. Some cross themselves and others pray, but no-one wants to touch him believing, somehow, that it will bring bad luck, for he was the mirror of their despair.

"Poor man," says a woman, standing nearby. But the relief in her face is plain.

1958: Refugees

Crowds of refugees clog the roads and sometimes it seems as if the whole country is on the move. Some seek refuge in churches and temples; others make for the camps where they hope to find missing relatives. Refugee camps are makeshift, overcrowded and badly-equipped, with endless queues at the stand-pipes and little food to go around.

In Colombo alone, the refugee population numbers twelve thousand. Yet, even here, in the cosmopolitan atmosphere of the capital, Sinhalese and Tamils are accommodated in separate camps. Even here, where the homeless, hungry and traumatised, are herded together like cattle, language is still regarded as a potentially explosive issue.

While visiting a camp, one politician notices that the sign for the men's lavatory is written in Tamil. He insists that it should be taken down immediately and replaced with an English sign. It is unclear whether his motive is due to racism, or a fear that a Tamil sign will attract new trouble from the goondas. However, a temporary return to the neutral language of the Empire is clearly regarded as preferable to the use of either Tamil or Sinhalese.

But such issues are of little consequence to those who have lost their homes, livelihoods and loved ones. Every day of trudging over hot tarmac, unprotected from the sun, carrying parcels of possessions, children, the sick or the old, tire them more, draining both body and soul. Their feet bleed and they become weak from lack of food. Water they get where they can: from wells, tanks, streams, even from puddles where nothing else is to hand and, inevitably, they become sick.

Country people, farm-workers and servants, fare best for they are used to long, back-breaking hours of physical labour. The blistering heat of the sun hardly seems to touch them. From childhood, they have trained themselves to deny the discomfort of fatigue so that they no longer feel it.

It is the middle classes who suffer the most; accustomed to regular meals, baths and freshly-laundered clothes, travel by car and taxi and servants to do their bidding. They have no way of dealing with the aches and pains of exhaustion, the sores on their feet, or the hunger in their bellies, because, until now, they have been used to dealing only with minor discomfort: the late running of a train, too much spice in their curry, a badly-pressed shirt. And there is something else that saps their energy more surely than physical pain, because it attacks the soul. The loss of status. For doctors, lawyers, teachers and civil servants, now form part of a new class: the homeless and dispossessed. As such, they are insignificant and of no account. They have as much, or as little, claim on other people's charity as the lowliest farm-worker.

It is a crippling blow to those who have been brought up to think of themselves as being entitled to a privileged place in society. The realisation that they are dependent on fate, not birth, for the necessities of food and water, enlightens some and destroys others.

Soldiers are handing out food from the back of a truck. They try to keep order but the crowd is impatient, pushing and squirming, arms outstretched; a thick, toiling mass coiled around the base of the truck, like a giant millipede. It is impossible for the people on the outer edges to break through, so the soldiers have to throw the food over the heads of those nearest them. A dozen hands reach for one loaf of bread, tearing it to pieces, none of them getting more than a mouthful.

There is much shoving and stamping while elbows are employed to manoeuvre a space a few inches closer to the truck. Squabbles break out, particularly among the women who are desperate to feed their children. The wives of doctors and peasants fight like fishwives, slapping and shrieking, tugging at small bags of rice or flour. Middle-class women, incensed that food has been snatched out of their hands, are the most vocal, while peasants simply hang on to their prizes with a look of deadly resolution. It is an expression that has developed through generations of famine and disease, a ruthless determination to survive.

On the fringe of the crowd, another fight has broken out. Three women are contesting ownership of a small loaf. They are middle-class women, not used to hardship, but they fight like cats, pulling at scarves and hair, gouging at eyes with varnished nails which now look like the nails of sluts because they are chipped and broken.

"Ha, ha, ha. Look at them!"

An old man with white hair and a concave chest is enjoying the spectacle. He is frail, hardly more than a skeleton wrapped in skin. His ribs stick out of his chest and, every so often, he has to stop laughing in order to breathe. He has the husky cackle of an asthmatic.

"Ha, ha, ha!"

He slaps his skinny side and wheezes with pleasure. He is pale, exhausted by the exertion of laughing, but his eyes twinkle spitefully. He gasps his remarks to a woman beside him. She is tall and thin, with protruding teeth and large feet; like a great, gaunt wading bird. She watches silently. It is impossible to tell from her face what she is thinking.

One of the women lands a blow on her rival's nose. It is a chance hit, but successful. There is a scream and the other woman puts her hand up to her face. Blood oozes through her fingers. She has a nosebleed, if not a broken nose. Weeping, she holds her hand to her face. The blood runs up her arm, off her elbow, then onto her sari, staining the expensive green silk with a tracery of crimson splashes.

"Look! Look!"

With delight, the old man elbows his neighbour, directing her gaze to the weeping woman who is now retiring into the crowd, the arm of an elderly lady draped protectively around her shoulders. The old woman is shouting something at the two remaining contenders, but the competition for the loaf is too fierce for them to listen.

One of the women is tall with long arms, but she is older, about forty, moving with the slow, stilted gait of a crane. The other woman is young, more flexible, in her early twenties. She has green eyes and thick, lustrous hair. Some might call her a beauty. She has a sinuous, leopard-like grace and a hungry, desperate need to win. Cat-like, she springs at the other woman, digging her nails into her face. The woman screams and tries to beat her off, shrieking with fear as the girl's fingers claw at her eyes. Struggling, she pushes her aggressor away, then runs into the crowd.

The girl picks up the loaf, glaring tigerishly at the onlookers, daring anyone to oppose her. She is slender and voluptuous, agile with a quality of danger. The men stare at her. For the first time in weeks, they feel the stirring of desire. But she is not interested in them.

Clutching the loaf to her breast, she pushes through the crowd to where another woman is waiting for her. The woman must be the girl's mother, for she has the same green eyes, but that is where the likeness ends. She has large elastic lips, painted bright red, even in this dismal place. Until recently, she was as fat as a marrow; but now, the skin hangs in pouches from her face. They quiver when she talks or moves, like the wattles of a turkey. She is holding a bundle, wrapped in a sari.

The girl hands the loaf to her mother and takes the bundle. Her expression changes instantly to one of tenderness. She pushes back the folds of cloth and looks inside. A tiny fist appears, flexes its fingers, clutches a strand of the girl's hair. She bends over and kisses it. Dalia has had her baby. By the roadside. With only her mother for company. For Michael never returned.

The soldiers are shouting something from the back of the truck. The crowd surges forward. The woman, recently beaten in the contest for the loaf, pushes past the old man and his companion.

"Hello Mrs Mahadeva."

The old man taunts the woman. She nods at him, then dives away. She does not want to be recognised. She still has enough self-respect to feel ashamed.

"Ha, ha, ha. See that! My doctor's wife. He treated me for many years and every time he saw me, he told me that it would be the last. A big strong fellow, he was. Half my age. Caught dengue fever on the road. Now he's gone and I'm still here."

The old man wheezes at the joke, enjoying the irony. His doctor has died while he has cheated death. It is a victory of sorts. His breath comes in shallow gasps, he coughs and his lips become wet with spittle. The woman by his side is silent. Ella has travelled many miles to reach this camp. It is one of the smaller camps, nameless, created by the army outside an insignificant village on some rough ground. Those who are lucky sleep under canvas, those who are not sleep exposed to the sky, wrapped only in their clothes.

Close by, another fight has broken out. Two more women fighting to the death over scraps. Ella watches them, scratching and biting, tearing each other's clothes. One is hit in the stomach and collapses, weeping. A soldier jumps down from the truck. The crowd parts to let him through. The army has threatened to fire on the crowds if things get out of hand. The soldier pushes his way to where the women are still fighting and breaks them up, pulling them roughly apart. They howl and spit. One scratches him. He slaps her. She screams in indignation.

"Do you know who my husband is?"

"No and I don't care."

The old asthmatic laughs until his lips are blue. Then, reaching into his clothes, he produces a crust of bread. Placing the end in his mouth, he sucks on it, like a child. His front teeth are gone and he cannot chew. He must make the bread wet before he can swallow. In a bag, strapped to his waist under the loose folds of his shirt, he has several other crusts.

He has food to spare, but he does not offer to share it. Years of illness have made him selfish. That is how he survives. But Ella has seen. She stares at him, her face impassive. He is hoarding. Even these few crusts are more than most people have. If word were to get out, he would not be able to protect his treasure. He looks into her eyes, cunning as an old fox.

"I will give you bread if you keep quiet"

Despite herself, she agrees. She is too hungry to refuse. Keeping her arm pressed to her side, so that no-one can see, she extends her fingers and feels the old man pressing a crust into her hand. With an almost imperceptible gesture of her head, she thanks him, then walks away from the crowd around the truck, unable to bear the sight of more fighting.

1958: Water

Early morning in the refugee camp. People are stirring, yawning, stretching. Despite the hard, stony ground, Ella has slept for many hours, although her sleep was disturbed by the sound of voices: her children. But it was just a dream. Her cheeks are wet with tears. Reluctantly, she opens her eyes.

A woman died in the night and is being carried away on a stretcher. The dead must be disposed of quickly to prevent the spreading of disease. There is no ceremony, no time to say goodbye. The bodies are simply disposed of. No-one knows how. No-one cares to ask. Even their grieving families acknowledge that no more can be done. There is no fuel for funeral pyres, no churches, no mosques. Christians, Buddhists, Hindus and Moslems must share the same fate.

Ella sits up and rubs her aching limbs. She is thirsty and must join the queue at the stand-pipe. It is early but, already, many people have gathered to wait. Water has leaked into the ground around the tap and been churned into mud by the refugees. Those returning from the stand-pipe have feet caked in brown slime. Soon it will dry and turn into a pale coating that, from a distance, resembles shoes. Some do not even bother to brush it off. What is the point when one must visit the stand-pipe several times a day?

Ella gets in line and waits patiently. Her head is still thick with sleep. She feels as if she is still dreaming, for she keeps hearing voices in her head. The voices of her children. There is a sudden wail at the front of the queue. A child is crying.

Ella feels a shiver passing up her spine. Suddenly galvanised, she throws herself forward, pushing through the crowd, not listening to the tut-tutting of the elderly matrons that she thrusts aside. It is like swimming through treacle. The people in front, thinking that she is jumping the queue, try to close ranks. But she knows that voice.

If people do not move, she pushes them aside, using her elbows, knees and feet to shift the most stubborn. She hears another voice. Her own. Calling the name of her child. A voice as wild as a madwoman. Screaming. Shrieking. Unearthly. Desperate. At last, she is at the front of the queue. And there, in front of her, is her mother and three of her children.

The sun slides into the sky and light trickles through the steaming canopy of the forest, waking the birds. Barbets, parakeets and hoopoes, all join the cacophony of screeching, squawking and squabbling that begins the day and, as light filters down through the trees, other forest-dwellers awake. Langur monkeys yawn and stretch, scratching themselves like old men, before gingerly feeling their way along the branches in search of food.

On the forest floor, strings of ants move in close formation, foraging, hunting, swarming over small creatures that have fallen in the night, delivering the coup de grâce where necessary: a mobile processing plant, delivering food to the masses with ruthless efficiency. Working as one, the ants scour the forest floor, clearing up the leavings of their neighbours, sometimes clearing up the neighbours themselves. A beetle, encountering some soldier ants, is flipped on its back and butchered, then quickly dispatched to the nest.

A stray ant, wandering away from its detachment, discovers an object of interest: immense, like a range of hills. It smells different. The ant pauses, its antennae trembling. The object does not have the pungent smell of soil, or the aromatic odour of bark or leaf. It is as large as a rock but, unlike stone, it varies in texture and colour. Propelled by instinct, the ant sets off to explore. Finding a convenient foothold, it begins to scale the mysterious object. Antennae waving furiously, the ant begins to decipher a subtle language of odours: salt, the sour tang of bacteria that feed on sweat and other aromas reminiscent of animals.

The ant runs about excitedly, here and there, picking up signals, both foreign and familiar, hostile and enticing. It finds a strange, brown growth: fungus-shaped, like the sort often found on a tree, its ridges and channels leading down to a dark, well-shaped hollow; a further opportunity for exploration. The ant circles the hollow, considering the best approach. Suddenly, the earth quakes under the ant's feet. A giant, flailing object falls from the sky and slaps at the ground, sending the ant flying into the undergrowth.

"Aaargh!" screams the object.

Tissa raises himself from where he has been lying, his hair and skin dusty with the fine earth on which he has slept. He wipes his face with his hands, grinding particles of dirt into his skin. Licking his lips, he tastes the musty flavour of soil. It is not unpleasant. Months ago, driven mad by the loss of Sriya, he took refuge in the forest, living like an outcast. Now, after a brief respite, he is an outcast again.

Everyone has deserted him: Anil, his men, Sriya. So, he has taken his revenge: raping village girls, torturing their men, killing whenever he can. At first, his venom was directed at Tamils but, lately, he has become less discriminating. Like a drunk with a hangover, he struggles to recall the events of the previous day. They return in fragments, both thrilling and disgusting.

He recalls a clearing at the edge of a village. There was a chicken scratching at the dirt in a yard. Tissa was hungry and without a second thought he had pounced on the bird and wrung its neck.

Next, he remembers a voice. An old man, shouting feebly, was hurrying towards him, waving a machete. The old man's legs were bowed, his feet large and bony, splayed outwards, paddling over the ground as if he were wading through a paddy field. Tissa had laughed.

Enraged, the old man had thrown himself upon the intruder, spluttering curses through his broken teeth. Tissa, still laughing, had caught him in his arms. The old man had struggled to get free.

"Now, Grandad, save your energy. Too much excitement is bad at your age."

"You young bastard," croaked the old man. "Let me go. Hey, hey. Help me someone."

He had swiped about with the machete and caught Tissa on the shin, splitting the skin and causing Tissa to yelp with pain.

"Hey ..."

The old man's cries for help were cut short. His neck had been snapped with the same cold efficiency as that of the hen. Tissa had dropped the body where he stood, not even bothering to hide it, and walked calmly into the forest, the dead bird dangling from one hand.

As he thinks of it, Tissa's member swells and, slipping his hand inside his sarong, he takes what comfort he can. When it is over, he lies gasping on the forest floor, then laughs till he cries.

**

Feeling hungry, Tissa searches in the canvas bag that he has been carrying with him; a trophy from an early raid on a Tamil store. He cooked the chicken over a small brush fire last night and has wrapped its remains in a palm frond. As he removes it from the bag, something catches his eye. He reaches in and takes it out. It is a mirror, the folding sort that a woman might carry. He does not know how it got there. He turns it over in his hand.

Then, he sees his reflection: red, inflamed eyes; hollow cheeks, a great gash running across one of them; and, a dishevelled mane of hair, coarse with dust and shreds of vegetation. The face of a demon. With a cry, he smashes the mirror against a stone and throws the remains into the bushes.

Well, let Sriya see him like this. That will teach her. And, if she rejects him, there is always something else, something that will make him irresistible.

1958: A broken home

After several days' rest, Asoka is well enough to leave the monastery. At dawn, he slips out of a side entrance, a parcel of rice and vegetables, saved from the previous night, tucked inside his clothes. Unlatching the heavy wooden door, he steps out into the world and, as he does so, his heart seems to catch light, blazing up within him. At last, he is going home. Soon, he will be re-united with Sriya and the child that he has not yet seen. It is like being reborn.

With his face raised to the sun, he pauses to admire the sky, taking a deep draught of cool morning air as he savours his freedom. He must get home. As soon as possible. He pulls the door shut behind him. It grumbles, grinding on its hinges. The iron latch drops with a sharp click, severing his link to the world within, a place of timeless peace that, for a short while, has been his haven. Asoka is thankful, but not sorry. It is no longer his world. Perhaps it never was. A life of prayer and solitary contemplation could never satisfy him; especially now, having tasted the joy of human love.

In the lee of the monastery wall, flower-sellers and beggars are taking up their positions for the day and the pavement glistens with patches of freshly-chewed betel; crimson stains, the colour of blood. Asoka drifts into the road, crossing to the shady side where he passes an elderly beggar, sitting under a tree, his scrawny arm stretched out for alms. The old man has long, yellow nails. A pye-dog is snuffling around his feet, scratching at the dirt with ragged claws. Companions of the street, they seem almost to be related.

Asoka passes by, trying not to catch the man's eye. He does not wish to be noticed. Although the police have other matters to attend to, he could still be arrested for Mennan's murder. Arjun gave him a reprieve, but not one that will count in law.

Asoka has directions from the young monk who befriended him in the monastery. The route will take him through a couple of towns and several villages. It will not be safe, nowhere is, but it is preferable to following hidden paths through the jungle. Only those with local knowledge can do that and, if anything, remote parts of the countryside offer less protection than urban areas.

In towns and cities, now patrolled by the army and police, the dusk to dawn curfew is strictly enforced. However, in rural areas, outside the immediate control of the authorities, the observance of curfew is more lax and many goondas are still at large, roaming the countryside in small bands, looking for easy pickings. Lawlessness has brought them a measure of freedom and they are reluctant to sink back into obscurity and the thankless drudgery of a labourer's life.

Asoka has no choice. He must risk a higher degree of visibility if he wishes to travel at all and keep to the high roads. He must trust his senses to warn him of danger and leave the road, to seek cover, whenever he hears the distant rumble of an engine.

***

He has not travelled far, but he is already tired. The lack of food and repeated beatings that he suffered on his forced march with Anil are still taking their toll. He finds a quiet street with one or two large, but decaying residences whose windows have been boarded up: old colonial buildings for which no-one seems to have any use. The once-elegant gardens are now overgrown with a tangle of vegetation, a rich hunting ground for pye-dogs and feral cats. The door of one building has been torn off its hinges and the interior is now open to the elements. Asoka climbs over the wall and makes his way up the gravel path which is covered with a tapestry of weeds. He climbs the steps and looks inside.

The building has been unoccupied for some time and, having been left open to the elements, has started to decay. Plaster is peeling from the walls and thick piles of droppings indicate that pigeons are nesting in the upper windows. Heat and humidity have rotted the wooden staircase that once led to the first floor. The planks, blackened and soft, will no longer hold the weight of a man. There is something strangely enticing about a staircase that can no longer be used and that, perhaps, leads nowhere. For, by the piles of rubble lying in the rooms adjoining the hall, it looks as if the ceilings have collapsed. The stairs will not only lead to empty rooms, but to empty space.

Asoka had thought to rest in here, away from prying eyes, but the atmosphere is stifling. To breathe the air here is to fill one's lungs with decay. And there is something else. A reflection of current circumstances; a message too close to home. These are not the elegant ruins of an ancient civilisation, but the rotting carcase of one that is newly-dead.

Asoka leaves the house, treading carefully over the gravel path whose undergrowth may conceal scorpions and spiders. Then, climbing back over the wall, he seats himself on a dusty knoll in the shade of a mango tree. A pall of silence hangs over this town, and only a few people have ventured onto the street. They creep furtively along the pavement, keeping to the shelter of the houses, forced out of their homes by the need to find food or relatives who have not returned home.

An elderly man, a basket on his back, his sarong hitched up over skinny knees, shuffles past, muttering to himself. The only one who seems untouched by fear or apprehension. He crosses to the middle of the street and stoops to examine something in the dust, falling on it with predatory glee. Pinching it delicately between thumb and forefinger, he holds the object up to the sunlight for a closer look.

Intrigued by the old man, Asoka wonders what it is that has such power to draw him out into the open and hold his attention. He squints into the sun, trying to get a better look. The old man cackles and, turning suddenly to Asoka, holds out his prize. But his hand is empty. Now Asoka understands the reason for the old man's lack of fear. Those who are deranged are immune to the madness of others. He probably continued to roam the streets during the riots, ignorant of the chaos around him, ignored by those who caused it. In such times, thinks Asoka, lunatics may be at an advantage.

The old man's face suddenly changes. The smile is replaced by a snarl. Through some change, apparent only to the madman's inner eye, Asoka has been transformed into an aggressor, one who covets his invisible prize. The old man spits and, producing a strange, low growl from the pit of his throat, sidles away, uttering curses that are no less potent for being incomprehensible.

But Asoka smiles, tolerant of the other man's weakness. He even feels a stab of envy. The beggar is unrestrained by thoughts of religion, race or politics. His unique view of the world gives him a certain liberty: freedom, regardless of circumstance, is sweet. The old man has moved on in search of fresh treasure, talking to himself as he rakes the gutter with his fingers. Getting to his feet, Asoka takes a last look at the building, before skirting the wall, then darting into the tangle of alleyways that lead eventually to the high road.

1958: Tracks

It is a small town. He does not know its name. He passes through streets, scarred and blackened from the recent violence, where fallen debris and smoking remains provide a hunting ground for scavengers, both human and animal. Inhabitants, who have lost their homes, have ventured from their hiding places and are sifting through piles of broken masonry. Each has a different method of searching: some turn the debris over with sticks, inserting them into crevices and holes, as if scared of what they might find; others, more reckless, pull the rubble apart with their hands, scrabbling among the remains like dogs; while others, their faces screwed up in disgust, poke at the debris with their toes.

Sometimes, there is a cry of joy as a blackened memento is retrieved from the ashes. A photograph in a charred frame, a baby's rattle, even a shoe, it does not matter. What matters is that something from a previous life remains intact. A sign of hope. Not everything has been destroyed. Such items become objects of wonder, passed around for inspection, scrutinised, commented on, admired, cradled in the owner's hands as if they were newborn children. Then, carefully wrapped in a fold of the owner's clothes, the treasure is carried away, to be kept in a safe place, a link with the past.

The sour taste of cinders taints Asoka's tongue and his feet throw up puffs of ash as he passes burned-out buildings. The sight of people digging in the remains, rejoicing over the discovery of some small useless item, brings tears to his eyes. But those who affect him the most are those who do not search. Still traumatised, they sit on the pavement where their homes previously stood, staring vacantly at passers-by, unable to comprehend their loss.

An old woman is squatting in the road, her head covered by her scarf, her withered hand held out, begging. A small boy of about six, stands behind her, his huge eyes, dark as liquorice, staring at the stranger. They have none of the guile of professional beggars and Asoka guesses that they are newly homeless, perhaps an orphan and his ageing grandmother, the very old and the very young with only each other for support.

With a shadow over his heart, Asoka passes on. The streets narrow until they are little more than alleys, snaking through hovels that cluster leech-like around the outskirts of the town. The atmosphere is quiet and menacing. Frightened faces peer from the dark recesses of tin shacks. Frightened eyes follow his progress along the road. His coming invokes terror. All sound is stifled, replaced by a silence in which no-one breathes or speaks. Then, after he has passed, the street comes back to life; behind him, always behind him, a dog barks, a child cries, or a pot clangs as it is stirred. Behind him is normality but, if he turns to look, it will disappear: always, in front of him, there is silence. The whole country is convulsed by fear.

He turns into a dark and noisome alleyway where shacks, constructed of planks and corrugated iron, huddle together like robbers. Sacking curtains hang over the doorways. Normally these places would be teeming with people, but they are quiet, deserted although, as he passes, Asoka hears soft movements within the shacks and, sometimes, he glimpses the pale outline of a face at a window before it is quickly withdrawn. The dirt track is wet in places, puddles covered with a layer of green slime that stink if disturbed. Sometimes, the puddle grows into a small lake and it is impossible to pick one's way around it.

Asoka's heart beats faster as he passes through this area. Residents living here might consider it easier to kill him than to wait for an attack. Such is the atmosphere of terror that even one man, if a stranger, is considered a threat. If he dies here, Sriya will never know. She will never get the letter.

Sweat trickles from Asoka's forehead into his eyes. A sacking curtain twitches to the side of him. He catches his breath. A small head peeps out. A child, no more than a toddler peers at him, inquisitive. The mother's face appears beside it, angry and frightened. Asoka smiles at her. She stares at him, her expression frozen, as if turned to stone. Then she pulls the child back inside. The sharp retort of a slap is followed by a wailing cry. He feels guilty. The child has been punished because of him.

Tears well up in his eyes. He wants to sob, tries to swallow the lump lodged in his throat, but still the tears come, coursing down his cheeks. He is quivering. A return of his weakness, perhaps. He has been walking for many hours. But he knows it is something else. He pushes forward, not looking where he puts his feet, smelling the terrible stink of rottenness as he splashes through the green pools scattered across the track.

The alleyway takes a slight, upward turn, then opens out onto a main road. Even the light seems different here, although the spectacle is still a bleak one. On the other side of a railway track, some weary-looking trees with limp branches screen a cemetery; but only partially. The trees are too few and too tired to serve any real purpose. A few shacks huddle beside the graveyard; the bare earth tracks which lead to them scored by deep ruts, filled with rubbish and brackish, rust-coloured water. At regular intervals, trains thunder past, blasting smoke and soot from their funnels, shaking the ground with their great metal wheels, disturbing the peace of the local inhabitants, both living and dead. It is a depressing sight.

Asoka trudges on, following the road which is busier than any he has seen so far. A few lorries pass him on their way into town, loaded with produce from the country: water-melons, leeks, carrots, onions and sacks of rice. It reminds him of home and he wonders if Prema has managed to harvest the rice on his own. He feels a small stab of guilt. Ridiculous, really. It was not his fault that he was abducted but, all the same, he is partly responsible for what happened. His previous life had not let him rest.

He glances at the shacks across the railway line. They are grey and stained with rust. Small children in ragged clothes play in the doorways. Poverty clings to people like clay. It can never be washed away entirely. Even if they escape the shanties, these people will carry the whiff of poverty with them. It is in their blood. Like one's misdeeds. Only, unlike Asoka, the shanty-dwellers have done nothing to deserve their fate. He sighs. Mennan's death still haunts him like a shadow.

The road is dusty and his throat is dry. He is hungry, too. He must find a well or a stand-pipe. Rest. Eat. Almost without thinking, he puts his hand up to his shirt. He has a parcel of food tucked inside. Something crackles. The letter to Sriya. He had forgotten. He will read it again before he gives it to her; make sure that he has told her everything. He needs to be sure that she loves him, truly, for what he is. He needs her forgiveness. Then, everything will be all right. He knows it.

Finally, the last signs of habitation disappear and Asoka is alone. The shanties have vanished and the road curves away from the rail-track, plunging into the green wilderness of the countryside. On either side of the road are coconut groves where men, carrying primitive tools, flit through the dappled light.

Asoka now walks in the shade of palm trees. Agitated by the breeze, their stiff leaves clatter gently overhead and beyond this sound, Asoka imagines that he can hear another: the hissing of waves breaking on a shore. Trees have many languages, all speaking of freedom. They whisper of things forgotten during his captivity: hope, love, joy. His heart leaps. Soon, he will see Sriya.

Many of the villages and hamlets, through which Asoka passes, bear the signs of devastation and yet, in the middle of it all, there are pockets which remain untouched. In one place, homes will have been burned and crops destroyed while, in another settlement, a mile or so down the road, it is as if nothing has happened. Violence seems to have erupted with sudden, primordial force; randomly, without warning, like molten lava surging from the earth's crust. But why here and not there? Why this place and not that?

The more he sees along the way, the more confused Asoka becomes. Were the Tamils the primary target; or even the only one? Did the violence have a single source or many? Having broken the surface, had one grievance acted as a catalyst, inflaming, igniting and reviving others? Was it all organised or, had some of it arisen spontaneously? He does not know.

In one place, white tapes and flags mark the site of a Buddhist funeral ground while, in another, freshly-turned mounds of earth bearing small wooden crosses, bear witness to Christian burials. All were recent; all hastily performed. And still, they are disposing of the dead: those who died, in flight, at the side of the road and others, who died in their homes. Asoka passes many funeral parties with widows, fathers, sisters and brothers, young and old, dressed in white, wailing with grief as they follow the bier.

His heart grows heavy at the sight of so much pain.

***

As he continues his journey, Asoka considers the theories of rebirth and renewal that he learned in his youth. The symbol of the wheel represented fate, life, Buddhist teaching, even political freedom. Strange how the simple turning of a wheel can have such profound meaning and yet, now he thinks of it, it makes sense.

There are many revolutions within the space of a single life. That is fate. But, if one is Buddhist, it does not end there. According to Buddhist belief, the soul is also subject to revolution, a cycle of birth, death and re-birth, repeated over and over until enlightenment is finally achieved, the wheel stops turning and the soul comes to rest.

When Asoka thinks of his country, he sees not one wheel, but many, all representing separate lives, all turning at different speeds, like the workings of a clock: spinning fly-wheels and slow, cumbrous cogs, all interdependent, each completing its own little orbit only to start again, each in constant motion, ceaselessly repeating the same cycle. No single component can operate this machine, but the failure of one can stop it. Gandhi knew that.

It is no coincidence that the wheel was adopted as an emblem of Indian nationality. The spinning wheel symbolised India's political freedom from the British. But the wheel also represents dharma, or religious teaching. And something else. One wheel for one nation. All the separate wheels of individual lives must work together to operate the great wheel of state. Of course, it did not work at first. On attaining Independence, the Indian sub-continent had divided into two nations – Pakistan and India – and there was terrible bloodshed. But did that not prove Gandhi's point? For a nation to survive, everyone must work together. Towards one goal. Not several.

Ceylon professes to be one nation but, at every level, people are striving to achieve different things. Buddhists, nationalists, Tamils, Communists: the list is endless. While all communities contain divisive elements, it is the job of the Government to unite them and direct them towards a single goal.

While India was, initially, subsumed in a bloodbath, it always had a single goal. One created by a visionary. But Ceylon has no Gandhi; nor even a Nehru, for that matter. Its Government is weak and all the individual cogs and wheels that should be working together to drive the nation forward, are operating separately, tearing it apart.

Asoka sighs. He can see no solution. Unless the people, themselves, can work a change. But that will take time. Perhaps, he thinks, he could begin in a small way. He will revive the little school that he started in his village. And Sriya will be at his side.

Just the thought of her warms his heart. It lights something within; a flame that burns steadily, inextinguishable despite the darkness and misery around him. He is going home. He will see her soon. He is gloriously, selfishly happy. Neither the aching of his limbs, nor the sharp stones that cut his feet can weary him. He has a new energy, a purpose, a strength that will carry him to the ends of the earth. If the path before him were covered in hot coals, he would step onto it without hesitation, in the knowledge that Sriya is at the end of it.

His heart races and he feels giddy, like a young man who has fallen in love for the first time. Everywhere he looks, he sees beauty: birds, trees, flowers, all painted in the brightest colours, all singing the sweetest songs. It has always been there, that beauty, but one has to lift one's eyes from the ugly deeds of men to see it.

Beyond the fighting, hatred and pain, there is harmony, immutable and eternal, encompassing the earth, reaching out beyond the stars, into the unknown infinity of space. A harmony that directs the tiny workings of ants and the graceful orbit of planets. Even men, wayward and wilfully cruel, are part of its endless cycle. The great revolution, the wheel, is reflected in his own life.

He understands now: the wheel of fate that, turning, has dragged him down and, having reached its lowest point, threatened to submerge him has, just as suddenly, pulled him up from the silty depths to which he descended, flinging him skywards, towards heaven, towards Sriya. Soon, he will return home, to her, and the circle will be complete.

With mounting excitement, Asoka contemplates their future: life within the family, sharing meals, eating, talking, working the fields together: and moments alone, with Sriya; evening walks in the palm groves, the setting sun reflected in the watery surface of paddy fields, the screech of roosting parrots. And, of course, there will be their child.

***

A harsh, carping cry shakes him from his reverie: a crow, black as a premonition, wings outstretched, stands before him. It has been feasting on the remains of a dead lizard, at the side of the road. Asoka's approach has disturbed it.

"Arkk, arkk," the creature croaks loudly, hopping and flapping, trying to scare the intruder away yet, at the same time, retreating a few feet from its prey. Head on one side, the crow eyes Asoka angrily, waiting for him to pass, daring him to steal its meal. The two gaze at each other for a moment.

"Strange creature," thinks Asoka with a shudder, "it seems to read my thoughts."

The bird glares at him, its black eye glittering with malevolence. Asoka hurries past. The bird darts forward and, seizing the lizard in its bill, takes to the air, flapping clumsily into the trees.

Asoka tries to regain the thoughts which filled him with such optimism a few minutes before, but they elude him. Without words, the crow has spoken; the hatred in its eyes unmistakeable, almost human. It reminds Asoka of things he would like to forget.

Unnerved, he tries to recapture his good humour. But he cannot. His meeting with the crow has a deeper significance, although, as yet, its meaning is obscure. The sun glints through the palm fronds, striking his face with bright rays but it fails to dispel the shadow of fear. Asoka turns and looks behind him. He feels as if something has slipped from the trees and is following him: a shape, the dark outline of a man, as insubstantial as shadow. Squinting against the light of the sun, Asoka slowly scans the trees, then the road. But he sees nothing.

"My imagination," he murmurs. But, as he turns, he thinks he catches something out of the corner of his eye. He spins round on his heel, walking quickly back down the road to where he thought he saw the shadow.

"Come out," he shouts to the trees.

"Arkk, ark!" comes the reply.

The crow, balanced uncomfortably in a branch, still holds the remains of the lizard in its claw. It looks down at him knowingly, its head cocked to one side.

"Arkk," it taunts him.

Asoka laughs uneasily and shakes his head.

"It was that bird," he mutters.

Under the watchful eye of the crow, he turns away and resumes his journey. Stirred by fear, his memory throws up images from its depths: a body dangling from a rope, a look of terror on its bloated face. Mennan. Still haunting him.

"We create demons for ourselves. Images onto which we project our own sin," thinks Asoka.

It is a rational explanation, yet it fails to comfort him. Still, he senses that something is pursuing him. Sometimes, this feeling becomes so strong that he stops to look over his shoulder. But he sees nothing. Just a ribbon of empty road and sunlight, glancing off the trees.

***

He begins to tire. His legs ache and the soles of his feet are sore. To the side of the road, he sees a pathway, leading into a grove. It looks shady and pleasant. He decides to rest for a while and follows the path, deep into the shadow. The ground is well-worn, bare of undergrowth and there is a slight hollow, sheltered from the road, in which he can lie, undetected.

As he shuffles around, trying to make himself comfortable, something scratches his skin. He reaches inside his shirt and pulls out a sheet of paper. It is the letter, written in the monastery, in which he has explained everything to Sriya, without excuse, telling her how much he loves her. Re-reading it, he smiles, calmed by the thought of her.

No need for this now, he thinks, and screws the letter up as if to throw it away but, just as he extends his hand to tuck the paper under the roots of a tree, he hears a noise. It is the rattling cough of a lorry approaching from the direction in which he was travelling. The vehicle churns along the road towards his hiding place, its gears scraping, threatening to stall any minute. As it approaches, he hears the voices of men, shouting, belligerent and most likely drunk. The lorry draws level and, with a metallic grinding and burst of fumes, it shudders to a halt. Instinctively, Asoka retreats into the hollow, lying flat, keeping out of sight.

"Tell that bastard to keep going. If he doesn't, I'll shoot him. I have a gun. And dynamite. That'll move his fat arse."

There is a ragged burst of laughter, then the same voice speaks again.

"Did you hear me, Mahesh? You're not driving a taxi now. Get this boneshaker moving. We want to go home."

A voice replies from inside the cab, but Asoka cannot hear what it says. There is a thud, followed by another, as two men jump down from the back of the lorry. Then he hears footsteps, a single set, heading directly for his hiding place. He holds his breath. The feet stop a couple of yards away, then there is the sound of liquid splashing on the ground. One of the men has stopped to relieve himself. The footsteps retreat. Asoka takes a small breath, letting the air leak into his lungs.

"Come on, stop dawdling," says another voice. "Come and give me a hand. Help me get this pile of junk moving."

He can hear the men grunting as they turn the crank handle. The others are shouting directions from the back of the lorry. They are getting restless and irritable.

"It was better when Anil was leading us," whines a high-pitched voice. "He would have known what to do. He would have stayed with us. Unlike his bloody lieutenant – or whatever he called himself. Bloody village idiot."

Asoka stiffens with fear at the mention of Anil's name. If these men knew what had happened to Anil – and Asoka's part in it – his fate would be certain, although death would not come quickly. His mind races, keeping time with his heart. He wonders who Anil's lieutenant could be. He is probably a peasant or a share-cropper of some sort. Tissa. Of course. But he is not with the men now. It sounds as if they parted on bad terms.

There is more shouting. Several men jump down and wander to the front of the lorry. The others, less interested, decide to explore their surroundings. If they come in his direction, he will be discovered. With beating heart, he listens for approaching footsteps. A few more feet and they will find him.

Then, suddenly, the vehicle coughs into life. The driver revs the engine and the men race to get back on board for fear of being left behind. There is a cloying stink of diesel that reaches Asoka where he lies and, after more crunching of gears, the lorry chugs reluctantly away.

Asoka lies prone for several minutes until the sound of the lorry's engine has faded into the distance, then he sits up and peers over the edge of the hollow. The road is empty. He sighs with relief and sits back. The letter, which he had meant to throw away, is still clutched tightly in his hand. He smoothes it out, re-folds it, then places it back inside his shirt.

1958: A mother's love

The smell of wood-smoke wafts through the door. The first fires of morning have been lit. The baby, having fed, has fallen asleep. Sriya holds him, nestled against her breast. Stroking the black down of his hair with one finger, she watches him. His hold over her is magnetic, like a lover. She cannot take her eyes away. Swaddling him in her arms, she steps into the patch of sunlight in the doorway and lets it bathe them.

Without opening his eyes, the baby, sensitive to warmth and light, lifts up a fist, as if to push it away. His soft lips part with the sound of a kiss and his mouth remains open as he falls into a deeper sleep. He lowers his fist and relaxes in Sriya's arms, soothed by the warmth of the sun. She hums, softly. Not a song exactly, but the sort of sound mothers make to their babies, telling them that there is nothing to fear.

She smiles as she looks into his sleeping face. He is the most beautiful thing she has ever seen. She is fascinated by him, addicted, almost unable to bear the explosive force of her love for him, a love so powerful that the slightest shift in its axis would lead her to the brink of destruction. Sometimes, she almost feels that she could eat him, so great is the desire borne of her love and she bites her own lip with pleasure as she traces the contour of his soft, round cheek. Love fills her up until she feels that she will burst open, scattering the seeds of her joy. It is a love sharpened by unbearable loss.

At night, she lies awake, looking at the moon from her window, wondering where Asoka is or, indeed, if he is still alive. She aches for him, physically and mentally and, when the pain becomes too much to bear, she consoles herself with the baby, picking him up from his basket, carrying him around the room, whispering to him or listening to the soft rhythm of his breathing.

"You must put him down sometimes," her mother says, but it is a half-hearted warning for her mother knows that, without the baby, Sriya's grief would have destroyed her. She saw the dead look in her daughter's eyes as she wept inwardly, dry-eyed and, to the outside world, seemingly untouched. She heard her crying softly at night, every night, whispering Asoka's name like a prayer, as if its mere repetition had the power to summon him. But he did not return. Hope died and Sriya had begun to fade, like a flower that keeps its shape, yet slowly loses its colour. The baby saved her.

Now, standing in the sunlight, clasping the baby to her, Sriya feels hope creeping back into her heart. Her father has recovered from the injury to his ankle and, with the help of neighbours, they have saved most of their harvest. Elsewhere, the violence is over. The country is returning to normal. Sriya's optimism is returning. Something good is about to happen. It is a feeling that has been growing, for several days. If only Asoka would return, her life would be perfect.

A faint smell of meat and spices fills the air. Even at this hour in the morning, her mother is at work in the kitchen, preparing the evening meal. A group of men trudge past the house on their way to the fields. One raises his arm, the others nod in greeting. Sriya smiles at them before turning back into the house.

In the yard, with hens scratching around her feet, she washes the baby in a large enamel bowl then, wrapping him in a fold of cloth, ties him to her back. It is her habit these days to work early in the chena garden. For some reason, it makes her feel closer to Asoka. Her mattock and hoe are lying by the fence where she left them yesterday. Tucking them under her arm, she shifts the baby so that he lies more comfortably on her back.

"Do you want to leave him with me?"

Her mother emerges from the back of the house where she has been chopping onions. Sriya shakes her head.

"No, thank you, Amma."

Every morning the same question and the same response: her mother always trying to persuade Sriya to leave the baby; Sriya refusing. He is her constant companion and wherever she goes, he watches her with the same dark eyes as his father. *He will be clever*, she thinks. Like Asoka.

"Will Thaatha come later?"

"Probably."

After breakfast, Prema usually joins Sriya in the chena garden, although he does little work. She knows that it is a plan by her parents to keep an eye on her, company being the best antidote to despair.

"You seem happy this morning."

Her mother, wiping her hands on a piece of cloth, is looking at her quizzically.

"Yes."

"Why is that?"

"I don't know."

Bemused, her mother withdraws into the shadows where she watches Sriya through the window.

"Perhaps," she thinks, hardly daring to hope, "she has ceased to grieve."

1958: The well

It is early morning and, after walking for several days, Asoka is nearing home. Within earshot of the village, he hears children laughing and can even identify some familiar voices. Women, left in charge of toddlers too young to be of use in the fields, have gathered round the well for the daily exchange of news and gossip. Hiding in the shadow of a tree, he stops to watch.

One of the younger women is drawing water from the well. She pulls down on a rope, one end of which is attached to a bucket, the other to the end of a long pole which is balanced on a primitive fulcrum. The rope is thick and coarse, but the woman's hands, calloused from much work, are impervious to blisters. She pulls down hard, ensuring that the bucket is fully immersed before giving the rope a tug. There is a sound of sloshing and gushing as the bucket, streaming and overfull, lurches from the water at the bottom of the well. After several dry weeks, the water-level has dropped. The reserve at the bottom of the well is becoming rank and the water has developed an earthy flavour.

Children, normally forbidden to go anywhere near the well, take the opportunity while in the company of their mothers, to peer into the depths. Leaning over the parapet, they squint into the blackness, holding their breath. When the well is full, they see their faces reflected in the water; small shimmering images that laugh and point, inviting them down to explore. But, now that the water level has dropped, they can see nothing, not even the occasional glint of light on water. It is the sign that the well will soon run dry. Rain must come. Soon.

Now, the heat is at its worst and the air so heavy that it feels like lead in the lungs. The atmosphere is tense as everyone awaits monsoon. Every morning, as they emerge from their homes, the villagers cast anxious eyes at the sky, examining it for omens of change. But, so far, there have been none. The sky remains clear, an immaculate blue without a wisp of cloud and, as yet, there has been no sighting of the outriders of monsoon: towering black thunderheads that roll across the sky like juggernauts. These are the signs for which everyone waits: within minutes of their appearance, the earth will be pelted with rain and pellets of dust, rising from the streets, will fall back as water.

The girl at the well gently pulls on the rope, raising the bucket. Her task is made easier by heavy stones tied to the end of the pole which act as counterweights. As the bucket surfaces, the other women gather round, helping the girl to guide the bucket over the side of the parapet where earthenware vessels have been lined up, ready for filling. The girl fills a large pot then, with the help of a friend, raises the vessel onto her head, balances it carefully, then carries it home. The empty bucket is dropped back over the side of the well, ready for the next user. The process will be repeated many times until all the pots have been filled and transported to homes throughout the village.

It is usually the younger women who disappear first, for they have more to do. The older women, enjoying the luxury of old age, make the most of their time. For them, sessions at the well last, not just minutes, but hours. The children in their care soon become bored. Unchecked, their hilarity increases to a raucous pitch.

Round and round they chase each other, in and out of the static pairings of adults who stand with their heads together, like groups of old trees, as loftily unconcerned by the children's activities as if they were ants on the forest floor. Occasionally, a child stops to catch its breath or massage a stitch in its side, then the frantic pursuit starts again. Only faster. Eventually, one falls over and cries, more from exhaustion than pain. He is lifted to his feet and his back rubbed by a gnarled hand. The old women, recalled to their duties, begin to make their way home, struggling under the weight of their water pots, one or two small children clinging to their skirts.

***

Once the women have gone, Asoka steps out of the shadows, walking cautiously to the well where he fills the bucket and helps himself to a drink. He has been listening carefully to the women's conversation, hoping to catch news of Sriya, but there has been no mention of her. At present, all the villagers' thoughts are concentrated on the weather. At home, in the fields, around the well, there is only one topic of conversation, characterised by two questions: when will the monsoon come and what will happen if it does not.

Asoka feels a little disappointed, although he cannot blame them. Having worked in the fields himself, he knows how dependent they are on the weather. The failure of just one crop can mean hardship, even hunger, for months. The mood of the whole village is governed by the clemency of the seasons. If the weather is kind and the crops flourish, then everyone is happy. But, if the rice fails, the gloom is palpable. Unable to accept the helplessness of their fate, the peasants seek reasons: they were sold bad seed; the priest made a bad job of blessing the crops, even the Government is blamed. Someone has to be responsible.

Splashing water over his face and hands, Asoka wonders how the villagers will greet him on his return. He had not thought of that. Will they welcome him, or treat him with mistrust? After all, he left them at one of the busiest times of the year. No doubt, some assume that he left of his own accord, simply ran away: the city boy, unable to cope with the hardships of peasant life, running back to a soft life in town. He will have a lot of explaining to do, but it is not the villagers' opinion of him that matters. It is Sriya's. Will she believe him? Can she ever forgive him?

I must find her. Now.

He empties the bucket into the well. Not a drop must be wasted. On a whim, he picks up a small stone and drops it over the parapet. The pebble hits the water with a faint splash, followed by an ominous echo. It has fallen deep. The well is nearly dry.

***

Not wanting to be seen, Asoka turns away from the road and slips through the trees following a track known only to the villagers. He knows where to find her. In the cool of the morning, Sriya will be working in the garden, tending her plants. He can already see her in his mind's eye and his heart begins to race. He hurries forward, then stops. For a second, he thought he saw a shadow, the dark form of a man, keeping pace with him. He looks about him, but can see nothing. The shadow has disappeared.

"My imagination. Too little sleep," he thinks, although the fleeting image disturbs him. It reminds him of the dark shadows he saw in the forest, human-looking, although they could have been trees, indistinct yet menacing. Phantoms.

786

"Ridiculous," he tells himself.

Yet, he cannot dispel the slight chill of apprehension that he feels. He stares hard into the trees. Scattered by the swaying fronds of palm, light flickers over the dry earth floor. Deep within the grove, Asoka can hear the shuffling of a small creature as it burrows into a pile of dry leaf waste: a mouse, perhaps, stripping threads from dry palm frond to line its nest. Familiar sounds come from the direction of the village: the lowing of cattle, a clink of pails, the high-pitched clucking of a hen. But nothing else. Nothing moves. Only the ever-changing patterns of light, filtering through the trees.

"I have been alone for too long," he murmurs.

Sriya. With her, he knows no fear. One sight of her will dispel all hauntings. Drawn on by the thought of her, he sets off at a run.

1958: Rain

Having left home early, Sriya is already at work, opening up a new section of the garden, hacking at the red soil with a small mattock, as the other women make their way to the fields. In the distance, she can hear the occasional lowing of buffalo as the milking herd is driven along the road by young boys with sticks.

The work is heavy and her arms are aching. She decides to try some lighter work and, exchanging her mattock for a hoe, Sriya starts weeding between the rows of carrots. The hoe slides effortlessly through the tilthy soil, but the earth is dry. She will have to walk back to the village to collect water for her plants. It will double, even treble the amount of work she has to do and she will crawl onto her mattress tonight, aching and exhausted. Life is at its hardest before monsoon and, like everyone else, she prays for rain.

"Let it come soon. Let it come soon," she thinks. And then, as they always do, the words change. *Let him come soon.*

Something thickens in her throat. The green tops of the carrots sway mistily at her feet. She blinks hard, trying to hold back the tears, but they splash onto the dry soil, like early drops of rain. What has happened to her new-found optimism? She awoke this morning, sure that everything would be different. But now, she has the dismal feeling that nothing will change. He will never come back.

With meaningful glances at Sriya, the village gossips tell tales of men who have mysteriously disappeared, only to emerge a few years later, in another place, with a new family. Her mother has told her to ignore them but, like poisoned darts, their words have wormed into her heart. She still trusts Asoka, sure of his love for her, but why has she not heard anything? Why has he sent no word? It can only mean one thing. He is dead. Death. That word. More poisonous and final than the rest. Nothing the others say can hurt her as much.

Alone in the middle of the field, she begins to sob: loud, ragged gulps of misery.

***

The baby is mewling, gently. She has placed him in an old log basket, under a tree, his carrying-cloth wound around him like a nest. He was asleep when she left home but now he is stirring, grinding one tiny fist into his eye and moaning softly. Soon he will start to whimper, then scream, if she fails to feed him.

Laying down the hoe, Sriya wipes her eyes and stepping over the rows of vegetables, walks over to where the baby lies, the dusty red earth rising with every footfall and sticking to the hem of her sari. He kicks his legs excitedly as she picks him up and, as she holds him and looks into his face, he smiles. Unmistakeable. The first time. She laughs. Sitting in the shade beside the basket, she unbuttons her chemise and holds him to her, feeling the pull of his mouth on her nipple. It soothes her as much as him and, for a short time, she forgets her sorrow, resting her head against the trunk of the tree.

She is awoken by a breath of air on her face. Looking up at the sky, she sees a huge black cloud rolling towards her. The air has cooled by several degrees and the earth seems to quicken around her. A drop of rain falls on her cheek.

Placing the baby back in the basket, she goes to collect her tools. There will be no more work today. The rain, when it comes, will be torrential and she does not want to be caught out in it. As she stoops to pick up the hoe, she becomes aware of someone approaching. She does not turn to look, assuming that it is her father.

"There's no point in working now. The rains are coming," she remarks, over her shoulder.

"No."

The voice is not her father's, but another, just as familiar. Did she imagine it? Straightening up slowly, she turns to look. A man has emerged from the trees and is standing at the edge of the garden, watching her. She catches her breath.

"Asoka," she murmurs. Then, louder: "Asoka."

She runs towards him, faster than she has ever run in her life. He runs also, his arms open, ready to catch her. They are close, so close, when she sees something else. Another figure emerging from the trees. A man. Familiar. Yet changed. A demon. His features distorted, without humanity, full of hatred. Tissa. Wearing the robes of a monk. He draws something out from the folds of cloth around his waist and raises his arm. Pointing at them. A cruel smile on his lips.

"Asoka. No."

She tries to warn him. But it is too late. There is a sharp report. Asoka continues to run forward, but then stumbles, his arms still outstretched. Sriya runs to him and drops to her knees. A dark stain has appeared on his shirt. At first a small and insignificant spot, it blooms outwards like a crimson flower.

"Sriya. I came back."

"Yes. I knew you would."

She cradles his head in her arms and is stroking his face.

"Do you still love me?"

"Of course. Always."

"Sriya ..."

He is trying to speak but his breath comes in short gasps.

"The letter. Read my letter."

His trembling hand clutches at the pocket of his shirt. She reaches in and draws out a blood-spattered sheet of paper.

"Read it."

"Yes. I will."

She unfolds the letter.

"Not now. Later."

He has taken hold of her hand and is squeezing it tight, clinging onto life.

"My beautiful wife."

She tries not to weep, brushing away the tears with her hand. She must not cry. She must see his face clearly. Try to remember him.

He reaches his hand up to her face and strokes her cheek.

"Do you forgive me?"

"For what?"

"For everything," he whispers.

"There is nothing to forgive."

"I made you unhappy."

"No, no."

Holding him in her arms, she rocks him gently, kissing his forehead.

Somewhere, close by, the baby begins to cry.

Too weak to speak, Asoka looks into Sriya's eyes.

"We have a son. Shall I get him?"

Asoka makes a slight motion with his head.

Laying him gently on the ground, Sriya runs to the basket, picks up the baby and brings him to his father. But it is too late. Asoka is dead.

"No," she howls as the wind whips the trees and tears at her hair. The first drops of rain begin to fall, hitting the ground like bullets.

Sriya drops to her knees, kissing Asoka's face, stroking his hair, unable to believe that he has left her so soon. Then, as the rain beats down, she bends over him, shielding his body with hers, their child in her arms.

***

Mute, Tissa watches from the trees. He meant to kill her too, but he cannot. The force of Sriya's grief has cowed him, touching a chord of sympathy, long dormant. It was not meant to be like this. He was supposed to kill her, or claim her. But he can do neither. Only watch knowing that her grief will soon turn to hatred. Of him. The one thing he cannot bear. All the callouses around his heart cannot protect him from that one hurt. He still loves her. He still wants her to love him. And now, she never will.

He watches her, bent over the body of Asoka and knows, as surely as he knows his own name, that she will never love again. Such love only comes once and it will be denied him. He feels her loss as surely as if the bullet had passed through his own heart.

He watches, slack-mouthed, his matted hair hanging around his face, his robes soaked with rain, the yellow dye dripping from his limbs. A creature, unloved and forgotten. No longer human.

The sun flashes through the trees, striking Arjun full in the face, as the army lorry speeds past villages and fields. Although Walter offered to drive Arjun home, the police advised against it. It is still not safe for civilians to travel by road, especially if the car they are travelling in belongs to the Government Agent's office. So, Nash's wife has used her influence to find Arjun another means of transport: some of the soldiers drafted into Polonnaruwa are returning to their barracks. It will be a long, circuitous route. There have been reports that some of the goonda bands are still active and the soldiers have been ordered to reconnoitre the outlying countryside. But, at least with them, Arjun's safety will be assured.

He is sitting in the cab, next to a sweating driver who smells strongly of garlic. However, this is better than sharing the humid, canvas-covered quarters at the back where he would be crammed in amongst the squaddies. Every time the lorry hits a pothole, there is a cheer from the back.

"They taunt me," smiles the driver, directing the lorry towards another pothole. "They say I am not a good driver."

There is a thud and the lorry bounces on its axle. This is followed by a cheer and the sound of applause. Grinning with satisfaction, the driver leans back in his seat. Like the other men in his platoon, he is in good spirits, relieved to be returning to barracks and leaving the sticky work of sorting out the country to the politicians.

They have already passed several villages, gutted by fire and fields, previously full of ripe sugar cane, that have been reduced to blackened wastes of charcoal. A fearful silence hangs over those places: deserted by living creatures, they now seem to repel all life. It reminds Arjun of a story that he was told in childhood.

A mischievous uncle had tried to scare the boy with tales of a haunted lake. It was said that no living being, human or animal, dared to go near it and any fisherman that rowed out on it in his boat was never seen again. The uncle had told Arjun that the lake covered the site of an ancient city whose columns and arches could still be seen beneath its waters. The city's ghostly inhabitants still walked its water-filled streets; hungry spirits, who, each night, left their watery graves and stalked the shores for live prey.

"Do you believe in ghosts?" Arjun asks the driver.

The man looks bemused.

"Nahh," he laughs, and shakes his head. "They will be back soon."

"Who?"

"People. People will come back here soon. They always do."

"What people?"

The driver shrugs. "Any people."

Not my people, thinks Arjun, although he takes some comfort from the young man's blunt optimism. People are just people to him, no matter what they call themselves, no matter what politics or religion they espouse. People, of one sort or another, will always be there to populate the villages and work the fields. The human race will continue its haphazard course and the land will not be handed over to ghosts or demons or haunted by superstition. Like the jungle, life itself cannot be repressed. Soon, it will return and, in a few years, the evil of this moment will be forgotten.

Arjun sees two little beggar children at the side of the road. Scores of them haunt the roads around the refugee camps: children who have lost, or become separated from, their parents; confused, hungry, unable to understand what they have seen or what has happened to them. He wonders what happened to Ella. He asked after her in the camps, but without success. No-one knows anyone else's name. Some cannot even remember their own. Individuals have lost their identity and been reduced to a few simple necessities: eat, sleep, survive.

Is Ella still alive? Has she found her children? He does not know. Perhaps he never will. He sighs and thinks how terrible it must be to lose one's loved ones and not know what has happened to them. Suddenly, his heart lurches. In all the chaos, it has simply not occurred to him. He just assumed, convinced himself that everything would be all right but, since he left home on his journey to the Government bungalow, he has had no contact with Neleni. Supposing, just supposing, something has happened?

Resting his elbow on the door, he stares from the window and is confronted by another scene of devastation. Pye-dogs and crows have gathered around the bloated corpse of a cow. Further along the road, a pile of feathers lies by the verge: the remains of several chickens, slaughtered but not eaten, left to rot in the sun.

"Pooh!" the driver winds up the window. The stench of rotting meat is everywhere. A pye-dog slinks into the undergrowth carrying what looks like a goat's head. All the domestic animals have been killed. Even if they return now, the villagers will have nothing to sustain them.

Arjun bites his knuckle, sickened by the stench and a newly-formed fear. *Please let her be safe. Please.* He shrinks within himself, stung by guilt. He has been too busy to think, or even worry. He has not even prayed for her. He had just assumed that she would be all right. But what if she has lost her home? What if something worse has happened?

"How far, now?" he asks, drumming his fingers nervously on the door.

"Not far," says the driver, laconically. "You're in a hurry. Got a girlfriend?"

"Yes," says Arjun, without thinking.

The driver chuckles. He is in his early twenties and has a pleasant face, plump and good-natured, full of good sense; a man incapable of evil.

"Are you Tamil?" ventures Arjun.

"Me? No, thank God. I wouldn't want to be one of those poor devils. Not for anything. Where my father lives, he had Tamil neighbours, but ..."

He shakes his head and sighs.

"What happened?"

"I don't know exactly. But they've gone. One day they were there, the next, their house was empty. Sinhalese have moved in there now."

"Already?"

"Mmm."

"What about the Tamils?"

The driver shrugs.

"I feel sorry for them. Don't get me wrong, but they brought it on themselves."

There is an embarrassed silence.

"You're Tamil, huh?" the driver asks.

"Yes."

"Don't worry. You'll be OK. A man like you, with connections, you'll be all right."

The young man's bluff assertion fails to comfort Arjun. It is obvious that he does not really believe what he says; his cheerfulness is merely a foil for embarrassment.

"Yes, of course."

Arjun replies politely but a shadow has fallen between them. He turns away and looks out of the window, returning to his former thoughts. What if the violence reached Neleni? A possibility he has not allowed himself to entertain. What if she has fled? How will he find her? What if … he cannot think of the other possibility. He suddenly finds himself choking back tears. He is desperate to get home, to find her, to be reassured of her safety.

While visiting the camps, he heard many tales of atrocities. He realises now that he tried to protect himself by creating an artificial distance between himself and the victims: they had lived in a different part of the country; they had attracted envy by their position or wealth. God forgive him, he even dismissed some stories as the kind of overblown rumours that trail a civil crisis, the result of panic and mass hysteria. But it is his present companion's reticence on the subject of his Tamil neighbours that finally prises Arjun from his cocoon. No-one is immune to the violence. Neither Tamil, nor Sinhalese. Not even Neleni.

The lorry bounces over a rough piece of track. The driver frowns, leaning over the wheel and pretending to concentrate on the road. The two men lapse into silence. Arjun stares from the window. The roads are quiet, with the exception of a few peasants, trudging along the verge. One carries a couple of live chickens, slung over his back, their feet tied together with string. Every so often the chickens flap their wings and squawk. In response, the man jerks the string and swears at them. The man is old, as thin as a cadaver, his cheeks hollow and his eyes sunken into dark pits. He is the effigy of death. Other peasants push their belongings in handcarts, their faces blank and without hope.

"They are travelling from nowhere to nowhere," thinks Arjun.

He wonders if, one day, he will share their fate.

***

The soldiers in the back are getting restless. It has been a long, uncomfortable journey and they still have miles to go. Their cheerful mood has turned to one of despondency. There is no more cheering as they run over potholes, just groans. The driver has ceased his pranks. During the last hour, the journey has become much smoother, although the roads have not visibly improved. The lorry chugs into town.

"Here. Just here!"

Arjun points, motioning the driver to stop.

The lorry halts at the end of the road, its sides quivering as the engine idles. Some of the soldiers take advantage of the break to jump out and stretch their legs. In the shade, one pees against a wall.

"Close enough?" the driver asks. It is a statement rather than a question.

"Yes, thank you."

The man smiles cheerfully at Arjun, then leans across him to unfasten the door.

"Handle's a bit tricky," he explains. But Arjun senses the man's eagerness to get rid of him. It is getting late and even soldiers cannot run the risk of getting ambushed in the dark.

"Thanks."

Arjun climbs out of the cab, hauling out the battered old bag, lent to him by Chitra, which contains a selection of mismatched clothes, some of them belonging to Nash. He did not want to accept, but she insisted. From the ground, he sees the driver's face above him, his arm stretched out, grasping the door-handle.

"Bye."

The man grins briefly before slamming the passenger door. As he walks up the road, Arjun can feel the soldiers' eyes upon him. One of them grumbles loudly, intending him to hear.

"Who's he, anyway? What's so special about him that he needs an armed escort?"

One of the others mutters something inaudible.

"Bloody Tamils," mutters the grumpy voice. "Always expecting special treatment."

As he sets off along the street, an image flashes through Arjun's mind. A young man, climbing down from a country bus, walking up the road with the eyes of others upon him. He was a stranger then, and he is a stranger now. But with a difference. Back then, he had been a newcomer to a small town. His arrival had been greeted with curiosity, rather than suspicion. He had been accepted with enthusiasm and learned to think of the place as home. But now, wherever he goes, he feels like a stranger, an alien in his own country; an object of mistrust, even hatred.

"Come on, you lot. Get back in."

The driver is calling to the soldiers. Boots thud as they climb back into the lorry. The engine chugs and the exhaust belches a cloud of grey smoke, filling the street with the hot smell of diesel. Then, turning slowly, the lorry pulls away. Just as the bus had done. Leaving him alone in the street.

1958: The temple tree

Arjun walks slowly along the road, stopping in front of a burned-out shop, gazing at the blackened remains. Among the piles of rubble, familiar shapes are still discernible: tins, their shiny metal oxidised by the heat; jars; even a tin bath. But no sign of the owners. Nothing to tell him what happened to them. Something slips from the wall and falls with a thud, sending up a cloud of grey ash.

Fear burns a hole in his stomach. He looks anxiously along the street but cannot see Neleni's house which is set a little way back from the pavement. He wants to run towards it, yet he does not want to arrive, for fear of what he might see.

Clenching his fist around the handle of his leather bag, he continues his journey. In one of the houses, he hears the murmur of voices. He looks around and thinks he sees a face retreating from a window. But he cannot be sure. This road, once full of people, is inhabited by ghosts.

As he draws closer, he can see the temple tree, its branches hanging over the pavement, in full bloom. His hopes raised, he walks more quickly, breaking into a run until, with a cry of joy, he sees the house, intact and undisturbed. Taking the front steps two at a time, he turns the handle of the front door and is surprised when it does not open. His stomach knots, all sorts of images race through his mind. Has she left? Is she safe?

Frantic, he hammers on the door with his fist. The house is silent. He runs to the side window and, with his hand up to his eyes, peers in; but it is dark inside and he cannot see much, only the edge of the table, the back of the sofa, the outline of a picture frame. Overcome with exhaustion and despair, he sits on the leather bag, his head in his hands, hot tears running down his cheeks and wetting his palms.

"Uncle Arjun?"

A voice so soft it might be his imagination. A hand pats his shoulder.

"Uncle Arjun, don't cry."

But he cannot stop. All the agony, uncertainty and pain, shelved during the troubles, all the relief that he now feels, overwhelm him. He feels helpless and ashamed, but he cannot move, just sits there weeping, with Rani's arm around his shoulders.

***

Once in control of himself, his first instinct is to run, find her, but the front door is still locked. Rani sees him looking at it.

"We use the back door, now. It's safer. I'll show you."

He rises to his feet and lets her lead him by the hand, along the narrow, overgrown passage and through the gate, still creaking on its hinges, across the back yard and into the kitchen. Unexpectedly, Raj is there, eating a late lunch at the kitchen table, Saro at his feet, playing with a doll.

"Arjun, brother. We have been so worried."

Raj's chair scrapes against the polished red floor as he pushes it back. In his hurry, he rises awkwardly, knocking the plate so that it spills food on the table. He flings his arms around Arjun's neck and, by the movement of his shoulders, Arjun can tell that he is weeping.

Arjun feels a rush of guilt, then irritation. He wants to see Neleni. Now. He wants to run to her, hold her in his arms, kiss her. But all that will have to wait. He must be polite, ask after each member of the family, listen carefully and show concern when, all the time, his heart is bursting to be with her.

"Sit down, brother. Sit down. You must tell me all that happened."

He is forced into a chair and plied with arrack. There will be no quick escape. He must tell his story in full. Raj shakes his head angrily when told of the Government Agent's murder.

"Those bastards," he murmurs, shaking his head.

Then Arjun tells him of Ella.

"So she is still alive."

"She was," corrects Arjun. "I saw her a few days ago, but then I lost contact."

"Happens to everyone," muses Raj. "Dalia's house was burned down and she and her mother were forced to hide in a neighbour's house. But then they left. The neighbour does not know where they went. Niran is mad with worry. Searching all the camps. And no-one has seen Michael. Niran thinks ..."

He stops. Rani is standing nearby, listening intently.

"Well, you know," Raj finishes, lamely.

Arjun lowers his head, trying to commiserate but, really, he is thinking of Neleni. He can wait no longer.

"How is ... your wife?"

He tries to keep the urgency out of his voice.

"Oh, of course. We haven't told you."

Arjun looks alarmed.

"No, nothing like that."

Raj laughs, waving his hand.

"We've had a son."

"My god!"

Tears prick Arjun's eyes.

"There, there, my boy. It's all right."

Raj pats him on the back.

"I know how you feel. Cried myself. Like a baby. Imagine it. A son. Here. Have another drink."

Sipping politely from the edge of the glass, Arjun feels as if the arrack will choke him.

"Can I see her?" he ventures, at last.

"Not at the moment," Raj laughs, jovially. "She's sleeping. Seems to need a lot these days. She'll wake up later. It usually takes a couple of hours. Go and see her then. I'm sure she'll be delighted to see you. I'll be back at work this evening. Extra shifts to clear the backlog. After the troubles. You know."

Raj shrugs by way of additional explanation. Then, as an afterthought, he adds: "She'll be glad of the company."

Arjun, impatient to see her, tries to smile, choking back his disappointment.

During her mother's indisposition, Rani has assumed the role of house-keeper. Now, putting on an apron, to give herself an air of adult authority, she hurries about the kitchen, returning from the stove with a plate piled with food.

Arjun has not eaten for many hours and now, when meat and rice are placed in front of him, he realises how hungry he is. As he eats, Rani chatters about what she calls their adventure. She tells him how she found the boy in the street, how bad men chased them back to the house but were repelled, magically, by the snake; using her innate skill as a storyteller to embellish the details. In fact, her story sounds more fabulous than factual and Arjun does not know which part to believe, if any. Yet, Raj sits beside them, sagely nodding his head, so it must be more or less correct.

"There was Amma, lying on the kitchen floor, about to have the baby, when the door knob started to turn. Ve-ery slowly."

Rani, her eyes as large as saucers, motions with her hand, as if turning the door knob.

"We thought the men had come back to kill us."

She pauses for effect. Arjun, places the ball of rice that he had been holding in his fingers back on the plate. He has suddenly lost his appetite. The thought of Neleni, alone and vulnerable, makes him feel sick. It raises the spectre of terrible stories, told by the refugees; things too terrible to think of, that should never be spoken. Images of their suffering begin to superimpose themselves on Rani's story. Neleni could have been one of those victims and, all the time, he had assumed she was safe. What arrogance to suppose that, simply because he loves her, she is a special case, entitled to safety where others have been brutalised and killed.

Sickened with guilt, Arjun hangs his head, his need to see her, even more desperate than before. How can he sit here, eating and chatting, as if nothing had happened? But he has to. Because no-one knows of their attachment. More than ever, he is oppressed by the secrecy with which they have surrounded themselves. It is like a physical weight bearing down upon him, stifling and crushing him until he can hardly breathe.

"Are you all right, Uncle?"

Rani places her hand on his arm, her plain little face twisted into a comical expression of concern.

"Uncle is tired. He needs to rest. Save your stories until later, child."

Raj waves her away.

"No, please. Tell me what happened."

Arjun holds onto Rani's hand to prevent her from leaving.

"Well, that's it," she says, deflated. "Amma had the baby."

"But who was at the door?"

Arjun has to exert all his self-control not to shout at her.

"Was it the bad men who had chased you in the street?"

"No," Raj roars with laughter. "It was me, brother. I was supposed to be away overnight, travelling to a post office up-country. But the roads were blocked and when I tried to return to Head Office the police told me that it was under attack. The rioters that had been here earlier had moved into the centre of town. So I came home early. Just as well. Neleni had the baby half an hour later. Here. On the kitchen floor."

"And ... she was all right."

"Of course. She has had two children before. It was not the first time. She was fine."

Arjun wants to hit Raj for his airy dismissal of Neleni's suffering. Then, he thinks guiltily of what he did. Leaving without saying goodbye. Intending to leave and never come back. She had run after him down the steps. In her condition. He had heard her, murmuring his name, imploring him to comfort her. But he had just walked away. Without turning back. Without speaking. He hurt her far more deeply than Raj ever could. He longs to go to her, tortured by the thought that she is only a few feet away. He must beg her forgiveness. But when? When will they have the chance to be alone?

Somewhere, in the distance, Raj is still talking. *She is fine. A son. A boy, at last.*

Needled by her father's previous interjection which, as usual, destroyed the dramatic impact of her story and, not a little jealous of his praise for the baby, Rani tries to pick up the thread of her narrative.

"But the boy wasn't fine, was he Appa?"

"Which boy?"

"The boy from the shop. The one I brought here. The one whose parents were murdered."

She relishes the last word as something almost too awful to be spoken.

"No," says Raj, looking uncomfortable. "He will not be fine."

Then, turning to Arjun, he adds a word of explanation

"The boy stayed with us for a while, but he never spoke in the whole time he was here. Then, his aunt and uncle came to find him. They took him away. But he still did not speak. Even to them."

Arjun shakes his head. He knows why the boy did not speak. There are no words for such unhappiness, none to express it. Words are simply inadequate. Just as they are for his own guilt and shame.

***

Eventually, Raj returns to work, wheeling his bike into the road, walking alongside it for a while, chatting to the neighbours, giving them the latest news of his baby son, although it is no different from what he told them yesterday, or the day before that. Nevertheless, they listen indulgently, many with genuine interest.

Once he is sure that Raj will not return, having forgotten, as he usually does, some trivial item, such as a handkerchief or a few rupees for the tea-seller, Arjun rises from the table, intent on seeing Neleni. But he is not to see her alone. Rani, still wearing her apron, now assumes the role of matron and insists on escorting him to her mother's room.

"It's very kind of you, but I know where she is," says Arjun with as much patience as he can muster.

"No, Uncle Arjun. I want to show you the baby. Please. Let me show you the baby."

She is so insistent, so desperate to please that he has not the heart to send her away. He has grown to love Rani like his own child. There is something about her that reflects his own sense of being an outsider. Hurting her would be like hurting himself because he knows how it would feel.

"All right, then. Show me the baby. I hope he is very handsome."

"Yes, very. Almost as handsome as you."

There. She has said it. She did not mean to. It just slipped out. She stands, looking up at him, her eyes glistening with adoration. Taken aback, Arjun does not know what to say. Then, he laughs. It is a childish crush. All girls of her age are like that. All the same, the intensity of her devotion disturbs him. He tries to pass it off, make a joke.

"Come on then, Nurse. Show me to the maternity ward."

Rani bustles along in front of him and, full of beaming, self-importance flings open the door to her mother's room. But she has forgotten to knock and they surprise Neleni, sitting up in bed, her hair dishevelled, the baby clinging to her breast.

"Oh."

She tries to pull her nightdress around her. Arjun thinks she has never looked more beautiful: her hair loose, hanging around her shoulders, thin tendrils curling around her face; her eyes wide and startled, like a gazelle; her skin gleaming, almost gold. Sitting there, her hand curled around the baby's head, she is as beautiful as any Madonna, glowing with the radiance of new motherhood.

"Arjun!"

Her eyes glitter, as they always do before they fill with tears.

"Rani. Will you be a special girl and get your Uncle some tea? I am still parched after that long journey."

Arjun gives Rani his most charming smile. The sort which women find irresistible. He feels guilty, imposing his will like this on a child, but he needs her out of the way. It works. Enthralled by this special attention, Rani turns on her heel and sets off smartly for the kitchen. Arjun pushes the door with his toe. It sticks, as usual, against the uneven floor, but at least they will have a little more privacy.

"My love!"

Tears are streaming down Neleni's cheeks. She holds out her hand to him.

"I thought you had left me. For good."

Sitting beside her on the bed, he puts his arms around her, pressing her head into his shoulder.

"Forgive me. I was such a fool. So selfish."

His voice catches in his throat. He must not cry. He must not. For her sake. She is sobbing quietly. He can feel her shaking, the fragile creature that he so nearly abandoned. He bites his lip, rocking her gently for comfort. His tears drop onto her hair, lying there like dewdrops. She swallows, takes a deep breath, pushes herself back so that she can look him in the eye.

"Arjun, there is something I must tell you."

"Shhh."

He tries to pull her back to him.

"Arjun, please. There isn't much time. Rani will be back in a minute."

He presses a finger to her mouth.

"It doesn't matter. Some things are better left unsaid. All I need to know is that you still love me. Do you?"

"Yes. Oh, yes."

She holds her face up to him and, holding it in his hands, he kisses it. Then their lips meet, fusing them into one inseparable unit, immune to pain, untouched by the world's sorrows, the baby still asleep, cradled between them.

***

Returning with the tea, Rani peers through the door and sees her mother kissing Arjun. The old pain returns, sharpened by jealousy, like a knife stabbing through her heart. In the gloomy passage, watched by the sepia images of her family, she leans against the wall and weeps.

1958: The owl's question

It is night-time and Mr Bandaranaike is in bed; his wife, Sirimavo, next to him. He listens to the gentle cadence of her breathing. She lies very still and seems, always, to wake in exactly the same position as she went to sleep. He envies her tranquillity.

The moon is nearly full. The small, bird-like figure of a bat flits past the window. It circles, disappears, then passes the window again. A larger figure swoops past. A few seconds later, an owl hoots from a nearby tree. Mr Bandaranaike recognises both the bat and the owl. Every night, they come to hunt in his garden. He has watched them on many occasions because, for many nights, he has lain awake, worrying, asking himself questions to which he has no answer.

He wants to be remembered as a great man. But there seems little likelihood of that now. He winces as he thinks of his disastrous address to the nation, rehearsing it again in his head as he has done every night since he sat at a desk in the radio station and spoke coolly into the microphone. He had blamed the Tamils for the death of Mr Seneviratne and used that event to explain the outbreak of violence. But why?

He can remember, quite clearly, what he said but, for the life of him, he cannot remember why he said it. He knows now that he was wrong. The violence had already broken out in another part of the country several days before Mr Seneviratne met his death and, although Mr Seneviratne was in a Tamil-dominated part of the country, there is still no clue as to who killed him; or why. It is a mystery.

The owl hoots again. A lonely, haunting sound. A warning? In other cultures, the owl is an omen of ill-luck. In Ancient Greece, it was the symbol of Athene, goddess of war. Mr Bandaranaike learned that at school. Having been educated in the European tradition, he bears the burden of not one culture, but two. He envies the ordinary Ceylonese their simplicity. It is easier for an ignorant peasant to acquire knowledge than for an educated man to forget what he knows.

Pride. He remembers another part of his education. His upbringing as a Christian. Pride is a sin and he is guilty of it. No matter that he is now a Buddhist. He cannot forget. He cannot unlearn what he was taught as a child. He is guilty of the sin of pride. He thought he knew best.

He remembers sitting at the microphone in the small, stuffy studio, full of self-confidence, surrounded by adoring lackeys. He had read his speech over to them many times before speaking on air. They had all approved it. *Tell the nation the truth*, they had said. *It is the only thing to do*. But, strangely, he cannot now recall who those men were or who, exactly, had fed him the information that he delivered in his speech. Perhaps no-one else is to blame. Perhaps it was all his own idea. Unthinkable. He would never do such a thing.

"Whoo-oo."

The owl sweeps past the window. There is a rustle and a squeak. A shadow passes, a limp shape dangling from its talons. Mr Bandaranaike shivers.

"Whoo-oo."

He sits up in bed. He can see the owl quite clearly from here, perched on the dead branch of a tree, tearing at a mouse with its beak. The owl looks up, momentarily, as if it knows it is being watched, then stoops over its prey, ripping into the warm flesh.

801

Other dark images come to mind. Murder and brutality. Beating, burning and people, thousands of them, crowding the roads, desperate to find safety, to escape the violence. Tamils and Sinhalese. Even Moslems, a harmless and insignificant minority. No-one has been spared.

Everyone, it seems, is either a perpetrator or a victim. Neutrality is impossible. Everyone has been forced to take sides. Fault-lines have opened up within communities, dividing people who have managed to co-exist peaceably for centuries. The nation is fractured. With the next tremor, or the one after that, it will fall apart.

"Whoo-oo," the owl cries, taunting him.

"Whoo-oo."

Who is to blame? It is the question that haunts him every night. Certainly the violence escalated after his speech. But he was innocent, wasn't he? He had simply relied on the information that he had been given by others. People he thought he trusted but whose names he cannot remember. Although, come to think of it, he has seen them whispering in corridors with Vimala Wijewardene. As he passed her the other day, she gave him a strange look; triumph mixed with derision. Vimala Wijewardene whose patron is Buddharakkita Thera. How many others are in the abbot's thrall?

The Prime Minister's skin tingles. He can feel it shrinking over his flesh, as if cold air has passed over him. But the room is hot and stuffy. It is fear, not the cold, that causes his skin to crawl. He has been trapped, manipulated, driven like a stupid animal. The abbot's revenge. Mr Bandaranaike folds himself in his arms. He cannot stop shaking.

"Pull yourself together," he tells himself.

It is something his father used to say. He can see him now, looking down at his son with disapproval, wondering how he had managed to sire such a puny boy. Mr Bandaranaike bites his lip to stop it from quivering, just as he did when he was a child.

"Oh god," he moans, his head in his hands.

Something moves in the corner of the room, near to the large hard-backed chair in which he sometimes sits, reading reports, before he retires to bed. Mr Bandaranaike peers into the gloom, then shakes his head. It must have been his imagination.

He does not see Hooniyam, sitting in the chair, watching him as he sits up in bed. In fact, Hooniyam has been there every night, making sure the Prime Minister does not sleep. It gives him satisfaction to see someone else suffer; distracts him from his own problems.

"Oh god," moans Mr Bandaranaike.

It is heartfelt. A prayer. Despite himself, Hooniyam is bound to respond.

"Be positive," whispers a small voice in Mr Bandaranaike's ear.

The Prime Minister forces himself to be optimistic. In his head, he lists the things that are positive. Despite the mayhem, order has now been restored. The armed forces have proved loyal and efficient although, just for a while, he had his doubts. Also, Governor General Goonetilleke has done a good job of keeping the press quiet. Nothing gets out without his censorship. That means nothing gets into the papers at all. With Goonetilleke's help, even the destruction of the Nagadipa temple has been kept secret. An extraordinary feat. So, perhaps, with a little clever manipulation, the Government can gloss over the violence altogether. After all, there have been civil disturbances before.

But, thinks Mr Bandaranaike, there have never been so many disastrous events in such a short space of time: Gal Oya, the Sri campaign, the violent suppression of the Communist gathering at Hyde Park, the crippling hartals – actual and threatened – all since Mr Bandaranaike came to power. His majority has ebbed away. The Cabinet has split into many factions. Vimala Wijewardene and her cronies are openly hostile, not bothering to hide their contempt. And his ally, the outspoken Marxist, Philip Gunawardene is threatening to go his own way. Added to this, politicians of other parties, who he had hoped would boost his majority, are openly courting the leader of the Opposition, Mr Jayawardene.

Mr Bandaranaike lapses into despair.

"Be positive," whispers the voice, again.

The Prime Minister rallies. He is a survivor. He must go on, recover, ensure his place in history, even, perhaps … No, that is too much even for him. He entertained that thought once before, in Hooniyam's temple. It came to him suddenly, like the sweet seductive scent of a temple tree. Immortality.

"But why not?" whispers the little voice in his head. "Why not? You are a great man. These are extraordinary times. Nothing is impossible."

Comforted, Mr Bandaranaike lies down, next to his wife. She is still sleeping quietly, in the same position. He listens to her breathing. It is regular and soft, like the distant sound of waves on a beach. He closes his eyes and soon falls into a peaceful sleep.

1958: The abbot and the monk

A single lamp burns in the abbot's window. From outside, the top of his bald head can be seen moving from one side of the window to the other, then back again. He is pacing his room, like a caged cat, full of malevolent energy. Since the Prime Minister refused his request for the Government rice contract, relations have soured between them.

According to Vimala Wijewardene, the Cabinet is deserting Mr Bandaranaike. But the abbot knows that already. He is in contact with a number of disgruntled politicians. Through them, he has succeeded in undermining the Prime Minister. He has even helped to orchestrate his public humiliation.

Buddharakkita smiles as he thinks of the information, fed through different channels, that insinuated itself into the Prime Minister's ear, then worked its way into his speech. That address to the nation nearly sparked a civil war. In the event, there was no war, but the unrest allowed the nationalists to gauge the depth of their support, test the mood of the country. They will now face the future with increased confidence. It is common belief that there will be no organised opposition to their policies, however aggressive or draconian.

The Government has survived the crisis, but only just. Mr Bandaranaike is fatally weakened although he, himself, cannot see it. Such is the man's arrogance that he thinks he can cling to power indefinitely. His future is hopeless. Yet, still, he rejects the abbot's help and is never at home when the abbot calls.

After his failed attempts at an audience, Buddharakkita has made it a habit to wait in the street. Several times, he has seen the Prime Minister leaving in his car, just minutes after his own departure. He was in the house all the time. Buddharakkita seethes with rage. That is no way for the Prime Minister to treat the man who brought him to power.

He has tried to contact Mr Bandaranaike by telephone, hoping to surprise him by using his direct number. On the first occasion, he got through, but he was greeted with silence, then a faint click as the receiver was put back in its cradle, followed by the 'burr' of a dead line.

The Prime Minister's telephone is now answered by a clerk. The man always recognises the abbot even though Buddharakkita attempts to disguise his voice. He has even got one of his monks to make the phone call. But to no avail. Each time, the abbot receives a polite refusal. The Prime Minister is out. Or busy. He will phone back later. But he never does.

The abbot does not bother to visit or telephone these days. It is like trying to save a drowning man who does not have the wit, or inclination, to grasp the life-line that is thrown to him. And Buddharakkita is a proud man. A powerful man. He will not accept rejection indefinitely. He will not allow himself to be insulted. It is not appropriate for someone of his status or disposition. But what is he to do? It is a question that has exercised Buddharakkita for many days and nights.

The Prime Minister is weak. His ministers have deserted him. Yet, he stubbornly rejects help from the only man who can save him; the man who brought him to power. Such ingratitude. Buddharakkita's rage boils over. He has done with these games. He will not suffer further insult. Even if begged, he will not lift a finger to help the Prime Minister.

But, the fact remains. While Mr Bandaranaike remains unco-operative – and in office – Buddharakkita's future looks bleak. His only hope of salvation lies in the Government rice contract. For the abbot's finances are in a dire state. He is virtually bankrupt. The court battle that he hoped would give him direct control of the temple's wealth is still grinding on without any promise of a speedy conclusion. He cannot wait any longer. If the Prime Minister will not help him, he must find someone else.

He must think. Hard. He paces up and down the room while bats whirl outside in the darkness, carving loops in the dark air. Then, he stops in front of the window, staring out into the darkness. Bandaranaike must go. That is clear. But he will not leave office of his own accord. Something must be done. But what?

Buddharakkita's reflection stares back at him from the window, distorted by a fault in the glass. The features look like melted wax. Only the colour and shape of the saffron robe is clear. It puts him in mind of someone else; a man with whom he spoke today.

Somarama Thera, a Buddhist monk and Ayurvedic practitioner, came to enlist the abbot's help. The man is about to lose his position at the local hospital. He is desperate. Buddharakkita saw it in his eyes. He recognises the look of a man who will do anything to get what he wants. And this nondescript little fellow with the wire-rimmed glasses is such a man. Fear and desperation are a potent mix. They can be used. To Buddharakkita's advantage.

The abbot pours himself a Scotch then, sitting in his large, executive chair, swings around to face the window. The saffron-robed image stares back at him, its features still cloudy but the folds of its garment as clear as if they had been etched in the glass. Pensively, Buddharakkita swirls the whisky around as he considers his next move. As he stares at the window, the face of another monk gradually appears, superimposed over the abbot's own, indistinct features, as if the other man inhabits his robes.

Instead of his own, round face, he sees that of a small, nervous man, peering through cheap spectacles, as short-sighted as a mole. He is insignificant. But there is no doubt about his feelings. Like all practitioners of traditional medicine, the monk resents the western-based practices now favoured by the Government. Like most Ayurvedic practitioners, he is Sinhalese and a fervent nationalist. Despite his unprepossessing appearance, he speaks with surprising fervour. He would do anything for his country. That's what he said. Buddharakkita has no reason to disbelieve him. He is a fanatic. A crank. Just the kind of fellow Buddharakkita needs.

A deal must be struck. Something must be offered to the monk. An inducement. Luckily, Buddharakkita is in a position to offer the fellow what he wants. The abbot sits on the hospital board. He can use his influence to secure the monk's post. In return for this favour, Buddharakkita may ask the monk to render a service, something that will benefit both his country and the abbot.

Buddharakkita leans forward and sees his own face staring back from the window. Everything has become clear. He looks at the clock on his desk. It is 2 a.m. No matter. The abbot picks up the telephone and orders his sleepy chauffeur to bring the car. It is time to visit Somarama Thera.

First light. The boy is eager to be gone. He has a new fishing rod, made by his uncle, and he is eager to try it. He spent all of last evening unravelling the line that his father gave him. Although twisted into many knots, it is still serviceable.

"It will be better than the one on uncle's rod," his father said.

There are weights, too. Small pieces of lead, shaped like teardrops, with a loop in one end that can be tied to the line. The boy has not slept all night, due to excitement. But neither has anyone else. At 3 a.m. the whole village was woken by the loud retort of a gun. Since then, no-one has slept. They have been lucky. So far. The violence that has scorched a trail across the country has passed them by, although they have heard that villages only a few miles away have been affected.

There is a radio in the headman's house, the only one in the village and, every night, they gather around it to hear the news. The voice from Colombo has told them that the violence is over; the Government has everything under control. But no-one knows what to believe. The elders are sceptical. Although uneducated, they are wise. They know that the radio is government-owned and are loathe to believe everything it tells them. Its calm pronouncements that order has returned are met with disbelief and mumbled comments: "They would say that, wouldn't they?"

No-one feels safe. No-one ventures far from the village unless they have to. Wives and mothers are visibly relieved when husbands and sons return from the weekly market and children are forbidden to play outside. The spirit of the village, once so open and trusting, has changed. Villagers speak only to each other and the few strangers that pass through meet with suspicion and silence.

The violence has not ended. It is still out there, stalking the shadows like a hungry beast, waiting to claim its next victim. The gunshot in the night has only confirmed their fears.

It sounded close, echoing through the night-time stillness, loud enough to wake them all. But no-one can tell exactly where it came from. Several of the men ran out of their houses to look, but nothing could be seen. Reluctantly, they parted company, returning alone to their homes where their wives and children were huddled together, their eyes glowing in the candlelight, huge with fear. Startled awake, the smaller children wept, but were soon lulled back to sleep while those of an age to understand kept vigil with their parents, anxiously watching the door, praying for dawn.

The boy has also stayed awake all night, excited by the prospect of a day's fishing. Now that dawn has arrived, he must get out early, before his mother has time to nag him. No doubt, she will try to stop him altogether or, at least, ensnare him with promises. He must not go too far. He must not fish where he cannot be seen. He must come back immediately if he sees anything suspicious. He must not stay out too long.

Fortunately, the boy has everything ready. He has wrapped the precious rod in a piece of rag and hidden it, along with a bag containing hooks, line and bait, in a secret place, at the side of the house. He sits up on the thin, straw-filled mattress that he shares with his brother and looks around. Exhausted by night fears, everyone has fallen asleep. Quietly, he rises to his feet and tiptoes across the floor, stepping lightly between the sleeping bodies. He has a twinge of conscience as he passes his mother. When asleep, her face is smooth and youthful; not lined, as it usually is, by anxiety. His father says that she worries too much. When he returns with his catch of fish, the boy will prove to her that there is nothing to worry about.

Softly, he steps from the door and retrieves his fishing tackle from the dirt hollow that he has dug at the side of the house. He sets out, with the rod propped on his shoulder, like a real fisherman. Up to now, he has only had a play-rod, made from a twig with a piece of string tied to the end. But this fine cane is a man's rod, made by an expert. It has been oiled and shaped. It has a proper handle, metal loops through which the line will pass and even a small reel. He steps out proudly on his way to the lake.

The morning is fresh and the sun is warm on his face. In his mind, he has already marked out the place where he will fish. There is a collection of rocks that form a small jetty. The water there is deeper and fish shelter and feed under the overhanging rock. He has been there with his uncle many times.

He can see the lake, shimmering in the distance. It is an artificial lake, a tank, built by one of the ancient kings, and the road runs up to it from a lower level. He cannot see the shore from here, only the glittering surface of the water. Something in his stomach skips with excitement. He cannot wait. He begins to run. Up the road. Towards the retaining wall. Then, all he will have to do is climb over onto the shoreline.

He is up on the wall, the sun full on his face, the water so bright it nearly blinds him. It is a beautiful morning. The best. His heart sings. He climbs down precariously with one hand, protecting the rod with the other. He would rather fall and break his leg than break that rod.

At last, he is down. He shades his eyes. He can see the pile of rocks where he will fish. He cannot get there quickly enough. He runs along the shoreline, breathless, tripping over his feet, then scrambles up the rocks to the place where his uncle taught him to cast. He is so intent on setting up the rod that he does not see what lies on the other side of the rocks, hidden from view.

He clips the reel onto the rod, feeds the line through the loops, fixes the bait to the hook, then casts with a fine swinging motion. The weight hits the water with a small splash and the reel unwinds, allowing the line to run free. It makes a soft, whining sound, then stops as the weight hits the bottom. The boy reels in the slack then, propping the rod between two rocks, sits back to enjoy the morning.

He looks up at the sky, cloudless and perfect, then lets his eyes follow the line of the hills, down to the lake, around the shore, back to where he is sitting. He catches his breath. Sits up, alert. He has seen something. Several yards away, on the other side of the rocks. It looks like a bundle of rags. He climbs down to investigate. The rags are saffron, the colour of a monk's robes. As he approaches, he sees a foot, then an arm. Perhaps the man is sleeping, or unwell. The boy treads nervously over the sharp stones, drawn on by curiosity. The man does not move. The boy walks up to him.

"Are you all right, Hamuduru?"

The man does not reply. Perhaps he has fainted. Kneeling down, the boy gently shakes his shoulder. The skin feels cool. The boy shakes him harder. Too hard. The man rolls onto his back and, it is only then, that the boy realises that half of his head is missing.

"Thaatha, Thaatha," the boy screams as he runs back along the beach.

He screams all the way back to the village. His precious rod left, forgotten, on the rocks.

Under the moonlight, Kasyapa paces the broken ramparts of his fortress, waiting for Hooniyam. He is lonely and, for once, has released the Maidens from their enchantment. He can hear them, splashing and giggling as they bathe in the tank, lit only by the stars. In their excitement and relief, they have put aside old enmities and are speaking to each other again. Yaani has even made a small bow to the one they call 'Queen mother', addressing her deferentially – at least in front of Kasyapa. All grudges have been forgotten – for now – and there is peace in the royal household.

But Kasyapa is under no illusion. This is a temporary truce. Soon, the women will be at war again, plotting, scheming and whispering. There will be tears and pleas for retribution and, once more, he will be obliged to confine them to their painted images high on the rock face. But this is a family, he tells himself. And all families are the same: prone to fighting and cruelty, greed, jealousy and opportunism. Just like any kingdom. Or state.

His eyes wander to the spot in the forest where Hooniyam has his lair. There have been signs of activity there recently, secret comings and goings which only Kasyapa, as a spirit, can see. But, still, Hooniyam has not visited the king. Kasyapa has been waiting for over a month. Something has gone wrong.

Kasyapa has no spies in the human world, no-one to tell him of the mayhem and bloodshed. He does not know that the country has turned on itself, like a dog biting its own tail, nor that it now lies wounded and panting, scored with many cuts that will never heal. Some day soon, the old enemy will return. Another army will arrive from India, responding to a plea from one of the warring factions, just as it did in Kasyapa's day, and there will be slaughter. But Kasyapa knows none of this.

Far below, in the forest, a pale light flickers between the trees. It is one of the minor demons, known to Kasyapa, who sometimes brings him news in return for permission to hunt in his grounds. Kasyapa puts his fingers to his lips and whistles. There is a puff of smoke and a small, rotund demon is deposited at the king's feet. The demon looks shifty and unusually fearful.

"Well?" says Kasyapa, as he towers over the demon, his hands resting on his hips.

The demon holds up two rabbits that he has caught in a snare.

"No, not that. I don't want your catch. I want to know what's going on."

The demon swallows hard. He feared as much. Kasyapa will not like what he has to say. For Hooniyam is in trouble with the gods.

"It was nothing to do with me," insists the demon, shifting uncomfortably from foot to foot. He is an unconvincing liar. But Kasyapa humours him. Keen to know more. Hooniyam, it seems, has been following a hidden agenda. He planned to overthrow the gods, placing himself at the head of the pantheon. But, at the last minute, his plot was uncovered. Filled with wrath, the god Vishnu has sworn to take revenge. He has armed himself for battle and, with a deadly weapon in each of his eight hands, he is flying around the country on the eagle, Garuda, searching for Hooniyam.

"It is only a matter of time," whispers the demon, his green eyes wide with terror. "Who knows what will happen when Vishnu finds him."

"Argh!" Kasyapa roars with rage.

Terrified and unable to control himself, the demon disappears with a loud 'pop', leaving behind an unpleasant smell. But the king has his mind on other matters. He paces the ramparts, storming up and down, cursing and snarling like a captured lion. When he catches sight of Hooniyam's lair, he stops and waves his fist.

"Damn you, Hooniyam. Damn you!"

This was never what Kasyapa planned. He should have known that he could not trust Hooniyam. He is furious at being deceived. But he is also afraid. He has killed his father, stolen a throne, committed every damnable crime known to Man, but never, has he attacked the gods. He knows his limits. Hooniyam, it seems, does not. Seating himself on a piece of fallen masonry, Kasyapa tries to think.

Now that the first flush of rage has passed, his thoughts run more clearly. At least, he did not take an active part in Hooniyam's plan. Perhaps no-one but the demon-god himself knows of the king's willingness to help. Kasyapa must hope that Hooniyam is not caught for, if he is questioned, the truth will come out. If Hooniyam escapes, there is a chance that Kasyapa will not be tainted with treachery. But there will be no return to glory.

Kasyapa sighs. Even now, despite all that has happened, he still feels the sting of disappointment. There will be no visit from Hooniyam: no armies, no elephants, no battles and no victories. At least, not for the time being. Kasyapa must remain an outcast, remembered not for his strengths as a king, or his vision as an architect, but for his crime as a son and the unforgiveable act of patricide.

The sound of women's laughter floats down from the bathing terrace. The Maidens are getting dressed. He can see them now, outlined against the moon, their wet skin radiant in the soft light. There is a flash of gemstones as jewels are applied to necks and fingers. Lengths of silk flutter in the air like banners as they are lifted, shaken, then wrapped with sensuous pride around shapely hips. Hair is combed, pinned and adorned.

There is more giggling as the Maidens admire themselves in a mirror. He can smell their perfume. They are nearly ready. Soon, they will come to find him. Calling his name, they will skip down the steps, ready to entertain him with their musical instruments and their ceaseless chatter. But he does not want their company. Not tonight.

Kasyapa descends to the cool, starlit garden where the water sings in stone channels and the monkeys sleep peacefully in the trees, their tails and limbs trailing from the branches. Here, there is peace and, as he wanders the moonlit groves, Kasyapa remembers a woman that he saw here a few months ago. She reminded him of the only love of his life, dead these many hundreds of years, whose image is captured on the sheer face of the Rock and who now passes the time, bathing with her sisters under the stars. She was a beautiful woman, and wise.

He wonders now whether he should have done things differently, given up his pretensions to power and simply contented himself with her love. Would it have been enough? He cannot tell. It was too long ago. He wonders what has happened to the woman he saw in the gardens and whether she has found happiness.

Part 7: 1968
Neleni

The temple tree is old. Although it knows no season, flowering continuously throughout the year, it has seen at least thirty summers. It has grown tall, almost blocking the light from the lower windows, and now its branches touch the roof. It is covered in blossom, its buds bunched together in tight clusters; the petals furled around each other in slender, green twists.

Every day, new flowers open to fill the spaces left by those that have dropped: full-blown blossoms do not die on the branch but float gracefully to the ground where they gather in drifts against the foot of the tree. The air is filled with their delicate scent. No passer-by can ignore it.

Some pause, taking deep breaths of the sweet perfume, while others hurry past, trying to dismiss the images of death that the tree evokes. For the temple tree is treacherous: its branches snap without warning and its sap burns the skin. Despite its beauty, few women wear its flowers in their hair, for it is the flower of funerals and graveyards. Nevertheless, there are those who love it and a tiny picture, painted in watercolours, hangs on the wall above Neleni's bed.

***

Click, click, click. Vijaya is playing jacks on the porch. Just like his sisters used to do. In fact, they have taught him to play, sitting in exactly the same spot as they did, all those years ago when they were little girls. Vijaya is ten years old now and, although Saro sometimes plays with him, she prefers her own friends – a bunch of giggling, self-conscious schoolgirls who have little time for small boys. Vijaya's older sister, Rani, is married with a home of her own. She is expecting her first child, but she still visits every day: cooking, washing, ironing clothes, taking him to school and teaching him games.

Click, click. Vijaya drops one of the jacks. He frowns. He is quite good at the game but not as good as his sisters with their long fingers and years of practice. Vijaya examines his hands. The fingers are square, not tapered, quite unlike those of his sisters. Sometimes, in play, the adults in the family hold their hands up against his, palm to palm, fingers splayed, comparing their size as adults and children do. But Vijaya has noticed that no-one has hands shaped like his. He wishes that he had his sisters' long fingers. Then, he could beat them at jacks.

A car draws up, sleek and shining, like a great black beetle. It is an Austin, very new, Uncle Arjun's car. Uncle Arjun gets out, waves at Vijaya, then walks around to the passenger side where he helps a young woman to climb out of the door. She is heavily pregnant and moves slowly. Her face is pale and there are dark rings around her eyes. She looks tired. She pauses for a moment, trying to re-arrange her sari which has come adrift somewhere around her middle. Then, she pushes her hair back from her face, tucking it behind her ears. Rani's hair always looks slightly unkempt. Unlike her sister, who is pretty and well-groomed. Saro is also Vijaya's favourite, although he would never dare to tell anyone for fear of causing an argument. Rani has a prickly temper and, if he is honest, he is a little scared of her.

Uncle Arjun guides Rani to the steps and offers to help her, but she pushes his hand away. She is like that. Amma says that she is independent. Others just say that she is difficult. Independence. Vijaya has heard that word applied to countries, but rarely to people. It is a word that confuses him. The teachers at school speak as if it is a good thing, but it always seems to be followed by trouble. There is fighting and people die. He does not know how such a word could apply to Rani, however difficult she may be.

Rani has climbed to the top of the stairs and is now resting against the post that supports the porch. Her hair has fallen out of place again and is hanging across her face in untidy wisps. She pushes her hands into her back and winces, as if in pain, then she shuffles forward, dragging her feet as if every step is an effort. She smiles at Vijaya as she passes him, but her eyes are distant. She is thinking of something else.

Having returned to the car to fetch a huge basket of fresh laundry, Uncle Arjun hurries up the steps behind her. At the top, he leans against the front door and pushes it open to let her in then, after placing the basket on the floor inside, he returns to Vijaya and, bending down, reaches into his pocket. He produces a parcel, loosely-wrapped in red tissue, and hands it to Vijaya who tears off the wrapping. Inside is a box with a cellophane window displaying a gleaming, red car. An E-type Jaguar. Vijaya gasps.

"Thanks, Uncle."

Uncle Arjun ruffles the boy's hair and smiles. He is greying around the temples, but still handsome. Vijaya notices that he looks sad. Everyone around him looks sad these days. All except Amma, who always smiles, although she rarely gets out of bed.

"Play quietly, now," warns Uncle Arjun.

Everyone always says that, too. It is because Amma is often sleeping. Vijaya has asked why she has to sleep so much. Because she is ill, they say. *But when will she be better?* No-one answers. They look away and will not meet his eyes. So he has stopped asking that question.

Vijaya opens the box and slides the car onto the porch. It rolls out, running smoothly across the wooden boards. He picks it up and examines it. Its tiny doors open. It even has a boot at the back. Every detail is perfect. He holds it up in his hands. The paint has a metallic finish and sparkles in the sunlight. He has never seen anything so beautiful.

Something pats him on the head. He reaches up. A temple flower has dropped from the tree and is resting in his hair. Irritated, he pulls it off, scrunching it up between his fingers before throwing it over the balcony, into the street.

***

Rani is sorting laundry in the kitchen, taking it out of the large basket and arranging it in piles: one for her father, one for her mother, one for Vijaya. Unable to persuade her to rest, Arjun has tried to make himself useful, boiling the kettle for her mother's tea, setting out the best cup and saucer. But he looks awkward. It is a change brought about by their marriage. For some time after their wedding, he was uncomfortable in her parents' house and always seemed anxious to leave.

It is strange when one thinks how many years he lived here, virtually a member of the family. Rani noticed that her husband's affliction was at its worst when her mother entered the room. There was a frostiness between them and he would look at his hands, fidgeting to get away, wishing to be gone. Rani took comfort from the estrangement between her mother and Arjun.

However, things have changed since her mother fell ill. Now Arjun brings Rani to visit her mother every day and is never in a hurry to leave. He makes excuses to go and see her mother, taking her tea or the thin broth that she sometimes drinks, holding her up in bed and feeding her patiently with a spoon. No-one complains. Being heavily pregnant, Rani tires easily and her father is not good in the sick-room. Everyone is grateful to Arjun for his kindness to her mother but, still, Rani wonders.

There is a knock at the door.

"Hello."

A muffled voice calls from the hallway. Another visitor.

"Can I come in?"

Arjun almost runs to the door.

"Another excuse," thinks Rani. "To see my mother."

***

Click, click. Click, click. Vijaya is playing jacks on the porch again. The small figure on the bed lies with her eyes closed, but she hears everything. She can identify people just by the sound of their feet. Outside, the clicking of the jacks has stopped. A soft voice is speaking to Vijaya, then someone raps on the door. A visitor. A woman's voice calls into the house. There is a brief silence, then she hears the voice of a man. It is him. Her heart leaps and, for a second, her pale cheeks flush with warmth. He is coming.

She waits, listening for their footsteps. At last, they arrive. She waits for the door to open before opening her eyes. It is such an effort. The woman is in front. She steps forward with a smile. Neleni smiles, too. But her smile is for him. He knows it and smiles back, holding her eyes. He draws up a chair for the visitor, close to the bed so that she does not have to speak too loud. He ensures that the other woman is comfortable, then squeezes Neleni's hand. He would like to stay, but the visitor has intimated that she has things to say, things that she wants only Neleni to hear. He walks reluctantly to the door. Then, he has an idea.

"Can I bring you some tea?"

He holds his breath, waiting for the answer. Neleni is still looking at him.

The woman hesitates.

"Yes," she says, after some thought. "That would be nice."

"Good."

He cannot hide his relief. He is rapturously happy. In just a few minutes, he will see her again.

***

While she talks, Dalia holds Neleni's hand, gently stroking her fingers. They have become friends. Dalia visits often and, to fill the long, empty hours of the sick-room, the two women reminisce.

812

1958. Everything changed in that year. Some lost their homes, others their lives but, for some, loss was the beginning of a transformation. Dalia is one of the latter. Now, she bears no resemblance to her former self, pampered and spoiled. Her looks have faded, but she has grown into someone better: a sensible, kind woman, strong and independent.

She does not live on the charity of others, but supports herself and her child by going out to work. She has to. Michael never returned. For years, they thought that he had died, ambushed in some lonely corner by rioters. It is that thought that has troubled her more than anything else. But, today, she has news. She strokes Neleni's hand, trying to keep her attention.

"Uncle Peter came to see me yesterday. He has seen Michael."

Neleni's eyes open wide. Her lips work, as if she wants to say something, but no words come out. Instead, she squeezes Dalia's hand, although the pressure that she exerts is almost imperceptible.

"It was in Canada. Toronto. A few weeks ago. Uncle Peter was there on business. After work, he went into a bar with some friends. And he met Michael."

She pauses, looking out of the window to where the temple tree is shedding its blossom over the street.

"He's been there for years. In fact, he arrived shortly after the riots. He's been running the bar with a woman. You know the one. You remember the overseer who was murdered. Well, it's his widow. They've been living together as husband and wife. She has even taken his name."

She stares out of the window again, her lips pressed tightly together.

"I'm going to write to him."

Neleni gives a slight moan.

"Don't worry, Aunty. I don't want him back. I'm going to write to him and ask for a divorce."

Neleni raises her eyebrows, enquiringly.

"Oh, I never really felt that he was dead, although I feared it. It's all been quite a relief. Poor Uncle Peter. He put off telling me for weeks. He feared that I would be upset. He couldn't understand why I was so happy. He just thought I had not heard all that he had said. But I had and I am still happy. Because, I've got other news."

She hesitates and looks deep into Neleni's eyes.

"I haven't told anyone else, yet."

She lowers her head, blushing, smiling, and is suddenly as beautiful as she was before she married. Only kinder, wiser.

"I've met someone."

She waits for Neleni's reaction. None comes.

"He works at the University. A lecturer in science. He's a good man. He knows everything and he still wants to marry me. There's just one thing."

She hesitates.

"He's Sinhalese. Do you think it will matter?"

Slowly, Neleni's lips part in a smile. She makes a slight movement of her head. No, it does not matter. She approves. It is a good thing.

"Thank you, Aunty."

Dalia's eyes have filled with tears, but she is smiling, happy. She leans forward and strokes Neleni's hair, kissing her forehead.

"Now, you get some rest. I've talked enough."

Neleni's eyelids flutter, then close. She has so little energy these days. Gently, Dalia lays Neleni's hand on the bed, then quietly tiptoes across the room. She has just closed the door behind her, when Arjun appears bearing a tray with tea and biscuits. She notes that there are three cups on the tray.

"She's sleeping," Dalia explains, apologetically.

"Oh."

Disappointed, he looks down at the tray. Dalia pats his arm. She has learned much in the last few years, including the silent language of pain.

***

"Vijaya. Come inside for your tea."

Someone is calling her son.

"But, Rani, just a few more minutes. Please."

"Vijaya!"

Vijaya. The prince from India, ship-wrecked on the shores of Ceylon, who overcame demons to win the throne. His name means victory. Neleni thought it a good name and chose it for her son. But the optimism that prompted her to choose that name was misplaced. For, it seems to her, that Vijaya's birth marked the beginning of her loss.

She sighs and tries to turn in the bed. She hardly has the energy to move any more and requires other people to help her change position. Her back is aching. She wishes he would return. She thought he was coming but, as usual, she fell asleep. When she awoke, Dalia was gone and the room was empty. It is lonely being ill. She feels forgotten and useless, lying here alone in the small narrow bed that they have brought to the front of the house so that she can get a little sun. She closes her eyes, squeezing them shut, trying to deny the self-pity that comes all too easily these days. A tear escapes from the corner of her eye and runs down her cheek.

"Vijaya!"

She remembers Raj proudly displaying the new baby, holding him up in his arms, showing him off. *My son. Look at my son.* She remembers the anguish on Arjun's face. His pain. She wanted to tell him her secret so badly, but he would not let her. He said that there were some things that were better left unsaid. At the time, she agreed but she has often wondered since whether she was wrong. Sometimes it is better to speak the truth, whatever the consequences. Secrets are like poison. If she had spoken, Arjun might not have married Rani. But, like all men, he wanted a son.

"Vijaya!"

Rani is getting angry. Neleni remembers her own anger when Arjun announced his intention of marrying her daughter. She was sitting at the table, painting temple flowers, when he told her. She was so angry that she threw a bottle of paint water at him. It hit the wall and dribbled down, leaving a red stain that looked like blood draining from a heart. The Sacred Heart. Her heart. She had refused to let Raj paint over it. She wanted to keep it. A memorial to her suffering. Every time she looked at it, her wound had opened a little wider. And she wanted it there to remind him. To make him suffer.

She had thought he was doing it to spite her, because she had never offered to leave Raj, to take the final test and give everything up for her lover. But it was the secret that had stopped her from leaving. Someone other than Raj would have suffered. But she could never explain because she believed that Arjun could not face the truth. So she stayed and kept silent until, at last, it was too late.

She attended his wedding with a bad grace and, for several months after that, they had not spoken. Then, she fell ill and everything changed. He came to see her, held her hand and wept. And she realised that she had misunderstood him. His marriage to Rani was motivated, not by spite, but by devotion. To Neleni.

He had always felt that his position within the family was a precarious one and, as the children grew up, it seemed even less secure. What would happen when they all left home? Would Raj still want a lodger in his house? Would other people find it strange that a man, unrelated to the family, continued to live with them? He would be forced to leave. The thought tormented him. He had to find a way to stay near her because he could not live without her.

And so, he had married Rani. He had committed himself to a loveless marriage, just as she had done, in order to be near her. After his confession, he had wept and she had rocked him in her arms, like a child, her eyes fixed on the wall and the stain that looked like a bleeding heart. Only it was his heart, not hers.

***

Now, he comes to see her every day. It was easier, at first, when she was able to sit in the living-room, propped up on the couch with many cushions. They spoke for hours, about everything and nothing, holding hands when they were alone. But still, the secret lay between them. She felt it, almost like a physical barrier. Even then, she was able to ignore it, pretend it was not there. But now, with time so short, it troubles her. She has seen a priest, confessed, asked his advice. After thinking for a minute, he patted her hand. *God is truth*, he said. And since then, she has thought of nothing else. Her time is coming. Her conscience must be clear.

"*... Only you ...*"

The faint strains of the gramophone float on the air. He is playing their song, the secret code by which they communicate.

"*... only you ...*"

Her lips move, shaping the refrain. She smiles. It is time. She must see him. It takes all her strength to reach for the bell on the bedside table. She pauses, wincing with pain, breathless with the effort. Feebly, she shakes it. Will he hear it over the gramophone?

She holds her breath, listening. Then, she hears his footsteps, coming along the passage. He is alone. Silently, she gives thanks, a prayer of relief. At last, she can tell him. And then, she must see Raj. Before the doctor comes with the morphine and it is too late.

***

Neleni is free, released from her burden. Her spirit soars from the house, leaving behind the bed in which she was confined, the body which had become her prison. Up, up, swirling like smoke, then swooping down, over the street with its tinkling bells and bicycles, over the market where the Moslem trader still sells sweets. Then back, for a few seconds, hovering over the house. Vijaya is playing on the porch, his new car, in its box, beside him. He is happy. Unaware of his loss.

815

But inside, things are different. Arjun sits at the kitchen table, weeping, his head buried in his hands. He has just gained a son for whom there will be no place in his home. Rani's ashen face tells him as much. In the bedroom, still clutching the hand of his dead wife, Raj weeps also. For he has just lost the two people that he loved the most. Before she died, Neleni told him that Vijaya was not his son. Soon, there will be tears and recriminations, arguments and harsh words. Then, after that, the adults will have to decide whether to reveal the secret or carry it, as she did, for the rest of their lives.

Neleni smiles, benignly. She loves them all, but it is no longer her business to care. She circles the house once more and is gone.

1968: Sriya

The woman sits on the steep bank beside the paddy field watching her son play with the other boys. They have been helping their fathers all morning, planting the new rice seedlings. The men have taken a break to eat their mid-day meal, some are even sleeping, stretched out on the bank, letting the sun tend to their aching limbs. But the boys' energy is limitless. They run, squealing through the water, throwing clumps of mud at each other, falling over, splashing and shouting.

They remind her of other boys, when she was young, who played just like this. Games are eternal, although those who play them tire and die. She thinks of another small boy who used to chase her through the paddy, laughing, his eyes shining, without a care in the world. He has been dead a long time now. They found him a few miles away, lying on the lake shore with a bullet through his skull. It seems that he died by his own hand. After killing her husband.

Her eyes mist over. When her husband died all those years ago, people told her that time would heal. But it has not. The wound is as deep as ever. The village holds many reminders of his presence, but she feels especially close to him when she is here, sitting by the paddy fields, the place where they used to sit together and watch the stars. Her wound will never heal, but she has tried to give it meaning.

After his death, she continued the informal classes that he had started for village children, fighting to get more funds, pleading with Government officials. Now, there is a proper school with classrooms and teachers. She is pleased with her achievement, but will take no credit for it. When villagers attempt to thank her, she reminds them that it was her husband's idea. Perhaps a school like that would have saved someone like Tissa. An education might have given him hope, other opportunities. Who knows?

She shudders. The memory of that terrible day, when she held her dying husband in her arms, is still fresh. It will never leave her. For part of her died with him. In the same instant that happiness returned, it was snatched away. It is something that no-one else can understand. Loneliness accompanies her suffering.

But she is not sorry for herself. She has an antidote. One that he taught her. Reading. She reaches into her basket and extracts a tattered newspaper from beneath the tiffin-boxes. She is still in the habit of gleaning old papers from the country bus. Her husband would laugh if he could see her. She opens the paper which is soft from much handling. There is a yellow thumb-print in the margin, probably made by a farmer. She is careful not to touch it. She turns the pages, skimming over stories about the present Prime Minister, Mr Dudley Senanayake, son of the revered D.S. Senanayake. He is not half the man his father was. At least, that is what her father says.

She glances towards the trees where her father is taking a nap. His wit is still as keen as ever, although he has slowed up considerably. It is a good thing that she has a son to help him. The Prime Minister is encouraging children to help in the fields and agriculture leads the curriculum in many schools. But whether or not this will mean a better life for the peasants, or increased drudgery, no-one yet knows.

She turns to a picture of Mrs Sirimavo Bandaranaike who has also served a term as Prime Minister. Surely, that must be a good thing for women. Like her, Mrs Bandaranaike is a widow. In 1959, just a few months after the riots, Mr Bandaranaike was assassinated, by a monk, in his own home, as he received guests on the verandah.

817

The monk and several other men, including Buddharakkita Thera, the abbot of Kelaniya, were put on trial for murder. Even a Cabinet member, Mrs Wijewardene was arrested, although she was later discharged. The five men, however, were all sentenced to death. The abbot appealed and his sentence was commuted to life imprisonment. But the monk was not so lucky. He was hanged in prison: his only memorial, a ribald song that told how he had been shot in the genitals by a police sentry.

Sriya remembers every detail of the assassination, even the name of the Prime Minister's residence – Temple Trees – because it is a story that reflects her own, acute pain. While other people overpowered the monk, Mrs Bandaranaike cradled her husband in her arms. Kneeling in a pool of blood, she held him to her, as Sriya held Asoka to her in the chena garden.

Although she does not know it, Mrs Bandaranaike has comforted Sriya because she knows what it is like. And Sriya has repaid the debt. She is proud to think that her vote helped Mrs Bandaranaike to power: a phoenix rising from the ashes of her husband's death. Thanks to Sirimavo, the Bandaranaikes have become a political dynasty.

Sriya turns the page. Despite her admiration for Mrs Bandaranaike, she does not like politics. Or politicians. In that, she agrees with her father, although she does not hold with his preferred solution of burying them all alive. She flicks to the back pages, to her favourite section which tells of births, deaths and marriage proposals.

In the column dealing with astrological predictions, a small article catches her eye. The print is tiny and smudged in places. It is evident that other people have read it. The article claims that Mr Bandaranaike has achieved reincarnation as the god Mangalanatha. In some measure, at least, he has achieved his wish. He is now immortal.

Sriya puts the paper aside and looks towards the horizon where the rock of Sigiriya stands dark and silent against the bright, blue sky. Centuries ago, King Kasyapa killed his father, then died by his own hand. The history of this country is steeped in blood. It is like the game played by the boys in the paddy field, renewing itself with every generation. She wonders if it will ever end.

"Mummy, Mummy look at me!"

Her son is turning cartwheels in the water. She laughs and claps. He waves then, seeing something, stoops down and dabbles, elbow-deep in the water.

"I've got something for you."

His voice is shrill with excitement. He races through the water, droplets flying from his legs like strings of crystal. He flings himself at the bank, scrabbling to climb up as the earth gives way under his feet.

"Here. I found something. It's for you."

He holds out a yellow stone: a piece of quartz that, in his child's eye, has been transformed into a precious jewel. Because that is what he wants. For his mother.

"It's beautiful, Asoka."

He grins. He has the deep set eyes of his father. She takes the pebble and opens her arms. The boy dives into her embrace, and she hugs him tight. He is muddy and his small, lithe body is as slippery as a fish. Yet, as she holds him, something ignites within her. There is still hope.

GLOSSARY OF TERMS

BHIKKU: A Buddhist monk.

BUDDHA JAYANTHI: 2,500 celebration of Buddha's death or parinibbana.

BURGHER: Originally the term for those of mixed Dutch and Ceylonese parentage. However, often used more loosely to describe those of mixed European and Ceylonese race.

CARROM: A traditional game in which counters are flicked across a polished board.

CHELVANAYAKAM, S.J.V.: Leader of the Tamil Federal Party.

CEYLON: The name by which Sri Lanka was known prior to 1972.

DALADA MALIGAWA: The famous Temple of the Tooth, Kandy.

DEVI: A Hindu goddess.

DHOBI WOMAN: A washerwoman.

GATHAS: Buddhist poems used in religious meditation.

GOONDA: Thug, hooligan, rabble-rouser.

HAMUDURU: A respectful term of address for a monk.

HANUMAN: Hindu monkey-faced god.

HOPPERS: Pancakes made with rice flour and leavened with toddy yeast.

ICARUS: Refers in this instance to a painting by Flemish artist Pieter Breughel.

JANSZ: Neleni's maiden name denoting her Burgher ancestry.

KATCHERI: A government department.

KALI: A Hindu goddess.

KATTIES: Knives.

KITTUL TREES: The leaves provide food for elephants while the sap of the flower is used to make kittul treacle, a substance similar to maple syrup.

LAKH: A term for the number 100,000.

LATHI: A baton used by the police.

LOKKA: The 'Boss'.

LUNGHI: A length of cloth, similar to a sarong, worn by women.

MACHAN: Tamil form of friendly address, equivalent to 'brother'.

MAHAVAMSA: A chronicle written by Buddhist monks c. 6th century.

MAHOUT: A man who trains, keeps and 'drives' a domesticated elephant.

"O": The Sinhalese word for 'yes'.

OFFICIAL LANGUAGE ACT: Another term for the Sinhala Only Act.

PARINIBBANA: Ultimate enlightenment achieved by Buddha.

PERAHERA: A religious procession.

PRINCE VIJAYA: An Indian prince who, according to the Mahavamsa, conquered Ceylon and founded the Sinhalese race.

PYE-DOG: A feral dog.

MAHATHAYA: A Sinhalese term of respect.

MUSTH: The time when a male elephant comes into season.

NAGA: Sanskrit term for snake (often a cobra). In Buddhism and Hinduism, nagas are deities or spiritual beings that take the form of a snake. Also the name of an Indian tribe.

RAJ: Means 'prince' or 'king'.

SANGHA: The Buddhist order of monks or bhikkus.

SARONG: A length of cloth tied around a man's waist covering the lower half of the body.

SERENDIPITY: A fortunate discovery derived from the ancient name for Ceylon, that is, 'Sarandip' (Persian) or 'Sarandib' (Arabic). The word in its current form was coined by Horace Walpole in his story, 'The Three Princes of Serendip', in 1754.

SLIPPERS: Flip-flops.

STRING HOPPERS: Fine rice noodles.

TANK: Reservoir, derived from the Portuguese word 'tanque'.

THAATHA: Sinhalese for 'Daddy'.

THAMBILI JUICE: Sweet juice from a coconut.

VADDA: Oldest ethnic community of Sri Lanka. Also known as the Wanniya-Laeto or forest-dwellers. Thought to be descendants of Neolithic people who inhabited the Island c. 16,000 B.C. Possibly identified in the Mahavamsa as the demons who inhabited Ceylon prior to the arrival of Prince Vijaya.

YAKKHA: A demon.

BIBLIOGRAPHY

HISTORY AND POLITICS
'Emergency '58' Tarzie Vittachi [Written by a journalist, this contemporary document provides invaluable eyewitness accounts of the civil disturbances of 1958 together with a detailed analysis of events.]
Buddharakkita Thero v. Wijewardena: NLR 49 of 62 [1960] LKSC 20; (1960) 62 NLR 49 (26 April 1960) [The Privy Council rejects Buddharakkita's attempt to claim the income from Helena Wijewardene's legacy of paddy land to the temple at Kelaniya.]
The Queen v Buddharakkita and 2 Others: NLR 433 or 63 [1962] LKHC 1; [1962] 63 NLR 433 (15 January 1962) [Buddharakkita's appeal against the death penalty to the Court of Criminal Appeal.]
The Mahavamsa Anon.
A History of Sri Lanka K.M. de Silva
Buddhism Betrayed? Stanley Jeyaraja Tambiah
Sri Lanka A History Chandra Richard de Silva
Ceylon of the early travellers H.A.J. Hulugalle
Sri Lanka: The Untold Story K.T. Rajasingham

CULTURE AND RELIGION
Buddhism Transformed R. Gombrich, G. Obeyesekere
Legends of People Myths of State Bruce Kapferer
Buddha Karen Armstrong

AGRICULTURE, FLORA AND FAUNA
Traditional agriculture in Sri Lanka Edward Goldsmith and Mudyanse Tenekoon
Nava Kekulam method of paddy cultivation G. K. Upawana
Snakebite in Sri Lanka Anslem de Silva
Birds of Sri Lanka Gehan de Silva Wijeyratne, Deepal Warakagoda, T.S.U. de Zylva

MAPS AND GENERAL INFORMATION
Insight Guides Sri Lanka Discovery Channel
Globetrotter Sri Lanka Robin Gauldie